RANDOM
HOUSE

LARGE
PRINT

The Snowman

The Snowman

JO NESBØ

Translated from the Norwegian by Don Bartlett

RANDOM HOUSE
LARGE PRINT

Translation copyright © 2010 by Don Bartlett

All rights reserved.
Published in the United States of America by
Random House Large Print in association with
Alfred A. Knopf, New York.
Distributed by Random House, Inc., New York.

Originally published in Norway as Snømannen by
H. Aschehoug & Co. (W. Nygaard), Oslo, in 2007.
Copyright © 2007 by Jo Nesbø. This translation was
originally published in Great Britain by Harvill Secker, an
imprint of the Random House Group Ltd., London, in 2010.

Cover design by Peter Mendelsund

Grateful acknowledgment is made to Bug Music for
permission to reprint lyrics from "Call Me on Your Way
Back Home" by Ryan Adams, copyright © 2000 by
Barland Music (BMI)/Administered by Bug Music. All
rights reserved. Reprinted by permission of Bug Music.

The Library of Congress has established a
Cataloging-in-Publication record for this title.

ISBN: 978-0-7393-7819-9

www.randomhouse.com/largeprint

FIRST LARGE PRINT EDITION

Printed in the United States of America

10 9 8 7 6 5 4 3 2 1

This Large Print edition published in accord with
the standards of the N.A.V.H.

For Kirsten Hammervoll Nesbø

Part One

I

The Snowman

It was the day the snow came. At eleven o'clock in the morning, large flakes had appeared from a colorless sky and invaded the fields, gardens and lawns of Romerike like an armada from outer space. At two, the snowplows were in action in Lillestrøm, and when, at half past two, Sara Kvinesland slowly and carefully steered her Toyota Corolla SR5 between the detached houses on Kolloveien, the November snow was lying like a down duvet over the rolling countryside.

She was thinking that the houses looked different in daylight. So different that she almost passed his driveway. The car skidded as she applied the brakes, and she heard a groan from the backseat. In the rearview mirror she saw her son's disgruntled face.

"It won't take long, my love," she said.

In front of the garage there was a large patch of black pavement amid all the white, and she realized that the moving van had been there. Her throat constricted. She hoped she wasn't too late.

"Who lives here?" came from the backseat.

"Just someone I know," Sara said, automatically checking her hair in the mirror. "Ten minutes, my love. I'll leave the key in the ignition so you can listen to the radio."

She went without waiting for a response, slithered in her slippery shoes up to the door she had been through so many times, but never like this, not in the middle of the day, in full view of all the neighbors' prying eyes. Not that late-night visits would seem any more innocent, but for some reason acts of this kind felt more appropriate when performed after the fall of darkness.

She heard the buzz of the doorbell inside, like a bumblebee in a jam jar. Feeling her desperation mount, she glanced at the windows of the neighboring houses. They gave nothing away, just returned reflections of bare black apple trees, gray sky and milky-white terrain. Then, at last, she heard footsteps behind the door and heaved a sigh of relief. The next moment she was inside and in his arms.

"Don't go, darling," she said, hearing the sob already straining at her vocal cords.

"I have to," he said in a monotone that suggested a refrain he had tired of long ago. His hands sought familiar paths, of which they never tired.

"No, you don't," she whispered into his ear. "But you want to. You don't dare any longer."

"This has nothing to do with you and me."

She could hear the irritation creeping into his voice at the same time as his hand, the strong but gentle hand, slid down over her spine and inside the waistband of her skirt and tights. They were like a pair of practiced dancers who knew their partner's every move, step, breath, rhythm. First, the white lovemaking. The good one. Then the black one. The pain.

His hand caressed her coat, searching for her nipple under the thick material. He was eternally fascinated by her nipples; he always returned to them. Perhaps it was because he didn't have any himself.

"Did you park in front of the garage?" he asked with a firm tweak.

She nodded and felt the pain shoot into her head like a dart of pleasure. Her sex had already opened for him. "My son's waiting in the car."

His hand came to an abrupt halt.

"He knows nothing," she groaned, sensing his hand falter.

"And your husband? Where's he now?"

"Where do you think? At work, of course."

Now it was she who sounded irritated. Both because he had brought her husband into the conversation and it was difficult for her to say anything at all about him without getting irritated, and because her body needed him, quickly. Sara Kvinesland opened his fly.

"Don't . . . ," he began, grabbing her around the wrist. She slapped him hard with her other hand. He looked at her in amazement as a red flush spread across his cheek. She smiled, grabbed his thick black hair and pulled his face down to hers.

"You can go," she hissed. "But first you have to fuck me. Is that understood?"

She felt his breath against her face. It was coming in hefty gasps now. Again she slapped him with her free hand, and his dick was growing in her other.

He thrust, a bit harder each time, but it was over now. She was numb, the magic was gone, the tension had dissolved and all that was left was despair. She was losing him. Now, as she lay there, she had lost him. All the years she had yearned, all the tears she had cried, the desperate things he had made her do. Without giving anything back. Except for one thing.

He was standing at the foot of the bed and taking her with closed eyes. Sara stared at his chest. At first she had thought it strange, but after a while she had begun to like the sight of unbroken white skin over his pectoral muscles. It reminded her of old statues on which the nipples had been omitted out of consideration for public modesty.

His groans were getting louder. She knew that soon he would let out a furious roar. She had loved that roar. The ever-surprised, ecstatic, almost pained expression as though the orgasm surpassed his wildest expectation each and every time. Now she was waiting for the final roar, a bellowing farewell to this freezing box of a bedroom, divested of pictures, curtains and carpets. Then he would get dressed and travel to a different part of the country, where he said he had been offered a job he couldn't say no to. But he could say no to this. This. And still he would roar with pleasure.

She closed her eyes. But the roar didn't come. He had stopped.

"What's up?" she asked, opening her eyes. His features were distorted, all right. But not with pleasure.

"A face," he whispered.

She flinched. "Where?"

"Outside the window."

The window was at the other end of the bed, right above her head. She heaved herself around, felt him slip out, already limp. The window above her head was set too high in the wall for her to see out. And too high for anyone standing outside to peer in. Because of the already dwindling daylight all she could see was the double-exposed reflection of the ceiling lamp.

"You saw yourself," she said, almost pleading.

"That was what I thought at first," he said, still staring at the window.

Sara pulled herself up onto her knees. Got up and looked into the yard. And there, there was the face.

She laughed out loud with relief. The face was white, with eyes and a mouth made with black pebbles, probably from the driveway. And arms made of twigs from the apple trees.

"Heavens," she gasped. "It's only a snowman."

Then her laugh turned into tears; she sobbed helplessly until she felt his arms around her.

"I have to go now," she sobbed.

"Stay for a little while longer," he said.

She stayed for a little while longer.

As Sara approached the garage she saw that almost forty minutes had passed.

He had promised to call her now and then. He had always been a good liar, and for once she was glad. Even before she got to the car she saw her son's pale face staring at her from the backseat. She pulled at the door and found to her astonishment that it was locked. She peered in at him through steamed-up windows. He opened it only when she knocked on the glass.

She sat in the driver's seat. The radio was silent and it was ice-cold inside. The key was on the passenger seat. She turned to him. Her son was pale, and his lower lip was trembling.

"Is there anything wrong?" she asked.

"Yes," he said. "I saw him."

There was a thin, shrill tone of horror in his voice that she couldn't recall hearing since he was a little boy jammed between them on the sofa in front of the TV with his hands over his eyes. And now his voice was changing, he had stopped giving her a good-night hug and had started being interested in car engines and girls. And one day he would get in a car with one of them and also leave her.

"What do you mean?" she said, inserting the key in the ignition and turning.

"The snowman . . ."

There was no response from the engine and panic gripped her without warning. Quite what she was afraid of she didn't know. She stared out the windshield and turned the key again. Had the battery died?

"And what did the snowman look like?" she asked, pressing the accelerator to the floor and desperately turning the key so hard it felt as though she would break it. He answered, but the response was drowned by the roar of the engine.

Sara put the car in gear and let go of the clutch as if in a sudden hurry to get away. The wheels spun in the soft, slushy snow. She accelerated harder, but the rear of the car slid sideways. By then the tires had spun their way down to the pavement and they lurched forward and skidded into the road.

"Dad's waiting for us," she said. "We'll have to get a move on."

She switched on the radio and turned up the volume to fill the cold interior with sounds other than her own voice. A broadcaster said for the hundredth time today that last night Ronald Reagan had beaten Jimmy Carter in the American election.

The boy said something again, and she glanced in the mirror.

"What did you say?" she said in a loud voice.

He repeated it, but still she couldn't hear. She turned down the radio while heading toward the main road and the river, which ran through the countryside like two mournful black stripes. And gave a start when she realized he had leaned forward between the two front seats. His voice sounded like a dry whisper in her ear. As if it were important no one else heard them.

"We're going to die."

2

Pebble-Eyes

Harry Hole gave a start and opened his eyes wide. It was freezing cold, and from the dark came the sound of the voice that had awoken him. It announced that the American people would decide today whether their president for the next four years would again be George Walker Bush. November. Harry was thinking they were definitely heading for dark times. He threw off the duvet and placed his feet on the floor. The linoleum was so cold it stung. He left the news blaring from the clock radio and went into the bathroom. Regarded himself in the mirror. November there, too: drawn, grayish pale and overcast. As usual, his eyes were bloodshot, and the pores on his nose large black craters. The bags under his eyes, with their light-blue alcohol-washed irises, would disappear after his face had been ministered to with hot water, a towel and breakfast. He assumed they would, that is. Harry was not sure exactly how his face would fare during the day now that he had turned forty. Whether the wrinkles would be ironed out and peace would fall over the hunted expression he woke with after nights of being ridden by nightmares. Which was most nights. For he avoided mirrors after he left his small, spartan apartment on Sofies Gate and transformed into Inspector Hole of the Crime Squad at the Oslo Police HQ. Then he stared into others' faces to find their pain, their Achilles' heels, their nightmares, motives and reasons for self-deception, listening to their fatiguing lies and trying to find a meaning in what he did: imprisoning people who were already imprisoned inside themselves. Prisons of hatred and self-contempt he recognized all too well. He ran a hand over the shorn bristles of blond hair that grew precisely seventy-five inches above the frozen soles of his feet. His collarbone stood out under his skin like a clothes hanger. He had trained a lot since the last case. In a frenzy, some maintained. As well as cycling he had started to lift weights in the fitness room in the bowels of the Police HQ. He liked the burning pain, and the repressed thoughts. Nevertheless, he just became leaner. The fat disappeared and his muscles were layered between skin and bone. And while before he had been broad-shouldered and what Rakel called a natural athlete, now he had begun to resemble the photograph he had once seen of a skinned polar bear: a muscular but shockingly gaunt predator. Quite simply, he was fading away. Not that it actually mattered. Harry sighed. November. It was going to get even darker.

He went into the kitchen, drank a glass of water to relieve his headache and peered through the window in surprise. The roof of the building on the other side of Sofies Gate was white and the bright reflected light made his eyes smart. The first snow had come in the night. He thought of the letter. He did occasionally get such letters, but this one had been special. It had mentioned Toowoomba.

On the radio a nature program had started and an enthusiastic voice was waxing lyrical about seals. "Every summer Berhaus seals collect in the Bering Strait to mate. Since the males are in the majority, the competition for females is so fierce that those males that have managed to procure themselves a female will stick with her during the whole of the breeding period. The male will take care of his partner until the young have been born and can cope by themselves. Not out of love for the female, but out of love for his own genes and hereditary material. Darwinist theory would say that it is natural selection that makes the Berhaus seal monogamous, not morality."

I wonder, thought Harry.

The voice on the radio was almost turning falsetto with excitement. "But before the seals leave the Bering Strait to search for food in the open sea, the male will try to kill the female. Why? Because a female Berhaus seal will never mate twice with the same male! For her this is about spreading the biological risk of hereditary material, just like on the stock market. For her it makes biological sense to be promiscuous, and the male knows this. By taking her life he wants to stop the young of other seals competing with his own progeny for the same food."

"We're entering Darwinian waters here, so why don't humans think like the seal?" another voice said.

"But we do, don't we! Our society is not as monogamous as it appears, and never has been. A Swedish study showed recently that between fifteen and twenty percent of all children born have a different father from the one they—and for that matter the postulated fathers—think. Twenty percent! That's every fifth child! Living a lie. And ensuring biological diversity."

Harry fiddled with the radio dial to find some tolerable music. He stopped at an aging Johnny Cash's version of "Desperado."

There was a firm knock on the door.

Harry went into the bedroom, put on his jeans, returned to the hall and opened up.

"Harry Hole?" The man outside was wearing blue overalls and looking at Harry through thick lenses. His eyes were as clear as a child's.

Harry nodded.

"Have you got fungus?" The man asked the question with a straight face. A long wisp of hair traversed his forehead and was stuck there. Under his arm he was holding a plastic clipboard with a densely printed sheet.

Harry waited for him to explain further, but nothing was forthcoming. Just this clear, open expression.

"That," Harry said, "strictly speaking, is a private matter."

The man gave the suggestion of a smile in response to a joke he was heartily sick of hearing. "Fungus in your apartment. Mold."

"I have no reason to believe that I do," said Harry.

"That's the thing about mold. It seldom gives anyone any reason to believe that it's there." The man sucked at his teeth and rocked on his heels.

"But?" Harry said at length.

"But it is."

"What makes you think that?"

"Your neighbor's got it."

"Uh-huh? And you think it may have spread?"

"Mold doesn't spread. Dry rot does."

"So then . . . ?"

"There's a construction fault with the ventilation along the walls in this building. It allows dry rot to flourish. May I take a peep at your kitchen?"

Harry stepped to the side. The man powered into the kitchen, where at once he pressed an orange hairdryer-like apparatus against the wall. It squeaked twice.

"Damp detector," the man said, studying something that was obviously an indicator. "Just as I thought. Sure you haven't seen or smelled anything suspicious?"

Harry didn't have a clear perception of what that might be.

"A coating like on stale bread," the man said. "Moldy smell."

Harry shook his head.

"Have you had sore eyes?" the man asked. "Felt tired? Had headaches?"

Harry shrugged. "Of course. For as long as I can remember."

"Do you mean for as long as you've lived here?"

"Maybe. Listen . . ."

But the man wasn't listening; he'd taken a knife from his belt. Harry stood back and watched the hand holding the knife being raised and thrust with great force. There was a sound like a groan as the knife went through the plasterboard behind the wallpaper. The man pulled out the knife, thrust it in again and bent back a powdery piece of plaster, leaving a large gap in the wall. Then he whipped out a small penlight and shone it into the cavity. A deep frown developed behind his oversize glasses. Then he stuck his nose deep into the cavity and sniffed.

"Right," he said. "Hello there, boys."

"Hello there who?" Harry asked, edging closer.

"**Aspergillus**," said the man. "A genus of mold. We have three or four hundred types to choose among and it's difficult to say which one this is because the growth on these hard surfaces is so thin it's invisible. But there's no mistaking the smell."

"That means trouble, right?" Harry asked, trying to remember how much he had left in his bank account after he and his father had sponsored a trip to Spain for Sis, his little sister, who had what she referred to as "a touch of Down syndrome."

"It's not like real dry rot. The building won't collapse," the man said. "But you might."

"Me?"

"If you're prone to it. Some people get ill from

breathing the same air as the mold. They're ailing for years, and of course they get accused of being hypochondriacs since no one can find anything and the other residents are fine. And then the pest eats up the wallpaper and the plasterboard."

"Mm. What do you suggest?"

"That I eradicate the infection, of course."

"And my personal finances while you're at it?"

"Covered by the building's insurance, so it won't cost you a krone. All I need is access to the apartment for the next few days."

Harry found the spare set of keys in the kitchen drawer and passed them to him.

"It'll just be me," the man said. "I should mention that in passing. Lots of strange things going on out there."

"Are there?" Harry smiled sadly, staring out of the window.

"Eh?"

"Nothing," Harry said. "There's nothing to steal here anyway. I'll be off now."

The low morning sun sparkled off all the glass on the Oslo Police HQ, standing there as it had for the last thirty years, on the summit of the ridge by the main street, Grønlandsleiret. Although this had not been exactly intentional, the HQ was near the high-crime areas in east Oslo, and the prison, located on the site of the old brewery, was its closest neighbor. The police station was surrounded by a brown withering lawn and maple and linden trees that had been covered with a thin layer of gray-white snow during the night, making the park look like a deceased's shrouded chattels.

Harry walked up the black strip of pavement to the main entrance and entered the central hall, where Kari Christensen's porcelain wall decoration with running water whispered its eternal secrets. He nodded to the security guard in reception and went up to the Crime Squad on the sixth floor. Although it had been almost six months since he had been given his new office in the red zone, he still often mistakenly went to the cramped, windowless one he had shared with Officer Jack Halvorsen. Now Magnus Skarre was in there. And Jack Halvorsen had been interred in the ground of Vestre Aker cemetery. At first the parents had wanted their son to be buried in their hometown, Steinkjer, as Jack and Beate Lønn, the head of Krimteknisk, the Forensics Unit, had not been married; they hadn't even been living together. But when they found out that Beate was pregnant and Jack's baby would be born in the summer, Jack's parents agreed that Jack's grave should be in Oslo.

Harry entered his new office. Which he knew would be known as that forever, the way the fifty-year-old home ground of the Barcelona football club was still called Camp Nou, Catalan for "New Stadium." He dropped into his chair, switched on the radio and nodded good morning to the photos perched on the bookcase and propped against the wall. One day in an uncertain future, if he remembered to buy picture hooks, they would hang on the wall. Ellen Gjelten and Jack Halvorsen and Bjarne Møller. There they stood in chronological order. The Dead Policemen's Society.

On the radio Norwegian politicians and social scientists were giving their views on the American presidential election. Harry recognized the voice of Arve Støp, the owner of the successful magazine **Liberal** and famous for being one of the most knowledgeable, arrogant and entertaining pundits in the country. Harry turned up the volume until the voices bounced off the brick walls, and grabbed his Peerless handcuffs from the new desk. He practiced speed-cuffing the table leg, which was already splintered as a result of this new bad habit of his. He had picked it up in the FBI course in Chicago and perfected it during lonely evenings in a lousy apartment in Cabrini-Green, surrounded by arguing neighbors and in the company of Jim Beam. The aim was to bang the cuffs against the arrestee's wrist in such a way that the spring-loaded arm closed around the wrist and the lock clicked on the other side. With the right amount of force and accuracy you could cuff yourself to an arrestee in one simple movement before he had a chance to react. Harry had never had any use for this on the job and only once for the other thing he had learned over there: how to catch a serial killer. The cuffs clicked around the table leg and the radio voices droned on.

"Why do you think Norwegians are so skeptical about George Bush, Arve Støp?"

"Because we're an overprotected nation that has

never fought in any wars. We've been happy to let others do it for us: England, the Soviet Union and America. Yes, ever since the Napoleonic Wars we've hidden behind the backs of our older brothers. Norway has based its security on others taking the responsibility when things got tough. That's been going on for so long that we've lost our sense of reality and we believe that the earth is basically populated by people who wish us—the world's richest country—well. Norway, a gibbering, pea-brained blonde who gets lost in an alley in the Bronx and is now indignant that her bodyguard is so brutal with muggers."

Harry dialed Rakel's number. Aside from Sis's, Rakel's telephone number was the only one he knew by heart. When he was young and inexperienced, he thought that a bad memory was a handicap for a detective. Now he knew better.

"And the bodyguard is Bush and the U.S.A.?" the host asked.

"Yes. Lyndon B. Johnson once said that the U.S. hadn't chosen this role, but he had realized there was no one else, and he was right. Our bodyguard is a born-again Christian with a father complex, a drinking problem, intellectual limitations and not enough backbone to do his military service with honor. In short, a guy we should be pleased is going to be re-elected president today."

"I assume you mean that ironically?"

"Not at all. Such a weak president listens to his advisers, and the White House has the best, believe you me. Even though from that laughable TV series about the Oval Office one may have formed the impression that the Democrats have a monopoly on intelligence, it is on the extreme right wing of the Republicans, surprisingly enough, that you find the sharpest minds. Norway's security is in the best possible hands."

"A girlfriend of a girlfriend has had sex with you."

"Really?" said Harry.

"Not you," Rakel said. "I'm talking to the other guy. Støp."

"Sorry," Harry said, turning down the radio.

"After a lecture in Trondheim. He invited her up to his room. She was interested, but drew his attention to the fact that she'd had a mastectomy. He said he would give that some thought and went to the bar. And came back and took her with him."

"Mm. I hope expectations were fulfilled."

"Nothing fulfills expectations."

"No," Harry said, wondering what they were talking about.

"What's happening this evening?" Rakel asked.

"Palace Grill at eight is fine. But what's all this garbage about not being able to reserve tables in advance?"

"It gives the whole place cachet, I suppose."

They arranged to meet in the bar area first. After they had hung up, Harry sat thinking. She had sounded pleased. Or bright. Bright and cheery. He tried to sense if he had succeeded in being pleased on her behalf, pleased that the woman he had loved so much was happy with another man. Rakel and he had had their time, and he had been given chances. Which he wasted. So why not be pleased that she was well, why not let the thought that things could have been different go, and move on with his life? He promised to try a bit harder.

The morning meeting was soon over. As head of the Crime Squad, Politioverbetjent—POB for short—Gunnar Hagen ran through the cases they were working on. Which were not many, as for the time being there weren't any fresh murder cases under investigation, and murder was the only thing that got the unit's pulse racing. Thomas Helle, an officer from the Missing Persons Unit of the uniformed police, was present and gave a report on a woman who had been missing from her home for a year. Not a trace of violence, not a trace of the perpetrator and not a trace of her. She was a housewife and had last been seen at the day-care center where she had left her son and daughter in the morning. Her husband and everyone in her closer circle of acquaintances had an alibi and had been cleared. They agreed that the Crime Squad should investigate further.

Magnus Skarre passed on regards from Ståle Aune—the Crime Squad's resident psychologist—whom he had visited at Ullevål University Hospital. Harry felt a pang of conscience. Ståle Aune was not just his adviser on criminal cases; he was his personal supporter in his fight against alcohol and the closest thing he had to a confidant. It had been more than a week since Aune had been admitted with some vague diagnosis, but Harry had still not overcome his reluctance to enter hospitals. Tomorrow, Harry thought. Or Thursday.

"We have a new officer," Gunnar Hagen announced. "Katrine Bratt."

A young woman in the first row stood up unbidden, but without offering a smile. She was very attractive. Attractive without trying, thought Harry. Thin, almost wispy hair hung lifelessly down both sides of her face, which was finely chiseled and pale and wore the same serious, weary features Harry had seen on other stunning women who had become so used to being observed that they had stopped liking or disliking it. Katrine Bratt was dressed in a blue suit that underlined her femininity, but the thick black tights below the hem of her skirt and her practical winter boots invalidated any possible suspicions that she was playing on it. She let her eyes run over the gathering, as if she had risen to see them and not vice versa. Harry guessed that she had planned both the suit and this little first-day appearance at the Police HQ.

"Katrine worked for four years at the Bergen Police HQ, dealing mainly with public-decency offenses, but she also did a stint at the Crime Squad," Hagen continued, looking down at a sheet of paper Harry presumed was her CV. "Law degree from University of Bergen 1999, the police academy and now she's an officer here. For the moment no children, but she's married."

One of Katrine Bratt's thin eyebrows rose imperceptibly, and either Hagen saw this or he thought this last scrap of information was superfluous, because he added, "For those who may be interested . . ."

In the oppressive and telling pause that followed, Hagen seemed to think he had made matters worse; he coughed twice with force and said that those who had not yet signed up for the Christmas party should do so before Wednesday.

Chairs scraped and Harry was already in the corridor when he heard a voice behind him.

"Apparently I belong to you."

Harry turned and looked into Katrine Bratt's face. Wondering how attractive she would be if she made an effort.

"Or you to me," she said, showing a line of even teeth but without letting the smile reach her eyes. "Whichever way you look at it." She spoke Bergen-flavored standard Norwegian with moderately rolled r's, which suggested, Harry wagered, that she was from Fana or Kalfaret or some other solidly middle-class district.

He continued on his way, and she hurried to catch up with him. "Seems the Politioverbetjent forgot to inform you."

She pronounced the word with a slightly exaggerated stress on all the syllables.

"But you should show me around and take care of me for the next few days. Until I'm up and running. Can you do that, do you think?"

Harry eased off a smile. So far he liked her, but of

course he was open to changing his opinion. Harry was always willing to give people another chance to wind up on his blacklist.

"I don't know," he said, stopping by the coffee dispenser. "Let's start with this."

"I don't drink coffee."

"Nevertheless. It's self-explanatory. Like most things here. What are your thoughts on the case of the missing woman?"

Harry pressed the button for Americano, which, in this machine, was as American as Norwegian ferry coffee.

"What about it?" Bratt asked.

"Do you think she's alive?" Harry tried to ask in a casual manner so that she wouldn't realize it was a test.

"Do you think I'm stupid?" she said and watched with undisguised revulsion as the machine coughed and spluttered something black into a white plastic cup. "Didn't you hear the Politioverbetjent say that I worked at the Sexual Offenses Unit for four years?"

"Mm," Harry said. "Dead, then?"

"As a dodo," said Katrine Bratt.

Harry lifted the white cup. He pondered the possibility that he had just been allocated a colleague he might come to appreciate.

Walking home in the afternoon, Harry saw that the snow was gone from the streets, and the light, flimsy flakes whirling through the air were eaten up by the wet sidewalk as soon as they hit the ground. He went into his regular music shop on Akersgata and bought Neil Young's latest even though he had a suspicion it was a stinker.

As he unlocked his apartment he noticed that something was different. Something about the sound. Or perhaps it was the smell. He pulled up sharp at the threshold to the kitchen. The whole of one wall was gone. That is, where early this morning there had been bright flowery wallpaper and plasterboard, he now saw rust-red bricks, gray mortar and grayish-yellow studwork dotted with nail holes. On the floor was the mold man's toolbox and on the countertop a note saying he would be back the following day.

He went into the sitting room and slipped in the Neil Young CD, then glumly took it out again after a quarter of an hour and put on Ryan Adams. The thought of a drink came from nowhere. Harry closed his eyes and stared at the dancing pattern of blood and total blindness. He was reminded of the letter again. The first snow. Toowoomba.

The ringing of the telephone interrupted Ryan Adams's "Shakedown on 9th Street."

A woman introduced herself as Oda, said she was calling from **Bosse** and it was nice to talk to him again. Harry couldn't remember her, but he did remember the TV program. They had wanted him to talk about serial killers, because he was the only Norwegian police officer to have studied with the FBI, and furthermore he had hunted down a genuine serial killer. Harry had been stupid enough to agree. He had

told himself he was doing it to say something important and moderately qualified about people who kill,
not so that he could be seen on the nation's most popular talk show. In retrospect, he was not so sure about
that. But that wasn't the worst aspect. The worst was
that he'd had a drink before going on the air. Harry
was convinced that it had been only one. But on the
program it looked as if it had been five. He had spoken with clear diction; he always did. But his eyes had
been glazed and his analysis sluggish, and he hadn't
managed to draw any conclusions, so the show host
had been forced to introduce a guest who was the new
European flower-arranging champion. Harry had not
said anything, but his body language had clearly
shown what he thought about the flower debate.
When the host, with a surreptitious smile, had asked
how a murder investigator related to flower arranging, Harry had said that wreaths at Norwegian burials
certainly maintained high international standards.
Perhaps it had been Harry's slightly befuddled, non-
chalant style that had drawn laughter from the studio
audience and contented pats on the back from the TV
people after the program. He had "delivered the
goods," they said. And he had joined a small group
of them at Kunstnernes Hus, had been indulged and
had woken up the next day with a body that
screamed, demanded, it had to have more. It was a
Friday and he had continued to drink all weekend.
He had sat at Schrøder's and shouted for beer as they
were flashing the lights to encourage customers to
leave, and Rita, the waitress, had gone over to Harry

and told him that he would be refused admission in the future unless he went now, preferably to bed. On Monday morning Harry had turned up for work at eight on the dot. He had contributed nothing useful to the department, thrown up in the sink after the morning meeting, clung to his office chair, drunk coffee, smoked and thrown up again, but this time in the toilet. And that was the last time he had succumbed; he hadn't touched a drop of alcohol since.

And now they wanted him back on the air.

The woman explained that the topic was terrorism in Arab countries and what turned well-educated middle-class people into killing machines. Harry interrupted her before she was finished.

"No."

"But we would so much like to have you. You are so . . . so . . . rock 'n' roll!" She laughed, with an enthusiasm whose sincerity he could not be sure of, but he recognized her voice now. She had been with them at Kunstnernes Hus that night. She had been good-looking in a boring, young way, had talked in a boring, young way and had eyed Harry hungrily, as though he were an exotic meal she was considering; was he **too** exotic?

"Try someone else," Harry said and hung up. Then he closed his eyes and heard Ryan Adams wondering, "Oh, baby, why do I miss you like I do?"

The boy looked up at the man standing beside him at the kitchen counter. The light from the snow-covered yard shone on the hairless skin drawn tightly around his father's massive skull. Mommy had said that Dad had such a big head because he was such a brain. He had asked her why she said he **was** a brain and not that he **had** a brain, and when she had laughed, she had stroked his forehead and said that was the way it was with physics professors. Right now the brain was rinsing potatoes under the tap and putting them straight into a pan.

"Aren't you going to peel the potatoes, Dad? Mommy usually—"

"Your mother isn't here, Jonas. So we'll have to do it my way."

He hadn't raised his voice, yet there was an irritation that made Jonas cringe. He never quite knew what made his father so angry. Or, now and then, even **whether** he was angry. Until he saw his mother's face with the anxious droop around the corners of her mouth, which seemed to make Dad even more irritable. He hoped she would be there soon.

"We don't use them plates, Dad!"

His father slammed the cupboard door and Jonas bit his bottom lip. His father's face came down to his. The square, paper-thin glasses sparkled.

"It's 'those' plates, not 'them' plates," his father said. "How many times do I have to tell you, Jonas?"

"But Mommy says—"

"Mommy doesn't speak properly. Do you understand? Mommy comes from a place and a family where they're not bothered about language." His father's breath smelled salty, of rotten seaweed.

The front door banged.

"Hello," she sang out from the hall.

Jonas was about to run to her, but his father held him by the shoulder and pointed to the unlaid table.

"How good you are!"

Jonas could hear the smile in her breathless voice as she stood in the kitchen doorway behind him while he set out glasses and cutlery as quickly as he could.

"And what a big snowman you've made!"

Jonas turned in surprise to his mother, who was unbuttoning her coat. She was so attractive. Dark skin, dark hair, just like him, and those gentle, gentle eyes she almost always had. Almost. She wasn't quite as slim as in the photos from the time she and Dad got married, but he had noticed that men looked at her whenever the two of them took a stroll in town.

"We didn't make a snowman," Jonas said.

"You didn't?" His mommy frowned as she unfurled the big pink scarf he had given her for Christmas.

Dad went over to the window. "Must be the neighbors' boys," he said.

Jonas stood up on one of the kitchen chairs and peered out. And, sure enough, there on the lawn in front of the house was a snowman. It was, as his mother had said, big. Its eyes and mouth were made with pebbles and the nose was a carrot. The snowman had no hat, cap or scarf, and only one arm, a thin twig Jonas guessed had been taken from the hedge. However, there was something odd about the snowman. It was facing the wrong way. He didn't know why, but it ought to have been looking out onto the road, toward the open space.

"Why—" Jonas began, but was interrupted by his father.

"I'll talk to them."

"Why's that?" Mommy said from the hall, where Jonas could hear her unzipping her high black leather boots. "It doesn't matter."

"I don't want that sort roaming around our property. I'll do it when I'm back."

"Why isn't it looking out?" Jonas asked.

In the hall, his mother sighed. "When will you be back, love?"

"Tomorrow sometime."

"What time?"

"Why? Have you got a date?" There was a lightness of tone in his father's voice that made Jonas shiver.

"I was thinking I would have dinner ready," Mommy said, coming into the kitchen, going over to the stove, checking the pans and turning up the temperature on two of the burners.

"Just have it ready," his father said, turning to the pile of newspapers on the countertop. "And I'll be home at some point."

"OK." Mommy went over to Dad's back and put her arms around him. "But do you really have to go to Bergen tonight?"

"My lecture's at eight tomorrow morning," Dad said. "It takes an hour to get to the university from the time the plane lands, so I wouldn't make it if I caught the first flight."

Jonas could see from the muscles in his father's neck that he was relaxing, that once again Mommy had managed to find the right words.

"Why is the snowman looking at our house?" Jonas asked.

"Go and wash your hands," Mommy said.

They ate in silence, broken only by Mommy's tiny questions about how school had been and Jonas's brief, vague answers. Jonas knew that detailed answers could evoke unpleasant questions from Dad about what they were learning—or not learning—at the "excuse of a school." Or quick-fire interrogation about someone Jonas mentioned he had been playing with, about what his parents did and where they were from. Questions that Jonas could never answer to his father's satisfaction.

When Jonas was in bed, on the floor below he heard his father say good-bye to his mother, a door close and the car start up outside and fade into the distance. They were alone again. His mother switched on the TV. He thought about something she had asked. Why Jonas hardly ever brought his friends home to play anymore. He hadn't known what to answer; he hadn't wanted her to be sad. But now he became sad instead. He chewed the inside of his cheek, feeling the bittersweet pain extend into his ears, and stared at the metal tubes of the wind chime hanging from the ceiling. He got out of bed and shuffled over to the window.

The snow in the yard reflected enough light for him to make out the snowman down below. It looked alone. Someone should have given it a cap and scarf. And maybe a broomstick to hold. At that moment the moon slid from behind a cloud. The black row of teeth came into view. And the eyes. Jonas automatically sucked in his breath and recoiled two steps. The pebble-eyes were gleaming. And they were not staring into the house. They were looking up. Up here. Jonas drew the curtains and crept back into bed.

3

Cochineal

Harry was sitting on a bar stool in the Palace Grill reading the signs on the walls, the good-natured reminders to clientele not to ask for credit, not to shoot the pianist and to be good or be gone. It was still early evening and the only other customers in the bar were two girls sitting at a table frenetically pressing the buttons of their mobile phones and two boys playing darts with practiced refinement of stance and aim, but poor results. Dolly Parton, who Harry knew had been brought back in from the cold by arbiters of good country-and-western taste, was whining over the loudspeakers with her nasal Southern accent. Harry checked his watch again and had a wager with himself that Rakel Fauke would be standing at the door at exactly seven minutes past eight. He felt the crackle of tension he always did at seeing her again. He told himself it was just a conditioned response, like Pavlov's dogs starting to salivate when they heard the bell for food, even when there wasn't any. And they wouldn't be having food this evening. That is, they would be having food, but **only** food. And a cozy chat about the lives they were leading now. Or, to be more precise: the life she was leading now. And about Oleg, the son she had had with her Russian ex-husband, from when she had been working at the Norwegian embassy in Moscow. The boy with the closed, wary nature whom Harry had reached, the boy with whom he had gradually developed bonds that in many ways were stronger than those Oleg had with his own father. And when Rakel had, in the end, been unable to tolerate any more and had left, he didn't know whose loss had been greater. But now he knew. For now it was seven minutes past eight and she was standing by the door with that erect posture of hers, the arch of her back he could feel on his fingertips and the high cheekbones under the glowing skin he could feel against his. He had hoped she wouldn't look so good. So **happy.**

She walked over to him and their cheeks touched. He made sure he let go first.

"What are you looking at?" she asked, unbuttoning her coat.

"You know," Harry said, and heard that he should have cleared his throat first.

She chuckled, and the laughter had the same effect on him as the first swig of Jim Beam; he felt warm and relaxed.

"Don't," she said.

He knew exactly what her "Don't" meant. Don't start, don't be embarrassing, we're not going there.

She had said it softly, it was practically inaudible, yet it felt like a stinging slap.

"You're thin," she said.

"So they say."

"The table . . ."

"The waiter will come and get us."

She sat down on the stool opposite him and ordered an aperitif. Campari, it went without saying. Harry used to call her "Cochineal" after the natural pigment that gave the spicy, sweet wine its characteristic color. Because she liked to dress in bright red. Rakel had herself claimed that she used it as a warning, the way animals use strong colors to tell others to keep their distance.

Harry ordered another Coke.

"Why are you so thin?" she asked.

"Fungus."

"What?"

"Apparently it's eating me up. Brain, eyes, lungs, concentration. Sucking out colors and memory. The fungus is growing, I'm disappearing. It's becoming me, I'm becoming it."

"What are you babbling on about?" she exclaimed with a grimace meant to denote disgust, but Harry caught the smile in her eyes. She liked to hear him talking, even when it was just gobbledygook. He told her about the mold in his apartment.

"How are you doing?" Harry asked.

"Fine. I'm good. Oleg's fine. But he misses you."

"Has he said that?"

"You know he has. You should keep tabs on him better."

"Me?" Harry looked at her, dumbfounded. "It wasn't my decision."

"So?" she said, taking the drink from the bartender. "Just because you and I are not together doesn't mean that you and Oleg don't have an important relationship. For you both. Neither of you finds it easy to commit to people, so you should nurture the relationships you do have."

Harry sipped his Coke. "How's Oleg getting on with your doctor?"

"His name's Mathias," Rakel said with a sigh. "They're working on it. They're . . . different. Mathias tries hard, but Oleg doesn't exactly make it easy for him."

Harry experienced a sweet tingle of satisfaction.

"Mathias works long hours as well."

"I thought you didn't like your men working," Harry replied, and regretted it the moment he had said it. But instead of getting angry, Rakel sighed sadly.

"It wasn't the long hours, Harry. You were obsessed. You **are** your job, and what drives you isn't love or a sense of responsibility. It's not even personal ambition. It's anger. And the desire for revenge. And that's not right, Harry—it shouldn't be like that. You know what happened."

Yes, thought Harry. I allowed the disease to enter your house as well.

He cleared his throat. "But your doctor is driven by . . . the right things, then?"

"Mathias used to do the night shift at the emergency room. Voluntarily. At the same time as lecturing full-time at the Anatomy Department."

"And he's a blood donor and a member of Amnesty International."

"B negative is a rare blood group, Harry. And you also support Amnesty—I know that for a fact."

She stirred her drink with an orange plastic stick that had a horse on top. The red mixture swirled around the ice cubes. Cochineal.

"Harry?" she said.

Something in her inflection made him tense up.

"Mathias is going to move in with me. Over Christmas."

"So soon?" Harry ran his tongue over his palate in an attempt to find moisture. "You haven't known each other for long."

"Long enough. We're planning to get married in the summer."

Magnus Skarre studied the hot water running over his hands and into the sink. Where it disappeared. No. Nothing disappeared—it was just somewhere else. Like these people about whom he had spent the past few weeks collecting information. Because Harry had asked him. Because Harry had said there might be something in it. And he had wanted Magnus's report before the weekend. Which meant that

Magnus had been obliged to work overtime. Even though he knew that Harry gave them jobs like this to keep them busy in these feet-on-desk times. The uniformed division's tiny Missing Persons Unit of three refused to delve into old cases; they had more than enough to do with the new ones.

In the deserted corridor on his way back to his office Magnus noticed that the door was ajar. He knew he had closed it, and it was past nine, so the cleaners had finished long before. Two years ago they had had problems with thieving from the offices. Magnus Skarre pulled the door open with a vengeance.

Katrine Bratt was standing in the middle of the room and glanced at him with a furrowed brow, as if it were he who had burst into her office. She turned her back on him.

"I just wanted to see," she said, casting her eyes over the walls.

"See what?" Skarre looked around. His office was like all the others except that it didn't have a window.

"This was his office, wasn't it?"

Skarre frowned. "What do you mean?"

"Hole's. This was his office for all those years. Even while he was investigating the serial killings in Australia?"

Skarre shrugged. "I think so. Why?"

Katrine Bratt ran a hand over the desktop. "Why did he change offices?"

Magnus walked around her and plopped down on the swivel chair. "It hasn't got any windows."

"And he shared the office, first with Ellen Gjelten

and then Jack Halvorsen," Katrine Bratt said. "And both were killed."

Magnus Skarre put his hands behind his head. This new officer had class. A league or two above him. He bet her husband was the boss of something or other and had money. Her suit seemed expensive. But when he looked at her a bit closer, there was a little flaw somewhere. A slight blemish he couldn't quite put his finger on.

"Do you think he heard their voices? Was that why he moved?" Bratt asked, scrutinizing a wall map of Norway on which Skarre had circled the hometowns of all the missing persons in Østland, eastern Norway, since 1980.

Skarre laughed but didn't answer. Her waist was slim and her back willowy. He knew she knew he was ogling her.

"What's he like, actually?" she asked.

"Why do you ask?"

"I suppose everyone with a new boss does, don't they?"

She was right. It was just that he had never thought of Harry Hole as a boss, not in that way. OK, he gave them jobs to do and led investigations, but beyond that all he asked was that they keep out of his way.

"He is, as you probably know, somewhat infamous," Skarre said.

She shrugged. "I've heard about his alcoholism, yes. And that he has reported colleagues. And that all the heads wanted him booted out, but the previous POB protected him."

"His name was Bjarne Møller," Skarre said, looking at the map, at the ring around Bergen. That was where Møller had been seen last, before he disappeared.

"And that people at HQ don't like the media turning him into a kind of pop idol."

Skarre chewed his lower lip. "He's a damn good detective. That's enough for me."

"You like him?" Bratt asked.

Skarre grinned. He turned and looked straight into her eyes.

"Like, dislike," he said. "I don't think I could say one or the other."

He pushed back his chair, put his feet on the desk, stretched and gave a semi-yawn. "What are you working on so late at night?"

It was an attempt to gain the upper hand. After all, she was only a low-ranking detective. And new.

But Katrine Bratt just smiled as if he had said something funny, walked out the door and was gone.

Disappeared. Speaking of which. Skarre cursed, sat up in the chair and went back to his computer.

Harry woke up and lay on his back, staring at the ceiling. How long had he been asleep? He turned and looked at the clock on his bedside table. A quarter to four. The dinner had been an ordeal. He watched Rakel's mouth speaking, drinking wine, chewing meat and devouring him as she told him about how she and Mathias were going to Botswana for a couple of years; the government had a good setup there to fight HIV but was short of doctors. She asked whether he was seeing anyone. And he answered that he had seen his childhood pals Øystein and Tresko. The former was an alcoholic, taxi-driving computer freak; the latter an alcoholic gambler who would have been the world poker champion if he had been as good at maintaining his own poker face as he was at reading others'. He even began to tell her about Tresko's fatal defeat in the world championships in Las Vegas before he realized he had told her before. And it wasn't true that he had seen them. He hadn't seen anyone.

He noticed the waiter pouring booze into the glasses on the adjacent table and for one crazy moment he thought about tearing the bottle out of his hands and putting it to his mouth. Instead he agreed to take Oleg to a concert the boy had begged Rakel to let him see. Slipknot. Harry had omitted telling her what kind of band she was letting loose on her son, since he fancied seeing Slipknot himself. Even though bands with the obligatory death rattle, satanic symbols and speeded-up bass drum usually made him laugh, Slipknot was in fact interesting.

Harry threw off the duvet now and went into the kitchen, let the water from the tap run cold, cupped his hands and drank. He had always thought water tasted better like that, drunk from his own hands, off his own skin. Then he suddenly let the water run into the sink again and stared at the black wall. Had he seen anything? Something moving? No, not a thing,

just movement itself, like the invisible waves underwater that caress the sea grass. Over dead fibers, fingers so thin that they can't be seen, spores that rise at
the smallest movement of air and settle in new areas
and begin to eat and suck. Harry switched on the
radio in the sitting room. It had been decided.
George W. Bush had been given another term in the
White House.

Harry went back to bed and pulled the duvet over
his head.

Jonas was awoken by a sound and lifted the duvet off
his face. At least he thought it had been a sound. A
crunching sound, like sticky snow underfoot in the
silence between the houses on a Sunday morning. He
must have been dreaming. But sleep would not return even when he closed his eyes. Instead fragments
of the dream came back to him. Dad had been standing motionless and silent in front of him with a reflection in his glasses that lent them an impenetrable,
icelike surface.

It must have been a nightmare, because Jonas was
scared. He opened his eyes again and saw that the
chimes hanging from the ceiling were moving. Then
he jumped out of bed, opened the door and ran
across the corridor. By the stairs to the ground floor
he managed to stop himself, looking down into the
darkness, then didn't pause again until he was in
front of his parents' bedroom and pressing down the
handle with infinite caution. Then he remembered

that his dad was away, and he would wake his mom whatever he did. He slipped inside. A white square of moonlight extended across the floor to the undisturbed double bed. The numbers on the digital alarm clock were lit up: 1:11. For a moment Jonas stood there, bewildered.

Then he went out into the corridor. He walked toward the staircase. The darkness of the stairs lay there waiting for him, like a vast open void. Not a sound could be heard from down below.

"Mommy!"

He regretted shouting the moment he heard his own terror in the brief, harsh echo. For now **it** knew, too. The darkness.

There was no answer.

Jonas swallowed. Then he began to tiptoe down the stairs.

On the third step down he felt something wet under his feet. The same on the sixth. And the eighth. As if someone had been walking with wet shoes. Or wet feet.

In the living room the light was on, but there was no Mommy. He went to the window to look at the Bendiksens' house. Mommy occasionally went over to see Ebba. But all the windows were dark.

He walked into the kitchen and over to the telephone, successfully keeping his thoughts at bay, not letting the darkness in. He dialed his mother's mobile phone number. And was jubilant to hear her soft voice. But it was a message asking him to leave his name and wishing him a nice day.

And it wasn't day, it was night.

On the porch he stuffed his feet into a pair of his father's large shoes, put on a padded jacket over his pajamas and went outside. Mom had said the snow would be gone by tomorrow, but it was still cold, and a light wind whispered and mumbled in the oak tree by the gate. It was no more than a hundred yards to the Bendiksens' house, and fortunately there were two streetlamps on the way. She had to be there. He glanced to the left and to the right to make sure there was no one who could stop him. Then he caught sight of the snowman. It stood there as before, immovable, facing the house, bathed in the cold moonlight. Yet there was something different about it, something almost human, something familiar. Jonas looked at the Bendiksens' house. He decided to run. But he didn't. Instead he stood feeling the tentative, ice-cold wind go right through him. He turned slowly back to the snowman. Now he realized what it was that had made the snowman so familiar. It was wearing a scarf. A pink scarf. The scarf Jonas had given his mother for Christmas.

4

The Disappearance

By the middle of the day the snow had melted in Oslo city center. But in Hoff there were still patches on lawns on both sides of the road as Harry Hole and Katrine Bratt drove along. On the radio Michael Stipe was singing about a sinking feeling, about what was bringing it on, knowing that something had gone wrong and about the boy in the well. In the middle of a quiet estate on an even quieter street Harry pointed to a shiny silver Toyota Corolla parked by the fence.

"Skarre's car. Park behind him."

The house was large and yellow. Too big for a family of three, Harry thought as they walked up the gravel path. Everything around them dripped and sighed. On the lawn stood a snowman with a slight list and poor future prospects.

Skarre opened the door. Harry bent down to study the lock.

"No signs of a break-in anywhere," Skarre said.

He led them into the living room, where a boy was sitting on the floor with his back to them watching a cartoon channel on TV. A woman got up off the sofa, shook hands with Harry and introduced herself as Ebba Bendiksen, a neighbor.

"Birte has never done this type of thing before," she said. "Not as long as I've known her, anyway."

"And how long's that?" Harry asked, looking around. In front of the TV were large pieces of heavy leather furniture and an octagonal coffee table of darkened glass. The tubular steel chairs around the dining table were light and elegant, the type Rakel liked. Two paintings hung on the walls, both portraits of bank-manager-like men staring down at him with solemn authority. Beside them, modernist abstract art of the kind that had succeeded in becoming unmodern and so very modern again.

"Ten years," said Ebba Bendiksen. "We moved into our house across the road the day Jonas was born." She nodded toward the boy, who was still motionless, staring at careering birds and exploding coyotes.

"I understand it was you who called the police last night?"

"Yes, that's right."

"The boy rang the bell at about a quarter past one," Skarre said, looking down at his notes. "Police were phoned at one-thirty."

"My husband and I went back with Jonas and searched the house first," Ebba Bendiksen explained.

"Where did you look?" Harry asked.

"In the cellar. In the bathrooms. In the garage. Everywhere. It's very odd that anyone would do a runner like that."

"Do a runner?"

"Disappear. Vanish. The policeman I spoke to on the phone asked if we could take care of Jonas, and said we should call everyone Birte knew and who she might be staying with. And then wait until early today to find out if Birte had gone to work. In eight out of ten cases, he explained, the missing person reappeared after a few hours. We tried to get hold of Filip—"

"The husband," Skarre interjected. "He was in Bergen lecturing. He's a professor of something or other."

"Physics." Ebba Bendiksen smiled. "However, his mobile phone was switched off. And we didn't know the name of the hotel where he was staying."

"He was contacted in Bergen this morning," Skarre said. "He should be here soon."

"Yes, thank God," Ebba said. "So when we called Birte's workplace this morning and she hadn't turned up at the customary time, we called you back."

Skarre nodded in confirmation. Harry signaled that Skarre could continue his conversation with Ebba Bendiksen, went over to the TV and sat down on the floor beside the boy. On the screen, a coyote was lighting the fuse on a stick of dynamite.

"Hello, Jonas. My name's Harry. Did the other policeman tell you that things like this almost always turn out fine? People disappear and then they turn up of their own accord?"

The boy shook his head.

"But they do," Harry said. "If you had to guess, where do you think your mother would be now?"

The boy shrugged. "I don't know where she is."

"I know you don't know, Jonas. None of us does right now. But what's the first place that would occur to you if she wasn't here or at work? Don't think about whether it's likely or not."

The boy didn't answer, just stared at the coyote desperately trying to throw away the stick of dynamite that had got stuck to his hand.

"Is there a cabin or something like that where you go?"

Jonas shook his head.

"A special place where she likes to go if she wants to be on her own?"

"She doesn't want to be on her own," Jonas said. "She wants to be with me."

"Just with you?"

The boy turned and looked at Harry. Jonas had brown eyes, like Oleg. And in the brown Harry saw the horror he had been expecting and the anger he had not.

"Why did they go?" the boy asked. "The ones who come back?"

Same eyes, Harry thought. Same questions. The important ones.

"For all sorts of reasons," Harry said. "Some got

lost. There are various ways of getting lost. And some only needed a break and went off to get some peace."

The front door slammed and Harry saw the boy start.

At that moment the dynamite exploded in the coyote's hand, and behind them the living-room door opened.

"Hello," a voice said. Sharp and controlled at the same time. "What's the latest?"

Harry turned in time to see a man of around fifty wearing a suit stride toward the coffee table and pick up the remote control. The next moment the TV picture imploded to a white dot as the set hissed in protest.

"You know what I've said about watching TV during the day, Jonas," he said with a resigned tone, as if to tell the others in the room what a hopeless job raising children was nowadays.

Harry stood up and introduced himself, Magnus Skarre and Katrine Bratt, who until now had merely stood by the door observing.

"Filip Becker," the man said, pushing his glasses although they were already high up his nose. Harry tried to catch his eye, to form the crucial first impression of a potential suspect, should it ever come to that. But his eyes were hidden behind the reflection from his glasses.

"I've spent my time calling everyone who might conceivably have been in contact, but no one knows anything," Filip Becker said. "What do you know?"

"Nothing," said Harry. "But the first thing you can

do to help us is to find out if any suitcases or clothes are missing, so that we can formulate a theory." Harry studied Becker before continuing. "As to whether this disappearance is spontaneous or planned."

Becker returned Harry's searching gaze before nodding and going upstairs.

Harry crouched down beside Jonas, who was still staring at the black TV screen.

"So you like roadrunners, do you?" Harry asked.

The boy shook his head mutely.

"Why not?"

Jonas's whisper was barely audible: "I feel sorry for Wile E. Coyote."

Five minutes later Becker came back down and said that nothing was missing, neither travel bags nor clothing, apart from what she was wearing when he left, plus her coat, boots and a scarf.

"Mm." Harry scratched his unshaven chin and glanced across at Ebba Bendiksen. "Can you and I go into the kitchen, Herr Becker?"

Becker led the way, and Harry signaled to Katrine to join them. In the kitchen the professor immediately began to spoon coffee into a filter and pour water into the machine. Katrine stood by the door while Harry went over to the window and looked out. The snowman's head had sunk between its shoulders.

"When did you leave last night and which flight did you take to Bergen?" Harry asked.

"I left at around nine-thirty," Becker said without hesitation. "The plane took off at eleven-oh-five."

"Did you have any contact with Birte after leaving home?"

"No."

"What do you think could have happened?"

"I have no idea, Inspector. I really don't."

"Mm." Harry glanced out into the street. Since they had been there, he hadn't heard a single car pass. A really quiet neighborhood. The peace and quiet alone probably cost half a million in this area of town. "What sort of marriage do you and your wife have?"

Harry heard Filip Becker stop what he was doing, and he added, "I have to ask because spouses do sometimes simply get up and leave."

Filip Becker cleared his throat. "I can assure you that my wife and I have a perfectly good marriage."

"Have you considered that she may be having an affair, unbeknownst to you?"

"That's out of the question."

"'Out of the question' is pretty strong, Herr Becker. And extramarital relationships are pretty common."

Filip Becker gave a weak smile. "I'm not naïve, Inspector. Birte's an attractive woman and a good deal younger than I. And she comes from a relatively liberal family, it has to be said. But she's not the type. And I have a relatively good perspective on her activities, if I may put it like that."

The coffee machine rumbled ominously as Harry opened his mouth to pursue the point. He changed his mind.

"Have you noticed any mood changes in your wife?"

"Birte is not depressed, Inspector. She has not gone into the forest and hanged herself or thrown herself into the lake. She's out there somewhere, and she's alive. I've read that people disappear all the time, and then they turn up again with a natural and fairly banal explanation. Isn't that so?"

Harry nodded slowly. "Would you mind if I had a look around the house?"

"Why's that?"

There was a brusqueness to Filip Becker's question that made Harry think he was a man who was used to being in control. To being kept informed. And that argued against his wife having left without a word. Which, for that matter, Harry had already excluded in his mind. Well-adjusted, healthy mothers do not abandon ten-year-old sons in the middle of the night. And then there was all the rest. Usually they used minimal resources at such an early stage of a missing-persons case, unless there were indications that suggested something criminal or dramatic. It was "all the rest" that had made him drive up to Hoff himself.

"Sometimes you don't know what you're looking for until you find it," Harry answered. "It's a methodology."

He caught Becker's eyes behind the glasses now. They were, unlike his son's, light blue and shone with an intense, clear gleam.

"By all means," Becker said. "Go ahead."

The bedroom was chilly, aroma-free and tidy. On the double bed was a crocheted quilt. On one bedside table a photograph of an elderly woman. The similarity led Harry to assume this side of the bed was Filip Becker's. On the other bedside table was a photograph of Jonas. There was a faint scent of perfume in the wardrobe containing ladies' clothing. Harry checked that the corners of the clothes hangers hung with equal distance from one another, as they would if they had been allowed to hang undisturbed for a while. Black dresses with slits, short sweaters with pink motifs and glitter. At the bottom of the wardrobe there was a drawer section. He pulled out the top drawer. Underwear. Black and red. Next drawer. Garter belts and stockings. Third drawer. Jewelry placed in holes in bright red felt. He noticed a large gaudy ring with precious stones that glittered and sparkled. Everything here was a bit Vegas. There were no empty gaps in the felt.

The bedroom had a door leading into a newly decorated bathroom with a steam shower and two steel washstands.

In Jonas's room, Harry sat down on a small chair by a small desk. On the desk there was a calculator with a series of advanced mathematical functions. It looked new and unused. Above the desk there was a poster with a picture of seven dolphins inside a wave and a calendar for the whole year. Several of the dates were circled and had tiny reminders added. Harry noted birthdays for Mommy and Grandpa, vacation in Denmark, dentist at ten o'clock and two July dates with DOCTOR above. But Harry didn't see any football matches, trips to the movies or birthday parties. He caught sight of a pink scarf lying on the bed. A color no boy of Jonas's age would be seen dead wearing. Harry lifted the scarf. It was damp, but he could still smell the distinctive fragrance of skin, hair and feminine perfume. The same perfume as in the wardrobe.

He went back downstairs. Stopped outside the kitchen and listened to Skarre holding forth on procedures regarding missing-persons cases. There was a clink of coffee cups inside. The sofa in the living room seemed enormous, perhaps because of the slight figure sitting there reading a book. Harry went closer and saw a photo of Charlie Chaplin in full regalia. Harry sat down beside Jonas.

"Did you know that Chaplin was a sir?" Harry asked. "Sir Charlie Chaplin."

Jonas nodded. "But they chucked him out of the U.S.A."

Jonas flicked through the book.

"Were you ill this summer, Jonas?"

"No."

"But you went to the doctor's. Twice."

"Mom wanted to have me examined. Mom . . ." His voice suddenly failed him.

"She'll be back soon, you'll see," Harry said, putting a hand on his narrow shoulders. "She didn't take her scarf with her, did she? The pink one on your bed."

"Someone hung it around the snowman's neck," Jonas said. "I brought it in."

"Your mother didn't want the snowman to freeze, then."

"She would never have given her favorite scarf to the snowman."

"Then it must have been your dad."

"No, someone did it after he left. Last night. The person who took Mom."

Harry nodded slowly. "Who made the snowman, Jonas?"

"I don't know."

Harry looked through the window to the yard. This was the reason he had come. An ice-cold draft seemed to run through the wall and the room.

Harry and Katrine drove down Sørkedalsveien toward Majorstuen.

"What was the first thing that struck you when we went in?" Harry asked.

"That the couple living there were not exactly soul mates," Katrine said, steering through the tollbooth without braking. "It may have been an unhappy marriage, and if so, she was the one who suffered more."

"Mm. What made you think that?"

"It's obvious." Katrine smiled, glancing in the mirror. "Clash of taste."

"Explain."

"Didn't you see the dreadful sofa and the coffee

table? Typical eighties style bought by men in the nineties. While she chose a dining table in white oiled oak with aluminum legs. And Vitra."

"Vitra?"

"Dining-room chairs. Swiss. Expensive. So expensive that with what she could have saved by buying slightly more reasonably priced copies, she could have changed all the damn furniture."

Harry noticed that "damn" didn't sound like a regular swear word in Katrine Bratt's mouth; it was a linguistic counterpoint that merely underlined her class affiliation.

"Meaning?"

"That big house, at that Oslo address, means it's not money that's the problem. She isn't **allowed** to change his sofa and table. And when a man with no taste, or no apparent interest in interior design, does that kind of thing, it tells me something about who dominates whom."

Harry nodded, mostly as a marker for himself. Her first impression had not been mistaken. Katrine Bratt was good.

"Tell me what **you** think," she said. "It's me who should be learning here."

Harry looked out the window at the old, traditional, though never particularly venerable café Lepsvik.

"I don't think Birte Becker left the house of her own free will," he said.

"Why not? There were no signs of violence."

"Because it was well planned."

"And who's the guilty party? The husband? It's always the husband, isn't it?"

"Yes," said Harry, aware his mind was wandering. "It's always the husband."

"Except that this one had gone to Bergen."

"Looks like it, yes."

"On the last plane, so he couldn't have come back and still managed to catch the first lecture." Katrine accelerated and raced across the Majorstuen intersection on yellow. "Had Filip Becker been guilty he would have taken the bait you set for him anyway."

"Bait?"

"Yes. The bit about her mood swings. You suggested to Becker that you suspected suicide."

"And so?"

She laughed. "Come on, Harry. Everyone, including Becker, knows that the police don't commit resources to a case resembling suicide. In a nutshell, you gave him the chance to espouse a theory that, if he'd been guilty, would have solved most of his problems. However, he replied that she was as happy as a lark."

"Mm. So you think the question was a test?"

"You test people all the time, Harry. Including me."

Harry didn't answer until they were well down Bogstadveien.

"People are often smarter than you think," he said, and then said nothing until they were in the Police HQ parking lot.

"I have to work on my own for the rest of the day."

And he said that because he had been thinking about the pink scarf and had come to a conclusion. That he urgently needed to go through Skarre's missing-persons report and he urgently needed to have his nagging suspicion confirmed. And if it was what he feared, he would have to go to POB Gunnar Hagen with the letter. That damn letter.

5

The Totem Pole

When William Jefferson Blythe III came into the world on August 19, 1946, in the little town of Hope, Arkansas, exactly three months had passed since the death of his father in a traffic accident. Four years later William's mother remarried and William took his new father's surname. And on a November night in 1992, forty-six years after his birth, white confetti fell like snow onto the streets of Hope in celebration of their own hope and hometown boy, William—or just Bill—Clinton, after he had been elected America's forty-second president. The snow falling on Bergen that same night did not reach the streets but melted in the air, as usual, and turned to rain over the town. This had been happening since mid-September. But as the following morning unfolded there was a nice sprinkling of sugar on top of the seven peaks guarding this beautiful town. And Inspector Gert Rafto had already arrived on the highest of them, Ulriken. He was breathing in the mountain air with a shiver, hunching up his shoulders around his broad head, his face so covered with folds of skin that it seemed to have been punctured.

The yellow cable car that had brought him and three Crime Scene officers from Bergen Police HQ up the 2,110 feet above the town was swaying gently from the solid steel wires, waiting. The service had been discontinued as soon as the first tourists who had dismounted onto the popular mountaintop that morning had sounded the alarm.

"Out and about," one of the crime scene officers let slip.

The town's tourism slogan had become such a parody of Bergen Norwegian that Bergensians had almost stopped using it. But in situations where fear prevails, your innermost lexicon takes over.

"Yes, out and about," Rafto repeated sarcastically, his eyes shining from behind the pancake batter of skin folds.

The body lying in the snow had been cut into so many pieces that it was only thanks to a naked breast that they had been able to determine the gender. The rest reminded Rafto of a traffic accident in Eidsvågneset the year before, when a truck coming around a bend too fast had lost its load of aluminum sheeting and had literally sliced up an oncoming car.

"The killer murdered her and carved her up right here," one of the officers said.

The information seemed somewhat superfluous to Rafto since the snow around the body was spattered with blood and the thick streaks to the side suggested that at least one artery had been cut while the heart was still beating. He made a mental note to find out when it had stopped snowing last night. The last cable car had left at five in the afternoon. Of course, the victim and the killer may have taken the path that wound up beneath the cable cars. Or they could have taken the Fløyen funicular up to Fjelltoppen beside it and walked from there. But they were demanding walks and his gut instinct told him: cable car.

There were two sets of footprints in the snow. The small prints were undoubtedly the woman's, even though there was no sign of her shoes. And the others had to be the killer's. They led to the path.

"Big boots," said the young technician, a hollow-cheeked coastal man from Sotra. "At least size thirteen. Guy must have been pretty beefy."

"Not necessarily," Rafto said, sniffing the air. "The print is uneven and yet the ground here is flat. That suggests the man's foot is smaller than his boot. Perhaps he was trying to fool us."

Rafto felt everyone's eyes on him. He knew what they were thinking. There he went again, trying to dazzle, the star of bygone times, the man the media had adored: big mug, hard face and driving energy to match. In short, a man made for headlines. But at some point he had become too grand for them, for all of them, the press and his colleagues. Indirect jibes had begun to circulate that Gert Rafto was thinking only about himself and his place in the limelight, that in his egotism he was treading on a few too many toes and over a few too many dead bodies. But he hadn't taken any notice. They didn't have anything on him. Not much, anyway. The odd trinket had disappeared from the crime scenes. A piece of jewelry or a watch belonging to the deceased, things you assumed no one would miss. But one day one of Rafto's colleagues had been searching for a pen and had opened a drawer in his desk. At least that was what he said. And found three rings. Rafto had been summoned to the POB and had explained himself, and had been told to keep his mouth shut and his fingers to himself. That was all. But the rumors had started. Even the media had picked up on it. So perhaps it was not so surprising that when charges of police brutality were leveled against the station, there was one man against whom concrete evidence was soon found. The man who was made for headlines.

Gert Rafto was guilty of the accusations; no one was in any doubt about that. But everyone knew that the inspector had been made a scapegoat for a culture that had permeated the Bergen police for many years. Just because he had signed a number of reports on prisoners—most of them child molesters and dope dealers—who had fallen down the ancient iron stairs to the remand cells and bruised themselves here and there.

The newspapers had been remorseless. The nickname they had given him, "Iron" instead of "Gert," was not exactly original, but nonetheless appropriate. A journalist had interviewed several of his long-standing enemies on both sides of the law and of course they had taken the opportunity to settle old scores. So when Rafto's daughter came home crying from school, saying she was being teased, his wife had said enough was enough, he couldn't expect her to sit and watch while he dragged the whole family through the mud. As so often before, he had lost his temper. Afterward she had taken their daughter with her, and this time she didn't return.

It had been a tough period, but he had never forgotten who he was. He was Iron Rafto. And when the quarantine period was over, he had gone for broke, worked day and night to regain lost ground. But no one was in a forgiving mood, the wounds were too deep, and he noticed the internal resistance to letting him succeed. Of course they didn't want him to shine again and remind them and the media of what they were so desperately trying to put behind them: photographs of battered bodies in handcuffs. But he would show them. Show them that Gert Rafto was not a man to let himself be buried before his time. That the town below belonged to him, not to the social workers, to the cream puffs, to the smooth talkers sitting in their offices with tongues so long they could lick the assholes of both the local politicians and the pinko journalists.

"Take a few snaps and get me an ID," Rafto said to the technician with the camera.

"And who'll be able to identify this?" The young man pointed.

Rafto didn't care for his tone. "Someone has reported or will soon report this woman missing. Just get on with it, junior."

Rafto went up to the peak and looked back across what Bergensians call **vidden**—the plateau. His gaze swept the countryside and stopped at a hill and what seemed to be a person on the summit. But, if so, he wasn't moving. Perhaps it was a cairn? Rafto squinted. He must have been there hundreds of times, walking with his wife and daughter, but he couldn't recall seeing a cairn. He went down to the cable car, spoke to the operator and borrowed his binoculars. Fifteen seconds later he established that it wasn't a cairn, just three large balls of snow that someone must have piled one on top of the other.

Rafto didn't like the sloping district of Bergen known as Fjellsiden, with its oh-so-picturesque, crooked, uninsulated timber houses with stairs and cellars, situated in narrow alleys where the sun never shone. Trendy children of rich parents frequently paid millions to own an authentic Bergen house, then did them up until there wasn't an original splinter left. Here, you no longer heard the sound of children's running feet on the cobblestones; the prices had driven young Bergensian families into the suburbs on the other side of the mountains a long time ago. Now it was as quiet and deserted as a barren row of shops. Nonetheless he had the feeling he was being observed as he stood on the stone steps ringing the bell.

After a while the door opened and a pale, anxious woman's face looked out at him with a startled expression.

"Onny Hetland?" Rafto queried, holding up his ID. "It's about your friend Laila Aasen."

The apartment was tiny and the layout baffling: the bathroom was located behind the kitchen and between the bedroom and living room. Amid the patterned burgundy wallpaper in the living room Onny Hetland had just managed to squeeze a sofa and a green and orange armchair, and on the little floor space that remained there was a pile of weekly magazines and heaps of books and CDs. Rafto stepped over an upturned dish of water and a cat to reach the sofa. Onny Hetland sat on the armchair, fidgeting with her necklace. There was a black crack in the green stone in the pendant. Maybe a flaw. Or perhaps it was meant to be like that.

Onny Hetland had learned about her friend's death early that morning, from Laila's husband, Bastian. But still her face displayed several dramatic changes as Rafto mercilessly spelled out the details.

"Dreadful," whispered Onny Hetland. "Bastian didn't say anything about that."

"That's because we didn't want to publicize it," Rafto said. "Bastian told me you were Laila's best friend."

Onny nodded.

"Do you know what Laila was doing up on Ulriken? Her husband had no idea, you see. He and the children were with his mother in Florø yesterday."

Onny shook her head. It was a firm shake. One that should not have left any doubt. It wasn't the shake that was the problem. It was the hundredth of a second's hesitation before it started. And this hundredth of a second was all Gert Rafto needed.

"This is a murder case, Frøken Hetland. I hope you appreciate the gravity of it and the risk you run by not telling me everything you know."

She shot the policeman with the bulldog face a perplexed look. He smelled prey.

"If you think you're being considerate to her family, you have misunderstood. These things will come out anyway."

She swallowed. She looked frightened, had already looked frightened when she opened the door. So he gave her the final nudge, this actually quite trifling threat that still worked so amazingly well on the innocent as well as the guilty.

"You can tell me now or come to the station for questioning."

Tears welled up in her eyes, and the barely audible voice came from somewhere at the back of her throat. "She was meeting someone there."

"Who?"

Onny Hetland inhaled with a tremble. "Laila told me only the first name and profession. And that it was a secret; no one was to know. Especially not Bastian."

Rafto looked down into his notebook to hide his excitement. "And the first name and profession were?"

He noted down what Onny said. Peered at his pad.

It was a relatively common name. And a relatively common profession. But since Bergen was a relatively small town, he thought this would be enough. He knew with the whole of his being that he was on the right track. And by "the whole of his being" Gert Rafto meant thirty years of police work and a knowledge of humanity based on general misanthropy.

"Promise me one thing," Rafto said. "Don't tell what you have just told me to a soul. Not to anyone in the family. Not to the press. Not even to any other police officers you might talk to. Do you understand?"

"Not to . . . police officers?"

"Definitely not. I'm leading the investigation, and I must have full control over this information. Until I tell you anything different, you know nothing."

At last, thought Rafto, standing outside on the step again. Glass glinted as a window swung open farther along the alley, and again he had the feeling he was being watched. But then so what? Revenge was his. His alone. Gert Rafto buttoned up his coat, hardly noticing the pissing rain as, in silent triumph, he strode down the slippery streets to the Bergen town center.

It was five o'clock in the afternoon, and the rain trickled over Bergen from a sky with a blown gasket. On the desk in front of Gert Rafto was a list of names he had requested from the professional organization. He had started looking for candidates with the right first name. Just three so far. It was only two hours since he had been with Onny Hetland, and Rafto was thinking that soon he would know who had killed Laila Aasen. Case solved in less than twelve hours. And no one could take that away from him—the honor was his, and his alone. Because he was going to inform the press in person. The country's major media had flown in over the mountains and were already besieging the Police HQ. The chief constable had given orders that no details about the body were to be released, but the vultures had already scented a bloodbath.

"There must have been a leak," the chief had said, looking at Rafto, who hadn't answered, or formed the grin that yearned to surface. They were sitting out there now, ready to file their reports. And soon Gert Rafto would be king of the Bergen Police HQ again.

He turned down the radio from which Whitney Houston had insisted all autumn that she would always love you, but before he could lift the telephone, it rang.

"Rafto," he said with irritation, impatient to get going.

"It's me you're looking for."

The voice was what immediately told the discredited detective that this was not just a hoax or a crank. It was cool and controlled with clear, businesslike diction, which excluded the usual nuts and drunks. But there was something else about the voice, too, which he couldn't quite place.

Rafto coughed aloud, twice. Took his time, as if to show that he had not been taken aback. "Who am I talking to?"

"You know."

Rafto closed his eyes and cursed silently and roundly. Damn, damn, damn, the killer was going to turn himself in. And that would not have anywhere near the same impact as if he, Rafto, arrested the perpetrator.

"What makes you think I'm looking for you?" the policeman asked between clenched teeth.

"I just know," said the voice. "And if we can do this my way, you'll get what you want."

"And what do I want?"

"You want to arrest me. And you'll be able to. Alone. Are you listening now, Rafto?"

The officer nodded before he could gather himself to say yes.

"Meet me by the totem pole in Nordnes Park," the voice said. "In exactly ten minutes."

Rafto tried to think. Nordnes Park was by the aquarium; he could get there in under ten minutes. But why meet there, of all places, in a park at the end of a headland?

"So that I can see if you come alone," the voice said, as if in answer to his thoughts. "If I see any other police or you're late, I'll be gone. Forever."

Rafto's brain processed, calculated and drew a conclusion. He would not be able to organize an arrest team in time. He would have to explain in his written report why he had been forced to undertake the arrest on his own. It was perfect.

"OK," said Rafto. "What happens now?"

"I'll tell you everything and give you the conditions for my surrender."

"What sort of conditions?"

"I don't want to wear handcuffs at the trial. The press will not be allowed in. And I serve my time somewhere where I don't have to mix with other prisoners."

Rafto almost choked. "OK," he said, looking at his watch.

"Wait, there are more conditions. TV in my room, all the books I might wish for."

"We'll arrange that," Rafto said.

"When you've signed the deal with my conditions, I'll go with you."

"What about—?" Rafto began, but an accelerated **beep-beep-beep** told him that the other person had hung up.

Rafto parked his car by the Bergen shipyard. It wasn't the shortest route, but it meant he would have a better view of Nordnes when he went in. The big park was on undulating terrain with well-trodden paths and hillocks of yellow withered grass. The trees pointed with black gnarled fingers to heavy clouds sweeping in from the sea behind the island of Askøy. A man hurried away behind a nervous Rottweiler on a taut lead. Rafto felt the Smith & Wesson revolver in his coat pocket as he strode past the Nordnes seawater pool; the empty white basin looked like an oversize bath by the water's edge.

Beyond the bend he could make out the thirty-three-foot-high totem pole, a two-ton gift from Seattle on the occasion of Bergen's nine hundredth anniversary. He could hear his own breathing and the squelch of wet leaves beneath his shoes. It started to rain. Small, pinlike droplets drove into his face.

A solitary figure stood by the totem pole, facing Rafto as if the person had known that Rafto would come from that direction and not the other end.

Rafto squeezed the revolver as he walked the last few steps. Six feet away, he stopped. Pinched his eyes against the rain. It could not be true.

"Surprised?" said the voice he could place only now.

Rafto didn't answer. His brain had started processing again.

"You thought you knew me," the voice said. "But it was just me who knew you. That was how I guessed you would try to do this alone."

Rafto stared.

"It's a game," the voice said.

Rafto cleared his throat. "A game?"

"Yes. You like playing games."

Rafto closed his hand around the stock of the revolver, held it in such a way he could be sure it would not snag on his pocket if he had to draw quickly.

"Why me, particularly?" he asked.

"Because you were the best. I only play against the best."

"You're crazy," Rafto whispered, regretting it immediately.

"Of that," the other said with a tiny smile, "there is little doubt. But you're also crazy, my man. We're all crazy. We're restless spirits that cannot find their way home. It's always been like that. Do you know why the Indians made these?"

The person in front of Rafto banged the knuckle of a gloved index finger against the tree; the carved figures perched on top of one another stared across the fjord with large, blind, black eyes.

"To watch over the souls," the person continued. "So that they don't get lost. But a totem pole rots. And it should rot—that's part of the point. And when it's gone, the soul has to find a new home. Perhaps in a mask. Perhaps in a mirror. Or perhaps in a newborn child."

The sound of hoarse cries came from the penguin run at the aquarium.

"Will you tell me why you killed her?" Rafto said, and noticed that he, too, had gone hoarse.

"Shame the game's over, Rafto. It's been fun."

"And how did you find out that I was on your trail?"

The other person raised a hand, and Rafto automatically stepped back a pace. There was something hanging from it. A necklace. At the end there was a green tear-shaped stone with a black crack. Rafto felt his heart pounding.

"In fact, Onny Hetland wouldn't say anything at first. But she allowed herself . . . how shall I say it? . . . to be persuaded."

"You're lying." Rafto said it without breathing and without conviction.

"She said you instructed her not to tell your colleagues. That was when I knew you would accept my offer and come here alone. Because you thought this would be the new home for your soul, your resurrection. Didn't you."

The cold, thin rain lay like sweat on Rafto's face. He had placed his finger on the trigger of his revolver and concentrated on speaking slowly and with restraint.

"You chose the wrong place. You're standing with your back to the sea and there are police cars on all the roads out of here. No one can escape."

The person facing him sniffed the air. "Can you smell it, Gert?"

"What?"

"Fear. Adrenaline has quite a distinctive smell. But you know all about that. I'm sure you smelled it on the prisoners you beat up. Laila smelled like that, too. Especially when she saw the tools I would use. And Onny even more. Probably because you told her about Laila, so she knew what would happen to her. It's quite a stimulating smell, don't you think? I've read that it's the smell some carnivores use to find their prey. Imagine the trembling victim trying to hide, but knowing that the smell of its own fear will kill it."

Rafto saw the other's gloved hands hanging down, empty. It was broad daylight, close to the center of Norway's second-largest city. Despite his age, after the last years without alcohol he was in good physical shape. His reflexes were fast, and his combat techniques were more or less intact. Drawing the revolver would take a fraction of a second. So why was he so frightened that his teeth were chattering in his mouth?

6

Cellular Phone

Police Officer Magnus Skarre leaned back in his swivel chair and closed his eyes. And the image that immediately appeared to him wore a suit and stood facing the other way. He opened his eyes again in a flash, and checked his watch. Six. He decided that he deserved a break since he had been through the standard procedure for locating missing persons. He had called all the hospitals to hear if they had admitted a Birte Becker. Called two taxi firms, Norgestaxi and Oslo Taxi, and checked the trips they had made near the Hoff address the previous night. Spoken to her bank and received confirmation that she had not taken out large amounts from her account before disappearing, nor were there withdrawals registered for the previous evening or today. The police at Gardermoen Airport had been allowed to see passenger lists for last night, but the only passenger named Becker they found was her husband, Filip, on the Bergen flight. Skarre had also spoken to the ferry companies sailing to Denmark and England, although she could hardly have gone to England if her husband kept her passport and had shown it to them. The ambitious officer had sent the usual security fax to all the hotels in Oslo and Akershus, and finally instructed all operational units, including the patrol cars, in Oslo to keep their eyes peeled.

The only thing left was the question of the mobile phone.

Magnus called Harry and informed him of the situation. The inspector was out of breath, and in the background he heard the shrill twittering of birds. Harry asked a couple of questions about the mobile before hanging up. Then Skarre got up and went into the corridor. The door to Katrine Bratt's office was open and the light was on, but no one was there. He climbed the stairs to the cafeteria on the floor above.

No food was being served, but there was warmish coffee in a thermos and crispbread and jam on a cart by the door. Only four people were sitting in the room, but one of them was Katrine Bratt, at a table by the wall. She was reading documents in a ring binder. In front of her was a glass of water and a lunch box containing two open sandwiches. She was wearing glasses. Thin frames, thin glass—you could hardly see them against her face.

Skarre poured himself some coffee and went over to her table.

"Planned to do some overtime, did you?" he asked, taking a seat.

Magnus Skarre thought he heard a sigh before she looked up from the sheet.

"How I guessed?" He smiled. "Homemade sandwiches. You knew before you left home that our cafeteria would close at five and you would be working late. Sorry, but that's how you get when you're a detective."

"Do you?" she said, without batting an eyelid, as she sought to return to the pages in her file.

"Yep," Skarre said, slurping his coffee and using the occasion to get a good look at her. She was leaning forward and he could see the lace trim of her bra down the front of her blouse. "Take this missing-persons case today. I don't have any information that anyone else hasn't got. Yet I'm sitting here and thinking that she might still be in Hoff. Perhaps she's lying under snow or foliage somewhere. Or perhaps in one of the many small lakes or streams there."

Katrine Bratt didn't answer.

"And do you know why I think that?"

"No," she answered in a monotone, without raising her eyes from the file.

Skarre stretched across the table and placed a mobile phone directly in front of her. Katrine raised her face with a resigned expression.

"This is a mobile phone," he said. "You think, I assume, it's a pretty new invention. But back in April 1973 the father of the mobile phone, Martin Cooper, had the first conversation on one, with his wife at home. And, of course, he had no idea that this invention would become one of the most important ways in which we in the police force can find missing persons. If you want to become an OK detective, you have to listen and learn these things, Bratt."

Katrine removed her glasses and looked at Skarre with a small smile that he liked, but couldn't quite interpret. "I'm all ears."

"Good," said Skarre. "Because Birte Becker is the owner of a mobile phone. And a mobile phone sends out signals that can be picked up by base stations in the area where it is located. Not only when you ring, but in fact when you carry a phone on you. That's why the Americans called it a cellular phone from the very start. Because it is covered by base stations in small areas—in other words, cells. I've checked with Telenor, and the base station covering Høff is still receiving signals from Birte's phone. But we've been through the whole house, and there's no phone. And she could hardly have lost it by the house—that would be too much of a coincidence. Ergo"—Skarre raised his hands like a conjurer after pulling off a trick—"after this coffee I'm going to contact the Incident Room and send out a search party."

"Good luck," Katrine said, passing him the mobile phone and turning the page.

"That's one of Hole's old cases, isn't it?" Skarre said.

"Yes, that's right."

"He thought a serial killer was on the rampage."

"I know."

"Do you? So perhaps you know that he was wrong as well? And it wasn't the first time. He's morbidly obsessed with serial killers, Hole is. He thinks this is the U.S.A. But he still hasn't found his serial killer in this country."

"There have been several serial killers in Sweden. Thomas Quick. John Ausonius. Tore Hedin . . ."

Magnus Skarre laughed. "You've done your homework. But if you'd like to learn a couple of things about proper crime detection, I suggest you and I go for a beer."

"Thank you, I'm not—"

"And maybe a bite to eat. It wasn't a big lunch box." Skarre finally caught her eye and kept it. Her gaze had a strange gleam, as if deep inside there was a fire smoldering. He had never seen a gleam like that before. And he thought he was responsible for it; he had lit the fire and through the conversation he had moved up into her league.

"You could view it as . . . ," he began, and pretended to be searching for the right word. "Training."

She smiled. A broad smile.

Skarre felt his pulse racing; he was hot, thinking he could already feel her body against his, a stockinged knee against his fingertips, the crackle as his hand slid upward.

"What do you want, Skarre? To check out the new skirt in the unit?" Her smile became even broader and the gleam even fiercer. "To fuck her as soon as you can, the way boys spit on the biggest slices of birthday cake so they can enjoy them in peace before the others?"

Magnus Skarre had a feeling his jaw had dropped.

"Let me give you a few well-intentioned tips, Skarre. Keep away from women at work. Don't waste your time drinking coffee in the cafeteria if you think you've got a hot lead. And don't try to tell me you can call the Incident Room. You call Inspector Hole, and he's the one who decides whether a search party will be set up. And then he'll call the Emergency Operations Center, where there are people ready, not just a team from here."

Katrine scrunched up the waxed paper from her sandwiches and lobbed it toward the garbage can behind Skarre. He didn't even need to turn to know that she hadn't missed. She packed her file and stood up, but by then Skarre had managed to collect himself to some degree.

"I don't know what you're imagining, Bratt. You're a married slut who maybe doesn't get enough at home and so you're hoping a guy like me can be bothered . . . can be bothered to . . ." He couldn't find the words. Shit, he couldn't find the words. "I'm just offering to teach you a thing or two, you whore."

Something happened to her face—it was like a curtain being drawn aside to allow him to see into the flames. For a moment he was convinced that she would hit him. But nothing happened. And when she spoke again, he realized that everything had happened in her eyes alone; she hadn't lifted a finger and her voice was totally under control.

"I beg your pardon if I've misunderstood you," she said, although her facial expression suggested she considered that highly improbable. "By the way, Martin Cooper did not call his wife; he called his rival, Joel Engel at Bell Laboratories. Do you think that was to teach him a thing or two, Skarre? Or to brag?"

Skarre watched her leave, watched her suit rubbing against her backside as she wiggled toward the cafeteria door. Shit, the woman was off her rocker! He felt like getting up and throwing something at her. But he knew he would miss. Besides, he didn't want to move; he was afraid his erection was still visible.

Harry felt his lungs pressing against the inside of his ribs. His breathing was beginning to settle. But not his heart, which was running like a hare in his chest. His training clothes were heavy with sweat as he stood at the edge of the forest by the Ekeberg restaurant. The functionalist restaurant built between the wars had once been Oslo's pride and joy, towering above the town on the precipitous ridge face in the east. But as customers had stopped taking the long trip up from the city center to the forest, the place had become unprofitable; it had declined and become a peeling shack for over-the-hill dance fiends, middle-aged drinkers and lonely souls on the lookout for other lonely souls. In the end, they had closed the restaurant. Harry had always liked driving up here above the town's layer of yellow exhaust fumes and running along the network of paths on the steep terrain that provided a challenge and caused the lactic acid to burn in his muscles. He had liked to stop by the crumbling beauty of a restaurant, sitting on the rain-wet, overgrown terrace overlooking the town that had once been his, but which was now emotionally bankrupt, all assets transferred, an ex-lover with new affections.

The town lay below in a hollow with ridges on all sides and a sole retreat via the fjord. Geologists said that Oslo was a dead volcanic crater. And on evenings like this Harry could imagine that the town's lights were perforations in the earth's surface with the glowing lava shining through. From Holmenkollen ski jump, which lay like an illuminated white comma on the ridge on the opposite side of the town, he tried to work out where Rakel's house was.

He thought about the letter. And the telephone call he had just received from Skarre about the signals transmitted by Birte's missing phone. His heart was beating slower now, pumping blood and transmitting calm, regular signals to the brain that there was still life. Like a mobile phone to a base station. Heart, Harry thought. Signal. The letter. It was a sick thought. So why hadn't he already dismissed it? Why was he already calculating how long it would take him to run to the car, drive to Hoff and check which of them was sicker?

Rakel stood by the kitchen window looking across her property to the spruce trees blocking her view of the neighbors. At a local residents' meeting she had suggested that some of the trees might be cut down to let in more light, but the unspoken absence of enthusiasm that greeted her was so obvious that she didn't even ask for a vote. The spruce trees prevented people from looking in, and that was how they liked it on Holmenkollen Ridge. The snow still lay on the ground here, high above the town, where BMWs and Volvos gently threaded their way up through the bends on their way home to electric garage doors and dinners on tables, prepared by fitness-center-slim housewives taking their career breaks with just a little help from nannies.

Even through the solid floors of the wooden house she had inherited from her father, Rakel could hear the music from Oleg's room above. Led Zeppelin and the Who. When she was eleven years old, it would have been unthinkable to listen to music from her parents' generation. But Oleg had been given these CDs by Harry and he played them with genuine love.

She thought about how thin Harry had become, how he had shrunk. Just like her memory of him. It was almost frightening how someone you have been intimate with can fade and vanish. Or perhaps that was why; you had been so close to each other that afterward, when you no longer were, it seemed unreal, like a dream you soon forgot because it had happened only in your head. Perhaps that was why it had been a shock to see him again. To embrace him, to smell his aroma, to hear his voice, not on the telephone, but from a mouth with those strangely soft lips in that hard and ever more lined face of his. To look into those blue eyes with the gleam that varied in intensity as he talked. Just like before.

Yet she was glad it was over, that she had put it behind her. That this man had become a person with whom she would not share her future, a person who would not bring his grubby reality into their lives.

She was better now. Much better. She looked at her watch. He would be here soon. For, unlike Harry, he tended to be on time.

Mathias had suddenly appeared one day. At a garden party under the auspices of the Holmenkollen Residents' Association. He didn't even live in the neighborhood—he had been invited by friends—and he and Rakel had sat talking almost the entire evening. Mostly about her, in fact. And he had listened attentively, a bit like doctors do, she had thought. But then he had called her two days later and asked her whether she would like to see an exhibition at the Henie Onstad Art Center in Høvikodden. Oleg was welcome to join them, because there was a children's exhibition, too. The weather had been terrible, the art mediocre and Oleg fractious. But Mathias had managed to lift the mood with his good humor and acid comments about the artist's talent. And afterward he had driven them home, apologized for his idea and promised with a smile never to take them anywhere ever again. Unless they asked him to, of course. After that Mathias had gone to Botswana for a week. And had called her the evening he came home to ask if they could go out again.

She heard the sound of a car shifting down to

tackle the steep driveway. He drove a Honda Accord of older vintage. She didn't know why, but she liked the idea of that. He parked in front of the garage, never inside. And she liked that, too. She liked the fact that he brought a change of underwear and a toilet kit in an overnight bag he then took away with him the next morning. She liked him asking her when she wanted to see him again and taking nothing for granted. That might change now, of course, but she was ready for it.

He stepped out of the car. He was tall, almost as tall as Harry, and smiled to the kitchen window with his open, boyish face, even though he must have been dead on his feet after the inhumanly long shift. Yes, she was ready for it. For a man who was present, who loved her and prioritized their little trio above everything else. She heard a key being turned in the front door. The key she had given him the previous week. Mathias had looked like one big question mark at first, like a child who had just received a ticket to a chocolate factory.

The door opened, he was inside and she was in his arms. She thought even his woolen coat smelled good. The material was soft and autumn-cold against her cheek, but the secure warmth inside was already radiating out to her body.

"What is it?" He laughed in her hair.

"I've been waiting for this for so long," she whispered.

She closed her eyes, and they stood like that for a while.

She released him and looked up into his smiling face. He was a good-looking man. Better-looking than Harry.

He freed himself, unbuttoned his coat, hung it up and walked over to the slop sink, where he washed his hands. He always did that when he came from the Anatomy Department, where they handled real bodies during the lectures. As indeed Harry always had when he came straight from murder cases. Mathias opened the cupboard under the sink, emptied potatoes from the bag into the kitchen sink and turned on the tap.

"How was your day, darling?"

She thought that most men would have asked about the previous night; after all, he knew she had met Harry. And she liked him for that, too. She talked while looking out the window. Her gaze ran across the spruce trees to the town beneath them, where lights had started to twinkle. He was down there somewhere now. On a hopeless hunt for something he had never found and never would. She felt sorry for him. Sympathy was all that was left. In truth, there had been a moment last night when they were both silent and their eyes had held each other, unable to free themselves right away. It had felt like an electric shock, but it had been over in an instant. Completely over. No lasting magic. She had made her decision. She stood behind Mathias, put her arms around him and rested her head on his broad back.

She could feel muscles and sinews at work under

his shirt as he peeled the potatoes and put them in the saucepan.

"We could do with a couple more," he said.

She became aware of a movement by the kitchen door and turned.

Oleg was standing there looking at them.

"Could you fetch some more potatoes from the cellar?" she said and saw Oleg's eyes darken.

Mathias turned. Oleg was still there.

"I can go," Mathias said, taking the empty bucket from under the sink.

"No," said Oleg, stepping forward two paces. "I'll go."

He took the bucket from Mathias, turned and went out the door.

"What was that about?" Mathias asked.

"He's just a bit frightened of the dark," Rakel sighed.

"I thought so, but why did he go anyway?"

"Because Harry said he should."

"Should do what?"

Rakel shook her head. "The things he's frightened of. And doesn't want to be frightened of. When Harry was here, he used to send Oleg down to the cellar all the time."

Mathias frowned.

Rakel put on a sad smile. "Harry's not exactly a child psychiatrist. And Oleg wouldn't listen to me if Harry had given his opinion first. On the other hand, there are no monsters down there."

Mathias turned a knob on the stove and said in a low voice, "How can you be so sure of that?"

"Mathias?" Rakel laughed. "Were **you** afraid of the dark?"

"Who's talking about **was**?" Mathias grinned mischievously.

Yes, she liked him. This was better. A better life. She liked him, yes she did, she did like him.

Harry pulled up in front of the Beckers' house. He sat in the car staring at the yellow light from the windows spilling onto the yard. The snowman had shrunk to a dwarf. But its shadow still extended to the trees and right over to the picket fence.

Harry got out of the car. The lament of the iron gate made him wince. He knew he ought to have called first; a yard was as much private property as a house was. But he had neither the patience nor the inclination to discuss anything with Professor Becker.

The wet ground was springy. He crouched down. The light reflected off the snowman as if it were matte glass. The thaw during the day had made the tiny snow crystals hook together into larger crystals, but now that the temperature had fallen again, the water vapor had condensed and frozen onto other crystals. The result was that the snow, which had been so fine, white and light this morning, was now coarse, grayish white and packed.

Harry raised his right hand. Clenched his fist. And punched.

The snowman's crushed head rolled off its shoulders and down onto the brown grass.

Harry punched again, this time from above and down through the neck. His fingers formed a claw and bored their way through the snow and found what they were searching for.

He pulled out his hand and held it up triumphantly in front of the snowman, the way Bruce Lee did, to show his adversary the heart he had just torn out of his chest.

It was a red and silver Nokia mobile phone. It was still switched on.

But the feeling of triumph had faded. For he already knew that this was not a breakthrough in the investigation, just a minor scene in a puppet show with someone else pulling invisible strings. It had been too simple. They had been meant to find it.

Harry walked to the front door and rang the bell. Filip Becker opened up. His hair was disheveled and his tie askew. He blinked hard several times as though he had been sleeping.

"Yes," he answered to Harry's question. "That's the kind of phone she's got."

"Could I ask you to call her number?"

Filip Becker disappeared into the house and Harry waited. Suddenly Jonas poked his face out of the porch doorway. Harry was about to say hi, but at that moment the red phone began to play a children's tune: **"Blåmann, blåmann, bukken min."** And

Harry remembered the next line from his school songbook: **Tenk på vesle gutten din.** Think about your little boy.

And he saw Jonas's face light up. Saw the inexorable process of reasoning in the boy's brain, the immediate bewilderment and then the joy of hearing his mother's ringtone fade into intense, naked fear. Harry swallowed. It was a fear he knew all too well.

As Harry let himself into his apartment he could smell the plaster and the sawdust. The plasterboard forming the corridor walls had been taken down and lay piled up on the floor. There were some light stains on the brick wall behind. Harry ran a finger over the white coating that had drifted onto the parquet floor. He put a fingertip into his mouth. It tasted salty. Did mold taste like that? Or was it just salt bloom, the structure sweating? Harry flicked a lighter and leaned over to the wall. Nothing to smell, nothing to see.

When he had gone to bed and was staring into the room's hermetically sealed blackness, he thought about Jonas. And his own mother. About the smell of illness and her face slowly fading into the pillow's whiteness. For days and weeks he had played with Sis, and Dad had gone quiet and everyone had tried to act as if nothing were happening. He thought he could hear a faint rustle outside in the hall. As if the invisible puppet strings were multiplying, lengthening and sneaking around as they consumed the darkness and formed a faint shimmering light that quivered and shook.

7

Hidden Statistics

The frail morning light seeped through the blinds in the POB's office, coating the two men's faces in gray. POB Hagen was listening to Harry with a pensive furrow over bushy black eyebrows that met in the middle. On the huge desk stood a small plinth bearing a white knuckle bone that, according to the inscription, had belonged to the Japanese battalion commander Yoshito Yasuda. In his years at the military academy, Hagen had lectured about this little finger, which Yasuda had cut off in desperation in front of his men during the retreat from Burma in 1944.

It was just a year since Hagen had been brought back to his old employer, the police, to head the Crime Squad, and, as a lot of water had passed under the bridge in the meantime, he listened with relative patience to his veteran inspector holding forth on the theme of missing persons.

"In Oslo alone, more than six hundred people are

reported missing every year. After a couple of hours only a handful of these are not found. As good as none remain missing for more than a couple of days."

Hagen stroked a finger over the hairs on the bridge of his nose. He had to prepare for the budget meeting in the chief constable's office. The theme was cutbacks.

"Most missing persons are escapees from mental institutions or elderly people suffering from dementia," Harry continued. "But even the relatively compos mentis who have run off to Copenhagen or committed suicide are found. Their names appear on passenger lists, they withdraw cash from an ATM or wash up on a beach."

"What's your point?" Gunnar Hagen said, looking at his watch.

"This," Harry said, tossing a yellow file that landed on the POB's desk with a smack.

Hagen leaned forward and flicked through the stapled documents. "My goodness, Harry. You're not normally the report-writing type."

"This is Skarre's work," Harry said, wasting no words. "But the conclusion is mine, and I'll give it to you now, orally."

"Make it brief, please."

Harry stared down at his hands, which he had placed in his lap. His long legs were stretched out in front of the chair. He took a deep breath. He knew that once he had said this out loud, there was no going back.

"Too many people have disappeared," Harry said.

The right half of Hagen's eyebrow shot into the air. "Explain."

"You'll find it on page six. A list of missing women aged between twenty-five and fifty from 1994 until today. Women who in the last ten years have never been found. I've been talking to the Missing Persons Unit, and they agree. It's simply too many."

"Too many in relation to what?"

"In relation to before. In relation to Denmark and Sweden. And in relation to other demographic groups. Married and cohabiting women are hugely overrepresented."

"Women are more independent than they used to be," Hagen said. "Some go their own way, break with the family, go abroad with a man, maybe. That has some bearing on statistics. So?"

"They've become more independent in Denmark and Sweden, too. But they find them again there."

Hagen sighed. "If the figures are so divergent from the norm, as you claim, why has no one discovered this before?"

"Because Skarre's figures are valid for the whole country, and usually the police look only at those missing in their own district. There is a national missing-persons register at Kripos that has eighteen hundred names, but it's for the last fifty years and includes shipwrecks and disasters like the Alexander Kielland oil rig. The point is that no one has looked at countrywide patterns. Not until now."

"Fine, but our responsibility is not for the country, Harry. It's for the Oslo Police District." Hagen smacked both palms down to indicate that the audience was over.

"The problem," Harry said, rubbing his chin, "is that it's come to Oslo."

"What it?"

"Last night I found Birte Becker's mobile phone in a snowman. I don't know quite what it is, boss. But I think we need to find out. Quickly."

"These statistics are interesting," Hagen said, absentmindedly taking Battalion Commander Yasuda's little finger and pressing his thumb into it. "And I also appreciate that this latest disappearance is grounds for concern. But it's not enough. So tell me: What was it that actually made you ask Skarre to write this report?"

Harry looked at Hagen. Then he pulled a dog-eared envelope from his inside pocket and passed it to Hagen.

"This was in my mailbox after I did the TV show at the beginning of September. Until now I had thought it was a madman's work."

Hagen took out the letter, and after reading the six sentences, shook his head at Harry. "The snowman? And what is/are the Murri?"

"That's exactly the point," Harry said. "I'm afraid this is the it."

The POB looked nonplussed.

"I hope I'm wrong," Harry said, "but I think we have some hellishly dark days ahead of us."

Hagen sighed. "What do you want, Harry?"

"I want an investigation team."

Hagen studied Harry. Like most other officers at the Police HQ, he regarded Harry as a self-willed, arrogant, argumentative, unstable alcoholic. Nevertheless, he was glad they were on the same side and that he wouldn't have this man snapping at his heels.

"How many?" he asked at length. "And for how long?"

"Ten detectives. Two months."

"Two weeks?" said Magnus Skarre. "And four people? Is **that** supposed to be a murder investigation?"

He looked around with disapproval at the other three squeezed into Harry's office: Katrine Bratt, Harry Hole and Bjørn Holm from Krimteknisk, the Forensics Unit.

"That's what Hagen's given me," Harry said, tipping back on his chair. "And this is not a murder investigation. For the moment."

"What is it, actually?" Katrine Bratt asked. "For the moment?"

"A missing-persons case," Harry said. "But one that bears a certain similarity to other recent cases."

"Housewives who one day in late autumn suddenly up and run?" asked Bjørn Holm with remnants of the rural Toten dialect he had added to the goods he had removed from the village of Skreia, along with an LP collection consisting of Elvis, hard-core hillbilly, the Sex Pistols, Jason & the Scorchers, three hand-sewn suits from Nashville, an American Bible, a slightly undersize sofa bed and a dining-room suite that had outlived three generations of Holms. All piled up on a trailer and towed to the capital by the last Amazon to roll off the 1970 Volvo assembly line. Bjørn Holm had bought the Amazon for 1,200 kroner, but even at that time no one knew how many miles it had gone because the odometer went up only to 100,000. However, the car expressed everything Bjørn Holm was and believed in; it smelled better than anything he knew, a mixture of imitation leather, metal, engine oil, sun-faded rear dash, Volvo factory and seats impregnated with "personality perspiration," which Bjørn Holm explained was not common body perspiration but a select veneer of all the previous owners' souls, karma, eating habits and lifestyles. The furry dice hanging from the mirror were original Fuzzy Dice, which expressed the right mix of genuine affection for and ironical distance from a bygone American culture and aesthetic that perfectly suited a Norwegian farmer's son who had grown up with Jim Reeves in one ear and the Ramones in the other, and loved both. Now he was sitting in Harry's office with a Rasta hat that made him look more like an undercover narcotics cop than a forensics officer. Two immense fire-engine-red cutlet-shaped sideburns framing Bjørn Holm's plump, round face emerged from the hat, and his slightly protruding eyes gave him a fishlike expression of constant wonderment. He was the only person Harry had insisted on having on his small investigation team.

"There's one more thing," Harry said, reaching out to switch on the overhead projector between the piles of paper on his desk. Magnus Skarre cursed and shielded his eyes as blurred writing suddenly appeared on his face. He moved, and Harry's voice came from behind the projector.

"This letter landed in my mailbox exactly two months ago. No address, postmarked Oslo. Produced on a standard inkjet printer."

Before Harry could ask, Katrine Bratt had pressed the light switch by the door, plunging the room into darkness. A square of light loomed up on the white wall.

They read in silence.

Soon the first snow will come. And then he will appear again. The snowman. And when the snow has gone, he will have taken someone else. What you should ask yourself is this: "Who made the snowman? Who makes snowmen? Who gave birth to the Murri?" For the snowman doesn't know.

"Poetic," mumbled Bjørn Holm.

"What's the Murri?" Skarre asked.

The monotonous whir of the projector fan was the answer.

"The most interesting part is who the snowman is," Katrine Bratt said.

"Obviously someone who needs his head examined," Bjørn Holm said.

Skarre's lone laughter was cut short.

"The Murri was the nickname of a person who is now dead," Harry said from out of the darkness. "A Murri is an Aborigine from Queensland in Australia. While this Murri was alive he killed women all over Australia. No one knows for certain how many. His real name was Robin Toowoomba."

The fan whirred and buzzed.

"Serial killer," said Bjørn Holm. "The one you killed."

Harry nodded.

"Does that mean you think we're dealing with one now?"

"As a result of this letter, we can't rule out the possibility."

"Whoa there. Hold your horses!" Skarre raised his palms. "How many times have you cried wolf since you became a celeb because of the Aussie stuff, Harry?"

"Three times," Harry said. "At least."

"And still we haven't seen a serial killer in Norway." Skarre glanced at Bratt as if to make sure she was following. "Is it because of that FBI course you took on serial killers? Is that what's making you see them everywhere?"

"Maybe," Harry said.

"Let me remind you that apart from that nurse fellow who gave injections to a couple of old fogies who were at death's door anyway, we haven't had a single serial killer in Norway. Ever. Those guys exist in the U.S.A., but even there usually only in films."

"Wrong," said Katrine Bratt.

The others turned to face her. She stifled a yawn.

"Sweden, France, Belgium, Britain, Italy, Holland, Denmark, Russia and Finland. And we're talking only solved cases here. No one utters a word about hidden statistics."

Harry couldn't see Skarre's flushed face in the dark, just the profile of his chin jutting forward aggressively in Bratt's direction.

"We haven't even got a body, and I can show you a drawer full of letters like this one. People who are a lot nuttier than this . . . this . . . snowguy."

"The difference," Harry said, getting up and strolling over to the window, "is that this head case is thorough. The name Murri was never mentioned in the papers at the time. It was the nickname Robin Toowoomba used when he was a boxer with a traveling circus."

The last of the daylight leaked out through a crack in the cloud cover. He looked at his watch. Oleg had insisted on going early so that they could take in Slayer as well.

"Where we gonna begin, then?" Bjørn Holm mumbled.

"Eh?" Skarre said.

"Where are we going to begin, then?" Holm repeated with exaggerated diction.

Harry went back to the desk.

"Holm goes over Becker's house and yard as if it were a murder scene. Check the mobile phone and the scarf in particular. Skarre, you make a list of ex-murderers, rapists, suspects in—"

"—comparable cases and other scum on the loose," Skarre said.

"Bratt, you go through the missing-persons reports and see if you can spot a pattern."

Harry waited for the inevitable question: What type of pattern? But it was not forthcoming. Katrine Bratt just gave a brief nod.

"OK," Harry said. "Get going."

"And you?" Bratt asked.

"I'm going to a gig," Harry said.

When the others had left the office, he looked down at his pad. At the only words he had jotted down. **Hidden statistics.**

Sylvia ran as fast as she could. She ran toward the trees where they were most dense, in the growing murk. She was running for her life.

She hadn't tied up her boots, and now they were full of snow. She held the little hatchet in front of her as she burst through layer after layer of low, leafless branches. The blade was red and sleek with blood.

She knew the snow that had fallen yesterday had melted in town, but even though Sollihøgda was barely half an hour's drive away, the snow could lie on the ground until spring up here. And right now she wished they had never moved to this godforsaken place, to this bit of wilderness by the town. She wished she were running on black pavement, in a city where the noise drowned out the sounds of escape and she could hide in the secure mass of humanity. But here she was completely alone.

No.

Not completely.

8

Swan Neck

Sylvia ran into the forest. Night was on the way. Usually she hated the way November evenings drew in so early, but today she thought the night couldn't come soon enough. She sought the darkness in the depths of the forest, the darkness that could erase her footprints in the snow and conceal her. She knew her way around here; she could find her bearings so that she didn't run back to the farm or straight into . . . into **its** arms. The problem was that the snow had changed the landscape overnight, covered the paths, the familiar rocks, and leveled out all the contours. And the dusk . . . everything was distorted and disfigured by the blackness. And by her own panic.

She stopped to listen. Her heaving, rasping breathlessness rent the tranquillity; it sounded as if she were tearing the waxed paper wrapped around her daughters' packed lunches. She managed to bring her breathing under control. All she could hear was the blood pounding in her ears and the low gurgle of a stream. The stream! They usually followed the stream when they were picking berries, setting traps or searching for chickens that in their heart of hearts they knew the fox had taken. The stream led down to a gravel road, and there, sooner or later, a car would pass.

She no longer heard any footsteps. No twigs cracking, no crunching of snow. Perhaps she had escaped? With her body hunched over, she moved swiftly toward the gurgling sounds.

The stream looked as though it were flowing over a white bedsheet.

Sylvia trampled straight in. The water, which reached mid-ankle, soon penetrated her boots. It was so cold that it froze her leg muscles. Then she began to run again. In the same direction as the water flowed. She made loud splashes as she lifted her legs for long, ground-gaining strides. No tracks, she thought triumphantly. And her pulse slowed, even though she was running.

That had to be a result of the hours she had spent on the treadmill at the fitness center last year. She had lost fifteen pounds and ventured to maintain that her body was in better shape than those of most thirty-five-year-olds. That was what he said, anyway, Yngve, whom she had first met at the so-called inspiration seminar last year. Where she had been all too inspired. My God, if only she could turn back the clock. Back ten years. All the things she would have done differently! She wouldn't have married Rolf. And she wouldn't have had an abortion. Yes, of course, it was an impossible thought now that the twins had come into the world. But before they were born, before she had seen Emma and Olga, it would have been possible, and she wouldn't have been in this prison that she had constructed around herself with such care.

She swept away the branches overhanging the stream, and from the corner of her eye she saw something, an animal, react with a startled movement and disappear into the gray gloom of the forest.

It went through her mind that she would have to be careful swinging her arms so that she didn't hit her leg with the hatchet. Minutes had passed, but it felt like an eternity since she had been standing in the barn slaughtering chickens. She had cut off two heads and had been about to cut off a third when she heard the barn door creak behind her. Of course she had been alarmed; she was alone and hadn't been aware of either footsteps or a car in the yard. The first thing she had noticed was the strange apparatus, a thin metal loop attached to a handle. It looked like the snares they used to catch foxes. And when the holder of this instrument began to talk, it slowly dawned on her that she was the prey, she was the one who was going to die.

She had been told why.

And she had listened to the sick but limpid logic as the blood slowed in her veins, as if it were already coagulating. Then she had been told how. In detail. And the loop had begun to glow, first red, then white. That was when she had swung her arm in horror, felt the recently sharpened hatchet blade cut through the material under the raised arm, seen the jacket and sweater open as if she had unzipped them and seen the steel slice a red line through the bare skin. As the figure had staggered backward and fallen onto the floorboards slippery with chickens' blood, she had raced to the door at the back of the barn. The one leading into the forest. Into the darkness.

The numbness had spread over her knees, and her clothes were soaked up to her navel. But she knew she would soon be on the gravel road. And from there it was no more than fifteen minutes to the nearest farm if she stayed at a run. The stream turned. Her left foot kicked something protruding from the water. There was a crack, as if someone had grabbed her foot, and the next moment Sylvia Ottersen was falling headlong. She landed on her stomach, swallowed water tasting of earth and rotten leaves, then pushed herself into a kneeling position. Once she knew she was still alone, and the first panic had passed, she discovered that her foot was trapped. She groped with her hand under the water, expecting to find entwined tree roots around her foot, but instead her fingers felt something smooth and hard. Metal. A metal ring. Sylvia's gaze scoured around for what she had kicked. And there on the snowy bank she saw it. It had eyes, feathers and a pale red cockscomb. She felt her terror mounting again. It was a severed chicken's head. Not one of the heads she had just cut off, but one of the ones Rolf used. As bait. After writing to the local council that a fox had killed sixteen chickens last year, they had been given permission to set a limited number of fox traps—so-called swan necks—at a certain radius around the farm, well off the beaten track. The best place to hide traps was underwater with the bait sticking up. After the fox had taken the bait, the trap snapped shut, breaking the neck of the animal and killing it instantly. At least in theory. She felt with her hand. When they had bought the traps at Jaktdepotet in Drammen, they had been told the springs were so strong that the jaws could break the leg of an adult, but she couldn't feel any pain in her frozen foot. Her fingers found the thin steel wire attached to the swan neck. She wouldn't be able to force open the trap without the lever, which was in the farm toolshed, and anyway they usually tied the swan neck to a tree with steel wire so that a half-dead fox, or anything else, would not be able to run off with the expensive equipment. Her hand traced the wire through the water and up onto the bank. There was the metal sign bearing their names, as per regulations.

She stiffened. Wasn't that a twig she heard breaking in the distance? She felt her heart pounding again as she stared into the dense murk.

Numb fingers followed the wire through the snow as she crawled up onto the bank of the stream. The wire was fastened around the trunk of a solid young birch tree. She searched for and found the knot under the snow. The metal had frozen into a stiff, unyielding lump. She had to open it, had to get away.

Another twig cracked. Closer this time.

She leaned against the trunk, on the opposite side

to where she had heard the sound. Told herself not to panic, that the knot would come loose after she had yanked at it for a while, that her leg was intact, that the sounds she heard coming closer were made by a deer. She tried pulling at one end of the knot and didn't feel the pain when a fingernail broke down the middle. But it was no use. She bent over and her teeth crunched as she bit into the steel. Shit! She could hear light, quiet footsteps in the snow and held her breath. The steps paused somewhere on the other side of the tree. She might have been imagining things, but she thought she could hear it scenting the air, inhaling the smell. She sat utterly motionless. Then it began to move again. The sounds were softer. It was going away.

She took a deep, quivering breath. Now she would have to free herself. Her clothes were soaked and she would certainly freeze to death at night if no one found her. At that moment she remembered. The hatchet! She had forgotten the hatchet. The wire was thin. Put it on a stone, a couple of well-aimed blows and she would be free. The hatchet must have fallen in the stream. She crawled back into the black water, put her hands down and searched the stony bottom.

Nothing.

In despair, she sank to her knees, scanning the snow on both banks. And then she caught sight of the blade poking up out of the water six feet in front of her. And already she knew, before she felt the wire jerk, before she lay down flat in the water with the melted snow gurgling over her, so cold that she thought her heart would stop, stretching like a desperate beggar for the hatchet, already she knew that it was a foot too far. Her fingers curled around air a foot and a half from the handle. Tears came, but she forced them back; she could cry afterward.

"Is this what you're looking for?"

She had neither seen nor heard a thing. But in front of her sat a figure, crouched down. **It.** Sylvia scrambled back, but the figure followed with the hatchet held out to her.

"Just take it."

Sylvia got to her knees and took the hatchet.

"What are you going to do with it?" the voice asked.

Sylvia felt the fury surge up inside her, the fury that always accompanies fear, and the result was ferocious. She lunged forward with the hatchet raised and swung low with an outstretched arm. But the wire tugged at her; the hatchet just sliced the darkness and the next moment she was lying in the water again.

The voice chuckled.

Sylvia fell onto her side. "Go away," she groaned, spitting pebbles.

"I want you to eat snow," the voice said, getting up and briefly holding the side where the jacket had been slashed open.

"What?" Sylvia exclaimed, in spite of herself.

"I want you to eat snow until you piss yourself." The figure stood slightly outside the radius of the steel wire, tilted its head and watched Sylvia. "Until your stomach is so frozen and full that it can't melt the snow any longer. Until it's ice inside. Until you've become your true self. Something that can't feel."

Sylvia's brain perceived the words, but could not absorb the meaning. "Never!" she screamed.

A sound came from the figure and blended into the gurgle of the stream. "Now's the time to scream, dear Sylvia. For no one will hear you again. Ever."

Sylvia saw it raise something. Which lit up. A loop formed the outline of a red, glowing raindrop against the dark. It hissed and smoked as it came into contact with the surface of the stream. "You'll choose to eat snow. Believe me."

Sylvia realized with a paralyzing certainty that her final hour had come. There was only one possibility left. In the past minutes night had fallen quickly, but she tried to focus her gaze on the figure between the trees as she weighed the hatchet in her hand. The blood tingled in her fingers as it streamed back, seeming to know that this was the last chance. They had practiced this, she and the twins. On the barn wall. And every time she had thrown and one of them had pulled the hatchet out of the fox-shaped target, they had cheered with jubilation: "You killed the beast, Mommy! You killed the beast!" Sylvia put one foot slightly in front of the other. A one-step run-up, that was the optimum to get the right combination of power and accuracy.

"You're crazy," she whispered.

"Of that," the figure said, and Sylvia thought she could discern a little smile, "there is little doubt."

The hatchet whirled through the thick, almost tangible darkness with a low hum. Sylvia stood perfectly balanced with her right arm pointed forward and watched the lethal weapon. Watched it whistle through the trees. Heard it cut off a thin branch. Watched it disappear into the darkness and heard the dull thud as the hatchet buried itself in the snow somewhere deep in the forest.

She leaned back against the tree trunk and slowly slumped to the ground. Felt the tears come without attempting to stop them this time. Because now she knew. There would be no afterward.

"Shall we begin?" the voice said softly.

9

The Pit

"Was that **great** or what?"

Oleg's enthusiastic voice drowned out the spitting fat in the kebab shop, which was crowded with people after the concert at the Oslo Spektrum. Harry nodded to Oleg, who was standing in his hoodie, still sweaty, still moving to the beat as he prattled on about the members of Slipknot by name, names Harry didn't even know since Slipknot CDs were sparing with personal data, and music magazines like **MOJO** and **Uncut** didn't write about bands like that. Harry ordered hamburgers and looked at his watch. Rakel had said she would be standing outside at ten o'clock. Harry looked at Oleg again. He was talking nonstop. When had it happened? When had the boy turned eleven and decided to like music about various stages of death, alienation, freezing and general doom? Perhaps it ought to have worried Harry, but it didn't. It was a starting point, a curiosity that had to be satisfied, clothes the boy had to try on to see if they fit. Other things would come along. Better things. Worse things.

"You liked it, too, didn't you, Harry?"

Harry nodded. He didn't have the heart to tell him the concert had been a bit of an anticlimax for him. He couldn't put his finger on what it was; perhaps it just wasn't his night. As soon as they had joined the crowd in the Spektrum, he had felt the paranoia that used to regularly accompany drunkenness but that during the last year had come when he was sober. And instead of getting into the mood, he had had the feeling he was being observed, and stood scanning the audience, studying the wall of faces around them.

"Slipknot rules," Oleg said. "And the masks were übercool. Especially the one with the long, thin nose. It looked like a . . . sort of . . ."

Harry was listening with half an ear, hoping Rakel would come soon. The air inside the kebab shop suddenly felt dense and suffocating, like a thin film of grease lying on your skin and over your mouth. He tried not to think his next thought. But it was on its way, had already rounded the corner. The thought of a drink.

"It's an Indian death mask," a woman's voice behind them said. "And Slayer was better than Slipknot."

Harry spun around in surprise.

"Lots of posing with Slipknot, isn't there?" she continued. "Recycled ideas and empty gestures."

She was wearing a shiny, figure-hugging, ankle-length black coat buttoned up to her neck. All you could see under the coat was a pair of black boots. Her face was pale and her eyes made up.

"I would never have believed it," Harry said. "You liking that kind of music."

Katrine Bratt managed a brief smile. "I suppose I would say the opposite."

She gave him no further explanation and signaled to the man behind the counter that she wanted a Farris mineral water.

"Slayer sucks," Oleg mumbled under his breath.

Katrine turned to him. "You must be Oleg."

"Yes," Oleg said sulkily, pulling up his army trousers and looking as if he both liked and disliked this attention from a mature woman. "How d'ya know?"

Katrine smiled. "'How d'ya know?' Living on Holmenkollen Ridge as you do, shouldn't you say 'How do you know?'? Is Harry teaching you bad habits?"

Blood suffused Oleg's cheeks.

Katrine laughed quietly and patted Oleg's shoulder. "Sorry, I'm just curious."

The boy's face went so red that the whites of his eyes were shining.

"I'm also curious," Harry said, passing a burger to Oleg. "I assume you've found the pattern I asked for, Bratt. Since you've got time to come to a gig."

Harry looked at her in a way that spelled out his warning: Don't tease the boy.

"I've found something," Katrine said, twisting the plastic top off the Farris bottle. "But you're busy, so we can sort it out tomorrow."

"I'm not **so** busy," Harry said. He had already forgotten the film of grease, the feeling of suffocation.

"It's confidential and there are a lot of people
here," Katrine said. "But I can whisper a couple of
key words."

She leaned closer, and over the fat he could smell
the almost masculine fragrance of perfume and feel
her warm breath on his ear.

"A silver Volkswagen Passat has just pulled up outside. There's a woman sitting inside trying to catch
your attention. I would guess it's Oleg's mother . . ."

Harry straightened up with a jolt and looked out
the large window toward the car. Rakel had wound
down the window and was peering in at them.

"Don't make a mess," Rakel said as Oleg jumped into
the backseat with the burger in his hand.

Harry stood beside the open window. She was
wearing a plain, light blue sweater. He knew that
sweater well. Knew how it smelled, how it felt against
the palm of his hand and cheek.

"Good gig?" she asked.

"Ask Oleg."

"What sort of band was it, actually?" She looked at
Oleg in the mirror. "Those people outside are a bit
oddly dressed."

"Quiet songs about love and so on," Oleg said,
sending a quick wink to Harry when her eyes were
off the mirror.

"Thank you, Harry," she said.

"My pleasure. Drive carefully."

"Who was that woman inside?"

"A colleague. New on the job."

"Oh? Looked as if you knew each other pretty well already."

"How so?"

"You . . ." She stopped in midsentence. Then she slowly shook her head and laughed. A deep but bright laugh that came from down in her throat. Confident and carefree at the same time. The laugh that had once made him fall in love.

"Sorry, Harry. Good night."

The window glided upward; the silver car glided off.

Harry walked the gauntlet down Brugata, between bars with music blaring out of open doors. He considered a coffee at Teddy's Softbar, but knew it would be a bad idea. So he made up his mind to walk on by.

"Coffee?" repeated the guy behind the counter in disbelief.

The jukebox at Teddy's was playing Johnny Cash, and Harry passed a finger over his top lip.

"You got a better suggestion?" Harry heard the voice that came out of his mouth; it was familiar and unfamiliar at the same time.

"Well," said the guy, running a hand through his oily, glistening hair, "the coffee's not exactly fresh from the machine, so what about a freshly pulled beer?"

Johnny Cash was singing about God, baptism and new promises.

"Right," Harry said.

The man behind the counter grinned.

At that moment Harry felt the mobile phone in his pocket vibrate. He grabbed it quickly and greedily, as though it were a call he had been expecting.

It was Skarre.

"We've just received a missing-persons call that fits. Married woman with children. She wasn't at home when the husband and children returned a few hours ago. They live way out in the woods in Solli-høgda. None of the neighbors have seen her and she can't have left by car because the husband had it. And there are no footprints on the path."

"Footprints?"

"There's still snow up there."

The beer was banged down in front of Harry.

"Harry? Are you there?"

"Yes, I am. I'm thinking."

"What about?"

"Is there a snowman there?"

"Eh?"

"Snowman."

"How should I know?"

"Well, let's go and find out. Jump in the car and pick me up outside Gunerius shopping center, on Storgata."

"Can't we do this tomorrow, Harry? I've got some action lined up for tonight, and this woman is only missing, so there's no immediate hurry."

Harry watched the foam coiling its way down the outside of the beer glass like a snake.

"Actually . . . ," Harry said, " . . . there's one hell of a hurry."

Amazed, the bartender looked at the untouched beer, the fifty-krone note on the counter and the broad shoulders making off through the door as Johnny Cash faded out.

"Sylvia would never have simply left," said Rolf Ottersen.

Rolf Ottersen was thin. Or, to be more precise, he was a bag of bones. His flannel shirt was buttoned all the way up, and from it protruded a gaunt neck and a head that reminded Harry of a wading bird. A pair of narrow hands with long, scrawny fingers that continually curled, twisted and twirled protruded from his shirtsleeves. The nails of his right hand had been filed long and sharp, like claws. His eyes, behind thick glasses in plain, round steel frames, the type that had been popular among seventies radicals, seemed unnaturally large. A poster on the mustard-yellow wall showed Indians carrying an anaconda. Harry recognized the cover of a Joni Mitchell LP from hippie Stone Age times. Next to it hung a reproduction of a well-known self-portrait by Frida Kahlo. A woman who suffered, Harry thought. A picture chosen by a woman. The floor was untreated pine, and the room was lit by a combination of old-fashioned paraffin lamps and brown clay lamps, which looked as if they might have been homemade. Leaning against the wall in the corner was a guitar with nylon strings, which Harry took to be the explanation for Rolf Ottersen's filed nails.

"What do you mean, she 'would never have left'?" Harry asked.

In front of him on the living-room table Rolf Ottersen had placed a photograph of his wife with their twin daughters, Olga and Emma, ten years old. Sylvia Ottersen had big, sleepy eyes, like someone who had worn glasses all her life and then started wearing contact lenses or had laser eye surgery. The twins had their mother's eyes.

"She would've said," Rolf Ottersen explained. "Left a message. Something must've happened."

In spite of his despair his voice was muted and gentle. Rolf Ottersen pulled a handkerchief from his trouser pocket and put it to his face. His nose seemed abnormally big for his narrow, pale face. He blew his nose in one single trumpet blast.

Skarre poked his head inside the door. "The dog patrol's here. They've got a cadaver dog with them."

"Get going, then," Harry said. "Have you spoken to all the neighbors?"

"Yep. Still nothing."

Skarre closed the door, and Harry saw that Ottersen's eyes had become even bigger behind the glasses.

"Cadaver dog?" Ottersen whispered.

"Just a generic term," Harry said, making a mental note that he would have to give Skarre a couple of tips on how to express himself.

"So you use them to search for living people as well?" From his intonation, the husband appeared to be pleading.

"Yes, of course," Harry lied, rather than tell him that cadaver dogs sniffed out places where dead bodies had been. They were not used for drugs, lost property or living people. They were used for deaths. Period.

"So you last saw her today at four," Harry said, looking down at his notes. "Before you and your daughters went to town. What did you do there?"

"I took care of the shop while the girls had their violin lessons."

"Shop?"

"We have a small shop in Majorstuen selling handmade African goods. Art, furniture, fabric, clothes, all sorts of things. They're imported directly from the artisans, and the artisans are paid properly. Sylvia is there most of the time, but on Thursdays we're open late, so she comes back home with the car and I go in with the girls. I'm at the shop while they have violin lessons at the Barrat Due Institute of Music from five until seven. Then I pick them up, and we come home. We were home a little after seven-thirty."

"Mm. Who else works in the shop?"

"No one."

"That must mean you're closed for a while on Thursdays. About an hour?"

Rolf Ottersen gave a wry smile. "It's a very small shop. We don't have many customers. Almost none until the Christmas sales, to be honest."

"How . . . ?"

"NORAD. They support shops and our suppliers as part of the government's trade program with Third World countries." He coughed quietly. "The message it sends is more important than money and short-sighted gain, isn't it?"

Harry nodded, even though he wasn't thinking about development aid and fair trade in Africa but about the clock and driving time in Oslo. From the kitchen, where the twins were eating a late snack, came the sound of a radio. He hadn't seen a TV in the house.

"Thank you. We'll carry on." Harry got up and went outside.

Three cars stood parked in the yard. One was Bjørn Holm's Volvo Amazon, repainted black with a checkered rally stripe over the roof and trunk. Harry looked up at the clear, starry sky arching over the tiny farm in the forest clearing. He breathed in the air. The air of spruce and wood smoke. From the edge of the wood he heard the panting of a dog and cries of encouragement from the policeman.

To get to the barn Harry walked in the arc they had determined so as not to destroy any clues they might be able to use. Voices were emanating from the open door. He crouched down and studied the footprints in the snow in the light from the outside lamp.

Then he stood up, leaned against the frame and tugged out a pack of cigarettes.

"Looks like a murder scene," he said. "Blood, bodies and overturned furniture."

Bjørn Holm and Magnus Skarre fell silent, turned and followed Harry's gaze. The big open room was lit by a single bulb hanging from a cable wrapped around one of the beams. At one end of the barn there was a lathe and, behind it, a board with tools attached: hammers, saws, pliers, drills. No electric gadgets. At the other end there was a wire fence and behind it chickens perched on shelves in the wall or strutted around, stiff-legged, on the straw. In the middle of the room, on gray, untreated, bloodstained floorboards, lay three headless bodies. Harry poked a cigarette between his lips without lighting it, entered, taking care not to step in the blood, and squatted down beside the chopping block to examine the chicken heads. The beam from his flashlight focused on matte-black eyes. First he held half a white feather that looked as if it had been scorched black along the edge, then he studied the smooth severing of the chickens' necks. The blood had coagulated and was black. He knew this was a quick process, not much more than half an hour.

"See anything interesting?" asked Bjørn Holm.

"My brain has been damaged by my profession, Holm. Right now it's analyzing chickens' bodies."

Skarre laughed and painted the newspaper headlines in the air: "SAVAGE TRIPLE CHICKEN MURDER. VOODOO PARISH. HARRY HOLE ASSIGNED."

"What I can't see is more interesting," Harry said.

Bjørn Holm raised an eyebrow, looked around and began to nod slowly.

Skarre looked at them skeptically. "And that is?"

"The murder weapon," Harry said.

"A hatchet," Holm said. "The only sensible way to kill chickens."

Skarre sniffed. "If the woman did the killing, she must have put the hatchet back in its place. Tidy types, these farmers."

"I agree," Harry said, listening to the cackle of the chickens, which seemed to be coming from all sides. "That's why it's interesting that the chopping block is upside down and the chickens' bodies scattered around. And the hatchet is not in its place."

"Its place?" Skarre faced Holm and rolled his eyes.

"If you can be bothered to take a peek, Skarre," Harry said without moving.

Skarre was still looking at Holm, who nodded toward the board behind the lathe.

"Shit," said Skarre.

In the empty space between a hammer and a rusty saw was the outline of a small hatchet.

From outside came the sound of a dog barking and whimpering, and then the policeman's loud shout, which was no longer encouraging.

Harry rubbed his chin. "We've searched the whole barn, so for the moment it looks as if Sylvia Ottersen left the place while slaughtering the chickens, taking the hatchet with her. Holm, can you take the body temperatures of these chickens and estimate the time of death?"

"Yup."

"Eh?" Skarre said.

"I want to know when she ran off," Harry said. "Did you get anything from the shoe prints outside, Holm?"

The forensic officer shook his head. "Too trampled, and I need more light. I found several of Rolf Ottersen's boot prints. Plus a couple of others going **to** the barn, but none **from** the barn. Perhaps she was carried out of the barn?"

"Mm. Then the prints of the carrier would have been deeper. Shame no one stepped in the blood." Harry peered at the dark walls outside the range of the bulb. From the yard they heard a dog's pitiful whine and a policeman's furious curses.

"Go and see what's up, Skarre," Harry said.

Skarre went, and Harry switched the flashlight back on and walked toward the wall. He ran his hand along the unpainted boards.

"What's . . . ," Holm began, but stopped when Harry's boot hit the wall with a dull thud.

The starry sky came into view.

"A back door," Harry said, staring at the black forest and the silhouette of spruce trees against the dome of dirty-yellow light from the town in the distance. He shone the flashlight on the snow. The beam immediately found the tracks.

"Two people," Harry said.

"It's the dog," Skarre said on his return. "It won't budge."

"Won't budge?" Harry lit up the trail of footprints.

The snow reflected the light, but the trail vanished in the darkness beneath the trees.

"The dog handler doesn't understand. He says the dog seems petrified. At any rate it refuses to go into the forest."

"Perhaps it can smell fox," Holm said. "Lots of foxes in this forest."

"Foxes?" Skarre snorted. "That big dog can't be afraid of foxes."

"Perhaps it's never seen a fox," Harry said. "But it knows it can smell a predator. It's rational to be afraid of what you don't know. The dog that isn't won't live long." Harry could feel his heart begin to quicken. And he knew why. The forest. The dark. The type of terror that was not rational. The type that had to be overcome.

"This is to be treated as a crime scene until further notice," Harry said. "Start work. I'll check where this trail leads."

"OK."

Harry swallowed before stepping out the back door. It had been more than thirty years ago. And still his body bristled.

He had been staying at his grandparents' house in Åndalsnes during his autumn vacation. The farm lay on a hillside with the mighty Romsdal Mountains towering above. Harry had been ten and had gone into the forest to look for the cow his grandfather was searching for. He wanted to find it before his grandfather, before anyone. So he hurried. Ran like a maniac over hills of soft blueberry bushes and funny, crooked dwarf birch trees. The paths came and went as he ran in a straight line toward the bell he thought he had heard among the trees. And there it was again, a bit farther to the right now. He jumped over a stream and ducked under a tree and his boots squelched as he ran across a marsh with a rain cloud edging toward him. He could see the veil of drizzle beneath the cloud showering the steep mountainside.

And the rain was so fine that he had not noticed the darkness descending; it slunk out of the marsh, it crept between the trees, it spilled down through the shadows of the mountainside like black paint and collected at the bottom of the valley. He looked up at a large bird circling high above, so dizzyingly high he could see the mountain behind it. And then a boot got stuck and he fell. Facedown and without anything to grab. Everything went dark, and his nose and mouth were filled with the taste of marsh, of death, decay and darkness. He could **taste** the darkness for the few seconds he was under. And then he came up again, and discovered that all the light had gone. Gone across the mountain towering above him in its silent, heavy majesty, whispering that he didn't know where he was, that he hadn't known for a long time. Unaware that he had lost a boot, he stood up and began to run. He would soon see something he recognized. But the landscape seemed bewitched; rocks had become heads of creatures growing up out of the ground, bushes were fingers that scratched at his legs and dwarf birch trees were witches bent with laughter as they pointed the way, here or there, the way home or the way to perdition, the way to his grandparents' house or the way to the Pit. Because adults had told him about the Pit. The bottomless swamp where cattle, people and whole carts vanished, never to return.

It was almost night when Harry tottered into the kitchen and his grandmother hugged him and said that his father, grandfather and all the adults from the neighboring farm were out looking for him. Where had he been?

In the forest.

But hadn't he heard their shouts? They had been calling Harry; she had heard them calling Harry all the time.

He didn't remember it himself, but many times later he had been told that he had sat there trembling with cold on the wooden box in front of the stove, staring into the distance with an apathetic expression on his face, and had answered: "I didn't think it was them calling."

"Who did you think it was, then?"

"The others. Did you know that darkness has a **taste**, Grandma?"

Harry had walked barely a few yards into the forest when he was overtaken by an intense, almost unnatural silence. He shone the flashlight down on the ground in front of him because every time he pointed it into the forest, shadows ran between the trees like jittery spirits in the pitch black. Being isolated from the dark in a bubble of light didn't give him a sense of security. Quite the opposite. The certainty that he was the most visible object moving through the forest made him feel naked, vulnerable. The branches scraped at his face, like a blind man's fingers trying to identify a stranger.

The tracks led to a stream whose gurgling noise drowned his quickened breathing. One of the trails disappeared while the other followed the stream on lower ground.

He went on. The stream wound hither and thither, but he wasn't concerned about losing his bearings; all he had to do was retrace his steps.

An owl, which must have been close by, hooted an admonitory **to-wit-to-woo.** The dial on his watch glowed green and showed that he had been walking for more than fifteen minutes. Time to go back and send in the team with proper footwear, gear and a dog that was not afraid of foxes.

Harry's heart stopped.

It had darted past his face. Soundless and so fast that he hadn't seen anything. But the current of air had given it away. Harry heard the owl's wings beating in the snow and the piteous squeak of a small rodent that had just become its prey.

He slowly let out the air from his lungs. Shone the flashlight over the forest ahead one last time and turned to go back. Took one step, then came to a halt. He wanted to take another, two more, to get out. But he did what he had to do. Shone the light behind him. And there it was again. A glint, a reflection of light that should not be there in the middle of the black forest. He went closer. Looked back and tried to fix the spot in his mind. It was about fifty feet from the stream. He crouched down. Just the steel stuck up, but he didn't need to brush away the snow to see what it was. A hatchet. If there had been blood on it after the chickens were killed, it was gone now. There were no footprints around the hatchet. Harry shone the flashlight and saw a snapped twig on the snow a few yards away. Someone must have thrown the ax here with enormous strength.

At that moment Harry felt it again. The sensation he had had at the Spektrum earlier that evening. The sensation that he was being observed. Instinctively, he switched off the flashlight, and the darkness descended over him like a blanket. He held his breath and listened. Don't, he thought. Don't let it happen. Evil is not a thing. It cannot take possession of you. It's the opposite; it's a void, an absence of goodness. The only thing you can be frightened of here is yourself.

Harry switched on the flashlight and pointed it toward the clearing.

It was her. She stood erect and immobile between the trees, looking at him without blinking, with the same large, sleepy eyes as in the photograph. Harry's first thought was that she was dressed like a bride, in white, that she was standing at the altar, here, in the middle of the forest. The light made her glitter.

Harry breathed in with a shiver and grabbed his mobile phone from his jacket pocket. Bjørn Holm answered after the second ring.

"Cordon off the whole area," Harry said. His
throat felt dry, rough. "I'm calling in the troops."

"What's happened?"

"There's a snowman here."

"So?"

Harry explained.

"I didn't catch the last part," Holm shouted. "Poor
coverage here . . ."

"The head," Harry repeated. "It belongs to Sylvia
Ottersen."

The other end went quiet.

Harry told Holm to follow the footprints and
hung up.

Then he crouched against a tree, buttoned his coat
right up and switched off the flashlight to save the
battery while he waited. Thinking he had almost forgotten what it tasted like, the darkness.

Part Two

10

DAY 4

Chalk

It was three-thirty in the morning and Harry was exhausted as he finally unlocked the door to his apartment. He undressed and went straight into the shower. Tried not to think as he let the burning jets of water numb his skin, massage his stiff muscles and thaw his frozen body. They had spoken to Rolf Ottersen, but the formal questioning would have to wait until the morning. At Sollihøgda they had quickly wrapped up the door-to-door inquiries with the neighbors; there weren't so many to ask. But the Crime Scene officers and the dogs were still at work and would be the whole night. They had a brief window of time before the evidence would become contaminated, melted or covered by snow. He turned off the shower. The air was gray with steam, and when he wiped the mirror a new layer of condensation immediately settled. It distorted his face and blurred the contours of his naked body.

Harry was brushing his teeth when the telephone rang. "Harry."

"Stormann, the mold man."

"You're up late," Harry said in surprise.

"Reckoned you were at work."

"Oh?"

"It was on the late-night news. Woman in Solli-høgda. Saw you in the background. I've got the results back."

"And?"

"You've got fungus. A hungry bugger, too. **Aspergillus versicolor.**"

"Which means?"

"That it can be any color. If and when it's seen. Apart from that, it means I'll have to take down more of your walls."

"Mm." Harry had a vague sense that he ought to show more interest and concern, or at least ask more questions. But he couldn't be bothered. Not at this hour.

"Feel free."

Harry hung up and closed his eyes. Waited for the ghosts, for the inevitable, just as long as he stayed away from the only medicine he knew for ghosts. Perhaps it would be a new acquaintance this time. He waited for her to come out of the forest, stumping along toward him on a huge white body without legs, a misshapen bowling ball with a head, black sockets with crows pecking at the remainder of her eyeballs, teeth bared after the foxes had helped themselves to the lips. Hard to know if she would come; the subconscious was unpredictable. So unpredictable that when Harry slept, he dreamed that he was lying in a bath with his head underwater listening to a deep rumble of bubbles and women's laughter. Sea grass grew on the white enamel, stretching out for him like green fingers on a white hand seeking his.

The morning light cast rectangles over the newspapers lying on POB Gunnar Hagen's desk. It lit up Sylvia Ottersen's smile and the headlines on the front pages. KILLED AND DECAPITATED, DECAPITATED IN THE FOREST and—the shortest and probably the best—DECAPITATED.

Harry's head had ached from the moment he woke up. Now he was holding it gingerly in his hands, thinking that he might as well have had a drink last night—it wouldn't have made the pain any worse. He wanted to close his eyes, but Hagen was staring straight at him. Harry noticed that Hagen's mouth kept opening, twisting and closing—in short that he was formulating words that Harry was receiving on a badly tuned frequency.

"The conclusion . . . ," Hagen said, and Harry knew it was time to prick up his ears, "is that this case has top priority from now on. And that means, of course, that we will increase the size of your investigation team immediately and—"

"Disagree," Harry said. Just articulating a single word invoked a sense that his cranium was exploding. "We can requisition more people as and when, but for the moment I don't want anyone else at the meetings. Four is enough."

Gunnar Hagen looked dumbfounded. In murder cases, even the straightforward ones, investigation teams always comprised at least a dozen people.

"Free thinking functions best in small groups," Harry added.

"Thinking?" Hagen burst out. "What about standard police work? Following up forensic evidence, questioning, checking tips? And what about the co-ordination of information? A total of—"

Harry held up a hand to stem the flow of words. "That's just the point. I don't want to drown in all that."

"Drown?" Hagen stared at Harry in disbelief. "I'd better give the case to someone who can swim, then."

Harry massaged his temples. Right now there was no one in the Crime Squad apart from Inspector Hole who could lead a murder case such as this one, and both Hagen and Harry knew it. Harry also knew that giving the case to the central investigation bureau, Kripos, would be such a huge loss of prestige for the new POB that he would rather sacrifice his extremely hirsute right arm.

Harry sighed. "Normal investigation teams fight to stay afloat in the stream of information. And that's when it's a **standard** case. With decapitations on the front pages . . ." Harry shook his head. "People have gone mad. We received more than a hundred calls just after the news item last night. You know, drunks slurring and the usual nuts, plus a few new ones. People telling you that the murder was described in the Book of Revelation, that sort of thing. So far today we've had two hundred calls. And just wait until it emerges that there may be several bodies. Let's say we have to set aside twenty people to take care of the calls. They check them out and write reports. Let's say that the team leader has to spend two hours every day physically going through the incoming data, two hours coordinating it and two hours assembling everyone in groups, updating them, answering their questions, and half an hour editing the information that can be revealed at the press conference. Which takes forty-five minutes. The worst part is"—Harry put his forefingers against his aching jaw muscles and grimaced—"that in a standard murder case this is, I suppose, a good use of resources. Because there will always be those out there who know something, who have heard or seen something. Information that we can painstakingly piece together or that enables us to magically solve the whole case."

"Exactly," Hagen said. "That's why—"

"The problem is," Harry continued, "this is not that kind of case. Not that kind of killer. This person has not confided in a friend or shown his face in the vicinity of the murder. No one out there knows anything, so the calls that come in won't help us, they'll just delay us. And any possible forensic clues we uncover have been left there to confuse us. In a nutshell, this is a different kind of game."

Hagen had leaned back in his chair and pressed his fingertips together, and, immersed in thought, he was now observing Harry. He blinked like a basking lizard, then asked: "So you see this as a game?"

As he nodded, Harry wondered where Hagen was going.

"What sort of game? Chess?"

"Well," Harry said, "blindfold chess, maybe."

Hagen nodded. "So you envisage a classic serial killer, a cold-blooded murderer with superior intelligence and a proclivity for fun, games and challenges?"

Now Harry had an idea where Hagen was going.

"A man straight from the serial killings you profiled in that FBI course? The kind you met in Australia that time? A person who"—the POB smacked his lips as if he were tasting the words—"is basically a worthy opponent for someone of your background."

Harry sighed. "That's not how I think, boss."

"Don't you? Remember, I've taught at the military academy, Harry. What do you think aspiring generals dream about when I tell them how military strategists have personally changed the course of world history? Do you think they dream about sitting around quietly hoping for peace, about telling their grandchildren that they just **lived,** that no one would ever know what they might have been capable of? They might say they want peace, but inside they dream, Harry. About having one opportunity. There's a strong social urge in man to be **needed.** That's why generals in the Pentagon paint the blackest scenario as soon as a firecracker goes off anywhere in the world. I think you **want** this case to be special, Harry.

You want it so much that you can see the blackest of the black."

"The snowman, boss. You remember the letter I showed you?"

Hagen sighed. "I remember a madman, Harry."

Harry knew he ought to give in now. Put forward the compromise suggestion he had already concocted. Give Hagen this little victory. Instead he shrugged. "I want to have my group as it is, boss."

Hagen's face closed, hardened. "I can't let you do that, Harry."

"Can't?"

Hagen held Harry's gaze, but then it happened. Hagen blinked; his eyes wandered. Just for a fraction of a second, but it was enough.

"There are other considerations," Hagen said.

Harry tried to maintain an innocent expression as he twisted the knife. "What sort of considerations, boss?"

Hagen looked down at his hands.

"What do you think? Senior officers. The press. Politicians. If we still haven't got the murderer after three months, who do you think will have to answer questions about the unit's priorities? Who will have to explain why we put four people on this case because small groups are better suited to"—Hagen spat out the words like rotten shrimps—"free thinking and games of chess? Have you considered that, Harry?"

"No," Harry said, crossing his arms on his chest. "I've thought about how we'll catch this guy, not about how I'm going to justify not catching him."

Harry knew it was a cheap shot, but the words hit home. Hagen blinked twice. Opened his mouth and shut it again, and Harry instantly felt ashamed. Why did he always have to instigate these childish, meaningless wall-pissing contests, just to have the satisfaction of giving someone else—anyone at all—the finger? Rakel had once said that he wished he'd been born with an extra middle finger that was permanently sticking up.

"There's a man in Kripos called Espen Lepsvik," Harry said. "He's good at leading large investigations. I can talk to him, get him to set up a group that reports to me. The groups will work in parallel and independently. You and the chief superintendent take care of the press conference. How does that sound, boss?"

Harry didn't need to wait for an answer. He could see the gratitude in Hagen's eyes. And he knew he'd won the pissing contest.

The first thing Harry did when he was back in his own office was to call Bjørn Holm.

"Hagen said yes, it's going to be as I said. Meeting in my office in half an hour. Will you call Skarre and Bratt?"

He put down the phone. Thought about what Hagen had said about hawks wanting their own war. And pulled out the drawer in a vain hunt for an aspirin.

"Apart from the footprints, we haven't found a single trace of the perp at what we assume is the crime

scene," Magnus Skarre said. "What's harder to understand is how we haven't found a trace of the body,
either. After all, he cut off the woman's head—there
ought to have been masses of evidence left behind.
But there was nothing. The dogs didn't even react! It's
a mystery."

"He killed and decapitated the woman in the
stream," Katrine said. "Her footprints came to an
end farther up the stream, didn't they? She ran in the
water so as not to leave prints, but he caught up with
her."

"What did he use?" Harry asked.

"Hatchet or a saw—what else?"

"What about the burn marks around the skin
where he cut?"

Katrine looked at Skarre and they both shrugged.

"OK, Holm, check that out," Harry said. "And
then?"

"Then maybe he carried her through the stream
down to the road," Skarre said. He had slept for two
hours and his sweater was on back to front, but no
one had had the heart to tell him. "I say **maybe** because we've found nothing there, either. And we
should have. A streak of blood on a tree trunk, a
lump of flesh on a branch or a shred of clothing. But
we found his footprints where the stream flows under
the road. And beside the road there were imprints in
the snow of what might have been a body. But, for
Christ's sake, the dogs didn't pick it up. Not even the
damn cadaver dog! It's a—"

"Mystery," Harry repeated, rubbing his chin. "Isn't

it pretty impractical to cut off her head while standing in a stream? It's just a narrow ditch. You wouldn't have enough elbow room. Why?"

"Obvious," Skarre said. "The evidence is carried away with the water."

"Not obvious," retorted Harry. "He left her head, so he's not worried about leaving any traces. Why there's no trace of her on the way down to the road—"

"Body bag!" said Katrine. "I've just been wondering how he managed to carry her so far in that terrain. In Iraq they used body bags with straps like a rucksack."

"Mm," Harry said. "That would explain why the cadaver dog didn't pick up a scent by the road."

"And why he could risk letting her lie there," Katrine said.

"Lie there?" Skarre queried.

"The imprint of a body in the snow. He put her there while he went to fetch his car. Which was probably parked somewhere near the Ottersen farm. That would've taken half an hour—don't you agree?"

Skarre mumbled a grudging "Something like that."

"The bags are black, look like run-of-the-mill garbage bags to anyone passing in a car."

"No one drove past," Skarre said sourly, stifling a yawn. "We've spoken to everyone up in that damn forest."

Harry nodded. "What should we think about Rolf Ottersen's story about him being in his shop between five and seven?"

"The alibi isn't worth shit if there weren't any customers," Skarre said.

"He might've driven there and back while the twins were having their violin lessons," Katrine said.

"But he's not the type," Skarre said, leaning back in the chair and nodding as if to corroborate his own conclusion.

Harry was tempted to make a sweeping statement about the prevailing assumption on the part of the police that they could tell a murderer when they saw one, but this was the phase when everyone was supposed to say what he or she thought without fear of contradiction. In his experience, the best ideas originated from flights of fancy, half-baked guesswork and erroneous snap judgments.

The door opened.

"Howdy!" sang out Bjørn Holm. "'Pologies all around, but I've been on the trail of the murder weapon."

He pulled off his waterproof jacket and hung it on Harry's coatrack, which was tilting wildly. Underneath he was wearing a pink shirt with yellow embroidery and a legend on the back proclaiming that Hank Williams—despite all evidence that he died in the winter of 1953—was alive. Then he flung himself down on the last free chair and looked at the others' upturned faces.

"What's up?" He smiled, and Harry waited for Holm's favorite one-liner. Which was not long in coming. "Someone die?"

"The murder weapon," Harry said. "Come on."

Holm grinned and rubbed his hands together. "I was wondering of course where the burn marks on Sylvia Ottersen's neck came from. The pathologist didn't have a clue. She just said that the small arteries had been cauterized, the same way you stop amputations from bleeding. Before the leg's sawn off. And when she talked about sawing, that made me think of something. As you know, I grew up on a farm . . ."

Bjørn Holm leaned forward, his eyes alight, reminding Harry of a father about to open a Christmas present, a big train set he has bought for his newborn son.

"If a cow was calving, and the calf was already dead, sometimes the carcass was too big for the cow to force out unaided. And if, on top of that, it was lying crooked, we couldn't get it out without risking injury to the cow. In that case the vet would have to use a saw."

Skarre grimaced.

"It's a sort of very thin, flexible blade-type thing you can put inside a cow, kind of around the calf, like a noose. And then you pull and wriggle the blade to and fro, and cut through the body." Holm demonstrated with his hands. "Until it's in two parts, and you can take out half the carcass. And then as a rule the problem's solved. As a rule. Because the blade sometimes cuts the mother too as it goes to and fro inside her, and the mother bleeds to death. So a couple of years ago some French farmers came up with a practical gadget that solved the problem. A looped electric filament that can burn through flesh.

There's a plain plastic handle with a dead thin, super-strong metal wire attached to each end of the handle, forming a loop you can put around whatever you want to cut off. Then you switch on the heat. The wire is white hot in fifteen seconds, and you press a button on the handle and the loop begins to tighten and cut through the body. There's no sideways movement and thus less chance of cutting the mother. And if you should cut her, there are two further advantages—"

"Are you trying to sell us this instrument or what?" Skarre asked with a grin, searching Harry's eyes for a reaction.

"Because of the temperature the wire is perfectly sterile," Holm continued. "It doesn't transmit bacteria or poisoned blood from the carcass. And the heat cauterizes the small arteries and restricts the bleeding."

"OK," Harry said. "Do you know for certain that he used a tool like this?"

"No," Holm said. "I could've tested it if I'd got hold of one, but the vet I spoke to said that electric cutting loops haven't been approved by the Norwegian Ministry of Agriculture yet." He looked at Harry with an expression of deep and heartfelt regret.

"Well," Harry said, "if it isn't the murder weapon, it would at least explain how he could have cut off her head while standing in the stream. What do the rest of you think?"

"France," Katrine Bratt said. "First the guillotine and now this."

Skarre puckered his lips and shook his head.

"Sounds too weird. Anyway, where did he get hold of this loop gizmo? If it isn't approved, I mean?"

"We can start looking there," Harry said. "Would you check that out, Skarre?"

"I said I don't believe all that stuff."

"Sorry, I didn't make myself clear. I meant to say: Check it out, Skarre. Anything else, Holm?"

"No. There must've been masses of blood at the crime scene, but the only blood we found was in the barn after the chickens had been slaughtered. Speaking of the chickens, their body temperatures and the room temperature showed that they were killed at approximately half past six. Bit unsure, though, 'cause one chicken was warmer than the other two."

"Must've been feverish." Skarre laughed.

"And the snowman?" Harry asked.

"You don't find fingerprints on piles of snow crystals changing form from one hour to the next, but you ought to be able to find scraps of skin, since the crystals are sharp. Possibly fibers from gloves or mittens, if he wore them. But we didn't find either."

"Rubber gloves," Katrine said.

"Otherwise not a sniff," Holm said.

"OK. At least we have a head. Have you checked the teeth—?"

Harry was interrupted by Holm, who had straightened up with an offended expression on his face. "For traces left on her teeth? Her hair? Fingerprints on her neck? Other things forensic officers don't think about?"

Harry nodded a "Sorry" and checked his watch.

"Skarre, even if you don't think Rolf Ottersen is the type, find out where he was and what he was doing at the time Birte Becker disappeared. I'll have a chat with Filip Becker. Katrine, you hunker down with all the missing-persons cases, including these two, and look for matches."

"OK," she said.

"Compare everything," Harry said. "Time of death, phase of moon, what was on TV, hair color of victims, whether any of them borrowed the same book from the library or attended the same seminar, the sum of their telephone numbers. We have to know how he selects them."

"Hang on a moment," Skarre said. "Have we already decided that there is a connection? Shouldn't we be open to all possibilities?"

"You can be as open as you fucking like," Harry said, getting up and making sure his car keys were in his pocket. "As long as you do what your boss says. Last person turns off the light."

Harry was waiting for the elevator when he heard someone coming. The footsteps stopped right behind him.

"I spoke to one of the twins during the school recess this morning."

"Oh, yes?" Harry turned to Katrine Bratt.

"I asked what they'd been doing on Tuesday."

"Tuesday?"

"The day Birte Becker disappeared."

"Exactly."

"She, her sister and her mother were in town. She

remembered that because they were at the Kon-Tiki Museum looking for a toy after a visit to the doctor. And they spent the night at an aunt's while their mother was visiting a girlfriend. The father was at home keeping an eye on the house. Alone."

She was standing so close that Harry could smell her perfume. It wasn't like anything he had ever known a woman to wear. Very spicy, nothing sweet about it.

"Mm. Which twin did you speak to?"

Katrine Bratt held his gaze. "No idea. Does it matter?"

A **pling** told Harry that the elevator had reached their floor.

Jonas was drawing a snowman. The idea was to make it smile and sing, to make it a happy snowman. But he couldn't get it right; it just stared back at him blankly from the enormous white sheet. Around him in the large auditorium, there was hardly a sound, just the scratch of his father's chalk, now and then a bang on the board in front of him and the whisper of students' ballpoint pens on paper. He didn't like pens. If you used a pen you couldn't rub it out, you couldn't change anything, what you drew was there forever. He had woken up today thinking that his mother was back, that everything was fine again, and he'd run into her bedroom. But his father had been in there getting dressed and he told Jonas to get dressed as well because he was going to the university today. Pens.

The room sloped down to where his father stood and was like a theater auditorium. His father had not said a word to the students, not even when he and Jonas entered. Just nodded to them, pointed to the seat where Jonas was to sit and went straight to the board and began to write. And the students were clearly used to that, for they had been sitting ready and started taking notes at once. The boards were covered with numbers and small letters and a few strange doodles that Jonas did not recognize. His father had once explained to him that physics had its own language, one that he used to tell stories. When Jonas asked if they were adventure stories, his father had laughed and said that physics could be used only to explain things that were true, that it was a language that couldn't lie if it tried.

Some of the doodles were funny. And very elegant.

Chalk dust floated down onto his father's shoulders. A fine white layer settled like snow on his jacket. Jonas looked at his father's back and tried to draw him. But this didn't turn out to be a happy snowman, either. And suddenly the lecture room went absolutely still. All the pens stopped writing. Because the piece of chalk had stopped. It stood motionless at the top of the board, so high up that his father had to stretch his arm over his head to reach. And now it looked as if the chalk was stuck and his father was hanging from the board, like when Wile E. Coyote was hanging from a tiny branch on a cliff face and it was a very, very long way down. Then his father's shoulders began to shake, and Jonas thought he was trying to free the chalk, get it to move again, but it wouldn't. A ripple ran through the auditorium as if all the students were opening their mouths and sucking in breath at the same moment. Then his father freed the chalk at last, walked to the exit without turning and was gone. He's going to get some more chalk, Jonas thought. The buzz of students' voices around him grew gradually louder. He caught two words: "wife" and "missing." He looked at the board, which was almost completely covered. His father had been trying to write that she was dead, but the chalk could say only what was true, so it had got stuck. Jonas tried to rub out his snowman. Around him people were packing up their things, and the seats banged as they got up and left.

A shadow fell over the failed snowman on the paper, and Jonas looked up.

It was the policeman, the tall one with the ugly face and the kind eyes.

"Would you like to come with me, and we'll see if we can find your father?" he asked.

Harry knocked gently on the office door with the sign saying PROF. FILIP BECKER.

As there was no answer, he opened it.

The man behind the desk raised his head from his hands. "Did I say you could come in . . ."

He paused when he saw Harry. And shifted his gaze down to the boy standing next to him.

"Jonas!" Filip Becker said, the tone somewhere between bewilderment and a reprimand. His eyes were red-rimmed. "Didn't I say you should sit quietly?"

"I brought him with me," Harry said.

"Oh?" Becker looked at his watch and stood up.

"Your students have left," Harry said.

"Have they?" Becker dropped back into his chair. "I . . . I only meant to give them a break."

"I was there," Harry said.

"Were you? Why . . ."

"We all need a break once in a while. Can we have a chat?"

"I didn't want him to go to school," Becker explained after sending Jonas into the coffee room with instructions to wait there. "All the questions, speculation; I quite simply didn't want it. Well, I'm sure you understand."

"Yes." Harry took out a pack of cigarettes, shot Becker a questioning look and put it back when the professor firmly shook his head. "That, at any rate, is much easier to understand than what was on the board."

"It's quantum physics."

"Sounds weird."

"The world of atoms is weird."

"In what way?"

"They break our most fundamental physical laws. Like the one about an object not being able to be in two places at the same time. Niels Bohr once said that if you aren't profoundly shocked by quantum physics, then you haven't understood it."

"But you understand it?"

"No—are you crazy? It's pure chaos. But I prefer that chaos to this chaos."

"Which one?"

Becker sighed. "Our generation has turned itself into servants and secretaries of our children. That applies to Birte as well, I'm afraid. There are so many appointments and birthdays and favorite foods and soccer practices that it drives me insane. Today someone rang from a doctor's office in Bygdøy because Jonas hadn't turned up for an appointment. And this afternoon he has training God knows where, and his generation has never heard of the possibility of catching a bus."

"What's wrong with Jonas?" Harry took out the notepad he never wrote in; in his experience it seemed to focus people's minds.

"Nothing. Standard checkup, I assume." Becker dismissed it with an irritated flick of the hand. "And I assume you're here for a different reason?"

"Yes," Harry said. "I want to know where you were yesterday afternoon and evening."

"What?"

"Just routine, Becker."

"Has this anything to do with . . . with . . ." Becker nodded toward the **Dagbladet** newspaper lying on top of a pile of papers.

"We don't know," Harry said. "Just answer me, please."

"Tell me, are you all out of your minds?"

Harry looked at his watch without answering.

Becker groaned. "All right, I do want to help you.

Last night I sat here working on an article about wavelengths of hydrogen, which I hope to have published."

"Any colleagues who can vouch for you?"

"The reason that Norwegian research contributes so little to the world is that the self-satisfaction of Norwegian academics is surpassed only by their indolence. I was, as usual, utterly on my own."

"And Jonas?"

"He made himself some food and sat watching TV until I got home."

"Which was when?"

"Just past nine, I think."

"Mm." Harry pretended to take notes. "Have you been through Birte's things?"

"Yes."

"Found anything?"

Filip Becker stroked the corner of his mouth with one finger and shook his head. Harry held his gaze, using the silence as leverage. But Becker had shut up shop.

"Thank you for your help," Harry said, stuffing his notepad into his jacket pocket and getting up. "I'll tell Jonas he can come in."

"Give me a moment, please."

Harry found the coffee room where Jonas was sitting and drawing, the tip of his tongue poking out from his mouth. He stood beside the boy, peering down at the paper on which, for the moment, were two uneven circles.

"A snowman."

"Yes," Jonas said, glancing up. "How could you see that?"

"Why was your mother taking you to the doctor's, Jonas?"

"Don't know." Jonas drew a head on the snowman.

"What's the name of the doctor?"

"Don't know."

"Where was it?"

"I'm not allowed to tell anyone. Not even Dad." Jonas leaned over the paper and drew hair on the snowman's head. Long hair.

"I'm a policeman, Jonas. I'm trying to find your mother."

The pencil scratched harder and harder, and the hair became blacker and blacker.

"I don't know what the place's called."

"Do you remember anything nearby?"

"The king's cows."

"The king's cows?"

Jonas nodded. "The woman sitting behind the window is called Borghild. I got a lollipop because I let her take blood with one of those needles."

"Are you drawing anything in particular?" Harry asked.

"No," Jonas said, concentrating on the eyelashes.

Filip Becker stood by the window watching Harry Hole cross the parking lot. Lost in thought, he slapped the small black notebook against the palm of his hand. He was wondering whether Hole had believed him when he pretended not to know that the policeman had attended his lecture. Or when he said he had been working on an article the previous evening. Or that he hadn't found anything among Birte's things. The black notebook had been in her desk drawer; she hadn't even made an attempt to conceal it. And what was written there . . .

He almost had to laugh. The simpleton had believed she could trick him.

II

DAY 4

Death Mask

Katrine Bratt was bent over her computer when Harry poked his head in.

"Find any matches?"

"Nothing much," Katrine said. "All the women had blue eyes. Apart from that they're all quite different in appearance. They all had husbands and children."

"I have somewhere we can begin," Harry said. "Birte Becker took Jonas to a doctor close to the 'king's cows.' That has to be the royal Kongsgården estate in Bygdøy. And you said the twins were at the Kon-Tiki Museum after a visit to the doctor's. Also Bygdøy. Filip Becker didn't know anything about the doctor, but Rolf Ottersen might."

"I'll call him."

"Then come and see me."

In his office Harry picked up the handcuffs, put one around his wrist and smacked the other against the table leg while listening to his voice mail. Rakel

said Oleg was bringing a pal along to the skating rink
Valle Hovin. The message was unnecessary. He knew
it was a reminder in disguise, in case Harry had forgotten the whole thing. To date, Harry had never forgotten an arrangement with Oleg, but he accepted
these little nudges that others might have taken as a
declaration of mistrust. Indeed, what was more, he
liked them. Because it said something about what
kind of mother she was. And because she disguised
the reminder so as not to offend him.

Katrine walked in without knocking.

"Kinky," she said, nodding toward the table leg
Harry was cuffed to. "But I like it."

"Single-handed speed-cuffing." Harry smiled.
"Some crap I picked up in the States."

"You should try the new Hiatt speed cuffs. You
don't even need to think whether you're going to approach from the left or the right—the cuff arm will
close around your wrist or whatever, so long as you
get a clean hit. And then you practice with two sets of
cuffs, one around each wrist, so that you have two attempts at hitting."

"Mm." Harry unlocked the handcuffs. "What's on
your mind?"

"Rolf Ottersen hasn't heard of any doctor's appointment or any doctor in Bygdøy. In fact, they
have their own doctor in Bærum. I can ask the twins
if either of them remembers the doctor, or we can call
the doctors in Bygdøy and check ourselves. There are
only four of them. Here."

She put a yellow Post-it on his desk.

"They aren't allowed to disclose names of patients," he said.

"I'll talk to the twins when they're back from school."

"Wait," Harry said, lifting the telephone and dialing the first number.

A nasal voice answered with the name of the practice.

"Is Borghild there?" Harry asked.

No Borghild.

At the second number an equally nasal answering machine said that the office received calls only during a restricted two-hour period, and this had passed some time ago.

Finally, at the fourth attempt, a chirpy, almost laughing voice gave him what he had been hoping for.

"Yes, that's me."

"Hello, Borghild, this is Inspector Harry Hole, Oslo Police."

"Date of birth?"

"Sometime in spring. I'm calling about a murder case. I assume you've read the papers today. What I want to know is whether you saw Sylvia Ottersen last week?"

There was silence at the other end of the line.

"One moment," she said.

Harry heard her getting up, and waited. Then she was back. "I'm sorry, Herr Hole. Information about patients is confidential. And I think the police know that."

"We do. But if I'm not mistaken, it's the daughters who are patients, not Sylvia."

"Nevertheless. You're asking for information that indirectly might reveal the identities of our patients."

"I would remind you that this is a murder investigation."

"I would remind you that you can come back to us with a search warrant. We might perhaps be more guarded with patient information than most, but that's the nature of our work."

"Nature of your work?"

"Our areas of expertise."

"Which are?"

"Plastic surgery and specialist operations. See our Web site—www.kirklinikk.no."

"Thank you, but I think I've learned enough for the time being."

"If you say so."

She put down the phone.

"Well?" Katrine asked.

"Jonas and the twins have been to the same doctor," Harry said, leaning back in the chair. "And that means we're in business."

Harry could feel the adrenaline rush, the trembling that always came when he got the first scent of the brute. And after the rush came the Great Obsession. Which was everything at once: love and intoxication, blindness and clear-sightedness, meaning and madness. Colleagues spoke now and then about excitement, but this was something else, something special. He had never told anyone about the Obsession or made any attempt to analyze it. He hadn't dared. All he knew was that it helped him, drove him, fueled the job he was appointed to perform. He didn't want to know any more. He really didn't.

"And now?" Katrine asked.

Harry opened his eyes and leapt off his seat. "Now we're going shopping."

The shop Taste of Africa was situated close to the busiest street in Majorstuen, Bogstadveien. But unfortunately its location fifty feet down a side street meant that it was still on the periphery.

A bell rang as Harry and Katrine entered. In the muted lighting—or, to be more precise, the lack of lighting—Harry saw brightly colored coarse-weave rugs, sarong-like materials, large cushions with West African patterns, small coffee tables that looked as if they had been carved straight out of the rainforest and tall, thin wooden figures representing Masai tribesmen and a selection of the savannah's best-known animals. Everything seemed carefully planned and executed: There were no visible price tags, the colors complemented one another and the products were placed in pairs as if in Noah's ark. In short, it looked more like an exhibition than a shop. A somewhat dusty exhibition. This impression was reinforced by the almost unnatural stillness after the door closed behind them and the bell stopped ringing.

"Hello?" called a voice from inside the shop.

Harry followed the sound. In the darkness at the

back of the room, behind an enormous wooden giraffe and illuminated only by a single spotlight, he saw the back of a woman who was standing on a chair. She was hanging up a grinning wooden black mask on the wall.

"What is it?" she said without turning.

She gave the impression she was conditioned to expect the unexpected, but not customers.

"We're from the police."

"Oh, yes." The woman turned and the spotlight fell on her face. Harry felt his heart stop, and he automatically took a step back. It was Sylvia Ottersen.

"Something wrong?" she asked with a frown between the lenses of her glasses.

"Who . . . are you?"

"Ane Pedersen," she said, instantly understanding the reason for Harry's perplexed expression. "I'm Sylvia's sister. We're twins."

Harry began to cough.

"This is Inspector Harry Hole," he heard Katrine say behind him. "And I'm Katrine Bratt. We were hoping to find Rolf here."

"He's at the funeral parlor." Ane Pedersen paused, and at that moment all three of them knew what the others were thinking: How do you actually bury a head?

"And you've stepped into the breach?" Katrine said, rallying.

Ane Pedersen smiled briefly. "Yes." She stepped down from the chair with care, still holding the wooden mask.

"Ceremonial or spiritual mask?" Katrine asked.

"Ceremonial," she said. "Hutu. Eastern Congo."

Harry looked at his watch. "When will he be back?"

"I don't know."

"Any guesses?"

"As I said, I don't—"

"That really is a beautiful mask," Katrine interrupted. "You've been to the Congo, and you bought it yourself, didn't you?"

Ane gave her a look of amazement. "How did you know?"

"I can see by the way you're holding it, not covering the eyes or mouth. You respect the spirits."

"Are you interested in masks?"

"Sort of," Katrine said, pointing to a black mask with small arms at the side and legs hanging underneath. The face was half human, half animal. "That's a Kpelie mask, isn't it?"

"Yes, from the Ivory Coast. Senufo."

"A power mask?" Katrine ran a hand over the stiff, greasy animal hair hanging off the coconut shell at the top of the mask.

"Wow, you do know a lot," Ane said.

"What's a power mask?" Harry asked.

"What it says," Ane answered. "In Africa masks like these are not just empty symbols. A person wearing this type of mask in the Lo community automatically has all executive and judicial power bestowed upon him. No one questions the authority of the wearer; the mask confers power."

"I saw two death masks hanging by the door," Katrine said. "Very beautiful."

Ane smiled in response. "I have several of them. They're from Lesotho."

"Can I have a look?"

"Of course. Wait here a moment."

She was gone, and Harry looked at Katrine.

"I just thought it might be useful to have a chat with her," she said, to answer his unspoken question. "To check if there were any family secrets, you understand?"

"I understand. And you'd do that best on your own."

"You've got something to do?"

"I'll be in my office. If Rolf Ottersen turns up, remember to get a written statement waiving patient confidentiality."

By the door, as he left, Harry cast a glance at the human faces, leathery, shrunken and frozen in a scream. He assumed they were imitations.

Eli Kvale trundled her shopping cart between the shelves of the ICA supermarket at Ullevål Stadium. It was huge. A bit more expensive than other supermarkets, but with a much better selection. She didn't come here every day, only when she wanted to make something nice. And tonight her son, Trygve, was coming home from the States. He was in his third year of economics at a university in Montana, but didn't have any exams this autumn and was going to study at home until January. Andreas would drive straight from the church office to pick him up at Gardermoen Airport. And she knew that by the time they were home they would be deep in conversation about fly-fishing and canoe trips.

She leaned over the freezer and felt the cold rise as a shadow passed her. And without looking up she knew it was the same one. The same shadow that had passed her when she was standing by the fresh-food counter, and in the parking lot when she was locking the car. It meant nothing. It was just the old stuff surfacing. She had come to terms with the fact that her fears would never quite let go, even though it was half a human lifetime away now. At the checkout she chose the longest line; her experience was that this was generally the quickest. Or at least she thought it was her experience. Andreas believed she was mistaken. Someone joined the line behind her. So there were more mistaken people, she noted. She didn't turn around, just thought the person must have been carrying a load of frozen goods: She could feel the cold on her back.

But when she did turn around, there was no longer anyone there. Her eyes wanted to scour the other lines. Don't start, she thought. Don't start this again.

Once outside, she forced herself to walk slowly to the car, not to look around, to unlock the car, put in the groceries, sit down and drive off. And as the Toyota slowly crawled up the long hills to the duplex apartment in Nordberg, her mind was on Trygve and

the dinner that had to be ready the moment he and
Andreas came in through the door.

Harry was listening to Espen Lepsvik on the telephone and gazing up at the photographs of his dead
colleagues. Lepsvik already had his group assembled
and was asking Harry for access to all the relevant information.

"You'll get a password from our IT boss," Harry
said. "Then you go into the folder labeled 'The
Snowman' on the Crime Squad network."

"The Snowman?"

"Got to be called something."

"OK. Thanks, Hole. How often do you want reports from me?"

"Just when you've got something. And, Lepsvik?"

"Yes?"

"Keep off our turf."

"And what exactly is your turf?"

"You concentrate on tips, witnesses and ex-cons
who might be possible serial killers. That's where the
brunt of the work lies."

Harry knew what the experienced Kripos detective
was thinking: the shit jobs.

Lepsvik cleared his throat. "So we agree there is a
connection between the disappearances?"

"We don't have to agree. You follow your instincts."

"Fine."

Harry hung up and looked at the screen in front of him. He had gone onto the Web site Borghild had recommended and seen pictures of female beauties and male-model types with dotted lines on their faces and bodies suggesting where their perfect appearance could still—if desired—be adjusted. The doctor, Idar Vetlesen, himself was smiling at Harry from a photograph, indistinguishable from his male models.

Under the picture of Vetlesen there was a résumé listing diplomas and courses with long names in French and English that, for all Harry knew, could have been completed in two months, but still gave you the right to add new Latin abbreviations to your doctorate. He had Googled Idar Vetlesen and come up with a list of results from what he thought were curling competitions, as well as an old Web site from one of his previous employers, the Marienlyst Clinic. It was when he saw the name beside Idar Vetlesen's that he thought it was probably true what people said: Norway is such a small country that everyone is, at most, two acquaintances from knowing everyone else.

Katrine Bratt came in and plumped down onto the chair across from Harry with a deep sigh. She crossed her legs.

"Do you think it's true that beautiful people are more preoccupied with beauty than ugly people?" Harry asked.

"I don't know," Katrine said. "But there's a kind of logic to it, I suppose. People with high IQs are so fixated on IQs that they have founded their own club, haven't they? I suppose you focus on what you have. I would guess you're fairly proud of your investigative talent."

"You mean the rat-catching gene? The innate ability to lock up people with mental illnesses, addiction problems, well-under-average intellects and well-above-average childhood deprivations?"

"So we're just rat-catchers, then?"

"Yep. And that's why we're so happy when once in a blue moon a case like this lands on our table. A chance to go big-game hunting, to shoot a lion, an elephant, a fucking dinosaur."

Katrine didn't laugh. On the contrary, she nodded her head gravely.

"What did Sylvia's twin sister have to say?"

"I was in danger of becoming her best friend." Katrine sighed, folding her hands over a stockinged knee.

"Tell me."

"Well," she began, and Harry noticed his "well" in her mouth, "Ane told me that both Sylvia and Rolf thought that Rolf had been the lucky one when they got together. While everyone else thought the opposite. Rolf had just finished qualifying as an engineer at the Technical University in Bergen and had moved to Oslo and a job with Kværner Engineering. Sylvia was apparently the type who wakes up every morning with a new idea about what she's going to do with her life. She had half a dozen different majors at the university and had never been in the same job for more than six months. She was stubborn, hotheaded, spoiled, a declared socialist and attracted by ideologies that preached the obliteration of the ego. The few girlfriends she had she manipulated, and the men she was involved with left her after a short while because they couldn't take it. Her sister thought that Rolf was so deeply in love with her because she represented his absolute opposite. You see, he had followed in his father's footsteps and become an engineer. He came from a family that believed in the unseen charitable hand of capitalism and middle-class happiness. Sylvia thought that we in the Western world were materialistic and corrupt as human beings, that we had lost touch with our real identity and the source of happiness. And that some king in Ethiopia was the reincarnated Messiah."

"Haile Selassie," Harry said. "Rastafarian beliefs."

"No flies on you."

"Bob Marley records. Well, that may explain the link with Africa."

"Maybe." Katrine shifted position in her chair, her left leg crossing her right now, and Harry directed his gaze elsewhere. "Anyway, Rolf and Sylvia took a year off and traveled around West Africa. It turned out to be a road to Damascus for them both. Rolf discovered that his vocation was to help Africa get back on its feet. Sylvia, who had a big Ethiopian flag tattooed on her back, discovered that everyone looked out for himself, even in Africa. So they started up Taste of Africa. Rolf to help a poor continent, Sylvia because the combination of cheap imports and government support seemed like easy money. She had the same motive when she was caught with a backpack full of marijuana at customs, returning from Lagos."

"There you go."

"Sylvia was given a short conditional sentence because she was able to sow seeds of doubt. She said she didn't know what was in the backpack, she had brought it with her as a favor for a Nigerian living in Norway."

"Mm. What else?"

"Ane likes Rolf. He's kind and thoughtful and has boundless love for the children. But apparently he's quite blind in all things Sylvia. Twice she fell in love with other men and left Rolf and the children. But the men left her and both times Rolf happily took her back."

"What was her hold over him, do you think?"

Katrine Bratt mounted a smile tinged with sadness and gazed into the air as her hand stroked the hem of her skirt. "The usual, I would guess. No one can leave someone they have good sex with. They can try, but they always go back. We're simple souls like that, aren't we?"

Harry nodded slowly. "And what about the men who left her and didn't come back?"

"It's different with men. Over the course of time some of them suffer from performance issues."

Harry eyed her. And decided not to pursue that subject.

"Did you see Rolf Ottersen?"

"Yes, he arrived ten minutes after you left," Katrine said. "And he looked better than last time. He'd never heard of the plastic surgery clinic in Bygdøy, but he signed the declaration of consent to waive doctor-patient confidentiality." She left the folded sheet on his desk.

An ice-cold wind blew over the low stands at Valle Hovin, where Harry sat watching the ice skaters gliding around the circuit. Oleg's technique had become more supple and effective in the last year. Every time his friend accelerated to pass him, Oleg sank lower, dug in harder and calmly sailed off.

Harry called Espen Lepsvik and they caught up on each other's news. Harry found out that a dark sedan had been seen entering Hoffsveien late on the night Birte disappeared. And it had returned the same way not long afterward.

"Dark sedan," Harry repeated with a grim shiver. "Sometime late that night."

"Yes, I know it's not a lot to go on." Lepsvik sighed.

Harry was stuffing the phone in his jacket pocket when he sensed that something was obscuring one of the floodlights.

"Sorry I'm a bit late."

He looked up into the jovial, smiling face of Mathias Lund-Helgesen.

Rakel's envoy took a seat. "Are you a winter sportsman, Harry?"

Harry noticed that Mathias had this direct way of looking at you, with an expression that was so intense it gave you the feeling he was listening even when he was talking.

"Not really. Bit of skating. And you?"

Mathias shook his head. "But I've decided that the day my life's work is done and I'm so ill I no longer want to live, I'll take the lift up to the top of the ski-jump tower on that hill there."

He jerked his thumb over his shoulder and Harry did not need to turn. Holmenkollen, Oslo's dearest monument and worst ski jump, could be seen from everywhere in town.

"And then I'll jump. Not on skis but from the tower."

"Dramatic," Harry said.

Mathias smiled. "A hundred-and-thirty-foot free fall. Over in seconds."

"Not imminent, I trust."

"With the level of anti-Scl-70 in my blood, you never know." Mathias laughed grimly.

"Anti-Scl-70?"

"Yes, antibodies are a good thing, but you should always be suspicious when they appear. They're there for a reason."

"Mm. I thought suicide was a heretical notion for a doctor."

"No one knows better than doctors what diseases involve. I agree with the stoic Zeno, who considered suicide a worthy action when death was more attractive than life. When he was ninety-eight years old he dislocated his big toe. This upset him so much that he went home and hanged himself."

"So why not hang yourself instead of going to all the trouble of climbing to the top of the Holmenkollen ski jump?"

"Well, death should be a sort of homage to life. Anyway, I have to confess that I like the idea of the publicity that would come in its wake. My research attracts very little attention, I'm afraid." Mathias's jolly laughter was slashed to pieces by the sound of swift-moving skate blades. "By the way, I'm sorry I bought new speed skates for Oleg. Rakel didn't tell me that you had planned to buy a pair for his birthday until afterward."

"No problem."

"He would have preferred to have them from you, you know."

Harry didn't answer.

"I envy you, Harry. You can sit here and read the paper, make a call on your phone, talk to other people; for him it's good enough that you're just **here**. When I cheer and shout and encourage him and do everything the manual says a good father should do, he just gets irritated. Did you know that he polishes his skates every day because he knows that you used to do that? And until Rakel demanded that skates had to be kept indoors, he insisted on leaving them outside on the steps because you once said that skate steel should always be kept cold. You're his role model, Harry."

Harry shuddered at the thought. But somewhere deep inside—no, not even that far—he was pleased to hear this. Because he was a jealous bastard who would have liked to imprecate a mild curse on Mathias's attempts to win over Oleg.

Mathias fidgeted with a coat button. "It's strange in these divorce-ridden times, with children and their deep awareness of their origins. The way a new father can never replace the real one."

"Oleg's real father lives in Russia," Harry said.

"On paper, yes," Mathias said with a crooked smile. "But not in reality, Harry."

Oleg sped past and waved to the two of them. Mathias waved back.

"You've worked with a doctor called Idar Vetlesen," Harry said.

Mathias eyed him with surprise. "Idar, yes. At Marienlyst Clinic. Goodness, do you know Idar?"

"No, I was Googling his name and found an old Web site listing doctors employed at the clinic. And your name was there."

"That's a few years ago now, but we had a lot of fun at Marienlyst. The clinic was started at a time when everyone believed that private health enterprises were bound to make a lot of money. And closed down when we saw things were not like that, of course."

"You went bust?"

"I think **downsized** was the term used. Are you a patient of Idar's?"

"No, his name came up in connection with a case. Can you tell me what kind of person he is?"

"Idar Vetlesen?" Mathias laughed. "Yes, I can say quite a bit about him. We studied together and hung around in the same crowd for many years."

"Does that mean you no longer have any contact?"

Mathias shrugged. "I suppose we were quite different, Idar and I. Most people in our crowd saw medicine as . . . well, as a calling. Apart from Idar. He made no bones about it. He was studying medicine because it was the profession that commanded most respect. At any rate, I admire his honesty."

"So Idar Vetlesen was preoccupied with earning respect?"

"There was money, too, of course. No one was surprised when Idar took up plastic surgery. Or that he ended up at a clinic for a select clientele comprising the rich and famous. He had always been attracted by that sort of person. He wants to be like them, to move in their circles. The problem is that Idar tries a bit too hard. I can imagine that these celebrities smile to his face, but behind his back they call him a clinging, pretentious jackass."

"Are you saying he's the kind who would go to great lengths to achieve his goals?"

Mathias mulled this over. "Idar has always searched for something that could bring him fame. Idar's problem is not that he isn't energetic, but that he's never found his mission in life. The last time I spoke to him he sounded frustrated, depressed, even."

"Can you imagine him finding a mission that would bring him fame? Something outside medicine, perhaps?"

"I haven't thought about it, but maybe. He's not exactly a born doctor."

"In what way?"

"In the same way that Idar admires the successful and despises the weak and infirm. He's not the only doctor to do so, but he's the only one to say so outright." Mathias laughed. "In our circle, we all started as out-and-out idealists who at some point or other became more preoccupied with consultant positions, paying off the new garage and overtime rates. At least Idar didn't betray any ideals; he was the same from the get-go."

Idar Vetlesen laughed. "Did Mathias really say that? That I haven't betrayed any ideals?"

He had a pleasant, almost feminine face, with eyebrows so narrow that one might have suspected him of plucking them, and teeth so white and regular that one might have suspected they were not his own. His complexion looked soft and touched up; his hair was thick and rippled with vitality. In short, he looked several years younger than his thirty-seven.

"I don't know what he meant by that," Harry lied.

They were each ensconced in a deep armchair in the library of a spacious white house, built according to the old, august Bygdøy style. His childhood home, Idar Vetlesen had explained as he guided Harry through the two vast, dark lounges and into a room whose walls were lined with books. Mikkjel Fønhus. Kjell Aukrust. Einar Gerhardsen's **Tillitsmannen.** A broad range of popular literature and political biographies. A whole shelf of yellowing issues of

Reader's Digest. Harry didn't see a single copy published after 1970.

"Oh, I know what he meant." Idar chuckled.

Harry had an inkling what Mathias had implied by the two of them having a lot of fun at the Marienlyst Clinic: They probably competed to see who could laugh the most.

"Mathias, the saintly bastard. Lucky bastard, more like. No, by Christ, I mean both." Idar Vetlesen's laughter pealed out. "They say they don't believe in God, but my God-fearing colleagues are terrified moral strivers accumulating good deeds because deep down they're petrified of burning in hell."

"And aren't you?" Harry asked.

Idar elevated one of his elegantly formed brows and eyed Harry with interest. Idar was wearing soft light-blue moccasins with loose laces, jeans and a white tennis shirt with a polo player over the left breast. Harry couldn't remember which brand it was, only that for some reason he connected it with bores.

"I come from a practical family, Inspector. My father was a taxi driver. We believe what we can see."

"Mm. Nice house for a taxi driver."

"He owned a taxi company, had three licenses. But here in Bygdøy a taxi driver is, and always will be, a plebeian."

Harry looked at the doctor and tried to determine whether he was on speed or anything else. Vetlesen was sitting back in his chair in an exaggeratedly casual fashion, as though anxious to hide a restless or excited state. The same thought had gone through Harry's mind when he had called to explain that the police wanted answers to a few questions and Vetlesen had extended an almost effusive invitation to his home.

"But you didn't want to drive a taxi," Harry said. "You wanted . . . to make people look better?"

Vetlesen smiled. "You could say that I offer my services in the vanity market. Or that I repair people's exteriors to soothe the pain inside. Take your pick. Actually, I don't give a damn." Anticipating a shocked reaction from Harry, Vetlesen laughed. When Harry did not take the bait, Vetlesen's expression became more serious. "I see myself as a sculptor. I don't have a vocation. I like to change appearances, to shape faces. I've always liked that. I'm good at it, and people pay me for it. That's all."

"Mm."

"But that doesn't mean that I'm without principles. And patient confidentiality is one of them."

Harry didn't answer.

"I was talking to Borghild," he said. "I know what you're after, Inspector. And I understand that this is a grave matter. But I can't help you. I'm bound by my oath."

"Not any longer." Harry took the folded sheet of paper out of an inside pocket and placed it on the table between them. "This statement, signed by the father of the twins, exempts you."

Idar shook his head. "That won't make any difference."

Harry frowned in surprise. "Oh?"

"I can't say who has been to see me or what they've

said, but I can say in general that those who come to a doctor with their children are protected by the oath of client confidentiality, even with respect to their spouse, if they so wish."

"Why would Sylvia Ottersen hide from her husband the fact that she'd been to see you with her twins?"

"Our behavior may seem rigid, but do remember that many of our clients are famous people who are exposed to idle gossip and unwanted press attention. Go to Kunstnernes Hus on a Friday evening and take a look around. You have no idea how many of them have had parts trimmed here and there at my clinic. They would swoon at the very idea that their visits here might become public knowledge. Our reputation is based on discretion. If it should ever come out that we are sloppy with client information, the consequences for the clinic would be catastrophic. I'm sure you understand."

"We have two murder victims and one single coincidence," Harry said. "They've both been to your clinic."

"That I neither will nor can confirm. But let us suppose for the sake of argument that they have." Vetlesen twirled a hand through the air. "So what? Norway is a country of few people and even fewer doctors. Do you know how few handshakes we all are from having met one another? The coincidence that they have been to the same doctor is no more dramatic than that they might have been on the same tram at some point. Ever met friends on a tram?"

Harry couldn't think of a single occasion. First off, he didn't take the tram that often.

"It was a long trip to be told that you won't tell me anything," Harry said.

"My apologies. I invited you here because I assumed that the alternative was the police station. Where, right now, the press is scrutinizing the comings and goings day and night. Yes, indeed, I know those people . . ."

"You are aware that I can get a search warrant, which would render your oath of confidentiality null and void?"

"Fine by me," Vetlesen said. "In that case the clinic will be on the side of the angels. But until then . . ." He closed an imaginary zipper across his mouth.

Harry shifted in his seat. They both knew that to get the courts to waive the oath of confidentiality, even for a murder case, the police would need clear evidence that the doctor's information would be of significance. And what did they have? As Vetlesen himself put it, a chance meeting on a tram. Harry felt a strong need to do something. To drink. Or to pump iron. With a vengeance. He breathed in.

"I'm still obliged to ask you where you were on the nights of the second and the fourth of November."

"I was counting on that." Vetlesen smiled. "So I had a think. I was here with . . . yes, and here she is."

An elderly woman with mousy hair hanging like a curtain around her head entered the room with mousy steps and a silver tray bearing two cups of coffee, which rattled ominously. The expression on her face suggested she was carrying a cross and a crown of thorns. She cast a glance at her son, who jumped up in a flash and took the tray.

"Thanks, Mother."

"Tie your shoelaces." She half turned to Harry. "Is anyone going to inform me who comes and goes in my house?"

"This is Inspector Hole, Mother. He'd like to know where I was yesterday and three days ago."

Harry stood up and stretched out his hand.

"I remember, of course," she said, giving Harry a resigned look and a hand covered in liver spots. "We watched that talk show featuring your curling friend. And I didn't like what he said about the royal family. What's his name again?"

"Arve Støp." Idar sighed.

The old lady leaned over toward Harry. "He said we should get rid of the royals. Can you imagine anything so dreadful? Where would we have been without the royal family during the war?"

"Right where we are now," Idar said. "Seldom has a head of state done so little during a war. And he also said that broad support for the monarchy was the final proof that most people believe in trolls and fairies."

"Isn't that dreadful?"

"Veritably, Mother." Idar smiled, placing a hand on her shoulder and simultaneously catching sight of his watch, a Breitling, which seemed large and unwieldy on his thin wrist. "My goodness! I have to go now, Hole. We'll have to hurry this coffee along."

Harry shook his head and smiled at Fru Vetlesen. "I'm sure it's delicious but I'll have to save it for another day."

She heaved a deep sigh, mumbled something inaudible, took the tray and shuffled out again.

When Idar and Harry were in the hall, Harry turned. "What did you mean by **lucky**?"

"Sorry?"

"You said Mathias Lund-Helgesen wasn't just a saintly bastard, he was lucky, too."

"Oh that! It's this woman he's fixed himself up with. Mathias is generally pretty helpless in this area, but she must have been with a couple of losers in her life. Must have needed a God-fearer like him. Well, don't tell Mathias I said that. Or actually even mention it."

"By the way, do you know what anti-Scl-70 is?"

"It's an antibody in the blood. May suggest the presence of scleroderma. Do you know someone who's got it?"

"I don't even know what scleroderma is." Harry realized he should let it go. He **wanted** to let it go. But he couldn't. "So Mathias said she had been with some losers?"

"My interpretation. Saint Mathias doesn't use expressions like **loser** about people. In his eyes, every human has the potential to become a better person." Idar Vetlesen's laughter echoed through the dark rooms.

After Harry had said his thank-yous, put on his boots and was standing on the step outside, he turned and watched—as the door slid closed—Idar sitting bent over, tying his shoelaces.

On the way back, Harry called Skarre and asked him to print out the picture of Vetlesen from the clinic Web site and go over to the Narcotics Unit to see if any of the undercover guys had seen him buying speed.

"In the street?" Skarre asked. "Don't all doctors have that kind of thing in their medicine cabinets?"

"Yes, but the rules governing the declaration of drug supplies are now so strict that a doctor would rather buy his amphetamines off a dealer in Skipper-gata."

They hung up, and Harry called Katrine in the office.

"Nothing for the moment," she said. "I'm leaving now. You on your way home?"

"Yes." Harry hesitated. "What do you think the chances are of the court ruling that Vetlesen can waive his Hippocratic oath?"

"With what we've got? Of course, I could put on an extra-short skirt, pop over to the courthouse and find a judge of the right age. But, to be frank, I think we can forget it."

"Agreed."

Harry headed for Bislett. Thinking about his apartment, stripped bare. He looked at his watch. Changed his mind and turned down Pilestredet toward the Police HQ.

It was two o'clock in the morning as, once again, Harry had Katrine, drowsy with sleep, on the phone.

"What's up now?" she said.

"I'm in the office and have had a look at what you've found. You said all the missing women were married with children. I think there could be something in that."

"What?"

"I have no idea. I just needed to hear myself say that to someone. So that I could decide if it sounded idiotic."

"And how does it sound?"

"Idiotic. Good night."

Eli Kvale lay with her eyes wide open. Beside her, Andreas was breathing heavily, without a care in the world. A stripe of moonlight fell between the curtains across the wall, on the crucifix she had bought during her honeymoon in Rome. What had woken her? Was it Trygve? Was he up? The dinner and the evening had gone just as she had hoped. She had seen happy, shiny faces in the candlelight, and they had all talked at the same time, they had so much to tell! Mostly Trygve. And when he talked about Montana, about his studies and friends there, she had stayed quiet just looking at this boy, this young man who was maturing into an adult, becoming whatever he would become, making his own life. That was what made her happiest: that he could choose. Openly and freely. Not like her. Not on the sly, in secret.

She heard the house creaking, heard the walls talking to one another.

But there had been a different sound, an alien sound. A sound from outside.

She got out of bed, went over to the window and opened the curtains a crack. It had snowed. The apple trees had woolen branches and the moonlight was reflected on the thin white ground covering, emphasizing every detail in the garden. Her gaze swept from the gate to the garage, unsure what it was she was looking for. Then it stopped. She gave a gasp of surprise and terror. Don't start this again, she told herself. It must have been Trygve. He's got jet lag, hasn't been able to sleep and has gone out. The footprints went from the gate to right under the window where she was standing. Like a line of black dots in the thin coating of snow. A dramatic pause in the text.

There were no footprints leading back.

12

The Conversation

"One of the Narc guys recognized him," Skarre said. "When I showed him the picture of Vetlesen, the detective said he'd seen him several times at the intersection of Skippergata and Tollbugata."

"What's at the intersection?" asked Gunnar Hagen, who had insisted on joining the Monday-morning meeting in Harry's office.

Skarre looked at Hagen uncertainly to check if the POB was joking.

"Dealers, whores, bookies," he said. "It's the new **in** place after we chased them out of Plata."

"Only there?" Hagen asked, jutting out his chin. "I was told it was more widespread now."

"It's like the center," Skarre said. "But of course you'll find them down toward the Stock Exchange and up toward Norges Bank. Around the Astrup Fearnley Museum of Modern Art, Gamle Logen concert hall and the Church Mission café . . ." He stopped when Harry yawned out loud.

"Sorry," Harry apologized. "It was a hard weekend. Go on."

"The detective couldn't remember seeing him buy dope. He thought Vetlesen was frequenting Hotel Leon."

At that moment Katrine Bratt came through the door. She was unkempt and pale, and her eyes were slits, but she sang out a cheery Bergensian greeting as she searched the room for a chair. Bjørn Holm leapt up from his, flourished a hand and went to look for another.

"Leon in Skippergata?" Hagen queried. "Is that a place they sell drugs?"

"Could well be," Skarre said. "But I've seen loads of black hookers going in there, so I suppose it must be a so-called massage place."

"Hardly," Katrine Bratt said, standing with her back to them as she hung her coat on the coatrack. "Massage parlors are part of the indoor market, and the Vietnamese have that now. They stay in the suburbs, in discreet residential areas, use Asian women and keep away from the territory of the African outdoor market."

"I think I've seen a poster for cheap rooms hanging outside," Harry said. "Four hundred kroner a night."

"That's right," Katrine said. "They have small rooms that are officially hired out by the day, but in practice on an hourly basis. Black money. Customers don't exactly ask for a receipt. But the hotel owner, who earns the most, is white."

"Lady's spot on." Skarre grinned at Hagen. "Strange

that the Bergen Sexual Offenses Unit should suddenly be so well up on Oslo brothels."

"They're the same everywhere," Katrine said. "Want to bet on anything I said?"

"The owner's a Pakistani," Skarre said. "Two hundred kronerooneys."

"Done."

"OK," Harry said, clapping his hands. "What are we sitting here for?"

The owner of the Leon Hotel was Børre Hansen, from Solør, in the east; his skin was as grayish white as the slush the so-called guests brought in on their shoes and left on the worn parquet floor underneath the sign saying RESEPTION in black letters. As neither the clientele nor Børre was particularly interested in spelling, the sign had remained there, uncontested, for as long as Børre had had it: four years. Before that, he had traveled up and down Sweden selling Bibles, trying his hand at border trade with discarded porno films in Svinesund and acquiring an accent, sounding like a cross between a jazz musician and a preacher. It was in Svinesund that he had met Natasha, a Russian erotic dancer, and they had escaped from her Russian manager only by the skin of their teeth. Natasha had been given a new name and now she lived with Børre in Oslo. He had taken over the Leon from three Serbians who, for a variety of reasons, were no longer able to stay in the country, and he continued where they left off, since there had been no reason to alter the business model: hiring out the rooms on a short-term—often extremely short-term—basis. The revenue generally came in the form of cash, and the guests were undemanding with regard to standards and maintenance. It was a good business. A business he did not want to lose. Consequently he disliked everything about the two people standing in front of him, most of all their ID cards.

The tall man with the cropped hair placed a picture on the counter. "Seen this man?"

Børre Hansen shook his head, relieved in spite of everything that it was not him they were after.

"Sure?" said the man, resting his elbows on the counter and leaning forward.

Børre looked at the picture again, thinking he should have scrutinized the ID card more closely; this guy seemed more like one of the dopeheads hanging around the streets than a policeman. And the girl behind him didn't look like a policewoman, either. True, she had that hard look, the whore look, but the rest of her was lady, all lady. If she got herself a pimp who didn't rob her, she could earn five times her wage, at least.

"We know you're running a brothel here," the policeman said.

"I'm running a legit hotel, I've got a license and all my papers are in order. Do you want to see?" Børre pointed to the little office directly behind the reception area.

The policeman shook his head. "You hire out rooms to prostitutes and their clients. It's against the law."

"Listen here," Børre said, swallowing. The conversation had taken the course he had feared. "I'm not interested in what my guests are up to so long as they pay their bills."

"But I am," said the policeman in a low voice. "Have a closer look at the picture."

Børre looked. The photo must have been taken some years before because he seemed so young. Young and carefree, without a trace of despair or anguish.

"Last time I checked, prostitution in Norway was not illegal," Børre Hansen said.

"No," the policewoman said. "But running a brothel is."

Børre Hansen did his best to assume an indignant expression.

"As you know, at regular intervals the police are obliged to check that hotel regulations are being complied with," the policeman said. "Such as emergency exits from all rooms in case of fire."

"Submission of foreign guests' registration forms," added the policewoman.

"Fax machine for incoming police inquiries about guests."

"VAT account."

He was teetering. The policeman delivered the knockout blow.

"We're considering bringing in the Fraud Squad to check the accounts you hold for certain customers whom undercover police have observed coming and going in recent weeks."

Børre Hansen could feel the nausea coming. Natasha. The mortgage. And incipient panic at the thought of freezing cold, pitch-black winter evenings on unfamiliar steps with Bibles under his arms.

"Or we might not," the policeman said. "It's a question of priorities. A question of how to use the police's limited resources. Isn't it, Bratt?"

The policewoman nodded.

"He rents a room twice a week," Børre Hansen said. "Always the same room. He's there all evening."

"All evening?"

"He has several visitors."

"Black or white?" the woman asked.

"Black. Only black."

"How many?"

"I don't know. It varies. Eight. Twelve."

"At the same time?" the policewoman exclaimed.

"No, they change. Some come in pairs. They're often in pairs on the street as well, of course."

"Jesus," the policeman said.

Børre Hansen nodded.

"What name does he sign in under?"

"Don't remember."

"But we'll find it in the guest book, won't we? And in the accounts?"

The back of Børre Hansen's shirt was soaked with sweat under his shiny suit jacket. "They call him Dr. White. The women who ask for him, that is."

"Doctor?"

"Nothing to do with me. He . . ." Børre Hansen hesitated. He didn't want to say any more than he had to. On the other hand, he wanted to show a willingness to cooperate. And this was already a lost customer. "He carries one of those big doctor's bags with him. And always asks for . . . extra towels."

"Oooh," said the woman. "Doesn't sound good. Have you seen any blood when you clean the room?"

Børre didn't answer.

"If you clean the room," the policeman corrected. "Well?"

Børre sighed. "Not much, not more than . . ." He paused.

"Than usual?" the woman asked sarcastically.

"I don't think he hurts them," Børre Hansen hastened to say, and regretted it instantly.

"Why not?" the policeman snapped.

Børre shrugged. "They wouldn't come back, I suppose."

"And it's just women?"

Børre nodded. But the policeman must have noticed something. A nervous tautening of his neck muscles, a little twitch in the bloodshot membrane of his eye.

"Men?" he asked.

Børre shook his head.

"Boys?" asked the policewoman, who clearly scented the same thing as her colleague.

Børre Hansen shook his head again, but with that little, almost imperceptible delay that arises when the brain has to choose between alternatives.

"Children," said the policeman, lowering his forehead as if about to charge. "Has he had children here?"

"No!" Børre shouted, feeling the sweat break out over his whole body. "Never! I draw the line at that. There have only been the two times . . . And they didn't come in. I threw them back out on the street!"

"African?" the man asked.

"Yes."

"Boys or girls?"

"Both."

"Did they come alone?" the woman asked.

"No, with women. The mothers, I believe. But, as I said, I didn't let them go up to his room."

"You said he comes here twice a week. Does he have fixed times?"

"Monday and Thursday. From eight to midnight. And he's always on time."

"Tonight, too?" the man said, looking at his colleague. "OK, thanks for your assistance."

Børre released the air from his lungs and discovered that his legs were aching—he had been standing on his toes the whole time. "Glad to help," he said.

The police officers walked toward the door. Børre knew he should keep his mouth shut, but he wouldn't be able to sleep if he didn't receive an assurance.

"But," he said as they were leaving, "but then, we have a deal, don't we?"

The policeman turned, with one eyebrow raised in surprise. "About what?"

Børre swallowed. "About these . . . inspections?"

The policeman rubbed his chin. "Are you implying that you have something to hide?"

Børre blinked twice. Then he heard his own high-pitched nervous laughter as he gushed: "No, no, of course not! Ha-ha! Everything here's in order."

"Excellent, so you have nothing to fear when they come. Inspections are not my responsibility."

They left with Børre opening his mouth, about to protest, to say something, he just didn't know what.

The telephone welcomed Harry on his return to the office.

It was Rakel wanting to give him back the DVD she had borrowed from him.

"**The Rules of Attraction?**" Harry repeated, taken aback. "Have you got it?"

"You said it was on your list of most underrated modern films."

"Yes, but you never like those films."

"That's not true."

"You didn't like **Starship Troopers**."

"That's because it's a crap macho film."

"It's satire," Harry said.

"Of what?"

"American society's inherent fascism. The Hardy Boys meet Hitler Youth."

"Come on, Harry. War on giant insects on a remote planet?"

"Fear of foreigners."

"Anyway, I liked that seventies film of yours, the one about bugging . . ."

"**The Conversation,**" Harry said. "Coppola's best."

"That's the one. I agree **that** is underrated."

"It's not underrated," Harry sighed. "Just forgotten. It was nominated for an Oscar for Best Film."

"I'm having dinner with some friends this evening. I can drop the film off on my way home. Will you be up at around midnight?"

"Might be. Why not drop by on your way to the meal instead?"

"Bit more stressful, but I can do it, of course."

Her answer had come fast. But not fast enough for Harry not to hear it.

"Mm," he said. "I can't sleep anyway. I'm inhaling fungus and I can't catch my breath."

"You know what? I'll pop it in the mailbox downstairs so you don't have to get up. OK?"

"OK."

They hung up. Harry saw that his hand was trembling. Concluded it had to be due to lack of nicotine and headed for the elevator.

Katrine came out of her office door as if she knew it was him stomping along. "I spoke to Espen Lepsvik. We can have one of his guys for the job tonight."

"Great."

"Good news?"

"What?"

"You're smiling."

"Am I? Must be happy, then."

"About what?"

He patted his pocket. "Cigarette."

· · ·

Eli Kvale was sitting at the kitchen table with a cup of tea, looking out at the yard and listening to the comforting rumble of the dishwasher. The black telephone was on the countertop. The receiver had grown hot in her hands, from squeezing it so tight, but it had been a wrong number. Trygve had enjoyed the fish au gratin—it was his favorite, he had said. But he said that about most things. He was a good boy. Outside, the grass was brown and lifeless; there were no signs of the snow that had fallen. And who knows? Perhaps she had just dreamed the whole thing.

She flipped aimlessly through a magazine. She had taken off the first few days that Trygve was at home so they could have some time together. Have a good talk, just the two of them. But now he was sitting with Andreas in the living room and they were doing what she had made space for. That was fine—they had more to talk about. They were so similar, after all. And in fact she had always liked the idea of a good talk more than the reality. Because the conversation always had to stop somewhere. At the huge, insurmountable wall.

Of course, she had agreed to name the boy after Andreas's father. At least let the boy take a name from Andreas's side. She had been close to spilling the beans before she was due to give birth. About the empty parking lot, about the darkness, about the black prints in the snow. About the knife to her neck and the faceless breath against her cheek. On the way home, with his seed running into her underwear, she had prayed to God that it would continue to run until it was all gone. But her prayers had not been answered.

Later she had often wondered how things would have been if Andreas had not been a priest and his view of abortion so uncompromising, and if she had not been such a coward. If Trygve had not been born. But by then the wall had already been built, an unshakable wall of silence.

That Trygve and Andreas were so similar was a silver lining. It had even sparked a little hope, so she had gone to a doctor's office where no one knew her, given them two strands of hair that she had taken from their pillows and that she had read were enough to find a code of something called DNA, a kind of genetic fingerprint. The doctor had sent the hairs to the Institute of Forensic Medicine at Rikshospitalet, which was employing this new method in paternity cases. And after two months, all doubt was gone. It had not been a dream: the parking lot, the black prints, the panting, the pain.

She looked at the telephone again. Of course it had been a wrong number. The breathing she had heard at the other end was the perplexed reaction to hearing an unexpected voice, indecision as to whether to put the receiver down or not. That was all.

Harry went into the hall and picked up the entry phone.

"Hello?" he shouted over Franz Ferdinand on the sitting-room stereo.

No answer, just a car whizzing past on Sofies Gate. "Hello?"

"Hi! It's Rakel. Were you in bed?"

He could hear from her voice that she had been drinking. Not much but enough for her pitch to be half a tone higher, and her laughter, that beautifully deep laughter, rippled over her words.

"No," he said. "Nice evening?"

"Quite."

"It's only eleven o'clock."

"The girls wanted an early night. It's a workday and so on."

"Mm."

Harry visualized her. The teasing look, the alcohol sheen in her eyes.

"I've got the film," she said. "If I'm going to drop it in the mailbox, I think you might have to open up."

"Right."

He raised his finger to press the bell to let her in. Waited. Knowing that this was a window of time. They had two seconds at their disposal. For the moment they had all the fall-back positions. He liked fall-back positions. And he knew very well that he didn't want this to happen—it was too complicated, too painful to go through again. So why was his chest heaving as if he had two hearts? Why hadn't he immediately pressed the button, so that she would have been in and out of the building and out of his head?

Now, he thought, placing the tip of his finger against the hard plastic of the button.

"Or," she said, "I could come up with it."

Harry already knew before speaking that his voice was going to sound strange.

"You don't need to," he said. "My mailbox is the one without a name. Good night."

"Good night."

He pressed the button. Went into the sitting room, turned up Franz Ferdinand, loud, tried to blast out his thoughts, forget the idiotic jangling of nerves, just absorb the sound, the jagged attack of guitars. Angry, frail and not especially well played. Scottish. But the feverish series of chords was joined by another sound.

Harry turned down the music. Listened. He was going to turn up the volume again when he heard a sound. Like sandpaper on wood. Or shoes shuffling on the floor. He went into the hall and saw a figure behind the door's wavy glass.

He opened up.

"I rang the bell," Rakel said, looking up at him apologetically.

"Oh?"

She waved a DVD box. "It wouldn't go in the slot."

He was going to say something, wanted to say something. But he had already thrust out his arm, caught her, pulled her to him, heard her gasp as he held her tight, saw her mouth opening and her tongue moving toward his, taunting and red. And basically there was nothing to say.

She snuggled up to him, soft and warm.

"Goodness," she whispered.

He kissed her on the forehead.

The sweat was a thin layer that both separated them and glued them together.

It had been exactly as he knew it would be. It had been like the first time, though without the nerves, the fumbling and the unspoken questions. It had been like the last time, without the sadness, without her sobbing afterward. You can leave someone with whom you have good sex. But Katrine was right; you always go back. But Harry knew this was different, too. For Rakel this was an essential, final visit to old pastures, a good-bye to what they had both called the great love of their lives. Before she entered a new era. To a lesser love? Maybe, but to an endurable love.

She was making purring sounds as she stroked his stomach. He could still feel the tension in her body. He could make it difficult or easy for her. He decided on the latter.

"Bad conscience?" he asked and felt her flinch.

"I don't want to talk about it," she said.

He didn't want to talk about it, either. He wanted to lie quite still, listen to her breathing and feel her hand on his stomach. But he knew what she had to do, and he didn't want any more postponements. "He's waiting for you, Rakel."

"No," she said. "He and the technician are preparing a body for an Anatomy Department lecture early tomorrow morning. And I told him he wasn't coming near me after touching a corpse. He'll sleep at his place."

"What about me?" Harry smiled in the dark, thinking that she had planned this, known it would happen. "How do you know I haven't touched a corpse?"

"Have you?"

"No," Harry said, thinking about the pack of cigarettes in the bedside-table drawer. "We don't have any corpses."

They fell silent. Her hand described ever larger circles on his stomach.

"I have a feeling I've been infiltrated," he said out of the blue.

"What do you mean?"

"I don't quite know. I just have the feeling someone is watching me the whole time, that someone is watching me now. I'm part of someone's plan. Do you understand?"

"No." She snuggled up closer to him.

"It's this case I'm working on. It's as though my person is involved in—"

"Shh." She bit his ear. "You're always involved, Harry. That's your problem. Relax."

Her hand placed itself on his flaccid member and he closed his eyes, listened to her whispers and felt his erection come.

At three o'clock she got out of bed. He saw her back in the light from the streetlamps through the window. The arched back and the shadow of her spine. And he fell to thinking about something Katrine had said, that Sylvia Ottersen had had the Ethiopian flag tattooed on her back; he would have to remember to mention that in the briefing. And Rakel was right: He never stopped thinking about cases; he was always involved.

He accompanied her to the door. She kissed him quickly on the mouth and dashed down the stairs. There was nothing to say. He was going to close the door when he saw wet boot prints outside the door. He followed them to where they disappeared down into the darkness of the stairwell. They must have been left by Rakel. And he thought about the Berhaus seals, about the female who finished mating with the male in the breeding period and never went back to him in the next breeding period. Because it wasn't biologically rational. The Berhaus seals must be clever creatures.

13

Paper

It was nine-thirty and the sun was shining on a solitary car negotiating the roundabout on the Sjølyst overpass above the highway. It turned up Bygdøyveien, which led to the idyllic rural peninsula located a mere five minutes' drive from the City Hall Square. It was quiet, there was almost no traffic, no cows or horses in the Kongsgården estate, and the narrow sidewalks where people made pilgrimages to the beaches in summer were deserted.

Harry steered the car around the bends in the rolling terrain and listened to Katrine.

"Snow," Katrine said.

"Snow?"

"I did as you said. I concentrated on the married women with children who had disappeared. And then I began to look at the dates. Most were in November and December. I isolated them and considered the geographical spread. Most were in Oslo; there were some in other parts of the country. Then it struck me, because of the letter you received. The part about the snowman reappearing with the first snow. And the day we were in Hoffsveien was the first snow in Oslo."

"Really?"

"I had the Meteorological Institute check the relevant dates and places. And do you know what?"

Harry knew what. And he should have known it long ago.

"The first snow," he said. "He kills them the day the first snow falls."

"Exactly."

Harry smacked the wheel. "Christ, we had it spelled out for us. How many missing women are we talking about?"

"Eleven. One a year."

"And two this year. He's broken the pattern."

"There was a murder and two disappearances when the first snow fell in Bergen in 1992. I think we should start there."

"Why's that?"

"Because the victim was a married woman with a child. And the woman who disappeared was her best friend. Thus we have one body, one crime scene and case files. As well as a suspect who vanished and has never been seen since."

"Who's that?"

"A policeman. Gert Rafto."

Harry glanced over quickly. "Oh, that case, yes. Wasn't he the one who stole stuff from crime scenes?"

"So it was rumored. Witnesses saw Rafto going

into the apartment of one of the women, Onny Hetland, a few hours before she disappeared. And extensive searches turned up nothing. He disappeared
without a trace."

Harry stared at the road, at the leafless trees along
Huk Aveny leading down to the sea and the muse-
ums for what Norwegians regarded as the nation's
greatest achievements: a voyage in a raft across the
Pacific Ocean and a failed attempt to reach the North
Pole.

"And now you think it's conceivable that he didn't
disappear after all?" he said. "That he might reappear
every year at the first sign of snow?"

Katrine hunched her shoulders. "I think it's worth
investing the time to find out what happened there."

"Mm. We'll have to start by asking Bergen for assistance."

"I wouldn't do that," she said quickly.

"Oh?"

"The Rafto case is still an extremely sensitive issue
for the police in Bergen. The resources they put into
that case were largely spent burying rather than investigating it. They were terrified of what they might
unearth. And since the guy had disappeared all by
himself . . ." She drew a big X in the air.

"I see. What do you suggest?"

"That you and I go on a little trip to Bergen and
do a bit of investigating on our own. After all, it's part
of an Oslo murder case now."

Harry parked in front of the address, a four-story
brick building right by the water, surrounded by a

mooring quay. He switched off the engine, but remained in his seat looking across Frognerkilen Bay to Filipstad Harbor.

"How did the Rafto case get onto your list?" he asked. "First of all, it's further back than I asked you to check. Second, I believe it's not a missing-persons case but murder."

He turned to look at Katrine. She met his gaze without blinking.

"The Rafto case was pretty famous in Bergen," she said. "And there was a photo."

"A photo?"

"Yes. All new trainees at Bergen Police Station are shown it. It was of the crime scene at the top of Ulriken Mountain and a kind of baptism of fire. I think most were so terrorized by the details in the foreground that they never looked at the background. Or maybe they had never been to the top of Ulriken. At any rate there was something there that didn't make sense, a mound farther back. When you magnify it, you can see quite clearly what it is."

"Oh?"

"A snowman."

Harry nodded slowly.

"Speaking of photos," Katrine said, taking a padded envelope from her bag and throwing it into Harry's lap.

The clinic was on the second floor, and the waiting room had been immaculately designed at horrendous expense with Italian furniture, a coffee table as low off the ground as a Ferrari, glass sculptures by Nico Widerberg and an original Roy Lichtenstein print showing a smoking gun.

Instead of the obligatory reception area with glass partition, a woman sat behind a beautiful old desk in the middle of the room. She was wearing an open white coat over a blue business suit and a welcoming smile. A smile that did not stiffen appreciably when Harry introduced himself and stated the purpose of their visit and his assumption that she was Borghild.

"Would you mind waiting for a moment?" she said, pointing to the sofas with the practiced elegance of a stewardess gesturing toward the emergency exits. Harry refused the offer of espresso, tea or water, and he and Katrine took a seat.

Harry noticed that the magazines laid out were up to date; he opened a copy of **Liberal** and his attention was caught by the headline in which Arve Støp claimed that politicians' willingness to appear on entertainment shows to "flaunt themselves" and assume the role of clown was the ultimate victory for government by the people—with the populace on the throne and the politician as the court jester.

Then the door marked DR. IDAR VETLESEN opened and a woman strode quickly through the waiting room, said a brief "Bye" to Borghild and was gone without so much as a glance left or right.

Katrine stared after her. "Wasn't that the woman from TV2 News?"

At that moment Borghild announced that Vetlesen

was ready to receive them, went to the door and held it open for them.

Idar Vetlesen's office was CEO–size, with a view of the Oslo Fjord. Framed diplomas hung on the wall behind the desk.

"Just a moment," Vetlesen said, without looking up from the computer screen. Then, with a triumphant expression, he pressed a final key, swiveled around in his chair and removed his glasses.

"Face-lift, Hole? Penis enlargement? Liposuction?"

"Thank you for the offer," Harry said. "This is Police Officer Bratt. We've come once again to request your help with information about Ottersen and Becker."

Idar Vetlesen sighed and began to clean his glasses with a handkerchief.

"How can I explain this to you in a way that you can understand, Hole? Even for someone like me, who has a genuine burning desire to help the police and basically couldn't care less about principles, there are some things that are sacrosanct." He raised an index finger. "In all the years I've worked as a doctor I have never, ever"—the finger wagged in time with his words—"broken my Hippocratic oath. And I do not intend to start now."

A long silence ensued in which Vetlesen just looked at them, clearly satisfied with the effect he had created.

Harry cleared his throat.

"Perhaps we can still fulfill your burning desire to help, Vetlesen. We're investigating possible child prostitution at a so-called hotel in Oslo, known as the Leon. Last night two of our officers were outside in a car taking photographs of people going in and out."

Harry opened the brown padded envelope he had been given by Katrine, leaned forward and placed the photographs before the doctor.

"That's you there, isn't it?"

Vetlesen looked as though something had become lodged in his gullet; his eyes bulged and the veins in his neck stuck out.

"I . . . ," he stuttered. "I . . . haven't done anything wrong or illegal."

"No, not at all," Harry said. "We're just considering summoning you as a witness. A witness who can say what's going on there. It's common knowledge that Hotel Leon is a center for prostitutes and their clients; what's new is that children have been seen there. And unlike other prostitution, child prostitution is, as you know, illegal. Thought we should inform you before we go to the press with the whole business."

Vetlesen stared at the photograph, rubbing his face hard.

"By the way, we just saw the TV2 News lady coming out," Harry said. "What's her name again?"

Vetlesen didn't answer. It was as if all the smooth youthfulness had been sucked out of him before their very eyes, as if his face had aged in the space of a second.

"Call us if you can find a loophole in the Hippocratic oath," Harry said.

Harry and Katrine were halfway to the door before Vetlesen stopped them.

"They were here for an examination," he said. "That's all."

"What kind of examination?" Harry asked.

"A disease."

"The same disease? Which one?"

"It's of no importance."

"OK," Harry said, walking to the door. "When you're summoned as a witness you can take that view. It's of no importance, either. After all, we haven't found anything illegal."

"Wait!"

Harry turned. Vetlesen was supporting himself on his elbows with his face in his hands.

"Fahr's Syndrome."

"Father Syndrome?"

"Fahr's. F-a-h-r. A rare hereditary disease, a bit like Alzheimer's. Motor skills deteriorate, especially in cognitive areas, and there is some spasticity of movement. Most develop the syndrome after the age of thirty, but it is possible to have it in childhood."

"Mm. And so Birte and Sylvia knew their children had this disease?"

"They suspected it when they came here. Fahr's Syndrome is hard to diagnose, and Birte Becker and Sylvia Ottersen had been to several doctors, although nothing conclusive was found in their children. I seem to remember that both of them had searched the Internet, typed in the symptoms and discovered Fahr, which matched alarmingly well."

"And so they contacted you? A plastic surgeon?"

"I happen to be a Fahr specialist."

"Happen to be?"

"There are around eighteen thousand doctors in Norway. Do you know how many known diseases there are in the world?" Vetlesen motioned with his head to the wall of diplomas. "Fahr's Syndrome happened to be part of a course I took in Switzerland about nerve channels. The little I learned was enough to make me a specialist in Norway."

"What can you tell us about Birte Becker and Sylvia Ottersen?"

Vetlesen hunched his shoulders. "They came here with their children once a year. I examined them and was unable to determine any deterioration of their conditions, and, apart from that, I know nothing of their lives. Or for that matter"—he tossed back his hair—"their deaths."

"Do you believe him?" Harry asked as they drove past the deserted fields.

"Not entirely," Katrine said.

"Nor I," Harry said. "I think we should concentrate on this and drop Bergen for the time being."

"No," said Katrine.

"No?"

"There's a link here somewhere."

"Which is?"

"I don't know. It sounds wild, but perhaps there's a link between Rafto and Vetlesen. Perhaps that's how Rafto's managed to hide all these years."

"What do you mean?"

"That he quite simply got himself a mask. An authentic mask. A face-lift."

"From Vetlesen?"

"It could explain the coincidence of having two victims with the same doctor. Rafto could have seen Birte and Sylvia at the clinic and decided they would be his victims."

"You're jumping the gun," Harry said.

"Jumping the gun?"

"This kind of murder investigation is like doing a jigsaw puzzle. In the opening phase you collect the pieces, play with them, are patient. What you're doing is trying to force the pieces into position. It's too early."

"I'm just saying things out loud to someone. To see if they sound idiotic."

"They sound idiotic."

"This isn't the way to the Police HQ," she said.

Harry could hear a curious quiver in her voice and glanced across at her, but her face gave nothing away.

"I'd like to check out some of the things Vetlesen told us with someone I know," he said. "And who knows Vetlesen."

Mathias was wearing a white coat and regulation yellow cleaning gloves when he received Harry and Katrine in the garage beneath Preclinical, the usual name for the brown building in the part of Gaustad Hospital that faces the Ring 3 highway.

He directed their car into what turned out to be his own unused parking space.

"I try to cycle as often as I can," Mathias explained, using his swipe card to open the door leading from the garage into a basement corridor in the Anatomy Department. "This kind of access is practical for transporting bodies in and out. Would have liked to offer you coffee, but I've just finished with one group of students and the next will be here shortly."

"Sorry for the hassle. You must be tired today."

Mathias sent him a quizzical look.

"Rakel and I were talking on the phone. She said you had to work late last night," Harry added, cursing himself inside and hoping his face gave nothing away.

"Rakel, yes." Mathias shook his head. "She was out late herself. Out with the girls and has had to take the day off work. But when I called her she was in the midst of a big cleanup at home. Women, eh! What can you say?"

Harry put on a stiff smile and wondered if there was a standard response to that question.

A man in green hospital gear trundled a metal table toward the garage door.

"Another delivery for the University of Tromsø?" Mathias asked.

"Say bye-bye to Kjeldsen," said the man in green with a smile. He had a cluster of small rings in one ear, a bit like a Masai woman's neck rings, except that these rings gave his face an irritating asymmetry.

"Kjeldsen?" Mathias exclaimed, and stopped. "Is that true?"

"Thirty years of service. Now it's Tromsø's turn to dissect him."

Mathias lifted the blanket. Harry caught sight of the body. The skin over the cranium was taut, smoothing out the old man's wrinkles into a genderless face, as white as a plaster mask. Harry knew that this was because the body had been preserved—that is, the arteries had been pumped full of a mixture of formalin, glycerin and alcohol to ensure that it did not decompose from inside. A metal tag with an engraved three-digit number had been attached to one ear. Mathias watched the assistant roll Kjeldsen toward the garage door. Then he seemed to wake up again.

"Sorry. It's just that Kjeldsen has been with us for so long. He was a professor at the Anatomy Department when it was down in the center of town. A brilliant anatomist. With well-defined muscles. We're going to miss him."

"We won't hold you up for long," Harry said. "We were wondering if you could tell us something about Idar's relationships with women patients. And their children."

Mathias raised his head and looked with surprise at Harry, then Katrine, and back again.

"Are you asking me what I think you're asking me?"

Harry nodded.

Mathias led them through another locked door. They entered a room with eight metal tables and a blackboard at one end. The tables were equipped with lamps and sinks. On each of the tables lay something oblong wrapped in white hand towels. Judging by the shape and the size, Harry guessed that today's theme was situated somewhere between hip and foot. There was a faint smell of bleach, but not nearly as pronounced as Harry was used to from the autopsy room at the Institute of Forensic Medicine. Mathias sank down onto one of the chairs and Harry sat on the edge of the lecturer's desk. Katrine walked over to a table and scrutinized three brains; it was impossible to say whether they were models or real.

Mathias thought a long time before answering. "Personally, I've never noticed or heard anyone suggest there was anything between Idar and any of his patients."

Something about the stress placed on **patients** brought Harry up short. "What about nonpatients?"

"I don't know Idar well enough to comment. But I know him well enough to prefer not to comment." He flashed a tentative smile. "If that's OK?"

"Of course. There was something else I was wondering about. Fahr's Syndrome—do you know what it is?"

"Superficially. A terrible disease. And unfortunately very much a hereditary—"

"Do you know of any Norwegian specialists in the disease?"

Mathias reflected. "None that I can think of, off the top of my head."

Harry scratched his neck. "OK, thanks for your help, Mathias."

"Not at all, a pleasure. If you want to know more about Fahr's Syndrome, you can call me tonight, when I have a few books around me."

Harry stood up. Walked over to Katrine, who had lifted the lid off one of the four large metal boxes by the wall, and peered over her shoulder. His tongue prickled and his whole body reacted. Not at the body parts immersed in the clear alcohol, looking like lumps of meat at the butcher's. But at the smell of alcohol. Forty percent.

"They start off more or less whole," Mathias said. "Then we cut them up as and when we need individual body parts."

Harry observed Katrine's face. She seemed totally unaffected. The door opened behind them. The first students came in and began to put on blue coats and white latex gloves.

Mathias followed them back to the garage. At the door, Mathias caught Harry's arm and held him back.

"Just a tiny thing I should mention, Harry. Or shouldn't mention. I'm not sure."

"Out with it," Harry said, thinking that this was it—Mathias knew about him and Rakel.

"I have a slight moral dilemma here. It's about Idar."

"Oh, yes?" Harry said, feeling disappointment rather than relief, to his surprise.

"I'm sure it doesn't mean anything, but it occurred to me that maybe it's not up to me to decide. And that you can't let loyalty take priority in such a terrible case. No matter what. Last year, when I was still working in the emergency room, a colleague who also knows Idar and I popped by Postcafeen to have breakfast after a night shift. It's a café that opens at the crack of dawn and serves beer, so a lot of thirsty early birds gather there. And other poor souls."

"I know the place," Harry said.

"To our surprise we found Idar there. He was sitting at a table with a filthy young boy slurping soup. On seeing us, Idar jumped up from the table in shock and came up with some excuse or other. I didn't think any more about it. That is, I believed I hadn't thought any more about it. Until what you just said. And I remembered what I'd been thinking at the time. That maybe . . . well, you understand."

"I understand," Harry said. And, seeing his interlocutor's tormented expression, added: "You did the right thing."

"Thank you." Mathias forced a smile. "But I feel like a Judas."

Harry tried to find something sensible to say, but all he could do was proffer his hand and mumble a "thanks." And shiver as he pressed Mathias's cold cleaning glove.

Judas. The Judas kiss. As they drove down Slemdalsveien, Harry thought about Rakel's hungry tongue in his mouth, her gentle sigh and loud groan, the pains in his pelvis as it banged against Rakel's, her cries of frustration when he stopped because he wanted it to last longer. For she wasn't there to make it last longer. She was there to exorcise demons, to purify her body so that she could go home and purify her soul. And wash every floor in the house. The sooner the better.

"Call the clinic," Harry said.

He heard Katrine's quick fingers and tiny beeps. Then she passed him the mobile phone.

Borghild answered with a studied mixture of gentleness and efficiency.

"This is Harry Hole speaking. Tell me, who should I see if I have Fahr's Syndrome?"

Silence.

"It depends," answered Borghild hesitantly.

"On what?"

"On the syndrome your father has, I suppose."

"Right. Is Dr. Vetlesen in?"

"He's gone for today."

"Already?"

"They've got a curling match. Try again tomorrow."

She radiated impatience. Harry assumed she was in the process of leaving for the day.

"Bygdøy Curling Club?"

"No, the private one. The one down from Gimle."

"Thanks. Have a good evening."

Harry gave Katrine the phone back.

"We'll bring him in," he said.

"Who?"

"The specialist who has an assistant who's never heard of the disease he specializes in."

After asking the way, they found Villa Grande, a luxurious property that, during the Second World War, had belonged to a Norwegian whose name, unlike those of the raft sailor and the Arctic explorer, was also widely known outside Norway: Quisling, the traitor.

At the bottom of the slope to the south of the building there was a rectangular wooden house resembling an old military barracks. As soon as you entered the building you could feel the cold hit you. And inside the next door the temperature fell further.

There were four men on the ice. Their shouts bounced off the wooden walls, and none of them noticed Harry and Katrine come in. They were shouting at a shiny stone gliding down the rink. The fifty pounds of granite, the type known as ailsite, from the Scottish island of Ailsa Craig, stopped against the guard of three other stones on the front edge of two circles painted into the ice. The men slid around the rink, balancing on one foot and kicking off with the other, discussing, supporting themselves on their brooms and preparing for the next stone.

"Snob sport," Katrine whispered. "Look at them."

Harry didn't answer. He liked curling. The meditative element as you watched the stone's slow passage, rotating in an apparently friction-free universe, like one of the spaceships in Kubrick's odyssey, accompanied not by Strauss but by the stone's quiet rumble and the furious sweeping of brooms.

The men had seen them now. And Harry recognized two of the faces from media circles. One was Arve Støp's.

Idar Vetlesen skated toward him.

"Joining us for a game, Hole?"

He shouted that from far away, as if it was meant for the other men, not Harry. And it was followed by seemingly jovial laughter. But the muscles outlined against the skin of his jaw betrayed the game he was playing. He stopped in front of them, and the breath coming from his mouth was white.

"The game's over," Harry said.

"I don't think so." Idar smiled.

Harry could already feel the cold from the ice creeping through the soles of his shoes and advancing up his legs.

"We'd like you to come with us to the Police HQ," Harry said. "Now."

Idar Vetlesen's smile evaporated. "Why?"

"Because you're lying to us. Among other things, you're not a Fahr's Syndrome specialist."

"Says who?" Idar asked, glancing at the other curling players to confirm that they were standing too far away to hear them.

"Says your assistant. Since she's clearly never even heard of the disease."

"Listen here," Idar said, and a new sound, that of despair, had crept into his voice. "You can't just come here and take me away. Not here, not in front of . . ."

"Your clients?" Harry asked and peered over Idar's shoulder. He could see Arve Støp sweeping ice off the bottom of a stone while studying Katrine.

"I don't know what you're after," he heard Idar say. "I'm happy to cooperate with you, but not if you're consciously setting out to humiliate and ruin me. These are my best friends."

"We'll keep going, Vetlesen . . . ," resounded a deep baritone voice. It was Arve Støp's.

Harry eyed the unhappy surgeon. Wondered what he understood by "best" friends. And thought that if there was the tiniest chance of gaining anything by fulfilling Vetlesen's wish, then it was worth their while.

"OK," Harry said. "We're off. But you have to be at the Police HQ in Grønland in exactly one hour. If not, we'll come looking for you with sirens and trumpet fanfares. And they're easy to hear in Bygdøy, aren't they?"

Vetlesen nodded and for a moment looked as though he would laugh from force of habit.

Oleg shut the door with a bang, kicked off his boots and ran upstairs. There was a fresh aroma of lemon and soap throughout the house. He stormed into his room, and the mobile hanging from the ceiling chimed in alarm as he pulled off his jeans and put on his sweatsuit bottoms. He ran out again, but as he grabbed the banister to take the stairs in two long strides, he heard his name from behind the open door of his mother's bedroom.

He went in and found Rakel on her knees in front of the bed with a long-handled scrubbing brush.

"I thought you did the cleaning over the weekend."

"Yes, but not well enough," his mother said, getting up and wiping a hand across her forehead. "Where are you going?"

"To the stadium. I'm going skating. Karsten's waiting outside. Be back home for dinner." He pushed off from the door and slid across the floor on stockinged feet, gravity low, the way Erik V, one of the skating veterans at Valle Hovin, had taught him.

"Wait a minute, young man. Speaking of skates . . ."

Oleg stopped. Oh, no, he thought. She's found the skates.

She stood in the doorway, tilted her head and scrutinized him. "What about homework?"

"Haven't got much," he said with a relieved smile. "I'll do it after dinner."

He saw her hesitate and added quickly: "You look so nice in that dress, Mom."

She lowered her eyes at the old sky-blue dress with the white flowers. And even though she gave him an admonitory look, a smile was playing at the corners of her mouth. "Watch it, Oleg. Now you're sounding like your father."

"Oh? I thought he only spoke Russian."

He hadn't meant anything with that comment, but something happened to his mother—a shock seemed to run through her.

He tiptoed. "Can I go now?"

"Yes, you can go?" Katrine Bratt's voice lashed the fitness-room walls in the basement at the Police HQ. "Did you really say that? That Idar Vetlesen could just go?"

Harry stared up at her face, which was bent over the bench he was lying on. The dome-shaped ceiling light formed a shining yellow halo around her head. He was breathing heavily because an iron bar was lying across his chest. He had been about to perform a bench press of two hundred pounds and had just lifted the bar off the stand when Katrine had marched in and ruined his attempt.

"I had to," Harry said, managing to push the bar a bit higher so that it was on his breastbone. "He had his lawyer with him. Johan Krohn."

"So what?"

"Well, Krohn started by asking what sort of methods we employed to blackmail his client. Then he said the buying and selling of sexual services in Norway is legal, and that our methods for forcing a respected doctor to break his Hippocratic oath would also be worth a headline."

"But damn it!" Katrine shouted in a voice that was shaking with fury. "This is a murder case!"

Harry hadn't seen her lose control before and answered in his gentlest voice.

"Listen, we can't link the murders to the illness or even make the connection seem a possibility. And Krohn knows that. And so I can't hold him."

"No, but you can't just . . . lie there . . . and do nothing!"

Harry could feel his breastbone aching, and it struck him that she was absolutely right.

She put both hands to her face. "I . . . I . . . I'm sorry. I just thought . . . It's been a strange day."

"Fine." Harry groaned. "Could you help me with this bar? I'm almost—"

"The other end!" she exclaimed, removing her hands from her face. "We'll have to begin at the other end. In Bergen!"

"No," Harry whispered with the last air he had left in his lungs. "Bergen's not an end. Could you . . ."

He looked up at her. Saw her dark eyes fill with tears.

"It's my period," she whispered. Then she smiled. It happened so fast that it was like another person was standing above him, a person with an odd sheen to her eyes and a voice under complete control. "And you can just die."

In amazement, he heard the sound of her footsteps fading away, heard his own skeleton crack and red dots begin to dance in front of his eyes. He cursed, wrapped his hands around the iron bar and, with a roar, pushed. The bar wouldn't budge.

She was right; he could in fact die like that. He could choose. Funny, but true.

He wriggled, tipped the bar to one side until he heard the weights slide off and hit the floor with a deafening clang. Then the bar hit the floor on the other side. He sat up and watched the weights careering around the room.

Harry showered, dressed and went upstairs to the sixth floor. Fell into the swivel chair, already feeling the sweet ache of his muscles, which told him that he was going to be stiff in the morning.

There was a message on his voice mail from Bjørn Holm telling him to call back ASAP.

Holm picked up and there was the sound of heartrending sobs accompanied by the slide tones of a pedal steel guitar.

"What is it?" Harry asked.

"Dwight Yoakam," Holm said, turning down the music. "Sexy bastard, ain't he?"

"I mean, what's the call about?"

"We've got the results for the Snowman letter."

"And?"

"Nothing special as far as the writing's concerned. Standard laser printer."

Harry waited. He knew Holm had something.

"What's special is the paper he used. No one at the lab here has seen this type before—that's why it's taken a bit of time. It's made with mitsumata, Japanese papyrus-like bast fibers. You can probably tell mitsumata by the smell. They use the bark to make the paper by hand, and this particular sheet is extremely exclusive. It's called Kono."

"Kono?"

"You have to go to a specialty shop to buy it, the sort of place that sells fountain pens for ten thousand kroner, fine inks and leather-bound notebooks. You know . . ."

"I don't, in fact."

"Me neither," Holm conceded. "But anyway, there is one shop on Gamle Drammensveien that sells Kono writing paper. I spoke to the owner and was told they rarely sold such things now, so it was unlikely they would reorder. People don't have a sense of quality the way they used to, he reckoned."

"Does that mean . . ."

"Yes, I'm afraid that means he couldn't remember when he last sold any Kono paper."

"Mm. And this is the only dealer?"

"Yes," Holm said. "There was one in Bergen, but they stopped selling it a few years ago."

Holm waited for an answer—or, to be more precise, questions—as Dwight Yoakam, at low volume, yodeled the love of his life into her grave. But none came.

"Harry?"

"Yes. I'm thinking."

"Excellent!" said Holm.

It was this slow inland humor that could make Harry chuckle long afterward, and even then without knowing why. But not at this moment. Harry cleared his throat.

"I think it's very odd that paper like this would be put into the hands of a murder investigator if you didn't want it to be traced back to you. You don't need to have seen many crime shows to know that we would check."

"Perhaps he didn't know it was rare?" Holm suggested. "Perhaps he hadn't bought it?"

"Of course that's a possibility, but something tells me that the Snowman wouldn't slip up like that."

"But he has."

"I mean I don't think it's a slip," Harry said.

"You mean . . ."

"Yes, I think he wants us to trace him."

"Why?"

"It's classic. The narcissistic serial killer staging a game, with himself in the principal role as the invincible, the all-powerful conqueror who triumphs in the end."

"Triumphs over what?"

"Well," Harry replied, saying it for the first time aloud, "at the risk of sounding narcissistic myself, me."

"You? Why?"

"I have no idea. Perhaps because he knows I'm the only policeman in Norway who has caught a serial killer, he sees me as a challenge. The letter would suggest that—he refers to Toowoomba. I don't know, Holm. By the way, have you got the name of the shop in Bergen?"

. . .

"Flab speaking!"

Or so it sounded. The word—**flæsk**—was articulated with Bergensian tones and gravity. That is, with a soft **l**, a long **æ** with a dip in the middle and a faint **s**. Peter Flesch, who voluntarily pronounced his name like the word for **flab,** was out of breath, loud and obliging. He was happy to talk; yes, he sold all types of antiques so long as they were small, but he specialized in pipes, lighters, pens, leather briefcases and stationery. Some used, some new. Most of his customers were regulars with an average age in line with his own.

To Harry's questions about Kono writing paper he answered, with regret in his voice, that he no longer had any such paper. Indeed, it had been several years since he had stocked it.

"This might be asking a bit too much," Harry said. "But since you have regular customers for the most part, is it possible that you might remember some of the ones who bought Kono paper?"

"Some maybe. Møller. And old Kikkusæn from Møllaren. We don't keep records, but my wife's got a good memory."

"Perhaps you could write down the full names, rough age and the address of those you can remember and e-mail them—"

Harry was interrupted by tut-tutting. "We don't have e-mail, son. Not going to get it, either. You'd better give me a fax number."

Harry gave the Police HQ number. He hesitated. It was a sudden inspiration. But inspiration never came without a reason.

"You wouldn't by any chance have had a customer a few years back," Harry said, "by the name of Gert Rafto, would you?"

"Iron Rafto?" Peter Flesch laughed.

"You've heard of him?"

"The whole town knew who Rafto was. No, he wasn't a customer here."

POB Møller always used to say that in order to isolate what was possible, you had to eliminate everything that was impossible. And that was why a detective should not despair, but be glad whenever he could discount a clue that did not lead to the solution. Besides, it had just been an idea.

"Well, thank you anyway," Harry said. "Have a good day."

"**He** wasn't a customer," Flesch said. "**I** was."

"Oh?"

"Yes. He brought me bits and bobs. Silver lighters, gold pens. That sort of thing. Sometimes I bought them off him. That was before I realized where they came from . . ."

"And where did they come from?"

"Don't you know? He stole them from crime scenes he worked on."

"But he never bought anything?"

"Rafto didn't have any need for the sort of thing that we had."

"But paper? Everyone needs paper, don't they?"

"Hm. Just a moment and I'll have a word with my wife."

A hand was placed over the receiver, but Harry

could hear shouting, then a slightly lower conversation. Afterward the hand was removed and Flesch trumpeted in elated Bergensian: "She thinks Rafto took the rest of the paper when we stopped selling it. For a broken silver penholder, she thinks. Helluva memory the wife has, you know."

Harry put down the telephone knowing he was on his way to Bergen.

At nine o'clock that evening night lights were still burning on the first floor of Brynsalléen 6 in Oslo. From the outside, the six-story building looked like any commercial complex, with its modern red brick and gray steel façade. And for that matter inside, too, as most of the more than four hundred employees had jobs as engineers, IT specialists, social scientists, lab technicians, photographers and so on. But this was nevertheless "the national unit for the combating of organized and other serious crime," generally referred to by its old name of Kriminalpolitisentralen, or in its abbreviated form, Kripos.

Espen Lepsvik had just dismissed his men after reviewing their progress on the murder investigation. Only two people were left in the bare, harshly illuminated meeting room.

"That was a bit thin," Harry Hole said.

"Nice way of saying **zilch,**" Espen Lepsvik said, massaging his eyelids with thumb and first finger. "Shall we go and have a beer while you tell me what you've unearthed?"

Harry told him while Espen Lepsvik drove them to the center and Kafé Justisen, which was on the way home for both men. They sat at the table at the back of the busy café, frequented by everyone from beer-thirsty students to even thirstier lawyers and police-men.

"I'm considering taking Katrine Bratt instead of Skarre to Bergen," Harry said, sipping from a bottle of carbonated water. "I checked her employment record before coming here. She's pretty green, but her file says that she worked on two murder cases in Bergen that I seem to remember you were sent over to lead."

"Bratt, yes, I remember her." Espen Lepsvik grinned and raised his index finger for another beer.

"Happy with her?"

"Extremely happy. She's . . . extremely . . . compe-tent." Lepsvik winked at Harry, who saw that the other man already had that glassy look of a tired de-tective with three beers inside him. "And if both of us hadn't been married, I think I'd have had a chance with her."

He drained his glass.

"I was wondering more if you thought she was sta-ble," Harry said.

"Stable?"

"Yes, there's something about her . . . I don't know quite how to explain it. Something intense."

"I know what you mean." Espen Lepsvik nodded slowly as his eyes tried to focus on Harry's face. "Her record's unblemished. But between you and me I heard one of the guys over there say something about her and her husband."

Lepsvik searched for some encouragement in Harry's face, found none, but continued anyway.

"Something . . . you know . . . that she likes leather and rubber. S and M. Apparently went to that kind of club."

"That's not my concern," Harry said.

"No, no, no, mine neither!" Lepsvik exclaimed, raising his hands in defense. "It's just a rumor. And do you know what?" Lepsvik sniggered, leaning forward across the table, so that Harry could smell his beery breath. "She can dominate me any day."

Harry realized that there must have been something in his eyes because Lepsvik immediately seemed to regret his openness and beat a quick retreat to his side of the table. And went on in a more businesslike tone.

"She's a professional. Clever. Intense and committed. Insisted with a bit too much vehemence that I should help her with a couple of cold cases, I remember. But not at all unstable—more the opposite. She's more the closed, sullen type. But there are lots like that. Yes, in fact I think you two could be a perfect team."

Harry smiled at the sarcasm and stood up. "Thanks for the tip, Lepsvik."

"What about a tip for me? Have you and she . . . got something going?"

"My tip," Harry said, throwing a hundred-krone note on the table, "is that you leave your car here."

14

Bergen

At precisely 8:26, the wheels of Flight DY 604 touched down on the wet tarmac at Flesland Airport, Bergen. So hard that Harry was suddenly wide awake.

"Sleep well?" Katrine asked.

Harry nodded, rubbed his eyes and stared out at the rain-heavy dawn.

"You were talking in your sleep," she said with a smile.

"Mm." Harry didn't want to ask about what. Instead he quickly went back over what he had been dreaming. Not about Rakel. He hadn't dreamed about her for nights. He had banished her. Between them they had banished her. But he had dreamed about Bjarne Møller, his old boss and mentor, who had walked onto the Bergensian plateaus and been found in Lake Revurtjern two weeks later. It was a decision Møller had made because he—just like Zenon, with the sore big toe—didn't think life was worth living any longer. Had Gert Rafto come to the same conclusion? Or was he really still out there somewhere?

"I called Rafto's ex-wife," Katrine said as they were walking through the arrivals hall. "Neither she nor the daughter wants to talk to the police again—they don't want to reopen old wounds. And that's fine. The reports from that time are more than adequate."

They got into a taxi outside the terminal.

"Lovely to be home?" Harry asked in a loud voice over the drumming of the rain and the rhythmic swish of the windshield wipers.

Katrine shrugged indifferently. "I always hated the rain. And I hated Bergensians who maintained it didn't rain here as much as eastern Norwegians made out."

They passed Danmarksplass, and Harry looked up at the top of Ulriken. It was covered with snow, and he could see the cable cars in motion. Then they drove through the viper's nest of service roads by Store Lungegårdsvann Bay and reached the center, which for visitors was always a welcome surprise after the drab approach.

They entered the SAS hotel by Bryggen on the harbor front. Harry had inquired whether she would stay with her parents, but Katrine had answered that for one night it would be too much stress—they would go to too much trouble, and in fact she hadn't even told them she was coming.

They were given key cards for their rooms, and in the elevator they were silent. Katrine looked at Harry and smiled as though silence in elevators were an implicit joke. Harry looked down, hoping his body wasn't sending false signals. Or real ones.

The doors finally slid open, and her hips sashayed down the corridor.

"Lobby in five," Harry said.

"What's the timetable?" he asked when they were sitting in the lobby six minutes later.

Katrine leaned forward from the deep armchair and flipped through her leather-bound diary. She had changed into an elegant gray suit, which meant she immediately blended in with the hotel's business clientele.

"You meet Knut Müller-Nilsen, the head of the Missing Persons and Violent Crime Unit."

"You're not coming with me?"

"I'd have to say hello and talk to everyone, and the whole day would be wasted. In fact, it would be good if you didn't mention my name at all. They'd just be pissed off that I hadn't dropped by. I'm heading for Øyjordsveien to have a word with the last witness to see Rafto."

"Mm. And where was that?"

"By the docks. The witness saw him leave his car and walk into Nordnes Park. No one returned for the car, and the area was gone over with a fine-toothed comb without yielding a thing."

"Then what do we do?" Harry ran his thumb and

middle finger along his jaw, thinking he should have shaved before making a trip out of town.

"You review the old reports with the detectives who were on the case and are still at the station. Get up to speed. Try to see it from a different angle."

"No," Harry said.

Katrine looked up from her diary.

"The detectives at the time drew their own conclusions and will just defend them," Harry explained. "I prefer to read the reports in peace and quiet in Oslo. And to spend my time here getting to know Gert Rafto a bit better. Can we see his possessions anywhere?"

Katrine shook her head. "His family gave everything he owned to the Salvation Army. It wasn't a great deal, apparently. Some furniture and clothes."

"What about where he lived or stayed?"

"He lived alone in an apartment in Sandviken after his divorce, but it was sold ages ago."

"Mm. And there's no childhood home, country cottage or cabin that's still in the family?"

Katrine hesitated. "The reports mentioned a little cabin in the police summerhouse quarter, on the island of Finnøy in Fedje. The cabins stay in the family in such cases, so maybe we can see it. I've got Rafto's wife's telephone number. I'll give her a call."

"I thought she wasn't talking to the police."

Katrine winked at him with a sly grin.

From the hotel reception Harry managed to borrow an umbrella, which turned inside out in the gusts before he got to Fisketorget—the harbor fish market—and looked like a tangled bat by the time he had jogged, head down, to the entrance of the Police HQ.

While Harry was standing in reception, waiting for POB Knut Müller-Nilsen, Katrine called him to say that the cabin on Finnøy was still in the Rafto family's hands.

"But his wife hasn't set foot there since the case. Nor her daughter, she thought."

"We'll go there," Harry said. "I'll be done here by one o'clock."

"OK, I'll get us a boat. Meet me at Zacharias wharf."

Knut Müller-Nilsen was a chuckling teddy bear with smiling eyes and hands the size of tennis rackets. The tall stacks of paper made him look as if he were snowed in at his desk, with his rackets folded behind his head.

"Rafto, hmm," Müller-Nilsen said, after explaining that it didn't rain in Bergen as much as eastern Norwegians made out.

"Seems like policemen have a tendency to slip through your fingers," Harry said, holding up the photo of Gert Rafto that came with the reports in his lap.

"Oh, yes?" Müller-Nilsen queried, looking at Harry, who had found a spindle-back chair in the one paper-free corner of the office.

"Bjarne Møller," Harry said.

"Right," said Müller-Nilsen, but the tentative delivery gave him away.

"The officer who disappeared from Fløyen," Harry said.

"Of course!" Müller-Nilsen slapped his forehead. "Tragic business. He had only been here a short time so I didn't manage to . . . The assumption was that he got lost, wasn't it?"

"That was what happened," Harry said, peering out the window and thinking about Bjarne Møller's path from idealism to corruption. About his good intentions. About the tragic errors. Which others would never know about. "What can you tell me about Gert Rafto?"

My spiritual doppelgänger in Bergen, Harry thought, after receiving Müller-Nilsen's description: unhealthy attitude toward alcohol, difficult temperament, lone wolf, unreliable, doubtful morality and very blemished record.

"But he had exceptional powers of analysis and intuition," Müller-Nilsen said. "And an iron will. He seemed to be driven by . . . something. I don't know quite how to express it. Rafto was extreme. Well, that goes without saying now that we know what happened."

"And what did happen?" Harry asked, catching sight of an ashtray amid the piles of paper.

"Rafto was violent. And we know he was in Onny Hetland's apartment just before she disappeared, and that Hetland might have had information that would have revealed the identity of Laila Aasen's killer. Furthermore, he disappeared immediately afterward. It's not improbable that he drowned himself. Anyway, we saw no reason to implement a large-scale investigation."

"He couldn't have fled abroad?"

Müller-Nilsen smiled and shook his head.

"Why not?"

"Let me say that in this case we had the advantage of knowing the suspect very well. Even though, in theory, he could well have left Bergen, he was not the type. Simple as that."

"And no relatives or friends have reported any signs of life?"

Müller-Nilsen shook his head. "His parents are no longer with us, and he didn't have many friends, Rafto. He had a strained relationship with his ex-wife, so he would hardly have contacted her anyway."

"What about his daughter?"

"They were close. Nice girl, clever. Turned out well, considering the upbringing she had, of course."

Harry noticed the implied common knowledge. "Turned out well, of course," a phrase typical of small police stations where you were expected to know most things about most things.

"Rafto had a cabin on Finnøy, didn't he?" Harry asked.

"Yes, and that could of course be a natural place to take refuge. To mull things over and then . . ." Müller-Nilsen made a gesture with one of his huge hands across his larynx. "We went through the cabin, searched the island with dogs and dragged the waters. Nothing."

"Thought I would take a look out there."

"Not a lot to see. We have a cabin just opposite Iron Rafto's, and unfortunately it's in total disrepair. It's a disgrace his wife doesn't give it up. She's never there." Müller-Nilsen cast an eye at the clock. "I have a meeting, but one of the senior officers on the case will go through the reports with you."

"No need," Harry said, looking at the photo on his lap. All of a sudden the face seemed strangely familiar, as if he had seen it not long ago. Someone in disguise? Someone he had passed in the street? Someone in a minor role he wouldn't have noticed, one of the traffic wardens sneaking around on Sofies Gate or an assistant at the Vinmonopol? Harry gave up.

"Not 'Gert,' then?"

"I beg your pardon?" Müller-Nilsen said.

"You said 'Iron Rafto.' You didn't call him just 'Gert,' then?"

Müller-Nilsen sent Harry a dubious look, ventured a chuckle, but then gave him only a wry smile. "No, I don't think that would ever have occurred to us."

"OK. Thanks for your help."

On his way out Harry heard Müller-Nilsen call, and he turned. The POB was standing in his office doorway at the end of the corridor and the words cast a brief vibrating echo between the walls.

"I don't think Rafto would have liked it, either."

Outside the Police HQ, Harry stood looking at the people bent double as they forced their way through the wind and rain. The sensation would not leave him. The sensation that something or someone was there, nearby, on the inside, visible, if he could only see things the right way, in the right light.

Katrine picked Harry up at the wharf, as arranged.

"I borrowed this from a friend," she said as she steered the twenty-one-foot so-called skerry jeep out of the narrow harbor mouth. As they rounded the Nordnes peninsula, a noise made Harry spin, and he caught sight of a totem pole. The wooden faces were screaming hoarsely at him with open mouths. A cold gust of wind swept across the boat.

"Those are the seals in the aquarium," Katrine said.

Harry pulled his coat tighter around him.

Finnøy was a tiny island. Apart from heather, there was no vegetation on the rain-lashed chunk of land, but it did have a quay, where Katrine expertly moored the boat. The residential area consisted of sixty wooden cabins in all, of doll's-house proportions, and reminded Harry of the miners' shacks he had seen in Soweto.

Katrine led Harry down the gravel path between the cabins and then walked up to one of them. It stood out because the paint was peeling. One of the windows was cracked. Katrine stretched up on tiptoes, grabbed the bulkhead light over the door and unscrewed it. A scraping sound came from inside as she rotated the dome and dead insects fluttered out. Plus a key, which she caught in midair.

"The ex-wife liked me," Katrine said, inserting the key in the door.

There was a smell of mold and damp wood inside. Harry stared into the semidarkness and heard the flick of a switch, and the light came on.

"She's got electricity, then, even if she doesn't use the cabin," he said.

"Communal," Katrine said, taking a slow look around. "The police pay."

The cabin was three hundred square feet and consisted of a sitting room–cum–kitchen–cum–bedroom. Empty beer bottles covered the countertop and sitting-room table. There was nothing hanging on the walls and there were no ornaments on the windowsills or books on the shelves.

"There's a cellar, too," Katrine said, pointing to a trapdoor in the floor. "This is your area. What do we do now?"

"We search," Harry said.

"What for?"

"That's the last of our thoughts."

"Why?"

"Because it's easy to miss something important if you're searching for something else. Clear your mind. You'll know what you're searching for when you see it."

"OK," Katrine said with exaggerated slowness.

"You start up here," Harry said, going to the trapdoor and pulling at the inset iron ring. A narrow staircase led down into the gloom. He hoped she didn't see his hesitation.

Dry cobwebs from long-dead spiders stuck to his face as he descended into the damp murk, which smelled of soil and rotten boards. The whole of the cellar was underground. He found a switch by the bottom of the staircase and pressed it, but nothing happened. The only light was the red eye at the top of a freezer by the side wall. He flicked on his flashlight, and the cone of light fell on a storeroom door.

The hinges screamed as he opened it. It was a carpenter's cubbyhole, full of tools. For a man with ambitions to do something meaningful, Harry thought. Besides catching murderers.

But the tools didn't look as if they had been used much, so maybe Rafto had realized that in the end he was no good at anything else; he wasn't the kind to make things, he was the kind to clear up afterward. A sudden noise made Harry whirl around. And he breathed out with relief when he saw that the freezer thermostat had activated the fan. Harry went into a second storeroom. A blanket had been spread over everything. He pulled it off, and the smell of damp and mildew hit him. The flashlight beam revealed a rotting parasol, a plastic table, a pile of freezer drawers, discolored plastic chairs and a croquet set. There was nothing else in the cellar. He heard Katrine rummaging around upstairs and was on the verge of closing the storeroom door. But one of the freezer drawers had slipped down into the doorway when he removed the blanket. He was about to nudge it back with his foot when he stopped and looked at it. In the light he could see the raised lettering on the side. ELECTROLUX. He walked over to the wall, where the fan on the freezer was still humming. It was an Electrolux. He grabbed the handle and pulled, but the door didn't budge. Beneath the handle he noticed a lock and realized that the freezer was simply locked. He went into the tool room to fetch a crowbar. As he returned, Katrine came down the stairs.

"Nothing up top," she said. "I think we should just go. What are you doing?"

"Breaking and entering," Harry said, with the tip of the crowbar inserted in the freezer door just above the lock. He put all his weight against the other end. It didn't give. He readjusted his grip, put one foot against the staircase and pushed.

"Goddamn—"

With a dry snap the door swung open and Harry fell headlong. He heard the flashlight hit the brick floor and felt the cold hit him, like the breath of a glacier. He was fumbling for the light behind him when he heard Katrine. It was a sound that chilled to the marrow, a deep-throated scream that passed into hysterical sobs, sounding like laughter. Then it went quiet for a couple of seconds as she drew breath, before it started again, the same scream, long and drawn out, like the methodical, ritual song of pain of a woman giving birth. But by then Harry had seen everything and knew why. She was screaming because after twelve years the freezer was still functioning perfectly and its internal light revealed something crammed inside, its arms to the fore, its knees bent and the head forced against one side. The body was covered with white ice crystals, as if a layer of white fungus had been feeding on it; and the distorted form was the visual representation of Katrine's screams. But that was not what had made Harry's stomach turn. Moments after the freezer broke open the body fell forward and the forehead hit the edge of the door, causing ice crystals to fall from the face and shower the cellar floor. That was how Harry could tell it was Gert Rafto grinning at them. However, the grin was not formed by the mouth, which was sewn up with coarse, hemplike thread zigzagging in and out of the lips. The grin traversed the chin and arced up to the cheeks and was drawn with a line of black nails that could only have been hammered in. What caught Harry's attention was the nose. He forced down the rising bile out of sheer defiance. The nasal bone and cartilage would have been removed first. The cold had sucked all the color from the carrot. The snowman was complete.

Part Three

15

Number Eight

It was eight o'clock in the evening, yet people walking down Grønlandsleiret could see that lights were burning on the whole of the sixth floor of the Police HQ.

In K1, Holm, Skarre, Espen Lepsvik, Gunnar Hagen and the chief superintendent sat in front of Harry. Six and a half hours had passed since they had found Gert Rafto on Finnøy, and four since Harry had called from Bergen to arrange a meeting for when he returned.

Harry had reported back on the discovery of the body, and even the chief superintendent had quailed in his chair when Harry showed the crime scene photos that the Bergen Police had e-mailed over.

"The autopsy report isn't ready yet," Harry said. "But the cause of death is fairly obvious. A firearm in the mouth and a bullet through the palate and out the back of the head. That happened at the crime scene; the Bergen guys found the bullet in the storeroom wall."

"Blood and cerebral matter?" Skarre asked.

"No," Harry said.

"Not after so many years," Lepsvik said. "Rats, insects . . ."

"There might have been residual traces," Harry said. "But I spoke to the pathologist and we agreed: Rafto probably helped so that it wouldn't be so messy."

"Eh?" Skarre said.

"Ugh," Lepsvik said with feeling.

Reality seemed to dawn on Skarre and his face crumpled in horror. "Oh, hell . . ."

"Sorry," Hagen said. "Can anyone explain to me what you're talking about?"

"This is something we occasionally experience with suicides," Harry said. "The poor soul sucks the air out of the barrel before shooting himself. The vacuum causes there to be less"—he searched for the word—"soiling. What happened here is probably that Rafto was ordered to suck out the air."

Lepsvik shook his head. "And a policeman like Rafto must have known exactly why."

Hagen paled. "But how . . . how on earth do you make a man suck . . ."

"Perhaps he was given a choice," Harry suggested. "There are worse ways of dying than shooting yourself through the mouth." A stunned silence fell over them. And Harry let it fill the void for a few seconds before going on.

"So far we've never found the bodies. Rafto was also hidden, but he would have been found quickly enough, had it not been for relatives shunning the cabin. This leads me to believe that Rafto was not part of the killer's project."

"And you believe this is a serial killer?" There was no defiance in the chief superintendent's tone, just a wish to have this confirmed.

Harry nodded.

"If Rafto is not part of this so-called project, what could the motive be?"

"We don't know, but when a detective is killed it's natural to think that he's come to represent a threat for the killer."

Espen Lepsvik coughed. "Sometimes the way bodies are treated can tell us something about the motive. In this case, for example, the nose has been replaced with a carrot. In other words, he's thumbing his nose at us."

"Making fun of us?" Hagen asked.

"Perhaps he's telling us not to stick our noses in?" Holm suggested tentatively.

"Exactly!" Hagen exclaimed. "A warning to others to keep their distance."

The chief superintendent lowered his head and looked at Harry from the corner of his eye. "What about the stitched-up mouth?"

"A message: Keep your mouth shut," Skarre crowed.

"Right!" Hagen exclaimed. "If Rafto was a rotten apple he and the killer were probably in cahoots in some way, and Rafto was threatening to expose him."

They all looked at Harry, who had not responded to any of the suggestions.

"Well?" growled the chief superintendent.

"You may well be right, of course," Harry said. "But I believe the only message he wanted to send was that the Snowman had been there. And he likes making snowmen. Period."

The detectives exchanged quick glances, but no one objected.

"We have another problem," Harry said. "The Bergen Police have released a statement saying that a person has been found dead on Finnøy, that's all. And I've asked them to withhold further details for the time being so that we have a couple of days to hunt for clues without the Snowman knowing the body has been found. Unfortunately two days is not so realistic. No police station is **that** watertight."

"The press have Rafto's name for release early tomorrow," said Espen Lepsvik. "I know the people on **Bergens Tidende** and **Bergensavisen**."

"Wrong," they heard behind them. "It'll be on the TV2 late news tonight. Not just the name but details of the crime scene and the link with the Snowman."

They turned around. In the doorway stood Katrine Bratt. She was still pale, though not as ashen as when Harry had watched her drive the boat from Finnøy, leaving him to wait for the police.

"So you know the TV2 people, do you?" asked Espen Lepsvik with a crooked grin.

"No," Katrine said, sitting down. "I know the Bergen Police Station."

"Where have you been, Bratt?" Hagen was asking. "You've been gone for several hours."

Katrine glanced at Harry, who sent her an imperceptible nod and cleared his throat. "Katrine's been doing a couple of jobs I gave her."

"Must have been important. Let's hear, Bratt."

"We don't need to go into it now," Harry said.

"I'm just curious," Hagen teased.

Mr. goddamn Armchair General, Harry thought. Mr. Punctuality, Mr. Debrief, can't you leave her alone, can't you see the girl's still in shock? You blanched yourself when you saw the pictures. She ran home, ducked everything. So what? She's back now. Give her a pat on the back rather than humiliate her in front of her colleagues. This went through Harry's mind, in loud, clear tones, as he tried to catch Hagen's eye and make him understand.

"Well, Bratt?" Hagen said.

"I've been checking a few things," Katrine said, raising her chin.

"I see. Such as . . ."

"Such as Idar Vetlesen being a medical student when Laila Aasen was murdered and Onny Hetland and Rafto disappeared."

"Is that relevant?" asked the chief superintendent.

"It's relevant," Katrine said. "Because he studied at the University of Bergen."

K1 went quiet.

"A medical student?" The chief looked at Harry.

"Why not?" Harry said. "He took up plastic surgery later, and he says he likes shaping faces."

"I checked the places where he trained as an intern and later worked," Katrine said. "They don't coincide with the disappearances of the women we believe the

Snowman has killed. But as a young doctor you quite often travel. Conferences, short, temporary posts."

"Damn shame Krohn won't let us talk to the guy," Skarre said.

"Forget it," Harry said. "We'll arrest Vetlesen."

"What for?" Hagen said. "Studying in Bergen?"

"For trying to buy sex from minors."

"On what basis?" asked the chief superintendent.

"We have a witness. The owner of the Leon. And we have photos connecting Vetlesen with the place."

"I hate to say this," said Espen Lepsvik, "but I know the Leon guy, and he will never testify. The case won't stick; you'll have to release Vetlesen within twenty-four hours, no question."

"I know," Harry said, looking at his watch. He was working out how long it would take to drive to Bygdøy. "And it's incredible what people can find to say in that space of time."

Harry pressed the doorbell once more, thinking it was like summer vacation when he was small and everyone had gone and he was the only boy left in Oppsal. When he had stood there ringing the bell at Øystein's place or one of the others', hoping by some miracle that someone would be at home and not with Grandma in Halden or in a cabin in Son or camping in Denmark. He had pressed the bells again and again until he knew that only one possibility re-mained. Tresko. Tresko, with whom Øystein and he never wanted to play, but who still hung around like a shadow waiting for them to change their minds, to bring him in from the cold, temporarily. He must have chosen Harry and Øystein because they weren't the most popular, either, so he reckoned if he was going to be accepted into a club this was where his greatest hope lay. And now this was his opportunity because he was the only one left, and Harry knew that Tresko was always at home because his family could never afford to go anywhere and he had no other friends to play with.

Harry heard slippers shuffling inside, and the door opened a crack. The woman's face lit up. Just like Tresko's mother's face had lit up when she saw Harry. She never invited him in, just called Tresko, went to get him, gave him an earful, shoved him into his ugly parka and pushed him out onto the step, where he stood looking sulkily at Harry. And Harry knew Tresko knew. And felt his mute hatred as they walked down to the kiosk. But that was fine. It helped time pass.

"I'm afraid Idar's not here," Fru Vetlesen said. "But won't you come in and wait? He was just going out for a little drive, he said."

Harry shook his head, wondering if she could see the blue lights piercing the evening darkness of Bygdøy on the street behind him. He bet it was Skarre who had put them on, the numbskull.

"When did he leave?"

"Just before five."

"But that's several hours ago," Harry said. "Did he say where he was going?"

She shook her head. "Never tells me anything. What do you think about that? Doesn't even want to let his own mother know what he's doing."

Harry thanked her and said he would be back later. Then he walked down the gravel path and the steps to the wicket gate. They hadn't found Idar Vetlesen at his office or at Hotel Leon, and the curling club had been shut up and dark. Harry closed the gate behind him and walked over to the car. The uniformed officer rolled down the window.

"Switch off the blue lights," Harry said, turning to Skarre in the backseat. "She says he's not at home, and she's probably telling the truth. You'll have to wait to see if he returns. Call the duty officer and tell him to mount a manhunt. Nothing over the police radio, OK?"

On the way back to town Harry called the Telenor switchboard, where he was informed that his contact Torkildsen had gone home for the day and that inquiries regarding the location of Idar Vetlesen's mobile phone would have to go through formal channels early the following morning. He hung up and turned up the volume of Slipknot's "Vermilion," but he wasn't in the mood and pressed the eject button to change to a Gil Evans CD he had rediscovered at the back of the glove compartment. The NRK twenty-four-hour news was jabbering away on the radio as he fidgeted with the CD cover.

"The police are searching for a male doctor in his thirties, a resident of Bygdøy. He is thought to be connected to the Snowman murders."

"Fuck!" Harry yelled, throwing Gil Evans at the windshield and showering the car with bits of plastic. The disc rolled into the foot well. In sheer frustration Harry stamped on the accelerator and passed a tanker, which was in the left lane. Twenty minutes. It had taken them twenty minutes. Why didn't they just give the Police HQ a microphone and live air-time?

The police cafeteria was closed and deserted for the evening, but that was where Harry found her, her and sandwiches at a table for two. Harry sat in the other chair.

"Thank you for not telling anyone I lost it on Finnøy," she said softly.

Harry nodded. "What did you do?"

"I checked out and caught the three o'clock flight. I just had to get away." She looked down into her cup of tea. "I'm . . . sorry."

"It's fine," Harry said, regarding her slim, bent neck, pinned-up hair and the petite hand placed on the table. He saw her differently now. "When the tough nuts crack, they crack in style."

"Why?"

"Perhaps because they haven't had enough practice at losing control."

Katrine nodded, still staring at the teacup with the police sports team logo.

"You're a control freak, too, Harry. Don't you ever lose it?"

She raised her eyes, and Harry thought it must have been the intense light in her irises that lent her whites a bluish shimmer. He groped for his cigarettes. "I've had masses of practice at it. I've hardly trained at anything else except freaking out. I've got a black belt in losing control."

She gave a faint smile by way of response.

"They've measured the brain activity of experienced boxers," he said. "Did you know that they lose consciousness several times in the course of a fight? A fraction of a second here, a fraction of a second there. But somehow they still manage to stay on their feet. As if the body knows it's temporary, assumes control and holds them up for as long as it takes them to regain consciousness." Harry tapped out a cigarette. "I also lost it at the cabin. The difference is that, after all these years, my body knows that control will return."

"But what do you do," Katrine asked, stroking a wisp of hair from her face, "not to be knocked out by the first blow?"

"Do what boxers do, sway with the punches. Don't resist. If any of what happens at work gets to you, just let it. You won't be able to shut it out in the long term anyway. Take it bit by bit, release it like a dam, don't let it collect until the wall develops cracks."

He poked the unlit cigarette between his lips.

"Yes, I know. The police psychologist told you all this when you were a cadet. My point is this: Even when you release it into real life you have to feel what it's doing to you, feel if it's destroying you."

"OK," Katrine said. "And what do you do if you feel it's destroying you?"

"Then you get yourself another job."

She gave him a long stare.

"And what did you do, Harry? What did you do when you felt it was destroying you?"

Harry bit lightly into the filter, feeling its soft, dry fiber rub against his teeth. Thinking she could have been his sister or daughter—they were made of the same stern stuff. Solid, heavy, ungiving building material with big cracks.

"I forgot to look for another job," he said.

She beamed. "Do you know what?" she whispered.

"What?"

She stretched out her hand, grabbed the cigarette from his mouth and leaned across the table.

"I think—"

The cafeteria door burst open. It was Holm.

"TV2," he said. "It's on the news now. Names and photos of Rafto and Vetlesen."

And with that came the chaos. Even though it was eleven o'clock at night, within half an hour the foyer of the Police HQ was full of journalists and photographers. They were all waiting for the Kripos head, Espen Lepsvik, or Hagen, the head of the Crime Squad, the chief superintendent, the chief constable, or basically anyone, to come down and say something. Mumbling among themselves that the police had to acknowledge their responsibility to keep the general public informed about such a serious, shocking and circulation-increasing matter.

Harry stood by the banister in the atrium looking down at them. They were circling like restless sharks, consulting one another, duping one another, helping one another, bluffing and scenting tidbits. Had anyone heard anything? Would there be a press conference tonight? Or at least an impromptu briefing? Was Vetlesen already on his way to Thailand? The deadline was looming; something had to happen.

Harry had read that the word **deadline** originated from the battlefields of the American Civil War, when, for lack of anything material to lock prisoners behind, the captors gathered together the prisoners and a line was drawn around them in the dirt. Which became known as the "dead line," and anyone who strayed beyond it was shot. And that was precisely what they were, the news warriors down there in the foyer: prisoners of war restrained by a deadline.

Harry was on his way to the meeting room with the others when his mobile phone rang. It was Mathias.

"Have you listened to the voice mail I left you?" he asked.

"Haven't had the chance—things are heating up here," Harry said. "Can we talk about it later?"

"Of course," Mathias said. "But it's about Idar. I saw on the news that he was a wanted man."

Harry shifted the phone to his other hand. "Tell me now, then."

"Idar called me earlier today. He was asking about

carnadrioxide. He often calls me to ask about medicines—pharmacy's not Idar's strong suit—so I didn't think too much about it at the time. I'm calling because carnadrioxide is an extremely dangerous medicine. Just thought you would want to know."

"Sure, sure," Harry said, rummaging through his pockets until he found a half-chewed pencil and a tram ticket. "Carna . . . ?"

"Carnadrioxide. It contains venom from the cone snail and is used as a painkiller for cancer and HIV patients. It's a thousand times stronger than morphine and just a tiny overdose will paralyze muscles with immediate effect. The respiratory organs and heart will stop and you will die instantly."

Harry made notes. "OK. What else did he say?"

"Nothing. He sounded stressed. Thanked me and hung up."

"Any idea where he was calling from?"

"No, but there was something odd about the acoustics. He certainly wasn't calling from his consulting room. It sounded as if he were in a church or a cave—do you understand what I mean?"

"I understand. Thank you, Mathias. We'll call you back if we need to know any more."

"Just happy to—"

Harry didn't catch the rest as he pressed the end-call button and the line went dead.

Inside K1, the whole of the small investigation team was sitting with cups of coffee—a fresh pot was simmering on the machine—and jackets were hanging from chairs. Skarre had just returned from Bygdøy. He reported back on the conversations he had had with Idar Vetlesen's mother, who had repeated that she didn't know anything and the whole thing must be an enormous misunderstanding.

Katrine had phoned his assistant, Borghild Moen, who had expressed the same sentiments.

"We'll question them tomorrow if need be," Harry said. "Now, I'm afraid, we have a more pressing problem."

The three others looked at Harry as he summarized the conversation with Mathias. Reading from the back of a tram ticket. Carnadrioxide.

"Do you think he murdered them?" Holm asked. "With paralyzing medicine?"

"There we have it," Skarre interrupted. "That's why he has to hide the bodies. So that the medicine isn't discovered at the autopsy and traced back to him."

"The only thing we know," Harry said, "is that Idar Vetlesen is out of control. And if he's the Snowman, he's breaking the pattern."

"The question," Katrine said, "is who he's after now. Someone's definitely going to die from that stuff soon."

Harry rubbed his neck. "Did you get a printout of Vetlesen's phone calls, Katrine?"

"Yes, I was given names for the numbers and went through them with Borghild. Most were patients. And there were two conversations with Krohn, his lawyer, and the one you just summarized with Lund-

Helgesen. In addition, there was a number registered under Popper Publishing."

"We haven't got much to work on," Harry said. "We can sit here and drink coffee and scratch our stupid heads. Or we can go home and return with the same stupid, but not quite so exhausted, heads tomorrow."

The others just stared at him.

"I'm not joking," he said. "Get the hell home."

Harry offered to drop Katrine off in the former workers' district of Grünerløkka, where, following her instructions, he stopped outside an old four-story building on Seilduksgata.

"Which apartment?" he asked, leaning forward.

"Second floor, on the right."

He peered up. All the windows were dark. He didn't see any curtains. "Doesn't look like your husband's at home. Or perhaps he's gone to bed."

"Perhaps," she said, not making a move. "Harry?"

He looked at her quizzically.

"When I said the question was who the Snowman was after now, did you know who I meant?"

"Maybe," he said.

"What we found on Finnøy was not the random murder of someone who knew too much. It had been planned long before then."

"What do you mean?"

"I mean that if Rafto had in fact been on his trail, then that was planned, too."

"Katrine . . ."

"Wait. Rafto was the best detective in Bergen. You're the best in Oslo. He could predict that it would be you who would investigate these murders, Harry. That was why you received the letter. I'm merely saying you should be careful."

"Are you trying to frighten me?"

She shrugged. "If you're frightened, do you know what that means?"

"No."

Katrine opened the car door. "That you should find yourself another job."

Harry unlocked his apartment door, took off his boots and stopped at the threshold to the sitting room. The room was completely dismantled now, like a building kit in reverse. The moonlight fell on something white on the bare red wall. He went in. It was a number eight, drawn in chalk. He stretched out his hand and touched it. It must have been done by the mold man, but what did it mean? Perhaps a code to tell him which liquid to apply there.

For the rest of the night wild nightmares racked Harry's body, turning him this way and that. He dreamed that something was forced into his mouth and he had to breathe through some kind of opening so as not to die from suffocation. It tasted of oil, metal and gunpowder, and in the end there was no more air left inside, just a vacuum. Then he spat the thing out and discovered it was not the barrel of a gun, but a figure eight he had been breathing through. An eight with a large circle below, a smaller one above. The big circle at the bottom, the little one at the top. Gradually the figure eight acquired a third, a smaller circle on top. A head. Sylvia Ottersen's head. She tried to scream, tried to tell him what had happened, but she couldn't. Her lips were sewn together.

When he awoke, his eyes were gummed up, he had a headache and there was a coating on his lips that tasted of chalk and bile.

16

Curling

It was a chilly morning in Bygdøy as Asta Johannsen unlocked the curling club at eight, as usual. The soon-to-be seventy-year-old widow cleaned there twice a week, which was more than sufficient, as the private little hall was not used by more than a handful of men and, moreover, it didn't have any showers. She switched on the light. From the cog-jointed timber walls hung trophies, diplomas, pennants adorned with Latin phrases and old black-and-white photographs of men wearing beards, tweeds and worthy expressions. Asta thought they looked comical, like those foxhunters in English TV series about the upper classes. She went through the door to the curling hall and knew from the cold inside that they had forgotten to turn up the thermostat for the ice, which they usually did to save electricity. Asta Johannsen flicked on the light switch and, as the neon tubes blinked and wrestled to decide whether they wanted to work, she put on her glasses and saw that the thermostat for the cooling cables was indeed too low, and she turned it up.

The light shone on the gray surface of ice. Through her reading glasses she glimpsed something at the other end of the hall, so she removed them. Slowly things came into focus. A person? She wanted to walk across the ice, but hesitated. Asta Johannsen was not at all the jittery type but she feared that one day she would break her thigh on the ice and have to stay there until the foxhunters found her. She gripped one of the brooms leaning against the walls, used it as a walking stick and, taking tiny steps, teetered across the ice.

The lifeless man lay at the end of the sheet with his head in the center of the rings. The blue-white gleam from the neon tubes fell on the face stiffened in a grimace. There was something familiar about his face. Was he a celebrity? The glazed eyes seemed to be looking for something behind her, beyond what was here. The cramped right hand held an empty plastic syringe containing a residue of red contents.

Asta Johannsen calmly concluded that there was nothing she could do for him and concentrated on making her way back over the ice to the nearest telephone.

After she had called the police and they had come, she went home and drank her morning coffee.

It was only when she picked up the **Aftenposten** newspaper that she realized who it was she had found.

. . .

Harry was in a crouch, examining Idar Vetlesen's boots.

"What does our pathologist say about the time of death?" he asked Bjørn Holm, who was standing beside him in a denim jacket lined with white teddy-bear fur. His snakeskin boots made almost no noise as he stamped them on the ice. Barely an hour had passed since Asta Johannsen had made her call, but the reporters were already assembled outside the red police cordon by the curling club.

"He says it's difficult to tell," Holm said. "He can only guess how fast the temperature of a body lying on ice in a much warmer room might fall."

"But he **has** made a guess?"

"Somewhere between five and seven yesterday evening."

"Mm. Before the TV news announcement about him. You saw the lock, did you?"

Holm nodded. "Standard Yale. It was locked when the cleaning lady arrived. I saw you looking at the boots. I've checked the prints. I'm pretty sure they're identical to the prints we've got from Sollihøgda."

Harry studied the pattern on the sole. "So you think this is our man, do you?"

"I would reckon so, yes."

Harry nodded, deep in thought. "Do you know if Vetlesen was left-handed?"

"Would doubt it. As you can see, he's holding the syringe in his right hand."

Harry nodded. "So he is. Check anyway."

Harry had never really managed to experience a sense of pleasure when, one day, cases he was working on reached a conclusion, were solved, were over. For as long as the case was under investigation this was his aim, but once it was achieved, he knew only that he hadn't arrived at his journey's end. Or that this was not the end he had imagined. Or that it had shifted, he had changed or Christ knows what. The thing was, he felt empty, success did not taste as promised, catching the guilty party always came loaded with the question So what?

It was seven in the evening, witnesses had been questioned, forensic evidence collected, a press conference held and in the Crime Squad corridors there was a burgeoning party atmosphere. Hagen had ordered cakes and beer and summoned Lepsvik's and Harry's teams to some self-congratulation in K1.

Harry sat in a chair eyeing a huge piece of cake someone had placed in his lap. He listened to Hagen speaking, the laughter and the applause. Someone nudged him in the back as he passed, but most left him in peace. There was a buzz of conversation around him.

"The bastard was a real loser. Chickened out when he knew we had him."

"Cheated us."

"Us? Do you mean that you Lepsvik crew—?"

"If we'd caught him alive, the court would have declared him insane and—"

"We should be happy. After all, we didn't have any conclusive evidence, just circumstantial."

Espen Lepsvik's voice boomed from the other side of the room. "OK, folks, shut up! A motion has been put forward, and passed, that we meet at Fenris Bar at eight to get seriously drunk. And that's an order. OK?"

Loud cheering.

Harry put the cake down and was standing up when he felt a light hand on his shoulder. It was Holm.

"I checked. It's as I said—Vetlesen was right-handed."

Carbon dioxide fizzed from a beer being opened, and an already tipsy Skarre put his arm around Holm's shoulder.

"They say that life expectancy is higher for right-handed people than for left-handed. Didn't apply to Vetlesen, though, did it? Ha-ha-ha!"

Skarre left to share his nugget of wisdom with others, and Holm asked Harry: "Are you off?"

"Going for a walk. Might see you at Fenris."

Harry had almost reached the door when Hagen grabbed his arm.

"Nice if no one left quite yet," he said quietly. "The chief constable said he would come down to say a few words."

Harry looked at Hagen, then realized that there must have been something in his eyes because Hagen let go of his arm as though he had been burned.

"Just going to the toilet," Harry said.

Hagen gave a quick smile and nodded.

Harry went to his office, got his jacket and walked slowly downstairs, out of the Police HQ and down to Grønlandsleiret. There were a few flakes of snow in the air, lights twinkled on Ekeberg Ridge, a siren rose and fell like the distant song of a whale. Two Pakistanis were having a good-natured argument outside Harry's local shops as the snow settled on their oranges, and a swaying drunk was singing a sea shanty in Grønlands torg. Harry could sense the creatures of the night sniffing the air, wondering if it was safe to come out. God, how he loved this town.

"You in here?"

Eli Kvale looked in surprise at her son, Trygve, who was sitting at the kitchen table reading a magazine. The radio was droning away in the background.

She was going to ask why he didn't sit in the living room with his father, but it struck her that it should be equally natural for him to want to talk to her. Except that it wasn't. She poured herself a cup of tea, sat down and watched him in silence. He was so good-looking. She had always believed she would find him ugly, but she had been wrong.

The voice on the radio said men were no longer the cause of women's inability to get into Norwegian boardrooms; companies were struggling to reach the legally determined quota of women because the majority seemed to have a chronic aversion to posts where they might be exposed to criticism, find themselves professionally challenged or have no one to hide behind.

"They're like kids who cry and cry to have a pistachio, but spit it out when they finally get it," the voice said. "Damn irritating to see. It's about time women took some responsibility and showed some guts."

Yes, thought Eli. It is about time.

"Someone came up to me in ICA today," Trygve said.

"Oh, yes?" Eli said, her heart in her throat.

"Asked me if I was your son, yours and Dad's."

"Uh-huh," Eli said softly, all too softly, feeling dizzy. "And what did you answer?"

"What did I answer?" Trygve looked up from his magazine. "I answered yes, of course."

"And who was the man who asked?"

"What's the matter, Mom?"

"What do you mean?"

"You're so pale."

"Nothing, my love. Who was he?"

Trygve went back to his magazine. "I didn't say it was a man, did I?"

Eli got to her feet, turned down the radio as a woman's voice was thanking the minister of industry and Arve Støp for the debate. She stared into the dark as a couple of snowflakes swirled hither and thither, aimless, unaffected by gravity and their own will, apparently. They would land wherever chance dictated. And then they would melt and vanish. There was some comfort in that.

She coughed.

"What?" Trygve said.

"Nothing," she said. "I think I'm getting a cold."

Harry drifted aimlessly, without any will of his own, through the streets of Oslo. It was only when he was standing outside the Hotel Leon that he realized that was where he had been heading. The prostitutes and the dope dealers had already taken up their positions in the neighboring streets. It was rush hour. Customers preferred to deal in sex and dope before midnight.

Harry walked into reception and saw from Børre Hansen's horrified expression that he had been recognized.

"We had a deal!" squealed the hotel owner, wiping the sweat from his brow.

Harry wondered why men who lived off others' urges always seemed to wear this glistening film of sweat, like a veneer of false shame at their unscrupulousness.

"Give me the key to the doctor's room," Harry said. "He's not coming tonight."

Three of the hotel-room walls had seventies wallpaper with psychedelic patterns of brown and orange, while the main bathroom wall was painted black and shot through with gray cracks and blotches where the plaster had fallen off. The double bed sagged in the middle. The needle-felt carpet was hard. Water and semen repellent, Harry assumed. He removed a threadbare hand towel from the chair at the foot of the bed and sat down. Listened to the rumbles of expectant excitement in the town and sensed that the dogs were back. They snapped and barked, pulled at the iron chains, shouting: Just one drink, just a shot so that we can leave you in peace and lie at your feet. Harry was not in a laughing mood, but laughed anyway. Demons had to be exorcised, and pain drowned. He lit a cigarette. The smoke curled up to the rice-paper lamp.

What demons had Idar Vetlesen been grappling with? Had he brought them here, or was this the sanctuary, the refuge? Perhaps he had discovered some answers, but not all of them. Never all of them. Like whether madness and evil are two different entities, or whether when we no longer understand the purpose of destruction we simply term it madness. We're capable of understanding that someone has to drop an atomic bomb on a town of innocent civilians, but not that others have to cut up prostitutes who spread disease and moral depravity in the slums of London. Hence we call the former realism and the latter madness.

Christ, how he needed a drink. Just one to take the edge off the pain, off this day, off this night.

There was a knock at the door.

"Yes," Harry yelled and started at the sound of his own anger.

The door opened and a black face came into view. Harry looked her over. Beneath the beautiful, strong head and neck she wore a short jacket, so short that the rolls of fat bulging over the top of her tight trousers could be seen.

"Doctor?" she asked in English. The stress on the second syllable gave the word a French timbre.

He shook his head. She looked at him. Then the door was closed and she was gone.

A couple of seconds passed before Harry got off his chair and went to the door. The woman had reached the end of the corridor.

"Please!" Harry shouted in English. "Please, come back."

She stopped and regarded him warily.

"Two hundred kroner," she said. Stress on the last syllable.

Harry nodded.

She sat on the bed and listened to his questions, perplexed. About Doctor, this evil man. About the orgies with several women. About the children he wanted them to bring. And with every new question she shook her head in incomprehension. In the end, she asked if he was from the police.

Harry nodded.

Her eyebrows puckered. "Why you ask these questions? Where is Doctor?"

"Doctor killed people," Harry said.

She studied him suspiciously. "Not true," she said at length.

"Why not?"

"Because Doctor is a nice man. He helps us."

Harry asked how Doctor helped them. And now he was the one to sit and listen as the black woman told him that every Monday and Thursday Doctor sat in this room with his bag, talked to them, sent them to the bathroom to provide urine samples, took blood samples and tested them for venereal diseases. He gave them pills and treatment if they had any of the usual sexual diseases. And the address of the hospital if they had the other one, the Plague. If there was anything else wrong with them, he gave them pills for that, too. He never took payment, and the only thing they had to do was promise that they wouldn't tell anyone apart from their colleagues on the street. Some of the girls had brought their children when they were ill, but the hotel owner had stopped them.

Harry smoked a cigarette as he listened. Was this Vetlesen's indulgence? The counterpoint to evil, the necessary balance. Or did it just accentuate the evil, set it into relief? Dr. Mengele was said to have been very fond of children.

His tongue kept growing in his mouth; it would suffocate him if he didn't have a drink soon.

The woman had stopped talking. She was fingering the two-hundred-krone note.

"Will Doctor come back?" she asked finally.

Harry opened his mouth to answer her, but his tongue was in the way. His mobile phone rang and he took the call.

"Hole speaking."

"Harry? This is Oda Paulsen. Do you remember me?"

He didn't remember her; anyway, she sounded too young.

"From NRK," she said. "I invited you to **Bosse** last time."

The researcher. The honey trap.

"We were wondering whether you would like to join us again, tomorrow. We'd like to hear about this Snowman triumph. Yes, we know he's dead, but nevertheless. About what goes through the head of this sort of person. If he can be called that—"

"No," Harry said.

"What?"

"I don't want to join you."

"It's **Bosse**," Oda Paulsen said with genuine bewilderment in her voice. "On NRK TV."

"No."

"But listen, Harry, wouldn't it be interesting to talk—"

Harry threw the mobile phone at the black wall. A chip of plaster fell off.

Harry put his head in his hands, trying to hold it together so that it didn't explode. He had to drink something. Anything. When he looked up again, he was alone in the room.

It might have been avoided if Fenris Bar had not served alcohol. If Jim Beam had not been on the shelf behind the bartender, screaming with its hoarse whiskey-voice about anesthesia and amnesty: "Harry!

Come here, let's reminisce about old times. About those awful ghosts we have dispelled, about the nights we could sleep."

On the other hand, perhaps it might not.

Harry hardly registered his colleagues, and they took no notice of him. When he had entered the garish bar with the plush red Danish ferry interior, they were already well on the way. They were hanging off one another's shoulders, shouting and breathing alcohol over one another, singing along with Stevie Wonder, who claimed he had just called to say he loved you. They looked and sounded, in short, like a football team who had won the cup. And as Stevie Wonder finished by stating that his declaration of love came from the bottom of his heart, Harry's third drink was placed in front of him on the bar.

The first drink had numbed everything; he had been unable to breathe and mused that that was how taking carnadrioxide must feel. The second had almost made his stomach turn. But his body had got over the first shock and known that it had received what it had been demanding for so long. And now it was responding with a murmur of well-being. The heat washed through him. This was music for the soul.

"Are you drinking?"

Katrine was standing by his side.

"This is the last," Harry said, his tongue no longer feeling thick, but smooth and supple. Alcohol just improved his articulation. And people hardly noticed that he was drunk, up to a certain point. That was why he still had a job.

"It's not the last," Katrine said. "It's the first."

"That's one of those AA precepts." Harry looked up at her. The intense blue eyes, the thin nostrils, the full lips. God, she looked so wonderful. "Are you an alcoholic, Katrine Bratt?"

"I had a father who was."

"Mm. Was that why you didn't want to visit them in Bergen?"

"You avoid visiting people because they have an illness?"

"I don't know. You may have had an unhappy childhood because of him or something like that."

"He couldn't have made me unhappy. I was born like that."

"Unhappy?"

"Maybe. What about you?"

Harry hunched his shoulders. "Goes without saying."

Katrine sipped her drink, a shiny number. Vodka shiny, not gin gray, he established.

"And what's your unhappiness due to, Harry?"

The words came out before he had time to think. "Loving someone who loves me."

Katrine laughed. "Poor thing. Did you have a harmonious start to life and a cheery disposition that was later destroyed? Or was your path marked out for you?"

Harry stared at the golden-brown liquid in his glass. "Sometimes I wonder. But not often. I try to think about other things."

"Like what?"

"Other things."

"Do you sometimes think about me?"

Someone bumped into her and she stepped closer. Her perfume intermingled with the aroma of Jim Beam.

"Never," he said, grabbing his glass and knocking back the contents. He stared ahead, into the mirror behind the bottles, where he saw Katrine Bratt and Harry Hole standing much too close to each other. She leaned forward.

"Harry, you're lying."

He turned to her. Her eyes seemed to be smoldering, yellow and blurred, like the fog lights on an approaching car. Her nostrils were flared, and she was breathing hard. There was a smell, as if she took lime in her vodka.

"Tell me exactly, in detail, what you feel like doing now, Harry." There was gravel in her voice. "Everything. And don't lie this time."

His mind went back to the rumor Espen Lepsvik had mentioned, about Katrine Bratt and her husband's predilections. Bullshit—his mind didn't go back, the thought had been too far forward in his cerebral cortex the whole time. He breathed in. "OK, Katrine. I'm a simple man with simple needs."

She had tipped back her head, as some animal species do to show submission. He raised his glass. "I feel like drinking."

A colleague unsteady on his legs knocked Katrine from behind and she was sent staggering toward

Harry. Harry broke her fall by grasping her left side with his free hand. Her face screwed up with pain.

"Sorry," he said. "An injury?"

She held her ribs. "Fencing. It's nothing. Sorry."

She turned her back on him and plowed a path through her colleagues. He saw several of the guys follow her with their eyes. She went into the bathroom. Harry scanned the room, saw Lepsvik look away as their gazes met. He couldn't stay here. There were other places he and Jim could chat. He paid and was about to leave. There was still a heeltap in his glass. But Lepsvik and two colleagues were watching him from the other side of the bar. It was just a question of some self-control. Harry wanted to move his legs, but they were stuck to the floor like glue. He took the glass, put it to his lips and drained the contents.

The cold night air was wonderful on his burning skin. He could kiss this town.

When Harry got home he tried to masturbate into the sink, but spewed instead and peered up at the calendar hanging on the nail under the top cupboard. He had been given it by Rakel for Christmas a few years ago. It had photos of all three of them. A photo for every month. November. Rakel and Oleg were laughing at him against a background of yellow autumnal foliage and a pale blue sky. As blue as the dress Rakel was wearing, the one with the small white flowers. The dress she had been wearing the first time. And he decided that tonight he would dream himself into that sky. Then he opened the cupboard under the counter, swept away the empty Coke bottles, which tipped over with a clatter, and—right at the back—there it was. The untouched bottle of Jim Beam. Harry had never risked being without alcohol in the house, not even in his most sober spells. Because he knew what he might do to get hold of the stuff once he had gone on a bender. As if to delay the inevitable, he ran his hand across the label. Then he opened the bottle. How much was enough? The syringe Vetlesen had used was still coated in red after the poison, showing that it had been full. As red as cochineal. My darling, cochineal.

He breathed in and raised the bottle. Put it to his mouth, felt his body tense, steel itself for the shock. And then he drank. Greedily and desperately, as if to get it over and done with. The sound from his throat between swigs sounded like a sob.

17

Good News

Gunnar Hagen strode down the corridor at speed.

It was Monday and four days since the Snowman case had been solved. They should have been four pleasant days. And there had been, it was true, congratulations, smiling bosses, positive comments in the press and even inquiries from foreign newspapers as to whether they could have the whole of the background story and the investigation from start to finish. And that was where the problem had started: The person who could have given Hagen the details of the success story had not been present. Four days had passed and no one had either seen or heard from Harry Hole. And the reason was obvious. Colleagues had seen him drinking at Fenris Bar. Hagen had kept this to himself, but the rumors had reached the ears of the chief superintendent. And Hagen had been summoned to his office that morning.

"Gunnar, this won't do anymore."

Gunnar Hagen had said there might be other explanations. Harry wasn't always that prompt at letting them know he was working away from the office. There was a lot of investigating left to do on the Snowman case even though they had found the killer.

But the chief superintendent had made up his mind. "Gunnar, we've come to the end of the road as far as Hole is concerned."

"He's our best detective, Torleif."

"And the worst representative for our force. Do you want that kind of role model for our young officers, Gunnar? The man's an alcoholic. Everyone in-house knows he was drinking at Fenris, and that he hasn't turned up for work since. If we tolerate that, we're setting a very low standard and the damage will be practically irreparable."

"But dismissal? Can't we—"

"No more warnings. The regulations regarding civil servants and alcohol abuse are abundantly clear."

This conversation was still reverberating in the POB's head as he knocked on the chief superintendent's door once again.

"He's been seen," Hagen said.

"Who?"

"Hole. Li called me to say he'd seen him go into his office and close the door behind him."

"OK," said the chief superintendent, getting to his feet. "Then let's go and have a talk with him right away."

They stomped through the Crime Squad, the red zone on the sixth floor of the Police HQ. And staff, as though scenting something in the air, came to the doors of their offices, poked their heads out and watched the two men walking side by side with stern, closed faces.

When they reached the door labeled 616, they stopped. Hagen took a deep breath.

"Torleif . . . ," he began, but the chief superintendent had already gripped the door handle and thrust it open.

They stood in the doorway, their eyes wide with disbelief.

"Good God," whispered the chief superintendent.

Harry Hole, in a T-shirt, sat behind his desk with an elastic band tightened around his forearm, his head bent forward. A syringe hung from the skin directly under the elastic band. The contents were transparent, and even from the door they could see several red dots where the needle had punctured the milky-white arm.

"What the hell are you doing, man?" hissed the chief superintendent, pushing Hagen in front of him and slamming the door behind them.

Harry's head bobbed up, and he looked at them from miles away. Hagen observed that Harry was holding a stopwatch. Suddenly Harry snatched out the syringe, looked at the remaining contents, threw aside the syringe and made notes on a piece of paper.

"Th-this makes it easier, in fact, Hole," the chief superintendent stammered. "Because we have bad news."

"I have bad news, gentlemen," Harry said, tearing a piece of cotton padding from a bag and dabbing his arm. "Idar Vetlesen can't possibly have committed suicide. And I presume you know what that means?"

Gunnar Hagen felt a sudden urge to laugh. The whole situation appeared so absurd to him that his brain simply could not come up with any other satisfactory reaction. And he could see from the chief superintendent's face that he didn't know what to do, either.

Harry looked at his watch and stood up. "Come to the meeting room in exactly one hour. Then you'll find out why," he said. "Right now I have a couple of other matters that need to be sorted out."

The inspector hurried past his two astonished superiors, opened the door and disappeared down the corridor with long, sinewy strides.

One hour and four minutes later Gunnar Hagen trooped into a hushed K1 with the chief superintendent and the chief constable. The room was filled to the rafters with officers from Lepsvik's and Hole's investigation teams, and Harry Hole's voice was the only thing to be heard. They found standing room at the back. Pictures of Idar Vetlesen were projected onto the screen, showing how he was found in the curling hall.

"As you can see, Vetlesen has the syringe in his right hand," Harry Hole said. "Not unnatural since he was right-handed. But it was his boots that triggered my curiosity. Look here."

Another picture showed a close-up of the boots.

"These boots are the only real forensic evidence we have. But it's enough. Because the print matches those we found in the snow at Sollihøgda. However, look at the laces." Hole indicated with a pointer. "Yesterday I carried out some tests with my own boots. For the knot to lie like that, I would have to do up my laces back to front. As if I were left-handed. The alternative would be to stand in front of the boot as if I were doing it for someone else."

A ripple of unease went through the room.

"I'm right-handed." It was Espen Lepsvik's voice. "And I tie my laces like that."

"Well, this may just be an oddity. However, it's this sort of thing that arouses a certain"—Hole looked as if he were tasting the word before he chose it— "disquiet. A disquiet that forces you to ask other questions. Are they really Vetlesen's boots? These boots are a cheap make. I visited Vetlesen's mother yesterday and got permission to see his collection of shoes. They're expensive, every pair, without exception. And, as I thought, he was no different from the rest of us—he sometimes kicked his shoes off without undoing the laces. That's why I can say"—Hole banged the pointer on the image—"that I know Idar Vetlesen did not tie his shoelaces like this."

Hagen glanced across at the chief superintendent, whose forehead was lined with a deep furrow.

"The question that emerges," Hole said, "is whether someone could have put the boots on Vetlesen. The same ones that the individual in question wore in Sollihøgda. The motive would be to make it seem as if Vetlesen were the Snowman, of course."

"A shoelace and cheap boots?" shouted an inspector from Lepsvik's team. "We have a sicko who wanted to buy the sexual favors of children, who knew both victims here in Oslo and whom we can place at the crime scene. All you have is speculation."

The tall policeman bowed his shorn skull. "That's correct, as far as it goes. But now I'm coming to hard facts. On the face of it, Idar Vetlesen took his own life with carnadrioxide by inserting a syringe with a very fine point into a vein. According to the postmortem, the concentration of carnadrioxide was so great that he must have injected twenty milliliters into his arm. That stacks up with the residue inside the syringe, which showed that it had been full. Carnadrioxide, as we now know, is a paralyzing substance, and even small doses can kill as the heart and respiratory organs are instantly incapacitated. According to the pathologist, it would take at most three seconds for an adult to die if that dose was injected into a vein, as was the case with Idar Vetlesen. And that simply does not make sense."

Hole waved a piece of paper on which Hagen could see he had jotted down some numbers in pencil.

"I've done some tests on myself with the same kind of syringe and needle that Vetlesen used. I injected a salt-water solution that matches carnadrioxide, in that all such solutions are at least ninety-five percent water. And I've kept track of the numbers. However hard I pressed, the narrow needle means that you can't inject twenty milliliters in less than eight seconds. Ergo . . ." The inspector waited for the inescapable conclusion to sink in before continuing. "Vetlesen would have been paralyzed before injecting a third of the contents. In short, he can't have injected everything. Not without help."

Hagen swallowed. This day was going to be even worse than he had anticipated.

When the meeting was over, Hagen saw the chief constable whisper something into the chief superintendent's ear, and the chief superintendent leaned over to Hagen.

"Ask Hole and his team to meet in my office now. And put a muzzle on Lepsvik and his lot. Not **one** word of this must get out. Understand?"

Hagen did understand. Five minutes later they were sitting in the chief superintendent's large, cheerless office.

Katrine Bratt closed the door and was the last person to sit down. Harry Hole had slid into his chair, and his outstretched legs rested directly in front of the chief superintendent's desk.

"Let me be brief," the chief superintendent said, running a hand across his face as if to erase what he saw: an investigation team back at square one. "Have you any good news, Hole? To sweeten the bitter fact that in your mysterious absence we have told the press that the Snowman is dead as a result of our un-flagging toil?"

"Well, we can assume that Idar Vetlesen knew something he should not have known, and that the killer discovered we were on his trail and therefore eliminated the possibility that he might be un-masked. If that's correct, it's still true that Vetlesen died as a result of our unflagging toil."

The chief superintendent's cheeks had gone rosy with the stress. "That's not what I mean by good news, Hole."

"No, the good news is that we're getting warmer. If not, the Snowman wouldn't have gone to such lengths to make it seem as if Vetlesen were the man we were hunting. He wants us to call off the investigation, believing we have solved the case. In short, he's under pressure. And that's when killers like the Snowman begin to make mistakes. In addition, it suggests that he dare not resume the bloodbath."

The chief superintendent sucked at his teeth and ruminated. "So that's what you think, is it, Hole? Or is it just what you hope?"

"Well," said Harry Hole, scratching his knee through the tear in his jeans, "you were the one who asked for good news, boss."

Hagen groaned. He looked out the window. It had clouded over. Snow was forecast.

Filip Becker gazed down at Jonas, who was sitting on the living-room floor with his eyes riveted to the TV screen. Since Birte had been reported missing the boy had sat for hours like this every single afternoon. As though it were a window into a better world. A world in which he could find her if only he looked hard enough.

"Jonas."

The boy glanced up at him obediently, but without interest. His face stiffened with horror when he spotted the knife.

"Are you going to cut me?" the boy asked.

The expression on his face and the reedy voice were so amusing that Filip Becker almost burst into laughter. The light from the lamp over the coffee table glinted on the steel. He had bought the knife from a hardware store in Storo Mall. Right after he had phoned Idar Vetlesen.

"Just a tiny bit, Jonas. Just a tiny bit."

Then he made an incision.

18

View

At two o'clock Camilla Lossius was driving home from the gym. She had, as usual, driven across town, to Oslo West, and the Colosseum Park fitness center. Not because they had different equipment from the gym near their house in Tveita, but because the people at Colosseum were more like her. They were West End types. Moving to Tveita had been part of the marriage deal with Erik. And she had needed to consider it as a whole package. She turned into the street where they lived. Saw the lights in the windows of the neighbors she had greeted, but with whom she had never really spoken. They were Erik's people. She braked. They weren't the only ones to have a two-car garage in this street in Tveita, but it was the only one with electric doors. Erik was obsessed by these things; she couldn't give a damn. She pressed the remote, the door tipped and rose and she depressed the clutch and slid in. As expected, Erik's car was not there; he was at work. She leaned over to the passenger seat, grabbed her gym bag and the groceries from ICA supermarket, snatched a customary glance at herself in the rearview mirror before getting out. She looked good, her friends said. Not yet thirty and a detached house, second car and country retreat outside Nice, they said. And they asked what it was like living in the East End. And how her parents were after the bankruptcy. Strange how their brains automatically linked the two questions.

Camilla looked in the mirror again. They were right. She did look good. She thought she saw something else, a movement at the edge of the mirror. No, it was just the door tipping back into position. She got out of the car and was searching for her house keys when she realized her mobile phone was still in the hands-free holder in the car.

Camilla turned and uttered a short scream.

The man had been standing behind her. Terrified, she took a step back with a hand over her mouth. She was about to apologize with a smile, not because there was anything to apologize for, but because he looked entirely innocuous. But then she caught sight of the gun in his hand. It was pointed at her. The first thing she thought was that it looked like a toy.

"My name's Filip Becker," he said. "I called. There was no one at home."

"What do you want?" she asked, trying to control the quiver in her voice as her instinct told her she must not show her fear. "What's this about?"

He flashed a quick smirk. "Whoring."

· · ·

In silence, Harry watched Hagen, who had interrupted the team meeting in Harry's office to repeat the chief superintendent's order that the "theory" of Vetlesen's murder was not to be leaked under any circumstances, not even to partners, marital or otherwise. At length, Hagen caught Harry's eye.

"Well, that was all I wanted to say," he concluded quickly and left the room.

"Go on," Harry said to Bjørn Holm, who had been summarizing their findings at the curling-hall crime scene. Or, to be more accurate, the lack of findings.

"We'd only just got going when it was determined it was a suicide. We didn't find any forensic evidence, and now the crime scene's contaminated. I looked this morning and there's not a lot to see, I'm afraid."

"Mm," Harry said. "Katrine?"

Katrine looked down at her notes. "Yes, well, your theory is that Vetlesen and the killer met at the curling club and this must have been prearranged. The obvious conclusion to draw is that they were in phone contact. You asked me to check the list of calls."

"Yes," said Harry, stifling a yawn.

She flicked through. "I got lists from Telenor for Vetlesen's clinic phone and mobile. I took them to Borghild's house."

"House?" Skarre queried.

"Of course—she doesn't have a job to go to anymore. She told me that Idar Vetlesen didn't have any visitors except for patients during the last two days. Here's a list of them."

She took a piece of paper from a file and placed it on the table between them.

"As I had presumed, Borghild has a good knowledge of Vetlesen's professional and social contacts. She helped me to identify practically all of the people on the call list. We divided them in two: professional contacts and social contacts. Both show phone numbers, the time and date of the call, whether it was incoming or outgoing and how long it lasted."

The other three put their heads together and studied the lists. Katrine's hand touched Harry's. He didn't detect any signs of embarrassment in her. Perhaps he had dreamed it all, the suggestion she had made at Fenris Bar. The thing was, though, that Harry didn't dream when he was drinking. That was the whole point of drinking. Nevertheless, he had woken up the next day with an idea that must have been conceived somewhere between the systematic emptying of the whiskey bottle and the pitiless moment of awakening. The idea of cochineal and of Vetlesen's full syringe. And that was the idea that had saved him from running straight to the liquor store on Thereses Gate, and instead propelled him back into work. One drug for another.

"Whose number is that?" Harry asked.

"Which one?" Katrine asked, leaning forward.

Harry pointed to a number on the list of social contacts.

"What makes you ask about that number in particular?" Katrine asked, peering up at him with curiosity.

"Because it's the social contact who called him, and not vice versa. We have to believe it's the killer who's stage-managing here, therefore he's the one who called."

Katrine checked the number against the list of names. "Sorry, but that person is on both lists, a patient as well."

"OK, but we have to start somewhere. Who is it? Man or woman?"

Katrine gave a wry grin. "Definitely a man."

"What do you mean?"

"Manly. As in macho. Arve Støp."

"Arve Støp?" Holm burst out. "**The** Arve Støp?"

"Put him at the top of our visiting list," Harry said.

When they had finished, they had a list of seven calls to investigate. They had the names to match all seven numbers except for one: a pay phone in Storo Mall the morning of Idar's murder.

"We've got the exact time," Harry said. "Is there a surveillance camera by the phone?"

"I don't think so," Skarre said. "But I know there's a camera at each entrance. I can check with the security firms whether they've got a recording."

"Monitor all the faces half an hour before and after," Harry said.

"That's a big job," Skarre said.

"Guess who you need to ask," Harry said.

"Beate Lønn," Holm said.

"Correct. Say hello."

Holm nodded, and Harry felt a pang of bad conscience. Skarre's mobile went off with the La's "There She Goes" as a ringtone.

They watched as Skarre listened. Harry reflected on how he had put off calling Beate for a long time now. Since the one visit in the summer, after the birth, he hadn't seen her. He knew she didn't blame him for Jack Halvorsen's being killed in the line of duty. But it had been a bit too much for him: seeing Beate and Halvorsen's child, the child the young officer never got to see, and knowing deep down that Beate was wrong. He could—he should—have saved Halvorsen.

Skarre hung up.

"A woman up in Tveita's been reported missing by her husband. Camilla Lossius, twenty-nine years old, no children. It came in only a couple of hours ago, but there are a few worrying details. There's a shopping bag on the countertop, nothing has been put in the fridge. The mobile phone was left in the car, and according to the husband she never goes anywhere without it. And one of the neighbors told the husband she saw a man hanging around their property and garage as if waiting for someone. The husband can't say whether anything's missing, not even toiletries or suitcases. These are the types who have a villa outside Nice and so many possessions they don't notice if something's missing. Understand what I mean?"

"Mm," Harry said. "What does the Missing Persons Unit think?"

"That she'll turn up. They just wanted to keep us posted."

"OK," Harry said. "Let's go on, then."

No one commented on the report for the rest of the meeting. However, Harry could feel it was in the air, like the rumble of distant thunder that might—or might not—come closer. After being allocated names off the call list, the group dispersed from Harry's office.

Harry went back to the window and gazed down at the park. The evenings were drawing in earlier and earlier; it was almost tangible as the days passed. He thought about Idar Vetlesen's mother when he had told her about the free medical help he had given to black prostitutes in the evenings. And for the first time she had dropped her mask—not in grief but in fury—and screamed it was lies, her son did not tend Negro whores. Perhaps it was better to lie. Harry thought about what he had told the chief superintendent the day before, that the bloodbath was over for the time being. In the gathering darkness beneath him he could just make it out under his window. The kindergarten classes often played there, especially if snow had fallen, as it had last night. At least that was what he had thought when he saw it on his way to work this morning. It was a big grayish white snowman.

Above the **Liberal** editorial offices in Aker Brygge, on the top floor, with a view of the Oslo Fjord, Akershus

Fortress and the village of Nesoddtangen, were situated 2,500 of Oslo's most expensive privately owned square feet. They belonged to the owner and editor of **Liberal,** Arve Støp. Or just Arve, as it said on the door where Harry rang the bell. The stairway and landing had been decorated in a functional, minimalist style, but there was a hand-painted jug on either side of the oak door, and Harry caught himself wondering what the net gain would be if he made off with one of them.

He had rung once, and now at last he could hear voices inside. One was a bright twitter, and one deep and calm. The door opened and a woman's laughter tinkled out. She was wearing a white fur hat—synthetic, Harry assumed—from which cascaded long blond hair.

"I'm looking forward to it!" she said, turning and only then catching sight of Harry.

"Hello," she said in a neutral tone, until recognition caused her to replace it with an enthusiastic "Well, hi!"

"Hi," said Harry.

"How are you?" she asked, and Harry could see she had just recalled their last conversation. The one that ended against the black wall in the Hotel Leon.

"So you and Oda know each other?" Arve Støp stood in the hallway with his arms crossed. He was barefoot and wearing a T-shirt with a barely perceptible Louis Vuitton logo and green linen trousers that would have looked feminine on any other man. For Arve Støp was almost as tall and broad as Harry and had a face an American presidential candidate would have killed for: determined chin, boyish blue eyes edged with laughter lines and thick gray hair.

"We've just exchanged greetings," Harry said. "I was on their talk show once."

"I have to go, guys," Oda said, imparting air-kisses on the run. Her footsteps drummed down the stairs as if her life depended on it.

"Yes, this was about that damn talk show, too," Støp said, beckoning Harry in and grasping his hand. "My exhibitionism is approaching pathetic levels, I'm afraid. This time I didn't even ask what the topic was before agreeing to take part. Oda was here doing her research. Well, you've done this, so you know how they work."

"In my case, they just phoned," Harry said, still feeling the heat from Støp's hand on his skin.

"You sounded very serious on the telephone, Hole. What can a miserable journalist help you with?"

"It's about your doctor and curling colleague, Idar Vetlesen."

"Aha! Vetlesen. Of course. Shall we go in?"

Harry wriggled out of his boots and followed Støp down the corridor to a living room that was two steps lower than the rest of the apartment. One look was enough to tell Harry where Idar had found the inspiration for his waiting room. The moonlight glittered on the fjord outside the window.

"You're running kind of an a priori investigation, I understand?" Støp said, flopping into the smallest item of furniture, a single molded plastic chair.

"I beg your pardon?" Harry said, sitting on the sofa.

"You're starting with the solution and working backward to find out how it happened."

"Is that what 'a priori' means?"

"God knows—I just like the sound of Latin."

"Mm. And what do you think of our solution? Do you believe it?"

"Me?" Støp laughed. "I don't believe anything. But that's my profession, of course. As soon as something begins to resemble an established truth, it's my job to argue against it. That's what liberalism is."

"And in this case?"

"Oof. I can't see that Vetlesen had any rational motive. Or was crazy in a way that would defy standard definitions."

"So you don't think Vetlesen is the murderer?"

"Arguing against the belief that the world is round is not the same as believing it to be flat. I assume you have evidence. An alcoholic beverage? Coffee?"

"Yes, coffee, please."

"I was teasing." Støp smiled. "I've got only water and wine. No, I tell a lie—I've got some sweet cider from Abbediengen Farm. And you have to taste that whether you want to or not."

Støp scuttled into a kitchen and Harry stood up to inspect his surroundings.

"Quite an apartment you've got here, Støp."

"It was in fact three apartments," Støp shouted from the kitchen. "One belonged to a successful shipowner who hanged himself out of boredom more or less where you're sitting now. The second, where I am, belonged to a stockbroker who was indicted for insider trading. He found deliverance in prison, sold the apartment to me and gave all the money to an Inner Mission preacher. But that's a kind of insider trading, too, if you know what I mean. Still, I've heard the man is a lot happier now, so why not?"

Støp came into the living room carrying two glasses with pale yellow contents. He passed one to Harry.

"The third apartment was owned by a plumber from Østensjø who decided when they were planning the Aker Brygge harbor area that this was where he would live. A kind of class journey, I guess. After scrimping and saving—or working in the black market and overcharging—for ten years, he bought it. But it cost so much he couldn't afford a moving company and did the move himself with a couple of pals. He had a safe weighing eight hundred pounds. I suppose he must have needed it for all his black market money. They had reached the final landing and there were only eighteen steps left when the infernal safe slipped. The plumber was dragged under it, broke his back and was paralyzed. Now he lives in a nursing home in the area he came from, with a view of Lake Østensjøvannet." Støp stood by the window, drank from his glass and gazed thoughtfully across the fjord. "True, it's only a lake, but it's still a view."

"Mm. We were wondering about your connection with Idar Vetlesen."

Støp spun around theatrically, as nimble in his

movements as a twenty-year-old. "Connection? That's a damned strong word. He was my doctor. And we happened to curl together. That is, **we** curled. What Idar did can at best be described as pushing a stone and cleaning the ice." He waved his hand dismissively. "Yeah, yeah, I know, he's dead, but that's how it was."

Harry put the glass of cider on the table untouched. "What did you talk about?"

"By and large about my body."

"Huh?"

"He was my doctor, for Christ's sake."

"And you wanted to change parts of your body?"

Arve Støp laughed heartily. "I've never felt a need for any of that. Of course I know that Idar performed these ridiculous plastic surgery operations, liposuction and all that, but I recommend prevention rather than repair. I play sports, Inspector. Don't you like the cider?"

"It contains alcohol," Harry said.

"Really?" Støp said, contemplating his glass. "That I can't imagine."

"So which parts of the body did you discuss?"

"The elbow. I have tennis elbow and it bothers me when we curl. He prescribed the use of painkillers before training, the idiot. Because it also suppresses inflammation. And therefore I strained my muscles every time. Well, I suppose I don't need to issue any medical warnings since we're talking about a dead doctor here, but you shouldn't take pills for pain. Pain is a good thing; we would never survive without it. We should be grateful for pain."

"Should we?"

Støp tapped his index finger on a windowpane so thick that it didn't let in a single sound from the town. "If you ask me, it's not the same as a view of fresh water. Or is it, Hole?"

"I haven't got a view."

"Haven't you? You should. A view gives perspective."

"Speaking of perspectives, Telenor gave us a list of Vetlesen's recent telephone calls. What did you talk about the day before he died?"

Støp fixed an inquisitive eye on Harry while leaning back and finishing off the cider. Then he took a deep, contented breath. "I had almost forgotten we spoke, but I suppose it was about elbows."

Harry's childhood friend Tresko had once explained that the poker player who bases his game on his ability to intuit a bluff is bound to lose. It's true that we all give ourselves away with superficial mannerisms when lying; however, you have no chance of exposing a good bluffer unless you coldly and calculatedly chart all these mannerisms against each individual, in Tresko's opinion. Harry tended to think Tresko was right. And so he didn't base his conviction that Støp was lying on the man's expression, his voice or his body language.

"Where were you between four and eight o'clock the day Vetlesen died?" Harry asked.

"Hey!" Støp raised an eyebrow. "Hey! Is there something about this case I or my readers ought to know?"

"Where were you?"

"That sounds manifestly like you haven't caught the Snowman after all. Is that right?"

"I would appreciate it if you would let me ask the questions, Støp."

"Fine, I was with . . ."

Arve paused. And his face suddenly lit up in a boyish smile.

"No, hang on a moment. You're insinuating that I could have had something to do with Vetlesen's death. If I were to answer I would be conceding the premise of the question."

"I can easily register that you refused to answer the question, Støp."

Støp raised his glass in a toast. "A familiar countermove, Hole. One that we press people use every single day. Hence the name. Press. People. But please note that I'm not refusing to answer, Hole. I'm just refraining from doing so at this minute. In other words, I'm giving it some thought." He nodded to himself. "I'm not refusing—I just haven't decided whether to answer or indeed what. And in the meantime you'll have to wait."

"I've got plenty of time."

Støp turned. "And I don't mean to waste it, Hole, but I have declared in the past that **Liberal**'s only capital and means of production is my personal integrity. I hope you appreciate that I as a pressman have an obligation to exploit this situation."

"Exploit?"

"Hell, I know I'm sitting on a little atomic bomb

of a news scoop here. I assume no newspapers have been tipped off that there's something fishy about Vetlesen's death. If I were to give you an answer now that would clear me of suspicion, I would have already played my hand. And then it's too late for me to ask for relevant information before I answer. Am I right, Hole?"

Harry had an inkling where this was leading. And that Støp was a smarter bastard than he had anticipated.

"Information isn't what you need," Harry said. "What you need is to be told that you can be prosecuted for consciously obstructing the police in the course of their duties."

"Touché." Støp laughed, distinctly enthusiastic now. "But as a pressman and a liberalist I have principles to consider. The issue here is whether I, as a declared anti-establishment watchdog, should unconditionally make my services available to the ruling power's forces of law and order." He spat out the words without concealing the sarcasm.

"And what would your preconditions be?"

"Exclusivity on the background information, of course."

"I can give you exclusivity," Harry said. "Together with a ban on passing the information to a single soul."

"Hm, well, that doesn't take us anywhere. Shame." Støp stuffed his hands in the pockets of his linen trousers. "But I already have enough to question whether the police have apprehended the right man."

"I'm warning you."

"Thank you. You've already done that." Støp sighed. "Consider, however, whom you're dealing with, Hole. On Saturday we're having the mother of all parties at the Plaza. Six hundred guests are going to celebrate twenty-five years of **Liberal.** That's not bad for a magazine that has always pushed the boundaries of our freedom of speech, that has navigated in legally polluted waters every day of its existence. Twenty-five years, Hole, and we have yet to lose a single case in the courts. I'll take this up with our lawyer, Johan Krohn. I fancy the police know him, Hole?"

Harry nodded glumly. Støp indicated with a discreet flourish toward the door that he regarded the visit over.

"I promise to assist in any way that I'm able," Støp said as they stood in the hall by the door. "If you in the force assist us."

"You know quite well that it's impossible for us to make such a deal."

"You have no idea what deals we've already made, Hole." Støp smiled, opening the door. "You really don't. I expect to see you again soon."

"I didn't expect to see you again so soon," Harry said, holding the door open.

Rakel trotted up the last steps to his apartment.

"Yes, you did," she said, stealing into his arms. Then she shoved him inside, kicked the door shut with her heel, grabbed his head with both hands and kissed him greedily.

"I hate you," she said while slackening his belt. "You know I didn't need this in my life right now."

"Go, then," Harry said, unbuttoning her coat and then her blouse. Her trousers had a zip at the side. He undid it and slipped his hand in, right to the bottom of her spine, over her cool, silky-smooth panties. It was quiet in the hall, just their breathing and a single click of her heel on the floor as she moved her foot to allow him in.

In bed afterward, sharing a cigarette, Rakel accused him of being a drug dealer.

"Isn't that how they do it?" she said. "The first doses are free. Until they're hooked."

"And then they have to pay," Harry said, blowing one large and one small ring toward the ceiling.

"A lot," Rakel said.

"You're only here for sex," Harry said. "Aren't you? Just so that I know."

Rakel stroked his chest. "You've got so thin, Harry."

He didn't answer. He waited.

"It's not working so well with Mathias," she said. "That is, he works well. He works perfectly. It's me who doesn't work."

"What's the problem?"

"If only I knew. I look at Mathias and I think, There's your dream guy. And I think, He lights my fire, and I try to light his, I almost attack him because

I want some pleasure—do you understand? It would be so good, so right. But I can't do it . . ."

"Mm. I have some difficulty imagining that, but I hear what you're saying."

She pulled his earlobe hard. "The fact that we were always hungry for each other wasn't necessarily a hallmark of quality for our relationship, Harry."

Harry watched as the smaller smoke ring caught up with the larger one and formed a figure eight. Yes, it was, he thought.

"I've started looking for pretexts," she said. "Take this amusing physical quirk that Mathias inherited from his father, for example."

"What?"

"It's nothing special, but he's a bit embarrassed about it."

"Come on, tell me."

"No, no, it has absolutely no significance, and to start with I thought his embarrassment was just sweet. Now I've started to think it's annoying. As if I'm trying to make a flaw out of this bagatelle of Mathias's, an excuse for . . . for . . ." She fell silent.

"For being here," Harry completed.

She hugged him tight. Then she got up.

"I'm not coming back," she said with a pout.

It was almost midnight when Rakel left Harry's apartment. Silent, fine drizzle made the pavement shine under the streetlamps. She turned onto Stensberggata, where she had parked the car. She got inside and was about to start the engine when she spotted a handwritten note placed under the windshield wiper. Opening the door a crack, she grabbed it and tried to read the writing that the rain had nearly washed away.

We're going to die, whore.

Rakel flinched. Looked around. But she was alone. All she could see on the street were other parked cars. Were there notes on them, too? She couldn't see any. It had to be chance; no one could have known where her car was. She rolled down the window, held the note between two fingers and let it go, started the engine and pulled out onto the road.

Just before the end of Ullevålsveien she suddenly had a feeling someone was sitting in the backseat staring at her. She looked and saw a boy's face. Not Oleg, but another boy's unfamiliar face. She slammed on the brakes and the rubber screamed on the pavement. Then came the angry sound of a car horn. Three times. She stared into her mirror as her chest heaved. And saw the face of the terrified young man in the car right behind her. Trembling, she put the car back into gear.

Eli Kvale stood in the hallway as if rooted to the floor. In her hand she was still holding the telephone receiver. She had not been imagining things, not at all.

Only when Andreas had said her name twice did she come to.

"Who was it?" he said.

"No one," she said. "Wrong number."

When they were in bed, she wanted to snuggle up to him. But she couldn't. Couldn't bring herself to do it. She was impure.

"We're going to die," the voice on the phone had said. "We're going to die, whore."

19

TV

By the time the investigation team was assembled the following morning they had checked out six of the seven names on Katrine Bratt's list. There was just one remaining.

"Arve Støp?" Bjørn Holm and Magnus Skarre queried in unison.

Katrine Bratt said nothing.

"OK," Harry said. "I've spoken to Krohn on the phone. He made it quite clear that Støp does not wish to answer the question of whether he has an alibi. Or any other questions. We can arrest Støp, but he is perfectly within his rights not to make a statement. The only thing we'll achieve by doing this is to announce to the world that the Snowman is still out there. The point at issue is whether Støp is telling the truth or this is all an act."

"But an A-list celebrity as a murderer," Skarre said with a grimace. "Who's ever heard of that?"

"O. J. Simpson," Holm said. "Phil Spector. Marvin Gaye's father."

"Who the hell's Phil Spector?"

"It'd be better if you all told me what you think," Harry said. "Straight from the hip, spontaneous. Has Støp got anything to hide? Holm?"

Bjørn Holm rubbed his cutlet-shaped sideburns. "It's suspicious that he doesn't wanna answer a question as specific as where he was when Vetlesen died."

"Bratt?"

"I think Støp just finds being under suspicion amusing. And as far as his magazine is concerned, it doesn't mean a thing. The opposite, in fact. It reinforces its outsider image. The great martyr standing firm against the current of opinion, as it were."

"Agreed," Holm said. "I'm changing sides. He wouldn't have taken this risk if he'd been guilty. He'd have gone for a scoop."

"Skarre?" Harry asked.

"He's bluffing. This is just bullshit. Did anyone actually understand the stuff about the press and principles?"

None of the others answered.

"OK," Harry said. "Assuming the majority is right and he's telling the truth, then we should eliminate him as quickly as possible and move on. Is there anyone we can think of who might have been with him at the time of Vetlesen's death?"

"Hardly," Katrine said. "I called a girl I know at **Liberal**. She said that outside working hours Støp isn't particularly sociable. By and large he keeps to himself in his apartment in Aker Brygge. Ladies excepted, that is."

Harry looked at Katrine. She reminded him of the overzealous student who is always a term ahead of the lecturer.

"Ladies in the plural?" Skarre asked.

"To quote my friend, Støp is notorious for buzzing around the honeypot. Right after she had rejected one of his advances, he told her in no uncertain terms that she wasn't living up to his expectations as a journalist and ought to think about grazing in new pastures."

"The two-faced bastard," Skarre said, snorting.

"A conclusion you and she share," Katrine said. "But the fact is she's a crappy journalist."

Holm and Harry burst into laughter.

"Ask your friend if she can name any of the lovers," Harry said, getting up. "And afterward call the rest of the staff at the magazine and ask them the same. I want him to feel us breathing down his neck. So let's get going."

"And what about you?" said Katrine, who had not moved.

"Me?"

"You didn't tell us if you think Støp is bluffing."

"Well." Harry smiled. "He's definitely not telling the whole truth."

The other three looked at him.

"He said he didn't remember what he and Vetlesen had been talking about during their last telephone conversation."

"And?"

"If you found out that a man you'd just been talking to was a wanted serial killer who'd now committed suicide, wouldn't you have instantly remembered the conversation, gone over it in great detail, asking yourself if you should have picked up anything?"

Katrine nodded slowly.

"The other thing I'm wondering," Harry said, "is why the Snowman would contact me to tell me to look for him. And when I get close, as he should have anticipated, why does he become desperate and try to make it look as if Vetlesen were the Snowman?"

"Perhaps that was the idea the whole time," Katrine said. "Perhaps he had a motive for pointing the finger at Vetlesen, some unsettled score between them. He led you that way right from the word go."

"Or perhaps that was how he was going to beat you," Holm suggested. "To force you to make mistakes. And then quietly enjoy the victory."

"Come on," Skarre said. "You're making this sound as if it's something personal between the Snowman and Harry Hole."

The other three eyed the detective in silence.

Skarre frowned. "Is it?"

Harry took his jacket from the coatrack. "Katrine, I want you to visit Borghild again. Say that we've got a warrant entitling us to look at patients' medical records. I'll take the rap if it comes. Then see what you can dig up on Arve Støp. Anything else before I go?"

"This woman in Tveita," Holm said. "Camilla Lossius. She's still missing."

"You go take a look, Holm."

"What are you going to do?" Skarre asked.

Harry gave a thin smile. "Learn to play poker."

Standing outside Tresko's door on the sixth floor of the only apartment building in Frogner Plass, Harry had that same feeling he had when he was small and everyone else in Oppsal was on vacation. This was the last resort, his last desperate action, having rung the doorbells at all the other houses. Tresko—or Asbjørn Treschow, which was his real name—opened up and stared sullenly at Harry. Because he knew now, just as he had then. Last resort.

The front door led straight into a three-hundred-square-foot living space one might call, charitably, a lounge with an open-plan kitchen, and uncharitably, an SRO. The stench was breathtaking. It was the smell of bacteria vegetating on damp feet and stale air, hence the vernacular but accurate Norwegian term **tåfis,** or toe-fart. Tresko had inherited his sweaty feet from his father. Just as he had inherited the sobriquet **tresko,** clogs, this dubious footwear he always wore in the belief that the wood absorbed the smell.

The only positive thing you could say about Tresko junior's foot odor was that it masked the smell of the dishes piled up in the sink, the overflowing ashtrays and the sweat-impregnated T-shirts drying over chair backs. It occurred to Harry that in all probability Tresko's sweaty feet had driven his opponents to the

edge of sanity on his passage through to the semifi-
nals of the world poker championship in Las Vegas.

"Been a long while," Tresko said.

"Yes. Great that you had some time for me."

Tresko laughed as if Harry had told him a joke.
And Harry, who had no desire to spend any longer
than necessary in the place, got straight to the point.

"So why is poker just about being able to see when
your opponent is lying?"

Tresko didn't seem to mind skipping the social
niceties.

"People think poker's about statistics, odds and
probability. But if you play at the highest level all the
players know the odds by heart, so that's not where
the battle takes place. What separates the best from
the rest is their ability to read others. Before I went to
Vegas I knew I was going to be up against the best.
And I could see the best playing on the Gamblers'
Channel, which I received on satellite TV. I recorded
it and studied every single one of the guys when they
were bluffing. Ran it in slow motion, logged what
went on in their faces down to the tiniest detail, what
they said and did, every repeated action. And after I'd
worked at it for long enough there was always something, some recurrent mannerism. One scratched his
right nostril; another stroked the back of the cards.
Leaving Norway, I was sure I was going to win. Sadly
it turned out I had even more telltale tics."

Tresko's grim laughter sounded more like a kind of
sobbing and caused his amorphous frame to shake.

"So if I bring a man in for questioning, you can see whether he's lying or not?"

Tresko shook his head. "It's not that simple. First of all, I need to have a recording. Second, I must have seen the cards so that I know when he's been bluffing. Then I can rewind and analyze what he does differently. It's like when you calibrate a lie detector, isn't it? Before you run the test, you get the guy to say something that is obviously true, such as his name. And then something that is obviously a lie. And afterward you read the printout so that you have points of reference."

"An obvious truth," Harry mumbled. "And an obvious lie. On a film clip."

"But, as I said on the phone, I can't guarantee anything."

Harry found Beate Lønn in the House of Pain, the room where she had spent most of her time when she had been working in the Robberies Unit. The House of Pain was a windowless office packed with equipment for watching and editing closed-circuit TV footage, blowing up images and identifying people in grainy shots or voices on fuzzy telephone recordings. But now she was head of the Forensics Unit, in Brynsalléen, and furthermore just back from maternity leave.

The machines were buzzing, and the dry heat had put roses in her almost transparent, pale cheeks.

"Hi," Harry said, letting the iron door close behind him.

The small, agile woman got up and they hugged,
both feeling a bit awkward.

"You're thin," she said.

Harry shrugged. "How's . . . everything going?"

"Greger sleeps when he has to, eats what he has to
and hardly ever cries." She smiled. "And for me that's
everything now."

He thought he should say something about
Halvorsen. Something to show that he hadn't forgotten. But the right words wouldn't come. And instead,
seeming to understand, she asked how he was.

"Fine," he said, dropping into a chair. "Not bad.
Absolutely dreadful. Depends on when you ask."

"And today?" She turned to the TV monitor and
pressed a button, and people on the screen started
running backward into the Storo Mall.

"I'm paranoid," Harry said. "I have the feeling I'm
hunting someone who is manipulating me, that
everything is chaotic and he is making me do exactly
what he wants. Do you know the feeling?"

"Yes," Beate said. "I call him Greger." She stopped
rewinding. "Do you want to see what I've found?"

Harry pushed his chair closer. It was no myth that
Beate Lønn had special gifts, that her fusiform gyrus,
the part of the brain that stores and identifies human
faces, was so highly developed and sensitive that she
was a walking index file of criminals.

"I went through the shots you have of those involved in the case," she said. "Husbands, children, witnesses and so on. I know what our old friends look like, of course."

She moved the images frame by frame. "There," she said, stopping.

The image was frozen and jumped on the screen, showing a selection of people in grainy black and white, out of focus.

"Where?" Harry said, feeling as witless as he usually did when he was studying pictures with Beate Lønn.

"There. It's the same person in this picture." She took out one of the photos from her file.

"Could this be the person who is tailing you, Harry?"

Harry stared at the photo in astonishment. Then he nodded slowly and grabbed his phone. Katrine Bratt answered after two seconds.

"Get your coat and meet me down in the garage," Harry said. "We're going for a drive."

Harry drove along Uranienborgveien and Majorstuveien to avoid the traffic lights on Bogstadveien.

"Was she really sure it was him?" Katrine said. "The picture quality on surveillance cameras—"

"Believe me," Harry said. "If Beate Lønn says it's him, it's him. Call directory assistance and get his home number."

"I saved it on my mobile," Katrine said, bringing it up.

"Saved?" Harry glanced at her. "Do you do that with everyone you encounter?"

"Yep. Put them in a group. And then I delete the group when the case is over. You should try it. It's a wonderful feeling when you press delete. Really . . . tangible."

Harry stopped across from the yellow house in Hoff.

All the windows were dark.

"Filip Becker," Katrine said. "Fancy that."

"Remember, we're just having a talk with him. He might have had quite understandable reasons for calling Vetlesen."

"From a pay phone in Storo Mall?"

Harry eyed Katrine. The pulse in the thin skin on her neck was visibly throbbing. He looked away and at the living-room window of the house.

"Come on," he said. The moment he seized the car-door handle his mobile rang. "Yes?"

The voice at the other end sounded excited, but still reported in short, concise sentences. Harry interrupted the stream with two **Mms,** a surprised **What?** and a **When?**

Then, at last, the other end went quiet.

"Call the Incident Room," Harry said. "Ask them to send the two nearest patrol cars to Hoffsveien. No sirens and tell them to stop at each end of the residential block . . . What? . . . Because there's a boy inside and we don't want to make Becker any more nervous than we have to. OK?"

Evidently it was OK.

"That was Holm." Harry leaned in front of Katrine, opened the glove compartment, rummaged through it and took out a pair of handcuffs. "His people have found quite a few fingerprints on the car in the Lossiuses' garage. They checked them against the other prints we have in the case."

Harry took the bunch of keys from the ignition, bent forward and produced a metal box from under the seat. Inserted a key in the lock, opened the box and lifted out a black short-barreled Smith & Wesson. "One off the windshield matched."

Katrine shaped her mouth into a mute O and inquired with a nod of her head if it was the yellow house.

"Yup," Harry responded. "Professor Filip Becker."

He saw Katrine Bratt's eyes widen. But her voice was as calm as before. "I have a feeling I'll soon be pressing delete."

"Maybe," Harry said, flipping open the cylinder of the revolver and checking that there were bullets in all the chambers.

"There can't be two men who kidnap women in this way." She tilted her head from side to side as if warming up for a boxing contest.

"A reasonable assumption."

"We should've known the first time we came here."

Harry observed her, wondering why he didn't share her excitement. What had happened to the intoxicating pleasure of making an arrest? Was it because he knew it would soon be replaced by the empty sensation of having arrived too late, of being a fireman sifting through the ruins? Yes, but it wasn't that. It was something else—he could sense it now. He had a nagging doubt. The fingerprints and the recordings from Storo Mall would go a long way in a court case, but it had been too easy. This killer wasn't like that; he didn't make such banal errors. This was not the same person who had placed Sylvia Ottersen's head on top of a snowman, who had frozen a policeman in his own freezer, who had sent Harry a letter saying, **What you should ask yourself is this: "Who made the snowman?"**

"What should we do?" Katrine asked. "Should we arrest him ourselves?"

Harry couldn't hear from the intonation whether this was a question or not.

"For the time being we wait," Harry said. "Until backup is in position. Then we'll ring the bell."

"And if he isn't at home?"

"He's at home."

"Oh? How do—"

"Look at the living-room window. Keep your eyes focused."

She watched. And when the white light changed behind the large panoramic window he could see she understood. The light came from a TV.

They waited in silence. There were no sounds. A crow screeched. Then it was quiet again. Harry's phone rang.

Their backup was in position.

Harry briefed them quickly. He didn't want to see any uniforms until they were summoned, except perhaps if they heard shots or shouting.

"Put it on vibrate," Katrine said after he had hung up.

He smiled briefly, did as she said and stole a glance at her. Thought about her face when the freezer door fell open. But now her face revealed no fear or tension, just concentration. He put the phone in his jacket pocket and heard it clunk against his revolver.

They got out of the car, crossed the road and opened the gate. The wet gravel sucked greedily at their shoes. Harry kept his eyes on the large window, watching for shadows and any movement toward the white wall.

Then they were standing on the doorstep. Katrine glanced at Harry, who nodded. She rang the bell. A deep, hesitant **ding-dong** sounded from inside.

They waited. No footsteps. No shadows against the wavy glass of the oblong window beside the front door.

Harry moved forward and placed his ear against the glass, a simple and surprisingly effective way of monitoring a house. But he could hear nothing, not even the TV. He took three paces back, grabbed the eaves that protruded over the front steps, held on to the gutter with both hands and pulled himself up until he was high enough to see the whole of the living room through the window. On the floor sat a figure, legs crossed, with its back to him, wearing a gray coat. A pair of enormous headphones encircled the cranium like a black halo. A cable stretched from the headphones to the TV.

"He can't hear us because he's got headphones on," Harry said, dropping down in time to see Katrine grip the door handle. The rubber seal around the frame released the door with a sucking noise.

"Seems we're welcome," Katrine said in a soft voice and entered.

Caught unawares and quietly cursing, Harry strode in after her. Katrine was already by the living-room door, and opened it. She stood there until Harry came alongside. She stepped back, banged into a pedestal where a vase teetered perilously until it decided to stay upright.

There were at least fifteen feet between them and the person still sitting with his back to them.

On the screen a baby was trying to walk while holding the index fingers of a smiling woman. The blue light of the DVD player button shone under the TV. Harry experienced a moment of déjà vu, a sense that a tragedy was going to repeat itself. Exactly like this: silence, home movie of happy times with the family, the contrast between then and now, the tragedy that has already been played out and just needs a conclusion.

Katrine pointed, but he had already seen it.

The gun was lying behind the figure, between a half-finished puzzle and a Game Boy, and looked like a toy. A Glock 21, Harry guessed, feeling queasy as his body geared up and more adrenaline entered his bloodstream.

They had a choice. Stay by the door, shout Becker's name and risk the consequences of confronting an armed man. Or disarm him before he saw them. Harry placed a hand on Katrine's shoulder and pushed her behind him while visualizing how long it would take for Becker to turn, pick up the gun, aim and fire. Four long strides would be enough, and there was no light behind Harry that would cast a shadow and too much light on the screen for him to be reflected there.

Harry took a deep breath and set off. Placed his foot as gently as possible on the parquet floor. The back did not react. He was in the middle of his second stride when he heard the crash behind him. And knew instinctively it was the vase. He saw the figure spin around, saw Filip Becker's agonized expression. Harry froze and the two of them stared at each other. The TV screen behind Becker went black. Becker's mouth opened as if he wanted to say something. The whites of his eyes contained rivers of red, and his cheeks were puffy, as though he had been crying.

"The gun!"

It was Katrine shouting and Harry automatically lifted his eyes and saw her reflection in the dark screen. She was standing by the door, legs apart with her arms stretched out in front, her hands squeezed around a revolver.

Time seemed to slow, to become a thick, shapeless material in which only his senses continued to function in real time.

A trained policeman like Harry should have in-

stinctively thrown himself to the ground and drawn
his gun. But there was something else, something
that was tardier than his instincts, but worked with
greater power. Harry would later change his opinion,
but at first he thought he acted as he did because of
another déjà vu experience, the sight of a dead man
on a floor struck by a police bullet because he knew
he had reached the end of the road, that he didn't
have the energy to grapple with any more ghosts.

Harry stepped to the right, into Katrine's line of
fire.

He heard a smooth, oiled click behind him. The
sound of the revolver hammer being uncocked, of
the finger easing the pressure on the trigger.

Becker's hand was pressed against the floor near
the pistol. His fingers and the flesh between them
were white. Which meant that Becker was supporting his body weight on them. The other hand—his
right—was holding the remote control. If Becker
went for his gun with his right hand as he was sitting
now, he would lose balance.

"Don't move," Harry said loudly.

Becker's only move was to blink twice, as though
wishing to erase the sight of Harry and Katrine. Harry
moved forward calmly but efficiently. Bent down to
pick up the gun, which was surprisingly light. So light
that it would have been impossible for there to have
been bullets in the magazine, he reflected.

Harry stowed the gun in his jacket pocket, beside
his own revolver, and crouched down. On the screen
he could see Katrine's gun pointed at them as she ner-

vously shifted her weight from foot to foot. He stretched out a hand to Becker, who retreated like a timid animal, and removed the man's headphones.

"Where's Jonas?" Harry asked.

Becker scrutinized Harry as if he understood neither the situation nor the language.

"Jonas?" Harry repeated. Then he shouted. "Jonas! Jonas, are you here?"

"Shh," Becker said. "He's asleep." His voice was somnambulant, as if he had taken tranquilizers.

Becker pointed to the headphones. "He mustn't wake up."

Harry swallowed. "Where is he?"

"Where?" Becker angled his head and looked at Harry, seeming only then to recognize him. "In bed, of course. All boys have to sleep in their own beds." His voice rose and fell as if he were quoting from a song.

Harry plunged his hand down into his other jacket pocket and took out the handcuffs. "Put out your hands," he said.

Becker blinked again.

"It's for your own safety," Harry said.

It was a well-used line, one they drilled into you back at the police academy, and was primarily intended to relax arrestees. However, when Harry heard himself say it, he knew at once why he had stepped into the firing line. And it was not because of ghosts.

Becker raised his hands to Harry as though in supplication, and the steel snapped shut around his narrow, hairy wrists.

"Stay where you are," Harry said. "She'll take care of you."

Harry straightened up and went toward the doorway where Katrine stood. She had lowered her gun, and she smiled at him with a curious gleam in her eyes. The coals deep inside seemed to be smoldering.

"Are you OK?" Harry asked in an undertone. "Katrine?"

"'Course." She laughed.

Harry hesitated. Then he continued up the stairs. He remembered where Jonas's room was, but opened the other doors first. Trying to delay the dreaded moment. Although the light was off in Becker's bedroom, he could make out the double bed. The duvet had been removed from one side. As if he already knew that she would never return.

Then Harry was outside Jonas's room. He emptied his mind of thoughts and images before opening the door. An off-key assortment of delicate tinkles rang out in the dark, and even though he couldn't see anything, he knew that the draft from the door had set off a small array of thin metal pipes, because Oleg had the same wind chimes hanging from the ceiling in his room. Harry went in and glimpsed someone or something under the duvet. He listened for breathing. But all he could hear was the tones continuing to vibrate, not wanting to die away. He placed his hand on the duvet. And for a moment he was numb with horror. Even though there was nothing in this room that presented a physical danger, he knew what he was afraid of. Because someone else, his old boss Bjarne Møller, had once formulated it for him. He was afraid of his own humanity.

Carefully, he pulled back the duvet from the body lying there. It was Jonas. In the dark he really did seem to be sleeping. Apart from his eyes, which were open and staring at the ceiling. Harry noticed a bandage on his forearm. He stooped over the boy's half-open mouth and touched his forehead. And gave a start when he felt warm skin and a current of air against his ear. And heard a sleepy voice mumble: "Mommy?"

Harry was completely unprepared for his own reaction. Perhaps it was because he was thinking of Oleg. Or perhaps because he was thinking of himself when once, as a boy, he woke up, thinking she was still alive, and charged into his parents' bedroom in Oppsal and saw the double bed with the duvet removed from one side.

Harry was unable to stem the flow of tears that suddenly welled up in his eyes, filling them until Jonas's face blurred before him, and they ran down his cheeks, leaving hot trails before finding grooves that led them to the corners of his mouth and Harry became aware of his own salty taste.

Part Four

20

The Sunglasses

It was seven o'clock in the morning when Harry unlocked Cell 23 in the custody block. Becker was sitting fully clothed on the prison bed, regarding him with a blank expression. Harry brought in the chair he had found in the duty room, sat astride it and offered Becker a cigarette from his crumpled Camel pack.

"Hardly legal to smoke here," Becker said.

"If I were sitting here awaiting a life sentence," Harry said, "I think I'd take the risk."

Becker just stared.

"Come on," Harry said. "You won't find a better place for a sly puff."

The professor smirked and took the cigarette Harry had flipped out.

"Jonas is fine, under the circumstances," Harry said, taking out his lighter. "I've spoken to the Bendiksens, and they've agreed to have him with them for a few days. I had to argue with social services a bit, but they went for it. And we haven't released news of your arrest to the press yet."

"Why not?" Becker asked, inhaling over the flame from the lighter with care.

"I'll come back to that. But I'm sure you understand that if you don't cooperate I can't continue to sit on the news."

"Aha, you're the good cop. And the one who questioned me yesterday is the bad cop, right?"

"That's right, Becker, I'm the good cop. And I'd like to ask you a few questions off the record. Whatever you tell me will not and cannot be used against you. Are you with me on this?"

Becker shrugged.

"Espen Lepsvik, who interviewed you yesterday, thinks you're lying," Harry said, blowing blue cigarette smoke at the smoke alarm on the ceiling.

"About what?"

"When you said you only spoke to Camilla Lossius in the garage and then you left."

"It's the truth. What does he think?"

"What he told you last night. That you kidnapped, killed and hid her."

"That's just crazy!" Becker erupted. "We were talking, that was all, and that's the truth!"

"Why are you refusing to tell us what you talked about?"

"It's a private matter. I've told you."

"And you admit that you called Idar Vetlesen the day he was found dead, but you regard that conversation as a private matter, too, I take it?"

Becker cast around as if thinking there ought to be an ashtray somewhere. "Listen, I haven't done anything illegal, but I didn't want to answer any more questions without my lawyer being present. And he's not coming until later today."

"Last night we offered you a lawyer who would have been able to come at once."

"I want to have a decent lawyer, not one of those . . . local government employees. Isn't it time you told me why you think I've done something to this wife of Lossius's?"

Harry was taken aback by the phraseology: "This wife of Lossius's."

"If she's missing, you should arrest Erik Lossius," Becker went on. "Isn't it always the husband who does it?"

"Yes, it is," Harry said. "But he has an alibi; he was working at the time she disappeared. The reason you're sitting here is that we think you're the Snowman."

Becker's jaw half dropped and he blinked as he had done in the living room on Hoffsveien the night before. Harry pointed to the spiraling cigarette smoke from between his fingers. "You'll have to inhale a bit so we don't set off the alarm."

"The Snowman?" Becker blurted. "That was Vetlesen, wasn't it?"

"No," Harry said. "We know it wasn't."

Becker blinked twice before bursting into laughter so dry and bitter that it sounded like coughing. "So that's why you haven't leaked anything to the press.

They can't find out that you've screwed up. And in the meantime you're desperate to find the right man. Or a potential right man."

"Correct," Harry said, sucking on his own cigarette. "And at the moment that's you."

"'At the moment'? I thought your role was to persuade me that you knew everything, so I might as well confess right away."

"But I don't know everything," Harry said.

Becker scrunched up one eye. "Is this a trick?"

Harry shrugged. "It's just a gut instinct. I need you to convince me that you're innocent. The short interview reinforced the impression that you're a man with a lot to hide."

"I had nothing to hide. I mean, I **have** nothing to hide. And I just don't see why I should tell you anything if I've done nothing wrong."

"Listen to me carefully, Becker. I don't think you're the Snowman or that you killed Camilla Lossius. And I think you're a rational, thinking person. The kind who can appreciate that it will damage you less if you reveal private matters to me here and now rather than read in tomorrow's papers that Professor Filip Becker has been arrested on suspicion of being Norway's most notorious killer. Because you know that even if you were cleared and released the day after tomorrow, your name would be forever connected with these headlines. And your son's."

Harry watched Becker's Adam's apple rise and fall in his unshaven neck. Watched his brain drawing the logical conclusions. The simple conclusions. And then it came, in an anguished tone that Harry initially thought was due to the unaccustomed cigarette.

"Birte, my wife, was a whore."

"Eh?" Harry tried to conceal his astonishment.

Becker dropped his cigarette on the floor, leaned forward and pulled a black notebook from his back pocket. "I found this the day after she disappeared. It was in her desk drawer, wasn't even hidden. At first sight it looked quite innocent. Commonplace memoranda to herself and telephone numbers. It was just that when I checked the numbers with directory assistance, they didn't exist. They were codes. But my wife wasn't much good at writing in code, I'm afraid. It took me less than a day to crack them all."

Erik Lossius owned and ran Rydd & Flytt, a moving company that had found a niche in an otherwise less than lucrative market by dint of standardized prices, aggressive marketing, cheap foreign labor and contracts that demanded cash payment as soon as the vehicles were loaded up but before they left for their destination. He had never lost any money on a customer, because, among other things, the small print stated that any complaints regarding damage or theft had to be made within two days, which in practice meant that 90 percent of the fairly numerous complaints came too late and could therefore be dismissed. As far as the final 10 percent were concerned, Erik Lossius had devised routines to make himself inaccessible or to slow the usual procedures, which became so draining that even those who had lost plasma TVs or had had pianos wrecked during the move gave up in the end.

Erik Lossius had started in the industry at a young age with the former owner of Rydd & Flytt. The owner was a friend of Erik's father, and his father had got him a job there.

"The boy's too restless to go to school and too smart to be a crook," the father had said. "Can you take him?"

As a salesman working on commission Erik soon distinguished himself with his charm, efficiency and brutality. He had inherited his mother's brown eyes and his father's thick curly hair and had an athletic build; women in particular decided not to collect quotes from other moving companies and signed on the spot. And he was intelligent and nifty with figures and ploys on the rare occasions the company was asked to bid for bigger jobs. The price was set low and the loss or damage excess set high. After five years the firm enjoyed a substantial profit and Erik had become the owner's right hand in most areas of the business. However, during a relatively easy job just before Christmas—moving a table up to Erik's new office next to the boss's on the first floor—the owner had suffered a heart attack and dropped dead. In the days that followed, Erik comforted the owner's wife as well as he was able—and he was well able—and a week after the funeral they agreed on an almost symbolic transfer sum that reflected what Erik had emphasized was "a little business in a less than lucrative market with high risks and nonexistent profit margins." But, he asserted, the most important thing for him was that someone would carry on her husband's life's work. A tear glistened in his brown eyes as he said that, and she laid a trembling hand on his and said that he personally should visit her to keep her informed. With that Lossius became the owner of Rydd & Flytt and the first thing he did was to throw all the letters of complaint into the garbage, rewrite the contracts and send circulars to all the households in Oslo's wealthy West End, where residents moved most frequently and were most price-sensitive.

By the time Erik Lossius was thirty, he had enough money to buy two BMWs, a summer residence to the north of Cannes and a five-thousand-square-foot detached house somewhere in Tveita, where the highrise flats he had grown up in didn't block the sun. In short, he could afford Camilla Sandén.

Camilla came from bankrupt clothing nobility in the West End, from Blommenholm, an area that was as alien to the workingman's son as the French wine he now had stacked a yard high in his cellar in Tveita. But when he entered the Sandéns' great house to give them a quote and saw all the things that had to be moved, he discovered what he still didn't have and therefore had to have: class, style, former splendor and a natural superiority that politeness and smiles only served to reinforce. And all this was personified in the daughter, Camilla, who sat on the balcony looking across Oslo Fjord through a pair of large sunglasses, which, for all Erik knew, could have been

bought at the local gas station, but which on her became Gucci, Dolce & Gabbana or whatever the other
brands were called.

Now he knew what all the other brands were
called.

He moved all their things, minus a couple of paintings that had to be sold, to a smaller house with a less
fashionable address and never received a loss report on
the one thing he had pinched off the load. Not even
when Camilla Lossius was standing outside the Tveita
church as a bride, with the high-rises as silent witnesses, did her parents show with so much as a moue
that they disapproved of their daughter's choice. Perhaps because they saw that Erik and Camilla complemented each other in a way; he lacked refinement and
she lacked money.

Erik treated Camilla like a princess, and she let
him. He gave her what she wanted, left her in peace
in the bedroom department whenever she wished
and demanded no more than that she should pretty
herself up when they went out or invited "couples
they were friendly with"—that is, friends from his
childhood—to supper. She wondered from time to
time whether he really loved her, and she slowly
began to develop a deep affection for the ambitious,
energetic Oslo East boy.

For his part, Erik was extremely happy. He had
known from the start that Camilla was not the hot-
blooded type; in fact, that was one of the things that,
in his eyes, placed her in a higher sphere than the girls
he was used to. He had his physical needs covered by

close customer contact anyway. Erik had come to the conclusion that there had to be something in the nature of moving that made people sentimental, distressed and open to new experiences. At any rate, he screwed single women, separated women, cohabiting and married women, on dining tables, on staircase landings, on plastic-wrapped mattresses and freshly washed parquet floors amid taped-up cardboard boxes and echoing bare walls while wondering what he would buy Camilla next.

The genius of the arrangement was that naturally he would never see these women again. They would move out and disappear. And they did. Apart from one.

Birte Olsen was dark-haired and sweet and had a **Penthouse** body. She was younger than he was, and her high-pitched voice and the language it produced made her seem even younger. She was two months into a pregnancy, moving into town from his part of Tveita to Hoffsveien with the child's father-to-be, a West End man she was going to marry. This was a move Erik Lossius could identify with. And—he realized after taking her on a plain spindle-back chair in the middle of the stripped room—sex he could not do without.

In a nutshell, Erik Lossius had met his match.

Yes, indeed, because he thought of her as a man, one who did not pretend she wanted anything different from what he wanted: to fuck the other person's brains out. And in a way they did just that. At any rate they began to meet in bare apartments, being moved out of or into, at least once a month, and always there was a distinct risk of being found out. They were quick and efficient and their rituals were fixed and without variation. Nevertheless, Erik Lossius looked forward to these assignations like a child to Christmas—that is, with unfeigned, uncomplicated joy that was increased only by the certainty that everything would be the same, that their expectations would be fulfilled. They lived parallel lives, had parallel realities, and that seemed to suit him as much as it suited her. And so they continued to meet, interrupted only by the birth—which, fortunately, was accomplished with a Cesarean section—some fairly long holidays and an innocent STD whose source he neither was able to nor attempted to trace. And now ten years had passed, and in front of Erik Lossius, sitting on a cardboard box in a half-emptied apartment in Torshov, a tall man with buzzed hair and a lawn-mower voice was asking if he had known Birte Becker.

Erik Lossius gulped.

The man had introduced himself as Harry Hole, an inspector from the Crime Squad, but he looked more like one of his moving men than an inspector of anything. The police officers Erik had spoken to after he had reported Camilla's disappearance were from the Missing Persons Unit. However, when this one had shown his ID, Erik's first thought had been that he had news of Camilla. And—since the officer in front of him hadn't called but tracked him down here—he feared it was bad news. Accordingly, he had sent his moving crew out and asked the inspector to take a seat while he found a cigarette and tried to prepare himself for what was to come.

"Well?" said the inspector.

"Birte Becker?" Erik Lossius repeated, trying to light his cigarette and think fast. He didn't manage either. Christ, he couldn't even think slowly.

"I appreciate that you have to compose yourself," the inspector said, taking out his own pack of cigarettes. "Take your time."

Erik watched the inspector light up a Camel and leaned over when he held the lighter out to Erik.

"Thanks," Erik mumbled, sucking so hard that the tobacco crackled. The smoke filled his lungs, and it was as if the nicotine were being injected into his bloodstream, clearing all the obstructions. He had always thought this would happen sooner or later, that the police would somehow discover a link between him and Birte and come asking questions. But at that time he had worried only about how he would keep it hidden from Camilla. Now everything was different. From right now, in fact. Because up until this moment he hadn't realized that the police might think there was a connection between the two disappearances.

"Birte's husband, Filip Becker, found a notebook in which Birte had entered a kind of easy, decipherable code," the policeman said. "There were telephone numbers, dates and tiny messages. Leaving little doubt that Birte had regular contact with other men."

"Men?" Erik let slip.

"If it's any consolation, Becker thought you were the one she met most often. At a huge variety of addresses, I'm led to believe," Harry added.

Erik, adrift in a boat watching a tidal wave growing on the horizon, didn't answer.

"So Becker found your address, took his son's toy gun along with him—a very authentic-looking imitation of a Glock 21—and went to Tveita to wait for you to come home. He wanted to see the fear in your eyes, he said. Threaten you to make you tell whatever you knew so that he could pass your name on to us. He followed the car into the garage, but it turned out your wife was driving."

"And he . . . he . . ."

"Told her everything, yes."

Erik rose from the cardboard box and walked over to the window. The apartment had a view of Torshov Park and an Oslo bathed in wan morning sun. He didn't like the old apartment buildings with views. They meant stairs. The better the view, the more stairs there were and the more exclusive the apartments, which meant heavier, more expensive goods, higher payouts for damage and more days with his men out sick. But that was the way it was when you exposed yourself to the risks of maintaining fixed low rates; you always won the competition for the worst jobs. Over time there is a price to pay with all risks. Erik took a deep breath and heard the policeman scuffing his feet on the wood floor. And he knew. This detective would not be worn down by any delaying tactics. This was one damage report he would not be throwing in the garbage. Birte Olsen, now Becker, was going to be the first customer he would suffer a loss on.

"Then he told me he'd been having an affair with Birte Becker for ten years," Harry said. "And that when they met and had sex for the first time she'd been pregnant with her husband."

"You're pregnant with a girl or a boy," Rakel corrected, patting down the pillow so that she could see him better. "Or by your husband."

"Mm," Harry said, levering himself up on his arm, stretching across her and grabbing the cigarette pack on the bedside table. "Not more than eighty percent of the time."

"What?"

"They said on the radio that somewhere between fifteen and twenty percent of all children in Scandinavia have a different father from the one they think." He shook a cigarette out of the pack and held it up against the afternoon light seeping in under the blind. "Share one?"

Rakel nodded without speaking. She didn't smoke, but this was something they had always done after making love: shared this one cigarette. The first time Rakel had asked to taste his cigarette, she had said it was because she wanted to feel the same as he did, to be as poisoned and stimulated as he was, to get as close to him as she could. And he had thought of all the girl junkies he had met who had had their first fix for the same idiotic reason, and refused. But she had persuaded him and eventually it had become a ritual. After they had made love slowly, lingering over it, the cigarette was like an extension of their lovemaking. At other times it was like smoking a peace pipe after a fight.

"But he had an alibi for the whole evening Birte disappeared," Harry said. "A boys' night in Tveita that started at six and lasted all night. At least ten witnesses, admittedly wasted for the most part, but no one had been allowed to go home before six in the morning."

"Why keep it a secret that Vetlesen wasn't the Snowman?"

"As long as the real Snowman thinks we think we've got the killer he'll lie low, hopefully, and won't commit any more murders. And he won't be so wary if he thinks the hunt has been called off. In the meantime we can quietly work our way closer at our leisure . . ."

"Do I hear irony there?"

"Maybe," Harry said, passing her the cigarette.

"You don't quite believe that, then?"

"I think our superiors have many reasons for concealing the fact that Vetlesen wasn't our man. The chief superintendent and Hagen held the press conference at the time when they were congratulating themselves on solving the case . . ."

Rakel sighed. "And yet still I do occasionally miss the Police HQ."

"Mm."

Rakel studied the cigarette. "Have you ever been unfaithful, Harry?"

"Define unfaithful."

"Having sex with someone other than your partner."

"Yes."

"While you were with me, I mean."

"You know I can't be absolutely certain."

"OK, sober, then."

"No, never."

"So what does that make you think of me? Being here now?"

"Is this a trick question?"

"I mean it seriously, Harry."

"I know. I just don't know if I feel like answering it."

"Then you can't have any more of the cigarette."

"Mm. All right. I think you believe you want me, but you wish you wanted him."

The words hung over them as if imprinted in the darkness.

"You're so damn . . . detached," Rakel erupted, handing Harry the cigarette and crossing her arms.

"Perhaps we shouldn't talk about it?" Harry suggested.

"But I have to talk about it! Don't you see? Otherwise I'll go out of my mind. My God, I'm already out of my mind, being here, now . . ." She pulled the duvet up to her chin.

Harry turned and slid over to her. Already before he had touched her she had closed her eyes and tipped back her head, and from between her parted lips he could hear her breathing accelerate. And he thought: How does she do it? From shame to sexual abandon in a flash? How can she be so . . . detached?

"Do you think . . . ," he said, seeing her open her eyes and stare at the ceiling in surprise and frustration at the caresses that hadn't materialized, "a bad conscience makes us wanton? That we're unfaithful not in spite of the shame but because of it?"

She blinked a couple of times.

"There's something in that," she said at length. "But it's not everything. Not this time."

"This time?"

"Yes."

"I asked you once and at that time you said—"

"I was lying," she said. "I've been unfaithful before."

"Mm."

They lay in silence listening to the distant drone of the afternoon rush hour on Pilestredet. She had come to him straight from work; he knew Rakel and Oleg's routines, and knew she would have to go soon.

"Do you know what I hate about you?" she said finally, giving his ear a tweak. "You're so goddamned proud and stubborn you can't even ask if it was to you."

"Well," Harry said, taking the half-smoked cigarette and admiring her naked body as she jumped out of bed, "why would I want to know?"

"For the same reason Birte's husband did. To reveal the lie. To have the truth out in the open."

"Do you think the truth will make Filip Becker any less unhappy?"

She pulled her sweater over her head, a tight-fitting black one in coarse wool that lay straight over her soft skin. It occurred to Harry that if he was jealous of anything, it was the sweater.

"Do you know what, Herr Hole? For someone whose job it is to uncover unpleasant truths, you certainly enjoy living a lie."

"OK," Harry said, stubbing the cigarette in the ashtray. "Out with it, then."

"It was in Moscow while I was with Fjodor. There was a Norwegian attaché at the embassy I had trained with. We fell head over heels in love."

"And?"

"He was also in a relationship. As we were about to finish with our respective partners, she got in first and told him she was pregnant. And since by and large I have good taste as far as men go"—pulling on her boots, she screwed up her top lip—"I had of course chosen someone who would not desert his responsibilities. He applied for a transfer back to Oslo, and we never saw each other again. And Fjodor and I got married."

"And right afterward you became pregnant?"

"Yes." She buttoned up her coat and looked down at him. "Now and then I've wondered whether it was to get over him. And whether Oleg was a product not of love but of lovesickness. Do you think he was?"

"I've no idea," Harry said. "I just know he's one great product."

She smiled down at him in gratitude and stooped to give him a kiss on the forehead. "We'll never see each other again, Hole."

"Of course not," he said, sitting up in bed and staring at the bare wall until he heard the heavy door to the street close behind her with a dull thud. Then he walked into the kitchen, turned on the tap and took down a glass from the top cupboard. While waiting for the water to run cold his gaze fell on the calendar with the picture of Oleg and Rakel in the sky-blue dress and then onto the floor. There were two wet boot prints on the linoleum. They must have been Rakel's.

He donned his coat and boots, was about to leave, then turned, fetched his Smith & Wesson service revolver from the top of the wardrobe and stuffed it in his coat pocket.

The lovemaking was still in his body like a quiver of well-being, a mild intoxication. He had reached the street door when a sound, a click, made him spin around and peer into the yard, where the darkness was denser than in the street. He was intending to go on his way, and would have, had it not been for the prints. The boot prints on the linoleum. So he went into the yard. The yellow lights from the windows above him bounced off the remnants of snow that still lay where the sun could not quite reach. It stood by the entrance to the cellar storerooms. A crooked figure with its head at an angle, pebbles for eyes and a gravel grin laughing at him. Silent laughter reverberated between the brick walls and blended into a hysterical shriek he recognized as his own as he grabbed the snow shovel beside the cellar steps and swung it in violent fury. The sharp metal edge of the shovel struck below the head, lifting it off the body and sending the wet snow flying against the wall. The next hefty swipe sliced the snowman's torso into two and the third scattered the remains across the black pavement in the middle of the yard. Harry stood there gasping for breath when he heard another click behind him. Like the sound of a revolver being cocked. In one smooth movement he swirled around, dropped the shovel and drew the black revolver.

Muhammad and Salma stood by the wooden fence, underneath the old birch, mutely staring at their neighbor with big, frightened children's eyes. In their hands they were holding dry branches. The branches looked as if they might have been elegant arms for a snowman, had Salma not snapped hers in two, out of sheer terror.

"Our . . . s-snowman," Muhammad stammered.

Harry returned the revolver to his coat pocket and closed his eyes. Cursing himself, he swallowed and instructed his brain to let go of the gun stock. Then he opened his eyes again. Tears were welling under Salma's brown irises.

"I'm sorry," he said softly. "I'll help you make another one."

"I want to go home," Salma whispered in a thick voice.

Muhammad took his little sister by the hand and accompanied her home, giving Harry a wide berth.

Harry felt the revolver grip against his hand. The click. He had thought it was the sound of the hammer being raised. But he was wrong, of course; this phase of the firing procedure is noiseless. What you hear is the sound of the hammer being cocked, the sound of the shot that has not been fired, the sound of being alive. He took out his service revolver again. Pointed it at the ground and pressed the trigger. The hammer still didn't move. Only when he had forced the trigger a third of the way back and he was thinking that the gun could fire at any moment did the hammer begin to rise. He let go of the trigger. The hammer fell back into position with a metallic click. And again he heard the sound. And realized that anyone who pressed the trigger so far back that the hammer rose intended to shoot.

Harry looked up at the windows of his apartment on the second floor. They were dark, and a thought struck him: He had no idea what went on behind them when he wasn't there.

Erik Lossius listlessly stared out the window in his office and mused about how little he had known of what went on behind Birte's brown eyes. About how it felt worse that she had been with other men than that she had disappeared and was perhaps dead. And wishing he had lost Camilla to a murderer than in this way. But mostly Erik Lossius was thinking that he must have loved Camilla. And still did. He had called her parents, but they hadn't heard from her, either. Perhaps she was living with one of those Oslo West girlfriends he knew about only from hearsay.

He gazed at the afternoon gloom slowly descending on Groruddalen as it became thicker and erased the detail. There was nothing more to do today, but he didn't want to go home to the much too large and empty house. Not yet. There was a case of assorted spirits in the cupboard behind him, the so-called slush fund from various liquor cabinets in transit. But no mixers. He poured gin into his coffee cup and managed a little sip before the phone on the desk rang. He recognized the French international code on the display. The number wasn't on the complaints list, so he took it.

He knew it was his wife from her breathing, even before she had spoken a word.

"Where are you?" he asked.

"Where do you think?" Her voice sounded a long way away.

"And where are you calling from?"

"From Casper."

That was the café two miles from their country house.

"Camilla, the police are looking for you."

"Are they?"

She sounded as if she were dozing on a sunbed. Bored, just going through the motions of being interested, with that polite but distant nonchalance he had fallen for all those years ago on the balcony in Blommenholm.

"I . . . ," he began. But stopped. What could he really say?

"I thought it was right to call you before our lawyer did," she said.

"**Our** lawyer?"

"My family's," she said. "One of the best at this kind of thing, I'm afraid. He'll go for a straightforward split down the middle as far as possessions and money are concerned. We'll ask for the house, and we'll get it, even though I'll make no secret of the fact that I intend to sell it."

Goes without saying, he thought.

"I'll be home in five days. By then I assume you'll have moved out."

"That's short notice," he said.

"You can do it. I've heard no one works faster or cheaper than Rydd and Flytt."

She pronounced the latter with such distaste that he shrank. The way he had shrunk ever since the conversation with Inspector Hole. He was a blanket that had been washed on too high a temperature; he had become too small for her, become unusable. And with the same certainty that he knew now, at this moment, that he loved her more than ever before, he knew that he had lost her irrevocably, that there would be no reconciliation. And when she had hung up he saw her squinting into the sunset on the French Riviera through a pair of sunglasses she had bought for twenty euros but on her they looked like three thousand kroners' worth of Gucci or Dolce & Gabbana or . . . he had forgotten what the other brands were called.

Harry had driven to the top of the Holmenkollen Ridge on the west side of town. He had parked his car at the sports center, in the large, deserted parking lot, and walked up Holmenkollen. There he had stood on the viewing promontory beside the ski jump, where he and a couple of out-of-season tourists were peering across at the grandstands grinning emptily on both sides of the landing slope, the pond at the bottom, which was drained in the winter, and the town stretching out to the fjord. A view gives perspective. They had no concrete evidence. The Snowman had been so close, it had felt as if all they had to do was reach out and arrest him. But then he had slipped from their grasp again, like a wily professional boxer. The inspector felt old, heavy and clumsy. One of the tourists was looking at him. The weight of his service revolver pulled his coat down on the right-hand side. And the bodies, where the hell were the bodies? Even buried corpses turned up again. Was he using acid?

Harry sensed the onset of resignation. No, he damn well didn't! At the FBI course they had examined cases where it had taken more than ten years to catch the killer. As a rule, it had been one tiny, random detail, it seemed, that had solved the case. However, what actually cracked it was the fact that they had never given up; they had gone all fifteen rounds, and if the opponent was still standing they screamed for a return fight.

The afternoon darkness stole upward from the town beneath, and the lights around him were slowly being switched on.

They had to start looking where there was light. It was a banal but important procedural rule. Begin wherever you have a clue. On this occasion it meant beginning with the least likely person you could imagine and the worst, the craziest idea he had ever had.

Harry sighed, took out his mobile phone and searched back through the list of calls. There weren't that many, so it was still there, the very short conversation at the Hotel Leon. He pressed OK.

Bosse researcher Oda Paulsen replied at once with the happy, animated voice of someone who views all incoming calls as an exciting new opportunity. And this time, in a sense, she was right.

21

DAY 18

The Waiting Room

It was the heebie-jeebies room. Perhaps that was why some people called it the "waiting room," as if you were at the dentist's. Or the "antechamber," as if the heavy door between the two Studio 1 sofas led to something important or even holy. But on the floor plan for the government-owned NRK's buildings in the Marienlyst district of Oslo, it was simply, and boringly, termed Lounge, Studio 1. Nevertheless, it was the most exciting room Oda Paulsen knew.

Most of the guests taking part in the evening's edition of **Bosse** had arrived. As usual, it was the guests who were least known and who would be appearing for the shortest time who had got there first. Now they were sitting on one of the sofas, made up, their cheeks flushed with tension as they chatted and sipped tea or red wine, their eyes inevitably seeking the monitor that gave a full view of the studio on the other side of the door. There, the audience had been admitted and the TV floor manager was instructing them on how to clap, laugh and cheer. The screen also showed the host's chair and four guests' chairs, empty, waiting for people, content and entertainment.

Oda loved these intense, nervous minutes before they went live. Every Friday, for forty minutes, this was as close to the center of the world as it was possible to get in Norway. Between 20 and 25 percent of the country's population saw the program, an insanely high viewing percentage for a talk show. Those working here were not only **where** it happened, they **were** what happened. This was celebrity's magnetic North Pole, which attracted everything and everyone. And because celebrity is an addictive drug and there is only one compass point from the North Pole—south, downward—everyone clung to his or her job. A freelancer like Oda had to deliver in order to be on the team next season, and that was why she was so happy, on her own behalf, to have received the call late yesterday afternoon, just before the editorial meeting. Bosse Eggen himself had smiled at her and said this was a scoop. Her scoop.

The evening's theme was to be adult games. It was a typical **Bosse** theme, suitably serious without being too weighty. Something about which all the guests could express a semiqualified opinion. Among the guests was a woman psychologist who had written a thesis on the topic, but the main guest was Arve Støp, who would be celebrating **Liberal**'s twenty-fifth anniversary the following day. Støp hadn't objected to the angle of the playful adult, the playboy, when Oda had had a preparatory meeting with him in his apartment. He had just laughed when she had drawn a parallel between him and an aging Hugh Hefner wearing a bathrobe and smoking a pipe at an eternal bachelors' party in his mansion. She had felt his eyes on her, inspecting, curious, right up to the moment she had asked him whether he regretted not having a child, an heir to the kingdom.

"Have **you** got any children?" he had asked.

And when she had replied in the negative, he had, to her astonishment, suddenly seemed to lose interest in both her and their conversation. She had therefore quickly finished up by giving him the usual information: arrival and makeup times, the request that he not wear striped clothing, the fact that themes and guests could change at short notice since this was a topical show, and so on.

And now here was Arve Støp in Lounge, Studio 1, straight from makeup, with his intense blue eyes and thick gray hair, which was groomed, but just long enough for the tips to bob up and down in suitably rebellious style. He was wearing a plain gray suit, which everyone knew cost an arm and a leg, though no one could say how he or she knew that. A tanned hand was already out to greet the psychologist, who was sitting on a sofa with peanuts and a glass of red wine.

"I didn't know psychologists could be so beautiful," he said to the woman. "Hope people can listen to what you say as well."

Oda watched the psychologist hesitate before beaming. And even though the woman clearly knew that Støp's compliment was a joke, Oda saw from the sparkle in her eyes that it had hit home.

"Hi, everyone—thank you all for coming!" This was Bosse Eggen sweeping into the room. He started with the guests on the left, shook hands, looked them in the eye, declared how happy he was to have them on board, told them that they could interrupt with questions for the other guests or make comments; it would enliven the conversation.

Gubbe, the producer, signaled that Støp and Bosse should withdraw into a side room to have a chat about the structure of the main interview and the introduction to the show. Oda checked her watch. Eight and a half minutes until they were live. She was just beginning to be concerned and wondered whether to phone reception to find out if he was waiting there: the real main guest. The scoop. But as she raised her eyes, there he was in front of her with one of the assistants, and Oda felt her heart skip a beat. He wasn't exactly good-looking, perhaps he was even ugly, but she was not ashamed to confess that she felt a certain attraction. And this had something to do with the fact that he was the guest all TV channels in Scandinavia wanted to get their hands on right now. For he was the man who had caught the Snowman, the biggest crime story in Norway for many years.

"I said I would be late," Harry Hole got in before she could utter a word.

She sniffed his breath. The last time he had been on the show he had been visibly drunk and had annoyed a whole nation. Or at least between 20 and 25 percent of it.

"We're just happy you're here," she chirped. "You'll be on second. Then you sit in for the rest of the show; the others will take their turns."

"Fine," he said.

"Take him to makeup," Oda said to the assistant. "Use Guri."

Guri wasn't just efficient, she knew how to make a worn face presentable for a TV audience with some simple, and some less simple, tricks.

They went off and Oda took a deep breath. She loved, loved the last edgy minutes when everything seemed to be chaos but still fell into place.

Bosse and Støp returned from the side room. She gave Bosse the thumbs-up. She heard the audience clapping as the studio door slid shut. On the monitor she saw Bosse taking his seat and knew that the floor manager had started the countdown. Then the signature tune began, and they were on air.

Oda realized something was amiss. The show had run like clockwork so far. Arve Støp had been brilliant and Bosse was reveling in it. Støp had said he was perceived as elitist because he was elitist. And that he wouldn't be remembered unless he suffered a real failure or two.

"Good stories are never about a string of successes but about spectacular defeats," Støp had said. "Even though Roald Amundsen won the race to the South

Pole, it's Robert Scott the world outside Norway remembers. None of Napoleon's victories is remembered like the defeat at Waterloo. Serbia's national
pride is based on the battle against the Turks at
Kosovo Polje in 1389, a battle the Serbs lost resound-
ingly. And look at Jesus! The symbol of the man who
is claimed to have triumphed over death ought to be
a man standing outside the tomb with his hands in
the air. Instead, throughout time Christians have preferred the spectacular defeat: when he was hanging
on the cross and close to giving up. Because it's always the story of the defeat that moves us most."

"And you're thinking of doing a Jesus?"

"No," Støp had answered, looking down and smiling as the audience laughed. "I'm a coward. I'm going
for forgettable success."

Støp had shown an unexpectedly likable, indeed
even humble, side of himself, instead of his notorious
arrogance. Bosse asked him whether he, as a single
man of many years' standing, didn't long for a
woman at his side. And when Støp answered yes,
Oda knew there would be an avalanche of marriage
proposals heading his way. The audience responded
with a long round of warm applause. Then Bosse dra-
matically announced: "Ever on the hunt, the lone
wolf of the Oslo Police, Inspector Harry Hole," and
Oda thought she caught an expression of astonishment as the camera rested on Støp for a second.

Bosse had evidently enjoyed the response he had
received to the question about a regular woman,
because he tried to maintain the thread by asking

Harry—since he knew he was also single—if he didn't long for a woman. Harry smirked and shook his head. But Bosse wouldn't let it drop and asked if there was perhaps someone special he was waiting for.

"No," Harry answered, short and sweet.

Usually this kind of rejection spurred Bosse to press further, but he knew he shouldn't spoil the party. The Snowman. So he asked Harry if he could tell them about the case all Norway was talking about, the nation's first real serial killer. Harry wriggled in his chair as if it were too small for his long body, while summarizing the chain of events in short, sculpted sentences. In recent years there had been some missing-persons cases with obvious similarities. All the missing women had been in relationships and had children, and there had never been a trace of the bodies.

Bosse assumed the grave expression that informed all and sundry that this was a flippancy-free zone.

"This year Birte Becker disappeared from her home in Hoff, here in Oslo, under similar circumstances," Harry said. "And soon afterward Silvia Ottersen was found dead in Sollihøgda outside Oslo. That was the first time we had found a body. Or at least part of it."

"Yes, because you found her head, didn't you?" Bosse interjected. Warily informative for those not in the know, and blood and tabloid for those who were. He was so professional that Oda immediately swelled with satisfaction.

"And then we found the body of a missing police

officer outside Bergen." Harry plowed on. "He'd been missing for twelve years."

"Iron Rafto," Bosse said.

"Gert Rafto," Harry amended. "A few days ago we found the body of Idar Vetlesen in Bygdøy. Those are the only bodies we have."

"What would you say has been the worst aspect of this case?" Oda could hear the impatience in Bosse's voice, probably because Harry had neither taken the "head" bait nor portrayed the murders in the gory detail Bosse would have hoped for.

"So many years passing before we realized that there was a connection among the disappearances."

Another dull answer. The floor manager signaled to Bosse that he had to start thinking about a link to the next topic.

Bosse pressed his fingertips together. "And now the case is solved and you're a star again, Harry. How does it feel? Do you get fan mail?" The disarming boyish smile. They were out of the flippancy-free zone.

The inspector nodded slowly and moistened his lips with concentration, as if how he phrased the answer was crucial. "Well, I got one letter earlier this autumn, but I'm sure Støp can say more about that."

Close-up of Støp as he looked at Harry with mild curiosity. Two long, silent TV seconds followed. Oda chewed her lower lip. What did Harry mean? Then Bosse swept in and tidied up.

"Yes, Støp does get a lot of fan mail, of course. And groupies. What about you, Hole? Have you got groupies, too? Do the police have their own groupies?"

The audience laughed cautiously.

Harry Hole shook his head.

"Come on," Bosse said. "A female recruit must sometimes come and ask for some extra lessons on body searches."

The studio was really laughing now. With gusto. Bosse grinned with pleasure.

Harry Hole didn't even crack a smile; he just looked resigned and cast a glance toward the exit. For one short, frantic moment Oda had visions of him getting up and leaving. Instead he turned to Støp in the chair beside him.

"What do you do, Støp? When a woman comes to you after a lecture in Trondheim, saying she has only one breast, but she would like to have sex with you. Do you invite her for a bit of extracurricular in your hotel room?"

The audience went deadly quiet, and even Bosse looked perplexed.

Only Arve Støp seemed to think the question was amusing. "No, I don't think I would do that. Not because sex wouldn't be fun with only one breast, but because the hotel beds in Trondheim are so narrow."

The audience laughed, though without conviction, mostly from relief that the exchange had not been more embarrassing. The psychologist was introduced.

They talked about playful adults, and Oda noticed that Bosse was navigating the conversation away from Harry Hole. He must have decided that the unpredictable policeman was not in good form today. And therefore Arve Støp, who definitely was in good form, had even more airtime.

"How do you play, Støp?" Bosse asked with an innocent expression underlining the noninnocent subtext. Oda rejoiced—she had written that question.

But before Støp could answer, Harry Hole leaned forward and asked him in loud, clear tones, "Do you make snowmen?"

And that was when Oda knew that something was amiss. Hole's peremptory, angry tone, the aggressive body language; Støp, who raised an eyebrow in surprise as his face seemed to shrink and tense up. Bosse paused. Oda didn't know what was going on, but counted four seconds, an eternity on live TV. Then she realized that Bosse knew what he was doing. For even though Bosse saw it as his duty to create a good atmosphere on the panel, he of course knew that the most important thing, his highest duty, was to entertain. And there is no better entertainment than people who are angry, cry, break down or in some other way display their feelings in front of a large audience on the air. Accordingly, he simply let go of the reins and just looked at Støp.

"Of course I make snowmen," Støp said after the four seconds were up. "I make them on the roof terrace beside my swimming pool. I make each one look like a member of the royal family. That way—when spring comes—I can look forward to the unseasonable elements melting and disappearing."

For the first time that evening Støp earned neither laughter nor applause. Oda thought Støp should have known that fundamentally antiroyalist comments never did.

Undaunted, Bosse broke the silence by introducing the pop star, who was to talk about her recent onstage breakdown and then conclude the show by singing the single that would be released on Monday.

"What the hell was that?" asked Gubbe, the producer, who had taken up a position directly behind Oda.

"Perhaps he isn't sober after all," Oda said.

"He's a fucking goddamn policeman!"

At that moment Oda remembered he was hers. Her scoop. "But, Jesus, can he deliver the goods."

The producer didn't answer.

The pop star talked about psychological problems, explaining that they were inherited, and Oda looked at her watch. Forty seconds. This was too serious for a Friday night. Forty-three. Bosse interrupted after forty-six.

"What about you, Arve?" Bosse was usually on first-name terms with the main guest by the end of the broadcast. "Ever experienced madness or a serious hereditary illness?"

Støp smiled. "No, Bosse, I haven't. Unless you count a craving for total freedom as an illness. In fact, it's a family weakness."

Bosse had come to round-up time; now he just had to sign off with the other guests before introducing the song. Final few words from the psychologist about the ludic in life. And then:

"And as the Snowman's no longer with us, I suppose you'll have time to play for a couple of days, Harry?"

"No," Harry said. He had slumped so far down into his chair that his long legs almost reached over to the pop star. "The Snowman hasn't been caught."

Bosse frowned, smiled and waited for him to go on, waited for the punch line. Oda hoped to God it was better than his opening line promised.

"I never said Idar Vetlesen was the Snowman," Harry said. "On the contrary. Everything points to the Snowman still being at large."

Bosse gave a little chuckle. It was the laugh he used to smooth over a guest's hapless attempt to be funny.

"I hope for the sake of my wife's beauty sleep that you're joking now," Bosse said mischievously.

"No," Harry said. "I'm not."

Oda looked at her watch and knew the floor manager was standing behind the camera now, shifting nervously as she ran a finger across her throat to show Bosse that they were running over and he would have to begin the song if they were to manage the first verse before the credits started rolling. But Bosse was the best. He knew that this was more important than all the singles in the world. Thus he ignored the raised baton and leaned forward in his chair to show those who might have been in any doubt about what this was. The scoop. The sensational announcement.

Here on his, on their, program. The quaver in his voice was almost genuine.

"Are you telling us here and now that the police have been lying, Hole? That the Snowman is out there and can take more lives?"

"No," Harry said. "We haven't been lying. New details have come to light."

Bosse swiveled around in his chair, and Oda thought she could hear the technical director shouting for camera one, and then Bosse's face was there, the eyes staring straight at them.

"And I would guess we'll hear more about those details on the news tonight. **Bosse** is back next Friday. Thank you for watching."

Oda closed her eyes as the band began to play the single.

"Jesus," she heard the producer wheeze behind her. And then, "Jesus fucking Christ." Oda just felt like howling. Howling with pleasure. Here, she thought. Here at the North Pole. We aren't **where** it happens. We **are** what happens.

22

Match

Gunnar Hagen was standing inside the door at Schrøder's, scanning the room. He had set out from home exactly thirty-two minutes and three telephone conversations after the credits had rolled on **Bosse**. He hadn't found Harry in his apartment, at Kunstnernes Hus or in his office. Bjørn Holm had tipped him off that he might try Harry's local, Schrøder's. The contrast between the young, beautiful and almost-famous clientele at Kunstnernes Hus and Schrøder's somewhat dissipated beer drinkers was striking. At the back, in the corner, by the window, alone at a table, sat Harry. With a large glass.

Hagen made his way to the table.

"I've been trying to call you, Harry. Have you switched off your mobile?"

The inspector looked up, bleary-eyed. "There's been so much hassle. Loads of fucking reporters suddenly after me."

"At NRK they said the **Bosse** crew and guests usually went to Kunstnernes Hus after the show."

"The press was standing outside waiting for me. So I cleared out. What do you want, boss?"

Hagen plumped down onto a chair and watched Harry raise the glass to his lips and the golden-brown liquid slip down into his mouth.

"I've been talking to the chief super," Hagen said. "This is serious, Harry. Leaking that the Snowman is still at large is a direct breach of his orders."

"That's right," Harry said, taking another swig.

"Right? Is that all you've got to say? But in the name of all that's sacred, Harry, why?"

"The public has a right to know," Harry said. "Our democracy is built on openness, boss."

Hagen banged his fist on the table and received a few encouraging looks from neighboring tables and an admonitory glance from the waitress passing them with an armful of sixteen-ounce glasses.

"Don't mess with me, Harry. We've gone public and said the case was solved. You've put the force in a very bad light—are you aware of that?"

"My job is to catch villains," Harry said. "Not to appear in a good light."

"It's two sides of the same thing, Harry! Our working conditions are dependent on how the public perceives us. The press is crucial!"

Harry shook his head. "The press has never hindered or helped me in solving a single case. The press is crucial only for individuals who want to be in the

limelight. The people you report to are just concerned with having concrete results that will give
them good press. Or prevent bad press. I want to
catch the Snowman, period."

"You're a danger to your colleagues," Hagen said.
"Do you know that?"

Harry seemed to be considering the statement,
then nodded slowly, drained his glass and signaled to
the waitress that he wanted another.

"I've just been talking to the chief superintendent
and the chief constable," Hagen said, bracing himself. "I was told to find you instantly to muzzle you.
From this very second. Understood?"

"Fine, boss."

Hagen blinked in amazement, but Harry's face
revealed nothing.

"As of this moment, I'm going to be very hands-
on, all the time," said the POB. "I want regular reports. I know that you won't do that, so I've spoken
to Katrine Bratt and given her the job. Any objections?"

"None at all, boss."

Hagen was thinking that Harry must be drunker
than he looked.

"Bratt told me you'd asked her to go and see this
assistant of Idar Vetlesen's to check Arve Støp's files.
Without going through the public prosecutor. What
the hell are you two doing? Do you know what we
would have been exposed to if Støp had found out?"

Harry's head shot up like a watchful animal's.
"What do you mean by if he **had** found out?"

"Fortunately there was no file on Støp. This secretary of Vetlesen's said they never kept one."

"Oh? And why not?"

"How should I know, Harry? I'm just relieved. We don't want any more trouble now. Arve Støp, my God! Be that as it may, from now on Bratt will dog your every step so that she can report to me."

"Mm," Harry said, nodding to the waitress, who set down another glass for him. "Hasn't she already been informed?"

"What do you mean?"

"When she started you told her I would be her—" Harry stopped in his tracks.

"Her what?" Hagen snapped.

Harry shook his head.

"What's up? Something wrong?"

"Nothing," Harry said, sinking half the glass in one big gulp and placing a hundred-krone note on the table. "Have a nice evening, boss."

Hagen sat at the table until Harry had left the restaurant. Only then did he notice that there were no carbon dioxide bubbles rising in the half-empty glass. He stole a few sidelong glances and put the glass cautiously to his lips. It tasted tart. Nonalcoholic cider.

Harry walked home through silent streets. The windows of the old, low buildings shone like cats' eyes in the night. He felt an urge to speak to Tresko to find out how things were going, but decided to let him have the night, as agreed. He rounded the corner to Sofies Gate. Deserted. He was heading for his building when he caught a movement and a tiny glint. Light reflecting off a pair of glasses. Someone standing by the line of vehicles parked along the pavement, apparently struggling to open a car door. Harry knew which cars generally parked at this end of the street. And this car, a blue Volvo C70, was not one of them.

It was too dark for Harry to see the face clearly, but he could tell from the way the person was holding his head that he was keeping an eye out for Harry. A journalist? Harry passed the car. In the side mirror of another, he glimpsed a shadow flit between the cars and approach from behind. Without any undue haste Harry slipped his hand inside his coat. Heard the footsteps coming. And his anger. He counted to three, then turned around. The person behind him froze on the pavement.

"Is it me you're after?" Harry growled, stepping forward with gun raised. He collared the man, dragged him sideways, knocking him off balance, and launched himself at him, sending both of them over the hood of a car. Harry pressed his forearm against the man's throat and thrust the barrel against one lens of his glasses.

"Is it me you want?" Harry hissed.

The man's answer was drowned out by the car alarm going off. The sound filled the whole street. The man tried to free himself, but Harry had him in a tight grip and he gave up. His head hit the car's hood with a soft thud and the light from the street-lamp fell on the man's face. Then Harry let go. The man doubled up, coughing.

"Come on," Harry shouted over the relentless howl, grabbed the man under the arm and dragged him over the road. He unlocked the front door and shoved the man inside.

"What the hell are you doing here?" Harry said. "And how do you know where I live?"

"I've been trying to call the number you gave me all evening. In the end I called directory assistance and got your address."

Harry observed the man. That is, he observed the ghost of the man. Even in the remand cell there had been more of Professor Filip Becker left.

"I had to switch off my mobile," Harry said.

Harry walked ahead of Becker up to his apartment, opened the door, kicked off his boots, went into the kitchen and switched on the kettle.

"I saw you on **Bosse** this evening," Becker said. He had come into the kitchen, still wearing his coat and shoes. His face was ashen, lifeless. "You were brave. So I thought I should be brave, too. I owe you that."

"Owe me?"

"You believed me when no one else did. You saved me from public humiliation."

"Mm." Harry pulled up a chair for the professor, but he shook his head.

"I'll be off in a minute, but I'll tell you something no one else must know. I'm not sure if it has anything to do with the case, but it's about Jonas."

"Uh-huh?"

"I took some blood from him the night I visited Camilla Lossius."

Harry remembered the bandage on Jonas's forearm.

"Plus a mouth swab. Sent it to the paternity section of the Institute of Forensic Medicine for DNA testing."

"Huh? I thought you had to go through a lawyer."

"You did before. Now anyone can buy the test. Twenty-eight hundred kroner per person. Bit more if you want a quick answer. Which I did. And the answer came today. Jonas"—Becker paused and took a deep breath—"Jonas is not my son."

Harry nodded slowly.

Becker rocked back on his heels as if about to start a race.

"I asked them to match him against all the data in the data bank. They found a perfect match."

"Perfect? So Jonas was in the bank?"

"Yes."

Harry pondered. It was starting to dawn on him what Becker meant.

"In other words, someone had already sent in a sample for Jonas's DNA profile," Becker said. "I was informed that the previous sample was seven years old."

"And they confirmed it was Jonas?"

"No, it was anonymous. But they had the name of the client who had ordered the test."

"And that was?"

"A medical center that no longer exists." Harry knew the answer before Becker said it. "Marienlyst Clinic."

"Idar Vetlesen," Harry said, angling his head as though studying a picture to see if it was hanging straight.

"Right," Becker said, clapping his hands together and smiling weakly. "That was it. All I wanted to say was that . . . I have no son."

"I'm sorry."

"Actually, I've had that feeling for a long time."

"Mm. Why the hurry to come here and tell me?"

"I don't know," Becker said.

Harry waited.

"I . . . I had to do something tonight. Like this. If I hadn't I don't know what I would've done. I . . ." The professor hesitated before going on. "I'm alone now. My life no longer has much meaning. If the gun had been real . . ."

"Don't," Harry said. "Don't even think it. The thought will only become more tempting the more you dwell on it. And you're forgetting one thing. Even if your life has no meaning for you, it has meaning for others. For Jonas, for example."

"Jonas?" Becker said with a bitter laugh. "The evidence of Birte's infidelity? 'Don't dwell on it'—is that what they teach you at the police academy?"

"No," Harry said.

They eyed each other.

"Whatever," Becker said. "Now you know."

"Thank you," Harry said.

After Becker had left, Harry was still sitting there, trying to decide if the picture was hanging straight, not noticing that the water had boiled, the kettle had switched itself off and the little red eye under the ON button was slowly dying.

23

Mosaic

The thick, fluffy clouds concealed the dawn as Harry entered the corridor on the sixth floor of the high-rise in Frogner. Tresko had left his door ajar, and when Harry entered, Tresko had his feet up on the coffee table, his ass on the sofa and the remote control in his left hand. The images that flicked backward across the screen dissolved into a digital mosaic.

"Don't want a beer, then?" Tresko repeated, lifting his half-empty bottle. "It's Saturday."

Harry thought he could discern bacterial gases in the air. Both ashtrays were full of cigarette butts.

"No thanks," Harry said, taking a seat. "Well?"

"Well, I've just had one night on it," Tresko said, stopping the DVD player. "It usually takes me a couple of days."

"This person's not a pro poker player," Harry said.

"Don't be too sure," Tresko said and took a swig from the bottle. "He bluffs a lot better than most card players. This is the place where you ask him the question you reckoned he would answer with a lie, isn't it?"

Tresko pressed PLAY and Harry saw himself in the TV studio. He was wearing a pinstriped suit jacket, a Swedish brand, slightly too tight. A black T-shirt that was a present from Rakel. Diesel jeans and Doc Martens boots. He was sitting in a strangely uncomfortable position, as if the chair had nails in the back. The question sounded hollow through the TV speakers. "Do you invite her for a bit of extracurricular in your hotel room?"

"No, I don't think I would do that," Støp answered, but froze as Tresko pressed the PAUSE button.

"And there you know he's lying?" Tresko asked.

"Yup," Harry answered. "He fucked a friend of Rakel's. Women don't usually like to boast. What can you see?"

"If I ran this on the computer I could enlarge the eyes, but I don't need to. You can see the pupils have dilated." Tresko pointed an index finger with a chewed nail at the screen. "That's the classic sign of stress. And look at the nostrils. Can you see they've flared a tiny bit? We do that when we're stressed and the brain needs more oxygen. But that doesn't mean he's lying; many people get stressed even when they're telling the truth. Or don't get stressed when lying. You can see, for example, that his hands are still."

Harry noticed that Tresko's voice had undergone a transformation; the jarring sounds were gone and it had become soft, almost pleasant. Harry looked at the screen, at Støp's hands, which lay still in his lap, the left hand over the right.

"I'm afraid there are no immutable signs," Tresko continued. "All poker players are different, so what you have to do is spot the differences. Find out what's different in a person from when he's lying and when he's telling the truth. It's like triangulation—you need two fixed points."

"A lie and an honest answer. Sounds easy."

"**Sounds** is right. If we assume he's telling the truth when he's talking about the founding of his magazine and why he hates politicians, we have the second point." Tresko rewound the clip and played it. "Look."

Harry looked. But obviously not where he was supposed to. He shook his head.

"The hands," Tresko said. "Look at his hands."

Harry looked at Støp's tanned hands resting on the chair arms.

"They're not moving," Harry said.

"Yes, but he isn't hiding them," Tresko said. "A classic sign of bad poker players with poor cards is all the effort they make to hide them behind their hands. And when they bluff they like to place an apparently pensive hand over their mouth to hide their expression. We call them hiders. Others exaggerate the bluff by sitting upright in the chair or leaning back to appear bigger than they are. They're the bluffers. Støp is a hider."

Harry leaned forward. "Did you . . ."

"Yes, I did," Tresko said. "And it runs all the way through. He takes his hands off the arms of the chair and hides the right one—I would guess he's right-handed—when he's lying."

"What does he do when I ask him if he makes snowmen?" Harry made no attempt to conceal his eagerness.

"He's lying," Tresko said.

"Which bit? The bit about making snowmen or making them on his roof terrace?"

Tresko uttered a short grunt, which Harry realized was meant to be laughter.

"This is not an exact science," Tresko said. "As I said, he's not a bad card player. In the first seconds after you asked the question he has his hands on the arms as if he's considering telling the truth. At the same time his nostrils flare as though he's becoming stressed. But then he changes his mind, hides his right hand and comes up with a lie."

"Exactly," Harry said. "And that means he has something to hide, doesn't it?"

Tresko pressed his lips together to show this was a tricky one. "It may also mean he's choosing to tell a lie he knows will be found out. To hide the fact that he could easily have told the truth."

"What do you mean?"

"When pro card players have good hands, some-times, instead of trying to bump up the pot, they bid high first time and give tiny signals that they're bluff-ing. Just enough to hook inexperienced players into believing they've spotted a bluff and to get them to join the bidding. That's basically what this looks like. A bluffed bluff."

Harry nodded slowly. "You mean he wants me to believe that he has something to hide?"

Tresko looked at the empty beer bottle, looked at the fridge, made a halfhearted attempt to lever his huge body off the sofa and sighed.

"As I said, this is not an exact science," he said. "Would you mind . . ."

Harry got up and went over to the fridge. Cursing inside. When he had rung Oda at **Bosse** he had known they would accept his offer to appear. And he had also known that he would be able to ask Støp direct questions unhindered; that was the format of the show. And that the camera would film the person answering, with close-ups or so-called medium shots—that is, the upper half of the body. All of this had been perfect for Tresko's analysis. And yet they had failed. This had been the last ray of hope, the last place to look where there was some light. The rest was darkness. And perhaps ten years of fumbling and praying for luck, serendipity, a slipup.

Harry stared at the neatly stacked rows of Ringnes beer bottles in the fridge, a comical contrast to the chaos reigning in the apartment. He hesitated. Then he took two bottles. They were so cold that they burned his palms. The fridge door was swinging shut.

"The only place where I can say with certainty that Støp is lying," Tresko said from the sofa, "is when he answers that there isn't any madness or hereditary illness in his family."

Harry managed to catch the fridge door with his foot. The light from the crack was reflected in the black, curtainless window.

"Repeat," he said.

Tresko repeated.

Twenty-five seconds later Harry was halfway down the stairs and Tresko halfway down the beer Harry had chucked him.

"Yes, there was one more thing, Harry," Tresko mumbled to himself. "Bosse asked you if there was someone special you were cooling your heels waiting for, and you answered no." He belched. "Don't take up poker, Harry."

Harry called from his car.

There was an answer before he could introduce himself. "Hi, Harry."

The thought that Mathias Lund-Helgesen either recognized his number or had his number listed made Harry shudder. He could hear Rakel's and Oleg's voices in the background. Weekend. Family.

"I have a question about the Marienlyst Clinic. Are there still any patient records from there?"

"I doubt it," Mathias said. "I think the rules say that sort of thing has to be destroyed if no one takes over the practice. But if it's important I'll check, of course."

"Thank you."

Harry drove past the Vinderen tram stop. A glimpse of a ghost fluttered by. A car chase, a collision, a dead colleague, a rumor that it had been Harry driving and he should have been forced to take a Breathalyzer test. That was a long time ago. Water under the bridge. Scars under the skin. Versicolor on the soul.

Mathias called back after fifteen minutes.

"I spoke to Gregersen—he was the boss of Marienlyst. Everything was deleted or destroyed, I'm afraid. But I think some people, including Idar, took their patient information with them."

"And you?"

"I knew I wouldn't go into private practice, so I didn't take anything."

"Can you remember any of the names of Idar's patients, do you think?"

"Some, maybe. Not many. It's a while ago, Harry."

"I know. Thank you anyway."

Harry hung up and followed the sign to Rikshospitalet. The collection of buildings ahead of him covered the low ridge.

Gerda Nelvik was a gentle, buxom lady in her mid-forties and the only person in the paternity department at the Institute of Forensic Medicine at Rikshospitalet this Saturday. She met Harry in reception and took him through. There was not much to suggest that this was where society's worst criminals were hunted. The bright rooms, decorated in homey fashion, were, rather, testimony to the fact that the staff consisted almost entirely of women.

Harry had been here before and knew the routines for DNA testing. On a weekday, behind the laboratory windows, he would have seen women dressed in white lab coats, caps and disposable gloves, bent over solutions and machines, busy with mysterious processes they called hair-prep, blood-prep and amplification, which would ultimately become a short report with a conclusion in the form of numerical values for fifteen different markers.

They passed a room fitted with shelves, on which lay brown padded envelopes marked with names of police stations around the country. Harry knew they contained articles of clothing, strands of hair, furniture covers, blood and other organic material that had been submitted for analysis. All to extract the numeric code that represented selected points on the mysterious garland that is DNA and identified its owner with a certainty of 99.999 . . . percent.

Gerda Nelvik's office was no larger than it needed to be to accommodate shelves of ring files and a desk with a computer, piles of paper and a large photograph of two smiling boys, each with a snowboard. "Your sons?" Harry asked, sitting down.

"I think so." She smiled.

"What?"

"Insiders' joke. You said something about someone submitting tests?"

"Yes. I'm anxious to know about all the DNA tests submitted by a particular institution. Starting from twelve years back. And who they were for."

"I see. Which institution?"

"The Marienlyst Clinic."

"The Marienlyst Clinic? Are you sure?"

"Why?"

She shrugged. "In paternity cases it's usually a court or a lawyer who submits the request. Or individuals directly."

"These aren't paternity suits but tests to establish possible family links because of the danger of hereditary medical conditions."

"Aha," Gerda said. "Then we've got them in the database."

"Is that something you can check on the spot?"

"Depends on whether you've got the time to wait"—Gerda looked at her watch—"for thirty seconds."

Harry nodded.

Gerda tapped away on the keyboard as she dictated to herself. "M-a-r-i-e-n-l-y-s-t C-l-i-n-i-c."

She leaned back in her chair and let the machine work.

"Terrible autumn weather we're having, isn't it," she said.

"Yes, it is," Harry answered, miles away, listening to the whirring of the hard drive as if that could reveal whether the answer was the one he was hoping for.

"The darkness can get to you," she said. "Hope snow is on its way soon. Then it'll brighten up, at least."

"Mm," Harry said.

The whirring stopped.

"There you go," she said, looking at the screen.

Harry took a deep breath.

"Yes, the Marienlyst Clinic has been a client here. But not for quite some time."

Harry tried to think back. When was it Idar Vetlesen had finished there?

Gerda furrowed her brow. "But before that there were a lot, I can see."

She hesitated. Harry waited for her to say it. And then she said: "An unusually high number for a medical center, I would say."

Harry had a feeling. This was the path they should take; this one led out of the labyrinth. Or to be more precise: into the labyrinth. Into the heart of darkness.

"Have you got any names or personal details of those tested?"

Gerda shook her head. "Usually we do, but in this case the center wanted them to be anonymous, evidently."

Fuck! Harry closed his eyes and deliberated.

"But you still have the test results? About whether individuals are fathers or not, I mean."

"Yes, indeed," Gerda said.

"And what do they tell you?"

"I can't give you an answer off the cuff. I'll have to go into each one, and that'll take more time."

"OK. But have you saved the DNA profiles of those you have tested?"

"Yes."

"And the test is as comprehensive as in criminal cases?"

"More comprehensive. To establish paternity beyond a doubt we require more markers, since half of
the genes are from the mother."

"So what you're saying is that I can collect a swab
from a specific person, send it here and have you
check it for any similarities with those you've checked
from the Marienlyst Clinic?"

"The answer is yes," Gerda said with an intonation
that suggested she would appreciate an explanation.

"Good," Harry said. "My colleagues will send you
some swabs from a number of people who are husbands and children of women who have disappeared
in recent years. To check whether they've been submitted before. I'll make sure this is authorized to receive top priority."

A light seemed to be switched on in Gerda's eyes.
"Now I know where I've seen you! On **Bosse.** Is this
about . . ."

Even though there were only two of them there,
she lowered her voice as if the name they had given
the monster was a curse, an obscenity, an incantation
that was not to be uttered aloud.

Harry called Katrine and asked her to meet him at the
Java café in St. Hanshaugen. He parked in front of an
old apartment building with a sign on the entrance
threatening that parked cars would be towed away, although the entrance was barely the width of a lawn
mower. Ullevålsveien was full of people hurrying up
and down doing their essential Saturday shopping.

An ice-cold northerly wind swept down from St. Hanshaugen, blowing black hats off a bowed funeral procession on its way to the Vår Frelsers cemetery.

Harry paid for a double espresso and a cortado, both in paper cups, and sat on one of the chairs on the pavement. On the pond on the other side of the road a lone white swan drifted around quietly with a neck formed like a question mark. Harry watched it and was reminded of the name of the fox trap. The wind blew goose pimples onto the surface of the water.

"Is the cortado still hot?"

Katrine was standing in front of him with outstretched hand.

Harry passed her the paper cup, and they walked to his car.

"Great that you could work on a Saturday morning," he said.

"Great that you could work on a Saturday morning," she said.

"I'm single," he said. "Saturday morning has no value for people like us. You, on the other hand, should have a life."

An elderly man stood glaring at their car as they arrived.

"I've ordered a tow truck," he said.

"Yes, I hear they're popular," Harry said, unlocking the door. "The only problem is finding somewhere to park them."

They got in and a wrinkled knuckle rapped on the glass. Harry rolled down the window.

"Truck's on its way," the old man said. "You've got to stay here and wait."

"Do I?" Harry said, holding up his ID.

The man ignored the card and glowered at his watch.

"Your space's too narrow to qualify as an entrance," Harry said. "I'm sending over a man from the traffic department to unscrew your illegal sign. I'm afraid there'll be a big fat fine, too."

"What?"

"We're police."

The old man snatched the ID card, looked suspiciously at Harry, at the card and back at Harry.

"That's fine this time. You can go," the man mumbled with a sour expression and gave back the card.

"It's not fine," Harry said. "I'm calling the traffic department now."

The old man stared at him with fury.

Harry twisted the key in the ignition, let the engine roar, then turned to the old man again. "And you are to stay here."

They could see his openmouthed expression in the rearview mirror as they drove off.

Katrine laughed. "You are **bad**! That was an old man."

Harry shot her a sidelong glance. Her facial expression was strange, as if it hurt her to laugh. Paradoxically, the episode at Fenris Bar had made her more relaxed with him. Perhaps that was a thing about attractive women: A rejection demanded their respect, made them trust you more.

Harry smiled. He wondered how she would have reacted if she had known that this morning he had woken with an erection and fragments of a dream in which he had fucked her while she was sitting on the sink with her legs wide apart in the Fenris Bar bathroom. Screwed her so hard the pipes creaked, water slopped in the toilet bowls and the neon tubes buzzed and flickered as he felt the freezing porcelain on his balls every time he thrust. The mirror behind her had vibrated so much his features had blurred as they banged hips, backs and thighs against taps, hand dryers and soap holders. Only when they had stopped did he see that it wasn't his but someone else's face in the mirror.

"What are you thinking about?" she asked.

"Reproduction," Harry said.

"Oh?"

Harry passed her a packet, which she opened. At the top was a piece of paper with the heading instructions for dna swabbing kit.

"Somehow this is all tied up with paternity," Harry said. "I just don't know how or why yet."

"And we're off to . . . ?" Katrine asked, lifting a small pack of Q-tips.

"Sollihøgda," Harry said. "To get a swab from the twins."

In the fields surrounding the farm the snow was in retreat. Wet and gray, it squatted on the countryside it still occupied.

Rolf Ottersen received them on the doorstep and offered them coffee. As they removed their outer clothing Harry told him what they wanted. Rolf Ottersen didn't ask why, just nodded.

The twins were in the living room knitting.

"What's it going to be?" Katrine asked.

"Scarf," the twins said in unison. "Auntie's teaching us."

They motioned to Ane Pedersen, who was sitting in the rocking chair knitting and smiling a "Nice to see you again" at Katrine.

"I just want a bit of spit and mucus from them," Katrine said brightly, raising a Q-tip. "Open wide."

The twins giggled and put down their knitting.

Harry followed Rolf Ottersen to the kitchen, where a large kettle had boiled and there was a smell of hot coffee.

"So you were wrong," Rolf said. "About the doctor."

"Maybe," Harry said. "Or maybe he has something to do with the case after all. Is it OK if I take a look at the barn again?"

Rolf Ottersen made a gesture inviting Harry to help himself.

"But Ane has tidied up in there," he said. "There's not a lot to see."

It was indeed tidy. Harry recalled the chicken blood lying on the floor, thick and dark, as Holm took samples, but now it had been scrubbed. The floorboards were pink where the blood had seeped into the wood. Harry stood by the chopping block and looked at the door. Tried to imagine Sylvia standing there and slaughtering chickens as the Snowman came in. Had she been surprised? She had killed two chickens. No, three. Why did he think it was two? Two plus one. Why plus one? He closed his eyes.

Two of the chickens had been lying on the chopping block, their blood pouring out onto the sawdust. That was how chickens should be slaughtered. But the third had been lying some distance away and had soiled the floorboards. Amateur. And the blood had clotted where the third chicken's throat had been cut. Just like on Sylvia's throat. He recalled how Holm had explained this. And knew the thought wasn't new; it had been lying there with all the other half-thought, half-chewed, half-dreamed ideas. The third chicken had been killed in the same way as Sylvia, with an electric cutting loop.

He went to the place where the floorboards had absorbed the blood and crouched down.

If the Snowman had killed the last chicken, why had he used the loop and not the hatchet? Simple. Because the hatchet had disappeared in the depths of the forest somewhere. So this must have happened after the murder. He had come all the way back here and slaughtered a chicken. But why? A kind of voodoo ritual? A sudden inspiration? Bullshit—this killing machine stuck to the plan, followed the pattern.

There was a reason.

Why?

"Why?" Katrine asked.

Harry hadn't heard her come in. She stood in the doorway of the barn, the light from the solitary bulb falling on her face, and she was holding up two plastic bags containing Q-tips. Harry shuddered to see her standing like that again, in a doorway with her hands pointing in his direction. Just like at Becker's. But there was something else, another realization, too.

"As I said," Harry mumbled, studying the pink residue, "I think this is about family relationships. About covering things up."

"Who?" she asked and moved toward him. The heels of her boots clicked on the wooden floor. "Who have you got in mind?"

She crouched down beside him. Her masculine perfume wafted past him, rising from her warm skin into the cold air.

"I haven't a clue."

"This is not systematic processing; this is an idea you've had. You've got a theory," she stated simply and ran her right index finger through the sawdust.

Harry held back. "It's not even a theory."

"Come on, out with it."

Harry took a deep breath. "Arve Støp."

"What about him?"

"According to Arve Støp, he went to Idar Vetlesen for medical help with his tennis elbow. But, according to Borghild, Vetlesen didn't have any records for Støp. I've been asking myself why that might be."

Katrine shrugged. "Perhaps it was more than an elbow. Perhaps Støp was afraid it might be documented that he was having cosmetic surgery."

"If Idar Vetlesen had agreed not to keep records for all the patients who were afraid of that, he wouldn't have had a single name in his files. So I thought it had to be something else, something that really couldn't bear close scrutiny."

"Like what?"

"Støp was lying on **Bosse.** He said there was no madness or hereditary illness in his family."

"And there is?"

"Let's assume there is, as a theory."

"The theory that's not even a theory?"

Harry nodded. "Idar Vetlesen was Norway's most secret expert on Fahr's Syndrome. Not even Borghild, his own assistant, knew about it. So how on earth did Sylvia Ottersen and Birte Becker find their way to him?"

"How?"

"Let's assume Vetlesen's specialty was not hereditary illness but discretion. After all, he said himself that's what his business was founded on. And that was why a patient and friend went to him and said he had Fahr's Syndrome, a diagnosis that he had been given somewhere else, by a real specialist. But this specialist did not have Vetlesen's expertise in discretion, and this was something that had to be kept secret. The patient insisted, perhaps paid extra for it. Because this person could really pay."

"Arve Støp?"

"Yes."

"But he's already been diagnosed by someone and that might leak out."

"This is not what Støp is primarily afraid of. He's afraid that it could come to light that he goes there with his offspring. Whom he wants checked to see if they have the inherited illness. And this has to be treated with the utmost confidentiality because no one knows they're his children. In fact there are some people who believe them to be their own. As indeed Filip Becker thought he was Jonas's father. And . . ." Harry nodded toward the farmhouse.

"Rolf Ottersen?" Katrine whispered, breathless. "The twins? Do you think"—she lifted the plastic bags—"that they have Arve Støp's genes?"

"Possibly."

Katrine looked at him. "The missing women . . . the other children . . ."

"If the DNA test shows that Støp is the father of Jonas and the twins, we'll do tests on the children of the other missing women on Monday."

"You mean . . . that Arve Støp has been bonking his way around Norway? Impregnating a variety of women and then killing them years after they've given birth?"

Harry rolled his shoulders.

"Why?" she asked.

"If I'm right, we're talking about madness, of course, and this is pure speculation. There's often a pretty clear logic behind madness. Have you heard about Berhaus seals?"

Katrine shook her head.

"The father of the species is cold and rational," Harry said. "After the female has given birth to their young and it has survived the first critical phase, the father tries to kill the mother. Because he knows she won't want to breed with him again. And he doesn't want other young seals to compete with his own off-spring."

Katrine seemed to be having trouble absorbing this.

"It's madness, yes," she said. "But I don't know what's more insane: thinking like a seal or thinking that someone's thinking like a seal."

"As I said"—Harry stood up with an audible creak of his knees—"it's not even a theory."

"You're lying," she said, peering up at him. "You're already certain that Arve Støp's the father."

Harry responded with a crooked smile.

"You're as crazy as I am," she said.

Harry subjected her to a searching gaze. "Let's get going. The institute is waiting for your Q-tips."

"On a Saturday?" Katrine ran her hand over the sawdust, smoothing over her doodles, and stood up. "Haven't they got a life?"

After delivering the plastic bags to the institute and receiving a promise that they would get back to him that evening or early the following morning, Harry drove Katrine home to Seilduksgata.

"No lights on in the windows," Harry said. "On your own?"

"Good-looking girl like me?" She smiled, grasping the door handle. "Never on my own."

"Mm. Why didn't you want me to tell your colleagues at the Bergen Police Station that you were there?"

"What?"

"Thought they would be amused to hear you were working on a big murder case in the capital."

She shrugged and opened the door. "Bergensians don't think of Oslo as a capital. Good night."

"Good night."

Harry drove to Sannergata.

He wasn't certain, but he thought he had seen Katrine stiffen. But what could you be certain of? Not even a click, which you took to be a gun being cocked but turned out to be a girl cracking a dry twig out of sheer fright. He couldn't pretend any longer, though, couldn't pretend he didn't know. Katrine had pointed her service revolver at Filip Becker's back that evening. And when Harry had stepped into her firing line he had heard the sound, the sound he had thought he heard when Salma cracked a twig in the yard. It was the lubricated click of a revolver hammer being released. Which meant that it had been raised, that Katrine had squeezed the trigger more than two-thirds of the way and that the gun could have gone off at any time. She had meant to shoot Becker.

No, he couldn't pretend. Because the light had fallen on her face in the doorway to the barn. And he had recognized her. And, as he had said to her, this was all about family relationships.

POB Knut Müller-Nilsen loved Julie Christie. So much that he had never dared to tell his wife the whole truth. However, since he suspected her of having an extramarital affair with Omar Sharif, he didn't feel too guilty as he sat beside her, devouring Julie Christie with his eyes. The only fly in the ointment was that his Julie at this moment was in a passionate embrace with said Sharif. And when the telephone on the living-room table rang and he answered, his wife pressed the PAUSE button, causing the frame of this wonderful yet unbearable moment of their favorite movie, **Doctor Zhivago**, to freeze in front of them.

"Well, good evening, Hole," said Müller-Nilsen after the inspector had introduced himself. "Yes, I imagine you've got enough to keep you busy for the time being."

"Have you got a minute?" asked the hoarse but soft voice at the other end.

Müller-Nilsen gazed at Julie's quivering red lips and raised misty eyes. "We'll take the time we need, Hole."

"You showed me a photo of Gert Rafto when I was in your office. There was something about it I recognized."

"Oh, yes?"

"And then you said something about his daughter. She had turned out very well, of course, you said. It was this understood 'of course.' As if this were information I already knew."

"Yes, but she did turn out well, didn't she?" said Müller-Nilsen.

"Depends on how you look at it," Harry said.

24

Toowoomba

There was an expectant buzz under the chandeliers in the Sonja Henie Ballroom at the Plaza Hotel. Arve Støp stood in the doorway where he had received the guests. His jaw was aching from all the smiling, and the glad-handing had given him back the sensation of tennis elbow. A young woman from the publicity firm who was responsible for logistics slid alongside him and told him that the guests were now seated around the table. Her neutral black suit and headset with its almost invisible microphone made him think of a female agent in **Mission Impossible.**

"We're going in," she said, adjusting his bow tie with a friendly, quasi-tender movement.

She wore a wedding ring. Her hips swayed in front of him toward the room. Had those hips given birth to a child? Her black trousers were tight against her well-exercised bottom, and Arve Støp visualized the same bottom, without trousers, in front of him on the bed in his Aker Brygge apartment. But she seemed too professional. It would be too much has-sle. Too much heavy persuasion. He met her eyes in the big mirror beside the door, knew he had been caught and beamed an apology. She laughed at the same time as a slightly unprofessional flush shot up into her cheeks. Mission impossible? Hardly. But not tonight.

Everyone at his table of eight rose as he entered. His dinner partner was his own assistant editor. A dull but necessary choice. She was married and had children and the ravaged face of a woman who worked twelve to fourteen hours every day. Poor kids. And poor him the day she found out that life con-sisted of more than **Liberal**. The table reacted with a **skål** for him as Støp's gaze swept across the room. The sequins, jewels and smiling eyes sparkled under the chandeliers. And the dresses. Strapless, shoulderless, backless, shameless.

Then the music erupted. The vast tones of "Also Sprach Zarathustra" boomed out of the loudspeak-ers. At the meeting with the publicists Arve Støp had pointed out that it wasn't exactly an original introduction—it was pompous and made him think of the creation of man. And was told that was the idea.

Onto the large stage, wreathed in smoke and light, stepped a TV celebrity who had demanded—and been given—a six-figure sum to be the master of cer-emonies.

"Ladies and gentlemen!" he shouted into a large cordless microphone that reminded Støp of a large, erect penis. "Welcome!" The celeb's famous lips were almost touching the black dick. "Welcome to what I promise you is going to be a very special evening!"

Arve Støp was already looking forward to it being over.

Harry stared at the photographs on the bookshelf in his office, the Dead Policemen's Society. He tried to think, but his mind was spinning, unable find a foothold, an entire image. He had felt the whole time that there was someone on the inside; someone had known what he would do at all times. But he hadn't expected it to be like this. It was so unimaginably easy. And at the same time so incomprehensibly complicated.

Knut Müller-Nilsen had told him that Katrine had been regarded as one of the most promising Crime Squad detectives at the Bergen HQ, a rising star. Never any problem. Yes, there was of course the incident that led to her application for a transfer to the Sexual Offenses Unit. A witness from a shelved case had called to complain that Katrine Bratt was still bothering him with new questions. She wouldn't stop, even though he had made it plain that he had already made a statement to the police. It came to light that Katrine had been independently investigating this case for months without notifying her superiors. As she had been doing it in her own free time, this would not normally have been a problem, but this particular case was not one they wanted her raking up. She had been made aware of this, and her reaction had been to point out several flaws in the original investigation, but she didn't gain a sympathetic ear, and in her frustration she had applied for a transfer.

"This case must have been an obsession for her," was the last Müller-Nilsen had said. "As far as I remember, that was the time her husband left her."

Harry got up, went into the corridor and over to Katrine's office door. It was, as office regulations stipulated, locked. He continued down the corridor to the photocopy room. On the lowest shelf beside the packs of paper he pulled out the guillotine, a large, heavy iron base with a mounted blade. It had never been used as far as he could recall, but now he carried it with both hands into the corridor and back to Katrine Bratt's door.

He raised the paper cutter over his head and took aim. Then he brought his arms down hard.

The guillotine hit the handle, knocking the lock into the frame, which split with a loud crack.

Harry just managed to shift his feet before the machine landed on the floor with a muffled groan. The door spat splinters of wood and swung open at the first kick. He picked up the guillotine and carried it inside.

Katrine Bratt's office was identical to the one he had shared with Jack Halvorsen in times gone by. Tidy, bare, no pictures or any other personal possessions. The desk had a simple lock at the top controlling all the drawers. After two doses of the guillotine, the top drawer and the lock were smashed. Harry rifled through, pushing papers to the side and rummaging through plastic folders, hole punches and other office equipment until he found a knife. He removed the sheath. The top edge was serrated. Definitely not a scout's knife. Harry pressed the blade into the pile of papers it was lying on and the knife sank without resistance into the wad.

In the drawer beneath there were two unopened boxes of bullets for her service revolver. The only personal belongings Harry found were two rings. One was studded with gems that glinted angrily in the light of the desk lamp. He had seen it before. Harry closed his eyes trying to visualize where. A large, gaudy ring. Las Vegas–style. Katrine would never have worn such a ring. And then he knew where he had seen it. He felt his pulse throbbing: hard, but steady. He had seen it in a bedroom. In Birte Becker's bedroom.

In the Sonja Henie Ballroom dinner was over and the tables were cleared away. Arve Støp leaned against the rear wall while staring toward the stage. The guests had huddled together next to it and were gazing in rapture at the band. It was a big sound. It was an expensive sound. It was the sound of megalomania. Arve Støp had had his doubts, but in the end the publicists had convinced him that investing in an experience was a way to buy his employees' loyalty, pride and enthusiasm for their workplace. And by buying a bit of international success he was underscoring the magazine's own success and building the **Liberal** brand, a product with which advertisers would want to be associated.

The vocalist held a finger against his earpiece as he attacked the highest note of their song, which had been an international hit in the eighties.

"No one hits a bum note as beautifully as Morten Harket," said a voice next to Støp.

He turned. And knew at once that he had seen her before, because he never forgot a beautiful woman. What he was beginning to forget more and more was who, where and when. She was slim and wearing a plain black dress with a slit that reminded him of someone. Of Birte. Birte had had a dress like that.

"It's scandalous," he said.

"It's a difficult note to hit," she said, without taking her eyes off the vocalist.

"It's scandalous I can't remember your name. I only know we've met before."

"We haven't met," she said. "You just gave me the once-over." She brushed her black hair off her face. She was attractive in a stern, classical way. Kate Moss–attractive. Birte had been Pamela Anderson–attractive.

"That, I think, can definitely be excused," he said, with a feeling that he was waking up, that his blood was beginning to surge through his body, bringing Champagne to parts of his brain that relaxed him rather than making him drowsy.

"Who are you?"

"I'm Katrine Bratt," she said.

"Oh, yes. Are you one of our advertisers, Katrine? A bank connection? A lessor? A freelance photographer?"

To every question Katrine shook her head with a smile.

"I'm a gate-crasher," she said. "One of your female journalists is a friend of mine. She told me who was playing after dinner, and said I could just put on a dress and slip in. Feel like throwing me out?"

She raised her Champagne glass to her lips. They weren't as full as he usually liked, but nevertheless deep red and moist. She was still looking at the stage, so he could study her profile at his leisure. The whole of her profile. The hollow back, the perfect arch of her breasts. No need for any silicone, maybe just a good bra. But could they have suckled a child?

"I'm considering the option," he said. "Any arguments you would like to put forward?"

"Will a threat do?"

"Perhaps."

"I saw the paparazzi outside waiting for your celebrity guests to emerge with the evening's catch. What if I told them about my journalist friend? That she was given to understand her prospects at **Liberal** were poor after she had rejected your advances?"

Arve Støp laughed aloud and from his heart. He saw that they had already been attracting inquisitive looks from other guests. Leaning toward her, he noticed that the aroma of her perfume was not unlike the cologne he used.

"First, I'm not frightened of a bad reputation, least of all among my colleagues in the gossip rags. Second, your friend is a useless journalist and third, she's lying. I've fucked her three times. And you can tell the paparazzi **that**. Are you married?"

"Yes," said the unknown woman, turning to the stage and shifting her weight so that the slit of her dress allowed a glimpse of a lacy garter. Arve Støp felt his mouth go dry and took a sip of Champagne. Watched the flock of tiptoeing women at the front of the stage. Breathed through his nose. He could smell pussy from where he was standing.

"Have you got any children, Katrine?"

"Do you want me to have children?"

"Yes."

"Why?"

"Because through creating life women have learned to subject themselves to nature, and that gives them a more profound insight into life than other women. And men."

"Bullshit."

"No, it makes you women less desperate to hunt for a potential father. You just want to enjoy the game."

"OK." She laughed. "Then I've got children. What games do you like to play?"

"Whoa," Støp said, looking at his watch. "We're moving too fast."

"What games do you like to play?"

"All of them."

"Great."

The singer closed his eyes, grabbed the microphone with both hands and attacked the song's crescendo.

"This is a boring party, and I'm going home." Støp put his empty glass on a tray whistling past. "I live in Aker Brygge. Same entrance as **Liberal**, top floor. Top bell."

She gave a thin smile. "I know where it is. How much of a head start do you want?"

"Give me twenty minutes. And a promise that you won't talk to anyone before you leave. Not even your girlfriend. Is that a deal, Katrine Bratt?"

He looked at her, hoping he had said the right name.

"Trust me," she said, and he noticed a strange gleam in her eyes, like that of a forest fire in the sky. "I'm just as keen as you that this stay between us." She raised her glass. "And, by the way, you fucked her four times, not three."

Støp enjoyed a last glance before making his way to the exit. Behind him the vocalist's falsetto was still quivering, almost inaudibly, under the chandeliers.

A door slammed and loud, enthusiastic voices reverberated down Seilduksgata. Four youths on their way from a party to one of the bars in Grünerløkka. They passed the car parked at the edge of the pavement without noticing the man inside. Then they rounded the corner, and the street was quiet again. Harry leaned toward the windshield and looked up at the windows of Katrine Bratt's apartment.

He could have called Hagen, could have sounded the alarm, taken Skarre along and a patrol car. But he might be wrong. And he had to be certain first; there was too much to lose, both for him and for her.

He got out of the car and went to the door and the unmarked second-floor bell. Waited. Rang once more. Then he went back to his car, fetched the crowbar from the trunk, returned to the door and rang the first-floor bell. A man answered with a sleepy **ja**, the TV droning in the background. Fifteen seconds later the man came down and opened up. Harry showed him his police ID.

"I didn't hear a domestic dispute," the man said. "Who called you?"

"I'll find my own way out," Harry said. "Thanks for your help."

The door on the second floor didn't have a nameplate, either. Harry knocked, rested his ear against the cold wood and listened. Then he inserted the tip of the crowbar between the door and the frame immediately above the lock. Since the blocks of apartment buildings in Grünerløkka had been built for workers in the factories along the Akerselva River with the cheapest possible materials, Harry's second forced entry in under an hour was easy.

He listened for a few seconds in the dark of the corridor before he switched on the light. Looked down at the shoe rack in front of him. Six pairs of shoes. None of them big enough to belong to a man.

He lifted one pair, the boots Katrine had worn earlier today. The soles were still wet.

He went into the living room. Switched on the flashlight instead of the ceiling light so that she wouldn't see from the street that she had a visitor.

The cone of light swept over the worn pine floor with large nails between the boards, a plain white sofa, low bookshelves and an exclusive Linn loudspeaker. There was an alcove in the wall, with a tidy, narrow bed, and a kitchenette with a stove and a fridge. The impression was austere, spartan and neat. Like his own place. The light had caught a face staring stiffly at him. And then another. And one more. Black wooden masks with carvings and painted patterns.

He looked at his watch. Eleven. He let the flashlight wander farther afield.

There were newspaper clippings pinned up above the only table in the room. They covered the wall from floor to ceiling. He went closer. His eyes skimmed them as he felt his pulse begin to tick like a Geiger counter.

These were murder cases.

Many murder cases, ten or twelve, some so old the newspaper had yellowed. But Harry could remember them all quite clearly. He remembered them because they had one thing in common: He had led the investigation.

On the table, beside a computer and a printer, lay a heap of folders. Case reports. He opened one of them. There weren't any reports of his cases, but Laila Aasen's murder on Ulriken Mountain was there. Another folder was of Onny Hetland's disappearance in Fjellsiden. A third was about a case of police violence in Bergen, about complaints against Gert Rafto. Harry flicked through. Found the same photograph of Rafto that he had seen in Müller-Nilsen's office. Looking at it now, he thought it was obvious.

Beside the printer was a pile of paper. Something was drawn on the top sheet. A quick, amateur penciled sketch, but the motif was clear enough. A snowman. The face was long, as if it had leaked, melted; the coal eyes had died and the carrot was long and thin and pointed downward. Harry leafed through the sheets. There were several drawings. All of snowmen, most just of the face. Masks, Harry thought. Death masks. One of the faces had a beak, small human arms at the side and bird feet at the bottom. Another had a pig's snout and a top hat.

Harry started to search the other end of the room. And told himself the same thing he had said to Katrine on the island of Finnøy: Empty your mind of expectations and look, don't search. He went through all the cupboards and drawers, rummaged through kitchen utensils and washing paraphernalia, clothes, exotic shampoos and bizarre creams in the bathroom, where the smell of her perfume hung heavily in the air. The floor of the shower was wet and on the sink there was a Q-tip stained with mascara. He came out again. He didn't know what he was after, just that it wasn't here. He straightened up and looked around.

Wrong.

It was here. He just hadn't found it yet.

He took the books off the shelves, opened the toilet cistern, checked whether there were any loose boards in the floor or the walls and turned the mattress in the alcove. Then he was finished. He had searched everywhere. Without any success, except for the most important premise of any search: What you **don't** find is just as important as what you do. And he knew now what he hadn't found. Harry looked at his watch. Then he began to tidy up.

It was only when he was putting the drawings in order that it occurred to him that he hadn't checked the printer. He pulled out the tray. The top sheet was yellowish and thicker than normal printer paper. He lifted it up. It had a particular aroma, as if it had been impregnated with a spice or burned. He turned on the desk lamp and held the sheet up to it as he hunted for the mark. And found it. Down in the bottom right-hand corner, a kind of watermark in between the fine paper fibers, visible if held against the lightbulb. The blood vessels in his throat seemed to widen; the blood was suddenly in a hurry, his brain screaming for more oxygen.

Harry switched on the computer. Checked his watch again and listened while it took an eternity for the operating system and programs to boot up. He went straight to the search function and typed in a single word. Clicked the mouse on SEARCH. An animated dog, in both senses, appeared, jumping up and down and barking soundlessly in an attempt to shorten the waiting time. Harry stared at the text flashing by as the documents were scanned. Shifted his gaze to the rubric where it said for the moment, **No items matched your search.** He examined the spelling of the search word. **Toowoomba.** He closed his eyes. Heard the deep purr of the machine, like an affectionate cat. Then it stopped. Harry opened his eyes. **One item matched your search.**

He placed the cursor over the Word icon. A yellow rectangular box popped up. **Date modified: September 9.** He felt his finger tremble as he double-clicked. The white background of the short text shone into the room. There was no doubt. The words were identical to those in the letter from the Snowman.

25

Deadline

Arve Støp was lying in a bed that had been sewn and weighed to customer specifications in the Misuku factory in Osaka and shipped already assembled to a tannery in Chennai, India, because the laws in the state of Tamil Nadu did not permit the direct exportation of this type of leather. It had taken six months from order to receipt of the goods, but it had been worth the wait. Like a geisha, it adapted perfectly to his body, supported him where necessary and allowed him to adjust it to every conceivable level or direction.

He watched the teak blades of the ceiling fan slowly rotate.

She was in the elevator on her way up to him. He had explained on the intercom that he was waiting for her in the bedroom, and had left the door ajar. He could feel the cool silk of his boxer shorts against his alcohol-warmed body. The music from a Café del Mar CD streamed out of the Bose audio system, with its small, compact speakers hidden in every room of the apartment.

He heard her heels clacking on the parquet floor of the living room. Slow but resolute footsteps. Just the sound made him go hard. If only she knew what was awaiting her . . .

His hand foraged under the bed; his fingers found what they were groping for.

And then she was in the doorway, silhouetted against the moonlight over the fjord, looking at him with a half-smile. She loosened the belt of her long black leather coat and let it fall. He gasped, but she was still wearing her dress beneath. She went over to the bed and passed him something rubbery. It was a mask. A pink animal mask.

"Put this on," she said in a neutral, businesslike voice.

"Well, well," he said. "A pig's face."

"Do as I say." Again this strange yellow gleam in her eyes.

"Mais oui, madame."

Arve Støp put it on. It covered his whole face and smelled like rubber gloves, and he could only just see her through the small slits for eyes.

"And I want you to—" he began and heard his own voice, encased and alien. That was as far as he got before he felt a stinging pain over his left eye.

"You shut your mouth!" she shouted.

Slowly it reached his consciousness that she had hit him. He knew he shouldn't—it would ruin her role play—but he could not help himself. It was too comical. A pig mask! A clammy, pink rubbery thing with pig ears, snout and overbite. He let out a guffaw. The next blow hit him in the stomach with shocking power, and he doubled up, groaned and fell back on the bed. He was unaware that he wasn't breathing until everything went black. Desperately he fought for air inside the tight-fitting mask as he felt her wrench his arms behind his back. Then, finally, oxygen reached his brain and the pain came at the same time. And the fury. Fucking cow, what did she think she was doing? He wriggled free and would have grabbed her, but couldn't move his hands; they were held tight behind his back. He jerked and felt something sharp cut into his wrists. Handcuffs? The perverted bitch.

She pushed him into a sitting position.

"Can you see what this is?" he heard her whisper.

But his mask had slipped sideways; he couldn't see anything.

"I don't need to," he said. "I can smell it's your cunt."

The blow hit him over the temple. It was like a CD skipping, and when he had the sound back he was still sitting upright in bed. He could feel something running down between his cheek and the inside of his mask.

"What the hell are you hitting me with?" he shouted. "I'm bleeding, you madwoman!"

"This."

Arve Støp felt something hard pressed against his nose and mouth.

"Smell," she said. "Isn't it good? It's steel and gun oil. Smith and Wesson. Smells like nothing else, doesn't it? The smell of powder and cordite is even better. If you ever get to smell it, that is."

Just a violent game, Arve Støp told himself. A role play. But there was something else, something in her voice, something about the whole situation. Something that put all that had happened in a new light. And for the first time in ages—so long ago he had to think back to his childhood, so long that initially he didn't recognize the feeling—Arve Støp noticed: he was frightened.

"Sure we shouldn't fire her up?" said Bjørn Holm, shivering and pulling the leather jacket around him more tightly. "When the Amazon came out she was well known for having a helluva heater."

Harry shook his head and looked at his watch. One-thirty. They had been sitting in Holm's car outside Katrine's apartment building for more than an hour. The night was blue-gray, the streets empty.

"She was actually California white," Holm continued. "Volvo color number forty-two. Previous owner sprayed it black. Qualifies as a veteran car and all that now. Mere three hundred and sixty-five kroner road tax a year. A krone a day . . ."

Bjørn Holm paused when he saw Harry's warning

look and instead turned up David Rawlings and Gillian Welch, which was the only new music he could tolerate. He had recorded it from a CD onto a cassette, not just so that it could play on the newly installed cassette player in the car, but because he belonged to that extremely small yet unbending faction of music lovers who opined that the CD had never managed to reproduce the cassette's uniquely warm sound quality.

Bjørn Holm knew he was talking too much because he was nervous. Harry hadn't told him any more than that Katrine had to be eliminated from some inquiries. And that Holm's daily grind for the next few weeks would be eased if he didn't know the details. And being the peaceful, laid-back, intelligent person he was, Holm didn't try to cause any trouble. That didn't mean he liked the situation, though. He checked his watch.

"She's gone back to some guy's place."

Harry reacted. "What makes you think that?"

"She's not married, after all. Wasn't that what you said? Single women are like us single guys nowadays."

"And by that you mean . . ."

"Four steps. Go out, observe the herd, select the weakest prey, attack."

"Mm, you need four steps?"

"The first three," said Bjørn Holm, adjusting the mirror and his red hair, "just cock-teasers in this town." Holm had considered hair oil, but concluded it was too radical. On the other hand, perhaps that was just what was needed. Go the whole hog.

"Fuck," Harry burst out. "Fuck, fuck, fuck."

"Eh?"

"Wet shower. Perfume. Mascara. You're right." The inspector had taken out his mobile, maniacally punched the numbers in and got an almost immediate answer.

"Gerda Nelvik? This is Harry Hole. Are you still doing the tests? . . . OK. Any preliminary results?"

Bjørn Holm watched as Harry mumbled two **mm**s and three **right**s.

"Thank you," Harry said. "And I was wondering if any other officers had called earlier this evening and asked you the same . . . What? . . . I see. Yes, just call me when the tests are finished."

Harry hung up. "You can start the engine now," he said.

Bjørn Holm twisted the key in the ignition. "What's the deal?"

"We're going to the Plaza Hotel. Katrine Bratt called the institute earlier this evening to ask about paternity."

"This evening?" Holm put his foot down and turned right, toward Schous Plass.

"They're running preliminary tests to establish paternity to ninety-five percent probability. Then they'll try to increase the certainty to ninety-nine point nine."

"And?"

"It's ninety-five percent certain that the father of the Ottersen twins and Jonas Becker is Arve Støp."

"Holy moly."

"And I think Katrine's followed your recommendations for a Saturday evening. And the prey is Arve Støp."

Harry called the Incident Room and asked for assistance as the old reconditioned engine roared through the night-still streets of Grünerløkka. And as they passed the Akerselva emergency room and skidded on the tram tracks on Storgata, the heater was indeed blowing red-hot air on them.

Odin Nakken, a newspaper reporter at **Verdens Gang,** stood freezing on the pavement outside the Plaza Hotel cursing the world, people in general and his job in particular. As far as he could judge, the last guests were leaving the **Liberal** celebration. And the last, as a rule, were the most interesting, the ones who could create the next day's headlines. But the deadline was approaching; in five minutes he would have to go. Go to the office in Akersgata a few hundred yards away and write. Write to the editor that he was a grown-up now, that he was fed up with standing outside a party like a teenager, with his nose pressed against the windowpane staring in and hoping someone would come out and tell him who had danced with whom, who had bought drinks for whom, who had been in a clinch with whom. Write that he was handing in his notice.

A couple of rumors had been floating about that had been too fantastic to be true, but naturally they couldn't print those. There was a limit, and there were unwritten rules. Rules to which, at least in his generation, journalists adhered. For what that was worth.

Odin Nakken took stock. There were only a couple of reporters and photographers still holding out. Or who had the same deadlines for celebrity gossip as his newspaper. A Volvo Amazon came hurtling toward them and pulled up to the curb with a squeal of brakes.

Out jumped a man from the passenger seat, and Odin Nakken immediately recognized him. He signaled to the photographer, and they ran after the police officer, who was sprinting for the door.

"Harry Hole," panted Nakken when he had caught up. "What are the police doing here?"

The red-eyed policeman turned to him. "Going to a party, Nakken. Where is it?"

"Sonja Henie Room on the first. But I reckon it's finished now."

"Mm. Seen anything of Arve Støp?"

"Støp went home early. What do you want with him?"

"Nothing. Was he alone?"

"To all outward appearances."

The inspector pulled up sharply and turned to him. "What do you mean?"

Odin Nakken angled his head. He had no idea what this was about, but he was in no doubt that there was something.

"A rumor was going around that he was negotiating with a pretty foxy lady. With fuck-me eyes. Nothing we can print, more's the pity."

"So?" growled the inspector.

"A woman answering the description left the party twenty minutes after Støp. She got into a taxi."

Hole was soon walking back the same way he had come. Odin hung onto his coattails.

"And you didn't follow her, Nakken?"

Odin Nakken ignored the sarcasm. It was water off a duck's back. Now.

"She wasn't a celebrity, Hole. A celeb screwing a non-celeb is non-news, if I can put it like that. Unless the lady decides to talk, of course. And this one's long gone."

"What did she look like?"

"Slim, dark. Good-looking."

"Clothes?"

"Long black leather coat."

"Thanks." Hole jumped into the Amazon.

"Hey," Nakken shouted. "What do I get in return?"

"A good night's sleep," Harry said. "The knowledge that you've helped to make our town a safer place."

Grimacing, Odin Nakken watched the old boat of a car embellished with rally stripes accelerate away with a throaty roar of laughter. It was time to get out of this. Time to hand in his notice. It was time to grow up.

"Deadline," the photographer said. "We'll have to go and write this shit up."

Odin Nakken heaved a sigh of resignation.

Arve Støp stared into the darkness of the mask wondering what she was doing. She had dragged him into the bathroom by the handcuffs, pressed what she claimed was a revolver against his ribs and ordered him into the bathtub. Where was she? He held his breath and heard his heart and a crackling electric hum. Was one of the neon tubes in the bathroom on its way out? The blood from his temple had reached the corner of his mouth; he could taste the sweet metallic tang with the tip of his tongue.

"Where were you the night Birte Becker disappeared?" Her voice came from over by the sink.

"Here in my apartment," Støp answered, trying to think. She had said she was from the police and then he remembered where he had seen her before: in the curling hall.

"Alone?"

"Yes."

"And the night Sylvia Ottersen was killed?"

"The same."

"Alone all evening, without talking to anyone?"

"Yes."

"So no alibi?"

"I'm telling you I was here."

"Good."

Good? thought Arve Støp. Why was it good that he didn't have an alibi? What was it she wanted? To force a confession out of him? And why did it sound as if the electric hum was getting louder as she came closer?"

"Lie down," she said.

He did as instructed and felt the cold bath enamel sting the skin of his back and thighs. His breath had condensed on the inside of the mask, made it wet, made it even more difficult to breathe. Then the voice was there again, close by now.

"How do you want to die?"

Die? She was out of her mind. Insane. Stark raving mad. Or was she? He told himself to keep a clear head; she was just trying to frighten him. Could Harry Hole be behind this? Could it be that he had underestimated the drunken asshole? But his whole body was shaking now, shaking so much that he could hear his TAG Heuer watch clink against the enamel, as if his body had accepted what his brain still had not. He rubbed the back of his head against the bottom of the tub, trying to straighten the pig mask so that he could see through the small holes. He was going to die.

That was why she had put him in the bathtub. So that there wouldn't be so much mess, so all the traces could be quickly removed. Bullshit! You're Arve Støp and she's with the police. They know nothing.

"OK," she said. "Lift up your head."

The mask. At last. He did as she said, felt her hands touch his forehead and at the back, but she didn't loosen the mask. Something thin and strong tightened around his neck. What the fuck? A noose!

"Don't . . . ," he began, but his voice died as the noose pressed against his windpipe. The handcuffs rattled and scraped against the bottom of the tub.

"You killed them all," she said, and the noose was tightened a notch. "You're the Snowman, Arve Støp."

There. She had said it out loud. The lack of blood to his brain was already making him dizzy. He shook his head frantically.

"Yes, you are," she said, and as she jerked the noose he felt as if his head were being severed. "You've just been appointed."

The darkness came all of a sudden. He raised a leg and let it fall again, the heel of his foot banging impotently against the bathtub. A hollow boom reverberated around.

"Do you know that rushing sensation, Støp? It's the brain not getting sufficient oxygen. Quite wonderful, isn't it? My ex-husband used to jerk himself off while I had him in a stranglehold."

He tried to scream, tried to force the little air that was left in his body past the iron grip of the noose, but it was impossible. Jesus, didn't she even want a confession? Then he felt it. A slight swishing sound in his brain, like the hiss of Champagne bubbles. Was that how it would happen? So easy. He didn't want it to be easy.

"I'm going to hang you in the living room," said the voice by his ear as a hand affectionately patted his head. "Facing the fjord. So that you have a view."

Then came a thin peeping sound, like the alarm on one of those heart monitors you see in films, he thought. When the curve flattens out and the heart no longer beats.

26

The Silence

Harry pressed Arve Støp's doorbell again.

A night owl was walking over the canal bridge and peering down at the black Amazon parked in the middle of the car-free square in Aker Brygge.

"Not gonna open up if he's got a dame there, I s'pose," Bjørn Holm said, looking up at the ten-foot-high glass door.

Harry pressed the other doorbells.

"Those are just offices," Holm said. "Støp lives alone at the top. I've read that."

Harry looked around.

"No," said Holm, who had guessed what he was thinking. "It won't work with the crowbar. And the steel glass is unbreakable. We'll have to wait until the care—"

Harry was on his way back to the car. And this time Holm was unable to follow the inspector's train of thought. Not until Harry got into the driver's seat and Bjørn remembered that the key was still in the ignition.

"No, Harry! No! Don't . . ."

The remainder was drowned in the roar of the engine. The wheels spun on the rain-slippery surface before gaining purchase. Bjørn Holm stood waving in the road, but caught a glimpse of the inspector's eyes behind the wheel and leaped out of the way. The Amazon's bumper hit the door with a muffled crash. The glass in the door turned to white crystals, as for one noiseless second it hovered in the air before tinkling to the ground. And before Bjørn could gauge the extent of the damage, Harry was out of the car and striding through the now-glassless entrance.

Bjørn ran desperately after him, cursing. Harry had grabbed a pot containing a six-foot-high palm tree, dragged it over to the elevator and pressed the button. As the shiny aluminum doors slid apart, he jammed the pot between them and pointed to a white door with a green exit sign.

"If you take the fire escape and I take the main stairs we have all the escape routes covered. Meet you on the sixth, Holm."

Bjørn Holm was drenched with sweat before he reached the second floor on the narrow iron staircase. Neither his body nor his head was prepared for this. He was a forensics officer, for Christ's sake! His bag was **re**constructing dramas, not constructing them.

He stopped for a moment. But all he could hear was the fading echo of his own footsteps and his own panting. What would he do if he met someone? Harry had told him to bring his service revolver along to Seildukgata, but had Harry meant that he would have to use it? Bjørn took hold of the railing and started running again. What would Hank Williams have done? Buried his head in a drink. Sid Vicious? Shown him a finger and legged it. And Elvis? Elvis. Elvis Presley. Right. Bjørn Holm wrapped his fingers around his revolver.

The steps finished. He opened the door and there, at the end of the corridor, was Harry, leaning back against the wall beside a brown door. He had his revolver in one hand and was holding the other to his mouth. Forefinger over his lips as he watched Bjørn and pointed to the door. It was ajar.

"We'll do it room by room," Harry whispered when Bjørn was alongside. "You take the ones on the left, I'll take the ones on the right. Same rhythm, back to back. And don't forget to breathe."

"Wait!" Bjørn whispered. "What if Katrine's there?"

Harry studied him and waited.

"I mean . . . ," Bjørn Holm went on, trying to articulate what he meant. "In a worst-case scenario would I shoot . . . a colleague?"

"In the **worst**-case scenario," Harry said, "a colleague would shoot **you**. Ready?"

The young forensics officer from Skreia nodded and promised himself that if this went well he would wear goddamned hair oil.

Harry silently prodded the door open with his foot

and went in. He felt the current of air at once. The draft. He reached the first door to the right and grabbed the handle with his left hand as he pointed the revolver. Pushed the door open and went in. It was a study. Empty. Over the desk hung a large map of Norway with pins stuck in it.

Harry walked back into the hall, where Holm was waiting for him. Harry motioned to Holm to keep his revolver raised the whole time.

They moved through the apartment with stealth.

Kitchen, library, fitness room, conservatory, guest room. All empty.

Harry felt the temperature drop. And as they came into the living room he saw why. The sliding door to the terrace and pool was wide open; white curtains flapped nervously in the wind. On either side of the room ran narrow pathways, each leading to a door. Harry pointed to Holm to take the door on the right while he took up position in front of the other.

Harry breathed in, huddled up to make the target as small as possible and opened.

In the darkness he could make out a bed, white linen and something that might have been a body. His left hand groped for a switch inside the door.

"Harry!"

It was Holm.

"Over here, Harry!"

Holm's voice was excited, but Harry turned a deaf ear and concentrated on the darkness in front of him. His hand found the switch, and the next moment the room was bathed in light from overhead spots. It was empty. Harry checked the closets, then left. Holm stood outside the other door with his gun pointing into the room.

"He's not moving," Holm whispered. "He's dead. He . . ."

"Then you needn't have called me so urgently," Harry said, walking to the bathtub, bending over the naked man and removing the pig mask. A thin red stripe ran around his neck, his face was pale and swollen and his eyes were bulging out from beneath the eyelids. Arve Støp was barely recognizable.

"I'll call the Crime Scene people," Holm said.

"Hang on." Harry held a hand in front of Støp's mouth. Then he took the editor's shoulder and shook him.

"What are you doing?"

Harry shook harder.

Bjørn laid a hand on Harry's shoulder. "But, Harry, can't you see . . ."

Holm recoiled. Støp had opened his eyes. And now he was drawing breath—like a skin diver breaking the surface—deep, painful and with a rattle in his throat.

"Where is she?" Harry said.

Støp was unable to focus his eyes, and short gasps were all that emerged from his mouth.

"Wait here, Holm."

Holm nodded and watched his colleague leave the bathroom.

· · ·

Harry stood on the edge of Arve Støp's roof terrace. Twenty-five yards below glittered the black water of the canal. In the moonlight he could discern the sculpture of the woman on stilts in the water and the deserted bridge. And there . . . something shiny bobbing on the surface of the water, like the belly of a dead fish. The back of a black leather coat. She had jumped. From the sixth floor.

Harry stepped up to the edge of the terrace, between the empty flower boxes. An image from the past flashed through his brain. Østmarka, and Øystein, who had dived from the mountain into Lake Hauktjern. Harry and Tresko dragging him to the shore. Øystein in bed at Rikshospitalet with what looked like scaffolding around his neck. What Harry had learned from this was that you should jump from great heights, not dive. And remember to keep your arms against your body so that you don't break your collarbone. But above all you have to make up your mind before you look down, and jump before terror has engaged your common sense. And that was why Harry's jacket slid to the terrace floor with a soft smack while Harry was already in the air, listening to the roar in his ears. The black water accelerated toward him. As black as pavement.

He put his heels together, and the next moment it was as if the air had been knocked out of him and a large hand were trying to tear off his clothes, and all sound was gone. Then came the numbing cold. He kicked and rose to the surface. Got his bearings, located the coat and began to swim. He had already started losing sensation in his feet and knew he only had a few minutes before his body would stop functioning in this temperature. But he also knew that if Katrine's laryngeal reflex was working and closed itself when it came into contact with water it would be the sudden cooling down that could save her; it would stop the metabolism, send the body's cells and organs into hibernation mode and allow the vital functions to survive on a minimum of oxygen.

Harry lunged and glided through the thick, heavy water toward the glistening leather.

Then he was there and he grabbed her.

His first unconscious thought was that she was already heaven-bound, consumed by demons. For only her coat was there.

Harry cursed, spun around in the water and stared up at the terrace. Followed the edge up to the eaves, the metal pipework and the sloping roofs that led down the other side of the building, to other buildings. Other terraces and the multitude of fire escapes and routes through the labyrinth of façades in Aker Brygge. He treaded water with legs that could no longer feel while confirming to himself that Katrine had not even underestimated him; he had fallen for one of the oldest tricks in the book. And for a moment of madness he considered death by drowning; it was supposed to be pleasant.

It was four o'clock in the morning, and on the bed in front of Harry, wearing a bathrobe, was a trembling

Arve Støp. The tan seemed to have been sucked from his complexion, and he had shrunk into an old man. But his pupils had regained their normal size.

Harry had taken a boiling hot shower and seated himself in a chair, wearing a sweater from Holm and sweatpants he had borrowed from Støp. In the living room they could hear Bjørn Holm trying to organize the hunt for Katrine Bratt via a mobile phone. Harry had told him to contact the Incident Room to put out a general alert; the police at Gardermoen Airport in case she attempted to take one of the early-morning flights; and the Special Forces Unit, Delta, to raid her apartment, even though Harry was fairly sure that they wouldn't find her there.

"So you think this was not just a sex game but Katrine trying to kill you?" Harry asked.

"Think?" Støp said with chattering teeth. "She was trying to strangle me!"

"Mm. And she asked you if you had an alibi for the times of the murders?"

"For the third time, yes!" Støp groaned.

"So she thinks you're the Snowman?"

"Christ knows what she thinks. The woman's obviously out of her mind."

"Maybe," Harry said. "But that doesn't prevent her from having a point."

"And what sort of point would that be?" Støp looked at his watch.

Harry knew that Krohn was on his way and that the lawyer would muzzle his client as soon as he got there.

He made up his mind and leaned forward. "We know that you're the father of Jonas Becker and Sylvia Ottersen's twins."

Støp's head shot up. Harry had to take a risk.

"Idar Vetlesen was the only person who knew. You're the one who sent him to Switzerland and paid for the Fahr's Syndrome course he enrolled in, aren't you? The disease you yourself inherited."

Harry could see he wasn't far off the mark by the way Arve Støp's pupils dilated.

"It's my guess Vetlesen told you we were putting the squeeze on him," Harry persisted. "Perhaps you were frightened he would crack. Or perhaps he was exploiting the situation to extort favors? Money, for example."

The editor stared at Harry in disbelief and shook his head.

"Nevertheless, Støp, you would obviously have had a lot to lose if the truth about these paternities had come out. Enough to give you a motive for killing those who could expose you: the mothers and Idar Vetlesen. Isn't that correct?"

"I . . ." Støp's gaze began to roam.

"You?"

"I have . . . nothing else to say." Støp fell forward and lowered his head into his hands. "Talk to Krohn."

"Fine," Harry said. He didn't have much time. Though he did have one last card. A good one. "I'll tell them you said that."

Harry waited. Støp was still bent forward, motionless. Then at last he raised his head.

"Who's **them?**"

"The press, of course," Harry said. "There is reason to believe they will give us quite a grilling, don't you think? This is what you people would call a scoop, wouldn't you?"

Something clicked behind Støp's eyes.

"How do you mean?" he asked, but with intonation that suggested he already knew the answer.

"A well-known figure thinks he's luring a young woman home, whereas in fact the opposite is the case," Harry said, studying the painting on the wall behind Støp. It seemed to represent a naked woman balancing on a tightrope. "He's persuaded to wear a pig mask in the belief that this is a sex game and this is how he's found by the police, naked and crying in his bathtub."

"You can't tell them that!" Støp exploded. "That . . . that's breaking the principle of client confidentiality."

"Well," Harry said, "it might be breaking the image you've built up around yourself, Støp. However, it doesn't break any obligation to remain silent. More the opposite."

"The opposite?" Støp almost yelled. The chattering of teeth was gone now and the color was back in his cheeks.

Harry coughed. "My only capital and means of production is my personal integrity." Harry waited until he saw that Støp was savoring his own words.

"And as a policeman that means, among other things, keeping the public informed to the extent that it is possible without damaging the investigation. In this case, it is possible."

"You can't do that," Støp said.

"I can, and I will."

"That . . . that would crush me."

"More or less the way **Liberal** crushes someone every week on its front page?"

Støp opened and closed his mouth like a fish in an aquarium.

"But of course, even for men with personal integrity there are compromises," Harry pointed out.

Støp studied him hard.

"I hope you appreciate," Harry said, smacking his lips as if to memorize the precise wording, "that as a policeman I have a duty to exploit this situation."

Støp nodded slowly.

"Let's start with Birte Becker," Harry said. "How did you meet her?"

"I think we should stop there," a voice said.

They turned to the door. Appearances suggested that Johan Krohn had found time to shower, shave and iron his shirt.

"OK," Harry said with a shrug. "Holm!"

Bjørn Holm's freckled face appeared in the doorway behind Krohn.

"Call Odin Nakken of **Verdens Gang**," Harry said, facing Arve Støp. "Is it all right if I return your clothes later today?"

"Wait," said Støp.

The room went silent as Arve Støp raised both hands and rubbed the backs of his hands against his forehead as though to start his blood circulating.

"Johan," he said at length, "you'll have to go. I can manage this on my own."

"Arve," the lawyer said, "I don't think you should—"

"Go home and sleep, Johan. I'll call you later."

"As your lawyer I have to—"

"As my lawyer you have to keep your mouth shut and go, Johan. Got that?"

Johan Krohn straightened up, mobilized the remainder of his wounded lawyer dignity, then changed his mind on seeing Støp's expression. Nodded quickly, turned and left.

"Where were we?" Støp asked.

"At the beginning," said Harry.

27

The Beginning

Arve Støp saw Birte Becker for the first time one cold winter's day in Oslo, during a lecture he was giving for a publicity firm at Sentrum Auditorium. It was a motivational seminar where companies sent their jaded employees for a so-called refresher course, that is, lectures intended to make them work even harder. In Arve Støp's experience most lecturers at this seminar were businessmen who had enjoyed a bit of success with not very original ideas, gold medalists from major championships in minor sports, or mountaineers who had made a career out of climbing up mountains and coming down them again to tell others about the experience. What they had in common was that they claimed that their success was a result of their very special willpower and morale. They were motivated. This was what was supposed to be motivating.

Arve Støp was last on the program—he always stipulated that as a prerequisite for his appearances. So that he could start by slating the other lecturers as greedy narcissists, divide them into the three above-mentioned categories and place himself in the first—success with a not very original business idea. The money that was spent on this motivational day was wasted; most people in the room would never advance that far because they were lucky enough not to have the abnormal drive for recognition that tormented those standing on the platform. Including himself. A condition that he said was caused by his father's lack of affection. So he had been obliged to seek love and admiration from others and he should therefore have become an actor or a musician, only he had no talent in those areas.

At this point in the lecture the audience's amazement had turned into laughter. And sympathy. And Støp knew this would culminate in admiration. For he stood there and shone. Shone because he and everyone else knew that whatever he said, he was a success, and you can't argue with success, not even your own. He stressed that luck was the most important factor in success, he played down his own talent and he emphasized that general incompetence and idleness in the Norwegian business sector ensured that even mediocrity can succeed.

At the end they gave him a standing ovation.

And he smiled as he eyed the dark-haired beauty in the first row who would prove to be Birte. He had noticed her the minute he had entered. He was aware that the combination of slim legs and large breasts was often synonymous with silicone implants, but Støp was no opponent of cosmetic surgery for women. Nail polish, silicone: In principle, what was the difference? With the applause pounding in his ears he simply stepped down from the stage, walked along the first row and began to shake hands with the audience. It was a fatuous gesture, something an American president could permit himself to do, but he didn't give a damn; if he could annoy someone he was happy. He stopped in front of the dark-haired woman, who glowed back at him with elated red cheeks. As he passed her, she curtsied as if for a royal, and he felt the sharp corners of his business card stick in his palm as he pressed it against hers. She looked for a wedding ring.

Her ring was lusterless. And her right hand narrow and pale, but it held his in an astonishingly firm grip.

"Sylvia Ottersen," she said with a foolish smile. "I'm a great admirer so I just had to shake hands."

That was how he had met Sylvia Ottersen for the first time, in her shop Taste of Africa one hot summer's day in Oslo. Her looks were run-of-the-mill. Married, though.

Arve Støp looked up at the African masks and asked about something so as not to make the situation any more awkward than it already was. Not that it was awkward for him, but he noticed that the woman at his side had stiffened when Sylvia Ottersen had shaken his hand. Her name was Marita. No, it was Marite. She had insisted on bringing him here to show him some zebra-skin cushions that Marite—or was it Marita?—thought he just **had** to have for the bed that they had left not long before and that now sported strands of long blond hair, which, he made a mental note, would have to be removed.

"We don't have any left in zebra," Sylvia Ottersen said. "But what about these?"

She walked over to a shelf by the window; the daylight fell on her curves, which, he reflected, were not bad at all. Her commonplace brown hair, however, was straggly and dead.

"What is it?" asked the woman whose name began with **M.**

"Imitation gnu skin."

"Imitation?" M. snorted, tossing her blond hair over her shoulder. "We'll wait until you get in more zebra."

"The zebra skin's imitation, too," Sylvia said, smiling the way you do at children when you have to explain that the moon isn't made of cheese after all.

"I see," M. said, breaking her red lips into a sour smile and hooking her arm under Arve's. "Thank you for letting us browse."

He hadn't liked M.'s idea of going out and parading around in public, and even less the grip she now had on his arm. She may have noticed his distaste when they were outside. At any rate, she let go. He glanced at his watch.

"Ooh," he said. "I've got a meeting."

"No lunch?" She regarded him with a surprised expression, quite able to hide how hurt she was.

"I'll call you, maybe," he said.

·   ·   ·

She called him. Only thirty minutes had passed since he had been standing on the Sentrum stage, and now he was sitting in a taxi behind a snowplow churning filthy snow onto the roadside.

"I was sitting right in front of you," she said. "I'd like to thank you for the lecture."

"Hope my staring wasn't too obvious," he shouted exultantly over the scraping of iron on pavement.

She chuckled.

"Any plans for the evening?" he asked.

"Well," she said, "none that can't be changed . . ." Beautiful voice. Beautiful words.

The rest of the afternoon he went around thinking about her, fantasizing about screwing her on the chest of drawers in the hallway, her head banging against the Gerhard Richter painting he had bought in Berlin. And thinking this was always the best bit: the wait.

At eight she rang the bell downstairs. He was in the hall. Heard the echo of the elevator's mechanical clicking, like a weapon being loaded. A humming tone that rose. The blood was throbbing in his dick.

And then there she stood. He felt as if he had been slapped.

"Who are you?" he said.

"Stine," she said and a mild expression of surprise spread across the smiling fleshy face. "I phoned . . ."

He scanned her from top to toe and for a moment considered the possibility regardless; every so often he was turned on by the ordinary and fairly unattractive type. However, he could feel his erection dwindling and rejected the idea.

"I'm sorry, but I was unable to get hold of you," he said. "I've just been summoned to a meeting."

"A meeting?" she said, quite unable to hide how hurt she was.

"An emergency meeting. I'll call you, perhaps."

He stood in the hallway and heard the elevator doors outside opening and closing. Then he began to laugh. He laughed until he realized he might never see the dark-haired beauty in the first row again.

He saw Sylvia again an hour later. After he had eaten lunch alone in the aptly named Bar&Restaurant, bought a suit at Kamikaze that he put on right away and twice walked past Taste of Africa, which was a refuge from the boiling hot sun. The third time he went in.

"Back already?" Sylvia Ottersen smiled.

Just as an hour before, she was alone in the cool, dark shop.

"I liked the cushions," he said.

"Yes, they're elegant," she said, stroking the imitation gnu skin.

"Do you have anything else you could show me?" he asked.

She put a hand on her hip. Tilted her head. She knows, he thought. She can smell.

"Depends what you want to see," she said.

He heard the quaver in his voice as he answered. "I'd like to see your pussy."

She let him fuck her in the back room and didn't even bother to lock the shop door.

Arve Støp came almost at once. Now and then the ordinary, fairly unattractive type made him so damned horny.

"My husband's in the shop on Tuesdays and Wednesdays," she said as he was leaving. "Thursday?"

"Maybe," he said and saw that his suit from Kamikaze was already stained.

The snow was swirling in flurries between the office buildings in Aker Brygge when Birte called.

She said she assumed he had given her his business card for her to contact him.

Sometimes Arve Støp asked himself why he had to have these women, these kicks, these sexual relations that were actually no more than ceremonial rituals of surrender. Hadn't he had enough conquests in his life? Was it the fear of getting old? Did he believe that by penetrating these women he could steal some of their youth? And why the hurry, the frenetic tempo? Perhaps it came from the certainty of the disease he was carrying; that before long he would not be the man he once was. He didn't have the answers, and what would he do with them anyway? That same night he listened to Birte's groans, as deep as a man's, her head banging against the Gerhard Richter painting he had bought in Berlin.

Arve Støp ejaculated his infected seed as the bell over the front door angrily warned them that someone was on his way into Taste of Africa. He tried to free himself, but Sylvia Ottersen grinned and tightened her grip around his buttocks. He tore himself free and pulled up his trousers. Sylvia slid down off the counter, adjusted her summer skirt and went around the corner to serve the customer. With his back to the room Arve Støp hurried over to the shelves of ornaments and buttoned up his fly. Behind him he heard a man's voice apologizing for being late; it had been difficult to find somewhere to park. And Sylvia had said in a sharp voice that he should have known; after all, the summer holidays were over now. She was meeting her sister and she was already late and he would have to take over with the customer.

Arve Støp heard the man's voice at his back. "May I help you?"

He turned and saw a skeleton of a man with unnaturally large eyes behind round glasses, a flannel shirt and a neck that reminded him of a stork.

He looked over his shoulder at the man, caught Sylvia going out the door, the hem of her skirt ridden up, a wet line running down the back of her bare knee. And it struck him that she had known this scarecrow, presumably her husband, would be coming now. She had **wanted** him to catch them at it.

"I'm fine, thank you. I got what I came for," he said, heading for the door.

Every once in a while Arve Støp imagined how he would react if he were told he had made someone pregnant. Whether he would insist on an abortion or that the child should be born. The only thing he was absolutely sure of was that he would insist on one or the other; leaving decisions to others was not in his nature.

Birte Becker had told him they didn't need to use contraception since she couldn't have children. When, three months and six acts of sexual intercourse later, she informed him with a rapturous smile that she could after all, he knew at once that she would have the baby. He reacted by panicking and insisting on the alternative option.

"I have the best contacts," he said. "In Switzerland. No one will ever know."

"This is my opportunity to become a mother, Arve. The doctor says it's a miracle that may never be repeated."

"Then I want to see neither you nor any children you may have again. Do you hear me?"

"The child needs a father, Arve. And a secure home."

"And you won't find either here. I'm the carrier of an awful inherited disease. Do you understand?"

Birte Becker understood. And since she was a straightforward but quick-witted girl with a drunkard of a father and a nervous wreck of a mother, accustomed from early years to coping on her own, she did what she had to do. She found her child a father and a secure home.

Filip Becker could not believe it when this beautiful woman he had wooed with such determination, yet to no avail, suddenly surrendered and set her heart on becoming his. And since he could not believe it, the seeds of suspicion were already sown. At the moment she announced that he had made her pregnant—only a week after she had given herself to him—the seeds were still well entrenched.

When Birte rang Arve to say that Jonas had been born and was the spitting image of him, Arve stood with his ear against the receiver staring into the air. Then he asked her for a photograph. It arrived in the mail, and two weeks later she was sitting, as arranged, in a coffee bar with Jonas on her lap and a wedding ring on her finger while Arve sat at another table pretending to read a paper.

That night he tossed and turned between the sheets, restlessly brooding over the disease.

It had to be handled with discretion, by a doctor he could trust to keep his mouth shut. In short, it would have to be the feeble, obsequious fool of a surgeon at the curling club: Idar Vetlesen.

He contacted Vetlesen, who was working at the Marienlyst Clinic. The idiot said yes to the job and yes to the money, and at Støp's expense traveled to Geneva, where the foremost Fahr's Syndrome experts in Europe gathered every year to hold a conference and present the latest discouraging findings from their research.

The first tests Jonas underwent revealed nothing wrong, but even though Vetlesen repeated that the symptoms usually came to light in adulthood—Arve Støp had himself been symptom-free until he was forty—Støp insisted that the boy be examined once a year.

Two years had passed since he had seen his seed running down Sylvia Ottersen's leg as she walked out of the shop and out of Arve Støp's life. He had quite simply never contacted her again, nor she him. Until now. When she called he said immediately that he was on his way to an emergency meeting, but she kept the message brief. In four sentences she told him that obviously not all his seed had dribbled out, she now had twins, her husband thought they were his and they needed a kindly disposed investor to keep Taste of Africa afloat.

"I think I've injected enough into that shop," said Arve Støp, who often reacted to bad news with witticisms.

"I could, on the other hand, raise the money by going to **Se og Hør.** They love these the-father-of-my-child's-a-celeb stories, don't they?"

"Bad bluff," he said. "You've got too much to lose by doing that."

"Things have changed," she said. "I'm going to leave Rolf if I can scrape together enough cash to buy him out of the shop. The problem with the shop is its location, so I will make it a condition that **Se og Hør** publishes pictures of the place to get it some decent publicity. Do you know how many people read the rag?"

Arve Støp knew. Every sixth Norwegian adult. He had never objected to a nice glitzy scandal every once in a while, but to be made to look like a slippery Lothario exploiting his celebrity status with an innocent married woman in such a craven way? The public image of Arve Støp as upright and fearless would be smashed, and **Liberal**'s morally indignant outbursts would be cast in a hypocritical light. And she wasn't even attractive. This was not good. Not good at all.

"What sort of money are we talking?" he asked.

Upon reaching agreement, he called Idar Vetlesen at the Marienlyst Clinic and explained that he had two new patients. They arranged to do the same as with Jonas, first make the twins take DNA tests and send them to the Institute of Forensic Medicine to confirm paternity, then start checking for symptoms of the unmentionable disease.

After hanging up, Arve Støp leaned back in the high leather chair and saw the sun shining on the treetops in Bygdøy and on the Snarøya peninsula, knowing he should feel deeply depressed. But he didn't. He felt excited. Yes, almost happy.

The distant memory of this happiness was the first thing that went through Arve Støp's mind when Idar Vetlesen phoned to tell him that the newspapers were alleging that the decapitated woman in Sollihøgda was Sylvia Ottersen.

"First Jonas Becker's mother disappears," Vetlesen said. "And then they find the mother of the twins killed. I'm no whiz at the calculus of probability, but we have to go to the police, Arve. They're anxious to find connections."

In recent years Vetlesen had made a lucrative career out of embellishing the appearances of celebrities, but in Arve Støp's eyes he was nevertheless—or perhaps as a consequence—a fool.

"No, we're not going to the police," Arve said.

"Oh? Then you'll have to give me a good reason."

"Fine. What sort of money are we talking about?"

"My God, Arve, I'm not trying to blackmail you. I just can't—"

"How much?"

"Stop it. Do you have an alibi or not?"

"I don't have an alibi, but I do have an awful lot of money. Tell me how many zeros and I'll think about it."

"Arve, if you have nothing to hide—"

"Of course I've got something to hide, you twat! Do you think I want to be publicly exposed as a home wrecker and murder suspect? We'll have to meet and talk this through."

"And did you meet?" Harry Hole asked.

Arve Støp shook his head. Outside the bedroom

window he could see the heralding of dawn, but the fjord was still black.

"We didn't get that far before he died."

"Why didn't you tell me any of this when I came here the first time?"

"Isn't it obvious? I don't know anything that may be of value to the police, so why should I interfere? Don't forget, I have a brand to attend to, and that is my name. This label is in fact **Liberal**'s only capital."

"I seem to remember you said the only capital was your personal integrity."

Støp shrugged his shoulders with displeasure. "Integrity. Label. It's the same thing."

"So if something looks like integrity, then it's integrity?"

Støp stared at Harry. "That's what sells **Liberal**. If people feel they're given the truth, they're satisfied."

"Mm." Harry glanced at his watch. "And do you think I'm satisfied now?"

Arve Støp didn't answer.

28

Disease

Bjørn Holm drove Harry from Aker Brygge to the Police HQ. The inspector had put on his wet clothes, and the artificial leather squelched as he shifted position.

"Delta raided her apartment twenty minutes ago," Bjørn said. "She wasn't there. They've left three guards on the door."

"She won't be back," Harry said.

In his office on the sixth floor Harry changed into the police uniform hanging on the coatrack; he hadn't worn it since Jack Halvorsen's funeral. He scrutinized himself in the mirror. The jacket hung off him.

Gunnar Hagen had been alerted and had come to the office on short notice. He sat behind his desk as Harry debriefed him. The story was so dramatic that he forgot to be irritated by the inspector's creased uniform.

"The Snowman's Katrine Bratt," Hagen repeated slowly, as if saying it aloud made it more comprehensible.

Harry nodded.

"And do you believe Støp?"

"Yes," Harry said.

"Can anyone corroborate his story?"

"They're all dead. Birte, Sylvia, Idar Vetlesen. He could have been the Snowman. That was what Katrine Bratt wanted to find out."

"Katrine? But you're saying she's the Snowman. Why would she . . . ?"

"I'm saying that she wanted to find out if he **could** be the Snowman. She wanted to set up a scapegoat. Støp says that when he said he had no alibi for the times of the murders she said, 'Good,' and told him he had just been appointed the Snowman. Then she started to strangle him. Until she heard the car crash into the front door, realized we were on the way and fled. The plan was probably that we would find Støp dead in the apartment and that it would look as if he had hanged himself. And we would relax in the belief that we had found the guilty party. Just as she killed Idar Vetlesen. And when she tried to shoot Filip Becker during his arrest."

"What? She tried . . . ?"

"She had her revolver pointed at him with the hammer cocked. I heard her release the hammer as I positioned myself in the firing line."

Gunnar Hagen closed his eyes and massaged his temples with the tips of his fingers. "I hear you. But for the moment all this is just speculation, Harry."

"And then there's the letter," Harry said.

"The letter?"

"From the Snowman. I found the document on her computer at home, dated before any of us knew anything about the Snowman. And the paper in the printer."

"Christ!" Hagen banged his elbows down hard on the desk and buried his face in his hands. "We employed the woman here! Do you know what that means, Harry?"

"Well, an almighty scandal. Lack of confidence in the whole police force. Heads will roll in the upper echelons."

A crack opened between Hagen's fingers and he squinted at Harry. "Thank you for being so explicit."

"My pleasure."

"I'll summon the chief superintendent and the chief constable. In the meantime I want you and Bjørn Holm to keep this under your hats. What about Arve Støp? Will he blab?"

"Hardly, boss." Harry smirked. "He's run out."

"Run out of what?"

"Integrity."

It was ten o'clock and from his office window Harry watched the pale, almost hesitant daylight settle on the rooftops and a Sunday-still Grønland. Several hours had passed since Katrine Bratt had vanished from Støp's apartment, and so far the search had borne no fruit. Of course she could still be in Oslo, but if she had been prepared for a strategic withdrawal she could well be over the hills and far away. Harry had no doubt that she had made preparations.

Just as he had no doubt now that she was the Snowman.

First of all, there was the evidence: the letter and the murder attempts. And all his instincts were confirmed: the feeling that he was being observed from close range, the feeling that someone had infiltrated his life. The newspaper clippings on the wall, the reports. Katrine had got to know him so well that she could predict his next moves, could use him in her game. And now she was a virus in his bloodstream, a spy inside his head.

He heard someone come in, but didn't turn around.

"We've traced her mobile phone," Skarre's voice said. "She's in Sweden."

"Huh?"

"Telenor says that the signals are moving south. The location and speed match the Copenhagen train that departed from Oslo Central Station at seven oh five. I've spoken to the police in Helsingborg; they need a formal application to make an arrest. The train's due to arrive in half an hour. What should we do?"

Harry nodded slowly, as though to himself. A seagull sailed past on stiff wings before suddenly changing direction and swooping down to the trees in the park. Perhaps it had spotted something. Or just changed its mind. The way humans do. Oslo Station at seven o'clock in the morning.

"Harry? She might make it to Denmark unless we—"

"Ask Hagen to talk to Helsingborg," Harry said, swiveling and grabbing his jacket from the coatrack in one quick movement.

Skarre watched in amazement as the inspector hurried down the corridor with long, purposeful strides.

Officer Orø at the equipment counter at the Police HQ looked at the tall inspector with undisguised astonishment and repeated: "CS? Gas, that is?"

"Two canisters," Harry said. "And a box of ammo for the revolver."

The officer limped to the supplies, mouthing imprecations. This Hole guy was a complete fruitcake—everyone knew that—but tear gas? If it had been anyone else at the station, he would have guessed that it was for a stag night with the pals. But from what he heard, Hole had no pals, at least not on the force.

The inspector coughed as Orø returned. "Has Katrine Bratt in Crime Squad requested any weapons here?"

"The woman from the Bergen Police Station? Only the one stipulated in the rule book."

"And what does the rule book say?"

"Return all weapons and unused ammo to the old police station upon departure and request a new revolver and two boxes of bullets from the new station."

"So she has nothing heavier than a revolver?"

Orø shook his head, mystified.

"Thank you," Hole said, putting the boxes of ammunition in a black bag beside the green cylindrical gas canisters.

The officer didn't answer, not until he had received Hole's signature for the delivery, then he mumbled, "Have a peaceful Sunday."

Harry was sitting in the waiting room at Ullevål University Hospital with the black bag beside him. There was a smell of alcohol, old people and slow death. A female patient had taken a seat opposite him and was staring at him as though trying to locate someone who was not there: a person she had known, a lover who had never materialized, a son she thought she recognized.

Harry sighed, glanced at his watch and visualized the police storming the train in Helsingborg. The engineer who was instructed by the stationmaster to stop the train half a mile before the station. The armed police dispersed along both sides of the track, standing by with dogs. The efficient inspection of the carriages, the compartments, the bathrooms. The terrified passengers reacting to the sight of armed police, still an unusual sight here in Scandinavian dreamland. The trembling, groping hands of women requested to present ID. The hunched shoulders of the police, the nervousness, but also the anticipation. Their impatience, doubt, irritation and ultimately their disappointment and despair that they didn't find what they were looking for. And, at the end, if they were lucky and competent, the loud curses when they found the source of the signals the base stations had picked up: Katrine Bratt's mobile phone in a bathroom garbage bin.

A smiling face appeared before him. "You can see him now."

Harry followed the clatter of clogs and broad, energetic hips in white trousers. She pushed open the door. "But don't stay too long. He needs rest."

Ståle Aune lay on the bed in a private room. His round, red-veined face was sunken and so pale it almost blended in with the pillowcase. Thin hair, like a child's, lay on the chubby sixty-year-old's forehead. Had it not been for the same sharp-eyed, jovial eyes, Harry would have believed he was looking at the corpse of the Crime Squad's resident psychologist and Harry's personal spiritual adviser.

"Goodness me, Harry," Ståle Aune said. "You look like a skeleton. Aren't you well?"

Harry had to smile. Aune sat up with a grimace.

"Sorry not to have visited you before," Harry said, dragging and scraping a chair along the floor to the bed. "It's just that the hospital . . . it . . . I don't know."

"The hospital reminds you of your mother when you were a boy. That's fine."

Harry nodded and dropped his gaze to his hands. "Are they treating you well?"

"That's what you ask when you're visiting people in prison, Harry, not in a hospital."

Harry nodded again.

Ståle Aune sighed. "I know you're concerned about me, Harry. But I know you too well, so I know this is not a courtesy visit. Come on, spit it out."

"It can wait. They said you weren't well."

"Being well is a relative thing. And, relatively speaking, I'm tremendously well. You should have seen me yesterday. By which I mean, you should **not** have seen me yesterday."

Harry smiled at his hands.

"Is it the Snowman?" Aune asked.

Harry nodded.

"At long last," Aune said. "I've been bored to death in here. Out with it."

Harry breathed in. Then he recited all that had happened in the case. Trying to trim the tedious, irrelevant information without losing the essential details. Aune interrupted him only a few times with pithy questions; otherwise he listened in silence with a concentrated, quasi-entranced expression on his face. And when Harry had finished, the sick man appeared to have perked up; there was color in his cheeks and he was sitting up straighter in bed.

"Interesting," he said. "But you already know who the guilty person is, so why come to me?"

"This woman is insane, isn't she?"

"People who commit such crimes are without exception insane. Though not necessarily in a criminal sense."

"Nevertheless, there are one or two things I don't understand about her," Harry said.

"Goodness me—there are only one or two things I **do** understand about people, so in that case you're a better psychologist than I."

"She was just nineteen years old when she killed the two women in Bergen and Gert Rafto. How can a person who is that crazy get through the psychological tests for the police academy and function in a job for all these years with no one being any the wiser?"

"Good question. Perhaps she's a cocktail case."

"Cocktail case?"

"Someone with a bit of everything. Schizophrenic enough to hear voices, but capable of concealing her illness from those around her. Obsessive-compulsive personality disorder mixed with a dash of paranoia, which creates delusions about the situation she is in and what she has to do to escape, but which to the outside world is simply perceived as a certain reticence. The bestial fury that emerges during the murders you describe tallies with a borderline personality, though one that can control its fury."

"Mm. In other words, you haven't a clue?"

Aune laughed. The laughter degenerated into a coughing fit.

"I'm sorry, Harry," he growled. "Most cases are like this. In psychology we have set up a number of corrals that our cattle refuse to be herded into. They're nothing less than impudent, ungrateful, muddle-headed creatures. Think of all the research we've done for them!"

"There's something else. When we stumbled on the body of Gert Rafto she was genuinely frightened.

I mean, she wasn't acting. I could see the shock; her pupils were still enlarged and black even though I was shining the flashlight straight into her face."

"Aha! This is interesting." Aune levered himself up higher. "Why did you shine the flashlight in her face? Did you suspect something even then?"

Harry didn't answer.

"You may be right," Aune said. "She may have repressed the murders; that is by no means untypical. You've told me that in fact she has been a great help in the investigation and hasn't sabotaged it. That may suggest she has a suspicion about herself and a genuine desire to uncover the truth. How much do you know about noctambulism—in other words, sleepwalking?"

"I know that people can walk in their sleep. Talk in their sleep. Eat, get dressed and even go out and drive a car in their sleep."

"Correct. The conductor Harry Rosenthal conducted and sang the parts of instruments for entire symphonies in his sleep. And there have been at least five murder cases in which the murderer has been acquitted because the court determined that he or she was a parasomniac, that is, a sufferer of sleep disorders. There was a man in Canada who, some years ago, got up, drove more than ten miles, parked, killed his mother-in-law, with whom he generally had an excellent relationship, almost strangled his father-in-law, drove home and went back to bed. He was acquitted."

"You mean she might have killed in her sleep? That she's one of these parasomniacs?"

"It's a controversial diagnosis. But imagine a person who regularly goes into a hibernation-like state and is subsequently unable to remember with any clarity what she has done. Someone who has a blurred, fragmented image of events, like a dream."

"Mm."

"And suppose that this woman in the course of the investigation has begun to realize what she has done."

Harry nodded slowly. "And realizes that to get away she needs a scapegoat."

"It's conceivable." Ståle Aune made a face. "However, most things are conceivable as far as the human psyche is concerned. The problem is that we cannot see the disorders we're talking about; we have to assume they exist based on the symptoms."

"Like mold."

"What?"

"What makes a person like this woman so psychologically sick?"

Aune groaned. "Everything in existence! And nothing! Nature and nurture."

"A violent, alcoholic father?"

"Yes, yes, yes. Ninety points for that. Add a mother with a psychiatric history, a traumatic experience or two in her childhood and you have the round hundred."

"Does it seem likely that if she had become stronger than her violent, alcoholic father she would try to hurt him? Kill him?"

"By no means impossible. I remember a ca—" Ståle Aune stopped midword. Stared at Harry. Then leaned forward and whispered with a gleam dancing wildly in his eyes. "Are you saying what I think you're saying?"

Harry Hole studied his fingernails. "I was given a photo of a man at the Bergen Police Station. It struck me there was something strangely familiar about him, as if I had met him before. I've only just figured out why. It was the family likeness. Before Katrine Bratt got married her name was Rafto. Gert Rafto was her father."

On his way to the airport express train Harry received a call from Skarre. He had been mistaken. They hadn't found her mobile phone in the bathroom; it had been on the luggage rack in one of the coaches.

Eighty minutes later he was enshrouded in gray. The captain announced that there were low-lying clouds and rain in Bergen. Zero visibility, Harry thought. They were flying on instruments alone now.

The front door was torn open seconds after Thomas Helle, from the Missing Persons Unit, had pressed the doorbell over the sign reading ANDREAS, ELI AND TRYGVE KVALE.

"Thank the Lord you came so quickly." The man standing in front of Helle looked over his shoulder. "Where are the others?"

"There's just me. You still haven't heard anything from your wife?"

The man, who Helle presumed was the Andreas Kvale who had called the HQ, stared at him in amazement. "She's gone, I told you."

"We know, but they usually come back."

"Who's **they**?"

Thomas Helle sighed. "May I come in, Herr Kvale? This rain . . ."

"Oh, sorry! Please . . ." The man in his fifties stepped aside, and in the gloom behind him Helle caught sight of a dark-haired man in his early twenties.

Thomas Helle decided to do the business standing in the hallway. They barely had enough staff to man the phones today; it was a Sunday and those who were on duty were out searching for Katrine Bratt. One of their own. It was all hush-hush, but the rumors going around suggested she might be involved in the Snowman case.

"How did you discover she was missing?" Helle asked, getting ready to take notes.

"Trygve and I just returned from a camping trip in Nordmarka today. We'd been away for two days. No mobile phone, just fishing rods. She wasn't here, no messages, and, as I said on the phone, the door was unlocked. It's always locked, even when she's at home. My wife is a very anxious woman. And none of her coats is missing. Nor her shoes. Only her slippers. In this weather . . ."

"Have you called everyone she knows? Including the neighbors?"

"Of course. No one has heard from her."

Thomas Helle took notes. A familiar feeling had already surfaced. Missing wife and mother.

"You said your wife was an anxious woman," he said. "So who might she have opened the door to? And who might she have let in?"

He saw father and son exchange glances.

"Not too many people," the father said with conviction. "It must have been someone she knew."

"Or someone she didn't feel threatened by, maybe," Helle said. "Like a child or a woman?"

Andreas Kvale nodded.

"Or someone with a plausible reason for coming in. Someone from the electric company to read the meter, for example."

The husband hesitated. "Perhaps."

"Have you seen anything unusual around the house?"

"Unusual? What do you mean?"

Helle bit his lower lip. Braced himself. "Something that may resemble a . . . snowman?"

Andreas Kvale looked at his son, who energetically shook his head, petrified.

"Just so that we can eliminate that from our investigation," Helle said conversationally.

The son said something. In a low mumble.

"What?" Helle asked.

"He said there isn't any more snow."

"No, of course not." Helle stuffed his notepad in his jacket pocket. "I'll radio the patrol cars. If she hasn't turned up by this evening we'll intensify the search. In ninety-nine percent of cases the person will have found her way home by then. So this is my card . . ."

Helle felt Andreas Kvale's hand on his upper arm.

"There's something I want to show you, Officer."

Thomas Helle followed Kvale through a door at the end of the hall and down a staircase into the cellar. He opened a door to a room that smelled of soap and clothes hanging out to dry. In the corner stood an old-fashioned clothes mangle beside an Electrolux washing machine of older vintage. The brick floor sloped down to a drain in the middle. The floor was wet and there was water on the wall, as though the floor had recently been sluiced with the green hose lying there. But that was not primarily what attracted Thomas Helle's attention. It was the garment hanging on the wash line, attached with a clothespin at each shoulder. Or, to be precise, what was left of it. It had been cut off under the chest. The edge was crooked and black with burned, shriveled threads of cotton.

29

Tear Gas

The rain leaked through the heavens down onto Bergen, which lay bathed in the blue afternoon dusk. The boat Harry had reserved was ready at the quayside by the foot of Puddefjord Bridge when his taxi stopped there.

The boat was a well-used twenty-seven-foot Finnish cabin cruiser.

"I'm going fishing," Harry said, pointing to the nautical chart. "Any submerged rocks or anything I ought to know about if I go here?"

"Finnøy island?" said the boat-rental man. "Take a rod with a sinker and a spinner, but the fishing's bad out there."

"Soon find out, won't I. How do you start this thing?"

As Harry chugged past the Nordnes headland in the gathering gloom, he could make out the totem pole among the bare trees in the park. The sea lay flat under the rain, which whipped up the surface and made it foam. Harry thrust the lever next to the wheel forward, the bow lifted—he had to take a step back for balance—and the boat powered away.

Fifteen minutes later Harry pulled the lever back and swung in toward a quay on the far side of Finnøy, hidden from Rafto's cabin. He moored the boat, took out the fishing rod and listened to the rain. Fishing was not his thing. The spinner was heavy, the hook got snagged at the bottom and Harry pulled up sea-weed that swirled around the rod as he tugged. He freed the hook and cleaned it. Then he tried to drop the spinner in the water again, but something in the reel had locked and the spinner hung ten inches under the tip of the rod and would go neither up nor down. Harry looked at his watch. If someone had been alerted by the throb of the boat engine he or she would have relaxed by now, and he had to get this done before dark. He placed the rod on the seat, opened his bag, removed the revolver and opened the box of bullets and eased them into the chamber. He then stuffed the thermos-like CS canisters in his pockets and went ashore.

It took him five minutes to reach the top of the de-serted island and descend to the cabins boarded up for the winter on the other side. Rafto's cabin stood before him, dark and uninviting. He found a place on a rock twenty yards away, from which he had a full view of all the doors and windows. The rain had seeped through the shoulders of his green military jacket a long time ago. He took out one of the CS canisters and removed the safety pin. In five seconds the spring-loaded valve would discharge and the gas would begin to hiss out. He ran toward the cabin with the canister held in his outstretched arm and hurled it at the window. The glass smashed, making a thin tinkling sound. Harry retreated to the rock and raised his revolver. Above the rain he could hear the canister hissing and he could see the inside of the window turning gray.

If she was there she wouldn't be able to stand more than a few seconds.

He took aim. Waited, with the cabin in his sights.

After two minutes still nothing had happened.

Harry waited for two more.

Then he prepared the second canister, walked toward the cabin with gun raised and tried the door. Locked. Flimsy, though. He stepped back four paces and then ran forward.

The door split off along the hinges, and he plunged into the smoke-filled room, right shoulder first. The gas immediately assailed his eyes. Harry held his breath as he groped his way to the cellar trap-door, flipped it up, pulled out the safety pin of the second canister and let it fall. Then he ran out again. Found a pool of water and sank to his knees with streaming nose and eyes, put his head in with both eyes open, as deep as he could, until his nose scraped the stones. Twice he repeated the shallow dip. His nose and palate still smarted like hell, but his eyes had cleared. He pointed the revolver toward the hut again. Waited. And waited.

"Come on! Come on, you bitch!"

But no one came out.

After fifteen minutes the smoke had stopped issuing from the hole in the pane. Harry went back down to the cabin and kicked open the door. Coughed and cast a final glance inside. Wasteland wreathed in mist. Flying on instruments. Fuck, fuck, fuck!

As he walked back to the boat it had become so dark that he knew he was going to have visibility problems. He untied the moorings, went on board and grasped the starter lever. A thought went through his mind: He hadn't slept for nearly thirty-six hours, hadn't eaten since early morning, was drenched to the skin and had flown to fucking Bergen for absolutely nothing. If this engine didn't start immediately he would pepper the hull with lead and swim ashore. The engine started with a roar. Harry almost thought it was a shame. He was just about to push the lever forward when he saw her.

She was standing right in front of him on the steps leading down below deck. Nonchalantly leaning against the door frame, in a gray sweater over a black dress.

"Hands up," she ordered.

It sounded so childish it seemed almost a joke. The black revolver pointing at him was not. Nor was the threat that followed. "If you don't do as I say I'll shoot you in the stomach, Harry. Which will smash the nerves in your back and paralyze you. Then one in the head. But let's start with the stomach . . ."

The gun barrel was lowered.

Harry let go of the wheel and the lever and put up his hands.

"Back off, if you would be so kind," she said.

She came up the stairs, and it was only now that Harry could see the gleam in her eyes, the very same he had seen when they arrested Becker, the very same he had seen in Fenris Bar. But sparks were flying from the quivering irises. Harry retreated until he felt the seat at the stern against his legs.

"Sit down," Katrine said, switching off the motor.

Harry slumped back, sat on the fishing rod and felt the water on the plastic seat soak through his trousers.

"How did you find me?" she asked.

Harry shrugged.

"Come on," she said, raising the gun. "Satisfy my curiosity, Harry."

"Well," Harry replied, trying to read her pale, drawn face. But this was unknown territory; the face of this woman did not belong to the Katrine Bratt he knew. Thought he knew.

"Everyone has a pattern of behavior," he heard himself say. "A game plan."

"I see. And what's mine?"

"Pointing one way and running the other."

"Oh?"

Harry sensed the weight of the revolver in his right jacket pocket. He raised his backside and moved the fishing rod, leaving his right hand on the seat.

"You write a letter from 'the Snowman,' send it to me and several weeks later stroll into the Police HQ.

The first thing you do is to tell me Hagen has said I should take care of you. Hagen never said that."

"All correct so far. Anything else?"

"You threw your coat into the canal in front of Støp's apartment and fled in the opposite direction, over the roof. The pattern, therefore, is that when you plant your mobile phone on an eastbound train, you flee west."

"Bravo. And how did I flee?"

"Not by plane, of course. You knew that Gardermoen would be under surveillance. My guess is that you planted the phone in Oslo Central Station well before the train was due to depart, crossed over to the bus terminal and caught an early bus west. I would guess you split the journey into various legs. Kept changing buses."

"The Notodden express," Katrine said. "The Bergen bus from there. Got off in Voss and bought clothes. Bus to Ytre Arna. Local bus from there to Bergen. Paid a fisherman at Zacharias wharf to bring me here. Not bad guesswork, Harry."

"It wasn't so difficult. We're pretty similar, you and I."

Katrine tilted her head. "If you were so sure, why did you come alone?"

"I'm not alone. Müller-Nilsen and his people are on their way by boat now."

Katrine laughed. Harry shifted his hand closer to his jacket pocket.

"I agree we're similar, Harry. But when it comes to lying, I'm better than you."

Harry swallowed. His hand was cold. Fingers had to obey. "Yes, I'm sure that comes easier to you," Harry said. "Like murder."

"Oh? You look as if you could murder me now. Your hand is getting alarmingly close to your jacket pocket. Stand up and remove your jacket. Slowly. And throw it here."

Harry swore inwardly, but did as she said. His coat landed on the deck in front of Katrine with a thud. Without taking her eyes off Harry, she grabbed it and slung it overboard.

"It was time you got yourself a new one anyway," she said.

"Mm," Harry said. "You mean one to match the carrot in the middle of my face?"

Katrine blinked twice and Harry saw what appeared to be confusion in her eyes.

"Listen, Katrine. I've come here to help you. You need help. You're sick, Katrine. It was the illness that made you kill them."

Katrine had started to shake her head slowly. She pointed to land.

"I've been sitting in the boathouse for two hours waiting for you, Harry. Because I knew you would come. I've studied you, Harry. You always find what you're looking for. That was why I chose you."

"Chose me?"

"Chose you. To find the Snowman for me. That was why I sent you the letter."

"Why couldn't you find the Snowman yourself? You didn't exactly have to go far."

She shook her head. "I've tried, Harry. I've tried for many years. I knew I wouldn't be able to do it on my own. It had to be you. You're the only person who's succeeded in catching a serial killer. I needed Harry Hole." She gave a sad smile. "A last question, Harry. How did you figure out that I had deceived you?"

Harry was wondering how this would end. A bullet to the forehead? The electric cutting loop? A trip out to sea and then death by drowning? He swallowed. He ought to be afraid. So frightened that he would be unable to think, so frightened that he would fall sobbing to the deck and implore her to let him live. Why wasn't he? It couldn't be pride; he had swallowed that with whiskey and spat it out again several times. It could of course be his rational brain working, knowing that being frightened wouldn't help; on the contrary, it would only shorten his life further. He concluded, however, it was the tiredness that did it. A profound, all-encompassing exhaustion that made him feel as if he just wanted to get it over and done with.

"Deep down I've always known that this all started a long time ago," Harry said, noting that he no longer felt the cold. "It was planned and the person behind it had managed to get into my head. There are not so many people to choose from, Katrine. And when I saw the newspaper clippings in your apartment, I knew it was you."

Harry saw her blinking, disoriented. And he felt a wedge of doubt being driven into his line of thought, into the logic he had seen so clearly. Or had he? Hadn't the doubt always been there? The steady drizzle gave way to a deluge; the water hammered down on the deck. He saw her mouth open and her finger curl around the trigger. He grabbed the fishing rod beside him and stared down the gun barrel. This was how it would end, in a boat on the western coast, without witnesses, without evidence. An image sprang into his mind. Of Oleg. Alone.

He swung the rod in front of him, at Katrine. It was a last desperate lunge, a pathetic attempt to turn the tables, to divert fate. The soft tip hit Katrine's cheek, not hard—she could hardly have felt it—and the blow neither hurt nor unbalanced her. In retrospect, Harry couldn't remember if what happened was intentional, half thought through or sheer unadulterated luck: The accelerated movement of the spinner caused the eight-inch-long stretch of line to wrap itself around her head in such a way that the spinner continued around and struck the front teeth in her open mouth. And when Harry pulled hard at the rod, the tip of the hook did what it was designed to do: it found flesh. It dug into the right-hand corner of Katrine Bratt's mouth. And Harry's despairing pull was so violent that, in consequence, Katrine Bratt's head was wrenched back and around to the right with such power that for a moment he had the impression that he was screwing the head off her body. After an infinitesimal lag, her body followed the head's rotation, first to the right, then propelled toward Harry. Her body was still spinning when she fell onto the deck in front of him.

Harry dropped onto her, knees first. They hit her on either side of the collarbone, and he knew he had rendered her arms immobile.

He twisted the revolver out of the paralyzed hand and pushed the barrel against one of her dilated eyes. The weapon felt light and he could see the iron pressing against her soft eyeball, but she didn't blink. Quite the opposite. She was grinning. A broad grin. From the ripped corner of her mouth and blood-stained teeth, which the rain was trying to wash clean.

30

Scapegoat

Knut Müller-Nilsen had appeared on the quay under Puddefjord Bridge in person as Harry arrived in the cabin cruiser. He, two police officers and the duty psychiatrist joined him below deck, where Katrine Bratt lay handcuffed to the bed. She was given a shot of an anti-psychotic tranquilizer and transported to a waiting vehicle.

Müller-Nilsen thanked Harry for agreeing to handle the matter with discretion.

"Let's try to keep this to ourselves," Harry said, looking up at the leaking heavens. "Oslo will want to take control if this is made public."

"'Course." Müller-Nilsen nodded.

"Kjersti Rødsmoen," said a voice that made them turn around. "The psychiatrist."

The woman peering up at Harry was in her forties, with light, tousled hair and a big bright red down jacket. She was holding a cigarette in her hand and didn't appear to be bothered that the rain was drenching both her and the cigarette.

"Was it dramatic?" she asked.

"No," Harry said, feeling Katrine's revolver pressing against his skin under his waistband. "She surrendered without resistance."

"What did she say?"

"Nothing."

"Nothing?"

"Not a word. What's your diagnosis?"

"Obviously a psychosis," Rødsmoen said without hesitation. "Which does not imply in any way that she's mad. It's just the mind's way of managing the unmanageable. Much the same as the brain choosing to faint when the pain is too great. I would conjecture that she's been under extreme stress for a lengthy period. Could that be correct?"

Harry nodded. "Will she be able to speak again?"

"Yes," Kjersti Rødsmoen said, gazing with disapproval at the wet, extinguished cigarette. "But I don't know when. Right now she needs rest."

"Rest?" Müller-Nilsen snorted. "She's a serial killer."

"And I'm a psychiatrist," Rødsmoen said, dispensing with the cigarette and departing in the direction of a small red Honda that even in the pouring rain looked dusty.

"What are you going to do?" Müller-Nilsen asked.

"Catch the last plane home," Harry said.

"No way. You look like a skeleton. The station's got a deal with the Rica travel hotel. We can drive you there and send on some dry clothes. They've got a restaurant, too."

Once Harry had checked in and was standing in front of the bathroom mirror in the cramped single room, he thought about what Müller-Nilsen had said about looking like a skeleton. And about how close he had been to death. Or had he? After taking a shower and eating in the empty restaurant he went back to his room and tried to sleep. He couldn't and switched on the TV. Crap on all the channels except NRK2, which was showing **Memento.** He had seen the film before. The story was told from the point of view of a man with brain damage and the short-term memory of a goldfish. A woman had been killed. The protagonist had written the name of the killer on a Polaroid, as he knew he would forget. The question was whether he could trust what he had written. Harry kicked off the duvet. The minibar under the TV had a brown door and no lock.

He should have caught the plane home.

He was on his way out of bed when his mobile phone rang somewhere in the room. He put his hand in the pocket of the wet trousers hanging over a chair by the radiator. It was Rakel. She asked where he was. And said they had to talk. And not in his apartment, but somewhere public.

Harry fell back on the bed with closed eyes.

"You're going to tell me we can't keep meeting?" he asked.

"I'm going to tell you we can't keep meeting," she said. "I can't take it."

"It's enough if you tell me on the phone, Rakel."

"No, it's not. It won't hurt enough."

Harry groaned. She was right.

They agreed on eleven o'clock the next morning by Bygdøy's Fram Museum, a tourist attraction where you could disappear in crowds of Germans and Japanese. She asked him what he was doing in Bergen. He told her and said she was to keep it to herself until she read about it in the papers after a couple of days.

They hung up, and Harry lay staring at the minibar as **Memento** continued its course in reverse chronological order. He had almost been killed, the love of his life didn't want to see him anymore and he had concluded the worst case in his experience. Or had he? He hadn't answered when Müller-Nilsen asked why he had chosen to hunt for Bratt on his own, but now he knew. It was the doubt. Or the hope. This desperate hope that it would not end up the way it seemed to be going. Hope that was still there. But now it had to be extinguished, drowned. Come on, he had three good reasons and a pack of dogs in the pit of his stomach all barking as though possessed. So why not just open the minibar anyhow?

Harry got to his feet, went to the bathroom, turned on the tap and drank, letting the jet of water gush over his face. He straightened up and looked into the mirror. Like a skeleton. Why won't the skeleton drink? Aloud, he spat out the answer to his face: "Because then it won't hurt enough."

· · ·

Gunnar Hagen was tired. Tired down to his soul. He looked around. It was almost midnight and he was in a conference room at the top of one of Oslo's central buildings. Everything here was shiny brown: the wood floor, the ceiling with the spotlights, the walls with painted portraits of former club chairmen who had owned the premises, the thirty-square-foot mahogany table and the leather blotting pad in front of each of the twelve men around it. Hagen had been phoned by the chief superintendent an hour earlier and summoned to this address. Some of the people in the room—such as the chief constable—he knew, others he had seen in newspaper photographs, but he had no idea who most of them were. The chief superintendent brought them up to date. The Snowman was a policewoman from Bergen who had been operating for a while from her post in the Crime Squad in Grønland. She had pulled the wool over their eyes, and now that she was caught, they would soon have to go public with the scandal.

When he had finished, the silence lay as thick as the cigar smoke.

The smoke was filtering upward from the end of the table, where a white-haired man leaned back in his chair, his face hidden in shadow. For the first time, he made a sound. Just a tiny sigh. And Gunnar Hagen realized that everyone who had spoken so far had turned to this man.

"Damned tedious, Torleif," said the white-haired man in a surprisingly high-pitched, effeminate voice. "Extremely damaging. Confidence in the system. We are at the top. And that means"—the whole room seemed to be holding its breath as the man puffed on his cigar—"heads will have to roll. The question is whose."

The chief constable cleared his throat. "Do you have any suggestions?"

"Not yet," said the white-hair. "But I believe you and Torleif do. Go ahead."

"In our view, specific mistakes have been made in the appointment and follow-up phases. Human blunders and not systemic flaws. Hence this is not directly a management problem. Therefore we propose that we make a distinction between responsibility and guilt. Management takes the responsibility, is humble and—"

"Skip the basics," said the white-hair. "Who's your scapegoat?"

The chief superintendent adjusted his collar. Gunnar Hagen could see that he was extremely ill at ease.

"Inspector Harry Hole," said the chief superintendent.

Again there was silence as the white-haired man lit his cigar anew. The lighter clicked and clicked. Then sucking noises issued from the shadows and the smoke rose again.

"Not a bad idea," said the high-pitched voice. "Had it been anyone other than Hole I'd have said you would have to find your scapegoat higher up in the system. An inspector is not fat enough as a sacrificial lamb. Indeed, I might have asked you to consider yourself, Torleif. But Hole is an officer with a profile; he's been on that talk show. A popular figure with a certain reputation as a detective. Yes, that would be perceived as fair game. But would he be cooperative?"

"Leave that to us," said the chief superintendent. "Eh, Gunnar?"

Gunnar Hagen gulped. His mind turned—of all things—to his wife. To the sacrifices she had made so that he could have a career. When they'd got married she had broken off her studies and moved with him to wherever the Special Forces, and later the police force, had sent him. She was a wise, intelligent woman, an equal to him in most areas, his superior in some. It was to her he went with both career and moral issues. And she always imparted good advice. Nevertheless, he had perhaps not succeeded in achieving the illustrious career for which they had both hoped. But now things were looking rosier. It was in the cards that his position as Crime Squad supremo would lead onward and upward. It was just a question of not putting a foot wrong. That needn't be so difficult.

"Eh, Gunnar?" repeated the chief superintendent.

It was just that he was so tired. So tired down to the soul. This is for you, he thought. This is what you would have done, darling.

31

The South Pole

Harry and Rakel stood at the bow of the wooden ship **Fram** in the museum, observing a group of Japanese tourists taking pictures of the ropes and masts as, with smiles and nods, they ignored the guide, who was explaining that this simple vessel had transported both Fridtjof Nansen on his failed attempt to be the first to the North Pole in 1893 and Roald Amundsen, when he beat Scott to the South Pole in 1911.

"I left my watch on your table," Rakel said.

"That's an old trick," Harry said. "It means you'll have to come back for it."

She laid a hand over his on the railing and shook her head. "Mathias gave it to me for my birthday."

Which I forgot, Harry thought.

"We're going out and he's going to ask, if I'm not wearing it. And you know what I'm like about lying. Could you . . . ?"

"I'll drop it off before four," he said.

"Thanks. I'll be working, but just put it in the birdhouse on the wall by the door. That's . . ."

She didn't need to say any more. That was where she had always put the house key when he got there after she had gone to bed. Harry slapped the railing with his hand. "According to Arve Støp, Roald Amundsen's problem was that he won. He thinks all the best stories are about losers."

Rakel didn't answer.

"I suppose it's a kind of consolation," Harry said. "Shall we go?"

Outside it was snowing.

"So it's over now?" she said. "Until next time?"

He shot her a quick glance to assure himself she was talking about the Snowman and not them.

"We don't know where the bodies are," he said. "I was with her in her cell this morning before going to the airport, but she won't say anything. Just stares into the air as if there's someone there."

"Did you tell anyone you were going to Bergen alone?" she asked out of the blue.

Harry shook his head.

"Why not?"

"Well," Harry said, "I might have been wrong. Then I could have returned quietly without losing face."

"That wasn't why," she said.

Harry glanced at her again. She looked more fed up than he did.

"To be frank, I have no idea," he said. "I suppose I hoped it wouldn't be her after all."

"Because she's like you? Because it could have been you?"

Harry couldn't even remember telling her they were similar.

"She looked so alone and frightened," Harry said as the snowflakes stung his eyes. "Like someone who'd got lost in the twilight."

Fuck, fuck, fuck! He blinked and felt the tears, like a clenched fist, trying to force their way up his windpipe. Was he having a breakdown? He froze as Rakel's warm hand caressed his neck.

"You're not her, Harry. You're different."

"Am I?" He smiled thinly, removing her hand.

"You don't kill innocent people, Harry."

Harry turned down Rakel's offer of a lift and caught the bus. He stared at the flakes falling and the fjord beyond the window, thinking how Rakel had inserted the word **innocent** only at the last minute.

Harry was about to open his front door on Sofies Gate when he remembered he didn't have any instant coffee, and walked the fifty yards to Niazi, the corner shop.

"Unusual to see you at this time of day," Ali said, taking the money.

"Day off," Harry said.

"What weather, eh? They say there's going to be a foot and a half of snow over the next twenty-four hours."

Harry fidgeted with the coffee jar. "I happened to

frighten Salma and Muhammad in the yard the other day."

"Yes, I heard."

"I'm sorry. I was a bit stressed, that's all."

"That's OK. I was just afraid you'd started drinking again."

Harry shook his head and gave a weak smile. He liked the Pakistani's direct approach.

"Good," said Ali, counting out the change. "How's the redecorating going?"

"Redecorating?" Harry took his change. "Do you mean the mold man?"

"The mold man?"

"Yes, the guy who's checking the cellar for fungus. Stormann or something like that."

"Fungus in the **cellar**?" Ali looked horrified.

"Didn't you know?" Harry said. "You're the chairman of the residents' committee. I'd have thought he would have spoken to you."

Ali shook his head slowly. "Perhaps he spoke to Bjørn."

"Who's Bjørn?"

"Bjørn Asbjørnsen, who's lived on the ground floor for thirteen years," Ali said, giving Harry a reproving look. "And has been the vice chair for just as long."

"Oh, right, Bjørn," Harry said, pretending to note the name.

"I'll check that out," Ali said.

Upstairs in his apartment, Harry pulled off his boots, headed straight for the bedroom and fell asleep. He had hardly slept at the hotel in Bergen. When he awoke his mouth was dry and he had stomach pains. He got up to drink some water and came to a sudden halt when he entered the hall.

He hadn't noticed when he got in, but the walls were back.

He walked from room to room. Magic. It had been done to such perfection that he could swear they hadn't been touched. No old nail holes visible, no lines askew. He touched the sitting-room wall as if to assure himself that this was not a hallucination.

On the sitting-room table, in front of the wing chair, there was a yellow piece of paper. A handwritten message. The letters were neat and strangely attractive.

It's gone. You won't see me anymore. Stormann.
P.S. Had to turn one of the boards in the
wall since I cut myself and blood got onto it.
When blood gets into untreated wood it's
impossible to wash off. The alternative would
have been to paint the wall red.

Harry fell into the wing chair and studied the smooth walls.

It was only when he went into the kitchen that he discovered the miracle was not complete. The calendar with Rakel and Oleg was gone. The sky-blue dress. He swore aloud and feverishly ransacked the wastepaper baskets and even the plastic garbage can in the yard before concluding that the happiest time of his life had been eradicated along with the fungus.

It was definitely a different workday for psychiatrist Kjersti Rødsmoen. And not just because the sun had made a rare appearance in the Bergen sky and was at this moment shining through the windows as she hurried along a corridor in Haukeland University Hospital's psychiatric department, in Sandviken. The department had changed its name so many times that very few Bergensians knew that the current official name was Sandviken Hospital. However, a closed ward was, until further notice, a closed ward, while Bergen waited for someone to claim that the terminology was misleading or at any rate stigmatizing.

She was both dreading and looking forward to the imminent session with the patient who was confined under the strictest security measures she could ever remember. They had reached agreement on the ethical boundaries and procedures with Espen Lepsvik from Kripos and Knut Müller-Nilsen from the Bergen Police. The patient was psychotic and could therefore not undergo a police interview. Kjersti was a psychiatrist and entitled to talk to the patient, but with the patient's best interests at heart, not in a way that might be construed as police questioning. And ultimately there was the issue of client confidentiality. Kjersti Rødsmoen would have to assess for herself whether any information that emerged from the conversation could have such great significance for the police that she should take it further.

And this information would have no validity in a court of law anyway, since it came from a psychotic person. In short, they were moving in a legal and ethical minefield where even the slightest slip might have catastrophic consequences, since everything she did would be scrutinized by the judicial system and the media.

A nurse and a uniformed policeman stood outside the door of the consulting room. Kjersti pointed to the ID card pinned to her white medical coat, and the officer opened the door.

The agreement was that the nurse would keep an eye on what was happening in the room and sound the alarm if necessary.

Kjersti Rødsmoen sat down on the chair and observed the patient. It was hard to imagine that she represented any danger, this small woman with hair hanging over her face, black stitches where her torn mouth had been sewn up and wide-open eyes that seemed to be staring with unfathomable horror at something Kjersti Rødsmoen could not see. Quite the contrary. The woman appeared so incapable of any action that you had the feeling she would be blown over if you so much as breathed on her. The fact that this woman had killed people in cold blood was quite simply inconceivable. But it always was.

"Hello," said the psychiatrist. "I'm Kjersti."

No response.

"What do you think your problem is?" she asked.

The question came straight from the manual governing conversations with psychotics. The alternative was: **How do you think I can help you?**

Still no response.

"You're quite safe in this room. No one will harm you. I won't hurt you. You're absolutely safe."

According to the manual, this solid statement was supposed to reassure the psychotic patient, because a psychosis is primarily about boundless fear. Kjersti Rødsmoen felt like a flight attendant running through the safety procedures before takeoff. Mechanical, routine. Even on routes crossing over the driest of deserts you demonstrate the use of the life jacket. Because the statement proclaims what passengers want to hear: You're allowed to be frightened, but we'll take care of you.

It was time to check her perception of reality.

"Do you know what day it is today?"

Silence.

"Look at the clock on the wall over there. Can you tell me what time it is?"

She received a hunted stare by way of an answer.

Kjersti Rødsmoen waited. And waited. The minute hand of the clock shifted with a quivering goose step.

It was hopeless.

"I'm going now," Kjersti said. "Someone will come fetch you. You're quite safe."

She went to the door.

"I have to talk to Harry." Her voice was deep, almost masculine.

Kjersti stopped and turned. "Who's Harry?"

"Harry Hole. It's urgent."

Kjersti tried to establish eye contact, but the woman was still staring into her own distant world.

"I'm afraid you'll have to tell me who Harry Hole is, Katrine."

"Crime Squad inspector in Oslo. And if you have to say my name, use my surname, Kjersti."

"Bratt?"

"Rafto."

"I see. But can't you tell me what you want to talk to Harry Hole about, so that I can pass it on—"

"You don't understand. They're all going to die."

Kjersti sank slowly back into the chair. "I do understand. And why do you think they're going to die, Katrine?"

And finally there was eye contact. And what Kjersti Rødsmoen saw made her think of one of those orange cards in the game of Monopoly she had in her vacation house: Your houses and hotels have all burned down.

"None of you understands anything," answered the low, masculine voice. "It's not me."

At two o'clock Harry pulled up to the curb in front of Rakel's timber house on Holmenkollveien. It had stopped snowing and he thought it wouldn't be wise to leave telltale tire prints on the driveway. The snow emitted soft, drawn-out screeches under his boots and the sharp daylight flashed against the sunglass-black windows as he approached.

He went up the steps by the front door, opened the hatch of the birdhouse, put Rakel's watch inside and closed it again. He had turned around to leave as the door behind him was wrenched open.

"Harry!"

Harry spun around, swallowed and essayed a smile. Before him stood a man naked but for a towel around his waist.

"Mathias," he said, bewildered, staring at the other man's chest. "You gave me a shock. Thought you'd be working at this time of day."

"Sorry." Mathias laughed, quickly crossing his arms. "I was working late last night. Day off today. I was on my way to the shower when I heard some noise at the door. I assumed it would be Oleg; his key sticks a bit, you see."

Sticks, Harry mused. That must mean Oleg has the key he used to have. And that Mathias has Oleg's. A woman's mind.

"Can I help you, Harry?" Harry noticed that his crossed arms were unnaturally high up on his chest, as though he was trying to hide something.

"Nope," Harry said casually. "I was just driving by and had something for Oleg."

"Why didn't you knock?"

Harry swallowed. "I suddenly realized he wasn't back from school yet."

"Oh? How did you know that?"

Harry nodded to Mathias, as though bestowing approval for an apposite question. There wasn't a shred of suspicion in Mathias's friendly, open face, only a genuine desire to have something clarified that he couldn't grasp.

"The snow," Harry said.

"The snow?"

"Yes. It stopped snowing two hours ago, and there are no prints on the steps."

"Well, I'll be damned, Harry," Mathias burst out enthusiastically. "Now that's what I call applying deductive reasoning to your everyday life. You're a detective, all right, no question about that."

Harry's laughter was strained. Mathias's crossed arms had sunk a little, and now Harry could see what Rakel must have meant by Mathias's physical quirk. Where you expected to see two nipples, the skin just continued, white and unbroken.

"It's hereditary," said Mathias, who had clearly been following Harry's eyes. "My father didn't have any, either. It's rare but quite harmless. And what are we men supposed to do with them anyway?"

"Indeed," Harry said, feeling his earlobes go warm.

"Would you like me to give the something to Oleg?"

Harry shifted his gaze. It settled instinctively on the birdhouse, then moved on.

"I'll drop it off another time," Harry said, grimacing in a way he hoped inspired trust. "You have a shower."

"OK."

"See you."

The first thing Harry did when he got back into the car was to smack both hands on the wheel and curse aloud. He had behaved like a twelve-year-old pilferer caught red-handed. He had lied to Mathias's face. Lied and crawled and been a shit.

He gunned the engine and let the clutch go with a jerk to punish the car. He didn't have the energy to think about it now. Had to focus on other things. But he couldn't, and his mind was racing in a chaotic chain of associations as he tore down to Oslo city center. He thought of blemishes, of flat, red nipples that looked like bloodstains on bare skin. Of bloodstains on untreated wood. And for some reason the mold man's words came into his head: "The alternative would have been to paint the wall red."

The mold man had bled. Harry half closed his eyes and visualized the cut. It must have been a deep cut to have made such a mess that . . . that the alternative would have been to paint the wall red.

Harry jumped on the brakes. He heard a horn, looked in the mirror and saw a Hiace sliding on new snow until the tires got a grip and it skidded alongside him and past.

Harry kicked open the car door, leaped out and saw that he was by the stadium at the bottom of Holmenkollveien. He took a deep breath and broke his tower of thoughts into pieces, dismantled it to see if he could reassemble it. Rebuilt it quickly, without forcing any of the parts. For they slotted in by themselves. His pulse was accelerating. If this made credible sense, everything was turned upside down. And it all fit, it fit that the Snowman had planned how to infiltrate Harry and had just walked in off the street and made himself comfortable. And the bodies—that would explain what had happened to the bodies. Trembling, Harry lit a cigarette and started to try to reconstruct what he had seen in a flash. The chicken feathers with blackened edges.

Harry didn't believe in inspiration, divine insights or telepathy. But he did believe in luck. Not the luck you were born with, but the systematic luck you earned through hard work and spinning yourself such a fine-meshed net that at some point chance would play into your hands. But this was not that kind of luck. This was just a fluke. An atypical fluke. If he was right, of course. Harry looked down and discovered that he was wading through snow. That in fact—quite literally—he had his feet on the ground.

He walked back to the car, took out his mobile phone and rang Bjørn Holm's number.

"Yes, Harry?" answered a sleepy, almost unrecognizable nasal voice.

"You sound hung over."

"I wish." Holm sniffled. "Goddamn cold. Freezing under two duvets. Ache all over—"

"Listen," Harry interrupted. "Do you remember when I asked you to take the temperature of the chickens to find out how long it had been since Sylvia had been in the barn slaughtering them?"

"Yes?"

"And you said afterward that one was warmer than the other two."

Bjørn Holm sniffed. "Yes. Skarre suggested it had a temperature. A theory that's perfectly plausible."

"I think it was warmer because it was killed after Sylvia was killed, in other words, at least an hour later."

"Oh? Who by?"

"By the Snowman."

Harry heard a long, loud snort as snot traveled backward before Holm answered. "You mean she took Sylvia's hatchet, went back and—"

"No, the hatchet was in the forest. I should have reacted when I saw it, but of course I'd never heard of this cutting loop when we were there looking at the chicken carcasses."

"And what did you see?"

"A sliced feather with a blackened edge. You see, I think the Snowman was using the cutting loop."

"Right," said Holm. "But why on earth would she kill a chicken?"

"To paint the whole wall red."

"Eh?"

"I've got an idea," Harry said.

"Shit," mumbled Bjørn Holm. "I suppose this idea means I have to get out of bed."

"Well . . . ," Harry began.

The snowy weather must have just been taking a breather, for at three it started again, and thick, furry flakes began to sweep down over Østland. A gray glazed coat of slush lay on Route E16, winding upward from Bærum.

At the highest point on the road, Sollihøgda,

Harry and Holm turned and skidded their way along the forest road.

Five minutes later Rolf Ottersen was standing in front of them in the doorway. Behind him, in the sitting room, Harry could see Ane Pedersen sitting on the sofa.

"We just wanted to have another look at the barn floor," Harry said.

Rolf Ottersen pushed his glasses back up his nose. Bjørn Holm let out a rasping chesty cough.

"Help yourselves," Ottersen said.

As Holm and Harry walked toward the barn Harry could feel that the thin man was still standing by the door watching them.

The chopping block was in the same place, but there was no sign of any chickens, living or dead. Leaning against the wall there was a spade with a pointed blade. To dig in the ground, not to shovel snow. Harry headed for the tool board. The outline of the hatchet that should have been hanging there reminded Harry of the chalk outlines after bodies have been removed from crime scenes.

"It's my belief the Snowman came here and slaughtered the third chicken to spray blood over the floorboards. The Snowman couldn't turn the boards and the alternative was to paint them red."

"You told me that in the car as well, but I'm still lost."

"If you want to hide red stains you can either remove them or paint everything red. I think the Snowman was trying to hide something. A clue."

"What kind of clue?"

"Something red that's impossible to remove because untreated wood soaks it up."

"Blood? She was trying to hide blood with more blood? Is that your idea?"

Harry snatched a broom and swept away the sawdust around the chopping block. He crouched down and felt Katrine's revolver pressing into him under his belt. Studied the floor. There was still a pink glow.

"Did you bring the photos we took?" Harry asked. "Start checking the places where there was the most blood. It was some way from the chopping block, around here."

Holm took the photos from his bag.

"We know that it was chicken blood on top," Harry said. "But imagine that the first blood that was spilled here had time to saturate the wood and be absorbed into it and therefore didn't mix with the new blood that was poured on top a good while later. What I'm wondering is whether you can still get samples of the first blood—in other words, the blood that soaked into the wood."

Bjørn Holm blinked in dismay. "What the fuck am I supposed to answer to that?"

"Well," Harry said, "the only answer I will accept is yes."

Holm responded with a prolonged fit of coughing.

Harry strolled over to the farmhouse. He knocked, and Rolf Ottersen came out.

"My colleague will be here for a while," Harry said.

"Would you mind if he popped in now and again to get warm?"

"Fine," Ottersen said with reluctance. "What are you digging for now?"

"I was going to ask you the same thing," Harry said. "I saw there was soil on the spade over there."

"Oh, that. Fence posts."

Harry scoured the snow-covered ground that stretched into the dense, dark forest. Wondering what it was Ottersen wanted to fence in. Or out. For he had seen it: the fear in Rolf Ottersen's eyes.

Harry motioned toward the sitting room. "You've got a visitor . . ." He was interrupted by a call on his mobile phone.

It was Skarre.

"We've found another one," he said.

Harry stared into the forest and felt the large snowflakes melting on his cheeks and forehead.

"Another what?" he mumbled in response, even though he had already heard the answer in Skarre's tone.

"Another snowman."

The psychiatrist Kjersti Rødsmoen contacted POB Knut Müller-Nilsen as he and Espen Lepsvik from Kripos were leaving the police station.

"Katrine Bratt has talked," she said. "And I think you should come to the hospital to hear what she has to say."

32

The Tanks

Skarre trod in the tracks in the snow leading to the trees, ahead of Harry. Early-afternoon darkness presaged that winter was on its way. Above them flashed the Tryvann communications tower, and below them twinkled Oslo. Harry had driven straight from Sollihøgda and parked in the large empty parking lot where new graduates collected like lemmings every spring for the obligatory enactment of adult rituals of the species: cavorting around a fire, stupefying themselves with alcohol and indulging in sex with wild abandon. Harry's graduation celebrations were different. He had had just two companions, Bruce Springsteen and "Independence Day," which shrieked from his boom box on top of the German bunker on Nordstrand beach.

"A hiker found it," Skarre said.

"And considered it necessary to report a snowman in the forest to the police?"

"He had a dog with him. It . . . well . . . you'll see for yourself."

They emerged into open terrain. A young man straightened up on catching sight of Skarre and Harry and came toward them.

"Thomas Helle, Missing Persons Unit," he said. "We're glad you're here, Hole."

Harry sent the young officer a look of surprise, but saw that he really meant it.

On a hill in front of him Harry watched the Crime Scene Unit at work. Skarre crawled under the red police cordon and Harry stepped over. A path marked out where they were to walk so as not to destroy any forensic evidence that had not already been destroyed. The Crime Scene officers became aware of Harry and Skarre's presence and silently moved aside to observe the newcomers. As if they had been waiting for this: a chance to display. To collate reactions.

"Oh, shit," Skarre said, recoiling a step.

Harry felt his head go cold, as if all the blood had drained from his brain, leaving a numb, dead sensation of nothing.

It was not the details, because at first glance the naked woman did not seem to have been brutally mutilated. Not like Sylvia Ottersen or Gert Rafto. What scared the living daylights out of him was the construction, the studied, cold-blooded nature of the arrangement. The body sat on top of two large balls of snow that had been rolled up against a tree trunk, one on top of the other like an incomplete snowman. The body leaned against the tree but any sideways movement would have been prevented by a steel wire attached to the thick branch over her head. The wire ended in a rigid noose around her neck, bent in such a way that it touched neither her shoulders nor her neck, like a lasso frozen in motion as it falls perfectly over the victim. Her arms were tied behind her back. The woman's eyes and mouth were closed, affording the face a peaceful expression; she could have been asleep.

It was almost possible to believe the body had been arranged with loving attention. Until the stitches on the naked, pale skin became evident. The edges of the skin under the nearly invisible thread were separated only by a fine, even join of black blood. One welt of stitches ran across her torso, just under her breasts. The other around her neck. Immaculate workmanship, Harry mused. Not a stitch hole visible, not a line askew.

"Looks like that abstract-art shit," Skarre said. "What's it called?"

"Installation art," said a voice behind him.

Harry cocked his head. They were right. But there was something that conflicted with the impression of perfect surgery.

"He chopped her up into chunks," he said in a voice that sounded as if someone had him in a stranglehold. "And reassembled her."

"He?" queried Skarre.

"Maybe to ease transportation," Helle said. "I think I know who she is. She was reported missing by her husband yesterday. He's on his way here now."

"Why do you think it's her?"

"Her husband found a dress with scorch marks." Helle pointed to the body. "Roughly where the stitches are."

Harry concentrated on his breathing. He could see the imperfection now. This was the unfinished snowman. And the knots and angles of the twisted wire were jagged. They seemed rough, arbitrary, tentative. As though this was a mock-up, a rehearsal. The first draft of an unfinished work. And why had he tied her hands behind her back? She must have been dead long before she came here. Was that part of the mock-up? He cleared his throat.

"Why wasn't I told about this before?"

"I reported it to my boss, who reported it to the chief superintendent," said Helle. "All we were told was that we should keep it under our hats until further notice. I assume that had something to do with"—he shot a quick glance at the Crime Scene officers—"this anonymous fugitive."

"Katrine Bratt?" Skarre suggested.

"I didn't hear that name," a voice behind them said.

They turned. The chief superintendent was standing with his hands in trench-coat pockets, legs apart. His cold blue eyes were examining the body. "That should have been in the autumn art exhibition."

The younger officers stared wide-eyed at the chief superintendent, who, unmoved, turned to Harry.

"A couple of words in your ear, Inspector."

They walked over to the police cordon.

"One hell of a mess," the chief superintendent said. He was facing Harry but his eyes wandered down to the carpet of lights below. "We've had a meeting. That's why I had to talk to you in private."

"Who's had a meeting?"

"That doesn't matter, Harry. The crux is that we've made a decision."

"Uh-huh?"

The chief superintendent stamped his feet in the snow, and Harry wondered for a moment if he should point out that he was contaminating a crime scene.

"I'd been thinking of discussing this with you tonight, Harry. In quieter, calmer surroundings. But the matter has become urgent with the discovery of this new body. The press will be on it within a couple of hours. And as we don't have the time we hoped for, we'll have to go live with naming the Snowman. And explain how Katrine Bratt managed to get her post and operate without our knowing. Top management has to take responsibility, of course. That's what management is for, goes without saying."

"What's this really about, boss?"

"The credibility of the Oslo Police. Shit is subject to gravity, Harry. The higher up it starts, the greater the soiling of the force as a whole. Individuals at a lower level can commit blunders and be forgiven. But if we lose people's confidence that the police are being governed with a modicum of competence, that we have some control, then we're lost. I assume you realize what's at stake, Harry."

"Time's pressing, boss."

The chief superintendent's gaze returned from its urban perambulations and locked on to the inspector. "Do you know what **kamikaze** means?"

Harry shifted his weight from one foot to the other. "Being Japanese, brainwashed and crashing your plane into an American aircraft carrier?"

"That's what I thought, too. But Gunnar Hagen says the Japanese never used the word themselves; the American code breakers misinterpreted it. **Kamikaze** is the name of a typhoon that rescued the Japanese in a battle against the Mongolians sometime in the thirteenth century. Literally translated, it means 'divine wind.' Quite picturesque, isn't it?"

Harry didn't answer.

"We need a wind like that now," said the chief superintendent.

Harry nodded slowly. He understood. "You want someone to take the blame for Katrine Bratt's appointment? For not checking her out? For the whole shitty mess, in short?"

"Asking someone to sacrifice himself in this way doesn't feel good. Especially when said sacrifice means your own skin is saved. Then you have to remember that this is all about something greater than the individual." The chief superintendent's gaze veered out over the town again. "The anthill, Harry. The hard work, the loyalty, the at times senseless self-denial. It's the anthill that makes it all worthwhile."

Harry ran a hand over his face. Treachery. Stabbed in the back. Cowardliness. He tried to swallow his fury. Told himself the chief superintendent was right. Someone had to be sacrificed and the blame had to be placed as low down in the hierarchy as possible. Fair enough. He should in fact have checked Katrine out before.

Harry straightened up. In a strange way it felt like a relief. For a very long time he had sensed it would end like this for him, so long that basically he had come to accept it. The way his colleagues in the Dead Policemen's Society had made their exit: without any fanfares and badges of honor, without anything except self-respect and the respect of those who knew them, the few who knew what it was all about. The anthill.

"I understand," Harry said. "And I accept. You'll have to instruct me on the manner in which you would like it to happen. However, I still believe we'll have to postpone the press conference for a few hours until we know a little more."

The chief superintendent shook his head. "You don't understand, Harry."

"There may be new factors in the case."

"You're not the one who will be taking the short straw."

"We're checking to see—" Harry paused. "What did you just say, boss?"

"That was the original suggestion, but Gunnar Hagen refused to go along with it. So he will accept the blame. He's in his office now, writing his letter of resignation. I just wanted to inform you so that you know when the press conference takes place."

"Hagen?" said Harry.

"A good soldier," said the chief superintendent, patting Harry on the shoulder. "I'm off now. The press conference is at eight in the Great Hall, OK?"

Harry watched the chief superintendent's back fade into the distance and felt his mobile phone vibrate in his jacket pocket. He read the display before deciding to answer.

"**Love me tender,**" Bjørn Holm said in English. "I'm at the institute."

"What have you got?"

"It was human blood in the floorboards. The lab lady here says that unfortunately blood is pretty overrated as a source of DNA, so she doubts we'll find any cell material for a DNA profile. But she checked the blood type and guess what we found."

Bjørn Holm paused before realizing that Harry had no intention of playing **Who Wants to Be a Millionaire,** and went on.

"There's one blood type that eliminates most people, let's put it like that. Two out of every hundred have it, and in the whole of the archives there are only a hundred and twenty-three criminals with it. If Katrine Bratt has this blood type it's an excellent indicator that she bled in Ottersen's barn."

"Check with the Incident Room. They've got a list of the blood types of every officer at the HQ."

"They do? Jeez, then I'll check them out right away."

"But don't be disappointed if you find out she's not B negative."

Harry enjoyed his colleague's speechless amazement and waited.

"How in Christ's name did you know it was B negative?"

"How quickly can you meet me at the Anatomy Department?"

It was six o'clock and employees not on flextime at Sandviken Hospital had gone home some time ago. But the light in Kjersti Rødsmoen's office was still burning. The psychiatrist saw that Knut Müller-Nilsen and Espen Lepsvik had their notebooks at the ready, then glanced at her own and started off.

"Katrine Rafto tells me she loved her father above all else." She peered up at the two men. "She was just a girl when he was hung out to dry in the newspapers as a man of violence. Katrine was hurt, frightened and very confused. At school she was bullied because of what was written in the press. Shortly afterward her parents split up. When Katrine was nineteen her father disappeared at the same time as one woman was killed in Bergen and another vanished. The investigation was dropped, but inside the police force and out it was thought her father had murdered the women and taken his own life, knowing that he couldn't get away with it. Katrine decided then and there that she would join the police, clear up the murders and avenge her father."

Kjersti Rødsmoen looked up. Neither of the two was taking notes; they were just watching her.

"So after her law degree she applied to the police academy," Rødsmoen continued. "And after finishing her training she was employed by the Crime Squad in Bergen. Where she soon started going through her father's case in her free time. Until this was discovered and stopped, and Katrine applied for a transfer to the Sexual Offenses Unit. Is that correct?"

"Affirmative," said Müller-Nilsen.

"It was seen to that she did not go anywhere near the investigation into her father, so instead she started to examine related cases. While she was going through the national missing-persons reports she made an interesting discovery. Namely, that in the years after her father's disappearance women were being reported missing under conditions that bore several points of similarity with the disappearance of Onny Hetland." Kjersti Rødsmoen flicked over the page. "However, to make any progress Katrine needed help, and she knew she wouldn't get this help in Bergen. Accordingly, she resolved to put someone on the case who had experience with serial killers. Though this had to happen without anyone knowing that she, Rafto's daughter, was behind it."

The Kripos officer, Espen Lepsvik, slowly shook his head as Kjersti continued.

"After thorough groundwork she decided on Inspector Harry Hole at the Crime Squad in Oslo. She wrote a letter to him under the mysterious-sounding sobriquet the Snowman, in order to awaken his curiosity, and because a snowman had been mentioned in several of the witnesses' statements connected with the disappearances. A snowman had also been mentioned in her father's notes on the Ulriken Mountain killing. When the Oslo Crime Squad advertised for a detective, stating a preference for a woman, she applied and was invited to an interview. She said they offered her the job more or less before she had even sat down."

Rødsmoen paused, but as the two men said nothing, she went on. "From the very first day, Katrine made sure that she came into contact with Harry Hole and was put onto the investigation. With all that she already knew about Hole and the case, it was relatively easy for her to manipulate him and steer him toward Bergen and her father's disappearance. And, with Hole's help, she also found her father. In a freezer on Finnøy."

Kjersti removed her glasses.

"You don't need much imagination to understand that an experience of this nature forms the basis of a psychological reaction. The stress became even worse when three times she thought the killer had been unmasked. First Idar Vetlesen, then a"—she squinted at her notes—"Filip Becker. And finally Arve Støp. Only to discover that it was the wrong person each time. She tried to force a confession out of Støp herself, but gave up when she realized that he was not the man she was hunting. She fled the place when she heard her colleagues approaching. She says she didn't want to be stopped until she had completed her mission. Which was to identify the perpetrator. At this point I think we can safely say that she was well into the psychosis. She returned to Finnøy, where she was convinced Hole would track her down. And, in fact, she turned out to be correct. When he appeared, she disarmed him to make him listen while she instructed him on what he had to do next in the investigation."

"Disarmed?" said Müller-Nilsen. "It's our understanding that she surrendered without any fuss."

"She says the injury to her mouth was caused by Harry Hole catching her off guard," said Kjersti Rødsmoen.

"Should we believe a psychotic?" Lepsvik asked.

"She's no longer psychotic," Rødsmoen stated with emphasis. "We ought to keep her under observation for a couple more days, but after that you should be prepared to take her back. If you still consider her a suspect, that is."

The last remark was left hanging in the air until Espen Lepsvik leaned across the table.

"Does that mean you think that Katrine Bratt is telling the truth?"

"That doesn't fall within my special field and I cannot comment," Rødsmoen said, closing her notebook.

"And if I were to ask you as a non-specialist?"

A brief smile played on Rødsmoen's lips. "I think you should continue to believe what you already believe, Inspector."

· · ·

Bjørn Holm had walked the short distance from the Institute of Forensic Medicine to its neighbor, the Anatomy Department, and was waiting in the garage when Harry arrived by car from Tryvann. Beside Holm was the green-overalled technician with earrings, the one who had been trundling a body away the last time Harry had been here.

"Lund-Helgesen's not here today," Holm informed him.

"Perhaps you can show us around, then," Harry said to the technician.

"We aren't allowed to show—," Green Overalls began, but was interrupted by Harry.

"What's your name?"

"Kai Robøle."

"OK, Robøle," Harry said, presenting his police ID. "I give you permission."

Robøle shrugged and unlocked the door. "You were lucky to find anyone in. It's always empty after five o'clock."

"I had the impression you people did a lot of overtime," Harry said.

Robøle shook his head. "Not in the cellar with all the stiffs, man. Here we like to work in daylight." He smiled, although he didn't seem to be amused. "What is it you'd like to see?"

"The most recent bodies," Harry said.

The technician unlocked and led them through two doors to a tiled room with eight sunken tanks, four on each side with a narrow aisle between. Each tank was covered with a metal lid.

"They're under there," Robøle said. "Four in each tank. The tanks are filled with alcohol."

"Neat," said Holm under his breath.

It was impossible to say whether the technician misunderstood on purpose, but he answered: "Forty percent, no mixers."

"Thirty-two bodies, then," Harry said. "Is that all?"

"We have around forty bodies, but these are the latest. They usually have them lying here for a year before we start to use them."

"How are they brought in?"

"By car from the funeral parlor. Some we collect ourselves."

"And you bring them in via the garage?"

"Yes."

"And what happens then?"

"What happens? Well, we preserve them, make an incision at the top of the thigh and inject a fixative. They keep well like that. Then we make metal tags and stamp the number that's in the paperwork."

"Which paperwork?"

"The paperwork that comes with the body. It's filed up in the office. We attach one tag to the toe, one to a finger and one to an ear. We try to keep the body parts registered, even when they've been split up, so that as much of the body can be cremated together as possible when the time comes."

"Do you regularly check the bodies against the paperwork?"

"Check?" He scratched his head. "Only if we have to transport bodies. Most bodies are bequeathed here in Oslo, so we supply universities in Tromsø, Trondheim and Bergen when they don't have enough."

"So it's conceivable that someone might be lying here who shouldn't be?"

"Oh, no. Everyone here has donated his body to the institute in a will."

"That's what I was wondering," Harry said, squatting down by one of the tanks.

"What?"

"Listen now, Robøle. I'm going to ask you a hypothetical question. And I want you to think carefully before you answer. OK?"

The technician gave a hurried nod.

Harry stood up to his full height. "Is it conceivable that anyone with access to these rooms could bring bodies here through the garage at night, put on a metal tag with a fictitious number, place the body in one of these tanks and assume with a relatively high degree of probability that it will never be discovered?"

Kai Robøle hesitated. Scratched his head a bit more. Ran a finger down the row of earrings.

Harry shifted his weight. Holm's mouth had slipped half open.

"In a sense," Robøle said. "There's nothing to stop it happening."

"Nothing to stop it happening?"

Robøle shook his head and gave a quick laugh. "No, not at all. It's perfectly feasible."

"In that case I'd like to see these bodies now."

Robøle looked up at the tall policeman. "Here? Now?"

"You can start at the back on the left."

"I think I'll have to call someone to give me authorization."

"If you want to delay our murder investigation, then be my guest."

"Murder?" Robøle screwed up one eye.

"Heard of the Snowman?"

Robøle blinked twice. Then he turned, walked over to the chains hanging from a motorized pulley in the ceiling, pulled them down to the tank with a loud rattle and attached the two hooks to the metal lid on the tank, grabbed the remote control and pressed. The pulley hummed and the chains began to coil. From the tank the lid slowly rose as Harry and Holm followed it with their eyes. Fixed to the underside of the lid were two horizontal sheets of metal, one beneath the other, separated by one vertical sheet. On each side of the central partition lay a naked white body. They resembled pale dolls, and this impression was reinforced by the rectangular black incisions on their thighs. When the bodies were at hip height the technician pressed the stop button. In the ensuing silence they could hear the deep sigh of dripping alcohol echoing around the white-tiled room.

"Well?" said Robøle.

"No," Harry said. "Next."

The technician repeated the procedure. Four new bodies rose from the neighboring tank.

Harry shook his head.

As the third quartet came into view Harry flinched. Kai Robøle, who misinterpreted Harry's reaction as horror, smiled with satisfaction.

"What's that?" Harry asked, pointing to the headless woman.

"Probably a return from one of the other universities," Robøle said. "Ours tend to be whole."

Harry bent down and touched the body. It was cold, and the consistency unnaturally firm because of the fixative. He ran a finger along the severed edge. It was smooth and the flesh pallid.

"We use a scalpel on the exterior and then a fine saw," the technician explained.

"Mm." Harry leaned across the body, grabbed the woman's right arm and pulled her over so that she was facing him.

"What are you doing?" screamed Robøle.

"Can you see anything on her back?" Harry asked Holm, who was standing on the other side of the body.

Holm nodded. "A tattoo. Looks like a flag."

"Which one?"

"Haven't a clue. Green, yellow and red. With a pentagram in the middle."

"Ethiopia," Harry said, letting go of the woman, who fell back into position. "This woman did not donate her body, but she has been donated, if I can put it like that. This is Sylvia Ottersen."

Kai Robøle kept blinking as though hoping something would go away if he blinked enough times.

Harry placed a hand on his shoulder. "Get hold of someone who has access to the paperwork for the bodies and go through all of them. Now. I have to be on my way."

"What's going on?" Holm asked. "I honestly can't get my head around this."

"Try," Harry said. "Forget everything you thought you knew and try."

"Right, but what's going on?"

"There are two answers to that," Harry said. "One is that we're closing in on the Snowman."

"And the other?"

"I don't know."

Part Five

33

The Snowman

It was the day the snow came. At eleven o'clock in the morning, large flakes had appeared from a colorless sky and invaded the fields, gardens and lawns of Romerike like an armada from outer space.

Mathias was sitting alone in his mother's Toyota Corolla in front of a house on Kolloveien. He had no idea what his mother was doing inside the house. She had said it wouldn't take long. But it had already taken a long time. She had left the key in the ignition and the car radio was playing "Under Snø," by the new girl group Dollie. He kicked open the car door and went out. Because of the snow an almost unnatural silence had settled over the houses. He bent down, picked up a handful of the sticky white stuff and cupped it into a snowball.

Today they had thrown snowballs at him in the school playground and called him "Mathias No-Nips," his so-called classmates in 7A. He hated secondary school, hated being thirteen years old. It had begun after the first gym class, when they found out he didn't have any nipples. According to the doctor, it could have been hereditary, and he had been tested for a number of illnesses. Mom had told him and Dad that her father, who died when Mom was small, didn't have any nipples, either. But looking through one of his grandmother's photo albums Mathias had found a picture of his grandfather during the mowing season in trousers and suspenders with a bare chest. And he definitely had nipples then.

Mathias packed the snowball harder between his hands. He wanted to throw it at someone. Hard. So hard that it hurt. But there was no one to launch it at. He could make someone to throw it at. He placed the packed snowball in the snow beside the garage. Started rolling it. The snow crystals hooked into one another. After he had done a circuit of the lawn, it already reached his stomach and had left a trail of brown grass. He continued to roll it. When he couldn't push it any farther, he started a new one. It was big, too. He just managed to lift it up onto the first one. Then he made a head, climbed up and placed it on top. The snowman stood by one of the windows in the house. Sounds were coming out. He broke a couple of twigs off the apple tree and stuck them in the snowman's sides. Dug up some gravel by the front steps, shinnied up again and made two eyes and a line of pebbles for a smile. Then he placed his thighs around the snowman's head, and, sitting on the shoulders, looked through the window.

In the illuminated room stood a man with a bare

chest thrusting his hips backward and forward with his eyes closed, as if he were dancing. From the bed in front of him protruded a pair of spread legs. Mathias couldn't see, but he knew that it was Sara. That it was his mother. That they were fucking.

Mathias tightened his thighs around the snow head, felt the cold in his crotch. He was unable to breathe; a steel wire seemed to tauten around his throat.

Again and again the man's hips banged against his mother. Mathias stared inside at the man's chest as the cold numbness spread from his crotch to his stomach and up until it reached his head. The man was thrusting his willy inside her. As they did in the magazines. Soon the man would be spraying sperm inside his mother. And the man didn't have any nipples.

Suddenly the man stopped. His eyes were open now. And they were looking at Mathias.

Mathias loosened his grip, slid down the back of the snowman, curled up and sat as quiet as a mouse, waiting. His mind was reeling. He was a smart boy, he'd always been told that. Strange, but with excellent mental faculties, the teachers had said. Thus all his thoughts were falling into place now, like pieces of a jigsaw he had been doing for a long time. But the picture that emerged was still incomprehensible, intolerable. It couldn't be right. It had to be right.

Mathias listened to his own breathless gasps.

It was right. He just knew it. Everything fit. His mother's coldness to his father. The conversations they thought he couldn't hear; his father's desperate threats and pleas for her to stay, not just for his sake but for Mathias's sake. Good God, they had a child together, didn't they? And his mother's bitter laugh. Grandfather in the photo album and Mom's lies. Of course, Mathias hadn't believed it when Stian from his class had said that Mathias No-Nips's mom had a lover living on the plateau—he said his aunt had told him. For Stian was just as stupid as the others and didn't understand anything. Not even when, two days later, Stian found his cat hanging from the top of the school flagpole.

Dad didn't know. Mathias could feel it in his whole body that Dad thought Mathias was . . . was his. And he must never know that he wasn't. Never. It would kill him. Mathias would rather die himself. Yes, that was exactly what he wanted. He wanted to die, wanted to go, to go away from his mother and the school and Stian and . . . everything. He got up, kicked the snowman and ran to the car.

He would take her with him. She would die, too.

When his mother came out and he unlocked the door, almost forty minutes had passed since she had gone into the house.

"Is there anything wrong?" she asked.

"Yes," Mathias said, moving on the backseat so that she could see him in the mirror. "I saw him."

"What do you mean?" she said, putting the key in the ignition and turning.

"The snowman . . ."

"And what did the snowman look like?" The engine started with a roar and she let the clutch go with such a jerk that he almost dropped the car jack he was clinging to.

"Dad's waiting for us," she said. "We'll have to get a move on."

She switched on the radio. Just an announcer droning on about the American elections and Ronald Reagan. Nonetheless she turned up the volume. They drove over the crest of the hill, down toward the main road and the river. In the field ahead of them stiff yellow straw poked through the snow.

"We're going to die," Mathias said.

"What did you say?"

"We're going to die."

She turned down the voice on the radio. He steeled himself. Leaned forward between the seats and raised his arm.

"We're going to die," he whispered.

Then he struck.

The jack hit the back of her head with a crunch. And his mother didn't seem to react, just sort of stiffened in her seat, so he hit her again. And again. The car jumped as her foot slid off the clutch pedal, but still no sound came from her. Perhaps the talking thing in her brain had been smashed, Mathias thought. At the fourth blow he could feel her head give; it seemed to have gone soft. The car rolled forward and picked up speed, but he knew she was no longer conscious. His mother's Toyota Corolla crossed the main road and continued across the field on the other side. The snow slowed the car but not enough for it to stop. Then it hit the water and glided out into the broad black river. It tilted and was motionless for a moment before the current caught it and spun it around. The water seeped in through the doors and the bodywork, through the handles and at the side of the windows as they gently floated downstream. Mathias looked out the window, waved to a car on the main road, but the driver didn't appear to have seen him. The water was rising in the Toyota. And suddenly he heard his mother mumble something. He watched her, saw the deep gashes under her bloodstained hair at the back of her head. She was moving under the seat belt. The water was rising quickly now; it was already up to Mathias's knees. He felt his panic mounting. He didn't want to die. Not now, not like this. He smashed the jack into the side window. The glass shattered and the water poured in. He jumped up onto the seat and squeezed his way through the gap between the top of the window and the mass of water flooding in. One of his boots got snagged on the frame; he twisted his foot and felt the boot float away. Then he was free and began to swim ashore. He saw that a car had stopped on the main road and two people had got out and were on their way through the snow to the river.

Mathias was a good swimmer. He was good at a lot of things. So why didn't they like him? A man waded out and dragged him ashore as he approached the riverbank. Mathias slumped into the snow. Not because he couldn't stand but because instinctively he knew it was the smartest thing to do. He closed his eyes and heard an agitated voice by his ear ask whether there was anyone else in the car. If there was they might still be able to save them. Mathias slowly shook his head. The voice asked whether he was sure.

The police would later ascribe the accident to the slippery road conditions and the drowned woman's head injuries to the impact from driving off the road and hitting the water. In fact the car was barely damaged, but in the end it was the only plausible explanation. Just as shock was the only possible explanation for the boy's answer when those first on the scene asked him several times whether there was anyone else in the car and he said at length: "No, only me. I'm alone."

"No, only me," Mathias repeated six years later. "I'm alone."

"Thanks," said the boy standing in front of him and putting down his tray on the cafeteria table that until then Mathias had had to himself. Outside, the rain was drumming its welcome march on the medical students in Bergen, a rhythmical march that would last until spring.

"You new to medicine as well?" the boy asked, and Mathias watched his knife cut the thick Wiener schnitzel.

He nodded.

"You've got an Østland accent," the boy said. "Didn't get into Oslo?"

"Didn't want to go to Oslo," Mathias said.

"Why not?"

"Don't know anyone there."

"Who do you know here, then?"

"No one."

"I don't know anyone here, either. What's your name?"

"Mathias. Lund-Helgesen. And you?"

"Idar Vetlesen. Have you been up Ulriken Mountain?"

"No."

But Mathias had been up Ulriken. And up Fløyen and Sandviksfjellet. He had been in the narrow alleyways, to Fisketorget, to Torgalmenningen—the main square, seen the penguins and the sea lions at the aquarium, drunk beer in Wesselstuen, listened to an overrated new band in Garage and seen SK Brann lose a football match at Brann Stadium. Mathias had found time to do all these things that you should do with student friends. Alone.

He did the circuit with Idar again and pretended it was the first time.

Mathias soon discovered that Idar was a social suckerfish, and by fastening onto him, Mathias found himself at the heart of all the action.

"Why did you choose to study medicine?" Idar asked Mathias at a party in an apartment belonging to a student with a traditional Bergensian name. It was the evening of the medical students' annual autumn ball, and Idar had invited two nice Bergen girls in black dresses and with pinned-up hair, who were leaning forward to hear what the two of them were saying.

"To make the world a better place," Mathias said,

drinking up his lukewarm Hansa beer. "What about you?"

"To earn money, of course," Idar said, winking at the girls.

One of them sat down beside Mathias.

"You've got a blood-donor badge," she said. "What blood type are you?"

"B negative. And what do you do?"

"Let's not talk about that. B negative? Isn't that extremely rare?"

"Yes. How did you know?"

"I'm training as a nurse."

"Oh," Mathias said. "Which year?"

"Third."

"Have you thought about what you're going to speciali—"

"Let's not talk about that," she said and placed a hot little hand on his thigh.

She repeated the same sentence five hours later while lying naked beneath him in his bed.

"That's never happened to me before," he said.

She smiled up at him and stroked his cheek. "So there's nothing wrong with me, then?"

"What?" he stammered. "No."

She laughed. "I think you're sweet. You're nice and thoughtful. What happened to these, by the way?"

She pinched his chest.

Mathias felt something black descend. Something nasty and black and wonderful.

"I was born like that," he said.

"Is it a disease?"

"It comes with Raynaud's phenomenon and scleroderma."

"What?"

"A hereditary disease causing connective tissue in the body to thicken."

"Is it dangerous?" She carefully stroked his chest with her fingers.

Mathias smiled and sensed an incipient erection. "Raynaud's phenomenon just means that your toes and fingers go cold and white. Scleroderma is worse . . ."

"Oh?"

"The thickened connective tissue makes the skin tighten. Everything is smoothed out and wrinkles disappear."

"Isn't that good?"

He was aware of her hand groping southward. "The tightened skin begins to hinder facial expressions—you have fewer of them. It's like your face is stiffening into a mask."

The hot little hand closed around his dick.

"Your hands and, in time, your arms are bent and you can't straighten them. In the end you're left standing there, quite unable to move, as if you're suffocated by your own skin."

She whispered breathlessly: "Sounds like a gruesome death."

"The best advice is to commit suicide before the

pain drives you insane. Would you mind lying at the end of the bed? I'd like to stand and do it."

"That's why you study medicine, isn't it?" she said. "To find out more. To find a way of living with it."

"All I want," he said, getting up and standing at the end of the bed with his erect penis swaying in the air, "is to find out when it's time to die."

The newly qualified Dr. Mathias Lund-Helgesen was a popular man in the Neurology Department of Bergen's Haukeland University Hospital. Both colleagues and patients described him as a competent, thoughtful person and, not least, a good listener. The latter was a great help, as he often received patients with a variety of syndromes, generally inherited and often without much prospect of a cure, only some relief. And when on rare occasions patients were diagnosed with the dreadful condition of scleroderma they were always referred to the friendly young doctor who was beginning to consider specializing in immunology. It was early autumn when Laila Aasen and her husband came to him with their daughter. The daughter's joints had stiffened and she was in pain; Mathias's first thought was that it could be Bekhterev's disease. Both Laila Aasen and her husband confirmed that there had been rheumatic illnesses on their side of the family, so Mathias took blood samples from them as well as from the daughter.

When the results came back Mathias was sitting at

his desk and had to read them three times. And the same nasty and black and wonderful feeling surged to the surface again. The tests were negative. Both in the medical sense—Bekhterev's disease could be eliminated as a cause of the afflictions—and in the more familiar sense, Herr Aasen could be eliminated as the girl's father. And Mathias knew he didn't know. But she knew; Laila Aasen knew. He had seen her face twitch when he asked for blood samples from all three of them. Was she still screwing the other man? What did he look like? Did he live in a detached house with a big front lawn? What secret flaws did he have? And how and when would the daughter find out that all her life she had been deceived by this lying whore?

Mathias looked down and realized he had knocked over his glass of water. A large wet stain was spreading across his crotch, and he felt the cold spread to his stomach and up toward his head.

He phoned Laila Aasen and informed her of the result. The medical result. She thanked him, audibly relieved, and they hung up. Mathias stared at the telephone for a long time. God, how he hated her. That night he lay unable to sleep on the narrow mattress in his apartment. He tried to read, but the letters danced in front of his eyes. He tried masturbating, which as a rule made him tired enough to sleep afterward, but he couldn't concentrate. He stuck a needle in the big toe that had gone completely white again, just to see if he had any sensation. In the end he huddled up under the duvet and cried until daybreak painted the night sky gray.

Mathias was also responsible for more general neurological cases, and one of them was an officer from the Bergen Police Station. After the examination, the middle-aged policeman stood up and dressed. The combination of body odor and boozy breath was numbing.

"Well?" growled the policeman, as if Mathias were one of his subordinates.

"First stages of neuropathy," Mathias replied. "The nerves under your feet are damaged. There is reduced sensation."

"Do you think that's why I've started walking like a goddamned drunk?"

"Are you a drunk, Rafto?"

The policeman stopped buttoning up his shirt and a flush rose up his neck, like mercury up a thermometer. "What did you say, you snot-nosed bastard?"

"As a rule too much alcohol is the cause of polyneuropathy. If you continue to drink, you risk permanent brain damage. Have you heard of Korsakoff, Rafto? You haven't? Let's hope you never do because if you hear his name it's generally in connection with an extremely unpleasant syndrome named after him. When you look in the mirror and ask yourself if you're a drunk, I don't know what you answer, but I suggest that next time you ask an additional question: Do I want to die now or do I want some more time?"

Gert Rafto scrutinized the young man in the doctor's coat. Then he swore under his breath, marched out and slammed the door behind him.

Four weeks later Rafto called. He asked if Mathias could come to see him.

"Drop in tomorrow," Mathias said.

"I can't. It's urgent."

"Then get yourself to the emergency room."

"Listen to me, Lund-Helgesen. I've been in bed for three days without being able to move. You're the only one who's asked me straight out if I'm a drunk. Yes, I am a drunk. And no, I don't want to die. Not yet."

Gert Rafto's apartment stank of garbage, empty beer bottles and him. But not of leftovers, for there was no food in the house.

"This is a B-one vitamin supplement," Mathias said, holding the syringe to the light. "It will get you back on your feet."

"Thank you," Gert Rafto said. Five minutes later he was asleep.

Mathias walked around the apartment. On the desk there was a photograph of Rafto with a dark-haired girl on his shoulders. Above the desk on the wall hung photographs of what must have been murder scenes. Many photographs. Mathias stared at them. Took a couple of them down and studied the details. Goodness, how sloppy they had been, the murderers. Their inefficiency was especially noticeable on the bodies with wounds from both sharp and blunt instruments. He opened drawers and looked for more photographs. He found reports, notes, a few valuables: rings, ladies' watches, necklaces. And newspaper clippings. He read them. Gert Rafto's name ran right through them, often with quotes from press conferences at which he talked about the murderers' stupidity and how he had caught them. Because it was clear he had caught them, every single one.

Six hours later, when Gert Rafto awoke, Mathias was still there. He was sitting by the bed with two murder reports in his lap.

"Tell me," Mathias said. "How would you commit a murder if you didn't want to get caught?"

"Avoid my beat," Rafto said, looking around for something to drink. "If the detective's good, you haven't got a hope in hell anyway."

"And if I still wanted to do it on the beat of a good detective?"

"Then I would cozy up to the detective before committing the murder," Gert Rafto said. "And then, after the murder, I would kill him, too."

"Funny," Mathias said. "That's just what I was thinking."

In the weeks that followed, Mathias made quite a few house calls to Gert Rafto. He recovered quickly and they talked often and at length about illness, lifestyle and death, and about the only two things Gert Rafto loved on this earth: his daughter, Katrine, who, incomprehensibly, returned his love, and the little cabin on Finnøy, which was the one place he could be sure of finding peace. Mostly, though, they talked about the murder cases Gert Rafto had solved. About the triumphs. And Mathias encouraged him, told him the fight against alcohol could be won, he could celebrate new triumphs so long as he kept off the bottle.

And by the time late autumn came to Bergen, with even shorter days and even longer showers, Mathias had his plan ready.

One morning he called Laila Aasen at home.

He gave his name, and she listened in silence as he explained the reason for his call. The daughter's blood sample had revealed new information and he now knew that Bastian Aasen was not the child's biological father. It was important that he be given the real father's blood sample. This would of necessity mean that the daughter and Bastian would be apprised of the relationship. Would she give her consent?

Mathias waited, allowing this to sink in.

Then he said that if she considered it important that the matter remain behind closed doors, he would still like to help, but it would have to be done "off the record."

"Off the record?" she repeated with the apathy of someone in shock.

"As a doctor I'm bound to observe ethical rules regarding candor to the patient, here, your daughter. But I'm researching syndromes and am therefore particularly interested in following up her case. If, with the utmost discretion, you could meet me this afternoon . . ."

"Yes," she whispered in a tremulous voice. "Yes, please."

"Good. Catch the last cable car of the day to the top of Ulriken. There we will be undisturbed and can walk back down. I hope you appreciate what I'm risking, and please don't mention this meeting to a living soul."

"Of course not! Trust me."

He was still holding the receiver to his ear after she had hung up. With his lips to the gray plastic, he whispered: "And why should anyone trust you, you little whore?"

It was only when she was lying in the snow with a scalpel to her throat that Laila Aasen admitted she had told a friend she was going to meet him. Because in fact they had originally had a dinner date. But she'd mentioned only his Christian name and not why they were meeting.

"Why did you say anything at all?"

"To tease her," Laila howled. "She's so nosy."

He pressed the thin steel harder against her skin and Laila sobbed her friend's name and address. After which she said no more.

When, two days later, Mathias was reading about the murder of Laila Aasen and the disappearances of Onny Hetland and Gert Rafto in the newspaper, he had mixed feelings. First of all, he was displeased with the murder of Laila Aasen. It had not gone as he had planned; he had lost control in a frenzy of fury and panic. Hence there had been too much mess, too much to clean up, too much that reminded him of the photographs in Rafto's apartment. And too little time to enjoy the revenge, the justice of it.

The murder of Onny Hetland had been even worse, nearly a catastrophe. Twice his courage had failed him as he was about to ring her doorbell, and he had walked away. The third time he had realized he was too late. Someone was already there ringing the bell. Gert Rafto. After Rafto had left he had rung and introduced himself as Rafto's assistant and had been let in. But Onny had said she wouldn't tell him what she had told Rafto; she had given a promise that the matter would stay strictly between them. Only when he had made an incision in her hand with the scalpel did she talk.

Mathias gleaned from what she said that Gert Rafto had decided to solve the case under his own steam. He wanted to rebuild his reputation, the fool!

There had been nothing to criticize about the disposal of Onny Hetland, however. Very little noise, very little blood. And the carving up of her body in the shower had been efficient and quick. He had packed all the parts in plastic and placed them in the large backpack and bag he had brought along for the purpose. On his visits to Rafto, Mathias had been told that one of the first things the police check in murder cases is cars observed in the vicinity and reg-istered taxi rides. So he walked the whole way back to his apartment.

All that remained now was the last part of Gert Rafto's instructions for the perfect murder: Kill the detective.

Strangely enough this was the best of the three murders. Strange because Mathias had no feelings for Rafto, none of the hatred that he had felt for Laila Aasen. It was more about him getting close, for the first time, to the aesthetics he had envisaged, to the idea he had of how the murder should be executed. His experience of the very act itself was above all as gruesome and heartrending as he had hoped it would be. He could still hear Rafto's screams echoing around the deserted island. And the strangest thing of all: On the way back he discovered that his toes were no longer white and numb; it was as if the grad-ual freezing process of his extremities had been halted for a moment, as if he had thawed.

Four years later, after Mathias had killed another four women, and he could see that all the murders were an attempt to reconstruct the murder of his mother, he concluded that he was mad.

Or, to be more precise, that he was suffering from a serious personality disorder. All the specialist litera-ture he had read certainly pointed to that. The ritual nature of the murders, their having to take place on the day the first snow of the year came, his having to build a snowman. And, not least, his growing sadism.

But this insight in no way prevented him from continuing. For time was short; Raynaud's phenomenon was already appearing with increasing frequency, and he thought he could detect the first symptoms of scleroderma: a stiffness in the face that would eventually give him the revolting pointed nose and the pursed carp mouth with which the worst afflicted were ultimately burdened.

He had moved to Oslo to continue his work on immunology and water channels in the brain, as the research center for this was the Anatomy Department in Gaustad. In addition he was working at the Marienlyst Clinic, where Idar was employed and had recommended him. Mathias also did night shifts at the emergency room since he couldn't sleep anyway.

It was not difficult to find victims. Initially it was the patients' blood samples that in many cases ruled out paternity, and then there were the DNA tests by the Paternity Unit at the Institute of Forensic Medicine. Idar, who had fairly limited competence even for a general practitioner, covertly took advice on all cases concerning hereditary illness and syndromes. And, if the patients were young people, Mathias's advice was invariably the same.

"Get both parents to appear at the first consultation, take mouth swabs from everyone, say it's just to check the bacterial flora and send the samples to the Paternity Unit so that we at least know we're working from an accurate starting point."

And Idar, the idiot, did as he was told. Which meant that Mathias soon had a little file on women with children who were sailing under a false flag, so to speak. And best of all was that there was no link between him and these women, since the mouth swabs were submitted under Idar's name.

The method for luring the women into the trap was the same as the one applied with such success to Laila Aasen. A telephone call and an agreement to meet at a secret location unknown to anyone. Only once had it happened that the appointed victim broke down on the phone and went to her husband to tell all. And that had ended with the family splitting up, so she had received her just deserts anyway.

For a long time Mathias had pondered how he could dispose of the bodies with increased efficiency. At any rate, it was obvious that the method he had used with Onny Hetland was not viable for the long term. He had done it piecemeal with hydrochloric acid in the bathtub in his apartment. It was a risky, laborious process and injurious to his health, and it had taken almost three weeks. So he was greatly pleased when he chanced upon the solution. The body storage tanks at the Anatomy Department. It was as brilliant as it was simple. Just like the cutting loop.

He had read about the loop in an anatomy journal; a French anatomist recommended it for use on bodies that had started to decompose, because the loop cut through soft, rotting tissue with the same precise efficiency as through bone, and because it could be used on several bodies at the same time without any danger of transmitting bacteria. He had realized right away that with a loop to cut up the victims, transportation would be radically simplified. Consequently he contacted the manufacturer, flew to Rouen and had the tool demonstrated, in halting English, one misty morning inside a whitewashed cowshed in northern France. The loop consisted of a plain handle shaped like—and the approximate size of—a banana furnished with a metal shield to protect your hand against burns. The wire itself was as thin as fishing line and ran into both ends of the banana, from which it could be tightened or slackened with a button. There was also an on-off switch that activated the battery-driven heating element and made the garrotelike wire glow white in seconds. Mathias was elated; this tool would be useful for more than carving up bodies. When he heard the price he almost burst out laughing. The loop cost Mathias less than the flight to Rouen had. Batteries included.

The publication of the Swedish study concluding that somewhere between 15 and 20 percent of all children had a different biological father from the one they thought reflected Mathias's own experiences. He was not alone. Nor was he alone in having to die a cruel, premature death because of his mother's whoring with tainted genes. But he would be alone in this: the act of cleansing, the fight against disease, the crusade. He doubted that anyone would thank or honor him. This he did know, however:

They would all remember him, long after his death. For he had finally found what was to be his fame for all posterity, the masterpiece, the final flourish of his sword.

It was chance that set the ball rolling.

He saw him on TV. The policeman. Harry Hole. Hole was being interviewed because he had hunted down a serial killer in Australia. And Mathias was reminded of Gert Rafto's advice: "Avoid my beat." He also recalled, however, the satisfaction of having taken the life of the hunter. The feeling of supremacy. The feeling of power. Nothing later had quite compared with the murder of the police officer. And this Herostratically famous Hole appeared to have something of Rafto about him, some of the same offhandedness and anger.

Nonetheless, he might have forgotten all about Harry Hole had it not been for one of the gynecologists at the Marienlyst Clinic mentioning in the cafeteria the next day that he had heard that this to all outward appearances solid detective was actually an alcoholic and a nutcase. Gabriella, a pediatrician, added that she had the son of Hole's girlfriend as a patient. Oleg, a nice boy.

"He'll be an alcoholic then, as well," said the gynecologist. "It's in the damn genes, you know."

"Hole's not the father," Gabriella countered. "But what's interesting is that the man who's registered as the father, some professor or other in Moscow, is also an alcoholic."

"Hey, I didn't hear that!" shouted Idar Vetlesen

over the laughter. "Don't forget client confidentiality, folks!"

Lunch carried on, but Mathias was unable to forget what Gabriella had said. Or, rather, the way she had expressed herself: "the man who's registered as the father."

Accordingly, after lunch, Mathias followed the pediatrician to her office, went in behind her and closed the door.

"May I ask you something, Gabriella?"

"Oh, hello," she said, and a flush of anticipation spread up her cheeks. Mathias knew she liked him; he supposed she thought he was handsome, friendly, funny and a good listener. She had even, indirectly, asked him out on a couple of occasions, but he had declined.

"As you may know, I'm allowed to use some of the clinic's blood samples for my research," he said. "And in fact I found something interesting in the sample of the boy you were talking about. The son of Hole's girlfriend."

"My understanding is that their relationship is now a thing of the past."

"You don't say? There was something in the blood sample, so I was wondering if there was anything in the family . . ."

Mathias thought he could discern a certain disappointment in her face. As for himself, he was far from disappointed by what she had to tell him.

"Thank you," he said, standing up and exiting. He could feel his heart pumping eager, life-giving blood, his feet propelling him forward without consuming any energy, his pleasure making him glow like a cutting loop. For he knew this was the beginning. The beginning of the end.

The Holmenkollen Residents' Association was having its summer party on a burning hot August day. On the lawn in front of the association pavilion the adults were sitting on camp chairs under umbrellas and drinking white wine while the children ran between tables or played football on the gravel field. Although she was wearing enormous sunglasses that concealed her face, Mathias recognized her from the photograph he had downloaded from her employer's Web site. She was standing on her own, and he went over to her and asked with a wry smile if he might stand beside her and pretend he knew her. He knew how to do this sort of thing now. He was not the Mathias No-Nips of old.

She lowered her glasses, scrutinizing him, and he established that the photograph had lied after all. She was much more beautiful. So beautiful that for a moment he thought Plan A had a weakness: It was not a foregone conclusion that she would want him; a woman like Rakel—single mother or not—had alternatives. Plan B had, to be sure, the same result as A, but would not be anywhere near as satisfying.

"Socially timid," he said, raising a plastic cup in an embarrassed gesture of greeting. "I was invited here by a friend living nearby, and he hasn't shown up.

And everyone else looks as if they know each other. I promise to decamp the second he appears."

She laughed. He liked her laugh. And knew that the critical first three seconds had gone in his favor.

"I just saw a boy score a fantastic goal on the field down there," Mathias said. "I wouldn't mind betting you're related to him."

"Oh? That might have been Oleg, my son."

She succeeded in hiding it, but Mathias knew from countless sessions with patients that no woman can resist praise of her child.

"Nice party," he said. "Nice neighbors."

"You like parties with other people's neighbors?"

"I think my friends are worried I'm spending too much time on my own," he said. "So they try to cheer me up. With their successful neighbors, for example." He took a sip from the cup. "And with the very sweet house wine. What's your name?"

"Rakel. Fauke."

"Hello, Rakel. Mathias."

He shook her hand. Small, warm.

"You don't have anything to drink," he said. "Allow me. House sweet?"

On his return, and after passing her the cup, he took out his pager and looked at it with a concerned expression.

"Do you know what, Rakel? I'd love to stay and get to know you better, but the ER is short-staffed and needs an extra man immediately. So I'll put on my Superman outfit and make my way into town."

"Shame," she said.

"You think so? It's only for a few hours. Are you going to be here long?"

"I don't know. It depends on Oleg."

"Right. We'll see, then. Anyway, it was nice to meet you."

Again he shook her hand. Then left, knowing he had won the first round.

He drove to his apartment in Torshov and read an interesting article about water channels in the brain. When he returned at eight she was sitting under one of the umbrellas, wearing a big white hat. She smiled as he sat down beside her.

"Saved any lives?" she asked.

"Mostly scrapes and grazes," Mathias said. "An appendicitis. The high point was a boy who'd got a lemonade bottle stuck up his nose. I told his mother he was probably too young to sniff Coke. Sad to say, people in that type of situation don't have much of a sense of humor . . ."

She laughed. That refined, trilled laugh, which almost made him wish the whole thing were for real.

Mathias had already observed the thickening of his skin in various areas, but in the autumn of 2004 he noticed the first signs that the disease was entering the next phase. The phase he did not want to be a part of. The tightening of his face. His plan had been that Eli Kvale would be the victim of the year, then the whores Birte Becker and Sylvia Ottersen in the years that followed. The interesting part would be to see whether the police would pick up on the connections between the latter two victims and the lecher Arve Støp. But, as it turned out, his plans would have to be pushed forward. He had always promised himself that he would call it a day once the pain came, he wouldn't wait. And now it was here. He decided to take all three of them. As well as the grand finale: Rakel and the policeman.

Previously he had worked undercover, and now it was time to exhibit his life's work. To do that he would have to leave clear clues, show them the connections, give them the bigger picture.

He started with Birte. They agreed to talk about Jonas at her house after her husband had gone to Bergen in the evening. Mathias arrived at the appointed time and she took his coat on the porch and turned to put it in the closet. It was rare for him to improvise, but a pink scarf was hanging on one peg and he grabbed it as if by instinct. He wound it twice before going up behind her and placing it around her neck. He lifted the little woman up and positioned her in front of the mirror so that he could see her eyes. They were bulging; she was like a fish that had been hauled up from the deep.

After depositing her in the car, he went onto the lawn to the snowman he had made the night before. He pressed the mobile phone into its chest, filled the cavity and knotted the scarf around its neck. It was past midnight by the time he arrived at the garage of the Anatomy Department, injected fixative into Birte's body, stamped the metal tags, tied them on and put her on an unoccupied ledge in one of the tanks.

Then it was Sylvia's turn. He called her and rattled off the usual spiel, and they arranged to meet in the forest behind the Holmenkollen ski jump, a place he had used on previous occasions. But this time there were people nearby and he wouldn't take the risk. He explained to her that Idar Vetlesen, unlike himself, was not exactly a specialist in Fahr's Syndrome, and they would have to meet again. She suggested he call her the following evening, when she would be at home on her own.

The next evening he drove out, found her in the barn and set on her on the spot.

But it had almost gone wrong.

The crazy woman had swung her hatchet at him, hit him in the side, cut open his jacket and shirt and severed an artery, with the result that his blood had gushed out all over the barn floor. B-negative blood. Two people in a hundred's blood. So after he had killed her in the forest and left her head on top of the snowman, he returned, slaughtered a chicken and sprayed its blood over the floor to cover up his own.

It was a stressful twenty-four hours, but the strange thing was that he felt no pain that night. And over the subsequent days he followed the case in the newspapers, quietly triumphant. The Snowman. That was the name they had given him. A name that would be remembered. He would never have guessed that a few printed words in a newspaper could afford such a feeling of power and influence. He almost regretted having operated clandestinely for so many years. And it was so easy! There he was going around thinking that what Gert Rafto said was true, that a good detective would always find the murderer. But he had met Harry Hole and had seen the frustration in the policeman's frazzled face. It was the face of someone who comprehended nothing.

But then, while Mathias was preparing his final moves, it came like a bolt from the blue. Idar Vetlesen. He called to say that Hole had visited him asking questions about Arve Støp and pressing him for the connection. And Idar himself wondered what was going on; after all, it was unlikely that the selection of the victims was arbitrary. And, apart from himself and Støp, Mathias was the only person who knew about the paternities, since Mathias, as usual, had helped him with the diagnosis.

Idar was rattled, of course, but fortunately Mathias managed to calm him down. He told Idar not to say a word to anyone and to meet him in a safe place where no one could see them.

Mathias was nearby laughing as he said it; it was practically word for word what he told his female victims. He supposed it must have been the tension.

Idar proposed the curling club. Mathias hung up and pondered his options.

It struck him that he could make it seem as if Idar were the Snowman and at the same time procure himself some downtime.

The next hour he spent sketching out the details of Idar's suicide. And even though he appreciated his friend in many ways, it was an oddly stimulating, indeed inspiring, process. As the planning of the great project had been. The last snowman. She would have to sit—as he had on the first day of snow so many years ago—on the snowman's shoulders, feel the cold through her thighs and watch through the window, watch the treachery, the man who would be her death: Harry Hole. He closed his eyes and visualized the noose over her head. It glinted and glowed. Like a fake halo.

34

Sirens

Harry got into the car in the garage at the Anatomy Department. Closed the doors and his eyes, and tried to think clearly. The first thing to do was find out where Mathias was.

He had deleted Mathias from his mobile phone and now called directory assistance, which gave him the number and the address. He tapped in the number, noticed while he was waiting that his breathing was accelerated and excited, and tried to calm down.

"Hi, Harry." Mathias's voice was low, but sounded pleasantly surprised, as usual.

"Sorry to bother you," Harry said.

"Not at all, Harry."

"Ah, OK. Where are you now?"

"I'm at home. I'm on my way down to see Rakel and Oleg."

"Great. I was wondering if you could deliver the something to Oleg for me."

There was a pause. Harry clenched his jaw, making his teeth crack.

"Of course," Mathias said. "But Oleg's at home now, so you can—"

"Rakel," Harry interrupted. "We . . . I don't feel like seeing her today. Could I pop over to your place for a moment?"

Another pause. Harry pressed the receiver against his ear and listened hard, as if to pick up what his interlocutor was thinking. But all he could hear was breathing and fragile background music, minimalist Japanese glockenspiel or something like that. He visualized Mathias in an austere, equally minimalist apartment. Not that big, maybe, but tidy—that was obvious—nothing left to chance. And now he had put on a neutral light-blue shirt and a fresh bandage on the wound in his side. Because, when he had been standing on the steps in front of Harry, he hadn't held his crossed arms high to hide his missing nipples. It had been to hide the hatchet wound.

"Of course," Mathias said.

Harry was unable to decide whether his voice sounded natural. The background music had stopped.

"Thank you," Harry said. "I'll be quick, but promise me that you'll wait."

"I promise," Mathias said. "But, Harry . . ."

"Yes?" Harry took a deep breath.

"Do you know what my address is?"

"Rakel told me."

Harry cursed inside. Why hadn't he said he got it from directory assistance? There was nothing suspicious about that.

"Did she?" Mathias asked.

"Yes."

"OK," Mathias said. "Come right in. The door's unlocked."

Harry hung up and stared at the telephone. He could find no rational explanation for his foreboding that time was short and that he had to run for his life before darkness fell. So he resolved that he was imagining things. That it didn't help, this type of fear, the terror that comes with the onset of night, when you can't see your grandparents' farm.

He punched in another number.

"Yes," Hagen answered. The voice was toneless, lifeless. The resignation-writing voice, Harry presumed.

"Drop the paperwork," Harry said. "You've got to call the chief constable. I need a firearms authorization. Arrest of suspected murderer on Åsengata 12, Torshov."

"Harry—"

"Listen. The remains of Sylvia Ottersen are in a tank at the Anatomy Department. Katrine is not the Snowman. Do you understand?"

Silence.

"No," Hagen confessed.

"The Snowman is a lecturer at the department. Mathias Lund-Helgesen."

"Lund-Helgesen? Well, I'll be damned. Do you mean the—"

"Yes, the doctor who was so helpful in focusing our attention on Idar Vetlesen."

Life had returned to Hagen's voice. "The chief is going to ask if it's likely that the man's armed."

"Well," Harry said, "as far as we know, he hasn't used a firearm on any of the people he's killed."

A couple of seconds passed before Hagen caught the sarcasm. "I'll phone him now," he said.

Harry hung up and turned the key in the ignition while calling Magnus Skarre with his other hand. Skarre and the engine responded in unison.

"Still in Tryvann?" Harry shouted above the roar.

"Yes."

"Drop everything and get yourself in a car. Meet me at the intersection of Åsengata and Vogts Gate. It's a bust."

"All hell's broken loose?"

"Yeah," Harry said. The rubber screamed on the concrete as he let the clutch go.

He thought of Jonas. For some reason he thought of Jonas.

One of the six patrol cars Harry had asked the Incident Room for was already at Åsengata as Harry came down Vogts Gate from Storo. Harry drove up onto the pavement, jumped out and went over to them. They rolled down the window and passed Harry the walkie-talkie he had requested.

"Switch off the blender," Harry ordered, pointing to the rotating blue light. He pressed the TALK button and told the patrol cars to turn off the sirens well before they got to the scene.

Four minutes later six patrol cars were assembled at the intersection. The police officers, among them Skarre and Ola Li from Crime Squad, had crowded around Harry's car, where he sat with a street map in his lap, pointing.

"Li, you take three cars to cut off any possible escape routes. Here, here and here."

Li leaned over the map, nodding.

Harry turned to Skarre. "The caretaker?"

Skarre raised the phone. "Talking to him now. He's on his way over to the main door with keys."

"OK. You take six men and position yourselves by the entrance, back stairs and, if possible, on the roof. And you bring up the rear, OK? Has the Delta car arrived?"

"Here." Two of the officers, identical to the others from the outside, signaled that they were driving the regular vehicle for Delta, the Special Forces Unit trained particularly for this kind of operation.

"OK, I want you in front of the main entrance now. Are you all armed?"

The officers nodded. Some of them were armed with MP5 machine guns. The others had only service revolvers. It was a fiscal matter, as the chief constable had once explained.

"The caretaker says Lund-Helgesen lives on the second floor," Skarre said, slipping the mobile phone into his jacket pocket. "There's just one apartment on each floor. No exits to the roof. To reach the rear staircase he'd have to go up to the third and through a locked attic."

"Good," Harry said. "Send two men up the rear stairs and tell them to wait in the attic."

"OK."

Harry took with him the two uniformed officers from the car that had arrived first. An older officer and a young, pimply kid, both of whom had worked with Skarre before. Instead of going into Åsengata 12, they crossed the street and went into the building opposite.

Both young boys from the Stigson family stared wide-eyed at the two uniformed men while their father listened to Harry explaining why they had to use their second-floor apartment for a short while. Harry entered the sitting room, pushed the sofa away from the window and took a closer look at the apartment on the other side of the street.

"Light's on in the living room," he said.

"Someone's sitting there," said the older officer, who had taken up a position behind him.

"I've heard your eyesight deteriorates by thirty percent after you hit fifty," Harry said.

"I'm not blind. In the big chair there you can see the top of his head and the hand on the armrest."

Harry squinted. Shit, did he need glasses? Well, if the old guy thought he saw someone, then he must be right.

"You stay here and radio if he moves. All right?"

"All right." The older man smiled.

Harry took the kid along with him.

"Who's sitting inside?" the young officer said in a loud voice over the clatter of their feet as they raced downstairs.

"Heard of the Snowman?"

"Oh, crap."

"That's right."

They sprinted across the street to the other building. The caretaker, Skarre and five uniformed policemen stood ready by the front door.

"I haven't got a key for the apartments," the caretaker said. "Only for this door."

"That's fine," Harry said. "Everyone got their weapons ready? We make as little noise as possible, OK? Delta, you stay with me . . ."

Harry took out Katrine's Smith & Wesson and signaled to the caretaker, who turned the key in the lock.

Harry and the two Delta men, both armed with MP5's, strode soundlessly up the stairs, three steps at a time.

They stopped on the second floor outside an unmarked blue door. One officer laid his ear against the door, faced Harry and shook his head. Harry had lowered the volume of the walkie-talkie to the very minimum, and now he raised it to his mouth.

"Alpha to"—Harry had not allocated call names and couldn't remember first names—"the window post by the sofa. Has the target moved? Over."

He let go of the button and there was a low crackle. Then came the voice:

"He's still sitting in the chair."

"Roger. We're going in. Over and out."

One officer nodded and produced a crowbar while the other backed away and braced himself.

Harry had seen the technique used before; one man prizes open the door so that the other can charge in. Not because they couldn't have broken it open, but because it is the effect of the loud bang, the power and speed, that paralyzes the target and in nine cases out of ten causes him to freeze on the chair, sofa or bed.

But Harry held up a restraining hand. He pressed the door handle and pushed.

Mathias hadn't lied; it was unlocked.

The door slid open without a sound. Harry pointed to his chest to say he would go first.

The apartment was not minimalist in the way that Harry had imagined.

It was minimalist in the sense that there was nothing there: no shoes in the hall, no furniture, no pictures. Only bare walls begging for new wallpaper or a lick of paint. It looked as if it had been abandoned for a substantial amount of time.

The living-room door was ajar, and through the gap Harry could see the arm of the chair, a hand on top. A small hand with a watch. He held his breath, took two long strides, gripped the revolver with both hands and nudged the door open with his foot.

He sensed the other two—who had moved into the edge of his vision—stiffen.

And heard a barely audible whisper. "Jesus Christ . . ."

A large illuminated chandelier hung above the armchair and lit up the person sitting there and staring straight at him. The neck bore bruising from strangulation, the face was pale and beautiful, the hair black and the dress sky blue with tiny white flowers. The same dress as in the photo on his kitchen calendar. Harry felt his heart explode in his chest as the rest of his body turned to stone. He tried to move, but could not tear himself away from her glazed eyes. The accusatory, glazed eyes. Which accused him of not having acted; he had known nothing of this, but he should have acted, he should have stopped this happening, he should have saved her.

She was as white as his mother had been on her deathbed.

"Check the rest of the apartment," Harry said in a thick voice, lowering his revolver.

He took an unsteady step toward the body and held her wrist in his hand. It was ice-cold and lifeless, like marble. Yet he could feel a ticking, a weak pulse, and for one absurd moment he thought she had only been made up to look dead. Then he looked down and saw it was the watch that was ticking.

"There's no one else here," he heard one of the officers behind him say. Then a cough. "Do you know who she is?"

"Yes," Harry said, running a finger over the watch face. The same watch he had been holding in his own hand a mere few hours ago. The watch that had been left in his bedroom. That he had put in the birdhouse because Rakel's boyfriend was taking her out this evening. To a party. To celebrate that from now on the two of them would be as one.

Again Harry looked at the eyes, her accusing eyes.

Yes, he thought. Guilty on all counts.

Skarre had come into the apartment and was standing behind Harry, staring over his shoulder at the dead woman in the chair. Beside him stood the two Delta officers.

"Strangled?" he asked.

Harry neither answered nor moved. One shoulder strap of the sky-blue dress had slipped down.

"Unusual to wear a summer dress in November," Skarre said, mostly for the sake of conversation.

"She usually does," Harry said in a voice that sounded as if it came from a long way away.

"Who does?" Skarre asked.

"Rakel."

The policeman gave a start. He had seen Harry's ex when she used to work for the police. "Is . . . is . . . that Rakel? But . . ."

"It's her dress," Harry said. "And her watch. He's dressed her up as Rakel. But the woman sitting there is Birte Becker."

Skarre eyed the corpse in silence. It didn't look like any other corpse he had seen. This one was as white as chalk and bloated.

"Come with me," Harry said, directing his attention to the two Delta officers before turning to Skarre. "You stay here and cordon off the apartment.

Call the Crime Scene Unit in Tryvann and tell them they've got another job waiting for them."

"What are you going to do?"

"Dance," Harry said.

The apartment went quiet after the three men had clattered down the stairs at a run. But seconds later Skarre heard a car starting and the scream of tires on the pavement of Vogts Gate.

The blue light rotated and lit up the road. Harry was sitting in the front passenger seat and listening to the phone ringing at the other end. Hanging from the mirror, two miniature bikini-clad women danced to the despairing lament of the siren as the police car slalomed between vehicles on the Ring 3.

Please, he implored. Please pick up, Rakel.

He looked at the metal dancers beneath the mirror, thinking he was like them: someone who danced impotently to another's tune, a comic figure in a farce in which he was always two steps behind events, always racing through doors a little too late and being met by the audience's laughter.

Harry cracked. "Fuck, fuck, fuck!" he yelled and slung the mobile phone at the windshield. It slid off the dashboard and down to the floor. The officer driving exchanged glances with the other officer in the mirror.

"Turn off the siren," Harry said.

It went quiet.

And Harry's attention was caught by a sound coming from the floor.

He picked up the phone.

"Hello!" he shouted. "Hello. Are you at home, Rakel?"

"Of course I am—you're calling the landline." It was her voice. A gentle, calm laugh. "Is something the matter?"

"Is Oleg at home, too?"

"Yes," she said. "He's sitting here in the kitchen eating. We're waiting for Mathias. What's up, Harry?"

"Listen to me carefully now, Rakel. Do you hear me?"

"You're frightening me, Harry. What is it?"

"Put the safety chain on the door."

"Why? It's locked and—"

"Put the safety chain on, Rakel!" Harry yelled.

"OK, OK!"

He heard her say something to Oleg, then a chair scraped and he heard running feet. When the voice was back it was trembling.

"Now tell me what's going on, Harry."

"I will. First, though, you have to promise me you won't let Mathias into the house under any circumstances."

"Mathias? Are you drunk, Harry? You have no right—"

"Mathias is dangerous, Rakel. I'm sitting here in a police car with two other officers on our way up to you now. I'll explain the rest later. Now I want you to look out of the window. Can you see anything?"

He heard her hesitate. But he said nothing further, just waited. For he knew with a sudden certainty that she trusted him, that she believed him, that she always had. They were approaching the tunnel by Nydalen. On the side of the road the snow lay like grayish-white wool. Then her voice was back.

"I can't see anything. But I don't know what I'm looking for, do I?"

"So you can't see a snowman?" Harry asked quietly.

He could tell from the silence that the whole thing was becoming clear to her.

"Tell me this isn't happening, Harry," she whispered. "Tell me this is just a dream."

He closed his eyes and considered whether she could be right. On his eyelids he saw Birte Becker in the chair. Of course it was a dream.

"I put your watch in the birdhouse," he said.

"But it wasn't there, it . . . ," she began, paused and let out a groan. "Oh, my God!"

35

Monster

From the kitchen Rakel had a view of all three sides from which a person might approach the house. At the back there was a short but precipitous rocky slope it was difficult to descend, especially now that the snow had settled. She went from window to window. Peered out and tested them to make sure they were firmly shut.

When her father had built the house after the war he had put the windows high in the wall, with iron bars covering them. She knew this had something to do with the war and a Russian who had sneaked into his bunker near Leningrad and shot all his sleeping comrades. Everyone apart from him, who had been asleep nearest the door, so exhausted that he hadn't woken up until the alarm was sounded and discovered that his blanket was strewn with empty cartridges. That was the last night he'd slept properly, he had always said. But she'd always hated the iron bars. Until now.

"Can't I go up to my room?" Oleg said, kicking the leg of the large kitchen table.

"No," Rakel said. "You have to stay here."

"What's Mathias done?"

"Harry will explain everything when he comes. Are you sure you've attached the safety chain properly?"

"Yes, Mom. I wish Dad was here."

"Dad?" She hadn't heard him use that word before. Except for Harry, but that was several years ago. "Do you mean your father in Russia?"

"He's not Dad."

He said it with a conviction that made her shiver.

"The cellar door!" she screamed.

"What?"

"Mathias has the cellar-door key, too. What should we do?"

"Simple," said Oleg, finishing his glass of water. "You put one of the garden chairs under the door handle. They're just the right height. No chance anyone could get in."

"Have you tried?" she asked, taken aback.

"Harry did it once when we were playing cowboys."

"Sit here," she said, heading for the hall and the cellar door.

"Wait."

She stopped.

"I saw how he did it," said Oleg, who had got to his feet. "Stay here, Mom."

She looked at him. God, how he had grown in this

last year; he would soon be taller than her. And in those dark eyes of his the childishness was giving way to what for the moment was youthful defiance, but would, she could already see, in time become adult determination.

She hesitated.

"Let me do it," he said.

There was a plea in his tone. And she knew this was important for him; it was about bigger matters. About coming to terms with childish fears. About adult rituals. About becoming like his father. Whoever he thought that was.

"Hurry," she whispered.

Oleg ran.

She stood by the window and stared out, listening for the sound of a car on the drive. She prayed that Harry would come first. Wondered about how quiet it was. And had no idea where the next thought came from: how quiet it would be.

But then she did hear a sound. A tiny sound. At first she assumed it came from outside. But then she was sure that it came from behind her. She turned. Saw nothing, just the empty kitchen. Then there was that sound again. Like the heavy tick of a clock. Or a finger tapping on a table. The table. She stared. That was where the sound was coming from. And then she saw it. A drop of water had landed on the table. She slowly raised her face to the ceiling. In the middle of the white paneling a dark circle had formed. And from the middle of that circle hung a shiny drop. It let go and landed on the table. Rakel saw it happen, yet the sound made her jump, as if she had received an unexpected slap to the head.

My God, it must be from the bathroom! Had she really forgotten to turn off the shower again? She hadn't been on the second floor since she came home; she had started cooking right away, so it must have been running since this morning. And it **would** have to happen now, in the midst of all this.

She went into the hall, dashed up the stairs and headed for the bathroom. She couldn't hear the shower. She opened the door. Dry floor. No water running. She closed the bathroom door and stood outside for a couple of seconds. Glanced at the adjacent bedroom door. Slowly walked over. Rested her hand on the handle. Hesitated. Listened again for cars. Then she opened the door. She looked inside the room. She wanted to scream. But instinctively she knew that she mustn't—she had to be quiet. Perfectly quiet.

"Fuck, fuck, fuck!" Harry screamed and banged a fist onto the dashboard, making it quiver. "What's going on?"

The traffic had ground to a halt in front of the tunnel. They had been there now for two long minutes.

The reason came over the police radio that second. "There's been a collision on the Ring 3 by the exit of the westbound tunnel at Tåsen. No injuries. Tow truck's on its way."

On a sudden impulse Harry snatched the micro-phone. "Do you know who it is?"

"We know it's two cars, both with summer tires," the nasal radio voice drawled laconically.

"November snow always brings chaos," the officer at the back said.

Harry didn't answer, just drummed his fingers on the dashboard. He weighed the alternatives. There was a barricade of cars in front of and behind them; all the blue lights and sirens in the world could not get them through. He could jump out, run to the end of the tunnel and radio a patrol car to meet him there, but it was more than a mile.

It was quiet in the car now; all that could be heard was the low hum of idling car engines. The van in front of them nudged forward a yard and the police driver followed. Didn't brake until he was almost on its rear bumper, as if afraid anything but aggressive driving would cause the inspector to explode again. The sudden braking made the two metal bikini-clad women jingle cheerfully in the silence that followed.

Harry thought about Jonas again. Why, though? What had made him think about Jonas when he was talking to Mathias on the phone? There was some-thing about the sound. In the background.

Harry studied the two dancers under the mirror. And everything clicked into place.

He knew why he had thought about Jonas. He knew what the sound had been. And he knew there wasn't a second to lose. Or—he tried to repress the thought—there was no need to hurry anymore. It was already too late.

Oleg hurried through the dark cellar corridor without looking left or right, knowing that the salt deposits on the brick walls were in the shape of white ghosts. He tried to concentrate on what he was going to do, tried not to think about anything else, not to let the wrong thoughts enter his mind. That was what Harry had said. It was possible to conquer the only monsters that existed, those inside your head. But you had to work at it. You had to confront them and fight them as often as you could. Minor skirmishes you could win. Then go home, bandage your wounds and try again. He had done it, he had been alone in the cellar many times, he had needed to be, of course, to make sure his skates were kept cold.

He grabbed the garden chair, dragged it after him for the noise to drown the silence. He checked that the cellar door was in fact locked. Then he wedged the chair under the handle and made sure it could not move. There we are. He stiffened. What was that? He looked up at the small window in the door. He couldn't hold back the thoughts any longer—now they flooded in. Someone was standing outside. He wanted to run away, but forced himself to stand his ground. Fought against the thoughts with other thoughts. I'm on the inside, he told himself. I'm as secure here as up there. He breathed in, felt his heart pounding like a runaway bass drum. Then he leaned forward and peered at the window. He saw the reflection of his own face. But above that he saw another face, a distorted face that was not his. And he saw hands, monster hands being raised. Oleg backed away, terrified. Bumped into something and felt hands close around his face and mouth. He was unable to scream. For he wanted to scream. He wanted to scream that this was not in his mind, this was the monster, the monster was inside. And they were all going to die.

"He's in the house," Harry said.

The other officers looked at him with incomprehension as Harry pressed the redial button on the phone. "I thought it was Japanese music, but it was metal wind chimes. The kind Jonas has in his room. And that Oleg has, too. Mathias has been there all the time. He told me himself, didn't he . . . ?"

"What do you mean?" the officer in the back ventured to ask.

"He said he was at home. And that's the house on Holmenkollveien now, of course. He even said he was on his way **down** to see Rakel and Oleg. I should have known. After all, Holmenkollen is up in relation to Torshov. He was on the second floor on Holmenkollveien. On his way down. We have to get them out of the house now. Answer, for Christ's sake!"

"Perhaps she's not near—"

"There are four telephones in the house. He's just cut the connection now. I have to get there."

"We can send another patrol car," the driver said.

"No!" Harry snapped. "It's too late anyway. He's got them. And the only chance we have is the final pawn. Me."

"You?"

"Yes. I'm part of his plan."

"You're **not** part of his plan, you mean, don't you?"

"No. I am part. He's waiting for me."

The two policemen exchanged glances as they heard the bleat of a motorbike worming its way forward between the stationary cars behind them.

"You think he is?"

"Yes," Harry said, catching sight of the bike in the side mirror. Thinking this was the only answer he could give. Because it was the only answer that offered any hope.

Oleg struggled with all his might, but went limp in the monster's iron grip when he felt the cold steel on his throat.

"This is a scalpel, Oleg." The monster had Mathias's voice. "We use it to dissect people. And you wouldn't believe how easy it is."

Then the monster told him to open wide, shoved a filthy cloth in his mouth and ordered him to lie on his stomach with his arms behind his back. As Oleg didn't obey at once, the steel was thrust in under his ear and he felt hot blood coursing over his shoulder and down the inside of his T-shirt. He lay on his stomach on the freezing cement floor, and the monster sat on top of him. A red box fell beside his face. He read the label. Plastic ties, the kind of thin ties you saw around cables and on toy packaging, which were so irritating because they could only be tightened, not loosened, and they couldn't be pulled apart however thin they were. He felt the sharp plastic cut into the skin around his wrists and ankles.

Then he was lifted up and dropped and there was no time to wait for the pain as he landed with a crunch. He stared up. He was lying on his back in the freezer; he could feel the ice that had broken off burn the skin on his forearms and face. Above him stood the monster, with his head angled to one side.

"Good-bye," he said. "We'll meet on the other side before very long."

The lid was slammed down and there was total darkness. Oleg could hear the key being turned in the lock and swift steps fading into the distance. He tried to lift his tongue, tried to get it behind the cloth, had to get it out. Had to breathe. Had to have air.

Rakel had stopped breathing. She stood in the bedroom doorway knowing that what she saw was insanity. An insanity that made her flesh creep, her mouth drop and her eyes bulge.

The bed and other furniture had been pushed against the walls, and the floor was covered by an almost invisible surface of water that was only broken when a new drop fell on it. But Rakel didn't notice; the only thing she saw was the enormous snowman dominating the center of the room.

The top hat above the grinning mouth almost touched the ceiling.

When she finally recovered her breathing and the oxygen rushed to her brain she recognized the smell of wet wool and wet wood and heard the sound of melting snow dripping. A wave of cold surged toward her, but this was not what gave her goose pimples. It was the body heat of the man standing behind her.

"Isn't it beautiful?" Mathias said. "I've made it just for you."

"Mathias . . ."

"Shh." He placed a kind of protective arm around her throat. She looked down. The hand was holding a scalpel. "Don't talk, my love. There's so much to do and so little time."

"Why? Why?"

"This is our day, Rakel. The rest of life is so unbelievably short, so let's celebrate, not waste time explaining. Please put your arms behind your back."

Rakel did as he said. She hadn't heard Oleg come up from the cellar. Perhaps he was still in the cellar; perhaps he could get out if she could just detain Mathias. "I'd like to know why," she said and could hear emotion tugging at her vocal cords.

"Because you're a whore."

She felt something thin and hard tighten around her wrists. Felt his warm breath on her neck. His lips.

And then his tongue. She gritted her teeth, knowing that if she screamed he might stop and she wanted him to go on, to waste time. The tongue worked its way around and up to her ear. A little nibble.

"And the son from your whoring is in the freezer," he whispered.

"Oleg?" she said, feeling herself lose control.

"Relax, my darling, he won't die of cold."

"Wo-won't he?"

"Long before his body has cooled down the son of a whore will have died from asphyxiation. It's simple mathematics."

"Mathema—"

"I did the calculations ages ago. It's all calculated."

A revving motorbike skidded up the winding roads of Holmenkollen in the dark. The roar reverberated between the houses and onlookers considered it madness in these snowy conditions. The rider should have his license taken away. But the rider didn't have one.

Harry accelerated up the drive to the black timber house, but in the sharp turn the wheels spun on the fresh snow and he felt the bike losing speed. He didn't try to correct the skid; he jumped off and the bike rolled down the slope, burst through a few low spruce branches before coming to a halt against a tree trunk, tipped onto its side and, spitting snow from the back wheel, breathed its last.

By then Harry was already halfway up the steps.

There were no footprints in the snow, neither to nor from the house. He took out his revolver as he bounded up to the door.

It was unlocked. As promised.

He slipped into the hall, and the first thing he saw was the cellar door wide open.

Harry stopped to listen. There was a noise, a kind of drumming. It seemed to be coming from the kitchen. Harry hesitated. Then he opted for the cellar.

With his revolver pointing in front of him, he sidled down the staircase. At the bottom he stopped to let his eyes get accustomed to the dark and listened. He had a sense that the whole room was holding its breath. He spotted the garden chair under the door handle. Oleg. His eyes delved further. He had decided to go upstairs again when his attention was caught by the dark stain on the brick floor by the freezer. Water? He took a step closer. It must have come from under the freezer. He forced his thoughts away from where they wanted to go and pulled at the lid. Locked. The key was in, but Rakel didn't usually lock the freezer. Images from Finnøy emerged in his brain, but he hurried, twisted the key and lifted the lid.

Harry just caught the glint of metal from the murky depths before a burning pain in his face made him throw himself backward. A knife? He had fallen on his back between two dirty-laundry baskets and a figure, speedy and nimble, was already out of the freezer and standing over him.

"Police!" Harry shouted and quickly raised his gun. "Don't move!"

The figure stopped with one hand raised over his head. "H-Harry?"

"Oleg?"

Harry lowered the revolver and saw what the boy was holding in his hand. A speed skate.

"I . . . I thought Mathias had come back," he whispered.

Harry got to his feet. "Where is Mathias?"

"I don't know. He said we would meet soon, so I assumed . . ."

"Where did the skate come from?" Harry tasted metallic blood in his mouth and his fingers found the cut on his face, which was bleeding profusely.

"It was in the freezer." Oleg gave a sly grin. "I was getting so much hassle for leaving the skates on the steps, so I keep them under the peas where Mom won't see them. We never eat peas, as you know."

He followed Harry, who was already on his way up the stairs.

"Luckily I'd had the blades sharpened, so I could cut the ties. The lock was impossible, but I managed to stab a couple of holes in the plate at the bottom to get some air. And I smashed the bulb so that the light wouldn't come on when he opened the lid."

"And your body heat melted the ice that ran out of the hole," Harry said.

They emerged in the hall, and Harry pulled Oleg over to the front door, opened it and pointed.

"See the neighbors' light? Run over and stay there until I come to get you. OK?"

"No!" said Oleg firmly. "Mom—"

"Shh! Now listen. The best thing you can do for your mom right now is to get away from here."

"I want to find her!"

Harry grabbed Oleg's shoulders and squeezed until tears of pain formed in the boy's eyes.

"When I say run, you run, you damn idiot."

He said it in a low voice but with such repressed fury that Oleg blinked in confusion and a tear rolled over his eyelashes and onto his cheek. Then the boy turned on his heel, rushed out the door and was swallowed up by the darkness and the driving snow.

Harry grabbed the walkie-talkie and pressed the talk button. "Harry here. Are you far away?"

"We're by the stadium. Over." Harry recognized Gunnar Hagen's voice.

"I'm inside," Harry said. "Drive up to the front of the house, but don't enter until I say. Over."

"Roger."

"Over and out."

Harry went toward the sound he'd heard earlier in the kitchen. From the doorway he watched the thin stream of water falling from the ceiling. It had been tinted gray by the dissolved plaster and was drumming furiously on the kitchen table.

Harry took the staircase to the second floor in four long strides. Tiptoed to the bedroom door. Swallowed. Studied the door handle. From outside he could hear the distant sound of police sirens approaching. Blood from his cut dripped onto the parquet floor with a gentle plop.

He could feel it now, as pressure on his temples;

this was where it would end. And there was a kind of logic to it. How many times had he stood like this in front of the bedroom door, at daybreak, after a night when he had promised to be at home with her, how often had he stood there with a bad conscience knowing she was inside asleep? Carefully he pressed the door handle, which he knew would creak halfway down. And she would wake up, look at him with sleepy eyes, try to punish him with her glare, until he slipped under the duvet, snuggled up to her body and felt its stiff resistance melt. And she would grunt with pleasure, but not too much pleasure. And then he would stroke her more, kiss and nibble at her, be her servant until she was sitting on him, no longer the queen in her slumbers, but purring and moaning, wanton and offended at the same time.

He closed his fist around the handle, noticed how his hand recognized the flat angular shape. He pressed with infinite care. Waited for the familiar creak. But it was not forthcoming. Something was different. There was resistance. Had someone tightened the springs? Gingerly, he let go. Stooped down to the keyhole and tried to peep in. Black. Someone had blocked the hole.

"Rakel!" he shouted. "Are you there?"

No answer. He placed his ear against the door. Thought he could hear a scratching sound, but wasn't sure. He held the handle again. Wavered. Changed his mind, let go and hastened into the adjacent bathroom. Pushed open the little window, forced his body through and leaned out backward.

Light was streaming from between the black iron bars of the bedroom window. He wedged his heels against the inside of the frame, tensed his leg muscles and stretched out of the bathroom and along the outside wall. His fingers groped in vain to find a hold between the rough logs as the snow settled on his face and melted into the blood running down his cheek. He applied greater force; the window frame was pressing into his leg so hard it felt as if the bone would crack. His hands crept along the wall like frenetic five-legged spiders. His stomach muscles ached. But it was too far—he couldn't reach. He stared down at the ground beneath him, knowing that under the thin layer of snow there was pavement.

He felt something cold against his fingertips.

An iron bar.

Got two fingers around the bar. Three. Then the other hand. Let his aching legs swing free, dangled and hurriedly found a foothold to relieve the pressure on his arms. At last he could see into the bedroom. And he saw. His brain struggled to absorb the sight while it knew immediately what it was looking at: the finished work of art, the prototype of which he had already seen.

Rakel's eyes were wide open and black. She was wearing a dress. Crimson. Like Campari. She was "cochineal." Her head strained toward the ceiling as though she were standing by a fence trying to see over, and from this position she stared down and out at him. Her shoulders were pulled back and her arms hidden. Harry assumed her hands were tied behind her back. Her cheeks bulged as though she had a sock or a cloth in her mouth. She sat astride the shoulders of an enormous snowman. Her bare legs were crossed in front of the snowman's chest, and he could see her tensed leg muscles quivering. She mustn't fall. She couldn't. For around her neck there was not a gray, lifeless wire, as with Eli Kvale, but a white glowing circle, like an absurd imitation of an old toothpaste advertisement promising a ring of confidence, good fortune in love and a long and happy life. A wire ran from the black handle of the cutting loop to a hook in the ceiling above Rakel's head. The wire continued to the other end of the room, to the door. To the door handle. The wire was not thick, but long enough to have provided noticeably more resistance when Harry had begun to press the handle. If he had opened the door, indeed if he had even pressed the handle right down, the white glowing metal would have cut into her throat, right under her chin.

Rakel was staring back at Harry without blinking. The muscles in her face were twitching, alternating between fury and naked fear. The loop was too narrow for her to remove her head unscathed; instead she held her head down so that it did not touch the death-bringing glow that hung almost vertically around her neck.

She looked at Harry, down at the floor and back to Harry. And Harry understood.

Gray clumps of snow were already lying in the water covering the floor. The snowman was melting. Fast.

Harry got a good foothold and shook the bars as hard as he could. They didn't budge, didn't even offer a hopeful creak. The iron was thin but firmly attached to the timber.

The figure inside was swaying.

"Hold on!" Harry shouted. "I'll be there soon!"

Lies. He wouldn't even be able to bend the bars with an iron lever. And he didn't have time to start sawing them off. Fuck her father, the crazy bastard! His arms were aching. He heard the ear-piercing siren of the first car turning into the drive. He looked around. It was one of Delta's special vehicles, a large, armored beast of a Land Rover. A man dressed in a green flak jacket jumped out of the passenger seat, took cover behind the vehicle and held up a walkie-talkie. Harry's handset crackled.

"Hello!" Harry shouted.

The man, taken aback, looked left and right.

"Up here, boss."

Gunnar Hagen straightened up behind the vehicle as a patrol car swung up in front of the house with the blue light swirling.

"Should we storm the house?" Hagen shouted.

"No!" screamed Harry. "He's got her strung up. Just . . ."

"Just?"

Harry raised his eyes, stared. Not down to the city, but up to the illuminated Holmenkollen ski jump farther up the ridge.

"Just what, Harry?"

"Just wait."

"Wait?"

"I have to think."

Harry rested his forehead against the cold bars. His arms were aching and he bent his knees to put most of his body weight on his legs. The cutting loop must have an off-switch. On the plastic handle, probably. They could smash the window and poke a long pole in with a mirror attached so that they could per-haps . . . But how the hell would they be able to press the off-switch without everything moving and . . . and . . . ? Harry tried not to think about the ludi-crously thin layer of skin and soft tissue that pro-tected the carotid artery. Tried to think constructively and ignore the panic that was roaring in his ears, telling him to get in and take control.

They could enter through the door. Without opening it. Just saw away the panel. They needed a chain saw. But who would have one? Only the whole of fucking Holmenkollen. After all, they all had a spruce forests in their yards.

"Get hold of a chain saw from the neighbor's house," Harry yelled.

Down below he heard the sound of running. And a splash inside the bedroom. Harry's heart stopped and he stared in. The snowman's whole left side was gone. It had sheared off and landed in the water. The snowman was collapsing. He saw Rakel's body trem-ble as she fought to maintain her balance to keep away from the white, tear-shaped gallows noose. They would never get back with the chain saw in time, let alone cut through the door.

"Hagen!" Harry heard the shrill hysteria in his own voice. "The patrol cars have a tow rope. Sling it up here and back the Land Rover up to the wall."

Harry heard a buzz of voices, the Land Rover's engine revving in reverse and a car trunk being opened.

"Catch!"

Harry let go of the bar with one hand and turned to see the coiled rope coming toward him. He lunged in the dark, caught it and held on as the rest unfurled and fell back down to the ground with a thud.

"Tie the end to the tow bar."

There was a carbine hook attached to his end of the rope. As quick as lightning he smacked the hook against the junction of the bars in the middle of the window and the lock snapped shut. Speed-cuffing.

Another splash from inside the bedroom. Harry didn't look. There was no point.

"Go!" he yelled.

Then he grabbed the edge of the gutter with both hands, using the bars as a ladder, and heard the Land Rover's revs increase as he swung himself onto the roof. With his chest on the roof tiles and his eyes closed he could hear the motor engage, the rev count fall and the iron bars groan. More groaning. And more. Come on! Harry was aware that time was passing more slowly than he thought. And yet not slowly enough. Then—as he was waiting for the auspicious crack—the rev count suddenly rose to a ferocious whine. Shit! Harry realized the tires of the Land Rover were spinning around helplessly.

A thought fluttered through his brain: He could

say a prayer. But he knew that God had made up His mind, that destiny was sold out, that this ticket would have to be bought on the black market. His soul wouldn't be worth much without her anyway. The thought was gone that very same second, interrupted by the sound of rubber, a sinking rev count and an increasing groan.

The big heavy tires had spun their way down to the pavement.

Then came the crack. The rev count roared and died. A second of total silence followed. And then a hollow crash as the bars hit the car roof below.

Harry pushed himself up. He stood with his back to the yard on the edge of the gutter and felt it give way. Then he bent down, grabbed the gutter with both hands and kicked off. Swung like a pendulum from gutter to window. Jackknifed. The moment the old, thin windowpane gave with a tinkle under his boots, Harry let go. And for a few tenths of a second he had no idea where he would land: down in the yard, on the jagged glass teeth of the window or in the bedroom.

There was a bang, a fuse must have been blown, and everything went black.

Harry sailed through a room of nothing, felt nothing, remembered nothing, was nothing.

And when the light came back on his only thought was that he wanted to return to that space. Pain radiated from all over his body. He was lying on his back in icy-cold water. But he must have been dead because he was looking up at an angel dressed in blood red, seeing her shining halo glow in the dark. Slowly sound returned. The scratching. The breathing. Then he saw the distorted face, the panic, the gaping mouth stuffed with the yellow ball, the feet scrambling up the snow. He just wanted to close his eyes. A noise, like low moaning. Wet snow crumbling.

In retrospect, Harry couldn't really account for what happened; he could remember only the nauseating smell as the cutting loop burned through flesh.

At the very moment the snowman collapsed he stood up. Rakel fell forward. Harry raised his right hand as he fastened his left arm around her thighs to hold her up. He knew it was too late. Flesh sizzled, his nostrils were filled with a sweet, greasy smell and blood ran down his face. He looked up. His right hand was situated between the white glow of the loop and her neck. The weight of her neck forced his hand down against the white-hot wire, which ate through the flesh of his fingers like an egg slicer through a hard-boiled egg. And when it was right through it would cut open her throat. The pain came, delayed and dull, like an initially reluctant then insistent steel hammer on an alarm clock. He fought to stay upright. Had to have his left hand free. Blinded by blood, he hauled her up onto his shoulders and stretched his free hand over his head. Felt her skin against his fingertips, her thick hair, felt the loop burn into his skin before his hand found the hard plastic, the handle. His fingers found a flip switch. Moved it to the right. But stopped as soon as the noose started tightening. His fingers found another switch and pressed. The sounds disappeared, the light flickered and he knew he was on the point of losing consciousness again. Breathe, he thought, the important thing was to get oxygen to the brain. But his knees were giving way, nevertheless. The white glow above him changed to red. And then gradually to black.

At his back he heard the sound of glass being crushed under several pairs of boot heels.

"We've got her," a voice said behind him.

Harry sank to his knees in the blood-tinged water, with clumps of snow and unused plastic ties floating around him. His brain engaged and disengaged as if the power supply to it were failing.

Someone said something behind him. He caught fragments of it, inhaled air and groaned, "What?"

"She's alive," the voice repeated.

His hearing stabilized. And sight. He turned. The two men clad in black had laid Rakel on the bed and cut the plastic ties. The contents of Harry's stomach came up without warning. Two heaves and it was all out. He stared down at the vomit floating in the water and felt a hysterical urge to laugh out loud. Because the finger seemed to have been spewed up with everything else. He lifted his right hand and looked at the bleeding stump as confirmation. It was his finger floating in the water.

"Oleg . . ." It was Rakel's voice.

Harry picked up a plastic tie, wrapped it around the stump of his middle finger and tightened it as hard as he could. Did the same with his index finger, which had been sliced through to the bone but was still firmly attached.

Then he went to the bed, spread the duvet over Rakel and sat beside her. The eyes staring up at him were large and black with shock, and blood ran from the wounds where the loop had come into contact with the skin on both sides of her neck. He took her hand with his uninjured left.

"Oleg," she repeated.

"He's OK," Harry said and responded to her hand pressure. "He's with the neighbors. It's over now."

He saw her trying to focus her eyes.

"Promise me?" she whispered, barely audible.

"I promise you."

"Thank God."

She sobbed once, buried her face in her hands and began to cry.

Harry looked down at his injured hand. Either the ties had stopped the bleeding or he was empty.

"Where's Mathias?" he said quietly.

Her head bobbed up, and she gaped at him. "You just promised me that—"

"Where did he go, Rakel?"

"I don't know."

"Did he say anything?"

Her hand squeezed his. "Don't go now, Harry. I'm sure someone else can—"

"What did he say?"

He could tell by the way her body recoiled that he had raised his voice.

"He said that it was finished now and he would

bring it to a conclusion," she said as tears welled in her dark eyes again. "And that the end would be an homage to life."

"An homage to life? Those were the words he used?"

She nodded. Harry loosened his hand from hers, stood up and went to the window. Scoured the night sky. It had stopped snowing. He looked up at the illuminated monument that could be seen from almost everywhere in Oslo. The ski jump. Like a white comma against the black ridge. Or a full stop.

Harry went back to her bedside, bent down and kissed her on the forehead.

"Where are you going?" she whispered.

Harry raised the bloodstained hand and smiled. "To see a doctor."

He left the room. Stumbled down the stairs. Came out into the cold, white darkness of the yard, but the nausea and giddiness would not release their grip.

Hagen stood beside the Land Rover talking on a mobile phone.

He broke off the conversation and nodded when Harry asked if they could drive him.

Harry sat in the back. He was thinking about how Rakel had thanked God. She couldn't know, of course, that someone else deserved her thanks. Or that the buyer had accepted the offer. And that payback time had already started.

"Down to the city center?" the driver asked.

Harry shook his head and pointed upward. The right index finger looked strangely alone between the thumb and the ring finger.

36

The Tower

It took three minutes to drive from Rakel's house to Holmenkollen ski jump. They drove through the tunnel and parked on the viewing promontory among the souvenir shops. The slope looked like a frozen white waterfall that plunged down between the stands and broadened into a flat out-run a hundred yards below.

"How do you know he's here?" Hagen asked.

"Because he told me he would be," Harry said. "We were sitting by a skating rink and he said the day his life's work was over and he was so ill he wanted to die he would jump from that tower there. As an homage to life." Harry pointed to the illuminated ski tower and the in-run soaring up against the black sky above them. "And he knew I would remember."

"Insane," whispered Gunnar Hagen, peering up at the darkened glass cage perched on the top of the tower.

"Could I borrow your handcuffs?" Harry asked, turning to the driver.

"You've already got some," Hagen said, nodding toward Harry's right wrist, where he had attached one cuff. The other hung open. "I'd like two pairs," Harry said, taking the leather case from the driver. "Can you help me? I'm a couple of fingers short here . . ."

Hagen shook his head as he attached half of the driver's handcuffs around Harry's other wrist.

"I'm not happy with you going on your own. It frightens me."

"There's not a lot of room up there and I can talk to him." Harry produced Katrine's revolver. "And I've got this."

"That's what frightens me, Harry."

Inspector Hole sent his boss a quick glance before twisting around and opening the car door with his healthy hand.

The police officer accompanied Harry to the entrance of the Ski Museum, which he had to pass through to get to the tower lift. They had taken along a crowbar to smash in the door. But as they approached, the flashlight caught fragments of glass glinting on the floor over by the ticket counter. A distant alarm from somewhere inside the museum was inhaling and exhaling with a howl.

"OK, so we know our man's here," Harry said, making sure his revolver was in position at the back of his waistband. "Place two men by the rear exit as soon as the next patrol car arrives."

Harry took the flashlight, stepped into the dark building and hurried past the posters and pictures of Norwegian ski heroes, Norwegian flags, Norwegian ski grease, Norwegian kings and Norwegian Crown princesses, all accompanied by succinct texts proclaiming that Norway was one hell of a nation, and Harry remembered why he had never been able to stomach this museum.

The elevator was right at the back. A narrow, enclosed space. Harry studied the elevator door. Felt the cold sweat on his skin. There was a steel staircase next to it.

Eight landings later he regretted his decision. The dizziness and nausea had returned and he was retching. The sound of footsteps on metal echoed up and down the flight of stairs, and the handcuffs dangling from his wrists played iron pipe music against the handrail. His heart ought to have been pumping adrenaline and preparing his body for action at this point. Perhaps he was too drained, too spent. Or perhaps he knew it was all over. The game was up, the outcome obvious.

Harry went on. Set his feet down on the steps, didn't even bother to try to be quiet, knew he had been heard ages ago.

The staircase led directly to the dark cage. Harry switched off his flashlight and felt a cold current of air as soon as his head appeared above the floor. Pale moonlight fell into the room. It was about forty square feet with glass all around and a steel railing that tourists clung to with a mixture of terror and joy as they enjoyed the view of Oslo or imagined what it must be like to set off down the in-run on skis. Or fall off the tower, sink like a stone toward the houses and be smashed between the trees far below them.

Harry climbed to the top step, turned to the silhouette outlined against the blanket of light that was the town beneath. The figure was sitting on the railing, by the large open window from where the cold air was flowing.

"Beautiful, eh?" Mathias's voice sounded light, almost cheerful.

"If it's the view you mean, I agree."

"I didn't mean the view, Harry."

One of Mathias's feet was dangling outside, and Harry was standing by the stairs.

"Did you or the snowman kill her, Harry?"

"What do you think?"

"I think you did it. After all, you're a clever guy. I was counting on you. Feels dreadful, doesn't it? Of course, it's not so easy to see the beauty then. When you've just killed the person you love most."

"Well," Harry said, taking a step closer, "I don't suppose you would know much about that, would you."

"Wouldn't I?" Mathias leaned his head back against the frame and laughed. "I loved the first woman I killed more than anything else on this earth."

"So why did you do it?" Harry felt a stab of pain as he moved his right hand behind his back and around the revolver.

"Because my mother was a liar and a whore," Mathias said.

Harry swung his hand around and raised the revolver. "Come down from there, Mathias. With your hands in the air."

Mathias eyed Harry with curiosity. "Do you know there's a twenty percent chance that your mother was the same, Harry? A twenty percent chance that you're the son of a whore. What do you say to that?"

"You heard me, Mathias."

"Let me make it easier for you, Harry. First, I refuse to obey. Second, you can say you couldn't see my hands, so I could have been armed. Fire away, Harry."

"Get down."

"Rakel was a whore, Harry. And Oleg's the son of a whore. You should thank me for letting you kill her."

Harry switched the gun to his left hand. The loose ends of the handcuffs banged against each other.

"Think about it, Harry. If you arrest me I'll be declared of unsound mind, pampered in some psychiatric ward for a few years before being released. Shoot me now."

"You want to die," Harry said, moving nearer. "Because you're going to die of scleroderma."

Mathias smacked a hand against the window frame. "Well done, Harry. You checked what I said about antibodies in my blood."

"I asked Idar. And afterward I researched scleroderma. If you've got the disease, it's easy to choose another death. For example, a spectacular death that would appear to crown this so-called life's work of yours."

"I can hear your contempt, Harry. But one day you'll understand, too."

"Understand what?"

"That we were in the same business, Harry. Fighting disease. But the diseases you and I are fighting can't be eradicated. All victories are temporary. So it's just the fight that is our life's work. And mine finishes here. Don't you want to shoot me, Harry?"

Harry met Mathias's eyes. Then he turned the revolver around in his hand. Held it out to Mathias, butt first. "Do it yourself, you bastard."

Mathias frowned. Harry saw the hesitation, the suspicion. Which gradually gave way to a smile.

"As you wish." Mathias stretched across the railing and took the weapon. Caressed the black steel.

"You made a great error there, my friend," he said, pointing the revolver at Harry. "You'll make a nice period at the end of the sentence, Harry. The guarantee that my work will not be forgotten."

Harry stared into the black muzzle, watching the hammer raise its ugly little head. Everything seemed to move slower and the room began to revolve. Mathias took aim. Harry took aim. And swung his right arm. The handcuff made a low whine through the air as Mathias pressed the trigger. The dry click was followed by a metallic smack as the open cuff struck his wrist.

"Rakel survived," Harry said. "You failed, you satanic bastard."

Harry saw Mathias's eyes widen. Then narrow. Saw them stare at the revolver that had not fired, at the iron around his wrist binding him to Harry.

"You . . . you removed the bullets."

Harry shook his head. "Katrine Bratt never had bullets in her revolver."

Mathias looked up at Harry and leaned backward. "Come on."

Then he jumped.

Harry was jerked forward and lost his balance. He tried to hold on but Mathias was too heavy and Harry a diminished giant, weakened by the loss of flesh and blood. The policeman screamed as he was dragged over the steel rail and sucked toward the window and the abyss. What he saw as he threw his free left arm above his head and behind him was a chair leg and himself sitting alone in a filthy, windowless Chicago apartment. Harry heard the sound of metal on metal, then he tumbled through the night in free fall. The game was at an end now.

Gunnar Hagen stared at the ski jump tower but the swirling snowflakes that had started again obscured his vision.

"Harry!" he repeated on his walkie-talkie. "Are you there?"

He released the button, but again the answer was intense, rustling nothingness.

There were four patrol cars in the open parking lot by the jump now, and total confusion had reigned when they had heard the scream from the tower a few seconds before.

"They fell," said the officer beside him. "I'm sure I saw two figures falling out of the glass cage."

Gunnar Hagen lowered his head in resignation. He didn't quite know how or why, but for a moment it seemed to him there was an absurd logic in things ending this way; there was a kind of cosmic balance.

Nonsense. What utter nonsense.

Hagen couldn't see the police vehicles in the drifting snow, but he could hear the lament of the sirens, like wailing women; they were already on their way. And he knew that the sound would attract the scavengers: the media vultures, the nosy neighbors, the bloodthirsty bosses. They would come to get their favorite tidbit off the body, their delicacy. And this evening's two-course meal—the repugnant snowman and the repugnant policeman—would be to their liking. There was no logic, no balance, just hunger and food. Hagen's walkie-talkie crackled.

"We can't find them! Over."

Hagen waited, wondering how he would tell his superiors that he had let Harry go alone. How he would explain that he was only Harry's superior, not his boss and never had been. And that there was a logic there, too, and that actually he didn't give a damn whether they understood or not.

"What's going on?"

Hagen turned. It was Magnus Skarre.

"Harry fell," Hagen said, nodding toward the tower. "They're searching for the body now."

"Body? Of Harry? No chance."

"No chance?"

Hagen turned to Skarre, who was squinting up at the tower. "I thought you'd have known the guy by now, Hagen."

Hagen could feel that despite everything he envied the young officer his conviction.

The walkie-talkie crackled again. "They're not here!"

Skarre turned to him, their eyes met and Skarre rolled his shoulders in a **What did I tell you?** shrug.

"Hey, you!" Hagen shouted to the Land Rover driver and pointed at the searchlight on the roof. "Shine it on the glass cage. And get hold of some binoculars for me."

A few seconds later a beam cut through the night.

"Can you see anything?" Skarre asked.

"Snow," Hagen said, pressing the binoculars against his eyes. "Shine a bit higher. Stop! Wait . . . my God!"

"What?"

"Well, I'll be damned."

At that moment the snow retreated like a theater curtain being drawn. Hagen heard several policemen shout. It looked like two men shackled together were dangling from the rearview mirror of a car. The lower of the two held a hand above his head in a kind of triumphant flourish; the other had both arms stretched out vertically as if he were being crucified sideways. And both were lifeless, with sunken heads as they slowly gyrated in the air.

Through the binoculars Hagen could see the handcuff holding Harry's left hand to the railing on the inside of the glass cage.

"Well, I'll be damned," Hagen repeated.

As chance would have it, the young officer from the Missing Persons Unit, Thomas Helle, was crouched down by Harry Hole when he regained consciousness. Four policemen had hauled him and Mathias Lund-Helgesen back up into the glass cage. And in the years to come Helle would tell the story of the infamous inspector's strange first reactions again and again.

"He was all wild-eyed and asked if Lund-Helgesen was still alive! As though he was terrified the guy had died. As though that was the worst thing that could have happened. And when I said yes and that he was being taken away in the ambulance he yelled that we had to remove Lund-Helgesen's shoelaces and belt and make sure he didn't commit suicide. Have you ever heard anything like it? Showing that much care for a guy who'd just tried to murder your ex?"

37

Dad

Jonas thought he had heard the metallic jangle of the wind chimes, but had gone back to sleep. It was only when he heard the choking sounds that he opened his eyes. There was someone in the room. It was Dad; he was sitting on the edge of his bed.

And the choking sounds were him crying.

Jonas sat up in bed. He placed a hand on his father's shoulder and felt it shaking. It was odd; he had never noticed that his father had such narrow shoulders.

"They . . . they've found her," he sobbed. "Mom's . . ."

"I know," Jonas said. "I dreamed it."

The father swiveled around in surprise. In the moonlight seeping through the curtains Jonas could see the tears running down his cheeks.

"It's just us now, Dad," he said.

His father opened his mouth. Once. Twice. But nothing came out. Then he stretched out his arms, wrapped them around Jonas and drew him close.

Held him tight. Jonas laid his head against his father's neck, felt the hot tears wetting his scalp.

"Do you know what, Jonas?" he whispered through the tears. "I love you so much. You're the dearest thing I have. You're my boy. Do you hear? My boy. And you always will be. We'll manage, won't we? Don't you think?"

"Yes, Dad," Jonas whispered. "We'll manage. You and me."

38

The Swans

It was December and the fields outside the hospital windows lay bare and brown under a steel-gray sky. On the highway, studded tires crunched on dry pavement and pedestrians scuttled across the footbridge with coat collars turned up and faced closed. But inside the walls of the building people huddled closer. And on the table in the ward the two candles marked the second Sunday of Advent.

Harry pulled up in the doorway. Ståle Aune was sitting up in bed and had obviously just made a joke because the head of the Forensics Unit, Beate Lønn, was still laughing. On her lap sat a red-cheeked baby, looking at Harry with big round eyes and an open mouth.

"My friend!" Ståle growled as he caught sight of the policeman.

Harry walked in, stooped, gave Beate a hug and offered Ståle Aune a hand.

"You look better than when I saw you last," Harry said.

"They say I'll be discharged before Christmas," Aune said and turned Harry's hand in his. "That's some fiendish claw. What happened?"

Harry allowed him to study his right hand. "The middle finger was chopped off and couldn't be saved. They sewed together the sinews in the index finger, and the nerve endings will grow a fraction of an inch a month and try to find each other. Though the doctors say I'll have to live with permanent paralysis on one side of it."

"A high price."

"No," Harry said. "Small beer."

Aune nodded.

"Any news about when the case is due to come up?" asked Beate, who had got to her feet to put the baby in the stroller.

"No," Harry said, watching the forensic officer's efficient movements.

"The defense will try to have Lund-Helgesen declared mad," Aune said, preferring the demotic form "mad," which, in his opinion, was not only a suitable description but also poetic. "And not to achieve that would take an even worse psychologist than me."

"Oh, yes, he'll get life anyway," Beate said, angling her head and straightening the baby's blanket.

"Just a shame life isn't life," Aune growled and put out a hand for the glass on his bedside table. "The more aged I become, the more I tend to the view that evil is evil, mental illness or no. We're all more or less disposed to evil actions, but our disposition cannot exonerate us. For heaven's sake, we're all sick with personality disorders. And it's our actions that define how sick we are. We're equal before the law, we say, but it's meaningless as long as no one is equal. During the Black Death seamen who coughed were immediately heaved overboard. Of course they were. For justice is a blunt knife, both as a philosophy and as a judge. All we have is fortunate or less fortunate medical prospects, my dears."

"Nevertheless," Harry said, staring down at the still-bandaged stump of a middle finger, "in this case, it'll be for life."

"Oh?"

"Unfortunate medical prospects."

The silence filled the room.

"Did I say that I was offered a finger prosthesis?" Harry announced, waving his right hand. "But basically I like my hand as it is. Four fingers. Cartoon hand."

"What did you do with the finger that was there?"

"Tried to donate it to the Anatomy Department, but they weren't interested. So I'll have it stuffed and put it on my desk, just like Hagen does with the Japanese little finger. Thought an upright middle finger might be a suitable Hole welcome."

The other two laughed.

"How are Oleg and Rakel doing?" Beate asked.

"Surprisingly well," Harry said. "Toughies."

"And Katrine Bratt?"

"Better. I visited her last week. She starts work again in February. Going back to her old unit in Bergen."

"Really? Didn't she almost shoot someone in her excitement?"

"Wrong call. Turns out she was walking around with an empty revolver. That was why she dared to press the trigger so far back. And I should have known that."

"Oh?"

"When you move from one police station to another you hand in your service revolver and get a new one with two boxes of ammo. There were two unopened boxes in her desk drawer."

A moment of silence followed.

"It's good she's well again," Beate said, stroking the baby's hair.

"Yes," Harry said absentmindedly, and it occurred to him that it was true; she did seem to be getting better. When he had visited Katrine in her mother's apartment in Bergen she had just had a shower after a long run on Sandviken Mountain. Her hair was still wet and her cheeks red as her mother served tea and Katrine talked about how her father's case had become an obsession. And she apologized for having dragged him into the matter. He didn't see any regret in her eyes, though.

"My psychiatrist says that I'm just a few notches more extreme than most people." She had laughed, and then shrugged. "But now I'm done with all that. It's pursued me from my childhood. Now he's finally had his name cleared and I can move on with my life."

"Shuffling papers for the Sexual Offenses Unit?"

"We'll start there, then we'll see. Even top politicians make comebacks."

Then her eyes glided toward the window, across the fjord. Toward Finnøy, perhaps. And as Harry left he knew the damage was there and always would be.

He looked down at his hand. Aune was right; if every baby was a perfect miracle, life was basically a process of degeneration.

A nurse coughed by the door. "Time for a few jabs, Aune."

"Oh, please let me off, sister."

"No one is let off here."

Ståle Aune sighed. "What is worse? Taking the life of a person who wants to live or taking death from a person who wants to die?"

Beate, the nurse and Ståle laughed, and no one noticed Harry twitch in his chair.

Harry walked up the steep hills from the hospital to Lake Sognsvann. There weren't many people around, only the loyal throng of Sunday walkers doing their fixed circuit around the lake. Rakel waited for him by the roadblock.

They gave each other a hug and started the circuit in silence. The air was sharp and the sun matte in a pale blue sky. Dry leaves crackled and disintegrated beneath their heels.

"I've been sleepwalking," Harry said.

"Oh?"

"Yes. And I've probably been doing it for a while."

"It's not so easy to be fully present all the time," she said.

"No, no." He shook his head. "Quite literally. I think I've been up and walking through the apartment at night. God knows what I've been up to."

"How did you find out?"

"The night after I came home from the hospital I was standing in the kitchen looking at the floor, at some wet footprints. And then I realized I didn't have a stitch on, except for my rubber boots, it was the middle of the night and I was holding a hammer in my hand."

Rakel smiled and looked down. Skipped a pace so that they were walking in rhythm. "I started sleepwalking for a while. Right after I became pregnant."

"Aune told me adults sleepwalk at times of stress."

They stopped at the water's edge. Watched a pair of swans float past, calm and noiseless, on the gray surface.

"I knew from the very first moment who Oleg's father was," she said. "But I didn't know that he and I were having a child when he was informed that his girlfriend in Oslo was pregnant."

Harry filled his lungs with the sharp air. Felt it bite. It tasted of winter. He closed his eyes to the sun and listened.

"By the time I found out, he had already made his decision and left Moscow for Oslo. I had two options. To give the child a father in Moscow who would love and look after him as if he were his own—so long as he thought he **was** his own—or for the child to have no father. It was absurd. You know how I feel about lying. If someone had told me that I—I, of all people—would one day choose to live the rest of my life based on a lie, I would of course have denied it vehemently. You think everything is simple when you're young; you know nothing about the impossible decisions you may have to face. And if I'd only had myself to consider, this would have been a simple decision, too. But there were so many things to take into account. Not only whether I would crush Fjodor and affront his family, but also whether I would destroy things for the man who had gone to Oslo and his family. And then there was Oleg to take into account. Oleg came first."

"I understand," Harry said. "I understand everything."

"No," she said. "You don't understand why I haven't told you this before. With you there was no one else to take into account. You must think that I've tried to appear to be a better person than I am."

"I don't think that," Harry said. "I don't believe that you're a better person than you are."

She rested her head on his shoulder.

"Do you believe it's true what they say about swans?" she asked. "That they're faithful to each other until death do them part?"

"I believe they're faithful to the promises they've made," Harry said.

"And what promises do swans make?"

"None, I would assume."

"So you're talking about yourself now? In fact, I liked you better when you made promises and broke them."

"Would you like more promises?"

She shook her head.

When they started walking again she hooked her arm under his.

"I wish we could begin afresh," she said with a sigh. "Pretend nothing had happened."

"I know."

"But you also know that that's no good."

Harry could hear that the intonation implied this was a statement; however, hidden somewhere there was still a tiny question mark.

"I've been thinking of going away," he said.

"Oh, yes? Where?"

"I don't know. Don't come looking for me. Especially not in North Africa."

"North Africa?"

"It's a Marty Feldman line in a film. He wants to escape and be found at the same time."

"I see."

A shadow flitted across them and over the gray-yellow leached forest floor. They looked up. It was one of the swans.

"How did it work out in the film?" Rakel asked. "Did they find each other again?"

"Of course."

"When are you coming back?"

"Never," Harry replied. "I'm never coming back."

In a cold cellar in a Tøyen high-rise two worried representatives of the residents' committee were looking
at a man in overalls wearing glasses with unusually
thick lenses. The breath was coming out of the man's
mouth like white plaster dust as he spoke.

"That's the thing about mold. You can't see it's
there."

He paused. Pressed his middle finger against the
wisp of hair that was stuck to his forehead.

"But it is."

Jo Nesbø is a musician, songwriter, economist and author. His first crime novel featuring Harry Hole was published in Norway in 1997 and was an instant hit, winning the Glass Key Award for best Nordic crime novel (an accolade shared with Henning Mankell and Stieg Larsson). His previous Harry Hole novels include **The Redbreast, Nemesis,** and **The Devil's Star.** He lives in Oslo.

Don Bartlett lives in Norfolk, England, and works as a freelance translator of Scandinavian literature. He has translated, or co-translated, Norwegian novels by Lars Saabye Christensen, Roy Jacobsen, Ingvar Ambjørnsen, Kjell Ola Dahl, Gunnar Staalesen and Pernille Rygg.

Praise for
VENONA: *Decoding Soviet Espionage in America*

"The full implications of Soviet espionage in the United States during and immediately after World War II are only now being realized. In yet another superbly fascinating volume, Haynes and Klehr make wondrous use of the evidence in the Venona cables to reveal the scope of this limited, but very real 'attack' which remained secret for too long."—Daniel Patrick Moynihan

"With unmatched knowledge of American communism and Soviet espionage in America, Haynes and Klehr settle some of the most persistent historical controversies of the domestic cold war."—Richard Gid Powers

"Probably the definitive public study of Soviet espionage in the United States."—Arnold Beichman, *Weekly Standard*

"The reverberations from this cool, balanced, and devastating appraisal will be heard for many years to come."—*Kirkus Reviews*

"A careful explanation of the greatest codebreak of the Cold War."
—David Ignatius, *Washington Monthly*

"Preeminent authorities on American communism provide the first comprehensive examination of these files, one of U.S. counter-intelligence's greatest achievements."—Rorin M. Platt, *Foreign Service Journal*

"Reads like a fast-paced spy novel."—John Hanchette, *Gannett News Service*

"May open a fundamental revision of U.S. history."—Gilbert Taylor, *Booklist*

"Better than anything John le Carré could produce, because in this case, truth is really stranger than fiction."—*Library Journal*

VENONA

VENONA

Decoding Soviet Espionage in America

John Earl Haynes and Harvey Klehr

Yale Nota Bene
Yale University Press
New Haven and London

To my wife, Marcia Steinberg

—HARVEY KLEHR

To my wife, Janette

—JOHN EARL HAYNES

First published as a Yale Nota Bene book in 2000.

For information about this and other Yale University Press publications, please contact:

  U.S. office   sales.press@yale.edu
  Europe office sales@yaleup.co.uk

Printed in the United States of America.

The Library of Congress has cataloged the hardcover edition as follows:

Haynes, John Earl.
    Venona: Decoding Soviet espionage in America / John Earl Haynes and Harvey Klehr.
      p. cm.
    Includes index.
    ISBN 0-300-07771-8

    1. Communist Party of the United States of America—History—Sources. 2. Espionage, Soviet—United States—History—Sources. 3. Communism—United States—History—Sources. 4. Spies—Soviet Union—History—Sources. 5. Spies—United States—History—Sources. 6. Cryptography—United States—History—Sources. I. Klehr, Harvey. II. Title.
    JK2391.C5H39   1999
    327.1247'073'0904—dc21 98-51464

ISBN 0-300-08462-5 (pbk.)

A catalogue record for this book is available from the British Library.

10 9 8 7 6 5 4 3

Contents

Acknowledgments

Everyone who studies Soviet espionage owes a debt of gratitude to Sen. Daniel Patrick Moynihan, who was instrumental in persuading the American intelligence community to expedite the release of the Venona material. We are also grateful for the work of Michael Lostumbo, a member of Senator Moynihan's staff, and Eric Biel, the director of the Commission on the Protection and Reduction of Government Secrecy. We are particularly appreciative of the help and encouragement we have received from Robert Louis Benson and the late Cecil Phillips of the National Security Agency. They not only patiently answered our sometimes naive queries about cryptology; they also read the manuscript and saved us from many errors. A number of scholars, writers, journalists, retired FBI agents and intelligence officers, and independent researchers helped us in a variety of ways. We are in their debt. They include Joseph Albright, Alan Cullison, Michael Dobbs, Fridrikh Igorevich Firsov, Robert Harris, David Horowitz, Gary Kern, Marcia Kunstel, Robert Lamphere, David McKnight, Harry Mahoney, Eduard Mark, Daniel Menaker, Hayden Peake, Richard Powers, Ronald Radosh, Rosalee Reynolds, Herbert Romerstein, Stephen Schwartz, Sam Tanenhaus, John Walsh, and Michael Warner. None of these people, however, is responsible for any of our interpretations, and our errors and mistakes are ours alone.

We remain indebted to our friends and colleagues at Yale University Press who have once again forced us to work much harder than we anticipated. Richard Miller's excellent editing sharpened our prose and organization. Jonathan Brent is a model of what a sponsoring editor should be. And we thank Susan Abel. Our families—particularly Amanda and Bill Haynes and Benjamin, Gabriel, and Joshua Klehr and Aaron Hodes—deserve lots of credit for tolerating six years of obsession with Moscow archives, decrypted cables, one-time pads, Communists, and Soviet spies.

A Note about Transcription of the Documents

American and Soviet intelligence agencies had the practice in written documents and messages of printing proper names, including cover names, completely in capital letters. This was done to signal that when one read "on Monday PILOT reported," the source of the report was not a real pilot. Persons not used to reading intelligence material, however, frequently mistake the purpose of such capitalization for emphasis. To avoid distraction, the practice will not be followed in this book; only the initial letter of a cover name will be capitalized.

The documents decrypted in the Venona Project were translated from Russian over the period 1946–1981. During that time National Security Agency practices on transliterating Russian words and names from the Cyrillic to the Latin alphabet changed several times. Furthermore, a portion of work was done by British linguists, who rendered the translations in British English rather than American English. To avoid distracting readers who will wonder, understandably, if the "Anatolii" of one document is the same person as the "Anatoly" of another, all such words will be rendered under a single standard of anglicization.

Every deciphered cable of the Venona Project is given a unique citation that identifies the message by the sending and receiving station, the date of transmission, the agency of transmission, and an "external" message number given to the cable by the National Security Agency.

(The NSA derived the external number from a sequential number actually placed in the outgoing cable by Soviet code clerks.) A citation of "Venona 722 KGB New York to Moscow, 21 May 1942" refers to a ciphered cable message sent by the KGB station in New York to the KGB headquarters in Moscow on May 21, 1942, and given the external number 722 by the Venona Project. Complete sets of the Venona messages are available at the Manuscript Division of the Library of Congress, at the NSA's National Cryptologic Museum, Fort Meade, Maryland, and, as of 1998, on the NSA's World Wide Web page (www.nsa.gov).

Glossary

Organizations and acronyms are identified when they are first used in the text. This glossary lists organizations mentioned in more than one chapter in order to minimize the need to search back for the original identification. See the appendixes for names of individuals.

Arlington Hall: informal name for the predecessors to the National Security Agency.

BEW: see Board of Economic Warfare.

Board of Economic Warfare (BEW): wartime U.S. agency that gathered information on and coordinated strategic international economic affairs.

Comintern: see Communist International.

Comparty: Comintern abbreviation for Communist party.

Coordinator of Information (Office of the Coordinator of Information): Set up by President Roosevelt in 1941, in 1942 this agency was split into two parts, the Office of Strategic Services and the Office of War Information.

Communist International (Comintern): founded by Lenin in 1919 as the international headquarters of all Communist parties.

CPSU: Communist Party of the Soviet Union.

CPUSA: Communist Party of the United States of America.

Daily Worker: flagship newspaper of the CPUSA.

Dies committee: Special Committee on Un-American Activities, a committee of the U.S. House of Representatives headed from 1938 to 1944 by Rep. Martin Dies (Democrat, Texas).

FBI: Federal Bureau of Investigation, chief American internal security agency.

FEA: see Foreign Economic Administration.

FOIA: Freedom of Information Act.

Foreign Economic Administration (FEA): wartime U.S. agency for foreign aid and successor to the Board of Economic Warfare. Coordinated strategic international economic affairs.

Great Terror: the most intense period of the Stalin-era purges of Soviet society, lasting roughly from 1936 to 1939.

GRU: Glavnoe razvedyvatelnoe upravlenie (Chief intelligence directorate of the Soviet general staff), the Soviet military intelligence agency, not part of the KGB.

House Committee on Un-American Activities: U.S. House of Representatives standing committee, created in 1945, that investigated subversion, sedition, espionage and terrorism.

HUAC: common acronym (from the informal name House Un-American Activities Committee) for the House Committee on Un-American Activities.

International Brigades: Comintern army of about thirty thousand foreign volunteers that fought in the Spanish Civil War of 1936–1939.

International Lenin School: Comintern school for mid- and upper-level foreign Communists and for Soviet Communists who worked with foreign Communists.

KGB: Komitet gosudarstvennoi bezopasnosti (Committee for state security), chief security service of the USSR. The KGB had a complex organizational history and in some periods the foreign intelligence apparatus was organizationally separated from the much larger internal security apparatus.

National Security Agency (NSA): chief American intelligence agency for signals and ciphers.

Naval GRU: Soviet naval intelligence agency (separate from the KGB).

NSA: see National Security Agency.

Office of Emergency Management: wartime economic mobilization agency, predecessor to the War Production Board.

Office of Price Administration (OPA): wartime agency to control prices and ration goods.

Office of Strategic Services (OSS): chief American intelligence and covert action agency in World War II. Officially disbanded in 1945; the remnants of its officers and functions were transferred either to the State Department or to the military Joint Chiefs of Staff and in 1947 transferred back to the newly organized Central Intelligence Agency.

Office of the Coordinator of Inter-American Affairs: wartime U.S. agency headed by Nelson Rockefeller that coordinated American diplomacy, information gathering, and propaganda in South and Central America.

Office of War Information (OWI): chief American propaganda agency in World War II, directed at both foreign and domestic audiences.

OPA: see Office of Price Administration.

OSS: see Office of Strategic Services.

OWI: see Office of War Information.

Popular Front: term used to describe the Communist political stance from 1935 to 1939 when Communists sought to create and lead a broad liberal-left alliance based on antifascism and reformist policies. Also used to describe similar stances in the 1942–1950 period.

Profintern: Krasnyi internatsional professional'nykh soiuzov (Red international of labor unions). The Profintern was the Comintern's trade union arm.

RTsKhIDNI: Rossiskii tsentr khraneniia i izucheniia dokumentov noveishei istorii (Russian center for the preservation and study of documents of recent history), archive holding records of the Comintern (1919–1943), the CPUSA up to 1944, and the CPSU up to 1953.

Senate Internal Security Subcommittee (SISS): informal name for the U.S. Senate Committee on the Judiciary's Subcommittee to Investigate the Administration of the Internal Security Act and Other Internal Security Laws.

SISS: see Senate Internal Security Subcommittee.

Trotskyists (Trotskyites): followers of Leon Trotsky, a Bolshevik leader defeated by Stalin in the struggle to succeed Lenin; accused of left-wing ultrarevolutionary ideological deviation.

United Nations Relief and Rehabilitation Administration (UNRRA): wartime U.S. agency that coordinated U.S. foreign economic aid and relief.

UNRRA: see United Nations Relief and Rehabilitation Administration.

War Production Board (WPB): U.S. wartime agency that controlled and coordinated military industrial production.

WPB: see War Production Board.

YCL: see Young Communist League.

Young Communist League (YCL): youth arm of the CPUSA.

INTRODUCTION: THE ROAD TO VENONA

For more than forty years, nearly three thousand telegraphic cables between Soviet spies in the United States and their superiors in Moscow remained one of the United States government's most sensitive secrets. Hidden away in guarded archives at Fort Meade in Maryland, these messages, decrypted shortly after World War II in an operation known as Venona, may change the way we think about twentieth-century American history.

Fort Meade is only a half-hour's drive from Washington, but our route to the Venona decryptions began with a nine-thousand-mile journey to a forbidding gray stone building that fills one block of Puskinskaia Street in central Moscow. This building houses archives of the Communist Party of the Soviet Union (CPSU) and the enormous records of the Communist International. The Comintern, as it is known, supervised Communist parties the world over from 1919 until Joseph Stalin dissolved it in 1943.

The CPSU kept tight control over which researchers would be allowed into its archive and what materials they would be allowed to see. As American scholars, neither of us ever expected to receive such permission. But in December 1991, the Soviet Union collapsed and the new Russian government of Boris Yeltsin seized the property of the Communist party. The archive, renamed the Russian Center for the Preservation and Study of Documents of Recent History (RTsKhIDNI, pronounced "ritz-kidney"), soon opened for the first time for research by Western scholars. In six visits to RTsKhIDNI, we spent many weeks requesting files, reading records, taking notes, and copying documents about the history of communism in America.

At first, the staff at RTsKhIDNI were hospitable and eager to accommodate our research needs. On later visits, however, one official in particular seemed bent on slowing our work by interpreting archival rules in the most restrictive ways possible. We came to call her a "remnant of the era of stagnation," using the Russian phrase for the stifling bureaucracy of the Brezhnev era. When we asked another RTsKhIDNI official why this change from warmth to frost, he replied that she had assumed we were American Communists at the time of our first visits but now realized that we were not. While most RTsKhIDNI staff members clearly welcomed the openness of the new Russia and were very helpful to our research, the "remnant" was not the only one who missed the old days. A larger-than-life statue of Lenin stared out over the spacious foyer of the RTsKhIDNI building, and some devotee of the old order kept putting fresh flowers at his feet every day. This Lenin, however, gazed down with his stony eyes on the office cubicles of that quintessential capitalist enterprise, a private bank, to which the archive had rented out half the foyer.

After our first visit to study the Comintern archives, RTsKhIDNI officials asked whether we might also be interested in the archive of the American Communist party, the CPUSA. That those records existed was a stunning revelation to us. No such collection exists in the United States, and although historians had joked that the CPUSA's records were hidden in Moscow, no one knew that to be true. The CPUSA archive, RTsKhIDNI staff explained, was stored at a remote warehouse because in the Soviet period it had rarely been consulted. Did the archive really have the files of the American Communist party's headquarters? Or was this just a small collection of CPUSA reports and yellowing copies of the *Daily Worker*? When the records arrived from the warehouse, an archivist wheeled in a cart with the first batch of what turned out to be more than forty-three hundred files. We blew the thick dust off the folders, untied the ribbons that bound them, and looked inside. There, just as the Russians had said, were the original records of the CPUSA, shipped secretly to Moscow many years ago.

Our research in that archive has produced two books, *The Secret*

World of American Communism (1995) and *The Soviet World of American Communism* (1998), which examine the relationship of the CPUSA to the Comintern and clarify contested parts of American Communist history. Early in our RTsKhIDNI research, we came across a series of queries about specific American Communists which had been sent in 1943 and 1944 to Georgi Dimitrov, then head of the Comintern. The queries ordered the Comintern to provide any background information it had on those Americans and were signed simply "Fitin." We were intrigued because we recognized the named individuals as Americans who had been accused of being Soviet spies in the late 1940s. The queries had been made by Pavel Mikhailovich Fitin, the Soviet Union's spymaster and head of the foreign intelligence section of the KGB from 1940 to 1946. The meaning of the messages to Dimitrov became clear: they were vetting inquiries. The KGB was in the process of recruiting American Communists as spies and was conducting background checks with the Communist International.

The subject of one of Fitin's inquiries, Judith Coplon, brought an obscure American code-breaking project into our research. Coplon, an analyst working in the Foreign Agents Registration section of the U.S. Justice Department, had access to FBI counterespionage files. The FBI had arrested her in 1949 in the act of handing over some of those files to Valentin Gubitchev, a KGB officer who nominally worked as an official of the United Nations. In his 1986 memoir, the retired FBI agent Robert Lamphere related that the FBI had been alerted that Coplon was a Soviet spy when the National Security Agency (the NSA) deciphered a 1944 KGB message regarding her recruitment. Lamphere also said that similar deciphered messages had led the FBI to identify Klaus Fuchs, a British physicist working on the atomic bomb project, as a spy, a discovery that ultimately brought about the arrests of Julius and Ethel Rosenberg on charges of espionage for passing atomic secrets to the Soviet Union. The deciphered messages that set all this in train, said Lamphere, were from the NSA code-breaking project. But he provided few details about the operation. David Martin, in his 1981 history of espionage, had also discussed a highly secret American code-breaking project that had provided key evidence against the Rosenbergs and other Soviet spies, a finding affirmed by the historians Ronald Radosh and Joyce Milton in their 1983 history of the Rosenberg case. Other histories of espionage gave the NSA project a name: Venona.[1]

Another message from Fitin to Dimitrov concerned the willingness of a French political leader, Pierre Cot, then in wartime exile in the United States, to assist the Soviet cause. Peter Wright, a retired officer for the British counterintelligence agency, MI5, reported in his 1987 memoir that deciphered messages of the Venona Project had led British and American security officials to identify Cot as a Soviet agent.[2]

We realized that the Fitin queries that we found in the RTsKhiDNI archives pointed to Venona. But what exactly was the Venona Project? Had the NSA deciphered only a few Soviet messages or many hundreds? Were other spies besides Cot, Coplon, and Fuchs identified? What did the messages say?

The NSA was notoriously closemouthed about its activities and by reputation far more secretive than either the Central Intelligence Agency or the FBI. During the height of the Cold War, Washington insiders joked that the initials "N.S.A." really stood for "No Such Agency." When we asked various government officials about Venona, we ran up against a stone wall. One official told us that yes, there had been a code-breaking project called Venona; yes, it had produced much valuable information that had never been made public; and yes, the project was old, with all its deciphered messages from the World War II era; but no, neither we nor anyone else would have access to Venona's records for many decades to come. Such cryptographic intelligence, we were told, was too sensitive to allow the public to examine.

In *The Secret World of American Communism* we presented RTsKhIDNI documents confirming that the CPUSA maintained an underground arm, a fact long denied by the party and by many historians. Other documents reproduced in the book showed that on several occasions the American Communist underground and high CPUSA officials had cooperated with Soviet intelligence agencies in espionage against the United States. That volume reproduces the full text of the Fitin messages about Judith Coplon and Pierre Cot and discusses the apparent tie between those Moscow documents and what little was known about Venona.

Soon after the book was published, we received a telephone call from Sen. Daniel Patrick Moynihan of New York. Senator Moynihan had read the book, wanted to discuss a few points, and also had a request. He noted that he chaired the newly established Commission on Protecting and Reducing Government Secrecy, consisting of eight persons selected by Congress and four appointed by President Bill Clinton. Moynihan thought that the end of the Cold War required a drastic revision of the regime of secrecy and security classification set up during the forty-five-year confrontation with the Soviet Union. He explained that in order to get across why the end of the Cold War should bring about a rethinking of secrecy policies, he wanted the commission to gain a better understanding of why those policies were established in the first place. To that end, he asked us to testify before the commission.

When the commission met in May 1995, we described the findings of our book. With reference to the documents tied to Venona, we observed that it seemed improper and ironic that American scholars could find messages linked to the Moscow end of the Soviet cable traffic in an *open* Russian archive but that the messages themselves were still locked up in *closed* American archives. With the Cold War ended and the messages more than forty years old, the rationale for continued secrecy, we asserted, seemed weak. Senator Moynihan then turned to his right and spoke to John Deutch, a presidential appointee to the commission, who was head of the Central Intelligence Agency (CIA) and hence the coordinator of all U.S. intelligence activities. Moynihan asked that Deutch discuss with the NSA what the status of Venona was and whether its secrecy might no longer be necessary. Deutch indicated that he would, but he made no promises regarding the outcome.

In view of the adamant refusals to consider declassifying Venona that we had met with earlier, we were not optimistic that even Senator Moynihan's influence and persuasiveness could pry Venona open. We were not aware that behind the outward wall of silence, figures inside the U.S. intelligence community had already been advocating opening Venona. The NSA, it turned out, had long ago decided that the project had ceased to have any operational value to American intelligence and had shut it down in 1980. It was, literally, history. James Angleton, the former head of CIA counterintelligence, had told colleagues before his death in 1987 that the deciphered Venona messages should be made public. Open the messages up, he had argued, and historians and journalists with perspectives different from those of professional security officers would probably be able to attach real names to the cover names of Soviet sources that the combined efforts of the FBI, the CIA, and the NSA had been unable to identify. His insight would prove to be correct.

Robert Louis Benson, an NSA officer who had an interest in the history of American counterintelligence, argued within the agency that the time was ripe for Venona to become public and for the record to be set straight about Soviet espionage. Cecil Phillips, a retired NSA officer who had been one of the earliest cryptanalysts (code-breakers) working on the project, spoke for many Venona veterans who hoped that their astounding success in breaking what the Soviets had believed to be an unbreakable cipher would become public before they all passed from the scene. Nor could it have been lost on senior security officials that Senator Moynihan hoped to persuade the Congress to support a bill mandating a drastic reduction in government secrecy. If executive-branch officials refused to voluntarily lift the secrecy on a project involving Soviet cables that were more than forty years old, they would appear intransigent and unreasonable and would risk having Congress mandate a more sweeping reduction in secrecy. Making Venona public would show that officials could act reasonably under the current system without statutory directives. Further, Venona had been a great success for American counterintelligence; opening it up would allow intelligence professionals to take a few bows in public—something they rarely had a chance to do.

None of this internal debate, however, was public knowledge. So it was a complete surprise when just two months after the secrecy commission hearing, we received calls inviting us to CIA headquarters in Langley, Virginia, on July 11, 1995, for the official disclosure of the Venona Project. At the public ceremony the heads of the CIA, FBI, and NSA, along with Senator Moynihan, jointly announced that Venona was being opened and gave the surviving members of the Venona code-breaking team, almost all of whom had retired from government service years earlier, some well-deserved public pats on the back. They also brought the first batch of Venona messages to the light of day. These forty-nine messages detailed Soviet atomic espionage and unmistakably showed that Julius Rosenberg was a Soviet agent, an assertion that some historians and much of the American public had rejected as unsupported by documentary evidence. Here, at last, was the evidence.

Over the next two years, the National Security Agency released the remaining messages, more than twenty-nine hundred, amounting to more than five thousand pages of text. Reading—and, more to the point, comprehending—these thousands of messages, all written in an abbreviated telegraphic style and strewn with cover names, many only partially deciphered, was difficult. But the effort was worthwhile, for the Venona decryptions fill in many gaps in the historical record and corroborate testimony from FBI files and congressional hearings. We also found that the new evidence required us to modify earlier judgments.

In 1992, before RTsKhIDNI was open and long before the Venona decryptions were made public, we published a one-volume history of the CPUSA, entitled *The American Communist Movement: Storming Heaven Itself.* In it we put forward convincing evidence that some American Communists had assisted Soviet espionage against the United States. But the limitations of the evidence then available made us cautious in our broader judgment of the American Communist party: "Ideologically, American Communists owed their first loyalty to the motherland of communism rather than to the United States," we wrote, "but in practice few American Communists were spies. The Soviet Union recruited spies from the Communist movement, but espionage was not a regular activity of the American C.P. The party promoted communism and the interests of the Soviet Union through political means; espionage was the business of the Soviet Union's intelligence services. To see the American Communist party chiefly as an instrument of espionage or a sort of fifth column misjudges its main purpose."[3]

As our computers correlated the evidence we found, first at RTsKhIDNI in Moscow and then in the Venona decryptions; as they printed out the names, not of "few," but of hundreds of American Communists who abetted Soviet espionage in the United States; as we read the deciphered messages showing that regional CPUSA officials, members of the party's most powerful body, the Politburo, and the party chief himself knowingly and purposely assisted Soviet spies, it became clear that espionage was a regular activity of the American Communist party. To say that the CPUSA was nothing but a Soviet fifth column in the Cold War would be an exaggeration; it still remains true that the CPUSA's chief task was the promotion of communism and the interests of the Soviet Union through political means. But it is equally true that the CPUSA was indeed a fifth column working inside and against the United States in the Cold War.

CHAPTER 1

VENONA
AND THE
COLD WAR

The Venona Project began because Carter Clarke did not trust Joseph Stalin. Colonel Clarke was chief of the U.S. Army's Special Branch, part of the War Department's Military Intelligence Division, and in 1943 its officers heard vague rumors of secret German-Soviet peace negotiations.[1] With the vivid example of the August 1939 Nazi-Soviet Pact in mind, Clarke feared that a separate peace between Moscow and Berlin would allow Nazi Germany to concentrate its formidable war machine against the United States and Great Britain. Clarke thought he had a way to find out whether such negotiations were under way.[2]

Clarke's Special Branch supervised the Signal Intelligence Service, the Army's elite group of code-breakers and the predecessor of the National Security Agency. In February 1943 Clarke ordered the service to establish a small program to examine ciphered Soviet diplomatic cablegrams. Since the beginning of World War II in 1939, the federal government had collected copies of international cables leaving and entering the United States. If the cipher used in the Soviet cables could be broken, Clarke believed, the private exchanges between Soviet diplomats in the United States and their superiors in Moscow would show whether Stalin was seriously pursuing a separate peace.

The coded Soviet cables, however, proved to be far more difficult to read than Clarke had expected. American code-breakers discovered that the Soviet Union was using a complex two-part ciphering system involving a "one-time pad" code that in theory was unbreakable. The Venona code-breakers, however, combined acute intellectual analysis with painstaking examination of thousands of coded telegraphic cables to spot a Soviet procedural error that opened the cipher to attack. But by the time they had rendered the first messages into readable text in 1946, the war was over and Clarke's initial goal was moot. Nor did the messages show evidence of a Soviet quest for a separate peace. What they did demonstrate, however, stunned American officials. Messages thought to be between Soviet diplomats at the Soviet consulate in New York and the People's Commissariat of Foreign Affairs in Moscow turned out to be cables between professional intelligence field officers and Gen. Pavel Fitin, head of the foreign intelligence directorate of the KGB in Moscow.[3] Espionage, not diplomacy, was the subject of these cables. One of the first cables rendered into coherent text was a 1944 message from KGB officers in New York showing that the Soviet Union had infiltrated America's most secret enterprise, the atomic bomb project.[4]

By 1948 the accumulating evidence from other decoded Venona cables showed that the Soviets had recruited spies in virtually every major American government agency of military or diplomatic importance. American authorities learned that since 1942 the United States had been the target of a Soviet espionage onslaught involving dozens of professional Soviet intelligence officers and hundreds of Americans, many of whom were members of the American Communist party (CPUSA). The deciphered cables of the Venona Project identify 349 citizens, immigrants, and permanent residents of the United States who had had a covert relationship with Soviet intelligence agencies (see appendix A). Further, American cryptanalysts in the Venona Project deciphered only a fraction of the Soviet intelligence traffic, so it was only logical to conclude that many additional agents were discussed in the thousands of unread messages. Some were identified from other sources, such as defectors' testimony and the confessions of Soviet spies (see appendix B).

The deciphered Venona messages also showed that a disturbing number of high-ranking U.S. government officials consciously maintained a clandestine relationship with Soviet intelligence agencies and had passed extraordinarily sensitive information to the Soviet Union that had seriously damaged American interests. Harry White—the second most powerful official in the U.S. Treasury Department, one of the most influential officials in the government, and part of the American delegation at the founding of the United Nations—had advised the KGB about how American diplomatic strategy could be frustrated. A trusted personal assistant to President Franklin Roosevelt, Lauchlin Currie, warned the KGB that the FBI had started an investigation of one of the Soviets' key American agents, Gregory Silvermaster. This warning allowed Silvermaster, who headed a highly productive espionage ring, to escape detection and continue spying. Maurice Halperin, the head of a research section of the Office of Strategic Services (OSS), then America's chief intelligence arm, turned over hundreds of pages of secret American diplomatic cables to the KGB. William Perl, a brilliant young government aeronautical scientist, provided the Soviets with the results of the highly secret tests and design experiments for American jet engines and jet aircraft. His betrayal assisted the Soviet Union in quickly overcoming the American technological lead in the development of jets. In the Korean War, U.S. military leaders expected the Air Force to dominate the skies, on the assumption that the Soviet aircraft used by North Korea and Communist China would be no match for American aircraft. They were shocked when Soviet MiG-15 jet fighters not only flew rings around U.S. propeller-driven aircraft but were conspicuously superior to the first generation of American jets as well. Only the hurried deployment of America's newest jet fighter, the F-86 Saber, allowed the United States to match the technological capabilities of the MiG-15. The Air Force prevailed, owing more to the skill of American pilots than to the design of American aircraft.

And then there were the atomic spies. From within the Manhattan Project two physicists, Klaus Fuchs and Theodore Hall, and one technician, David Greenglass, transmitted the complex formula for extracting bomb-grade uranium from ordinary uranium, the technical plans for production facilities, and the engineering principles for the "implosion" technique. The latter process made possible an atomic bomb using plutonium, a substance much easier to manufacture than bomb-grade uranium.

The betrayal of American atomic secrets to the Soviets allowed the Soviet Union to develop atomic weapons several years sooner and at a substantially lower cost than it otherwise would have. Joseph Stalin's knowledge that espionage assured the Soviet Union of quickly breaking the American atomic monopoly emboldened his diplomatic strategy in his early Cold War clashes with the United States. It is doubtful that Stalin, rarely a risk-taker, would have supplied the military wherewithal and authorized North Korea to invade South Korea in 1950 had the Soviet Union not exploded an atomic bomb in 1949. Otherwise Stalin might have feared that President Harry Truman would stanch any North Korean invasion by threatening to use atomic weapons. After all, as soon as the atomic bomb had been developed, Truman had not hesitated to use it twice to end the war with Japan. But in 1950, with Stalin in possession of the atomic bomb, Truman was deterred from using atomic weapons in Korea, even in the late summer when initially unprepared American forces were driven back into the tip of Korea and in danger of being pushed into the sea, and then again in the winter when Communist Chinese forces entered the war in massive numbers. The killing and maiming of hundreds of thousands of soldiers and civilians on both sides of the war in Korea might have been averted had the Soviets not been able to parry the American atomic threat.

Early Soviet possession of the atomic bomb had an important psychological consequence. When the Soviet Union exploded a nuclear device in 1949, ordinary Americans as well as the nation's leaders realized that a cruel despot, Joseph Stalin, had just gained the power to destroy cities at will. This perception colored the early Cold War with the hues of apocalypse. Though the Cold War never lost the potential of becoming a civilization-destroying conflict, Stalin's death in March 1953 noticeably relaxed Soviet-American tensions. With less successful espionage, the Soviet Union might not have developed the bomb until after Stalin's death, and the early Cold War might have proceeded on a far less frightening path.

Venona decryptions identified most of the Soviet spies uncovered by American counterintelligence between 1948 and the mid-1950s. The skill and perseverance of the Venona code-breakers led the U.S. Federal Bureau of Investigation (FBI) and British counterintelligence (MI5) to the atomic spy Klaus Fuchs. Venona documents unmistakably identified Julius Rosenberg as the head of a Soviet spy ring and David Greenglass, his brother-in-law, as a Soviet source at the secret atomic bomb facility at Los Alamos, New Mexico. Leads from decrypted telegrams exposed the senior British diplomat Donald Maclean as a major spy in the British embassy in Washington and precipitated his flight to the Soviet Union, along with his fellow diplomat and spy Guy Burgess. The arrest and prosecution of such spies as Judith Coplon, Robert Soblen, and Jack

Soble was possible because American intelligence was able to read Soviet reports about their activities. The charges by the former Soviet spy Elizabeth Bentley that several dozen mid-level government officials, mostly secret Communists, had assisted Soviet intelligence were corroborated in Venona documents and assured American authorities of her veracity.

With the advent of the Cold War, however, the spies clearly identified in the Venona decryptions were the least of the problem. Coplon, Rosenberg, Greenglass, Fuchs, Soble, and Soblen were prosecuted, and the rest were eased out of the government or otherwise neutralized as threats to national security. But that still left a security nightmare. Of the 349 Americans the deciphered Venona cables revealed as having covert ties to Soviet intelligence agencies, less than half could be identified by their real names and nearly two hundred remained hidden behind cover names. American officials assumed that some of the latter surely were still working in sensitive positions. Had they been promoted and moved into policy-making jobs? Had Muse, the unidentified female agent in the OSS, succeeded in transferring to the State Department or the Central Intelligence Agency (CIA), the successor to the OSS? What of Source No. 19, who had been senior enough to meet privately with Churchill and Roosevelt at the Trident Conference? Was the unidentified KGB source Bibi working for one of America's foreign assistance agencies? Was Donald, the unidentified Navy captain who was a GRU (Soviet military intelligence) source, still in uniform, perhaps by this time holding the rank of admiral? And what of the two unidentified atomic spies Quantum and Pers? They had given Stalin the secrets of the uranium and plutonium bomb: were they now passing on the secrets of the even more destructive hydrogen bomb? And how about Dodger, Godmother, and Fakir? Deciphered Venona messages showed that all three had provided the KGB with information on American diplomats who specialized in Soviet matters. Fakir was himself being considered for an assignment representing the United States in Moscow. Which of the American foreign service officers who were also Soviet specialists were traitors? How could Americans successfully negotiate with the Soviet Union when the American negotiating team included someone working for the other side? Western Europe, clearly, would be the chief battleground of the Cold War. To lose there was to lose all: the task of rebuilding stable democracies in postwar Europe and forging the NATO military alliance was America's chief diplomatic challenge. Yet

Venona showed that the KGB had Mole, the appropriate cover name of a Soviet source inside the Washington establishment who had passed on to Moscow high-level American diplomatic policy guidance on Europe. When American officials met to discuss ser.sitive matters dealing with France, Britain, Italy, or Germany, was Mole present and working to frustrate American goals? Stalin's espionage offensive had not only uncovered American secrets, it had also undermined the mutual trust that American officials had for each other.[5]

The Truman administration had expected the end of World War II to allow the dismantling of the massive military machine created to defeat Nazi Germany and Imperial Japan. The government slashed military budgets, turned weapons factories over to civilian production, ended conscription, and returned millions of soldiers to civilian life. So, too, the wartime intelligence and security apparatus was demobilized. Anticipating only limited need for foreign intelligence and stating that he wanted no American Gestapo, President Truman abolished America's chief intelligence agency, the Office of Strategic Services. With the coming of peace, emergency wartime rules for security vetting of many government employees lapsed or were ignored.

In late 1945 and in 1946, the White House had reacted with a mixture of indifference and skepticism to FBI reports indicating significant Soviet espionage activity in the United States. Truman administration officials even whitewashed evidence pointing to the theft of American classified documents in the 1945 *Amerasia* case (see chapter 6) because they did not wish to put at risk the continuation of the wartime Soviet-American alliance and wanted to avoid the political embarrassment of a security scandal. By early 1947, however, this indifference ended. The accumulation of information from defectors such as Elizabeth Bentley and Igor Gouzenko, along with the Venona decryptions, made senior Truman administration officials realize that reports of Soviet spying constituted more than FBI paranoia. No government could operate successfully if it ignored the challenge to its integrity that Stalin's espionage offensive represented. In addition, the White House sensed that there was sufficient substance to the emerging picture of a massive Soviet espionage campaign, one assisted by American Communists, that the Truman administration was vulnerable to Republican charges of having ignored a serious threat to American security. President Truman reversed course and in March 1947 issued a sweeping executive order establishing a comprehensive security vetting program for U.S. government employees. He also created the Central Intelligence Agency, a stronger and larger version of the OSS, which he had abolished just two years earlier. In 1948 the Truman administration followed up these acts by indicting the leaders of the CPUSA under the sedition sections of the 1940 Smith Act. While the Venona Project and the decrypted messages themselves remained secret, the substance of the messages with the names of scores of Americans who had assisted Soviet espionage circulated among American military and civilian security officials. From the security officials the information went to senior executive-branch political appointees and members of Congress. They, in turn, passed it on to journalists and commentators, who conveyed the alarming news to the general public.

Americans' Understanding of Soviet and Communist Espionage

During the early Cold War, in the late 1940s and early 1950s, every few months newspaper headlines trumpeted the exposure of yet another network of Communists who had infiltrated an American laboratory, labor union, or government agency. Americans worried that a Communist fifth column, more loyal to the Soviet Union than to the United States, had moved into their institutions. By the mid-1950s, following the trials and convictions for espionage-related crimes of Alger Hiss, a senior diplomat, and Julius and Ethel Rosenberg for atomic spying, there was a widespread public consensus on three points: that Soviet espionage was serious, that American Communists assisted the Soviets, and that several senior government officials had betrayed the United States. The deciphered Venona messages provide a solid factual basis for this consensus. But the government did not release the Venona decryptions to the public, and it successfully disguised the source of its information about Soviet espionage. This decision denied the public the incontestable evidence afforded by the messages of the Soviet Union's own spies. Since the information about Soviet espionage and American Communist participation derived largely from the testimony of defectors and a mass of circumstantial evidence, the public's belief in those reports rested on faith in the integrity of government security officials. These sources are inherently more ambiguous than the hard evidence of the Venona messages, and this ambiguity had unfortunate consequences for American politics and Americans' understanding of their own history.

The decision to keep Venona secret from the public, and to restrict knowledge of it even within the government, was made essentially by senior Army officers in consultation with the FBI and the CIA. Aside from the Venona code-breakers, only a limited number of military intelligence officers, FBI agents, and CIA officials knew of the project. The CIA in fact was not made an active partner in Venona until 1952 and did not receive copies of the deciphered messages until 1953. The evidence is not entirely clear, but it appears that Army Chief of Staff Omar Bradley, mindful of the White House's tendency to leak politically sensitive information, decided to deny President Truman direct knowledge of the Venona Project.[6] The president was informed about the substance of the Venona messages as it came to him through FBI and Justice Department memorandums on espionage investigations and CIA reports on intelligence matters. He was not told that much of this information derived from reading Soviet cable traffic. This omission is important because Truman was mistrustful of J. Edgar Hoover, the head of the FBI, and suspected that the reports of Soviet espionage were exaggerated for political purposes. Had he been aware of Venona, and known that Soviet cables confirmed the testimony of Elizabeth Bentley and Whittaker Chambers, it is unlikely that his aides would have considered undertaking a campaign to discredit Bentley and indict Chambers for perjury, or would have allowed themselves to be taken in by the disinformation being spread by the American Communist party and Alger Hiss's partisans that Chambers had at one time been committed to an insane asylum.[7]

There were sensible reasons (discussed in chapter 2) for the decision to keep Venona a highly compartmentalized secret within the government. In retrospect, however, the negative consequences of this policy are glaring. Had Venona been made public, it is unlikely there would have been a forty-year campaign to prove that the Rosenbergs were innocent. The Venona messages clearly display Julius Rosenberg's role as the leader of a productive ring of Soviet spies.[8] Nor would there have been any basis for doubting his involvement in atomic espionage, because the deciphered messages document his recruitment of his brother-in-law, David Greenglass, as a spy. It is also unlikely, had the messages been made public or even circulated more widely within the government than they did, that Ethel Rosenberg would have been executed. The Venona messages do not throw her guilt in doubt; indeed, they confirm that she was a participant in her husband's espionage and in the recruitment of her brother for atomic espionage. But they suggest that she was essentially an accessory to her husband's activity, having knowledge of it and assisting him but not acting as a principal. Had they been introduced at the Rosenberg trial, the Venona messages would have confirmed Ethel's guilt but also reduced the importance of her role.

Further, the Venona messages, if made public, would have made Julius Rosenberg's execution less likely. When Julius Rosenberg faced trial, only two Soviet atomic spies were known: David Greenglass, whom Rosenberg had recruited and run as a source, and Klaus Fuchs. Fuchs, however, was in England, so Greenglass was the only Soviet atomic spy in the media spotlight in the United States. Greenglass's confession left Julius Rosenberg as the target of public outrage at atomic espionage. That prosecutors would ask for and get the death penalty under those circumstances is not surprising.

In addition to Fuchs and Greenglass, however, the Venona messages identify three other Soviet sources within the Manhattan Project. The messages show that Theodore Hall, a young physicist at Los Alamos, was a far more valuable source than Greenglass, a machinist. Hall withstood FBI interrogation, and the government had no direct evidence of his crimes except the Venona messages, which because of their secrecy could not be used in court; he therefore escaped prosecution. The real identities of the sources Fogel and Quantum are not known, but the information they turned over to the Soviets suggests that Quantum was a scientist of some standing and that Fogel was either a scientist or an engineer. Both were probably more valuable sources than David Greenglass. Had Venona been made public, Greenglass would have shared the stage with three other atomic spies and not just with Fuchs, and all three would have appeared to have done more damage to American security than he. With Greenglass's role diminished, that of his recruiter, Julius Rosenberg, would have been reduced as well. Rosenberg would assuredly have been convicted, but his penalty might well have been life in prison rather than execution.[9]

There were broader consequences, as well, of the decision to keep Venona secret. The overlapping issues of Communists in government, Soviet espionage, and the loyalty of American Communists quickly became a partisan battleground. Led by Republican senator Joseph Mc-Carthy of Wisconsin, some conservatives and partisan Republicans launched a comprehensive attack on the loyalties of the Roosevelt and Truman administrations. Some painted the entire New Deal as a disguised Communist plot and depicted Dean Acheson, Truman's secretary of state, and George C. Marshall, the Army chief of staff under Roosevelt and secretary of state and secretary of defense under Truman, as participants, in Senator McCarthy's words, in "a conspiracy on a scale so immense as to dwarf any previous such venture in the history of man. A conspiracy of infamy so black that, when it is finally exposed, its principals shall be forever deserving of the maledictions of all honest men."[10] There is no basis in Venona for implicating Acheson or Marshall in a Communist conspiracy, but because the deciphered Venona messages were classified and unknown to the public, demagogues such as McCarthy had the opportunity to mix together accurate information about betrayal by men such as Harry White and Alger Hiss with falsehoods about Acheson and Marshall that served partisan political goals.[11]

A number of liberals and radicals pointed to the excesses of McCarthy's charges as justification for rejecting the allegations altogether. Anticommunism further lost credibility in the late 1960s when critics of U.S. involvement in the Vietnam War blamed it for America's ill-fated participation. By the 1980s many commentators, and perhaps most academic historians, had concluded that Soviet espionage had been minor, that few American Communists had assisted the Soviets, and that no high officials had betrayed the United States. Many history texts depicted America in the late 1940s and 1950s as a "nightmare in red" during which Americans were "sweat-drenched in fear" of a figment of their own paranoid imaginations.[12] As for American Communists, they were widely portrayed as having no connection with espionage. One influential book asserted emphatically, "There is no documentation in the public record of a direct connection between the American Communist Party and espionage during the entire postwar period."[13]

Consequently, Communists were depicted as innocent victims of an irrational and oppressive American government. In this sinister but widely accepted portrait of America in the 1940s and 1950s, an idealistic New Dealer (Alger Hiss) was thrown into prison on the perjured testimony of a mentally sick anti-Communist fanatic (Whittaker Chambers), innocent progressives (the Rosenbergs) were sent to the electric chair on trumped-up charges of espionage laced with anti-Semitism, and dozens of blameless civil servants had their careers ruined by the smears of a professional anti-Communist (Elizabeth Bentley). According to this version of events, one government official (Harry White) was killed by a heart attack brought on by Bentley's lies, and another (Laurence Duggan, a senior diplomat) was driven to suicide by more of Chambers's malignant falsehoods. Similarly, in many textbooks President Truman's executive order denying government employment to those who posed security risks, and other laws aimed at espionage and Communist subversion, were and still are described not as having been motivated by a real concern for American security (since the existence of any serious espionage or subversion was denied) but instead as consciously anti-democratic attacks on basic freedoms. As one commentator wrote, "The statute books groaned under several seasons of legislation designed to outlaw dissent."[14]

Despite its central role in the history of American counterintelligence, the Venona Project remained among the most tightly held government secrets. By the time the project shut down, it had decrypted nearly three thousand messages sent between the Soviet Union and its embassies and consulates around the world. Remarkably, although rumors and a few snippets of information about the project had become public in the 1980s, the actual texts and the enormous import of the messages remained secret until 1995. The U.S. government often has been successful in keeping secrets in the short term, but over a longer period secrets, particularly newsworthy ones, have proven to be very difficult for the government to keep. It is all the more amazing, then, how little got out about the Venona Project in the fifty-three years before it was made public.

Unfortunately, the success of government secrecy in this case has seriously distorted our understanding of post–World War II history. Hundreds of books and thousands of essays on McCarthyism, the federal loyalty security program, Soviet espionage, American communism, and the early Cold War have perpetuated many myths that have given Americans a warped view of the nation's history in the 1930s, 1940s, and 1950s. The information that these messages reveal substantially revises the basis for understanding the early history of the Cold War and of America's concern with Soviet espionage and Communist subversion.

In the late 1970s the FBI began releasing material from its hitherto secret files as a consequence of the passage of the Freedom of Information Act (FOIA). Although this act opened some files to public scrutiny, it has not as yet provided access to the full range of FBI investigative records. The enormous backlog of FOIA requests has led to lengthy delays in releasing documents; it is not uncommon to wait more than five years to receive material. Capricious and zealous enforcement of regulations exempting some material from release frequently has elicited useless documents consisting of occasional phrases interspersed with long sections of redacted (blacked-out) text. And, of course, even the unexpurgated FBI files show only what the FBI learned about Soviet espionage and are only part of the story. Even given these hindrances, however, each year more files are opened, and the growing body of FBI documentation has significantly enhanced the opportunity for a reconstruction of what actually happened.

The collapse of the Union of Soviet Socialist Republics in 1991 led to the opening of Soviet archives that had never been examined by independent scholars. The historically rich documentation first made available in Moscow's archives in 1992 has resulted in an outpouring of new historical writing, as these records allow a far more complete and accurate understanding of central events of the twentieth century. But many archives in Russia are open only in part, and some are still closed. In particular, the archives of the foreign intelligence operations of Soviet military intelligence and those of the foreign intelligence arm of the KGB are not open to researchers. Given the institutional continuity between the former Soviet intelligence agencies and their current Russian successors, the opening of these archives is not anticipated anytime soon. However, Soviet intelligence agencies had cooperated with other Soviet institutions, whose newly opened archives therefore hold some intelligence-related material and provide a back door into the still-closed intelligence archives.

But the most significant source of fresh insight into Soviet espionage in the United States comes from the decoded messages produced by the Venona Project. These documents, after all, constitute a portion of the materials that are still locked up in Russian intelligence archives. Not only do the Venona files supply information in their own right, but because of their inherent reliability they also provide a touchstone for judging the credibility of other sources, such as defectors' testimony and FBI investigative files.

Stalin's Espionage Assault on the United States

Through most of the twentieth century, governments of powerful nations have conducted intelligence operations of some sort during both peace and war. None, however, used espionage as an instrument of state policy as extensively as did the Soviet Union under Joseph Stalin. In the late 1920s and 1930s, Stalin directed most of the resources of Soviet intelligence at nearby targets in Europe and Asia. America was still distant from Stalin's immediate concerns, the threat to Soviet goals posed by Nazi Germany and Imperial Japan. This perception changed, however, after the United States entered the world war in December 1941. Stalin realized that once Germany and Japan were defeated, the world would be left with only three powers able to project their influence across the globe: the Soviet Union, Great Britain, and the United States. And of these, the strongest would be the United States. With that in mind, Stalin's intelligence agencies shifted their focus toward America.

The Soviet Union, Great Britain, and the United States formed a military alliance in early 1942 to defeat Nazi Germany and its allies.[15] The Soviet Union quickly became a major recipient of American military (Lend-Lease) aid, second only to Great Britain; it eventually received more than nine billion dollars. As part of the aid arrangements, the United States invited the Soviets to greatly expand their diplomatic staffs and to establish special offices to facilitate aid arrangements. Thousands of Soviet military officers, engineers, and technicians entered the United States to review what aid was available and choose which machinery, weapons, vehicles (nearly 400,000 American trucks went to the Soviet Union), aircraft, and other matériel would most assist the Soviet war effort. Soviet personnel had to be trained to maintain the American equipment, manuals had to be translated into Russian, shipments to the Soviet Union had to be inspected to ensure that what was ordered had been delivered, properly loaded, and dispatched on the right ships. Entire Soviet naval crews arrived for training to take over American combat and cargo ships to be handed over to the Soviet Union.

Scores of Soviet intelligence officers of the KGB (the chief Soviet foreign intelligence and security agency), the GRU (the Soviet military intelligence agency), and the Naval GRU (the Soviet naval intelligence agency) were among the Soviet personnel arriving in America.[16] These

intelligence officers pursued two missions. One, security, was only indirectly connected with the United States. The internal security arm of
the KGB employed several hundred thousand full-time personnel, assisted by several million part-time informants, to ensure the political
loyalty of Soviet citizens. When the Soviets sent thousands of their citizens to the United States to assist with the Lend-Lease arrangement,
they sent this internal security apparatus as well. A significant portion
of the Venona messages deciphered by American code-breakers reported
on this task. The messages show that every Soviet cargo ship that arrived at an American port to pick up Lend-Lease supplies had in its
crew at least one, often two, and sometimes three informants who reported either to the KGB or to the Naval GRU. Their task was not to
spy on Americans but to watch the Soviet merchant seamen for signs
of political dissidence and potential defection. Some of the messages
show Soviet security officers tracking down merchant seamen who had
jumped ship, kidnapping them, and spiriting them back aboard Soviet
ships in disregard of American law. Similarly, other messages discuss
informants, recruited or planted by the KGB in every Soviet office in
the United States, whose task was to report signs of ideological deviation or potential defection among Soviet personnel.

A second mission of these Soviet intelligence officers, however, was
espionage against the United States, the size and scope of which is the
principal subject of this book. The deciphered Venona cables do more
than reveal the remarkable success that the Soviet Union had in recruiting spies and gaining access to many important U.S. government agencies and laboratories dealing with secret information. They expose beyond cavil the American Communist party as an auxiliary of the
intelligence agencies of the Soviet Union. While not every Soviet spy
was a Communist, most were. And while not every American Communist was a spy, hundreds were. The CPUSA itself worked closely with
Soviet intelligence agencies to facilitate their espionage. Party leaders
were not only aware of the liaison; they actively worked to assist the
relationship.

Information from the Venona decryptions underlay the policies of
U.S. government officials in their approach to the issue of domestic
communism. The investigations and prosecutions of American Communists undertaken by the federal government in the late 1940s and
early 1950s were premised on an assumption that the CPUSA had assisted Soviet espionage. This view contributed to the Truman adminis-

tration's executive order in 1947, reinforced in the early 1950s under the Eisenhower administration, that U.S. government employees be subjected to loyalty and security investigations. The understanding also lay behind the 1948 decision by Truman's attorney general to prosecute the leaders of the CPUSA under the sedition sections of the Smith Act. It was an explicit assumption behind congressional investigations of domestic communism in the late 1940s and 1950s, and it permeated public attitudes toward domestic communism.

The Soviet Union's unrestrained espionage against the United States from 1942 to 1945 was of the type that a nation directs at an enemy state. By the late 1940s the evidence provided by Venona of the massive size and intense hostility of Soviet intelligence operations caused both American counterintelligence professionals and high-level policy-makers to conclude that Stalin had already launched a covert attack on the United States. In their minds, the Soviet espionage offensive indicated that the Cold War had begun not after World War II but many years earlier.

This book describes Soviet espionage in the United States in the 1930s and 1940s. It concentrates on operations during World War II, the most aggressive and effective phase of Soviet activity. It also shows how the success of the wartime espionage offensive rested on the extensive base prepared in the 1930s by the Communist International and the American Communist party. Separate chapters deal with the role of American Communists in Soviet espionage, Elizabeth Bentley's extensive spy rings, the lesser but still significant American activities of Soviet military intelligence (GRU and Naval GRU) compared with that of the larger KGB, the broad scope of Soviet industrial and scientific espionage, and the Soviet Union's waging of a secret war on American soil against its ideological enemies: Trotskyists, Zionists, defectors, and Russian exiles of various types. The Venona decryptions are central to documenting this activity, and the next chapter details the history of that highly successful and long-secret project.

CHAPTER 2

BREAKING THE CODE

Soviet agencies in the United States during World War II used three channels to communicate with Moscow. Most material went by diplomatic pouch and courier. But in wartime the pouch, though secure, was quite slow, often taking many weeks and sometimes months to reach its destination. For time-sensitive material the Soviets had a choice of in-house short-wave radio, commercial radiograms, or international commercial telegraphic cables. None of these, however, was totally secure. Radio messages could be intercepted by anyone with the proper equipment and sufficient listening personnel, while messages sent by telegraphic cable could be copied easily by authorities in any nation through which the cable passed. And during the war, the United States and other nations routinely kept copies of international cables as a military precaution.[1]

The solution to the lack of security of radio and cable was encryption. If messages were sent in a code that other parties could not read, then it was largely a matter of indifference to the Soviets if they were intercepted. For communications with their offices in the United States, the Soviets usually chose commercial cable and radiogram rather than in-house radio transmission. The Venona messages discussed in this book were sent largely by commercial telegraphic cable, although some went as commercial radiograms. For simplicity, all will be referred to as cables.

The technology of the early 1940s did not allow for reliable short-wave radio links between Moscow and North America unless one was using a large and powerful transmitting station, which the Soviets could not build within the confines of their diplomatic compounds. Further, such transmitters were illegal in the United States. The Soviets equipped their American diplomatic posts with short-wave stations but rarely used them. The transmitters appear to have been established chiefly as backup for emergencies such as breakdowns in commercial telegraphic traffic.

One Soviet agency, the Communist International (Comintern), had made heavy use of short-wave radio in the 1930s for communications with the foreign Communist parties that it supervised. But most of this radio traffic was with Central and Western European parties, radio links far more reliable than those with more distant North America. Nonetheless, the Comintern maintained a clandestine radio link with the American Communist party (CPUSA) in the 1930s. The records of the Comintern in the RTsKhIDNI archive in Moscow contain hundreds of decoded radio messages that passed between the CPUSA and the Communist International.

Throughout much of the 1930s, the Comintern's radio link to the United States ran through a resident agent operating under a false identity. His real name was Solomon Vladimirovich Mikhelson-Manuilov. Numerous decoded cables between Moscow and Mikhelson-Manuilov show him supervising the distribution of Comintern funds to the United States, overseeing the arrival from and departure to Moscow of CPUSA and Comintern couriers, passing along Moscow's orders to the CPUSA leadership, and answering requests from Moscow for information about CPUSA activities. The CPUSA and the Comintern maintained two covert short-wave sending-and-receiving stations in the United States, one primary (in New York City) and one backup (on Long Island), both unlicensed and illegal. Mikhelson-Manuilov supervised their operation, but the stations were usually manned by trusted American Communists. One man, Arnold Reid, submitted to the Comintern's International Brigades an autobiography that proudly noted, as a sign of the CPUSA's confidence in him, his assignment to set up and run the covert radio station on Long Island in 1935.[2]

The Comintern's radio links to foreign parties, however, also illustrate the vulnerability of that medium. In late 1997 the Government Communications Headquarters (GCHQ), the British equivalent of the American National Security Agency, released for public access thousands of these messages. GCHQ's 1930s predecessor had intercepted the broadcasts from 1934 to 1937 and broken the Comintern's code in a project given the name Mask.[3]

The Comintern was hardly the only agency to have its messages intercepted and its code broken. Several of the greatest successes of the Allied powers in World War II had their origins in code breaking. The American breaking of one of the Japanese navy's chief radio codes helped U.S. Navy forces to maximize their limited resources and reverse the tide of war in the Pacific at the Battle of Midway. Similarly, British success in breaking a key German machine-generated cipher called Enigma allowed the Royal Air Force to concentrate its resources to best advantage and turn back the numerically superior Luftwaffe in the Battle of Britain.

Soviet diplomatic offices and the intelligence officers who operated out of them were well aware of the vulnerability of coded messages to being broken and read. Nonetheless, they sent thousands of coded cables, many containing highly sensitive information, even about Soviet espionage against other nations. They did so because they were using a coding system that was far more difficult to break than that used by the Germans and the Japanese (or the Comintern radio code)—an encryption system that, if employed correctly, was unbreakable.

The Soviet Code and Cipher System

The following description of probable Soviet encryption procedures is constructed from comments by National Security Agency cryptanalysts who worked on the Venona Project, from information supplied by defecting Soviet code clerks, and from the knowledge of functions necessary in encoding and decoding texts and then further enciphering them with a one-time pad.[4]

The Soviet intelligence officer first writes out his message in Russian in as concise a form as possible, to reduce the cipher clerk's work and the expense of transmitting the cable. (The exact texts of the outgoing messages were prepared in the code clerk's office, and incoming texts were kept in that office, with the intelligence officer only permitted to bring in or take out notes or extracts of texts.) Proper names of people and places were replaced with cover names by the intelligence officer—both to conceal their identity from intermediaries who might see the text and, perhaps, to make the identity more specific to the receiving intelligence officer.

Using a code book, the code clerk converts the message text into four-digit numerical codes. The code book is a sort of dictionary that contains numerical groups for letters, syllables, words, entire phrases—even for punctuation and for numbers. If a word or phrase is not present in the code book, it is spelled out using letter or syllable equivalents. If the word is a name spelled with Latin letters, it is spelled out using a separate "spell table."[5]

Let's say the KGB receives a report from one of its spies, in this case William Ullmann, who provided information on U.S. Army Air Force experiments on a new rocket. (Ullmann was an Army Air Force officer assigned to the Pentagon.) The KGB sends Ullmann's detailed report about the rocket experiment to Moscow by diplomatic pouch. But it notifies Moscow by cable that Ullmann's report is on the way. The KGB officer might originally write (in Russian), "Ullmann delivered report about rockets." He then (or at the time of writing) substitutes Ullmann's cover name (Pilot) and hands the cipher clerk a message saying, "Pilot delivered report about rockets." The cipher clerk then consults his code book and converts the message to four-digit numbers:

Pilot	delivered	report	about	rockets
7934	2157	1139	3872	2166

The clerk then converts these four-digit groups into five-digit groups by shifting a digit from the second group to the first, and so on: 79342 15711 39387 22166.

Next the cipher clerk turns to the one-time pad. Each page of the pad contains 60 five-digit numerical groups, called the additive or the key. The clerk takes the first group in the upper lefthand corner of the page (26473 in this illustration) and writes it down as the first group of the message before he enciphers any text. This serves to tell the deciphering clerk on the receiving end (who has the same pad) which page to use or, more precisely, to confirm that the message he has just received was enciphered on the next page of the one-time pad.[6]

Starting with the second five-digit group on the key page, the code clerk places the numbers from the pad beneath the numbers from the code book. He then adds the numbers together; if the sum is greater than 9, nothing is carried (8 plus 6 yields 4, not 14, because the 1 is not carried). This produces a new set of enciphered five-digit numbers, which are placed after the first group from the key page, which serves as an indicator.

From the code book:		79342	15711	39387	22166
From the one-time pad:	26473	56328	29731	35682	23798
The enciphered message:	26473	25660	34442	64969	45854

Finally, the five-digit groups are converted to five-letter groups by the code clerk using the following substitution to Latin letters: 0=O, 1=I, 2=U, 3=Z, 4=T, 5=R, 6=E, 7=W, 8=A, 9=P.[7] This produces:

UETWZ UREEO ZTTTU ETPEP TRART . . . TEERP 23412

At the end of the message text he enters the next five-digit group from the one-time pad after the last one actually used for encipherment (46659 in the letter form of TEERP) and also enters *as digits* a five-digit group (23412 in this illustration), of which the first three digits are a serial number for all of the messages on that circuit and the last two digits are the date of encipherment.[8]

In Moscow the cable is determined to be KGB by an initial receiving point and then routed to the KGB cipher office and converted back to:

(26473) 25660 34442 64969 45854 . . . (46659)

The deciphering clerk then goes to his copy of the one-time pad. If no messages have been reordered in transmission, the group 26473 should confirm that he has the proper page for decipherment. Further, if the group 46659 appears at a point that corresponds exactly to the number of cipher groups received, it confirms that all cipher groups have been received. The clerk then subtracts the five-digit numbers given by the one-time pad. When the number to be subtracted is larger than the number being subtracted from, ten is added without borrowing (4 minus 6 yields 8). If the clerk does his arithmetic correctly, he now has the original five-digit groups: 79342 15711 39387 22166. After rebreaking this string of numbers into four-digit groups—essentially reversing the encryption procedure—he consults the code book and uncovers the message:

7934	2157	1139	3872	2166
Pilot	delivered	report	about	rockets

The message is then passed to the appropriate KGB officer at headquarters. The officer consults his own records and converts the cover name to the real name, Ullmann.[9]

Compromise of the Soviet Cipher System

Cecil Phillips, one of the American cryptanalysts who eventually broke the Soviet cipher, described the Soviet system: "The messages broken by the Venona program were both coded and enciphered. When a code is enciphered with a one-time pad, the cryptographer who designed the system expects the encipherment to provide absolute security—even if an adversary somehow obtains an underlying codebook or debriefs a defecting code clerk. . . . The security of such an encipherment-decipherment system depends on both the randomness (that is, unpredictability) of the "key" on the one-time pad pages and the uniqueness of the one-time pad sets held by the sender and the receiver."[10] If constructed correctly, each message in the Soviet one-time pad system was in a unique cipher. There was no repetition of the random cipher in any other message, which meant there was no way for the code-breaker (cryptanalyst) to decipher the message.

But this total security had a price. Because each coded message was further enciphered by a unique additive key (the one-time pad page) and there were hundreds of thousands of messages produced in wartime, the code-makers (cryptographers) had to manufacture hundreds of thousands of unique, nonrepeating key pages.[11] To be unbreakable, the key pages truly had to be used just one time. In an era before high-speed digital computers, this put a tremendous strain on code-makers to produce one-time pads.

German and Japanese cryptographers were as aware of the unbreakability of the one-time pads as were the Soviets. But in view of the daunting requirements for skilled personnel to produce huge quantities of one-time pads, each page containing a unique random-number cipher, they chose another route. They developed ciphers that, while theoretically less secure than one-time pads, could be much more easily manufactured and used. The German "Enigma" machine cipher, for example, was produced by a primitive electromechanical computer. Both the Germans and the Japanese believed that these ciphers, while in theory vulnerable to cryptanalysis, were as a practical matter unbreakable. Their error, based on an underestimation of the capabilities of British and American code-breakers, contributed to their defeat in the war.

The Soviets, who had a well-deserved reputation for obsession with secrecy, chose to do things the hard way, using one-time pads and paying the price of employing a small army of code-makers. For a while, though, Soviet cryptographers were unable to produce new key pages fast enough to meet demand. In June 1941 Adolf Hitler broke his alliance with Joseph Stalin and invaded the USSR. Overnight the production of ciphered messages by Soviet diplomatic and intelligence offices skyrocketed. It is not known for certain, but it appears that the existing stock of one-time pads began to melt away, and the Soviet cryptographic office in Moscow faced an emergency. Individuals who failed to meet military production quotas faced severe, sometimes mortal consequences, so the crisis was not only national but also personal. The solution, in early 1942, was to produce duplicate key pages. Whether this expedient was introduced intentionally by a panicky senior official or a desperately overworked staff of cryptographers is not known. In any case, tens of thousands of duplicate key pages were bound in one-time pads during 1942.[12]

Thus, for a period Soviet cryptographers doubled their output by duplicating cipher pages, almost certainly by the simple expedient of using extra carbon sheets in the machines that typed out the key pages. This, of course, turned their one-time key pages into two-time key pages. Perhaps they thought the risk minimal. Many professional cryptographers believed that a single duplication, while voiding the theoretical unbreakability of the cipher, in practice only marginally degraded the security of the system. Further, for a duplication to be of any use to cryptanalysts, both messages using the duplicated key page had to be copied, and some strategy had to be developed to establish that both messages had used the same key. To minimize this risk, the Soviets did not duplicate entire pads. Rather, they duplicated individual pages, then shuffled them into different pads, often with different page numbers, and distributed them to Soviet offices across the globe. Only a code-breaking agency with extensive sources throughout the world would be in a position to gather enough of the duplicated messages even to attempt to attack the Soviet cipher. And the attack itself would require resources to deploy a team of cryptanalysts of the highest order for many years.

The National Security Agency of the United States (NSA), however, had those resources. The NSA originated as the Army's Signal Intelligence Service. Before World War II, the Army had only a limited cryptographic capacity. In September 1939, when Germany invaded Poland, the entire staff of the Signal Intelligence Service numbered merely nineteen. By the time of the Japanese attack on Pearl Harbor, more than two years later, the staff had grown to nearly four hundred; yet this included not just code-makers and code-breakers but also large radio interception staffs in Washington and in various field locations, support personnel, and the headquarters section. With America in the war, however, the Army quickly added thousands of staff members to its communications intelligence and code-breaking effort, and the service's personnel grew to more than ten thousand by 1945. To accommodate its greatly enlarged staff, the Signal Intelligence Service took over Arlington Hall, the campus of a private girls' preparatory school in northern Virginia, across the Potomac River from Washington, D.C. For many years the agency was informally known within the government as Arlington Hall, if for no other reason than that its formal title kept changing. In 1949, when signals and cryptographic intelligence units from the Navy and Air Force were added, Arlington Hall was transformed into the Armed Forces Security Agency, removed from Army control, and placed under the Joint Chiefs of Staff. In 1952 the agency was given its current name, the National Security Agency, and came under the supervision of the secretary of defense. It also moved to a new site, at Fort George Meade, Maryland, outside Washington. For simplicity, the name National Security Agency will be used throughout this book.

The prewar Army's few professional cryptographers were vastly outnumbered by the new staff mobilized for World War II. These new code-breakers came from a variety of backgrounds: philologists and linguists with a range of foreign language skills, mathematicians to whom numerical ciphers were a technical challenge, engineers and technicians who worked on radio interception and construction of cipher machines, and English majors with a love for puzzles. Arlington Hall veterans note that card games emphasizing mathematical skills, such as bridge, as well as the maddeningly difficult crossword puzzles of the *London Times* and the *New York Times*, were a common form of relaxation among staff. Much of the new staff was female because the uniformed services took so many males for other military duties. Almost all the new personnel had to be taught, or in many cases had to teach themselves, the skills and principles of cryptography. Very quickly, though, Arlington Hall scored valuable successes against both German and Japanese ciphers. By the end of World War II this little-known agency, built almost from the ground up by wartime amateurs, rivaled the British Government Communications Headquarters as the most skilled code-breaking agency in the world.

The NSA's predecessors began to collect enciphered Soviet and other telegrams in 1939. But for several years little was done with the Soviet messages because German and Japanese codes had a higher priority and because American cryptanalysts had made very little headway against Soviet ciphers in the past. In 1942, however, NSA success against the Japanese military attaché code stimulated a second look at Soviet messages. The NSA deciphered cables between the Japanese army's general staff and its military attachés in Berlin and Helsinki regarding the work of Finnish cryptanalysts on Soviet ciphers. The Finns had an excellent cryptographic staff that concentrated almost entirely on the Soviet Union, the chief threat to Finland. The Finns had not broken any of the Soviet diplomatic ciphers, but they had developed a partial understanding of their external characteristics and were able to sort most diplomatic messages into a series of identifiable variants. They relayed the information to the Japanese, who shared the Finns' antipathy toward the Soviets.[13]

This Finnish-Japanese information allowed American cryptanalysts to separate messages into homogeneous sets—a prerequisite to starting any cryptanalytic attack. It also suggested—incorrectly—that the Russians employed reusable key tables rather than one-time pads. This may have encouraged American cryptanalysts to believe that the Soviet cipher might yield rapidly to their analysis. It was at this time, in 1943, that Carter Clarke of the Army's Special Branch authorized the examination of the Soviet cables. Initially the project had no special name and was referred to by such phrases as the "Russian diplomatic problem." The deciphered messages themselves later received a formal code name—first Jade, then Bride, then Drug, and finally, in 1961, Venona. Eventually the entire code-breaking effort became known as the Venona Project.

NSA analysts soon identified five variants of the Soviet one-time pad cipher. One was called Trade, because it carried the traffic of Amtorg, the Soviet trading agency, and the Soviet Government Purchasing Commission, which oversaw Soviet receipt of American Lend-Lease aid. A second variant was used by diplomats in the Soviet foreign ministry.

The other three variants, however, were used by officers of the three Soviet intelligence agencies: the KGB, the GRU, and the Naval GRU. These intelligence officers were operating out of the Soviet embassy and consulates as well as Amtorg and purchasing commission offices in Washington, New York, and San Francisco.

A breakthrough came in autumn 1943, when Lt. Richard Hallock, analyzing Trade messages, demonstrated that the Soviets were making extensive use of duplicate key pages assembled in separate one-time pad books. The work of Hallock and his colleagues opened the first crack in the walls of the Soviet code and yielded methods for discovering duplicate pages.[14] Over time, and after a prodigious amount of analytic work, American cryptanalysts showed that even a single duplication of a one-time pad cipher rendered the messages vulnerable to decryption.

As World War II was drawing to a close, the staff working on Venona increased as cryptanalysts who had been assigned to Japanese and German ciphers sought new projects. One of these newcomers was a brilliant and innovative cryptanalyst named Samuel Chew. Working on Trade traffic, he discovered some highly predictable patterns in the shipping messages. Many of the Trade messages were time-sensitive but otherwise routine notifications to Moscow that certain ships were leaving American ports with specified cargoes of Lend-Lease supplies.

Chew's work had a dramatic impact on the efforts of those who were recovering cipher keys. They were now able to solve or remove the one-time pad cipher for stretches of Trade code text and thereby to reveal significant strings of KGB code. These strings, though still in digital code-group form for which the Russian meanings were unknown, accumulated rapidly in the latter half of 1945 as the work effort was sharply increased thanks to staff coming off the Japanese code and cipher problems.

While breaking the one-time pad cipher was a key to the success of Venona, it was not the end of the code-breaking project, because the Soviets used a two-stage system. The Soviet code clerk first encoded the message from a code book and then further complicated the code by use of the one-time pad cipher. The duplicated cipher pages allowed the NSA to break the second part, but not the first. To solve the first part and make the message readable, cryptolinguists had to re-create the Soviet code book.[15]

Although Chew developed a fair amount of Russian language skill, solving the underlying coded text called for a full-time linguist "book-breaker." In the parlance of cryptography, a book-breaker seeks to establish the textual meanings of numerical ciphers by "breaking" into the code book used by the opponent. It was at this time, early in 1946, that Meredith Gardner transferred to the Venona Project and became the principal book-breaker for all the codes of the Soviet cable project. A tall, gangling, soft-spoken Southerner, Gardner read German, Sanskrit, Lithuanian, Spanish, and French and had taught languages at universities in Texas and Wisconsin. Shortly after Pearl Harbor, the Army had recruited him to work on German and Japanese codes, and he had taught himself Japanese in the process. In 1946 he began a new language, Russian. His linguistic work was helped by the now expanding body of plain code groups (what was left when the overlying one-time pad cipher was removed) being extracted from Trade and KGB messages that had used the duplicate key pages. By about mid-summer 1946, Gardner had recovered enough code groups and text to be sure that the messages involved Soviet espionage. By the end of 1946, he had broken out the text of a message that revealed Soviet atomic spying.

Eventually it would become clear that Gardner had reconstructed the code book used by the KGB from November 1943 into early 1946. This work allowed the reading of hundreds of KGB messages from that period and provided some of the most complete text that the Venona Project produced. It also became clear, however, that the KGB had used a different code book for 1942 and most of 1943. NSA analysts made little progress on those messages for several years. Then in late 1953 Samuel Chew was able to solve a set of code clerk "key-saving" cases that Cecil Phillips had identified earlier.[16] This breakthrough afforded significant progress on earlier messages.

Shortly after Chew's analysis, the NSA also determined that a copy of a badly burned Soviet code book in American hands contained some of the code used in these earlier KGB messages. Finnish troops had captured the code book when they overran the Soviet consulate at Petsamo, Finland, in June 1941.[17] The Germans then obtained the book from the Finns. In May 1945 a U.S. Army intelligence team headed by Lt. Col. Paul Neff found a copy at a German signals intelligence archive located in a castle in Saxony, Germany. The archive was in territory assigned to the Soviet zone of occupation, and Neff's team removed the copy only a day before the Soviets pushed into the area.[18] Although badly damaged, the book assisted Meredith Gardner in reconstructing part of the KGB code book for the earlier years. The reconstruction, however, was not as complete as that achieved for the KGB code book for November 1943–1946, and the decryptions for that earlier period are less complete.

This burned code book is not the same as the code and cipher materials that were obtained from Finnish officers by another American intelligence agency, the Office of Strategic Services, in late 1944. In that case, the State Department learned of the matter and, in a remarkably naive act, successfully urged President Roosevelt to order the OSS to hand the material over to the KGB as a gesture of goodwill. So far as is known, the OSS did not even keep a copy.[19]

The third of the five main Soviet systems to be breached successfully was that used by the diplomats of the Soviet foreign ministry. A small amount of progress in finding duplicate key pages among messages was made in late 1946, but these instances were essentially unexploitable. Real success in deciphering foreign ministry messages was achieved by the mathematician Richard Leibler in 1950. Leibler's work led to finding a large number of duplicate key pages among foreign ministry messages, and between foreign ministry messages and other systems, and ultimately pointed the way to the success in decrypting some GRU and Naval GRU messages.

The nature of the key page indicator (used to identify messages ciphered from duplicate key pages) and the underlying code made both the GRU and Naval GRU systems more resistant to NSA analysis than the KGB system was. It was not until 1952 that computer assaults, devised by the mathematician Hugh Gingerich on the basis of Leibler's earlier work, allowed duplicate key pages to be found among a limited number of GRU messages. The attack was grounded in observations of code practices made by the cryptolinguist Charles Condray and others. It was even later, in 1957, that Naval GRU messages gave way, in the face of an analytic offensive by British cryptanalysts who were working with the Venona Project.

Although from the late 1940s through the 1970s many hundreds of messages were entirely or almost entirely read, a significant number were only partially decrypted. Analysis yielded a paragraph or two, or several sentences and partial phrases split up by the cryptanalyst's bracketed comment "[37 unrecovered code groups]," "[two unrecovered code groups]," or some other total of numerical code groups that the NSA was never able to render into readable prose. In the Venona Project more than twenty-nine hundred messages amounting to more than five thousand pages of text were decrypted and read. But as impressive as that feat was, the messages represented only a fraction of the total Soviet cable traffic. Venona uncovered, in whole or in part, roughly half (49 percent) of the messages sent in 1944 between the KGB New York office and its Moscow headquarters, but only 15 percent of the messages from 1943 and a mere 1.8 percent of the messages from 1942 (only twenty-three out of nearly thirteen hundred). Only 1.5 percent of the 1945 traffic between the KGB Washington office and Moscow was deciphered. Venona cryptanalysts read half of the Naval GRU's Washington traffic in 1943 but not a single Naval GRU message for any other year.

The National Security Agency also established relations with Britain's highly regarded cryptographic service (GCHQ), and several of their linguists and analysts joined the Venona Project in 1948. (The British contribution can be observed in a number of messages that are rendered into British English rather than into American idiom.) Initially, of course, the NSA had copies of ciphered Soviet cables sent to and from Soviet diplomatic offices in the United States. Through a variety of means the NSA garnered ciphered Soviet cables from other nations as well, eventually including Soviet offices in Canada, Great Britain, France, the Netherlands, Sweden, Germany, Czechoslovakia, Bulgaria, Turkey, Iran, Japan, Manchuria, Ethiopia, South Africa, Australia, Chile, Uruguay, Colombia, Mexico, and Cuba. The Venona Project continued until October 1, 1980, although on a reduced scale in the 1970s. But even in the last year new messages, thirty-nine in all, were broken. By that point, the NSA deemed the material so old that it no longer had operational value to American intelligence, and the project ended. Its product, however, remained secret until 1995.

Until late 1947 the NSA worked virtually alone on Venona and shared it with only a few officials in Army intelligence. But at that point Carter Clarke, now a general and the Army's deputy G-2 (military intelligence), concluded that the information required wider dissemination if it were to be properly understood and used. In particular, while some of the identities of cover names in the Venona traffic were obvious, others were not. For example, by mid-1947 Gardner had broken messages that discussed a Soviet agent who at first had the cover name Antenna and later was called Liberal. Gardner did not know his identity, but one of the decrypted messages from the New York KGB office to Moscow reported that Liberal's wife of five years was named Ethel and was twenty-nine years old.[20] These investigative leads required further work. The NSA, however, was a cryptologic agency: it did not have street investigators who could check on candidates for Antenna/Liberal and see which one had a wife named Ethel.

General Clarke spoke with S. Wesley Reynolds, the FBI liaison with Army G-2. Initial cooperation was tentative, but in October 1948 Reynolds brought Special Agent Robert Lamphere to the Venona Project as its full-time FBI liaison. The result was a fruitful partnership that allowed rapid progress in identifying cover names in Venona. Gardner handed over deciphered Venona messages showing cover-named Soviet agents at certain places on certain days, holding certain jobs, with certain family circumstances and individual characteristics. In turn, the FBI looked at its own investigative files and undertook new checks to identify persons who fit the information provided by the deciphered Venona messages. Over the next years hundreds of cover names were identified. In 1950 this cooperation allowed the NSA and the FBI to identify Antenna/Liberal as Julius Rosenberg, who in the right year had married Ethel Greenglass, who was the right age.

Cover names played a security role in obscuring the identity of a person. But they also were used because they lessened the work of code clerks and promoted clarity. Proper names and other words not found in the code book had to be laboriously spelled out letter by letter from a table that had two-digit code groups for each letter. This was further complicated by having to convert English names from the Latin alphabet to the Cyrillic. It was easier to establish a cover name that was in the code book, or at least to use a short cover name, than to spell out a lengthy name. Use of cover names also minimized the risk of confusion that might result from spelling out similar names, particularly non-Russian ones.

The Soviets believed that the real security of their cables lay in their use of the unbreakable one-time pad cipher, not in the lesser security device of cover names. Consequently, although cover names predominate in the Venona messages, the real names of agents on occasion also appear in clear text. Often, when the KGB in the United States established a relationship with a new source, it would send a message to Moscow giving the agent's real name and then stating a new cover name that would be used in the future.[21] Cover names frequently hinted at a person's profession or character—a serious error if security is a primary consideration. George Silverman, a Soviet source in the U.S. Army

Air Force, had the cover name Aileron. Harold Glasser, a Soviet agent in the U.S. Treasury, received the cover name Ruble, the name of the Soviet currency. One writer has waggishly referred to the "semiotics of Venona," referring to the way Soviet intelligence officers indulged in insider humor and, consciously or unconsciously, expressed their attitudes by their choices of cover names.[22] The KGB gave Trotskyists and Zionists, both hated enemies, the cover names Polecats and Rats, respectively. Expressing their view that American intelligence and counterintelligence agencies were unsophisticated compared with themselves, the KGB assigned to the OSS the name Izba, the Russian word for log cabin, while the FBI received the similarly belittling designation Khata, or the Hut. KGB cables used the cover name Babylon for San Francisco, an obvious reference to the city's cultural reputation, while Washington, as the capital of the United States, received the name Carthage—and we know what happened to Carthage.

In a later era, when the Cold War led to heightened sensitivity about communications security, both Soviet and American security practices required that cover names be purely random. Several American agencies even had computers generate a random cover name when needed to ensure that a human choice might not unconsciously produce a cover name that would give an enemy clues to what or who was being camouflaged. Certainly the assistance provided to American counterintelligence by the Soviets' frequent disregard for security in choosing Venona cover names was an object lesson in why such practices were later adopted.

Venona provided the FBI with information that allowed it to neutralize several major Soviet espionage networks and scores of individual agents. (In most cases the Soviet agents were not prosecuted, for reasons that we discuss later.) But Venona did more than that. It identified, on a smaller scale, Soviet agents operating in Britain, Canada, Australia, and other nations. American authorities shared information with appropriate national counterintelligence agencies, and these agents, too, were largely neutralized. Australia was a striking example of the power of Venona's deciphered messages to convince otherwise skeptical politicians to take action. Rather like the Truman administration in the United States, Australia's left-of-center Labour government in 1946 abolished its wartime internal security apparatus, not wishing a rerun of the 1920s and 1930s, when Australia's conservative governments had used the internal security agencies to harass left-wing groups. Internal security became simply a secondary task of the Commonwealth Investigation Branch, the police section of the attorney general's office charged with a broad array of criminal investigative tasks. The same Labour government, however, reversed direction in 1949 when the United States and Great Britain handed over to the Australian government deciphered KGB messages (Venona decryptions) from the Soviet embassy in Canberra that pointed to well-placed Soviet sources inside the Australian government. Both countries also informed the Australians that unless the leaks were dealt with, Australia could not expect a significant role in British and American atomic research or other high-level security matters. In response the Labour government created the Australian Security Intelligence Organization, with responsibility for counterespionage and internal security and a specific mandate to track down the real identities of the spies in the KGB's Canberra traffic.[23]

Venona provided the FBI and the CIA with crucial information about the professional practices and habits of Soviet intelligence agencies—"tradecraft" in espionage jargon. It also revealed details about scores of professional Soviet intelligence officers who would be the West's opponents in the espionage arena of the Cold War. Young intelligence officers who show up often in Venona continued to serve with the KGB into the 1980s.

Most of all, American intelligence agencies used Venona as a standard against which to judge information from less reliable sources. One of the major sources of intelligence and counterintelligence information was the testimony of defectors: former Soviet intelligence officers, former Soviet spies, and former Soviet officials of various sorts. But defectors were driven by a variety of motives: ideological conversion, personal spite, fear, or greed. Most were voluntary, but some were coerced or blackmailed into defection. Many were truthful, but some otherwise truthful defectors had limited understanding of what they were reporting and inadvertently misled American intelligence officers. Others told the truth about some matters but also exaggerated their own importance or inflated the value of what they knew or lied about other things if it served their interests. And, of course, there were fake defectors, Soviet agents who pretended to defect in order to subvert American intelligence with false and misleading information.

Often defectors in the early decades of the Cold War gave information about topics or persons who were the subject of Venona messages, in particular the assignments and careers of Soviet intelligence officers in the 1940s. In those cases, American intelligence could compare what the defector said with what was known from Venona. If the defector's story matched the Venona information, it showed that on those matters he was telling the truth and gave a basis for confidence in his story on other matters. If, on the other hand, the defector's information was contradicted by Venona, his credibility plummeted. As an NSA-CIA history of Venona stated, "Venona thus became a touchstone of American counter-intelligence—a kind of super-secret central reference point for FBI and CIA leaders to use in judging the accuracy of subsequent information."[24]

Venona and Historical Documentation

Some of those who do not wish to believe the evidence of Venona have denied that the messages are authentic. They have maintained that the Venona messages are forgeries wholly or partially concocted by the American government.[25] A number of points, however, substantiate the authenticity of Venona.

First, the accusation of forgery, while easily made, is most unlikely in regard to the Venona decryptions. There are cases where U.S. government agencies prepared and distributed forged documents in deception operations during World War II and the Cold War. In wartime, forged documents may be successfully foisted on an enemy when that party must make a quick decision, lacks the opportunity to seek corroborative evidence, and is denied the clarity of hindsight.

Successfully forged *historical* documents, however, are much more difficult to prepare. The likelihood of the forger's making a mistake that will lead to exposure is high. Errors in formatting, in language and nomenclature, in references to individuals and events, and in printing, handwriting, and typefaces are common. Moreover, scholars examining historical documents are not under time pressure, have the opportunity to seek corroborative evidence, and will judge the document in the light of how it fits with independently derived historical knowledge. There are, to be sure, cases of forgery of historical documents, but they tend to center on a very small number of documents—often a single one. In the case of Venona, there are more than five thousand pages of messages. A successful forgery of historical documents in this quantity that could not be easily exposed is not only unprecedented, it is as a practical matter impossible.

Forgers of historical documents attempt to disguise the documents' origins in order to deflect critical attention from the true source. In the case of Venona, however, the origins are openly proclaimed and the identity of the chief cryptanalysts, linguists, and investigators in the project are known. Though some are dead, others are still alive and have made themselves available to scholars investigating the Venona messages. Venona could only be a forgery if it had been supported by a massive conspiracy involving hundreds of people. Further, over the more than three decades of its operation, the Venona Project employed many who later left government service and hence are under no legally enforceable restraint to remain silent about what would be a criminal enterprise under cover of government authority.

Second, in this book Venona is not treated in isolation. The documentation of Venona is integrated with a broad range of other corroborative evidence, including testimony, both written and oral, by a wide variety of persons over many decades. It includes voluntary statements from defectors from Soviet intelligence, reluctant testimony from persons under legal compulsion, and candid discourse gathered by listening devices, as well as information available in published works. The corroborative documentation also includes written primary material from a range of public and private archives as well as contextual historical material from the work of earlier scholars. As we shall see, the documentation of Venona fits, and fits very well, with this other evidence.

Ultimately the authenticity of Venona will be confirmed when Soviet-era intelligence archives are opened. Although unrestricted access seems unlikely in the near future, some documents have been released. The Russian Foreign Intelligence Service, successor to the KGB, has provided selected documents to current and retired Russian intelligence officers to publish narratives of certain aspects of KGB history. The largest opening from the KGB archive came in early 1999 with the publication of *The Haunted Wood: Soviet Espionage in America—The Stalin Era* by the American historian Allen Weinstein and the retired KGB officer Alexander Vassiliev.[26] These documents confirm the participation in Soviet espionage of fifty-eight persons identified in Venona.[27] They also establish the real identity of nine persons who were hidden behind cover names in the Venona messages, as well as uncovering other Soviet spies who are entirely absent from Venona.

There is also a back door into the Soviet intelligence archives, and we have already located documentary corroboration for Venona in those Moscow archives that are open, documents that would not exist if the claims that Venona is a forgery had any basis in reality.

Corroboration for Venona: Moscow Documents

From 1919 until 1943, the Communist International (Comintern), headquartered in Moscow, supervised the activities of Communist parties throughout the world. After the Comintern dissolved in 1943, its records were stored in an archive that in late 1991 became RTsKhIDNI, the Russian Center for the Preservation and Study of Documents of Recent History. This archive holds the bulk of the records of the central bodies of the Communist Party of the Soviet Union (CPSU) from the early 1920s to Stalin's death in 1953.

The records of the Comintern deal chiefly with its main task, the promotion of communism and world revolution by political means. The Comintern, although not itself an arm of Soviet intelligence, nonetheless cooperated with Soviet intelligence agencies. After Venona was made public, it was discovered that the Comintern's records contained communications with the KGB and GRU that corroborated a number of Venona documents.[28]

The case of Anwar Muhammed illustrates how Comintern records verify the authenticity of Venona. One deciphered Venona cable, from the New York KGB station to the KGB Moscow headquarters in July 1943, reports that the station has been unable to gather any information about Muhammed.[29] It also notes that Jacob Golos, the CPUSA's chief liaison with the KGB, reported that he knew nothing of Muhammed. The footnotes to this message by NSA and FBI analysts show that they were never able to identify Muhammed and had no idea why the New York KGB was interested in him.

A document found in 1993 in the RTsKhIDNI archive, however, explains the matter. In January 1943 the Comintern received an inquiry about Muhammed from a Soviet official named Sharia.[30] Sharia is unknown, and the agency on whose behalf he was writing is not clearly identified, although it was likely the KGB. Sharia stated that his agency's office in Kabul, Afghanistan, reported that Anwar Muhammed, director of a Kabul teachers' school, wanted to visit Moscow. Before this visit was approved, Sharia wanted to confirm Muhammed's claim that he was a Communist of some years' standing. Muhammed had told Soviet officials in Kabul that he held a doctorate in biochemistry from the Johns Hopkins University in Baltimore and that while a student at Johns Hopkins he had been recruited into the CPUSA through Albert Blumberg, head of the Maryland Communist party and a Johns Hopkins faculty member. Muhammed also said that his wife was an American and a fellow Communist. Sharia asked if the Comintern had any records that might verify Muhammed's claims.

The RTsKhIDNI document clarifies the meaning of the deciphered Venona message and verifies its authenticity. The Moscow KGB had asked its New York office, just as it had asked the Comintern, to corroborate Muhammed's story. In its July 1943 message the New York KGB reported that neither it nor the CPUSA was able to provide the requested confirmation.

Another objection to the Venona evidence is that in order to impress their Moscow superiors, KGB officers in the United States might exaggerate and falsely claim to have recruited as sources entirely innocent people they had casually met. This is very unlikely. Soviet intelligence officers could not simply report that they had recruited John Smith as a source. The KGB had elaborate procedures governing source recruitment.

A field officer who had spotted a candidate for recruitment had first to review the case with the head of the KGB station and receive permission to proceed. The next step was the "processing" of the candidate, to use Soviet tradecraft jargon. The intelligence officer gathered background information from various sources to verify the individual's biography and assess his or her fitness for espionage work. The CPUSA's liaisons with the KGB, Jacob Golos and Bernard Schuster on the East Coast and Isaac Folkoff on the West Coast, were often called upon to provide background material on prospective recruits. Sometimes the reports were not satisfactory and a candidate was dropped. If they were positive, the head of the KGB station would endorse the field officer's recommendation and ask the KGB Moscow headquarters for "sanction" to proceed with "signing-on," as the KGB called the formal recruitment of a source.

Moscow's sanction for a recruitment was not automatic or routine. Often the KGB headquarters asked its American station for additional documentation of a candidate's fitness. The KGB headquarters also did its own independent checking, sending queries to the Communist International to see if its extensive records on the American Communist movement contained relevant information. One case involved Marion

Davis, a candidate then working for the Office of the Coordinator of Inter-American Affairs in Washington, whom the New York KGB wanted to recruit. The field officer's report noted that she had earlier worked at the U.S. embassy in Mexico City and had had contact with Soviet diplomats. Not only did General Fitin of the KGB request Comintern records on Davis, but he refused to sanction her recruitment until he received a report from the head of the KGB station in Mexico City.

Once Moscow sanctioned a recruitment, the actual signing-on usually consisted of a meeting between the candidate and a professional KGB officer or, more rarely, one of the KGB's full-time American agents. The officer who conducted the signing-on then filed a report with Moscow confirming that recruitment had been completed. The Moscow KGB expected its field officers to provide regular reports on a source's productivity. The head of the KGB station in the United States also periodically shifted responsibility among his field officers for contact with sources. Under these circumstances, a faked or exaggerated source would show up quickly and might entail severe consequences for the offending officer. In most cases Moscow expected the delivery of actual or filmed documents or reports written personally by the source. Those were delivered to Moscow by diplomatic pouch; and when a source failed to deliver material, Moscow demanded an explanation. The KGB station in the United States sometimes transmitted only reports of verbal briefings by a source. Under special circumstances, this was acceptable to Moscow, but usually it was not. In 1945, for example, General Fitin became irritated that KGB field officers dealt with one of their most highly placed sources, the White House aide Lauchlin Currie, only through intermediaries provided by the Silvermaster network of American Communists. Further, Currie usually gave only verbal briefings. KGB officers were reluctant to press Currie because he was not under CPUSA discipline and cooperated with the KGB cautiously and on his own terms. Fitin demanded direct KGB contact with Currie, and his order was carried out. These KGB tradecraft practices greatly reduce the possibility that the Venona messages are replete with field officer braggadocio.

Finally, the Venona decryptions, while they contain extraordinary information, are otherwise an ordinary set of archival documents with all of the strengths and weaknesses of such records. They ought to be treated and judged in the same way that similar historical records are dealt with. Historical scholarship must be based on documentary records. One or another document may occasionally mislead or be misinterpreted, but in time other documents from other archives or reexamination by other scholars will bring about correction of errors. That is the normal course of historical scholarship, and is as true in this case as it is in others.

The Zubilin Affair

On August 7, 1943, the director of the FBI received an anonymous letter written in Russian.[31] It purported to name leading KGB officers operating under diplomatic cover in Soviet offices in the United States, Canada, and Mexico and charged that they were engaged in espionage on a broad scale. The letter stated that the chief KGB officer in the United States was Vasily Zubilin, that Zubilin's real name was Zarubin, and that his wife, Elizabeth, was also a KGB field officer running her own network of American sources.[32] Other KGB officers named in the letter were Pavel Klarin and Semyon Semenov, officials at the Soviet consulate in New York; Vasily Dolgov and Vasily Mironov, officials at the Soviet embassy in Washington; Grigory Kheifets, Soviet vice-consul in San Francisco; Leonid Kvasnikov, an engineer with Amtorg; Andrey Shevchenko and Sergey Lukianov, officials with the Soviet Government Purchasing Commission; Vladimir Pavlov, second secretary of the Soviet embassy in Canada; and Lev Tarasov, a diplomat at the Soviet embassy in Mexico.[33]

The FBI was, not surprisingly, perplexed by the letter and suspicious that it was a fraud. But an investigation of the activities of the Soviet diplomatic personnel named in the letter quickly convinced the bureau that they probably were indeed Soviet intelligence officers. Years later, the deciphered Venona messages further confirmed the accuracy of the identifications provided in the letter.

The motive behind the letter was clear: the anonymous author hated Vasily Zubilin and accused him of a variety of sins, including participating in the murder of thousands of Polish prisoners of war in the Katyn forest. This last accusation caught the attention of American authorities because at that time they were not sure what had happened at Katyn, and out of nowhere came a letter asserting inside knowledge about one of the participants in the Katyn action. Only a few months earlier, the German government had announced that it had uncovered a mass grave containing the bodies of thousands of executed Polish military officers in the Katyn forest near Smolensk, on Soviet territory overrun by Nazi forces. According to the Nazis, the Soviet Union had captured these Poles in 1939 when it conquered eastern Poland under the terms of the Nazi-Soviet Pact. The USSR blamed the mass murder on the Nazis, saying that the Germans had captured the Poles alive when they overran Soviet prisoner-of-war camps and had subsequently murdered them. In fact, the Soviets had murdered the Poles: on March 5, 1940, Stalin ordered the KGB to shoot 14,700 Polish prisoners of war.[34]

The anonymous letter also correctly asserted that Zubilin had some role in the KGB's Katyn operation. The FBI had no way to verify it at the time, but eventually the Venona Project deciphered a KGB cable in which Zubilin himself confirmed having played a role. On July 1, 1943, he reported to Moscow that he thought he had noticed surveillance of his activities by a hostile intelligence agency and speculated that it had found out about his 1940 service at one of the camps at which the Poles had been murdered.[35]

But while the claim that Zubilin had taken part in the Katyn massacre was accurate, the letter also contained the outlandish claim that he had betrayed the Soviet Union and was spying on the United States in the service of Japan. It urged American authorities to reveal Zubilin's treachery to Soviet authorities and asserted that when his betrayal was revealed, one of the other KGB officers, Vasily Mironov, would surely execute Zubilin on the spot. Mironov, nominally a Soviet diplomat, was described as a patriotic KGB colonel who hated Zubilin.

The FBI suspected that the author of the anonymous letter was a disgruntled KGB officer, but it was never sure of his identity. A passage in the 1994 memoir of a retired KGB general, Pavel Sudoplatov, suggests that Mironov wrote the letter. Sudoplatov, who held a headquarters role in KGB foreign intelligence operations during World War II, states that Mironov, a KGB lieutenant colonel, had sent a letter to Stalin denouncing Zarubin (the anonymous letter was correct about Zubilin's real name) as a double agent. Sudoplatov explains that "Mironov's letter caused Zarubin's recall to Moscow. The investigation against him and Elizabeth lasted six months and established that all his contacts were legitimate and valuable, and that he was not working with the FBI. Mironov was recalled from Washington and arrested on charges of slander, but when he was put on trial, it was discovered that he was schizophrenic. He was hospitalized and discharged from the service."[36]

Although Mironov had denounced Zubilin both to the FBI and to Joseph Stalin for imaginary crimes, virtually everything else in the letter has been independently documented as accurate.

Not only did the anonymous letter arrive in 1943, but that same year the FBI also opened, probably not coincidentally, an investigation labeled the Comintern Apparatus, which grew into a file containing thousands of pages of reports and memorandums. In December 1944 it completed a massive internal study entitled "Comintern Apparatus Summary Report."[37] More than six hundred pages, this report reviewed what the FBI knew at that point about Soviet espionage and about its overlap with the American Communist party.

The FBI understood that the Soviet Union, in alliance with the American Communist party, was mounting a major espionage attack on the United States. But although the bureau grasped the broad outlines of the espionage offensive, its knowledge of specific operations was spotty and its understanding of Soviet intelligence practices limited. Though convinced that espionage was taking place, in most cases the FBI did not feel it had sufficient evidence to bring successful criminal prosecutions. A tone of frustrated resignation pervaded the report; leading policy-makers in the government would not want trials and public revelations of Soviet espionage to threaten the wartime political alliance with the USSR.[38] In 1944 the FBI still regarded the Soviet Union as a secondary threat to American security; there was little sense of urgency about Soviet espionage.

The FBI also had difficulty sorting out the activities of American Communists and Soviet spies. Some of the CPUSA activities highlighted in the report as involving espionage certainly did not. This clarity, however, exists only in retrospect. And other CPUSA activities that the report mentions clearly did involve spying on the U.S. government. Espionage, of course, is not a mass movement, and most individuals who joined the CPUSA did not directly participate in espionage. Even many party leaders and officials never directly assisted Soviet intelligence. But there was no fire wall between the CPUSA's work in politics, in the trade union movement, or in other arenas, on the one hand, and its assistance to Soviet espionage, on the other. Rather, the transition between these activities was seamless. Scores of CPUSA members and officials were engaged both in political or labor organizing and in assistance to the intelligence services of a foreign power. Nor was this latter assistance provided by individual Communists. The American Communist party as an organization covertly cooperated with Soviet espionage. The CPUSA made party members available to Soviet intelligence when they were needed. For the FBI, and for all later observers, the overlap between the activities of the CPUSA and Soviet intelligence presented a difficult analytic problem. With no clear line of separation, it was easy to overstate or understate the extent to which the two intermeshed.

When Did the Soviets Learn of Venona?

Soviet cryptographic officials had great confidence in the unbreakability of their one-time pad system and appear to have done little about early reports of attacks upon it. In late 1941 a Soviet agent in Berlin informed Moscow that the Germans had obtained a copy of the Petsamo code book from the Finns. Confident that the overlying one-time pad cipher would protect the system, the Soviets did not get around to replacing the code book until 1943. They appear to have learned of the existence of the NSA's Venona Project within a year and a half of its origin. Elizabeth Bentley told the FBI that in the spring of 1943 Lauchlin Currie, one of the sources in her KGB-CPUSA network, reported that the United States was on the verge of breaking the Soviet code. Currie, one of President Roosevelt's assistants, may well have heard an overly optimistic report sent to the White House about the early Venona effort.[39]

There is evidence of what may have been a Soviet reaction to Currie's report. But the change was superficial, the sort made to placate nervous higher-ups by professionals who think their superiors' worries are unjustified. In late April 1944 the KGB issued a circular to all stations to use a new message starting-point or key page indicator in ciphered cables. This minor change was easily made, allowing KGB cryptographic officers to report to superiors that they had altered their system. Whatever the reason for the alteration in procedure, it backfired disastrously for the Soviets. Cecil Phillips, then a nineteen-year-old cryptanalyst newly assigned to the Venona Project, noticed the change in message formatting and after a few months identified the first five-digit cipher group as the key-page indicator. Consequently, when any two messages were found to have the same initial five-digit cipher group, the two were identified as having been enciphered using the duplicated one-time pages. Phillips's insight enabled American cryptanalysts to examine their collection of intercepted Soviet cables and rapidly find duplication of key pages between KGB messages and Trade messages, a fundamental step in breaking into the KGB traffic.[40]

There is also evidence, although it is not conclusive, that Currie attempted to kill the Venona Project before it revealed the contents of Soviet cable traffic. Col. Harold Hayes and Lt. Col. Frank Rowlett, senior officers at Arlington Hall, reported that in 1944 Colonel Clarke, their Army Special Branch supervisor, told them that he had received instructions from the White House to cease work on Soviet ciphers. Clarke, however, advised the two not to take the instruction seriously and to continue the Venona Project. Independently, veterans of the OSS counterintelligence branch also reported that in 1944 they received instructions from the White House to stop collecting information on Soviet intelligence operations. The OSS appears to have taken the order more seriously than the Army's Special Branch. It did not protest, and it obeyed the White House and State Department order to give Soviet officials cipher material on Soviet codes that the OSS had obtained from Finland. Nor did the OSS counterintelligence branch establish a Russian desk.[41]

No written record exists of these instructions to halt work on Soviet ciphers, and the memory of OSS and Arlington Hall veterans attributed them to the White House and not to anyone in particular. But in view of Bentley's testimony about Currie's knowledge of the attack on the Soviet codes, and Currie's intervention to frustrate counterintelligence investigations of KGB spy Gregory Silvermaster (chapter 5), Lauchlin Currie would be the most likely White House initiator.[42]

Shortly after the close of World War II, Soviet intelligence received two more warnings about their wartime cipher that surely must have seized their attention. One was from William Weisband. Born in Egypt to Russian parents, Weisband came to the United States in the 1920s and gained American citizenship in 1938. He joined the Army in 1942, and his considerable linguistic skills and an Officer Candidate School commission earned him an assignment to the Signals Security Agency, one of the NSA's earlier incarnations. His wartime duties took him to North Africa and Italy. In late 1944, however, he returned to the United States, and in 1945 he received an assignment as a "roving" language consultant assisting various NSA projects, including Venona. Meredith Gardner, the chief code-breaker on the Venona Project, remembered consulting Weisband on obscure points of Russian grammar and recalled that Weisband was present in late 1946 when he read a 1944

KGB espionage message about scientists working on the atomic bomb project. Although Weisband was never directly involved in the Venona Project, his position gave him some knowledge of its activities. Cecil Phillips, one of Venona's leading cryptanalysts, commented that Weisband "managed to roam around with great ease. He cultivated people who had access to sensitive information. He used to sit near the boss's secretary, who typed everything we did of any importance."[43]

Venona, however, also led indirectly to the unmasking of Weisband's treachery. Weisband himself is not clearly identified in Venona, although he is a candidate for the unidentified cover name Link.[44] Link occurs in three Venona messages, but two are very fragmented and give few clues to Link's identity. In the third, dated June 23, 1943, the New York KGB reported that Link had completed a language course in Italian in Arlington, Virginia, and was expected to be sent overseas shortly. It then gave recognition signals for the London KGB to contact Link when he passed through there. These details fit Weisband, who was at an Army language school in Arlington in June 1943 and then shipped out to Britain in July. From there he later went to North Africa and Italy. This message, however, was not fully broken until 1979 and played no role in Weisband's identification as a Soviet agent.[45]

What put the FBI on to Weisband was not the Link messages but the deciphering of fourteen Venona messages discussing a KGB agent with the cover name Nick. These messages provided enough information for the FBI to identify Nick as Amadeo Sabatini. The FBI also found that years earlier, during routine surveillance of Soviet diplomats, its agents had observed that Sabatini "exchanged envelopes and packages on the streets of Los Angeles with Kheifets."[46] Grigory Kheifets was a KGB officer who operated out of the Soviet consulate in San Francisco under diplomatic cover. At that time, however, the bureau had lacked sufficient evidence regarding Sabatini to proceed further.

Sabatini had joined the CPUSA in 1930 and soon earned selection to the governing board ("district buro") of the party's Pennsylvania district. By 1935 he had shifted from open political work for the CPUSA to covert work as an international courier for the Comintern. He joined the International Brigades in 1937 and fought in the Spanish Civil War. Records in Moscow show that among his assignments was membership in the CPUSA "Control Commission," which exercised political discipline over American Communists serving with the International Brigades. After his return from Spain he undertook assignments for the

KGB, including serving on a team that shadowed Walter Krivitsky, a high-ranking GRU defector who publicly exposed several Soviet intelligence operations. Krivitsky died in 1940, probably a suicide, although there were some puzzling aspects to his death that suggested murder.[47]

Venona shows that in the early 1940s Sabatini became a highly active courier linking the KGB to its American sources. He lived in Los Angeles and worked for the Bohn Aluminum and Brass Company, which made parts for aircraft plants. Sabatini used that position to develop and service Soviet industrial and technical espionage contacts in the aviation industry. The KGB reimbursed him for travel and living expenses and paid a monthly stipend to his wife. The FBI confronted Sabatini in 1949. Under questioning he denied much, but the FBI had enough on him that he conceded some matters and pointed the FBI toward a second Soviet agent, an aircraft engineer named Jones York. York was also identified in four deciphered Venona messages under the cover name Needle.[48]

The FBI tracked down York, and under questioning he provided considerable information about his role in Soviet espionage. He stated that in 1935, when working for Douglas Aircraft's El Segundo Division, he met a group of visiting Soviet engineers. One in particular, Stanislau Shumovsky, befriended him and convinced him to turn over Douglas Aircraft technical information in return for payment. Shumovsky was a KGB officer operating under cover of the Soviet Government Purchasing Commission. He specialized in industrial espionage, and York was but one of his recruits. York admitted that he continued to sell technical intelligence to the Soviets until late 1943, when he lost touch with them. During eight years of spying he went through a number of Soviet contacts, most known to him only by pseudonyms: Brooks, Werner, Bill, and a woman whose name York had forgotten.

York, however, provided a number of details about Bill. Bill bought him an expensive camera for photographing documents and paid him about fifteen hundred dollars over the year they were in contact. York said he had given Bill a number of rolls of film of technical documents he had photographed. The only particulars he could remember concerned technical documents about the P-61, an advanced night-fighter developed by Northrop Aircraft. (One Venona message, from 1943, shows York handing over to the Soviets, through Sabatini, five rolls of film, including several on the design and motors for the experimental

XP-58 aircraft.) York stated that he had met with Bill about ten times, three or four of them at York's residence, and that they had developed a friendly and relaxed relationship. He remembered that Bill had admired a poem York had written about the Soviet resistance to the Nazi invasion and had taken a copy to show his Soviet superiors. York also recalled that during their chats Bill had mentioned his family name, which York thought was something like Villesbend.[49]

In 1950 the FBI had York observe an individual walking along a street. York identified him as the man he had known as Bill. It was William Weisband. Weisband was repeatedly interviewed by the FBI. In 1950 he denied any participation in espionage but refused to sign a statement to that effect. He also refused to obey a grand jury subpoena. He was sentenced to a year in prison for contempt of court and lost his job with the NSA. Reinterviewed in 1953, he admitted to knowing York but refused to explain the circumstances. This time he declined to either affirm or deny involvement in espionage.[50] Considering his position inside America's chief cryptologic agency, there is every reason to assume that he did significant damage to American security. Weisband certainly was in a position to tell the KGB a good deal about the NSA's success against the KGB system used for most of 1944 and 1945. He was exposed, however, before any breakthroughs on earlier KGB traffic or on GRU and Naval GRU cables, and the Soviets may have thought those still immune.

The second major breach of Venona's secrecy came through H. R. "Kim" Philby, a senior British intelligence officer and also a longtime Soviet agent. In 1949 the British Secret Intelligence Service sent Philby to Washington for a tour as its liaison with American intelligence agencies. British cryptanalysts of GCHQ were partners in the Venona Project and shared in its product, and GCHQ's liaison with the NSA gave summaries to Philby. Philby also visited the NSA's Arlington Hall facility for discussions with its officials. He quickly informed the KGB that American code-breakers were beginning to read wartime KGB cables between New York and Moscow. A London KGB report from February 1950 laid out the dire situation:

Stanley [Kim Philby] asked to communicate that the Americans and the British had constructed a deciphering machine which in one day does "the work of a thousand people in a thousand years." Work on deciphering is facilitated by three factors: (1) A one-time pad used twice;

(2) Our cipher resembles the cipher of our trade organization in the USA; (3) A half-burnt codebook has been found in Finland and passed to the British and used to decrypt our communications. They will succeed within the next twelve months. The Charles [Klaus Fuchs] case has shown the counter-intelligence service the importance of knowing the past of civil servants. . . . Stanley, Paul [Guy Burgess], and Yan [Anthony Blunt] consider that the situation is serious.[51]

It was particularly serious because some of those early Venona successes of which Philby received summaries struck very close to Philby himself. Philby, Donald Maclean, Guy Burgess, John Cairncross, and Anthony Blunt are known in KGB lore as "the Magnificent Five," among the most productive moles ever developed within the governing establishment of a major Western nation. The first four had all been students at Cambridge University in the early 1930s; Blunt, a Cambridge don and art expert, recruited prospective spies from among the students. Philby became a high-ranking professional British intelligence officer, Maclean joined the foreign office and became a senior diplomat, Burgess transferred back and forth between British intelligence and the foreign office, and Cairncross worked for British intelligence and on military and intelligence matters for the British Treasury. In addition to his work as talent-spotter and recruiter, Blunt also did wartime service for British counterintelligence (MI5), thus greatly enhancing his value to Moscow as a spy. After the war Blunt became chief art adviser to the British monarch and acted as intermediary between Burgess and the KGB.[52]

As soon as Philby arrived in Washington, in the fall of 1949, the FBI discussed with him Venona decryptions about a KGB agent with the cover name Homer who appeared to be connected with the British embassy in 1945–1946. The initial decryptions about Homer provided few details, and there were hundreds of candidates for Homer among the many British subjects who had served at the United Kingdom's diplomatic office in Washington in that period. Philby, however, immediately recognized Homer as his friend and fellow spy Maclean and warned Moscow.

The son of a prominent British Liberal party politician, Donald Maclean had become a Communist by 1933 and was quickly convinced to forego political activity and serve the cause by becoming one of Stalin's agents inside the British government. In 1935 he placed highly in the British foreign service exam and coolly told his questioners, who had heard of his student radicalism, that he had been working to shake off his Communist views but had not yet entirely succeeded. They bought his deception, and he joined the diplomatic corps in late 1935. In 1944 he was posted to the British embassy in Washington; for much of his four-year stay he held the senior position of first secretary. In that capacity he had access to virtually everything passing through the embassy.

Maclean and his wife arrived in the United States on May 6, 1944. By the end of June he was in touch with Vladimir Pravdin, a KGB officer operating under the cover of a journalist for the TASS news agency. The New York KGB station cabled Moscow on June 28 that Pravdin had met with Homer/Maclean three days previously and would see him again on the thirtieth in New York, where his wife was living with her mother. Although Maclean lived and worked at the Washington embassy, his wife, who was American and pregnant, lived in New York to enable Maclean to have a plausible excuse to travel there to meet his Soviet controller. After the birth of their son, Maclean and his wife moved to Washington.

Nearly a dozen Venona messages over the next year and a half detail the rich haul of intelligence that Maclean provided to the KGB. He offered details of secret telegrams between Prime Minister Winston Churchill and President Roosevelt, discussions of military plans, and synopses of issues they discussed at their Quebec meeting in September. Maclean also provided details of British plans for dealing with Greece, which had been under German occupation until late 1944. Chaos reigned in the wake of the German retreat, as pro- and anti-Communist Greek resistance forces and the Greek government-in-exile battled for control. British forces were entering the country to stabilize the situation and had no intention of allowing Communists to seize power. The New York KGB station told Moscow that in regard to the latter, "Homer hopes that we will take advantage of these circumstances to disrupt the plans of the British."[53]

One long, only partially decrypted New York KGB cable from August 1944 illustrates the wide range of sensitive material to which Maclean had access and which he passed on to the KGB. The cable reported that British and American officials were establishing a high-level joint commission to decide on political and economic policies for those areas of Western Europe then being liberated by advancing American and British troops. The cable reported that in regard to the commission almost all the work is done by H. [Homer/Maclean] who is present at all the sessions. In connection with this work H. obtains secret documents . . . including the personal telegraphic correspondence of Boar [Churchill] with Captain [Roosevelt]. . . . H. was entrusted with the decipherment of a confidential telegram from Boar to Captain which said that [British general Henry] Wilson and other generals of the Island [Great Britain] were insisting strongly on a change in the plan to invade the South of France, suggesting instead an invasion through the Adriatic Sea, Trieste and then north-eastwards. Boar supported this plan. From the contents of the telegram it is clear that Boar did not succeed in overcoming the strong objection of Captain and the Country's [America's] generals. Yesterday H. learnt of a change in the plans . . . and Anvil [Anglo-American invasion of southern France] will be put into effect possibly in the middle of August.[54]

Among his other duties Maclean represented Great Britain as diplomatic liaison between the American atomic bomb program, the Manhattan Project, and its British counterpart in 1944 and 1945. In 1946 he continued this role as the British liaison with the U.S. Atomic Energy Commission (AEC), the successor to the Manhattan Project. He made at least twenty visits to the AEC in 1947 and 1948, including one conference to discuss what atomic bomb data should not be declassified. Maclean continued to provide the Soviet Union with reports about the British and American discussions of early Cold War policy until his reassignment and departure in September 1948.

Although the initial deciphered message about Homer in 1949 provided few clues to his identity, as more messages were broken the list of possibilities began to narrow. With MI5 and the FBI cooperating, the hundreds of possibilities of 1949 declined to thirty-five by the end of 1950 and to fewer than a dozen by the spring of 1951. As Philby well knew, Maclean was on the rapidly shrinking list. In April 1951 a newly decrypted Venona message noted that in June 1944 Homer was traveling back and forth between New York and Washington to see his pregnant wife, who was living with her mother. That settled it. There was only one name on the list that fit: Donald Maclean. Philby, as British intelligence liaison, immediately learned that his comrade was in danger. But MI5 had to gather evidence to support an arrest, a delay that Philby used to his advantage. Guy Burgess, who was then working at the British embassy in Washington and lodging with the Philbys, was returning to London in disgrace after a drunken escapade. Philby briefed Burgess and told him to leave at once and contact their KGB controller in London to arrange Maclean's escape. He did, and on May 25 Maclean and Burgess took a channel ferry to St.-Malo, picked up false papers from a waiting KGB contact, and traveled on to Moscow.

After Maclean and Burgess fled, both American and British counterintelligence wondered who had warned them. Suspicion quickly fell on Philby because of his close relationship with the two, particularly Burgess. The evidence against Philby was largely circumstantial. The CIA, however, demanded that the British find a new liaison officer, and Philby was withdrawn from Washington. MI5 thought him guilty but also concluded that it had insufficient evidence for a criminal charge. The Secret Intelligence Service ordered Philby into retirement in December 1951. Philby then worked as a journalist, but he remained under suspicion and as time went on, evidence accumulated pointing to his treachery. In 1963 he too fled to Moscow. Philby's access to Venona information ended in the summer of 1951. Like Weisband's information, Philby's probably indicated to the KGB that the NSA's success to that point was confined to messages from 1944 on and did not reach back to earlier KGB cables or to GRU and Naval GRU messages.[55]

Weisband's and Philby's information about Venona did not appear to trigger any sudden changes in Soviet diplomatic cryptographic habits. Nor should it have. After all, the vulnerability of the Soviet code was limited to the duplicate one-time pad pages produced in 1942. By 1946 most of these had already been used, although a few would turn up in outlying Soviet stations as late as 1948. But the warnings of the three about the NSA breakthrough did allow the KGB to alert agents who were at risk of exposure to prepare for FBI scrutiny and, if they were still active, to cease any espionage activity that could be uncovered and used against them in a criminal trial. Philby, for example, warned Moscow that British and American counterintelligence had identified one of the atomic spies in the Venona traffic as the British scientist Klaus Fuchs. This information allowed Moscow to withdraw at least one and perhaps several of its officers operating covertly in the West who might be compromised when Fuchs was arrested.[56] The KGB also warned a number of its American agents who were linked directly or indirectly to Fuchs. Several of them fled to the Soviet Union (Morris and Lona Cohen, Joel Barr, and Alfred Sarant), others were arrested while in flight (Morton Sobell was caught and returned after fleeing to Mexico) or when preparing to leave the United States (Julius and Ethel Rosenberg), and several attempted to ride out the investigation (David and Ruth Greenglass and William Perl).

Even after it sank in at the NSA, sometime in the 1950s, that Venona had been exposed by Weisband and Philby, the agency still had reasons for keeping the project highly secret. It did not want Moscow to learn of its subsequent success with GRU, Naval GRU, and the earlier KGB traffic. Nor did it want Moscow to know the extent of the NSA's success: it did not want Soviet intelligence to find out which messages had been read and which remained opaque. American interests, at least in the short run, were served by Moscow's uncertainty over how much the United States had really learned. That uncertainty enhanced the ability of American intelligence and counterintelligence agencies to use Venona as a standard for evaluating other sources of intelligence information.

CHAPTER 3

THE AMERICAN COMMUNIST PARTY UNDERGROUND

The size and success of the Soviet espionage offensive in World War II rested on the preparatory work of the CPUSA in the 1930s. The American Communist party was born as the organizational center of a revolutionary movement. The manifesto of the movement's 1919 founding convention declared that "Communism does not propose to 'capture' the bourgeoisie parliamentary state, but to conquer and destroy it. . . . It is necessary that the proletariat organize its own state *for the coercion and suppression of the bourgeoisie.*"[1]

Initially, American communism operated legally. American Communists proclaimed their revolutionary goals at an open convention. Official harassment was limited to the ripping down by irritated Chicago police of the convention's red rose floral arrangements and pictures of Marx, Trotsky, and Lenin. Spurred on, however, by a series of left-wing terrorist bombings a few months later, the federal government began arresting radical noncitizens and deporting them. Since the overwhelming majority of the new American Communist movement consisted of immigrants without U.S. citizenship, this response posed a direct threat, and the movement went underground. Members of the nascent American Communist party, in any case, needed little encouragement to operate clandestinely. With the model of the conspiratorial

Bolshevik party in Tsarist Russia in mind, most regarded underground activity as the natural mode for a revolutionary Marxist movement.[2]

By 1921 the postwar fear that Bolshevism was about to sweep the world had subsided, and the federal government ceased taking much of an interest in the Communist party. American Communists, enthralled by the Bolshevik model, nevertheless insisted on staying underground. In fact, the Communist International, the Soviet agency that supervised all foreign Communist parties and ensured their fealty to Moscow, had to order the American party to surface, as it did in 1922.[3] In the 1920s a few state and city governments undertook sporadic harassment of Communists, but in most places the Communist movement was free to operate openly and legally. It did so even while continuing to proclaim revolution and the abolition of constitutional liberties as its mission. In 1928 William Z. Foster, then the CPUSA's presidential candidate and one of the top party leaders until his death in 1961, told cheering American Communists, "When a Communist heads a government in the United States—and that day will come just as surely as the sun rises [Applause]—that government will not be a capitalistic government but a Soviet government and behind the government will stand the Red Army to enforce the Dictatorship of the Proletariat."[4] The CPUSA would later downplay and even deny its commitment to revolution and one-party rule, but it was an open aim as late as the early 1930s. In 1932 Foster, again running for president on the CPUSA ticket, foretold a Communist future for Americans:

> One day, despite the disbelief of the capitalists . . . the American workers will demonstrate that they, like the Russians, have the intelligence, courage and organization to carry through the revolution. . . .
>
> By the term "abolition" of capitalism we mean its overthrow in open struggle by the toiling masses, led by the proletariat. . . . To put an end to the capitalist system will require a consciously revolutionary act by the great toiling masses, led by the Communist party; that is, the conquest of the State power, the destruction of the State machine created by the ruling class, and the organization of the proletarian dictatorship. . . .
>
> Under the dictatorship all the capitalist parties—Republican, Democratic, Progressive, Socialist, etc.—will be liquidated, the Communist party functioning alone as the Party of the toiling masses. Likewise will be dissolved all other organizations that are political props of the bourgeois rule, including chambers of commerce, employers' associations, rotary clubs, American Legion, Y.M.C.A., and such fraternal orders as the Masons, Odd Fellows, Elks, Knights of Columbus, etc. . . .

The press, the motion picture, the radio, the theatre, will be taken over by the government.[5]

Even though the U.S. government treated Foster's revolutionary threats with indifference, the party always feared that authorities might decide that tolerating an antidemocratic and anticonstitutional movement was dangerous. Consequently, the CPUSA always kept the need for illegal operations in mind. The movement's commitment to maintaining an underground arm was reinforced by the instructions of the Communist International. Under Comintern orders American Communists created "illegal departments" charged with protecting the party's internal security, preserving its ability to function in the event of government repression, infiltrating non-Communist organizations for political purposes, and otherwise using clandestine means to serve the interests of the world revolution. These Communist party underground organizations were not primarily espionage or intelligence agencies. But, as we shall see, it was relatively easy for such underground apparatuses to move from assisting the world revolution politically to helping the homeland of the world revolution through espionage.

The Communist International itself was not primarily an intelligence organization, but it too was linked to Soviet intelligence. Within the Comintern the OMS (International Liaison Department) oversaw the covert financing of foreign parties and the activities of Comintern emissaries. Numerous American Communists worked for this agency, which served as the Comintern's own covert apparatus. In the course of its mission to secretly transfer Comintern agents and money around the world, it produced false passports, developed mail drops, procured safe-houses, and established systems of coded telegraphic and radio communications. The OMS was supervised by the "Illegal Commission," made up of senior Comintern officials but usually including an official of the foreign intelligence arm of the KGB as well. In 1923, for example, the Illegal Commission consisted of two senior Cominternists along with Mikhail Trilisser, the KGB's foreign intelligence chief in the 1920s. In May of that year it met to consider whether the American Communist party was maintaining the proper balance between legal and illegal work. After a discussion with Israel Amter, the CPUSA's representative to the Comintern, it issued a number of directives designed to enhance the CPUSA's capacity for "secret work."[6]

In 1929 the CPUSA's flagship newspaper, the *Daily Worker,* announced that the party had undertaken to "make all necessary preparations for illegal functioning of the leading organs of the Party." It was, however, a symptom of the indifference of the American authorities toward the CPUSA at the time and the sense of security of CPUSA officials that its newspaper openly published a resolution about its intent to form a secret organization. In 1930 the Comintern again reminded American Communists that "legal forms of activity must be combined with systematic illegal work." The Comintern reinforced the point with another memo to the CPUSA noting that "all legal Parties are now under the greater responsibility in respect to the creation and strengthening of an illegal apparatus. All of them must immediately undertake measures to have within the legally existing Party committees an illegal directing core." The next year, 1931, Solomon Lozovsky, head of the Profintern, urged Communist trade unionists to disregard the "mystic secrecy" of governmental institutions and expose the secrets of capitalist nations by operating "in the holy of holies of capitalist society, in the armed forces and diplomatic service," and another Comintern official, Boris Vasiliev, reminded Communists that "it is obvious that any secret treaties, government proposals and military orders which by one means or another fall into the hands of Communist Party organizations must be published without delay."[7]

During the 1920s the American party had an underground, but, distracted as it was by its vicious internal factional battles, its covert apparatus was not carefully maintained. This debilitating factionalism, however, ended in 1929 after the systematic expulsion of Trotskyists, Lovestoneites, and other dissidents had produced a thoroughly Stalinized party. The person chosen to revitalize the CPUSA's secret apparatus for the 1930s was Josef Peters.[8]

J. Peters and the Secret Apparatus

J. Peters, as he was known in Communist ranks, was an example of the professional revolutionaries of European origin who populated the Communist underground and intelligence world of the 1930s and 1940s. During his life he used a variety of names—Alexander Goldfarb, Isador Boorstein, and Alexander Stevens. Born in Cop, then part of the Austro-Hungarian empire, into a working-class Jewish family, he dropped out of college because of lack of funds and went to work in an office. Peters served in the Austro-Hungarian army during World War I and was made an officer because he was a high school graduate.

When the Austro-Hungarian empire collapsed in 1918, the newly formed Communist party briefly seized power in newly independent Hungary. Peters, on furlough at the time and caught up in the revolutionary fervor, joined the Communists, organized railroad workers, and fought the White (anti-Communist) armies. He continued his party work after the defeat of the Hungarian Communists and held several minor positions in the regional party organization. In 1924 he moved to the United States and worked in a New York factory for eight months before becoming an organizer for the Hungarian-language federation of the CPUSA.[9]

By the end of the decade, Peters was the leading functionary in the Hungarian federation and had been a delegate to the Sixth Congress of the Comintern in Moscow. The CPUSA was convulsed by factional warfare in 1929, and dozens of leading party functionaries loyal to the party leader, Jay Lovestone, were expelled. Peters, who had been a Lovestoneite, made his peace with the new leadership and was appointed head of the CPUSA's National Minorities Department at the end of 1929. Shifted to mainline party work in 1930, he became organizational secretary of the New York Communist party, the CPUSA's largest regional unit. In that capacity he was responsible for building an illegal apparatus for the New York organization.

In 1931 Peters was sent to Moscow for training with the Communist International. He worked at the Comintern's Anglo-American Secretariat as a senior intern and late in 1932 returned to the United States, where the Central Committee, in the words of a Comintern document, "assigned him to work in the secret apparatus. He was at this post until June of 1938."[10] Peters's headquarters was in the CPUSA main office at Union Square in New York City.

The secret apparatus under Peters's leadership carried out a variety of tasks. Some of these concerned party security: to detect surveillance by hostile police, expose infiltrators, and protect special party assets, such as sensitive records, from seizure. The secret apparatus was also responsible for preparing the party to function underground. Peters purchased printing presses that were secretly stored around the country to be used for printing Communist material in an emergency. One, for example, was located at the back of the Intimate Bookshop in Chapel Hill, North Carolina. This press had been bought by Alton Lawrence, ostensibly a member of the Socialist party but actually a secret Communist, with funds provided by Peters.[11] In an offensive mode the secret apparatus carried out the surveillance, infiltration, and disruption of rival groups such as the Socialist party and the Socialist Workers party (Trotskyist).

The Washington Communist Underground

Another of Peters's duties was maintaining contact with sensitive groups of secret party members in Washington. In the 1930s the CPUSA recruited several hundred persons among the many thousands of new employees hired by the federal government under the impact of the New Deal's rapid expansion of governmental programs. While the CPUSA operated legally in the 1930s, federal regulations forbade partisan political activity by federal employees, and open membership in the Communist party brought discharge. The CPUSA evaded the law by organizing caucuses of government employees that met in secret, studied party literature, paid dues, and listened to visiting party officials explain party policies.

The existence of a significant Washington Communist underground in the 1930s became a matter of public debate in 1948 when Whittaker Chambers described his role in it. Chambers related how in the spring of 1934 Peters introduced him to Harold (Hal) Ware in New York and soon afterward the three of them met again in Washington to coordinate the activities of what came to be known as the Ware group. Ware was the CPUSA's point man for farm issues, and the Ware group initially consisted of young lawyers and economists hired by the Agricultural Adjustment Administration (AAA), a New Deal agency that reported to the secretary of agriculture but was independent of the long-established Department of Agriculture bureaucracy. In origin the Ware group was a secret Communist political club. Espionage on behalf of the USSR was not part of its agenda, although from the beginning its members gave inside government information to the CPUSA.

By the time Chambers became involved, the Ware group had grown to about seventy-five persons and was in the process of being broken up into smaller, more manageable units. It leading figures were Alger Hiss, Lee Pressman, John Abt, Charles Kramer, and Nathan Witt, who all originally worked for the AAA, as well as Henry Collins of the National Recovery Administration (the NRA was the leading New Deal agency for reorganizing industry), George Silverman, an economist with the Railroad Retirement Board, Marion Bachrach (John Abt's sister), Donald Hiss (Alger's brother and also a government attorney), and Victor Perlo, a statistician for the NRA. After Harold Ware's death in an automobile accident in 1935, Peters took over direct supervision of Ware's Washington underground organization. Although based in New York, Peters served on the CPUSA's Baltimore district committee, making frequent trips to the Washington area to meet with members of the growing group of government employees that Ware had put together.

When Chambers first discussed the Washington Communist underground in 1948, those he named as members either flatly denied that it existed or refused to say anything at all. While some people believed Chambers, others thought the idea of a CPUSA underground nothing but a paranoid fantasy. But over the years the accumulated evidence has become overwhelming. In 1950 Lee Pressman testified that he had been a formal, albeit secret member of the CPUSA in 1934 and 1935 and, although no longer officially a party member, a firm ideological Communist from 1936 to 1950. He agreed that there had been a group in the AAA which had met with Peters. Although he depicted the group as an innocuous study club of government employees who got together to discuss political theory, he admitted that several of its leading figures (he, Nathan Witt, John Abt, and Charles Kramer) were Communists. Later, he privately admitted to Jerome Frank, a leading AAA official, that the group had been a Communist party enterprise. Also in 1950, Nathaniel Weyl, a former AAA economist, stated that he had been an original member of the Ware group, and that it was a Communist caucus that met to discuss how CPUSA policies could be applied to the agricultural issues with which they dealt.[12]

Another of the original members of the Ware Group was John Abt, a lawyer for the AAA. In his posthumously published autobiography, Abt, who admitted to party membership only when he was eighty years old, acknowledged that Hal Ware invited him to join the CPUSA in 1934 and he had accepted. He also said that Ware had recruited his sister, Marion Bachrach, as well. According to Abt, the party decided to keep his membership a closely held secret in order to protect his usefulness during his government service and, later, as a leading labor lawyer. After Hal Ware's death, Abt wrote, J. Peters would come to the capital once a month to meet the group members. Although Abt denied that he and his comrades had engaged in espionage, he admitted that they provided Communist party leaders with information about government policies.[13]

Another member of the Ware group was John Herrmann, the husband of the radical writer Josephine Herbst. Herbst's biographer wrote of Herrmann: "From early 1934 until the summer of 1935 he was a paid courier for the Communist Party whose job was to deliver to New York material emanating from the secret cells of sympathetic government employees being cultivated by Harold Ware. . . . John's superior in the network was Whittaker Chambers. . . . According to his widow, whom I met in 1974, John Herrmann was the man who introduced Chambers to Alger Hiss."[14]

The most intimate look at the CPUSA Washington underground and the Ware group in the 1930s comes from Hope Hale Davis in her *Great Day Coming: A Memoir of the 1930s*. She and her husband, Hermann Brunck, both worked for the National Recovery Administration, and both were recruited into the CPUSA and its underground organization. Davis wrote that her unit, led by Charles Kramer, was a subgroup of what had been the Ware group. From her initial group meeting she retained a vivid memory of Victor Perlo lecturing earnestly about Mao Tse-tung's Long March in China. Her husband was soon passing sensitive, confidential documents from the National Labor Relations Board (NLRB), then part of the NRA, and from the NRA's shipping industry regulatory board to the CPUSA to assist its union organizing efforts. She noted that Peters appeared from time to time at her group meetings, not as an education lecturer, as Pressman and Abt claimed, but as the authoritative head of the party underground.

By the late thirties, Davis explained, the original Ware group had evolved into a large number of small secret Communist clubs operating in a great variety of federal agencies, including congressional committee staffs. These clubs were linked to each other and to the CPUSA through a hierarchy of intermediary leaders. Victor Perlo had several of these small caucuses reporting to him. For example, Herbert Fuchs headed one of the CPUSA's secret caucuses at the National Labor Relations Board from 1937 to 1942, a period in which his unit grew from four members to seventeen. He said that his NLRB unit's link to the larger apparatus was initially through Perlo. Davis and her husband eventually became heads of their own subgroups, and her residence was used to store documents kept by a mysterious Latvian immigrant whom she understood to be connected with some sort of anti-Trotsky operation.[15]

These secret Washington Communist caucuses were not formed for espionage. Instead, they were engaged in politics, albeit secret politics, and political subversion, inasmuch as they attempted to secretly manipulate government decisions, to serve Communist party interests.[16] However, such covert organizations were adaptable to espionage operations. Whittaker Chambers's account of his role in Soviet espionage in the mid-1930s is one example of such adaptation.

Peters's secret apparatus was the CPUSA's covert arm, and Peters reported to Earl Browder, head of the CPUSA. On Browder's direction Peters also cooperated with Soviet intelligence. In the 1930s the chief Soviet intelligence agency operating in the United States was the GRU, Soviet military intelligence. Chambers explained that Peters recognized that the network of secret Communists in government agencies offered espionage potential and that he had selected a few people who held sensitive positions as possible intelligence sources. Among other goals, he hoped that the Soviets would pay for services rendered and thereby assist in meeting the high costs of the party's underground operations. In early 1936 Peters had Chambers obtain documents from two secret Communist sources, Julian Wadleigh in the State Department and Ward Pigman at the National Bureau of Standards. Peters then offered these documents to his chief GRU contact, known to Chambers only by the pseudonym Bill, who was unenthusiastic about Peters's plans but agreed to send the documents to Moscow for review.

Two examples of documents stolen by secret Communists in the U.S. State Department in this era were found in the CPUSA's own records, which were surreptitiously shipped to Moscow decades ago and only opened to research after the collapse of the USSR. One is a copy of an October 19, 1936, letter from William Dodd, the U.S. ambassador to Germany, to President Roosevelt. Dodd reports on conversations he had with Hjalmar Schacht, president of the Reichsbank and Hitler's chief economic adviser, Hans Heinrich Dieckhoff, shortly to become the German ambassador to the United States, and Baron Konstantin von Neurath, then German foreign minister. The other document, from an unidentified source in the State Department, is entitled "Excerpt of a letter enclosed to Judge Moore of the State Department and written by Ambassador Bullitt, written confidentially." It quotes from a letter from

William Bullitt, the U.S. envoy to France, to Assistant Secretary of State R. Walton Moore regarding how economic conditions in Europe might affect growing international tensions. The document then quotes from Moore's written comment on Bullitt's observations and notes that Moore's comment was also confidential. The thief who stole the document also offered his own judgment that the quoted remarks are "interesting and important because they show attitudes of men in key positions. . . . Moore has great influence on President Roosevelt. And Bullitt is not undangerous in Paris." Both documents are from the fall of 1936 and are date-stamped as reaching the CPUSA on January 5, 1937—swift work by the CPUSA source.[17]

In late 1936 Bill was replaced by a new GRU officer, Col. Boris Bykov, who endorsed the espionage project (possibly Moscow had found the sample documents of interest). Chambers soon found himself the link between Bykov and a network of sources in various U.S. government agencies drawn from the CPUSA underground but essentially transferred to a GRU-supervised espionage apparatus.[18]

By late 1937 Chambers had lost much of his once fervent ideological loyalty to communism and was increasingly disturbed by rumors that Soviet intelligence officers and agents were being recalled to Moscow and vanishing. The rumors were well founded. Stalin used his Great Terror not only to purge the Soviet Communist party and the Soviet state of all possible opposition to his rule but to clean out his own security agencies as well. Hundreds of officers of the KGB's internal security apparatus found themselves facing the same fate to which they had sent hundreds of thousands: the labor camps of the Gulag or a bullet in the back of the head. Nor were the foreign intelligence arms of the KGB and the GRU exempt, and their senior officials and scores of their field officers also fell victim to the Terror.

Chambers, however, did not publicly renounce the Communist party, nor did he contact U.S. authorities. Given American politics at the time, he thought little would result from either course and did not wish to risk imprisonment for espionage if he were to turn himself in and confess. Instead, in April 1938 he simply dropped out of Soviet espionage and the CPUSA in a way he hoped would protect himself and his family and allow him to reenter normal life. Fearing immediate retaliation, he initially fled to Florida with his family and remained in seclusion for several months. Through intermediaries he got word back to his former colleagues that if they left him alone he would not go to the authorities. He also warned that he had hidden material that would embarrass them if any move were made against him. By the end of the year he felt that it was safe to gradually reenter society and moved his family to a farm in Maryland. Reviving old journalistic contacts from the 1920s, he sought and found a position with *Time* magazine.

Chambers's defection caused considerable turbulence in the organization of Soviet espionage and the CPUSA underground. Potentially he could compromise a number of Soviet officers and American sources. Someone had to take the blame, and one victim was J. Peters. In June, two months after Chambers disappeared and a frantic search by underground Communists failed to locate him, Peters was removed as head of the secret apparatus and replaced by Rudy Baker. After Chambers's story became public in 1948, Peters, then using the name Alexander Stevens, was subpoenaed by a congressional investigating committee. He refused to answer any questions. He had never gained American citizenship and was deported to Communist Hungary.

Rudy Baker and the Secret Apparatus

Although he served as head of the secret apparatus from 1938 through the end of World War II, Rudy Baker always remained in the Communist shadows. Baker was never called before a congressional committee, never drew the attention of the media, and was never deported from the United States. Instead he quietly slipped out of the country in the late 1940s: not even the year he left is certain. But he later turned up in Communist Yugoslavia as a translator for a state publishing house and a government research institute.

Rudy Baker's anonymity was well planned. In a 1939 report to the Comintern, he identified one of the weaknesses of the secret apparatus: "The problem with this work was that it became generally known that this work was being directed by Peters." He noted that in choosing him as the new head of the underground, Earl Browder "was above all concerned that this work be passed on to me in such a way that my participation in the work of the special apparatus not become generally known, as had been the case with Com. Peters." To hide his "special work," Baker was also given other party assignments, which, while taking up time and energy, achieved the aim that his "special work goes unnoticed and unknown."[19] The plan succeeded. Not only did Baker's role remain secret within the CPUSA, but the FBI took a very long time to identify him. The Comintern Apparatus file shows that from 1943 on, the FBI was trying to identify "Al," the cover name for the head of the apparatus. Later it identified Al as Ralph Bowman, but this too was a pseudonym. Not until several years later did it identify Al/Ralph Bowman as Rudy Baker.

Like the man he replaced, Rudy Baker was an immigrant from Eastern Europe and a veteran of Communist organizing in the United States. Baker was born in 1898 in Vukovar, Croatia, probably under the name of Rudolph Blum. He arrived in the United States with his family in 1909. He had little formal education, having finished four years of primary school and briefly attended an evening technical school. He became a radical militant at an early age and was arrested during a Westinghouse strike in Pittsburgh. Convicted of inciting to riot, he was jailed for a year and a half. Released from prison in May 1918, he was arrested in August for further radical agitation, held as an enemy alien (his native Croatia was part of the Austro-Hungarian empire, with which the United States was at war), but released after two months. Baker joined the Communist party when it was founded in 1919. He worked as a machinist until 1926, when he became the party's district organizer in Detroit. From 1927 to 1930 he studied at the Comintern's prestigious International Lenin School in Moscow, where he became a member of the Soviet Communist party.[20]

A biography found in the Comintern's archives shows that after returning from the International Lenin School in 1930, Baker directed the CPUSA's organizational department for a period and carried out unspecified "illegal work" in Korea, Canada, and England. For much of the 1930s Baker directed the clandestine work of the San Francisco bureau of the Pan-Pacific Trade Union Secretariat, a covert agency of the Profintern (the Comintern's trade union arm) which sought to promote Communist unionism in those Asian countries where Communist organizing was illegal or restricted. With its heavy shipping traffic with China, Japan, and other Asian ports, San Francisco was one of the secretariat's key regional offices. In 1938 Baker told the Comintern that this work had kept him out of CPUSA activities since 1932, and this low profile would assist in keeping his role as head of the CPUSA's covert arm a secret.[21]

Baker became head of the CPUSA underground in late 1938 and lived in Peekskill, New York, as a gentleman farmer with his wife, Lilly (the former wife of J. Peters). He had a desk at the New York City offices of the CPUSA's literary-intellectual magazine, *New Masses,* and publicly carried out several minor Communist party tasks while at the same time directing a large clandestine organization. Because it was a "secret apparatus" that was largely successful in maintaining its secrecy, many details of Baker's organization remain unknown. There is now enough evidence, however, from recently declassified FBI files, recently unearthed Comintern files, and the recently released Venona decryptions to provide an outline of the apparatus, identify some of its personnel, and describe some of its methods.

Baker visited Moscow in January 1939 to confer with Comintern officials regarding his new post as head of the underground. Shortly after returning to the United States, he began to communicate via coded radio and telegraphic cables with Georgi Dimitrov, head of the Communist International. Copies of some of these messages were located in Comintern archives. During World War II he also sent reports to the Comintern by diplomatic pouch via the KGB. There are two mentions of Baker in deciphered Venona cables. In one the New York KGB station reports receiving a letter from him that it was forwarding to Moscow. In the other the New York KGB notes that it had received a cable for Baker from Moscow and requested instructions on whether its agents should deliver the message or whether Soviet diplomats could be used for the chore.[22]

Moscow absorbed a significant share of the cost of the CPUSA's secret apparatus. In November 1939 Baker and Browder sent Dimitrov a message requesting that he "send several 1000 bill every 2 or 3 weeks" hidden inside the cover of a book and addressed to a mail drop in the Bronx; another message from Baker repeated the plea for money and gave a different address. In early 1942 Baker alerted Dimitrov that he had received "85" during 1941. From the context, it seems likely that this meant Baker had gotten $85,000. Baker reported that of this total $35,000 had gone to Alexander Trachtenberg, head of International Publishers, while Baker had retained $10,000. Baker was forwarding the remainder to sites abroad, mostly stations in Latin America. Early in 1943 Baker wrote a report, transmitted to the Comintern, on his apparatus's activities during the preceding year, indicating expenditures of $11,311 in 1942 with $18,834 remaining for 1943 operations. The total 1942–1943 sum in Baker's report, $30,145, would be more than $200,000 in 1998 dollars.[23]

These coded messages were sometimes addressed to Browder and

Baker separately and sometimes jointly. Similarly, the messages to the Comintern were signed by them separately and jointly. In his 1943 report to Dimitrov, Baker explained that although for security reasons "our apparatus is kept strictly isolated from party . . . periodically all questions are discussed and considered by son [Baker] and father [Browder]."[24] And in the report itself Baker discussed several matters about the secret apparatus's work that he had referred to Browder for an authoritative decision.

One of Baker's tasks as head of the secret apparatus was to ensure communications with the Soviet Union. Immediately after the Nazi-Soviet Pact, on September 2, 1939, Dimitrov had informed him and Browder, "According to the new situation I propose that the automobile man start to work with us from the tenth this month"—"automobile" being a Comintern cover term for clandestine short-wave radio operations. Two weeks later Dimitrov sent a second message to Baker and Browder, repeating his earlier admonition: "The new situation demands also from us new methods of connections. It is of great importance to organize with the necessary reserves the automobile connections."[25] The Comintern also used Baker and the CPUSA secret apparatus to maintain clandestine short-wave radio links to Communist parties in Latin America and Canada. One section of Baker's 1942 end-of-year report to the Comintern was devoted to one of his short-wave radio operators with the cover name Louis. Baker told Dimitrov:

> *Louis:* Your suggestion of more than year ago that he set up auto [short-wave radio] in Argentina had been conveyed to him and 5,000 sent to him as per your suggestion. We also invited him to come to Gilla [unknown location] but he informed us that if he left he could not return. Now your present suggestion that he organize auto in Gilla is very much along same lines. Insofar as his trip to Gilla will mean that he loses his connection in South American countries and cannot return[,] Father [Browder] is firmly opposed to his leaving. More than one years [*sic*] ago son [Baker] reported to you that our comrades in Gilla investigated problem of auto and reported that it would cost about $4000 which is over five times its cost here. . . . We will send person to Gilla to work on this problems [*sic*] from here again.[26]

In addition to radio links, Baker also established other communication ties to Moscow. In the 1930s only a few countries subjected international mail to close scrutiny. American authorities rarely looked at international mail unless the sender or the recipient was on a special watch list. Consequently, the CPUSA used mail drops, generally inactive rank-and-file Communist party members who had never attracted official attention, to receive letters from the Comintern. Once World War II began, however, government authorities everywhere began to examine international mail more closely. In early 1940 Baker informed the Comintern that he would be using microdots for sending "largess [*sic*] possible quantity mail," and a later message read, "Please acknowledge receipt invisible micro under stamps. Letters in future examine all envelopes, some of them will have micro under flaps or postage stamps."[27]

In addition to radio and microdots, Baker also used sailors as couriers to carry messages and material to Moscow. The Comintern was used to seaman couriers, and in September 1939 Dimitrov, while urging more work on the short-wave radio link, had told Browder and Baker that "it is good to utilize the sailors."[28] The Comintern archives also turned up this 1942 Dimitrov message to Baker: "We think that now is just [the] time to organize a courier connection between you and us using some comrades among ship crew on U.S. cargo steamers that come every week from American ports to South Persia ports with munitions for Russia. We hope that you find trustworthy boys among crews who could deliver us your mail and take back. We shall secure transit connections through Persia with our man who will meet your mailmen in Persian Ports. Please inform us can you organize this business."[29] In April 1943 Baker told Moscow that the system was in place. "After long delay," he wrote, "am now able to ship material through Persia," and he named a crew member of a U.S. ship then bound for Persia carrying material for transmission to Moscow.[30]

The Comintern and the CPUSA had, in fact, employed Communist seamen to transport political literature, messages, and information for years. In 1932 George Mink, former head of the CPUSA's Marine Workers Industrial Union, was in Moscow preparing for a tour as a maritime organizer for the Profintern, which had long encouraged the establishment of clandestine seaman courier networks. Mink assured them that as head of the Marine Workers Industrial Union he had been "in charge of maintaining contact through the seamen, with India and Cuba, Mexico" and that he had "secured many passports for our work."[31]

The FBI's 1944 "Comintern Apparatus Summary Report" (chapter 2) devoted one section to the Communist seaman courier network. It identified the chief overseers of the system as Frederick "Blackie" Myers (vice-president of the National Maritime Union), Joseph Kenegsberg (or Koenigsberg, a long-time official of the San Pedro Club of the Los Angeles Communist party), Rudy Lambert (head of the California Communist party labor commission), and Albert Lannon (a key Communist maritime organizer on the East Coast).[32] The FBI could not, however, differentiate between sailors who were carrying batches of Communist and maritime union agitational literature to foreign ports (of little interest to the FBI) and those who were carrying clandestine party communications to other Communist parties and the Comintern. But it knew that Communist sailors returning from foreign ports who were seen delivering letters to CPUSA officials or Soviet consulate staff were not carrying routine political literature.

J. Peters had met directly and frequently with Soviet intelligence officers while he was supervising the CPUSA secret apparatus. This is one reason that Chambers's defection initially panicked both the Soviets and the CPUSA underground. Chambers not only could compromise the agents and the Soviet controllers of his own particular network but, owing to his association with Peters, he also threatened the entire CPUSA underground and other Soviet intelligence officers and operations to which Peters was directly linked. Rudy Baker was far more circumspect. It appears that after he took over the CPUSA secret apparatus, direct liaison with Soviet intelligence on the East Coast was assigned to another senior CPUSA official, Jacob Golos, so that the link between the head of the CPUSA underground and Soviet intelligence became less direct.

Connections between the CPUSA's secret apparatus and Soviet intelligence ran through the most senior Soviet intelligence officers in the United States. In the Comintern archive is a copy of an October 1941 message, in poor English, that Dimitrov sent to Baker: "One of our friends name cooper who works in your county and whom [we] trust is authorized to establish [contact] wi[th] your .... We gave him the address. ... His slogan by meeting you: 'I have something for your from brother, some greetings.' After you established direct connections with him continue this connections not directly but through one of your secret comrades. Acknowledge."[33]

Cooper and Baker did establish contact. In Baker's end-of-year report on 1942 activities he told Dimitrov that because the war had made use of the regular international mail too insecure, "this year we began sending mail through Cooper." Later in the report Baker stated that "we are also cooperating very closely with Cooper which accounts also for his helpful aid in communication with you." As an example of the cooperation, Baker cited his agent George, whom he described as having been "loaned . . . to Cooper for auto building work"—short-wave radio operations.[34]

Was Cooper another Comintern representative sent to promote communism as a political movement? In April 1943 Steve Nelson, the West Coast head of the CPUSA secret apparatus, received a visitor named Cooper. The FBI, which had bugged Nelson's house, recognized Cooper as Vasily Zubilin, nominally a Soviet diplomat. It assumed that Zubilin was a Soviet intelligence officer, but only years later would it become clear that he was the chief of KGB operations in the United States.

Nelson and Cooper/Zubilin, using guarded language, discussed espionage and how Nelson's West Coast underground, which they referred to as the apparat, could assist Soviet intelligence. They referred to Rudy Baker ("Al") and to Earl Browder's support for cooperation between Soviet intelligence and the CPUSA underground. Nelson told Zubilin that between thirty and forty-five seamen were available for courier activities for the Communist party between West Coast ports and the Pacific rim and assured Zubilin of their availability for Soviet use. Nelson, however, also complained to Cooper/Zubilin that there were too many cases of Soviet intelligence officers co-opting West Coast CPUSA members to assist their operations without coordinating with Nelson. Zubilin handed over a sum of cash, although the amount is not known. Whether Zubilin was transmitting funds from the Comintern or providing a KGB subsidy is unclear. By this time the Comintern was preparing for its dissolution and the KGB was taking over selected parts of the Comintern's covert operations.[35] In any case, the links between Rudy Baker and Steve Nelson of the CPUSA and Zubilin illustrate the tie between Soviet intelligence and the American Communist party.

American Communists on Intelligence Missions Abroad

In the 1930s the CPUSA supplied several recruits for Soviet intelligence operations abroad. Two of them, Robert Switz and Arvid Jacobson, landed in European jails. And one, sent to Asia, paid with his life.

Born in Japan in 1903, Yotoku Miyagi immigrated to the United States in 1919. An aspiring painter, he graduated from the San Diego

Public Art School in 1925. Already by that time he had developed chronic tuberculosis. He settled in Los Angeles and in the late 1920s he joined the Proletarian Art Society, a CPUSA affiliate. He formally joined the CPUSA in 1931 and was quickly spotted by Tsutomu Yano, who had arrived in California in the early 1930s to help revive the CPUSA's languishing Japanese section. But Yano's duties also included recruiting agents to assist Soviet intelligence. Yano recruited Miyagi in 1931 and in 1933 sent him back to Japan, where he became part of a Soviet spy ring headed by Richard Sorge. Sorge, a German Communist operating under the cover of being a pro-Nazi German journalist stationed in Japan, became an unofficial adviser to Germany's ambassador. Sorge's access to the German embassy and that of his subagents to the Japanese government allowed him to provide the Soviets with highly valuable intelligence on both Japan and Germany.

Miyagi was one of Sorge's chief assistants, but his CPUSA past was the undoing of the Sorge ring. Japanese security police in 1940 began to look for Communists among expatriates who had returned to Japan. The investigation turned up a returnee who had joined the CPUSA in Los Angeles at the same time as Miyagi and knew him as a fellow Communist. On the basis of that information Japanese police put Miyagi under surveillance and arrested him in October 1941. He attempted suicide by leaping head-first from an upper-storey window of the police station, but shrubbery broke his fall. Under torture he confessed, and the security police rolled up the rest of the Sorge network, including Sorge himself. Miyagi, in poor health even before his arrest, died in prison in 1943.[36]

During World War II the CPUSA secret apparatus supplied personnel for clandestine Soviet operations in Europe. In September 1940 Dimitrov, by ciphered message, told Earl Browder, "It is of great importance to have some of your peoples not known as members of Party in the organization that have to be organized in your country for various relief to people of Europe." Dimitrov explained that those picked "have to be very carefully chosen from the well developed, absolutely sure" in order "to penetrate committees we propose to utilize for the international connection work." By "international connection work" Dimitrov meant that these persons, serving as relief officials, would use their freedom of movement among the warring nations of Europe (America was not yet a belligerent) to act as covert couriers for the Soviets.[37]

One month after Dimitrov's message to Browder, Noel Field, a secret American Communist who worked on disarmament issues for the League of Nations, resigned his post. He then went to work for an international relief organization, the Unitarian Service Committee, and began work in early 1941 directing their refugee services in Europe from offices in Marseilles. Field used that position to serve as a courier for the underground German Communist party and to convey messages to and from representatives of the Hungarian, Polish, Bulgarian, and Yugoslav parties as he traveled around Europe on refugee business.

Field was not new to Soviet and Communist clandestine work. A mid-level State Department official in the 1930s, he had been the object of a tug of war between two separate Soviet espionage networks. Hede Massing, who worked then for the KGB, later wrote that she had attempted to recruit Field but he had told her he preferred to work with his old friend Alger Hiss, who was part of a GRU network. (Field left the State Department to work for the League of Nations in 1936.)[38]

After the Hiss case became public in 1948, Field, fearing he would be called to testify against his old comrade, fled to Eastern Europe with several members of his family. His timing, however, was poor. Joseph Stalin was then purging the leadership of the Communist regimes in Hungary and Czechoslovakia. Field, in his clandestine role for the Comintern, had also been in touch with underground Communists, including many targeted for liquidation in the late 1940s. During World War II Field had provided information on conditions in Nazi-occupied Europe to Allan Dulles, the American OSS station chief in Switzerland. At the time, this activity was compatible with his Communist loyalties. Those conducting Stalin's purges, however, found Field a convenient way to link their targets to American intelligence. Although he was in fact a Soviet spy, Field, his wife, his brother, and a foster daughter were all arrested and imprisoned by Hungary's Communist regime as American spies, and Field's activities were cited in the indictments of Hungarian and Czechoslovak officials imprisoned or executed in the purges. After Stalin's death in 1953, Field was released and rehabilitated. Despite his imprisonment Field remained a loyal Communist. He never returned to the United States. He died in Hungary in 1970.[39]

Field was only one of the reliable comrades Dimitrov had asked Browder to find for infiltration of international relief agencies. A memorandum sent from the foreign intelligence directorate of the KGB to the Comintern in 1942 suggests that Browder may have found at least one more. General Fitin informed Dimitrov that someone on the staff of the Unitarian Service Committee, identified only as "Doctor Joe," had successfully delivered letters from the CPUSA to the Communist Party of Great Britain.[40] Nothing else, however, is known of Doctor Joe.

On September 13, 1939, Dimitrov also ordered the CPUSA "to select two comrades with good bourgeois references as salesmen or journalists of a solid bourgeois newspaper who will be able to live in Europe and to move from one country to the other. They have to go to Stockholm and wait there for our instructions." Dimitrov supplied the passwords and meeting places they were to use.[41]

Shortly after this cable was sent, the CPUSA handed over a young Communist journalist working for the *Brooklyn Eagle*, Winston Burdett, to the Comintern for clandestine work. Burdett had secretly joined the CPUSA in 1937. Early in 1940 a fellow reporter, Nathan Einhorn, who was then serving as executive secretary of the New York local of the American Newspaper Guild and was also a secret Communist, asked Burdett to meet with Joseph North, a prominent Communist and editor of *New Masses*. North informed Burdett that "we" had a mission for him and introduced him to a man whose name Burdett was not told. Burdett later identified a photograph of Jacob Golos as the man he had met. Golos, a shadowy figure in the CPUSA's leadership, was also the liaison between the CPUSA and the KGB. Golos instructed the young reporter that he should persuade the *Eagle* to give him credentials as a foreign correspondent, with Burdett financing his own way (Golos promised to furnish the funds) and the *Eagle* paying only for those stories it used. Golos told Burdett to suggest as his first assignment going to Finland to cover the war that had just broken out between the Finns and the Soviets. Golos also had Burdett turn in his CPUSA membership card, hand over photographs of himself (for use by Soviet agents to identify him), and write out an autobiography, the latter a standard Soviet intelligence practice for new agents.[42]

The *Eagle* was delighted to obtain a war correspondent on the cheap, and Golos provided Burdett with funds and instructions for a covert meeting with a Soviet contact in Stockholm. Burdett left the United States in February 1940. When he reached Stockholm he cabled confirmation of his arrival to a name he recalled only as that of a woman and sounding Anglo-Saxon, with an address in New York City. He met his Soviet contact in Stockholm and was instructed to use his position as a reporter to find out about the morale of the Finnish population and its psychological willingness to continue fighting. (Finland was vastly overmatched by the USSR, and the Soviets had been shocked when the Finns not only failed to collapse after the Soviet invasion but halted the initial Soviet assault.) His Stockholm contact also handed over more funds to supplement those Golos had provided to him.

After the Finnish-Soviet war ended in March 1940, Burdett made a final report to his Stockholm contact and received an additional payment. He then undertook other journalistic assignments for American newspapers, reporting from Norway, Romania, Yugoslavia, and Turkey, all the while meeting with Soviet intelligence contacts as well. Burdett gradually grew dissatisfied with his clandestine work, and his ideological loyalty to Communism weakened. He quietly dropped his ties to Soviet intelligence in 1942 when he went to work for CBS Radio News, where he eventually became a prominent correspondent.

When Elizabeth Bentley, the Soviet spy and former associate of Jacob Golos, defected in late 1945, she told the FBI that in 1940 she had received a cable from Burdett which was a signal to Golos that he had reached Stockholm. The FBI interviewed Burdett in 1951. He initially admitted being close to the CPUSA in the 1930s but denied any knowledge of Bentley, Golos, or Soviet intelligence. Upon being reinterviewed, however, he admitted that in the early 1940s he had furnished the Soviets with information while overseas. In 1955 he testified to a congressional committee about his recruitment through Einhorn and North and his work for the Soviets.

In his testimony Burdett mentioned in passing that while in Stockholm in early 1940 he had run into another American reporter, Peter Rhodes, who then worked for the United Press wire service. Burdett said he knew nothing about Rhodes except that from talking to him it was obvious that he was pro-Communist. Burdett did not know it, but Rhodes, like himself, was a clandestine contact of the Soviets via the CPUSA and Golos. The Comintern archive contains a February 1940 coded cable to Dimitrov in which Rudy Baker reports that Peter Rhodes had not gone to Bucharest as planned earlier and his scheduled contact there with Soviet agents had to be rescheduled. A year later, while conducting a surveillance of Jacob Golos, the FBI observed him meeting with Peter Rhodes and his wife, Ione.[43]

Rhodes's attachment to communism was of some years' standing. After attending Oxford University from 1934 to 1936, he joined the

United Press. He wrote extensively about the Americans fighting with the International Brigades in Spain and became an ardent partisan of their cause, to the point of serving as an American delegate to the International Coordinating Committee for Aid to Republican Spain. A German Communist who had been with the International Brigades even entered the United States illegally using Rhodes's passport. In 1939 and 1940 Rhodes signed nominating petitions to put Communist party candidates on the New York State ballot. After America entered the war Rhodes first worked for the Foreign Broadcasting Monitoring Service of the Federal Communications Commission and then transferred to the Office of War Information; by 1944 he was the chief of its Atlantic News Section.

In August 1944 Ione Rhodes met with Bernard Schuster, then the CPUSA liaison with the KGB (replacing Golos). A deciphered Venona message of the New York KGB reported that Mrs. Rhodes had told Schuster that her husband had lost contact with Soviet intelligence.[44] Schuster recommended that the KGB reestablish contact and reminded the KGB that earlier Rhodes had been in liaison with them through Jacob Golos.

Ione Rhodes's reference to her husband's having lost contact most likely points to Golos's death in 1943. When Elizabeth Bentley defected in 1945, she told the FBI that Golos had described Peter Rhodes as one of his covert contacts and had met with him on a number of occasions in 1941 and 1942. Bentley also said that though she had met Ione Rhodes, she had had no personal contact with her husband and did not know what sort of information he provided. She said that from her contact with Ione and from what Golos had said, she knew that the Rhodeses were secret Communists, that he had been born in the Philippines and she in Belgium. Bentley also understood that Rhodes was a journalist who later became a government official involved in broadcasting, and that there had been a family tragedy: Rhodes's mother had killed his father. The FBI checked Bentley's knowledge about the Rhodeses' background and found it accurate.[45]

Bentley's statement to the FBI also demonstrated that the KGB attempted, although without any immediate success, to follow up on Schuster's recommendation of reestablishing contact with Rhodes. Bentley reported that in early 1945 one of her KGB contacts, Joseph Katz, directed her to reapproach Ione Rhodes. Bentley said she tried to do so but that Ione was wary and refused to meet. A few months later, Anatoly Gromov, who had replaced Katz as her KGB liaison, again asked her to contact Ione. Bentley, who was only a few months from her own defection, declined, citing Ione's suspicious attitude.[46]

The FBI interviewed Peter Rhodes in June 1947. He flatly denied ever having met Jacob Golos and claimed not to recognize his photograph. The FBI had observed Golos meeting with the Rhodeses in 1941, so it knew this statement to be false. Much of the rest of Rhodes's statement also lacked credibility. He denied knowing that his friends from the International Brigades were Communists and dismissed the matter of the fraudulent use of his passport as something that he did not need to explain. He also left his interviewers flabbergasted by delivering a strident defense of the Nazi-Soviet Pact.[47]

The CPUSA Secret Apparatus and False Passports

In the early and mid-1930s, the CPUSA's secret apparatus under J. Peters engaged in the wholesale procurement of false American passports for use by American Communists traveling abroad and by Soviet intelligence for espionage purposes. This task was largely dropped when Baker took over in mid-1938, for reasons that will become obvious.

American passports were greatly prized in the intelligence world because of their international acceptability to most border authorities. Moreover, because of the polyglot population of the United States, agents from a variety of ethnic and racial backgrounds and speaking English with all kinds of accents could plausibly claim to hold valid American passports.

The lack of a system of national identification in the United States made obtaining false passports relatively easy. In 1938, shortly after his defection, Whittaker Chambers wrote an essay about this aspect of Soviet espionage and gave it to an old friend and journalist colleague, Herbert Solow. Signed by "Karl," Chambers's pseudonym in the underground, it was entitled "The Faking of Americans." Chambers claimed that in 1932 a Latvian agent of the KGB, known as Ewald, arrived in New York to assume responsibility for the production of false passports. Chambers never knew Ewald's real name, but documents that have surfaced in Russian archives identify him as Arnold Ikal. Chambers wrote that Ewald's chief contact was a man Chambers called Sandor, "the organizer of most of the illegal activities of the Communist Party of America."[48] From this and other descriptive phrases Chambers provided, it is clear that Sandor was Chambers's pseudonym for J. Peters.

In his 1938 essay Chambers asserted that producing fake passports was a source of money for the secret apparatus: "The greatest handicap to Sandor's expensive work is lack of funds and here was a sizable slice of the secret service budget at his disposal." Peters and Ewald/Ikal struck a deal: "The Party supplied the secret service with naturalization papers, birth certificates, business and social fronts, cover addresses and reliable contacts of various kinds. And the Soviet Government pumped life-blood into the underground Communist Party in the form of money payment for such services."[49]

Members of Peters's secret apparatus looked in the genealogical division of the New York Public Library for the names of dead children. The researcher would obtain a copy of the child's birth certificate, which would then be used to apply for a false passport. The CPUSA underground also provided witnesses who would falsely swear to the identity of the applicant before a passport official. By the time Ikal was arrested in Moscow in 1937, he had received hundreds of fraudulent American passports from the CPUSA underground.[50]

The productivity of the CPUSA-Soviet passport fraud ring is illustrated by the arrest in 1935 in Denmark of George Mink, Leon Josephson, and Nicholas Sherman. Mink, born in Russia in 1899, came to the United States in 1912. He was a leading CPUSA maritime union organizer in the 1920s and for a time headed its Marine Workers Industrial Union. In the early 1930s he became an operative for the Profintern, coordinating Communist trade union activities in the maritime field around the world.

When he was arrested in Denmark, Mink had in his possession four American passports, one in his name, one fraudulent passport with his photograph but in the name of Al Gottlieb, one for Harry H. Kaplan, and one for Abraham Wexler. The Kaplan passport was authentic; when American authorities asked Harry Kaplan how his passport had gotten into Mink's hands, Kaplan stated that it had been stolen from him by Barney Josephson, Leon Josephson's brother. The Wexler passport was also authentic; Wexler claimed it had been stolen but could not say when, where, or by whom. Wexler was a member of the small Marine Workers Industrial Union, of which Mink was the first national chairman, and Kaplan was an associate of the Josephson brothers and Mink. The obvious inference was that both had turned their passports over to Mink for later alteration by insertion of new photographs.[51] A Danish court convicted Mink of espionage, and he served eighteen months in prison. He was then deported to the USSR. His history after that time is unclear.[52]

Leon Josephson, who had been arrested with Mink, spent four months in jail. At that point a Danish court decided that the evidence was insufficient to proceed, and Josephson returned to America. State Department handwriting experts later determined that the application for the fraudulent Gottlieb passport carried by George Mink was in Josephson's hand. Nor was this Josephson's only venture into the illegal passport business. An analysis of the application for a fraudulent American passport in the name of Samuel Liptzen carried by Gerhart Eisler, the Comintern's illegal representative in the United States in the mid-1930s, was in Josephson's hand, as was the statement of a witness falsely vouching for Liptzen's identity.[53]

Josephson had joined the CPUSA in 1926. He was a lawyer and in the late 1920s represented Amtorg and the party's interests in a variety of legal proceedings. In 1930 he was one of a group of Communist lawyers helping several unionists convicted of killing a local sheriff during a textile strike in Gastonia, North Carolina. Those convicted jumped bail and fled to the Soviet Union. One of them, Fred Beal, later returned to the United States, announced his disillusionment with communism, and served his prison sentence. He stated that Josephson had arranged for the false passports that he and the others had used to flee.[54]

The third person arrested with Mink and Josephson claimed to be Nicholas Sherman. He carried a U.S. passport in that name but also had in his possession a Canadian passport in the name of Abraham Goldman and a German passport in the name of Wilhelm Brettschneider. The Sherman passport was fraudulent, obtained by using the naturalization papers of a man who had died in 1926 and a false witness supplied by Peters's secret apparatus. When arrested, Sherman had on him correspondence from a business firm operated by Harry Kaplan, the same Kaplan whose passport was in Mink's possession. The Danish court convicted Sherman of espionage; he served eighteen months in prison and was deported to the USSR.

Who was the fake Nicholas Sherman? Robert Switz, an American who worked for Soviet military intelligence in the 1930s, later identified a photograph of Sherman as that of a senior GRU officer operating illegally in the United States whose name was Aleksandr Petrovich Ulanovsky. Whittaker Chambers, who worked for Ulanovsky's GRU espionage apparatus in the early 1930s, discussed him in detail in his memoir, *Witness*.[55]

The arrest of Mink, Josephson, and Sherman/Ulanovsky demonstrates not only the productivity of the CPUSA-Soviet fraudulent passport operations. Traveling together and arrested together were a CPUSA unionist and Profintern operative (Mink), a CPUSA lawyer and associate of its clandestine arm (Josephson), and a GRU officer and professional spy (Ulanovsky). Communist trade unionism, the CPUSA (aboveground and below), and Soviet espionage were intermingled. To use the jargon of Cold War espionage, there was no "compartmentalization." In the 1930s and early 1940s the organizational blending of these different aspects of the Communist movement allowed the Soviet Union to maximize its return on the assets it possessed. But after World War II, when American authorities belatedly started to pay attention and the FBI began an aggressive investigation, the vulnerability of this arrangement also became clear. An organization as large as the CPUSA had too many areas of weakness. Many party-linked espionage operations were exposed and neutralized by American counterintelligence in the late 1940s and 1950s. And of course the CPUSA itself became tainted with disloyalty. That, however, was for the future. In 1935 the State Department noticed the Danish arrests and began to look into the matter of false passports, but follow-up was slow, the Justice Department had little interest in prosecuting Soviet espionage, and the popular press paid scant attention.

Nor was much notice taken in 1936 when two Comintern agents, Arthur Ewert and his wife, Elsie, turned up in Brazil with fake American passports. Ewert, a German Communist leader in the early and mid-1920s, became a covert Comintern agent in the late 1920s. In the mid-1930s he and his wife arrived by separate routes in Brazil. Arthur Ewert's American passport gave his name as Harry Berger, while his wife's American passport was in the name of Machla Lencsyski. The real Berger had died as an infant; the CPUSA passport ring had again simply used the infant's birth certificate and provided witnesses who falsely swore that Ewert was Berger. Elsie Ewert's passport had been gained by using the naturalization papers of Machla Lencsyski. When the passport fraud came to light, the real Lencsyski claimed that her naturalization papers had been lost and she had no idea how they had come to be used to obtain a fake passport. Her brother, however, was one of the perjuring witnesses to the fake Berger passport and part of the CPUSA fake passport apparatus.

The Ewerts were in Brazil to assist a Communist-backed insurrection against the authoritarian Vargas regime. The insurrection failed when it was uncovered by Brazilian police, and the Ewerts were arrested. The U.S. embassy initially took an interest in their fate when it was thought that they were American citizens. Once it became clear the two were using fraudulent passports and were not Americans, U.S. diplomats withdrew from the matter.[56]

The passport issue gained more attention in 1937 with the arrest of Arnold Ikal, the GRU's contact with Peters's passport operation. Ikal was not, however, arrested in the United States for his role in the wholesale faking of American passports. Diplomats at the U.S. embassy in Moscow got word that an American woman, Mrs. Donald L. Robinson, needed assistance at the nearby Hotel National. They visited the distraught woman, who said that her husband, also an American, had disappeared. The officials returned to the embassy to check their records, then went back to the hotel, only to find the room occupied by a new person and the hotel staff claiming that Mrs. Robinson had departed without leaving a forwarding address. The American chargé d'affaires, Loy Henderson, refused to accept that story, went to Soviet authorities, and insisted that Mrs. Robinson be located and that embassy officials be allowed to speak to her. After lengthy delays, Henderson was allowed to visit Mrs. Robinson, in a Moscow prison. She told Henderson that she neither needed nor wanted American diplomatic assistance.

Meanwhile, a search of State Department passport records showed that the Robinsons also possessed a second set of passports, as Mr. and Mrs. Adolph A. Rubens. The wife of a former U.S. diplomat at the American consulate in Latvia also recognized the photograph of Donald Robinson as that of a Latvian believed to have been a Soviet intelligence agent. It turned out that the real Donald Robinson was born in Queens in 1905 and had died in 1909. Mrs. Robinson, meanwhile, had used the birth certificate of Ruth Norma Birkland, who was born in 1909 and died in 1915, for her passport. At this point Henderson concluded that the two were not innocent Americans but Soviet agents of some sort caught up in the nightmarish purges then sweeping the Soviet Union and saw little reason for the U.S. embassy to pursue the case.

The Moscow incident, however, generated considerable press coverage and interest in how the Rubenses got two sets of false American passports. Chambers's friend, Herbert Solow, used the Rubens case and the information Chambers provided as the basis of an article, "Stalin's American Passport Mill," in the popular *American Mercury,* which outlined the sizable joint CPUSA-Soviet passport forgery operation.[57]

Ikal was merely one of many hundreds of KGB, GRU, and Comintern agents who in the late 1930s fell victim to Stalin's Terror. When recalled to Moscow in 1937, he was arrested by his colleagues and charged with being part of a Trotskyist-fascist plot to destroy the Soviet Union. Like many of those arrested during the Terror, Ikal signed a false confession, admitting to having made contacts with the American followers of Leon Trotsky on behalf of Latvian fascists, at whose head stood Gen. Yan Berzin, head of the GRU. Ikal's confession also claimed that through Philip Rosenblit, a New York dentist and participant in the CPUSA underground, he had funneled money to James Cannon, head of the American Trotskyist movement (Cannon and Rosenblit were married to sisters). Rosenblit, who in the 1920s had played a key role in the clandestine transfer of Comintern subsidies to the CPUSA and had been part of the CPUSA underground that had assisted the GRU in the early 1930s, had unwisely emigrated to the USSR in the mid-1930s. He disappeared in 1937, the same year as Ikal's faked confession, having been either executed or sent to the Gulag.

As for Ikal, after signing the confession he went to the Gulag. In 1939, no longer under immediate threat of execution, he repudiated his 1937 confession, strenuously denied any ideological deviation, and asked for reconsideration of his sentence. He remained in prison, however, and died in the camps. His wife, although holding two false American passports, really was an American. Her true name was Ruth Buerger, and she was a Communist. After she cooperated with Soviet authorities by declining American diplomatic assistance, she was released from Soviet prison but not allowed to leave the USSR. Her family in the United States received a visit from an intermediary for the Soviets who warned that they should make no public outcry about their daughter's fate. They did not, and she was allowed to live out her natural life in the Soviet Union.[58]

Although fake American passports had surfaced by this time in the hands of Comintern and Soviet intelligence agents in Denmark, Brazil, and Moscow, the U.S. government still did little about the matter until war broke out in Europe in September 1939. Authorities then launched an investigation that included the seizure of the records of World Tourists, a travel agency headed by Jacob Golos. These documents showed that World Tourists had provided travel services for at least sixteen persons who possessed false American passports, and that the passage tickets and other charges for these persons were assigned to two special accounts, one labeled George Primoff and the other A. Blake. Charges to these accounts, it turned out, were actually paid by the American Communist party.[59]

On the basis of the passport investigation in 1939, the Justice Department launched several prosecutions. Most prominently, it indicted Earl Browder, head of the CPUSA, for use of fraudulent passports. He was arrested in October 1939, tried, convicted, and, after his appeals failed, imprisoned in 1941. Although he was sentenced to four years in prison, after Browder had served fourteen months President Roosevelt commuted his sentence as a gesture of goodwill toward the Soviet Union, by that time an ally of the United States against Nazi Germany. William Weiner, the CPUSA's national treasurer, was also convicted, but the court suspended his sentence when he claimed to have a life-threatening heart condition. The government indicted the party official Harry Gannes for passport fraud, but his case was repeatedly delayed, and he died in 1941 before trial. Virtually all the other Communists identified in the investigation as having obtained fraudulent passports, as well as the many witnesses who falsely vouched for them, escaped prosecution.

Jacob Golos and World Tourists were also indicted, but they got away remarkably lightly. Under a plea bargain, on March 14, 1940, Golos pled guilty to failing to register as the agent of a foreign power, namely, the USSR. He was fined five hundred dollars and given a suspended jail sentence.

American Counterespionage: Other Priorities

With the exception of jailing Earl Browder, the government's response to the CPUSA-Soviet passport fraud operation was anemic, and it was symptomatic of the disarray in American counterintelligence. In the 1930s the U.S. government had a hodgepodge of internal security laws, no clear executive order on what constituted government secrets, no clear policy on the security fitness of government personnel with access to sensitive information, and divided and unclear authority as to which government agencies were responsible for internal security enforcement.

This disarray had historical precedents. America had entered World War I in 1917 with a governmental structure ill-prepared for a major international conflict. Nor had the nation's history given it any serious experience with the espionage, sabotage, or political subversion linked to a foreign power. Yet these became legitimate concerns, if in retrospect exaggerated, when the United States entered the war against Imperial Germany. In 1917 and 1918 the government under emergency wartime conditions created a large security system based on the Justice Department's Bureau of Investigation (predecessor to the FBI) and the counterintelligence sections of Army military intelligence and the Office of Naval Intelligence. Unable to expand its own agencies rapidly enough, the federal government also sponsored the creation a series of state and local authorities (for example, the New York City Committee on Aliens) as auxiliaries of the national government. The federal government also sanctioned an array of quasi-private organizations manned by eager volunteers (the American Protective League and the American Defense Society were among the largest) that watched for sabotage, espionage, or other acts of resistance to the war effort.[60]

This hastily created arrangement worked. German government financial support for American antiwar activities, significant before the United States entered the war, was stopped and its recipients were largely silenced. German intelligence made a number of efforts to penetrate the United States, but most were blocked or thwarted. Domestic resistance to conscription was also suppressed. The cost, however, had been high. The hastily thrown-together arrangements were inefficient, inconsistent, and prone to abuse. Several of the state-level security agencies became tools of partisan politics. The Minnesota Commission of Public Safety, for example, used its extensive official power to suppress the political ambitions of Minnesota's Non-Partisan League, a populist farm organization that threatened the position of the dominant Republican party. Several of the private organizations that received federal government support also ventured into vigilante justice and engaged in egregious violations of basic legal norms.

After the war ended in November 1918, some parts of the wartime security apparatus continued to operate, turning their attention to Bolshevism, which seemed on the threshold of sweeping Europe. But the

panic over the new Red threat receded by 1921, and the Harding administration completed the dismantling of the wartime security apparatus. The Bureau of Investigation withdrew almost entirely from the
internal security field.[61] The military's intelligence agencies shrank drastically in size. Both the Army's and the Navy's counterintelligence
branches continued to monitor domestic radicalism, but neither service
had any jurisdiction to prosecute espionage or subversion that did not
directly involve military personnel. Their reports went largely unread
by military commanders and usually were not shared with civilian agencies that might actually have had jurisdiction.

In the mid-1930s President Roosevelt, concerned about the pro-Nazi
German-American Bund and domestic fascist groups such as the Silver
Shirts and the Black Legion, ordered the Federal Bureau of Investigation
to reenter the domestic security field. Bureau head J. Edgar Hoover did
so eagerly and included American Communists among those under observation. The FBI of the 1930s, however, was very small, with barely
three hundred agents in 1933 and fewer than nine hundred even by the
end of the decade. While the agency had become skilled in criminal
investigation, it took some years for its agents to develop knowledge
and procedures geared to counterintelligence activities.

Internal security concerns grew in the late 1930s when it appeared
that fascists had created a new strategy of combining internal subversion with external military aggression. During the Spanish Civil War
the Nationalist forces of Gen. Francisco Franco, backed by Nazi Germany and Fascist Italy, advanced in four columns on Madrid, the be-
sieged capital of the Spanish Republicans. The Nationalist general directing the offensive, Emilio Mola, boasted that he had a secret "fifth
column" of fascists inside the city sowing disaffection and defeatism
which would assail the Republicans from within as his troops assaulted
the city's defenses from without. Thus was born the image of the "fifth
column" as a clandestine underground that spread subversion, engaged
in sabotage and espionage, and prepared the way for military conquest.
Fifth-column imagery grew stronger as Hitler used covertly organized
Nazi sympathizers, first in Austria and then in Czechoslovakia, to pave
the way for German conquest.

As a consequence, the FBI devoted more of its resources to internal
security. Both the Army and the Navy also expanded their efforts, although all three agencies were still on Depression-era austerity budgets
with limited personnel until mobilization began in earnest in 1941. The

State Department took an interest in the area, and the Treasury Department, which oversaw the Secret Service, thought it might have a role as well. Even the Post Office claimed a role with its jurisdiction over the mail, and the Commerce Department, concerned about foreign trade manipulation, asserted an interest. It became clear to Attorney General Frank Murphy that the overlapping and uncoordinated efforts in this field were wasting what limited resources the government had. In 1939 he asked President Roosevelt to issue an order clarifying the situation. The president did so in a June 26, 1939, confidential memorandum to the secretaries of state, treasury, war, navy, and commerce and to the attorney general and postmaster general: "It is my desire that the investigation of all espionage, counterespionage, and sabotage matters be controlled and handled by the Federal Bureau of Investigation of the Department of Justice, the Military Intelligence Division of the War Department, and the office of Naval Intelligence of the Navy Department. . . . [Y]ou will instruct the heads of all other investigative agencies other than the three named, to refer immediately to the nearest office of the Federal Bureau of Investigation any data, information, or material that may come to their notice bearing directly or indirectly on espionage, counterespionage, or sabotage."[62]

Roosevelt's order imposed some system on the threatening chaos of American counterintelligence operations. As it worked out, the Navy and the Army would take care of internal security for their own personnel, bases, and facilities. The FBI would cover everything else. There was overlap in regard to war plants and civilian workers as American military mobilization got under way, and the military agencies kept a finger in civilian counterintelligence, but the main jurisdictional lines were clear. Interagency cooperation, however, continued to be poor.[63]

The system worked fairly well on its chief targets. After the invasion of Poland in 1939, German intelligence made repeated efforts to establish espionage and sabotage networks in the United States, with little success. In a 1940 report Hoover boasted, with justifiable pride, that the FBI had so infiltrated German intelligence networks that a German clandestine short-wave radio was run by FBI penetration agents. He noted that "all material furnished by German Agents through their complicated channels of communication to this station for transmittal to Europe is cleared by State, War and Navy Department officials prior to the time that it is actually transmitted to Germany."[64] Once the United States entered the war in December 1941, German and Japanese intelligence networks were easily rolled up, and new penetrations were few. Dozens of Americans who had covertly accepted German and Japanese money between 1939 and 1941 to finance pro-Nazi propaganda, anti-intervention literature, or antisemitic publications were prosecuted or silenced. The German-American Bund collapsed and its chief figures were imprisoned. Pro-Mussolini Italian-American networks were dispersed. Key leaders of other domestic fascist organizations were also imprisoned, or they faced such strict official attention that their ability to impede the war effort was reduced to nil. With the glaring exception of the internment of West Coast Japanese-Americans, an act that Hoover and the FBI advised against, the internal security regime in World War II also worked with much greater sensitivity to individual rights and democratic liberties than did the security regime in World War I. Because of the abuses that had occurred, the World War I experience of delegating internal security authority to semi-autonomous state and local governmental entities or semi-private volunteer organizations was not repeated.

It would be poor history to use the clarity of hindsight to fault officials for not giving Soviet espionage priority consideration in this era. German, Italian, and Japanese espionage was the overriding concern of security officials in the late 1930s and during World War II, and rightly so. But even though Soviet intelligence operations in the United States were a secondary or even a tertiary concern, the American response to Soviet espionage was noticeably weak, and the limited follow-through on the uncovering of the massive CPUSA-Soviet passport operation was but one example.

The Missed Opportunity: Whittaker Chambers in 1939

During most of 1939 Whittaker Chambers continued his effort to reenter normal life. He solidified his position at *Time* magazine and managed to avoid both public and official notice. The Nazi-Soviet Pact in August 1939, however, caused Chambers to change his stance. He realized that the pact made war inevitable and that the Soviet Union had become a de facto nonbelligerent ally of Nazi Germany. He anticipated, correctly, that the pact would put Soviet supporters in the United States in conflict with American national policy. Isaac Don Levine, a journalist who wrote extensively on communism and had a rough idea of what Chambers had been involved in, convinced him that he had to alert

American authorities. Chambers agreed, with the proviso that he wanted immunity from prosecution. Levine approached Marvin McIntyre, the White House appointments secretary, summarized Chambers's story, and asked for a meeting with President Roosevelt himself. McIntyre declined a meeting with FDR but arranged for Levine to take Chambers to see Assistant Secretary of State Adolf Berle.

Levine and Chambers met with Berle on the evening of September 2. A day earlier Nazi armored columns had smashed into Poland. Soviet Red Army forces would wait two weeks and then, with the Poles fully engaged in the west, would strike from the east and annex half of Poland. Chambers told Berle a large part, although not all, of the story of the CPUSA-GRU network of which he had been a part. Concerned about his own vulnerability to imprisonment, he held back how deeply he himself had been involved in spying. There was no doubt, however, that Berle understood that he was being told of espionage. Berle kept written notes of the meeting, headed "Underground Espionage Agent." They show that Chambers gave him the names and provided short descriptions of a number of mid-level government officials whom he described as secret Communists and members of covert CPUSA caucuses operating within the U.S. government. He also provided the names of persons outside the government who supported the operations of the CPUSA underground. In several cases, according to Berle's notes, Chambers implied that the person in question might be engaged in espionage against the United States as well as in covert Communist activity.

The Venona decryptions confirm that eight of those whom Chambers named in September 1939 later cooperated with Soviet espionage against the United States.[65] They were Alger Hiss, then a mid-level State Department official; Laurence Duggan, then head of the State Department's Division of the American Republics, which supervised diplomatic relations with Central and South America; Frank Coe, a Treasury Department official who worked in international economics; Charles Kramer, on the staff of the National Labor Relations Board; John Abt, a prominent labor lawyer with wide contacts in the Congress of Industrial Organizations; Isaac Folkoff, a senior leader of the California Communist party; Lauchlin Currie, recently brought into the White House as a senior aide to President Roosevelt; and Harry Dexter White, assistant to the secretary of the Treasury. (Isaac Don Levine also kept notes on the meeting, and his notes contain White's name. Berle's notes do not. Chambers, in his memoir, names White as an espionage contact but thought he had not mentioned him to Berle.)

In addition to these eight, five others named by Chambers and listed in Berle's notes are confirmed to have participated in Soviet espionage by evidence other than that of Venona.[66] These were Julian Wadleigh, a State Department official who confessed to his role in Soviet espionage in 1949; Vincent Reno, a civilian official at the Army's Aberdeen Proving Grounds who also confessed in 1949 to his role in spying for the Soviets; Noel Field, who had been a State Department official in the mid-1930s; Solomon Adler, a senior Treasury Department official whom Elizabeth Bentley would later name as one of the sources for her CPUSA-KGB network; and Philip Rosenblit. Unknown to Chambers, by this time Rosenblit had fallen victim to Stalin's terror and was no longer a threat to the United States.

In accordance with Roosevelt's 1939 order, the president's appointments secretary should have sent Levine and Chambers to the FBI. Similarly, Assistant Secretary of State Berle, once he understood that Chambers was raising an issue of possible espionage, had a responsibility under Roosevelt's order, as well as by common sense, to notify the FBI. He did not. Exactly why he did not is not clear, but it certainly had nothing to do with any sympathy for the Soviet cause. Berle was, and was known to be, a firm anti-Communist, which is why Levine and Chambers felt comfortable discussing these issues with him. In his diary for that night Berle recorded that he had met with Levine and Chambers regarding what he described as "Russian espionage" and that "it becomes necessary to take a few simple measures."[67]

The measures he took were simple, but they were also ineffective. He did not file a report on the interview with the FBI, either military counterintelligence agency, or even the State Department's own personnel security office, although Chambers's information dealt with several State Department employees. In March 1941, more than a year after the interview, Berle checked on Chambers's veracity by asking the FBI if it was investigating Chambers or had information on him. The bureau told Berle that it was not investigating Chambers and only had him on a list that noted past participation in radical activities. Berle did not pass on Chambers's warnings or explain why he wanted to know about Chambers. His diary also shows that he discussed the matter with Marvin McIntyre, but not until 1942, and Berle did not know if McIntyre ever told President Roosevelt.[68]

As the years passed, several sources told FBI agents that Whittaker Chambers, by then a senior *Time* journalist, had information worth hearing. In May 1942 the FBI interviewed Chambers, who told them that he had already given all the information he had to Berle in 1939. The FBI contacted Berle and, a year later, in June 1943, his notes finally reached the FBI.[69] Even then the matter had a low priority, and nothing was done for many months—only after other evidence, the Katherine Perlo letter (chapter 5) and the FBI's own Comintern Apparatus investigation of 1944 (chapter 2) produced a body of corroborative documentation. And still the FBI accorded little urgency to the matter until Elizabeth Bentley turned herself in to the FBI in the fall of 1945.

Chambers had given the assistant secretary of state a list that included no fewer than thirteen persons, eight of them serving officials, several of them senior officials of the U.S. government who had had compromising relationships with Soviet intelligence. But the government did not act, in part because the information did not reach the proper agency for more than three and a half years, and even then the follow-up was slow. Had the government acted on Chambers's information in 1939, significant damage to U.S. national interests would have been avoided and a great deal of the basis for the bitter postwar domestic controversy about communism and subversion would have been removed.

CHAPTER 4

THE GOLOS–BENTLEY NETWORK

The American Communist party's secret apparatus under Josef Peters and Rudy Baker performed a multitude of tasks. It protected the CPUSA from infiltrators, hunted down internal ideological deviators, infiltrated and disrupted left-wing rivals and right-wing enemies, and maintained contact with secret party caucuses of members who were government employees. Not the least of its duties, however, was assisting the Comintern in its international operations and helping Soviet intelligence with its espionage activities.

After war broke out in 1939, and particularly after Nazi Germany invaded the Soviet Union in June 1941, sections of the CPUSA's underground shifted from being party networks to being primarily Soviet espionage networks. The most extensive of these ran through Jacob Golos and his assistant and successor, Elizabeth Bentley. It was not, in fact, a single apparatus, but several networks and a number of singleton agents, all of whom at some point were linked to Soviet intelligence through Golos and Bentley.

Jacob Golos

The story of the Golos-Bentley networks begins with Jacob N. Golos. A good deal about Golos's life remains unknown or unclear. He was born

Jacob Raisen in 1890 in what today is Ukraine. He later told Elizabeth Bentley that he had been involved in radical agitation against the Russian government at an early age, and was imprisoned and sent into Siberian exile. After several years he escaped via Japan and came to the United States to join his parents, who in the meantime had emigrated. The details and dates are unclear, but he or his parents arrived in the United States about 1908, and one source states that he became a naturalized citizen in 1915. In any event, around that time Golos became active in the Russian-language federation of the Socialist party, the core of its growing left-wing faction from which the American Communist movement developed. When the left wing was ejected from the Socialist party in 1919, it formed two rival organizations, the Communist Labor party and the Communist Party of America. Raisen went with the latter. (The two parties merged in 1921.) Raisen, then, had the status of a founding member of the American Communist party. Like many Communists of that era, he also adopted a new name, Golos, the Russian word for "voice." (In an obvious play on his name, the KGB in the Venona cables gave him the cover name Zvuk, or "sound" in Russian.)[1]

Golos's activities in the early 1920s are murky. He told Bentley that he returned to his native Russia in 1919 to work for several years for the Bolshevik regime, serving for a time as a foreman in a Siberian coal mine but also joining the Cheka, the powerful political police of the Soviet state and predecessor of the KGB. If Golos had been a "Chekist," it would have prepared him for his later role as a liaison between the CPUSA and the KGB.

The records of the Comintern in Moscow contain an autobiographical questionnaire that Golos filled out. It is undated, but the information on it indicates that he wrote it at some point after 1927. Unfortunately, the questionnaire was an American party form, and its questions related to American matters. Golos's answers refer to his birth in Russia and, in response to a question about his arrest record, states that he had been jailed for three years in Russia, probably a reference to his internal exile under the Tsarist regime. Otherwise the questionnaire is silent on whether Golos was in the Soviet Union in the early 1920s. It does state that he became a "full time functionary" (employee) of the CPUSA in 1923, so if he had gone to Russia in 1919, he was back four years later.[2]

After 1923 Golos worked for *Novy Mir,* one of the CPUSA's Russian-language journals, served as a party organizer in Detroit and

Chicago, and rose to the position of secretary (chief administrator) of the Society for Technical Aid to Soviet Russia, an organization that recruited technicians and specialists for work in Russia and shipped machinery, tools, and other needed goods to the new Soviet state.

His work for the Communist movement took a new direction in 1927. That June, Golos was one of the incorporators of World Tourists, a travel agency, and became its chief official, serving in that position until his death from a heart attack in 1943. All of World Tourists' officers and key staff were members of the CPUSA, and its capital was covertly provided by the party as well. On paper Golos was the principal owner of its stock.

World Tourists had a contractual relationship with Intourist, the official Soviet travel agency, and its chief business was the selling of Intourist services on commission. These included travel tickets, customs services, and documentation for transport to and from the USSR as well as lodging, travel, and tourist services inside the Soviet Union. It also arranged the shipment of parcels to the USSR, a major source of business because of the large number of immigrants who had family in the Soviet Union. Like any travel agency, it sold travel arrangements for other destinations as well. World Tourists' arrangement with Intourist guaranteed the agency a steady flow of business because Intourist was the only agency allowed to provide commercial tourist services inside the USSR. Further, Amtorg, the Soviet Union's trading arm, encouraged American businessmen seeking to do business with the Soviet state to make their travel arrangements through World Tourists. World Tourists, then, provided a method for the Soviet Union to indirectly subsidize the American Communist movement because the agency's covert owner was the CPUSA itself.

World Tourists also served the CPUSA in other ways. American Communists on party business, seeking to avoid notice by both American officials and those of foreign nations, often traveled abroad carrying false passports and deceptive travel documents. World Tourists not only never raised questions about the authenticity of the documents offered to it by CPUSA personnel; it also assisted in the subterfuge. It provided this service not only for the American party but even for foreign Communists on missions for the Communist International or Soviet intelligence agencies who were using false American travel documents.

At this point the story of Jacob Golos and World Tourists overlaps with that of the American Communist party's underground. The services Golos and World Tourists provided for the CPUSA secret apparatus and for Soviet intelligence resulted in World Tourists' indictment and plea bargain in 1940 as an unregistered agent of a foreign power.

Although the government's prosecution of World Tourists amounted to little more than a slap on the wrist, it signaled that authorities were not entirely blind to Golos's activities. So Golos changed his mode of operations in several ways. First, with World Tourists tainted as an agent of a foreign power, he and the CPUSA created a new cover business: U.S. Service and Shipping Corporation. Second, fearing himself under surveillance, he made Elizabeth Bentley, then unknown to the FBI, his courier and assistant for his covert operations.

U.S. Service and Shipping Corporation

To function as a new cover, U.S. Service and Shipping Corporation also needed a respectable head. Earl Browder arranged for a socially prominent and wealthy party sympathizer, John Hazard Reynolds, to become the president of the new company. To finance it the CPUSA put up fifteen thousand dollars as initial capital, delivered in cash to Reynolds, who laundered the funds through his own accounts. Although Reynolds put in only five thousand dollars of his own money, he initially held all of the company's stock. As a front man, he was far better than Golos, who was a Russian immigrant, an open although little-known CPUSA official, and a convicted criminal. Reynolds, by contrast, was from a wealthy Long Island family, his father was a New York judge, and his wife, Grace Fleischman, was an heiress to the Fleischman Yeast fortune. In the 1920s Reynolds, a member of the New York Stock Exchange, had by good luck or good judgment cashed in most of his holdings before the 1929 crash; he had also inherited a healthy share of the family's wealth in 1930. He had served as an Army officer in World War I and, taking a commission in the finance corps, became a lieutenant colonel in the Army in World War II.

Despite his elite background, Reynolds had been a Soviet sympathizer since the early 1920s. Although he never joined the CPUSA, he lent his name and some of his wealth to party-linked causes. One was the journal *Soviet Russia Today,* which promoted Stalin's USSR as a place where the idealistic goals of socialism had actually been realized. Theodore Bayer, president of the CPUSA-aligned Russky Golos Publishing Company, managed this journal, got to know Reynolds, and recommended him to Browder.[3] Lemuel Harris, a long-time CPUSA agricultural specialist who shared Reynolds's elite social background, served as the chief link between the party and Reynolds.

In 1947, when the FBI questioned Reynolds about U.S. Service and Shipping, he confirmed much of what Bentley had earlier told them but put it in a benign light. Reynolds explained that Bayer, whom he described as a friend, had introduced him to Browder and Golos, who had suggested the venture that became U.S. Service and Shipping. But, he assured the FBI, it had been purely a business enterprise. He denied that there were any party funds involved in the company and explained that the fifteen thousand dollars he had accepted from Lemuel Harris was a personal loan, not a CPUSA investment. Although insisting that all of this was strictly business, Reynolds also admitted that Harris's loan had not been accompanied by a written loan agreement, promissory note, or other documentation. The FBI did not believe him.[4]

When U.S. Service and Shipping was organized in 1941, Elizabeth Bentley was named vice-president. De facto she was the manager of the company, because Reynolds took little interest in its day-to-day affairs and, after he resumed Army duty in late 1942, was absent in any case. Bentley was Golos's proxy within U.S. Service and Shipping and the link to World Tourists, which Golos continued to head and which did much of the work for U.S. Service and Shipping on what amounted to a subcontractor basis.

The importance of U.S. Service and Shipping to Soviet intelligence as a cover is illustrated by two decrypted KGB messages from late 1944. Several persons connected with Russian War Relief, a major supplier of donated goods to the USSR, asked Amtorg to authorize other firms to offer the same services as did the U.S. Service and Shipping/World Tourists combination. The New York KGB urged its Moscow headquarters to derail this proposal because it "directly threatens the existence of Myrna's cover" and from the KGB's view it was "essential to continue the contract with Myrna's firm."[5] Myrna was the cover name used by the KGB at that time for Elizabeth Bentley.

Elizabeth Bentley

Elizabeth Bentley, born in 1908 in Connecticut, came from a socially respectable but not wealthy family. She graduated from Vassar, went to Italy on a student exchange program, and earned a master's degree from Columbia University. While at Columbia she joined the American League Against War and Fascism. This organization was covertly controlled by the CPUSA, and Bentley was drawn to the Communists within the league, all of whom kept their party membership secret. After she had proved her worth, they sponsored her for membership in the party in 1935.[6]

Over the next several years Bentley gradually moved into the CPUSA's underground. The CPUSA initially used Bentley for its basic covert work, infiltrating and reporting on organizations of interest to it. In 1938 Bentley got a job at the Italian Library of Information, a pro-Mussolini institution. Her reports on the pro-fascist propaganda put out by the library, however, did not seem to arouse much interest in the CPUSA. One of the party officials she reported to, however, took an interest in *her*. It was Jacob Golos. Golos had a wife and son, but both had emigrated to the Soviet Union in the mid-1930s. By the time Bentley met him Golos was lonely, and the two formed a romantic attachment. They would remain together until Golos's death in 1943.

Golos also began to use Bentley as an assistant in his covert work, although initially her tasks were minor. In 1939 she acted as a mail drop for Golos, receiving letters from Sam Carr and Tim Buck of the Canadian Communist party. (The Canadian government later imprisoned Carr, the national organizing secretary of the Communist Party of Canada, for espionage.) She also acted as a go-between for another Golos mail drop, Rose Arenal, who received mail for Golos from her brother-in-law, Leopolo Arenal, a Mexican Communist. Arenal helped to organize and participated in an armed assault in 1940 on the Mexican home of Leon Trotsky, the exiled Soviet leader. Trotsky escaped assassination then, but the assailants murdered one of Trotsky's guards, a young American.[7]

In late 1939 Golos also infiltrated Bentley into the office of the Mc-Clure newspaper syndicate to check on rumors that its chief was a Nazi agent. Bentley, who had taken a secretarial job, found no indication that he was, and she left the job early in 1940. Meanwhile, the government's legal attack on World Tourists had begun, and Golos started to suspect that he was under FBI surveillance. He responded by creating U.S. Service and Shipping and by increasingly relying on Bentley to meet with his sources and contacts.

Early in 1941 Golos, fearing that his trips outside New York would be watched, made Bentley his courier to his sources who were now located in Washington. One was Mary Price, secretary until mid-1943 to one of America's most respected press commentators, Walter Lippmann. Lippmann had wide access to the nation's decision makers, and Price furnished Golos with items that Lippmann chose not to write about or the names of Lippmann's sources, often not carried in Lippmann's stories but useful to the Soviets for weighing Lippmann's comments on American foreign policy.

Mary Price: The Spy as Secretary

Price shows up in the Venona traffic in mid-1943.[8] The two versions of what happened at that time, one from Bentley and the other from the KGB cables, do not contradict each other as concerns the facts. The two differ, however, with regard to the motives Bentley attributes to the KGB and those the KGB attributes to Bentley. Bentley told the FBI that Price had recurrent bouts of ill health exacerbated by the nervous strain of her espionage work. She left Lippmann's employ and went for an extended visit to Mexico to recover her health. Bentley's view was that the burden of the covert world was getting to be too much for Price and she should be withdrawn. Bentley claimed, though, that in early 1944 the KGB officer known to her as Bill pressed her to turn over Price to direct KGB control. From her description of Bill and Bill's wife, the FBI later concluded that Bill was Iskhak Abdulovich Akhmerov, a senior KGB officer. This identification is confirmed by deciphered Venona messages.[9] Bentley told the FBI that for some months in 1944 she and Bill/Akhmerov argued about Price's next mission, and she suspected him of reserving Price for "honey-trap" assignments, using sex as a means of recruiting sources. In the meantime Price was used as an intermediary with members of Bentley's network.

The Venona cables cast the same story in a different light. In June 1943, when Price was preparing for her extended vacation in Mexico, the New York KGB made a preliminary move to take her under its direct control and out of the Golos-Bentley network, reporting that it planned to have her courier material to its agent Nora (unidentified) in Mexico. In two decrypted KGB cables in April and May of 1944, Akhmerov reported to Moscow that he had met with Price and been at her New York apartment. (After returning from Mexico, Price had moved from Washington to New York.) Then in a July Venona message Akhmerov reported on his feud with Bentley about Price. He said that Browder and Bentley, citing Price's health and strained nerves, were insisting that she be withdrawn from intelligence work and given CPUSA political assignments. Akhmerov agreed to try to persuade Browder to turn Price over to the KGB, explaining he did not want to lose someone who "has been working for a long time and has acquired considerable experience."[10] He said that even if Price's health was delicate, her apartment could be used as a safe-house and she could function as an intermediary. Akhmerov made no comments that would support Bentley's suspicions that he meant for Price to do honey-trap work. Although Bentley attributed her stance to concern for Price, Akhmerov told Moscow that he thought Bentley had taken a personal dislike to Price and wanted her out of intelligence work for that reason.

In Bentley's account, she finally persuaded Earl Browder to her way of thinking. The decrypted Venona messages in fact confirm that in mid-1944 Browder told the KGB he was withdrawing Price from the underground and assigning her to political work, and the KGB finally acquiesced. Price became director of the Legislative and Educational Department of the Communist-dominated United Office and Professional Workers of America, a small CIO union, in 1945. In 1946 she moved to North Carolina to serve as secretary-treasurer of the North Carolina Committee of the Southern Conference for Human Welfare and ran for governor on the Progressive party ticket in 1948. Both of those organizations had numerous hidden Communists in their top leadership.

Although the Soviets found the information from Lippmann's files of interest, scavenging was not Price's most important work for them. Price acted as liaison with Maurice Halperin, one of the most productive agents in the Golos-Bentley networks, and assisted in recruiting one of their most highly placed sources, Duncan Lee.

Maurice Halperin: The Scholar Spy

Like almost everyone in the Golos-Bentley apparatus, Halperin came to Soviet espionage through the CPUSA. In the 1930s he was a Latin American specialist at the University of Oklahoma and at some point secretly joined the Communist party. Nathaniel Weyl and his wife knew him as a party member in 1936–1937 when Sylvia Weyl became organizational secretary of the Texas-Oklahoma district of the CPUSA.[11]

Although he kept his party membership secret, Halperin was a highly visible champion of far-left political causes. In 1940, with Communists subject to public opprobrium over the Nazi-Soviet Pact, this activism got him into trouble at the University of Oklahoma. Although he vigorously (and falsely) denied CPUSA membership, the Oklahoma legislature pushed for his dismissal. The university's president, however, believed Halperin and arranged a soft landing for him: a fully paid sabbatical, followed by Halperin's resigning rather than being fired. Almost immediately, in the late summer of 1941, a new federal agency, the Office of the Coordinator of Information, offered Halperin a position in its research section. This agency, renamed the Office of Strategic Services, became the U.S. government's chief intelligence arm in World War II, and Maurice Halperin became head of the Latin American division of its research and analysis section.

Halperin's party membership was secret, and he now worked for a sensitive government agency, so he did not approach the open CPUSA organization in Washington. According to Bentley, he made contact with the party through Bruce Minton, an editor of the party's literary intellectual journal, *New Masses*. Minton, recognizing his potential, notified Jacob Golos. Golos arranged for Bentley to contact Halperin at the Washington residence of his friend and fellow Latin American specialist, Willard Park, who worked for another federal agency, the Office of the Co-ordinator of Inter-American Affairs. Park, although not a CPUSA member, was a sympathizer. Initially, Bentley presented herself as a covert party contact (rather than an espionage link) and, using Mary Price's apartment as a meeting place, collected dues from Halperin and donations from Park. But she soon pressed them to deliver documents and information. She said that Park's material was of low quality, and eventually he ceased providing information. Halperin, however, was a fountain of material. Initially he delivered information to Mary Price, who passed it on to Bentley, although on occasion he handed his material directly to Bentley. Deciphered KGB messages confirm Bentley's account of Halperin's productivity as a spy: Halperin "reports," Halperin "has handed over material," "according to the information of" Halperin, Halperin "handed over . . . telegrams," Halperin "handed over a copy of an 'Izba' [OSS] document," "according to information sent to the 'Bank' [U.S. State Department] . . . and received by us from" Halperin, and so on.[12]

Halperin was particularly assiduous in getting copies of sensitive

U.S. diplomatic dispatches that were furnished to the OSS. Bentley rarely read them, and later she could tell the FBI only that there were a lot of them. The twenty-two Venona messages about Halperin's espionage alerted Moscow to the subjects dealt with in the stolen documents that the CPUSA was sending by diplomatic pouch. Halperin handed to the Soviets U.S. diplomatic cables regarding Turkey's policies toward Romania, State Department instructions to the U.S. ambassador in Spain, U.S. embassy reports about Morocco, reports from Ambassador John Winant in London about the internal stance of the Polish government-in-exile toward negotiations with Stalin, reports on the U.S. government relationship with the many competing French groups and personalities in exile, reports of peace feelers from dissident Germans being passed on by the Vatican, U.S. perceptions of Tito's activities in Yugoslavia, and discussions between the Greek government and the United States regarding Soviet ambitions in the Balkans.[13]

Nor did Halperin confine his work on behalf of the Soviets to collecting information. A number of the OSS reports written under his supervision were distorted to reflect Communist views. One Halperin OSS report depicted the Movimiento Nacionalista Revolucionario, which took power in Bolivia in 1943, as dangerous and pro-Nazi. Another described exiled Trotskyists and European anti-Stalinist Socialists in Mexico as pro-Hitler and linked the Socialist Workers party, the chief Trotskyist organization in the United States, to the Gestapo. In pursuit of a claim that a Roman Catholic political movement in Mexico was pro-Nazi, Halperin had OSS agents intercept and read mail between Mexican Catholic clergy and leading bishops and cardinals in the United States in hopes of finding evidence that the American church was aiding a pro-Nazi movement. All of these claims were false but fully in accord with CPUSA and Soviet stances.[14]

Halperin stayed with the OSS until it dissolved in 1945, but he was able to transfer to the State Department and continue to work on Latin American questions. By 1946, however, as American-Soviet tensions rose, and probably warned by the KGB of Bentley's defection to the FBI, he concluded that his days were numbered, and resigned. When the FBI interviewed Halperin in 1947, he emphatically denied that he was a Communist, that he had ever met Elizabeth Bentley, and that he had had any contact with Soviet intelligence. Many years later Halperin contradicted his FBI statement, telling a biographer that on the recommendation of an unnamed relative of Bruce Minton, he had met with

Bentley on several occasions, including at his residence. But, he insisted, she was simply a research assistant to Earl Browder who was interested in Latin America, and their conversations were innocent.[15]

Bentley's statements about Halperin became public in 1948, but press attention centered on others, and in the elite academic world in which Halperin moved, Bentley was widely dismissed as a fantasist. By 1953 Halperin was head of the Latin American regional studies program at Boston University. In that year the Senate Internal Security Subcommittee called him to testify. He promptly refused, citing his Fifth Amendment rights. When called to appear before a Boston University committee he once again refused to answer questions. The academic leadership at the university, however, did not want to press the matter and worked out a compromise whereby Halperin told the committee he was not a member of the CPUSA and the committee mildly criticized him for not being more forthcoming, but he kept his job and his position as head of the Latin American studies program.

The issue received more attention when Attorney General Herbert Brownell made public a 1945 FBI report specifically naming Halperin as a Soviet spy. University authorities privately told Halperin that its committee would like to discuss the matter with him once more. Halperin did not wait; he and his family left abruptly for Mexico. Once there, he refused a university offer to pay his way back to Boston to talk over his status. He was then discharged, not for taking the Fifth but for abandoning his job. He remained in Mexico until 1958 and then, fearing he might be deported to the United States, moved to Moscow. There the Soviets gave him a position with their leading scholarly institution, the Academy of Sciences. By 1962, disillusioned with Soviet communism, he moved to Cuba in hopes that the Castro variety might come closer to his ideals. He worked for the government Central Planning Commission and taught at the University of Havana.

By 1967, soured on Castroist communism as well, he moved yet again, to Canada to teach at Simon Fraser University in British Columbia. In his later years he wrote critically of both Soviet and Castroist communism. Don Kirschner, a colleague of Halperin's at Simon Fraser, described him as having become a "New Deal liberal" who was "immovably hostile to any variant of socialism." Halperin continued, however, to deny that he had ever cooperated with Soviet intelligence. After his death Kirschner published *Cold War Exile: The Unclosed Case of Maurice Halperin,* which appeared before the Venona decryptions became available. Kirschner wrote that his study had been "a distressing exercise" because, as he marshaled the evidence about Bentley's statements and Halperin's life, he had concluded, "In the essentials of the story, I believe the lady."[16] Venona shows that his judgment was correct.

Duncan Lee: The Ivy League WASP Spy

Duncan Chaplin Lee was descended from the Lees of Virginia. His father was an Episcopal priest and rector for many years at Chatham Hall, an elite girls' school in Virginia. Duncan attended the equally prestigious St. Alban's preparatory school in Washington, went to Yale, played football, and was graduated first in his class in 1935. He then went to Oxford as a Rhodes scholar, returned to Yale to get a law degree, and in 1939 joined the prominent Wall Street law firm Donovan, Leisure, Newton and Lumbard. In 1942 he accepted a commission in the Office of Strategic Services, an agency whose upper echelons included many Yale alumni who shared Lee's high-establishment background, a fact that inspired a witticism from the regular military that OSS stood for "Oh So Social."

Initially Lee served as an aide and adviser to Gen. William Donovan, head of the OSS and the senior partner of Lee's law firm. Later Lee took an OSS field assignment in China. (Lee's parents had served many years in China as missionaries, and he had lived there until he was twelve.) Most OSS officials held Army rank, and by the time the war ended he had become a lieutenant colonel.

Lee, however, was a secret Communist. It is not known when he became one, although mostly likely it was at Oxford. There he met and married Ishbel Gibb, whose hard-left sympathies were unconcealed. Oxford possessed a highly active Communist student group in the mid-1930s, and it may or may not be a coincidence that no fewer than four young Americans who attended Oxford in the mid-1930s (a time when Americans at Oxford were rare) had compromising relationships with Soviet intelligence: Duncan Lee, Peter Rhodes, Donald Wheeler, and Carl Marzani.

In 1940, just as Lee was completing his final year at Yale Law School, a neighbor notified the FBI that the Lees were Communists, citing the accumulation of party literature in their residence and their political statements. At the time, anxious citizens were deluging the FBI with reports on suspected Nazi and Communist fifth columnists, and the New Haven FBI office simply filed a brief report with the New York office, which in turn filed the statement away: the politics of a newly minted lawyer were not of interest to the FBI. Once established in New York, Duncan Lee worked during the day for various Wall Street clients. On his own time, however, he volunteered his services to CPUSA causes. By the end of 1941 he was the legal adviser to Russian War Relief, and early in 1942 he was on the executive board of the China Aid Council. The council, which directed assistance to Chinese organizations aligned with the Chinese Communist party, was headed by Mildred Price, Mary Price's sister and an ardent secret Communist.[17]

Bentley explained that Mary Price had met Lee through his association with her sister and, having learned that General Donovan had asked him to join the OSS, brought this to Golos's attention. Golos directed Price to develop Lee as a source. She did so, but according to Bentley the information Price passed on from Lee was limited in both quality and quantity. Hoping for more, Golos had Bentley meet Lee in Washington. Lee, she discovered, was willing to help but very cautious. She told the FBI, "After my initial meeting with Lee, he began to supply me with O.S.S. information of a varied nature. These data were always given by him orally, and he would never furnish any thing in writing, nor would he allow me to make notes of the information he gave me." All the time she dealt with him he remained "extremely apprehensive about the possibility of being under FBI surveillance."[18]

Bentley recalled that Lee furnished much information about OSS operations in Europe that might adversely affect Soviet interests and identified OSS sources in foreign countries. In her November 1945 FBI deposition she gave as an example Lee's "mentioning O.S.S. agents being parachuted into Hungary and Yugoslavia and peace maneuvering going on between the satellite Axis nations through the medium of O.S.S. representatives."[19] The FBI attached no special significance to this remark, and neither did Bentley. What neither Bentley nor the FBI knew was that she had referred to a highly secret OSS project, the Sparrow mission, designed to persuade the Hungarian government to surrender to the Allies in the fall of 1944 and collapse the entire Nazi position in the Balkans.[20]

When Bentley's statements became public in 1948, many OSS veterans refused to believe that one of their leading officers, one who so embodied the OSS's Ivy League WASP image, could have betrayed them. Similarly, much of the press treated Bentley's charges about Duncan Lee as preposterous on the face of it. Lee did not resort to the Fifth Amendment when called to testify and firmly denied the charges. He was not pressed, however, about his background or the circumstances of his relationship with Bentley. This omission helped to maintain the facade of his innocence because the story he had told the FBI when it interviewed him was not one that inspired belief. Lee admitted meeting with Bentley on a number of occasions over a period of two years, both in Washington and during trips to New York. But, he insisted, he had known Bentley only as "Helen." As for Golos, Lee admitted he had met Helen's friend "John," and the description matched that of Jacob Golos. He said he never knew Helen's last name and knew nothing of her activities. Helen, said Lee, was simply a social acquaintance he had met through his friend Mary Price. That a highly placed OSS officer engaged in intelligence work in wartime would over two years meet privately with someone and never learn that person's full name or occupation strains credibility. Lee also claimed that he was a New Deal liberal. He did not disclose, and the FBI at the time did not know, that when the Lees married in the 1930s they honeymooned in Moscow.[21] As the public controversy over domestic communism and Soviet espionage grew in the early 1950s, Duncan Lee left the United States. Although he returned for periods, he largely lived abroad for the rest of his life.[22]

Decoded KGB cables show Lee reporting to the Soviets about British and American diplomatic strategy for negotiating with Stalin over the fate of postwar Poland, American diplomatic activities in Turkey and Romania, and OSS operations in China and France. Venona confirms Bentley's comment about Lee's caution. In May 1943 the New York KGB office informed Moscow that "we discussed with Koch [Lee] the question of his removing documents for photographing. Koch said that in some cases he agrees to do this, but as a rule he considers it inexpedient."[23] In discussing Lee's espionage, Bentley wrote:

When we discovered he had access to the [OSS] security files, we had asked him to bring us information that might be of value. Thereupon, he had given me a slip of paper on which he had written down the names of people that the O.S.S. considered dangerous risks, divided into three categories—"known Soviet agents," "known Communists," and "Communist sympathizers." In the first group were three names—none of whom I knew; in the second was an active member of the Perlo group, and in the third, Maurice Halperin. We had quite promptly alerted Maurice and told him to be careful; the other since he was more reckless, we had "put on ice" and told to abstain from any activities for a six-month period.[24]

Three Venona messages confirm the essential elements of this passage unambiguously. A September 15, 1944, New York KGB message states:

> According to Koch's [Lee's] advice, a list of "reds" has been compiled by the Security Division of Izba [OSS]. The list contains 4 surnames of persons who are supplying information to the Russians. . . .
>   The list is divided into two categories: 1. Open Fellowcountrymen [Communists] (among them "Izra" [Donald Wheeler]) and 2. Sympathizers, left-wing liberals etc. (among them "Hare" [Halperin]). Koch is trying to get the list.[25]

Lee did get the list, and it constituted the text of a follow-up message of September 22.[26]

These messages confirm Bentley's statement that Lee supplied an OSS security list containing three elements: names of persons OSS security had identified as Soviet sources, names of Communists serving in the OSS, and names of Soviet sympathizers. The only difference from Bentley's FBI statement, made several years after the event in question, is that the Venona messages show the names of four suspected Soviet sources on the list, whereas she had remembered it as containing only three, and that she characterized the list as having three categories, whereas the messages refer to two categories and a third element, the designation of four persons as Soviet sources.

Bentley also wrote that the list had named Maurice Halperin. Venona confirms this. Bentley said the list contained the name of a source who was part of the Perlo group (discussed in chapter 5). Venona confirms that too, as Donald Wheeler was part of that network. A third Venona message, from the KGB headquarters in Moscow, further corroborates Bentley's account. This message of September 20, in reply to the New York message of September 15 about Lee's list, advises the New York KGB to "tell 'Myrna' [Bentley] to cease liaison with 'Izra' [Wheeler] and 'Hare' [Halperin]. In future liaison may be re-established only with our permission."[27] Bentley's version largely conforms to this one, stating that Wheeler was placed on inactive status for six months but that Halperin was simply warned to be careful.

In late 1944 the OSS sent Lee to China to supervise an attempt to penetrate Japan via Japanese-occupied China and Korea. A decoded Venona message shows that Bentley made arrangements with Lee so that Soviet agents in China could approach him and he could continue his service to the Soviet cause.

Julius Joseph: From Political Subversion to Espionage

Julius Joseph was yet another of Bentley's sources within the OSS. In 1938 he received a master's degree in economics and public administration from the University of Michigan, and in 1940 he got a job with the government's National Resources Planning Board. From there he went in 1941 to the Federal Security Agency (a welfare agency) and the Social Security Board, in 1942 to the Office of Emergency Management (war industries mobilization), and in 1943 to the Labor War Manpower Commission, where he became a senior administrative officer. He was also a not-too-secret Communist, writing for the *Daily Worker* in 1936, signing New York electoral petitions for the CPUSA in 1940, and speaking at a forum of the Communist-aligned *Science and Society* in 1942.[28]

In 1942 Joseph contacted the CPUSA with government information he thought of value. Bentley picked up material from him during the next two years, chiefly information on labor-related matters of interest to the CPUSA's labor cadre inside the CIO but not to Soviet intelligence. In May 1943, however, Joseph was drafted. At Golos's urging he applied for and got a position with the Office of Strategic Services, as did his wife, Bella: he in the Far Eastern section, she in the motion picture and publicity divisions. By 1945 Joseph was deputy chief of his section, working chiefly on Japanese intelligence. Bentley said that he supplied useful OSS information, not only on the work of the Far Eastern section but also on the Russian section of the OSS, on the basis of his discussions with colleagues in that division. Joseph shows up in two Venona cables, once in a June 1943 report on Soviet agents the New York KGB office maintained in the OSS, and once in a 1944 cable reporting information on the OSS Russian section that Joseph had learned from a pro-Soviet OSS staff member.[29]

After the OSS dissolved, Joseph went to work for the United Nations Relief and Rehabilitation Administration and then directed the New York Committee for the Arts, Sciences, and Professions, a Popular Front political advocacy group. He was later called to testify about his wartime activities by the Senate Internal Security Subcommittee, in 1953. He declined to answer key questions, taking the Fifth.[30]

Joseph's sister, Emma, was also a Communist and also worked for the OSS. Although Bentley never mentioned it to the FBI, deciphered Venona messages show that in 1944 Bentley informed the KGB that Emma Joseph was well suited for KGB work and Bentley would give her recognition procedures so that she could be contacted by the KGB when she reached Ceylon on her next OSS assignment.[31]

Cedric Belfrage: Betrayer of Two Nations

One of the more unusual sources of the Golos-Bentley network was a British intelligence officer. Cedric Belfrage was born and grew up in Great Britain, first came to America in the mid-1920s, and returned on frequent visits while pursuing a career as a writer and journalist. He secretly joined the CPUSA in 1937 and filed an intent to become an American citizen with U.S. immigration authorities, but he never completed his naturalization. After the Nazi attack on the USSR, he went to work for the British Security Coordination Office, an arm of British intelligence under the direction of William Stephenson. Stephenson's agency acted as British intelligence liaison with the American OSS and FBI.

Elizabeth Bentley told the FBI that starting in late 1942 or early 1943 Belfrage met on a number of occasions with Jacob Golos. She remembered that either Earl Browder or V. J. Jerome (a senior CPUSA official) brought Belfrage to Golos. Bentley recalled Belfrage's turning over to Golos a variety of items that came to him at the British Security Coordination Office, both material on British concerns and American material that had been given to the British. She also said that after Golos died, the KGB in 1944 asked her to establish contact with Belfrage. Bentley, however, had replied that she had not dealt with him directly, being aware of his activities only through Golos, and that Belfrage would be wary of her. At the direction of the KGB, she contacted Browder because Belfrage had come to Golos through the CPUSA and his material was shared with Browder himself. But Browder refused to put Bentley in touch with Belfrage, stating that Belfrage should be kept out of further espionage. Later, at KGB insistence, she found out where Belfrage was living but did not make contact with him and did not know if the KGB reestablished contact.[32]

When the war ended Belfrage took a position with the Allied occupation government in Germany. He returned to the United States as a founder of the *National Guardian,* which first appeared in 1948 and for a number of years was the most influential journal on the Popular Front left.

In 1947 the FBI asked Belfrage about Bentley's statements. Belfrage told the bureau that in 1942 he had met with Earl Browder and a man whose name he did not know but who, he admitted, looked a great deal like the FBI's photograph of Jacob Golos. He also said that in 1943 he had met with V. J. Jerome eight or nine times. As to the purposes of these meetings, Belfrage explained that he met with Jerome "with a view to finding out what I could about Communist and Russian politics." Belfrage reported that in order to induce Jerome to provide him with information, he answered Jerome's questions about British policy toward the Soviet Union while the latter took notes and "I supplied him with information about Scotland Yard surveillances and also with some documents relative to the Vichy Government in France, which were of a highly confidential nature with respect to their origin but which contained information of no value whatever." Belfrage did not know it, but his statement about giving Jerome material on Scotland Yard surveillance matched closely with a Bentley statement that among the documents Belfrage had handed over was a British security service manual on procedures and techniques for the proper running of agents. He also insisted that he was not and never had been a Communist.[33]

The FBI did not find Belfrage's statement very credible. Belfrage did not provide any explanation about why he would be attempting to learn about Russian politics from Jerome, whose longtime area of responsibility in the CPUSA was supervising American intellectuals allied with the party, and Belfrage did not relate anything of interest that he learned from Jerome. He also admitted that his contact with Jerome and his turning over of British Security Coordination documents was not authorized by his superiors, that he never told his superiors what he had done, and that he might be subject to prosecution under British law.

The decrypted Venona cables show that the bureau's skepticism was well founded.[34] Belfrage lied. The cables show Belfrage giving the KGB an OSS report that British intelligence had received on the anti-Communist Yugoslav resistance forces of Gen. Draza Mihailovic, then in competition with the Communist resistance led by Josip Tito; reporting on the contacts and activities of British Security Coordination's own Yugoslav specialist; telling the Soviets what his superior, William Stephenson, had said about British policy on a second front after a meeting with Prime Minister Churchill; describing the sometimes tense relationship between British Security Coordination and the FBI over the former's U.S. activities; offering to establish covert contact with the Soviets if he were assigned to permanent duty in Britain; and delivering to Golos documents he had obtained during a visit to London. The subject matter of the London documents was not described, but the New York KGB reported that it was sending them to Moscow by diplomatic pouch. The Venona cables also corroborate Bentley's story that Golos shared Belfrage's information with Browder. One Venona message noted Golos's irritation over Belfrage's insistence on a personal meeting with Browder.

The FBI informed U.S. immigration authorities of its view that Belfrage had had a compromising relationship with Soviet intelligence. The Immigration and Naturalization Service then moved to deport Belfrage to Great Britain. He fought the action in court and in public, proclaiming his innocence and depicting the deportation order as political persecution. In 1955, however, he accepted voluntary deportation and returned to England. He later published two books, *The Frightened Giant: My Unfinished Affair with America* and *The American Inquisition, 1945–1960,* describing American concern about Soviet espionage as baseless paranoia.[35]

Bentley's Other Singleton Agents

Bentley told the FBI of several other individual espionage contacts who reported to her. These included Helen Tenney of the OSS and Michael Greenberg, a China specialist who worked for the Board of Economic Warfare and its successor agency, the Foreign Economic Administration, as well as Joseph Gregg and Robert T. Miller, both of the Office of the Coordinator of Inter-American Affairs.[36] This latter body was one of the hybrid wartime agencies created by the White House. Headed by Nelson Rockefeller, it supervised economic warfare, propaganda, and intelligence operations in Central and South America. In addition to a research staff in Washington, it had representatives working out of various American embassies.

In 1942 Grace Granich, a CPUSA and Comintern veteran, called Golos's attention to Helen Tenney, a secret Communist who worked

for Short Wave Research, a firm on contract for the Office of War
Information to recruit people with foreign language skills. Golos recruited Tenney as a source, but Short Wave Research soon disbanded.
Golos then encouraged her to seek a job with OSS headquarters in
Washington. Tenney had excellent Spanish language skills and in late
1942 got a job in the Spanish section of the OSS. Bentley arranged for
Tenney to sublet the Washington apartment of Mary Price, who was
then returning to New York. Wartime Washington suffered from an
acute housing shortage, and this arrangement made it easier for Tenney
to take a Washington job with the OSS—and kept the apartment available for use as an espionage safe-house by the Golos-Bentley network.
(When interviewed by the FBI, Price denied that Bentley had any role
in Tenney's getting her apartment, claiming that Tenney had simply
been the first person to answer a newspaper ad.) In Venona, Tenney
appears under the cover name Muse. A 1943 OSS report on Spain,
marked secret, found in the Moscow archives of the Communist International may be among the fruits of Tenney's espionage. The report
was an appraisal of the strength of the Communist party in Catalonia.[37]

After the FBI became convinced of Bentley's bona fides and began
to follow up on the various Soviet sources she had named, the bureau
found Tenney ensconced in the State Department. After the OSS disbanded, Tenney was able to move with one of its surviving offices to a
newly created State Department research section assigned to analyze
American intelligence on the Soviet Union. The FBI quietly had her
fired, and the State Department revoked her passport. Tenney realized
that she was under suspicion and suffered a partial nervous collapse.
Friends had her hospitalized briefly in January 1947 when she started
babbling about Soviet spies and being under FBI surveillance. This was
not paranoia, as her worried friends thought: she really was under FBI
surveillance and she really was a Soviet spy.[38]

The FBI thought that perhaps she would break if Bentley, then cooperating with the bureau, approached her. Bentley did so in early February 1947. Tenney, clearly unaware that Bentley had defected, said
that she had been out of touch with the Soviets for some time. The
isolation from her Soviet contact, along with her sense that the FBI was
closing in, had produced a sense of abandonment, and she hoped that
Bentley was reestablishing Soviet contact. Tenney, however, did not
indicate any disaffection with the Soviet cause, and the FBI dropped
hopes of turning her. Later, when the bureau formally interviewed her,

Tenney denied having done any work for the Soviets. Apparently unaware that their meeting just a few months earlier had been observed by FBI agents, she admitted knowing Bentley, but under another name and only during 1942 and 1943.[39]

Tenney's loss of her KGB liaison in 1946 is evidence that the Soviets, realizing that Bentley's networks had been compromised, had cut off contact with her sources. In most cases Soviet intelligence appeared to have succeeded in warning its sources of what was happening, but for some reason the KGB was unable to brief Tenney.

Michael Greenberg had become a secret Communist while a student at Cambridge University in the 1930s. Born in Britain, he immigrated to the United States in 1939 and became editor of *Pacific Affairs,* a prestigious journal published by the Institute of Pacific Relations. His tenure, however, caused one trustee of the institute to complain that Greenberg had imposed a pro-Communist slant on the journal's articles. In 1942 he became a China specialist for the Board of Economic Warfare and an assistant to that agency's de facto head, Lauchlin Currie. (Currie's links to Soviet intelligence are discussed in chapter 5.) Bentley stated that she never met directly with Greenberg but received his information via Mary and Mildred Price.[40]

Civil Service Commission security officials learned something of Greenberg's Communist background and wanted him discharged as a security risk. He appealed, and naive superiors overruled the security officials. In 1945 he won a transfer to the State Department. He resigned in 1946, however, probably after being warned that Bentley's network had been compromised. When questioned by the FBI in 1947, Greenberg agreed that he knew the Price sisters and had met with them on a number of occasions but denied passing them any information. He had no explanation for how Elizabeth Bentley had come to know of his relationship with the Price sisters. Although he had become a U.S. citizen in 1944, shortly after the FBI interview he moved back to Britain.[41]

Robert T. Miller III had visited the Soviet Union in 1934 and liked it well enough to stay in Moscow, supporting himself by becoming a part-time correspondent for an American newspaper. He also met his wife there, Jenny Levy, who worked for the English-language *Moscow News,* a pro-Soviet paper. He left Moscow in 1937 to become press agent for the Spanish Republican government. After the Spanish Civil War ended, Miller teamed up with an American veteran of the International Brigades, Jack Fahy, to found Hemispheric News Service, which concentrated on Latin American affairs. Miller served as president, Fahy as vice-president, and Jenny Levy Miller as secretary. In 1941 the firm moved to Washington and Joseph Gregg joined as its manager. Gregg had also served in the Comintern's International Brigades during the Spanish Civil War. Under the name of Export Information Bureau, their agency first became a contract research arm of the Office of the Coordinator of Inter-American Affairs and then was entirely absorbed by it. Fahy, meanwhile, was recruited by the Naval GRU as one of its spies.

Bentley said that Gregg and Miller were recruited by Golos via the CPUSA and handled as separate agents, and that neither knew that the other was in touch with the KGB.[42] Gregg, she said, was the more active, turning over to the Soviets U.S. naval intelligence, military intelligence, and FBI reports on Soviet and Communist activities in Central and South America. Gregg transferred to the State Department in late 1944, concealing on his employment form his service with the International Brigades.[43]

Miller also transferred to the State Department in 1944, obtained a position working on Soviet-American diplomatic matters, and rose to the position of assistant chief of the Division of Research and Publication. Probably warned that Bentley's defection had compromised him, he resigned in December 1946. When questioned by the FBI, Miller admitted knowing Bentley under the name Helen, acknowledged that both he and his wife met her on several occasions in New York and Washington, and allowed that he may have casually discussed confidential information with her. Miller also took the same bizarre position that Duncan Lee had, insisting that although he had met Helen/Bentley repeatedly and perhaps even discussed confidential information with her, he had never known her family name.[44]

Greenberg, Gregg, and Miller are not identified in those KGB cables that were deciphered in the Venona Project. Given, however, the high degree of corroboration of Elizabeth Bentley's testimony, her statements about these persons must be regarded as having great credibility. There are, moreover, numerous unidentified cover names in Venona that one or more of these persons might hide behind, such as Charlie (provided the KGB with government reports on China), Dodger (provided diplomatic information), Eagle, Fakir (provided diplomatic information), Harold, Hedgehog, Horus, Levi, Mirage (provided diplomatic information), Reed, Robert, Vick, Vita, and Whitefish. The information supplied in the cables was sufficient to identify these cover names as Americans who passed information to the KGB but was insufficient to identify who precisely was spying for the Soviet Union.

CHAPTER 5

FRIENDS IN HIGH PLACES

Elizabeth Bentley ran two networks of American Communist party members employed in the federal government. The Perlo group developed Soviet sources on the War Production Board, on a key Senate committee, and in the Treasury Department. The Silvermaster group established contacts not only in Treasury and the Army Air Force but in the White House itself. These were small groups of Communists who had known each other for years, socialized together, met secretly to discuss party policy and pay their party dues, helped each other get jobs and promotions in the government, and dreamed together of the day when America would attain the perfection already achieved by Russia under Stalin.

The Perlo Group

Victor Perlo was one of the original members of the Ware group of young Communist professionals that Whittaker Chambers met when he arrived in Washington in 1934. Perlo's parents were immigrants from Russia, and he attended Columbia University, gaining bachelor's and master's degrees in mathematics. After leaving Columbia he became a statistician for the National Recovery Administration and transferred to the Federal Home Loan Bank Board in 1935. In 1937 Perlo-went to the Brookings Institution for two years to hone his credentials as an economist. He reentered government employment in 1939 at the Commerce Department. In 1940 he moved to an agency that eventually became the wartime Office of Price Administration, and three years later he became a senior economist at the War Production Board. In 1945, with the wartime agencies disbanding, he transferred to the Division of Monetary Research at the Treasury Department, then headed by Frank Coe, a fellow secret Communist.

The accounts of Hope Davis and Herbert Fuchs depict Perlo as a senior member of the Communist underground in Washington in the late 1930s. Perlo is mentioned in numerous deciphered KGB cables of the Venona Project and was a central figure in Elizabeth Bentley's account of Soviet espionage in the 1940s.[1]

Bentley said that in November 1943 Earl Browder put Golos in touch with a group of Washington Communists that she later came to designate as the Perlo group. Golos met once in New York with the leading figures of the group to discuss their cooperation with his espionage apparatus. He died the same month, however, before a second meeting. Bentley at that point had not met any of its members and knew little about them.

Since Bentley had been acting as Golos's assistant and courier to many of his sources, both the KGB and Earl Browder initially welcomed her taking over much of Golos's role. Early in 1944 Browder urged her to renew Golos's attempt to approach the Perlo group and arranged a meeting, which most likely took place on Sunday, March 5.[2]

Bentley met the group at the New York apartment of John Abt, who had been the intermediary between Browder and this Washington-based group. Abt, however, was an increasingly visible labor lawyer, and both he and Browder thought it wise to withdraw him from covert activity. Bentley explained that Abt had introduced her to the group and from that point on had no contact with her espionage apparatus. In addition to Abt, she recalled that Perlo (War Production Board), Charles Kramer (Senate Subcommittee on War Mobilization), Edward Fitzgerald (War Production Board), and Harry Magdoff (War Production Board) had all traveled to New York from Washington for the meeting.

Bentley learned at this meeting that other members of the group included Donald Wheeler (Office of Strategic Services) and Allan Rosenberg (Foreign Economic Administration). Later she was told that the group included among its contacts Harold Glasser (Treasury), Sol Leshinsky (United Nations Relief and Rehabilitation Administration), and George Perazich (United Nations Relief and Rehabilitation Administration).

Three deciphered KGB cables corroborate Bentley's account. In these Venona cables of April 27, May 13, and May 30, 1944, the KGB officer Iskhak Akhmerov reported on the reorganization of the KGB system of collecting intelligence from the American Communist party after Golos's death. Golos had worked with Soviet intelligence for a very long time, at least since the mid-1930s and probably earlier, had been born and raised in Russia, and was an "Old Bolshevik" who had been part of the movement before the 1917 revolution and, if the story he told Bentley is true, even a veteran Chekist (Soviet secret policeman). His death disrupted long-established relationships and required shifting arrangements regarding who reported to whom.

These three cables are Akhmerov's initial report on the Perlo group.[3] Akhmerov stated that after Golos's death, Bentley, acting on Browder's instructions, had taken over liaison with two covert Communist groups in Washington that had reported information to the CPUSA. The messages are not completely deciphered and contain several garbled passages. But in regard to the Perlo group the messages show that Bentley established contact through John Abt. The readable sections of the April 27 KGB cable name as part of the group Charles Kramer, Victor Perlo, Charles Flato, Harold Glasser, and Edward Fitzgerald and state that several other, unnamed persons belonged as well. Flato, an official in the Board of Economic Warfare, is unusual in that he was not named by Bentley in her deposition to the FBI or in her memoir *Out of Bondage*. Bentley either forgot about him or chose for some reason not to disclose his name. The May 13 message adds this judgment: "They are reliable Fellowcountrymen [Communists], politically highly mature; they want to help with information." It also names Harry Magdoff as a participant.

That Abt's name does not occur in any readable Venona messages after those of April 27 and May 13 conforms to Bentley's account that he handed over the Perlo group and then left clandestine work. Of the ten persons she named as members of the Perlo group (Abt, Perlo, Kramer, Fitzgerald, Magdoff, Wheeler, Glasser, Rosenberg, Leshinsky, and Perazich), the first seven come up in the three deciphered Venona messages discussed here as well as in numerous others.[4]

An eighth, Allan Rosenberg, appears in a partly deciphered December 1944 KGB message noting the acquisition of a State Department report and promising that a full translation would be forwarded to Moscow by courier. Rosenberg is named in clear text, apparently as the source of the report. Rosenberg's close relationship with others in the Perlo group went back to the early days of the Communist underground in Washington. When John Abt became chief attorney for the Civil Liberties Subcommittee of the Senate Education and Labor Committee in 1935, he saw to it that his staff included several of his fellow secret Communists—Rosenberg, Kramer, and Flato. Rosenberg later joined the legal staff of the National Labor Relations Board, where Herbert Fuchs knew him as one of the members of his secret Communist caucus. When a congressional committee questioned Rosenberg about these matters, he refused to answer.[5]

The April Venona message on the Perlo group also stated that aside from those specifically named, two or three other persons were part of the group. Bentley's two remaining names, Leshinsky and Perazich, were probably among them. The first Akhmerov report (April 27) on the Perlo group has all of the names in clear text because, obviously, cover names had not yet been assigned, except in the case of Glasser, who had been designated Ruble during earlier work with Soviet intelligence. By Akhmerov's second and third reports, cover names had been assigned to most and were easily identified: Kramer was Plumb; Fitzgerald was Ted; Magdoff was Kant; Perlo was Raider; and Wheeler was Izra.

But in Akhmerov's reports of May 13 and 30, one unidentified cover name, Storm, is connected to the Perlo group in an unspecified fashion. Storm is unlikely to have been Rosenberg, whose name occurred in later Venona messages in the clear, or Abt, because his name occurs in the clear in the May 13 message also mentioning Storm. Possibly Storm was Flato, but the cable of May 30 includes a partially decrypted sentence with a partially deciphered name, beginning "Char . . ." The text at that point describes Char . . . as a very close friend of another Soviet agent, Jane Foster, who in her autobiography calls Charles Flato one of her closest friends of that period.[6] If "Char . . ." was Charles Flato, then Storm was not Flato. Leshinsky and Perazich are obvious candidates for Storm, but there are other possibilities as well. The deciphered Venona messages show that Bentley did not remember all the Soviet sources with whom she had had contact.

Another possibility for Storm is Josef Peters. When Peters headed the CPUSA's underground in the mid-1930s, he cooperated with both the GRU and the KGB and knew the KGB officer Iskhak Akhmerov. Akhmerov's cables to the KGB in 1938 used Storm as Peters's cover name.[7] Usually cover names for active sources were changed from time to time, but the cover names of KGB officers changed only at great intervals. Peters was not a source but a CPUSA staff officer, and it is therefore possible that his cover name was not changed. Akhmerov is also the author of both of the 1944 messages that used the cover name Storm.

Peters was removed as head of the CPUSA secret apparatus after Chambers's defection in 1938, but he continued to work on the CPUSA's Central Committee staff on what a 1947 Soviet Communist party personnel report guardedly called "special assignments" and may have continued to act as a liaison with some of the party underground groups in Washington not then connected with Soviet intelligence.[8] An examination of the Comintern's records turned up two 1943 messages from the GRU (Soviet military intelligence) referring to a GRU officer in Washington as having come across "a group of workers singled out by the American Comparty CC [Central Committee] for informational work and headed by the CC worker 'Peter.' " Though usually called "Peters" in the United States, in Comintern records Peters's name is often rendered as "Peter."[9] "Informational work" was GRU jargon for clandestine intelligence activity. The GRU asked the Comintern whether its officer had stumbled on a Comintern apparatus. The messages have the look of the GRU's appraising a covert CPUSA group for possible takeover into its own espionage work.

Another of the GRU messages reported that "certain workers in that group are unhappy with 'Peter,' since he pays almost no attention to informational work and takes no interest in the information received."[10] This complaint sounds remarkably close to that reported by Akhmerov in April 1944 about the Perlo group. He told Moscow that Bentley reported that during her first meeting with the Perlo group "they told her that this group was neglected and that nobody was interested in them."[11] Mention of Storm appears in deciphered KGB cables about the Perlo group only in Akhmerov's two May 1944 reports on the group's background as the KGB prepared to take it over. Storm never occurs later as a source. The passages in which Storm is named are sufficiently garbled that a firm judgment cannot be made; but it is possible that Storm was Peters and the references to Storm are references to his earlier relationship with the group before its absorption by Bentley's KGB-connected apparatus.[12]

Akhmerov said something else in his April 27 report to the KGB in Moscow in regard to the group: "For more than a year Maksim [Zubilin] and I tried to get in touch with Perlo and Flato. For some reason Helmsman [Browder] did not come to the meeting and has just decided to put Clever Girl [Bentley] in touch with the whole group. If we work with this group, it will be necessary to remove her."[13] And remove her they did. Bentley first met with the Perlo group in March 1944. By the end of the year, on Soviet orders, she had cut all ties to it. Bentley reported constant pressure by her Soviet contacts during 1944, particularly by Akhmerov, to gain direct control not only of the Perlo group but of all of the sources that Golos had built up and she had taken over.

Bentley essentially functioned as a transitional figure. She took a group that had reported to the CPUSA directly and to Soviet intelligence only through intermediaries (Browder and Golos) and transformed it into one that reported directly to Soviet intelligence, initially through her. The KGB clearly intended to remove her as intermediary as soon as it was practical to do so. On orders from her KGB contacts Bentley prepared biographies of those sources she knew best, a preliminary step for reducing the need to keep her involved. Also as part of the KGB vetting process, in September 1944 General Fitin of the KGB asked Dimitrov of the Comintern to "provide any information at your disposal on the following members of the Comparty of America. 1. Charles . . . Flato, in 1943 worked at the US Office of Economic Warfare. 2. Donald Wheeler . . . , works in the Office of Strategic Services. 3. Kramer, works in a government institution in Washington. 4. Edward Fitzgerald, works on the WPB. 5. Magdoff, works on the WPB. 6. Harold Glas[s]er, currently on assignment abroad. 7. P[e]rlo, works on the WPB."[14]

The KGB was satisfied with the checking of the Perlo network, and it proceeded to phase Bentley out. In December 1944 she met covertly with Anatoly Gromov, the chief of the KGB Washington office and Zubilin's successor as head of KGB operations in the United States. In her memoir Bentley reconstructed the conversation: "[Gromov:] We have at last decided what to do about all the contacts that Golos handled. You cannot, obviously, continue to handle them; the set-up is too full of holes and therefore too dangerous. I'm afraid our friend Golos was not too cautious a man, and there is the risk that you, because of your connection with him, may endanger the apparatus. You will therefore turn them over to us; we will look into their backgrounds thoroughly and decide which ones we will keep."[15] He ordered Bentley to inform her sources of the pending change and to confine her activity to the U.S. Service and Shipping Corporation. Gromov also suggested that later she would be removed from that task as well and placed on inactive status for a period.

Bentley's memory of the KGB's concern that Golos's practices did not meet its increasingly professional security standards is corroborated by Venona. In October 1944 a deciphered KGB message reports that Gregory Silvermaster, head of another and larger network managed by Golos and Bentley, was resisting KGB advice that the group be broken into smaller units and that the KGB establish direct liaison with key agents. Akhmerov complained to Moscow that Silvermaster's reluctance unfortunately showed that Golos's "education is making itself felt."[16]

The logic of the KGB's position was clear. Bentley simply was not attuned to the rules of espionage tradecraft it was implementing. Golos, Bentley, and their agents moved back and forth between CPUSA political activities and Soviet espionage, readily socialized with one another, and only barely disguised their political attitudes. In the 1930s and early 1940s, with government policy-makers largely oblivious to Soviet espionage and the FBI's then-limited resources focused elsewhere, these amateurish practices had had few serious consequences. But the KGB feared that this era was ending and a higher professional standard of tradecraft was needed.

The KGB, however, did not handle Bentley well in this transition. Bentley had been in love with Jacob Golos and had sustained a great loss when he died in late 1943. She had then thrown herself into continuing his work. But by the end of 1944 the KGB had taken that away. In 1945 it further urged her to give up the U.S. Service and Shipping Corporation, the only thing she had left of her life with Golos. Her morale hit rock bottom. By the late summer of 1945 she was convinced that the FBI was closing in. It was not, but her fear of arrest and her disillusionment led her to defect. The KGB had pushed Bentley out because it wanted a more secure system. What it got by doing so was the exposure and neutralization of the very networks it was trying to protect.

The Perlo Group's Espionage

The extent of the espionage performed by the spies of the Perlo group is not clear. Bentley collected documents and reports from her sources but usually did not read them, and kept no notes or copies; she provided to the FBI only general descriptions and a few specifics that stuck in her memory. She told the FBI that she had met with Perlo and other members of his group at Mary Price's apartment, where they handed over documents. She remembered memoranda on aircraft production (from Perlo), OSS intelligence summaries and OSS copies of State Department cables (from Wheeler), and plans for the occupation of Germany (from Rosenberg). She reported that Leshinsky, although a member of the group, never handed over documents during her tenure. She said that, through Perlo, Perazich supplied some information on Yugoslavia and that she thought the KGB had made arrangements to contact him when he traveled to that country for the United Nations Relief and Rehabilitation Administration.

The decrypted Venona cables provide more definite information, but they are only brief summaries of much more voluminous information sent by courier. In any case, the Venona Project decrypted only a portion of all KGB traffic from the United States to Moscow. The readable Venona messages on the Perlo group corroborate Bentley's recollection of the types of information that Perlo group sources provided. Wheeler of the OSS, for example, passed information to the Soviets regarding the organization and policies of the British intelligence services, with which the OSS had a close relationship and which the Soviets regarded at that time as a more serious opponent than American intelligence. Perlo, an economist with the aircraft production division of the War Production Board, supplied data on aircraft production and U.S. shipments to various fronts and reports about development difficulties for a jet engine for America's first and very secret jet fighter, as well as information on clashes between U.S. military and civilian policy-makers over allocation of economic resources.

Charles Kramer: The Spy as Congressional Aide

A number of members of the CPUSA underground in the 1930s worked at one time or another for a congressional committee. Marion Bachrach, one of the original Ware group members (and John Abt's sister), was the chief aide to one member of Congress, Rep. John Bernard, a Farmer-Labor party member elected from Minnesota in 1936 for a single term. Bernard was unusual in that he himself was secretly a Communist.[17] Charles Kramer, however, was more than an underground Communist. He was a Soviet spy. He also worked for four congressional committees in his career, the Senate Civil Liberties Subcommittee in the 1930s, the Senate Subcommittee on War Mobilization and the Senate Subcommittee on Wartime Health and Education during the war, and the Senate Labor and Public Welfare committee after the war. His congressional employment was interspersed with work in the executive branch, including the Agricultural Adjustment Administration, the National Labor Relations Board, and the Office of Price Administration (OPA).

Fellow members of the CPUSA underground assisted him in obtaining all his jobs. Abt hired Kramer for the Civil Liberties Subcommittee, Nathan Witt (another Ware group veteran) helped him get the job with the NLRB, and at the OPA Victor Perlo signed his job performance rating and was listed as an employment reference. During this period Kramer publicly posed as a committed liberal Democratic political activist, and he took time off in 1944 to work for the Democratic National Committee and in 1946 to assist the reelection campaign of California Democratic representative Ellis Patterson.[18] After Kramer's exposure by Bentley, he abandoned the Democratic party to work for the Progressive party and was far more open about his radical loyalties, although he never admitted CPUSA membership.

Venona cables show Kramer, from his position as a professional staff member of the Senate Subcommittee on War Mobilization, providing information about the dispute among American policy-makers concerning what the U.S. attitude should be toward Charles de Gaulle's Free French movement and an internal U.S. government investigation of German corporate links to American companies. After Roosevelt's death, the cables show that Kramer passed on to the KGB insider political information from the Democratic National Committee about

President Truman's likely changes in State Department leadership and appraisals of Truman by U.S. senators with whom Kramer had contact.

Harold Glasser: The Discreet Stalinist

Although not in the top tier of American government, Harold Glasser was nonetheless a very important bureaucrat. He had joined the Treasury Department in 1936 as an economist and had risen to the position of assistant director of the Division of Monetary Research by late 1938. The Treasury and the State Department sent Glasser to Ecuador in 1940 to act as the chief American economic adviser to its government. He served there until 1942. After that he held increasingly high-level wartime positions: vice-chairman of the War Production Board, economic adviser to American forces in North Africa, U.S. Treasury representative to the United Nations Relief and Rehabilitation Administration, and Treasury representative to the Allied High Commission in Italy. Immediately after the war he became economic adviser to the American delegation at the Council of Foreign Ministers meeting in Moscow in 1947 and economic adviser to the Treasury secretary at the board of governors meeting of the World Bank. When he resigned in December 1947 Glasser was serving as assistant director of Treasury's Office of International Finance.

When Glasser left government service, Treasury secretary John Snyder wrote a glowing letter of recommendation, assuring Glasser's prospective employers that he "has no hidden facets to his personal qualities."[19] Snyder could not have been more mistaken. Throughout Glasser's distinguished career with the U.S. government he was an underground Communist and a Soviet source.

A decrypted 1944 Venona message from the New York KGB station stated that "Harold Glasser is an old fellow countryman," the latter the standard KGB term for a Communist party member.[20] But exactly how old a Communist is not clear. When questioned by the FBI in 1947, Glasser would admit only to having had a casual curiosity about communism in the early 1930s. When asked later about these matters under oath, he declined to answer.[21]

Glasser shows up as a trusted member of the CPUSA underground in 1937. In that year Whittaker Chambers's CPUSA-GRU network had as one of its sources Harry Dexter White, then assistant director of the

Division of Monetary Research in the Treasury Department. Chambers, however, thought that White was providing less material than he expected both in quality and in quantity. Chambers recalled that his GRU controller, Boris Bykov, "fumed" that White should supply more. But White was not a CPUSA member, only a sympathizer. Though he was willing to cooperate with Soviet espionage, he did so on his own terms and did not respond to orders as committed CPUSA members did. Chambers discussed the problem with Josef Peters, and Peters transferred to Chambers's network Harold Glasser, who was a member of the party's covert organization but had not been linked to Soviet intelligence. Chambers had Glasser, then in his second year as an economist at Treasury, check on the sort of material to which White had access. Glasser reported that, as far as he could ascertain, White was providing everything of importance. This task done, Chambers cut off his contact with Glasser and after 1937 knew nothing more of his activities.[22]

That Glasser continued to work for Soviet intelligence is clear from a Moscow document obtained by the historian Allen Weinstein: an April 1945 memo from Pavel Fitin, head of KGB foreign intelligence, to Vsevolod Merkulov, then head of the overall KGB organization. Fitin asked for equitable treatment in terms of awards for a longtime KGB agent, Ruble. The Venona decryptions indicate that Ruble was Harold Glasser. Fitin informed Merkulov that Ruble/Glasser had worked for Soviet intelligence since May 1937, usually for the KGB but also at times for the GRU. The 1937 dating coincided, of course, with Chambers's account.

Fitin went on to explain that one of those tours with the GRU had led to his agent Ruble/Glasser's being slighted in regard to Soviet awards. (For ideologically motivated agents, Soviet decorations had great psychological value.) Fitin stated that "the group of agents of the 'military' neighbors [GRU] whose part Ruble was earlier, recently was decorated with orders of the USSR. Ruble learned about this fact from his friend Ales [Alger Hiss], who is the head of the mentioned group." Fitin asked, in view of Glasser's valuable work for the KGB and because only "as a result of transfer to our station [KGB], Ruble [Glasser] was not decorated together with other members of the Ales group," that the KGB put him in for the Order of the Red Star.[23]

Glasser appears in two KGB Venona cables in July 1943.[24] At the time of these messages he was the U.S. Treasury representative to American military forces in North Africa. The cables are only deciphered in part but appear to say that Glasser had been asked to give an opinion on Eugene Dennis or about something in which Dennis was involved, or possibly that Dennis had asked that Glasser be told of something. Dennis was one of the leading figures in the CPUSA and became its head (general secretary) in 1946. He was also involved in the party's covert activities during World War II and maintained contact with secret Communists in the Office of Strategic Services and the Office of War Information.

Glasser came to Elizabeth Bentley's attention in mid-1944, after he returned from a wartime Treasury mission to Italy. Bentley told the FBI that Victor Perlo had informed her that Glasser had reestablished contact. Perlo explained that Glasser had been part of the group earlier, before Bentley had been involved with it. He had been transferred to assist another Soviet network, but that task had ended, and he wished to work once more with the Perlo group. Bentley mentioned that Perlo did not know who headed the network to which Glasser had been temporarily transferred, but Charles Kramer told her that it was Alger Hiss in the State Department. This story is corroborated by the Fitin-Merkulov document just discussed.[25]

Glasser came back into the Perlo group but then went abroad on another Treasury assignment, and by the time he returned, the KGB had taken direct control of the Perlo group and had restricted Bentley's work to the U.S. Service and Shipping Corporation. Consequently, she had no direct knowledge of what sort of espionage tasks Glasser performed in this period. Several decrypted Venona cables, however, allude to his work.

One cable from March 28, 1945, shows Glasser working as a talent-spotter. Glasser reported that in April the Treasury Department was sending a young lawyer, Josiah DuBois, to Moscow to serve as its representative on the American delegation to the Allied Reparations Commission meeting. Glasser explained that he had established "most friendly relations" with DuBois and judged him to be ideologically a Communist, although he was not a CPUSA member. Glasser stated that he had counseled DuBois to be more "discreet" in expressing his left-wing views and noted that his personal relationship with DuBois was such that he could "normally obtain by asking" anything he wanted.[26]

Three June 1945 KGB cables report Glasser's handing over a State Department analysis of Soviet war losses, a State Department report on a Finnish company that was believed to be hiding Nazi financial assets, and an OSS report on the movement of Nazi gold through Swiss banks. In a fourth June cable Glasser reported that he had won a seat on the Treasury committee advising Supreme Court justice Robert Jackson, the U.S. member of the Allied War Crimes tribunal.

Although Glasser was an able economist, his rise in the Treasury Department was assisted by the network of fellow underground Communists inside Treasury. At various times in his Treasury career, his promotions and job ratings were determined by fellow Communists Frank Coe and William Ullmann. His promotions and job ratings were also reviewed and backed by Harry Dexter White, director of the Division of Monetary Research and later assistant secretary of the Treasury. Coe, Ullmann, and White, like Glasser, cooperated with the KGB.[27] This hidden network also helped Glasser when security officers first ran across evidence of his Communist background. In December 1941 the Secret Service, the Treasury Department's investigative arm, forwarded a report indicating that it had evidence of Glasser's involvement in Communist activities. Had the report been acted on, Glasser's subsequent work for Stalin's intelligence agencies might never have taken place. The report, however, went to Harry White, and nothing happened.[28]

Neutralization of the Perlo Group

By 1947 the FBI was convinced that the Perlo group's members had spied during World War II, but the authorities also judged that without additional evidence successful prosecution was unlikely. The bureau decided the only practical step it could take was to remove the opportunity for the members of the Perlo group to damage the United States further. In the case of those still working for the U.S. government, the FBI alerted appropriate officials to its findings. It was all done quietly; those involved were allowed to resign, or their posts were abolished, rather than being publicly fired for cause. Perlo lost his job with the Division of Monetary Research, Magdoff and Fitzgerald resigned from the Commerce Department, Kramer left the staff of the Senate Labor and Public Welfare Committee, and Glasser was forced out of his high-ranking Treasury post. For many years Perlo refused to admit that he was a Communist, declining to answer questions about CPUSA membership when asked by congressional committees and stating that he had only been "helping in my humble way to carry out the great New Deal program under the leadership of Franklin D. Roosevelt." In 1981, however, he discarded his pretense of having been just another New Deal liberal; he emerged openly as a member of the national leadership of the CPUSA. When the American Communist party split between hard-line Marxist-Leninists and supporters of Gorbachev's attempt to democratize Soviet communism in 1991, Perlo, a member of the CPUSA's National Board, sided with the hard-liners and denounced Gorbachev's reforms as "treachery" and "betrayal."[29]

None of the Perlo group members were ever prosecuted for espionage; some of the key evidence against them could not be used in court, and what could was not sufficient to gain their conviction. But material from Moscow's archives, and particularly the evidence of Venona, make their culpability very clear.

The Silvermaster Group

While the Perlo group provided the Soviets with useful information, it was easily outdone by another network, the Silvermaster group, that reported to the Soviets first through Jacob Golos and then through Elizabeth Bentley.

Bentley told the FBI that in the late summer of 1941 Golos had sent her to establish contact with a network that had been reporting to the CPUSA but which, in view of the recent Nazi invasion of the Soviet Union, was being made available for espionage. Gregory Silvermaster, assisted by his wife, Helen, and William Ullmann, a close family friend who lived with them, led the group. Bentley herself dealt chiefly with the Silvermasters and Ullmann, who passed on material from a diverse group of sources, most of whom Bentley rarely met and some of whom she never met face to face. These other sources included Solomon Adler, William Taylor, George Silverman, Frank Coe, William Gold, Sonia Gold, Irving Kaplan, Norman Bursler, Lauchlin Currie, Anatole Volkov, and Harry Dexter White.

Bentley said she traveled frequently to Washington, sometimes every month, sometimes twice a month, to pick up material from this group until it was fully turned over to direct Soviet control in 1944. The volume of material grew so great that Ullmann obtained a high-quality camera and set up a darkroom in the Silvermaster residence so that documents could be photographed rather than laboriously copied by hand. Bentley explained that initially she had picked up material and delivered it to Golos, who turned it over to the Soviets. Later, she herself met with a KGB contact and delivered the material. She also reported that after Golos's death the KGB repeatedly pressed her and Browder to transfer the group to its direct control. She said that they were reluctant to do so, but in mid-1944 Browder agreed, and the transfer was made over a period of months.

Eighty-five deciphered KGB cables, dating from 1942 to 1945, mention one or more of the persons Bentley named as members of the Silvermaster group. Eleven of the fourteen persons she named feature in Venona messages: both Silvermasters, Ullmann, Silverman, Coe, both Golds, Bursler, Currie, Adler, and White.[30] Not identified in any deciphered Venona messages are three members of the group: Kaplan, Taylor, and Volkov.

An unidentified cover name, El, is associated with the Silvermaster group in several Venona messages, but it is difficult to tell whether El is a source or someone assisting Iskhak Akhmerov, the KGB officer, in managing the group. It is possible that El was merely a shortened form of Elsa, the cover name for Akhmerov's wife and espionage assistant, Helen Lowry. Finally, the unidentified cover name Tur appears in a message alongside those of Gregory Silvermaster and Ullmann, but it is not clear whether Tur is a fellow member of the Silvermaster network or an independent source supplying the KGB with the same information—in this case, news of a delay in the Anglo-American invasion of southern France.

Various deciphered KGB cables corroborate details of Bentley's story about her relationship with the Silvermaster group. Several cables noting members of the Silvermaster group as the source of information refer to Golos as the intermediary. The first reference to Bentley in a Venona message occurs in December 1943, after Golos's death. The message, though only partly deciphered, indicates that Bentley had met Earl Browder and would "continue work"—presumably Golos's work.[31] In February 1944 the New York KGB reported to Moscow that the information coming from the Silvermaster network flowed through Bentley and then to Akhmerov. Several messages also report Akhmerov's irritation that Bentley was dragging her feet about implementing his plan to take direct control over the Silvermaster apparatus, and note her unhappiness when in mid-1944 Browder agreed to KGB absorption of the group.

One New York message notes that the KGB was sending by diplomatic pouch fifty-six "films"—probably rolls of film—delivered by the Silvermaster network.[32] Bentley said that she rarely picked up fewer than two or three rolls on her visit to the Silvermasters and remembers being given forty rolls on one visit. The KGB cable said that these films included photographic copies of seventeen different stolen American reports, including Board of Economic Warfare reports on Germany and the Far East, a memo from President Roosevelt regarding Lend-Lease policy toward France, a related Lend-Lease Administration report on its plans for France as well as one on Italy, a report by the U.S. embassy in Spain on German assets located there, an analysis of German industrial organization, an analysis of American military industrial capacity, and American plans for the dissolution of the Nazi party. Later, when the Silvermasters advertised their Washington home for sale, the real estate ad noted the extra amenity of a superbly equipped darkroom.[33]

Gregory Silvermaster: The Spy with Friends in High Places

Nathan Gregory Silvermaster was born in Russia in 1898 and came to the United States in 1914. He attended the University of Washington, where he established a record as a exceptional student and earned a bachelor's degree in philosophy in 1920. He also secretly joined the Communist party. The poet Kenneth Rexroth, in *An Autobiographical Novel,* described his experiences in Seattle's heady radical milieu during that era and noted that the theoretician of the nascent Communist movement there was a brilliant philosophy student at the University of Washington. Rexroth did not name him, but the details of the description clearly point to Silvermaster.[34] He became a U.S. citizen in 1926 and went on to graduate study in economics, receiving a doctorate at the University of California, Berkeley, in 1932; his dissertation was entitled "Lenin's Economic Thought Prior to the October Revolution." In 1935 he received an appointment as an economist with the Resettlement Administration, a New Deal agency attached to the Department of Agriculture. In 1938 he moved on to the U.S. Maritime Labor Board, and in 1940 to the Farm Security Administration (formerly the Resettlement Administration), where he stayed until 1944. Late that year he transferred to the War Assets Division of the Treasury Department. Silvermaster was transferred, along with the rest of the division, in mid-1945, first to the Commerce Department and later to the Reconstruction Finance Corporation, where it became the War Assets Corporation.

Though nominally remaining on the employment rolls of the Farm Security Administration, in 1942 Silvermaster arranged through contacts of his espionage apparatus to be detailed to the Board of Economic Warfare. The transfer, however, triggered objections from the Office of Naval Intelligence and from War Department counterintelligence. Neither agency had evidence that Silvermaster was engaged in espionage, but both believed that he was a hidden Communist and regarded him as a security risk at an agency with access to U.S. intelligence information.

Silvermaster flatly denied any Communist beliefs, past or present, and appealed to Under Secretary of War Robert Patterson to overrule the security agencies.[35] Silvermaster also called upon hidden Communists and Soviet sources within the government to bring pressure on Patterson. Harry White, then assistant to the secretary of the Treasury, got in touch with Patterson and told him that the suspicions about Silvermaster were baseless. White was a secret admirer of Stalin's regime and cooperated with the Soviets through Silvermaster's network. Lauchlin Currie, a presidential aide who also cooperated with Soviet intelligence, personally phoned Patterson and urged a reconsideration of Silvermaster's case. Calvin B. Baldwin, head of the Farm Security Administration and Silvermaster's superior, also vouched for him. Baldwin, while no spy, was a secret Communist. Patterson chose to trust and accommodate these highly placed persons and overruled military counterintelligence.[36] His naive decision facilitated the work of a man who headed one of the largest and most productive spy rings that Stalin's espionage agencies maintained inside the U.S. government. It would also provide substance to the postwar Republican charge that high officials in the Roosevelt and Truman administrations aided Soviet espionage against the United States.

The Silvermaster group's success in manipulating the under secretary of war illustrated as well the continued gaps in U.S. internal security procedures. The evidence that military counterintelligence possessed about Silvermaster was incomplete. Neither Naval nor Army intelligence knew that Silvermaster had come to the attention of the FBI as a contact of Gaik Ovakimian, a KGB officer who directed Soviet espionage from 1933 to 1941 under cover of being an Amtorg official.[37] Nor did Patterson, when weighing Currie's and White's support for Silvermaster, have knowledge that in 1939 Whittaker Chambers had informed Assistant Secretary of State Adolf Berle that both of them had cooperated with the CPUSA's Washington underground in the 1930s.

Silvermaster's security problems did not, however, end in 1942. Although detailed to the Board of Economic Warfare, he was still officially on the employment rolls of the Department of Agriculture. Its personnel office and the Civil Service Commission were not under Patterson's jurisdiction, and they opened an inquiry on Silvermaster in 1943 and called in the FBI. Once more, Silvermaster's high-placed friends swung into action. Lauchlin Currie assured the FBI that there was no basis for the suspicions that Silvermaster was a Communist. And the FBI had yet to get Berle's notes with their indication that Whittaker Chambers had identified Currie as an ally of the Communist underground in 1939. The FBI also appears to have been unaware of the details of the earlier Naval and Army counterintelligence investigations of Silvermaster. The FBI investigation produced nothing concrete, and the matter was dropped. In 1944 Silvermaster's tenure at the Board of Economic Warfare (by then merged into the Foreign Economic Administration) was ending, and he sought a new post. Although no adverse action had been taken in the Agriculture Department security probe, a security cloud surrounded him. White and Currie again intervened, and Under Secretary of Agriculture Paul Appleby sent a memo to his subordinates:

> The other day when Harry White, of the Treasury Department, was in to see me on other business, he lingered to ask whether or not I could do anything about placing Gregory Silvermaster, who has been in Farm Security Administration for some years. . . . Silvermaster has been under some attack by the Dies committee, I believe, principally or exclusively because he happens to have been born in Russia and has been engaged most of his life as an economist and more particularly a labor economist. He is a highly intelligent person and is very close both to Harry White and to Lauch Currie. There is no reason to question his loyalty and good citizenship.[38]

Appleby's statement was inaccurate. The Dies committee (House Special Committee on Un-American Activities) had raised questions about Silvermaster's having concealed Communist loyalties, not about his birth or occupation. It is unlikely, however, that Appleby was lying. He was neither a Communist nor even a fellow traveler but merely gullible. He was easily manipulated by men as unscrupulous as Currie and White, and his memo reflected his naive trust in their honesty.

Silvermaster briefly returned to the Department of Agriculture, but White soon found him a better post in the War Assets Division of his own Treasury Department.

In 1943 Lauchlin Currie reported to the Silvermaster network that the FBI had interviewed him about Silvermaster's Communist sympathies. The network passed this report on to the New York KGB, which informed Moscow. From the nature of the FBI inquiries to Currie and its questions to Silvermaster himself, the KGB deduced correctly that American authorities were suspicious of his Communist convictions but had not as yet picked up evidence of espionage. Consequently, the KGB decided that although increased caution was needed, Silvermaster could continue his work.

In her November 1945 statement to the FBI Bentley had said that Akhmerov had sought to convince Silvermaster of the need for direct KGB contact with the network's chief sources, but that Silvermaster had long resisted the move. The deciphered Venona cables confirm Bentley's recollection. Several Venona messages show Akhmerov urging Silvermaster to split his large network into smaller groups and to allow the KGB to take several members under its direct supervision. The New York KGB, however, told Moscow that Akhmerov described Silvermaster as "jealous about encroachments" on his apparatus and that "an attempt to 'remove members of the group, however, circumspectly, will be received . . . unfavorably by Robert [Silvermaster].' "[39]

Although seeking to convince him of the advisability of a change, Akhmerov was aware that Silvermaster had created and managed an espionage network of impressive size. He informed Moscow that "it is doubtful whether we [the KGB] could get same results as Robert [Silvermaster]." He gave the example of two Treasury Department employees, William and Sonia Gold, who were Silvermaster network "probationers," the KGB term for agents who were not professional KGB officers. Akhmerov described them as devoted to the Communist cause but difficult to manage because of unspecified "caprices." He told Moscow that "it costs Robert great pains to keep the couple and other Probationers in line. Robert being their leader in the CPUSA line helps him give them orders." Akhmerov stressed that Silvermaster's position as an underground CPUSA leader added to his ability to direct such ideologically motivated agents, noting "that our workers [KGB officers] would not manage to work with the same success under the CPUSA flag." Akhmerov further reported that he was at pains to convince Silvermaster that the breaking up of the network into smaller groups was a security measure, not a reflection on Silvermaster's leadership, and that Silvermaster would "retain general direction."[40]

Elizabeth Bentley wrote that Helen Witte Silvermaster was an active partner in her husband's work, did much of the copying, met sources to pick up material, and passed on material to Bentley herself. Helen Silvermaster was Russian-born, like her husband. She had immigrated to the United States in 1923 and become a U.S. citizen in 1930. Her marriage that year to Gregory Silvermaster was her second, and she had a son from her first marriage, Anatole Volkov. Bentley reported that Volkov, born in 1924, had occasionally performed courier duties for the Silvermaster network but dropped out of the picture when he was drafted into military service. Under the cover name Dora, Helen Silvermaster shows up in the deciphered KGB cables as a fully knowledgeable assistant in her husband's work. When she was interviewed by the FBI in 1947, she denied any belief, past or present, in communism, complaining that "anyone with liberal views seemed to be called a Communist now-a-days." She agreed that she had known Elizabeth Bentley and that Bentley had often met with her and stayed overnight at the Silvermaster residence, but claimed that she had believed Bentley to be an OSS speech writer collecting material for speeches for U.S. government officials.[41]

The deciphered Venona cables show that, in recognition of their hard work, the KGB provided Silvermaster with a regular stipend and in late 1944 paid him a bonus of three thousand dollars. This KGB cable is partially garbled, but it appears that the KGB also gave Silvermaster a Soviet medal for his service to the USSR. Akhmerov reported that "Robert [Silvermaster] is sincerely overjoyed and profoundly satisfied with the reward given him in accordance with your instructions. As he says his work for us is the one good thing he has done in his life. He emphasized that he did not take this only as a personal honor, but also as an honor to his group. He wants to see the reward and the book."[42]

It is impossible to differentiate between what information Silvermaster provided in his own right and what he delivered from the various members of his group. Deciphered Venona messages mentioning Silvermaster, sixty-one in total, report his handing over huge quantities of War Production Board data on weapons, aircraft, tank, artillery, and shipping production; Board of Economic Warfare documents on

German industry and on American reserves of manpower, foodstuffs, and raw materials; summaries and copies of U.S. diplomatic cables, particularly those dealing with American negotiations with the USSR; OSS reports on a wide variety of subjects; analyses of rivalries inside the U.S. government and of the increasingly tense relations between Secretary of State Cordell Hull and President Roosevelt; American reports about British intentions in the Balkans after Hitler's defeat; and postwar U.S. military planning documents. Silvermaster also accepted KGB requests for specific items of information. One KGB cable, for example, reported that he delivered requested technical and operating manuals for various models of American bombers and attack aircraft. Probably these were supplied by William Ullmann, then an officer with the Army Air Force headquarters at the Pentagon.[43]

William Ullmann: The Spy as Family Friend

William Ullmann was born to a prosperous Missouri family in 1908. He graduated from Harvard Business School in 1932 and arrived in Washington in 1935 to take a job with the National Recovery Administration. At that time he also met the Silvermasters. In 1938 they jointly bought a house that they shared until Ullmann and Gregory Silvermaster were forced out of the government in 1947. All three then moved to Harvey Cedars, New Jersey, where they were partners in a building construction firm.

Ullmann transferred to the Resettlement Administration (which later became the Farm Security Administration) in 1937. In 1939 Harry White, director of Treasury's Division of Monetary Research, hired him. Ullmann received a strong recommendation for the position from C. B. Baldwin, then assistant administrator of the Farm Security Administration. His immediate supervisor at Treasury was Frank Coe. White later told the FBI that he hired Ullmann on the recommendation of his close friend George Silverman. As noted earlier, Baldwin was a secret Communist, and White, Coe, and Silverman were all part of Silvermaster's espionage network. Ullmann worked in White's office until 1942, when he was drafted. He then obtained a commission in the Army Air Force. Bentley told the FBI that Silverman, then a civilian official in the Army Air Force, had arranged for Ullmann to be assigned to work in his division at the Pentagon, an assignment that allowed him to resume living in the Silvermaster/Ullmann residence and carrying on his espionage activities. When interviewed by the FBI in 1947, Ullmann confirmed that Silverman had arranged his assignment to the Pentagon.

Ullmann is mentioned in twenty-four deciphered Venona messages under the cover names Pilot and Donald and was clearly both a major source in his own right and Silvermaster's partner in managing the rest of the network.[44] After his military duty he returned to the Treasury Department, where he worked under Harold Glasser, yet another Soviet agent, until he was quietly forced to resign in 1947.[45]

George Silverman: The Link to Highly Placed Sources

Abraham George Silverman's roots in the CPUSA underground of the 1930s were deep. When Hope Hale Davis and her husband joined in the mid-1930s, he was already a leading member. In early 1935 her husband, Hermann Brunck, had written an economic study concluding that the New Deal's reforms were beginning to work. Such a position was a serious ideological error before the CPUSA's shift to a Popular Front position (late 1935) in support of Roosevelt, and Silverman ferociously attacked Brunck's findings at a meeting of their underground Communist group.[46]

Whittaker Chambers knew Silverman as a secret Communist and as a contact of the espionage network that he had supervised in the mid-1930s. Chambers noted that Silverman, along with Alger Hiss, Harry White, and Julian Wadleigh, had been a recipient of expensive Bokhara rugs, which he distributed to leading figures of his network in January 1937. (The giving of New Year's presents, a sort of Christmas bonus, to agents was common Soviet intelligence practice in the 1930s and early 1940s. Bentley in her testimony reported the same custom.) Chambers explained that the rugs were shipped to Silverman's residence, from which they were then distributed. Chambers said that Silverman was a close friend of White, and his chief task for the network was keeping White in a cooperative mood. It was Silverman, according to Chambers, who actually delivered the rug to White.

Silverman later admitted knowing Chambers in the 1930s but described him as only a casual social acquaintance. Silverman also admitted having received two rugs from him, but he said they were repayment for a seventy-five-dollar loan he had made to Chambers. In Silverman's version he paid Chambers three hundred dollars for the rugs in addition to canceling the debt. He could not, however, produce any receipts for the loan to Chambers or his payment to Chambers for the rugs.[47]

Silverman worked as an economist and statistician for a variety of government agencies in the 1930s: the National Recovery Administration, the Tariff Commission, and the Railroad Retirement Board. While he had been active in the CPUSA underground and assisted Chambers's GRU-linked network, none of these positions offered significant access to information of intelligence interest. This changed, however, in 1942, when Silverman became civilian chief of analysis and plans in the office of the assistant chief of the Army Air Force Air Staff for Material and Service. He brought William Ullmann into this division. In the Venona cables, where he has the cover name Aileron, Silverman furnished the KGB with reports on American aircraft production and allocation and on training and provisioning of air crews.[48]

Although this information was of intelligence value to the Soviets, Silverman's close association with two highly placed government officials, Harry White and Lauchlin Currie, remained his most critical work for Soviet intelligence. Bentley told the FBI that Silverman was the network's chief link to both, although Gregory Silvermaster himself developed a close relationship with the two men as well.

Harry Dexter White: A Most Highly Placed Spy

Among all the covert sources that Stalin possessed in the American government, none held a higher position than Harry Dexter White, assistant secretary of the Treasury. He joined the Treasury Department in 1934, and his brilliance as an economist and his ability to explain and propose solutions to complex monetary issues to nontechnically trained policy-makers soon made him one of the department's most influential officials. Secretary of the Treasury Henry Morgenthau's extensive and detailed diary shows that no individual had greater influence on Morgenthau's own thinking in the late 1930s and during World War II than White.

Rising steadily, White became director of monetary research in 1938 and assistant to the secretary of the Treasury in 1941. He and John Maynard Keynes were the chief architects of the historic Bretton Woods monetary agreement in 1944 that structured international monetary policy for decades to come, and he became assistant secretary of the Treasury, the second-ranking position in the department, in 1945. The next year President Truman appointed him the American director of the International Monetary Fund, one of the chief institutional pillars of the postwar international economic order. He came close to rising even higher. Henry Wallace, vice-president from 1941 to 1945 and a candidate for president in 1948, told the press that White was his first choice for secretary of the Treasury. Had Roosevelt died a year earlier or not decided to replace Wallace on the ticket in the 1944 election, Wallace would have become president.[49]

Whittaker Chambers stated that in the mid-1930s White was valued because of his talent and potential, but that he was not a very productive source for Chambers's GRU-CPUSA network. He was then only establishing his influence at Treasury and, in any case, at that time the Treasury Department was not involved in issues of much intelligence interest to the Soviets. Chambers also noted that White was not a CPUSA member; he cooperated with the Communist underground on his own terms and could not be ordered to do anything in particular.

Although White was not one of Chambers's most productive sources in the mid-1930s, he was nonetheless a source. After Alger Hiss sued Chambers for slander in 1948, Chambers responded by producing a collection of documents and microfilm that he had hidden in 1938. Most of the material had come from Hiss, but it also included a long memo in Harry White's own handwriting.

Chambers later wrote that when he stopped spying for the Soviets he met briefly with his chief sources and urged them to cease as well, hoping that they would either rethink their loyalties or at least break contact out of fear of exposure. Elizabeth Bentley heard that White did draw back after Chambers's defection. She said that Silvermaster told her that White "had been giving information to the Russians during the thirties but ceased abruptly when his contact ... turned 'sour' in 1938."[50] But, Silvermaster explained to Bentley, in 1940 White had renewed his ties with the CPUSA underground in Washington.

White facilitated Soviet espionage by sponsoring government employment of a number of Soviet sources. Working for the Treasury Department during his tenure as one of its most powerful officials were at least eleven Soviet sources: Frank Coe, Harold Glasser, Ludwig Ullmann, Victor Perlo, Sonia Gold, Gregory Silvermaster, George Silverman, Irving Kaplan, William Taylor, and Solomon Adler. He also used his position to protect Silvermaster and Glasser when they came under security scrutiny.

In addition, in 1941 White successfully urged the Chinese Nationalist government's Ministry of Finance to employ in a senior position Chi Ch'ao-ting, a Chinese national trained as an economist in the United States. Chi Ch'ao-ting was educated at Tsinghua College in Peking and then attended the University of Chicago and Columbia University. He also secretly joined the American Communist party in 1926 and was part of its Chinese bureau until 1941. He worked as an interpreter for the Communist International in Moscow in the late 1920s and was a member of the Chinese Communist party's delegation to the Sixth Congress of the Comintern in 1928. In the United States in the 1930s he wrote for the *Daily Worker, Amerasia,* and other publications under the pseudonyms of Hansu Chan, R. Doonping, Huang Lowe, and Futien Wang. Chi's Communist activities, however, were secret.

In 1940 Chi traveled to Chungking, the capital of China after the capture of Beijing by the Japanese. Comintern records show that in August Mao Tse-tung informed Georgi Dimitrov that Chi had met with Chou En-lai, Mao's chief lieutenant and representative in Chungking. Mao asked Dimitrov to inform Earl Browder that Chi would be returning to the United States to recruit Japanese-American Communists for espionage against the Japanese forces in China, oversee a courier system using American Communist seamen to link the Chinese Communist party via Hong Kong with Japan, the Philippines, and the United States, and supervise a program by the CPUSA's Chinese Bureau to collect funds from Chinese immigrants that would go to the Chinese Communists. Chi's return to the United States was brief, however. With U.S. government support, arranged through White, Chi returned to Chungking in 1941 to become an official of the Chinese government's finance ministry. There he supplied the Chinese Communists with information and disrupted Chiang Kai-shek's regime from within. When Chiang and his Nationalist government retreated to Taiwan in 1949, Chi stayed on the mainland, openly announcing his status as a veteran Chinese Communist party operative, and became a senior official of Mao Tse-tung's government.[51]

There are fifteen deciphered KGB messages during 1944 and 1945 in which White was discussed or which reported information he was providing to Soviet intelligence officers.[52] The KGB mentioned that White offered advice concerning how far the Soviets could push the United States on abandoning the Polish government-in-exile (which was hostile to Stalin) and assured the Soviets that U.S. policy-makers, despite their public opposition, would acquiesce to the USSR's annexation of Latvia, Estonia, and Lithuania. White was also a senior adviser to the U.S. delegation at the founding conference of the United Nations in San Francisco in May 1945. During the negotiations on the UN charter he met covertly with Soviet intelligence officers and provided them with information on the American negotiating strategy. He assured the Soviets that "Truman and Stettinius want to achieve the success of the conference at any price" and advised that if Soviet diplomats held firm to their demand that the Soviet Union get a veto of UN actions, that the United States "will agree."[53] He offered other tactical advice on how the Soviets might defeat or water down positions being advanced by his own government and that of Great Britain. The KGB officer meeting with White even carried with him a questionnaire on a variety of issues about which Soviet diplomats wanted to know the American negotiating strategy; White answered in detail.

In November 1944 the KGB told Moscow that Silvermaster had spoken with Terry Ann White, Harry's wife. She told him that her husband was considering a position in private business in order to finance college education for one of their daughters. Silvermaster, according to a Venona decryption, responded that the KGB "would willingly have helped them and that in view of all the circumstances would not allow them to leave Carthage [Washington]. Robert [Silvermaster] thinks that Richard [Harry White] would have refused a regular payment but might accept gifts as a mark of our gratitude for [unrecovered code groups] daughter's expenses which may come to up to two thousand a year. Albert [Akhmerov] said to Robert that in his opinion we would agree to provide for Richard's daughter's education."[54] The New York KGB endorsed Akhmerov's offer to finance the college education of White's daughter and asked for Moscow's sanction. (Moscow's reaction, however, is not among the Venona messages decrypted.)

The Venona messages show that Silvermaster had protested the KGB's bypassing him and meeting directly with White, an objection that was overridden. White did not meet just with Americans who were part of Soviet intelligence, but also directly with Soviet intelligence officers. An August 1944 deciphered cable reported on a July meeting between Kolstov, the cover name of an unidentified KGB officer, and Jurist, White's cover name at the time:[55]

As regards the technique of further work with us Jurist said that his wife was ready for any self-sacrifice; he himself did not think about his personal security, but a compromise would lead to a political scandal and the discredit of all supporters of the new course, therefore he would have to be very cautious. He asked whether he should [unrecovered code groups] his work with us. I replied that he should refrain. Jurist has no suitable apartment for a permanent meeting place; all his friends are family people. Meetings could be held at their houses in such a way that one meeting devolved on each every 4–5 months. He proposes infrequent conversations lasting up to half a hour while driving in his automobile.[56]

In addition to these particular examples of White's espionage, he also attempted—sometimes successfully, sometimes not—to influence American policy to serve Communist interests. One case of White's acting as an agent of influence is the matter of a Soviet loan for postwar reconstruction. On January 3, 1945, the USSR asked the United States to give it a loan of six billion dollars repayable under generous terms: over thirty years at a rate of $2\frac{1}{4}$ percent. A week later White, then assistant secretary of the Treasury, persuaded Secretary Morgenthau to urge President Roosevelt to offer Stalin an even larger loan on even more generous terms: ten billion dollars repayable over thirty-five years at a rate of 2 percent. Internal U.S. government discussions about a Soviet loan were highly sensitive and were kept secret, or so government officials thought. White, however, was a central participant in these conversations, and several KGB cables in January 1945 relay information from White on these discussions, including his and Morgenthau's loan proposal. The State Department, however, opposed any postwar loan as ill-advised at that time, as did President Roosevelt, and the idea was dropped. If the loan proposal had moved to the point of serious negotiations, the Soviets would have been in the enviable position of having covert communications with a leading member of the American negotiating team who was their secret partisan.

Another case in point is the Chinese gold loan. In 1942 the U.S. Congress authorized a $500 million loan to Nationalist China. In 1943 the Chinese government asked for a $200 million delivery of gold to be charged against this loan. China's currency was inflating rapidly under wartime conditions, with great damage to that country's economy. A supply of gold to back the currency would assist in slowing inflation, which was rising to ruinous levels. Roosevelt approved the gold loan, and in July 1943 Secretary Morgenthau signed a letter to the Chinese government pledging transfer of the gold.

White, with the assistance of Frank Coe (director of the Division of Monetary Research) and Solomon Adler (Treasury representative in China), opposed carrying out the transfer and repeatedly won Morgenthau's support for delaying delivery, arguing that pervasive corruption in the Nationalist government and its failure to adopt financial reforms would result in the gold's doing little good. By July 1945, two years later, only $29 million in gold had been sent to China. Meanwhile, the hyperinflation of this period, more than a thousand percent a year, did immense damage to the Chinese economy and severely weakened the standing of the Nationalist government when civil war with the Chinese Communists resumed at the end of 1945.

White, Coe, and Adler were right about the corruption of the Nationalist regime, but their position that China needed to institute a monetary reform in the midst of World War II, with the Japanese occupying China's most productive regions, was an excuse rather than a reason. They effectively delayed the transfer while only going through the motions of offering alternatives. By mid-1945 Morgenthau, who had supported delaying the transfer, realized that he had been misled on key points. He told Coe, White, and the others that they had put him "in an absolutely dishonorable position, and I think it's inexcusable."[57] Morgenthau, however, thought his aides had merely mishandled the gold transfer but were well motivated, and he never suspected that they had an entirely separate agenda from his.[58]

Frank Coe was one of the persons Whittaker Chambers had identified as a covert Communist to Assistant Secretary of State Berle in 1939. Frank Coe had the cover name Peak, which appears in four deciphered Venona cables.[59] Only one conveys much of the substance of Coe's work, a New York KGB message in December 1944 informing Moscow that five reels of filmed documents provided by Peak/Coe were on the way. The cable briefly described the documents as reports and memoranda about American Lend-Lease plans and negotiations with the British.

After White became the American director of the International Monetary Fund in 1946, he found a post for Coe there. In 1947 the FBI interviewed Coe, and he denied any participation in Soviet espionage, any sympathy for communism, or any association with Communists. In

1948 he testified to the House Committee on Un-American Activities and denied Elizabeth Bentley's statements about his activities. When American authorities decided to force those identified as Soviet agents from public employment in 1947, Coe's position at the International Monetary Fund put him beyond immediate firing. But by 1950 American pressure forced Coe out. In 1952 he was called before a congressional investigating committee. Considerable evidence had accumulated since he had testified in 1948, and this time he chose not to take a chance that a perjury charge might be brought. He refused to answer most questions, citing the right not to provide evidence against himself. In 1956 he was once more called to testify. He denied having engaged in espionage but again refused to answer questions on most specifics, including his relationship with the CPUSA. He then moved permanently to Communist China in 1958 to work for Mao Tse-tung's government. By 1959 he was writing articles justifying the "rectification campaign," a massive Maoist purge of Chinese society instituted the previous year, and claiming that the resulting Marxist-Leninist ideological purification had led to prodigious increases in economic production.[60]

Solomon Adler is identified under the cover name of Sachs as a member of the Silvermaster network in a deciphered Venona message regarding delivery of information about China. Elizabeth Bentley remembered Adler as a source who had been in China during part of the war but little else about him. She did not even recall meeting him. When interviewed by the FBI in late 1947, Adler stated that he had met Bentley, introduced to her by Ludwig Ullmann at a social occasion also attended by Helen Silvermaster. Adler denied any sympathy or association with Communists. The FBI wanted him fired from his senior Treasury post, but its evidence was not as strong as for other members of the Silvermaster group, and he kept his job until 1950. By then the evidence accumulated by the FBI convinced Treasury Department authorities, and he quietly resigned under pressure. At that time he also obtained a passport and left the United States, traveling initially to Britain. (Adler had been born in Britain and had become a U.S. citizen in 1936, the same year he became a U.S. government employee.) He remained abroad for more than three years and allowed his American passport to expire. This subjected him to denaturalization and he lost his American citizenship.[61]

At some point in the 1950s Adler also emigrated to the People's Republic of China. Sidney Rittenberg, another American Communist who emigrated to China, wrote in a memoir that in 1960 Adler, Coe, and he were working together on translating Mao's writings into English. In 1983 a Chinese Communist journal identified Adler as having worked for twenty years for the Chinese Communist party's Central External Liaison Department, an agency that included among its duties foreign espionage. He also appeared in a photograph in a memoir published in China as a colleague of Henshen Chen, a senior official in Mao's government who had worked as an intelligence operative in the United States from the late 1930s until the Communist victory in China in 1949. In his memoir Chen described how during that period he, Chen, had worked as an agent for the Chinese Communist party and its liaison with the CPUSA, while using as cover the position of editor at *Pacific Affairs* and researcher for the Institute of Pacific Relations.[62]

In the late 1940s and 1950s some Republicans charged that a cabal of secret Communists in the Roosevelt and Truman administrations had "lost China" to the Communists.[63] The duplicitous role that White, Coe, and Adler played in the matter of the Chinese gold loan figured among the particulars of the charge. This was exaggeration for partisan purposes. The chief reasons for China's fall to Mao's forces lay in China. The obstruction of the gold loan made a minor, not a major, contribution to Mao's victory. White, Coe, and Adler were minor actors, but actors they were, and China's Communist government showed its gratitude by hiring the latter two as advisers. Both spent the rest of their lives in Communist China, Coe dying there in 1980, Adler in 1994.

Lauchlin Currie: White House Aide as Soviet Spy

Harry White and Alger Hiss were the two most highly placed Soviet sources in the American government. Lauchlin Currie, however, was a close third. Born in Nova Scotia and educated at the London School of Economics, he went to Harvard to pursue a doctorate in economics and became an American citizen in 1934. He became a U.S. government employee the same year, working with Harry White in Treasury's Division of Research and Statistics before moving to the Federal Reserve Board.

These technical positions ended in 1939 when he joined the White House staff as a senior administrative assistant to the president. The growth in the White House staff was just getting under way; presidential aides were few and exercised significant authority. Roosevelt sent Currie to China in 1942 for a brief period as his personal representative and head of the American economic mission to the Nationalist government. In 1943 the Board of Economic Warfare, part of the Lend-Lease Administration, and several other war agencies merged to form the Foreign Economic Administration. Currie was detailed from the White House to serve as deputy administrator and day-to-day head of the agency. Currie was, then, a powerful figure in wartime Washington, both as a presidential aide and as an administrator of an agency.

His ties to the Washington Communist underground went back to the mid-1930s. Chambers described him in his memoir as working with the underground as a fellow traveler rather than a party member, in the same manner as Harry White. Adolf Berle's 1939 notes on his conversation with Chambers describe Currie as someone who cooperated with the underground but who "never went the whole way."[64] Bentley also described his relationship with the Silvermaster group as cautious and calibrated by Currie himself. She remembered Currie as providing only verbal briefings, through George Silverman and Gregory Silvermaster, and refraining from handing over documents. She also said that Akhmerov had urged Silvermaster to arrange for direct KGB contact with Currie, but that Silvermaster had resisted. She recalled Currie's warning that American cryptanalysts were on the verge of breaking the Soviet diplomatic code, an apparent reference to the origins of the Venona Project. Otherwise the only specifics Bentley remembered were Currie's intervention to assist Silvermaster with his security probes and his helping various Soviet intelligence contacts get jobs in the government.

There are nine deciphered Venona messages that discuss Currie, who had the cover name Page.[65] They show that Currie gave assistance to Soviet intelligence cautiously and on a limited basis, just as Bentley said. The KGB cables also demonstrate that, although Bentley did not know or did not remember, on occasion he did turn over documents to the KGB. An August 1943 New York KGB cable reports to Moscow that Currie had given Silverman a memorandum on a political subject, otherwise unspecified, that was either from or for the State Department. In June 1944 the New York KGB reported receipt of two items from Currie. One was information on President Roosevelt's reasons for keeping Charles de Gaulle at arm's length. The other, however, was of greater importance to Stalin. Currie told the Soviets that Roosevelt was willing to accept Stalin's demand that the USSR keep the half of Poland that it had received under the Nazi-Soviet Pact of 1939 and that FDR would put pressure on the Polish government-in-exile to make concessions to the Soviets. In public the United States was supporting the Polish government-in-exile, and President Roosevelt had personally assured Polish-Americans, prior to the 1944 election, of his support for the Polish cause. Currie's private information let Stalin know that he could disregard these public stands and need not make serious concessions to the Poles.

The Venona cables also confirm Bentley's statement that the Soviets sought direct contact with Currie. In February 1945 the Moscow KGB headquarters reminded its officers in the United States to find out from Akhmerov and Silvermaster "whether it would be possible for us to approach Page [Currie] direct."[66] The cables also show that by this point Moscow had begun to grow impatient. General Fitin, head of KGB foreign intelligence, told its New York office in March that it wanted more out of Currie. Fitin acknowledged that "Page trusts Robert [Silvermaster], informs him not only orally, but also by handing over documents"—further confirmation that Currie delivered documents to Soviet intelligence. But, said Fitin, "up to now Page's relations with Robert were expressed, from our point of view, only in common feelings and personal sympathies. [unrecovered code groups] question of more profound relations and an understanding by Page of Robert's role. If Robert does not get Page's transfer to our worker, then he [unrecovered code groups] raising with Page the question of Page's closer complicity with Robert."[67]

Fitin was being unduly harsh on his New York station, since earlier messages show Currie doing much more than merely expressing personal sympathies. But it served to make the point about Moscow's expectation that Currie could do much more. This March 1945 message was the last concerning Currie that the National Security Agency deciphered, so Venona does not show the New York KGB's response. There is, however, other evidence that Moscow's instruction to establish direct contact between Currie and its officers, bypassing Silverman and Silvermaster, was carried out. After Bentley defected in late 1945, the FBI opened an investigation of her Soviet supervisor at the time, Anatoly Gromov, a KGB officer operating out of the Soviet embassy in Washington under the guise of being a Soviet diplomat. A report on the investigation in February 1946 cited several meetings between Gromov and Currie. In 1947 the FBI interviewed Currie, who stated that he had met twice with Gromov in early 1945, once at Gromov's residence and once at his, and that they had had at least two other meetings after his leaving government service in June 1945. He described them as innocent discussions of cultural matters and denied any knowledge that Gromov was a KGB officer. Many years later it was discovered that Currie had also met with Vasily Zubilin, Gromov's predecessor as KGB station chief, in 1943. White House records show that Currie gave an innocuous reason for his meeting with Zubilin, who was nominally a Soviet diplomat. But the date, August 1943, coincides with that of the "anonymous Russian letter" (chapter 2) in which a Soviet KGB officer stated that Zubilin "has some high level agent in the office of the White House."[68]

The FBI also asked whether Currie had ever discussed with George Silverman the possibility that American code-breakers were close to breaking Soviet codes, one of the few specifics of his espionage that Bentley had remembered. Currie's answer was peculiar; he stated that while he did not specifically remember discussing breaking Soviet codes with Silverman, he might have done so casually because Silverman was a trusted friend. He further admitted that he might have been indiscreet on various other matters, all of which suggests that he was setting up a claim of carelessness as his defense against an espionage charge.

Indeed, the more the FBI learned of Currie's activities over the years, the more that "indiscreet" seemed a mild term for his behavior. In early 1941, for example, the Washington Committee for Aid to China planned to raise funds for victims of the Japanese war. It announced that Paul Robeson would sing at a fund-raising concert under the sponsorship of Cornelia Pinchot, the social-activist wife of Gifford Pinchot, the respected conservationist and former Republican governor of Pennsylvania, and Eleanor Roosevelt, the First Lady.[69] What neither Mrs. Pinchot nor Mrs. Roosevelt knew was that the CPUSA controlled the Washington Committee for Aid to China. They also did not know until a few days before the concert that only half the funds were to go to the Chinese relief; the rest would go to the National Negro Congress. Communists covertly led the latter organization, and in accordance with the requirements of the Nazi-Soviet Pact it had spent the last year and a half denouncing President Roosevelt in harsh terms.[70]

When Mrs. Pinchot and Mrs. Roosevelt discovered that they had been misled and manipulated, they demanded that either the concert go forward as they had originally been told (all funds to China) or that they not be named as sponsors. At that point Lauchlin Currie, who was a member of the Washington Committee for Aid to China, intervened and urged the two to avoid controversy and allow half the funds to go to an avowedly anti-Roosevelt organization. They refused, and issued a public statement withdrawing their sponsorship. That a Roosevelt aide should act in such a manner seems bizarre, unless his secret ties to the CPUSA are understood.[71]

The FBI lacked sufficient direct evidence to sustain a criminal prosecution against Currie. Bentley had dealt with him only through Silverman and Silvermaster and could not personally testify about his actions. Even if she had, it still came down to her word against his, not nearly enough to win a conviction. Venona would later provide more direct evidence, but Venona was a secret and could not be cited in court.

In 1948 Currie testified before the House Committee on Un-American Activities. Perhaps realizing that the FBI had only Bentley's indirect evidence, he shifted from his defensive stance in the 1947 interview with the FBI to a more aggressive posture. He rejected any possibility of indiscretion on his part and stated that he had no reason to suspect that Silvermaster, Silverman, Ullmann, Coe, and Glasser, whom he readily acknowledged as close friends and associates, had any Communist sympathies. Currie claimed that he had intervened with Under Secretary of War Patterson at the request of an official whose name he could not remember. He said that in his call to Patterson he had not urged a favorable consideration, and he also insisted that it was "customary procedure" in Roosevelt's White House for presidential aides to get in touch with officials at Patterson's level about individual personnel security investigations. This was false: it was unusual for one of the president's half-dozen administrative assistants to intervene in such a matter, but only one member of the committee, Richard Nixon, taxed Currie with the weaknesses of his explanation.[72]

Indeed, one of the committee's most vocal and reactionary members, Democratic representative John Rankin of Mississippi, rushed to Currie's defense. Rankin was an ardent racist who believed that slavery had been a blessing for African Americans. The chief object of his hatred, however, was Jews. He identified the New Deal, liberalism, racial equality, and communism as a Jewish conspiracy. Communism in itself was not really of interest to Rankin unless he could connect it with Jews; he even occasionally had kind words for Stalin, in whom he recognized a fellow anti-Semite. When Bentley testified that Currie had provided information to her espionage network through Silverman and Silvermaster, Rankin lashed out at her for "smearing Currie by remote control through two Communists." Rankin readily believed that Silverman and Silvermaster were Communists because they were Jews. But he could not believe Bentley about Currie because, as Rankin twice said, Currie was a "Scotchman" and therefore ethnically immune to communism.[73]

By 1950, however, Currie felt more vulnerable. The FBI had accumulated more evidence and the then-secret Venona Project had confirmed much of Bentley's story. Exactly what precipitated his decision is unclear, but in late summer of that year he emigrated to Colombia and a few years later renounced his American citizenship.[74]

Bentley's Defection

Although Elizabeth Bentley thought the FBI was closing in, it actually knew nothing about her when she suddenly appeared at an FBI office in August 1945. Was she a defector or a lunatic confessing to imaginary crimes? After several extensive interviews with Bentley and some quick checking on parts of her story, by the late fall of 1945 the FBI became convinced that she was genuine and had been deeply involved in espionage.

One item the FBI discovered was that it already had in hand a letter from Katherine Perlo that had made accusations about some of the same people that Bentley named. Katherine had married Victor Perlo in 1933, but in 1943 he divorced her. Distraught and bitter, in April 1944 Mrs. Perlo sent an unsigned letter to President Roosevelt denouncing her former husband and others as participants in clandestine Communist activities in Washington in the 1930s. The FBI traced the letter back to her, and she confirmed when interviewed that she had written it. In addition to her husband, she named George Silverman, John Abt, Charles Kramer, Harold Glasser, Harry White, Hermann Brunck, Hope Brunck (Hope Hale Davis), and Henry Collins.[75]

Bentley did not defect until more than six months after the KGB had taken over her networks, severed her contact with her agents, and changed her status to inactive. Once she had been replaced as their liaison, her former sources would have regarded any contact by her as a sign that something was amiss and would have been put on their guard. The FBI did, of course, begin extensive surveillance of those she named, in hopes of observing contact with Soviet agents and evidence of criminal activity. But by late 1945, when the FBI began surveillance of those Bentley named, the Soviets appeared to have suspected that their networks had been compromised and warned their sources to cease activity.

Indeed, one contact between a Bentley source and a Soviet intermediary that the FBI did observe appears to have been the actual delivery of a KGB warning that the network was in danger and that contact was being cut. One of the earliest Bentley contacts put under surveillance was Gregory Silvermaster. On December 1, 1945, bureau agents noted a man meeting with Gregory and Helen Silvermaster for several hours. The man was followed, and FBI suspicions were heightened when on his journey back to New York he "executed a number of diversionary maneuvers which appeared to the surveilling Agents to be calculated to ascertain the presence of a surveillance." The FBI identified the man as Alexander Koral, a Communist and maintenance engineer working for the New York City school system.[76]

The FBI had come across Koral several years earlier when it placed Gaik Ovakimian under surveillance. Ovakimian, an Amtorg official, had worked in the United States from 1933 to 1941. After the Nazi-Soviet Pact and the start of World War II, the U.S. government, which had paid little attention to Soviet espionage, belatedly looked into the matter briefly and spotted Ovakimian as an intelligence officer. He was arrested in May 1941 as an unregistered foreign agent. The FBI wanted him prosecuted, but the State Department negotiated an agreement that allowed him to leave the United States in return for the release of six Americans or spouses of Americans whom Soviet authorities had refused to allow out of the USSR. Although the FBI did not know it at the time, Ovakimian was the head of KGB operations in the United States. During its surveillance the FBI noted that Ovakimian met on a number of occasions with Koral and, although nothing could be proved, it was assumed that a Soviet intelligence officer and a school district maintenance man were not meeting for benign purposes.[77]

Confronted by the FBI in 1947, Koral admitted that from 1939 to 1945 he had worked as a clandestine courier. He explained that he had been paid two thousand dollars by someone known to him only as Frank to travel to different cities in order to pick up and deliver small packages and envelopes to different persons, including the Silvermasters. Koral stated that at his last meeting with Gregory Silvermaster, the one observed by the FBI in December 1945, he had also delivered a verbal message from his employer that "no more visits would be made to him." This was probably the KGB's message breaking contact with those compromised by Bentley's defection.[78]

Koral identified a photograph of Semyon Semenov, a KGB officer in New York working under Amtorg cover, as one of the persons to whom he delivered material. Koral's admissions, however, were a strategic retreat, acknowledging what he feared the FBI had observed. He then attempted to put his admissions in a context that would protect him from criminal prosecution. He hid his ties to the CPUSA, apparently unaware that the FBI already knew of his Communist background. He denied all knowledge of the content of the packages and messages he couriered. He presented himself simply as someone doing an odd job on the side for extra money and suggested that those he dealt with were involved in some sort of shady business deals over government war contracts.

The deciphered Venona cables show that Alexander Koral was part of a husband-and-wife KGB courier team. He, under the cover name Berg, and she, under the names Miranda and Art, show up in eleven KGB cables during 1944 and 1945.[79] These cables show that the KGB paid each a regular stipend of a hundred dollars a month in 1945. The cables also show Helen Koral (or more likely the Korals jointly) as one of three KGB courier links assigned to pick up material from the Silvermasters and as a link between Olga Valentinovna Khlopkova, a KGB officer working under diplomatic cover, and the KGB's illegal officer Iskhak Akhmerov. In the latter case, the arrangement usually was for Olga Khlopkova to meet with Helen Koral, who would also meet with Helen Lowry, Akhmerov's wife and assistant. The KGB assumed that these meetings would appear to be normal female socializing and would be less likely to attract FBI attention than contact between male links.

Alexander Koral's work for the KGB as a liaison agent also showed up in statements made to the FBI by Michael Straight. The son of wealthy American liberals who had founded the magazine the *New Republic*, Straight attended Cambridge University in England in 1934 and joined the Communist Party of Great Britain in 1935. He also developed a friendship with Anthony Blunt, the art expert, Cambridge don, and KGB recruiter. Soviet documents made public in 1998 include a 1943 autobiographical report that Blunt made to the KGB in which he discussed his "trying to combine the difficult task of not being thought left-wing and at the same time being in the closest contact with all left-wing students in order to spot likely recruits for us. As you already know the actual recruits whom I took were Michael Straight and . . ."[80] Straight gave his version of what happened in his memoir *After Long Silence*. He said that early in 1937 Blunt ordered him to drop his open Communist connections, return to the United States, and use his family connections to establish a career as a Wall Street banker while secretly working for the Communist cause. Straight protested that he had little interest in business and planned to stay in England and become a British subject. He recorded this conversation with Blunt:

> "Our friends have given a great deal of thought to it. . . . They have instructed me to tell you that that is what you must do."
> "What *I* must do? . . . What friends have instructed you to tell me—"
> "Our friends in the International. The Communist International."[81]

According to Straight, Blunt promised that his objections would be considered. A week later Straight met with Blunt again and learned the party's decision. "If I refused to become a banker that would be accepted. But my appeal was nonetheless rejected. I was to go back to America, and I was to go underground. . . . That was the bargain that was offered to me. I accepted it."[82] Straight publicly distanced himself from his student Communist connections, and shortly before he left Great Britain Blunt introduced him to a "stocky, dark-haired Russian," who gave him a brief introduction to conspiratorial technique.[83]

Through his family connections Straight met with both President Roosevelt and Mrs. Roosevelt to discuss his employment prospects and was hired as an unpaid assistant at the State Department in the fall of 1937. In late 1938 he accepted a paid job as a presidential speechwriter while nominally an employee of the Interior Department. There in 1939 he worked closely with Roosevelt's chief speechwriters and political advisers, James Rowe, Tom Corcoran, and Ben Cohen. In 1940 he returned to the State Department, this time as a regular employee of its European division. In 1941, however, he left State to take a post with the *New Republic* and remained there until he entered the military in 1942.

Meanwhile, early in 1938 Straight was contacted by a Soviet agent who identified himself as Michael Green. For the next four years, Straight says, he met occasionally with Green. At several of these meetings, he gave Green memoranda and reports that he had written at the

State Department and at Interior, none of which were important, he says. Michael Green was an alias, one of the several used by Iskhak Akhmerov, the KGB's leading illegal officer in the United States.

In espionage parlance, a "legal" intelligence officer is one who operates under diplomatic cover. Officers of the KGB working at the Soviet embassy or other recognized agencies of the Soviet government, such as Amtorg, were "legal" officers. Although they pretended to be diplomats or trade officials and often went by false names, they were openly Soviet officials, and their presence in the United States was part of a recognized Soviet activity. Vasily Zubilin, nominally a Soviet diplomat with the Soviet embassy, was a "legal" officer. "Illegals" such as Akhmerov are the classic spies of espionage novels, who have no diplomatic status, no official connection with the Soviet government, and a wholly false identity, often including a false nationality as well.

According to a biography prepared by the Russian Foreign Intelligence Service, Iskhak Abdulovich Akhmerov, born in 1901, was of Tartar background and joined the Communist party in 1919, shortly after the Bolshevik revolution. Recognizing his talent, in 1921 the party sent him to the Communist University of Toilers of the East, a school that principally served the USSR's Asian nationalities, and later to the elite Moscow State University, where he specialized in international relations. He joined the KGB immediately after graduating and served initially in its internal security arm aiding in the suppression of anti-Soviet movements in the USSR's Central Asian republics. He transferred to foreign intelligence in 1932 and served as a legal intelligence officer in Turkey under diplomatic cover. In 1934 he became an illegal officer and, using false identity papers, entered China, where he enrolled at an American-run college in order to improve his English and prepare for his next assignment. He entered the United States in 1935 with false identity documents and remained there for ten years, serving as the chief of the KGB's illegal station from 1942 to 1945. The admiring biography from the Russian Foreign Intelligence Service credits him with having "recruited a number of agents in the State Department, the Treasury Department, and the intelligence services" from whom "important political, scientific-technical, and military information" was obtained. He returned to the USSR in 1945 and became deputy chief of the illegals branch of the KGB's foreign intelligence arm, receiving the rank of full colonel and numerous medals, including the Badge of Honor, two Orders of the Red Banner, and the title of Honored Chekist.[84]

Those Americans who had contact with Akhmerov report that his English, while good, was accented and clearly not native, so most likely he pretended to be an immigrant. Some of the aliases he used are known, but what sort of false identity documents he kept and what profession he claimed are not, although American counterintelligence officers found indications that he maintained a business front as a clothier. He lived on the East Coast, probably in New York, and there are reports that he moved to Baltimore in 1945 shortly before he was withdrawn from the United States. His secret move to the USSR at that time was probably a reaction to concern that Bentley's defection would eventually lead the FBI to him, although there are also some indications that he was in poor health.[85]

Michael Straight records that he once had dinner with Green/Akhmerov and his wife, whom he described as a native-born American with a Midwestern accent. Mrs. Akhmerov, certainly, was a major contributor to Akhmerov's success as an illegal. She was a full partner in his espionage work and acted as his liaison with many of the sources he developed. As a native-born American and a woman, she attracted far less attention than he. She is known to have used the name Helen Lowry. According to several Soviet and American sources, she was also the niece of the CPUSA leader Earl Browder, although through which of his siblings the relation went is unclear. The Browder family was from Kansas (Earl himself never lost his Kansas accent), and Straight's description of Mrs. Akhmerov's accent and origins is compatible with the claim that she was Browder's niece. Bentley also knew the Akhmerovs, as Bill and Catherine. Like Straight, she knew that Bill was Russian and his wife American. Both Iskhak Akhmerov and Helen Lowry show up in scores of Venona messages.[86]

In his memoir Straight, making light of his connections with Soviet intelligence, insists that his contacts with Akhmerov were intermittent and largely inconsequential and that he never committed espionage. Although the KGB archive is not open for research, it has released selected documents, some of which deal with Michael Straight. In 1938 Straight was fresh out of college and working at the State Department job that the White House had arranged for him. In May Akhmerov sent a cable to Moscow informing his KGB superiors that Nigel (Straight's cover name at the time) had recommended one of the State Department rising stars, Alger Hiss, as someone with "progressive" (i.e., pro-Communist) views. Akhmerov, who knew that Hiss was already working for Soviet intelligence through the GRU, appeared to fear that Straight's youthful enthusiasm might compromise an already productive Soviet agent. Akhmerov reported to Moscow that he faced a dilemma because if he told Straight to stay away from Hiss, "he might guess that Hiss belongs to our family." He also worried that from the other side the GRU might order Hiss to recruit Straight and "in this case 'Nigel' would find out Hiss's nature." The message implied that Akhmerov expected the Moscow KGB to make contact with the GRU and make sure that their respective networks did not start tripping over each other. It also suggested that Akhmerov thought it unwise for Straight, a young and undeveloped contact, to know too much about Hiss, a Soviet source of proven reliability and great promise.[87]

Straight claimed that he was appalled by the Nazi-Soviet Pact. By late 1939 he felt himself increasingly estranged from communism and identifying himself inwardly as well as outwardly as a New Deal liberal. He had left government service, he wrote, to extricate himself from his link to Soviet intelligence, but he continued to meet Akhmerov until 1942, when he entered the U.S. armed forces. Unbeknownst to Straight, the KGB had dispatched Arnold Deutsch, a KGB illegal officer who had operated in England from 1934 to 1937, to the United States to renew contact with him and several other sources. Deutsch, however, died when the Soviet ship on which he was traveling was sunk in the Atlantic by a German U-boat in 1942.[88]

After World War II, Straight visited Britain and met his old friend and KGB recruiter, Anthony Blunt. KGB documents show that Blunt informed Moscow that Straight "in principle remains our man," but that he was increasingly disenchanted with the CPUSA.[89] Straight still had a sufficiently Popular Front orientation to align himself with Henry Wallace. When Straight was publisher of the *New Republic* he gave Wallace an editorial position that served as a platform for launching his Progressive party campaign for the presidency in 1948. But Straight was repelled by the CPUSA's secret leading role in the Progressive party, distanced his journal from it, and subsequently moved toward mainstream liberalism. In 1960 he supported John Kennedy, an exemplar of anti-Communist liberalism. In 1963 President Kennedy asked him to chair the Advisory Council on the Arts. Faced with an FBI security check, Straight informed Arthur Schlesinger, Jr., then working in the Kennedy White House, of his past and soon told his story to the FBI. The bureau arranged for him to tell British counterintelligence, MI5, about his contact with Anthony Blunt. Although MI5 had long suspected Blunt of espionage, it had had no firm evidence. With Straight's information in hand, British authorities confronted Blunt, and he confessed his guilt, although he provided few details. The confession and Blunt's spying were kept secret but were exposed by British journalists in 1979, at which time Straight's role also became public.[90]

Straight added to the picture of Alexander Koral as a KGB liaison agent, a go-between linking KGB officers to their sources. Straight told the FBI that because their face-to-face meetings were infrequent, Akhmerov also provided him with a telephone contact: Alexander Koral. The New York School Board later fired Koral when he refused to testify to a congressional investigating committee. The dismissal led one writer in the 1970s to present Koral as a victim of McCarthyism. He was, in fact, a spy, and his loss of public employment was a remarkably light penalty given the seriousness of his offense.[91]

In addition to Koral's meeting with the Silvermasters, the FBI in 1946 may have gotten a second indication that Bentley's various sources had been warned. FBI agents watching Charles Kramer, identified by Bentley as a member of the Perlo network, observed him leaving his residence carrying packages. He then proceeded to an isolated bus stop some distance from his residence and disposed of the material in a streetside trash can. The agents were understandably curious about what he had disposed of in so surreptitious a manner. They checked the can and found an accumulation of CPUSA literature. The obvious conclusion was that he was preparing for a possible search of his home.[92]

It is not known how the KGB learned about Bentley's defection and proceeded to warn her former sources of the need to break contact and cease activity.[93] Shortly after Bentley made contact with the FBI, it arranged for her to schedule a meeting with her KGB supervisor, Anatoly Gromov, head of the KGB office operating out of the Soviet embassy. The FBI observed the meeting on November 21, 1945. It is possible that KGB countersurveillance detected the FBI's surveillance or that Gromov surmised from his discussion with Bentley that she had turned. A still stronger possibility is that a Soviet agent within the Justice Department warned the KGB. Among the earliest Venona messages deciphered (late 1946 or early 1947) was one referring to a Soviet source hired by the Justice Department in 1944 who had access to counterintelligence information. Not surprisingly, that message initiated a crash FBI program to find the rotten apple in its own barrel, and in December 1948 it identified Judith Coplon, an analyst who had been working since early 1945 in the Foreign Agents Registration section of the Justice Department.

Fourteen deciphered KGB Venona messages, a KGB document regarding Coplon found in a Moscow archive, and the Justice Department's prosecution of her provide a fairly complete picture of Coplon's betrayal of the United States.[94] She attended Barnard College and was graduated in 1943. As an undergraduate she participated in the Communist student group at the school. Coplon got her first job in 1944, working for the New York office of the Economic Warfare Section of the Justice Department. A routine personnel security check at the time of her hiring noted her undergraduate Communist activities, but most personnel security offices were on the lookout for Nazi sympathizers, and Coplon's Communist links neither disqualified her nor even earned a flag on her file for future reference. Among Coplon's friends was another young Communist, Flora Wovschin, who already worked for the KGB. Coplon's new job had obvious intelligence interest, and Wovschin sounded her out and reported to the KGB that she was an excellent prospect. The New York office of the KGB agreed, and in July 1944 it requested Moscow's permission to recruit her as an agent.

The New York KGB temporarily suspended further action on her case when a change in personnel forced a reassignment of responsibilities for contact with various covert agents. The KGB headquarters did not get around to Coplon's case for several months. It was not until October that General Fitin sent an inquiry to the Comintern asking if it had any background information on Coplon.[95] Wovschin reported in November that Coplon was impatient for direct contact, and in December the New York KGB office, having received Moscow's approval, announced that it was proceeding and that Coplon's espionage potential had greatly increased since she had obtained a transfer to the Foreign Agents Registration section of the Justice Department.

Vladimir Pravdin, a KGB officer who worked under the cover of a journalist for the TASS news agency, met with Coplon in January 1945 and reported to Moscow that she was a "serious person who is politically well developed and there is no doubt of her sincere desire to help us. She had no doubts about whom she is working for."[96] Pravdin went on to say that he expected that Coplon would provide the KGB with highly valuable information on FBI operations. The remaining deciphered Venona messages regarding Coplon, all from the first half of 1945, report that she was working well, but the KGB had advised her initially to refrain from stealing documents until she was confident that she had consolidated her position at Justice.

In one Venona cable the New York KGB reported that Coplon was studying Russian to assist in getting assigned to work on Soviet-related matters. This gambit succeeded, and she gained access to files on FBI operations directed at possible Soviet agents. There is every reason to believe that Coplon gave the KGB early warning of many FBI counterintelligence operations from 1945 until she was identified in late 1948. Her alerts allowed the KGB to warn its sources to cease activity and break contact. Consequently, as in the Bentley case, by the time a case got to the point of the FBI's instituting surveillance in order to produce enough evidence to bring a criminal charge, the sources were forewarned and surveillance produced little.

The FBI arrested Coplon in 1949 in the act of handing over Justice Department counterintelligence files to Valentin Gubitchev, a KGB officer working under cover of being an official of the United Nations. Gubitchev claimed diplomatic immunity and was allowed to return to Moscow. Coplon, though, was tried and convicted of espionage.[97]

Coplon's trial, however, illustrated the difficulties of successfully prosecuting an espionage case under peacetime conditions. Coplon's defense attorneys, by insisting that the government add to the public record the counterintelligence files that Coplon had been transferring to Gubitchev when they were arrested, gave the Soviets in open court the confidential information that their arrested source had stolen. One document, for example, may have surprised key members of the CPUSA's underground arm. It was an FBI report that in 1944 its agents had surreptitiously entered the residence of Philip Levy, a member of the Communist underground apparatus. Among other things, the agents reported discovering that Levy was storing files belonging to Leon Josephson, a figure in the party underground (chapter 3). Josephson's files contained material that had been stolen in 1938 from the residence of Jay Lovestone, a leading opponent of the CPUSA. Thus, a Soviet agent's theft of government files produced a report of an FBI burglary of a Communist's residence that had turned up the booty of an earlier CPUSA theft of the files of one of its critics.[98]

Once they paid the price of revealing some of the secrets they wanted to protect, government prosecutors had little difficulty winning a conviction. Coplon, after all, had been arrested while actually passing documents to a Soviet official. But though the evidence was clear, its admissibility under the complex standards of U.S. criminal justice was not. The government had no intention of revealing that the FBI had initiated surveillance and wiretaps of Coplon in response to its having broken the cipher to KGB cables that the Soviets believed unbreakable. Authorities feared that if the Soviets learned of the success of American code-breakers, they would end contact with their sources and close down operations revealed in the cables. Such an outcome would prevent the FBI from doing what it had done with Coplon: using Venona to identify a Soviet agent, institute surveillance, and catch the spy in the act. But because the government did not produce Venona as the basis for its actions, an appeals court held that the reasons the government did give lacked probable cause for the surveillance and arrest, and ordered a new trial.

The government reformulated its evidence to avoid the legal technicality that had voided the first trial, but still it did not reveal Venona. For a second time the government tried and convicted Coplon of espionage. But for a second time an appeals court found key evidence inadmissible, owing to lack of probable cause, and returned the case to the trial court. Utterly frustrated, prosecutors had to allow a Soviet agent to walk away free. The only punishments they could inflict were that Coplon lost her job working for the Justice Department and her indictment remained alive, keeping the door open for a third trial. In fact, however, she was never retried. The case also left the public in a sour mood because most people were enraged that an obviously guilty spy had escaped punishment.

As the Coplon case showed, the requirements for a successful criminal prosecution under the American legal system were high—too high for the evidence that the government could produce in court against most of those Elizabeth Bentley had named. And in most instances the government had less direct proof than it did against Coplon: only the testimony of a single witness, Bentley, an admitted ex-spy, whose credibility was vulnerable to attack by a defense attorney. There was a great deal of supporting evidence, but it was largely circumstantial and concerned actions several years in the past. There were no stolen documents or other direct physical evidence of spying. As one FBI official bitterly commented about the Bentley investigation in early 1947, "The subjects in this case are extraordinarily intelligent, at least they are unusually well educated, and include some very prominent people, including Harry Dexter White. It can be expected that some of the finest legal talent in the country would be retained for their defense in the event of prosecution. With the evidence presently available, the case is nothing more than the word of Gregory [Bentley's FBI cover name] against that of the several conspirators. The likely result would be an acquittal under very embarrassing circumstances."[99]

The FBI concluded that its only chance for conviction would be to interview the suspects and hope that "one of the subjects of this case, probably the weakest sister," would break and give them a second witness to join Bentley, or that those interviewed would make provably false statements that would allow a prosecution for perjury.[100] It did not, however, expect this to happen, and with one exception it did not.

When interviewed, most of those whom Bentley had named gave evasive answers or refused to say anything at all, and most refused to sign statements. Later, they would be called before grand juries and congressional committees. There, under oath and conscious that a false answer might result in a perjury charge, most refused to testify, relying on their right under the Fifth Amendment not to incriminate themselves. Four of those Bentley named did testify, denied her charges, but then put themselves beyond prosecution for perjury by leaving the United States: Maurice Halperin, Duncan Lee, Frank Coe, and Lauchlin Currie. Two others, Michael Greenberg and Solomon Adler, left the United States, never to return, before they could be called to testify.

The prudence of these actions is illustrated by the fate of one of those Bentley named who failed to take the Fifth or to leave the United States. Bentley stated that one of her less important sources was William Remington, an employee of the War Production Board when she had contact with him. She explained that one of the CPUSA talent-spotters, Joseph North, an editor of *New Masses,* had introduced Remington to Jacob Golos. Golos completed his recruitment, and Bentley later testified that Remington had furnished information on airplane production, high-octane gasoline, and synthetic rubber and paid her his CPUSA dues money. Bentley described Remington as very nervous about his covert work and as not a major source, and she explained that contact had ceased when he entered the Navy in 1944.[101]

As a result of Bentley's information, the FBI interviewed Remington in 1947. He confirmed that he had known North and that North had introduced him to Golos and Bentley, known to him only as John and

Helen. He even agreed that he had met with Helen/Bentley and given her information. He insisted, however, that none of this was espionage, that he had thought Bentley was a journalist and that he had only handed over publicly available information. He agreed that he had paid Bentley money, but said it was not CPUSA dues but payment for copies of newspapers she had given him. As for North and Golos, he described his meetings with them as innocuous and claimed that only much later did he realize that Joseph North might be a Communist. To prove his loyalty, Remington offered to work as an FBI informant, meet with North, and trap him into making compromising statements. Remington denied that he had ever been a Communist and insisted that although he had been a member of the Communist party's antiwar front group, the American Peace Mobilization, during the period of the Nazi-Soviet Pact, he had actually opposed the group's positions.

Remington's motive for his not very credible statements is unclear. When the FBI interviewed him in 1947, Remington was in the process of applying for a job with the Atomic Energy Commission. He may have tried to account for Bentley's evidence because he hoped that it might still be possible to pursue a government career if he convinced the FBI of his innocence. What he did not know was that the FBI had become convinced of his guilt even before the interview and had already torpedoed a previous attempt of his to get an important government job. After his wartime naval duty, Remington had gotten a position with the Office of War Mobilization and Reconversion. In December of 1946 the FBI learned that Remington was about to be transferred to a professional position in the White House as an aide to one of President Truman's special assistants. An FBI warning that Remington was a suspected Soviet agent put an end to that promotion. The FBI was equally unenthusiastic about the prospect that a Soviet intelligence contact would get a job at the Atomic Energy Commission, and that bid also came to nothing.[102]

Called before a grand jury, Remington did not invoke the right against self-incrimination when asked about his Communist background. In the course of his testimony he made statements that the government was able to prove to have been false. Among other points, Remington denied having taken part in Communist activities, a fact the government easily refuted with, among other evidence, the testimony of his former wife. He was convicted of perjury and imprisoned. Espionage, however, played only a background role in his perjury trial.[103]

Another person named by Bentley was imprisoned under special circumstances. In 1954 Congress passed the Compulsory Testimony Act, which granted authorities the option of offering immunity from prosecution in exchange for testimony. Immunity, of course, removed grounds for taking the Fifth. Edward Fitzgerald, one of those whom Bentley had named as a Soviet source, was given immunity. Fitzgerald still refused to testify and went to jail.

Aside from these two, however, none of the several dozen persons whom Bentley named as spies was tried, much less convicted and imprisoned. Because there were no trials, the FBI's collaborative evidence, impressive in its totality, remained confidential, kept secret in the FBI's files for more than three decades. Congressional investigative committees, chiefly the House Committee on Un-American Activities and the Senate Internal Security Subcommittee, called many of those whom Bentley had named to testify, but again most invoked the Fifth Amendment to avoid testifying. The committees put on the record some of the evidence corroborating Bentley's story, but it was incomplete, only part of what the FBI had accumulated. Further, the congressional investigative committees became enmeshed in partisan politics; a large segment of the public and many commentators dismissed anything brought out in the hearings as suspect. In light of these factors, the doubt that many people came to feel about Bentley's story produced, as one scholar wrote, the consensus that Bentley's charges were the "imaginings of a neurotic spinster."[104] The consensus, however, was wrong. The deciphered Venona cables show that Elizabeth Bentley had told the truth.

CHAPTER 6

MILITARY ESPIONAGE

Most examinations of Soviet espionage focus on Soviet spies linked to the foreign intelligence arm of the KGB. But the KGB's predominance was of recent origin, dating from the early years of World War II.[1] In the 1920s and 1930s the intelligence branch of the Soviet army, the GRU (Glavnoe razvedyvatelnoe upravlenie, or chief intelligence directorate of the Soviet general staff), had more extensive foreign intelligence operations than the KGB.[2] In the late 1920s the GRU had set up the first organized Soviet espionage operation in the United States. Alfred Tilton, a Latvian, and Lydia Stahl, a Russia-born American citizen, put together a courier service and photographic facilities and sought out military information. Tilton also recruited Nicholas Dozenberg, the first American GRU agent about whom much is known.

Nicholas Dozenberg

Born in Latvia in 1882, Nicholas Dozenberg immigrated to the United States in 1904. He joined the radical Lettish Workingmen's Society, the Latvian-language affiliate of the Socialist party, which split from that party in 1919 to form the new American Communist movement. By 1923 Dozenberg held the position of literature director of the Workers party, as the CPUSA then termed itself. He dropped out of open party work in 1927 to become an agent of the GRU under Alfred Tilton.[3]

Over the next decade Dozenberg carried out a variety of tasks for Soviet intelligence. Several involved use of American territory as the staging grounds for Soviet espionage operations aimed at foreign nations, particularly France and Romania. (In that era those nations as well as others were of higher priority to Soviet intelligence than was the United States.) He also assisted a Soviet GRU officer in obtaining American identity documents and a U.S. passport as Frank Kleges (the real Kleges was dead). The fake Kleges then proceeded to France to carry out GRU operations there under cover of his American identity. While working for the GRU, Dozenberg also established cover offices in China, representing an American radio manufacturer, and in the Philippines, marketing Bell and Howell motion picture equipment.

The ease with which Dozenberg was able to gain a Bell and Howell franchise for a cover business illustrates another aspect of Soviet intelligence operations in the United States in the 1930s. Dozenberg received authorization to represent Bell and Howell with the assistance of William Kruse, head of the company's film division.[4] Like Dozenberg, Kruse had been a mid-level CPUSA leader in the 1920s and had also served with the Comintern in Moscow for a time. In 1929 Jay Lovestone and several hundred of his adherents, including Kruse, were expelled for ideological deviation. For several years Lovestone and his followers termed themselves the "Communist Party (Opposition)" and continued to proclaim their loyalty to the Soviet Union, which several covertly demonstrated by assisting Soviet espionage.[5] Dozenberg had entered GRU service before Lovestone was expelled from the CPUSA, but he had been aligned with Lovestone and made full use of the continued willingness of some of Lovestone's followers to undertake Soviet intelligence tasks.

In the late 1930s Stalin unleashed a purge of the Soviet intelligence services in which hundreds of GRU and KGB officers were executed. Numerous Soviet intelligence officers serving abroad were recalled and arrested. Fearing for their lives, some dropped out of Soviet service. Whittaker Chambers, who worked for a GRU network in the United States, attributed his defection in part to fear of being called to Moscow. Nicholas Dozenberg also dropped out in the late 1930s. He attempted to live quietly in Oregon, but a more vocal GRU defector, Walter Krivitsky, exposed him as a GRU agent in an article published in the *Saturday Evening Post*. Arrested in December 1939, Dozenberg confessed, in exchange for being allowed to plead guilty to a single charge of using a false passport, and was sentenced to a year in prison in 1940. Dozenberg's statement confirmed, among other points, that Philip Rosenblit, a Communist dentist in New York, was part of the courier system for delivering Soviet money to Soviet intelligence networks in the United States as well as funds to subsidize the CPUSA itself. Dozenberg also stated that he had recruited Philip Aronberg, a veteran American Communist, for GRU assignments.[6]

Other American Agents of the GRU in the 1930s

A surprising fallout from Dozenberg's confession, however, was that what had earlier been regarded as an ordinary case of currency counterfeiting turned out to be part of a Soviet intelligence operation. In 1933 the U.S. Secret Service, which had jurisdiction over counterfeiting, traced some counterfeit money through an intermediary to Dr. Valentine Burtan, who refused to reveal to authorities the source of nearly $100,000 in counterfeit bills. He received a sentence of fifteen years. After Dozenberg's arrest in 1940 and his confession to having been a GRU agent, Burtan talked. He told the FBI that Dozenberg had been his source and that the money was to be used to finance Soviet covert operations. In addition to his role in the failed counterfeiting scheme, Burtan had been Dozenberg's partner in the American Rumanian Film Corporation, one of the business covers that Dozenberg had established to assist Soviet intelligence infiltration of Romania. Burtan had been a member of the CPUSA in the 1920s and had been expelled with Lovestone in 1929.[7]

Burtan's work for the GRU earned him reentry into the Communist movement. While in federal prison in 1935 he received a visit from a jeweler named Julius Heiman. In the early 1920s some of the Soviet subsidies provided to the American Communist movement had been in the form of jewelry rather than cash, and Heiman, a secret party member, was one of the outlets the CPUSA had used to convert the jewelry into currency. Max Bedacht, a senior CPUSA official, raised funds to assist Burtan's wife and family while he was in prison. William Edward Crane, who worked for the GRU in the 1930s—he was one of Whittaker Chambers's photographers—told the FBI that he remembered taking money, at the request of either Chambers or Boris Bykov, his GRU controller, to a woman in upper Manhattan who he thought was the wife of someone in jail for counterfeiting money. It was probably Mrs. Burtan. After Burtan left prison (he was paroled after ten years), he reestablished ties with the CPUSA.[8]

In the early 1930s the GRU replaced Tilton as head of its U.S. operations with Mark Zilbert, also known as Moishe Stern and later, in the Spanish Civil War, as General Kleber. One of his major operations was foiled when a source he had recruited to steal military secrets went to the Office of Naval Intelligence and for months turned over faked material to the Russians. One of Zilbert's successors was Aleksandr Ulanovsky, who supervised Whittaker Chambers's early espionage endeavors. Another of Ulanovsky's contacts was Robert Gordon Switz, son of wealthy American parents, who obtained military plans pertaining to the Panama Canal through a network of American Communists. One of Switz's sources, U.S. Army corporal Robert Osman, was convicted of taking defense information but won reversal of the verdict on appeal. The Army, however, discharged him. Switz, arrested in 1933 while on a mission to France by French counterintelligence, made a full confession.[9] Another GRU agent, the Finnish-American Communist Arvid Jacobson, was also arrested, when he went on a GRU mission to Finland in 1933.

Some of the GRU's known activities in the United States during World War II are not mentioned in the decrypted Venona cables. Undoubtedly, these are among the thousands of cables that were never deciphered. But enough was decrypted to give a picture that looks remarkably like the outlines of the activities of the KGB, but on a smaller scale. In particular, like the KGB, the GRU habitually used ideologically motivated American Communists (Dozenberg and Chambers, for example) and veterans of the International Brigades as sources and agents.

Alger Hiss

A prime example of ideologically driven espionage was the activity of the most infamous Soviet spy linked to the GRU, Alger Hiss. Hiss was one of the original members of the Ware group of young American Communists in the Agricultural Adjustment Administration in the early 1930s, and he became a valued member of the CPUSA-GRU network managed by Whittaker Chambers. Hiss was only a mid-level State Department official at the time of Chambers's defection in 1938, but he was already marked as a rising star. And rise he did. By the end of World War II he was a senior assistant to the secretary of state and part of the American diplomatic delegation that accompanied President Roosevelt to Yalta in 1945 to negotiate the final stages of the war with Joseph Stalin and Winston Churchill. He headed the State Department's Office of Special Political Affairs, which oversaw United Nations diplomacy, and he presided at the founding conference of the UN in San Francisco in 1945. He left the State Department in 1946 to lead the prestigious Carnegie Endowment for International Peace.

Hiss was a highly respected member of the Washington establishment. Unbeknownst to the public and the press, however, Hiss had been very quietly eased out of the government by Truman administration officials who feared that he was a security risk and might become an embarrassment because of accumulating indications that he was in covert contact with Soviet intelligence. In 1945 Igor Gouzenko, a GRU cipher clerk who had defected in Ottawa, handed over to Canadian authorities more than a hundred Soviet military intelligence documents and his personal knowledge of GRU operations. Shocked Canadian authorities learned that the Soviets had used their wartime alliance with Canada as an opportunity to launch extensive espionage operations on Canadian soil. Gouzenko's documents and information allowed Canadian authorities to break up several GRU spy networks, discharge a number of government employees who had surreptitiously assisted the Soviets, and send five Soviet spies to prison. Those imprisoned included Allan Nunn May (a British scientist working in Canada on part of the British-American atomic bomb project), Fred Rose (a Communist member of the Canadian parliament), and Sam Carr (the national organizing secretary of the Communist Party of Canada). Canadian prime minister Mackenzie King contacted President Truman, and the Royal Canadian Mounted Police shared with American officials those parts of the Gouzenko investigation that bore on American matters. One of these was that Gouzenko had heard other GRU officers bragging that the agency had a source who was an assistant to the American secretary of state.[10] In the same year, and independently of Gouzenko, Elizabeth Bentley told the FBI that one member of the Perlo group had earlier been part of a separate Soviet network headed by Alger Hiss. And, of course, by this time the FBI had begun to pay attention to Chambers's 1939 information, given to Assistant Secretary of State Berle, that Hiss had been part of a covert Communist group.

Chambers told the House Committee on Un-American Activities in 1948 that Hiss had been a member of the Ware group in the early 1930s. Initially he did not accuse Hiss of espionage, only of having been a Communist. Hiss demanded and got an opportunity to reply. He flatly denied any Communist links and denied even knowing Chambers. Hiss's rebuttal carried the day with the press, but the committee persisted, and Hiss's story began to crumble. Chambers provided details of a close relationship with the Hiss family during the 1930s, and Hiss began to backtrack, stating that he had known Chambers, but under a different name and only casually. He continued to deny any Communist connections.

Hiss increasingly found himself on the defensive. Chambers said, for example, that Hiss had given the Communist party an old car he no longer needed for use by a party organizer. Hiss testified that he had sold the car to Chambers as part of a deal in which Chambers rented an apartment from Hiss. Congressional investigators, however, produced motor vehicle records bearing Hiss's signature to show that ownership of the auto had been signed over to an official of the Communist party. Press coverage began to shift from overwhelmingly pro-Hiss to a more neutral stance. Chambers was protected from a slander suit when testifying before a congressional committee, and Hiss then attempted to regain the offensive with a challenge to Chambers to repeat his claims outside of a congressional hearing. It was an ill-advised ploy. Chambers repeated his charges on the television program *Meet the Press*. After a three-week delay that caused consternation among his supporters, Hiss sued.

In preparation for the slander trial, Hiss's lawyers demanded that Chambers produce any documents relevant to his charge that Hiss had been a Communist. Chambers, to the lawyers' surprise, did have documents, ones he had not discussed with the House Committee on Un-American Activities. They included four sheets of paper in Hiss's handwriting with summaries of State Department information, sixty-five typewritten pages copied from confidential State Department material that had passed through Hiss's office in 1938 (and many pages that experts identified as having been typed on Hiss's typewriter kept at his residence), and two microfilm strips of State Department documents from 1938 with Hiss's initials on them. Although the documents did not prove that Hiss had been a Communist, they were powerful evidence that he been a spy. A grand jury looked into the matter and indicted Hiss for perjury. The statute of limitations had expired for an espionage charge, but the charge of having lied under oath to the grand jury when he made statements to the effect that he had never passed documents to Chambers was a way of getting at the same offense. After one hung jury, Hiss was convicted in 1950 and imprisoned for three and a half years.

The evidence at the trial and that which has appeared subsequently from Russian archives firmly establishes Hiss's espionage on behalf of the Soviet Union in the 1930s.[11] But what was until recently left open was whether Hiss's betrayal of the United States continued beyond the 1930s. Chambers's personal knowledge and the documents he produced were all from that decade. A number of persons who spied for the Soviet Union in those years later deserted the Communist cause. Some, like Chambers, later publicly acknowledged their role. Others quietly dropped out of espionage.

Some commentators have thought Hiss belonged to the latter group and speculated that when the Nazi-Soviet Pact was concluded in 1939, someone of Hiss's idealism would have seen that his faith in the Soviet cause was misplaced. In 1990, however, a onetime KGB officer, Oleg Gordievsky, stated that Hiss had continued to work for the Soviets in the 1940s.[12] The Venona decryptions support his claim. Hiss is named openly in one message, a 1943 GRU cable noting that a KGB report about the State Department mentioned Hiss. The remainder of the message was undeciphered and the significance of the cable unknown.[13] The Venona Project also deciphered a KGB message about a meeting between a KGB officer and a GRU source with the cover name Ales. And Ales, the evidence indicates, was Alger Hiss. While the KGB, GRU, and Naval GRU tended to keep their networks independent of each other, cross-agency contacts were far from rare. Further, the KGB had the authority to poach on the territory of the GRU and Naval GRU, appropriating their sources if it wished. In the history of Soviet espionage, the most notable example of this is atomic spying. The GRU penetrated Britain's early atomic bomb program and developed one of the Soviets' most important sources, Klaus Fuchs. But when Stalin made atomic espionage a priority, the KGB took over much of the GRU's atomic espionage operation, and when Fuchs came to work on the American atomic bomb program, he was already firmly under KGB jurisdiction.[14]

Before dealing with the Venona message on Ales, however, we should take note of a KGB document located by the historian Allen Weinstein. This cable, dated March 5, 1945, from the KGB office in Washington to Moscow, states that the Washington office had asked one of its agents, Ruble, to report on Ales. Ruble was the cover name in the Venona traffic for Harold Glasser, a Treasury Department official who spied for the Soviets. According to the cable, " 'Ruble' gives to 'Ales' an exceptionally good political reference as to a member of the Communist Party. 'Ruble' informs [me] that 'Ales' is a strong, determined man with a firm and resolute character."[15] Glasser, who, like Hiss, had been an active member of the Washington Communist underground in the 1930s, would have been qualified to give this evaluation of Hiss.

The March 5 cable is then followed by a deciphered March 30 Venona message about Ales. The NSA/FBI footnote to the Ales message identifies Ales as "probably Alger Hiss." It was not a difficult identification to make. The description of Ales in the KGB message fits Hiss, and it is difficult to imagine its fitting anyone but Hiss.[16]

"As a result of A.'s chat with Ales," the report notes, "the following has been ascertained: 1. Ales has been working with the Neighbors continuously since 1935." The Neighbors was KGB jargon for the GRU. Chambers had Hiss entering the CPUSA underground in 1934 and beginning to steal documents in 1935, and contended that Hiss was part of a group that came under GRU supervision. A. is unidentified, but the context of other KGB Venona messages suggests that it was the initial of Albert, the cover name of the illegal officer Iskhak Akhmerov. (The defector Gordievsky had linked Akhmerov to Hiss.)

"2. For some years past he has been the leader of a small group of the Neighbors' probationers, for the most part consisting of his relations." "Probationers" was standard KGB jargon for agents. Hiss's closest associates in his espionage work were his wife, Priscilla, who typed many of the documents he stole from the State Department, and his brother Donald, who also worked for the State Department for a time.

"3. The group and Ales himself work on obtaining military information only. Materials on the Bank allegedly interest the Neighbors very little and he does not produce them regularly. 4. All the last few years Ales has been working with Pol [unidentified] who also meets other members of the group occasionally. 5. Recently Ales and his whole group were awarded Soviet decorations." This passage indicates that Ales worked for the State Department (Bank), as Hiss did. It also says that the Neighbors/GRU were pressing Ales to produce military rather than the diplomatic information more readily available to him. In the 1920s and early 1930s, when the GRU dominated Soviet foreign intelligence operations, its networks sought political and strategic information as well as more narrowly defined military intelligence. But as the KGB established its supremacy in foreign intelligence, the GRU's jurisdiction was steadily narrowed. It had to get its agents to produce more strictly military information or risk losing them to the KGB. The GRU's stress on military intelligence may explain the extraordinary proposal Hiss made in September 1945, that the State Department create a new post, that of "special assistant for military affairs" linked to his Office of Special Political Affairs. The GRU's need for military intelligence also explains why when security officers belatedly began to look closely at Hiss in 1946 they discovered that he had obtained top secret reports "on atomic energy . . . and other matters relating to military intelligence" that were outside the scope of his Office of Special Political Affairs, which dealt largely with United Nations diplomacy.[17]

"6. After the Yalta Conference, when he had gone on to Moscow, a Soviet personage in a very responsible position (Ales gave to understand that it was Comrade Vishinski [the deputy Soviet foreign minister]) allegedly got in touch with Ales and at the behest of the Military Neighbors passed on to him their gratitude and so on." This passage indicates that Ales had been at the Yalta conference and had returned to the United States through Moscow. After the Yalta conference, most of the American delegation returned directly to the United States via Iran. Those Americans attending from the U.S. embassy in Moscow returned to Moscow but did not, as Ales did, then proceed quickly to the United States. (This message came only a month after the Yalta conference ended.) There was, however, a small party of four State Department officials who flew to Moscow to wrap up some details with the Soviets and then proceeded after a brief layover to Washington. There has never been any allegation or evidence that three of them—Secretary of State Edward Stettinius, Director of the Office of European Affairs H. Freeman Matthews, and Wilder Foote, Stettinius's press aide—were Soviet agents. The fourth official was Alger Hiss.[18]

Another illustration of the overlap and mutual corroboration of the testimony of Whittaker Chambers, various Venona messages (that on Ales/Hiss discussed in this chapter and those on Glasser, Victor Perlo, and Charles Kramer discussed in chapter 5), and the KGB documents cited by Weinstein is a passage from Elizabeth Bentley's FBI deposition in 1945:

> Referring again to Harold Glasser, I recall that after his return from his assignment in Europe, probably in Italy, for the United States Treasury Department, Victor Perlo told me that Glasser had asked him if he would be able to get back in with the Perlo group. I asked Perlo how Glasser happened to leave the group and he explained that Glasser and one or two others had been taken sometime before by some American in some governmental agency in Washington, and that this unidentified American turned Glasser and the others over to some Russian. Perlo declared he did not know the identity of this American, and said that Charley Kramer, so far as he knew, was the only person who had this information. Sometime later I was talking with Kramer in New York City, and brought up this matter to him. At this time Kramer told me that the person who had originally taken Glasser away from Perlo's group was named Hiss and that he was in the U.S. State Department.[19]

Between Bentley's testimony, the Ales Venona cable, and the new KGB documents Weinstein located in Moscow, there is little doubt that Hiss's service to Soviet intelligence continued beyond the 1930s and at least until 1945.

Arthur Adams

Arthur Adams was a long-term Soviet agent whose American ties went back to the earliest years of a Soviet presence in the United States. The connections he developed immediately after the formation of the Soviet Union enabled him to build an agent network that paid dividends in the 1940s. While the FBI apparently was able to neutralize his efforts at atomic espionage far more successfully than it countered the KGB's, many of the details of his network of agents and their activities remain obscure. Adams himself was not identified in the Venona messages, nor were several of his close collaborators. Either they are among the cover names that have never been identified or else the messages dealing with them were never decrypted.

Adams was an Old Bolshevik. Born either in one of the Scandinavian countries or the Baltic regions of the Russian empire, he knew Lenin from pre-revolutionary days in Russia. He entered the United States in 1910 as an immigrant and first came into public view as the head of the "technical department" of the Soviet Russian Information Bureau during 1919–1921. The United States did not officially recognize Lenin's new Soviet regime, and the Information Bureau was the Soviet government's unofficial embassy. The head of the Information Bureau, Ludwig Martens, said that Adams had been born in Russia but had acquired British citizenship and was a graduate of the School of Science in Kronstadt, Russia, and the University of Toronto. The U.S. government expelled Martens and Adams in 1921 and ordered the Information Bureau closed.[20]

Adams returned to the United States in the 1920s and 1930s, ostensibly on missions for Amtorg but actually in his role as a GRU officer. In the 1920s he also divorced his first wife (who had arrived in the United States in 1914) and married Dorothea Keen, the American-born daughter of a Russian immigrant, who had also been on the staff of the Soviet Russian Information Bureau. Adams entered the United States through Canada with a false passport in 1938. Soon afterward he set up a business called Technological Laboratories with a New Jersey man named Philip Levy. On the surface Levy, born in Russia in 1893, was a respectable businessman, the president of Federated Trading Corporation in New York, a textile firm engaged in import-export. In 1935, however, an associate of his, Leon Josephson, was arrested in Copenhagen and charged with espionage on behalf of the Soviet Union. Josephson claimed he was on a business trip in connection with Levy's firm. One of the men arrested with Josephson was traveling under a false American passport made out to Nicholas Sherman. Sherman was Aleksandr Ulanovsky, the GRU officer who directed Soviet espionage in the United States in the early 1930s. Levy did more than merely provide a business cover for Josephson's covert activities. Josephson's files and those of other members of the CPUSA's underground arm were hidden in Levy's residence, where they were found in a secret FBI search in 1944. Levy, however, told a congressional committee that he was not aware of Josephson's activities, and he also denied knowing anything about Technological Laboratories, the firm headed by Adams, although Levy was one of the company's officers.[21]

Adams had other associates who were part of the CPUSA underground. Just like Akhmerov, the KGB's leading illegal officer, the GRU's Adams treated the CPUSA as a recruiting pool for the GRU and the party's underground as an auxiliary to his espionage activities. When the FBI undertook surveillance of Adams during World War II, its agents observed that Adams visited Victoria Stone, owner of the Victoria Stone Jewelry Corporation, almost daily either at her home or at her store on Madison Avenue. In 1935 Stone had approached an attorney to get legal help for Dr. Valentine Burtan, the Lovestoneite who had been convicted of involvement in a counterfeiting scheme run by the GRU agent Nicholas Dozenberg. Julius Heiman, who visited Burtan in prison, was the secretary-treasurer of Stone's jewelry company. Heiman, as noted above, had arranged to convert jewels sent by the Comintern in the early 1920s into cash for the CPUSA. Still another business associate of Adams in the late 1930s was M. G. Kahn, who had been arrested in 1919 for smuggling jewels into the United States from Russia.[22]

The FBI became interested in Adams in 1943 when he was observed attempting to recruit as sources several scientists working at the Manhattan Project's Chicago laboratories. After observing these meetings, FBI and Manhattan Project security men surreptitiously entered Adams's apartment in New York. They discovered very sophisticated camera equipment, materials for constructing microdots, and notes on aspects of experiments being conducted at the atomic bomb laboratories at Oak Ridge, Tennessee.[23]

As cover for his espionage activities, Adams was employed by two companies headed by Communists. The Electronics Corporation of America, led by Sam Novick, held Navy contracts for the manufacture of radar. Novick, who had signed Adams's immigration papers when he entered the United States illegally from Canada in 1938, had falsely stated that Adams had been employed by him for ten years. The Keynote Recording Company, headed by Eric Bernay, a former editor of *New Masses,* paid Adams a salary. Early in 1945 Bernay helped Adams escape FBI surveillance and leave New York. Adams left Victoria Stone's apartment and walked a dog up a one-way street, then hailed a taxicab and fled before FBI agents could follow. He then boarded a train with Bernay. The FBI picked them up in Chicago, trailed Adams to Portland, and prevented him from boarding a Soviet ship. The State Department, fearful of offending the Soviets, ordered the FBI not to arrest him but also not to let him leave the country. Adams, however, later evaded FBI surveillance, disappeared, and presumably returned to the USSR.[24]

Joseph Bernstein and *Amerasia*

Although Adams's activities are not visible in the few GRU messages deciphered by the Venona Project, other GRU agents were identified. One agent whose activities were exposed was Joseph Bernstein, whose cover name in Venona is Marquis. Bernstein was a suspect in the first major post–World War II espionage case, the *Amerasia* affair, but was never indicted. Venona documents Bernstein's other activities on behalf of Soviet intelligence, while throwing some light on *Amerasia* itself.

Security officers from the Office of Strategic Services, investigating how portions of a secret report had come to be printed in the journal *Amerasia,* which was published by the wealthy, pro-Soviet greeting-card entrepreneur Philip Jaffe, secretly entered the magazine's offices in the spring of 1945 and discovered hundreds of classified government documents. When the case was turned over to the FBI, it wiretapped and bugged several of the editors and their contacts in Washington. One such bug, in a Washington hotel room occupied by Jaffe on May 7, 1945, picked up a conversation with Andrew Roth, a lieutenant in the Office of Naval Intelligence assigned as a liaison officer to the State Department. Jaffe mentioned to Roth that Joseph Bernstein, a former *Amerasia* employee, had told him that for many years he had worked for Soviet intelligence. According to Jaffe, Bernstein had said, "I would like to ask you whether you are willing to give me the dope you get on Chungking out of the Far Eastern Division of the State Department."[25]

Jaffe was willing to help Bernstein, but he insisted on checking his bona fides as a Soviet agent. The day after Bernstein's request, Jaffe visited first John Stuart, a writer for *New Masses,* and then Earl Browder at his home in Yonkers. Although the FBI observed Jaffe's meetings with Bernstein, Stuart, and Browder, it was not able to overhear the conversations. But Jaffe recounted them to Roth and to the hidden FBI microphones. Browder had advised Jaffe to insist on meeting Bernstein's Soviet contact. If he was genuine, "he'll find a way to prove it. If he can't find a way, don't deal with him. It may be that he [Bernstein] is ... on his own, and he just wants to put a feather in his own cap, if he can get a little something. And if it's just personal, nothing doing. Don't touch it."[26]

Although Jaffe and Bernstein held several more meetings, monitored by the FBI, and may even have exchanged some information, Bernstein apparently had not yet been able to arrange a meeting between Jaffe and his Soviet superiors when Jaffe, Roth, and several associates were arrested on June 6 on charges of conspiracy to commit espionage. Although the FBI believed that Bernstein was a Soviet agent, it never arrested him, in part because the stenographer who transcribed the bugged conversation rendered his name as Bursley and perhaps because the evidence gained by bugging was inadmissible in court.[27]

Confirmation that Bernstein was a GRU agent comes from the Venona decryptions. They make clear that he provided the GRU with information he received from several sources. And they shed light on the activities of two other spies, Philip and Mary Jane Keeney, who worked for both the KGB and the GRU.

There are five decrypted messages mentioning Marquis/Bernstein, all from 1943.[28] In one, Pavel Mikhailov, the GRU chief in New York, noted that Marquis had reported that he had become friends with T. A. Bisson, who was named in plain text and then given the cover name Arthur. Bisson had just left the Board of Economic Warfare and was with the Institute of Pacific Relations and "in the editorial office of Marquis's periodical."[29] Bernstein was then working for *Amerasia,* and Bisson was a close collaborator of Jaffe's. Bisson, who had been a staunch supporter of the Chinese Communists for many years, had been a founding editorial board member of both *China Today* and *Amerasia.* He was also a leading promoter of the view that the Chinese Communists under Mao Tse-tung were not real Marxist-Leninists. He wrote that the correct terminology for "so-called Communist China" was "democratic China," and that the system in place in Mao's areas was "in fact, the essence of *bourgeois* democracy."[30] When he testified before the Special Committee on Un-American Activities in 1943, Bisson denied Communist sympathies. All of his activities, he swore, had been devoted to promoting greater understanding of the USSR and China in the United States. Presumably in the interest of promoting greater understanding, Bisson turned over confidential Board of Economic Warfare reports to Bernstein in 1943, and the GRU dispatched them by diplomatic pouch, meanwhile notifying Moscow by cable that the reports included a valuable joint British-American evaluation of the military situation on the Russian-German front as well as reports on American troops shipped to China, a report by the Chinese embassy in Washington about trade between Chinese industrialists and the Japanese in China, and a report by the American consul on conditions in Vladivostok.[31]

In another message, Bernstein reported on the views of William Phillips, FDR's special envoy to India, and provided information about material *Amerasia* had received from a journalist who had interviewed the Chinese minister of war. A third Venona message contained more information from Bisson about Chiang Kai-shek's efforts to combat the Chinese Communists and discussions within the U.S. government about making direct contact with the Chinese Communists to arrange the establishment of air bases on territory they controlled.[32]

The Librarian Spies: Philip and Mary Jane Keeney

Bernstein also supervised another pair of agents with interesting radical credentials—Philip and Mary Jane Keeney. The Keeneys were librarians who first came to prominence in 1937 when Philip's firing by the president of the University of Montana for radical activity elicited widespread protests. While awaiting resolution of their court challenge to the dismissal, the Keeneys lived in Berkeley, California, and were in frequent contact with Communists; indeed, Mary Jane's diaries indicate that they were members of the Marin County CPUSA club. In 1940 Philip was hired at the Library of Congress and soon transferred to the Office of Strategic Services, where he served as a librarian. Mary Jane worked for the Board of Economic Warfare during World War II. Both were active in CPUSA fronts in Washington and friendly with many of those later accused of espionage, including the Silvermasters, William Ullmann, and Maurice Halperin. On November 1, 1945, Mary Jane left for Europe, where she worked for the Allied Staff on Reparations. Philip, meanwhile, left for Tokyo, where he worked on General MacArthur's staff, helping rebuild the Japanese library system. Mary Jane Keeney returned to the United States on March 9, 1946, to be met by the GRU agent Joseph Bernstein. Philip came home in the fall before returning to Japan in January 1947.[33]

The Keeneys are mentioned in three deciphered Venona messages.[34] The first is a KGB message from General Fitin in Moscow to Vasily Zubilin in New York in May 1942. The message has been only partially deciphered, but it appears to contain either suggestions by the Moscow KGB headquarters on persons who might be used to penetrate the OSS or comments by Moscow on suggestions made earlier by Zubilin. At that time a large section of the OSS staff was housed at the Library of Congress, and the cable mentions that Jacob Golos met Philip Keeney there. In response, on May 22 Zubilin noted that Keeney "is being entrusted to our agentura," a statement that his recruitment would be undertaken.[35] Keeney, however, was not recruited by the KGB in 1942. The reason may be that he was already working for the GRU. Sergey Kurnakov, a Russian immigrant and one of the KGB's most industrious agents, noted in a report in 1944 that "Keeney and his wife were signed on apparently by the Neighbors [GRU] for work in 1940."[36]

In 1944, however, the KGB decided that it was time to push the GRU out of the picture. Through "a highly confidential source," an FBI euphemism for a break-in, the bureau obtained a copy of Mary Jane Keeney's diaries from 1938 to 1945. It also intercepted and read correspondence between Mary Jane and Philip. This material chronicles Kurnakov's takeover of the two for the KGB. One month before Kurnakov's report about their GRU affiliation, the Keeneys had dinner with someone identified in the diaries as Colonel Thomas. Thomas "takes us to dinner and then discovers he came on a wild goose chase," in Mary Jane's words.[37] Thomas was, the FBI determined, Mary Jane's cover name for Kurnakov. One factor identifying Kurnakov as Thomas was that the diary records Colonel Thomas's leaving the United States to return to his homeland at the same time as Kurnakov returned to the Soviet Union. Several letters refer to Thomas's impending departure. On December 20 Philip noted in regard to Thomas, "It is wonderful for him that he is returning. It makes me green with envy." A handwritten note from Thomas was found indicating that around January 10, 1946, he would be going home. Kurnakov left the United States in January 1946. The "wild goose chase" was, of course, Thomas's discovery that the Keeneys were already working for Soviet intelligence.

Kurnakov, however, was not deterred by the GRU connection, and sometime between August 1944 and November 1945 the Keeneys went to work for the KGB. In November Philip was in New York, preparing to leave for Japan. He wrote Mary Jane several letters that make his intentions and loyalties clear. On November 22 he noted that "our friends, including Thomas, have made it clear there is a job to do and it falls to my lot to do it." On November 24 he indicated that while in New York he intended to see Colonel Thomas and Joe Bernstein. On November 29 he proudly wrote that he had spent several hours "with Col. Thomas which is a pass word to use in the higher circles." On December 1: "Last night I had a long session with Col. Thomas and I left with a terrible sense of responsibility."[38]

Philip Keeney had been recruited by the KGB but had not yet provided intelligence information when he went to Japan. Several letters to his wife suggested that his work for Soviet military intelligence under Joseph Bernstein had not been very productive. On February 2, 1946, he wrote to Mary Jane from Tokyo that "I presume word from Col. Thomas will be reaching us both in due course. I am certain we will be reached when something turns up for us to do. I have the feeling, at any rate, that we are both on call now which is more that I have felt for months past." And, two months later, he reflected that "probably, I might not have come to Japan, had it not been for my serious confabs with Col. Thomas. Now that I am here it seems as if I were repeating the long dry spell that twice occurred when we were part of Joe B's plans. I should have followed Greg's advice and relaxed."[39]

The Keeneys' equanimity was disturbed by the escalating investigations into Soviet espionage in 1946, prompted by Elizabeth Bentley's defection and that of Igor Gouzenko in Canada. In March 1946 Mary Jane sent a letter to Philip in Japan via a friend, warning him to be careful of what he wrote to such old acquaintances as the Silvermasters. Their friends were afraid they were being wiretapped and their mail examined. She concluded that "Joe told me to be on the lookout as well as several others in New York. There is no reason for alarm on your part or mine only it is well to remember that it's better to be safe than sorry." Two months later she wrote that their old GRU contact was temporarily on ice: "Joe B. [Bernstein] doesn't expect to be back in the swim for a long long time. He says that the Canadian affair will have a very lingering effect."[40] The "Canadian affair" was a reference to Gouzenko's defection in Ottawa.

The Keeneys both lost their government jobs but never were prosecuted for their espionage. Mary Jane secured a job at the United Nations, from which she was also fired under pressure from the American government. They were called to testify to a congressional investigating committee, were uncooperative and convicted of contempt of Congress. The convictions, however, were reversed on appeal. The two then opened an art film club. Joseph Bernstein, their original GRU handler, also escaped prosecution and worked as a translator and writer.

The GRU and the Lincoln Battalion

Several GRU agents identified in Venona were veterans of the Abraham Lincoln battalion. There is only one Venona message about Daniel Abraham Zaret, named in plain text in a message from New York to Moscow. Zaret, who served as aide-de-camp to the commander of the International Brigades' Fifteenth Division in Spain, returned to the United States in November 1938. Until August 1943 he worked in various explosives factories, at the last one as assistant director in Williamsport, Pennsylvania. He was slated to become production safety inspector in the Explosives Division of the War Department in Chicago when the New York GRU office informed Moscow that Zaret had already passed on to his GRU contact some data on material being used for shells, bombs, and torpedoes.[41]

Other information came to the GRU from Thomas Babin, a Communist organizer and Spanish Civil War veteran. Babin, born in 1901 in Croatia, was deported from the United States for Communist activities in 1925 but reentered by 1928 and remained illegally, serving as a leader of the Croatian Communists in America and one of the CPUSA leaders on the New York waterfront. He served in Spain from 1937 to 1939, first in a Balkan unit and then in the Abraham Lincoln battalion. During World War II Babin worked as a longshoreman in Hoboken, New Jersey, and briefly served in the OSS.[42]

Under the cover name Brem in Venona, Babin kept the GRU closely informed about his OSS activities.[43] Babin was apparently being trained, along with a group of other Yugoslavs, to be sent first to Cairo and then to Yugoslavia itself as liaison with anti-Nazi partisans. Babin vouched for several of his fellow trainees as potential GRU contacts, but an illness or injury prevented him from accompanying them when they left the United States. In one message, in July 1943, the New York GRU station queried Moscow: "Since they were recommended to the school by Brem [Babin] at our request, he asks what is to be done if they go without him."[44] Apart from his activities with the OSS, Babin provided a steady stream of information to the GRU about American shipping in New York harbor. The data on cargoes, types of ships, and destinations probably came to Babin from a network of Communist sailors and longshoremen.

Leonard Mins: The Spy Who Was Hard to Miss

The most blatant GRU agent was Leonard Mins. That he could ever have been in a position to provide classified information to the Soviet Union testifies to the ease with which the American government could be infiltrated. Mins worked for the OSS for a little over a year, from 1942 to late 1943, spending most of his time on a survey of strategic minerals and oil reserves in Asia and the USSR. He was called before the Dies Committee in 1943. He flatly denied being a member of the CPUSA or a Communist of any kind, but Mins conceded that he had taught at the Communist-controlled Workers School, served on the editorial board of *Partisan Review* when it was under party control, been a member of the CPUSA's John Reed Clubs, written for the CPUSA's *New Masses,* and been a member of the CPUSA-aligned League of American Writers. He admitted living in Moscow from 1934 to 1936 but insisted that he had done nothing more than undertake translations for the Soviet Academy of Sciences.[45]

His testimony was difficult to believe, and within a few months the OSS fired Mins. His record was more incredible than even the Dies Committee had thought. Although he had testified that he had been working for the Soviet Academy of Sciences during his time in Moscow, actually he was working for the Communist International. In 1935 the American representative to the Comintern asked the CPUSA to corroborate information that Mins had provided to the Comintern in Moscow. Mins had told the Comintern that he had joined the CPUSA in 1919, worked for the Communist movement in Germany in 1920 and 1921, worked for the Executive Committee of the Comintern as a translator in 1924 and 1925, worked for the Communist movement in Germany from 1925 to 1927, done party work in the United States from 1927 to 1932, and had transferred his party membership to the Communist Party of the Soviet Union in 1934.[46] Mins was in France in 1938 working with exiled anti-Nazi German writers, one of whom was the father of the later notorious East German spymaster and Stasi (secret political police) officer Markus Wolf. In his memoirs Wolf recalled his old friend Leonhard [Leonard] Mins, "a Communist exile who had been my parents' close friend" in Russia. "He had been the channel through which my father was able to communicate with us during his internment in France."[47]

Elizabeth Bentley later wrote that one member of her network had run into Mins at OSS headquarters and was afraid to be seen in his company, as he was such a well-known Communist. Bentley complained to Golos, who agreed that it was folly to use Mins as a spy: he was so obviously a Communist "that he might just as well go around

Washington with the hammer and sickle painted on his chest and waving a red flag."[48]

Nonetheless, Mins, who had the cover name Smith in the GRU Venona messages, worked in the Russian section of the OSS.[49] The messages show him reporting to the GRU on the training of American military intelligence officers to break Soviet codes, and trying to obtain a highly secret OSS report on discussions between President Roosevelt and Prime Minister Churchill concerning the USSR.

Mins also worked as a talent-spotter for other potential Soviet sources. He told the GRU that one of his friends, Isador Steinberg, had been hired "in the War Department as a member of the publications bureau and expert on military publications matters." Steinberg, Mins reported, "is a Corporant [GRU term for CPUSA members] and owner of the firm Production Illustration in New York." Mins, who had known Steinberg for fifteen years, strongly recommended him for recruitment. The New York GRU station commented, "We consider that the latter [Steinberg] will be useful to us both as a source for secret publications of the War Department and for general military and political information."[50] Another message reported the potential recruitment of an unidentified government employee given the cover name Clarke, and observed that Clarke was not a Communist and that Mins was approaching him cautiously. A further GRU message reported that Mins had met with a U.S. Army lieutenant colonel and had suggested an economics professor in Nashville as a possible recruit. Because of the OSS investigation of Mins, the New York GRU noted that he had "been instructed to refrain for the moment from private meetings" with these potential sources.[51]

An August 1943 GRU message demonstrated Mins's attitudes toward loyalty and betrayal. After General Donovan fired Mins from the OSS, Mins appealed for reinstatement to the Civil Service Commission. In this message Mins proudly reported to Soviet intelligence that six of his OSS colleagues, including Arthur Robinson, chief of the OSS Russian Section, testified that Mins was loyal and could be trusted.

The GRU Mole

The GRU also planted in the United States at least one long-term penetration agent, the classic "mole" of espionage fiction. Although he posed as an immigrant, he was actually a professional GRU officer. He appeared in Los Angeles in 1938 claiming to be a Canadian immigrant of Polish birth and carrying a Canadian passport identifying him as Ignacy Witczak. He enrolled in the University of Southern California, earned bachelor's and master's degrees in political science, and was admitted to a doctoral program. He had a wife and young child. He was exposed in 1945 when Igor Gouzenko, a GRU code clerk, defected from the Soviet embassy in Canada. Gouzenko was familiar with Witczak because of an error the GRU had made in creating his fake identify.

The GRU's Witczak (his real name is unknown) had taken the passport of a real person of Polish birth who had immigrated to Canada in 1930 and become a Canadian citizen in 1936. The real Ignacy Witczak had also fought in Spain with the International Brigades, which had collected the passports of many of its American and Canadian volunteers and turned them over to Soviet intelligence for their use. The GRU had thought that Witczak had died in Spain and so appropriated his identity for one of their agents. The real Witczak, however, had survived and returned to Canada. This produced a problem in 1945 when the fake Witczak's Canadian passport expired. Renewal of the passport could trigger a discovery that there were two Witczaks. GRU officers directed Sam Carr, head of the Canadian Communist party and a Soviet agent, to pay a bribe of three thousand dollars to a Canadian official to take care of the problem. Less than a week after this successful transaction, Gouzenko defected and alerted Canadian authorities to the scheme.

Informed of the Witczak matter by the Canadians, the FBI put him under surveillance. The bureau discovered that although his only known employment since 1938 was as a part-time instructor at the University of Southern California with an annual salary of $1,700, he had banked $16,000. Witczak traveled from Los Angeles to New York and Washington in 1946, all the while under FBI surveillance. He was observed passing material to an attorney, Leonard Cohen, who worked for the Interior Department and whom he appeared to have met by prearrangement at the Library of Congress. In New York FBI agents surreptitiously searched his hotel room and turned up a notebook with names and addresses, one of which was that of the family residence of Winston Burdett (chapter 3). Probably alerted about Gouzenko's defection, Witczak appeared to have detected the surveillance and vanished in late 1945 and is presumed to have returned to the Soviet Union.

Gouzenko had the impression that Witczak was establishing a deep-cover reserve espionage apparatus to be activated if a break in American-Soviet diplomatic relations or some other trauma disrupted the networks run by GRU officers operating under diplomatic cover. According to the retired FBI agent Robert Lamphere, the bureau had located several persons in California whom Witczak had recruited and obtained confessions from some of them, although none was ever prosecuted. Dr. Arnold Krieger, a former Communist, later testified that Witczak had attempted to recruit him for secret missions in Asia and Latin America. Although not identified by NSA/FBI analysts, Witczak is almost surely the Soviet illegal officer identified in the Venona traffic only by the initial "R." The San Francisco KGB reported to Moscow in January 1946 that R.'s family had surreptitiously boarded the Soviet ship *Sakhalin* and left the United States. Inasmuch as FBI surveillance of Witczak's wife, Bunia, who also had a false Canadian passport, and their American-born son indicated that they had slipped aboard the *Sakhalin* at that time, it is very likely that R. was Witczak.[52]

One Canadian GRU agent mentioned in the decrypted Venona documents was Fred Rose, a leader of the Canadian Communist party. Born in Poland, Rose had become a Canadian citizen in 1926. Early in the 1940s he was in secret communication with Jacob Golos. Elizabeth Bentley reported that Sam Carr and Rose turned over several Canadians to Golos for liaison with the KGB. One was Hazen Sise, a veteran of the Spanish Civil War who worked in the Canadian Film Bureau Office in Washington.[53] Rose was elected to the House of Commons in 1943 as a candidate of the Labor-Progressive party, the political arm of the Canadian Communists at the time. In a message dated August 12, 1943, Pavel Mikhailov, the GRU station chief in New York, proudly cabled Moscow that "Fred, our man in Lesovia ["Forestland," i.e., Canada] has been elected to the Lesovian parliament."[54] Rose was arrested after Gouzenko's disclosures and sentenced to six years in prison. After his release in 1951 he left for Communist Poland, where he died in 1983.

Other American Agents of the GRU in the 1940s

Another ring of GRU agents was connected with Charles Irving Velson, a member of the Communist party's secret apparatus. Velson had a distinguished Communist pedigree. His mother, Clara Lemlich Shavelson, was a rank-and-file garment worker, whose impassioned speech in

1909 was credited with sparking an industry-wide walkout led by the International Ladies Garment Workers' Union. She went on to a long career as a Communist. Charles Velson (he changed his name in 1939 or 1940) was a machinist who worked at the Brooklyn Navy Yard from 1931 to 1938. Congressional investigators believed that while there he was a mail drop for J. Peters, who headed the secret apparatus, and that Velson was also involved in Cpl. Robert Osman's espionage activities on behalf of the GRU in the Panama Canal Zone. The latter suspicion is supported by Robert Gladnick, a former CPUSA functionary and Lincoln Brigade veteran who knew Velson. He wrote that in the early 1930s Velson assisted Bernard Chester, then director of the CPUSA's antimilitarist work, in a program to develop secret Communist groups among American military personnel. In the mid-1930s, Gladnick said, Velson replaced Chester as head of the antimilitarist effort. (Chester was the party name of Bernard Schuster, who in the early 1940s became the liaison between the CPUSA and the KGB.) When a congressional committee asked him about his relationship with Peters, Velson refused to answer.[55]

The deciphered Venona messages show Velson performing a number of tasks for the GRU.[56] In one he is assigned to approach a prospective Soviet source. In another he reports that he has heard about some experiments dealing with the testing of a seventy-five-millimeter cannon but has thus far been unable to get the data. One message notes that Velson has endorsed the request of another GRU agent, Milton Schwartz, for a GRU loan of $1,200 to pay off debts incurred in taking care of his sick father.

The Naval GRU

Soviet naval intelligence, known as the Naval GRU, was the smallest of the three Soviet spy agencies, much smaller than the Soviet army's intelligence arm, the GRU, and only a fraction of the size of the KGB. Nonetheless, it maintained a station in the United States and developed a number of valuable sources. One was Jack Fahy, who came into the Soviet orbit through service with the Comintern's International Brigades in the Spanish Civil War. Born in Washington, D.C., in 1908, he grew up in New York, where his father was senior partner of Walter J. Fahy and Co., a stock exchange firm. After working for Sen. George Moses and campaigning for Herbert Hoover's election to the presidency in

1928, Fahy joined the family firm. The stock market crash of 1929 jolted him out of Republicanism, and he joined the Socialist party. Fahy was both adventurous and peripatetic; at various times he attended New York University, the Institute of International Affairs in Geneva, San Marcus University in Peru, Black Mountain College in North Carolina, and Montana State University, where he took courses in animal husbandry. He established several small companies, including a food business in Peru in 1933. In 1937 he went to Spain to fight in the International Brigades but did so under the auspices of the Socialist party, not the Communist party.[57]

Fahy served as a truck driver in Spain, was wounded in 1938, and returned to the United States. He quickly quarreled with Norman Thomas, head of the Socialist party, over policy toward the Spanish Civil War and publicly resigned from the Socialist party in a letter published in the Communist *Daily Worker*. In the summer of 1939 Fahy met Robert Miller, a onetime Moscow correspondent, who had worked for the Spanish republic as a propagandist. Miller and Fahy set up the Hemisphere News Service to provide American newspapers with information from Latin America, with much of the money coming from Miller's family inheritance. They hired Joseph Gregg, who had served as a truck driver with Fahy in Spain, to handle the business side of Hemisphere. The company limped along until 1941, when it gained a contract from and was later absorbed by the Office of the Coordinator of Inter-American Affairs, a wartime agency that coordinated diplomacy, propaganda, and economic warfare in Central and South America.[58]

Fahy soon left the Office of the Co-ordinator of Inter-American Affairs and moved on to the Board of Economic Warfare, where he held a position as "Principal Intelligence Officer." In 1943, just as he was about to move to the Department of the Interior to become chairman of the Territorial Affairs Bureau, Rep. Martin Dies included him on a list of government employees suspected of communism. Fahy testified before the Kerr Commission set up to investigate the charges. He claimed that his letter of resignation from the Socialist party was "silly and foolish" and described his past association with Communists as a youthful misadventure. The commission agreed, concluding that after 1938 he "returned to his affairs, has joined no organizations, written no articles and made no speeches" and noted that many persons had testified to his good character. It praised his "loyal service" and concluded that he "has not been guilty of any subversive activity."[59] Deciphered Venona cables show that the Kerr Commission could not have been more mistaken.[60] Almost precisely when he was denying before a congressional committee any Communist involvement and proclaiming his divorce from political activity, Fahy was transmitting material to Georgy Stepanovich Pasko, secretary to the Soviet Naval attaché in Washington and a Naval GRU officer. In January 1943 the Naval GRU in Moscow approved a special payment to Maxwell, Fahy's cover name, as recognition of his service. In February two messages emphasized the importance of Fahy's information; the Naval GRU commander in Moscow directed the Naval GRU station in Washington to "communicate each item of information from Maxwell [Fahy] on political questions to the Master [Soviet ambassador] and telegraph it to me with the postscript 'reported to the Master.' "[61]

Eugene Franklin Coleman never held an important government position, was never hauled before a congressional committee, and was never pulled from obscurity into the limelight by charges by an ex-Communist or anti-Communist. But Venona documents indicate that he was an important Soviet agent. In August 1942 the Naval GRU sent a query to the Comintern asking for any information it had about Coleman; it described him as an employee for a telephone company and a Communist.[62] Coleman, an electrical engineer, is the subject of six Venona messages. They show that the Naval GRU was still considering in early 1943 whether to recruit him and made a final decision to go ahead in July. By this point he was working for an RCA laboratory in New Jersey on devices to assist in radio navigation for high-altitude aerial bombardment. Indeed, according to one cable, he was engaged in writing the manual for the equipment. In addition, Coleman furnished the Naval GRU with the names and backgrounds of four other Communist engineers who were working at various defense establishments, as possible intelligence sources. Given its limited staff, Naval GRU asked the KGB in Washington to check up on these potential sources.[63]

The Naval GRU also had to ask for assistance with another project, an effort to smuggle an illegal officer into the United States. Called the Australian Woman or Sally in the deciphered Venona messages, her real name was Francia Yakilnilna Mitynen, and once in the United States she assumed a false identity, that of Edna Margaret Patterson. A Soviet citizen born in Australia, Sally/Mitynen was the subject of nineteen decrypted messages. In December 1942 the Washington Naval attaché sent a lengthy cable to Moscow detailing what was necessary for the "dispatch and legalization of the Australian Woman." He included information about such documents as birth certificates and driver's licenses, problems associated with smuggling her off a Soviet ship (he pointed out, among other problems, that Soviet women sailors stood out from Americans "because of their stockings, their berets . . . their handbags and their untidiness. They do not take any trouble over their hair or their make-up"), the advantages and disadvantages of using San Francisco or Portland, and the options for traveling across country to New York.[64]

Over the next several months the details were ironed out. San Francisco was chosen as the port of arrival, arrangements were made for contacts in San Francisco and New York, code words and recognition signals were set up, appropriate American clothes were purchased, and a detailed "legend" was constructed for the illegal agent. But the Naval GRU had to seek assistance. On June 10, 1943, Moscow angrily complained, "You have had eight months to prepare for Sally's reception at the port of disembarkation, and when, moreover, you have so many people of your own, you should be ashamed to turn to the Neighbors [KGB or GRU] for help." It demanded final details, for Sally was leaving the USSR that day. Sally arrived in August 1943 and was successfully inserted into American society under her false identity; the FBI later learned that she left the United States in 1956. Her mission here remains unknown.[65]

There were other GRU sources in the United States. Two more were identified either by name in cables or through counterintelligence work: Theodore Bayer, editor of *Russky Golos* and a senior Communist party official, and "L. Gordon," a female Communist functionary being considered to head a group of GRU sources in New York. Although L. Gordon is not identified in the Venona decryptions, she is probably Lottie Gordon. In the 1930s she served in Ohio as organizational secretary of the Young Communist League. Her husband, David, was a veteran of the Abraham Lincoln Brigade.[66]

Twenty-five other GRU sources were never identified by the FBI or the NSA. They ranged from Cerberus, a Treasury Department employee who lost touch with the GRU and in 1945 was trying to reestablish contact via the CPUSA, to Jack, who provided information on American testing of guided bombs.[67] Others served in the War Production Board, the U.S. Navy, the Board of Economic Warfare, and the Bureau of Shipping or worked as journalists. The GRU might not have run as many spies as the KGB, but nonetheless it procured a steady stream of important information from the United States.

CHAPTER 7

SPIES IN THE U.S. GOVERNMENT

The Soviet intelligence community enjoyed the cooperation of key persons in high positions in the U.S. government—among them, Harry White (assistant secretary of treasury), Alger Hiss (assistant to the secretary of state), and Lauchlin Currie (administrative assistant to the president). But just as impressive is the number of lower-ranking officials in virtually all major U.S. government agencies, civilian and military, who passed information to Soviet intelligence. This chapter will survey, agency by agency, Soviet penetration of the federal government for purposes of espionage.

Office of Strategic Services

At the start of the war in Europe, American leaders recognized that the United States possessed limited foreign intelligence capability. The intelligence branches of the Army and the Navy were oriented toward military applications, chiefly combat and signals intelligence, and had only limited capability to carry out political, diplomatic, and economic intelligence. The State Department had an interest in diplomatic and strategic intelligence but did not regard covert and clandestine information gathering as part of its mission. Nor did any of these established agencies have much capacity for behind-the-lines commando and guerrilla operations or propaganda and psychological warfare. Consequently, in mid-1941, before the attack on Pearl Harbor, President Roosevelt authorized Gen. William Donovan to establish the Office of the Coordinator of Information to deal with these matters. In 1942 Donovan's agency, which had grown enormously since the United States entered the war, was split; its propaganda operations aimed at domestic and Allied audiences were broken off to form the Office of War Information and some analysis and propaganda operations aimed at Central and South America assigned to the Office of the Coordinator of Inter-American Affairs, headed by Nelson Rockefeller. The FBI also had responsibility for intelligence gathering in Central and South America. The core of foreign intelligence gathering and analysis, covert action and commando operations, and propaganda aimed at enemy nations remained under General Donovan and was named the Office of Strategic Services (OSS).

Donovan's OSS developed the nation's first capacity for analytic strategic intelligence by bringing in hundreds of academic specialists (economists, political scientists, historians, psychologists, anthropologists, and sociologists) and supplying them with information from both covert and overt sources. The resulting intelligence estimates then supported the strategic decision making of the president, the military Joint Chiefs of Staff, and the State Department. The OSS also established a network of field officers who recruited and ran clandestine agents in Europe and Asia, trained and supplied anti-Nazi partisans in occupied Europe and anti-Japanese guerrillas in Asia, parachuted sabotage teams into occupied Europe, and beamed radio propaganda and dropped into enemy areas leaflets designed to dishearten enemy forces and arouse the resistance of those under German or Japanese occupation. The Office of Strategic Services became the chief American foreign intelligence agency in World War II and the predecessor to the contemporary Central Intelligence Agency.

In March 1945 a congressional committee, concerned by rumors of Communists in the OSS, asked Donovan about four OSS officers. Milton Wolff, Vincent Lossowski, Irving Fajans, and Irving Goff were International Brigade veterans then serving with the OSS in Italy. General Donovan testified that he had investigated all four and "did not find that they were Communists. I found that they were not." He was also asked whether any of the four had been in the Young Communist League; he said no.[1] In fact, all were Communists and three of the four,

Fajans, Wolff, and Lossowski, had been Young Communist League members in the 1930s.[2]

Donovan assured the Committee on Military Affairs that everyone in the OSS had been vetted: "I try to determine whether a man is or is not a Fascist or a Communist—I have never taken a man of whom I had any doubt." One congressman asked whether, perhaps because of the highly special qualifications needed for some types of intelligence work, Donovan had recruited someone even though "he had been a member of the Communist Party . . . or a contributor to . . . some Communistic magazine." Donovan, offered wiggle room, rejected it: "I should say right here no such case has ever happened."[3]

Donovan lied to the Congress. From the origins of his agency in mid-1941 he recruited dozens of persons he knew to be Communists. Through Milton Wolff, Donovan recruited veterans of the Comintern-led International Brigades for OSS commando operations in occupied Europe. Most were Communists, but they had attributes Donovan needed for OSS personnel working with various resistance and guerrilla forces: foreign language skills, experience working with foreign soldiers, and combat experience. In some cases the resistance groups with which the OSS wanted to establish contact were Communist-led, and having some OSS officers who shared that loyalty offered advantages.

After World War II some former senior OSS officers kept up Donovan's deception that the OSS had never recruited Communists and that only a handful had ever succeeded in joining the organization. Others were more candid and did not deny that they recruited Communists, explaining that they used Communists when the individuals in question had the appropriate skills, did not conceal their Communist background, and were willing to subordinate themselves to OSS policies. Indeed, it is known that Donovan discharged several OSS employees for concealing Communist membership or for allowing Communist loyalties to interfere with OSS goals. Among these was Stephen Dedijer, a Serbian recruited for OSS work in occupied Yugoslavia. The OSS released Dedijer when it concluded that he was a Comintern agent sent to the United States to edit a Serb-language Communist newspaper and that his brother was an aide to the Yugoslav Communist leader Tito. OSS officials decided that Dedijer's Communist partisanship was so blatant that he could not work successfully with non-Communist Yugoslavs.[4] Another example, discussed in chapter 6, was Donovan's firing of Leonard Mins for lying about his Communist connections.

With more honesty than when testifying to the Congress, Donovan once remarked to an aide, "I'd put Stalin on the OSS payroll if I thought it would help us defeat Hitler."[5] Between those who were known to be Communists when Donovan recruited them and those whose Communist affiliation was unknown when they were hired, it could be said that Donovan did put Stalin on the payroll: researchers have identified Communists in the Russian, Spanish, Balkan, Hungarian, and Latin American sections of the OSS's Research and Analysis Division and its operational Japanese, Korean, Italian, Spanish, Hungarian, Indonesian, and German divisions.[6] There is no exact count of the number of Communists who worked for the OSS, but the total was easily more than fifty and probably closer to a hundred or even more.

In the midst of World War II, when Hitler was the main enemy, General Donovan's attitude was a justifiable one, but it was also fraught with risk. Although the arrangement allowed the OSS to make use of Communists, the price of using their talents was high because it also facilitated KGB and GRU recruitment of sources within America's chief intelligence agency. Donovan's decision to employ Communists was defensible, but his egregious dishonesty when testifying to the people's elected representatives was not. Nor was his policy in accord with official government rules. Early in the war, in 1942, a Roosevelt administration task force authorized immediate discharge of Communists from government service. Later, in 1944, a directive specified that Communists could serve in the military but were to be excluded from duty in posts dealing with highly secret military technologies, cryptography, and intelligence.[7]

Other chapters in this book identify twelve Soviet agents within the OSS.[8] The deciphered Venona cables also have the cover names of four other Soviet intelligence contacts within the OSS, one whose real identity has not been established, and three whose real names are known.[9] The unidentified KGB source in the OSS had a cover name whose numeric cipher was never broken to yield a legible word. Referred to by the NSA as "unbroken cover name No. 6," this person was a member of an OSS team in Algeria in 1943. The KGB cable reporting on No. 6 suggests that this person was one of the veterans of the International Brigades serving with an OSS field unit in Algeria. These units chiefly worked with resistance forces in Italy and the Balkans.

The three additional identified sources are Franz Neumann, Linn Farish, and John Scott. Neumann, cover name Ruff, fled Germany in the early 1930s, reached the United States in 1936, and became a naturalized American citizen. An economist, he joined the OSS in 1942 as a member of its German section. Farish, cover name Attila, was an OSS officer who served as OSS liaison with Tito's Partisan forces in Yugoslavia. He died in a aircraft crash in the Balkans in September 1944. As for Scott, in a report discussing the Russian section of the OSS sent in May 1942, Vasily Zubilin noted that "our source Ivanov" was an OSS analyst on Soviet industry.[10] The son of radical writer Scott Nearing, he never publicly admitted CPUSA membership but was an organizer for the CPUSA's Trade Union Unity League in the late 1920s and early 1930s. He migrated to the USSR in 1932 and worked for much of the decade in Magnitogorsk, created under Stalin's five-year plans to be the Soviet Union's premier steel-making city. He returned with a Russian wife and in 1942 published *Behind the Urals: An American Worker in Russia's City of Steel,* recording his personal observations on the building of Magnitogorsk and presenting it as an awe-inspiring triumph of collective labor. Scott's book, however, was not a pure propaganda piece. He also described the painful human price of industrial accidents, overwork, and the inefficiency of the hyperindustrialization program, the wretched condition of peasants driven from the land in the collectivization program and coerced into becoming industrial workers, and the harshness of the ideological purges. These experiences, however, did not disillusion him with Soviet communism. He stated that the Soviet people believed (and Scott indicated he shared this belief) that "it was worthwhile to shed blood, sweat, and tears" to lay "the foundations for a new society farther along the road of human progress than anything in the West; a society which would guarantee its people not only personal freedom but absolute economic security."[11]

In addition, Venona has several unidentified cover names of Soviet sources who may have worked for the OSS or who may have been employed by another wartime agency with access to OSS material. A single 1945 message, for example, reported the delivery of an OSS document by a KGB source identified only by the initial "I." A 1943 KGB message noting KGB assets in the Office of Strategic Services and the Office of War Information included one unidentified cover name. This "unbroken cover name no. 19" (the numeric code was never converted to a readable name) was in one of the agencies, but which one is not clear.[12] Horus also reported what may have been OSS information to the New York KGB. Khazar was a naturalized American citizen, probably of Yugoslav origin, who gave the KGB information on OSS personnel inserted into occupied Yugoslavia. One message reported that the OSS discussed with Khazar his participation in such an operation. It is not clear, however, whether he became an OSS operative. Finally, Okho (possibly Ojo, Spanish "eye"), an asset of the New York KGB, furnished information on the OSS in 1944, but whether Okho was actually in the OSS is unclear.

How many Soviet agents operated inside the OSS? Because of the possibility of duplication between some unidentified cover names in Venona and persons otherwise established as Soviet sources, the exact number cannot be stated. There were at least fifteen Soviet agents inside the OSS, with the actual number probably being about twenty. These numbers may also be on the low side, because most GRU and many KGB messages were never deciphered. Since the total number of Communists in the OSS was at least fifty and perhaps as high as a hundred, at least one in seven and perhaps as many as one in three Communists in the OSS were spies.[13]

The Office of War Information

The Office of War Information (OWI) was America's chief propaganda agency in World War II. Originally part of Donovan's Office of the Coordinator of Information in 1941, it was broken off in June 1942 and placed under the direction of Elmer Davis, a prominent radio commentator and ardent Roosevelt supporter. The OWI's duties included providing supportive and motivational war information by print, radio, film, and all other media to domestic audiences and to audiences in Allied and neutral nations abroad. The task of preparing propaganda aimed at enemy nations remained largely with Donovan's OSS. While the OWI lacked formal censorship powers over domestic media, it monitored the domestic press and informally pressured U.S. newspapers and magazines that failed to conform to its guidelines. In the case of nonconforming radio broadcasts, its pressure included threats to urge the Federal Communications Commission, which regulated radio broadcasting, to lift a station's broadcasting license.

Like the OSS, the OWI hired Communists. Eugene Dennis sent a message to the Soviets informing them that the party was maintaining contacts with staff members in the propaganda sections of the OWI and the OSS. Both during and after World War II several congressmen and others complained that the OWI had allowed Communists on its staff to shape its policies on several matters in a way that served Soviet interests. In 1943 Rep. John Lesinski, a Michigan Democrat with a Polish-American constituency, warned OWI head Elmer Davis in a speech on the House floor that several members of the OWI's Polish-language section were pro-Soviet. Davis received a similar but private warning from Ambassador Jan Ciechanowski of the Polish government-in-exile. Infuriated by the criticism, Davis blasted Lesinski's speech for containing "more lies than were ever comprised in any other speech made about the Office of War Information" and rebuked Ambassador Ciechanowski for interfering with internal American matters. But after the war several members of the OWI's Polish-language section emerged as defenders of the Communist takeover of Poland and as close relatives of officials in the new Polish Communist regime; one section official, Arthur Salman, became chief editor of *Robotnik* (Worker), a leading Communist newspaper in Warsaw. In addition, the head of the OWI's Czechoslovak desk in New York emerged as a high-ranking Czechoslovak Communist and became the ambassador to France of the Czechoslovak Communist regime.[14]

Vanni Montana, an official of the International Ladies Garment Workers' Union and a former Communist, visited liberated Italy in 1944 and reported finding a number of American Communists on the staff of Radio Italy, a propaganda station operated by the Office of War Information. Montana complained that Radio Italy's programs, beamed toward Nazi-occupied northern Italy, supported the political ambitions of Italian Communists in postwar Italy.[15]

After World War II Elmer Davis testified to Congress that he had fired about a dozen OWI employees, including the head of the OWI's labor news desk and its Greek desk in New York, when evidence surfaced that they were actively involved in Communist party activities while working for the OWI. But he refused to concede anything about the Polish issue and, dismissing evidence about OWI employees who were Communists as unimportant, he flatly denied that any could have influenced OWI activities. The congressional committee specifically asked Davis about OWI treatment of the matter of the Soviet murder of some fifteen thousand captured Polish officers at Katyn and other prisoner-of-war camps. The OWI had endorsed the Soviet story that the Nazis had executed the Poles, and it pressured several domestic radio stations to stop carrying commentaries suggesting that the Soviets were responsible for the Katyn massacre. Davis explained that he had believed the Soviet explanation, and he denied that Communists in the OWI influenced acceptance of the Soviet cover story.

Venona contains the unidentified cover names of several Soviet espionage contacts in the Office of War Information. These include Philosopher (OWI French section), Fred, and Leona.[16] The KGB stated that Philosopher was being used for "processing"—that is, providing background information and character appraisals—of OWI personnel. Fred was an employee of a U.S. government agency and supplied information about Austria. The OWI is most likely the agency for which he worked, but there are other possibilities as well. The KGB described Leona as the wife of a New York radio journalist and said that she was attempting to get an OWI job. It is not clear that Leona got the post.

The most active Soviet agent in the OWI revealed in Venona was Flora Wovschin. Twenty KGB cables deciphered by the Venona Project detail her service to Soviet intelligence.[17] Both her mother, Maria Wicher, and her stepfather, Enos Regnet Wicher, were active members of the CPUSA. The Wichers, in addition to being Communists, appear in deciphered Venona messages as KGB contacts.[18] Maria Wicher had the cover name Dasha in the Venona traffic and was aware of both her husband's and her daughter's work. Enos Wicher received the cover name Keen. His liaison with the KGB ran through the KGB agent Sergey Kurnakov. Enos Wicher was a source for information on American military electronics. At that time he worked for the Wave Propagation Group of Columbia University's Division of War Research. In July 1945 Wicher reported to his KGB controller that his supervisor had shown him a letter from Army counterintelligence indicating that he was suspected of having concealed Communist ties. Enos told the KGB that the letter even listed the pseudonym he had used many years earlier when he worked as a CPUSA organizer in Wisconsin.

Flora Wovschin was a far more active spy than the Wichers. She got a job with the Office of War Information in September 1943 and worked there until February 1945. The Venona messages show her performing a variety of tasks for Soviet intelligence. In 1943 the KGB was considering recruiting a young radio engineer who worked in the design office of Hazeltine Electronics Corporation. It assigned Wovschin the task of checking on his background. She also spotted and carried out the recruitment of at least two other Soviet agents: Marion Davis and the invaluable Judith Coplon, both of whom had been fellow students of hers at Barnard College.

While not as valuable a source as Coplon, Marion Davis was a useful addition to Soviet espionage. The earliest record of the KGB's interest in Davis was found in the archives of the Communist International and dates from September 1944. The KGB's General Fitin asked the Comintern if it had any information about "*Marion Davis,* an employee of the American embassy in Mexico."[19] Davis at that time worked on the staff of the Office of Naval Intelligence at the U.S. embassy in Mexico. Fitin's message was one of a series of requests for background checks on Americans whom the KGB was considering for recruitment. Given later Venona messages describing Wovschin as the KGB's initial link to Davis, it seems likely that she suggested Davis as a prospect.[20]

Three deciphered Venona messages discuss Davis's recruitment. She was back in the United States at the end of 1944 and in touch with Flora Wovschin. A New York KGB message on December 5 states that Wovschin was "drawing [Davis] into active work" and told Moscow that the KGB planned "to entrust to Zora [Wovschin] after Lou [Davis] gets work of interest to us (Zora all the time is aiming Lou at this) the gradual preparation of Lou's signing on."[21] "Signing on" referred to formal recruitment as an active KGB agent. These messages also indicate that the KGB office in Mexico City had earlier entered into preliminary contacts with Davis. In response to its New York office's plans to go forward with her formal signing on, the KGB headquarters in Moscow on December 8 ordered Lev Tarasov, head of the Mexico City office, to send an appraisal of Davis based on his meetings with her. In January 1945 the New York KGB told Moscow that Davis was reporting for a new assignment with the Office of the Coordinator of Inter-American Affairs in Washington. It asked sanction for Wovschin to complete Davis's recruitment, stating that "since Lou [Davis] is beginning to work it is extremely important to direct her efforts from the very beginning along a line which we need and for this direct contact and leadership are necessary."[22]

As for Wovschin, her KGB controllers were pleased with her dedication. One KGB officer who met with her praised her for being "extremely serious, well-developed and understand[ing] her tasks."[23] Her KGB controllers were also impressed by the volume of her production.

An August 1944 New York KGB cable reported that it had shipped to Moscow a batch of OWI material that Wovschin had gathered. Then in November, in slightly amazed tones, the New York KGB reported that already "in her apartment are lying a lot of materials that she is supposed to turn over to us but up to now has not had an opportunity."[24] In December 1944 it reported that it had taken possession of Wovschin's new collection of OWI documents. It noted, however, that the material she had turned over was not of high value because her OWI job "is poor in opportunities for our line." Consequently, the New York KGB urged Wovschin to find a position that would better serve Soviet interests and reported that the ever-responsive young woman was "in search of work that would suit us."[25] She succeeded and in February 1945 transferred from the OWI to the U.S. State Department, a far more profitable intelligence target.

Wovschin's productivity was indeed impressive. Venona messages refer to the New York KGB office's forwarding to Moscow four reports she wrote in January and February 1945 alone. Nor did the reports go unread. The Moscow KGB headquarters ordered its New York office to follow up on a report about Ralph Bowen, a State Department economics official. Wovschin, it noted, had known Bowen and his wife in the Young Communist League.

By the end of March, however, someone in the Moscow KGB headquarters concluded that her energy had crossed over into impetuousness and that the New York KGB, impressed with her productivity, had let security slip. Appalled officials at KGB headquarters told their field officers that Wovschin's reports, written by her and not by her KGB controllers, used standard KGB cover names for various American agencies: Bank for the U.S. State Department, Cabaret for the Office of the Coordinator of Inter-American Affairs, and others. Only KGB officers, not their American agents, were supposed to know these cover names. Other items in her reports indicating that she was pressing various persons for information and initiating risky contacts were also cited.

Warning that it could lead to "serious political complications" between the USSR and the United States if her promiscuous espionage became public, Moscow ordered the New York KGB to see that steps were "taken to curtail Zora's [Wovschin's] dangerous activities." It further ordered the New York KGB to admonish the KGB officer who supervised Wovschin about his mistakes, "forbid Zora [Wovschin] to recruit all her acquaintances one after the other," and "as an ultimatum warn Zora that if she does not carry out our instructions and if she undertakes steps without our consent, we shall immediately terminate all relations with her."[26]

This message from March 1945 was the last KGB cable regarding Wovschin deciphered in the Venona Project, so the New York response is not documented. Wovschin continued to work for the State Department until September 1945. Only a few points about her subsequent life are known. When the Venona Project deciphered the KGB messages about Wovschin in the late 1940s, the FBI tried to find her but could not. In 1949 the FBI forwarded a memo to the National Security Agency stating that its information indicated that at some point, probably 1946 or 1947, she fled to the Soviet Union and renounced her American citizenship, and that she later married a Russian. The timing of her flight suggests that in reaction to Elizabeth Bentley's defection, the subsequent increase in FBI counterintelligence activity, and possibly knowledge that the Venona Project was under way, the KGB withdrew Wovschin from the United States because it expected her to be uncovered. In 1954 a postscript added to the 1949 FBI memo stated that information had been received that Wovschin had later gone to Communist North Korea to work as a nurse and had died there.[27]

The State Department and Wartime Diplomatic Agencies

While the U.S. Department of State was America's chief diplomatic agency, during World War II President Roosevelt created a number of temporary specialized wartime agencies that conducted war-related diplomatic and foreign affairs tasks. These included the Board of Economic Warfare (BEW), which later became part of the Foreign Economic Administration (FEA), the Office of the Coordinator of Inter-American Affairs, and the United Nations Relief and Rehabilitation Administration (UNRRA). At the end of World War II most of these agencies were dissolved and their remnants merged into the State Department.

In addition to Flora Wovschin (State) and Marion Davis (Inter-American Affairs), eighteen other sources within these foreign relations agencies are discussed elsewhere in this book.[28] The deciphered Venona cables identify three other Soviet sources in the diplomatic community. The most important was Laurence Duggan, a respected member of the Washington establishment. He had joined the U.S. State Department in 1930 and was chief of the Division of American Republics from 1935 until 1944. After leaving the State Department he served as a diplomatic adviser to the United Nations Relief and Rehabilitation Administration and then as president of the Institute for International Education. He was a close adviser on foreign policy to former vice president Henry Wallace.

The FBI interviewed Duggan in late 1948 about whether he had had contact with Soviet intelligence in the 1930s. Duggan admitted that during his tenure as a State Department official he twice had been the object of recruitment by Soviet intelligence, once by Henry Collins and once by Frederick Field, but he could not offer a satisfactory explanation for why he never reported either approach to the State Department, as had been his duty.[29] He denied participation in espionage but cut short the interview. Ten days later he fell to his death from a window of his sixteenth-floor office.

Sumner Welles, FDR's former under secretary of state, Eleanor Roosevelt, the poet and former Librarian of Congress Archibald MacLeish, and the influential journalists Drew Pearson and Edward R. Murrow all defended Duggan's reputation and denounced suspicions of his involvement in espionage as baseless. Even Attorney General Tom Clark, who should have known why Duggan was under suspicion, announced that Duggan was "a loyal employee of the United States Government."[30] His death closed access to investigatory files for several decades, and in many historical accounts Duggan has been presented as a loyal and innocent public servant driven to suicide by unfounded accusations. In fact he was a KGB agent.

Duggan's role in the CPUSA's underground and in Soviet espionage was first brought to the attention of Assistant Secretary of State Adolf Berle by Whittaker Chambers in September 1939. Chambers explained that in the mid-1930s his GRU-CPUSA network had tabbed Duggan as a Communist sympathizer. Henry Collins, a member of the CPUSA underground and one of Chambers's contacts, had been a friend of Duggan's at Harvard and knew his views. Collins approached Duggan about assisting the underground, but he seemed uninterested. Boris Bykov, the GRU officer who supervised Chambers's network, thought Duggan too good a prospect to ignore and ordered a second try. This time Frederick Field, a socially prominent figure in diplomatic circles and a secret Communist, pressed Duggan and found out that he was already working for the Soviets, having been recruited by Hede Massing for a KGB-linked network. In 1947 the FBI interviewed Massing, who had quietly defected in 1938, and she confirmed Chambers's story. In 1997 KGB documents from Moscow appeared that further confirm Massing's account.[31]

Deciphered Venona cables provide ample evidence that Duggan continued his cooperation with Soviet espionage into the 1940s. Nine cables from 1943 and 1944 show Duggan reporting to Soviet intelligence officers about Anglo-American plans for the invasion of Italy, consideration of an invasion of Nazi-occupied Norway (a plan later canceled), U.S. diplomatic approaches to Argentina's military government, and secret discussions regarding a common Anglo-American policy toward Middle Eastern oil resources.[32]

Duggan resigned from the State Department in mid-1944. He had been a protégé of Under Secretary of State Sumner Welles, and most likely his resignation was a result of the feud between Welles and Secretary of State Cordell Hull, which led Welles to resign earlier, at the end of 1943. In a July 22 Venona cable the New York KGB office reported the resignation of their source "Frank" (Duggan's cover name at the time) from the State Department. (Duggan officially resigned on July 18.) The cable glossed over the loss of this asset with an assurance to Moscow that "prospects for the future are being looked into." An August 4 message then reported that Frank/Duggan had gotten a new post with the United Nations Relief and Rehabilitation Administration. (Duggan officially received his appointment to UNRRA in late July 1944.) The New York KGB also reported that before his resignation from the State Department, Duggan had warned his Soviet controller, the illegal KGB officer Akhmerov, that his position was precarious. The text of the August 4 message was partially garbled owing to some unbroken code groups, but it appears to indicate that Akhmerov had told Duggan to hold on at State as long as possible.

In a November 18 cable Soviet officers reported their expectation that President Roosevelt would shortly remove Secretary of State Hull and speculated that Duggan might then be able to reenter the State Department in "a leading post." The hope was based on the rumor, reported in the same cable, that Roosevelt might name Henry Wallace secretary of state as recompense for having dropped him as vice president in the 1944 election. Even if Wallace did not get the State Department appointment, the cable went on to say, Duggan could still aid the Soviets by "using his friendship" with Wallace for "extracting . . . interesting information" that would inevitably come to someone of

Wallace's political standing. Roosevelt did in fact replace Hull after the 1944 election but installed Edward Stettinius as secretary of state. Wallace received the lesser position of secretary of commerce.

The earliest Venona cable mentioning Duggan is dated June 30, 1943. Only parts of the long message have been deciphered and are readable, but the cable appears to give what the message itself describes as Duggan's resume. It refers to someone as "by profession an authoress," which would be a reference to Duggan's mother, who was an established writer. The presence of the resume may indicate a routine re-vetting, or it may mean that Duggan had been a source who had been kept on the shelf for a period and had just been revived. It is very likely that after Chambers's defection in 1938, the GRU and the KGB put those who had been in contact with Chambers into "cold storage," to use Soviet intelligence jargon, until it was learned whether he had gone to authorities. Possibly Duggan was among them.

The second diplomatic source identified in Venona is Helen Keenan, a free-lance journalist active in the CPUSA in the 1930s, who went to work for the Coordinator of Inter-American Affairs as a writer and editor in January 1945.[33] By mid-1945 it was clear that this office would be dissolved at the war's end, and Keenan found a position with the Office of U.S. Chief of Counsel for Prosecution of Axis War Criminals. The Washington KGB office told Moscow that it approved the change because "there is certainly no doubt that while working for this commission El [Keenan] will have access to material of interest to us and with skillful guidance will be able to be [unrecovered code groups] of us."[34] The Washington KGB provided Moscow with recognition signs so that KGB agents could make contact with her when she reached Europe.

The third diplomatic source identified in Venona was Samuel Rodman, a UNRRA employee. In late 1944 the New York KGB reported that its CPUSA liaison, Bernard Schuster, had been in contact with Rodman, a CPUSA member, and arranged for him to gather information during a trip that Rodman was making on behalf of UNRRA to Yugoslavia.[35]

In addition to identified Soviet sources, Venona contains a number of cover names of sources within American diplomatic agencies whose identities were never established by American analysts.[36] In several cases it is difficult to tell whether the cover-named person is an original source within an American government agency or an intermediary passing on information from a source. These cover names include, for the KGB, Dodger (who provided information on American diplomats specializing in Soviet matters), Fakir (who passed along State Department documents and was considered for an assignment in Moscow by his agency), Flora (who supplied information on UNRRA), Godmother (who provided diplomatic information on American policy toward the USSR), and Mirage (who reported on U.S. diplomatic activities in Latin America).[37]

The Venona cables also describe cover names of two GRU sources among these diplomatic agencies.[38] These were "Source No. 12" (the GRU on occasion used numeric cover names), whose information and documents suggest he was with the Board of Economic Warfare. The second GRU source is described in a 1945 KGB cable under the KGB cover name Robert. Robert had appeared on a list of targets for recruitment at the U.S. State Department, but the Moscow KGB told its New York office that it had learned he was already a GRU source.

An intriguing but unidentified and ambiguous cover name in Venona related to diplomacy is "Source No. 19." This name occurs in a single KGB message in May 1943. The KGB only rarely used numeric cover names, and it is possible that here the New York KGB was reporting about a GRU contact. Source No. 19 reported on a private conversation he had had with President Roosevelt and Prime Minister Churchill during the just-ended "Trident" conference of the two Allied powers in Washington. The message, from the New York KGB office to Moscow, is signed by the KGB illegal officer Iskhak Akhmerov. It states that "19 reports that Kapitan [Roosevelt] and Kaban [Churchill], during conversations in the Country [USA], invited 19 to join them and Zamestitel." Unfortunately, much of the subsequent text is only partially deciphered. It is clear, however, that Source No. 19 reported Churchill's views that an Anglo-American invasion of continental Europe in 1943 was inadvisable. The message also reported that Zamestitel supported a second front and that it appeared that Roosevelt had been keeping Zamestitel in the dark about "important military decisions."[39]

There is too little material for a firm judgment on the identity of Source No. 19. It appears that this source was at the Trident conference or one of its ancillary events and was very highly placed, since he was asked to join a private conversation with Roosevelt and Churchill. Beyond that, however, it is difficult to get much of a clue about No. 19's identity. It is not even clear that Source No. 19 was American: possibly he was part of the British delegation that accompanied Churchill, and a few Trident events were attended by senior officials of other Allied powers and several governments-in-exile. Unfortunately, the deciphered parts of the message do not give the exact date of Source No. 19's conversation with Roosevelt and Churchill.

Nor is it known who Zamestitel was. The word *zamestitel* means "deputy" in Russian, and originally analysts thought it referred to Vice President Henry Wallace. In five later Venona messages, however, Wallace was clearly designated by the cover name Lotsman.[40] While the KGB had a practice of changing the cover names of its covert sources for security reasons, it rarely changed the cover names used in its cable traffic for institutions or individuals who were written of frequently but were not covert sources. The KGB, for example, used the cover names Captain (Kapitan) and Boar (Kaban) for Roosevelt and Churchill throughout the span of Venona traffic. Having second thoughts about the Zamestitel identification, analysts later added an annotation to the message from Source No. 19 suggesting that Zamestitel might be Harry Hopkins, Roosevelt's chief aide, rather than Wallace. But Hopkins's name appears in the clear in several later Venona messages, whereas Zamestitel never again occurs.[41] Although KGB cipher clerks did not always use a cover name when one had been set, the fact that they generally did suggests that Zamestitel was not Hopkins.

One is left, then, with the knowledge that at the Trident conference the Soviets had a very high level contact, Source No. 19, who reported on a sensitive political and diplomatic conversation between Roosevelt, Churchill, and a third high American official, possibly Wallace or Hopkins.[42]

Military and War Production Agencies

The KGB and the GRU maintained a plethora of sources in the American military and war industrial production agencies. Twenty-six of these are discussed elsewhere in this book.[43] Elizabeth Bentley identified two additional minor sources in military-related agencies: Vladimir Kazakevich, an instructor at a wartime U.S. Army school, and Bernice Levin, a clerical employee of the Office of Emergency Management and the Office of Production Management.[44]

Venona also has a number of unidentified cover names for Soviet sources within various American military and war economic agencies.

The unidentified KGB sources were Iceberg (who provided information about the movement of American aircraft in Asia), Liza (a secretary in the War Department), Nelly (who reported on the Lend-Lease Administration), Staff-Man (someone in the U.S. Army who was valuable enough for the KGB to assign him a cipher), and Tur (who reported on U.S. plans for the invasion of France). The GRU cover names that were not identified were Donald (a U.S. Navy captain), Farley (who delivered information from the War Production Board and the War Department), and an unidentified clerk in the Strategic Directorate of the Allied Joint Staff.[45]

Treasury and Other Agencies

Eight Soviet sources in the U.S. Treasury are discussed in the chapters dealing with the Perlo and Silvermaster groups.[46] In addition, one 1945 KGB message mentioned Cerberus, an employee of the U.S. Treasury Department who was a GRU asset. He had, however, lost touch with his GRU contact and was attempting to reestablish a connection through the Communist party. The KGB heard of this through its CPUSA contacts and reported it to Moscow.[47]

Other Government Agencies

Soviet sources were also scattered thoughout other sections of the U.S. government. The KGB maintained two sources, William Gold and Charles Kramer, on the staff of the Senate Subcommittee on War Mobilization, a rich source of military information. Both are discussed in earlier chapters on the Perlo and Silvermaster groups. Also discussed elsewhere are Norman Bursler (anti-trust section of the Justice Department), Judith Coplon (Foreign Agent Registration section of the Justice Department), James Walter Miller (postal censorship) Ward Pigman (National Bureau of Standards), and Jack Fahy (Interior Department). Two other unidentified Soviet sources inside the government were noted in Venona. An October 27, 1944, New York KGB message refers to a Soviet source in the FBI. It is unclear, however, whether this was a reference to Judith Coplon or to another Soviet source.[48] A 1943 GRU message also notes information from an unidentified source in the Bureau of Shipping.[49]

FELLOW-COUNTRYMEN

CHAPTER 8

Earl Browder: Helmsman

The KGB in its coded cables gave Earl Browder, who headed the CPUSA from 1930 to 1945, the cover name Helmsman. It was, of course, a reference to his leadership of the party. But it was also appropriate in that Browder's own involvement with Soviet intelligence set the example for other Communists.

Margaret Browder, Earl's sister, was herself a Soviet intelligence operative. In January 1938 Earl Browder sent a memorandum to Georgi Dimitrov, head of the Comintern:

> For about 7 years my younger sister, Marguerite Browder, has been working for the foreign department of the NKVD [KGB], in various European countries. I am informed that her work has been valuable and satisfactory, and she has expressed no desire to be released. But it seems to me, in view of my increasing involvement in national political affairs and growing connections in Washington political circles, it might become dangerous to this political work if hostile circles in America should by any means obtain knowledge of my sister's work in Europe and make use of this knowledge in America. I raise this question, so ... steps can be taken by you to secure my sister's release from her present work.[1]

Dimitrov agreed and wrote to Nikolai Yezhov, then head of the KGB: "I am forwarding you [this] note from Comrade Browder. . . . I, for my part, consider it politically expedient to relieve his sister of her duties in the foreign department of the NKVD."[2]

Browder's concern that his sister's work as a Soviet agent might become public and embarrass him may have been prompted by the late 1937 defection of Walter Krivitsky, a senior Soviet military intelligence officer. Margaret had for a time been part of an operation supervised by Krivitsky. If this was the cause of Browder's fear, it was well founded. In 1939 Krivitsky publicly revealed that Margaret Browder, using a fraudulent American passport identifying her as Jean Montgomery, had worked as a Soviet espionage agent in Europe.[3]

The House Special Committee on Un-American Activities questioned Browder and his brother William about their sister in 1939, but their responses were carefully phrased. Asked whether she was employed by either the Comintern or the Soviet government, Earl answered, "I think not. . . . To the best of my knowledge, she is not now and has not in the past been officially connected with any government institution." William Browder testified that "to the best of my knowledge and belief," his sister did not work for the Soviet government.[4] When examining the CPUSA's fraudulent passport operations, government investigators determined that the photograph for an American passport issued to "Jean Montgomery" was that of Margaret Browder and that the signature on her passport application that purported to be that of Jean Montgomery's brother was in the handwriting of William Browder.[5]

The Browders were also in contact with Vasily and Elizabeth Zubilin, both senior KGB officers, over a lengthy period. Margaret later admitted knowing Vasily Zubilin in Germany under the name Herbert. She also identified a picture of Zubilin and his wife and told the FBI that she had met them both at the home of William and Rose Browder sometime in the late 1930s. She claimed that Zubilin was merely a talent scout for a movie studio and that she knew them in the United States as Poppy and Mommy. Although Margaret Browder denied meeting with the Zubilins in 1942, Lucy Booker, a former Soviet agent who later cooperated with the FBI, told the bureau that in 1942 she and Margaret had spent a weekend with the Zubilins at an estate on Long Island. A Venona message confirms meetings in 1943 and 1944 between Zubilin and William Browder.[6]

Twenty-six deciphered Venona messages mention Earl Browder.[7] Some of the references are trivial, others show the KGB acting as the communications link between the CPUSA and the Comintern over political matters, but a number document Browder's personal involvement in Soviet espionage against the United States.

In some deciphered cables Browder passes on to the KGB diplomatic and political information he had gained through the CPUSA's own contacts. In May 1943, for example, he delivered a report on what Under Secretary of State Sumner Welles had told an influential writer about turmoil inside the Italian government. Occasionally, the cables show intelligence information going *to* Browder rather than coming from him. In January 1945 the KGB illegal officer Iskhak Akhmerov reported that Solomon Adler, a source of the Silvermaster group, demanded that certain information on Chinese matters he had obtained be shared with Browder.[8] This attitude was one left over from the CPUSA's Washington underground of 1930s, when many of the KGB's sources got their introduction to the secret world. As John Abt, one of the leaders of the Washington underground, later admitted in his autobiography, the secret CPUSA caucuses inside government agencies provided "the national Party leadership" with "commentary and analyses" of government plans and programs.[9] The intent, of course, was to assist the CPUSA's political activities. Even after these networks were shifted to Soviet espionage control in the 1940s, some of their members had difficulty understanding why the results of their espionage should not be made available to the CPUSA as well; in their eyes, it was all part of the same struggle.

Akhmerov cabled Moscow about Adler's demand because such sharing was, as he stated, "an exception" to KGB tradecraft. The KGB's policy, however, was of recent origin. Elizabeth Bentley related that when Jacob Golos had been the chief link between the KGB and several CPUSA espionage networks, he regularly met with Browder to discuss the information being obtained and provided him with summaries or copies of material of interest to the American Communist party.[10] But Golos was of the old school of Soviet espionage. He was an open CPUSA official and had spent his entire adult life working for the party. He mixed open Communist activity, underground party work, and Soviet espionage in a way that the increasingly professional KGB of the 1940s thought risky.

In her FBI deposition Bentley stated that the day after Golos's death

Arlington Hall, headquarters of the Army's code-breaking operations and the Venona Project, in 1944.

A deciphered Venona message. The New York KGB station reports to Moscow headquarters that Liberal (Julius Rosenberg) and his wife (Ethel) recommend recruiting Ruth Greenglass, Ethel's sister-in-law, as a Soviet agent. The local KGB stations in the United States had to request formal permission from Moscow for recruitments. Venona 1340 KGB New York to Moscow, 21 September 1944.

Courtesy National Security Agency

Army cryptanalysts at work at Arlington Hall in 1944. The man at the far left is Meredith Gardner, who in 1946 became the chief book-breaker (a cryptolinguist who breaks codes) on the Venona Project. The vast majority of code-breakers were young women.

Courtesy National Security Agency

Cecil Phillips in Paris in 1946. Phillips came to Arlington Hall at age eighteen. In 1944 he made the breakthrough in cracking the Soviet code by identifying Soviet cables that were vulnerable to cryptanalysis.

Courtesy National Security Agency

Carter Clarke, chief of the Special Branch of the Army Military Intelligence Division. Clarke initiated the Venona Project in 1943.

Courtesy National Security Agency

William Weisband, the Arlington Hall linguist who in the late 1940s alerted the Soviets that the Venona Project had succeeded in deciphering messages about Soviet espionage in the United States. After Weisband was identified as a KGB agent, he was fired from his job at the National Security Agency and imprisoned for refusing to obey a grand jury subpoena.

Courtesy National Security Agency

Vasily Zubilin (Zarubin), chief of KGB espionage operations in the United States from late 1941 to early 1944.

Courtesy National Security Agency

Elizabeth Bentley in 1948, around the time of her testimony before the House Committee on Un-American Activities. An American Communist and a KGB agent, Bentley turned herself in to the FBI in 1945 and identified scores of Soviet sources.

Courtesy Library of Congress

Duncan Lee being asked to identify a photo of Jacob Golos in 1948 for the House Committee on Un-American Activities. Lee insisted that his relationship with Bentley was purely social.

UPI/Corbis-Bettmann

Judith Coplon reading accounts of her conviction for espionage in 1949. Coplon was convicted twice, but both verdicts were overturned on technicalities.

UPI/Corbis-Bettmann

Victor Perlo appearing before the House Committee on Un-American Activities in 1948. In response to questions from committee members, Perlo, the leader of a large espionage cell, invoked the Fifth Amendment protection against self-incrimination.

Gregory Silvermaster appearing before the House Committee on Un-American Activities in 1948. He was called to respond to Elizabeth Bentley's charges that he supervised an extensive ring of U.S. government employees who spied for the Soviet Union. Silvermaster refused to testify, invoking the Fifth Amendment protection against self-incrimination.

Laurence Duggan testifying before a Senate committee in 1946. Duggan had first begun turning information over to Soviet agents in the mid-1930s. In 1948 he fell to his death, an apparent suicide, after having been questioned by the FBI.

UPI/Corbis-Bettmann

Lauchlin Currie in 1945. An administrative assistant to President Franklin Roosevelt, Currie was also a secret Soviet sympathizer and a source for the KGB. After denying any involvement in Soviet espionage, he left the United States in the early 1950s and renounced his American citizenship.

Courtesy Library of Congress

Harry White in 1946. Assistant secretary of the Treasury in the Roosevelt administration, White was the KGB's highest-ranking source in the U.S. government. He passed information to Soviet intelligence and used his position to promote more than a dozen KGB sources within the federal government. He died of a heart attack in 1948, shortly after denying that he had participated in espionage.

Alfred and Martha Dodd Stern, socially prominent millionaires and secret Communists who assisted Soviet intelligence operations in the United States. They fled, first to Mexico and then to Czechoslovakia, to avoid indictments for espionage.

David Greenglass preparing to testify in 1951 that his sister and brother-in-law, Ethel and Julius Rosenberg, recruited him to pass along atomic secrets from Los Alamos.

UPI/Corbis-Bettmann

Ruth Greenglass testifying that she assisted her husband in atomic espionage at the request of the Rosenbergs.

UPI/Corbis- Bettmann

in November 1943 she met with Browder at his office, and he urged her not to turn over Golos's sources directly to the Russians. Bentley continued to meet Browder about every two weeks at his office. Three imperfectly decrypted cables dealing with Golos went from the KGB in New York to Moscow in the weeks after his death. Zubilin reported to General Fitin that Bentley had twice seen Earl Browder to consult with him about Golos's networks.[11] But Bentley lacked Golos's standing in both the party and the intelligence world to negotiate successfully with the Soviets or to serve as the party's liaison with the KGB. While the KGB kept Bentley in the role of liaison with Golos's networks, from the start it intended her role to be a transitional one as it took direct control.

Browder also acted as a talent-spotter for the KGB. In the fall of 1940 he delivered a report regarding Pierre Cot, a member of the Radical party in France who had served in more than half a dozen of the short-lived French cabinets of the 1930s. A passionate supporter of a Franco-Soviet alliance against Germany, Cot was accused of handing over to the Soviet Union secret information he had obtained in his capacity as aviation minister during the Spanish Civil War. When Walter Krivitsky defected in 1937, he named Cot as a Soviet source within the French government. After the fall of France in 1940 Cot fled to London but was rebuffed in his efforts to join General de Gaulle's Free French movement, which regarded him as an embarrassment.[12]

In September 1940 Cot arrived in the United States, where he quickly established contact with Earl Browder. Browder's report on the meeting originally went via KGB cable from General Fitin, head of the KGB's foreign intelligence directorate, to Lavrenty Beria, chief of the KGB, who briefed both Stalin and Molotov about its contents and forwarded it to the Comintern, in whose archive it was eventually found. Browder reported that Cot had asked him to notify the USSR that he continued to work "for a full alliance between France and the Soviet Union," a coalition that could "be achieved only through the French Comparty [Communist party]." He also passed on that Cot "wants the leaders of the Soviet Union to know of his willingness to perform whatever mission we might choose, for which purpose he is even prepared to break faith with his own position"[13]—a reference to the politics of the Nazi-Soviet Pact. After the pact was concluded in August 1939, the French Communist party had dropped its bellicose anti-Hitler stance and adopted a defeatist attitude toward France's decision to go to war with Nazi Germany. After France's surrender in mid-1940, French Communists did not actively support the pro-Nazi Vichy regime, but neither did they oppose it. Moreover, French Communists were hostile to de Gaulle and his supporters, who refused to recognize the surrender and continued the fight against Hitler. Cot, too, had refused to accept the surrender or the Vichy regime and fled into exile. Through Browder, however, he offered to give up this position if that was the Soviets' wish. (After the Nazi attack on the Soviet Union in June 1941, the French Communist party reversed its stance: it opposed the Vichy regime, sought an alliance with de Gaulle's Free French, and became a major element in the anti-Nazi resistance in the German-occupied areas of France.)

The KGB followed up on Browder's report. Vladimir Pravdin, a KGB officer with a cover as a Soviet journalist, took advantage of a speech Cot gave in June 1942 to meet him. A decrypted Venona message indicates that Cot welcomed the overture. In response to this message, on July 1, 1942, Moscow cabled "about the signing on of Pierre Cot (henceforth 'Daedalus')."[14] For at least the next year, KGB contact with Cot was under the direct supervision of Vasily Zubilin. A number of deciphered KGB messages show that Cot turned over reports on his activities and analyses of events throughout 1943.[15] In addition to cooperating with the KGB, he worked closely with the Comintern and the French Communist party; one KGB cable from San Francisco refers to a message for Cot from the French Communist leader and Comintern official André Marty. In one imperfectly decoded message, dated July 1, 1943, Zubilin relayed a report in which Cot offered to go to Algiers to assist on some problem; Zubilin noted that Cot "will obey unquestionably." Cot also sent analyses of exiled French politicians with whom he had contact in French North Africa and in the United States. After World War II he successfully reentered French politics and briefly served once again as aviation minister. He continued to champion French-Soviet friendship and in 1953 received the Stalin Peace Prize. By the time the Venona documents revealing his cooperation with Soviet intelligence were decrypted, his political career was over, and French authorities chose to keep secret his relationship with the KGB.[16]

Although Browder performed many valuable services for Soviet intelligence, he also inadvertently provided it with misinformation about President Roosevelt. In July 1943 both the KGB and the GRU in the United States informed their superiors in Moscow that a friend of Browder's who was a secret member of the CPUSA was surreptitiously meeting with Franklin Roosevelt, who was using her as a back channel to communicate with Browder.

In a message to Moscow on July 18, a senior KGB officer in New York, Pavel Klarin, stated that Jacob Golos had told the New York KGB that Roosevelt had informed Browder that the invasion of Sicily was a prelude to a large-scale invasion of Europe during the summer, but that Churchill was objecting. In addition, according to Golos, the president was pleased with the positions of the CPUSA in New Jersey politics.[17] The very next Venona message, sent the same day, begins by stating that Browder had asked the KGB to get a message to Dimitrov. Most of the remainder of the lengthy cable, nearly two hundred code groups, was not deciphered, except that the name Carnero appears.[18]

Located in the archive of the Comintern in Moscow are two related documents, a covering note from General Fitin and a Browder report for the Comintern sent through the New York KGB station, both dated July 23, 1943, five days after the two Venona cables. The report discussed, among other points, American plans for following up on the invasion of Sicily, Churchill's reluctance to launch a continental assault, and Roosevelt's praise for the CPUSA's position in New Jersey. A section about Mexico notes the role of Carnero, a leading Mexican Communist, in party factionalism.[19] These documents in the Comintern's archive obviously derive from the two earlier cables that were later partially deciphered in the Venona Project. The report Fitin forwarded to Dimitrov was an in-clear version of the second, and largely undeciphered, Venona cable of July 18. The striking point about the version in the Comintern archive is its statement that President Roosevelt had conveyed the comments on the Sicilian invasion and on New Jersey politics to Browder "verbally."

Just one day after the KGB in New York sent along its information on FDR, Soviet military intelligence in New York also cabled Moscow. Although only fragments of the message were decoded by American cryptanalysts, it too appears to be about some Communist source with access to President Roosevelt. Two weeks later, obviously in response to queries from Moscow, Pavel Mikhailov, the GRU chief in New York, cabled Moscow that his source for the story was Theodore Bayer, cover name Simon. A Communist who headed the Russky Golos Publishing Company, Bayer described the CPUSA source near Roosevelt as a woman "from an aristocratic family, [who] has known the President and his wife for a long time, evidently a secret member of the Corporation [CPUSA]." Mikhailov passed along from Bayer gossipy tidbits from the woman's alleged conversations with Roosevelt, including praise of Stalin's leadership and the claim that Mrs. Chiang Kai-shek was "a narcotics addict," but he said that Bayer had not provided her name. Mikhailov warned that the information was thirdhand but speculated that FDR might be trying to improve his political standing "with the masses before the 1944 election" by lauding the CPUSA (a sign of how little the GRU officer understood American politics). In mid-August Mikhailov cabled that he had gotten the name of the woman: Josephine Treslow.[20]

Who was Josephine Treslow? The GRU in Moscow did not know. On August 21 it sent this memo to Dimitrov: "According to information we have received, an American citizen, Josephine Treslow, on instructions from Browder is meeting systematically with the president of the U.S. Roosevelt. Please advise whether this is in fact the case, and whether you have any information on this issue."[21]

The memo's Josephine Treslow was Josephine Truslow Adams, born in Brooklyn in 1897. From 1934 to 1941 she taught art at Swarthmore College and, without openly acknowledging her Communist loyalties, joined numerous Communist-led organizations. Adams's contact with the Roosevelt family began when she was commissioned to paint a picture for Eleanor Roosevelt. When Mrs. Roosevelt visited Swarthmore in 1941, they met. Adams then sent Mrs. Roosevelt another painting and began bombarding her with long letters.[22] Among the subjects Adams stressed was the advisability of freeing Earl Browder from federal prison, where he was serving a sentence for use of fraudulent passports; Adams was a mainstay of the Citizens' Committee to Free Earl Browder. President Roosevelt released Browder in May 1942, as a goodwill gesture to the Soviet Union at the time of Molotov's arrival in Washington and as a reward to Communists for their recent support for his war policies. There is no evidence that Josephine Truslow Adams's lobbying had any effect on the president's decision. Earl Browder, however, thought otherwise. He met with her at a Communist gala in July 1942 and believed her story that she had met with President and Mrs. Roosevelt on many occasions, had become an intimate family friend, and had successfully lobbied for his release.

Adams misled Browder not least because she suffered from delusions. By 1956 she was in and out of hospitals for psychiatric treatment.

In 1943, however, her mental delusions were not so manifest, and Browder believed he had a private pipeline to the White House. Browder gave Adams material on various political matters to discuss with President Roosevelt during their (as he thought) frequent chats. Actually, Browder's political information became the texts of the letters Adams continued to send Mrs. Roosevelt, who recognized the political interest of some of Adams's letters and forwarded them to her husband—noting on one, however, "I know nothing of her reliability." Mrs. Roosevelt sent polite responses to Adams, the most encouraging being a note that "your letters go directly to the president. What then happens I do not know."[23] That, however, is not what Josephine Adams told Earl Browder. She represented that she met in person with FDR, and she gave Browder substantive messages that she said were the president's responses to Browder. Adams in fact simply made up FDR's responses, basing them on the analysis offered by political commentators and on what Browder wanted to hear.[24]

Convinced that he had Roosevelt's blessing for his effort to build closer ties between American Communists and the Democratic party, and encouraged by the dissolution of the Comintern and by the Teheran meetings of Roosevelt, Churchill, and Stalin in 1943 that promised postwar cooperation among the Allies, Browder put American communism on a new course in 1944. He converted the American Communist party into the Communist Political Association and set out to make it the left wing of the Democratic party. Browder's influence also appeared in the CPUSA's decision to oppose New Jersey reformers' attempt to create a third party, the decision of Communists who secretly controlled Minnesota's Farmer-Labor party to merge it with the Democratic party in 1944, and the decision in early 1945 of the secret Communists who controlled the Washington (State) Commonwealth Federation to end its separate existence and attempt to integrate it into the Washington Democratic party.[25]

The Soviets, however, did not approve of Browder's new tack. Dimitrov warned Browder that he was veering away from Moscow's guidance, but Browder pushed ahead anyway. It is not known whether the KGB ever learned that Browder had been systematically misled by Adams. Did the Soviets worry that Browder had become too close to FDR? Or did they conclude that he had been played for a fool? In any case, sometime in the fall of 1944 someone in Moscow drafted what became known as the Duclos article, which harshly criticized Browder's policies.

After it was published in the spring of 1945, American Communists realized that their leader no longer had Moscow's approval. The Communist Political Association called an emergency convention, transformed itself back into the CPUSA, removed Earl Browder from its leadership, and later expelled him altogether.[26]

Adams not only encouraged Browder to travel down a path that proved disastrous for him but also contributed to the souring of postwar American politics. Browder would often hint at his relationship with Roosevelt. Rumors of his back channel to the White House circulated in the upper levels of the CPUSA. From there the story seeped out to Popular Front liberal allies of the party, who were thus reassured that there was nothing improper in their own relationship with the CPUSA. The rumors also reached anti-Communists; in some cases Communists who had become disillusioned and quit the party carried with them what they thought was inside knowledge of a Browder-Roosevelt relationship.[27] Many anti-Communists discounted the rumors, but some conservative anti-Communists who intensely disliked both FDR and the CPUSA found a Roosevelt-Browder connection believable. They were wrong, but their belief was based on credible sources from within the Communist party itself. Thus, Josephine Adams's fantasies and Browder's credulity misled some liberals into believing that association with the CPUSA had Roosevelt's backing and promoted the belief among some conservatives that Roosevelt had a conspiratorial relationship with the CPUSA. This perception in turn contributed to partisan divisiveness about the nature of the domestic Communist problem in the postwar period.

As for Adams, after Earl Browder was expelled from the CPUSA, she also drifted away from the party. The FBI interviewed her several times and examined her papers but concluded that she was unreliable. While in a New York mental hospital in late 1956, she got through to the staff of the Senate Internal Security Subcommittee and said she wanted to reveal her role as the secret link between President Roosevelt and the Communist party. She also asserted that "Communist doctors" were giving her shock treatments, drugs, and lobotomies to convince her she was mentally ill. That should have been a clue to her reliability, but nonetheless she was invited to Washington and testified in executive session in January 1957. Excerpts of her testimony were released in February and provided a sensation for those who believed that the New Deal was essentially a Communist conspiracy. In the excerpts Adams claimed to have had nearly forty personal meetings with the president at Hyde Park or the White House.[28]

The sensation, however, was brief. Following her testimony, Adams signed a book contract and hired Isaac Don Levine, the veteran anti-Communist journalist, as her ghostwriter. When Adams sent a file of what she said were letters between herself and President Roosevelt to Levine, however, he became suspicious. Included in Adams's material were more than a score of letters from FDR to Adams, displaying the irreverence and flightiness that characterized Adams's style, not FDR's. Further, of the twenty-one dates on which FDR supposedly wrote from Washington, Levine discovered that the president was not there on ten. Levine confronted Adams, who eventually admitted that the letters were forgeries. The planned book, tentatively entitled *I Was Roosevelt's Secret Emissary*, was dropped. Adams drifted deeper into her delusional world and in 1958 was committed to Norristown sanitarium in Pennsylvania, where she remained until her death in 1969.

Eugene Dennis and Infiltration of the OSS and OWI

Next to Earl Browder, Eugene Dennis was the most important figure in the CPUSA during World War II. Born Francis Waldron in 1905 in Seattle, he had become a full-time organizer shortly after joining the party in 1926. He fled to Moscow in 1930 after being indicted for criminal syndicalism in California in connection with Communist union organizing, changed his name to Tim Ryan, and undertook a series of covert tasks for the Comintern in China, South Africa, and the Philippines. Using the name Gene Dennis and leaving his American-born son behind in Moscow to be raised in Comintern boarding schools as a Russian, he arrived in Wisconsin in 1935 to serve as district organizer. Two years later he was back in the USSR as the CPUSA's representative to the Communist International for one year. On his return to the United States, he became a member of the national party leadership; he was ordered underground in 1940 in anticipation of a move to illegality if the U.S. government suppressed the party because of its support for the Nazi-Soviet Pact. The following year he once again visited Moscow to consult with Comintern leaders. When Browder was ousted from the party leadership in 1945, Dennis was selected to succeed him; he remained general secretary until 1959, when, in poor health, he was replaced by Gus Hall.

Louis Budenz, a former CPUSA leader turned anti-Communist, charged in 1948 that during World War II Dennis had directed a ring of Communist agents in the Office of Strategic Services (OSS) that included Carl Marzani.[29] In the 1920s Budenz had been a labor activist, an early official of the American Civil Liberties Union, and a supporter of the Socialist party. In the 1930s he moved to the left, first joining the American Workers party, led by the independent radical A. J. Muste; but Muste's radicalism was insufficient for Budenz, and he moved to the CPUSA. Budenz rose rapidly to membership on the Communist party's New York state committee, then on the national central committee. In 1941 he became managing editor of the *Daily Worker* and was on the fringe of the CPUSA's top leadership, even irregularly attending meetings of the party's ruling Political Bureau. In 1945, however, Budenz underwent a spiritual crisis, left the CPUSA, and was received into the Roman Catholic Church. He then joined the faculties of Notre Dame and Fordham universities and wrote, lectured, and testified widely about communism as a subversive threat.[30] Many scholars scoffed at Budenz's assertions, but documents found in Russian archives and deciphered material from Venona demonstrate that Budenz was correct about Dennis: he oversaw a CPUSA operation that placed Communists in the OSS during World War II.

In November 1941 Col. William Donovan, head of the OSS, approached Milton Wolff, the last commander of the Abraham Lincoln battalion in Spain. Wolff had been a member of the Young Communist League in the United States and the Communist Party of Spain.[31] When he returned to the United States he became the commander of the Veterans of the Abraham Lincoln Brigade, which encompassed all Americans who had served in the International Brigades as well as veterans of the Abraham Lincoln battalion. As its commander he steered it firmly in line with the policies of the Communist party. During the period of the Nazi-Soviet Pact, this meant that the Veterans of the Abraham Lincoln Brigade opposed any U.S. assistance to Britain in its war with Germany. Once Germany attacked the USSR in June 1941, however, the organization became an enthusiastic supporter of such aid. Donovan wanted Wolff to recruit Spanish Civil War veterans to serve with British commando units being prepared for operations in occupied Europe. (America was officially neutral at that time, but President Roosevelt was offering Britain all possible aid short of U.S. entry into the war.) Wolff agreed to Donovan's plan. After Pearl Harbor and America's declaration of war in December, Donovan redirected Wolff's recruits to his own agency, where several dozen International Brigades veterans served in the OSS units that worked with resistance forces in enemy-occupied areas.

On April 3, 1942, Dimitrov sent a coded cable to the CPUSA leadership that "we have information that Wolff, repeat Wolff, from Abraham Lincoln Brigade is recruiting comrades from this brigade for special work" in the name of the Communist party. "Special work" was a euphemism for intelligence work. Dimitrov instructed CPUSA leaders to "examine carefully this question and inform us urgently."[32] A week later Gene Dennis responded with a brief coded cable, assuring Dimitrov that "Wolff has our approval working for government."[33] Some weeks later Dennis met with a KGB officer in New York and delivered a more detailed report for forwarding to Moscow. In this report, found in the Comintern's archive, Dennis described Donovan's approach to Wolff the previous November and explained that Donovan had "proposed selecting dependable veterans and putting them at the disposal of the British for deployment in the interior of the Axis countries for diversionary work. Wolff conveyed this proposal by the intelligence service to the Comparty [CPUSA] and was given a sanction for it. . . . By the time the US entered the war, Wolff had provided the British with 12 Yugoslavs, 3 Czechs, and 1 Italian. . . . Wolff has provided American intelligence with 10 Americans, 1 Greek, and 3 Yugoslavs, who are considered on active duty in the army and undergoing training in special ('commando') groups." All were Communists, Dennis reported, but in addition Wolff had also handed over from among the veterans of the International Brigades "6 nonparty Hungarians and 4 Czechs to American intelligence." The report went on to explain that in December 1941 the CPUSA had appointed Dennis to negotiate with Donovan about the party's cooperation with the OSS. It noted that Dennis had provided the OSS with a "selection of Italian and German immigrants for the compilation of propagandistic materials and radio broadcasting."[34]

On May 13 General Fitin, head of KGB foreign intelligence, sent a sobering memo to Dimitrov. He noted that the KGB "regard[s] this entire matter as a political mistake by the leadership of the US Comparty, thanks to which the American and British intelligence services have been given the opportunity to infiltrate not only American Comparty channels but also the Comparty organizations of other countries."[35] (Fitin's fears were misplaced: as a matter of policy the OSS made no attempt to penetrate the CPUSA or Soviet intelligence.)[36] Dimitrov was not one to disagree with the KGB, and the same day he responded by telling Fitin that he agreed that "allowing Wolff to recruit people for English and American intelligence [was] a mistaken policy" and suggested "curtailing that recruitment and all connection with the indicated intelligence services." A handwritten note by Dimitrov on Fitin's memo said, "A directive has been given to New York for the discontinuation of this work."[37] Dennis, too, toed the line: on June 1 he sent a message to Dimitrov through the KGB: "We fully agree with your proposals regarding the activities of Wolff and we have taken all necessary measures for their discontinuation."[38] Wolff promptly closed down his recruiting operation.

Still, that left a body of Communists who had already been recruited. Via the KGB, Dennis explained to Dimitrov: "We are in contact with the department of foreign propaganda and with the information coordinator of the US. That department is one of three departments in the so-called *Donovan* Committee and is directly controlled by the White House. We also have several persons working in the Czech and Italian radio-broadcast sections of that department and influencing certain broadcasts in Germany [in German], although not in the overall program. We consider it expedient to prolong that contact and keep these persons in the radio-broadcast section, if, of course, you are in agreement. We have a similar contact with the inter-American Committee."[39]

In the last message Dennis was telling Dimitrov and the KGB that the CPUSA planned to retain contact with party members in the U.S. Office of Strategic Services, the Office of War Information, and the Office of the Coordinator of Inter-American Affairs. One Venona message from 1943 lists six Soviet agents working in the OSS and the OWI. The message was only partially decrypted, but five of the Soviet sources can be identified: Maurice Halperin, Duncan Lee, Franz Neumann, Bella Joseph, and Julius Joseph, all of whom worked with Elizabeth Bentley. One possibility for the unidentified source is the man Budenz named: Carl Marzani, who was hired by the Presentation Division of the OSS in 1942.[40]

Born in Italy, Marzani emigrated to the United States in 1924. After graduating from Williams College in 1935, he won a scholarship to attend Oxford in England. A member of the English Communist party, he went to Spain to fight but, oddly enough, enlisted in an anarchist rather than a Communist battalion. Back in the United States, Marzani joined the CPUSA on the day the Nazi-Soviet Pact was signed. Under the name of Tony Whales, he worked fervently for the party on the Lower East Side of New York. He insisted in his autobiography that he quit the party in 1941 and that when he joined the OSS he told people that he was an ex-Communist. After World War II he became a State Department official but was later convicted of making false statements in denying that he was a Communist when he joined the OSS. After his jail term he headed Marzani and Munsell, a left-wing publishing house. A retired KGB officer in 1994 identified Marzani as a contact and a recipient of KGB subsidies for his publishing house in the 1960s.[41]

Dennis is mentioned in only two Venona messages, and in neither one was enough of the message deciphered to make much sense of what it concerned. In both messages he is linked to Harold Glasser, a member of the Silvermaster espionage network.[42]

KGB Liaison with the CPUSA

In June 1943 Vasily Zubilin cabled Moscow regarding a realignment of liaison for several of the New York KGB's major contacts. He specified that his wife would supervise contact with Jacob Golos but would use an intermediary for communication. He would retain as his own liaisons three major contacts: Pierre Cot, Iskhak Akhmerov, and Earl Browder.[43] Very shortly thereafter, however, Moscow ordered a general reorganization of KGB contact with Communist parties around the world. In September General Fitin sent a circular order to KGB stations in Australia, Canada, and the United States warning that by continuing to meet with Communist party leaders, regional KGB offices risked giving Russia's allies the impression that the Comintern's recent dissolution had been a sham. He ordered his officers to stop meeting with prominent Communist party officials and no longer to routinely accept Communist party material for forwarding to Moscow. Henceforth all meetings had to take place "only with special reliable undercover contacts of the Fellowcountryman [Communist party] organizations" and were to be "exclusively about specific aspects of our intelligence work, acquiring [unbroken code group] contacts, leads, rechecking of those who are being cultivated, etc."[44]

The subsequent reorganization of liaisons was further complicated by the death of Jacob Golos in November 1943. By early 1944 there was a new liaison between the CPUSA and the KGB, Bernard Schuster or, as he was known in the CPUSA, Bernard Chester. A soft-spoken man of average height and build, Schuster was, according to FBI agents who watched him in 1945, "suspicious, nervous, tail conscious."[45] He had good reason to be. Venona cables clearly demonstrate that in the next two years he became deeply enmeshed in KGB operations, including atomic bomb espionage.

Schuster was born October 14, 1904, in Warsaw and came to the United States in 1921 with his father. He graduated from New York University in 1925, but mediocre grades discouraged his plans for medical school. Instead, he became an accountant. He may have worked for Amtorg in 1930. In the early 1930s he directed the CPUSA's antimilitarist work, a program to develop secret Communist groups among American military personnel. By 1935 he was treasurer of the Wholesale Book Corporation, which distributed Communist literature. In the next few years Schuster became a director, along with William Browder, of the Commonwealth Minupress Company, which printed party literature. He also formed the Bernador Sales Company and became co-owner of National Mercantile Trading Company, an import-export firm serving clients in Mexico, Uruguay, and Argentina, and a limited partner in Screenmakers, Inc., manufacturers of radio equipment.

Schuster's business interests were probably all fronts for the Communist party, which he served in a variety of second-rank positions. In 1938, as Bernard Chester, he was New York state membership director of the Communist party; the following year he was president of the Fifth Assembly District Club of the Communist party in the Bronx. By 1943 he was treasurer of the New York state Communist party and was often dispatched to do special audits by Charles Krumbein, the party's national treasurer. Several ex-Communists briefly mentioned Schuster in their memoirs. Louis Budenz identified "Comrade Chester" as the "man in charge of secret work in the New York district" in the late 1930s. Elizabeth Bentley recalled "Berny Schuster" as old friend of Jacob Golos's who had "turned contacts for espionage over to us." Bella Dodd, a New York Communist activist turned anti-Communist, wrote about "Chester," whom she knew as the head of the party's intelligence service. Chester, according to Dodd, received reports from secret Communist agents in other left-wing organizations and government agencies and collected money from various businesses with ties to the CPUSA.[46]

The Venona decryptions confirm Bernard Schuster's critical role in Soviet espionage in America. He is mentioned in more than three dozen messages from 1944 and 1945.[47] In line with Fitin's directive of September 1943, the New York KGB used Schuster as its intermediary with Earl Browder rather than meeting with him directly, as had been done earlier, and often checked with Moscow first when it needed to approach Browder through Schuster. Browder also went through Schuster when he passed on to the Soviets his assessment of political conditions in the United States. And Schuster passed along Browder's request that the Soviets approve the new theoretical positions he was developing about postwar détente between the USA and the USSR.[48]

A number of Venona messages dealt with KGB requests that Schuster check on potential recruits. In one cable, Soviet intelligence asked what the CPUSA knew about Marion Schultz, a Russian-born American working as a mechanic in the Philadelphia shipyards and active in Russian War Relief and Slavic organizations.[49] When Mary Ann Grohl, an American Communist once employed by the Joint Anti-Fascist Refugee Committee, moved to Mexico to live with a KGB agent who was being prepared for an assignment, Schuster told the KGB that she had been fired for incompetence.[50] Schuster arranged for Samuel Rodman, an employee of the United Nations Relief and Rehabilitation Administration leaving for Yugoslavia, to provide information to the KGB.[51] Schuster assured the KGB that Joseph Rappoport, a long-time party member active in Russian War Relief, was "a reliable and responsible comrade."[52] Sometimes he reported that a potential recruit was not known to the party.[53] The Soviets refused to maintain contact with an agent code-named Phloke and her husband until it received a report about them from Schuster, and it was through Schuster that Earl Browder warned the KGB about potentially unreliable or untrustworthy sources.[54]

Schuster's liaison role brought him into the KGB's efforts to steal scientific information and American atomic bomb secrets. (See chapter 10.) He met regularly with Julius Rosenberg to receive his CPUSA dues. The New York KGB office told Moscow that Schuster wanted to know whether the KGB was satisfied with the work of the Rosenberg apparatus. A number of Communist party members were working as scientists and engineers on projects relating to the atomic bomb, and the Communist-dominated Federation of Architects, Engineers, Chemists and Technicians (FAECT), to which Rosenberg belonged, was a natural recruiting ground for the KGB. When Schuster investigated a possible candidate for recruitment and reported that the individual was a disruptive force in the FAECT, the KGB decided not to approach him and instead to "find another candidate" from the union. Schuster had been so helpful that the New York office requested permission from Moscow to ask Schuster "through Liberal [Julius Rosenberg] about leads from among people who are working on Enormous [the Manhattan Project] and in other technical fields."[55] When Saville Sax and Theodore Alvin Hall—both young Communists—approached the KGB with the news that Hall, a physicist, was being dispatched to Los Alamos to work on the atomic bomb, Schuster was entrusted with the task of checking up on their backgrounds.[56]

Schuster also located safe-houses where KGB officers could meet in secrecy with their sources, and provided them with the names of two long-time CPUSA members, Louis Horvitz and Paul Burns. New York sent this information to Moscow on August 16, 1944; three days later General Fitin of the KGB directed a memo to Dimitrov asking for information on Horvitz, identified as working in a judicial office, and Paul Burns, a social worker and Lincoln battalion veteran.[57] Leonid Kvasnikov, a KGB officer, used the apartment of a CPUSA member for his first meeting with one source at the end of 1944, although it is not clear whether the apartment was Horvitz's or Burns's.[58]

Toward the end of 1944 Schuster began to balk at the demands placed on him by the KGB. His reasons are not clear. The CPUSA had recently been dissolved and replaced by the Communist Political Association. Possibly Earl Browder may have developed doubts that continued extensive American Communist involvement in Soviet espionage was compatible with moving communism into the mainstream of American politics. In any case, in October 1944 the New York KGB complained to Moscow that Schuster had begun to refuse to carry out assignments. During a meeting with the KGB agent Joseph Katz, Schuster declined several assignments, stating that his position within the Communist Political Association did not give him the authority to obtain safe-houses, find candidates to infiltrate the FBI, or perform other tasks. Schuster suggested that the KGB ask Browder "for a responsible worker to be assigned to us, one who is capable of carrying out the necessary measures without asking permission from the authorities each time."[59] In another message the KGB passed along Schuster's complaint that he could work effectively only within the New York area and that for anything else he had to go to Browder and get specific approval.[60] Both messages noted Schuster's claim that getting Communist party members to carry out espionage tasks for the KGB had become more difficult since Browder's reforms. (This latter observation did not, of course, recommend Browder's new course to Moscow and may have contributed to its decision to reverse the reforms.)

Moscow's response clearly demonstrated that the KGB had little use for any show of independence by an American Communist. The Communist party's secret apparatus was beholden not to the party leader, Earl Browder, but to the KGB. General Fitin angrily ordered the New York KGB to tell Schuster that "henceforth he must carry out our tasks without resorting to the help of Helmsman [Browder]."[61] Following this order Schuster took a holiday in Mexico from November 1944 to January 1945. While he was gone, the KGB planned his future assignments; the New York office reported that he would be asked to obtain information about the structure of the OSS. When he returned, Schuster desisted from complaining and once again began carrying out the tasks allotted to the Communist party by the KGB.[62] And, of course, via the Duclos article, by mid-1945 Moscow had disposed of Browder and his reforms, and the Communist Political Association had once more become the Communist Party of the USA.

Schuster's foot-dragging also coincided with a disagreement within the KGB about how crucial CPUSA cooperation was to intelligence operations in America. In 1944 Stepan Apresyan headed the KGB's New York station, but he did not have the broad authority over all KGB operations that his predecessor had had. Vasily Zubilin's move from New York to Washington in 1943 indicated that the senior KGB officer in the United States would henceforth be in the capital. Zubilin was hastily recalled from the United States in 1944, however, after his subordinate, Vasily Mironov, accused him of treason (chapter 2). Until the arrival of Anatoly Gromov several months later as Zubilin's replacement, this gap temporarily left uncertain who was the chief of KGB activity, and Vladimir Pravdin, the head of TASS in the United States and a senior KGB officer, asserted authority independently from Apresyan. Each sent a cable to Moscow accusing the other of poor performance. Apresyan denounced Pravdin for believing that "without the help of the Fellowcountrymen [American Communists] we are completely powerless." Apresyan disagreed: although "we shall have to have recourse to the Fellow Countrymen [American Communists] . . .

they ought not to be the one and only base especially if you take into account the fact that in the event of Kulak's [Thomas Dewey's] being elected [U.S. president] this source may dry up."[63]

Apresyan's irritation at the CPUSA and Browder was undoubtedly related to the KGB's effort to take direct control of the sources previously supervised by Jacob Golos, particularly the large Silvermaster group. Some of the group's activities, set up and run by enthusiastic but amateur spies, appalled the professional KGB officers. Its members socialized with each other, mixed Communist party activity with intelligence work, violated elementary rules of security, kept documents in the Silvermaster home, and even planned to buy a farm together. Akhmerov tried to professionalize the group's operations but ran into resistance from Gregory Silvermaster, who explained "that he did not believe in our orthodox methods."[64] One KGB initiative resisted by members of the Silvermaster group was the attempt to stop the sharing of espionage with the CPUSA leadership. As already noted, Akhmerov had to ask Moscow to make an exception to its rule and allow him to transmit some information to Browder. Otherwise, the frustrated Akhmerov stated, the "Fellow Countrymen [American Communists] may try to realize transmission passing us by," which would be even more insecure than if Akhmerov did it.[65]

The West Coast

There was a separate California branch of the CPUSA's secret apparatus, dating from the early 1930s. Its head in those years was a longtime Communist, Isaac Folkoff, often called Pop Folkoff. Born January 10, 1881, in Lutzin (Latvia), Folkoff came to the United States in 1904 and became a citizen in 1912. A charter member of the CPUSA, Folkoff kept a low profile until 1932, although the FBI believed that he had visited the Soviet Union in the early 1920s. Folkoff was a partner in the Model Embroidery and Pleating Company in San Francisco. For much of the 1930s he was the chairman of the Finance Committee of the California Communist party. While head of the West Coast party underground, Folkoff worked with Whittaker Chambers, and, like J. Peters, he was removed from his position after Chambers's defection in 1938 put him at risk of exposure. Indeed, Chambers identified him to Under Secretary of State Berle in 1939.[66]

Another West Coast figure was William Crane, a newspaper reporter who had worked for the *Wall Street Journal* in San Francisco and joined the Communist party in 1932. Crane, a native of Minnesota, had graduated from Stanford. His stay in the aboveground party was brief, however. He told the FBI years later that Pop Folkoff introduced him to John Loomis Sherman (just as Max Bedacht introduced Chambers to Sherman), who asked him to drop out of the CPUSA "in order to engage in special work." For the next several years Crane assisted Sherman in several operations that benefited both the party and Soviet intelligence. His first assignment was a survey of the Japanese and Chinese populations on the West Coast. Next, he taught English to a Japanese Communist whom he knew only as Joe. The FBI suspected that it was Joe Koide, an immigrant who worked for the Profintern's Pan-Pacific Trade Union Secretariat in the 1930s. Crane and Sherman also published a small Japanese newspaper in Los Angeles. In 1934 Crane, who was receiving $125 a month for his underground work, went to New York and met Whittaker Chambers, as well as the Soviet officer who headed the GRU apparatus in the United States.[67]

When he returned to San Francisco, Crane became more involved in Soviet intelligence operations. He served as the contact for Morris Asimow, who was originally used as a mail drop but who began to supply industrial formulas he obtained from his work at U.S. Steel in 1936. Asimow later acknowledged to American authorities that he had supplied Crane information about an industrial steel alloy. Crane also picked up materials from Vladimir De Sveshnikov, a ballistics expert employed by the U.S. government. In 1949 De Sveshnikov confirmed to the FBI that he had been recruited by the Soviets in the mid-1920s and regularly received a hundred dollars a month in return for patent information and American military journals dealing with artillery and engineering. He handed over material regularly throughout the 1930s. Crane also received from Lester Marx Huettig, who worked for Remington Arms in Bridgeport, Connecticut, the blueprints for automatic shell loaders, which Crane turned over to Boris Bykov of the GRU.[68]

Chambers was dispatched to San Francisco in 1935 with a money belt containing approximately twenty thousand dollars. He contacted Crane, whom he knew by the pseudonym Keith. Crane, in turn, introduced Chambers to Pop Folkoff, who took the money belt. Chambers assumed that the money was for the Pan-Pacific Trade Union Secretariat courier system to Japan; for some reason it was not used, and in 1935 Crane returned it to him in New York. Crane began working as a photographer for Chambers's Washington, D.C., espionage ring in 1937. He left the apparatus at the end of 1937 and returned to California; under the name Will Morgan he resumed activity in the aboveground CPUSA, writing for its West Coast newspaper, *People's World*. Not until 1947 did he break with the party. When the FBI found him in 1948, he confirmed Whittaker Chambers's story of espionage, although they differed on small details.[69]

After the KGB began operating out of the Soviet consulate in San Francisco in the early 1940s, Folkoff began to appear in Venona messages—more than a dozen from 1943 to 1946. He is portrayed as doing many of the same things as Bernard Schuster did on the East Coast. He arranged meetings for KGB officers with West Coast Communists they wanted to contact, such as Nat, described in the deciphered message as a leading Communist in the San Francisco area.[70] Folkoff, under the cover name Uncle, also passed along to the KGB the names of likely candidates for recruitment. In February 1944, for example, Uncle/Folkoff suggested as a likely source an engineer named Darcy Henwood, who worked for Standard Oil. The KGB message mentioning Henwood also indicated that Folkoff was being paid five hundred dollars. Another 1944 message suggests that Folkoff was helping the Soviets recruit Bay Area longshoremen, among whom the CPUSA had many supporters.[71]

One of Folkoff's most valuable agents was James Walter Miller, a Russian-language translator with the financial and trade section of the U.S. government wartime mail censorship office. With its legal access to mail and to U.S. security agencies' watch list of mail to be given special scrutiny, this office was of considerable interest to Soviet intelligence.[72] A Russian native, Miller had been a member of the Communist party in Los Angeles under the name of Victor Milo. He had worked for the party's *Russky Golos* and the American-Russian Institute and done translating for the *People's World*. Several times in 1943 Folkoff gave the KGB material he had received from Miller. In November San Francisco requested permission from Moscow "to sign on Vague [Miller]" but warned that because he was "talkative" it wanted to have Folkoff arrange for him to pass his material through Communist party contacts, so that he "will have no inkling that the information is coming to us." Because Miller was so eager to help, the KGB worried that he might be a double agent, but Grigory Kheifets, the KGB's San Francisco chief, reported that "the Fellowcountrymen [CPUSA] categorically rule out such an assumption."[73]

Miller was soon passing information to the KGB through an old friend at the *People's World,* Harrison George, himself a veteran of the Comintern's Pan-Pacific Trade Union Secretariat. One message indicated that Miller had enabled some KGB operation in Mexico to proceed with assurances that its communications had not been compromised. Late in 1943 Miller was able to warn his contacts that the Mail Censor's office had found secret writing upon opening a letter that a Naval GRU officer had sent to Moscow. The KGB warned Moscow to make sure the Naval GRU was alerted. Miller, however, came into the sights of the FBI in 1944 during its "Comintern Apparatus" investigation. His CPUSA membership was barely concealed. The bureau also observed Miller meeting the KGB officer Kheifets at least six times in the early months of 1944. The two would often walk along deserted streets, Miller talking and Kheifets taking notes. Under prompting from the FBI, Miller's superiors subjected his activities to extra scrutiny. When they found that he had copied a letter without authority to do so, they forced him to resign.[74]

Another important West Coast CPUSA official linked to Soviet espionage was Steve Nelson, who had years of experience in clandestine work. A native of Croatia, he joined the Young Communist League in 1923 in Philadelphia. After working in Pittsburgh, Nelson was encouraged to move to Detroit by Rudy Baker, a fellow Yugoslav with whom he shared an apartment before Baker went off to the International Lenin School in Moscow. By 1929 Nelson had become a full-time functionary (Communist party professional). The CPUSA sent him to the Lenin School in 1931 at Baker's suggestion. During his two-year stay there, Nelson was sent on clandestine missions to Germany, Switzerland, France, India, and China, while his wife also served in the Comintern's courier service. After another sojourn organizing within the United States, Nelson went to Spain to serve as political commissar of the Abraham Lincoln battalion. Nelson had traveled under false passports to the Soviet Union and to Spain.[75]

Nelson proved to be an effective political commissar, and upon his return to the United States the CPUSA, having marked him as an up-and-coming leader, sent him to southern California as a party functionary. He headed a covert special commission that both ferreted out infiltrators of the CPUSA and stole the files of hostile organizations. In 1939 the Civil Liberties Subcommittee of the U.S. Senate Education and Labor Committee, headed by Wisconsin Progressive senator Robert

La Follette, held hearings on labor relations in California. As part of its investigation the La Follette subcommittee subpoenaed the records of the Associated Farmers, a leading employer group in California that was hostile to the Communist role in the California CIO.

Committee investigators seized the records to ascertain the Associated Farmers' role in the use of labor spies and physical assaults on farm unionists in California. As part of its anti-Communist campaign the Associated Farmers had gathered extensive documentation on Communist activities. Eager to learn what the Associated Farmers knew (and to learn the identity of its informants), Nelson's apparatus secretly stole, photographed, and returned the subpoenaed records.[76] He also worked with Japanese-American Communists to produce propaganda and arranged with longshoremen and sailors to smuggle it onto ships bound for Japan. Transferred to San Francisco in the fall of 1939, Nelson went underground early the next year, preparing to function illegally in case the CPUSA was outlawed.

During World War II Nelson served as head of the local Communist party organizations in San Francisco and Oakland. Early in 1943 Rudy Baker informed Dimitrov that "we have assigned one responsible person in California (Mack) to be responsible for all our work from there." Although there is no direct evidence that Nelson was Mack, a bugged conversation between Nelson and Vasily Zubilin in April 1943 indicated that Nelson had been appointed to head the West Coast apparatus late in 1942. And although Nelson's name does not appear among the decrypted agent names in Venona, he is a candidate for Butcher, a KGB source on the West Coast, who identified possible recruits in the aviation and oil industries in California.[77] One part of Nelson's task was to gather information on the atomic bomb project. He was seen and overheard meeting with young Communist scientists working at the radiation laboratory at Berkeley. Information gleaned from FBI bugging and wiretaps indicated that several had discussed the atomic bomb project with him. Nelson made notes of what the scientists told him regarding their work, and he was subsequently observed passing materials, which the FBI assumed were his notes, to a Soviet intelligence officer operating under diplomatic cover at the USSR's San Francisco consulate.

The FBI's listening devices overheard Nelson meeting with Zubilin, the KGB's senior officer in the United States, on April 10, 1943. The conversation opened with Zubilin counting out a roll of bills and passing it to Nelson, who responded, "Jesus, you count money like a banker." Zubilin answered, "Vell, you know I used to do it in Moskva." Nelson and Zubilin discussed the role of Al, the head of the CPUSA's secret apparatus in the United States, whom the FBI later identified as Rudy Baker. Nelson indicated that Earl Browder knew about his activities and the work of the apparatus on behalf of the Soviet Union. Nelson also went into considerable detail about his underground party work on the West Coast. Although most of the members of the secret apparatus were referred to by code names, Nelson openly identified Dr. Frank Bissell and his wife, Nina. Both were active Communists who had served in medical units in the Spanish Civil War.[78]

Nelson had a number of complaints about the operations of his own apparatus and the way it was being used by Soviet intelligence. He was dissatisfied with courier operations to the South Pacific and contacts with Japanese Communists in the relocation camps. Two members of the underground apparatus, George and Rapp, came in for particularly strong condemnation. Nelson felt that George (later identified as Getzel "Joe" Hochberg) and Rapp (Mordecai "Morris" Rappaport) were inefficient. Hochberg was an intermediary with Earl Browder on secret apparatus matters. Rappaport supervised the West Coast seamen couriers. Soon after this conversation, Hochberg, who had previously been employed by the Jewish Communist newspaper *Die Freiheit* and had traveled as a bodyguard for Earl Browder, was transferred from New York to Detroit and stripped of his party responsibilities.[79]

Morris Rappaport was a far more prominent party figure, but Nelson's complaint ended his leadership role. A longtime party functionary, he had directed Communist activities in the Pacific Northwest for much of the 1930s. Born November 1, 1893, in Ekaterinoslav, Russia, Rappaport came to the United States by way of Vancouver in 1922. The government had unsuccessfully attempted to deport him in 1930, when he left no doubt about his beliefs. Questioned whether he believed in the overthrow of the government by force and violence, he replied that "in the interest of the working class of the government, I think it would be historically necessary to overthrow it by revolution." Rappaport was arrested for deportation again in 1941 and let out on bail. He then vanished to assume a leading role in the party underground. After Nelson's complaint, he was transferred from San Francisco to Los Angeles, where FBI agents located him in 1944 living under the name of John Fox and running a retail cigar and candy store. He was still in touch with Communists known to have ties to the underground, including

Leo Baroway and Rudy Lambert, and the head of the California Communist party, William Schneiderman. Rappaport never resumed a public leadership role in the CPUSA, although he remained active in the party in Petaluma, California, where he owned a chicken farm. He died in 1982.[80]

Nelson's most significant complaint to Zubilin reflected just how aggressive Soviet intelligence had become. Soviet intelligence agents were directly approaching Communist party members in California and asking for their help on specific assignments. Nelson was upset, not that Communists were being asked to work for the KGB, but that the KGB was bypassing the CPUSA organization when making the requests. According to an FBI summary of the conversation, "Nelson suggested to Zubilin that in each important city or State, the Soviets have but one contact who was trustworthy, and [that they] let that man handle the contact with party members who were to be given special assignments by the Soviets."[81]

One of the close contacts of Grigory Kheifets, the KGB San Francisco chief, was a wealthy San Francisco Communist, Louise Bransten—so close that she was frequently referred to as Kheifets's mistress. Born in San Francisco in 1908, the only child of a wealthy Jewish merchant who founded a produce company, Louise Rosenberg inherited more than a million dollars from her parents. Married to and then divorced from Richard Bransten, a prominent Communist journalist, she was active in the American-Russian Institute in San Francisco. The FBI, which closely monitored her activities during World War II, described her as "the hub of a wheel, the spokes thereof representing the many facets of her pro-Soviet activities, running from mere membership in the Communist Party . . . to military and industrial espionage and political and propaganda activities."[82]

The FBI observed her making contact with a remarkable number of Soviet agents. In addition to her relationship with Kheifets, Bransten was a longtime friend of Gregory Silvermaster and visited him in Washington. She met frequently with Pop Folkoff. Willard Park and Mary Price, both named by Bentley as sources, were friends. Martin Kamen, an atomic scientist who had been observed by the FBI meeting with the KGB officer Kheifets and who admitted providing information to him, met with Bransten. So did Haakon Chevalier, who approached Robert Oppenheimer to pass on atomic bomb data. Two of her friends at the

American-Russian Institute were Dolly Eltenton and Rose Isaak. The former's husband, a chemist at Shell Development Laboratories, had asked Chevalier to approach Oppenheimer about providing information to the Soviets. Rose Isaak advised the KGB in 1945 that she intended to resign from her job at the American-Russian Institute and "henceforth not to communicate with us."[83]

Still another contact of Bransten's was Vladimir Pozner, a Russian émigré.[84] Pozner's family had fled the Bolshevik Revolution, but Pozner became a Communist sympathizer while living in Europe. Pozner was chief engineer of the European branch of Metro-Goldwyn-Mayer in Paris in 1938. He fought in the French army until its defeat and then fled to the United States with his French wife and son in 1941. In 1943 he headed the Russian section of the film department of the U.S. War Department. A Venona message that year noted that "we are planning to use Vladimir Aleksandrovich Pozner (henceforth Platon)," discussed his background, and lauded his extensive connections. The same message noted that one of his secretaries was being "redeveloped by us for use in connection with Platon" and asked Moscow to "check Platon and sanction his use as a probationer [agent] and a source of leads."[85]

Although Bransten's name was not among those identified in Venona, she is a candidate for an unidentified agent with the cover name Map. The subject of half a dozen messages from the San Francisco KGB, Map served as a liaison between the KGB and several intelligence sources.[86]

Senior CPUSA Figures and Soviet Espionage

A substantial number of senior American Communists had compromising relationships with Soviet intelligence. These include Rudy Baker (Central Control Commission), Theodore Bayer (president of the Russky Golos Publishing Company), Max Bedacht (head of International Workers Order), Earl Browder (general secretary), William Browder (assistant to Earl Browder), Morris Childs (Illinois Communist party leader), Eugene Dennis (Political Bureau), Nicholas Dozenberg (National Literature Director), Isaac Folkoff (California Communist party treasurer), Jacob Golos (Central Control Commission), Bruce Minton (an editor of *New Masses*), Steve Nelson (Bay Area Communist party head), Joseph North (an editor of *New Masses*), Josef Peters (head of the Organizational Department), and Bernard Schuster (New York Communist party treasurer).[87]

In addition, deciphered Venona cables show that Boleslaw (Bill) Gebert, a CPUSA district organizer for many years, actively assisted the KGB. Gebert had immigrated from Poland in 1918 and gone to work as a miner. A charter member of the CPUSA, he had headed the Polish-language bureau of the party in the late 1920s before moving into a leadership role as district organizer in Chicago and Pittsburgh in the 1930s. When the CIO was formed, Gebert used his position as head of the Communist fraternal society Polonia to mobilize ethnic steelworkers to join the organization. After World War II Gebert returned to Communist Poland, where he assumed a leading position in the state-controlled labor unions. He came back to the United States in 1950 as UN representative of the Communist-dominated World Federation of Trade Unions and later served as a Polish ambassador. Louis Budenz claimed that Gebert engaged in espionage. He charged that during World War II Gebert, the district organizer in Detroit, frequently visited Chicago to meet covert contacts in the Slavic community. According to Budenz, there was conflict between Gebert and Morris Childs (district organizer for Illinois) over Gebert's intrusion into Chicago and, in particular, over a "Czech comrade who was doing vital underground work for Gebert."[88]

Budenz was right about Gebert; he appears in nine Venona messages written between May and October 1944.[89] In one, the KGB in New York gave Gebert's real name and cover name—Ataman—in plain text, noting that his father was a peasant of German background and his mother was Polish. Several of the messages dealt with political developments within the Polish-American community; others involved Gebert's transfer to another control agent. In one message it is reported that the New York KGB had promised Gebert a subsidy of one thousand dollars to publish a Polish-language book but had paid only five hundred dollars and Gebert was now demanding the rest. The most interesting cables dealt with Gebert's cultivation of Oskar Lange, a prominent Polish-American intellectual and economist. They also bear on the contentious issue of the postwar Polish government and the "betrayal" of Poland to Stalin.

Well known as a left-wing socialist critical of Stalinism, Oskar Lange, who was born in Poland in 1904, had achieved renown as an economist before moving to the United States in 1937. He taught at the University of Chicago and became an American citizen in 1943, when he began to involve himself in Polish émigré and diaspora politics. Most American Poles were vehemently anti-Communist and supported the London-based exile government of Prime Minister Stanislaw Mikolaj-czyk. In March 1944 an array of Polish-American groups formed the Polish American Congress to support Poland's independence from Soviet domination. Two smaller groups supported the Soviet Union and endorsed its demands to annex large portions of eastern Poland and provide eastern Prussia as compensation to Poland: the Kosciuszko League, based in Detroit and led by Father Stanislaw Orlemanski, and the American Slav Congress, led by the pro-Communist labor leader Leo Krzycki. As the Red Army moved into Poland in 1943, Lange emerged from political obscurity and attached himself to the pro-Soviet forces. By 1944 Joseph Stalin was suggesting to a slightly shocked American ambassador Averell Harriman that Lange, Krzycki, and Or-lemanski, all American citizens, become members of an entirely new Polish government. Although the Roosevelt administration was unenthusiastic, it did expedite a trip by Orlemanski and Lange to Moscow in April and May of 1944.[90]

While in Moscow, Lange met with Molotov and Stalin. The same day as the meeting with Stalin, the KGB in New York sent a cable with information that Bill Gebert felt was essential for Lange to have during his Moscow visit about internal émigré politics in the United States. At the end of May, Gebert provided information to the KGB about Lange. Although the beginning of the cable was poorly deciphered, it suggests that Lange's change of heart toward the USSR had come in 1943. At that point Lange had no cover name.[91] Lange returned to the United States at the end of May, met with Polish prime minister Mikolajczyk, who was in Washington, to stress how reasonable Stalin was prepared to be, and with a State Department official to urge that the United States put pressure on the exiled Poles (particularly Mikolajczyk) to cooperate with the Soviet Union. The Venona documents suggest that Oskar Lange had reached a tacit agreement with the Soviets, via the KGB, even before he went to Moscow in 1944. At that time the KGB also gave Lange a cover name—Friend—and told Moscow that he would "undoubtedly play a political role in Poland in the future."[92] In 1945 Oskar Lange renounced his American citizenship and returned to Poland. He was not out of the United States long, though. He came back to Washington as the first ambassador of Communist Poland to the United States.

The CPUSA, Journalists, and Espionage

As the CPUSA grew in the 1930s, it acquired adherents from all walks of life, including journalism. Journalists were of interest to Soviet intelligence as sources of information; reporters were, after all, in the business of finding out what was happening. Journalism also provided a convenient cover profession for espionage. Two of Jacob Golos's agents, Winston Burdett and Peter Rhodes, were journalists recruited through the CPUSA. Joseph Bernstein of the GRU was also a reporter by trade.

The *Daily Worker*'s Moscow correspondent, Janet Weaver Ross, illustrates one kind of assistance that Communist journalists provided to the USSR. Janet Ross accompanied her husband, Nat, to Moscow in 1939. In the early 1940s Nat Ross was the highest-ranking CPUSA member stationed in Moscow. Janet attended press briefings at the American embassy, was accorded interviews with American diplomats, and was given invitations to "Americans only" social events. But she did not just file her stories with the *Daily Worker;* she used her access to the American embassy to prepare secret reports for the Comintern about what she had heard. Georgi Dimitrov then forwarded her reports to Molotov, the Soviet foreign minister. A number of such reports, dated from August 1942 to June 1943, when the Rosses left the USSR to return to the United States, were located in the files of the Comintern. While Ross did not commit espionage—she conveyed no secret information and stole no embassy files—she functioned as an informer for the Soviet Union. As Dimitrov noted to Molotov when he sent one of Ross's reports, she was "*our* American correspondent comrade Janet Ross."[93]

Other Communist journalists also assisted the KGB's activities, either by providing information or by working to discredit anti-Communists. During Whittaker Chambers's years at *Time* magazine, he became a fierce anti-Communist. For a period in 1944 and 1945, Chambers was in charge of the foreign news department, where his editing of stories to bring out matters that depicted the USSR in a poor light enraged several correspondents, who demanded that publisher Henry Luce remove him. Two of the most hostile were John Scott and Richard Lauterbach. Lauterbach, described by one scholar as "the correspondent Chambers trusted least," had been *Time*'s correspondent in Moscow.[94] Two Venona cables refer to Lauterbach. The KGB agent Jack Soble reported in December 1944 that Lauterbach was a secret member of the CPUSA, had just returned from the USSR, and had passed on to Soble the information that *Time* (Chambers, most likely) had pressured him to write an anti-Soviet series but that he had refused and threatened to resign. Impressed by Lauterbach's defense of the USSR, Soble "recommends drawing him in" to the KGB apparatus. Vladimir Pravdin had started to study him, and the cable asked Moscow to check on his activities while he had been in the Soviet Union. It assigned him the cover name Pa. A few weeks later, another cable asked Moscow to "please expedite checking and telegraph your instructions about Pa," because he might soon be leaving on another foreign assignment. Moscow's response was not decrypted.[95]

As discussed above, John Scott, another of Chambers's enemies on *Time,* had been an active KGB source when he worked for the OSS. Whether Scott continued to provide assistance to the KGB after he joined *Time* is not clear.[96]

Another influential figure at *Time* was Stephen Laird, who for a period supervised *Time* foreign correspondents. Half a dozen deciphered Venona cables show that he, too, was a KGB agent.[97] In August 1944 the New York KGB station handed liaison with Laird over to a new case officer, Konstantin Shabenov. He cabled Moscow his assessment of his new charge:

> Yun [Laird] gives the impression of a politically well-developed person who wishes to help us. However, he considers his potentialities to be limited, for he deals only with technical work on the magazine. He can pass on correspondents' telegrams but we receive them from other sources. Using his connections among journalists and studying the magazine's materials he could draw up political reports for us but he lacks perseverance for that. Besides, [unrecovered code group] breakup with his wife. Yun declares that he is used to reporters' work and would like to go abroad again, but the owner of the magazine will not send him because he disapproves of his radical views. The other day the film company RKO took him on as a film producer, which he succeeded in getting thanks to social connections in actor and producer circles. Ac-

cording to Yun's words, Vardo [Elizabeth Zubilin] in her time did not object to such a maneuver and afterwards it may give him an opportunity to make trips to Europe and do work useful to us. In the middle of September Yun is moving to Hollywood. We consider it expedient to continue liaison with him in Hollywood. Telegraph whether a new password should be agreed upon.[98]

Subsequent cables show that the KGB gave Laird verbal recognition signals for use when the KGB made contact after his move to Hollywood. (He was to meet his KGB contact at the Beverly Hills Hotel.) Before he left for Hollywood, Laird turned over to the Soviets material obtained by a *Time* correspondent on diplomatic negotiations between the United States and Portugal over American use of the Azores as a military base.

While pursuing a Hollywood career, Laird also continued to work as a journalist and to promote Soviet causes. When the 1947 election in Poland was held, almost all American correspondents described it as a fraud preceded by a campaign of terror, intimidation, and coercion. Laird, however, did not see it that way. In the *New Republic* he insisted that the election was free, saw no reason to doubt the Communist regime's claim of having won 85 percent of the vote, and favorably compared the extent of political democracy in Communist Poland with that in the United States.[99] (One amusing note is that in 1945 Stepan Apresyan, then the San Francisco KGB chief, used the difficulty of meeting Laird in automobile-oriented Los Angeles as an argument for an adjustment in his budget so that he could have a car. He told Moscow, "In a town like Caen [Los Angeles] I should be simply walked off my feet.")[100]

Another Communist journalist mentioned in Venona was Walter Sol Bernstein, better known today as a screenwriter with such credits as *Fail Safe, The Front, The Molly Maguires,* and *Semi-Tough.* Bernstein's Communist loyalties led to his blacklisting by Hollywood studios in 1950. For the next decade he was forced to use "fronts" to survive professionally. In his 1996 memoirs Bernstein wrote that he had joined the Young Communist League while a student at Dartmouth in 1937. A writer for the *New Yorker* for several years, during World War II he was a correspondent for *Yank* in Europe and the Middle East. His greatest coup came in 1944, when with help from Communist contacts he became the first Western correspondent to obtain an interview with Josip Tito, the leader of the Yugoslav Communist Partisans.

In his memoirs Bernstein noted that after he returned to New York in 1944, his aunt, who worked in Communist party headquarters, asked if he would meet with some party leaders who wanted information on Tito. Gene Dennis and Avrom Landy, who supervised the party's work with ethnic minorities, came to his apartment. "I told them what I knew," Bernstein recalled, "which was no more that what I had already written. They asked intelligent questions, refused a drink and left with thanks." And Bernstein admitted, "I had myself been approached at a party by an affable secretary from the Soviet Embassy. I was still in uniform and what he wanted to know was trivial; what I thought about the morale of American troops. He knew me as a friend of the Soviet Union and if I would just write a few words on the subject. . . . I declined as politely as I could, feeling vaguely guilty afterward. Was I betraying the cause? The Russians were allies; where was the harm? I had gone against American policy in Yugoslavia, acting subversively in a time of war. What was the difference now? Should I have told my superior officer? (I didn't.)"[101]

Bernstein's story about his own brush with Soviet officialdom is given a different twist in one Venona message. In October 1944 the New York KGB reported to Moscow that a certain Khan had met with Bernstein, whose name is given in plain text. Bernstein "welcomed the re-establishment of liaison with him and promised to write a report on his trip by the first of November."[102]

Even though NSA and FBI analysts were never able to identify Khan, he is probably Avrom Landy. The other mentions of Khan—or Selim Khan, as he was later called in Venona—show him to be a liaison between the KGB and agents with connections in the CPUSA's ethnic societies. Khan handled liaison with Bill Gebert, Albert Kahn, and Mikhail Tkach, all of whom Landy would have met naturally in the course of his duties in the CPUSA. Moreover, Elizabeth Bentley reported that Landy had been recruited by Jacob Golos as a "look-out" for likely espionage recruits.[103]

Landy, born in 1902 to poor Russian immigrants, attended Ohio State University and the University of Wisconsin, earning election to Phi Beta Kappa. He was an editor on the *Daily Worker* in the early 1930s and educational director of the CPUSA before World War II. After his stint in charge of minority work for the party, Landy became co-publisher of International Publishers. He quietly dropped out of the CPUSA sometime in the late 1940s or early 1950s and died in 1992.

The October 1944 KGB cable is not necessarily in conflict with the story Bernstein told in his memoirs. The message noted that Bernstein welcomed the "re-establishment" of contact with the KGB. It is, of course, possible that Bernstein believed that he was merely resuming contact with the CPUSA. But it is also clear that Khan, the KGB contact, regarded the incident as a reestablishment with his agency.

Johannes Steele, a radio commentator and columnist known for his pro-Communist views, was the subject of several Venona cables.[104] One, from July 1944, shows Steele serving as a talent scout for the KGB. Vladimir Pravdin of the New York KGB told Moscow that for some time he had been deflecting the efforts of Roman Moszulski, director of the Polish Telegraphic Agency (a Polish-language wire service, aligned with the Polish government-in-exile) in the United States, to meet him. Then Steele, code-named Dicky, told Pravdin that Moszulski was secretly pro-Soviet and wanted to make contact with the KGB. Steele said he had known him for several years—that he was critical of "Polish fascists" and wanted to quit his job.

Steele had suggested to Moszulski that he remain where he was, to counteract the efforts of Polish reactionary propaganda. Steele set up a meeting with Pravdin at which Moszulski explained that he realized the future of Poland rested on its having good relations with the USSR and, "having thought over the full seriousness and the possible consequences of his step, he was putting himself at our disposal and was ready to give the Communists all the information he had and to consult with us on questions concerning his activities." Moszulski explained to Pravdin that he realized he could win the KGB's confidence only by deeds and that he would have to prove himself, given that Steele's endorsement of his bona fides was insufficient. "In reply he was told that we welcomed people well-disposed towards us and that naturally the proof of his sincerity would depend on himself."[105] Moszulski, attempting to provide the proof, delivered to the KGB the next month a list of Polish exiles and Polish-Americans, including an evaluation of how they stood on Polish-Soviet relations.[106]

Journalists who covered foreign news were useful to Soviet intelligence as couriers and intermediaries between KGB stations in the United States and elsewhere. Ricardo Setaro, deputy chief of the Latin American department of CBS Radio, functioned in those roles.[107] A deciphered 1943 Venona message identifies him as a way station for KGB funds for use in its Central and South American operations. In response to an inquiry from Moscow, an August 1944 message from the New York KGB station summarized his work: "Gonets [Setaro] is working as deputy chief of the Provincial [Latin American] department of the 'Columbia Broadcasting System.' He was used by us earlier for the most part on liaison with Arthur, as a meeting point for couriers. At the same time we used him on the processing of Provincial [seventeen unrecoverable code groups] as a Fellowcountryman [Communist]. We are using him here on the processing of the CBS and of the diplomatic representation of the Country [United States] in the Provinces [Latin America]."[108] By "processing," the KGB meant providing background information. Arthur, the person with whom Setaro was a liaison for the KGB, was not identified by NSA and FBI analysts. He occurs in dozens of Venona messages and appears to have been the principal courier between KGB stations in the United States and its stations in various Latin American capitals.

Newsmen are obvious targets for espionage recruitment. A reporter legitimately searching for legally available information has excellent cover for spying out secrets. Even when Soviet intelligence recognized that particular journalists were impossible targets for recruitment as spies under discipline, it cultivated them to obtain inside information or insights into political affairs. Walter Lippmann, for example, had no sympathy for communism. Golos's CPUSA-KGB network, however, placed Mary Price in his office as a secretary in order to find out what sources and additional information lay behind the prominent journalist's columns.

Another example of the KGB's cultivation of journalists as "legal" sources occurs in a fall 1944 deciphered Venona message. At that time the New York KGB station sent a message to Moscow about the activities of Vladimir Pravdin, a TASS correspondent and a senior KGB officer. The cable reported that several of his journalist "acquaintances are persons of great interest from a legal point of view. They are well informed and although they do not say all they know, nevertheless they provide useful comments on the foreign policy" of the United States. The message specifically named Joseph Barnes, an official in the OWI and later foreign editor of the *New York Herald Tribune*. Barnes was often accused of being a Soviet agent; he denied it under oath, and this Venona cable supports that denial. The message stated that "the signing up of Barnes is obviously not only inadvisable but unrealizable; however, it is desirable to use him without signing him up."[109]

Even without being agents, journalists had access to a great deal of information, their stock in trade. They knew many more things than they could print. In 1945, when Philip Jaffe, the editor of *Amerasia*, was trying to persuade his friend, Navy lieutenant Andrew Roth, to cooperate in spying for the USSR, Roth raised several objections. He was, naturally, worried whether Jaffe's contact with Soviet intelligence (Joseph Bernstein) was sincere or whether he was an American counterintelligence plant. But, he also suggested to Jaffe that it would be less risky to simply publish classified information in *Amerasia* and other media outlets as a way of informing the Soviets: "This country is so wide open and obvious, and [it is] so easy for dozens of newspapermen to get the information, and they proceed to state it very openly in dozens of forms, that I don't see why I shouldn't." After some additional argument, however, Roth gave in, reasoning that since TASS no doubt forwarded summaries of the contents of *Amerasia* to Soviet leaders anyway, Jaffe might as well go ahead and deal directly with Bernstein. He agreed that "if the situation warrants it, whenever anything comes up that you feel is significant, you can tell Joe [Bernstein]."[110]

Another Communist journalist who played a key role in the KGB's efforts to find journalistic informants and agents was Samuel Krafsur, an American who worked for TASS. Not much detail is available about his background and life. He was born in Boston around 1911 and attended Northeastern University for one year. Krafsur was a member of the CPUSA and fought with the International Brigades in Spain, where he was wounded in 1937. Krafsur went to work for TASS in 1941, first in New York and then in Washington, where he was assistant head of the local bureau. After leaving TASS in 1949 he worked in a toy factory. Krafsur was subpoenaed by the House Committee on Un-American Activities but was uncooperative.

Venona makes clear that Krafsur was an important Soviet agent, first recruited by the TASS correspondent and KGB officer Vladimir Pravdin.[111] Krafsur was particularly valued for the extensive contacts he had developed as a newsman. In May 1944, the New York KGB cabled Moscow to report that after months of study it proposed to use Krafsur, who was given the cover name of Ide, "for cultivating newspapermen's circles in Washington." Krafsur was described as a Communist, a Lincoln battalion veteran, and "absolutely devoted to the USSR, [someone who] always zealously carries out minor tasks" given by Pravdin to obtain information. Work with his wide circle of friends "will give opportunities for obtaining valuable information and also of studying individual subjects for signing on."[112] After checking with the Comintern about Krafsur's background, the KGB headquarters in Moscow approved his recruitment.[113]

The Venona cables show that Krafsur provided at least twenty leads for the KGB. One was Joseph Berger, a personal aide to the chairman of the Democratic National Committee. There is no evidence that Soviet intelligence succeeded in recruiting Berger, but the KGB clearly targeted him. A message one year later noted that Berger had left for Moscow as an American delegate to the Reparations Commission and discussed his background.

Joseph Berger was born in 1903 in Denver, Colorado. He graduated from the University of Missouri School of Journalism in 1924 and took a job as a reporter on the *Kansas City Star*. In 1934 he came to Provincetown, Massachusetts, with his wife and young daughter and worked as a free-lance writer. The Bergers lived in extreme poverty for a year, begging food from local residents. His fortunes changed when he got a job with the Federal Writers' Project under the Works Progress Administration, writing for the American Guide Series. Berger's *Cape Cod Pilot*, published in the series under the by-line Jeremiah Digges, won great praise, enabling Berger to obtain a Guggenheim Fellowship and launching his writing career. One of his many children's books detailed the adventures of a mythical figure, Bowleg Bill, an eight-foot bronco buster from Wyoming.[114]

In 1941 Berger moved to the Democratic National Committee (DNC), where he worked as a speechwriter for Pres. Franklin Delano Roosevelt, Sen. Harry Truman, Rep. Lyndon Johnson, and other national Democratic figures. In 1945 he served as a member of the Reparations Commission and traveled to Moscow. According to one KGB message, Robert Hannegan, the DNC chairman who had been appointed postmaster general, had hired Berger at ten thousand dollars a year to serve as his special assistant when he returned from Moscow. After leaving the government, Berger wrote scripts for daytime television shows. In 1950 he became a speech writer for the March of Dimes but continued to write short stories and articles until his death in 1971.[115]

In his 1945 message to Moscow about Berger, who had just left for the Soviet Union with the Reparations Commission, Pravdin reported that Krafsur had known Berger for five years and described him as a progressive and as well disposed toward the Soviet Union. According to Krafsur, Berger had expressed a desire to live in the USSR and maintained contact with the CPUSA. The message noted that given his connections and future job, "he could be a valuable probationer [agent]. I would recommend using B.'s trip to Smyrna [Moscow] for working on him and possibly signing him on." Pravdin also noted that Berger had met with Krafsur just before leaving and "insistently inquired" about what friends he should meet in Moscow.[116]

There are no further decrypted messages indicating whether Berger was actually recruited by the KGB. And the fact that he left government service and political work in 1946 suggests that in any case he might not have had access to sensitive information. Indeed, it is possible that Berger's decision to leave government work was linked to a desire not to have anything to do with Soviet espionage.

The cable requesting permission to sign up Krafsur noted that one of his leads, in addition to Joseph Berger, was "[deleted]- brother of the well-known journalist [deleted]. Ide [Krafsur] is very friendly with them both." In its notes to the cable, the NSA blacked out both names of the brother journalists, but noted that the well-known one was born in 1897 and his brother in 1899. Very likely these references are to Drew Pearson, born in 1897, and his younger brother, Leon, also a journalist. Leon worked for Drew until they had a falling-out and he pursued an independent career in journalism. He accompanied Secretary of State James Byrnes to Moscow in 1945 and later headed the International News Service's Paris Bureau and did newscasts for NBC Radio.

There is no evidence that Leon Pearson responded to a KGB approach, if one was ever made. Drew Pearson wrote in his diaries that in 1951 the FBI approached several persons and asked if Leon knew an unnamed Russian and "a newspaperman named Barger." Lou Nichols, a high-ranking FBI official, told Drew Pearson that "questions were asked about Leon's friends because they are trying to track down a Russian agent in this country who knew Leon. However, Leon is in no way involved." Quite likely the cable referring to the KGB's interest in Leon Pearson had been partially decrypted by 1951, and the FBI was trying to learn about his connections with Joseph Berger, Samuel Krafsur, and Vladimir Pravdin.[117]

Krafsur also pointed the KGB toward an associate of Drew Pearson. In a badly broken message from June 1944 Pravdin told Moscow about "information received by Ide [Krafsur] from the journalist David

Karr."[118] David Karr was at that time the chief aide to Pearson, one of America's most widely read columnists. His incredible career, which included important positions in American industry and friendships with some of America's most distinguished politicians, was dogged by accusations that he was a Soviet agent. The one Venona document in which his name is mentioned is not clear enough to determine whether in passing information to Krafsur he was innocently sharing material with a fellow journalist or knowingly supplying reports to a Soviet agent. Karr's life, however, suggests the latter.

David Karr was born in Brooklyn in 1918 into a middle-class family. As a young man he wrote articles and book reviews for the *Daily Worker,* attended CPUSA meetings, and befriended Communists. In later years, he always denied joining the CPUSA and maintained that his ties to the Communists were a consequence of his fervent antifascism.

In 1943 Karr, then working for the Office of War Information, was among a group of government employees attacked by Rep. Martin Dies, chairman of the House Special Committee on Un-American Activities, for their Communist ties. He appeared before the committee, insisted that his associations were entirely innocent, and falsely claimed to have been an FBI informant. A special congressional investigation exonerated him at the same time as the Civil Service Commission was concluding that he was both untruthful and unreliable.[119] Karr resigned from the OWI and went to work for Drew Pearson. An indefatigable investigator, Karr earned a reputation as an unscrupulous and unrelenting reporter, who eavesdropped on conversations, read documents upside down on people's desks, and misrepresented himself to sources. He was active politically as well, providing advice and help in Henry Wallace's effort to remain on the presidential ticket in 1944.

The FBI investigated Karr twice during the war, once for obtaining a confidential report on Stalin written by Oskar Lange for President Roosevelt by claiming to be on Vice President Wallace's staff and once because he was the recipient of leaked material from several of those charged in the *Amerasia* spy case. In 1950 Sen. Joseph McCarthy launched a bitter attack on Pearson, in the course of which he denounced Karr as the columnist's "KGB controller" and accused him of orchestrating the character assassination of a string of prominent anti-Communists. Conservative columnists like Westbrook Pegler hammered at Karr as a Communist for the next decade.[120]

During the 1950s Karr became involved in corporate intrigue and wrote a book about the use of public relations in business takeovers. He soon moved from theory to practice. In 1959, following a corporate raid, Karr became chief executive officer of the Fairbanks-Whitney Corporation, a large defense contractor whose divisions included Colt Firearms. After three rancorous years, a stockholders' revolt pushed him out. Karr dabbled in the movie and hotel businesses before becoming associated with Armand Hammer in 1972. Through Hammer, who had long-standing ties to the USSR (he had laundered Soviet money for the CPUSA in the 1920s and assisted Soviet intelligence agencies for years), Karr made valuable connections in the Soviet Union. Within a few years, he was brokering deals for Western firms in the USSR, most notably the construction of the $175 million dollar Kosmos Hotel in Moscow.[121]

The approach of the 1980 Moscow Olympics provided numerous opportunities for profit to Western businessmen with good connections to influential Soviet figures. Karr, a close friend of Dzherman Gvishiani, a son-in-law of Soviet president Aleksei Kosygin, obtained North and South American rights to Misha the Bear, the mascot of the games. Along with Hammer, he formed a joint venture to make and sell Olympic commemorative coins, an enterprise estimated to be worth some $200 million.

David Karr's connections in the Soviet Union were matched by his entrée to prominent American politicians. He boasted of his close ties and substantial campaign contributions to prominent U.S. senators and presidential candidates. He also claimed to have carried messages and information back and forth between the Soviet and American governments on such issues as détente, trade, strategic-arms negotiations, and emigration of Soviet Jews.

In 1979, shortly after returning to his Paris home from Moscow, Karr suddenly died. Amid charges that Karr had been murdered, his widow halted the burial so that an autopsy could be performed. One claim was that Karr had been swindling his Russian partners. Shortly before his death, in secret testimony before the Securities and Exchange Commission, he had implicated Hammer in the bribery of Soviet officials. Rumors circulated linking his friend Gvishiani to bribery scandals. Israeli intelligence officials spread rumors that Karr had been involved in secret Russian arms sales to Libya and Uganda. After the collapse of the Soviet Union a Russian journalist, citing a KGB file as her source, published an article in *Izvestia* charging that Karr was "a competent KGB source" who "submitted information to the KGB on the technical capabilities of the United States and other capitalist countries."[122]

Another Krafsur candidate for recruitment was I. F. "Izzy" Stone. Charges and countercharges about whether Stone had been a KGB agent roiled intellectual circles in the 1990s. By that time Stone, who had died in 1989, was a cultural hero. That a journalist celebrated for his fierce independence and iconoclastic writings about American government officials could have collaborated with the Soviet government was regarded by many on the American left as impossible, and they dismissed the charge as a McCarthyite smear.

Born Isidor Feinstein in Philadelphia in 1907 to Jewish immigrants from Russia, Stone dropped out of the University of Pennsylvania to become a journalist. He wrote for the *New York Post*, the *Nation*, and *PM*, before beginning *I. F. Stone's Weekly*, a highly regarded muckraking newspaper, in 1953. Stone was briefly a member of the Socialist party in the 1930s and was long sympathetic to the Soviet Union. In *The Hidden History of the Korean War* Stone spread the falsehood that it was South Korea that had sparked the war by invading the North with American backing. Although he was occasionally critical of aspects of Soviet policy, it was not until the mid-1950s that he lost his illusions about the Soviet regime, but he remained extremely critical of the United States and its policies throughout his life. In retirement Stone learned classical Greek and wrote a book on Socrates and Athens, part of his lifelong concern with issues of free speech and dissent.[123]

The question of Stone's relationship with the KGB heated up in 1992 when Oleg Kalugin, a retired KGB general, told a British journalist that "we had an agent—a well-known American journalist—with a good reputation, who severed his ties with us after 1956. I myself convinced him to resume them. But in 1968, after the invasion of Czechoslovakia . . . he said he would never again take any money from us." Herbert Romerstein, a former staff member of the House Committee on Un-American Activities, identified the journalist in question as Stone. The British journalist then reinterviewed Kalugin, who admitted that he had been referring to Stone but denied that Stone was a spy. Later, in his autobiography, Kalugin characterized Stone as a fellow traveler "who had made no secret of his admiration for the Soviet system" before the mid-1950s. He wrote that when he was asked to re-establish contact with Stone, KGB headquarters in Moscow "never said that he had been an agent of our Intelligence service, but rather that he was a man with whom we had regular contact."[124]

When Kalugin was stationed in the United States in the 1960s, he regularly met with journalists to glean their insights into the political scene. Since he was the official press attaché at the Soviet embassy, Kalugin had valid reasons to meet with American journalists, Stone's defenders noted. Even if Stone knew that Kalugin was a KGB officer, there was no evidence that Stone had done anything more than talk to him. Because Stone was not privy to government secrets, there was no illegality in his actions. Kalugin wrote that after the Soviet invasion of Czechoslovakia, Stone denounced the USSR, refused to meet with him again, and would not allow him to pick up the restaurant check, which Kalugin had customarily done.

The Venona decryptions provide a more complex background to this controversy. The KGB, it appears, had marked Stone as a promising source for recruitment. In September 1944 the New York KGB reported to Moscow that Stone "occupies a very prominent position in the journalistic world and has vast connections." In order to figure out "precisely his relations to us we will commission Echo to make a check." Echo was Bernard Schuster, the CPUSA's liaison to Soviet intelligence. Both Krafsur and Pravdin made several attempts to contact Stone, but to the former he was "coy" and to the latter he pleaded the press of business.[125]

Finally, in October 1944, Pravdin met with Stone, to whom the KGB gave the cover name Bliny, or Pancake. Stone knew he was not dealing with an ordinary journalist and told Pravdin "that he had noticed our attempts to contact him, particularly the attempts of Ide [Krafsur] and of people of the Trust [Soviet embassy] but he had reacted negatively fearing the consequences. At the same time he implied that the attempts at rapprochement had been made with insufficient caution and by people who were insufficiently responsible. To Sergey's [Pravdin's] reply that naturally we did not want to subject him to unpleasant complications, Pancake gave him to understand that he was not refusing his aid but one should consider that he had three children and did not want to attract the attention of the FBI."[126]

The tenor of this message suggests that Stone was flirting with the KGB. Had he thought he was simply dealing with TASS employees, he would hardly have been so cautious or frightened. No left-wing or even mainstream journalist in America would have been afraid to meet a

TASS correspondent or think that meeting with one in 1944 would incur the wrath of the FBI. Stone was perfectly willing to meet with Kalugin regularly during the 1960s, when the climate for Soviet government officials was far less hospitable. There is no evidence in Venona that Stone ever was recruited by the KGB, but Kalugin's comments in the 1990s that he "reestablished" contact leave open the possibility that Stone may have met with KGB agents on some basis after the meeting documented in Venona.

CHAPTER 9

HUNTING STALIN'S ENEMIES ON AMERICAN SOIL

In the 1930s and 1940s the Soviet Union carried out a maniacal campaign against Stalin's arch-rival, Leon Trotsky, and others abroad who posed ideological threats to Soviet communism. The foreign intelligence arm of the KGB spied on, infiltrated, and on occasion assassinated those Soviet dissidents who had been able to go into exile, as well as their foreign comrades and political allies.

The Venona decryptions, together with newly released FBI files, document the extensive involvement of the CPUSA and its secret apparatus in Trotsky's 1940 murder, as well as efforts to free his assassin and to spy on Stalin's ideological enemies. A dedicated revolutionary and brilliant Marxist theoretician who organized the Red Army and engineered its victory over the Whites in the civil war of 1918–1920, Leon Trotsky had appeared to many to be Lenin's obvious successor. He could not, however, match Stalin in the ruthless bureaucratic struggle inside the Soviet Communist party that followed Lenin's death in 1924. He and his supporters were subjected to a furious political attack both within the party and before the Soviet public. There was no free press in the USSR, and Trotsky was denied the right to reply. His ideas became thought crimes, and he was expelled from the Communist party and sent into internal exile. By the end of the 1920s very little remained of the once sizable Trotskyist faction.

For reasons that are not clear, Stalin allowed Trotsky to go into foreign exile in 1929. But thereafter Stalin's fury seemed to grow. By the mid-1930s it had reached nightmarish proportions, and Stalin set out to obliterate Trotsky and Trotskyism in both an ideological and a physical sense. Trotsky, to be sure, hoped to see Stalin overthrown and then to return to the Soviet Union in triumph as its new leader. He attempted to maintain contacts with supporters within the USSR, but in time few escaped imprisonment or execution. For example, when Trotsky initially went into exile in Turkey, the KGB learned that one of its senior officers there, Jacob Blumkin, was quietly communicating with Trotsky. Blumkin was recalled to the Soviet Union and shot. (There is also a minor American aspect of this affair. Blumkin was betrayed by his lover, Lisa Gorskaya. She was herself a KGB officer and later married Vasily Zubilin. As Elizabeth Zubilin she would serve with him in the United States as an effective espionage operative.)

Soviet pressure soon led the Turks to ask Trotsky to move on. As he wandered across Europe looking for a refuge, the campaign to destroy him escalated. Soviet intelligence operatives infiltrated his entourage, reported on his activities, stole his archives, and murdered a number of his associates. The campaign culminated in Mexico in 1940, when a KGB assassin smashed Trotsky's skull with an axe. Even Trotsky's murder, however, did not end Stalin's obsession with his movement and his small band of followers. Soviet intelligence continued to spy on Trotsky's widow and his associates and mounted a major clandestine campaign to free his assassin from a Mexican prison.

Infiltrating the Trotskyists

A long-standing Soviet counterintelligence tactic was to infiltrate and disrupt dissident organizations. As Trotsky struggled to establish a network of supporters from his exile in Prinkipo, Turkey, he was already encircled by KGB agents. Two of the earliest were a pair of Lithuanian Communist brothers, known in America as Jack Soble and Robert Soblen, recruited by the KGB to infiltrate the nascent European Trotskyist movement in the late 1920s. They were born in Lithuania to a wealthy Jewish family with the name Sobolevicius, which they anglicized slightly differently when they came to the United States. Their path through Europe and America spanned more than two decades of service to the Soviet Union.

Jack was born in 1903 and went to Leipzig in 1921 to attend college. There he joined the German Communist party at the age of eighteen. Graduating in 1927, he traveled to the USSR, where he married. Returning to Germany, he studied at the University of Berlin, becoming a Trotskyist and being expelled from the Communist party in 1929. When he testified at his brother's espionage trial in 1961, he claimed that he was recruited by the KGB in 1931 after his wife returned to the USSR to see her sick mother; he maintained he was summoned to the Soviet embassy and coerced into espionage with threats against his wife. The truth of this claim, however, is unclear, and there is evidence he was in Stalin's service by 1927, before he nominally became a Trotskyist.

Known as Abraham Senin in the European Trotskyist movement, Jack Soble visited Trotsky in Prinkipo in 1931 and in Copenhagen in 1932. Both he and his brother, known as Roman Weil to the Trotskyists, were important figures among German Trotskyists until 1932, when Trotsky grew suspicious of their maneuverings and ousted them. Robert Soblen/Roman Weil then openly emerged as a Stalinist and joined the German Communist party in 1933. Jack Soble returned to the USSR in 1933 and worked for a Profintern publication. He was apparently considered a possible witness in one of the Soviet purge trials but was spared.[1]

Lavrenty Beria, head of the KGB, personally allowed the entire Soble family to leave Russia in 1940. Three generations were sent across Siberia to Vladivostok, then on to Japan and into Canada. Soon afterward, Jack and Robert entered the United States to resume their espionage careers. Robert Soblen practiced medicine (he was a graduate of the University of Bern medical school) and assisted his brother in espionage. Jack Soble supervised a major KGB intelligence network that specialized in infiltration of the Trotskyists and other Russian exiles in America. In the deciphered KGB messages they are referred to by names derived from the false identities they had used while operating inside the European Trotskyist movement—Jack was called Abram (from Abraham Senin) and Robert was Roman (from Roman Weil).

The ouster of Jack Soble and Robert Soblen in 1932 did not leave the KGB without highly placed operatives among the Trotskyists. In 1956 Mark Zborowski, a prominent American anthropologist, confessed that he had worked as a KGB spy within the European Trotskyist movement in the 1930s.

Mark Grigorievich Zborowski was born in Uman, Russia, on January 21, 1908. He moved to Poland in 1921 and then went to France in 1928. The KGB's own file on Zborowski indicates that he had joined the Communist party in 1926 in Lodz, Poland, had been arrested in 1930, and had fled to Germany and then France after being sentenced to prison. Having been assigned to infiltrate the Trotskyist movement, he began working for the KGB in France in 1932. Zborowski, known in the movement as Etienne, worked for several years as a volunteer inside its Paris headquarters and became a close friend and confidant of Leon Sedov, Trotsky's son. He, Sedov, and Lilia Estrine Dallin were joint editors of the *Bulletin of the Opposition,* the authoritative voice of the Trotskyist movement. When the Fourth International (Trotsky's pale answer to the Communist International) was founded in 1938, he was its designated reporter on Russian issues, which were its chief concern at the time.[2] Zborowski, obviously, was in a position to report to the KGB on many of the details of the Trotskyist movement. To cite one example, his information is credited with enabling Soviet intelligence to steal a portion of Trotsky's archives.[3]

After Sedov took the lead in exposing Stalin's mass terror in Russia in 1937, the KGB targeted him for elimination. In 1938 he entered a French clinic suffering from abdominal pains, and after a routine appendectomy he died. Zborowski had alerted the KGB to the location of the clinic, owned by a Russian refugee, and later investigations established that Stalinist agents had been in and out of the clinic after Sedov was admitted. It may, of course, have been a natural death, but the KGB's activity surrounding the matter also raises the possibility that Sedov may have been medically murdered.

Following his secret defection in 1938, Aleksandr Orlov, a senior KGB officer, wrote an anonymous letter to Trotsky warning him about a KGB agent named Mark who had been close to his son. Convinced that the warning was an KGB provocation, Trotsky ignored it, but other Trotskyists became increasingly mistrustful of Mark Zborowski. He drifted away from the movement and finished his degree in anthropology at the Sorbonne. In 1941 he immigrated to the United States, where he was soon returned to work for the KGB.

Zborowski and Kravchenko

Nearly two dozen Venona messages discuss Zborowski's work in the United States under the code names Tulip and Kant.[4] Although the Venona traffic shows that originally the KGB directed Zborowski to spy on the Trotskyists, he then by chance became the lead agent in the KGB's effort to deal with Victor Kravchenko, a defector who deeply embarrassed the Soviets. A Soviet engineer and mid-level bureaucrat, Kravchenko arrived in Washington in 1943 as a member of the Soviet Government Purchasing Commission. Already secretly hostile to Stalin, he carefully prepared to defect. On April 3, 1944, he held a news conference, denounced the USSR's oppressive government and placed his life "under the protection of American public opinion."[5] Kravchenko was an embarrassment not only to the Soviets but to those in the U.S. government who did not want the image of a major American military ally sullied. He came very close to being handed back to the Soviets. But his public defection and the ties he developed with sympathetic journalists kept him safe from deportation.

He was, however, subject to a ferocious attack by the Soviet government and the CPUSA. Over the next several years, Kravchenko was harassed and threatened. Undaunted, he wrote *I Chose Freedom* (1946), a searing indictment of the Soviet Union as a terrorized and repressed society. Kravchenko's book became a best-seller, and the Soviet assault on his credibility intensified. In 1949 the French Communist journal *Les Lettres Françaises* published an article by Siam Thomas, identified as an American journalist, asserting that Kravchenko's book was a fraud manufactured by American intelligence agencies. Kravchenko, however, sued in a French court, established that Siam Thomas did not exist, and turned the trial into an indictment of Stalinism by calling as witnesses Russian refugees who testified to the accuracy of his assertions about the brutal collectivization campaigns, purges, and concentration camps of the 1930s. Numerous Communists and fellow travelers, on the other hand, testified in defense of the honor of Stalin's USSR. Kravchenko won his court case.[6]

One American witness against Kravchenko in Paris was Albert Kahn, a left-wing journalist and secret CPUSA member. Elizabeth Bentley told the FBI that in 1942 Jacob Golos had taken her to Kahn's home in New York and that he had provided them with information he had gathered on exiled anti-Soviet Ukrainian nationalists. According to Bentley, her contacts with Kahn ended in 1943. Kahn is a likely match for an unidentified KGB asset with the cover name Fighter, whom the Venona cables show to have been recruited in 1942. Fighter provided the KGB with information on émigré Ukrainian groups and the political leanings of American journalists. He was put "in cold storage" in 1944.[7]

Although he did not know what he had stumbled on, in 1944 Zborowski actually gave the KGB advance warning of Kravchenko's defection. Zborowski lived in the same apartment building as David and Lilia Estrine Dallin. One day in March, Zborowski spoke to a Russian who was looking for the Dallin residence. Later, the Dallins told Zborowski about a potential Soviet defector whom they had met, but they did not reveal his name. Lilia Dallin had never believed the rumors that Zborowski had KGB links. When General Orlov had written Trotsky warning about Mark, she had believed that the letter was a provocation. She also had sponsored the Zborowski family's entry into the United States in 1941. Her husband, David, was friendly with many exiled Russian Mensheviks (Social Democrats) and wrote voluminously on Soviet repression. Given the Dallins' standing as proven anti-Stalinists, their friendship protected Zborowski from suspicion. Zborowski repaid them by reporting on their activities to the head of his KGB network, Jack Soble. Soble passed Zborowski's news of a potential defector along, prompting a panicky Vasily Zubilin to visit Soble, demanding information about the threatened defection.[8] Kravchenko, however, defected before his identity was uncovered.

When Kravchenko defected in early April 1944, the KGB assigned Zborowski to befriend him. (In a not unusual display of KGB attitudes, in their cables the KGB gave Kravchenko the cover name Gnat.) A few weeks later, despite his best efforts, Zborowski had still not been able to meet Kravchenko, and he was afraid to push the Dallins too hard for information lest they become suspicious.[9] The KGB also received information about Kravchenko's defection from a source, identified as Green, who furnished the KGB with the unwelcome news that Kravchenko had been meeting with Eugene Lyons and Joseph Shaplen, two prominent anti-Stalinist journalists.[10] Lyons, a former Associated Press correspondent in Moscow, later translated Kravchenko's book into English and helped edit it. Shaplen, a *New York Times* reporter, advised Kravchenko on how best to present himself to the American press so as to promote widespread news coverage.

The KGB also received information from one of its agents in the U.S. Office of War Information, Christina Krotkova. Like Zborowski, Krotkova had cultivated Lilia Dallin as a way to gain information on anti-Stalinist Russian refugees. Krotkova got one Russian immigrant, a U.S. Marine sergeant who had played a role in Kravchenko's defection, drunk in order to get information about Kravchenko's intentions. She also met with Shaplen and, the KGB office in New York reported, "has been given the task of cautiously endeavoring to enter into closer relations" with him to get more information.[11] Another Soviet agent, Vasily Sukhomlin, a staff member of the Czechoslovak government-in-exile, reported to the KGB that Kravchenko was living in Connecticut in a cottage owned by Aleksandr Kerensky, the exiled leader of the Russian Provisional Government overthrown by Lenin in 1917.[12]

Zborowski, meanwhile, was also reporting what he heard from the Dallins. He had learned that Kravchenko had been an adherent of the views of Nikolai Bukharin, who, like Trotsky, had been a contender to succeed Lenin and had lost out to Stalin. (Stalin executed Bukharin in 1938.) Zborowski, confirming Green's information, reported that Kravchenko was dictating a manuscript to Lilia Dallin, writing an exposé of Soviet misuse of Lend-Lease aid, and seeing Isaac Don Levine, the energetic anti-Stalinist journalist. More ominously, Zborowski reported that Kravchenko was "well informed about the Krivitsky case."[13] Walter Krivitsky, a defector who had been a high-ranking Soviet military intelligence officer, had been found dead in a Washington hotel room in 1941, an apparent suicide, but suspicions that he had been murdered were widespread.

The suggestion that Kravchenko knew anything about Krivitsky must have alarmed both the KGB and Zborowski. Shortly after Krivitsky defected in France in 1937, he sought help from Leon Sedov and the Trotskyists. Sedov appointed Zborowski as Krivitsky's bodyguard, and he undoubtedly fed information about him to the KGB. Just before Krivitsky defected, his boyhood friend and fellow Soviet intelligence agent, Ignace Reiss, also broke with Stalin's regime. Reiss, a KGB officer, sent a defiant letter to the Central Committee of the Soviet Communist party in 1937 denouncing Stalin for betraying the ideals of the Bolshevik Revolution. The KGB caught up with him in Switzerland a few months later and murdered him. Else Bernaut, Reiss's widow, later charged in her autobiography that Zborowski had had a role in delivering her husband to the KGB murder squad.[14]

Finally, in late June 1944 Zborowski reported to the KGB that he had succeeded in meeting Kravchenko in the Dallins' apartment; their conversation began at nine in the evening and ended at four in the morning in Zborowski's nearby flat. One of Zborowski's tasks was to discover who had assisted Kravchenko in his defection. He was able to tell his KGB superiors that Kravchenko had told him the story of a Russian friend he identified only as Konstantin Mikhailovich, a winner of a Stalin Prize in metallurgy, who had been arrested in 1936 by the KGB. Set free in 1938, he had met Kravchenko in Moscow and encouraged him to work against the Soviet Union. In *I Chose Freedom,* Kravchenko identified his friend as Konstantin Mikhailovich Kolpovsky but made no mention of Kolpovsky's anti-Soviet views. With Zborowski's information in hand, the KGB presumably did not have to wait for the book to appear before dealing with Kolpovsky.[15]

Both Zborowski and Christina Krotkova continued to supply information about Kravchenko into 1945. Krotkova even became Kravchenko's typist and one of his translators in 1945. Zborowski reported gossip about Kravchenko's relationship with Isaac Don Levine, as well as his panic in early 1945 over reports that the U.S. government might hand him back to the Soviets and his well-founded fear that he was being shadowed by the KGB. The KGB concluded that Zborowski "is carrying out the task very diligently."[16]

Mark Zborowski continued to monitor the activities of other Soviet exiles and Trotskyists for the KGB. In late 1944 he reported on a conversation with Else Bernaut, the widow of the KGB defector murdered in Switzerland, and in 1945 he was accumulating information on the proposed trip to France of a Trotskyist leader. Zborowski never held any government jobs, nor did he steal government documents or industrial secrets: his espionage career was limited to betraying his friends and personal associates who were critics of Stalin. As a reward for his dedicated services, the KGB arranged with the CPUSA to enroll Zborowski as a member of the American Communist party. Bernard Schuster, the CPUSA's liaison with the KGB, reported that he would have to fill out an application and questionnaire, but if the KGB vouched for him, his membership would be approved and his real identify known only to Schuster and one other person.[17]

Jack Soble later testified that after 1945 Zborowski became a less productive agent and his regular KGB stipend was reduced. His growing prominence in American academic circles, however, easily compensated. After his arrival in America, he had worked at a screw factory in Brooklyn, but by 1944 Zborowski found employment compiling a Russian-American dictionary. In 1946 he went to work at the Yivo Scientific

Institute as a librarian. After meeting the well-known anthropologist Ruth Benedict, Zborowski became a consultant at Columbia University's Institute on Contemporary Culture and obtained a government grant, which led to the publication in 1952 of *Life Is with People,* a groundbreaking study of the Jewish shtetls of Eastern Europe. He then became study director of the American Jewish Committee. A series of grants enabled Zborowski to undertake projects on how people responded to pain. When published, the studies were well received and further enhanced his scholarly reputation.

Zborowski was exposed after Aleksandr Orlov went public in 1954. Orlov had remained in hiding in the United States ever since his defection in 1938. Following Stalin's death, he published an account of the dictator's crimes and offered a highly sanitized version of his own past.[18] Orlov met the Dallins and discovered that Mark, the KGB agent about whom he had warned Trotsky, was Mark Zborowski and lived in the United States. He told the FBI. Zborowski was interviewed and two years later testified before a Senate committee. Although he admitted spying on Trotskyists in Europe, he denied working for the KGB in the United States. He claimed that when the KGB had made contact with him in New York in 1941, he had refused to deal with them: "At this time, I became almost—I was almost hysterical and I remember well, I hit my fist on the table and said, 'I will not do anything with you any more.' And I walked out. Since then, I have not seen anyone."[19] Zborowski admitted that he was asked to spy on Kravchenko but claimed that he refused to do so. The deciphered Venona messages demonstrate that this statement, and much of the rest of his testimony, was false.

Convicted and sentenced to five years in jail for perjury, Zborowski successfully appealed on procedural grounds that his defense had not had access to certain information held by the prosecution. Retried in 1962 after having been given access to the contested information, he was again convicted and sentenced to three years and eleven months in prison. After serving his sentence, he moved to San Francisco, where he worked as a medical anthropologist at Mount Zion Medical Center.[20]

Spying on Other Enemies

Even when the KGB was not plotting the murder of Stalin's enemies, Soviet intelligence wanted to know what they were doing and with whom they were in contact. In some cases, infiltration of exile communities was designed to identify individuals as possible recruits for intelligence work. In others, there were efforts to discredit or disrupt their activities. One KGB circular order shows the broad sweep of Soviet interest; sent to KGB stations in New York, Mexico City, and Paris in 1945, it ordered forwarding of material on "old and new Russian and nationalist émigrés, the Russian, Armenian and Mohammedan clergy, Trotskyites and Zionists."[21]

Within the United States, the KGB had agents reporting on many of these groups. One unidentified agent, Alexandrov, reported on Russian émigrés, received a subsidy, and was promised Soviet citizenship. Another, Eugénie Olkhine, reestablished contact with the KGB in 1945 after a long break and supplied information about the Russian Orthodox Patriarch in the United States. She, too, was promised Soviet citizenship. Arrow (unidentified) worked among Carpatho-Russians, as did Eufrosina Dvoichenko-Markov, who also reported on Romanians and on several State Department employees with whom she had contact. Her son, Demetrius, was a U.S. Army sergeant on duty in Alaska. He was assigned to military counterintelligence duties and obtained some sort of manual that he turned over to the KGB. The KGB thought Demetrius had prospects, and it had a plan to fund his college education after the war.[22]

One of the most important Soviet agents working among émigrés was Sergey Kurnakov, a former tsarist cavalry officer who had immigrated to the United States and later became an ardent but undeclared Communist.[23] In addition to providing information about his fellow immigrant Russians, Kurnakov was a highly active KGB liaison agent. As a reward for his services, the KGB arranged for Kurnakov and his son to return to the USSR. The KGB also had sources who trolled for information about Bessarabians and Ukrainians. Mikhail Tkach edited a pro-Communist Ukrainian-language newspaper and supervised a small network of subagents. Tkach's daughter, Ann Sidorovich, and her husband, Michael, were part of Julius Rosenberg's espionage network.[24]

Several agents were assigned to infiltrate Jewish organizations. If the cover name Polecats, which the KGB used for Trotskyists, reflected Stalin's disdain for his ideological arch-enemy, the cover name for the Zionists in the KGB cables, Rats, was likewise a reflection of the Stalinist opinion of Jews. During World War II, for tactical reasons, the USSR encouraged the formation of Jewish groups in Russia that appealed to world Jewry for assistance. Always wary of Jewish nationalism, however, the KGB monitored all their activities. In 1943 Solomon Michoels and Itzhak Feffer, representatives of the USSR's Jewish Anti-Fascist Committee, toured the United States to great acclaim in Jewish communities. Feffer was himself a KGB agent. In 1947 Grigory Kheifets, who had run the KGB office in San Francisco for much of World War II, became Feffer's deputy. Kheifets's timing, however, was poor, as Soviet postwar purges took on an antisemitic air. Stalin had Michoels murdered in a fake accident, executed Feffer, and imprisoned Kheifets.[25]

The 1943 Michoels-Feffer tour of the United States was arranged by Ben-Zion Goldberg, son-in-law of the famed Yiddish writer Sholem Aleichem. Goldberg, born in Russia, returned there for a visit in 1945. During Stalin's purge of Soviet Jewish writers in the late 1940s, he was accused of being an American espionage agent, and several Soviet writers were executed because of their contacts with him. In fact, his situation resembles that of Noel Field (chapter 3). In *Out of the Red Shadows: Anti-Semitism in Stalin's Russia,* the Russian historian Gennady Kostyrchenko details how the KGB used contact with Goldberg by prominent Soviet Jews as evidence of complicity in American espionage, even though its own records stated that Goldberg had been a "foreign agent of the MGB [KGB] of the USSR abroad."[26]

The Venona messages confirm that the KGB maintained a number of informants in the Jewish community. Mark, a Jewish journalist (Menashe Unger is a likely candidate for Mark), reported not only on Jewish groups but also on exiled Social Democrats and Socialists. Mark was put on inactive status in 1944 because his information was of limited value. Hudson, the cover name of an unidentified American KGB agent, supervised a small group of subagents in various Jewish and Zionist organizations.[27] Esther Rand was one agent supervised by Hudson. A longtime Communist activist, Rand was born in Russia in 1907 and came to the United States as an infant. She moved to New York from Massachusetts in 1940. Rand had worked in 1944 for the United Jewish Appeal but in that capacity could report only on Zionist activity. The KGB encouraged her to obtain a position as administrative secretary to a group described as a "committee of Jewish writers and artists" where "she will be able to expand her opportunities for using Jewish organizations and prominent figures."[28] It is not clear that she got that position, inasmuch as she worked in Italy and Israel for the United

Jewish Appeal after World War II. Rand was named as an unindicted co-conspirator in the Soblen espionage case.[29]

Spying on the Socialist Workers Party

The KGB's infiltration of Jewish groups, however, was minor compared with that directed against American Trotskyists. James Cannon, one of the founders of the American Communist movement (and the party's chairman for a period in the early 1920s), had led about a hundred followers of Trotsky out of the CPUSA in 1928. Cannon's group went through a number of organizational permutations before becoming in the late 1930s the Socialist Workers party (SWP), the American affiliate of Trotsky's Fourth International. Without the prestige in radical circles of support by the USSR, and lacking the generous subsidies the Soviets provided the CPUSA, the American Trotskyist movement was never large, a few thousand members at its peak and barely more than a hundred militants. It never seriously challenged the many-times-larger and organizationally stronger Communist party for leadership of the revolutionary left in America. Nevertheless, the tiny Socialist Workers party was a prime target of the KGB.

In 1937 Louis Budenz was a rising CPUSA official on the fringe of the party's top leadership. Just before he went to Chicago to become editor of the *Midwest Daily Record,* a regional Communist newspaper, Budenz was asked by one of the CPUSA's Soviet intelligence contacts, Dr. Gregory Rabinowitz, to find someone there to infiltrate the Trotskyist headquarters in New York. The notion was that SWP activists would be likely to spot an infiltrator from New York's Communist community, but one from Chicago could more easily pass as a sincere Trotskyist. Jack Kling, head of the Young Communist League in Chicago, introduced Budenz to Sylvia Callen, a young Communist social worker who was eager to help. Her married name was Sylvia Franklin; her husband, Zalmond Franklin, already worked for the KGB. Budenz later testified that he had been told that Zalmond Franklin had done "secret work" in Spain and after his return had been sent on clandestine missions to Canada on behalf of Soviet intelligence. Budenz recalled that after Sylvia had successfully infiltrated the New York SWP headquarters, the KGB set up Zalmond in a separate apartment where the two could meet.[30]

A May 1944 Venona message documents essential points of Budenz's recollections of Zalmond Franklin. The message—a report from Bernard Schuster, the CPUSA's liaison with the KGB—described a complaint about Franklin from Nathan Einhorn, head of the American Newspaper Guild in New York and a secret Communist. After the Franklins divorced in 1943, Zalmond had married Rose Richter, whose sister, Frieda, was Einhorn's wife. Einhorn told Schuster that Zalmond was bragging to his new relations about his connection with the KGB. Einhorn thought this loose talk ill advised, although everyone in the family circle was a Communist. The KGB, too, thought it unwise. The New York KGB told Moscow that it was ordering Franklin to finish a report on his last assignment and then it would remove him from active work.[31] It also said that it would have Schuster keep an eye on Franklin in case of more insecure talk. An FBI inquiry into Zalmond Franklin's background also confirmed that he had served in the Spanish Civil War, working at least part of the time as a bacteriologist at a Spanish Loyalist hospital. He had worked in Alberta, Canada, in 1943. Michael Straight also told the FBI that during the period when he had been associated with the KGB, Franklin had been one of those with whom he was in contact.[32]

As for Sylvia Callen, she joined the Socialist Workers party in Chicago under the name of Sylvia Caldwell, according to instructions from the CPUSA. Following Rabinowitz's instructions, she moved to New York shortly afterward, assiduously undertook volunteer clerical tasks for the Trotskyist movement, and was rewarded by an appointment as secretary to the leader of the SWP, James Cannon. Callen later testified to a grand jury that she had provided information from the SWP offices to Rabinowitz, known to her as Jack. Jack, she stated, was later replaced by someone she knew as Sam, who was later identified as Jack Soble.[33] In confirmation, Callen turns up under the cover name Satyr in a number of deciphered Venona messages as a valuable KGB source in the Soble network that, as the KGB put it, "deals with the Polecats [Trotskyists]."[34] The Venona messages show her turning over to the KGB copies of the correspondence of SWP leaders, information on the household, health, and finances of Natalia Trotsky (Leon Trotsky's widow), and reports on the internal finances of Trotskyist groups.

Sylvia Callen dropped out of the SWP in 1947, a year before Louis Budenz, by then a Communist defector, exposed her as a Stalinist agent in the Trotskyist ranks. Her Trotskyist comrades, however, refused to believe Budenz's story. In 1954 Callen, then known as Sylvia Doxsee and living in Chicago, was called before a grand jury. Invoking the Fifth Amendment, she refused to answer questions about her membership in the SWP, her relationship to the KGB, Louis Budenz, or anything else bearing on her activities in New York. She was called back to another grand jury in 1958. This time she was more cooperative, confessing that she met regularly with Rabinowitz and Soble to pass on confidential Trotskyist material at an apartment rented by a woman named Lucy Booker. Callen was named as an unindicted co-conspirator when Robert Soblen was charged with espionage in 1960, but she never publicly testified.[35]

Lucy Booker, whose apartment had been used for meetings between Callen and Soble, was also named as an unindicted co-conspirator in the Soblen case. Booker had worked for Soviet intelligence in Germany in the 1930s along with Margaret Browder, sister of the head of the CPUSA. Booker returned to the United States in 1939 but lost touch with the KGB. In 1941 Jacob Golos told Elizabeth Bentley that he had been ordered to reestablish ties. Golos did so, and Booker worked at various times under the supervision of Golos, the longtime KGB liaison agent Joseph Katz, and the Soble-Soblen brothers. Jack Soble testified that Vasily and Elizabeth Zubilin had introduced him to Booker; he regularly paid her between $100 and $150 a month for her work. She cooperated with the FBI and was never called as a witness in a public forum.[36]

Still another Communist assigned to infiltrate the Socialist Workers party was Floyd Cleveland Miller, known in the SWP as Mike Cort. Miller confessed his activities to the FBI in 1954 and appeared as a witness in Robert Soblen's espionage trial in 1961. The story he told government investigators and the jury is confirmed by numerous decrypted Venona documents.[37]

Born in South Bend, Indiana, Miller went to school in Michigan and in 1934 moved to New York, where he found a job writing soap operas for radio station WMCA. He joined the CPUSA in 1936. Only a few months later, Gregory Rabinowitz recruited him to do "opposition work," as the CPUSA called covert action against rival political organizations. Miller's first assignment, which lasted a year, was to listen to a wiretap on James Cannon's home. Next he joined the SWP and became one of its activists, all the while writing up reports for the CPUSA and the KGB. The Trotskyists assigned him to the Sailors Union of the

Pacific in 1941, and he became editor of the union's journal, in addition to writing on military affairs for the *Fourth International,* a Trotskyist journal, during World War II. The Sailors Union of the Pacific, led by firm anti-Communists, challenged the Communist-led International Longshoremen's and Warehousemen's Union for leadership of maritime labor on the West Coast. Miller's position gave Communist unionists a spy in the upper ranks of a chief rival union. He later stated, "My job as a Stalinist was to keep track of the sailing of all Trotskyite seamen so a Stalinist agent would be at the port and have a surveillance on whatever Trotskyites entered the Soviet Union."[38]

Miller's primary KGB contacts were Joseph Katz, who himself had installed the listening device in Cannon's residence, and a woman he knew as Sylvia Getzoff. She has the cover name Adam in the deciphered Venona cables and is identified there as Rebecca Getzoff.[39] The Venona cables about Getzoff show that in addition to collaborating with Miller, she worked with Mark Zborowski, Joseph Katz, and Amadeo Sabatini (chapter 2). She was named as an unindicted co-conspirator in the Soblen indictment, but very little information about her was made public.

The Socialist Workers party decided to send Miller to Mexico in the spring of 1944 to meet with Natalia Trotsky and to show her a microfilm of the page proofs of her late husband's biography of Stalin. Before leaving, Miller met in New York with Jack Soble, and Soble copied the film for the KGB. Three Venona messages from that spring deal with the preparations for his trip and the methods by which he could best extract information of interest to the KGB about Trotskyist activity in Mexico. The New York KGB office asked Moscow's advice on whether Miller should arrange to spend time with Natalia Trotsky and collect information about the physical arrangements of her residence. One complication to his trip was that the FBI had Miller on a surveillance list because of his Trotskyist activities; KGB officials worried that he might be watched by American counterintelligence in Mexico, thus making more difficult its own contact with him.

These messages offer an example of KGB tradecraft of that era. The New York KGB reported Miller's departure for Mexico on June 11 and sent passwords and recognition codes to Moscow for transmittal to the Mexico City KGB. Miller would phone the Soviet embassy precisely at 9:30 A.M., ask for the ambassador's secretary, and identify himself as Mr. Leonard. This would mean he was setting up a meeting for seven o'clock that evening at the entrance to a specified movie house, where he would be holding a copy of *Life* magazine and wearing glasses, which he would periodically remove and wipe. His KGB contact should hold a copy of *Time* and ask in English, "Are you Mr. Toren?" to which Miller would reply, "No, my name is Charles Bruno."[40] Officials of the Mexico City KGB, however, were not impressed by the meeting place chosen by their New York colleagues. Mexico City complained to Moscow that the rendezvous New York had assigned to Miller was in full view of a café frequented by political émigrés who might spot the man meeting Miller as a Soviet embassy officer.[41]

Miller testified in 1961 that his 1944 Mexican assignment for the KGB had included investigating reports of a budding alliance between Trotskyists and anarchists and other radicals grouped around the exiled French writer Victor Serge. Miller admitted, and Venona cables confirm, that he had been given a contact at the Soviet embassy in Mexico City. He spent six weeks living in the Trotsky household and determined that no such alliance of radicals was brewing. Upon returning to New York, Miller delivered a written report on his mission to a KGB contact.[42] The New York KGB informed Moscow on August 10, 1944, that Miller had returned from Mexico and turned in a detailed report that not only described the relationship between the Trotskyists and Serge but also divulged the names and addresses of most of the active Trotskyists in Mexico. The cable also discussed future use of Miller. To avoid the military draft, he had taken a job as a seaman on a coastal steamer that would temporarily interrupt his spying on the Trotskyists. Nonetheless, "we will continue to put him forward for the staff [SWP headquarters] and strengthen his authority with the Polecats [Trotskyists]."[43]

Miller also testified that he was introduced to Lucy Booker, who served as a courier between him and Soble in 1945; his reports on the Trotskyists were typed in her apartment. In 1945 Soble informed Miller that he was being transferred to another controller and introduced him to his "cousin," who turned out to be Robert Soblen. A Venona message from May 1945 confirms that Jack Soble had handed over his agents in the Polecats and Rats to Robert Soblen. Miller insisted that he stopped working for Soviet intelligence in 1945, thereafter turning his energies to writing children's books.[44]

When he returned from Mexico, Floyd Miller expressed concern to the KGB that his true allegiance might be exposed to the Trotskyists. Another KGB agent pretending sympathy for the Trotskyist Fourth International, a friend of Miller's named Robert Owen Menaker, had returned to New York from Latin America. Menaker, Miller learned, had told some of his relatives that he was not a Trotskyist but associated with them on a Communist assignment. Miller, the KGB reported, "is afraid that this may get to the ears of the Polecats and they may become suspicious of Khe . . . [Miller] as he came to them through Bob [Menaker]."[45]

Robert Owen Menaker came from a radical family. His father, imprisoned for revolutionary activities in Russia, prospered in America as co-owner of a handkerchief factory. Determined not to exploit his workers, he abandoned manufacturing for farming. He named his sons after revolutionaries and radicals—Peter Kropotkin Menaker, William Morris Menaker, Robert Owen Menaker. One of Robert's brothers, Frederick Engels (Enge) Menaker, an openly Communist journalist, ran a League of American Writers home for anti-Nazi refugees in France. When the house was closed, he arranged shelter for some of the exiles in the home of the Arenal family in Mexico City, where he cooked for them. Years later, Enge's nephew and Robert's son, Daniel Menaker, wrote an affectionate portrait of his Communist uncle.[46]

In his account of his family Daniel Menaker noted that the Communist party had sent his father to Mexico "to keep an eye on Trotsky in exile."[47] He certainly did that, but more as well, although exactly what Menaker's assignment was is not clear from the sixteen Venona messages in which he is mentioned. As was noted in the Venona message just quoted, he assisted Floyd Miller's infiltration of the Socialist Workers party. Several of the messages relate to Menaker's employer, Michael Burd, owner of the Midland Export Corporation of New York. In 1944 and 1945 Menaker represented Midland in Chile, where he was associated with Christian Casanova Subercaseaux, a Chilean diplomat. Both Burd and Subercaseaux were KGB agents; Burd used his business to transfer large amounts of money to agents throughout Latin America and aided the KGB in a complicated effort to obtain American transit visas for Nicholas and Maria Fisher, the names used by two KGB illegal officers claiming Swiss citizenship who were to go to Mexico via the United States. Subercaseaux assisted in transferring funds and couriering messages and documents throughout Latin America.[48]

Menaker had difficulties as an agent. In 1944 he returned from a trip to Chile and tried to find permanent employment in the United States. Michael Burd complained to the New York KGB office that

Menaker had alienated several companies with whom he did business. The New York KGB station chief cabled Moscow that in working with Menaker "allowances should be made," since he had not been thoroughly trained or screened prior to being given his assignment.[49]

Later messages are only slightly clearer about Menaker's tasks. In one message the KGB speculated about the possibility that Laurence Duggan, one of its sources who had recently resigned from the State Department, might obtain a job in Chile to do some unspecified work with, or in place of, Menaker. A partially decrypted cable from October 1944 suggests that Menaker was distributing money to someone in Chile but also noted that "relations of Bob and X" (X was its veteran agent Joseph Katz) were "not quite normal." The cable asked for instructions about what should be done about Menaker's salary and noted that someone would be paying him thirty thousand dollars but that he might not receive it for a year.[50] Joseph Katz owned the Tempus Import Company in Manhattan in 1944; it is possible that Menaker was somehow connected with that firm.

Like his friend Floyd Miller, Robert Menaker apparently cooperated to some extent with the FBI in the 1950s. His name never surfaced in connection with investigations of Soviet espionage; he was never indicted or questioned by congressional committees. His son wrote of the frequent presence in the household in the 1950s of a friendly FBI agent, but his father never spoke about precisely what he did in Mexico or what he told the FBI.[51]

Katz, with whom Menaker was associated for a time, was one of the KGB's most active liaison agents. An immigrant to the United States (he was born in Lithuania in 1912), he is referred to in thirty-three deciphered Venona messages as the contact between Soviet KGB officers and numerous Soviets sources.[52] He went to work for Soviet intelligence in 1938 and at various times was the KGB go-between with such important contacts as Earl Browder, Elizabeth Bentley, Flora Wovschin, Harry Gold, Thomas Black, and Bernard Schuster. Deciphered Venona messages suggest that the KGB provided some of the capital for the business firms (Tempus Import Company and, earlier, Meriden Dental Laboratories) that afforded Katz cover for his work during World War II. Katz left the United States at some point after the war, probably in 1948, when the KGB decided that Bentley's defection or the Venona Project placed him in danger. He worked for Soviet intelligence in Europe but in 1950 had a falling out with his KGB superiors, dropped out of Soviet service, and emigrated to Israel.[53] He never talked to American authorities about his work for Soviet intelligence.

The Soble Apparatus

While one part of Jack Soble and Robert Soblen's apparatus concentrated on spying on Trotskyists and other political opponents, a second part ranged more widely. This group of agents infiltrated the OSS and created business covers for Soviet intelligence. In 1957 three of its principals—Jack and Myra Soble and Jacob Albam—pleaded guilty to espionage. Four years later, Robert Soblen was convicted of espionage. Several other members of the ring fled the United States and were never brought to trial. And one, Boris Morros, turned out to be a double agent working for the FBI.

Born in St. Petersburg in 1895, Boris Morros was a musical prodigy. He left Russia in 1922 and made his way to the United States. For sixteen years he was a producer and music director at Paramount Studios in Hollywood, responsible for such movies as *Flying Deuces*, which starred Stan Laurel and Oliver Hardy, and *Second Chorus* with Paulette Goddard and Fred Astaire. Morros aided the careers of stars such as Bing Crosby, Ginger Rogers, and Rudy Vallee. Morros later claimed that he agreed at first to help the KGB in order to ensure that the parcels of food he sent to his brothers and aged parents in the Soviet Union were delivered. A Russian he knew as Edward Herbert, claiming to be involved in anti-Nazi activities, used Morros in 1936 to obtain cover as a Paramount talent scout in Germany. Herbert once again approached Morros in 1942, identified himself as Vasily Zubilin, and obtained Morros's cooperation in return for allowing his father to immigrate to the United States.[54]

Morros later insisted that he resisted Zubilin's efforts to get him to hire and provide business cover for Soviet agents. But the anonymous Russian letter received by the FBI in 1943 (chapter 2), while asserting that a number of Americans cooperated with the KGB, specifically named only two—Earl Browder and Boris Morros. The letter identified Elizabeth Zubilin as the KGB officer who dealt with Morros. So it is likely that Morros was performing more important functions for the KGB than those he discussed in his exculpatory autobiography.

Morros's own story is that he attempted to discourage use of his company as cover for KGB operations by telling Zubilin that it was too small, but Zubilin had a solution. He informed Morros in the fall of 1943 that he had found a wealthy couple willing to invest in a sheet music company that would serve as cover for Soviet espionage. That December Zubilin drove Morros to Connecticut, where they met with Alfred and Martha Dodd Stern, who invested $130,000 in the Boris Morros Music Company.[55]

The Sterns were the epitome of Communist fellow-traveling chic. Alfred Stern, born in 1897, was educated at Phillips Exeter Academy and Harvard. In 1921 he married Marion Rosenwald, daughter of the head of Sears, Roebuck and Company, and directed the Rosenwald Foundation for a decade. After divorcing his wife in 1936 and receiving a million-dollar settlement, Stern met and married Martha Dodd, daughter of America's ambassador to Nazi Germany from 1933 to 1937.

Born in 1908, Martha Dodd was a femme fatale of the 1930s. Her long list of lovers included Carl Sandburg and Thomas Wolfe. She had shocked the diplomatic community in Germany with her torrid love affairs with Rudolf Dies, head of the Nazi Gestapo, and Boris Vinogradov, first secretary of the Soviet embassy. Vinogradov and Dodd asked the Soviet government for permission to marry in 1936, but they were turned down. Vinogradov returned to Moscow and their relationship came to an end. Decades later she learned from Soviet contacts that he had been executed in 1938. Although it is not certain, Vinogradov most likely was a KGB officer, and his execution was part of Stalin's late-1930s purge of his intelligence agencies. Jack Soble later testified that Martha Dodd had told him that she had worked as a Soviet source while at the U.S. embassy in Berlin and during her relationship with Vinogradov.[56]

After their marriage in 1938, Alfred and Martha Stern devoted themselves to promoting far-left causes, using both their wealth and their talents. In 1939 Martha Dodd published a best-selling book, *Through Embassy Eyes,* on her experiences in Berlin and the developing horror of the Nazi regime. She and her brother, William Dodd, Jr., published in 1941 an edited version of their deceased father's diaries of his time as ambassador. It, too, offered a revealing look at the nature of the Nazi regime and was a publishing success. The younger Dodd was himself a controversial figure. He had been an active participant in the late 1930s in such Communist front organizations as the American Friends of the Soviet Union and had worked for the American League for Peace and Democracy. He published an article in the March 1938 issue of *Champion,* the journal of the Young Communist League. He was a national sponsor of the League of American Writers annual conference in 1941, at a time when it was supporting the Nazi-Soviet Pact with such vehemence that most of its non-Communist members had long since departed. When a congressional investigating committee questioned him in 1943 about his activities, Dodd, then an assistant news editor for the U.S. government Foreign Broadcasting Monitoring Service, denied any Communist ties. He claimed not to know that *Champion* had connections with the Young Communist League and to be equally ignorant of any Communist role in the other organizations to which he belonged. His denials availed him little; Congress refused to appropriate money to pay his salary.[57]

William Dodd, Jr., is the subject of one Venona message. The KGB in New York asked Moscow in 1944 if it would allow Dodd, who had the cover name Sitsilla, to take a temporary job with TASS, the Soviet news agency. He had, it explained, worked for the Office of War Information, had supplied information in the past, and had most recently worked for Russian War Relief.[58]

Early in 1944 Jack Soble replaced the Zubilins as Morros's KGB contact. Several Venona messages detail the increasingly fractious business relationship between Morros and the Sterns, who were concerned that their KGB-inspired investment was being poorly managed. In four separate cables the New York KGB station informed Moscow that Alfred Stern, cover-named Louis, believed Morros had squandered large amounts of money and that he, Stern, refused to put any more cash into the business. In one message Stern linked the problems to the Zubilins' departure from the United States. He had been ordered not to make any contacts until the KGB got in touch with him, but the situation had become critical: "I want to reaffirm my desire to be helpful. My resources are sufficient for any solid constructive business but I don't intend to maintain silence when my resources, time and efforts are being spent for nothing." One of Stern's memos, given to Helen Lowry, Browder's niece and Akhmerov's wife, for transmittal to Elizabeth Zubilin, complained that the entire $130,000 initial investment had vanished: "In view of the poor business management and misguided artistic temperament unsuitable for conducting a very systematic business this sum is not enough. . . . My partner ignores my advice; my endeavors lead almost or completely to nothing and even evoke disdain."[59]

Jack Soble came to California in March 1945 to adjudicate the dispute between Stern and Morros. In April the partnership was dissolved and Morros repaid Stern $100,000 for his one-quarter interest in the company. The Sterns continued their socialite lives at their elegant Connecticut estate and New York apartment. A friendly journalist described the heady company: "Lillian Hellman, Marc Blitstein, Paul Robeson, Margaret Burke-White, Clifford Odets, and Isamu Noguchi were regular guests at the Sterns' parties, along with members of the Soviet and Eastern European diplomatic set. One evening a guest looked around the Stern's living room and, half in jest, dubbed the crowd 'La Très Haute Société Communiste.' "[60]

Morros, meanwhile, was brooding about his treatment and threats from Jack Soble that any lack of cooperation might result in trouble for his brothers back in the Soviet Union. He went to the FBI in 1947, confessed, and agreed to work as a double agent.[61] From then on he provided the U.S. government with information on the activities of Soble, while the FBI put the Soble network's members under periodic surveillance.

At the same time, the Sterns' work as highly visible advocates of Soviet causes attracted the attention of a congressional investigating committee. After they were subpoenaed by the House Committee on Un-American Activities in 1953, the Sterns fled to Mexico rather than testify. The government was finally ready to move against the Soble ring in 1957. Jack Soble and his wife, Myra, Jacob Albam (then Soble's assistant), and the Sterns were indicted for espionage.

Fearing extradition from Mexico, the Sterns fled to Communist Czechoslovakia. In the 1960s they moved for a time to Castro's Cuba but returned to Prague. Their indictments were dismissed in 1979, but they never returned home and died in Prague.

With the assistance provided by Morros, the government had ample evidence against Jack Soble, and he decided not to risk trial. He, his wife, and Jacob Albam pleaded guilty. Soble also made a detailed statement of his past activities. In addition to testifying about Mark Zborowski, he assisted the government in convicting his brother, Robert Soblen, of espionage in 1961. Sentenced to life in prison and suffering from leukemia, Soblen jumped bail and fled to Israel using a passport issued to a dead relative. The Israelis, however, refused to admit him and put him on a plane to the United States. During the flight he attempted suicide and the plane landed in London, where he underwent medical treatment and launched another battle for asylum. When he was ordered deported to the United States, Soblen took a large dose of barbiturates and died.

Two other members of the Soble network, Jane Foster and her husband, George Zlatowski, were also indicted in 1957. They were living in France at the time and refused to return home to face trial; the French government declined to extradite them, possibly because in return they provided information about Soviet espionage in France. Jane Foster was the daughter of a wealthy businessman. After graduating from Mills College in 1935, she toured Europe, married a Dutch government official in 1936, and moved with him to the Dutch East Indies (Indonesia). On a visit to her parents in California in 1938, she joined the American Communist party and soon afterward divorced her husband. Shortly after she moved to New York in 1941, friends introduced her to George Zlatowski. A Minnesotan, Zlatowski had joined the Young Communist League in 1937 and then went to Spain to fight with the International Brigades.[62] They married, but George was soon drafted.

Around the same time, Foster met Alfred and Martha Stern and became friends with them. She also met William Browder, the brother of the head of the CPUSA. She later wrote that both he and Martha told her "not to be so open in my Party work, as I could be more helpful to the Party if I were more discreet." Foster felt this was "a welcome suggestion." With George off on military duties, Jane moved in 1942 to Washington, where she rented a room from Henry Collins and his wife, Susan B. Anthony II, active members of the CPUSA Washington underground. In her autobiography Foster admitted that before she had left New York, William Browder had introduced her to a young woman (unnamed) who would visit her occasionally in Washington "so that I could still keep in touch with the Party."[63] With her Indonesian experience and Malay language skills Foster soon found work in the Netherlands Study Unit, a wartime agency set up to coordinate intelligence on the Dutch East Indies; the agency was later absorbed by the Board of Economic Warfare. She wrote that at the board her closest friend was the KGB agent Charles Flato. She transferred to the Office of Strategic Services in the fall of 1943, and early in 1944 she was sent to Ceylon.

According to Boris Morros, Jane Foster told him she had been recruited as a Soviet agent by Martha Dodd Stern in 1938. (Foster dated her acquaintance with the Sterns to the early 1940s.) In her autobiography Foster denied being a Soviet agent and offered a convoluted explanation of her relationships with Jack Soble and Boris Morros. In her telling, they were both unscrupulous businessmen who took advantage of her and her husband. She wrote that she had met Jack Soble in 1946, after returning to the United States, and had loaned him eighteen hundred dollars for a business venture in France, though she never later produced a receipt or an IOU. She also said that she had given him a copy of one of her OSS reports on Indonesia, labeled top secret, although she denied that it was really secret. Meanwhile her husband, George, had earned an officer's commission, and in 1946 he attended the U.S. Army Intelligence School. (The Army was then unaware of his Communist background.) George Zlatkowski became an interrogator with U.S. military intelligence in Austria. He was released from Army duty in 1948. In her account, what Morros had reported as Soble's espionage subsidies to the Zlatowskis was simply his belated repayment of her 1946 loan. She agreed that Soble had introduced her and her husband to Boris Morros, but said that the connection was entirely innocent and that they had even loaned Morros money.

Deciphered Venona messages show that Jane Foster lied in her autobiography. KGB cables prove that she was a spy, but that Morros was either mistaken or misinformed about when she was recruited. Zubilin notified Moscow in June 1942: "[Unrecovered code group] Liza [Martha Stern], we are cultivating the American Jane Foster with a view to signing her on. She is about 30 years old and works in Washington in the Dutch [two unrecovered code groups] translator of Malay languages. . . . She is a Fellowcountrywoman [CPUSA member]. She is described by the Fellowcountrymen [CPUSA] as a [unrecovered code group], dedicated person."[64] Under the cover name of Slang, she is mentioned in subsequent deciphered Venona messages from 1943 and 1944 as engaged in transmitting information and in other espionage tasks.[65]

The grand jury in the Soble case listed a number of other persons as coconspirators in the espionage network but did not indict them, because they either were foreigners no longer in the United States, were dead, had cooperated with the prosecution, or had spied on Trotskyists or Zionists but not the United States government. Spying on Trotskyists and Zionists on behalf of the USSR might be reprehensible, but it was not a criminal violation of federal law.

Three of those named were Germans: Johanna Koenen Beker (daughter of the prominent German Communist William Koenen), Hans Hirschfeld (a consultant for the OSS during World War II), and Horst Baerensprung (another OSS consultant). After the Nazi seizure of power in Germany, Johanna Beker, whose father had held high positions in the Comintern, moved to Moscow, where she worked as a translator for American businessmen. By her own testimony, she was recruited by the KGB in 1937 to spy on visiting Americans and then sent to the United States in 1939. Zubilin introduced her in 1942 to Robert Soblen, for whom she worked as a courier. Soblen paid her between thirty-five and forty dollars a month. Her regular job was as a file clerk in a New York law firm.[66]

Beker testified at the Soblen trial that Hirschfeld and Baerensprung had passed information to her for transmittal to Soblen. Baerensprung, she said, had supplied information on German émigré groups and biographical material from OSS files. After the war ended, Baerensprung returned to the Soviet occupation zone and became a police official in the new East German regime, but he died before the Soble case broke in the United States. Beker said that Hirschfeld also had given her material on other German émigrés, including their fields of interest and their political views, and had passed on information he had heard about the development of a new American weapon. After the war Hirschfeld moved to West Berlin, and in 1960 he became press chief for West Berlin mayor Willy Brandt. From West Berlin Hirschfeld denied Beker's charges but refused to return to the United States to testify unless he were granted complete immunity from prosecution. The U.S. government offered him only limited immunity: his testimony could not be used as evidence against him, but he would be liable to perjury charges if it could be shown that he had testified falsely. Faced with the possibility of an indictment for perjury if he denied Beker's testimony, he remained in Germany. In an interview with American intelligence agents, he admitted to "extended illegal activity and contacts with Communist agents in Europe prior to 1940" but again denied Beker's statements about his activities after that time. He resigned his position with Mayor Brandt.[67]

The Venona messages shed little light on this portion of Soble's ring. Johanna Beker probably appears in three Venona messages, under the cover names Clemence and Lee, although the identification is not certain.[68] Clemence/Lee is identified as an agent assigned to work among German immigrants and exiles and as the hostess of a safe-house. One Venona message, largely undecrypted except for a handful of names, refers to Robert Soblen's making a proposal to his brother Jack about Hans Hirschfeld and other German immigrants.[69]

Two mysterious figures listed in the Soble network indictment were Dr. Henry Spitz and his wife, Dr. Beatrice Spitz. Both physicians and naturalized citizens, in 1950 they lived in Albuquerque, New Mexico, where they allegedly took photographs of a military base where atomic weapons research was done and passed it to Dr. Soblen. That year they left for their native Austria; following Soblen's arrest they renounced their American citizenship.[70]

One other relative of Robert Soblen and Jack Soble also served as a member of their espionage ring. Ilya Wolston was the son of one of Robert and Jack's sisters. Boris Morros wrote in his autobiography that Jack Soble had told him that Ilya, whose cover name Morros remembered as Slava, had done work for the Russians in Alaska. Venona shows that Morros was correct.

Ilya Elliott Wolston entered the U.S. Army in World War II and became a military intelligence officer. He promptly began reporting to the KGB on the organization, curriculum, and personnel of the Army's intelligence school at Fort Ritchie, Maryland. In the Venona cables he describes the training that he and other American intelligence officers underwent as specialists in Soviet affairs. The deciphered KGB cable suggests that one of his missions was to spot other officers who might be susceptible to recruitment as Soviet agents. The KGB valued his position inside American military intelligence, and the New York KGB assured Moscow that "Slava was warned about appropriate secrecy and caution."[71]

After graduating, Wolston was posted to Alaska on an assignment to Army counterintelligence dealing with Soviet matters. At the time Soviet Lend-Lease traffic, both naval and air, through Alaska was heavy. Thus a Soviet spy was given what was from the point of view of the KGB a dream assignment, protecting the United States from Soviet spies. There are no Slava/Wolston Venona messages from his Alaska period. But cover names were changed from time to time, and he seems a likely candidate for Skrib, the cover name of an unidentified agent in a Venona cable who wrote to Frost (Boris Morros) from Alaska in December 1944 announcing that he was "ready to work if we want."[72]

After the war Wolston worked for the KGB network run by his uncle Jack. By the 1950s, however, he developed health problems and became a rural recluse. He ignored six subpoenas to testify before a federal grand jury. Tried for contempt, he pleaded guilty but claimed mental illness as a mitigating circumstance. He was given a one-year suspended sentence.

Most of the other unindicted co-conspirators in the Soblen case were people who had infiltrated the Trotskyists or Zionists: Floyd Miller, Sylvia Callen Franklin, Esther Rand, Sylvia Getzoff, and Lucy Booker. Infiltration of the Trotskyist movement, however, was not enough for Joseph Stalin. He wanted Trotsky dead. And the plan to murder Leon Trotsky and then to free his killer from prison had depended on the cooperation of members of the American Communist party's secret apparatus with the KGB.

Americans and Trotsky's Assassination

Pavel Sudoplatov, a senior KGB officer who had several successful KGB assassinations to his credit, was summoned to a meeting with Stalin and KGB head Lavrenty Beria in March 1939 and appointed deputy director of the KGB foreign department, with orders to eliminate Trotsky. Sudoplatov enlisted Leonid Eitingon, a veteran KGB officer, to run the operation. (Eitingon shows up in the Venona traffic under the cover name Tom.)[73] Another veteran Soviet intelligence officer, Lev Vasilevsky, who used the name Tarasov when in North America, helped coordinate the operation's communications and was posted to Mexico City, where Trotsky then lived in exile. Eitingon arrived in New York in October 1939 and set up an export-import company as a cover.[74]

Eitingon and Sudoplatov established several networks aimed at killing Trotsky. Eitingon had served in the Spanish Civil War under the name of General Kotov and supervised the training of special units of the International Brigades for commando and sabotage missions. He drew on those contacts for personnel for the anti-Trotsky operation. Caridad Mercader, a wealthy Spanish Communist, headed one of the networks, and Eitingon recruited her son, Ramón, to play the chief role in this network's mission. The internationally acclaimed Mexican mural painter David Siqueiros headed a second apparatus. Eitingon may have had still another apparatus prepared to eliminate Trotsky if these efforts failed. Thomas Black, an American Communist, testified that Gaik Ovakimian, the KGB chief in New York, had recruited him for industrial espionage in the mid-1930s. Black said that the KGB ordered him to join the Trotskyists in 1937 and prepare to go to Mexico to join the Trotsky household. He later learned that he was to be part of an assassination attempt. For personal reasons, however, Black was unable to go to Mexico and took little part in the anti-Trotsky operation.[75]

The Siqueiros group struck first. Approximately twenty Spanish and Mexican Communists, many of them veterans of the Spanish Civil War, launched an armed raid on Trotsky's villa in May 1940; although one of Trotsky's American bodyguards, Robert Sheldon Harte, was killed, the operation failed to kill Trotsky.[76] Siqueiros, himself an International Brigades veteran, was arrested and insisted that the raiders, who had fired several hundred bullets, were merely trying to gather evidence of Trotsky's counterrevolutionary activities in Mexico. After being released on bail, he was spirited out of the country with the assistance of Pablo Neruda, a Communist and future Nobel Prize laureate in literature, then a Chilean diplomat in Mexico.[77]

Two of the gunmen named in the Mexican press as the murderers of Robert Harte were Leopolo and Luís Arenal, members of a wealthy Mexican family. (Harte was not killed in the gun battle at the Trotsky residence but was taken away by the raiders and murdered later.) In the spring of 1939 Jacob Golos had introduced Elizabeth Bentley to Leopolo Arenal. Leopolo's brother Luís was married to an American, Rose Biegel Arenal, who lived in New York. An Arenal sister, Angelica, was married to David Siqueiros. Golos had arranged for Bentley to pick up mail sent by Leopolo to Rose and deliver it to him. Rose Arenal later admitted to the FBI that she had received such letters, which she turned over to Bentley and Jacob Golos; although she never opened the letters, she assumed they might have had to do with the Trotsky assassination plot.[78]

Although Rose Arenal professed to be shocked by her possible involvement in murder, deciphered Venona cables show that she remained in touch with the KGB. She told a KGB officer in New York in July 1943 about Elena (identified by analysts as Elena Huerta Muzquiz), who needed financial help and who, evidently having some claim on the Soviets, was planning to appeal to Konstantin Umansky, Soviet ambassador to Mexico. Rose told the KGB that she had advised Elena against this course and asked the KGB to "report on the situation." She also alerted the KGB to an opportunity to recruit still another member of the Arenal family. She had received a letter from Mexico with news that her husband's cousin, Capt. Alberto Arenal, had been appointed a member of a Mexican military mission and would soon be leaving for New York. Alberto was "an honorable man and sympathetic to us," she told her KGB contact.[79]

The failure of the Siqueiros apparatus to kill Trotsky led Sudoplatov and Eitingon to put in motion an alternative plan using the Mercader group, whose elements had been carefully nurtured for several years. Louis Budenz later testified that one of the American Communists he had introduced to Gregory Rabinowitz in 1938 was Ruby Weil, a member of the CPUSA's secret apparatus. Weil had been cultivating a friendship with Sylvia Ageloff, an ardent Trotskyist who did not know that Weil was a secret Stalinist. On a trip to Paris in 1938 to attend an international Trotskyist meeting, Weil introduced Sylvia Ageloff to "Jacques Mornard," the alias being used by Ramón Mercader. Mornard pursued Ageloff, and they became lovers. After Ageloff returned to the United States, Mornard visited her in September 1939 in New York on his way to Mexico. A few months later, Sylvia Ageloff traveled to Mexico to do volunteer work for Trotsky and to join her boyfriend. (Much of Trotsky's household and office staff in Mexico consisted of young American Trotskyists who volunteered a few months' work. The murdered Harte was one such volunteer.) Mornard then used Ageloff's position in the Trotsky household to gain entrance to the residence and became acquainted with Trotsky's guards and aides. Presenting himself as interested in Trotsky's ideas but still working out his own views, he arranged a private meeting in August 1940 with Trotsky himself to discuss a philosophical manuscript he had prepared. Once alone with Trotsky, Mornard used a small ax to smash in Trotsky's skull.[80]

Mornard had planned to kill Trotsky silently and escape, but his victim had cried out, and he was seized by Trotsky's guards. Convicted of murder by a Mexican court, Mornard maintained that he was a disaffected Trotskyist, and initial efforts to ascertain his true identify were fruitless. He had entered Mexico using an altered Canadian passport belonging to a man who had served in the International Brigades. Despite widespread suspicion that he was a Soviet agent, there was no proof, nor even any firm evidence of his real nationality.

When he was captured, Soviet intelligence immediately set in motion plans to free him. Known in the Venona messages as the Rita Project, later as the Gnome Project—both names were used as cover names for Mercader—it involved Russian, Mexican, and American Communists. Just as the assassination of Trotsky depended on the cooperation of American Communists, the plot to free his killer revealed a large group of CPUSA members who worked for the KGB as agents, mail drops, and couriers. The extensive operation is the subject of dozens of cables from Moscow, New York, and Mexico City.

The KGB had used Rose Arenal as a mail drop in New York before the assassination. Afterward it employed a separate network of American Communists. Between November 1941 and November 1943 the FBI intercepted twenty-four messages in cipher or concealed writing that had been sent by mail and courier between the United States and Mexico. The FBI files released thus far do not indicate how the bureau first learned of the messages. The individuals who served as mail drops all lived in New York and Mexico City and were longtime members of the Communist party. The first mail drop discovered by the FBI was Lydia Altschuler, an immigrant from Germany and employee of Consumers Union. Before taking that job, Altschuler had worked for a distributor of Soviet films in the United States.[81]

Other mail drops included Pauline Baskind (wife of a New York attorney), Frances Silverman (member of the Communist-dominated New York Teachers Union), Louis Bloch (a New York motion picture operator employed by the Soviet government), Fanny McPeek (a clerk at Washington Irving High School), Barnett Shepard, and Ethel Vogel (her husband, Sidney, had served in the International Brigades as a medical doctor). Helen Levi Simon, a columnist at the *Daily Worker*, traveled to Mexico City in August 1943 to attend a Joint Anti-Fascist Refugee Conference and sent $3,700 to Mexico City in February 1944 for Mercader's use.[82]

The FBI followed Anna Colloms, whose address had been used as a mail drop, on a trip to Mexico in August 1943. She was carrying secret messages concealed in a box of blank stationery. United States Customs officials, having confiscated the box on August 15 when she left the United States, deciphered the messages and returned the box to her on her way home. The FBI laboratory discovered that all the messages dealt with efforts to free Mercader.[83]

A teacher at Washington Irving High School and a member of the CPUSA, Colloms continued her journey to Mexico City, where she made a half-hearted effort to get in touch with an American named Jacob Epstein, whom she had known previously. (Colloms must have suspected that she was under surveillance when Customs seized her stationary.) After picking up the seized material upon reentering the United States on September 16, 1943, she returned to New York and gave the stationery box to Ethel Vogel, her sister-in-law, who handed it over to Ruth Wilson Epstein, Jacob's wife. When asked in 1950 about her activities, Colloms took the Fifth.[84]

Several decrypted Venona messages reveal that both Lydia Altschuler and Anna Colloms had been used extensively as mail drops for KGB operations throughout Latin America, and that the KGB quickly learned that one of its mail drops had been compromised after her trip to Mexico. On December 6, 1942, a KGB agent in Buenos Aires cabled to New York that several of his letters sent to Lydia Altschuler had been intercepted by American mail censorship. He warned New York to "take measures with Lidia." The letters, which indeed had been seized by the government, had dealt with the movement of agents, the transfer of money, the setting up of clandestine radio contact and contacts for KGB agents in several South American countries.[85] On February 1, 1943, the New York KGB warned Buenos Aires to stop writing to one address and "for the time being use only Anna Collums' address." But on September 29, 1943, just two weeks after Colloms returned to New York, the New York KGB warned Buenos Aires, "Do not write any more to the address of Ana Colloms. Warn Alexander [unidentified] about this."[86] Colloms's trip was also the subject of a 1944 Venona message which reported that the KGB had spotted "surveillance of Non [Ruth Epstein] and the courier "A" [Anna Colloms] who came to the Countryside [Mexico] for liaison with Harry [Jacob Epstein] but achieved nothing." The message assured Moscow that appropriate measures were being taken to shake surveillance.[87]

Jacob and Ruth Wilson Epstein were Soviet agents whose activities are the subject of a number of Venona messages. Jacob Epstein, who was stationed in Mexico City, was born in Brooklyn to Russian parents on November 10, 1903. He attended public schools in New York and was graduated from Cornell University, where he met Anna Colloms, also a student, in 1924. He worked for several clothing companies in New York from 1924 to 1938, when he enlisted in the International Brigades. In the fighting Epstein was badly wounded. While recuperating, he met and married Ruth Beverly Wilson, who was serving as a nurse.[88]

While it is not clear whether Epstein was first recruited by the KGB in Spain or after his return to the United States, there is one intriguing bit of evidence that he was associated with the CPUSA's secret apparatus in 1941. When he applied for his passport for Mexico, one of his witnesses was Abraham Held, who was a business associate of J. Peters from 1939 to 1941. Jacob entered Mexico on a tourist visa in 1941. The following year he was granted resident status as representative of a business called Aldon Rug Mills, run by James Lewis Marcus, that served as a Soviet intelligence front. In 1943 he applied for and was granted student status, but later in the year his request to engage in the furniture business was denied by the Mexican government. Epstein's primary business in Mexico, however, was not tourism, schooling, or business. Epstein was in charge of the Gnome Project—the effort to free Mercader from his Mexican jail cell.[89]

Epstein reported to a series of senior Soviet intelligence officers. Lev Tarasov, nominally first secretary of the Soviet embassy but in reality a professional KGB officer, had been sent to Mexico to support Trotsky's assassination and was the KGB station chief in Mexico City. Pavel Klarin, another senior KGB officer, arrived from New York in November 1943 to supervise the jailbreak. And, from Moscow, Leonid Eitingon oversaw the entire operation. But despite the elaborate preparations, the escape attempt never took place.[90]

The first reference to Epstein's activities in the deciphered Venona documents came in a cable of May 28, 1943. Two days later, another message reported that Harry (Epstein) had placed two agents in the prison where Mercader was being held—one as a "consultant" and the other as a "patient." (The KGB adopted medical pseudonyms for this project. The Mexican prison, for example, was called the Hospital.) Arrangements were being made to transport Mercader out of Mexico once he was freed from jail, and other agents were being deployed. But Klarin admitted to Moscow from New York that planning was going "extremely slowly."[91]

The discovery by American counterintelligence of the couriers carrying secret messages between Klarin in New York and Epstein in Mexico persuaded Klarin that he had to travel to Mexico City to oversee the operation directly. He arrived on November 23, 1943, ostensibly as second secretary of the Soviet embassy. A December 23, 1943, cable from Tarasov in Mexico City to Beria in Moscow indicated that "the surgical operation is planned by the Doctors" to take place in four days and requested the immediate transfer of twenty thousand dollars to pay expenses.[92]

Less than a week later, however, Tarasov reported failure. The escape had been scheduled to occur when Mercader was being taken from prison to a courthouse. Epstein's team had bribed some of the guards to inform them of which of nine possible routes would be used to transport Mercader. KGB combat teams would then ambush the caravan, free Mercader, take him to a hiding place, and transport him out of Mexico. Several obstacles had derailed the operation. A key meeting between Klarin, Epstein, and Juan Godoy, a taxicab driver and the leader of a group of Mexican KGB agents providing much of the personnel, had not taken place. Other unspecified snags had arisen, and the operation had had to be scrapped.[93]

Epstein's usefulness to the KGB in Mexico also had come to an end. The KGB had discovered that he was being watched in Mexico and that his wife was under surveillance in New York. It decided that his continued presence in Mexico jeopardized the eventual success of the Gnome Project. Epstein left for the United States in May 1944. Nothing more is known of Epstein's activities at the time, but his wife remained in touch with Soviet intelligence into 1945.[94]

After the operation was aborted, on Eitingon's instructions, Klarin decided to disband the combat groups set up to carry out the original escape plan and inaugurated a long and fruitless search for alternatives. Tarasov identified two in a March 29, 1944, cable. The first possibility was to take advantage of relaxed security at the jail on Easter Sunday. An unidentified employee of the prison, with the cover name Kite, would enlist the help of a senior guard to free Mercader. The second option was to rely on a member of the Mexican Department of Justice cover-named Lord.[95]

Neither of these plans succeeded. Klarin departed from Mexico on May 24. In June, Tarasov sent a long message to Moscow describing a new plan using Invention, an agent in the prison who was close to the governor of the state of Hidalgo, Dr. Javier Rojo Gomez. Much of this message was not deciphered, but it appeared to involve a Communist doctor, Esther Chapa, who was then treating Mercader. The message contained a few cryptic references to getaway vehicles. This plan also failed.[96]

The KGB had still not given up hope of freeing Trotsky's assassin. Caridad Mercader surreptitiously entered Mexico in 1945 to look into her son's situation. Moscow ordered "a detailed study of Gnome's hospital [prison] routine and activities, what sort of watch is kept on him by the special agents of the Competitors [Mexican counterintelligence]," and warned that he was so well known that even genuine travel documents might not suffice to get him out of the country through legal checkpoints. Nothing availed; Mercader remained in a Mexican prison until he had finished serving his sentence and was released in 1960. He eventually retired to the Soviet Union on a KGB pension.[97]

Kitty Harris and the KGB in Mexico

Because the Mexican Communist party was small, the KGB found it convenient to seek links to other political forces in the country. The most significant was the powerful labor leader Vicente Lombardo Toledano, president of the Confederación General de Obreros y Campesinos de Mexico, Mexico's largest labor confederation. Toledano was the most prominent pro-Soviet figure in Mexican political life but remained aloof from the Mexican Communist party.

Toledano himself regularly provided political information and resources to the KGB and helped to obtain papers and visas for its agents. Toledano, whose Venona cover name was only partially decrypted (Sh . . .), worked very closely with one of the more fascinating Soviet KGB agents, an American woman named Kitty Harris, who worked for the Comintern and Soviet intelligence on several continents and through several decades. Thanks to the Venona decrypts another portion of her remarkable intelligence career has been uncovered, although some mysteries remain.

Kitty Harris was born in London around the turn of the century to Russian parents and came to the United States with her family by way of Canada. Kitty and several of her brothers and sisters became active Communists in the 1920s. One of Kitty's brothers and two of her brothers-in-law fought in the International Brigades in Spain. Another brother and a sister worked for Amtorg, while a second sister worked for TASS, the Soviet news agency.[98]

Kitty Harris joined the CPUSA in 1923. Soon afterward she became Earl Browder's lover and accompanied him to China in 1928. They lived together in Shanghai, and she assisted his work on behalf of the Pan-Pacific Trade Union Secretariat, a Comintern organization engaged in clandestine labor organizing. At that time she briefly irritated some of her fellow Comintern agents by failing to vacate her residence as quickly as she was ordered to after the Shanghai police got wind of Browder's activity and began hunting for him. Browder and Harris returned separately to the United States in 1929 and went their separate ways: he to the public leadership of the CPUSA, she deeper into the Communist underground. When she tried to renew her passport in 1932, American authorities turned her down; she was deported to Canada (she had never gained official U.S. citizenship) and dropped out of sight. In 1997 a nephew reported that family lore held that she had died while on a mission abroad for the Soviet Union in the 1930s.[99]

Whatever she was doing from 1932 to 1943, Kitty Harris was in Mexico in 1943, living under false papers and acting as a KGB contact with Vicente Toledano. What name she used and what position she occupied are unclear.[100]

Just as she had in China, Harris could display an independent streak in Mexico that exasperated her superiors. One of the projects on which Harris worked was a complicated effort by the KGB to obtain legal American transit documents for a couple, Nicholas and Maria Fisher, cover-named the Pair and the Reef. The mysterious Fishers, assumed to be KGB illegal officers, must have been important agents, because Moscow devoted much money and considerable effort to try to getting them through the United States with valid transit documentation and into Mexico. In Mexico, the KGB worked through Adolfo Orive de Alba, a Mexican politician. Alba was a member of the National Irrigation Commission; in December 1946 he was appointed minister of irrigation. In one message Moscow ordered Tarasov to "set Sh . . . [Toledano] the task through Ada [Harris] of organizing with Okh's [Alba's] help" in obtaining entry and transit visas for the Fishers.[101] Tarasov gave Alba money for his help, but Toledano "forbade him to take the money and explained to us" that it was well known that Alba lived on his salary alone and would not be able to account for a sudden windfall.[102] Michael Burd, the business partner of Robert Menaker, used his connections in Washington and appealed to David Niles, a presidential aide, for assistance in getting the transit visas, at first to no avail but at last successfully. (Burd claimed to have bribed political associates of Niles.) Even Niles's intervention, however, did not end the saga. As late as January 1945, the FBI was still holding up issuance of visas because of questions about how the Fishers had obtained their alleged Swiss citizenship in 1942. A KGB cable explained that the bureau paid careful attention to Mexico because it considered the country "one of the focal points for [KGB] intelligence organizations."[103]

Toledano's reluctance to allow his associate Alba to accept Soviet money was characteristic of his caution in his dealings with Soviet intelligence. Kitty Harris was apparently his only direct liaison with the KGB. When Toledano left for a visit to the United States in April 1944, Tarasov informed Moscow that Harris did not think it advisable, as had been suggested, to put him in touch with another agent. On another occasion, General Fitin instructed Tarasov not to risk meeting Toledano himself but to have him relay his information through Ambassador Umansky, who could meet Toledano in the regular course of his diplomatic duties.[104]

Several other messages indicate that Toledano set strict limits on what he would do for the KGB, limits that sometimes irritated Moscow. One of the major tasks of the Mexico City KGB residency was to "legalize" a number of agents, many of them Spanish refugees, who were being prepared for intelligence assignments in other countries. In one cable, Moscow, eager to obtain papers for someone code-named Patriot, ordered Mexico City to "approach Sh . . . [Toledano] through Ada [Harris]" for help in using Alba to obtain papers.[105] Harris, however, refused to approach Alba because "Sh . . . has forbidden her without his knowledge to approach" anyone. (Toledano was in the United States on a visit at the time.)[106] The implication that its agent deferred to Toledano angered Harris's superiors in Moscow. They quickly fired off a cable ordering Tarasov to tell Harris "that we require our orders to be carried out without any discussion. Explain to her that she receives instructions and tasks only from you and carries them out at your request." Harris was to be ordered once again to obtain the needed papers.[107]

Harris also engaged in incautious behavior that provoked Moscow. She was secretly communicating with members of her family in the United States. Harris underwent operations for appendicitis and removal of a tumor in December 1943. Early in 1944 Moscow learned that, perhaps because of her illness, she was in contact with one of her sisters. The security break was a source of concern to Moscow, which announced that "we absolutely forbid Ada [Harris]" to communicate with her family. Whether owing to her prior loyal work or to humanitarian concern, Moscow finally approved a method by which she could send and receive letters to this sister through secure KGB channels.[108]

It was not her communicating with her family, however, that brought an end to Harris's service for the KGB in Mexico. In June 1944 Tarasov warned Moscow that through carelessness on the part of Toledano and Vasily Zubilin, Alejandro Carrillo, editor of *La Popular* and a deputy in the Mexican Parliament, "has been put in the picture about the work of our illegal, Ada." In response, Moscow issued orders to "carefully work out a new cover-story for her."[109]

Later the KGB decided to end Harris's contact with Toledano. A message from Moscow in May 1945 has a partial sentence that warns "not to let Sh . . . feel a break in liaison"—a suggestion that Harris would no longer be his contact. A later message from Moscow requests ideas on "how she should be used in future and also state how you are thinking of completing or putting through her legalization." The last Venona message referring to Kitty Harris is dated April 28, 1946; Moscow inquired how preparations for her departure from Mexico were progressing. Her destination and fate are not known.[110]

CHAPTER 10

INDUSTRIAL AND ATOMIC ESPIONAGE

Theft of scientific and technical information constituted the earliest and perhaps the most widespread form of Soviet espionage in the United States. It ranged from stealing commercially valuable industrial secrets to penetrating America's most closely guarded military scientific secret, the atomic bomb.

As in other areas, the Soviets relied heavily on ideological sympathy as a lure for industrial spies. Recruitment was assisted by a shift in the demographic makeup of American Communists. In the 1920s the CPUSA's membership consisted largely of first-generation immigrants with limited formal education and little access to leading-edge technology. By the 1930s, however, its membership was mainly native-born, the level of education had increased markedly, and the CPUSA attracted scientifically and technically trained professionals. American Communists regarded the capitalist corporations they worked for as morally illegitimate institutions. Consequently, when Soviet intelligence officers approached and asked that the scientific secrets of these corporations be shared with the Soviet Union, referred to by Communists as "the Great Land of Socialism," few had any moral objections. The willingness of American Communists to turn over the technical secrets of their corporate and government employers further increased when the USSR faced possible defeat by Nazi Germany in World War II. When the homeland of communism was threatened, the "fellowcountrymen," as the KGB referred to American Communists, were eager to help in any way they could.

Harry Gold is an example of a Soviet agent whose espionage career was largely devoted to industrial spying. Arrested and convicted of espionage, he made a full confession of his activities. Gold's parents were Russian Jews. He was born in Switzerland in 1912 and brought to the United States before he was two. After graduation from high school, he worked as a laboratory assistant for Pennsylvania Sugar Company and entered the University of Pennsylvania in 1930. Money difficulties, however, forced him to drop his studies in 1932. Later that year he was also laid off from Pennsylvania Sugar. Entranced by the vision that the USSR had created a just society without unemployment or antisemitism, he considered emigrating to Birobidzhan, an area of the USSR that the Soviets had declared to be an autonomous Jewish region. But a friend and fellow chemist, Thomas Black, found him another job until Pennsylvania Sugar reinstated him.

Black also worked to recruit Gold into the CPUSA, but Gold had found party activities dull and declined formal membership. Black himself dropped out of the CPUSA in 1934 and ceased urging Gold to join. In 1935, however, Black approached Gold again. He explained that he had left the open party to take up secret work for Amtorg, the USSR's foreign trade agency. Black argued that while Gold may have found the CPUSA a dreary organization, as a sympathizer with Communist ideals he owed it to the Soviets to promote their economic success by handing over the scientific secrets of the capitalists to the world's only socialist state. Gold later remarked, "The chance to help strengthen the Soviet Union appeared as such a wonderful opportunity."[1]

Initially, Gold's espionage was confined to stealing the chemical processes developed at the laboratories of Pennsylvania Sugar, but later the Soviets expanded his work by making him their contact with a far-flung network of industrial spies. In his confession Gold described his life as a spy as one of continuous hard work:

> The planning of a meeting with a Soviet agent; the careful preparation for obtaining data from Penn Sugar, the writing of technical reports and the filching of blueprints for copying (and then returning them); the meetings with Paul Smith or Ruga or Fred or Semenov, in New York or Cincinnati . . . the cajoling of Brothman to do work and the outright blackmailing of Ben Smilg for the same purpose; and the many

lies I had to tell at home, and to my friends, to explain my whereabouts during these absences from home (Mom was certain that I was carrying on a series of clandestine love affairs and nothing could have been farther from the truth); the hours of waiting on street corners, waiting dubiously and fearfully in strange towns where I had no business to be, and the uneasy killing of time in cheap movies.[2]

Nonetheless, Gold kept at it, and his KGB controllers became his friends and confidants. When he had doubts about the cause, as he did over the Nazi-Soviet Pact, they assuaged his concerns and assured him that in the end Soviet communism would sweep all before it. By 1942 Gold worked under the direction of Semyon Semenov, a KGB technical and industrial intelligence specialist.[3] Semenov told Gold in 1943 that he, Gold, was being transferred to more important work and someone else would take over his existing sources. Gold was to be used once more as a go-between, but this time on a special project involving highly placed scientists. The chief one was Klaus Fuchs, a Soviet source within the American atomic bomb project.

What the deciphered Venona cables confirm about Gold's involvement in atomic espionage is discussed later in this chapter. Venona, however, also deals with Gold's industrial espionage.[4] One 1944 New York KGB message asked for Moscow's approval of a proposal that its industrial sources report to Gold (cover name Goose and later Arnold) and to Smart, the cover name of an agent who has never been identified. The message also noted that Gold was pressing for an explanation for the delayed delivery of his $100 monthly stipend. A December cable of the same year reported that Gold wanted to set up his own laboratory to work on thermal diffusion of gases and had asked the KGB for a $2,000 subsidy. The New York office, however, thought that Gold had underestimated the capital needed for the laboratory. The KGB declined to provide the subsidy, and Gold went to work for a firm headed by Abraham Brothman.

Gold identified Brothman as one of his chief associates in industrial espionage. He was a chemist who originally started spying for the Soviets when he worked for Republic Steel, supplying blueprints and documents on industrial processes. Among other points, Gold said that Brothman had helped to deliver industrial processes to the USSR for producing synthetic rubber and developing industrial aerosols. Venona has two 1944 KGB messages identifying Brothman, under the cover names Expert and Constructor, as one of Gold's sources. The messages report that Brothman was setting up a new engineering firm after leaving the company where he had been working on synthetic rubber and "the Aerosol problem (the work has partly been sent you)."[5] After Gold confessed in 1950, Brothman and an associate, Miriam Moskowitz, were convicted and jailed for obstruction of justice for lying to a grand jury about these activities.

Gold also identified Alfred Slack, a chemist, as one of his sources of technical espionage. Slack provided information from Eastman Kodak in Rochester, New York, on the recovery of silver from used film and on color photography as well as information on explosives developed at Holston Ordnance Works in Kingsport, Tennessee. After Gold identified him, Slack confessed and received a fifteen-year prison sentence.[6]

Another Soviet agent named by Gold was the man who recruited him into espionage, Thomas Lessing Black. When confronted by the FBI in 1950, Black confirmed Gold's account of his recruitment and admitted to industrial espionage, an activity whose legal status was unclear at that time and rarely prosecuted. He denied, however, any participation in espionage involving government secrets. Given his cooperation in corroborating Gold's testimony and the difficulty of establishing criminality in the case of industrial espionage, Black escaped prosecution.[7]

Black's own story was that he had joined the CPUSA in 1931 and in late 1933 or early 1934 approached Amtorg to inquire about employment opportunities in the USSR. He talked to Gaik Ovakimian, nominally an Amtorg official but actually a KGB officer.[8] Ovakimian told him that before he could be considered for employment in the Soviet Union, he had to prove his worth by supplying technical information. Once he began doing so, however, the KGB kept putting off discussion of his move, and he became caught up in his role as a full-time Soviet agent. On KGB instructions, he dropped out of the CPUSA and worked on industrial espionage.

Black also took on other assignments. The Soviets had him join the American Trotskyist movement around 1937. Black said that at one point his Soviet contact considered sending him to Mexico to attempt to infiltrate Trotsky's Mexican residence, but nothing came of the idea. (The KGB also briefly assigned Harry Gold to anti-Trotskyist work.) In 1940 Joseph Katz became his chief KGB contact. Black claimed that he actually met with Katz only a few times during World War II and that his last meeting was in 1946.[9]

Black is the subject of seven deciphered KGB messages.[10] They show that, probably seeking to avoid prosecution for espionage, he significantly understated his service to the Soviets during World War II. Chiefly, he appears to have worked as go-between for a network of Soviet sources. As far as can be discerned (several of the messages are incompletely deciphered), his sources appear to have engaged in the theft of industrial secrets. One message, however, states that Black had a source at the U.S. Bureau of Standards, which during World War II was deeply involved in high-technology military projects.

Harry Gold was not the only KGB agent who requested KGB funding to set up his own business. Another Soviet industrial source also asked for clandestine Soviet capital. William M. Malisoff was born in Russia and immigrated to the United States at an early age, obtaining citizenship through his father's naturalization. He held a doctorate from Columbia University and ran his own company, United Laboratories in New York. He was also a highly active Soviet source and the subject of nine Venona messages. In 1944 Leonid Kvasnikov, a KGB officer who specialized in scientific-technical espionage, reported to Moscow that he had met with Malisoff twenty times in the preceding year alone.[11]

In mid-1944 Malisoff asked the KGB for a large infusion of capital to add a manufacturing component to his firm. He was turned down, and the New York KGB cabled Moscow that "Anton [Kvasnikov] has informed Talent [Malisoff] of the impossibility of large-scale one-time aid. Just as we expected, Talent took this announcement exceptionally morbidly." The New York KGB noted that in addition to pleading with Kvasnikov, Malisoff had raised the subsidy issue with two of Kvasnikov's predecessors, Mikhail Shalyapin and Ovakimian. The New York KGB said that Malisoff complained "that the materials handed over by him on one question alone—oil, by his estimate had yielded the [Soviet] Union millions during past years and the aid requested by him was trifling." Offended that he had been turned down again, Malisoff threatened that in the future it would be "impossible to expect much help from him." Kvasnikov noted that "one cannot put him into cold storage in this condition, it will look like an attempt to get rid of him altogether." He recommended being patient and continuing contact until Malisoff had calmed down.[12]

While Gold and Malisoff were turned down for capital subsidies, others were not. The KGB set up at least two enterprises in New York using Soviet seed money. One, headed by an agent who had the cover name Odessan, was given a budget of two thousand dollars in KGB funds to purchase a camera, fans, printing press, cash register, studio fittings, shop window fittings, and stock. Another unidentified agent, with the cover name Second Hand Bookseller, was picked to head a second subsidized enterprise. The two enterprises were related in some fashion, and several messages suggest that they were engaged in producing false documents and photographing intelligence material.[13]

In addition to Gold, Brothman, and Black, the deciphered cables name numerous other sources of industrial and scientific intelligence. These included Aleksandr Belenky (a Russian immigrant working at a General Electric plant, who provided material to the KGB through another immigrant), Michael Leshing (superintendent of Twentieth Century Fox film laboratories, who in 1943 provided the Soviets with documents and a formula for color motion pictures and other film-processing technology), Frank Dziedzik (an employee of National Oil Products Company who supplied documents on medical compounds), Herman Jacobson (an employee of the Avery Manufacturing Company), Burton Perry (who gave the KGB the technical particulars of a radar-guided glide bomb), Kenneth Richardson (an employee of World Wide Electronics), Eugene Franklin Coleman (an electrical engineer who worked for Bell Telephone and RCA), Jones Orin York (an aircraft engineer who provided information on both civilian and military aviation design from 1935 to 1944), and Daniel Abraham Zaret (a safety inspector for the U.S. Army's Explosives Division).[14] Aside from sources identified in Venona, two other Soviet technical intelligence sources were Otto Alleman (a chemist who worked for Du Pont) and Arthur Gerald Steinberg (a zoologist who worked for the U.S. Office of Scientific Research and Development).[15]

Venona also provides the cover names of a number of Soviet technical sources whose identity has not been determined. These included Bolt (who provided documents on radio control technology in 1944), Brother (who engaged in aviation-related technical espionage), Oppen (a military industrial source of the New York GRU in 1943), Emulsion (who provided information on the military aircraft industry in 1944), Fisherman (a liaison with subagents involved in industrial espionage), I. (the initial of the name of a New York KGB asset working in industrial espionage, possibly with the oil industry), Serb (who was in contact with Leonid Kvasnikov), Jack (a GRU source who passed information on testing of guided bombs and was a liaison with the CPUSA), Johnny (a GRU source who delivered a 150-page technical report), Octane (active at least from 1943 to 1945 and perhaps as early as 1939), and Karl (who appears to have been engaged in technical espionage for the New York KGB; Karl may have been a member of a covert CPUSA apparatus, inasmuch as the New York KGB asked Moscow about the advisability of its picking up material that Karl had delivered to Earl Browder).[16]

One KGB industrial espionage effort that the FBI partly neutralized involved the military aviation industry in New York State. The United States provided the USSR with thousands of aircraft under the Lend-Lease program during World War II. One of the suppliers was Bell Aircraft, which produced the Bell Airacobra fighter (P-39) that saw extensive use on the eastern front. The Soviet Government Purchasing Commission, the conduit for American Lend-Lease aid, assigned an aviation inspector, Andrey Ivanovich Shevchenko, to the Bell Aircraft plants at Buffalo to approve aircraft before shipment to the USSR. He arrived in the United States in mid-1942 and remained until early 1946.

Trained as an aviation engineer, Shevchenko was a professional KGB officer charged with stealing secrets from the American aviation industry. He recruited and developed a number of sources in Bell Aircraft and in New York aviation plants. (Unlike many of the other Soviet sources, most of those recruited by Shevchenko do not appear to have had any links to the CPUSA.) It is not clear exactly when and how the FBI concluded that Shevchenko was a spy. It may well have been the anonymous August 1943 Russian letter (chapter 2) that caused the FBI to put him under surveillance. This letter named Shevchenko as a KGB officer and identified his place of work (Buffalo) and his cover (the Soviet Government Purchasing Commission). The FBI observed him meeting with Leona and Joseph Franey on July 26, 1944. Leona was chief librarian at Bell Aircraft, while Joseph worked in the rubber section of nearby Hooker Electro-Chemical. The bureau observed a second liaison on July 30, during which Shevchenko met the Franeys on the parkway near Niagara Falls and then took them to a leisurely dinner.

The FBI suspected that Shevchenko was cultivating the Franeys for possible recruitment. The bureau made contact with them in August 1944, and they agreed to assist the U.S. government. They reported that Shevchenko, whom Leona had met the previous November when he first began using the Bell Aircraft library, gave them theater tickets and small gifts, took them out to dinner, and related how social conditions in the USSR were superior to those in the United States. At the FBI's request, the Franeys allowed themselves to be recruited as spies, and in 1949 they testified to a congressional committee about their work as double agents. They stated that the KGB gave them cash bonuses and provided a camera to photograph the secret documents to which Leona had access in the secure section of Bell Aircraft's library. Shevchenko was particularly interested in material on Bell's development of one of the prototype American jet aircraft (the P-59), technical questions about jet engine design, and design problems with the innovative swept-back wing. Of course, the material the Franeys furnished was reviewed and sanitized by the FBI.[17]

The Venona Project eventually deciphered five KGB cables about Shevchenko and the Franeys.[18] The earliest, dated July 4, 1944, noted that Shevchenko had been cultivating Leona with small presents and wanted sanction to attempt recruitment. Both that cable and one on July 25 state that even prior to formal recruitment Leona had been persuaded to hand over one batch of secret material on jet aircraft development. This was before the FBI contacted the Franeys in August and puts a slightly different light on their subsequent role as double agents. It may indeed have been based on a patriotic desire to help the U.S. government, but their realization that they were already implicated in espionage may have encouraged cooperation.

The FBI also interviewed another potential Shevchenko recruit, Loren Haas, a Bell engineer who assisted in the technical training of Soviet personnel. Haas agreed to assist the FBI and allowed Shevchenko to recruit him. As with the Franeys, Shevchenko provided Haas with a camera to assist his espionage. One late 1944 Venona message notes that Haas had turned over to Shevchenko detailed drawings of a jet engine under development. Haas left Bell in 1945 to take a position with Westinghouse, soon to become a major producer of jet aircraft engines. Shevchenko renewed contact with Haas when he was at Westinghouse, and he continued to function as a double agent for the FBI.[19]

There is no indication in the twenty-nine deciphered Venona messages mentioning Shevchenko that the KGB ever suspected that he was under surveillance or that three of his sources were FBI counterintelligence contacts. The FBI wanted to arrest and either try or expel Shevchenko, but to its frustration the State Department objected that such action might upset Soviet-American relations. Shevchenko was allowed to continue his espionage, and the bureau had to content itself with neutralizing his activities to the extent it could.[20]

Aside from the Franeys and Haas (all working for American counterintelligence), Venona shows that Shevchenko's other sources included Aleksandr Petroff (an employee of Curtiss-Wright Aircraft Corporation who provided information on aircraft production methods), William Pinsly (also a employee of Curtiss-Wright), and William Plourde (an engineer with Bell Aircraft). In addition, Venona gives five cover names of unidentified Shevchenko sources: Spline, Splint, Bugle, Armor, and someone whose first initial was B.[21] Armor was clearly a source at Bell Aircraft. B. worked at Republic Aviation and provided information on research on the American equivalent of the German V-1, the first practical cruise missile. It is not clear which aircraft companies employed the other three sources.

Julius Rosenberg's Network of Communist Engineers

Julius Rosenberg is best known for his role in Soviet atomic espionage. But he was more important to the KGB as a source of nonatomic technical intelligence than for his role in stealing American atomic bomb secrets. Rosenberg had been an engineering student at the College of the City of New York (CCNY) in the late 1930s, one of the central figures of a close group of engineering students who were members of the Young Communist League. He later recruited many of them into Soviet espionage.[22]

Elizabeth Bentley told the FBI that in 1942 someone named Julius had contacted Jacob Golos to offer the services of a group of engineers to the Soviet cause. Golos handled them initially but in 1943 turned them over to the KGB. Bentley did not know Julius's family name, his address, or where he worked, and it would take the FBI five years to figure it out, but Bentley's physical description fit Julius Rosenberg precisely. How did Rosenberg know to contact Golos? One fellow Communist engineer later told the FBI that Rosenberg had simply kept approaching CPUSA officials until he found one who referred him to the right person.[23]

Twenty-one deciphered KGB cables, all from 1944 and 1945, discuss Julius Rosenberg. The first, from May 5, 1944, and the second, from May 22, 1944, show that the Rosenberg apparatus was already well in operation by that time. In the first, the New York KGB asked

Moscow to "carry out a check and sanction the recruitment of Alfred Sarant," provided a brief description of Sarant's background, and noted that he "is a lead of Antenna"—Rosenberg's cover name.[24] In the second, the New York KGB told Moscow that in view of the volume involved and in light of periodic FBI surveillance of official Soviet offices, it had concluded that its officers' practice of bringing stolen documents to the Soviet consulate for filming ought to be changed. The New York office reported that it was arranging for several officers to get cameras and to film at their own apartments the material that their sources brought. But in addition to decentralizing filming, "we consider it necessary to organize the filming of Antenna's Probationers' [agents'] materials by Antenna himself."[25] The two messages show that Julius Rosenberg's network was well established and produced enough material to justify its own filming operation. The KGB trusted Rosenberg sufficiently to assign the filming to him and to accept and pass on to Moscow his recommendation for a new agent.

A KGB message of July 26, 1944, deciphered by the Venona Project in 1950, allowed the identification of Julius Rosenberg as the man behind the cover name Antenna. In this message the New York KGB reported that Antenna had been to Washington to explore recruitment of a new source. The cable named the candidate for recruitment in plain text as Max Elitcher and described him as a old friend of Antenna's, an electrical engineering graduate of CCNY, and added that both Elitcher and his wife were Communists. It noted that Mrs. Elitcher worked for the War Department and that Elitcher himself headed a section of the U.S. Bureau of Standards working on a fire control system for heavy naval guns. Antenna said of Elitcher that "he has access to extremely valuable materials."[26]

When the NSA's cryptanalysts deciphered this message, neither the NSA nor the FBI knew who Antenna was. But Elitcher was a different matter. His name appeared in clear text. The government had already had its suspicions about his loyalty. The Office of Naval Intelligence had noted in 1941 that Elitcher and his friend Morton Sobell had attended a rally of the American Peace Mobilization, a CPUSA front. Naval intelligence investigated, but Elitcher denied any Communist links and the matter was dropped.

Elitcher, however, had been a party member and had participated in a secret caucus of Communists employed by the Navy Department and the Bureau of Standards. Armed with what it had learned from Venona, the FBI confronted Elitcher in 1950, and he broke. He admitted that he had been a Communist and said that in the summer of 1944 his old friend Julius Rosenberg had visited him in Washington and asked him to spy for the Soviet Union. Elitcher said that he had declined to make a decision at the time, and Rosenberg had repeated his recruitment appeal six or eight times between the years 1944 and 1948. He also said that Morton Sobell, another engineering colleague, was already a member of Rosenberg's network. Elitcher related how he had accompanied Sobell to a rendezvous in New York when Sobell furtively dropped off film to Julius Rosenberg. Sobell worked at the time for Reeves Electronic, which held U.S. government contracts for secret military research. It is another illustration of the laxness of American internal security practices in the 1940s that Sobell, whom Naval Intelligence had marked as a supporter of the American Peace Mobilization, who had worked as a counselor at a Communist youth camp, and whose admiration for Stalin was hardly camouflaged, received a security clearance to work on American defense contracts as late as 1949.

In 1997 Aleksandr Feklisov, one of the KGB officers who supervised Rosenberg's espionage apparatus, assessed Alfred Sarant and Joel Barr as among the most productive sources of the group.[27] Both were among Rosenberg's circle of young Communist engineers: Barr had been at CCNY with Rosenberg, while Sarant got his training at Cooper Union, also in New York City. The two electrical engineers were close friends and shared an apartment during part of their espionage career. During World War II, both also worked on military radar at the U.S. Army Signal Corps laboratories at Fort Monmouth, New Jersey. Barr lost his job at Fort Monmouth in 1942 when Army counterintelligence came across evidence of his Communist allegiance. But because concern about Communist espionage in that period was so uneven, Barr had no difficulty getting a job with Western Electric for a project developing the highly secret radar bombsight. Sarant also lost his position with the Signal Corps, but because of disruptive union activity rather than out of concern about his Communist leanings. He, too, then moved on to Western Electric to continue his work on radar.

There are seven deciphered KGB messages about Barr and four about Sarant. The KGB treated them as a team, and often both were discussed in the same cable. The first deciphered message about either is that of May 5, 1944, which discussed the recruitment of Sarant, who had not yet been assigned a cover name. The other messages, however, use their cover names. (Sarant was Hughes, and Barr had the cover name Scout, later changed to Meter.)[28]

The New York KGB reported to Moscow on November 14, 1944, that Julius Rosenberg "has safely carried through the contracting of Hughes [Sarant]," who, it noted, was a good friend of Meter [Barr]. "Contracting" was Sarant's formal recruitment as an active agent. The New York KGB proposed "to pair them off and get them to photograph their own materials having [been] given a camera for this purpose. Hughes [Sarant] is a good photographer, has a large darkroom and all the equipment but he does not have a Leica."[29] Later, when the FBI interviewed Sarant, he confirmed that he was an amateur photographer and had equipped one room in his apartment as a darkroom. He also said that Barr, his roommate, shared an enthusiasm for photography. He stated that Barr eventually obtained a Leica, but that he (Sarant) owned a less sophisticated camera.

The KGB cable went on to say that Rosenberg would pick up the film from the two and deliver it to the KGB. In addition, it pointed out that although Rosenberg was the chief link with Sarant and Barr, the two had also met with Harry Gold, another frequent intermediary between the KGB and its technical spies. Film of technical documents that the two stole was forwarded to Moscow for evaluation and use and was not usually commented on by the New York office. In one message, however, the New York KGB boasted that Hughes [Sarant] had just "handed over 17 authentic drawings relating to the APQ-7."[30] The APQ-7 was an advanced and secret airborne radar system jointly developed for the U.S. military by the Massachusetts Institute of Technology and Western Electric.

After World War II Sarant and Barr set up an engineering firm (Sarant Laboratories) that sought U.S. defense contracts, but it failed to prosper, and they went their separate ways. In 1946 Sarant moved to Ithaca, New York, where he worked in the physics laboratories at Cornell University and lived in a house next to Philip Morrison, a Cornell physicist and former Manhattan Project scientist who was a personal and political friend. (Morrison joined the Young Communist League in 1938 and the American Communist party in 1939 or 1940 while studying physics at the University of California, Berkeley.)[31] Barr worked on secret military radar systems for Sperry Gyroscope in late 1946, but lost his job a year later when the Air Force denied him a security clearance. He moved to Europe in 1948 to continued his graduate engineering studies.

The FBI arrested Harry Gold in late May 1950. The next month it arrested David Greenglass, Julius Rosenberg's brother-in-law. Joel Barr, living in Paris, disappeared around the same time. He told no one of plans to leave, and he abandoned his apartment without taking his clothes and other personal possessions. The FBI arrested Julius Rosenberg on July 17. Two days later, the bureau interviewed Alfred Sarant. Unsure of Sarant's role, the FBI did not arrest him but did warn him that he was the subject of an investigation and should notify the bureau of travel plans. Sarant told the FBI on July 25 that he was driving to Long Island for a week's vacation with relatives. Once there, however, he was joined by Carolyn Dayton, an Ithaca neighbor with whom he was romantically involved. With the help of his relatives Sarant evaded FBI surveillance, and the two took off on what he told his relatives was a cross-country vacation. In mid-August they entered Mexico (Sarant used the name of Carol's husband when crossing the border) and vanished. Both abandoned their spouses and children.

Nothing more was known of Sarant and Barr until 1983, when Mark Kuchment, a Russian émigré at Harvard University's Russian Research Center, read about Sarant and Barr in *The Rosenberg File* and linked them to two leading Soviet scientists who were native speakers of English. One, Joseph Berg, claimed to be a South African; the other, Philip Georgievich Staros, claimed to be of Canadian background. Later, another Russian immigrant scientist identified a photograph of Sarant as the man he had known in the USSR as Staros. (Staros/Sarant died of a heart attack in the the Soviet Union in 1979.)

Carolyn Dayton, who had had the name Anna Staros in the USSR, returned to the United States in 1991, and Barr came back in 1992. Only then did the rest of the story emerge. After reaching Mexico in 1950, Sarant and Dayton, fearing FBI surveillance, had avoided the Soviet embassy and reached the Soviets through the Polish embassy, had crossed over to Guatemala, and then had flown to Communist Poland. After six months in Warsaw, they traveled on to Moscow, where they caught up with Barr, who had arrived in the USSR via Czechoslovakia. Soviet intelligence gave them new identities as Joseph Berg and Philip Staros and set them up as electrical engineers in Communist Czechoslovakia. Sarant and Dayton, although never officially married, lived as the Staroses; Barr/Berg married a Czech woman.

In 1956 the Soviets transferred Sarant and Barr to Leningrad, put them at the head of a military electronics research institute, and provided them with the benefits of membership in the Soviet elite: government cars, large apartments, and substantial salaries. They were credited with founding the Soviet microelectronics industry, and Barr claimed that they created the first Soviet radar-guided anti-aircraft artillery and surface-to-air missiles, weapons that proved highly effective against American aircraft in the Vietnam War. Sarant was admitted to the Communist Party of the Soviet Union and in 1969 was awarded a state prize for his contributions to Soviet science.

After returning to the United States in 1992, Barr denied any participation in Soviet espionage, as did Dayton on Sarant's behalf. Both insisted that their covert flights to the USSR had been motivated by fear of American anticommunism. Despite these protestations of innocence, the deciphered Venona messages, along with other accumulated evidence, show that Barr and Sarant were among the KGB's most valuable technical spies.[32]

Morton Sobell also tried to disappear but did not succeed. At the same time Barr vanished in Paris, Sobell, who was working at Reeves Electronics, asked for leave, claiming a medical emergency. He hastily settled his private affairs and flew to Mexico with his family. Once there, he tried to make arrangements to reach the Soviet bloc but was hampered because he had not had time to obtain American passports. (Passports had not been needed to enter Mexico.) Before he could travel farther, Mexican police picked him up and delivered him to the U.S. border, where American authorities arrested him. Tried for espionage, he was convicted and sentenced to thirty years in prison.

Another member of the Rosenberg network, William Perl, was warned but, hoping to bluff it out, chose not to flee. He almost succeeded. Perl was a brilliant and highly placed aeronautical scientist who had taken part in a series of highly secret American military projects since the early 1940s. Another one of Rosenberg's engineer acquaintances, he had graduated from CCNY in 1940. His talent immediately earned him a position with the National Advisory Committee for Aeronautics, predecessor to the National Aeronautics and Space Administration. He worked first at Langley Field, Virginia, then at the Lewis Flight Propulsion Laboratory in Cleveland, Ohio. The National Advisory Committee for Aeronautics sent him to Columbia University in 1946 for doctoral work with Theodore von Karman, then chairman of the Air Force Scientific Advisory Board. In 1948 Perl was back at the Lewis Flight Propulsion Laboratory, where he supervised a fifteen-person group studying jet propulsion and supersonic flight. In 1950, when the FBI first began to understand the extent of Rosenberg's apparatus, Perl was under consideration for an appointment to a sensitive scientific post with the Atomic Energy Commission.

Perl did not get the appointment. Instead, on July 20, 1950, he got an interview with the FBI, who asked questions about his subletting of Sarant's New York City apartment several years earlier. At that point the FBI was interested only in what Perl might know about Sarant, Barr, and Julius Rosenberg. It did not suspect Perl of espionage, but Perl thought the FBI was toying with him. He approached the FBI on July 24 and told agents about a visit the previous day from Vivian Glassman, a visit he evidently thought the FBI had observed. (It had not; he was not even under surveillance.) He explained that he had known Glassman as Joel Barr's fiancée. He said she had acted strangely, chatted about trivial matters, mentioned Julius Rosenberg, and given him a sheet of paper. She had then urged him to leave the United States at once; the paper provided directions for fleeing to Mexico and offered two thousand dollars if he would go immediately. Perl told the FBI that he had no idea what any of this was about and had rejected all of Glassman's suggestions.

The FBI interviewed Vivian Glassman, and she presented herself as an innocent bystander. She said that a man whose identity she didn't know had persuaded her to go to Cleveland and offer Perl two thousand dollars to go to Mexico for an unknown purpose. After Perl had refused to take the money, she had traveled back to New York and returned the money to the unknown man, accepting no payment or reimbursement for her expenses. This was not very believable, but neither was it the sort of evidence that would convince a jury to send Glassman or Perl to prison. Perl, however, overstepped himself when called before a federal grand jury. Under oath he denied that he had ever known Julius Rosenberg or Morton Sobell. The government easily established that his statements were lies. Considering the government's unwillingness to expose Venona in court, had Perl admitted to knowing Rosenberg and Sobell, it is doubtful that charges would have been brought against him. His lies, however, resulted in a perjury indictment. Perl was convicted and sent to prison in 1953.

The Venona Project deciphered fourteen KGB cables that refer to William Perl.[33] They show that he was a productive and highly valuable source of secret technical information. Chronologically, the first, a New

York KGB report of May 10, 1944, referred to information Perl provided on a long-distance fighter under development by Vultee Aircraft and on a prototype American jet aircraft. Ten days later he provided information on the jet engine under development by Westinghouse. The New York KGB told Moscow in July 1944 that it had forwarded Perl's reports on the work of the National Advisory Committee for Aeronautics by diplomatic pouch. In September the New York KGB told Moscow that Perl thus far had received reimbursement only for the extra expenses incurred in his espionage work, but that it felt his productivity merited a bonus of five hundred dollars, similar to that granted other veteran sources of Rosenberg's network.

Moscow agreed to the bonus, and with good reason. In February the Moscow KGB told the New York KGB that evaluators had judged Perl's material to be "highly valuable."[34] In April some of his latest material was called "valuable" and the rest "highly valuable."[35] The FBI later determined that Perl had gained access to numerous files on advanced military aircraft research which did not appear to have relevance to his own research. On one special trip in 1948 from Cleveland to Columbia University, he removed classified files on the development of jet turbine–powered helicopters and the results of expensive wind-tunnel tests of prototype aircraft and airfoil designs.[36] Perl's position allowed him to deliver to the Soviets some of the most advanced aeronautical research undertaken by the United States, particularly in the development of high-performance military jet aircraft.

The New York KGB told Moscow in November 1944 that Perl's information was both valuable and ample enough to warrant sending a liaison team to Cleveland dedicated to handling Perl's intelligence information. Julius Rosenberg recommended Michael and Ann Sidorovich. The New York KGB concurred and told Moscow that Rosenberg had described Michael Sidorovich as follows: "Fellow Countryman [CPUSA member], was volunteer in Spain, lives in Western NY, no political work last three years, Liberal [Rosenberg] known him since childhood, including his political work, says he and wife are devoted. Wife is dressmaker who can open a shop in city for cover.... Liberal says Linza [Michael Sidorovich] ready to renew contact with us."[37]

The New York KGB also asked Moscow to arrange for the KGB station in Mexico to provide Leica film cassettes, in short supply in the

United States, both for the Rosenberg apparatus in New York City and for Sidorovich in Cleveland. It also reported in December that the Sidoroviches had sold their New York home and moved to Cleveland. They had received a $500 bonus for undertaking the liaison job, and Rosenberg was traveling to Cleveland to arrange an introductory meeting between Perl and the Sidoroviches. When the FBI later investigated the Rosenberg network, it found that the Sidoroviches owned a Leica and in 1945 had paid for an automobile in cash without having to withdraw any funds from their bank account.[38]

The Moscow KGB headquarters sanctioned a New York KGB plan in March 1945 to make more extensive use of Ann Sidorovich and pay her a monthly stipend of fifty dollars. Like her husband, she also had an background in the American Communist movement. She was the daughter of Mikhail Tkach, editor of the CPUSA's Ukrainian-language newspaper and himself a KGB asset, who reported on Ukrainian immigrants and functioned as an intermediary with several KGB sources.

The Rosenberg network was a large one. It included six sources: Barr, Perl, Sarant, Sobell, David Greenglass, and an unidentified source with the cover name Nile.[39] In addition to these sources, the network maintained two active liaison-couriers, Michael and Ann Sidorovich, and three others who carried out support work: Vivian Glassman, Ruth Greenglass, and Ethel Rosenberg.

In addition to running the network, Julius Rosenberg was also a source in his own right. For much of the war Rosenberg worked as a engineering inspector for the Army Signal Corps, checking on electronic equipment and projects under contract to the Signal Corps. This job gave him access to a wide array of secret American military technology. Army counterintelligence, however, came across evidence of his Communist loyalties in 1944 and forced him out. But as with Joel Barr, the hit-or-miss quality of American security procedures allowed Rosenberg to quickly find another job at Emerson Radio working on classified military projects. There he achieved a singular espionage coup, stealing a working sample of the proximity fuse, one of the most innovative advances of American military technology in World War II.[40] There is no doubting the value the Soviets saw in Rosenberg. Moscow ordered its New York office to award him a $1,000 bonus in March 1945 in recognition of his achievements and authorized smaller sums for his agents.[41]

Giving Stalin the Bomb

Even before the 1995 release of the Venona cables, several books reported rumors that deciphered Soviet cables had played a critical role in uncovering atomic spies.[42] Not only were the rumors true, but the decryptions exposed several theretofore-unknown Soviet agents responsible for the remarkable success of the USSR's atomic bomb program.

Klaus Fuchs and Harry Gold

The British began their atomic bomb program before the United States, and the Soviets quickly developed a key source within the project. One of the scientists enlisted to work on the British bomb project was a naturalized British subject and brilliant young physicist named Klaus Fuchs. A refugee from Nazi Germany, Fuchs had also been a member of the German Communist party. After he joined the British atomic project in 1941, Fuchs contacted a refugee German Communist leader, Jürgen Kuczynski, and offered to spy for the Soviets. Kuczynski put Fuchs in touch with a contact at the Soviet embassy, and Fuchs was soon reporting the secrets of the British bomb project to the GRU through Ursula Kuczynski (Jürgen's sister). After America entered the war, the British threw their resources into the U.S. bomb program, whose immense industrial capacities would be more likely to develop a practical atomic weapon swiftly.[43]

Fuchs arrived in the United States in late 1943, part of a contingent of fifteen British scientists augmenting the Manhattan Project. (By this point the KGB had also taken over control of Fuchs from the GRU.) Initially he worked with a Manhattan Project team at Columbia University, which was experimenting with uranium separation through gaseous diffusion.

Uranium in its natural state consists of two isotopes, U-235 and U-238. U-235 is highly radioactive and better suited for achieving an atomic explosion, but it accounts for less than 1 percent of natural uranium. The two isotopes are chemically identical, so their physical separation is difficult and constituted one of the major technical barriers to building an atomic bomb. The Manhattan Project developed several separation methods. One of them, gaseous diffusion, converted solid uranium into a gas and then pumped it through a porous screen through which the lighter U-235 isotope would diffuse faster than (and thus be separated from) the heavier U-238. The physics of the procedure was complex, and in that day many scientists thought the process impractical.

After his work on gaseous diffusion, Fuchs was transferred in August 1944 to Los Alamos, the top-secret heart of the U.S. atomic bomb project, to join its theoretical division. He continued working at Los Alamos until mid-1946, when he returned to England as one of the leaders of the once-again-independent British atomic bomb program. He also continued his work as a spy for the Soviet Union.

In late 1948 the FBI turned over to its British counterparts the Venona decryptions and the supporting evidence that Fuchs was a Soviet agent.[44] The British were convinced. In December officers of MI5 began to question Fuchs. Under interrogation, he collapsed quickly and began his confession on January 24, 1950, which led to his trial and conviction on charges of espionage. Released in 1959 after serving nine years of a fourteen-year sentence, Fuchs moved to Communist East Germany, where he became director of a nuclear research institute.

Because he did confess, the Venona cables serve primarily to confirm and enrich the story Fuchs told. They also corroborate the confession of Harry Gold, the American who was the chief link between Fuchs and the KGB. Gold first appears in the Venona cables in 1944 in connection with his work as the liaison with Fuchs. As noted earlier, Gould had been working as an industrial spy for the Soviets for nine years. On the basis of information from Fuchs's confession and on decrypted Venona cables, the FBI confronted Gold in 1950 and found ample evidence in his house of his long work as a Soviet agent. Like Fuchs, Gold easily broke and confessed. He received a thirty-year sentence for his crimes and served sixteen years before receiving a parole in 1966.

A February 1944 New York KGB message told Moscow that Fuchs, who had arrived in the United States in December 1943, and Gold had firmly established their relationship. Fuchs, the cable said, had turned over information about the organization of the U.S. atomic project and work on uranium separation, both gaseous diffusion and an alternative method, electromagnetic separation, developed at the University of California Radiation Laboratory at Berkeley. Other KGB messages report that Fuchs delivered information on the progress of the project and more technical details about gaseous diffusion. The New York KGB was so pleased by the quality of his information that it planned to give Fuchs a $500 bonus.

In August, however, the New York KGB reported that Fuchs had failed to show up for several meetings with Gold. Initially the KGB thought that Fuchs might have returned to Britain, but it sent Gold to see Fuchs's sister, who lived near Boston, and find out what had happened to him. Gold learned that Fuchs had been transferred to Los Alamos, where tight security had cut him off from his KGB links. Fuchs was able to phone his sister, however, while on a business trip to Chicago. Informed of Gold's inquiries, Fuchs told his sister to tell Gold that when he got leave from Los Alamos at Christmas he would reestablish contact. Once he did, Fuchs continued his espionage, this time from Los Alamos itself.[45]

Fuchs's transfer to Los Alamos increased the range of secrets he turned over to the Soviets. In addition to his long-standing work on uranium separation, he now gained access to work on the development of plutonium as an alternative to uranium U-235 as a bomb fuel and on the implosion mechanism as a way to detonate plutonium.

The Manhattan Project developed two different types of atomic bombs. The first, dropped on Hiroshima, was a pure uranium bomb with a "gun-type" detonator. The second, dropped on Nagasaki, was a plutonium bomb with an implosion detonator. In the first type, a small amount of U-235 is fired down a barrel at tremendous speed to hit another piece of uranium. The collision sets off a fission chain reaction that produces an atomic explosion. One of the difficulties with this type of atomic bomb is that it depends on the rare U-235 isotope, and the separation methods required the expenditure of tremendous industrial resources.

In the face of the daunting problem of obtaining enough U-235, the Manhattan Project developed an alternative. A team of Berkeley scientists in 1941 used a cyclotron to create (transmute) a new element that did not exist in nature: plutonium. Plutonium, they discovered, was more fissionable than U-235 and could be created in quantity in a nuclear reactor. This greatly reduced (although it did not eliminate) the need for laborious uranium separation.

A practical plutonium bomb, however, required a different method of detonation. Plutonium was so unstable that in a gun-type bomb system plutonium would began a premature chain reaction before the two pieces of plutonium were fully fused. A premature chain reaction would destroy the rest of the plutonium before it could be affected, thus producing a small nuclear explosion (a "fizzle") rather than a city-destroying blast. The solution worked out was implosion. An explosive sphere is shaped around a central core of plutonium. The sphere is then set off by a system of detonators that essentially allow all parts of the sphere to explode simultaneously. The result is that the core of plutonium is squeezed from all directions at the same time by a uniform force, and simultaneously all parts of the squeezed plutonium core undergo fission.

Fuchs's assignment to the theoretical division at Los Alamos gave him access to information on the plutonium bomb and use of implosion in a detonation device. Given Fuchs's position at Los Alamos, it is no surprise that messages from the Moscow KGB show intense interest in Fuchs and his work. Indeed, the messages from Moscow to the New York KGB attest not only that the KGB received the information but also that it quickly turned the information over to Soviet scientists working on an atomic bomb, because Moscow sent technical follow-up questions with instructions that the queries be passed to Fuchs and other Soviet sources inside the Manhattan Project.

Fuchs's confession in Britain led the FBI to Harry Gold in the United States. Gold's confession, in turn, uncovered other Soviet agents. The credibility of Gold's confession has been harshly attacked by those who refuse to believe that there was significant Soviet espionage in the United States. The Venona cables, however, offer independent confirmation of many points Gold made.

Greenglass and the Rosenbergs

Harry Gold's confession did more than corroborate Klaus Fuchs's story. Although most of his trips to New Mexico had been to get material from Fuchs, on one trip he picked up documents from another Soviet source at Los Alamos, whom he described, in the words of his FBI interrogators, as "a soldier, non-commissioned, married, no children (name not recalled.)"[46] Gold's description quickly led the FBI to Sgt. David Greenglass, a machinist working at one of Los Alamos's secret laboratories. Greenglass confessed to espionage and also implicated his wife, Ruth, and his brother-in-law, Julius Rosenberg. Ruth Greenglass also confessed, corroborating David's testimony that Julius Rosenberg had recruited David as a Soviet source. Under further interrogation, the Greenglasses implicated David's sister Ethel (Julius's wife) in espionage. Simultaneously the FBI was comparing the decrypted Venona cables containing their cover names with the confessions of Fuchs, Gold, and the Greenglasses and with the results of their investigative work. Fuchs, it had been determined earlier, had the cover names Rest and Charles, while Harry Gold was known as Goose and Arnold in the Venona traffic. By the latter half of June, the FBI and the NSA had identified the cover names Antenna and Liberal as Julius Rosenberg, Caliber as David Greenglass, and Osa as Ruth Greenglass.[47]

David and Ruth Greenglass were both fervent Communists who had joined the Young Communist League as teenagers. David had ambitions to become a scientist, but the need for a job forced him to drop out of Brooklyn Polytechnic Institute after only one semester. Just a few months after his marriage in late 1942 he was drafted. After he entered the Army, the young soldier's letters to his bride mixed declarations of love and longing with equally ardent profession of loyalty to Marxism-Leninism. One letter declared, "Victory shall be ours and the future is socialism's." Another looked to the end of the war when "we will be together to build—under socialism—our future." In yet another David wrote of his proselytizing for communism among his fellow soldiers: "Darling, we who understand can bring understanding to others because we are in love and have our Marxist outlook." And in a June 1944 letter he reconciled his Communist faith with the violence of the Soviet regime: "Darling, I have been reading a lot of books on the Soviet Union. Dear, I can see how farsighted and intelligent those leaders are. They are really geniuses, everyone of them. . . . I have come to a stronger and more resolute faith in and belief in the principles of Socialism and Communism. I believe that every time the Soviet Government used force they did so with pain in their hearts and the belief that what they were doing was to produce good for the greatest number. . . . More power to the Soviet Union and a fruitful and abundant life for their peoples."[48]

At the time David Greenglass wrote this last letter, he was a skilled machinist in an Army ordnance unit that was preparing to go overseas. But he was unexpectedly transferred to work on a secret project. By August he was in Los Alamos and assigned to work in a facility that made models of the high-technology bomb parts being tested by various scientific teams; specifically he worked on models of the implosion detonators being developed for the plutonium bomb.[49]

Through phone calls and letters David let Ruth know something about what he was working on. She, in turn, informed David's older sister, Ethel Rosenberg, and her husband, Julius. Although they did not know the details, both of the Greenglasses were aware that Julius was involved in secret work with concealed Communist engineers who worked in defense plants. Julius immediately understood the importance of the project on which David was working. He quickly reported this to the KGB. A September 1944 cable from the New York KGB states: "Liberal [Rosenberg] recommended the wife of his wife's brother, Ruth Greenglass, with a safe flat in view. She is 21 years old, a Townswoman [U.S. citizen], Gymnast [Young Communist]. Liberal and wife recommend her as an intelligent and clever girl. . . . Ruth learned that her husband was called up by the army but he was not sent to the front. He is a mechanical engineer and is now working at the Enormous [atomic bomb project] plant in Santa Fe, New Mexico."[50]

The Rosenbergs suggested to the Greenglasses that David should put the knowledge he was gaining in the service of the Soviet Union. David worked under secure conditions at Los Alamos, so in the initial approach guarded language was used in phone calls and letters. Nevertheless, in early November 1944 David wrote a letter to Ruth in which he said plainly that he would "most certainly will be glad to be part of the community project that Julius and his friends have in mind."[51]

Shortly afterward, David got five days of leave, and Ruth prepared to visit him in Santa Fe, the city nearest to the secret Los Alamos facility. She testified that she had dinner with the Rosenbergs just before she left. Julius and Ethel both pushed her to press David to take part in Julius's plan for espionage. According to those who believe the Rosenbergs to be innocent, Ruth's testimony was phony and there had been no such discussion. Among the Venona cables, however, there is a KGB message dated November 14, 1944, and devoted entirely to the work of Julius Rosenberg. Among other matters, it reported that Ruth Greenglass had agreed to assist in "drawing in" David, and that Julius would brief her before she left for New Mexico.[52]

As for Ethel's role, the same September KGB cable that first noted the contact with Ruth Greenglass stated that Ethel had recommended recruitment of her sister-in-law. Both Greenglasses later testified that Ethel was fully aware of Julius's espionage work and assisted him by typing some material. The only other deciphered reference to Ethel in the Venona cables came in November 1944, when the New York KGB responded to a Moscow headquarters inquiry about her: "Information on Liberal's wife. Surname that of her husband, first name Ethel, 29 years old. Married five years. Finished secondary school. A Fellow-countryman [CPUSA member] since 1938. Sufficiently well developed politically. Knows about her husband's work and the role of Meter [Joel Barr] and Nil [unidentified agent]. In view of delicate health does not work. Is characterized positively and as a devoted person."[53]

A December 13 KGB cable stated that the New York office had decided to designate Julius Rosenberg as the liaison with the Greenglasses rather than to shift them to another KGB link. A few days later, on December 16, a triumphant New York KGB reported that Ruth had returned from Sante Fe with the news that David had agreed to become a Soviet source and that he anticipated additional leave and would be visiting New York soon. The cable noted that Julius Rosenberg felt technically inadequate to ask the right scientific questions and wanted assistance in debriefing David during his visit. Finally, in a January 1945 Venona cable, the New York KGB reported that while David Greenglass had been on leave in New York, his recruitment had been completed and arrangements for delivery of material made. He had also given an initial report on his implosion detonator work. All this information matches the later testimony of both David and Ruth Greenglass.

The Venona cables greatly assisted the FBI's investigation by providing a documentary basis against which interrogators could check Fuchs's, Gold's, and Greenglass's confessions and the statements made by others. It provided leads for follow-up questions and the tracking down of additional witnesses. Because of the policy decision not to reveal the Venona secret, prosecutors could not use the cables as evidence in court. Nonetheless, they provided the FBI and other Justice Department officials with the sure knowledge that they were prosecuting the right people.

Initially, the FBI's investigation gave promise of being a classic case of "rolling up" a network link by link. First Fuchs was identified, and he confessed. His confession led to Gold, and Gold's confession led to David Greenglass. Greenglass then confessed, followed swiftly by his wife Ruth. But there it ended. The next link in the chain was Julius Rosenberg, and he refused to admit anything. So did Ethel.

The government charged Julius and Ethel Rosenberg with espionage. They were swiftly convicted, even without use of the deciphered Venona cables. The eyewitness testimony of David and Ruth Greenglass, the eyewitness testimony of Max Elitcher, the corroborative testimony of Harry Gold, and an impressive array of supporting evidence led to a quick conviction. David Greenglass was sentenced to fifteen years in prison. In view of her cooperation and that of her husband, Ruth Greenglass escaped prosecution. Morton Sobell was tried with the Rosenbergs and also refused to confess, but Elitcher's testimony and his flight to Mexico led to Sobell's conviction and to a term of thirty years.

The stonewalling by the Rosenbergs and Sobell took its toll, however, on the ability of the government to prosecute additional members of the Rosenberg network. William Perl was convicted, but only of perjury rather than of espionage. Barr and Sarant secretly fled to the USSR and avoided arrest. Others suffered nothing more than exclusion from employment by the government or by firms doing defense work.

The government asked for and got the death penalty for the Rosenbergs, and they were executed on June 19, 1953. It appears that government authorities, hoping to use the death sentences as leverage to obtain their confessions and roll up other parts of the Soviet espionage apparatus, did not expect to carry out the executions. But the Rosenbergs were Communist true believers and refused to confess.

The deciphered KGB messages of the Venona Project do more than confirm the participation of Fuchs, Greenglass, and Rosenberg in Soviet atomic espionage. They also show that the Soviet Union's intelligence services had at least three additional sources within the Manhattan Project.

Quantum: The Unidentified Atomic Spy of 1943

The New York KGB reported in a message of June 21, 1943, that a source, given the cover name Quantum, had met with Soviet officers in Washington a week earlier, on June 14.[54] The message is only partially decrypted, but several points are clear. The cable shows that Quantum met initially with a high-ranking Soviet diplomat. The New York KGB referred to the official as "Grandfather's deputy." Grandfather was the KGB cover name for the Soviet ambassador to the United States, Maksim Litvinov. Analysts at the NSA and the FBI concluded that the reference to his deputy was most likely to Andrey Gromyko, Litvinov's chief aide and his eventual successor. After a short discussion Gromyko turned Quantum over to Egor. Egor has never been identified, but another cable shows that it was the cover name for a KGB officer at the Soviet embassy. Egor heard out Quantum and then (this is unclear owing to the incomplete decryption) either brought in immediately or later consulted Semyon Semenov, a KGB officer who worked on scientific intelligence. Semenov also had long been involved in the Soviet program to penetrate Enormous, the KGB cover name for the U.S. atomic bomb project.

The KGB cable reported that Quantum was "convinced of the value of the materials and therefore expects from us a similar recompense for his labor—in the form of a financial reward." The reference to "materials" indicates that Quantum not only provided a verbal briefing but brought documents with him as well. Asking for money was unusual. While the cables show that the KGB habitually gave its productive sources annual gifts of some sort, rewarded many with cash bonuses, and provided regular stipends for those with heavy work loads or expenses, in this period money was not the usual inducement for betrayal of the United States. Ideological sympathy for communism—not greed— was the most common motivation for treachery. Monetary payment for specific deliveries was not the usual practice.

Because only a portion of all KGB cables has been decrypted, we cannot be sure when Quantum first made contact with the Soviets. The partial decryption of the June 21 message further hampers a firm conclusion. But the June 14 meeting appears to have been, if not the first, then a very early contact. Egor called on Semenov to evaluate the information; had Quantum been a developed source, his material would have been dealt with more routinely. Further, the nature of the contact suggests an early meeting, perhaps even a "walk-in." Though Soviet diplomats cooperated with the KGB, both they and the KGB avoided becoming directly involved in meeting with spies; diplomats regarded direct involvement in espionage as interfering with their main work, and the KGB did not care to deal with persons not under its direct control. Yet on June 14 Quantum met first with a senior Soviet diplomat. Possibly Quantum had no established contact with the KGB before that time, came to the Soviet embassy, and secured a meeting with a senior diplomat. Once he realized that espionage was on Quantum's mind, the diplomat turned him over to a KGB officer.

Semenov was impressed with Quantum's material and quickly paid him three hundred dollars. A lengthy second message, sent in three parts over the next two days, shows why Semenov was pleased.[55] Quantum had turned over a detailed scientific description of one variant of the difficult process of uranium separation through gaseous diffusion. Russian scientists working on a Soviet bomb in 1942 and early 1943 had thought the process of separation through gaseous diffusion to be not worth pursuing.[56] Espionage changed their minds. Not only did the Soviet intelligence agencies learn that in both Britain and America scientists had devised a practical method, but the KGB handed the process to their own scientists on a platter. Quantum was one of the sources.

Who was Quantum? The FBI never identified him. He probably was a scientist or engineer of some sort, for it seems unlikely that someone without a sophisticated technical background would have realized the importance of gaseous diffusion. Quantum's ability to win an audience with a senior Soviet diplomat and to persuade a KGB officer also suggests someone with scientific credentials and some professional standing. The cover name Quantum seems to point to a physicist. None of this is certain, however. The only thing that can be said with confidence is that Quantum had access to highly valuable scientific information on the U.S. atomic bomb project and handed it over to the Soviet Union at a meeting at the Soviet embassy on June 14, 1943.

What happened to Quantum? In August another cable mentioned in passing the report of mid-June. But Quantum does not appear again in the Venona cables. Possibly he is mentioned later under another cover name or in cables never deciphered. Possibly his handover of June 14 was a one-time act of perfidy for cash. Perhaps the KGB, as surely it would have tried to do, developed Quantum into a long-term asset. We cannot tell.

Fogel/Pers: The Unidentified Atomic Spy of 1944

A second unidentified Soviet source shows up in several 1944 New York KGB cables. This source initially had the cover name Fogel, changed in September 1944 to Pers, Russian for Persian.[57] The New York KGB sent Moscow a very lengthy report in February 1944 on the sort of atomic bomb information that was being turned in by Fogel. Unfortunately, only a few parts of the report were deciphered. There was enough to see that it was technical in nature, but the details are unknown. A June message from the New York KGB noted that it was forwarding to Moscow a layout of one of the Manhattan Project's manufacturing facilities that Fogel had provided. The facility was not specified, but what is known of the intelligence information turned over to Soviet scientists at this time suggests that the plans were of one of the plants at the Manhattan Project's Oak Ridge, Tennessee, facility.[58] Finally, a December message dealt with Fogel's work. The actual description was not decrypted, but it does associate Fogel with Camp-1, the KGB cover name for Oak Ridge. All that can be said about Fogel with certainty is that he had access to technical information about the atomic bomb project; very probably he was an engineer or scientist of some sort, but even that is a guess.

Youngster: The Treachery of Theodore Hall

The greatest surprise in the Venona traffic was that it revealed the identity of a major Soviet spy who, although long known to U.S. authorities, was unknown to the general public, had never been prosecuted, and was living in comfortable and respected retirement in England. In its initial release of the Venona cables in 1995 the NSA blacked out its footnote giving the identity of a Soviet agent with the cover name Youngster. The text of the messages, however, provided sufficient information about Youngster to enable a *Washington Post* reporter, Michael Dobbs, to break the story of the espionage carried out by Theodore Alvin Hall.[59] The NSA, which apparently had already made a decision to withdraw it redaction, did so, and the footnotes showed that the U.S. security officers had identified Hall as a Soviet spy long ago. In September 1997 a new book, *Bombshell,* appeared that focused on Theodore Hall's role as a Soviet source.[60] The authors, Joseph Albright and Marcia Kunstel, based the book on the Venona decryptions, hours of interviews with Hall himself, and other documentation and interviews.

Eight KGB cables deal with Theodore Hall, covering his initial recruitment in November 1944 through his work as a source at Los Alamos in July 1945.[61] An intellectual prodigy, Hall graduated from Harvard in 1944 at age eighteen. Not surprisingly, Manhattan Project talent hunters recruited this young star physicist to work on the program. Hall was dispatched to Los Alamos early in 1944 and assigned to a team attempting to master the physics of implosion, the key to the U.S. plutonium bomb.

Los Alamos was under tight security, and Hall could not communicate easily with anyone about what he was working on. But in October 1944 he returned home to New York on leave and spoke with his best friend and Harvard roommate, Saville Sax. One of the bonds between Hall and Sax was that both were fervent young Communists.

The two agreed that the Soviet Union ought to have the secrets with which Hall had been entrusted. (Like Fuchs, Hall was a volunteer: he made contact with the Soviets, not the other way around.) Sax then visited the CPUSA headquarters in New York City. At one point he tried to obtain an appointment with Earl Browder, head of the CPUSA, but the Harvard student, even if he was a young Communist, could not talk his way past Browder's secretary. Eventually, though, someone sent him to the right man. In this case it was Sergey Kurnakov, a journalist who wrote on military affairs for the CPUSA's *Daily Worker,* as well as for more mainstream publications. He was also a KGB agent.[62]

Kurnakov heard Sax out and then met with Hall. The New York KGB told Moscow that Kurnakov reported Hall to have "an exceptionally keen mind and a broad outlook," and to be "politically developed," meaning that Hall was a loyal Communist.[63] The historian Allen Weinstein gained access to the detailed written report that Kurnakov submitted to the KGB, which was sent to Moscow via diplomatic pouch. Quoting from Kurnakov's 1944 report, Weinstein wrote:

> Hall also "proposed organizing meetings, if needed, to inform [us] about the progress of . . . practical experiments on explosion [*sic*] and its control, the shell's construction, etc . . . ."
> Kurnakov was fascinated but still cautious, possibly fearing that this off-the-street agent might have been planted by the FBI so he asked Hall: "Do you understand what you are doing? Why do you think it is necessary to disclose U.S. secrets for the sake of the Soviet Union?" Hall responded: "There is no country except for the Soviet Union which could be entrusted with such a terrible thing."[64]

At this first meeting Hall gave Kurnakov a report he had prepared on the Los Alamos facility, the progress of the research, and the roles of the chief scientists working on the bomb. Kurnakov had immediately reported to his KGB superiors, Anatoly Yatskov, a KGB officer who specialized in scientific intelligence, and the chief of the New York KGB office, Stepan Apresyan, both nominally Soviet diplomats. The New York KGB had to act quickly because Hall was about to return to Los Alamos. On Apresyan's instructions, Kurnakov met again with Hall, reached an initial understanding, and picked up a photograph to assist the KGB in future contacts. Because it had to act rapidly and without the usual background checks, the KGB decided to use Sax as its initial liaison with Hall rather than risk one of its regular agents. As the contact man, Sax traveled to New Mexico to pick up material from Hall.

Later Lona Cohen, an American Communist and career KGB agent, made at least one trip to New Mexico for Hall's material in the late spring of 1945.

Other deciphered messages show the KGB carrying out its background checks on Sax and Hall through its CPUSA liaison, Bernard Schuster. The KGB gave Hall the cover name Mlad, meaning Youngster in Russian (Hall was only nineteen at that point), while his friend Sax was named Star, or Oldster. Hall delivered reports on the implosion detonation system for the plutonium bomb and on the methods the Manhattan Project had developed to separate the needed uranium U-235 from the unneeded U-238. While not a senior scientist like Klaus Fuchs, Hall held a very sensitive position at Los Alamos, and his access to highly valuable secret material was broad. Moscow told the New York KGB office in March 1945 that Hall's material was of "great interest."[65] The basis for the KGB's opinion was an evaluation of Hall's material by Igor Kurchatov, the scientific head of the Soviet atomic bomb project.[66] Hall was also drafted into the Army while at Los Alamos, but given his scientific talent he was immediately offered a commission. He accepted and swore the oath of true faith and allegiance to the United States required of all officers. He then returned to Los Alamos and proceeded to break his oath.

After the war ended, Hall was released from the atomic bomb program. He attended the University of Chicago and received a doctorate in physics in 1950. His research interests also turned toward radiobiology and the medical uses of X rays, and he later worked at the Sloan-Kettering Institute for Cancer Research. In 1962 he moved to Great Britain to take a position as a biophysicist at the Cavendish Laboratories at Cambridge University, where he still lives in retirement. Hall's espionage continued beyond the period documented by Venona, into the early 1950s, and included his recruitment in the late 1940s of two other American atomic scientists to work for the KGB.

Theodore Hall and Saville Sax came to the attention of the FBI in 1949, when an early, partially decrypted Venona message produced both their names in clear text. (In this initial New York KGB report on the first contact with Hall and Sax, the two had not yet been given cover names.) The FBI interviewed Sax and Hall in 1951. Neither, however, broke under interrogation, and both denied any contact with Soviet intelligence. Hall also repeatedly accused the FBI of harassing him simply because of his progressive political beliefs. Given the decision not to reveal the Venona cables in court and the absence of alternative evidence of their crimes of five years earlier, prosecution was not practical. In addition, by this time Hall was no longer involved in military-related science, nor was there evidence that either Sax or Hall was then currently involved in espionage. The FBI dropped its interest in the two in 1952. Although later additional Venona decryptions would further document Hall's and Sax's guilt, the matter was not reopened. Indeed, FBI policies kept their treachery secret from the American people until the release of the Venona cables in 1995.[67]

Atomic Espionage and Morris and Lona Cohen

In the aftermath of the collapse of the Soviet Union, the Russian Foreign Intelligence Service, successor to the foreign intelligence section of the KGB, released selected documents to the Russian press. These documents and the stories that accompanied them by retired Soviet and active Russian intelligence officers highlighted past successful intelligence operations. One of the operations praised for its success was Soviet penetration of the American atomic bomb project during World War II.

Col. Vladimir Chikov, a press officer with the Russian intelligence service, wrote a lengthy article in 1991 about Soviet atomic espionage which singled out two Americans who worked for Soviet intelligence, Morris Cohen and his wife, Lona (Leontine).[68] The Russian Foreign Intelligence Service has been adamant in continuing to protect the identities of Soviet agents, whether living or dead, and within Russia uses legal sanctions to prevent disclosure of Soviet-era foreign agents. The only exceptions are agents who publicly identified themselves or who had been identified by the Soviet government for reasons of state. The Cohens, who cooperated with Chikov's research, fell into both categories. They secretly left the United States in 1950 and went to the Soviet Union. There they prepared for a new assignment and, holding fraudulent New Zealand passports, reappeared a few years later in London as antiquarian book dealers under the names of Peter and Helen Kroger. In 1961 British security officials arrested the two as part of a Soviet espionage network that had penetrated the British navy. The Cohen residence housed the ring's elaborate radio and microfilming equipment.[69]

The Cohens stuck to their cover and insisted that their name really was Kroger. But British security had been in touch with the FBI and identified them as the Cohens. The FBI had stumbled onto the Cohens when an informant in 1953 mentioned having known Morris Cohen as an ardent Communist. The FBI routinely checked on him and found that he and his wife had vanished in September 1950. Morris, a New York City school teacher, had abruptly resigned, and the couple also abandoned their furniture in the apartment they vacated. They had told their relatives that they were moving to the West, but correspondence from them had been brief, had not provided a new address, and had then ceased. The FBI thought this chain of events suspicious but had no reason to treat it as other than a routine matter until 1957, when the bureau arrested KGB colonel Rudolf Abel, a Soviet spy operating under a false identity in the United States. In his safe-deposit box the FBI discovered photographs of the Cohens, along with recognition phrases used to establish contact between agents who have not met previously. Not surprisingly, that discovery spurred a major FBI effort to find out more about the Cohens. The investigation generated information on their backgrounds but no real clues to what had happened to the couple after September 1950. There the matter had stood until 1961, when British security arrested the Krogers, whose photographs and fingerprints identified them as the long-missing Cohens.[70]

A British court convicted and imprisoned the Cohens for espionage. In an extraordinary act, the Soviet government in 1967 admitted that the two were Soviet agents and obtained their release by exchanging them for a British subject held by the Soviet Union. The Cohens then lived in Moscow on KGB pensions until their deaths—Lona in 1992 and Morris in 1995.

In writing about the Cohens, consequently, Chikov was not revealing previously unknown spies but praising acknowledged KGB agents who had spent a lifetime in the service of the Soviet Union. The Cohens, indeed, were treated as heroes by both the KGB and the successor Russian Foreign Intelligence Service. During the Soviet era both received the Order of the Red Banner and the Order of Friendship of Nations for their espionage work. After the collapse of the USSR they also were given the title of Heroes of the Russian Federation by the Yeltsin government.[71]

Chikov claimed key roles for the Cohens in Soviet penetration of the Manhattan Project. He stated that in 1942 Morris, who then had the cover name Louis, personally recruited a key scientist working on the U.S. atomic bomb project. Chikov published a 1942 message from a KGB officer in the United States that said, "The physicist . . . contacted our source 'Louis,' an acquaintance from the Spanish civil war. . . . We propose to recruit him through 'Louis.' 'Louis' has already carried out a similar task, and very successfully."[72] One of the cover names given this physicist, according to Chikov, was Perseus. Morris Cohen was drafted in mid-1942 and was unavailable for espionage until released from duty in 1945. Chikov credited Lona with acting as the courier to Perseus, including making trips to New Mexico to pick up Perseus's material from Los Alamos. Support for these claims also came from the retired KGB officer Anatoly Yatskov, a senior KGB officer in the United States during World War II.[73] Both Chikov and Yatskov refused to identify the physicist, Chikov saying only that Morris had originally met him in some connection during the Spanish Civil War.

In fact, it was in Spain that Cohen became a spy. Cohen had joined the American Communist party in 1935, at age twenty-five. Two years later he was among the more than two thousand young American Communists who traveled to Spain to fight with the Communist-led International Brigades. He served with the Mackenzie-Papineau battalion, a nominally Canadian but largely American unit. Always an ideological militant, he quickly became one of the battalion's Communist political officers. During fighting at Fuentes del Ebro in October 1937, Cohen was wounded and hospitalized. When he recovered, rather than being returned to the front, he was sent to a secret Soviet-run school in Spain for training in covert radio operations and recruited as a Soviet agent. After returning to the United States, Morris Cohen worked at the Soviet exhibit at the 1939 New York World's Fair and later for Amtorg. He also worked as a substitute teacher in the New York schools. These, however, were his "day" jobs. He also served KGB officer Semyon Semenov as a courier and talent-spotter for new sources. In 1941 he married Lona Petka, a fellow Communist, and she soon became a full partner in his espionage work.[74]

There are difficulties in relying on Chikov's account about the details of Perseus. His articles and his book were reviewed by the Russian Foreign Intelligence Service, and any material it found objectionable was removed or changed. Chikov's account appeared before the Venona cables, original documents not sanitized by the Russian Foreign Intelligence Service, became public. Their evidence is far more reliable than Chikov's censored and deliberately distorted secondary account. The cables reveal that Chikov provided a mixture of truth, half-truth, and deliberate deception. With regard to Perseus, Chikov states that this cover name was later changed to Youngster. But Youngster, as Venona shows, was actually the cover name of Theodore Alvin Hall. Hall/ Youngster was not recruited until late 1944, and the Cohens had no role in his recruitment. When Chikov prepared his articles and book, Hall was still alive and had never been publicly identified as a Soviet agent. Chikov's claim that Perseus and Youngster were one and the same has the look of an attempt by the Russian Foreign Intelligence Service to muddy the historical waters and obscure the identity of as yet unexposed agents.

One is then left with the problem of deciding what can be trusted in Chikov's account. That the Cohens were valuable Soviet spies is surely true. The highly unusual Soviet decision to acknowledge their service and get the Cohens out of prison through a spy exchange is evidence of their value. That the Cohens had some role in Soviet atomic espionage is true as well. Albright and Kunstel in *Bombshell* detail the evidence that Lona Cohen acted as a courier in 1945 at least once and perhaps twice to Hall in New Mexico. But beyond that, the particulars provided by Chikov cannot be relied upon. The Perseus of Chikov's account may have been constructed out of the stories of two different agents, Fogel/Pers and Youngster, and perhaps of a third altogether unknown spy.

An intriguing part of Chikov's story is that he puts the recruitment of the unidentified physicist in the first half of 1942, at the earliest stages of the Manhattan Project. Given what is known of Soviet atomic espionage, it is very likely that the Soviets had penetrated the U.S. project in 1942, but the identify of the source is unknown. Klaus Fuchs did not arrive in the United States until the end of 1943. The unidentified Quantum appeared in mid-1943, and Fogel/Pers was present only in 1944. Hall and David Greenglass are figures from late 1944 and 1945. Gen. Pavel Sudoplatov, the retired KGB officer who for a time supervised atomic espionage, wrote in his memoirs that Semyon Semenov had a valued source inside the Manhattan Project in the latter half of 1942. Sudoplatov asserted that the source provided a full report on the achievement of the first controlled nuclear chain reaction at the project's University of Chicago facility. This and other stolen atomic material were among the information that Stalin's aide Vyacheslav Molotov turned over to the Soviet nuclear physicist Igor Kurchatov in February

1943. Molotov had just picked Kurchatov to head the Soviet atomic bomb program. Hence Chikov's claim of a 1942 recruitment of a source in the Manhattan Project is probably accurate, but Morris Cohen's role is uncertain, and the identify of the source remains a mystery.[75]

As for the Cohens, they make only the briefest appearances in the Venona cables, in part because Morris was drafted and unavailable for espionage during the period covered by most of the deciphered messages. Here Chikov's account does give some assistance. Chikov notes that Lona had the cover name Lesley for a period and that the apparatus set up by the Cohens was called the Volunteers. Albright and Kunstel in their research found that Morris himself had the cover name Volunteer and that Lona was Lesley. A 1945 Venona message relayed a report that Volunteer had been killed while on Army duty in Europe.[76] Chikov's account, which appeared before Venona was made public, provides corroboration, because he wrote that in 1945 Lona was briefly grief-stricken when a erroneous report came that Morris had been killed. Lona shows up in Venona cables of the New York KGB office both under the cover name Lesley and as "Volunteer's wife."[77]

None of these Venona messages, however, reveal anything of substance about the work of the Cohens. Both Albright and Kunstel and Chikov reported that Lona was running a network that included engineers and technicians at munitions and aviation plants in the New York area while Morris was on military duty. One of her sources even smuggled a working model of a new machine gun out of his plant. The FBI later learned that Lona had herself worked at two defense plans, the Public Metal Company in New York City in 1942 and the Aircraft Screw Products plant on Long Island in 1943. In a 1993 interview released by the Russian Foreign Intelligence Service, Morris Cohen alluded to contact with Hall in the late 1940s, noted that he had developed several of his fellow International Brigades veterans as Soviet espionage contacts, and referred briefly to his and Lona's postwar work with Rudolph Abel.[78]

Checking on the Smyth Report

In the fall of 1945 Gen. Leslie Groves, military director of the Manhattan Project, supervised the preparation and public release of a technical report on the development of the atomic bomb. Written by physicist Henry D. Smyth, it appeared under the title *General Account of the Development of Methods of Using Atomic Energy for Military Purposes*. The Smyth report was intended to satisfy the need for some sort of technical explanation for public consumption, but Groves also wanted to use the report to establish a maximum limit on what technical information the many scientists involved in the project could talk about without damaging American security and giving away the crucial secrets of the bomb.

Soviet scientists working on the atomic bomb read the Smyth report with great interest.[79] Soviet intelligence suspected that the report did not merely leave out certain highly sensitive information but also contained disinformation designed to lead the Soviets down technical blind alleys. Deciphered Venona messages show that the KGB sent an agent with the cover name Erie (later changed to Ernest) to check on this matter.[80] A November 1945 San Francisco KGB cable reported that Ernest had been sent to meet Morris Perelman, an engineer with the Los Alamos atomic bomb project, and a professor whose name was not recovered, both of whom had been in contact with Smyth regarding the report's authenticity. Ernest's mission was to find out what the two had to say about the report. There is no reason to suspect that either Perelman or the professor realized he was talking to a Soviet agent rather than to a fellow American scientist discussing something of mutual professional interest. Ernest also met with a third scientist, identified in the deciphered portions of the KGB's cable only by the initial D. Whoever he was, D. supplied Ernest with some of the information deliberately left out of the Smyth report. The portions of the KGB cable that can be read suggest that D. knew he was assisting Soviet espionage, as in a KGB reference to D.'s willingness to "turn [technical information] over to us at any time."[81]

The CPUSA and Attempted Recruitment for Atomic Espionage

The KGB used the American Communist party as its vehicle for an attempt to recruit Clarence Hiskey. A chemist, Hiskey had been doing research at Columbia University until September 1943, when he joined the Metallurgical Laboratory, a part of the atomic bomb project, at the University of Chicago. Hiskey had been active in the Communist party while in graduate school at the University of Wisconsin and was a natural target of KGB interest.[82] A May 1944 New York KGB message reported that Bernard Schuster, the CPUSA's liaison with the KGB, had been to Chicago at the KGB's direction. The cable passed on Schuster's description of those he had met: "Olsen is district leader of the Fraternal [Communist party] in Chicago. Olsen's wife, who has been meeting Ramsey [Hiskey], is also an active Fellowcountryman [Communist] and met Ramsey on the instructions of the organization. At our suggestion Echo [Schuster] can get a letter from Olsen with which one or other of our people will meet Ramsey and thereafter will be able to strike up an acquaintance."[83] Analysts at the NSA and the FBI did not identify Olsen, but it may have been the cover name or the party name of Morris Childs, at that time the head of the Communist party in Illinois. The message stated that Olsen's wife had been cultivating Hiskey, and the KGB wanted to use the relationship to put one of its agents in contact with him.

In July the New York KGB reported a follow-up to this May message.[84] It told Moscow that Schuster had passed along copies of two letters that had been sent to Hiskey by Victor (an unidentified cover name) and Rose Olsen. Rose, however, is probably not Morris Childs's wife but his sister-in-law, Roselyn. Roselyn's husband, Jack Childs, was a full-time CPUSA functionary whose work for the party was obscure and probably connected with its underground. The section of the cable describing the content of the letters was not deciphered. There was a garbled indication, however, that one of the KGB's veteran liaison agents, Joseph Katz, had been assigned to the Hiskey case. On September 18, 1944, the New York KGB office sent a cable responding to several inquiries from Moscow, one of which was about the status of the approach to Hiskey. The New York KGB deferred its report, on the grounds that its intermediaries in the matter, Bernard Schuster and Joseph Katz, were out of New York at the time and that Rose Olsen, at that point designated by the cover name Phlox, and her husband had traveled to "Ramsey's area."[85]

Finally, the New York KGB told Moscow in December 1944 that "Dick [Joseph Katz] is directly in touch with Phlox's husband and not with Phlox [Rose Olsen] herself. The intention of sending the husband to see Ramsey [Hiskey] is explained by the possibility of avoiding a superfluous stage for transmitting instructions."[86] Here the New York KGB is conveying its decision to Moscow that Jack Childs would make the approach to Hiskey. So far as is known, the approach, if carried out, was unsuccessful.[87]

The KGB's use of the CPUSA in its search for information on the

U.S. atomic program is reflected as well in a garbled November 1945 report from the San Francisco KGB station. The cable said that Jerome Callahan, a ship's clerk judged "trustworthy," had advised the KGB regarding something from (or about) Rudolph Lambert, head of the California Communist party's labor activities and chief of the party's security commission. The unrecovered sections of the message make it difficult to read, but it appears that Callahan and Lambert were the sources of information about uranium deposits. Neither Lambert nor Callahan would have been likely to take any interest in uranium ore had not the KGB put out feelers through the CPUSA.[88]

Other Facets of Soviet Atomic Espionage

Only a few GRU espionage cables were decrypted, yet it is clear from other sources that Soviet military intelligence also penetrated the Manhattan Project. Several attempted and probably partially successful penetrations were through an illegal GRU officer, Arthur Adams (chapter 6), who entered the United States in the late 1930s using a fraudulent Canadian passport.

By 1944 American counterintelligence had identified Adams as a Soviet agent and observed him meeting with Clarence Hiskey, the same Manhattan Project scientist the KGB had attempted to approach. Security officers suspected that his furtive meetings with an illegal GRU officer suggested espionage. They neutralized the situation by drafting Hiskey in mid-1944 and assigning him to routine Army duty in Alaska for the duration of the war. While Hiskey was en route to Alaska, American counterintelligence surreptitiously searched his belongings and found seven pages of classified notes on his work at the Metallurgical Laboratory. On a follow-up search, however, the notes were missing. Hiskey had either passed the information to a Soviet contact or, suspecting that he was under surveillance, destroyed them.[89]

Before Hiskey left for Army duty he made contact with John H. Chapin, a chemical engineer who also worked on the atomic bomb project, and arranged for him to meet with Adams. Security officials, however, observed the meeting. When questioned, Chapin admitted that Hiskey had told him that Adams was a Soviet agent, but he denied actually passing any secrets to him. Hiskey also put Edward Manning, a technician working on the bomb project, in touch with Adams. As with Hiskey, authorities had insufficient evidence for criminal charges and had to be content with simply neutralizing Manning and Chapin.[90]

Another Adams effort to penetrate the Manhattan Project took place in the winter of 1944. A counterintelligence officer caught one of Adams's contacts, Irving Lerner, an employee of the Motion Picture Division of the OWI, attempting to photograph the cyclotron at the University of California at Berkeley without authorization. (The cyclotron had been used in the creation of plutonium.) Again there was insufficient evidence for criminal action. Lerner resigned under pressure and went to work for Keynote Recordings, where Arthur Adams was employed.[91]

No Venona messages clearly refer to Adams, Chapin, Lerner, or Manning. One GRU message, however, may be related to Adams's attempts to obtain information at the Metallurgical Laboratory at the University of Chicago. In August 1943 Pavel Mikhailov, the GRU station chief in New York who met with Adams, sent a message to Moscow about William Malisoff, owner of Unified Laboratories in New York and a KGB spy. Mikhailov noted that Malisoff "knows people in Eskulap wife's special field and can recommend reliable people as candidates for her post in Chicago University." Eskulap was never identified. But, the frustrated Mikhailov reported, the GRU could not follow up on this possible lead because its agent Achilles—who may have been Arthur Adams—"was forbidden to meet Malisov [Malisoff] since the latter is connected with the Neighbors [KGB]."[92]

The GRU also attempted and achieved at least a limited penetration, and perhaps more, through the Radiation Laboratory at the University of California at Berkeley. Steve Nelson was both an open CPUSA official and a West Coast leader of its covert apparatus. The FBI placed listening devices in Nelson's residence and in October 1942 overhead Giovanni Lomanitz, a young scientist at the Radiation Laboratory, tell Nelson he was working on a highly secret weapon, a reference to the atomic bomb project. Nelson indicated prior knowledge of the project and advised Lomanitz, a Communist, to be discrete and to consider himself a undercover member of the party. In March 1943, another young Communist physicist, Joseph W. Weinberg, visited Nelson's home and talked about his confidential work at the Radiation Laboratory. Nelson took notes and several days later met with Peter Ivanov, nominally vice-consul at the Soviet consulate in San Francisco but in reality a GRU officer. Nelson gave Ivanov a package, believed by American security officers who watched the exchange to be his notes from Weinberg's briefing. When later asked by authorities about these events, Nelson took the Fifth, while Weinberg simply lied, denying that any meetings had occurred.[93]

Lomanitz and Weinberg were part of a group of a half-dozen Communist scientists working on the atomic bomb project at Berkeley's Radiation Laboratory. All were also active in attempts to establish a Radiation Laboratory local of the Federation of Architects, Engineers, Chemists, and Technicians (FAECT), a small white-collar CIO union, dominated by Communists, that shows up in several Soviet approaches to the atomic bomb project.

Although Nelson worked as a link between young Communist scientists at the Berkeley Radiation Laboratory and the Soviet intelligence officers, one chemist, Martin Kamen, met directly with Grigory Kheifets and Grigory Kasparov, KGB officers at the Soviet consulate in San Francisco. He was fired from the project in 1944 when security officers overheard him discussing the atomic bomb project with Kheifets. Unaware that they had been listening, he lied when questioned about the conversation.[94]

In August 1943 the New York KGB cabled to Moscow that it would approach a scientist, described as a "progressive professor" and one of the directors of a major radiation laboratory. The KGB said that the approach could be made through Paul Pinsky, a CPUSA member and organizer for FAECT in northern California. None of the subsequent deciphered Venona traffic, however, discusses the matter further.[95] Use of FAECT as a channel for Soviet espionage did not go unnoticed by American security officials. They made their concerns known to the White House, which got in touch with Philip Murray, national president of the CIO. He forced FAECT to cease organizing at the Radiation Laboratory for the duration of the war. Paul Pinsky attempted to delay the action, but he was overruled. The FBI later observed the GRU officer Ivanov visiting Pinsky's home in October 1943.[96]

It may be that FAECT also is the vaguely described organization in a September 1945 Venona message from the New York KGB to Moscow, which largely deals with the work of Julius Rosenberg but also mentions a source given the cover name Volok. Volok was a Communist working at an unidentified Manhattan Project facility. Unfortunately, the message noted, just a day earlier Volok had "learned that they had dismissed him from his work. His active work in progressive organizations in the past was the cause of his dismissal."[97] The passage immediately before the description of Volok was undeciphered, so it is not certain that Volok was a Rosenberg contact. Yet both the passage immediately before the undeciphered section and that immediately following the portion of the Volok passage that was decrypted deal with the Rosenberg ring. "Progressive" was standard Communist terminology for any Communist-aligned organization. Several engineers and scientists were dropped from the Manhattan Project when security officers discovered they were or had been FAECT militants, and FAECT would be a candidate for one of the "progressive organizations" referred to by this message.

The San Francisco office of the KGB also had a source, identified only by the cover name Brother-in-Law, who provided information on Lt. Col. Boris T. Pash, the U.S. Army counterintelligence officer who directed security for the atomic bomb program.[98] This assignment, too, reflects the intensity of the KGB interest in the Manhattan Project. In a poorly decrypted section of a 1944 message, the San Francisco KGB also appears to have discussed the possibility of approaching Frank Oppenheimer, brother of the scientific head of the Manhattan Project, J. Robert Oppenheimer. Frank, also a physicist, was a member of the Communist party. This cable, however, appeared to warn Moscow that Frank Oppenheimer was under close U.S. security surveillance.[99]

And what of J. Robert Oppenheimer himself? In the postwar period he came under suspicion when it was realized that the Manhattan Project had been penetrated by Soviet intelligence. The basis for the suspicion was Oppenheimer's background, ambiguous conduct, and reticence about his involvement with the CPUSA. He had been an ardent Popular Front liberal and an ally of the Communist party from the late 1930s until early 1942—an indication that his attachment to the Communist cause was strong enough to withstand the news of a Nazi-Soviet alliance in August 1939. Over that period Oppenheimer had given generous monetary contributions to the CPUSA, which he had often delivered to Isaac Folkoff, a senior leader of the California Communist party who also functioned as the party's West Coast liaison with the KGB. Further, until shortly before joining the Manhattan Project, Oppenheimer had socialized with Steve Nelson, another senior West Coast Communist, a leader of its secret apparatus, and, like Folkoff, a party contact with the KGB.

Oppenheimer's brother Frank and Frank's wife were concealed Communist party members. Frank vehemently denied Communist party membership until 1949. He then admitted he had joined the party in 1937 and remained a member until 1941. Robert's own wife, Katherine, had been a Communist and married to Joseph Dallet, a full-time functionary of the Communist party who had died while serving as a Communist political commissar with the International Brigades in the Spanish Civil War.

In addition to his background, Robert Oppenheimer's own conduct compounded counterintelligence concerns. Oppenheimer informed Manhattan Project security officers in August 1943 that he had indirect information that someone had approached several Manhattan Project scientists with requests that they provide sensitive information to the USSR. Pressed for details, Oppenheimer changed his story: the approach had been made directly to him. According to Oppenheimer's new version, Haakon Chevalier, a professor of Romance languages at the University of California, had asked him to divulge atomic bomb secrets in early 1943. Chevalier, a leading figure in Oppenheimer's Popular Front political circle of the late 1930s and early 1940s, said that he had been approached by George Eltenton, a chemical engineer who had worked in the Soviet Union. Eltenton asked Chevalier to act as an intermediary to feel out a number of Manhattan Project scientists about sharing information (a polite euphemism for spying) with the USSR. Oppenheimer said that he had rejected Chevalier's approach but had difficulty explaining why he had not reported the incident until months later and why his initial report had been a distortion. He than went on to supply information about several Manhattan Project scientists, including Giovanni Lomanitz, Joseph Weinberg, and David Bohm, whom he knew to be close to the Communist party and whose ideological loyalties raised questions about their trustworthiness.[100] (The three were among the young Communist scientists who had met with Steve Nelson.) To complicate matters more, Oppenheimer later made comments that repudiated parts of his revised statement about what happened.

Chevalier contested Oppenheimer's story. He denied Communist loyalties and said that he had only casually mentioned Eltenton's scheme to Oppenheimer and had rejected it at once. He also admitted meeting with Ivanov and Kheifets but insisted he had no idea that the two were Soviet intelligence officers. In looking back at the evidence, it is clear that Chevalier was a concealed Communist. Further, Eltenton was also a concealed Communist, whom U.S. security officers observed meeting on several occasions in 1942 with Peter Ivanov, the GRU officer operating out of the Soviet consulate in San Francisco.[101]

These circumstances contributed to Oppenheimer's losing his security clearance in 1954 and to suspicion that he had participated in espionage. What do the Venona cables have to say about J. Robert Oppenheimer? Directly, very little, but indirectly perhaps a bit more.

Oppenheimer's name appears in several messages in clear text where various Soviet sources reported on which scientists were supervising various aspects of the Manhattan Project. These are reports about him by Soviet spies, not reports from him. None suggests any compromising relationship with Soviet intelligence.[102] Two messages mention the cover name Veksel, whom FBI analysts identified as Robert Oppenheimer. These references also are benign. In one case Veksel is mentioned as directing a Manhattan Project facility to which the KGB had given the cover name Reservation, and the messages suggest that Reservation is Los Alamos, which Oppenheimer then directed.[103] In the other message, Moscow directed the New York KGB to send one of its agents, Huron, to Chicago to "renew acquaintance" and "reestablish contact" with two scientists working on the Manhattan Project, one of whom was Veksel. The other was Hyman H. Goldsmith, a physicist who worked at the Metallurgical Laboratory in Chicago. The most straightforward interpretation of this message is that the KGB hoped that Huron, who has never been identified but who was probably a scientist himself, was someone who had known the two in the past and would be able to learn something useful. Nothing in the message indicated that Goldsmith and Veksel had a compromising relationship with the KGB.[104]

In addition to what was said about Oppenheimer in Venona, what was not said is significant. Because only a portion of KGB cable traffic has been decrypted, silence on a particular person or subject often means nothing. The KGB traffic was not silent, however, on atomic espionage, on Los Alamos, or on J. Robert Oppenheimer. The messages on those subjects were written in a manner that suggests the absence of so knowledgeable a source as the director of Manhattan Project.

Another silence has to be taken into consideration. Although the archives of the Soviet intelligence agencies remain closed to research, the Russian government has released some documents dealing with the content of the intelligence delivered to the Soviet atomic bomb project. These documents do not provide much in the way of direct clues about who gave the information to the USSR but do show that the KGB and GRU sources provided the Soviets with rich and highly valuable information.[105] Oppenheimer, however, did not know just the secrets of some parts of the atomic bomb project. As scientific director at Los Alamos he knew all the secrets, and knew them nearly as soon as they came into being. Had Oppenheimer been an active Soviet source, the quality and quantity of what the Soviet Union learned would most likely have been greater than they actually were. Further, even in regard to what secrets the USSR did learn, if Oppenheimer had been a source, the Soviets would have learned them significantly sooner than they actually appear to have done.

The evidence suggests that Oppenheimer's ties to the Communist party up through 1941 were very strong. He was not simply a casual Popular Front liberal who ignorantly bumped up against the party in some of the arenas in which it operated. Until he went to security officials in 1943, Oppenheimer's attitude toward possible Communist espionage against the Manhattan Project came very close to complete indifference. It was as if in mid-1943 his views changed and he realized that there actually was a serious security issue involved. Even then, it appeared that he wanted only to give security officials enough information to bring about a neutralization of the problem but not enough to expose associates to retribution for what they might have already done. Throughout his life Oppenheimer declined to provide a detailed or accurate accounting of his relationship with the CPUSA in the late 1930s and early 1940s and of his knowledge of Communists who worked on the Manhattan Project. While the preponderance of the evidence argues against Oppenheimer's having been an active Soviet source, one matter cannot be ruled out. The possibility exists that up to the time he reported the Chevalier approach to security officials in mid-1943, he may have overlooked the conduct of others whom he had reasonable grounds to question, a passivity motivated by his personal and political ties to those persons.[106]

CHAPTER 11

SOVIET ESPIONAGE AND AMERICAN HISTORY

The deciphered cables of the Venona Project reveal that hundreds of Americans had formal ties to Soviet intelligence services in the 1930s and 1940s. Soviet intelligence achieved its greatest espionage success in hastily created wartime agencies that hired large numbers of people under procedures that bypassed normal Civil Service hiring practices. America's World War II intelligence agency, the Office of Strategic Services, was home to between fifteen and twenty Soviet spies. Four other wartime agencies—the War Production Board, the Board of Economic Warfare, the Office of the Coordinator of Inter-American Affairs, and the Office of War Information—included at least half a dozen Soviet sources each among their employees.

Although more established government agencies were less susceptible to penetration, they were not immune. At least six sources worked in the State Department. The two highest-ranking among these officials, Alger Hiss and Laurence Duggan, both aided Soviet intelligence for a decade. Thanks to the influence of Assistant Secretary Harry D. White, the Treasury Department was a congenial home for Soviet agents. Six of the eight known Soviet sources in the department were connected with the Division of Monetary Research, headed first by White and then by a second Soviet source, Frank Coe, after White moved farther up in the Treasury hierarchy.

The USSR's sources were impressive in their quality as well as their number. They included a presidential administrative assistant (Lauchlin Currie), scientists working at the heart of the atomic bomb project (Theodore Hall and Klaus Fuchs), a senior aide to the head of the Office of Strategic Services (Duncan Lee), an assistant secretary of the Treasury (Harry White), the secretary of state's assistant for special political affairs (Alger Hiss), the head of the State Department's Division of American Republics (Laurence Duggan), and dozens of well-placed mid-level officials scattered throughout the government.

Not all the Americans who cooperated with Soviet espionage were sources. For every Gregory Silvermaster or Maurice Halperin—frontline spies stealing secret documents—there were support and liaison agents, such as Amadeo Sabatini and Elizabeth Bentley, who made it possible for the actual sources to do their work. Every source must be supported by an elaborate apparatus: talent-spotters who suggest likely candidates for recruitment, vetters who check on the background of prospective sources, couriers who carry documents and instructions, and others to supply safe-houses, provide mail drops, help set up cover businesses, and assist in procuring fraudulent identifications. All are necessary parts of the espionage enterprise.

While the Venona cables document Soviet penetration of the American government, they are of less assistance in determining how much damage Soviet spies did to American security. Very little of the substantive information passed to Soviet intelligence agencies by their spies was transmitted to Moscow by the cables deciphered in the Venona Project. The bulk of the reports from sources and copies of stolen documents were sent by courier and resides in still-closed Russian archives. Only occasional items of exceptional interest or time-sensitive information were cabled. The Venona messages, the testimony of defectors, and the confessions of apprehended spies provide general descriptions of the type of information that was being transmitted but few details and, of course, little about what the Soviets did with the information.[1] The lack of specificity about the actual substance of the intelligence gathered by Soviet spies and the use to which the USSR put it renders an assessment of the extent of the damage to American interests tentative. That the damage was at the very least significant, however, is clear enough.[2]

The major exception to the lack of specific knowledge bears on atomic espionage. Since the collapse of the Soviet Union, Russian sources have made available a significant proportion of the intelligence "take" of the Soviet atomic spies. Given time and resources, the USSR's talented scientists and engineers would certainly have been able to construct an atomic bomb without assistance from spies. But because of the information gained from Klaus Fuchs, David Greenglass, Theodore Hall, and several as-yet-unidentified spies, the Soviet Union did not need to explore all the technical blind alleys that American and British scientists went down first; espionage revealed what worked and what did not. They did not have to expend enormous resources on the design and development of crucial technologies; espionage revealed the technical approaches that were practical and provided the data from expensive experiments free of charge. They did not have to depend on scientific insight for key conceptual breakthroughs; espionage revealed that implosion and plutonium offered tremendous savings in time and resources over the manufacture of a pure uranium bomb. Espionage saved the USSR great expense and industrial investment and thereby enabled the Soviets to build a successful atomic bomb years before they otherwise would have.

During World War II the CPUSA had more than fifty thousand members. Although, as we have noted, most American Communists were not spies, when the KGB and the GRU looked for sources and agents in the United States, they found the most eager and qualified candidates in the ranks of the American Communist party. Most of the Americans who betrayed their country and handed over its industrial, military, and governmental secrets to a foreign power did so not because they were blackmailed or needed money or were psychological misfits but out of ideological affinity for the Soviets. Throughout this book are examples of valuable Soviet sources, such as Theodore Hall, Klaus Fuchs, Julius Rosenberg, Gregory Silvermaster, Charles Kramer, and Victor Perlo, who were not recruited but who, prompted by ideological loyalty to communism, themselves sought out KGB or GRU contacts and volunteered to assist Soviet espionage. Others sources, of course, were approached and recruited. And though some American Communists who were asked to spy for the Soviet Union declined out of fear of being caught, there are no examples of Communists who indignantly rejected such overtures as unethical and reported the approaches to the U.S. authorities.[3]

The Soviet agents and sources came especially from three areas. First, there were the bright young idealists who had flocked to Washington in the heady days of the early New Deal. Several hundred of them had joined the Communist party and been assigned to secret party clubs. Many of these willingly turned government information over to the party in hopes of assisting Communist political goals or its labor cadre inside the CIO. And of this group a few score went further. When they found themselves in positions with access to secret government information helpful to the USSR, they did not hesitate to give it to Soviet intelligence officers. The Silvermaster and Perlo networks, among the largest Soviet spy rings, were both products of the Washington Communist underground. Second, several thousand young American Communists volunteered to fight in Spain in 1937–1938 in the ranks of the Comintern's International Brigades. The American volunteers sustained harrowing combat losses, but of those who survived, nearly a score enthusiastically continued their service to the cause by working in Soviet spy rings. One of them, Morris Cohen, became a career KGB officer who devoted his entire life to Soviet espionage. Third, several hundred committed CPUSA members worked for years in its "secret apparatus" which ensured internal security, prepared the CPUSA for the possibility of legal repression, and engaged in the infiltration and disruption of non-Communist organizations targeted by the party. The CPUSA functioned as an auxiliary to Soviet intelligence agencies, and its leading figures, such as Steve Nelson in California, performed a variety of tasks to assist Soviet espionage.

Why did American Communists spy for the USSR? The answer, at least in part, lies in the nature of American communism. We have read the remarks in which such spies as Theodore Hall, Gregory Silvermaster, David Greenglass, and Harry Gold professed their enthusiasm for Soviet communism and expressed their gratitude for the opportunity that espionage afforded to help strengthen the Soviet state. These attitudes were promulgated by the American Communist party. In 1935 a CPUSA spokesman wrote that Stalin "has directed the building of Socialism in a manner to create a rich, colorful, many-side cultural life among one hundred nationalities differing in economic development, language, history customs, tradition, but united in common work for a beautiful future. . . . [He is a] world leader whose every advice to every Party of the Comintern on every problem is correct, clear, balanced, and points the way to new, more decisive class battles."[4] In 1940 the American Young Communist League's journal, Clarity, proclaimed: "EVERY ONE OF COMRADE STALIN'S UTTERANCES IS A MIGHTY SEARCH-

LIGHT LIGHTING UP THE PATH OF THE REVOLUTIONARY YOUTH MOVE-
MENT. . . . The young workers and toilers of the capitalist countries who
are groaning under the yoke of capitalism look with great love and hope
to Comrade Stalin. . . . They see and know that the people of the Soviet
Union, whose happy life is for them a bright beacon, are indebted to
the Bolshevik Party and its great leader, Comrade Stalin, for the flour-
ishing of their youth and their happiness. Stalin rears the young generation like a careful, experienced gardener."[5]

In 1941 the party's theoretical journal, the *Communist,* declared
that Stalin was the "greatest man of our era. . . . With every passing
hour the titanic figure of this magnificent leader becomes more inextri-
cably bound up with the very destiny of world humanity."[6] In 1943
V. J. Jerome, the party's liaison with intellectuals, announced that "Stalin is the true forward-looking son of his epoch . . . the individually
gifted and socially endowed fighter for freedom."[7] And in 1949 Alexander Bittleman, one of the party's chief ideologists, asserted: "Stalin's
greatness and genius stand out so clearly and beautifully that progressive humanity has no difficulty in recognizing them. . . . To live with
Stalin in one age, to fight with him in one cause, to work under the
inspiring guidance of his teachings is something to be deeply proud of
and thankful for, to cherish."[8] Those who believed these statements had
no difficulty spying for Stalin's USSR if the opportunity presented itself.[9]

In some cases, the ideological attraction to the USSR was reinforced
by residual Russian patriotism, although of a nontraditional form. Some
of the Americans who spied for the Soviet Union were immigrants from
Russia or the children of immigrants. The parents of Saville Sax, a
young American Communist who worked for the KGB, were radical
Russian immigrants whom their grandson remembers as living in an
apartment building with similar families. The Sax family, he said, had
"barricaded themselves" in this "very closed community" that "identified American society with the people who were responsible for per-
secuting the Jews in czarist Russia."[10] Meanwhile, they believed that,
back in their native land, all that had been unjust had been made right
by the Bolshevik regime. The twin attraction of Communist and Russian
loyalties produced in these immigrants and their children a form of
Soviet patriotism that overwhelmed their weak ties to American national traditions.

By abetting Soviet espionage, these Communists and the CPUSA
itself laid the basis for the anti-Communist era that followed World

War II. The investigations and prosecutions of the American Communist movement undertaken by the federal government in the late 1940s and early 1950s were premised on an assumption that the CPUSA had assisted Soviet espionage. This view contributed to President Truman's executive order in 1947, reinforced in the early 1950s by President Eisenhower, that U.S. government employees be subjected to loyalty-security investigations. It also lay behind the 1948 decision by the Truman administration to prosecute Eugene Dennis and other CPUSA leaders under the sedition sections of the Smith Act. The government's loyalty-security program in the late 1940s had a rational basis—but that is not to say that the program was well designed or administered with skill and discretion, or that there were not serious abuses and injustices.[11]

With the advent of the Cold War, the decrypted Venona texts became a security nightmare. The identities of more than half the Americans who the deciphered Venona cables indicate cooperated with Soviet intelligence remained hidden behind cover names. How many of those nearly two hundred persons were still working in sensitive positions? Were they holding policy-making jobs? The hunt for these real but unidentified Soviet sources consumed the time and attention of hundreds of security officers for many years and subjected thousands of individuals to investigation. Particularly in the realm of diplomacy and defense policy-making, the knowledge that these unidentified Soviet agents existed diminished the mutual trust with which American officials could deal with each other. Further, the issue lent itself to partisan political exploitation. Republicans sought to discredit Democrats by painting the response of Democratic executive-branch officials as inadequate or even as constituting complicity in espionage. Democrats responded sometimes by covering up the problem, as in the *Amerasia* case, but more often, as with President Truman's personnel security order, by preempting the issue by taking a hard line against Communist subversion and spying.

By the mid-1950s American authorities understood that William Weisband and Kim Philby had betrayed to the Soviets the secret that Venona had succeeded in decrypting Soviet messages. American security officials calculated, however, that Soviet uncertainty about exactly what the Americans knew and what percentage of its wartime traffic had been penetrated was important, and Venona remained a closely held secret. But Venona's utility as a basis for gauging the accuracy or reliability of data from Soviet defectors diminished with time. The grounds for Venona's secrecy were much reduced by the 1970s, and its continued secrecy in the 1980s and until 1995 denied Americans a much-needed resource for understanding their own history.

Taken as a whole, the new evidence—from the deciphered Venona documents, the FBI files released in the past decades under the Freedom of Information Act, and the newly available documents from those Russian archives opened since the collapse of the USSR—along with the information produced earlier from defectors from Soviet espionage such as Whittaker Chambers and Elizabeth Bentley, testimony before various congressional committees, and the trials of major Soviet spies, shows that from 1942 to 1945 the Soviet Union launched an unrestrained espionage offensive against the United States. This offensive reached its zenith during the period when the United States, under President Franklin D. Roosevelt, adopted a policy of friendship and accommodation toward the USSR. The Soviet assault was of the type a nation directs at an enemy state that is temporarily an ally and with which it anticipates future hostility, rather than the much more restrained intelligence-gathering it would direct toward an ally that is expected to remain a friendly power. Stalin's espionage offensive was also a significant factor contributing to the Cold War. By the late 1940s the evidence provided by Venona and other sources of the massiveness and the intense hostility of the Soviet espionage attack caused American counterintelligence professionals and high-level American policy-making officials to conclude that Stalin was carrying out a covert assault on the United States. The Soviet espionage offensive, in their minds, indicated that the Cold War was not a state of affairs that had begun after World War II but a guerrilla action that Stalin had secretly started years earlier. They were right.

Source Venona: Americans and U.S. Residents Who Had Covert Relationships with Soviet Intelligence Agencies

This annotated list of 349 names includes U.S. citizens, noncitizen immigrants, and permanent residents of the United States who had a covert relationship with Soviet intelligence that is confirmed in the Venona traffic. It does not include Soviet intelligence officers operating legally under diplomatic cover but does show four Soviet intelligence officers operating illegally and posing as immigrants.

Of these 349 persons, 171 are identified by true names and 178 are known only by a cover name found in the Venona cables. A great many cover names were never identified. Many of these, however, are not listed here because the context indicates that the cover names refer to Soviet personnel operating under legal cover or because no judgment about the status of the person behind the cover name is possible. Only unidentified cover names that probably refer to Americans are included here.

Because cover names were changed from time to time, it is possible that a few of the unidentified cover names refer to persons known by another cover name or to persons named in the clear in another message. Some of the persons behind these unidentified cover names are very likely to be identified in appendix B as Americans who had a compromising relationship with Soviet intelligence but are not known to be documented in the Venona decryptions.

The persons identified in appendixes A and B represent only a partial listing of the total number of Americans and others who provided assistance to Soviet espionage in the Stalin era. The National Security Agency followed Soviet intelligence cable traffic only for a few years in World War II and decrypted only a small portion of that traffic.

Notes cite Venona messages regarding the person in question. Those persons whose activities are discussed in the text are provided with brief annotations, while those who are not are given fuller description. The Perlo and Silvermaster groups, to which some of these persons belonged, were founded as covert CPUSA networks but eventually were turned over to the KGB. Cover names are given in italic type, and true names are given in roman type.

A.: see Colloms, Anna.

Abram: see Soble, Jack.

Abt, John: labor lawyer and concealed Communist who turned the Perlo group over to the KGB in 1944.[1]

Achilles: unidentified asset of the New York GRU active 1941–1943 and involved in scientific-technical espionage at the University of Chicago. May be the illegal GRU officer Arthur Adams (see appendix B).[2]

Acorn: see Gold, Bela (William).

Ada: see Harris, Kitty.

Adam: see Getzoff, Rebecca.

Adler, Solomon. Treasury Department official and secret Communist. Source for the Golos-Bentley network. Cover name Sachs.[3]

Aida: see Rand, Esther Trebach.

Aileron: see Silverman, Abraham George.

Akhmed: unidentified asset reporting to the New York KGB office in 1944 and 1945. Provided information on senior American journalists, reported on the activities of anti-Soviet émigrés, assisted in tracking the Soviet defector Victor Kravchenko, and served as the KGB liaison to a subset of other Soviet agents. Given the nature of his work, *Akhmed* may have been an immigrant from the USSR. Also carried under the cover name Thrush.[4]

Akhmerov, Iskhak Abdulovich: senior KGB illegal officer posing as an immigrant to America. Operated in the United States from the mid-1930s to the end of World War II. Credited by the KGB with the recruitment of scores of American sources. Known to have used the names William Grienke and Michael Green. Cover names in the Venona traffic are Mayor and Albert. On Akhmerov's full KGB career, see appendix E.[5]

Albert: see Akhmerov, Iskhak Abdulovich.

Aleksandr (Alexander): unidentified asset recruited by the New York KGB office in 1942 and mentioned in partially decrypted messages in 1943 and 1944. The 1943 message suggests some connection with KGB activities in Mexico.[6]

Aleksandrov (Alexandrov): unidentified asset for the New York KGB office who reported on anti-Soviet émigrés in 1944 and 1945. Also accepted payment. One message suggests that Aleksandrov was the father of Eugénie Olkhine (below).[7]

Ales: see Hiss, Alger.

Alma: see Levanas, Leo.

Altschuler, Lydia: functioned as a mail drop for the American end of the KGB's anti-Trotsky operations in Mexico. Cover name Lidia.[8]

Antenna: see Rosenberg, Julius.

Arena: unidentified asset of the New York KGB holding a mid-level position in an unidentified government agency. Met directly with Vasily Zubilin. His residence was used as a safe-house.[9]

Armor: unidentified asset of the KGB who was employed at Bell Aircraft. Also had the cover name Stamp.[10]

Arnold: see Fakir; Gold, Harry.

Arrow: unidentified asset of the KGB who carried out tasks among immigrants. Worked specifically among the Carpatho-Russians.[11]

Art: see Koral, Helen.

Arthur: see Bisson, Thomas Arthur.

Aster: unidentified asset of the KGB who may have worked on anti-Trotskyist tasks.[12]

Ataman: see Gebert, Boleslaw K.

Attila: see Farish, Linn Markley.

Augur: unidentified Soviet contact who lived in Chicago and with whom the KGB had no direct liaison. The New York KGB had difficulty approaching Augur and asked Moscow if it could use Soviet diplomats to establish contact.[13]

Australian Woman: see Mitynen, Francia Yakilnilna.

Author: see Morkovin, Vladimir Borisovich.

B.: initial of an unidentified KGB source at Republic Aviation who provided the New York KGB with information on American development of an equivalent of the German V-1, an early cruise missile.[14]

Babin, Thomas: reported to the New York GRU office on ships leaving the United States in 1943 and on his work with the OSS. Cover name Brem.[15]

Baker, Rudy: head of the CPUSA's underground apparatus from 1938. Baker shows up in the Venona traffic only under the cover name Son. (Also see *Rudi.*) The identification comes from coded correspondence between the Comintern and the CPUSA in Russia's RTsKhIDNI archive (495-184), which contains dozens of messages from Brother in Moscow to Father and Son in the United States. Annotations on these messages identify Brother as Dimitrov and Father as Earl Browder. In these messages Son is the head of the CPUSA's covert arm, which Baker had taken over in mid-1938. None of the Comintern messages to Son were sent until after Baker had been to Moscow in January 1939 and had briefed Comintern officials on his assumption of the leadership of the CPUSA secret apparatus. Further, a May 1942 message from General Fitin, head of the KGB's foreign intelligence directorate, to Dimitrov (in another Comintern collection) states, "We are forwarding a telegram we received from New York addressed to you from Rudy," and the telegram is signed "Son."[16]

Barash, Vladimir: Russian immigrant who approached a KGB asset and offered his services to the Soviet Union.[17]

Bark: unidentified asset who reported to the New York KGB office in 1943 and 1944. Checked out a Soviet sympathizer who worked for a major New York radio broadcaster as a candidate for KGB infiltration into the Office of War Information.[18]

Barr, Joel: concealed Communist, engineer, and part of the Rosenberg ring that reported to the New York KGB office. Cover names Scout and Meter (Metre).[19]

Barrows, Alice: employee of the Office of Education from 1919 to 1942, On the staff of the CPUSA's Abraham Lincoln School in Chicago in 1944. The KGB reported in 1945 that she gave Charles Kramer, one of its sources, some unspecified information.[20]

Bass: see Burd, Michael.

Bayer, Theodore: president of the Russky Golos Publishing Company, which published *Russky Golos,* the Russian-language newspaper allied to the CPUSA. Reported in 1943 to the New York GRU. Cover name Simon.[21]

Beam: unidentified asset of the New York KGB who appeared to work among immigrant groups, particularly Poles. In 1944 his work was of sufficient quality that the New York KGB proposed to Moscow that he receive a cash bonus.[22]

Beaver-Cloth: unidentified asset of the New York KGB who worked with the KGB illegal officer Iskhak Akhmerov in 1943.[23]

Beck: see Kurnakov, Sergey Nikolaevich.

Beer: see *El.*

Beiser, George: Bell Aircraft engineer who provided Andrey Shevchenko with information on machine tools. Described as a "left-winger" and an "idealist." Shevchenko was an inspector at Bell Aircraft, and Beiser may not have realized that he was also a KGB agent.[24]

Belenky, Aleksandr: Russian immigrant working at a General Electric plant. Provided material to the KGB through another immigrant.[25]

Belfrage, Cedric: journalist and concealed Communist, born in Britain, lived in the United States for many decades. Worked for British Security Co-ordination, a branch of British intelligence, in the United States during World War II. Reported both British and American information to the New York office of the KGB. Designated by Unbroken Cover Name No. 9.[26]

Ben: unidentified asset reporting to the New York KGB office in 1944. Worked with Joseph Katz, one of the KGB's most active American agents.[27]

Bentley, Elizabeth: joined the CPUSA in the mid-1930s and became part of its secret apparatus. Reported to the New York KGB office from 1943 to 1945 and managed several large rings (the Silvermaster group and the Perlo group) of secret CPUSA members who worked for the U.S. government. Cover names Clever Girl and Myrna.[28]

Berg: see Koral, Alexander.

Bernstein, Joseph Milton: journalist who reported to the GRU's New York office in 1943. Worked as GRU contact with Soviet agents employed in U.S. government agencies. Cover name Marquis.[29]

Bernstein, Walter Sol: journalist who the KGB said reestablished contact with the KGB in October 1944 and was preparing a report based on what he had learned during a trip abroad. Maintained in a memoir that he had met with representatives of the CPUSA at this time but denied any contact with Soviet intelligence.[30]

Bibi: unidentified asset who reported to the KGB New York office in 1943 and 1944. Worked for the economic mission of Charles de Gaulle's Free French movement in Washington, D.C., in 1944 and from that post sought to develop sources in the U.S. government's Lend-Lease Administration and Foreign Economic Administration. Also reported extensively on internal politics within the Free French movement. Appears to have been American but may have been French; gender unknown.[31]

Bisson, Thomas Arthur: Asia specialist, reported to the New York GRU office in 1943. Worked for the U.S. government's Board of Economic Warfare and for the private Institute for Pacific Relations. Cover name Arthur.[32]

Black: see Black, Thomas Lessing.

Black, Thomas Lessing: chemist engaged in industrial espionage on behalf of the Soviet Union starting in the mid-1930s. Cover names Black and Peter.[33]

Block: see *Osprey.*

Bob: see Menaker, Robert Owen.

Bolt: unidentified asset who provided the New York KGB office with documents on radio control technology in 1944.[34]

Borrow, Robinson: asset of the New York GRU in 1943. Cover name Richard.[35]

Bredan: unidentified asset of the New York KGB in 1942 who maintained contact with a target for Soviet recruitment.[36]

Brem: see Babin, Thomas.

Brook: unidentified asset for the Naval GRU office in Washington in 1943. Activities unknown.[37]

Brother: unidentified asset of the New York KGB office who appeared to have been involved in technical/scientific espionage, probably in the aviation industry. Also had the cover name Thomas.[38]

Brother-in-Law (Svoyak): unidentified asset of the San Francisco KGB in

1944 who provided information about U.S. atomic bomb project security.[39]

Brothman, Abraham: chemist and long-time KGB asset engaged in industrial espionage. Cover names Constructor, Chrome Yellow, and Expert.[40]

Browder, Earl: head of CPUSA from 1930 to 1945. Oversaw party's co-operation with Soviet espionage in the United States. Cover name Helmsman.[41]

Browder, Rose: courier between the CPUSA and the KGB. Wife of William Browder.[42]

Browder, William: Earl Browder's brother and longtime assistant. Met on several occasions with the head of the New York KGB office.[43]

Bugle: unidentified asset of the New York KGB office in 1944. Controlled by Andrey Shevchenko, a KGB officer who worked as an inspector at Bell Aircraft.[44]

Bumblebee: see Greenglass, David.

Burd, Michael: head of Midland Export Corporation. Played a key role in a complex KGB operation to arrange U.S. transit visas for Nicholas and Maria Fisher, two KGB agents. His firm also transmitted large amounts of money for the KGB. Cover names Tenor and Bass.[45]

Burns, Paul: member of the CPUSA secret apparatus and veteran of the International Brigades. Provided a safe-house for the KGB at the request of the CPUSA. Later became an employee of Soviet news agency TASS.[46]

Bursler, Norman: member of the Silvermaster group. Mid-level Justice Department official.[47]

Butcher: unidentified asset of the San Francisco KGB office in 1944. Identified possible recruits for Soviet espionage in the California oil and aviation industries. May be Steve Nelson (see appendix B).[48]

Caliber: see Greenglass, David.

Callahan, James: ship's clerk. Provided information in 1945 to the San Francisco KGB, which described him as "trustworthy."[49]

Callen, Sylvia: infiltrated the American Trotskyist movement on behalf of the CPUSA in the late 1930s and early 1940s. Later became part of the Soble espionage ring. Also used the surnames Franklin, Caldwell, and Doxsee. Cover name Satir (Satyr).[50]

Carmen: unidentified female courier who worked for the New York KGB office in 1942 and 1944. May have worked in the KGB's extensive Latin American operations in 1942 and 1943 but in 1944 was in New York, where the local KGB office planned to assign her to work with agents within the United States.[51]

Carter: see Coleman, Eugene Franklin.

Catalyst: unidentified asset of the New York KGB whom the Soviets were considering whether to continue to use in December 1942.[52]

Cautious: see Joseph, Julius J.

Cavalryman: see Kurnakov, Sergey Nikolaevich.

Cedar: see Perry, Burton.

Cerberus: unidentified employee of the U.S. Treasury Department. In a 1945 KGB message was identified as a GRU asset who in the view of the KGB had lost touch with the GRU and was attempting to reestablish contact through the CPUSA.[53]

Char . . . : partial decryption of the name of a member of one of Elizabeth Bentley's rings of former CPUSA covert sources taken over by the KGB in 1944. From description may be Charles Flato.[54]

Charlie: unidentified source of the New York KGB who provided sensitive official information on China and other subjects. May be Abraham Weinstein (see appendix B).[55]

Chef: unidentified asset of the New York KGB office in 1944. May have been a courier between KGB officers and their sources.[56]

Chen: (1) unidentified asset of the New York KGB in 1943 who reported information about the Czechoslovak government-in-exile and about the attitude of the U.S. State Department toward exile German groups.[57] (2) See Franklin, Zalmond David.

Chester: see Schuster, Bernard.

Chrome Yellow: see Brothman, Abraham.

Clemence: asset of the New York KGB who worked among German immigrants and exiles and ran a safe-house. Cover name later changed to Lee. May be Johanna Beker (see appendix B).[58]

Clever Girl: see Bentley, Elizabeth.

Coe, Virginius Frank: director of the Division of Monetary Research in the Treasury Department and after World War II a leading official of the International Monetary Fund. Member of the Silvermaster ring. Cover name Peak.[59]

Cohen, Lona: CPUSA activist, recruited into Soviet espionage by her husband, Morris. An active career agent in her own right, including as a courier on one mission to pick up reports from a Soviet spy working at the atomic bomb facility at Los Alamos. Cover name Lesley, also called Volunteer's Wife.[60]

Cohen, Morris: CPUSA activist and International Brigades veteran and career KGB spy. Cover name Volunteer.[61]

Coleman, Eugene Franklin: electrical engineer, secret CPUSA member recruited as a source by the Washington Naval GRU office in 1943. Cover name Carter.[62]

Colleague: see Joseph, Bella.

Colloms, Anna: New York City schoolteacher, worked as a courier linking the American and Mexican anti-Trotsky KGB operations. Called A. in a 1944 Venona cable reporting on her arrival in Mexico from the United States.[63]

Condenser: see Richardson, Kenneth.

Constructor: see Brothman, Abraham.

Coplon, Judith: concealed Communist and KGB asset in the Foreign Agents

Registration section of the Justice Department, where she had access to FBI counterintelligence information. Cover name Sima.[64]

Cora: member of CPUSA recruited by the New York KGB office in December 1944. Her husband and son-in-law were also party members. Iskhak Akhmerov was interested in using her and proposed drawing in her husband as well. Akhmerov planned to withdraw both of them gradually from CPUSA activities and move them to another city for KGB work. Subsequent activities unknown. Husband's cover name was Roy.[65]

Cork: see Pinsly, William.

Corporant: GRU cover name for member of the CPUSA or the CPUSA itself.

Costra, Louis: Puerto Rican Communist and International Brigades veteran whose address was proposed as a mail drop by a KGB asset.[66]

Crow: unidentified asset recruited by the New York KGB office in 1945. Nothing else known.[67]

Cupid: unidentified recruit of the New York KGB office in 1944. Considered for use as a "communications girl," possibly meaning a courier in the network supervised by Jack Soble. Also had the cover name Jeannette.[68]

Currie, Lauchlin B.: senior administrative assistant to President Roosevelt who served in a variety of positions, including that of the president's special representative to China and deputy administrator of the Foreign Economic Administration. Cooperated with Elizabeth Bentley's CPUSA-KGB Silvermaster network. Cover name Page.[69]

Czech: see Menaker, Robert Owen, and Soble, Jack.

D.: initial of a KGB source, probably a knowing one, who furnished information on the Manhattan Project.[70]

Danilov: see Mok.

Dasha: see Wicher, Maria.

Dauber, M.: of the Dauber and Pine Bookshop in New York City. Provided a mail drop for a KGB contact.[71]

Daughter: see Voge, Marietta.

Davis: (1) unidentified source of the New York KGB, possibly involved in industrial espionage.[72] (2) See *Long* and *Spark.*

Davis, Marion: KGB source in the Office of the Coordinator of Inter-American Affairs Cover name Lou.[73]

Dennis, Eugene: senior member of the CPUSA leadership, in contact with a group of concealed Communists in the Office of Strategic Services and the Office of War Information.[74]

Dick: see Schuster, Bernard.

Dicky: see Steele, Johannes.

Dinah: see Kahn, Mrs. Ray (Gertrude).

Dir: see Price, Mary Wolfe.

Dodd, William E., Jr.: Popular Front activist. Father had been Roosevelt's ambassador to Nazi Germany. In 1944 the New York KGB asked Moscow if it was permissible, in light of Dodd's relationship to the KGB, for him to take a public job with TASS, the Soviet press agency. Cover name Sitsilla.[75]

Dodger: unidentified asset of the New York KGB who provided diplomatic information in 1943.[76]

Donald: unidentified U.S. Navy captain described by the Naval GRU in 1943 as "loyal to us." The description was part of a lengthy message about U.S. naval personnel in close contact with Soviet naval personnel in the United States. Unclear whether Donald is a real name or a cover name.[77]

Donald: (1) unidentified asset of the New York office of the GRU recruited in 1943 by the GRU agent Irving Velson.[78] (2) See Ullmann, William Ludwig.

Dora: see Silvermaster, Helen Witte.

Douglas: see Katz, Joseph.

Drugstore: unidentified asset recruited by the New York KGB office in 1945. Activities unknown.[79]

Duggan, Laurence: KGB asset beginning in the mid-1930s, headed the South American desk at the State Department until 1944. Served with the United Nations Relief and Rehabilitation Administration. Cover names Frank, Prince, and Sherwood.[80]

Duke: unidentified asset of the New York office of the KGB. The Russian name used in the messages is Gertsog, which means "duke" but may also transliterate the name Herzog. Appears to have been in or had some sort of contact with the French section of the OWI.[81]

Duya's son: unidentified son of Duya (also unidentified). In 1944 the New York KGB said that Duya's son was not now but had in the past been one of its assets. Duya is most likely a cover name.[82]

Dvoichenko-Markov, Demetrius: asset of the New York KGB 1943–1945, U.S. Army sergeant. Obtained, while assigned to military counterintelligence in Alaska, some sort of book or manual for the KGB. Cover name Hook. His mother, Eufrosina, also worked for the KGB.[83]

Dvoichenko-Markov, Eufrosina: asset of the New York KGB 1943–1945, provided information on exile groups in the United States, particularly Romanians and Carpatho-Russians, as well as on State Department personnel with whom she had contact. Cover name Masha.[84]

Dziedzik, Frank: employee of National Oil Products Company who supplied documentation on medical compounds to a KGB industrial espionage specialist.[85]

Eagle: unidentified asset of the New York KGB in 1944. In June 1944 placed by the KGB in cold storage for later use. Activities unknown.[86]

Echo: see Schuster, Bernard.

Economist: asset of the KGB likely involved in infiltration of the American Trotskyist movement.[87]

Egorn: see Einhorn, Nathan.

Einhorn, Nathan: journalist and executive secretary of the American Newspaper Guild in New York from 1938 to 1946. Helped to link CPUSA members to Soviet intelligence. Cover name Egorn.[88]

El: unidentified asset who worked with the Soviet illegal officer Iskhak Akhmerov in Washington, D.C., in connection with the Silvermaster group, as well as reporting to the New York KGB office in 1944 and 1945. Cover name changed to Beer in October 1944. Because of close relationship to Akhmerov, it is possible that El was merely a shortened form of Elsa, the cover name of Akhmerov's wife, Helen Lowry. El, which in Russian means "fir" or "spruce," is also used as a cover name for other unidentified persons and for Helen Keenan.[89]

Eleanor: asset of the Naval GRU in 1943 described as the daughter of Frank Gertsog, an immigrant from Russia in 1934 who became a naturalized U.S. citizen in 1935. Activities unknown.[90]

Ellis: unidentified female asset of the Naval GRU's Washington office in 1943. Passed on to the Naval GRU diplomatic information she had received from a luncheon with a "deputy minister of agriculture," presumably a deputy or assistant secretary of agriculture. Other activities unknown.[91]

Elsa: see Lowry, Helen.

Emilia: see *Stella.*

Emulsion: unidentified asset of the New York KGB in the military aircraft industry in 1944. Later had the cover name Signal.[92]

Engineer: unidentified asset of the KGB in 1944. The New York KGB feared that U.S. authorities had placed him under surveillance and observed him delivering documents to Amadeo Sabatini, one of its most active couriers. Sabatini was living on the West Coast at that time, so the document hand-over may have been there, suggesting that Engineer may also have been a West Coast resident. See York, Jones Orin.[93]

Epstein, Jacob: American Communist who had served with the International Brigades. Worked throughout 1943 and 1944 for the Mexico City KGB in its unsuccessful efforts to free Trotsky's assassin from a Mexican prison. Cover name Harry.[94]

Erie: see *Ernest* (KGB).

Ernest: unidentified asset of the New York KGB. Involved in scientific and technical espionage and may have been a scientist. Also had the cover name Erie.[95]

Ernest or *Ernst:* unidentified asset of the Naval GRU in 1943. Activities unknown.[96]

Expert: see Brothman, Abraham.

Express Messenger: see Setaro, Ricardo.

Fahy, Jack Bradley: asset of the Naval GRU. Worked for the Office of the Coordinator of Inter-American Affairs, the Board of Economic Warfare, and the Interior Department. Cover name Maxwell.[97]

Fakir: unidentified asset of the New York KGB office, 1943–1945. The KGB messages report that Fakir turned over State Department material to the KGB, discussed a contemplated trip to Moscow on behalf of an unnamed institution or agency, but also spoke of possibly taking a job with a CPUSA journal. Also had the cover name Arnold, and one KGB message makes a reference to information learned from an "officer" in "the statistical branch of Arnold's division," suggesting that Fakir/Arnold worked for a government agency.[98]

Fan: unidentified asset of the New York KGB in 1942 who provided vetting reports.[99]

Farish, Linn Markley: Communist, OSS officer, liaison with Tito's Partisan forces in Yugoslavia, and a KGB asset. Cover name Attila.[100]

Farley: unidentified asset of the New York office of the GRU, 1942–1943. Delivered information from the War Production Board and from the War Department.[101]

Farmhand: KGB contact of a KGB technical intelligence specialist. Described as having been on a long visit to a factory in New England in 1944.[102]

Fellowcountryman: generally a KGB term for any CPUSA member, but used in two 1944 messages as a cover name for a specific but unidentified asset of the New York KGB.[103]

Ferro: see Petroff, Aleksandr N.

Fighter: unidentified asset of the New York KGB who was recruited in 1942. Provided information on immigrant Ukrainians in the United States and Canada and investigated the attitudes of American journalists toward the Soviet Union. May be Albert Kahn (see appendix B).[104]

Fin: see Petroff, Aleksandr N.

Fir (or *Spruce*): see Keenan, Helen Grace Scott.

Fitzgerald, Edward J.: member of the Perlo group. Worked in the War Production Board. Cover name Ted.[105]

Flato, Charles: member of the Perlo group. Worked in the Board of Economic Warfare.[106]

Flora: New York KGB source who provided information on the United Nations Relief and Rehabilitation Administration.[107]

Fogel: unidentified asset of the New York KGB. Provided technical intelligence on the Manhattan Project and was most likely a scientist of some kind. Also had the cover name Pers or Persian.[108]

Folkoff, Isaac: senior member of the California Communist party and West Cost liaison between the KGB and the CPUSA. Worked as a courier passing information to and from Soviet sources, and as a talent-spotter and vetter of potential espionage recruits. Supervised several subagents. Cover name Uncle.[109]

Foster, Jane: a concealed Communist, worked for the Board of Economic Warfare in 1942 and then in the Indonesian section of the Office of Strategic Services from 1943 to 1947. After World War II became a member of the Soviet espionage ring managed by Jack Soble. Cover name Slang.[110]

Frank: see Duggan, Laurence, and Moosen, Arthur.

Franklin, Zalmond David: a CPUSA member and KGB asset, put into cold storage in 1944. Married at one time to Sylvia Callen. Cover name Chen.[111]

Fred: unidentified asset of the New York KGB who had a position in an unidentified U.S. government agency and dealt with Austria. May have been in the Office of War Information or had close contact with it.[112]

Friend: see Lange, Oskar.

Frost: see Morros, Boris Mikhailovich.

Gallardo, Isabel: Chilean, married to the American Lorren Hay, a Marine captain. Worked for the KGB on projects involving Chile.[113]

Gebert, Boleslaw K.: Communist union organizer and leader of pro-Communist activities among Polish-Americans. Reported to the KGB on the Polish-American community. Was a national officer of the Polonia Society of the International Workers Order. Cover name Ataman.[114]

Gel: unidentified asset of the New York KGB, 1942–1943. A journalist, worked for an unidentified magazine in 1943.[115]

George, Harrison: senior CPUSA figure, edited the party's West Coast newspaper, *People's World*. Assured the San Francisco KGB of the Communist loyalties of a target of KGB recruitment.[116]

Getzoff, Rebecca: KGB asset engaged in its anti-Trotskyist effort. Cover name Adam.[117]

Girl Friend: unidentified asset of the New York KGB, put into cold storage in 1944.[118]

Glasser, Harold: member of the Perlo group. An economist, worked in the Treasury Department. Cover name Ruble.[119]

Glory: see Wolston, Ilya Elliott.

Gnome: see Perl, William.

Godmother: asset of the New York KGB with access to diplomatic information.[120]

Gold, Bela (William): member of the Silvermaster group. Worked for the Senate Subcommittee on War Mobilization and Office of Economic Programs in the Foreign Economic Administration. Husband of Sonia Gold. Cover name Acorn.[121]

Gold, Harry: recruited in the mid-1930s for Soviet industrial espionage operations in the United States. Active courier for the New York KGB's scientific-technical espionage operations as well as liaison for several sub-agents. Cover names Goose and Arnold.[122]

Gold, Sonia Steinman: member of the Silvermaster group. Worked for the Division of Monetary Research of the Treasury Department. Wife of Bela Gold. Cover name Sonya (Sonia).[123]

Golos, Jacob: longtime senior official of the CPUSA and head of several groups of concealed party members within the U.S. government. Delivered information from his apparatus, spotted and vetted potential KGB recruits, and acted as a link between the KGB and the leadership of the CPUSA. Cover name Sound.[124]

Goose: see Gold, Harry.

Gorchoff, George: asset of the New York GRU in 1943. Cover name Gustav.[125]

Gordon, L.: asset of the New York GRU office described as female and a former CPUSA officer. Most likely Lottie Gordon, a former CPUSA official in Ohio. The GRU planned to establish Gordon as the head of a group of GRU sources in New York City and to provide her with a regular stipend.[126]

Green: provided information to the KGB about the Soviet defector Victor Kravchenko. May have been a cover name or possibly Abner Green, executive director of the American Committee for the Protection of the Foreign Born.[127]

Greenglass, David: member of the Young Communist League, recruited into Soviet espionage through the New York KGB office by his wife, Ruth, his sister, Ethel Rosenberg, and Ethel's husband, Julius. A soldier machinist working on the Manhattan Project at Los Alamos. Cover names Bumblebee and Caliber.[128]

Greenglass, Ruth: member of the Young Communist League, recruited into Soviet espionage through the New York KGB office by her sister-in-law, Ethel Rosenberg, and Ethel's husband, Julius. Assisted in drawing in her husband, David. Cover name Wasp.[129]

Growth: see *Odessan.*

Gustav: see Gorchoff, George.

Gymnast: KGB cover name for member of the Young Communist League.

Hall, Theodore Alvin: young physicist and Communist at Harvard, recruited to work on the Manhattan Project at Los Alamos. Volunteered to spy for the KGB and was an important Soviet atomic source. Cover name Youngster.[130]

Halperin, Maurice: secret Communist, became a KGB asset after obtaining the post of chief of the Latin American Division of the Research and Analysis section of the Office of Strategic Services, 1943–1945. After World War II, became a Latin American specialist for the State Department, 1945–1946. Cover names Hare and Stowaway.[131]

Hare: see Halperin, Maurice.

Harold: the New York KGB asked Moscow for permission to complete his recruitment in May 1944.[132]

Harris, Kitty: asset of the Mexico City KGB during World War II. Born in England, moved with her family to the United States via Canada, had close ties to the CPUSA. Joined the CPUSA in 1923, became a Comintern operative in the late 1920s, and at some point transferred to the KGB. Cover name Ada.[133]

Harry: see Epstein, Jacob.

Havre: cover name in the Venona cables for a person who worked for

British Security Coordination, a branch of British intelligence operating in the United States. The KGB reported that Havre delivered reports on the Czechoslovak government-in-exile and was a go-between with Cedric Belfrage, another officer of British Security Coordination who spied for the KGB. It is unclear whether Havre was American or British.[134]

Hedgehog: unidentified courier working for the New York KGB.[135]

Helmsman: see Browder, Earl.

Henry: see Malisoff (Malisov), William Marias.

Henwood, William: engineer for Standard Oil in California. Born in South Africa, became a naturalized U.S. citizen. Isaac Folkoff, the CPUSA West Coast liaison with Soviet intelligence, put Henwood in touch with the San Francisco KGB office in 1944.[136]

Hiss, Alger: senior American diplomat and important asset of the GRU. Cover name Ales.[137]

Hook: see Dvoichenko-Markov, Demetrius.

Horus: unidentified asset of the New York KGB, may have been in the Office of Strategic Services.[138]

Horvitz, Louis D.: member of the CPUSA secret apparatus and veteran of the International Brigades who provided a safe-house for the KGB at the request of the CPUSA.[139]

Hudson: unidentified asset of the New York KGB. Also had the cover name John. Activities included working in the KGB's "first line" (political intelligence), placing Soviet sources in Jewish and Zionist organizations, and maintaining liaison with various Soviet sources.[140]

Hughes: see Sarant, Alfred Epaminondas.

Huron: unidentified asset of the New York KGB, 1944–1945. Involved in scientific and technical espionage, may have been a scientist, perhaps Bruno Pontecorvo.[141]

I.: (1) unidentified asset of the New York KGB working in a scientific or technological field, possibly dealing with the oil industry. In 1944 the KGB said that I.'s coworkers made him useless for the moment, although he remained "loyal to the USSR."[142] (2) Unidentified asset of the Washington KGB who in 1945 delivered a secret Office of Strategic Services cable reporting on OSS operations in Yugoslavia.[143]

Iceberg: unidentified asset of the New York KGB. Provided information about the movement of American aircraft in Asia.[144]

Ide: see Krafsur, Samuel.

Informer: see Katz, Joseph.

Ipatov: unidentified contact in Chicago of the New York KGB.[145]

Isaak, Rosa: executive secretary of the American-Russian Institute. In 1945 advised the San Francisco KGB that she intended to resign from her job and would be breaking off contact with Soviet intelligence.[146]

Ivanov: see Scott, John.

Ivanova: female KGB asset who worked in the French section of the Office of War Information. Appears to have been an immigrant who applied for American citizenship in 1943.[147]

Ivy: see Joseph, Emma Harriet (appendix D).

Izra: see Wheeler, Donald Niven.

Jack: unidentified asset of the New York GRU in 1943 who provided information on the U.S. testing of guided bombs and shipping cargoes. Also vetted prospects for GRU recruitment. Was also an intermediary between the GRU and the CPUSA.[148]

Jacob: see Perl, William.

Jacobson, Herman R.: employee of Avery Manufacturing Company, worked with the New York KGB office. Cover name S-1.[149]

Jean: see Setaro, Ricardo.

Jeanne: see Krotkova, Christina.

Jeannette: (1) see *Cupid*. (2) Unidentified asset of the New York KGB in 1944.[150]

John: see *Hudson*.

Johnny: unidentified asset of the New York GRU office. In 1943 delivered a 150-page technical report.[151]

Joseph, Bella: secret Communist. Worked for the motion picture division of the Office of Strategic Services. Wife of Julius Joseph. Cover name Colleague.[152]

Joseph, Julius J.: secret Communist and member of the Golos-Bentley network who worked for the Far Eastern section (Japanese intelligence) of the Office of Strategic Services (1943–1945). Cover name Cautious. His wife also worked for the OSS.[153]

Julia: contact of Iskhak Akhmerov, a KGB illegal officer, described in a 1944 message as having been out of contact for several years and as living near Lake Geneva in New York on the resources of a wealthy father.[154]

Jupiter: unidentified asset of the New York KGB in 1944. Later had the cover name Original (or Odd Fellow).[155]

Jurist: see White, Harry Dexter.

Kahn, Mrs. Ray (Gertrude): suggested for foreign work by Moscow. The New York KGB told Moscow that this was unwise and advised that she was best used in a "passive" role. Cover name Dinah.[156]

Kant: see Magdoff, Harry Samuel, and Zborowski, Mark.

Karl: unidentified asset of the New York KGB in 1944. Appears to have been engaged in scientific-technical espionage. May have been a former member of a covert CPUSA apparatus inasmuch as in one message the New York KGB asks Moscow headquarters about the advisability of its picking up material Karl had delivered to Earl Browder. Also had the cover name Ray.[157]

Karr, David: journalist and asset of the New York KGB.[158]

Katz, Joseph: one of the KGB's most active American assets. Served as a courier to many Soviet sources, also vetted prospective recruits, photographed material, and carried messages to and from the CPUSA leadership. Cover names Informer, Douglas, and X.[159]

Keen: (1) see Wicher, Enos Regent. (2) See *Osprey.*

Keenan, Helen Grace Scott: asset first of the New York KGB office and then of the Washington KGB. Worked in 1945 for the Office of U.S. Chief of Counsel for Prosecution of Axis War Criminals, initially run by the OSS. Cover name Fir (or Spruce).[160]

Keeney, Mary Jane: secret Communist, recruited (along with her husband, Philip) by the GRU in 1940. Worked for the Board of Economic Warfare and, after World War II, for the United Nations. Taken over by the KGB in 1945.[161]

Keeney, Philip Olin: secret Communist, recruited (along with his wife, Mary Jane) by the GRU in 1940. Worked for the Office of the Coordinator of Information (later the Office of Strategic Services) in 1941. Taken over by the KGB in 1945.[162]

Khan: unidentified KGB asset who linked Soviet KGB officers with KGB sources, a number of whom were CPUSA activists (Albert Kahn, Boleslaw Gebert, Eufrosina Dvoichenko-Markov) involved in ethnic minority work. May be Avram Landy, a senior CPUSA official who supervised party work among ethnic groups. Also had the cover name Selim Khan.[163]

Khan's wife: wife of KGB asset Khan. Kept watch over a Finnish-American woman whom the KGB had recruited for intelligence work but had decided not to use, because she expressed doubts about the justice of Stalin's purges.[164]

Khazar: unidentified asset of the New York KGB. A naturalized American citizen, probably of Yugoslav origin. Provided information on Office of Strategic Services personnel being inserted into occupied Yugoslavia. Not clear whether he became an OSS operative.[165]

Khe . . . : see Miller, Floyd Cleveland.

Kinsman: see *Solid.*

Klara: see Stridsberg, Augustina.

Klo: see Rand, Esther Trebach.

Koch: see Lee, Duncan Chapin.

Koral, Alexander: CPUSA member who worked as a KGB courier along with his wife, Helen. Cover name Berg.[166]

Koral, Helen: asset of the New York KGB. Assisted the KGB illegal officer Iskhak Akhmerov and received a regular stipend. Cover names Miranda and Art.[167]

Krafsur, Samuel: CPUSA member and veteran of the International Brigades, an asset of the New York KGB working as a journalist for the Soviet news agency TASS. Used by the KGB to cultivate American journalists, with an eye to recruiting as KGB sources. Cover name Ide.[168]

Kramer, Charles: member of the Perlo group. An economist, worked for the Senate Subcommittee on War Mobilization and the Office of Price

Administration. Before the war, worked for the National Labor Relations Board. Cover names Plumb, Lot, and Mole.[169]

Krotkova, Christina: KGB asset who worked for the Office of War Information. Her chief target was the Soviet defector Victor Kravchenko. Cover names Jeanne and Ola.[170]

Kurnakov, Sergey Nikolaevich: former Czarist cavalry officer who had immigrated to the United States and become a Communist. Spied on Russian immigrants, served as a courier to various KGB sources, and acted as both a talent-spotter and a vetter of potential recruits. Cover names Cavalryman and Beck.[171]

Kurt: see *Plucky.*

Laird, Stephen: radio broadcaster, journalist, and filmmaker, KGB source in 1944 and 1945. Cover name Yun.[172]

Lambert, Rudolph Carl: California Communist party labor director and head of its security arm. Named in a garbled 1945 San Francisco KGB cable discussing information about uranium deposits in Western states.[173]

Lange, Oskar: Polish immigrant who became a naturalized citizen, A leading advocate of American support for a pro-Soviet Polish government, functioned as an agent of influence. Cover name Friend.[174]

Laszl: unidentified source of the New York GRU in 1943. Described as a friend of the GRU agent Joseph Bernstein. Unclear whether Laszl was a cover name or a real name, and unclear whether Laszl was a witting or unwitting source for Bernstein.[175]

Lava: see Schultz, Marion Miloslavovich.

Lawyer: see White, Harry Dexter.

Lee: see *Clemence.*

Lee, Duncan Chapin: highly placed officer of the Office of Strategic Services, serving as an assistant to William Donovan, head of the OSS, and as an OSS field officer in China. Came under KGB control via a CPUSA covert network. Cover name Koch.[176]

Lens: see Sidorovich, Michael.

Leona: unidentified female asset of the New York KGB. Attempted to get a job with the Office of War Information. Her husband appears to have been an employee of a large New York radio station and to have been aware of his wife's connection with Soviet intelligence. Activities unknown.[177]

Leshing, Michael S.: superintendent of Twentieth Century Fox film laboratories. In 1943 provided the Soviets with documents and formula for developing color motion pictures and other film-processing technology.[178]

Lesley: see Cohen, Lona.

Levanas, Leo: chemist with Shell Oil. After a meeting with a KGB agent, asked to meet with the head of the San Francisco KGB office to "explore helping us." Cover name Alma.[179]

Levenson, L.: employee of Electro-Physical Laboratories of New York City, provided a mail drop for a KGB contact.[180]

Levi: unidentified asset of the Washington KGB office who in 1945 delivered political intelligence. Possibly a real name.[181]

Lewis (*Luis* or *Louis*): unidentified asset recruited by the New York KGB in 1942. In 1944 and 1945 Alfred Stern had the cover name Louis, but it is unclear that this is the same person. In the Venona messages a different Luis (or Lewis or Louis) is also involved in the KGB's Latin American operations.[182]

Libau, Morris: German immigrant, a "walk-in" who in 1944 offered the Soviets information on the eastern front. The KGB turned him over to the GRU.[183]

Liberal: see Rosenberg, Julius.

Lidia (or *Lydia*): see Altschuler, Lydia.

Lily: see Olkhine, Eugénie.

Link: unidentified asset of the KGB New York, 1943–1944. Held some position in the U.S. government, most likely in the military but possibly in the Office of Strategic Services. According to one 1943 KGB message, Link completed a course in Italian, was on leave, and was expected to be sent to Britain shortly. (The KGB arranged a password allowing a KGB officer to approach Link in Britain.) In 1944 passed information to the New York KGB via his brother to Lona Cohen, a KGB asset. May be William Weisband (see appendix B).[184]

Lira: see Strong, Anna Louise.

Liza: unidentified asset of the New York KGB, a secretary in the War Department to Vladimir Pozner, and the link between him and the KGB.[185]

Liza: see Stern, Martha Dodd.

Loesh: unidentified asset of the GRU. In 1943 given $12,083 by the GRU. Activities unknown. It is not clear whether Loesh is a cover name or a real name.[186]

Long: unidentified asset of the New York KGB office, at least as early as 1941 and perhaps earlier. In 1941 changed residences and lost contact with the KGB when his Soviet controller, Gaik Ovakimian, was arrested by the FBI for espionage. In 1944 the New York KGB renewed contact through the KGB officer Aleksandr Raev, who reported that Long was apprehensive but had accepted five hundred dollars in payment and wanted more. Also had the cover name Davis.[187]

Lot: see Kramer, Charles.

Lou: see Davis, Marion.

Louis: see Stern, Alfred Kaufman.

Lowry, Helen: wife of Iskhak Akhmerov, the leading KGB illegal officer operating in the United States. Served as a courier between her husband and the KGB. Cover name Elsa. See also El.[188]

Lynch: provided to a KGB officer, according to a 1943 GRU message, information he had learned from a meeting with the vice-chairman of the War Production Board. Unclear whether informant acted wittingly or unwittingly. Unclear whether Lynch was a cover name or a real name.[189]

Lyuba: unidentified female asset of the New York KGB in 1944, connected in some way to the CPUSA. In New York City in 1944 but was planning to return to her permanent residence unless the KGB had an assignment in the near future.[190]

Mabel: unidentified asset of the Naval GRU in 1943.[191]

Mackey, William: resident of Portland, Oregon, who was doing some unspecified work for Isaac Folkoff, a senior Communist and liaison with the KGB. The San Francisco KGB appeared to be considering taking Mackey under its direct control.[192]

Magda: unidentified female asset of the New York KGB, 1944–1945, with links to journalists and *Time* magazine.[193]

Magdoff, Harry Samuel: member of the Perlo group, worked for the War Production Board and the Office of Emergency Management. Cover names Kant and Tan.[194]

Malisoff (Malisov), William Marias: KGB asset and owner of United Laboratories in New York City. Cover names Talent and Henry.[195]

Map: unidentified female asset of the San Francisco KGB, 1943–1945. Acted as a liaison between KGB officers and several intelligence sources. May be Louise Bransten (chapter 8).[196]

Margarita: KGB asset. Identified by NSA/FBI analysts, who redacted her real name in its release of the messages. Born in the United States to Finnish immigrant parents and emigrated with them in 1933 to settle in Soviet Karelia. Later worked for the *Moscow Daily News,* a Soviet-controlled English-language newspaper. After returning to the United States, she worked for the wartime U.S. government mail and press censorship office and for the United Nations Relief and Rehabilitation Administration. The KGB established a relationship with her through one of its agents, Joseph Katz. Although pro-Soviet, Margarita expressed anger about the treatment of the Finnish-Americans who had settled in Karelia and deep resentment about the conduct of the KGB during the purges. (Many Finnish-American immigrants had been executed or imprisoned during Stalin's Terror.) Under the circumstances, the KGB decided not to continue using her as an agent. Because its contacts with her might have made her a security risk, the New York KGB raised with Moscow the option of luring her back to the USSR through a letter from her brother, who had been wounded while fighting in the Red Army. The New York KGB noted that "this solution of the problems would be the most radical"—an understatement, because her return would certainly have resulted in imprisonment, given that the KGB had her on record as voicing anti-Soviet sentiments. In the end, however, the New York KGB decided that she was still sufficiently pro-Soviet that this plan was not necessary. Instead, she was put in cold storage and her activities were observed for signs that she might go to American authorities.[197]

Mark: asset of the New York KGB. Reported on Jewish and Zionist groups and on exiled European Social Democrats and Socialists. One message suggests that Mark was Menashe Unger, chairman of the American Committee of Jewish Writers, Artists, and Scientists. In 1944, put in cold storage by the KGB.[198]

Marquis: see Bernstein, Joseph Milton.

Masha: see Dvoichenko-Markov, Eufrosina.

Master (or *Master Craftsman*): see Sheppard, Charles Bradford.

Mateo: unidentified KGB asset who worked on obtaining false documents and arranging U.S.-Mexico border crossings. An asset of the Mexico City KGB. Unclear whether he was Mexican or American.[199]

Matvey: see Schwartz, Milton.

Max: unidentified asset of the New York GRU in 1943.[200]

Maxwell: see Fahy, Jack Bradley.

Mayor: see Akhmerov, Iskhak Abdulovich.

Menaker, Robert Owen: KGB asset involved in U.S. and Latin American operations. Cover names Bob and Czech.[201]

Meri: unidentified asset of the New York KGB in 1944. Activities unclear, but the messages suggest a close connection with the CPUSA.[202]

Meter: see Barr, Joel.

Miller, Floyd Cleveland: major KGB asset within the American Trotskyist movement. Also known as Mike Cort. Cover name in KGB messages, only partially deciphered, was Khe . . .[203]

Miller, James Walter: asset of the San Francisco KGB, 1943–1945. Recruited for Soviet intelligence by Isaac Folkoff of the CPUSA. Worked for the U.S. government wartime mail censorship office. Cover name Vague.[204]

Mins, Leonard Emil: concealed Communist and GRU agent. Held a position in the Russian section of the research and analysis division of the Office of Strategic Services. Cover name Smith.[205]

Mirage: unidentified asset of the New York office of the KGB in 1943. Was an employee either of the State Department or of an agency that received State Department documents. Provided the KGB with information about U.S. diplomatic activities in Latin America. May be Charles Page (chapter 7).[206]

Mirage's wife: provided information to the KGB on the pending trip to Sweden of an American journalist of interest to the KGB. May be Mary Page, wife of Charles Page and an employee of the postal censorship office.[207]

Miranda: see Koral, Helen.

Mitron: unidentified asset of the New York GRU in 1943.[208]

Mitynen, Francia Yakilnilna: illegal officer of the Naval GRU who was smuggled into the United States in 1943. Used the name Edna Margaret Patterson until she left in 1956. Cover names Sally and Australian Woman.[209]

Mok: GRU illegal operating under a false identify. Extracted from the United States in 1943 and returned to the USSR. Activities unknown.

May have been the GRU officer Vladimir V. Gavrilyuk. The KGB noted his removal under the cover name Danilov.[210]

Mole: see Kramer, Charles.

Moosen, Arthur: asset of the New York GRU in 1943. Cover name Frank.[211]

Morkovin, Vladimir Borisovich: aeronautical engineer at Bell Aircraft who provided technical information to Andrey Shevchenko, a KGB agent operating as an inspector at Bell. Shevchenko described Morkovin as cautious and as friendly to the Soviet Union but unaware that Shevchenko was a Soviet intelligence officer. Cover name Author.[212]

Morros, Boris Mikhailovich: Russian immigrant and Hollywood producer, was an asset of the New York KGB and later became an FBI double agent. Cover names Frost (the Russian word for frost is *moroz*) and a name with the initial V.[213]

Muse: see Tenney, Helen.

Musician: unidentified asset of the San Francisco KGB, 1943–1944.[214]

Myrna: see Bentley, Elizabeth.

Napoli, Nicola: president of Artkino, distributor of Russian films. Passed on information from the CPUSA to a KGB asset about people seeking contact with the KGB.[215]

Nat: unidentified asset of the San Francisco KGB, 1945–1946. Identified as a leading official of the Communist party in the San Francisco Bay Area. May be Nat Yanish.[216]

Needle: see York, Jones Orin.

Nelly: unidentified asset of the New York KGB in 1944 who appeared to be employed by the U.S. Lend-Lease Administration.[217]

Nemo: see Pinsly, William.

Neumann, Franz: KGB source working for the Office of Strategic Services. Cover name Ruff.[218]

Nick: see Sabatini, Amadeo, and Velson, Irving Charles.

Nile (or *Neil* or *Neale*): unidentified asset of the New York KGB. Originally passed material to the KGB through the CPUSA. Later appeared to have become part of the Rosenberg apparatus. Also had another cover name that was only partially deciphered: Tu . . . [219]

Nina: unidentified asset of the New York KGB in mid-1944.[220]

NN-32: unidentified asset of the New York KGB, 1943–1944. Put in cold storage in 1944. Allowed by the KGB to set up a mail drop for correspondence from Spain, and messages also suggest some connection with the International Brigades.[221]

Noah: unidentified asset of the New York KGB office, 1943–1945. The New York KGB regarded his reports about American data on internal German political conditions as "valuable."[222]

Noise: see Splint.

Nona: see Wilson, Ruth Beverly.

Octane: unidentified cover name of an asset in contact with Semyon Semenov, a KGB officer who specialized in scientific-technical intelligence. Active from 1943 to 1945 and perhaps as early as 1939.[223]

Odessan: unidentified asset of the New York KGB office, 1944–1945. Appeared to be engaged in scientific-technical espionage, maintained some sort of enterprise that was subsidized by the KGB. Also had the cover name Growth.[224]

Okho (possibly *Ojo*, Spanish "eye"): unidentified cover name for an asset of the New York KGB who furnished information on the OSS in 1944.[225]

Ola: see Krotkova, Christina.

Old (or *Oldster*): see Sax, Saville.

Olkhine, Eugénie: KGB asset. The KGB reestablished liaison with her in 1945 after a prolonged absence. American born of a Russian father, perhaps Aleksandrov. The KGB considered attempting to plant her in the FBI. Provided information on immigrant Russians and was promised Soviet citizenship by the KGB. Cover name Lily.[226]

Olsen: provided a letter of introduction for a KGB agent seeking in 1944 to contact a scientist working on the Manhattan Project. The scientist had been cultivated by members of the CPUSA, and Olsen was described as head of the Illinois Communist party. May be Morris Childs, head of the CPUSA in Illinois in 1944. Olsen may be a party name rather than a cover name.[227]

Olsen, Rose: See *Phlox.*

Oppen: unidentified asset of the New York office of the GRU in 1943. Provided information on U.S. military technology and assisted in recruiting new GRU agents.[228]

Original (or *Odd Fellow*): see *Jupiter.*

Orloff, Nicholas W.: asset of the New York KGB. Russian immigrant, member of the tsarist aristocracy. Received a regular KGB stipend, provided information on immigrant groups, and acted as a talent-spotter for new sources. In 1944 the KGB reported that he was applying for U.S. citizenship and hoped to get a job with the Office of Strategic Services or the State Department, and that he had told his wife, a native-born American, that he was breaking off all connections with Soviet intelligence in order to reduce the chance that she might turn him in to American authorities. According to OSS records, he obtained American citizenship in mid-1944 and, shortly thereafter, applied for a position with the OSS, citing his fluency in several European languages and his many years of residence in Europe. It appears, however, that his application was rejected. Cover name Osipov.[229]

Osipov: see Orloff, Nicholas W.

Osipovich, Nadia Morris: Asset of the San Francisco KGB. Naturalized American citizen living in Portland, Oregon. Cover name Watchdog.[230]

Osprey: unidentified asset of the New York KGB office who in 1944 was rewarded with a monthly stipend. Also had the cover names Block and Keen.[231]

Padva's wife (or *Padua*'s wife): in late 1944 Padva (otherwise unidentified) approached a KGB officer at the Soviet consulate about his wife, who, he explained, had once been in touch with another KGB officer and had material to give the Soviets.[232]

Page: see Currie, Lauchlin B.

Painter: unidentified asset of the New York KGB in 1944. Delivered documents and headed a group of sources in New York.[233]

Pal: see Silvermaster, Nathan Gregory.

Patriarch: unidentified asset of the New York KGB in 1944. Duties included providing background information on people of interest to the KGB, particularly American merchant seamen.[234]

Peak: see Coe, Virginius Frank.

Perch: see Tkach, Mikhail.

Perl, William: aeronautical scientist working on advanced-technology military projects, particularly jet aircraft. Member of the Rosenberg network of the KGB. Cover names Gnome and Jacob.[235]

Perlo, Victor: head of the Perlo group. An economist, during World War II worked for the Advisory Council of National Defense of the Office of Price Administration and the War Production Board. After the war, worked for the Division of Monetary Research of the Treasury Department. Cover name Raider.[236]

Perry, Burton: asset of the San Francisco office of the KGB. In 1944 Perry gave the KGB the technical particulars of a radar-guided glide bomb whose testing he was part of. Cover name Cedar.[237]

Pers (or *Persian*): see *Fogel*.

Peter: see Black, Thomas Lessing.

Petroff, Aleksandr N.: employee of Curtiss-Wright Aircraft, provided the KGB with information on aircraft production methods. Cover names Fin and Ferro.[238]

Phil: unidentified GRU liaison agent who linked sources within the U.S. military to Soviet military intelligence in 1943.[239]

Philip: unidentified contact of the San Francisco KGB in 1946 who met with a KGB officer and senior West Coast CPUSA officers.[240]

Philosopher: unidentified asset of the New York KGB, 1943–1944. Worked in the French section of the Office of War Information.[241]

Phlox: CPUSA contact in Chicago of the New York KGB used in an attempt to approach a senior Manhattan Project scientist targeted for recruitment. Also referred to in the Venona cables as Rose Olsen, likely a CPUSA party name. May be the wife of Jack Childs or Morris Childs.[242]

Phlox's husband: In 1944 the New York KGB told Moscow that it intended to use him to approach a senior Manhattan Project scientist targeted for recruitment. May be either Jack Childs, a full-time CPUSA functionary working in its underground apparatus, or his brother, Morris Childs, head of the Illinois Communist party.[243]

Pillar: unidentified asset of the New York KGB. Activities unknown. After the return to the USSR of Pavel P. Klarin, a senior KGB officer who had had been Pillar's liaison, the New York KGB had difficulty developing a replacement.[244]

Pilot: see Ullmann, William Ludwig.

Pinsky, Paul: California Communist trade union official whom the KGB planned to use to approach a scientist working on the Manhattan Project.[245]

Pinsly, William: employee of Curtiss-Wright Aircraft in Williamsville, New York, an asset of the New York KGB office in 1944. Cover names Cork and Nemo.[246]

Plato: see Pozner, Vladimir Aleksandrovich.

Plourde, William Alfred: engineer with Bell Aircraft in Buffalo, New York, who was in contact with the KGB in 1944.[247]

Plucky: unidentified asset for the New York KGB office, 1941–1944. Worked for the KGB for four years, but the only clear report about his work refers to information he provided on exiled Bessarabians. Also had the cover name Kurt.[248]

Plumb: see Kramer, Charles.

Pozner, Vladimir Aleksandrovich: asset of the New York KGB. Russian immigrant who headed the Russian division of a photographic section of the U.S. War Department. Cover name Plato.[249]

Pratt, Gertrude: active with the Student Antifascist Committee. In 1943 the KGB proposed to use Pratt to "process" (gather background information about) Eleanor Roosevelt.[250]

Price, Mary Wolfe: part of a CPUSA covert apparatus run by Jacob Golos that was taken over by the KGB. A secretary of the journalist Walter Lippmann, she acted as a courier to several Soviet sources. Cover name Dir.[251]

Prince: see Duggan, Laurence.

Purser: KGB asset with whom the KGB lost contact when he entered the Navy.[252]

Quantum: unidentified asset of the New York KGB. Provided highly technical information on the Manhattan Project at an early date, June 1943, and appears to have been a scientist.[253]

R.: see Witczak, Ignacy.

Raider: see Perlo, Victor.

Rand, Esther Trebach: asset of the New York KGB who spied on Zionists, part of the Soble espionage ring. Cover names Aida and Klo.[254]

Randolph: unidentified asset of the New York office of the GRU, 1943. Appears to have been based in New York but made regular trips to Washington, D.C. May have been a journalist, inasmuch as he reported on what he had learned from prominent political and governmental figures as well as from major journalists.[255]

Ray: see Karl.

Redhead: Unidentified contact, mentioned in 1944 Venona cable, whom the illegal KGB officer Iskhak Akhmerov had known as early as 1940 and perhaps earlier. Possibly Hede Massing (appendix B), who is known to have had this cover name in 1936 when she supervised a KGB network in the United States.[256]

Reed: unidentified asset of the New York KGB. May have been a resident of Washington, D.C., where his KGB contact was assigned for a time.[257]

Relay: unidentified asset of the New York KGB in 1944, courier to several Soviet sources. Described as living in Philadelphia and having an artificial leg or foot. Cover name later changed to Serb.[258]

Rhodes, Peter: journalist and employee of the Foreign Broadcasting Monitoring Service, the psychological warfare section of Allied Military Headquarters in London, and the Office of War Information. In 1944 the New York KGB informed its headquarters that Rhodes had been connected with the KGB in earlier years through a CPUSA network but that the connection had been broken. The CPUSA's liaison with the KGB recommended that the connection be reestablished.[259]

Rich, Stephan: asset of the New York GRU in 1943. Cover name Sandi.[260]

Richard: see Borrow, Robinson, and White, Harry Dexter.

Richardson, Kenneth: employee of World Wide Electronics. Involved in scientific-technical intelligence with the New York KGB, 1943–1945. Cover name Condenser.[261]

Rit: unidentified asset of the New York KGB who was being replaced in 1944.[262]

Robert: (1) unidentified asset of the GRU in 1945. Name occurs in a list of KGB targets, most of whom have some State Department connection. The Moscow KGB headquarters warned its New York office away from him with the comment that he already was a GRU asset.[263] (2) See Silvermaster, Nathan Gregory.

Rodman, Samuel Jacob: journalist who for a time worked for the United Nations Relief and Rehabilitation Administration. In 1944 the KGB's CPUSA contact reported that Rodman was on his way to Yugoslavia on a UNRRA mission and that he had arranged for Rodman to gather information and carry out some unspecified task.[264]

Roman: see Soblen, Robert.

Rosenberg, Allan: member of the Perlo group. Rosenberg worked in the Board of Economic Warfare/Foreign Economic Administration.[265]

Rosenberg, Ethel: Communist and the wife of Julius Rosenberg. KGB messages show that she was fully informed about her husband's espionage activities and assisted in recruiting her brother and sister-in-law, David and Ruth Greenglass. She and her husband were convicted of espionage and executed in 1953.[266]

Rosenberg, Julius: engineer and concealed Communist who recruited a ring of engineers, most of whom were also concealed Communists, who gathered military scientific-technical intelligence for the New York KGB. He and his wife were convicted of espionage and executed in 1953. Cover names Antenna and Liberal.[267]

Ruble: see Glasser, Harold.

Rudi: unidentified contact of the New York GRU in 1943. Appears to have had responsibility for liaison with other sources, including some in Canada, and direct links with the CPUSA. May be Rudy Baker.[268]

Ruff: see Neumann, Franz.

S-1: see Jacobson, Herman R.

S-2: unidentified asset of the New York KGB. Described by the KGB in 1944 as female and forty-five years old. Appears to have been associated with Herman Jacobson (S-1).[269]

S-8: unidentified asset of the New York KGB in 1945.[270]

Sabatini, Amadeo: CPUSA member and veteran of the International Brigades, was one of the KGB's most active couriers and liaison agents. The KGB reimbursed him for travel and living expenses and paid a monthly stipend to his wife. Lived in California, and many of his assignments were in the West. Cover name Nick.[271]

Sachs: see Adler, Solomon.

Sally: see Mitynen, Francia Yakilnilna.

Sam: asset of the San Francisco KGB. Described as the younger brother of Burton Perry and helped to convince him to turn over the plans of a radar-guided glide bomb to the Soviets.[272]

Sandi: see Rich, Stephan.

Sarant, Alfred Epaminondas: concealed Communist, engineer, and part of the Rosenberg ring that reported to the New York KGB. Worked on military radar at the U.S. Army Signal Corps laboratories at Fort Monmouth, New Jersey. Cover name Hughes.[273]

Satir (Satyr): see Callen, Sylvia.

Sax, Saville: member of the Young Communist League at Harvard, roommate of Theodore Hall. Worked as a courier between Hall and the KGB. Cover name Old (or Oldster).[274]

Schultz, Marion (Marian) Miloslavovich: immigrant from Russia, an asset of the New York KGB for work among immigrants. Was a mechanic in a Philadelphia shipyard and chair of the United Russian Committee for Aid to the Native Country. Cover name Lava.[275]

Schuster, Bernard: official of the New York Communist party's internal security apparatus, also liaison between the New York KGB and the CPUSA national leadership. Performed a variety of other tasks for the KGB, including vetting potential KGB recruits and arranging for the use of CPUSA members for KGB courier work. Cover names Chester (his CPUSA party name), Echo, Dick, and South.[276]

Schwartz, Milton: asset of the New York GRU in 1943. The nature of Schwartz's work for the GRU is unknown, but he believed it valuable enough to ask the GRU for $1,200 to help him get out of a personal difficulty. Cover name Matvey.[277]

Scott, John: former Communist trade union organizer and asset of the New York KGB after he began work in the Russian section of the Office of Strategic Services. Cover name Ivanov.[278]

Scout: see Barr, Joel.

Second-Hand Bookseller: unidentified asset of the New York KGB in 1944. Put in cold storage in mid-1944 but brought back in the fall to assist with what appeared to be establishing a front enterprise for scientific-technical espionage. Also had close ties to the CPUSA.[279]

Selim Khan: see Khan.

Serb: asset of the New York KGB in 1945, In contact with Leonid Kvasnikov, a KGB officer who specialized in scientific-technical intelligence.[280]

Serpa: unidentified Soviet source. In 1944 the KGB headquarters told the New York KGB office to evaluate the information he was turning in and decide whether it wished to run him directly or indirectly, through its CPUSA liaison.[281]

Setaro, Ricardo: deputy chief of the Latin American department of CBS, a concealed Communist, and an asset of the New York office of the KGB, 1943–1944. Cover names Express Messenger and Jean.[282]

Sheppard, Charles Bradford: radio engineer working on radar in the design office of Hazeltine Electronics. Asked the KGB to arrange Soviet citizenship for him and his family and their eventual emigration to the USSR. Cover name Master or Master Craftsman.[283]

Sherwood: see Duggan, Laurence.

Sidorovich, Anne: member of the Rosenberg ring and the wife of Michael Sidorovich. Assisted her husband and received a monthly KGB stipend. Cover name Squirrel.[284]

Sidorovich, Michael: member of the Rosenberg ring. Did a great deal of courier work to sources, photographing their material and delivering to the KGB. Cover name Lens.[285]

Silverman, Abraham George: member of the Silvermaster group. During the war Silverman was an economic adviser to an assistant chief of the Army Air Force. Cover name Aileron.[286]

Silvermaster, Helen Witte: Active assistant in the management of the large Silvermaster group, headed by her husband, Nathan Silvermaster. Cover name Dora.[287]

Silvermaster, Nathan Gregory: head of the large and productive Silvermaster group of Soviet spies. An economist, his positions in the U.S. government during the war included posts with the Board of Economic Warfare/Foreign Economic Administration and the War Assets Administration. Cover names Pal and Robert.[288]

Sima: see Coplon, Judith.

Simon: see Bayer, Theodore.

Sitsilla: see Dodd, William E., Jr.

Skrib: unidentified KGB asset in Alaska in late 1944.[289]

Slang: see Foster, Jane.

Smart: asset of the New York KGB who worked on technical intelligence in 1944. Not clear whether Smart was an American or a Soviet. The KGB also arranged for Smart to make contact with the GRU.[290]

Smith: see Mins, Leonard Emil.

Sobell, Morton: engineer and member of the Rosenberg apparatus. Worked for General Electric and Reeves Electronics on military and government contracts. Convicted of espionage against the United States in 1951 and imprisoned. That Sobell was a Soviet spy is clear, but it is not certain that he appears in the Venona cables. A New York KGB cable dated July 11, 1944, about providing a camera to a member of the Rosenberg apparatus with the cover name Relay is, according to an NSA/FBI footnote, a reference to Sobell. However, the footnote mentions that a September cable changes the cover name Relay to Serb, and the later occurrence of Serb is in the view of NSA/FBI not a reference to Sobell. A July 4, 1944, cable also uses the cover name Relay, and this Relay was not linked to the Rosenberg apparatus and had personal characteristics that rule out Sobell.[291]

Soble, Jack: long-term KGB agent who infiltrated the Trotskyist movement in the 1930s and early 1940s. In mid-1945 the KGB shifted Soble's emphasis from spying on Trotskyists to monitoring other targets. Brother of Robert Soblen. Cover names Abram and Czech.[292]

Soblen, Robert: long-term KGB agent who infiltrated the Trotskyist movement in the 1930s and early 1940s. Convicted of espionage in 1961. Brother of Jack Soble. Cover name Roman.[293]

Solid: unidentified asset of the New York KGB. Also had the cover name Kinsman.[294]

Son: see Baker, Rudy.

Sonya (or *Sonia*): see Gold, Sonia Steinman.

Sound: see Golos, Jacob.

Sounding Board: unidentified asset of the New York KGB.[295]

Source No. 12: GRU asset in 1943 who, from the nature of his reports and the documents he turned over, was probably on the Board of Economic Warfare.[296]

Source No. 13: asset of the New York GRU who, after repeated prodding, provided information in 1943.[297]

Source No. 19: unidentified highly placed asset who at the time of the Trident conference in 1943 reported to the KGB on a conversation with Roosevelt and Churchill.[298]

South: see Schuster, Bernard.

Spark: unidentified asset of the New York KGB who operated in the United States and Canada from 1943 to 1945. Activities unclear but appears to have had some quasi-public role: the KGB asked the CPUSA to check the authenticity of reports that while Spark's public statements were pro-Soviet, privately he was the source of anti-Soviet rumors. Also had the cover name Davis.[299]

Spline: source of KGB officer Andrey Shevchenko in the aircraft industry in New York in 1944. Also had the cover name Noise.[300]

Spruce: see Keenan, Helen Grace Scott.

Squirrel: see Sidorovich, Anne.

Staff-Man: unidentified asset of the New York KGB. In the U.S. Army in 1944. Provided with a KGB cipher to use for communications. Nothing else known.[301]

Stamp: see *Armor.*

Steele, Johannes: immigrant German journalist who arranged a meeting between a KGB officer and an exiled Polish journalist who offered his services to the USSR. Cover name Dicky.[302]

Stella: unidentified asset of the Naval GRU. Received a regular stipend and among other tasks assisted in vetting potential Soviet sources and served as a contact between the Naval GRU and its sources. Also had the cover name Emilia.[303]

Stern, Alfred Kaufman: wealthy Popular Front activist in Illinois. With his wife, Martha, invested in Boris Morros's Hollywood music publishing company. Cover name Louis.[304]

Stern, Martha Dodd: daughter of William Dodd, U.S. ambassador to Germany in the 1930s, and a prominent writer and Popular Front activist. Wife of Alfred Stern. Cover name Liza.[305]

Stevens, Edmund: journalist, secret Communist, and KGB contact.[306]

Storm: unidentified person connected with the Perlo group. May be Josef Peters.[307]

Stowaway: see Halperin, Maurice.

Stridsberg, Augustina (formerly Augustina Jirku): asset of the KGB in 1943 and 1944. Cover name Klara. Her daughter, Marietta Voge, also worked for the KGB.[308]

Strong, Anna Louise: radical journalist who championed the Soviet and Chinese Communist revolutions. Denied accusations of being a Communist and of being involved in Soviet espionage. Planned in 1944 to travel to Moscow. Messages show that she had some kind of relationship with the KGB, and the San Francisco KGB arranged with her a password that would allow her to identify her Moscow KGB contact. Cover name Lira.[309]

Suk: unidentified asset of the New York KGB, 1944–1945. Provided information on senior American journalists and senior Republicans close to Sen. Tom Dewey. Was probably a journalist.[310]

Talent: see Malisoff (Malisov), William Marias.

Tan: see Magdoff, Harry Samuel.

Ted: see Fitzgerald, Edward J.

Tenney, Helen: secret Communist and analyst in the Spanish section of the OSS. Source for the Golos-Bentley network. Cover name Muse.[311]

Tenor: see Burd, Michael.

Thomas: unidentified asset of the New York KGB in 1944. Earlier given the cover name Brother and was controlled by a KGB officer who concentrated on aviation technology intelligence. Activities unknown[312]

Thrush: see *Akhmed.*

Tkach, Mikhail: editor of the *Ukrainian Daily News* and a Communist activist. Carried out KGB tasks among Ukrainian immigrants and ran a group of subagents. Cover name Perch.[313]

Trio: unidentified asset of the New York KGB in 1943 who was reported not to have had any contact with the CPUSA. May be Frederick Thompson (see appendix D).[314]

Tu . . . : see *Nile.*

Tulip: see Zborowski, Mark.

Tur: unidentified source who reported on U.S. plans for the invasion of France.[315]

Tuvin: unidentified asset of the KGB. Appears to have been a pro-Communist activist among Polish-Americans. A 1944 KGB message notes that he was in difficulty because he was no longer being subsidized.[316]

Ullmann, William Ludwig: member of the Silvermaster group. Worked for the Division of Monetary Research of the Treasury Department and for the Material and Service Division of the Army Air Corps headquarters at the Pentagon. Cover names Pilot and Donald.[317]

Unbroken Cover Name No. 6: unidentified New York KGB asset. In mid-1943 was in Algeria with an Office of Strategic Services unit.[318]

Unbroken Cover Name No. 9: see Belfrage, Cedric.

Unbroken Cover Name No. 13: unidentified asset personally controlled by the head of the New York KGB in 1943.[319]

Unbroken Cover Name No. 14: unidentified asset of the New York KGB who provided liaison between the KGB and the CPUSA, 1943–1945.[320]

Unbroken Cover Name No. 19: a KGB asset in either the Office of Strategic Services or the Office of War Information in 1943. May be Julia Older (see appendix B.)[321]

Unbroken Cover Name No. 22: a KGB asset in touch with the illegal KGB officer Akhmerov. Anticipated being sent to Stockholm in 1943 as a press correspondent. The NSA deciphered enough of the cover name to determine that the last syllable was "gel."[322]

Uncle: see Folkoff, Isaac.

Unidentified KGB asset connected with the Council for Public Relations and described by the New York KGB as a "friend and fellow-countryman [Communist]." Warned the KGB that the State Department was asking questions about the brother of one of the KGB's American agents.[323]

Unidentified major in the U.S. Army Special Services Division who provided information on American industrial conditions to the Washington office of the Naval GRU in 1943. Unclear whether this source was witting or unwitting.[324]

Unidentified officer in the press section of the office of the U.S. Army Chief of Staff who provided information on discussions between Gen. George Marshall, President Roosevelt, and Prime Minister Churchill on the issue of a second front in October of 1943. Unclear whether this source was witting or unwitting.[325]

Unidentified source in the FBI. An October 27, 1944, New York KGB message refers to a Soviet source in the FBI. Unclear whether this was a reference to Judith Coplon or to another Soviet source.[326]

Unidentified source of the New York GRU in the U.S. Bureau of Shipping in 1943.[327]

Unidentified source working as a clerk in the Strategic Directorate of the Allied Joint Staff. Provided the Naval GRU in 1943 with American diplomatic reports from the U.S. embassy in Finland.[328]

V.: see Morros, Boris Mikhailovich.

Vague: see Miller, James Walter.

Valentina: unidentified asset of the KGB probably involved in infiltration of the American Trotskyist movement.[329]

Velson, Irving Charles: asset of the New York GRU. Among his duties was to control subagents and recruit additional Soviet sources. Also reported on weapons technology. Cover name Nick.[330]

Vick: unidentified asset of the New York KGB in 1943. Had contact with State Department officials and may have been a State Department employee.[331]

Vita: unidentified asset of the New York KGB put into cold storage in 1944.[332]

Voge, Marietta: née Jirku (see Stridsberg, Augustina). An asset of the San Francisco KGB. Cover name Daughter.[333]

Volunteer: see Cohen, Morris.

Volunteer's wife: see Cohen, Lona.

Vuchinich, George Samuel: of Serb ethnicity and an officer in the Office of Strategic Services. Provided information to Thomas Babin, a GRU asset and fellow OSS agent also assigned to duties dealing with Yugoslavia. Not clear whether a witting or an unwitting source.[334]

Wasp: see Greenglass, Ruth.

Watchdog: see Osipovich, Nadia Morris.

Wedge: unidentified asset of the New York KGB put into cold storage in mid-1944.[335]

Wheeler, Donald Niven: member of the Perlo group. Worked for the Research and Analysis Division of the Office of Strategic Services. Cover name Izra.[336]

White, Harry Dexter: member of the Silvermaster group. Assistant secretary of the Treasury and, later, director of the International Monetary Fund. Arguably the KGB's most valuable asset and the subject of a number of KGB cables. Cover names Jurist, Lawyer, and Richard.[337]

Whitefish: unidentified asset of the New York KGB in 1944. First provided information to the KGB via the CPUSA before it took over direct contact.[338]

Wicher, Enos Regent: onetime CPUSA organizer in Wisconsin, in 1945 was a KGB asset and worked for the Wave Propagation Group, Division of War Research, Columbia University. Wife (Maria Wicher) and stepdaughter (Flora Wovschin) were also KGB assets. Cover name Keen.[339]

Wicher, Maria: a Communist and a KGB asset, as were her husband (Enos Regent Wicher) and daughter (Flora Wovschin). In 1944 was in contact with KGB agent Sergey Kurnakov. Cover name Dasha.[340]

Wilson, Ruth Beverly: assisted her husband, the KGB asset Jacob Epstein, and had her own direct connections with the KGB. Cover name Nona.[341]

Witczak, Ignacy: illegal GRU officer who posed as a Canadian immigrant and lived quietly in Los Angeles from 1938 until identified by the FBI in 1945. Subsequently disappeared. Cover name identifed only by the initial R.[342]

Wolston, Ilya Elliott: KGB asset who was a U.S. Army military intelligence officer. He provided the KGB with details on the Army's military intelligence school and on soldiers being trained for intelligence work in areas of interest to the Soviets. Cover name Glory.[343]

Wovschin, Flora Don: asset of the KGB, 1943–1945, first in New York and then in Washington, where she worked for the Office of War Information. Mother (Maria Wicher) and stepfather (Enos Regent Wicher) were also KGB assets. Cover name Zora.[344]

X: see Katz, Joseph.

York, Jones Orin: aviation engineer and asset of the San Francisco KGB, first recruited in the mid-1930s. Gave the KGB microfilm of plans for experimental aircraft and was heavily subsidized. Cover name Needle. May also be Engineer.[345]

Youngster: see Hall, Theodore Alvin.

Yun: see Laird, Stephen.

Yur: asset of the New York KGB, 1943–1944, who worked on ethnic and émigré intelligence.[346]

Zaret, Daniel Abraham: safety inspector for the U.S. Army's Explosives Division. Turned over documents on explosives technology to the GRU. Was a Communist and a former officer in the International Brigades.[347]

Zborowski, Mark: long-term KGB infiltrator of the Trotskyist movement assigned by the KGB to get close to Victor Kravchenko, a Soviet defector. Cover names Tulip and Kant.[348]

Zone: unidentified cover name of a female asset of the New York KGB in 1944. The KGB lost contact with her and planned to reestablish contact through Earl Browder, who knew her. Browder, however, judged her untrustworthy and recommended that the KGB not reestablish contact.[349]

Zora: see Wovschin, Flora.

Americans and U.S. Residents Who Had Covert Relationships with Soviet Intelligence Agencies but Were Not Identified in the Venona Cables

The evidence for the covert relationship of these 139 persons with Soviet intelligence comes from sources other than the Venona decryptions. For those discussed in the text, documentation is cited there; otherwise, it is cited here. This list does not include Soviet intelligence officers operating under legal diplomatic cover. It is likely that some of the persons listed here are behind the unidentified cover names in appendix A. The list includes five Soviet illegal officers who posed as immigrants. Of the 139 persons, five are identified only by cover names (in italics).

Adamic, Louis: writer and spokesman for Yugoslav immigrants. During World War II, advised the OSS on Balkan questions. Minor source for Golos-Bentley network via Louis Budenz.[1]

Adams, Arthur: illegal GRU officer posing as an immigrant in the United States from 1938 to 1945. May be Achilles (see appendix A).[2]

Aden: unidentified KGB source recruited by Theodore Hall. Nuclear scientist, possibly working at the Hartford, Washington, facility that produced bomb-grade plutonium.[3]

Albam, Jacob: chief assistant to Jack Soble in the Soble espionage apparatus of the KGB in the postwar period. Pled guilty to espionage in 1957.[4]

Alleman, Otto: chemist who worked for Du Pont. Before 1945, was a contact of the KGB officer Gaik Ovakimian and was probably involved in industrial espionage. Employed in 1945 by an import company and suspected by the FBI of assisting in the covert transfer of Soviet intelligence funds.[5]

Anta: unidentified KGB source recruited by Theodore Hall. Nuclear scientist, or possibly the wife of a nuclear scientist (see *Aden*), working perhaps at the Hartford, Washington, facility that produced bomb-grade plutonium.[6]

Arenal (neé Biegel), Rose: American wife of Luís Arenal of Mexico. Lived in New York and was a communications link and mail drop between Jacob Golos and Mexican Communists working on the operation to murder Leon Trotsky.[7]

Aronberg, Philip: mid-level CPUSA activist in the 1920s. Undertook courier and other assignments for the Comintern, the GRU, and the KGB in the 1930s and early 1940s.[8]

Asimow, Morris: industrial spy for the Soviets at U.S. Steel in 1936.[9]

Baskind, Pauline: part-time New York schoolteacher who provided a mail drop for the American end of the KGB's anti-Trotsky operations in Mexico.[10]

Bedacht, Max: founding member of the CPUSA and part of its top leadership in the 1920s. In the early 1930s, oversaw the transfer of several party members from open party work to the underground and provided support for various Soviet intelligence missions.[11]

Beker, Johanna Koenen: daughter of the German Communist leader Wilhelm Koenen. Immigrated to the United States in 1938. Member of the Soble spy ring. May be Clemence and Lee (see appendix A).[12]

Bernay, Eric: Communist, headed Keynote Recording Company. Assisted in providing the illegal GRU officer Arthur Adams with a business cover and helped him to escape FBI surveillance in 1945.[13]

Bloch, Louis: New York film projectionist who provided a mail drop for the American end of the KGB's anti-Trotsky operations in Mexico.[14]

Booker, Lucy: worked for Soviet intelligence in the 1930s on missions to Germany, studied at the University of Berlin. Jacob Golos told Elizabeth Bentley that the KGB had temporarily lost touch with Booker and that he was assigned to reestablish contact. In 1951 Floyd Miller, a KGB agent, identified her as one of the intermediaries between him and Jack Soble, a KGB officer who supervised anti-Trotskyist work.[15]

Bransten, Louise: wealthy San Francisco–area Communist who linked Soviet intelligence officers working at the Soviet consulate to CPUSA members and sympathizers who were of intelligence value. May be Map (see appendix A).[16]

Browder, Margaret: sister of CPUSA leader Earl Browder, worked for the KGB in Europe in the 1930s.[17]

Budenz, Louis: editor of the *Daily Worker,* passed information from CPUSA members and sympathizers to the Golos-Bentley network.[18]

Buerger, Ruth Marie: active in the Communist-led Unemployment Councils in the early 1930s. American wife of Arnold Ikal, a GRU officer operating illegally in the United States in the 1930s.[19]

Burdett, Winston: journalist, recruited by Golos in 1940, worked for Soviet intelligence in Europe. Broke with the Communists in 1944 and later cooperated with U.S. authorities.[20]

Burtan, Valentine (William G.): born in Russia in 1900, came to the United States in 1907, and became a naturalized citizen in 1921. A CPUSA member in the 1920s, he was expelled in 1929 as a Lovestone supporter. Assisted Nicholas Dozenberg in establishing a cover business for Dozenberg's GRU work and attempted to launder $100,000 in counterfeit U.S. currency furnished by Dozenberg, for which he went to prison.[21]

Chambers, Whittaker: CPUSA activist in the late 1920s. Dropped out of open party work in the early 1930s and joined its underground apparatus, later supervised a network of sources that reported to the GRU. Defected in 1937 but did not approach U.S. authorities until 1939 and did not reveal the full extent of his role in Soviet espionage until 1948.[22]

Chapin, John Hitchcock: scientist at the Chicago Metallurgical Laboratory, part of the Manhattan Project. Met covertly with the illegal GRU officer Arthur Adams.[23]

Chapman, Abraham: journalist and official of the New York Communist party. In 1950 he and his family left the United States in panic for Mexico, where they lived in hiding. Soviet intelligence then covertly moved them to Czechoslovakia, where they received false identities and began a new life. Appears to have been withdrawn because of his knowledge of or participation in espionage operations in the United States. Activities unknown.[24]

Chevalier, Haakon: secret Communist and French professor at the University of California, Berkeley. Attempted to recruit J. Robert Oppenheimer as a Soviet source.[25]

Cohen, Leonard: attorney working for the Interior Department. Was a contact and exchanged material with the GRU illegal officer Ignacy Witczak.[26]

Collins, Henry: member of the CPUSA Washington underground and talent-spotter for Soviet intelligence.[27]

Crane, William: joined the CPUSA in 1932 and entered its underground almost immediately. Worked as a courier and as a photographer for the GRU-linked network that Whittaker Chambers supervised. Confessed after he was identified to authorities by Chambers in 1949.[28]

De Sveshnikov, Vladimir V.: ballistics expert who worked for the U.S. government. Supplied Soviet intelligence with American military information from the mid-1920s through the 1930s.[29]

Devyatkin, Boris: born in Russia in 1888, arrived in the United States in 1923, and became a naturalized citizen in 1929. Under the name Dick Murzin he assisted Moishe Stern, an illegal GRU officer in the United States in the late 1920s and early 1930s.[30]

Dozenberg, Nicholas: Latvian immigrant, founding member of the CPUSA, and mid-level party official in the 1920s. Became a GRU agent in 1928. Arrested in 1939, he confessed and on a plea bargain went to prison on a false passport charge.[31]

Eltenton, George Charles: chemist at Shell Oil in California, British subject who had worked for some years in the Soviet Union. Activist in the United States in the Federation of Architects, Engineers, Chemists and Technicians, a small Communist-led union. In 1942 met with Peter Ivanov, a Soviet diplomat and GRU officer, then approached, directly or through intermediaries such as Haakon Chevalier, several scientists working on the Manhattan Project regarding furnishing information to the Soviet Union.[32]

Feierabend, Albert: naturalized American citizen from Latvia, member of the CPUSA, Comintern courier. Worked with Nicholas Dozenberg's GRU apparatus. Arrested on smuggling charges in 1930 when returning from abroad. At that time claimed his name was Jacob Kreitz and carried a small, easily concealed white cloth ribbon signed by Max Bedacht, then a member of the CPUSA's executive secretariat, which stated that "the bearer of this credential is thoroughly trustworthy and should be given all possible support so that he may effectively accomplish the mission he is engages in." Arrested again in 1933 when arriving from abroad carrying a false American passport and $28,000 in cash, Soviet subsidies either for the CPUSA or for Soviet espionage operations. Skipped bail and was never apprehended.[33]

Field, Frederick Vanderbilt: secret Communist and a prominent Popular Front liberal. Acted as a recruiter for the CPUSA-GRU underground of which Whittaker Chambers was a part in the mid-1930s. Also provided his residence as a safe-house for a 1945 meeting between Elizabeth Bentley, then supervising of a CPUSA-KGB espionage network, and Earl Browder.[34]

Field, Noel: secret Communist, recruited by Hede Massing for a KGB network in the mid-1930s when he held a mid-level post in the State Department's West European division.[35]

Frankfurter, Gerta: part of Hede Massing's KGB network in the 1930s.[36]

Gayn, Mark: left-wing journalist, assisted Philip Jaffe in the *Amerasia* case.[37]

Glassman, Vivian: carried a warning and money from Soviet intelligence to William Perl urging him to flee to Mexico when the FBI began to roll up the Rosenberg network.[38]

Goldberg, Ben-Zion: journalist, identified in Soviet documents as a Soviet agent. Activities unknown.[39]

Granich, Grace: veteran CPUSA leader, acted as a talent-spotter for Jacob Golos.[40]

Greenberg, Michael: mid-level official specializing in Chinese matters for the Board of Economic Warfare and the Foreign Economic Administration and source for Golos-Bentley network.[41]

Gregg, Joseph: veteran of the International Brigades, source for Golos-Bentley network. Worked for the Office of the Coordinator of Inter-American Affairs and for the State Department.[42]

Hammer, Armand: son of a founding member of the American Communist movement. Laundered Soviet subsidies for the CPUSA in the 1920s and later used his position as a wealthy businessman with ties to the USSR to assist Soviet intelligence.[43]

Heiman, Julius: immigrant from Russia and a naturalized citizen, in the early 1920s worked in the jewelry business and was a secret Communist. Converted Soviet subsidies that came in the form of jewelry into cash. In the 1930s and early 1940s, undertook a variety of support tasks for GRU operations in the United States, most notably as an associate of the GRU illegal officer Arthur Adams.[44]

Heller, Ferdinand: son of a wealthy American Communist. Admitted to the FBI that he was recruited into Soviet industrial espionage in 1935 by Gaik Ovakimian.[45]

Hiskey, Clarence: scientist at the Chicago Metallurgical Laboratory, part of the Manhattan Project. Met covertly with the GRU illegal officer Arthur Adams. Hiskey was also a target of KGB recruitment and appears in KGB cables under the cover name Ramsey.[46]

Huettig, Lester M.: industrial spy at Remington Arms who supplied Soviet intelligence with blueprints for automatic shell loaders in the 1930s.[47]

Hutchins, Grace: socially prominent writer and secret Communist, assisted the CPUSA-GRU apparatus of which Whittaker Chambers was a part. After Chambers defected and was in hiding, she delivered an indirect warning to his brother-in-law that if he revealed Chambers's location to her, she would guarantee the safety of Chambers's wife and children.[48]

Ikal, Arnold: illegal GRU officer in the United States from the early 1930s to 1937. Married to an American Communist.[49]

Inslerman, Felix: part of the GRU-CPUSA network supervised by Whittaker Chambers. Later, in cooperating with U.S. authorities, stated that he had left Soviet service in 1939.[50]

Jacobson, Arvid: Finnish-American Communist, recruited for Soviet espionage in Finland by the CPUSA-GRU network of which Whittaker Chambers was a part. Arrested in Finland in 1933.[51]

Jaffe, Philip: longtime friend of Earl Browder and the CPUSA. As editor and publisher of *Amerasia,* illegally procured thousands of pages of classified government documents and attempted to make them available to Soviet intelligence. Convicted of unauthorized possession of government documents.[52]

Jerome, V. J.: veteran CPUSA leader chiefly involved in party work among intellectuals. Acted as a talent-spotter for Golos.[53]

Josephson, Leon: veteran Communist attorney and part of the CPUSA-Soviet false-passport operation in the 1930s.[54]

Kahn, Albert: journalist and secret member of the CPUSA, suggested for recruitment by the San Francisco KGB in 1946. However, Elizabeth Bentley told the FBI that in 1942 she and Jacob Golos had met with Kahn, who furnished information on immigrant Ukrainians hostile to the Soviets. May be Fighter (see appendix A).[55]

Kahn, M. G.: assisted in providing business cover for the illegal GRU officer Arthur Adams. Involved in smuggling jewels from the Soviet Union in 1919.[56]

Kamen, Martin: chemist working at the Radiation Laboratory at the University of California, Berkeley. Met with Grigory Kheifets and Grigory Kasparov, KGB officers at the Soviet San Francisco consulate. Fired from the Manhattan Project in 1944 when security officers overheard him discussing atomic research with Kheifets.[57]

Kaplan, Irving: secret Communist working at the War Production Board, source for Golos-Bentley network.[58]

Kazakevich, Vladimir: instructor at a wartime U.S. Army school, contact of Golos-Bentley network.[59]

Kent, Tyler: code clerk at the U.S. embassies in Moscow (1934–1939) and London (1939–1940). Arrested by British security officials in 1940 for theft of Roosevelt-Churchill correspondence. Convicted and imprisoned until 1945. American security officials later concluded that while serving in Moscow he had been compromised by the KGB and had provided the Soviets with American diplomatic communications. Kent's recruitment resulted not from ideological conviction but from a "honey trap," wherein a female KGB agent used sex to induce cooperation. His activities in London were not on behalf of the Soviets but stemmed from his opposition to possible American entry into that war and his involvement with antisemitic and pro-Nazi circles in Britain.[60]

Kowan, Maurice: Chicago doctor and Communist, acted as a mail drop for William Crane and John Loomis Sherman.[61]

Kruse, William: mid-level Communist activist in the 1920s. A Lovestoneite, he left the party in 1929 but in the 1930s assisted Nicholas Dozenberg in establishing a cover business for his GRU activities in the Philippines.[62]

Landy, Avram: senior CPUSA official chiefly involved in work with ethnic minorities. Acted as a talent-spotter for Golos. May be Khan (see appendix A).[63]

Larsen, Emmanuel: State Department researcher, one of Philip Jaffe's sources for stolen government documents in the *Amerasia* case. Convicted of illegal procurement of government documents, he lost his job with the State Department.[64]

Lerner, Irving: associate of the illegal GRU officer Arthur Adams and an employee of the Motion Picture Division of the Office of War Information. Attempted to photograph the cyclotron at the University of California without authorization.[65]

Leshinsky, Sol: official of the United Nations Relief and Rehabilitation Administration, member of the Perlo group, part of the Golos-Bentley network.[66]

Levin, Bernice: clerical employee of the Office of Emergency Management and the Office of Production Management. Minor source for Golos-Bentley network.[67]

Levy, Philip: secret Communist, close associate of Leon Josephson. His residence was used to store documents stolen by the CPUSA underground from the party's critics.[68]

Lieber, Maxim: literary agent, born in 1897 in Russian Poland, naturalized U.S. citizen. Active member of the CPUSA-GRU network of which Whittaker Chambers and John Loomis Sherman were members.[69]

Lomanitz, Giovanni Rossi: scientist working at the Berkeley Radiation Laboratory, met in 1942 with Steve Nelson of the CPUSA to discuss his work on the Manhattan Project.[70]

Lovestone, Jay: head of the CPUSA in the late 1920s, expelled in 1929. For a few years he and some of his followers assisted Soviet intelligence in hopes that this would win them readmission to the Communist movement.[71]

Marcus, James Lewis: headed Aldon Rug Mills, a firm that provided business cover for Soviet agents.[72]

Marzani, Carl: joined the Office of Strategic Services in 1942 and by 1945 had become deputy chief of the presentation branch, which prepared charts, graphs, and other pictorial displays of OSS information. Transferred to the State Department when the OSS dissolved. Convicted in 1947 of fraud for concealing his Communist party membership on various State Department employment documents.[73]

Massing, Hede: supervised a KGB network in the 1930s that included two State Department officials, Noel Field and Laurence Duggan. She and her husband dropped out of intelligence work for the Soviets and later broke entirely with communism. Went to the FBI in 1947. May be Redhead (see appendix A).[74]

Massing, Paul: KGB agent working in partnership with his wife, Hede.[75]

McPeek, Fanny: clerk at a New York City school, provided a mail drop for the American end of the KGB's anti-Trotsky operations in Mexico.[76]

Miller, Jenny Levy: wife of Robert T. Miller and a contact of Elizabeth Bentley. Worked for the Chinese Government Purchasing Commission in Washington during World War II.[77]

Miller, Robert T.: official of the Office of the Coordinator of Inter-American Affairs, source for Golos-Bentley network.[78]

Mink, George: American Communist union organizer in the 1920s. Worked on maritime unionism for the Comintern in the 1930s and assisted in its establishment of a covert courier system using Communist seamen. Arrested and imprisoned in Denmark for espionage.[79]

Minton, Bruce: editor of the CPUSA's literary-intellectual journal, *New*

Masses. Worked as a talent-spotter and put Jacob Golos in touch with Maurice Halperin, an OSS official who was one of the most productive spies the Soviets developed during World War II.[80]

Mitchell, Kate: co-editor of *Amerasia,* assisted Philip Jaffe.[81]

Miyagi, Yotoku: immigrated to the United States from Japan in 1919 as a teenager, joined the CPUSA in 1931 and was recruited for Soviet intelligence work through a Japanese Comintern agent assisting the CPUSA's work among Japanese-Americans. Returned to Japan in 1933 as part of a Soviet spy network headed by the KGB officer Richard Sorge. Arrested by Japanese police in 1941 and died in prison in 1943.[82]

Morgan, Will: seaman courier for the CPUSA secret apparatus carrying material via Iran for the Comintern in 1943.[83]

Morris: KGB contact originally made in Great Britain in the mid-1930s who moved to the United States. The KGB sought to reestablish contact in 1942 by sending its illegal officer Arnold Deutsch (who had known Morris) to the United States. Deutsch, however, died en route when his ship was sunk by a German U-boat.[84]

Moskowitz, Miriam: associate of Abraham Brothman. Convicted of obstruction of justice for her role in attempting to conceal Brothman's industrial espionage.[85]

Nelson, Steve: CPUSA official and figure in its secret apparatus. Assisted KGB and GRU officers. May be *Butcher* (see appendix A).[86]

North, Joe: senior CPUSA official and editor of the journal *New Masses.* Worked as a talent-spotter for Soviet intelligence, recruiting (among others) Winston Burdett and William Remington.[87]

Novick, Sam: Communist and head of Electronics Corporation of America. Provided business cover for the illegal GRU officer Arthur Adams and helped him to enter the United States using false documents in 1938.[88]

Older, Julia: Office of Strategic Services employee, dismissed for attempting to gain access to a file on Ukrainian nationalists on behalf of Albert Kahn. Reinstated on appeal but transferred to the Office of War Information. Lived in Moscow in the 1930s and worked for numerous CPUSA-linked bodies. Her brother, Andrew Older, was a secret party member and journalist. May be Unbroken Cover Name No. 19 (see appendix A).[89]

Osman, Robert: U.S. Army corporal assigned to the Panama Canal Zone, provided military documents to a GRU network.[90]

Park, Willard: employee of the Office of the Coordinator of Inter-American Affairs and later of the United Nations Relief and Rehabilitation Administration. Minor source for Golos-Bentley network.[91]

Perazich, George: official of the Yugoslav section of the United Nations Relief and Rehabilitation Administration. Minor source for Golos-Bentley network.[92]

Peters, Josef: head of the CPUSA secret apparatus from the early 1930s to mid-1938 and liaison with the GRU and the KGB. May be Storm (appendix A).[93]

Pigman, William Ward: secret Communist source at the National Bureau of Standards in the mid-1930s for Whittaker Chambers's CPUSA-GRU network.[94]

Poyntz, Juliet Stuart: founding member of the CPUSA, directed its women's department and the New York Workers School in the 1920s. On the staff of the Friends of the Soviet Union and International Labor Defense. In 1934 she dropped out of open party activities and into Soviet intelligence work. She disappeared from her New York City residence in 1937, and a police investigation turned up no clues to her fate. In early 1938 Carlo Tresca, a leading Italian-American radical, publicly accused the Soviets of kidnapping Poyntz in order to prevent her defection. He said that before she disappeared, she had come to him to talk over her disgust at what she had seen in Moscow in 1936 in the early stages of Stalin's Great Terror. Elizabeth Bentley, who had known her as Juliet Glazer, stated that in the late 1930s Jacob Golos and in 1945 the KGB officer Anatoly Gromov had told her that Poyntz had been a traitor and was dead. Whittaker Chambers related that he had heard that Poyntz had been killed for attempted desertion, and that this rumor had contributed to his caution when he defected in 1938.[95]

Price, Mildred: sister of Mary Price and leader of the China Aid Council. Talent-spotter for Golos-Bentley network.[96]

Rabinowitz, Gregory: KGB agent in the late 1930s who assisted in its anti-Trotsky campaign, including the American end of the KGB's murder of Leon Trotsky.[97]

Redmont, Bernard: journalist and official of the Office of the Coordinator of Inter-American Affairs. Minor source for Golos-Bentley network.[98]

Remington, William: official of the War Production Board, minor source for Golos-Bentley network. Convicted of perjury and murdered in prison in 1954.[99]

Reno, Vincent: employee at the U.S. Army proving grounds at Aberdeen, Maryland. Provided military information to the CPUSA-GRU network that Whittaker Chambers supervised. Later cooperated with U.S. authorities.[100]

Rivkin, Ruth: employee of a predecessor to the United Nations Relief and Rehabilitation Administration. Minor source for Golos-Bentley network.[101]

Rosenberg, Simon: naturalized American from Poland, engineer employed by Amtorg in the early 1930s and engaged in industrial espionage under the direction of the illegal KGB officer Gaik Ovakimian.[102]

Rosenblit, Philip: Communist dentist in New York, part of the courier system for delivering Soviet money to Soviet intelligence networks in the United States as well as funds to subsidize the CPUSA.[103]

Roth, Andrew: Office of Naval Intelligence liaison officer with the State Department, cooperated with Philip Jaffe in the *Amerasia* case.[104]

Salich, Hafis: naturalized American citizen from Russia who worked for the Office of Naval Intelligence. Recruited by Soviet intelligence in 1938. In 1939 he and his Soviet controller, Mikhail Gorin, head of the Los Angeles Intourist office, were arrested and convicted of espionage. Salich went to prison. Gorin, a Soviet national, was given probation; he paid a $10,000 fine and returned to the Soviet Union.[105]

Schuman, Irving George: used by the KGB agent Joseph Katz in surveillance of the Soviet defector Walter Krivitsky.[106]

Shepard, Barnett: provided a mail drop for the American end of the KGB's anti-Trotsky operations in Mexico.[107]

Sherman, John Loomis: CPUSA activist in the late 1920s, expelled from the party as a Lovestoneite in 1929 but almost immediately recruited to underground party work. Worked chiefly for the GRU in association with Whittaker Chambers and William Crane. Abandoned Soviet intelligence work in the late 1930s but remained a Communist.[108]

Silverman, Frances: CPUSA militant in the New York City teachers union, provided a mail drop for the American end of the KGB's anti-Trotsky operations in Mexico.[109]

Simon, Helen Levi: columnist for the CPUSA's *Daily Worker,* acted as a conduit for funds to assist Ramón Mercader, Trotsky's murderer.[110]

Slack, Alfred D.: chemist, in the early 1940s supplied information to the industrial espionage apparatus of which Harry Gold was a part. After Gold identified him, he confessed and received a fifteen-year prison sentence.[111]

Soble, Myra, wife of the KGB agent Jack Soble. Pled guilty to charges of espionage in 1957.[112]

Source No. 19: cover name of a KGB contact originally made in Great Britain in the mid-1930s who moved to the United States. The KGB sought to reestablish contact in 1942 by sending its illegal officer Arnold Deutsch (who had known this source) to the United States. Deutsch, however, died en route when his ship was sunk by a German U-boat in 1942. Unlikely to be the same as Source No. 19 in appendix A.[113]

Spiegel, William: Communist who made his apartment available for photographic work to the GRU-CPUSA network supervised by Whittaker Chambers.[114]

Spitz, Beatrice: physician and naturalized citizen. See Spitz, Henry.[115]

Spitz, Henry: physician and naturalized citizen, he and his wife, Beatrice, moved to Albuquerque, New Mexico, in 1950 and took photographs of atomic weapons research facilities that they passed to Robert Soblen of the KGB.[116]

Stahl, Lydia: American assistant to Alfred Tilton, an illegal GRU officer in the United States in the late 1920s.[117]

Steinberg, Arthur Gerald: Canadian, Columbia Ph.D. (1940) in zoology, worked for the U.S. Office of Scientific Research and Development in 1945. Source for a Canadian GRU network.[118]

Stenbuck, Joseph: acted as a mail drop and receiver of stolen blueprints for Robert Osman in 1933.[119]

Stern, Moishe (also known as Mark Zilbert): illegal GRU officer in the United States in the late 1920s and early 1930s.[120]

Stone, Victoria Singer: Communist who undertook a variety of support tasks for GRU operations in the United States, most notably as an associate of the GRU illegal officer Arthur Adams.[121]

Straight, Michael: American, became a secret Communist while at Cambridge University in the mid-1930s. Protégé of the Soviet spy Anthony Blunt, encouraged to return to the United States in a covert role. Became a speech writer for President Roosevelt, met on several occasions with Iskhak Akhmerov, an illegal KGB officer, but broke off the relationship in 1942.[122]

Switz, Robert Gordon: worked in the early 1930s as a clandestine photographer and courier for the GRU in the United States. Intermediary between Robert Osman and the GRU.[123]

Tamer, Joshua: member of the CPUSA-GRU network of which Whittaker Chambers was a part in the early 1930s.[124]

Taylor, William: Treasury Department official, source for Golos-Bentley network. Sued the publisher of Elizabeth Bentley's autobiography, who, over Bentley's objection, settled out of court. Presented a lengthy attack on Bentley's credibility. The FBI supported Bentley and prepared a detailed rebuttal to his attack.[125]

Tilton, Alfred: illegal GRU officer in the United States in the late 1920s. Posed as a Canadian immigrant with the name Joseph Paquett.[126]

Ulanovsky, Aleksandr Petrovich: illegal GRU officer operating in the United States in the early 1930s. Used, among others, the identity of Nicholas Sherman, an American.[127]

Ulanovsky, Nadezhda: illegal GRU officer and the wife of Aleksandr Ulanovsky.[128]

Unidentified Radar Source: recruited by the KGB agent Morris Cohen in the spring of 1942. The KGB officer Aleksandr Feklisov stated of this unidentified source that "every year he transmitted to us two or three thousand pages of photographs of secret materials [on radar development], the majority of which were appraised as either 'valuable' or 'extremely valuable.' "[129]

Vogel, Ethel: provided a mail drop for the American end of the KGB's anti-Trotsky operations in Mexico.[130]

Volkov, Anatole: son of Helen Silvermaster and stepson of Gregory Silvermaster, acted for a short time as a courier between the Silvermasters and the Golos-Bentley network.[131]

Wadleigh, Julian: mid-level State Department official, part of the CPUSA-GRU network that Whittaker Chambers supervised. Later cooperated with U.S. authorities.[132]

Weil, Ruby: secret Communist who infiltrated the American Trotskyist movement. Part of the KGB operation that murdered Leon Trotsky.[133]

Weinberg, Joseph W.: physicist and secret Communist at the Radiation Laboratory at the University of California, Berkeley. Met secretly with Steve Nelson, a CPUSA West Coast official, and gave him documents regarding the Manhattan Project. Nelson then met with Peter Ivanov, a Soviet intelligence officer under diplomatic cover at the Soviet consulate in San Francisco.[134]

Weinstein, Abraham: New York dentist who provided dental services for many CPUSA officials involved in its clandestine work as well as for many government employees who spied for the Soviets. The FBI concluded that Weinstein acted as a communications intermediary, that many of the dental visits were a cover for the passing of information to Weinstein, who then passed the information on to another party. Elizabeth Bentley identified a contact of Jacob Golos's who was a dentist and whom she knew only as Charlie. From her description, the FBI concluded that Weinstein was Charlie. May be Charlie in Venona (see appendix A).[135]

Weisband, William: linguist working for the U.S. Army Signals Security Agency during World War II, later joined the Venona Project. Fired in 1950 when another Soviet agent, Jones York, identified him as his Soviet contact in the early 1940s. Imprisoned for a year when he refused to answer a U.S. grand jury summons. May be Link (see appendix A).[136]

Yano, Tsutomu: Japanese-American CPUSA official who in 1931 recruited Yotoku Miyagi, a young Japanese-American, for Soviet intelligence work in Japan.[137]

Zilbert, Mark: See Stern, Moishe.

Zimmerman, David: mid-level official of the CPUSA in Maryland. Using the name David Carpenter, he was part of the GRU-CPUSA network supervised by Whittaker Chambers.[138]

Zlatowski, George: veteran of the International Brigades and secret Communist, became a U.S. Army intelligence officer. Married to Jane Foster (see appendix A), a Soviet agent in the Office of Strategic Services. Indicted on charges of espionage when the Soble spy ring was broken up after World War II. Abroad at the time and refused to return to the United States.[139]

Foreigners Temporarily in the United States Who Had Covert Relationships with Soviet Intelligence Agencies

These thirty-three foreigners and persons of unknown nationality temporarily resident in the United States had covert relationships with Soviet intelligence. Not included are nearly a hundred Soviet citizens, chiefly professional intelligence officers, who carried out espionage against the United States while on American soil under diplomatic cover. Cover names appear in italics.

Great Britain

Burgess, Guy: British diplomat and long-term Soviet spy who served in the British embassy in Washington, 1950–1951. Fled to Moscow in 1951.[1]

Eduard: KGB asset described in the Venona traffic as having served in Washington from 1939 until February 1945 and having contacts with prominent political figures. Likely but not certain to have been a British national.[2]

Fuchs, Emil Julius Klaus: part of the British contingent sent to assist the Manhattan Project. Confessed to espionage in 1950 and was imprisoned in Britain. Cover names Rest and Charles.[3]

Maclean, Donald: British diplomat and longtime Soviet spy who served in a senior position at the British embassy in Washington from 1944 to 1948. When British security began to close in on him in 1951, he fled to Moscow. Cover name Homer.[4]

Philby, H. R. (Kim): a senior British intelligence officer and also a longtime

Soviet agent who served as liaison with American intelligence in the late
1940s and early 1950s. Fled to Moscow in 1963.[5]

Canada

Losey, Mary [Mrs. Spencer Mapes]: employee of the Canadian National
Film Board's office in Washington, D.C. Recruiter for a Canadian GRU
network.[6]

May, Allan Nunn: part of the British contingent sent to assist the Manhattan Project. Worked chiefly in Canada but visited several American
atomic research facilities. His role as a Soviet spy was revealed when Igor
Gouzenko, a GRU code clerk at the Soviet embassy, defected in 1945
and identified several Soviet espionage sources. Confessed to espionage
and was imprisoned.[7]

Pontecorvo, Bruno: refugee Italian physicist who was part of the British
contingent inside the Manhattan Project. Worked largely in Canada and
reported to the KGB through its Ottawa station. Moved in the late 1940s
to England to work on the British atomic weapons program. Fled to the
USSR after Fuchs was arrested in 1950. May be Huron (appendix A).[8]

Size, Hazen: secret Canadian Communist and veteran of the Spanish Civil
War (medical unit), in Washington during World War II as a representative of the Canadian National Film Board. Minor source of Canadian
and British embassy information for the Golos-Bentley network.[9]

France

Cot, Pierre: French political figure and KGB contact. Cover name Daedalus.[10]

Eliacheff, Boris: French diplomat born in Russia, longtime Soviet spy.
Cover name Palm.[11]

Central and South America

Arthur: unidentified asset of the KGB. Central figure in the KGB's Latin
American operations who came to New York frequently and reported to
the New York KGB office. Link between the KGB and Soviet sources
spread all over Central South America, with contacts in Spain as well.
Probably held a position in government or industry that allowed extensive travel. May have been an illegal KGB officer.[12]

Muzquiz, Elena Huerta: resident of New York City, used for KGB Latin
American operations. Cover name Southerner.[13]

Subercaseaux, Christian Casanova: Chilean diplomat and KGB asset involved in Latin American operations who traveled between New York,
Portugal, and South America. Cover name Carlos.[14]

Romania

Davila, Carol A.: Romanian diplomat recruited as a KGB agent in 1944. Cover name Docker.[15]

Czechoslovakia

Fierlinger, Jan: information officer of the New York consulate of the Czechoslovak government-in-exile. Source for the KGB in 1943. Most of his reports dealt with diplomatic contacts between the United States and Britain and the Czechoslovak government-in-exile. Cover name Officer.[16]

Sukhomlin, Vasily: Russian Socialist Revolutionary exile, employed by the Czechoslovak Information Service (an arm of the Czechoslovak government-in-exile) in the United States, 1941–1945. KGB asset who reported to the New York KGB about the activities of the Czechoslovak government-in-exile and about other exiled European political figures in the United States, particularly exiled Social Democrats. Received a KGB stipend and was promised Soviet citizenship. Cover name Mars.[17]

Germany

Baerensprung, Horst: German refugee and former German police official, consultant to the Office of Strategic Services on German matters.[18]

Hirschfeld, Dr. Hans E.: German refugee, consultant to the Office of Strategic Services on German matters.[19]

Lund: unidentified illegal KGB officer inserted into the United States in 1943. Described as a German. Mission unknown.[20]

Mann, Heinrich Ludwig: reported to the San Francisco KGB about talks between the U.S. government and exiled German government officials.[21]

Poet: identified by the FBI as either Bertolt Brecht or Berthold Viertel. Brecht, the renowned German playwright, had entered the United States in mid-1941 and declared his intention (never carried out) to become an American citizen. He later became a leading intellectual figure under the East German Communist regime. Viertel, a writer who was a close friend and associate of Brecht, was also a German refugee. He entered the United States in 1942. In 1943 Poet supplied the San Francisco KGB with information about exiled German political figures.[22]

Poland

Moszulski, Roman: official of the Polish Telegraph Agency, a de facto arm of the Polish government-in-exile. Became a KGB asset in 1944. Cover name Canuck.[23]

Yugoslavia

Ivancic, Anton S.: KGB asset who arrived in the United States in 1940 and became active in Yugoslave exile politics. Early in 1944 he became head of the Yugoslav Seamen's Union in New York City. Cover name Crucian.[24]

Kosanovic, Sava N.: Yugoslav journalist and a politician in the Yugoslav government when Germany invaded. KGB asset, active figure in Yugoslav exile politics in the United States. After World War II he became an official in the Tito government. Cover name Kolo.[25]

Subasic, Ivan: exiled Yugoslav politician who became a KGB asset. Carried out KGB tasks among exiled Yugoslavs, reported on the initiatives of the U.S. government toward the exiles, and took part in the maneuvering for control of Yugoslavia after the defeat of the Nazis. Cover name Seres.[26]

The Netherlands

Dutch Naval Attaché in Washington (unidentified). In 1943 the Naval GRU office in Washington, which received information from him, referred to him as "loyal to us."[27]

Unknown Nationality

Contact: unidentified asset of the New York KGB who was part of a group of émigré agents.[28]

Dan: Agent with a U.S. connection to be greeted in London with the pass phrase "Didn't I meet you at Vick's restaurant on Connecticut Avenue?"[29]

Guard: unidentified asset of the New York KGB. Reported from Britain with information on British shipping and forwarded microfilm with encrypted letters to New York through Switzerland. One KGB cable also refers to "Guard's people" in Antwerp.[30]

Saffian, Alexander: appeared to represent either a foreign government or a foreign business firm in the United States. Reported to the New York KGB about negotiations regarding Middle Eastern oil concessions involving American companies. Cover name Contractor.[31]

Señor: unidentified cover name for someone who arrived in the United States from Denmark in September 1944 (but may have been in the United States earlier) and who was an active asset of the New York KGB during late 1944 and 1945. Received a monthly subsidy. Cover name changed to Berg in the fall of 1944.[32]

Yur: unidentified asset of the New York KGB who was part of a group of emigre agents.[33]

Americans and U.S. Residents Targeted as Potential Sources by Soviet Intelligence Agencies

The Venona decryptions and documents from Russian archives show that twenty-four persons were targeted by Soviet intelligence as candidates for some sort of relationship. There is no corroborative evidence, however, that their recruitment was accomplished. In several cases there is evidence that recruitment was not carried out, and in others it is likely that recruitment was aborted at an early stage when KGB approaches showed the target to be loyal to the United States. Cover names appear in italics.

Bachrach, Marion: sister of John Abt (see appendix A). Secretly joined the CPUSA in the early 1930s. Personal secretary and congressional office manager to Rep. John Bernard (Farmer-Labor, Minnesota) in 1937–1938 and correspondent for the newspaper *PM*. In 1942 the foreign intelligence arm of the KGB requested a background report on her from the Comintern and received a positive report.[1]

Barnes, Joseph: prominent journalist, former official of the Office of War Information, and manager of the foreign news department of the *New York Herald Tribune*. The KGB considered attempting to recruit Barnes because he had a number of friends in or close to the CPUSA, but it concluded that "the signing up of Barnes is not only inadvisable but unrealizable."[2]

Berger, Joseph Isadore: former assistant of the chairman of the Democratic National Committee and DNC speechwriter (1941–1946), U.S. delegate to the Allied Reparations Commission (1945). Cultivated by KGB agents for several years.[3]

Bloomfield, Samuel: staff member of the Eastern European division of the Research and Analysis section of the Office of Strategic Services in 1942, Also a secret Communist. The KGB, in reporting on him to Moscow, noted that he was also the manager of the Washington Progressive Book Store, a CPUSA-aligned firm. The U.S. government, however, noticed his Communist undertakings and opened an investigation into his activities. Left the OSS in 1943 for a job with the British Information Service in San Francisco.[4]

Bowen, Ralph: State Department economist. He and his wife were former members of the Young Communist League (YCL) and friends of the KGB agent Flora Wovschin, also a State Department employee and former YCL colleague. Cover name Alan.[5]

Breit, Gregory: émigré from Russia and a scientist working on the Manhattan Project. Mentioned in a 1945 cable in which the Moscow KGB headquarters lists possible targets for the New York KGB to consider. Unbeknownst to the Moscow KGB, Breit was a strong supporter of Manhattan Project secrecy and had left the project to protest what he regarded as loose security.[6]

Clarke: prospective GRU recruit who appears to have held a responsible position in a government agency, perhaps the Office of Strategic Services, inasmuch as one of the GRU agents who was engaged in feeling out his attitudes was Leonard Mins. All that is known about Clarke is that although pro-Soviet, he was not a CPUSA member. It is not known whether Clarke is a real name or a cover name.[7]

DuBois, Josiah Ellis: assistant to the secretary of the Treasury and a member of the U.S. delegation to the Allied War Reparations Commission meeting in Moscow in 1945. Harold Glasser, a senior Treasury Department official and a KGB spy, recommended DuBois to the KGB for consideration.[8]

Elitcher, Max: engineer with the Naval Ordnance Section of the National Bureau of Standards. Concealed member of the CPUSA. In 1944 Julius Rosenberg reported to the KGB that he had met with Elitcher and felt that Elitcher's response was sufficiently positive that recruitment should be pursued.[9]

Joseph, Emma Harriet: Communist and contact of the New York KGB via Elizabeth Bentley's apparatus. Worked for the OSS and in late 1944 received an assignment to go to Ceylon. Sister of the KGB agent Julius Joseph. Cover name Ivy.[10]

Larin: unidentified scientist or engineer considered for recruitment but rejected. Described as a CPUSA member, but a check by the KGB's CPUSA liaison showed that in the Federation of Architects, Engineers, Chemists and Technicians, a Communist-led union, Larin was "self-willed" and did not always carry out orders. On the basis of that report the New York KGB dropped its interest in recruiting him. It is not clear whether Larin is a cover name or a real name.[11]

Lauterbach, Richard T.: journalist and concealed Communist who worked for *Time* magazine. A leading KGB agent, Jack Soble, had a discussion with Lauterbach that led Soble and the New York KGB to ask the Moscow KGB headquarters to sanction his formal recruitment. Moscow's reply, however, was not among the Venona messages that were deciphered. Cover name Pa.[12]

Magidov, Nila: writer whom the *American Magazine* planned to send to the USSR as its correspondent for a year. In 1944 the New York KGB suggested that Moscow consider "eventually signing [her] on."[13]

Oppenheimer, Frank: physicist, secret Communist, brother of J. Robert Oppenheimer.[14]

Oppenheimer, J. Robert: physicist, supporter of the CPUSA until 1941, scientific head of the Manhattan Project.[15]

Rappoport, Joseph: veteran Communist party member. He and his wife, who had the cover name Lanya, appear to have been considered for recruitment in 1945.[16]

Roy: husband of Cora (see appendix A), whom Iskhak Akhmerov, the KGB's illegal agent, planned to use for KGB work.[17]

Steinberg, Isadore N.: artist-illustrator working for the Publications Division of the War Department. Concealed member of the CPUSA. Leonard Mins, a GRU agent working in the Office of Strategic Services, recommended his recruitment.[18]

Stone, Isidor Feinstein ("I. F."): journalist and commentator whom the KGB repeatedly attempted to approach. Cover name Pancake.[19]

Tanz, Alfred: lawyer and CPUSA member who, when serving with the Comintern's International Brigades in Spain, was identified in 1937 by Russian authorities as a "reliable" comrade and a candidate for "organizational-technical work." In 1943 the KGB's foreign intelligence arm sent a message to the Comintern inquiring about Tanz's background and received back a positive report.[20]

Thompson, Frederick: scion of a wealthy San Francisco area family, secret Communist. In May 1943 the KGB asked the Comintern for information on his activities during the Spanish Civil War, when he had worked with the Comintern. The message is typical of KGB messages of that period in which a candidate is being vetted for recruitment. May be Trio (see appendix A).[21]

Traugott, Lillian: official in the labor section of the Office of Strategic Services with assignments to OSS missions in England, Sweden, Norway, and France. Received in 1945 an assignment to watch for signs of Communist infiltration of the labor movement of liberated Norway. In 1944 the foreign intelligence arm of the KGB asked for a Comintern background report on Traugott. The Comintern reported that her brother was an "active member" of the CPUSA and that she was believed to have been a CPUSA member since 1937. The OSS appears to have been unaware of her links to the CPUSA. After World War II, she joined the national headquarters staff of the National Citizens Political Action Committee, a prominent Popular Front political group, and in 1948 became an assistant to and later married C. B. Baldwin, national presidential campaign manager for Henry Wallace.[22]

Tuzov: candidate for recruitment developed by the KGB agent Nicholas Orloff. In the final stages of recruitment Tuzov expressed fear of the consequences and indicated that he was reluctant to work for the KGB. The New York KGB decided that given that Tuzov was also elderly, it was inexpedient to pursue recruitment further.[23]

Volok: unidentified engineer or scientist who was fired from the Manhattan Project, reportedly for working for a "progressive organization." Reported by the KGB to be a concealed CPUSA member. The discussion of Volok occurs in a KGB message reporting on the activities of Julius Rosenberg's apparatus and his plans to recruit Communist engineers.[24]

Biographical Sketches of Leading KGB Officers Involved in Soviet Espionage in the United States

Career information is taken largely from *Veterany Vneshnei Razvedki Rossii* (Moscow: Russian Foreign Intelligence Service, 1995).

Akhmerov, Iskhak Abdulovich (1901–1975): of Tartar background, joined the Bolshevik party in 1919, attended the Communist University of Toilers of the East and the First State University [Moscow State University] and graduated from the latter's School of International Relations in 1930. Joined the KGB in 1930 and participated in the suppression of anti-Soviet movements in the USSR's Bukhara Republic (1930–1931). Transferred to the KGB foreign intelligence arm in 1932 and served as a legal intelligence officer under diplomatic cover in Turkey. Became an illegal field officer in China in 1934, entered the United States with false identify papers in 1935, and acted as head of the KGB illegal station in the United States from 1942 to 1945. In late 1945 or early 1946 he returned to the USSR and became deputy chief of the KGB's illegal intelligence section. Attained the rank of colonel and was awarded the Order of the Red Banner (twice), the Order of the Badge of Honor, and the badge of Honored Chekist.

Fitin, Pavel Mikhailovich (1907–1971): graduated from an engineering program at the Timiryazev Agricultural Academy in 1932, served in the Red Army, and worked as an editor for the State Publishing House for Agricultural Literature. In 1938 the CPSU selected him for a special course in foreign intelligence at the KGB's training institute. Made deputy chief of the KGB's foreign intelligence arm in 1938 and became its chief in

1939, at the age of thirty-one. The Russian Foreign Intelligence Service credits Fitin with rebuilding the purge-depleted foreign intelligence department and providing ample warning of the German attack in June 1941. Only the actual invasion saved Fitin from execution for providing Beria, head of the KGB, with information that Stalin did not want to hear and would not believe. Beria retained Fitin as chief of foreign intelligence until the war ended but then demoted him. In 1951 Beria discharged Fitin from the KGB and denied him a pension. Fitin was unable to find other employment until Beria himself was executed in 1953. Attained the rank of lieutenant-general and was awarded the orders of the Red Banner (twice), the Red Star, and the Red Banner of Tuva.

Gromov, Anatoly, pseudonym in the United States of Anatoly Veniaminovich Gorsky (dates unknown): joined the KGB in 1928 and worked in its internal political police section until transferring to foreign intelligence in 1936. Became deputy chief of the KGB station in London in 1936 and chief in 1940. Managed the "Cambridge Five" and the initial KGB penetration of the British atomic bomb project. Was recalled to the USSR in 1944 for work at the central KGB headquarters but was then hastily sent to Washington to become chief of the KGB station in the United States after the sudden recall of Vasily Zubilin. Returned to Moscow in 1947 to take a supervisory position in foreign intelligence and in 1953 shifted to internal security work. Attained the rank of colonel and was awarded the orders of the Red Banner, the Red Banner of Labor, the Badge of Honor, and the Red Star.

Kvasnikov, Leonid Romanovich (1905–1993): graduated with honors from the Moscow Institute of Chemical Machine-Building in 1934 and worked as an engineer for several years. Returned for postgraduate engineering studies and in 1938 entered the KGB as a specialist in scientific-technical intelligence, undertaking short-term assignments in Germany and Poland and rising swiftly to become deputy chief and then chief of the KGB scientific intelligence section. The Russian Foreign Intelligence Service credits Kvasnikov with sparking the KGB's interest in atomic research in 1940 when he noticed that British, American, and German scientists who had regularly published their findings on uranium and related atomic research had ceased to publish. Supervised from Moscow the initial KGB penetration of the British and American atomic bomb projects and in 1943 went to New York under diplomatic cover to supervise scientific-technical espionage with special attention to the atomic bomb project. Returned to the USSR in 1945 and in 1948 again became chief of KGB scientific intelligence, a position he held until 1963. Attained the rank of colonel and was awarded the orders of Lenin, the Red Banner of Labor (twice), and the Red Star (twice).

Ovakimian, Gaik Badalovich (b. 1898): of Armenian background, he joined the KGB in 1931 while a graduate student at Moscow's Bauman Higher Technical School and went immediately into foreign intelligence.

Undertook an assignment in Germany emphasizing scientific-technical espionage. Returned to the USSR in 1932 for advanced technical training at the Workers' and Peasants' Red Army Military-Chemical Academy. Went to the United States in 1933 as deputy head of the KGB's scientific-technical intelligence section, operating under the cover of being an engineer for Amtorg. Became chief of scientific intelligence in the United States in 1939 and also undertook study for a doctorate in chemistry at a New York university. Arrested in 1941 during a meeting with an agent who had been turned by the FBI. After the Nazi invasion of the USSR, the United States agreed to forgo prosecution and allowed him to return to Moscow. Became deputy chief of the KGB's foreign intelligence arm in 1943 and attained the rank of major-general. Left the KGB in 1947 for full-time scientific work.

Semenov, Semyon Markovich (1911–1986): graduated from the Moscow Textile Institute in 1936 with a specialty in power engineering. Joined the KGB in 1937 and was immediately sent to the United States as an intelligence officer. Enrolled at the Massachusetts Institute of Technology, from which he graduated in 1940. Worked under the cover of an Amtorg engineer while specializing in scientific and technical espionage. A Russian Foreign Intelligence Service history quotes his KGB personnel files as stating, "While working from 1938 through 1944 in the United States, Major Semenov showed himself to be one of the most active workers in the *rezidentura* [station]. He practically created the line followed by scientific-technical intelligence during the prewar years. He obtained valuable materials from dozens of agents dealing with explosives, radar technology, and aviation." Later undertook assignments in France and in Moscow and rose to the rank of lieutenant-colonel. Fired from the KGB in 1953 during an antisemitic purge. Rehabilitated in the 1970s.

Yatskov, Anatoly Antonovich (d. 1993): graduated from the Moscow Printing Institute in 1937 and, after joining the KGB in 1939, attended the KGB's training institute. Sent to the United States in 1940 or 1941 as a junior intelligence officer working under diplomatic cover. Specialized in scientific-technical intelligence. After the war he undertook numerous intelligence assignments and headed one of the schools of the KGB's Andropov Red Banner Institute for training of KGB personnel. Attained the rank of colonel and was awarded the orders of the October Revolution, the Red Banner of Labor, the Patriotic War, and the Red Star.

Zubilin, Elizabeth, pseudonym in the United States of Elizaveta Yulyevna Zarubina, and also known as Lisa Gorskaya (1900–1987): born in Russia of Romanian background, she attended universities in Russia, France, and Austria. Joined the Austrian Communist party in 1923 and became an agent of the KGB in 1925, working for its Vienna station until 1928. Undertook several short-term foreign assignments, including one to Turkey. There she alerted Moscow that Jacob Blumkin, a senior KGB officer with whom she was romantically involved, was in communication with Leon Trotsky. Blumkin was recalled and executed. Shortly thereafter she married Vasily Zubilin and, continuing to serve as a KGB officer, accompanied and assisted him in his many intelligence assignments, although occasionally undertaking independent missions. Credited by the Russian Foreign Intelligence Service with recruiting twenty sources for Soviet intelligence during her tour of duty in the United States in the early 1940s.

Zubilin, Vasily, pseudonym in the United States for Vasily Mikhailovich Zarubin (1894–1972): served with the Russian Imperial Army from 1914 to 1917 (wounded) and with the Red Army from 1918 to 1920. Joined the KGB in 1920 and served in its internal security section until 1925, when he transferred to foreign intelligence. Served as a legal officer in China (1925), a legal officer in Finland (1926), an illegal officer in Denmark and Germany (1927–1929), an illegal officer in France (1929–1933), and an illegal officer in Germany (1933–1937). Returned to the USSR in 1937 for work with the KGB's central apparatus. In 1940 he survived an accusation of working for Germany and had some unclear association with the KGB's murder at Katyn of more than fifteen thousand Polish prisoners of war (see chapter 2). Undertook an assignment in China in 1941 and is credited with obtaining information from a high-ranking German adviser to Chiang Kai-shek about Hitler's plans to attack the USSR in mid-1941. Became the chief of the KGB station in the United States in the fall of 1941. Recalled in 1944 to face a second accusation of working for the Germans, which he survived. Became deputy chief of foreign intelligence, attained the rank of major general, and was awarded the orders of Lenin (twice), the Red Banner (twice), and the Red Star.

Notes

Introduction: The Road to Venona

1. Robert Lamphere and Tom Shachtman, *The FBI-KGB War: A Special Agent's Story* (New York: Random House, 1986), 78–98; Ronald Radosh and Joyce Milton, *The Rosenberg File: A Search for the Truth* (New York: Holt, Rinehart and Winston, 1983; New Haven: Yale University Press, 1997), 130; David Martin, *Wilderness of Mirrors* (New York: Ballantine Books, 1981), 39–45. Martin also reported that deciphered messages had pointed to the British diplomat Donald Maclean as a spy. Christopher Andrew and Oleg Gordievsky, *KGB: The Inside Story* (New York: Harper-Collins, 1990), 373–376, 446–447.

2. Peter Wright, *Spy Catcher: The Candid Autobiography of a Senior Intelligence Officer* (New York: Viking, 1987), 239–241.

3. Harvey Klehr and John Earl Haynes, *The American Communist Movement: Storming Heaven Itself.* (New York: Twayne, 1992), 108.

Chapter 1: Venona and the Cold War

1. The basis for the rumors regarding a new Nazi-Soviet Pact is discussed in Vojtech Mastny, *Russia's Road to the Cold War: Diplomacy, Warfare, and the Politics of Communism, 1941–1945* (New York: Columbia University Press, 1979), 77–78, 83–84, 162.

2. Robert Louis Benson and Michael Warner, eds., *Venona: Soviet Espionage and the American Response, 1939–1957* (Washington, D.C.: National Security Agency, Central Intelligence Agency, 1996), xiii.

3. For a summary of Fitin's KGB career, see appendix E.

4. The KGB (Komitet Gosudarstvennoi Bezopasnosti or Committee for State Security) and its foreign intelligence arm have a complex organizational history. The pred-

ecessors to the KGB, which came into existence in 1954, include the Cheka (All-Russian Extraordinary Commission to Combat Counterrevolution and Sabotage), GPU (State Political Directorate), OGPU (United State Political Directorate), NKVD (People's Commissariat of Internal Affairs), GUGB (Main Administration of State Security), NKGB (People's Commissariat of State Security), MGB (Ministry of State Security), KI (Committee of Information), and MVD (Ministry of Internal Affairs). For simplicity, throughout this volume the term KGB will be used to designate these various predecessor organizations.

5. Muse and Mole were eventually identified, but not until many decades later—in Muse's case, not until 1998. After the dissolution of the OSS, Muse (Helen Tenney) had succeeded in transferring to the State Department, where she became a Soviet analyst, a perfect position for a Soviet spy. Mole (Charles Kramer) had become a senior staff member on a Senate committee. Although their Venona cover names were not broken at the time, both were identified as Soviet agents by Elizabeth Bentley, a defector from Soviet espionage, and they were quietly forced to resign. But security officers continued to hunt for Muse and Mole, not realizing that they had already been found.

6. Daniel Patrick Moynihan, *Secrecy: The American Experience* (New Haven: Yale University Press, 1998), 70–71; Benson and Warner, *Venona*, xxiv, xxx.

7. On White House consideration of these actions, see George Elsey to Clark Clifford, 16 August 1948, Clark M. Clifford papers, Harry S. Truman Library, "Loyalty Investigations," box 11, reproduced in Benson and Warner, *Venona*, 117.

8. See chapter 10.

9. It is likely that had the Venona messages been available to the public, both Rosenbergs would have escaped the death penalty, but it should also be kept in mind that both would have been spared execution had they confessed.

10. Joseph McCarthy speech, U.S. Senate, 14 June 1951, *Congressional Record*, vol. 97, part 5, p. 6602.

11. The authors have several times been asked if Senator McCarthy had knowledge of the Venona decryptions, perhaps leaked to him by a security official frustrated by the decision to keep the information secret. There is no evidence that McCarthy had any such information. The targets he picked for his accusations do not suggest Venona as a source. Further, McCarthy was not one to keep politically explosive information secret.

12. Richard M. Fried, *Nightmare in Red: The McCarthy Era in Perspective* (New York: Oxford University Press, 1990); David Caute, *The Great Fear: The Anti-Communist Purge under Truman and Eisenhower* (New York: Simon and Schuster, 1978), 11.

13. Caute, *The Great Fear*, 54. In italics in the original.

14. Ibid., 11.

15. To be exact, the USSR was only half an ally until the final weeks of the war. The Soviet Union stayed neutral in the Pacific theater until after the dropping of the atomic bomb on Japan. Britain and the United States, however, fought two-front wars in both Europe and Asia.

16. The GRU (Glavnoye Razvedyvatelnoye Upravleniye or Chief Intelligence Directorate of the Soviet General Staff) and Naval GRU were military agencies separate from the intelligence arm of the KGB, the Soviet secret political police. These two military intelligence agencies also went through complex organizational and title changes. For a brief period, in 1937 and 1938, the Soviet military intelligence agency even reported to the chief of the NKVD (a predecessor to the KGB), as did the NKVD's own foreign intelligence branch. It was, however, put back in the military chain of command. To avoid confusion, throughout this book the various predecessors to the two military intelligence agencies will be referred to as the GRU and the Naval GRU.

Chapter 2: Breaking the Code

1. This section follows the history of Venona in Robert Louis Benson and Michael Warner, eds., *Venona: Soviet Espionage and the American Response, 1939–1957* (Washington, D.C.: National Security Agency, Central Intelligence Agency, 1996), and in the NSA historical monographs prepared by Robert Louis Benson: "Introductory History of VENONA and Guide to the Translations" (1995), "The 1942–43 New York–Moscow KGB Messages" (1995), "The 1944–45 New York and Washington–Moscow KGB Messages," (1996), "The KGB in San Francisco and Mexico, The GRU in New York and Washington" (1996), "The KGB and GRU in Europe, South America, and Australia" (1996), and "VENONA: New Releases, Special Reports, and Project Shutdown" (1997).

2. A number of the Comintern radio messages and Mikhelson-Manuilov's background are discussed in Harvey Klehr, John Earl Haynes, and Kyrill M. Anderson, *The Soviet World of American Communism* (New Haven: Yale University Press, 1998). On Reid, see "Datos Biogr ficos de Arnold Reisky (nombre del Partido Arnold Reid)," circa 1937–1938, Archive of the International Brigades, RTsKhIDNI 545-3-453. The International Brigades were a Comintern-controlled military formation that fought with the Spanish Republican government in the Spanish Civil War. Reid was killed during that war.

3. Among other points, Mask messages destroy the view that foreign Communist parties were independent of the Comintern. Sets of the Mask messages are maintained in the United Kingdom by the Public Record Office and in the United States by the National Cryptologic Museum, Fort Meade, Md.

4. For an explanation by one of the Venona program's leading cryptanalysts, see Cecil James Phillips, "What Made Venona Possible?" in Benson and Warner, *Venona*, xv. The Soviet defectors are Igor Gouzenko, a GRU code clerk who defected in Canada in 1945, and Vladimir and Evdokia Petrov, the former a mid-level KGB officer and the latter a KGB code clerk who defected in Australia in 1954. Vladimir Petrov had also been a code clerk earlier in his KGB career. The Petrovs' defection is summarized in David McKnight, *Australia's Spies and Their Secrets* (St. Leonards, Australia: Allen & Unwin, 1994), 59–76. Gouzenko is discussed later in this book. Also see Igor Gouzenko, *Iron Curtain* (New York: Dutton, 1948).

5. The KGB procedure used a two-digit spell table for such names. The GRU used a spell table of mixed one- and two-digit entries for Latin-alphabet names, with a separate but similar table for Cyrillic words or names.

6. The pages of a one-time pad are always used in order, but since messages may be transmitted out of order it is important to have a way of identifying the correct page. Most of the Soviet diplomatic systems provided a page number running from 01 to 35 or from 01 to 50. However, on May 1, 1944, the KGB shifted to the procedure described here of using the first numerical key group on the page rather than a page number to tell the deciphering clerk what key page to use.

7. At one time it was less expensive to transmit letters than numbers. This practice probably originated when messages were transmitted by Morse code rather than teletype machine.

8. This is the "external" number from which is derived the NSA message number used in citing Venona messages.

9. The steps described above are intended to show each of the discrete processes that must be performed. According to Gouzenko, the encoding, encipherment, and typing of the cipher text into the ten-letter substitution was performed as a single operation because the code clerk was not allowed to write down either plain code or the enci-

pherment key, to prevent transmitting anything but fully completed cipher. For anyone working with such a system regularly, performing the encoding, encipherment, and conversion to letters as a single step would not have been difficult. The hardest part would have been keeping track of one's place in the one-time pad. This would have been aided by marking off the groups in the pad as they were used.

10. Phillips, "What Made Venona Possible?" The Army had recruited Phillips, an eighteen-year-old college sophomore, for work in its cryptographic operation at Arlington Hall in 1943 and assigned him to what became the Venona Project in May 1944. His talent was such that he became one of the National Security Agency's long-serving senior cryptanalysts.

11. The Soviet international diplomatic cable traffic during World War II was between 200,000 and 300,000 coded and enciphered messages.

12. Phillips, "What Made Venona Possible?" The NSA identified the use of thirty-five thousand duplicate key pages, but the total number was estimated at perhaps twice that.

13. One of the deciphered Japanese cables based on what had been learned from the Finns is Japanese Army General Staff to Berlin and Helsinki, Tokyo circular 906, 6 October 1942, reproduced in Benson and Warner, Venona, 43–45. See also U.S. Army Signals Security Agency, "Memorandum on Russian Codes in the Japanese Military Attaché System," 9 February 1943, excerpt reproduced in ibid., 47–48.

14. Phillips, "What Made Venona Possible?" Hallock, a Signal Corps reserve officer, had been an archeologist at the University of Chicago.

15. Among the leading cryptanalysts who contributed to breaking the overlying one-time pad cipher were Richard Hallock, Cecil Phillips, Genevieve Feinstein, Frank Lewis, Frank Wanat, and Lucille Campbell.

16. In these cases, to reduce the rapid depletion of one-time pad pages, when the KGB cipher clerks had used only part of a page they did not destroy it but used the rest of the page to encipher a second message. Phillips showed how these could be identified and a search for messages relying on the same page could be made.

17. The USSR had attacked and defeated Finland in the "Winter War" of 1939–1940, forcing the Finns to cede considerable territory. When Nazi Germany invaded the USSR in 1941, the Finns joined the attack in the hope of regaining their lost land.

18. Lt. Oliver Kirby recovered related cryptographic material on a similar mission in Schleswig, Germany. Neff and Kirby later became senior NSA officials.

19. Edward Stettinius, Jr., memorandum for the President, "Soviet Codes," 27 December 1944, President's Secretary's Files, "Russia—1944," box 49, Franklin D. Roosevelt Library. Before the NSA released Venona in 1995 and provided accurate information about the history of the project, one rumor (reported in several books, including one by these authors) erroneously conflated the 1944 OSS Finnish material with that obtained by Army intelligence in 1945.

20. Venona 1657 KGB New York to Moscow, 27 November 1944.

21. Meredith Gardner memorandum, "Covernames in Diplomatic Traffic," 30 August 1947, reprinted in Benson and Warner, Venona, 93–104.

22. Stephen Schwartz, "La Venona Mexicana," Vuelta (Mexico) (August 1997), 19–25.

23. McKnight, Australia's Spies and Their Secrets, 6–25; David McKnight, "The Moscow-Canberra Cables: How Soviet Intelligence Obtained British Secrets through the Back Door," Intelligence and National Security 13, no. 2 (Summer 1998), 159–170; Desmond Ball and David Horner, Breaking the Codes: Australia's KGB Network (St. Leonard's, Australia: Allen & Unwin, 1998).

24. Benson and Warner, *Venona,* xxxi.

25. Victor Navasky, publisher of *The Nation,* derided the decryptions as part of a sinister government covert project "to enlarge post–cold war intelligence gathering capability at the expense of civil liberty." The lawyer-activist William Kuntsler wrote that the messages should be treated as frauds because of their derivation from U.S. government agencies. Victor Navasky, "Tales from Decrypts," *The Nation* (28 October 1996), 5–6; William Kuntsler, letter to the editor, *The Nation* (16 October 1995).

26. Allen Weinstein and Alexander Vassiliev, *The Haunted Wood: Soviet Espionage in America—The Stalin Era* (New York: Random House, 1999). These comments are based on uncorrected proof made available to us by Allen Weinstein.

27. They are Solomon Adler, Iskhak Akhmerov, Joel Barr, Elizabeth Bentley, Abraham Brothman, Earl Browder, William Browder, Frank Coe, Lona Cohen, Morris Cohen, Judith Coplon, Lauchlin Currie, William Dodd, Edward Fitzgerald, Klaus Fuchs, Rebecca Getzoff, Harold Glasser, Bella Gold, Harry Gold, Sonia Gold, Jacob Golos, David Greenglass, Ruth Greenglass, Theodore Hall, Maurice Halperin, Alger Hiss, Julius Joseph, Irving Kaplan, Joseph Katz, Alexander Koral, Charles Kramer, Sergey Kurnakov, Duncan Lee, Donald Maclean, Harry Magdoff, Boris Morros, Victor Perlo, Mary Price, Allan Rosenberg, Ethel Rosenberg, Julius Rosenberg, Saville Sax, Bernard Schuster, George Silverman, Gregory Silvermaster, Helen Silvermaster, Jack Soble, Myra Soble, Alfred Stern, Martha Dodd Stern, Michael Straight, Helen Tenney, William Ullmann, William Weisband, Donald Wheeler, Harry White, Jones York, and Mark Zborowsky.

28. Almost all the KGB messages found in the Comintern records are signed by Lt. Gen. Pavel Mikhailovich Fitin, head of the KGB's First Chief Directorate, the KGB's foreign intelligence arm, from 1940 to 1946. These RTsKhIDNI documents will be described and cited along with the matching deciphered Venona messages in later chapters when we discuss KGB or GRU links with Josephine Adams, Rudy Baker, Earl Browder, Paul Burns, Norman Bursler, Eugene Coleman, Judith Coplon, Pierre Cot, Marion Davis, Edward Fitzgerald, Charles Flato, Harold Glasser, Louis Horvitz, Samuel Krafsur, Charles Kramer, Harry Magdoff, Victor Perlo, Peter Rhodes, and Donald Wheeler. A detailed examination of corroboration of Comintern documents and deciphered Venona cables is in John Haynes and Harvey Klehr, "Venona and the Russian Archives: What Has Already Been Found," a paper presented to the Seventh Symposium on Cryptologic History, 30 October 1997, Fort Meade, Maryland.

29. Venona 1253 KGB New York to Moscow, 30 July 1943.

30. Sharia to Dimitrov, 27 January 1943, Archive of the Dimitrov Secretariat of the Comintern, RTsKhIDNI 495-73-188.

31. Anonymous Russian letter to Hoover, 7 August 1943, reproduced in Benson and Warner, *Venona,* 51–54.

32. Zubilin headed the New York KGB station in 1942 and 1943, operating out of the Soviet consulate, and his move to Washington to work from the Soviet embassy in the second half of 1943 signaled the transfer of the headquarters of KGB operations in America. The New York station, however, remained a major KGB office. Zubilin's immediate replacement in New York was Pavel Klarin, followed in 1944 by Stepan Apresyan, both of whom officially held the title of Soviet vice-consul. Elizabeth Zubilin eventually attained the KGB rank of colonel. For summaries of the KGB careers of the Zubilins, see appendix E.

33. Kheifets, officially Soviet vice-consul, headed the KGB station in San Francisco from 1941 to 1944, when he was replaced by Grigory Kasparov. In 1945 Stepan Apresyan took over as head of the KGB's San Francisco office.

34. Secretary of the Central Committee, All-Union Communist Party [CPSU] to

Beria-NKVD, 5 March 1940, reproduced in Diane Koenker and Ronald D. Bachman, eds., *Revelations from the Russian Archives: Documents in English Translation* (Washington, D.C.: Library of Congress, 1997), 167–168. The Nazis announced the discovery in hopes of stirring up conflict between the anti-Nazi allies. It did. When the Polish government-in-exile refused to accept the Soviet declaration of innocence, the Soviets broke off diplomatic relations.

35. Venona 1033 KGB New York to Moscow, 1 July 1943.

36. Pavel A. Sudoplatov and Anatoli Sudoplatov, with Jerrold L. Schecter and Leona P. Schecter, *Special Tasks: The Memoirs of an Unwanted Witness* (New York: Little, Brown, 1994), 196–197. It is possible that Mironov's real name was Markov. See Ben Fischer, " 'Mr. Guver': Anonymous Soviet Letter to the FBI," *Newsletter of the Center for the Study of Intelligence,* no. 7 (Winter–Spring 1997), 10–11. Sudoplatov also confirmed that Zubilin had been involved in the Katyn operation, but said that Zubilin's role was to select a few of the condemned Polish officers as recruits for the KGB, and that he did not directly take part in the murder operation (pp. 277–278). See also a brief mention of Zubilin in Allen Paul, *Katyn: Stalin's Massacre and the Seeds of Polish Insurrection* (Annapolis, Md.: Naval Institute Press, 1996), 77–78.

37. FBI Comintern Apparatus file (FBI file 100-203581), serial 3378, 1 November 1944; FBI Comintern Apparatus file, serial 3702, "Comintern Apparatus Summary Report," 15 December 1944. This and other FBI files cited herein were obtained through Freedom of Information Act requests or are available at the FBI reading room at the FBI headquarters in Washington, D.C.

38. Frustration with the Justice Department's reluctance to prosecute may have contributed to the willingness of some FBI and other security officials to leak information on Soviet espionage to sympathetic journalists and members of Congress.

39. Benson and Warner, *Venona,* xiv, state that a reference (in Venona 441 KGB San Francisco to Moscow, 31 October 1943) to a new code book to replace the "Pobjeda" code was almost certainly to the replacement of the code book found by the Finns at Petsamo. Elizabeth Bentley FBI deposition, 30 November 1945, FBI file 65-14603, obtained under the Freedom of Information Act. The text of this deposition is also present in the Silvermaster file (FBI file 65-56402).

40. Moscow circular, 25 April 1944, reprinted in Benson and Warner, *Venona,* 259.

41. Clarke's discussion with Rowlett and Hays was reported to Robert Louis Benson in a 1992 interview with Rowlett and Oliver Kirby; see Michael Warner and Robert Louis Benson, "Venona and Beyond: Thoughts on Work Undone," *Intelligence and National Security* 12, no. 3 (July 1997), 1–13. The warning off of the OSS was reported in Timothy J. Naftali, "X-2 and the Counterintelligence Response to Soviet Espionage," a paper presented at the "Venona Conference," 4 October 1996, Washington, D.C.

42. Currie's intervention on behalf of Silvermaster was verbal, and a record exists only because two of the recipients of his efforts made written records of the contacts.

43. Michael Dobbs, "The Man Who Picked the Lock," *Washington Post* (19 October 1996); Benson and Warner, *Venona,* xxviii.

44. Venona messages regarding Link are cited in appendix A.

45. Benson and Warner, *Venona,* xxviii.

46. Larry Kerley testimony, 15 September 1949, "Communist Activities Among Aliens and National Groups," U.S. Congress, Senate, Committee on the Judiciary, Subcommittee on Immigration and Naturalization, 81st Cong., 1st sess., part 2, 811. Venona messages regarding Sabatini are cited in appendix A.

47. Mask 1959/H, Comintern Moscow to Amsterdam 13, 5 January 1935, and

Mask 3760/H, Comintern Moscow to Amsterdam 326, 3 September 1935, Mask collection, National Cryptologic Museum, Fort Meade, Md.; Roster and assignment list of American Communists with the International Brigades, Archive of the International Brigades, RTsKhIDNI 545-6-846; FBI memorandum, "Existing Corroboration of Bentley's Overall Testimony," 6 May 1955, FBI Silvermaster file (FBI file 65-56402), serial 4201.

48. Venona messages regarding York are cited in appendix A.

49. Jones York statement of 6 October 1953, in William Wolf Weisband background memo, 27 November 1953, in Office of Security, National Security Agency, reproduced in Benson and Warner, *Venona*, 167-169.

50. Weisband background memo in Benson and Warner, *Venona*, 170; also see xxviii. Weisband's wife, also an NSA employee, lost her job as well.

51. From a KGB document released in 1998, quoted in Nigel West and Oleg Tsarev, *The Crown Jewels: The British Secrets at the Heart of the KGB Archives* (London: HarperCollins, 1998; New Haven: Yale University Press, 1999), 182. Venona Project cryptanalysts comment that Philby's explanation, although adequate for warning Moscow that its cable traffic had been broken into, reflected a layman's muddled understanding of cryptanalysis in that it exaggerated the assistance provided by early computers in sorting messages for duplications, overplayed how the burnt code book (which was in American, not British, hands) had been used up to that time (only as a model of Soviet code-making), and misunderstood the way Trade messages assisted solutions.

52. There are many detailed books on the five; summaries of their espionage careers appear in Christopher Andrew and Oleg Gordievsky, *KGB: The Inside Story* (New York: HarperCollins, 1990), and West and Tsarev, *The Crown Jewels*. Burgess, the student, actually first recruited Blunt, the don.

53. Venona 1271-1274 KGB New York to Moscow, 7 September 1944. Venona messages regarding Maclean are cited in appendix C.

54. Venona 1105-1110 KGB New York to Moscow, 2-3 August 1944.

55. On the damage done to American security by the three, see Vern W. Newton, *The Cambridge Spies: The Untold Story of Maclean, Philby, and Burgess in America* (Lanham, Md.: Madison Books, 1991).

56. Based on KGB documents released in 1998, Nigel West concluded that Philby's warning about Fuchs, passed on to Guy Burgess in September 1949, did not reach Moscow until February 1950, by which time MI5 already had Fuchs under surveillance. The delay was due to poor microfilming and carelessness on Burgess's part, brought about by his alcoholism and increasingly erratic mental state. West and Tsarev, *The Crown Jewels*, 180-181.

Chapter 3: The American Communist Party Underground

1. "Communist Party Manifesto," reprinted in Joint Legislative Committee Investigating Seditious Activities, *Revolutionary Radicalism, Its History, Purpose and Tactics, with an Exposition and Discussion of the Steps Being Taken and Required to Curb It* (Albany: J. B. Lyon, 1920), 782. Emphasis in the original.

2. On the early history of the American Communist movement, see Harvey Klehr and John Earl Haynes, *The American Communist Movement: Storming Heaven Itself* (New York: Twayne, 1992); Theodore Draper, *The Roots of American Communism* (New York: Viking, 1957); Theodore Draper, *American Communism and Soviet Russia, The Formative Period* (New York: Viking, 1960).

3. On the relationship of the American Communist party to the Comintern in light

of documents from Russian archives, see Harvey Klehr, John Earl Haynes, and Kyrill M. Anderson, *The Soviet World of American Communism* (New Haven: Yale University Press, 1998).

4. Quoted in Theodore Draper, *American Communism and Soviet Russia*, 298.

5. William Z. Foster, *Toward Soviet America* (New York: International Publishers, 1932), 67, 212–213, 275, 317.

6. Protocol II, Session of the Illegal Commission, 4 May 1923, Archive of the Illegal Commission of the Comintern, RTsKhIDNI 495-27-1.

7. *Daily Worker* (17 October 1929); "Resolutions of the Political Secretariat of the ECCI on the Situation and Tasks of the CPUSA," folder 1, box 1, and B. Vasiliev, "How the Communist International Formulates at Present the Problem of Organization," folder 21, box 1, Theodore Draper papers, Emory University Library, Atlanta, Ga.; Lozovsky, "The Trade Unions and the Coming War," and Vasiliev, "The Communist Parties on the Anti-Militarist Front," both in *Communist International* 8, no. 14 (15 August 1931).

8. A detailed account of the CPUSA's underground, based on documents from Russian archives, can be found in Harvey Klehr, John Earl Haynes, and Fridrikh Igorevich Firsov, *The Secret World of American Communism* (New Haven: Yale University Press, 1995).

9. "Autobiography of J. Peter of C.P.U.S.A.," 25 January 1932, and "Report Peters, Joseph . . . ," 15 October 1947, both in Archive of Personnel Files of the Comintern, RTsKhIDNI 495-261-5584.

10. "Brief on the Work of the CPUSA Secret Apparatus," 26 January 1939, Archive of the Dimitrov Secretariat of the Comintern, RTsKhIDNI 495-74-472. Rudy Baker, Peters's successor as head of the secret apparatus, prepared this memo for the Comintern.

11. Paul Crouch testimony, "Communist Underground Printing Facilities and Illegal Propaganda," U.S. Congress, Senate, Committee on the Judiciary, Subcommittee to Investigate the Administration of the Internal Security Act and Other Internal Security Laws, 83d Cong., 1st sess., 4–9, 24–63.

12. On the Ware group, see Earl Latham, *The Communist Controversy in Washington: From the New Deal to McCarthy* (Cambridge: Harvard University Press, 1966), 101–123; Joseph Lash, *Dealers and Dreamers* (New York: Doubleday, 1988), 218. After leaving the AAA, Weyl directed the CPUSA's "School on Wheels," a mobile classroom that toured agricultural areas tutoring farmers in communism. He left the CPUSA in 1939 in reaction to the Nazi-Soviet Pact and broke his silence after the Korean War began. He wrote two books: *Treason: The Story of Disloyalty and Betrayal in American History* (Washington, D.C.: Public Affairs Press, 1950) and *The Battle Against Disloyalty* (New York: Crowell, 1951).

13. John Abt with Michael Myerson, *Advocate and Activist: Memoirs of an American Communist Lawyer* (Urbana: University of Illinois Press, 1993), 39–46.

14. Elinor Langer, "The Secret Drawer," *The Nation* (30 May 1994), 756.

15. The Nazi-Soviet Pact initiated a rethinking on Davis's part that led her out of the party. Earlier her husband had developed mental problems and killed himself. Hope Hale Davis, *Great Day Coming: A Memoir of the 1930s* (South Royalton, Vt.: Steerforth Press, 1994), 30–40, 66–69, 81, 98, 222, 331–332; Testimony of Herbert Fuchs, 13 December 1955, "Investigation of Communist Infiltration of Government," U.S. Congress, House of Representatives, Committee on Un-American Activities, 84th Cong., 1st sess., part 1, 2955–3033.

16. For documentation on the manipulation of government agencies see Klehr,

Haynes, and Firsov, *The Secret World of American Communism,* 96–106; Earl Latham, *The Communist Controversy in Washington,* 124–150.

17. Unsigned [William Dodd] to Mr. President, 19 October 1936, Archive of the Communist Party of the USA, RTsKhIDNI 515-1-4077. Dodd's copy of this letter is in box 49, William E. Dodd papers, Manuscript Division, Library of Congress, Washington, D.C. "Excerpt of a Letter Enclosed to Judge Moore," date-stamped 5 January 1937, archive of the CPUSA, RTsKhIDNI 515-1-4077. The description of Bullitt as "not undangerous" referred to his anti-Soviet attitudes. Bullitt was the first U.S. ambassador to Moscow following Roosevelt's diplomatic recognition of the Soviet Union in 1933. He began his service in Moscow as an enthusiastic supporter of American-Soviet friendship but ended it highly suspicious of Stalin's foreign policy. Among FDR's close advisers Bullitt was one of the strongest anti-Soviet voices.

18. Chambers's CPUSA-GRU network is described in great detail in Whittaker Chambers, *Witness* (New York: Random House, 1952), Sam Tanenhaus, *Whittaker Chambers: A Biography* (New York: Random House, 1997), and Allen Weinstein, *Perjury: The Hiss-Chambers Case* (New York: Random House, 1997), see particularly 115, 137, 204–211.

19. "Brief on the Work of the CPUSA Secret Apparatus."

20. New York FBI memo, 10 February 1947, Comintern Apparatus file (FBI file 100-203581), serial 5392.

21. Baker biographical report, January 1939, Archive of the Dimitrov Secretariat of the Comintern, RTsKhIDNI 495-74-472; "Brief on the Work of the CPUSA Secret Apparatus." On Baker's role in the Pan-Pacific Trade Union Secretariat, see Klehr, Haynes, and Firsov, *The Secret World of American Communism,* 59–60.

22. Venona 1043 KGB New York to Moscow, 25 July 1944; 1286 KGB New York to Moscow, 8 September 1944. Baker occurs in the Venona traffic only under his cover name, Son. NSA/FBI analysts never identified Son as Baker because the two messages about Son provided few clues to his identity. For the identification of Son as Baker see appendix A.

23. Father and Son to Brother, "We discussed . . . ," 13 February 1940, and "Propose you again . . . ," undated, both in Archive of the Secretariat of the Executive Committee of the Communist International: coded correspondence with Communist parties (1933–1943), RTsKhIDNI 495-184-4 (1939–1940 file); Son to Brother, 2 April 1942, RTsKhIDNI 495-184-19 (1942 files); Son to Brother with attached "Son Financial Statement for 1942," Archive of the Dimitrov Secretariat of the Comintern, RTsKhIDNI 495-74-480.

24. Son to Brother with attached "Son Financial Statement for 1942."

25. Brother to Son and Earl, 2 September 1939, and Brother to Earl for Son, 15 September 1939, both in Archive of the Secretariat of the Executive Committee of the Communist International: coded correspondence with Communist Parties (1933–1943), RTsKhIDNI 495-184-8 (1939 file).

26. Son to Brother with attached "Son Financial Statement for 1942."

27. Father and Son to Brother, "We discussed . . . ," 13 February 1940, and Son to Comintern, 22 February 1940, both in Archive of the Secretariat of the Executive Committee of the Communist International: coded correspondence with Communist Parties (1933–1943), RTsKhIDNI 495-184-4, 1939–1940 file. Microdots were extremely tiny bits of microfilm, generally holding the image of a single sheet of paper. They could be glued under a stamp or envelope flap or otherwise hidden in a letter so as to escape all but the most rigorous examination by a government inspector checking international mail.

28. Brother to Earl, 15 September 1939, Archive of the Secretariat of the Executive Committee of the Communist International: coded correspondence with Communist Parties (1933–1943), RTsKhIDNI 495-184-8 (1939 file).

29. Brother to Son, July 1942, Archive of the Secretariat of the Executive Committee of the Communist International: coded correspondence with Communist Parties (1933–1943), RTsKhIDNI 495-184-5 (1942 file).

30. Son to Dimitrov, 19 April 1943, Archive of the Secretariat of the Executive Committee of the Communist International: coded correspondence with Communist Parties (1933–1943), RTsKhIDNI 495-184-7 (1943 file).

31. George Mink autobiographical statement, 29 April 1932, Archive of Personnel Files of the Comintern, RTsKhIDNI 495-261-1667.

32. "Comintern Apparatus Summary Report," 15 December 1944, FBI Comintern Apparatus file, serial 3702.

33. Brother to Son, 2 October 1941, Archive of the Secretariat of the Executive Committee of the Communist International: coded correspondence with Communist Parties (1933–1943), RTsKhIDNI 495-184-3 (1941 file).

34. Son to Brother with attached "Son Financial Statement for 1942."

35. The FBI summary of the recorded conversation is found in "Interlocking Subversion in Government Departments," U.S. Congress, Senate, Committee on the Judiciary, Subcommittee to Investigate the Administration of the Internal Security Act and Other Internal Security Laws, 83d Cong., 1st sess., part 15, 1050–1051. See also Federal Bureau of Investigation, *Soviet Activities in the United States,* 25 July 1946, Clark M. Clifford papers, Harry S. Truman Library, Independence, Mo.; FBI memo on Nelson-Zubilin meeting, 22 October 1944, Comintern Apparatus file, serial 3515; J. Edgar Hoover to Harry Hopkins, 7 May 1943, and CIA memorandum "COMRAP—Vassili M. Zubilin," 6 February 1948, both reproduced in Robert Louis Benson and Michael Warner, eds., *Venona: Soviet Espionage and the American Response, 1939–1957* (Washington, D.C.: National Security Agency, Central Intelligence Agency, 1996), 49–50, 105–115.

36. A transcript of Miyagi's statement to Japanese security police about his recruitment by Yano is reprinted in "Hearings on American Aspects of the Richard Sorge Spy Case," U.S. Congress, House of Representatives, Committee on Un-American Activities, 82d Cong., 1st sess., 1190–1193. Also see discussions of Miyagi's role in the Sorge network in Gordon W. Prange with Donald M. Goldstein and Katherine V. Dillon, *Target Tokyo: The Story of the Sorge Spy Ring* (New York: McGraw-Hill, 1984); "The Case of Richard Sorge," in *Covert Warfare,* vol. 7, John Mendelsohn, ed. (New York: Garland, 1989); and Chalmers Johnson, *An Instance of Treason: Ozaki Hotsumi and the Sorge Spy Ring* (Stanford: Stanford University Press, 1990).

37. Dimitrov to Browder, 21 September 1940, Archive of the Secretariat of the Executive Committee of the Communist International: coded correspondence with Communist Parties (1933–1943), RTsKhIDNI 495-184-15 (1940 file).

38. Hede Massing, *This Deception* (New York: Duell, Sloan and Pearce, 1951), 164–178. KGB documents confirming Massing's account are cited in Weinstein, *Perjury,* 182–184.

39. Flora Lewis, *Red Pawn: The Story of Noel Field* (New York: Doubleday, 1965).

40. Fitin to Dimitrov, 2 November 1942, Archive of the Secretariat of the Executive Committee of the Communist International: coded correspondence with Communist Parties (1933–1943), RTsKhIDNI 495-74-485.

41. Brother to Earl, 13 September 1939, Archive of the Secretariat of the Executive

Committee of the Communist International: coded correspondence with Communist Parties (1933–1943), RTsKhIDNI 495-184-8 (1939 file).

42. FBI memorandum, "Existing Corroboration of Bentley's Overall Testimony"; Elizabeth Bentley, *Out of Bondage: The Story of Elizabeth Bentley* (New York: Ivy Books, 1988), 254–255, 327; Winston Burdett testimony, 29 June 1955, Hearings, Strategy and Tactics of World Communism, Recruiting for Espionage, U.S. Congress, Senate, Committee on the Judiciary, Subcommittee to Investigate the Administration of the Internal Security Act and Other Internal Security Laws, 84th Cong., 1st sess., part 14, pp. 1324–1363.

43. Son [Rudy Baker] to Comintern, 22 February 1940, Archive of the Secretariat of the Executive Committee of the Communist International: coded correspondence with Communist Parties (1933–1943), RTsKhIDNI 495-184-4 (1939–1940 file); New York FBI office memorandum, 3 December 1945, serial 292; Washington FBI office memo, 1 November 1946, serial 464; Scheidt to Hoover, 31 January 1947, serial 1976, all in FBI Silvermaster file (FBI file 65-56402).

44. Venona 1221 KGB New York to Moscow, 26 August 1944.

45. Rhodes background report, 16 November 1945, FBI Silvermaster file, serial 108.

46. Elizabeth Bentley FBI deposition, 30 November 1945, FBI file 65-14603.

47. Scheidt to Hoover, 3 June 1947, serial 2504; Rhodes interview report, 7 June 1947, serial 2583, both in FBI Silvermaster file.

48. Karl [Whittaker Chambers], "The Faking of Americans," Herbert Solow papers, Hoover Institution on War, Revolution and Peace, Stanford University, Stanford, Calif.

49. Karl, "The Faking of Americans."

50. Chambers, *Witness*, 355–356; Karl, "The Faking of Americans."

51. U.S. Department of State Passport Division brief on a conspiracy charge against World Tourists and the CPUSA, prepared in 1939–1940 by Anthony J. Nicholas, reprinted in "Scope of Soviet Activity in the United States," U.S. Congress, Senate, Committee on the Judiciary, Subcommittee to Investigate the Administration of the Internal Security Act, 85th Cong., 1st sess., appendix I, part 23-A, A8, A84, A85, A87, A94, A102, A116, A117, A121, A124.

52. Several Americans who served in the International Brigades in Spain reported seeing Mink there as an officer of the military security police, a body supervised by Aleksandr Orlov, a senior KGB officer. Some sources have it that Mink was later executed or imprisoned in the USSR in Stalin's purge of the International Brigades veterans who had sought exile in the Soviet Union in 1939. On Mink's later fate see Dorothy Gallagher, *All the Right Enemies: The Life and Murder of Carlo Tresca* (New Brunswick, N.J.: Rutgers University Press, 1988), 158–161; Testimony of William C. McCuiston, 12 April 1940, "Investigation of Un-American Propaganda Activities in the United States," U.S. Congress, House of Representatives, Special Committee on Un-American Activities, part 13, 7826–7828; Herbert Romerstein and Stanislav Levchenko, *The KGB Against the "Main Enemy"* (Lexington, Mass.: Lexington Books, 1989), 140.

53. State Department passport brief, A115–A116. Josephson's role in procuring Eisler's fraudulent passport is elaborated in "Investigation of Un-American Propaganda Activities in the United States," hearings of 6 February 1947, U.S. Congress, House of Representatives, Committee on Un-American Activities, 80th Cong., 1st sess., 14–19.

54. "Investigations of Un-American Propaganda Activities in the United States (Regarding Leon Josephson and Samuel Liptzen)," U.S. Congress, House of Representatives, Committee on Un-American Activities, 80th Cong., 1st sess., 5 and 21 March 1947.

55. FBI memorandum, "John Loomis Sherman Background and Personal History," FBI file 65-14920, serial 3221; Chambers, *Witness,* 52–54, 290–310; Weinstein, *Perjury,* 99, 105–110, 171, 204, 281; Allen Weinstein, "Nadya: A Spy Story," *Encounter* (June 1977); Tanenhaus, *Whittaker Chambers,* 85–86, 89–90; William Crane FBI file 74-1333, serial 2706.

56. Passport Division brief, A80, A89–90; David Hornstein, *Arthur Ewert: A Life for the Comintern* (Lanham, Md.: University Press of America, 1993), 153–154, 244–258.

57. Herbert Solow, "Stalin's American Passport Mill," *American Mercury* (July 1939).

58. Alan Cullison, "How Stalin Repaid the Support of Americans," Associated Press story, *Washington Times* (9 November 1997); Chambers, *Witness,* 355–357, 399–400; Weinstein, *Perjury,* 544n; Arnold Ikal suppression file, interrogation by NKVD [KGB], 8 January 1939. The authors thank the Associated Press reporter Alan Cullison for access to his copy of Ikal's NKVD suppression file.

59. Passport Division brief, A5-A32.

60. Two case studies of the mixture of success and excess of this system are Carl H. Chrislock's *Watchdog of Loyalty: The Minnesota Commission of Public Safety During World War I* (St. Paul: Minnesota Historical Society Press, 1991) and, on the American Protective League, Joan M. Jensen, *The Price of Vigilance* (Chicago: Rand McNally, 1968).

61. The titles of the FBI predecessors were the Bureau of Investigation, from 1908 to 1933, and the Division of Investigation, from June 1933 to July 1935.

62. Roosevelt to the Secretary of State et al., 26 June 1939, President's Secretary's Files (Confidential File), "State 1939–40," box 9, Franklin D. Roosevelt Library, Hyde Park, New York, reproduced in Benson and Warner, *Venona,* 13.

63. This description refers to security or counterintelligence. In regard to the gathering of foreign intelligence, FDR assigned chief responsibility to the Army for Europe, to the Navy for the Pacific, and to the FBI for the Western Hemisphere. The later creation of the Office of Strategic Services, however, would confuse this division of responsibility.

64. Hoover memo, "Present Status of Espionage and Counter Espionage Operations of the Federal Bureau of Investigation," 24 October 1940, attached to Hoover to Maj. Gen. Edwin Watson (secretary to the president), 25 October 1940, White House Official Files, "Justice Department—FBI Reports," box 12, FDR Library, reproduced in Benson and Warner, *Venona,* 15–26. On American counterintelligence against German and Japanese espionage, see Frank J. Rafalko, ed., *A Counterintelligence Reader,* vol. 2, *Counterintelligence in World War II* (n.p.: U.S. National Counterintelligence Center, 1998).

65. The Venona cables that deal with each of these persons are cited in appendix A.

66. For citations to the espionage activities of these persons see appendix B.

67. Berle diary entry of 2 September 1939, quoted in Weinstein, *Perjury,* 58. Berle's notes of his meeting with Chambers are reproduced in "Interlocking Subversion in Government Departments," 6 May 1953, part 6, 329–330. Levine's notes of the meeting are in the Chambers file of the Isaac Don Levine Papers, Emory University Library, Atlanta, Ga.

68. Joseph Lash, *Dealers and Dreamers,* 442.

69. For a chronology of the contact between Berle, Chambers, and the FBI, see Ladd to Hoover, 29 December 1948, reproduced in Benson and Warner, *Venona,* 121–128.

Chapter 4: The Golos-Bentley Network

1. Jacob Golos autobiographical questionnaire prepared by Golos, undated but information indicates post-1927, Archive of Personnel Files of the Comintern, RTsKhIDNI 495-261-466; Elizabeth Bentley, *Out of Bondage: The Story of Elizabeth Bentley* (New York: Ivy Books, 1988), 143–144; Anthony Cave Brown and Charles B. MacDonald, *On a Field of Red: The Communist International and the Coming of World War II* (New York: Putnam, 1981), 340–342, 345. Golos's birth name is sometimes rendered Rasin. One 1946 FBI background memo on Golos puts his Siberian experience and escape via Japan in 1916–1918, but this dating seems erroneous; it was probably earlier. New York Field Office report, 7 January 1946, FBI Silvermaster file (FBI file 65-56402), serial 420.

2. One indirect (and inconclusive) piece of evidence supporting his having been in the Soviet Union in 1919–1923 is a 1928 letter from the Kuzbas Autonomous Industrial Colony to the Comintern. This colony had been founded in the early 1920s in the Kuzbas region of Siberia and consisted of coal mining and associated industrial projects staffed by American radicals who sought to bring American technology to the aid of the new socialist state. The letter announced that the project needed a new administrator and suggested that the Comintern consider Golos because he understood both American and Russian conditions. Possibly this is a reference to his having been in the Soviet Union in the early 1920s and even having been at the Kuzbas project itself; the story he told Bentley included his having been in Siberia and at a coal mine. L. J. Rutgers to Comintern, 8 October 1928, Archive of the Communist Party of the USA, RTsKhIDNI 515-1-507.

3. Jacob Golos later told Bentley that Bayer was part of a Soviet military intelligence (GRU) network. This is confirmed by Venona, in which three GRU messages refer to Bayer as a GRU source under the cover name Simon. Venona messages regarding Bayer are cited in appendix A.

4. FBI interview with John Reynolds, 7 June 1947, FBI Silvermaster file, serial 2503.

5. Venona 1673 KGB New York to Moscow, 30 November 1944; 1802 KGB New York to Moscow, 21 December 1944.

6. Elizabeth Bentley deposition, 30 November 1945, FBI file 65-14603; Bentley, *Out of Bondage,* 108, 176–177.

7. Rose Arenal later confirmed Bentley's story. FBI memorandum, "Existing Corroboration of Bentley's Overall Testimony," 6 May 1955, FBI Silvermaster file, serial 4201.

8. Venona messages regarding Price are cited in appendix A.

9. For a summary of Akhmerov's KGB career see appendix E. Venona messages about him are cited in appendix A.

10. Venona 1065 KGB New York to Moscow, 28 July 1944.

11. Don S. Kirschner, *Cold War Exile: The Unclosed Case of Maurice Halperin* (Columbia: University of Missouri Press, 1995), 130–131, 314–316.

12. Venona 887 KGB New York to Moscow, 9 June 1943; 921–922, 924 KGB New York to Moscow, 16 June 1943; 931 KGB New York to Moscow, 17 June 1943; 1019, 1021, 1024, 1034 KGB New York to Moscow, 29 June 1943; 1106 KGB New York to Moscow, 8 July 1943; 1162 KGB New York to Moscow, 17 July 1943; 1189 KGB New York to Moscow, 21 July 1943. See also Hayden B. Peake, "OSS and the Venona Decrypts," *Intelligence and National Security* 12, no. 3 (July 1997).

13. Venona messages regarding Halperin are cited in appendix A.

14. Kirschner, *Cold War Exile,* 76–77, 86–94, 98–104.

15. FBI report, 29 May 1947, FBI Silvermaster file, serial 2540; FBI report, 7 June 1947, FBI Silvermaster file, serial 2583; Kirschner, *Cold War Exile,* 282–288.

16. Kirschner, *Cold War Exile,* 272, 324.

17. Washington Field Office report, "Re: Lt. Col. Duncan C. Lee," 28 January 1946, FBI Silvermaster file.

18. Bentley deposition.

19. Bentley deposition.

20. Hitler got wind that his Hungarian allies were considering surrender, and in October 1944 German forces occupied Hungary, took direct control of its government, and imprisoned the OSS agents in Hungary who were negotiating the deal. The authors are grateful to Robert Goldberg, son of Arthur Goldberg (future Cabinet member and Supreme Court justice), one of the OSS authors of the Sparrow mission, for sharing his research into his father's suspicion that the Soviets, alerted to the Sparrow mission by Lee, deliberately leaked it to the Nazis to ensure that Hungary and the Balkans would come under Soviet domination.

21. Duncan Lee interview report, 4 June 1947, FBI Silvermaster file, serial 2530. Robert Goldberg brought the Lees' Moscow honeymoon to our attention.

22. Venona messages regarding Lee are cited in appendix A.

23. Venona 782 KGB New York to Moscow, 26 May 1943.

24. Bentley, *Out of Bondage,* 182.

25. Venona 1325–1326 KGB New York to Moscow, 15 September 1944.

26. Venona 1354 KGB New York to Moscow, 22 September 1944. In an act that is a serious barrier to historical accuracy, the NSA redacted—that is, blacked out—the names of Communists and Soviet sources contained in this message, with the single exception of the name of Donald Wheeler.

27. Venona 954 KGB Moscow to New York, 20 September 1944.

28. Testimony of Julius J. Joseph, 26 April 1953, "Interlocking Subversion in Government Departments," U.S. Congress, Senate, Committee on the Judiciary, Subcommittee to Investigate the Administration of the Internal Security Act and Other Internal Security Laws, 83d Cong., 1st sess., part 10, 605–621; FBI memo, "Underground Soviet Espionage Organization (NKVD) in Agencies of the United States Government," enclosed with D. M. Ladd to Director, 21 February 1946, serial 573, Hottel to Director, 13 January 1947, serial 2034, and Hottel to Hoover, 17 November 1947, serial 3009, all in FBI Silvermaster file.

29. Bentley deposition; Venona messages regarding Julius and Bella Joseph are cited in appendix A.

30. Julius Joseph testimony, 26 May 1953, "Interlocking Subversion in Government Departments," part 10, 615.

31. Venona 1464 KGB New York to Moscow, 14 October 1944. It is not known whether the KGB made contact with her in Ceylon.

32. Bentley deposition; Bentley, *Out of Bondage,* 139–140.

33. Cedric Belfrage interview, 8 June 1947, FBI Silvermaster file, serial 2522; Cedric Belfrage statement, 3 June 1947, FBI Silvermaster file, serial 2583.

34. Venona messages regarding Belfrage are cited in appendix A.

35. Cedric Belfrage, *The Frightened Giant: My Unfinished Affair with America* (London: Secker and Warburg, 1957) and *The American Inquisition, 1945–1960* (Indianapolis: Bobbs-Merrill, 1973).

36. Bentley deposition.

37. Bentley, *Out of Bondage,* 138–139; Bentley deposition; OSS report, secret, "Spain, Communist Party of Catalonia," 8 July 1943, archives of the Dimitrov Secretariat of the Comintern, RTsKhIDNI 495-74-481; Ladd memo on Mary Price interview, 18 April 1947, FBI Silvermaster file, serial 2340. Venona messages regarding Tenney are cited in appendix A.

38. Strickland memo on Tenney, 6 June 1946, FBI Silvermaster file, serial 1195; Ladd to Director 15 January 1947, FBI Silvermaster file, serial 2081.

39. Scheidt to Hoover, 12 February 1947, FBI Silvermaster file, serial 2407; Ladd to Hoover, 6 June 1947, FBI Silvermaster file, serial 2547; Bentley, *Out of Bondage,* 209–210.

40. Bentley deposition; Earl Latham, *The Communist Controversy in Washington: From the New Deal to McCarthy* (Cambridge: Harvard University Press, 1966), 306–307.

41. Michael Greenberg interview, 7 June 1947, FBI Silvermaster file, serial 2583.

42. Nor did either know that one of Miller's subordinates at the Office of the Coordinator of Inter-American Affairs, Charles Flato, was also a Soviet agent.

43. FBI report on Joseph Gregg, 11 March 1946, FBI Silvermaster file, serial 674.

44. FBI memo on Robert Talbott Miller III, 24 January 1948, FBI Silvermaster file, serial 3085; Robert T. Miller interview, 21 April 1947, FBI Silvermaster file, serial 2349.

Chapter 5: Friends in High Places

1. Venona messages regarding Perlo are cited in appendix A.

2. Bentley could not clearly remember the date, except that it was a rainy Sunday in March. She had also remembered that one participant, Harry Magdoff, had been on sick leave recovering from an operation and was about to return to work at the War Production Board. The FBI checked and found that Magdoff had been on sick leave from January 10 to March 7 for a gall bladder operation, and that it had rained in New York on both Sunday, February 27, and March 5. The bureau was inclined to regard the latter date as the most likely. Elizabeth Bentley FBI deposition, 30 November 1945, FBI file 65-14603; Elizabeth Bentley, *Out of Bondage: The Story of Elizabeth Bentley* (New York: Ivy Books, 1988), 163–165; New York FBI memo, 16 January 1947, FBI Silvermaster file (FBI file 65-56402), serial 1936.

3. Venona 588 KGB New York to Moscow, 29 April 1944; 687 KGB New York to Moscow, 13 May 1944; 769 and 771 KGB New York to Moscow, 30 May 1944.

4. Venona messages regarding each person are cited in appendix A.

5. Testimony of Herbert Fuchs, "Investigation of Communist Infiltration of Government"; Testimony of Allan Rosenberg, 21 February 1956, "Investigation of Communist Infiltration of Government," U.S. Congress, House of Representatives, Committee on Un-American Activities, 84th Cong., 2nd sess., part 4, 3300–3307; Earl Latham, *The Communist Controversy in Washington: From the New Deal to McCarthy* (Cambridge: Harvard University Press, 1966), 121–131.

6. Jane Foster, *An Un-American Lady* (London: Sidgwick and Jackson, 1980), 105.

7. Akhmerov's Storm/Peters cable is quoted in Allen Weinstein, *Perjury: The Hiss-Chambers Case* (New York: Random House, 1997), 184.

8. "Report Peters, Joseph . . . ," 15 October 1947, Archive of Personnel Files of the Comintern, RTsKhIDNI 495-261-5584.

9. The quoted material is from Bolshakov to Dimitrov, 5 May 1943, Archive of the Dimitrov Secretariat of the Comintern, RTsKhIDNI 495-74-486.

10. Ilichev to Dimitrov, 5 March 1943, Archive of the Dimitrov Secretariat of the Comintern, RTsKhIDNI 495-74-486. General Ilichev headed the GRU.

11. Venona 588 KGB New York to Moscow, 29 April 1944.

12. Also strengthening the possibility that Storm is Peters is the relationship with John Abt. In late 1943 the FBI opened an investigation of Abt, the intermediary with this group before it was handed over to Bentley and her CPUSA/KGB network. Its surveillance showed frequent meetings in the early months of 1944 between Abt and a man then known as Alexander Stevens, one of the several pseudonyms used by Josef Peters. New York FBI report, 9 April 1944, John Jacob Abt FBI file 100-236194, serial 6.

13. Venona 588 KGB New York to Moscow, 29 April 1944.

14. Fitin to Dimitrov, 28–29 September 1944, Archive of the Dimitrov Secretariat of the Comintern, RTsKhIDNI 495-74-485.

15. Bentley, *Out of Bondage,* 184. Given that Bentley reconstructed the conversation from memory, this should not be treated as if it were a transcript of Gromov's remarks.

16. Venona 1388–1389 KGB New York to Moscow, 1 October 1944.

17. On Bernard's secret relationship with the CPUSA and his later emergence as an open party member decades later, see John Earl Haynes, *Dubious Alliance: The Making of Minnesota's DFL Party* (Minneapolis: University of Minnesota Press, 1984), 29, 37, 55, 59, 224n.

18. Charles Kramer testimony, 6 May 1953, "Interlocking Subversion in Government Departments," Subcommittee to Investigate the Administration of the Internal Security Act and Other Internal Security Laws, U.S. Senate Committee on the Judiciary, 83d Cong., 1st sess., part 6, 327–381. Patterson had been discreetly allied with the CPUSA since the late 1930s. Harvey Klehr, *The Heyday of American Communism: The Depression Decade* (New York: Basic Books, 1984), 271–272, 403.

19. John Snyder to H. L. Lurie, 26 December 1947, reproduced in "Interlocking Subversion in Government Departments," part 2, 100.

20. Venona 769 and 771 KGB New York to Moscow, 30 May 1944.

21. Ladd to Director, 1 May 1947, serial 2380, memo on Glasser interview, 13 May 1947, serial 2429, both in FBI Silvermaster file; Glasser testimony, 14 April and 2 June 1953, "Interlocking Subversion in Government Departments," part 2, 53–100.

22. Whittaker Chambers, *Witness* (New York: Random House, 1952), 430.

23. Weinstein, *Perjury,* 326–327. The identification of Ales as Hiss is discussed in chapter 6.

24. Venona messages regarding Glasser are cited in appendix A.

25. Bentley deposition.

26. Venona 1759 KGB Washington to KGB Moscow, 28 March 1945.

27. Transcripts of Glasser's promotions and job rating forms signed by Coe, Ullmann, and White are in "Interlocking Subversion in Government Departments," part 2, 81–82, 98–99.

28. Hottel to Hoover, 14 January 1947, FBI Silvermaster file, serial 2028.

29. Edward Fitzgerald testimony, Harry Magdoff testimony, 1 May 1953, "Interlocking Subversion in Government Departments," part 5, 241–326; Perlo testimony, "Hearings Regarding Communist Espionage in the United States Government," U.S. Congress, House of Representatives, Committee on Un-American Activities, 80th Cong., 2d sess., 699–700; Victor Perlo, "Imperialism—New Features," *Political Affairs* (May 1981), 3; Vic Perlo, "Reply to Herbert Aptheker," *Political Affairs* (June 1992), 26.

30. Venona messages regarding these persons are cited in appendix A.

31. Venona 2011 KGB New York to Moscow, 11 December 1943.

32. Venona 1469 KGB New York to Moscow, 17 October 1944.

33. Real estate ad for 5515 30th Street, N.W., Washington, D.C., *Washington Star* (3 May 1947).

34. Kenneth Rexroth, *An Autobiographical Novel* (Santa Barbara, Calif.: Ross-Erikson, 1978), 278–279. The FBI's Seattle office identified Silvermaster as a Communist in 1922. See Silvermaster background memo, 16 November 1945, FBI Silvermaster file, Serial 26XI.

35. Patterson later became secretary of war under President Truman.

36. File card of Patterson contacts in regard Silvermaster, box 203, Robert P. Patterson papers, Library of Congress; General Bissell to General Strong, 3 June 1942, Silvermaster reply to Bissell memo, 9 June 1942, Robert P. Patterson to Milo Perkins of Board of Economic Warfare, 3 July 1942, all reprinted in "Interlocking Subversion in Government Departments," 30 August 1955, 84th Cong., 1st sess., part 30, 2562–2567; Lauchlin Currie testimony, 13 August 1948, U.S. Congress, House of Representatives, Committee on Un-American Activities, 80th Cong., 2d sess., 851–877. On Baldwin's secret Communist allegiances, see John Gates to Joseph Starobin, undated, box 10, folder 2, Philip Jaffe papers, Emory University Library, Atlanta, Ga.

37. Ladd to Hoover, 12 December 1945, FBI Silvermaster file, serial 235.

38. Paul Appleby to L. C. Martin and J. Weldon Jones, 23 March 1944, reprinted in "Interlocking Subversion in Government Departments," part 30, xii.

39. Venona 1388–1389 KGB New York to Moscow, 1 October 1944.

40. Venona 12, 13, 15, 16 KGB New York to Moscow, 4 January 1945.

41. Venona messages regarding Helen Silvermaster are cited in appendix A. Helen Silvermaster interview report, 21 April 1947, FBI Silvermaster file, serial 2349.

42. Venona 1635 KGB New York to Moscow, 21 November 1944. The reference to Silvermaster's wanting to "see the reward and the book" is to seeing the actual Soviet decoration and the official certificate ("book") in which the decoration is awarded to an individual. This was not the only KGB recognition Silvermaster received. He was at one time the only American citizen featured in the KGB's secret Hall of Fame in Moscow.

43. Venona messages regarding Gregory Silvermaster are cited in appendix A.

44. Venona messages regarding Ullmann are cited in appendix A.

45. Ladd to Hoover on White interview, 5 September 1947, FBI Silvermaster file, serial 2787; Ullmann interview report, 21 April 1947, FBI Silvermaster file, serial 2349.

46. Hope Hale Davis, "Looking Back at My Years in the Party," *New Leader* (11 February 1980).

47. Chambers, *Witness;* Weinstein, *Perjury,* 190–191.

48. Venona messages regarding Silverman are cited in appendix A.

49. Malcolm Hobbs, "Confident Wallace Aides Come Up with Startling Cabinet Notions," Overseas News Service dispatch, 22 April 1948, reprinted in "Interlocking Subversion in Government Departments," part 30, 2529–2530.

50. Bentley, *Out of Bondage,* 113.

51. Harvey Klehr and Ronald Radosh, *The Amerasia Spy Case: Prelude to McCarthyism* (Chapel Hill: University of North Carolina Press, 1996), 21–22, 37, 197, 159, 171–172. Mao Tse-tung and Chou En-lai to Dimitrov, 19 August 1940, Archive of the Secretariat of the Executive Committee of the Communist International: coded correspondence with Communist Parties (1933–1943), RTsKhIDNI 495-184-15, 1940 file.

52. Venona messages regarding White are cited in appendix A.

53. Venona 235–236 KGB San Francisco to Moscow, 5 May 1945.

54. Venona 1634 KGB New York to Moscow, 20 November 1944.

55. In the Venona cables White's cover name was first Jurist, then Lawyer, and finally Richard.

56. Venona 1119-1121 KGB New York to Moscow, 4-5 August 1944. The "new course" referred to a policy of American accommodation of Soviet foreign policy goals. Kolstov does not appear to have been a regular officer of the KGB stations in New York or Washington, but one visiting the United States from Moscow, probably posing as a diplomat in a high-level Soviet delegation, who could meet with a man of White's standing without attracting security attention.

57. Insert of 9 May 1945, *Morgenthau Diary (China),* vol. 2, hearing of 5 February 1965, U.S. Congress, Senate, Subcommittee to Investigate the Administration of the Internal Security Act and Other Internal Security Laws, 89th Cong., 1st sess., 1043.

58. In regard to White as an agent of influence, Vladimir Pavlov, a retired KGB officer, published a description of a clandestine meeting with White in 1941. Pavlov stated that he had met with White on KGB orders to urge him to promote a stern American policy toward Japan in order to relieve Japanese pressure on the USSR. While denying that White was a spy, Pavlov said that White had been in contact with the KGB through Iskhak Akhmerov and that the meeting itself was arranged by a Soviet spy who worked at the U.S. Treasury. V. Pavlov, "The Time Has Come to Talk about Operation 'Snow,' " *Novosti razvedki i kontrrazvedki* (News of intelligence and counterintelligence, Moscow, in Russian), nos. 9-10 and 11-12, 1995. Pavlov, under the cover of being the second secretary of the Soviet embassy in Ottawa, was the chief of the KGB Canadian station from 1942 to 1946. Pavlov is vague—purposefully misleading, it appears—on dates and other matters regarding the operation. The article was one of a number sanctioned by the Russian Foreign Intelligence Service which praised historic Soviet intelligence successes. Pavlov's essay portrayed the KGB as having saved Russia from a two-front war by promoting via White a tough American policy that provoked Japan into attacking south against the United States rather than north against the USSR. This is certainly an exaggeration of White's influence, although White did provide memorandums supporting a firm stand to Treasury Secretary Morgenthau to assist him in his discussion with other Roosevelt administration officials on what stance to take against Japan in the latter half of 1941. Like the similar Chikov article discussed in chapter 10, the mixture of truth, half-truth, and deliberate distortion in the essay makes Pavlov's reliability on any particular point uncertain.

59. Venona messages regarding Coe are cited in appendix A. His full name was Virginius Frank Coe.

60. Frank Coe testimony, 13 August 1948, "Hearings Regarding Communist Espionage in the United States Government," U.S. Congress, House of Representatives, Committee on Un-American Activities, 80th Cong., 2nd sess., 914-928; Frank Coe interview, 4 June 1947, FBI Silvermaster file, serial 2530; Benjamin Mandell report on Frank Coe, 12 November 1953, "Interlocking Subversion in Government Departments," part 16, 1073; Robert Alden, "Frank Coe Lauds Red China's Work," *New York Times* (21 February 1959), 4.

61. Solomon Adler interview, 19 December 1947, FBI Silvermaster file, serial 3030; Robert Morris statement, 18 November 1953, "Interlocking Subversion in Government Departments," part 16, 1163-1165.

62. Sidney Rittenberg and Amanda Bennett, *The Man Who Stayed Behind* (New York: Simon and Schuster, 1993), 251; *Selected Shanghai Culture and History Materials* (in Chinese), issue 43, April 1983, Shanghai People's Press; Henshen Chen, *Sige shidai de wo* (My life during four ages, in Chinese) (Beijing: Chinese Culture and History Press,

1988). The authors thank Professor Maochun Yu for calling our attention to the latter two Chinese sources. When the United States established diplomatic relations with the People's Republic of China, Adler petitioned for and received restoration of his American citizenship.

63. Anthony Kubek in *How the Far East Was Lost: American Policy and the Creation of Communist China, 1941–1949* (Chicago: Regnery, 1963) presents a scholarly version of this theme.

64. Chambers, *Witness,* 468; Berle's notes, reproduced in "Interlocking Subversion in Government Departments," 6 May 1953, part 6, 329–330.

65. Venona messages regarding Currie are cited in appendix A.

66. Venona 143 KGB Moscow to New York, 15 February 1945.

67. Venona 253 KGB Moscow to New York, 20 March 1945.

68. "Underground Soviet Espionage Organization (NKVD) in Agencies of the United States Government," 21 February 1946, FBI Silvermaster file, serial 573; Report on Currie interview, 31 July 1947, FBI Silvermaster file, serial 2794; Michael Warner and Robert Louis Benson, "Venona and Beyond: Thoughts on Work Undone," *Intelligence and National Security* 12, no. 3 (July 1997), 10–11; Anonymous Russian letter to Hoover, 7 August 1943, reproduced in Robert Louis Benson and Michael Warner, eds., *Venona: Soviet Espionage and the American Response, 1939–1957* (Washington, D.C.: National Security Agency, Central Intelligence Agency, 1996), 51–54.

69. Although an open ally of the CPUSA and an ardent Stalinist, Robeson refused to acknowledge his membership in the CPUSA during his lifetime. In 1998, however, the CPUSA announced that he had been a secret member. "World to Honor Robeson May 3," *People's Weekly World* (21 March 1998).

70. In the late 1930s the National Negro Congress grew rapidly and had prospects of becoming a major influence among African Americans. The CPUSA's insistence, however, that it follow the policy requirement of the Nazi-Soviet Pact caused many black activists who had joined it to leave in disgust, including the organization's most prominent figure, A. Philip Randolph.

71. Zola Clear, a member of the executive committee of the Washington Committee for Aid to China, resigned to protest the group's treatment of Pinchot and Roosevelt and testified to the Dies Committee with material supplied by Cornelia Pinchot. Clear to Pinchot, 6 October 1941, and Pinchot to Clear, 17 October 1941, both in the Washington Committee for Aid to China folders, box 398, Cornelia Pinchot Papers, Manuscript Division, Library of Congress; Zola Clear testimony and insert of 13 April 1941 statement of Cornelia Bryce Pinchot, 7 August 1941, "Investigation of Un-American Propaganda Activities in the United States," U.S. Congress, House of Representatives, Special Committee on Un-American Activities, 78th Cong., 2d sess., 2361–13881.

72. Currie testimony, U.S. Congress, House of Representatives, Committee on Un-American Activities, 13 August 1948, 80th Cong., 2d sess., 851–877.

73. Bentley and Rankin exchange, 31 July 1948, "Hearings Regarding Communist Espionage in the United States Government," 557–558.

74. The year 1950 was a high point in Soviet intelligence contacts' fleeing the United States. In addition to Currie, also emigrating that year (some publicly and some secretly) were Solomon Adler, Morris and Lona Cohen, Joseph Barr, Alfred Sarant, Henry and Beatrice Spitz, and Abraham Chapman. Also in 1950 the physicist Bruno Pontecorvo, a Soviet source who had worked on the American atomic bomb project, fled to the Soviet Union from Britain, where he then lived.

75. When the Bentley and Chambers cases became public, the FBI considered using

Katherine Perlo as a witness. Her mental condition, though, was poor: she had been admitted for a time to a mental institution, and she was likely to be an easy target for an aggressive defense lawyer. She was never called to testify. FBI background memo, 16 November 1945, FBI Silvermaster file, serial 26x1; Washington FBI Field Office to Hoover, 3 April 1947, FBI Silvermaster file, serial 2448.

76. New York FBI memo, 7 December 1945, FBI Silvermaster file, serial 248.

77. Ladd to Hoover, 12 December 1945, FBI Silvermaster file, serial 235.

78. Koral statement, 11 June 1947, FBI Silvermaster file, serial 2608; Alexander Koral interview summary, 9 June 1947, FBI Silvermaster file, serial 2571; FBI memorandum, "Existing Corroboration of Bentley's Overall Testimony," 6 May 1955, FBI Silvermaster file, serial 4201.

79. Venona messages regarding Alexander and Helen Koral are cited in appendix A.

80. Nigel West and Oleg Tsarev, *The Crown Jewels: The British Secrets at the Heart of the KGB Archives* (London: HarperCollins, 1998), 112, 116, 130, 133–134. Blunt's report is quoted on p. 130.

81. Michael Straight, *After Long Silence* (New York: Norton, 1983), 102.

82. Straight, *After Long Silence,* 104.

83. Straight, *After Long Silence,* 121.

84. Veterany Vneshney Razvedki Rossii (Veterans of Russian Foreign Intelligence Service), Russian Foreign Intelligence Service, Moscow, 1995. This biography states that while resident in the United States Akhmerov also undertook short-term missions to Europe and China.

85. On Akhmerov, see Robert Louis Benson, "The 1942–43 New York–Moscow KGB Messages" (NSA, 1995), and "The 1944–45 New York and Washington–Moscow KGB Messages" (NSA, 1996).

86. On Lowry as Browder's niece, see Christopher Andrew and Oleg Gordievsky, *KGB: The Inside Story* (New York: HarperCollins, 1990), 286; Pavel A. Sudoplatov, Anatoli P. Sudoplatov, with Jerrold L. Schecter and Leona P. Schecter, *Special Tasks: The Memoirs of an Unwanted Witness* (New York: Little, Brown, 1994), 83; Robert Louis Benson, "The 1944–45 New York and Washington–Moscow KGB Messages." A "J. C. Lowry" is one of the identifying witnesses for a passport obtained by Bill Browder, Earl's brother. Whether this person was related to Helen Lowry is unknown. U.S. Department of State Passport Division brief on a conspiracy charge against World Tourists and the CPUSA, reprinted in "Scope of Soviet Activity in the United States," U.S. Congress, Senate, Committee on the Judiciary, Subcommittee to Investigate the Administration of the Internal Security Act, appendix I, part 23-A (1957), A9.

87. Weinstein, *Perjury,* 183–184. Also see Vern W. Newton, *The Cambridge Spies: The Untold Story of Maclean, Philby, and Burgess in America* (Lanham, Md.: Madison Books, 1991), 218–221.

88. West and Tsarev, *The Crown Jewels,* 112–113. This account tends to support Straight's claims that he never became the spy that the KGB had hoped, because it appears that Deutsch was dispatched with a view to getting more out of him than Akhmerov had (p. 134).

89. West and Tsarev, *The Crown Jewels,* 174.

90. Straight had also known Guy Burgess as a fellow Cambridge Communist and likely an espionage recruit of Blunt's. He later wrote that in 1947 and 1949 he suspected that Burgess, then a British diplomat, might have been assisting Soviet intelligence and extracted promises from Burgess to leave the British Foreign Office. Burgess did not do so, and Straight did nothing.

91. David Caute, *The Great Fear: The Anti-Communist Purge under Truman and Eisenhower* (New York: Simon and Schuster, 1978), 156. Koral is named as "Koval" in Caute's book. The Akhmerovs and Alexander Koral were not the only members of the Bentley story for whom Straight gave corroboration. He also told the FBI that in 1938, during a period when he was out of touch with Akhmerov, Solomon Adler had approached him with the advice that he should "lay low" but that contact would be resumed. This was just after Chambers had dropped out of Soviet espionage, and his former contacts, of whom Akhmerov was one, feared he might go to government authorities. Straight also told the FBI that at his final meeting with Akhmerov in 1942, just before he entered the armed forces and severed contact with the KGB, he was asked about other possible contacts and mentioned another name that shows up in Bentley's story, Michael Greenberg. John Costello, *Mask of Treachery* (New York: Morrow, 1988), 380–381, 480–481. Straight initially remembered the name of the person who approached him as Solomon Leshinsky but identified a photograph of Solomon Adler as the man who had made contact with him. Bentley had named both Solomon Leshinsky and Solomon Adler as members of her network, and Straight had confused his Solomons.

92. Hoover to George Allen, 31 May 1946, FBI Silvermaster file, serial 1160.

93. On the FBI's conclusion that the Soviets warned Bentley's former contacts, see Hayden B. Peake, "Afterword," in Bentley, *Out of Bondage,* 290.

94. Venona messages regarding Coplon are cited in appendix A.

95. Fitin to Dimitrov, 19 October 1944, Archive of the Dimitrov Secretariat of the Comintern, RTsKhIDNI 495-74-485.

96. Venona 27 KGB New York to Moscow, 8 January 1945.

97. The FBI investigation of Coplon and the subsequent trial are discussed in Robert J. Lamphere and Tom Shachtman, *The FBI-KGB War: A Special Agent's Story* (New York: Random House, 1986), 97–125, and Sanche de Gramont [Ted Morgan], *The Secret War* (New York: Putnam, 1962).

98. Lovestone had publicly accused Leon Josephson of stealing his records, and in September 1938 Pat Toohey, the CPUSA's representative in Moscow, bragged to the Comintern that the party had carried out the theft. Toohey to Dimitrov, 19 September 1938, Archive of the Dimitrov Secretariat of the Comintern, RTsKhIDNI 495-74-466. The FBI report on the Levy entry was exhibit 119 in *United States* v. *Judith Coplon* (criminal case 381-49), United States District Court for the District of Columbia, 10 June 1949.

99. E. Morgan to H. H. Clegg, 14 January 1947, serial 2077. Other FBI expressions of the likelihood that prosecution would not be successful include Tamm to Director, 23 January 1947, serial 2007, and Nichols to Tamm, 14 February 1947, serial 2166. All three are in FBI Silvermaster file (65-56402).

100. Morgan to Clegg, 14 January 1947, FBI Silvermaster file, serial 2077.

101. Bentley deposition, 48; Bentley, *Out of Bondage,* 123–124.

102. FBI letter to John Steelman, 19 December 1946, FBI Silvermaster file, serial 2097x; regarding FBI interview with William Remington, 21 April 1947, FBI Silvermaster file, serial 2349; regarding FBI interview with William Remington, 28 April 1947, FBI Silvermaster file, serial 2381.

103. Gary May, *Un-American Activities: The Trials of William Remington* (New York: Oxford University Press, 1994). Remington was later killed in a prison fight.

104. Latham, *The Communist Controversy in Washington,* 160. Latham noted that he did not share the general view.

Chapter 6: Military Espionage

1. This shift is reflected in coded Soviet cable traffic. In 1940 the GRU transmitted nearly three times as many messages from New York to Moscow as did the KGB (992 versus 335). By 1942, however, the KGB had taken over many GRU agents, and its message traffic easily surpassed that of its brother agency. During most of World War II the GRU was clearly the lesser Soviet intelligence agency. The KGB had many more agents, developed a much more sophisticated support system of handlers and espionage controllers in the United States, and gathered more and better raw intelligence. Still, the relative inattention to GRU intelligence activity is partly due to the paucity of counter-intelligence information about GRU operations. There were no defectors from the GRU comparable in importance to the KGB defector Elizabeth Bentley, and the agents that Whittaker Chambers exposed were (with the exception of Alger Hiss) from the KGB. Also, far fewer GRU messages were successfully decrypted by the Venona Project.

2. Robert Louis Benson, "The 1942–43 New York–KGB Messages" (NSA, 1996), 2.

3. Inserted statement of Nicholas Dozenberg, hearings of 8 November 1949, U.S. Congress, House of Representatives, Committee on Un-American Activities, 81st Cong., 1st and 2d sess.

4. "Comintern Apparatus Summary Report," 15 December 1944, FBI Comintern Apparatus file (FBI file 100-203581), serial 3702.

5. Lovestone later became a leading anti-Communist. On his links to Soviet intelligence in the 1930s, see Harvey Klehr, John Earl Haynes, and Fridrikh Igorevich Firsov, *The Secret World of American Communism* (New Haven: Yale University Press, 1995), 128–131.

6. On Rosenblit and Aronberg, see Klehr, Haynes, and Firsov, *The Secret World of American Communism*, 25–26, 46–49; Whittaker Chambers, "Statements to the Federal Bureau of Investigation," January–April 1949, 58–59; Adolf Berle memo of 1939 interview with Whittaker Chambers, "Interlocking Subversion in Government Departments," Subcommittee to Investigate the Administration of the Internal Security Act, Senate Committee on the Judiciary, part 6 (Washington, D.C.: GPO, 1953), 328–330; Allen Weinstein, *Perjury: The Hiss-Chambers Case* (New York: Random House, 1997), 106–107.

7. Testimony of William G. Burtan, 8 November 1949, U.S. Congress, House of Representatives, Committee on Un-American Activities, 81st Cong., 1st and 2d sess.

8. "Comintern Apparatus Summary Report." On Heiman's role in converting jewelry, see Benjamin Gitlow testimony, 11 September 1939, "Investigations of Un-American Propaganda Activities in the US," U.S. Congress, House of Representatives, Special Committee on Un-American Activities, 76th Cong., 1st sess., vol. 7, 4687–4688; William Crane memorandum, 14 February 1949, William Crane FBI File 74-1333, serial 213; Herbert Romerstein and Stanislav Levchenko, *The KGB Against the "Main Enemy"* (Lexington, Mass.: Lexington Books, 1989), 12–13.

9. For information on early Soviet military espionage, see David Dallin, *Soviet Espionage* (New Haven: Yale University Press, 1955). On the Osman case, see Louis Waldman, *Labor Lawyer* (Dutton: New York, 1944), 221–257. Waldman, Osman's lawyer, takes the view that his client was used by Communists, particularly Robert Switz, as an unwitting tool for espionage.

10. On the Gouzenko case, see Igor Gouzenko, *Iron Curtain* (New York: Dutton, 1948); Robert Bothwell and J. L. Granatstein, eds. *The Gouzenko Transcripts* (Ottawa: Deneau, 1982); and Royal Commission (Canada), *The Report of the Royal Commission,*

Appointed Under Order in Council P.C. 411 of 5 February 1946, to Investigate the Facts Relating to and the Circumstances Surrounding the Communications, by Public Officials and Other Persons in Positions of Trust, of Secret and Confidential Information to Agents of a Foreign Power, 27 June 1946 (Ottawa: Edmond Cloutier . . . Controller of Stationery, 1946).

11. The two most complete accounts of the Hiss-Chambers case are Allen Weinstein, *Perjury,* and Sam Tanenhaus, *Whittaker Chambers: A Biography* (New York: Random House, 1997). The 1997 edition of Weinstein's *Perjury* includes new evidence from Russian archives confirming Hiss's guilt.

12. Christopher Andrew and Oleg Gordievsky, *K.G.B.: The Inside Story* (New York: HarperCollins, 1990), 285–286.

13. Venona 1579 GRU New York to Moscow, 28 September 1943.

14. Richard Rhodes, *Dark Sun: The Making of the Hydrogen Bomb* (New York: Simon & Schuster, 1995), 54–47, 103–104.

15. Weinstein, *Perjury,* 326. Weinstein does not identify Ruble as Glasser. This identification is from Venona. Weinstein also quotes from KGB messages from 1936 that identify Hiss as a GRU agent (pp. 182–184).

16. Venona 1822 KGB Washington to KGB Moscow, 30 March 1945.

17. Tanenhaus, *Whittaker Chambers,* 519; Weinstein, *Perjury,* 321–322.

18. The April 1945 cable from Fitin to Merkulov (Weinstein, *Perjury,* 326–327), discussed in chapter 5, further corroborates that Ales is Alger Hiss.

19. Bentley deposition (FBI file 65-14603).

20. On Adams, see New York FBI report, 28 April 1945, serial 4378, and "Comintern Apparatus Summary Report," 15 December 1944, serial 3702, both in FBI Comintern Apparatus file, no. 100-203581, and Larry Kerley testimony, 15 September 1949, "Communist Activities Among Aliens and National Groups," Subcommittee on Immigration and Naturalization of the Committee on the Judiciary, 81st Cong., 1st sess., part 2, 803–805, 822.

21. Klehr, Haynes, and Firsov, *The Secret World of American Communism,* 129–132; Philip Levy testimony, 28 October 1953, "Interlocking Subversion in Government Departments," part 15, 1039–1045.

22. Benjamin Gitlow, *The Whole of Their Lives: Communism in America—A Personal History and Intimate Portrayal of Its Leaders* (New York: Scribners, 1948), 45; "Comintern Apparatus Summary Report."

23. On the surveillance of Adams and entries into his apartment see the FBI Comintern Apparatus file, serials 3428, 3434, and 3460.

24. "Comintern Apparatus Summary Report"; Kerley testimony, "Communist Activities Among Aliens and National Groups," 805.

25. Attention: Inspector M. E. Gurnea, 17 May 1945, FBI file 100-267360, serial 221, box 117, folder 4, and Washington FBI memo, 26 May 1945, FBI file 100-267360, serial 237, box 117, folder 6, Philip Jaffe papers, Emory University Library, Atlanta, Ga.

26. Ibid.

27. For a detailed examination of the *Amerasia* case, see Harvey Klehr and Ronald Radosh, *The Amerasia Spy Case: Prelude to McCarthyism* (Chapel Hill: University of North Carolina Press, 1996).

28. Venona messages regarding Bernstein are cited in appendix A.

29. Venona 927–928 GRU New York to Moscow, 16 June 1943. Mikhailov was officially a Soviet vice-consul. His true name is believed to have been Menshikov or Meleshnikov.

30. Emphasis in the original. T. A. Bisson, "China's Part in a Coalition War," *Far Eastern Survey* (July 1943), 139.

31. Bisson testimony, 9 April 1943, "Investigation of Un-American Propaganda Activities in the United States," U.S. Congress, House of Representatives, Special Committee on Un-American Activities, 78th Cong., 1st sess., vol. 7, 3467–3480; Venona 938 GRU New York to Moscow, 17 June 1943. Bisson is also mentioned in plain text in one KGB Venona message, but the deciphered portion is fragmentary and not revealing. Venona 1064 KGB New York to Moscow, 3 July 1943.

32. Venona 1103 GRU New York to Moscow, 8 July 1943; 1348 GRU New York to Moscow, 16 August 1943.

33. Background memorandums of Philip and Mary Jane Keeney, FBI Silvermaster file (FBI file 65-56402), serial 2127. Mary Jane Keeney's diary for June 17, 1939, notes: "Get to Mill Valley at 2:00. C.P. Marin County branch membership meeting from 2:00 to 6:00 P.M."

34. Venona messages regarding the Keeneys are cited in appendix A.

35. Venona 726–729 KGB New York to Moscow, 22 May 1942. The reply is very fragmentary, and the translator's note indicates that the material is not very firm. In both messages Keeney's name is in plain text.

36. Venona 1234 KGB New York to Moscow, 29 August 1944.

37. Excerpts from Mary Jane Keeney's diary and from the Keeneys' correspondence are in FBI Silvermaster file, serial 938 and 2661.

38. Ibid.

39. Ibid. Greg is Gregory Silvermaster.

40. Ibid.

41. Venona 1325 GRU New York to Moscow, 11 August 1943.

42. "Comintern Apparatus Summary Report"; Investigation of Un-American Propaganda Activities in the United States (Hearings Regarding Toma Babin), 27 May and 6 July 1949, U.S. Congress, House of Representatives, Committee on Un-American Activities, 81st Cong., 1st sess.

43. Venona messages regarding Babin are cited in appendix A.

44. Venona 1249 GRU New York to Moscow, 29 July 1943. In fact, Babin's group seems to have had its orders changed and been sent to England. In Venona 1350 GRU New York to Moscow, 17 August 1943, Mikhailov noted that consequently "the question of their being developed by us falls to the ground."

45. Testimony of Leonard Mins, 8 April 1943, "Investigations of Un-American Propaganda Activities in the U.S.," vol. 7, 3415–3437.

46. CPUSA Comintern Representative to CPUSA, 26 January 1935, Archive of the Communist Party of the USA, RTsKhIDNI 515-1-3750. In the document he is identified as L. Minz.

47. Markus Wolf, *Man Without a Face* (New York: Times Books, 1997), 304.

48. Elizabeth Bentley, *Out of Bondage: The Story of Elizabeth Bentley* (New York: Ivy Books, 1988), 111.

49. Venona messages regarding Mins are cited in appendix A.

50. Venona 1350 GRU New York to Moscow, 17 August 1943.

51. Venona 1373 GRU New York to Moscow, 23 August 1943.

52. New York FBI report, 5 April 1946, Comintern Apparatus file, serial 5236; FBI report, "Soviet Espionage Activities," 19 October 1945," attached to Hoover to Vaughan, 19 October 1945, President's Secretary's Files, Harry S. Truman Library, Independence, Mo.; FBI report, "Soviet Activities in the United States," 25 July 1946, Clark M. Clifford papers, Truman Library; Dallin, *Soviet Espionage,* 286; Robert J. Lam-

phere and Tom Shachtman, *The FBI-KGB War: A Special Agent's Story* (New York: Random House, 1995), 34–36. Venona 3, 4, 5 KGB San Francisco to Moscow, 2 January 1946; 25 KGB San Francisco to Moscow, 26 January 1946. The authors thank retired FBI agent John Walsh, who in 1946 tried to spot Bunia Witczak and her son on the deck of the *Sakhalin* when it docked in a South American port, for noting the likelihood that R. was Witczak.

53. Elizabeth Bentley FBI deposition, 30 November 1945, FBI file 65-14603; also see James Barros, *No Sense of Evil: Espionage, The Case of Herbert Norman* (Toronto: Deneau, 1986).

54. Venona 1328 GRU New York to Moscow, 12 August 1943.

55. Testimony of Charles I. Velson, 26 September 1951, "Unauthorized Travel of Subversives Behind the Iron Curtain on United States Passports," U.S. Congress, Subcommittee to Investigate the Administration of the Internal Security Act, Senate Judiciary Committee, 207–217; Robert Gladnick, "I Was a Fifth Columnist," Gladnick folder, Isaac Don Levine papers, Emory University Library, Atlanta, Ga.

56. Venona messages regarding Velson are cited in appendix A.

57. Martin Dies statement, *Congressional Record* (1 February 1943), 504–516; FBI memo, 17 June 1946, FBI Silvermaster file, serial 1364.

58. *Daily Worker* (17 October 1938): Hottel to Director, 28 February 1947, FBI Silvermaster file, serial 2437; Memo on Fahy, 17 April 1946, FBI Silvermaster file, serial 1364. Miller and Gregg became KGB sources.

59. Jack Fahy testimony, 8 April 1943, "Investigation of Un-American Propaganda Activities in the United States," vol. 7, 3453–3465; Kerr Commission report, 14 May 1943, box 856, Clinton Anderson papers, Library of Congress. The commission consisted of Representatives John H. Kerr (Democrat, North Carolina), Albert Gore (Democrat, Tennessee), Clinton P. Anderson (Democrat, New Mexico), D. Lane Powers (Republican, New Jersey), and Frank B. Keefe (Republican, Wisconsin).

60. Venona messages regarding Fahy are cited in appendix A.

61. Venona 115 Naval GRU Moscow to Washington, 20 January 1943; 360 Naval GRU Moscow to Washington, 26 February 1943; 366 Naval GRU Moscow to Washington, 28 February 1943.

62. Investigative administration, Main Naval Staff, USSR Navy to Dimitrov, 15 August 1942, Archive of the Dimitrov Secretariat of the Comintern, RTsKhIDNI, 495-74-478.

63. Venona messages regarding Coleman are cited in appendix A.

64. Venona 2505–2512 Naval GRU Washington to Moscow, 31 December 1942. Venona messages regarding Mitynen cited in appendix A.

65. 1006 Naval GRU Moscow to Washington, 10 June 1943; Robert Louis Benson, "The KGB in San Francisco and Mexico, the GRU in New York and Washington" (NSA Historical Monograph, 1996), 9.

66. Venona messages regarding Bayer and Gordon are cited in appendix A. *People's Weekly World,* 1 May 1993.

67. Venona 82 New York to Moscow, 18 January 1945; 927–928 GRU New York to Moscow, 16 June 1943.

Chapter 7: Spies in the U.S. Government

1. William Donovan testimony, 13 March 1945, unpublished report of proceedings of hearing held before the Special Committee of the Committee on Military Affairs,

vol. 3, 189–190, Record Group 233, Center for Legislative Archives, National Archives, Washington, D.C.

2. The backgrounds of the four are discussed in Harvey Klehr, John Earl Haynes, and Fridrikh Igorevich Firsov, *The Secret World of American Communism* (New Haven: Yale University Press, 1995), 259–286. Fajans joined the Young Communist League in 1932, Lossowski in 1935, and Wolff in 1936. Goff was already a member of the CPUSA when he arrived in Spain in 1937 and after World War II became a full-time official of the CPUSA. Wolff joined the Spanish Communist party when in Spain and was commended by the Communist political committee in the International Brigades for his work in "executing a correct Party line." List of American Communists serving with the International Brigades, undated but probably 1938, Archive of the International Brigades, RTsKhIDNI 545-6-846; Milton Wolff biographical questionnaire for the Comisariado de Guerra de las Brigadas Internacionales, 1 November 1938, RTsKhIDNI 545-6-1015; Brigade party committee to Communist Party of Spain Central Committee, Milton Wolff evaluation, partly illegible date 1938, RTsKhIDNI 545-6-1015.

3. Donovan testimony, 179, 182.

4. After leaving the OSS, Dedijer joined the U.S. Army, became a paratrooper, and, to the amusement of his fellow troopers, when jumping insisted on shouting "Long Live Stalin!" After World War II, Dedijer directed atomic energy research for the Yugoslav government but later broke with Tito and left the country. R. Harris Smith, *OSS: The Secret History of America's First Central Intelligence Agency* (Berkeley and Los Angeles: University of California Press, 1972), 135.

5. Robert Hayden Alcorn, *No Bugles for Spies* (New York: David McKay, 1962), 134.

6. OSS Communists are identified or their role is discussed in Smith, *OSS;* Barry M. Katz, *Foreign Intelligence: Research and Analysis in the Office of Strategic Services, 1942–1945* (Cambridge: Harvard University Press, 1989); Earl Latham, *The Communist Controversy in Washington: From the New Deal to McCarthy* (Cambridge: Harvard University Press, 1966); Christopher Andrew and Oleg Gordievsky, *KGB: The Inside Story* (New York: HarperCollins, 1990); Robin W. Winks, *Cloak and Gown: Scholars in the Secret War, 1939–1961* (New York: Quill, 1988); Anthony Cave Brown, *The Last Hero: Wild Bill Donovan* (New York: Times Books, 1982).

7. Interdepartmental Committee on Investigations Pursuant to Public No. 135, "membership in the Communist Party or German American Bund as ground for dismissal from Federal employment," 18 May 1942, and "Disposition of Subversive and Disaffected Military Personnel," 5 February 1944, both in Record Group 226, OSS Washington Director's Office records, microfilm series M1642, reel 56, National Archives and Records Administration, Archives II, College Park, Md.

8. These included KGB assets Horst Baerensprung (OSS consultant on Germany), Jane Foster (OSS Far Eastern and Indonesian section), Maurice Halperin (chief of the Latin American Division of OSS Research and Analysis), Hans Hirschfeld (OSS consultant on Germany), Bella Joseph (motion picture section of OSS), Julius Joseph (OSS Far Eastern section), Duncan Lee (counsel to General Donovan and the OSS's Japanese intelligence section), Helen Tenney (OSS Spanish section), Donald Wheeler (OSS Research and Analysis), as well as GRU assets Thomas Babin (OSS section working with Yugoslav resistance), Philip Keeney (OSS librarian), and Leonard Mins (Russian section of OSS Research and Analysis).

9. Venona messages regarding all of the persons discussed here are cited in appendix A.

10. Venona 726–729 KGB New York to Moscow, 22 May 1942. Venona 387 KGB New York to Moscow, 12 June 1942 deals with Scott but is badly garbled.

11. John Scott, *Behind the Urals: An American Worker in Russia's City of Steel* (Boston: Houghton Mifflin, 1942), 248.

12. Venona messages regarding all these cover names are cited in appendix A.

13. The KGB assigned the task of preparing a report on the structure of the OSS in late 1944 to Bernard Schuster, its CPUSA liaison, a decision that probably reflects the Communist party's multiple sources inside the OSS. Venona 1668 KGB New York to Moscow, 29 November 1944.

14. Remarks of Representative Lesinski, *Congressional Record* (17 June 1943), 5999–6003; Elmer Davis testimony, 11 November 1952, "Hearings Before the Select Committee to Conduct an Investigation of the Facts, Evidence, and Circumstances of the Katyn Forest Massacre," U.S. House of Representatives, Select Committee, part 7, 1987–1994. Salman was also known as Stefan Arski. Irene Belinska, a member of the Polish section of the Office of War Information, was the daughter of Ludwig Rajchman, who became a high-ranking official of the Polish Communist regime. After World War II Belinska worked for a Polish-language newspaper aligned with the CPUSA. After the war, the husband of another staff member of the Polish OWI section, Mira Zlotowski, became a mid-level official in the Polish Communist government.

15. Ronald L. Filippelli, "Luigi Antonini, the Italian-American Labor Council, and Cold-War Politics in Italy, 1943–1949," *Labor History* 33, no. 1 (Winter 1992), 102–125.

16. Venona messages regarding these cover names are cited in appendix A. Several Soviet intelligence contacts—Peter Rhodes (chief of OWI's Atlantic news section), Christina Krotkova (it is unclear which OWI section employed her), and Irving Lerner (OWI's motion picture division)—were discussed in earlier chapters. As noted above, Unbroken Cover Name No. 19 denoted an unidentified Soviet agent in either the OWI or the OSS.

17. Venona messages regarding Wovschin are cited in appendix A.

18. Venona messages regarding the Wichers are cited in appendix A.

19. Fitin to Dimitrov, 24 September 1944, Archive of the Dimitrov Secretariat of the Comintern, RTsKhIDNI 495-74-485. Emphasis in original.

20. Venona messages regarding Davis are cited in appendix A.

21. Venona 1714 KGB New York to Moscow, 5 December 1944.

22. Venona 55 KGB New York to Moscow, 15 January 1945.

23. Venona 1714 KGB New York to Moscow, 5 December 1944.

24. Venona 1587 KGB New York to Moscow, 12 November 1944. Initially, in August, the New York KGB reported sending some UNRRA material from Wovschin, but in a September message it made the correction that the material was from the OWI.

25. Venona 1714 KGB New York to Moscow, 5 December 1944.

26. Venona 284–286, KGB Moscow to New York, 28 March 1945.

27. Lamphere to Gardner, memorandum on Flora Don Wovschin, 9 May 1949, reproduced in Robert Louis Benson and Michael Warner, eds., *Venona: Soviet Espionage and The American Response, 1939–1957* (Washington, D.C.: National Security Agency, Central Intelligence Agency, 1996), 131.

28. These sources include Thomas Bisson (BEW), Lauchlin Currie (FEA), Noel Field (State), Jack Fahy (Inter-American Affairs and BEW), Bela Gold (FEA), Michael Greenberg (BEW), Joseph Gregg (Inter-American Affairs and State), Maurice Halperin (OSS

and State), Alger Hiss (State), Mary Jane Keeney (BEW and the United Nations), Sol Leshinsky (UNRRA), Robert Miller (Inter-American Affairs), Willard Park (Inter-American Affairs and UNRRA), George Perazich (UNRRA), Allan Rosenberg (BEW/FEA), Gregory Silvermaster (BEW/FEA), Helen Tenney (OSS and State), and Julian Wadleigh (State). To this group one can add Ruth Rivkin (UNRRA) and Bernard Redmont (Inter-American Affairs), both minor sources of the CPUSA/KGB network supervised by Golos and Bentley.

29. Allen Weinstein, *Perjury: The Hiss-Chambers Case* (New York: Random House, 1997), 22, 175.

30. Weinstein, *Perjury*, 269.

31. Whittaker Chambers, *Witness* (New York: Random House, 1952), 30, 334, 339, 341, 381–382, 467, 469; Massing discussed her recruitment of Duggan in her 1951 memoir: Hede Massing, *This Deception* (New York: Duell, Sloan and Pearce, 1951), 206–211. Weinstein, *Perjury*, 181–183.

32. Venona messages regarding Duggan are cited in appendix A.

33. Venona messages regarding Keenan are cited in appendix A. See also Keenan section of "Underground Soviet Espionage Organization (NKVD) in Agencies of the United States Government," 21 February 1946, FBI Silvermaster file (FBI file 65-56402), serial 573.

34. Venona 3614, 3615 KGB Washington to KGB Moscow, 22 June 1945.

35. Venona 1553 KGB New York to Moscow, 4 November 1944. See also Rodman section of Robert Miller background memo, 26 December 1945, FBI Silvermaster file, serial 356.

36. Venona messages regarding these cover names are cited in appendix A.

37. A candidate for Mirage is Charles Albert Page, a mid-level cultural affairs officer for the State Department and the OWI in World War II who worked chiefly on South American matters. In 1945 he was assigned to the U.S. embassy in France. In 1944 the FBI identified Page as part of a shadowy Communist network but was unable to clearly distinguish between espionage activities and clandestine Communist political activities. He had access to the sort of information Mirage provided to the KGB. "Comintern Apparatus Summary Report," 15 December 1944, FBI Comintern Apparatus file (FBI file 100-203581), serial 3702; Larry Kerley testimony, 15 September 1949, "Communist Activities Among Aliens and National Groups," U.S. Congress, Senate, Committee on the Judiciary, Subcommittee on Immigration and Naturalization, 81st Cong., 1st sess., part 2, 810, 182.

38. Venona messages regarding Robert and Source No. 12 are cited in appendix A.

39. Venona 812 KGB New York to Moscow, 29 May 1943.

40. In one other message Wallace is designated by "Botsman" (Russian for Boatswain) but this may be simply an error by the cipher officer for "Lotsman." Venona 1625 KGB New York to Moscow, 3 October 1943. The messages in which Lotsman designates Wallace are Venona 1025, 1035–1936, KGB New York to Moscow, 30 June 1943; 590 KGB New York to Moscow, 29 April 1944; 744 and 746 KGB New York to Moscow, 24 May 1944; 759–760 KGB New York to Moscow, 27 May 1944; 1613 KGB New York to Moscow, 18 November 1944.

41. Venona 1350 KGB New York to Moscow, 23 September 1944; 1838 KGB New York to Moscow, 29 December 1944; 781–787 KGB New York to Moscow, 25–26 May 1945.

42. The historian Eduard Mark argues, on the basis on a close reading of the attendance records of the Trident conference and other archival evidence that most likely Deputy (Zamestitel) was Wallace and Source No. 19 was Hopkins. He concludes, fur-

ther, that the readable portions of the message do not allow a a clear determination of whether Hopkins/19 was a Soviet covert source or a benign "back-channel" diplomatic contact between Roosevelt and the Soviets. We agree that the partial decryption and ambiguity of the message does not allow a confident judgment on Source No. 19's relationship with the Soviets; while impressed by Mark's analysis, we view the evidence as too slim to enable us to reach a judgment about Source No. 19's identity. Edward Mark, "Venona's Source 19 and the Trident Conference of May 1943: Diplomacy or Espionage?" *Intelligence and National Security* 13, no. 2 (April 1998), 1–31.

43. Other chapters discuss the KGB sources Joel Barr (Army Signal Corps laboratories), Demetrius Dvoichenko-Markov (Army intelligence), Edward Fitzgerald (War Production Board), Klaus Fuchs (Manhattan Project), David Greenglass (Army/Manhattan Project), Theodore Hall (Army/Manhattan Project), Irving Kaplan (War Production Board), Charles Kramer (Office of Price Administration), Harry Magdoff (War Production Board and the Office of Emergency Management), William Perl (National Advisory Committee for Aeronautics), Victor Perlo (War Production Board), Vladimir Pozner (War Department), William Remington (War Production Board), Julius Rosenberg (Army Signal Corps), Alfred Sarant (Army Signal Corps laboratories at Fort Monmouth), George Silverman (Army Air Force), Ludwig Ullmann (Army Air Force), William Weisband (Army Signal Intelligence), Ilya Wolston (Army intelligence), and George Zlatovski (Army intelligence). Six GRU sources are also discussed elsewhere: John H. Chapin, (Manhattan Project), Clarence Hiskey (Manhattan Project), Edward Manning, (Manhattan Project), Robert Osman (Army, Panama Canal Zone), Vincent Reno (Aberdeen Army Proving Grounds), and Daniel Abraham Zaret (Army's Explosives Division).

44. Elizabeth Bentley FBI deposition, 30 November 1945, FBI file 65-14603; Elizabeth Bentley testimony, 13 May 1949, "Communist Activities Among Aliens and National Groups," Subcommittee on Immigration and Naturalization of the Committee on the Judiciary, U.S. Senate, 81st Cong., 1st sess., part 1, 106–123; FBI Washington Field Office memo, 26 August 1948, FBI Silvermaster file, serial 3430.

45. Venona messages regarding these cover names are cited in appendix A.

46. They include Solomon Adler (Treasury representative in China), Frank Coe (Division of Monetary Research), Sonia Gold (Division of Monetary Research), Victor Perlo (Division of Monetary Research), Gregory Silvermaster (War Assets Division), William Taylor (Division of Monetary Research, Treasury representative to China), Ludwig Ullmann (Division of Monetary Research), and Harry White (assistant secretary of the Treasury).

47. Venona 82 KGB New York to Moscow, 18 January 1945.

48. Venona 1522 KGB New York to Moscow, 27 October 1944.

49. Venona 1204 GRU New York to Moscow, 22 July 1943.

Chapter 8: Fellowcountrymen

1. Browder to Dimitrov, 19 January 1938, and reproduced in Harvey Klehr, John Earl Haynes, and Fridrikh Igorevich Firsov, *The Secret World of American Communism* (New Haven: Yale University Press, 1995), 241. At different times Margaret Browder adopted different spellings of her name.

2. Dimitrov to Yezhov, 24 January 1938, Archive of the Dimitrov Secretariat of the Comintern, RTsKhIDNI 495-74-465.

3. Walter G. Krivitsky, *Inside Stalin's Secret Service* (New York: Harper, 1939), 258–259.

4. Earl Browder testimony, 5 September 1939, William Browder testimony, 12 September 1939, "Investigations of Un-American Propaganda Activities in the United States," U.S. Congress, House of Representatives, Special Committee on Un-American Activities, 76th Cong., 1st sess., vol. 7, 4439, 4830.

5. U.S. Department of State Passport Division brief on a conspiracy charge against World Tourists and the CPUSA, prepared in 1939–1940 under the direction of Ashley J. Nicholas, reprinted in "Scope of Soviet Activity in the United States," U.S. Congress, Senate, Committee on the Judiciary, Subcommittee to Investigate the Administration of the Internal Security Act, 85th Cong., 1st sess., appendix I, part 23-A, A8, A93–A94, A107.

6. Report on New York FBI Interview with Margaret Browder dated 10 July 1951, SAC New York to FBI Director with report on Margaret Browder interview, and SAC New York to FBI Director dated 15 December 1952 with a Report on Margaret Browder Grand Jury Testimony, all in FBI file 100-59645; New York FBI synopsis of interview with Margaret Browder, 29 October 1957, FBI file 100-287645, serial 143. In the 1930s Zubilin used the cover of a Hollywood talent scout, a status provided by Boris Morros's film company. After the initial admissions to the FBI Margaret Browder refused to elaborate and in subsequent interviews refused to admit knowing the Zubilins. When she appeared before a grand jury she invoked the Fifth Amendment to refuse to testify. Booker had met the Zubilins and Margaret Browder in Berlin in the 1930s. On William Browder's meetings with Zubilin, see Venona 196 KGB New York to Moscow, 9 February 1944.

7. Venona messages regarding Browder are cited in appendix A.

8. Venona 14 KGB New York to Moscow 4 January 1945.

9. John Abt with Michael Myerson, *Advocate and Activist: Memoirs of An American Communist Lawyer* (Urbana: University of Illinois Press, 1993), 42.

10. Elizabeth Bentley FBI deposition, 30 November 1945, FBI file 65-14603.

11. Bentley deposition; Venona 2013 KGB New York to Moscow, 11 December 1943; 2011 KGB New York to Moscow, 11 December 1943; 2101 KGB New York to Moscow, 29 December 1943.

12. Jean Lacouture, *De Gaulle* (New York: New American Library, 1966), 79, 90.

13. Beria to Dimitrov, 29/30 November 1940, with attached Fitin memorandum, "The Secretary of the CC of the American Comparty . . . ," Archive of the Dimitrov Secretariat of the Comintern, RTsKhIDNI 495-74-478.

14. Venona 424 KGB Moscow to New York, 1 July 1942.

15. Venona messages regarding Cot are cited in appendix C.

16. Peter Wright, *Spy Catcher: The Candid Autobiography of a Senior Intelligence Officer* (New York: Viking, 1987), 239–241. Other KGB documents regarding Cot are cited and quoted in Thierry Wolton, *Le grand recrutement* (Paris: Grasset, 1993).

17. Venona 1163 KGB New York to Moscow, 18 July 1943. The latter point refers to the decision of the CPUSA to oppose an effort by New Jersey reformers and labor activists to split away from the Democratic party (dominated by Frank Hague's corrupt political machine) and form a new party modeled on the American Labor party of New York.

18. Venona 1164 KGB New York to Moscow, 18 July 1943.

19. Fitin to Dimitrov, 23 July 1943, and attached NKVD report "On 14 June of the Year, Com. Browder . . . ," Archive of the Dimitrov Secretariat of the Comintern, RTsKhIDNI 495-74-484.

20. Venona 1169 GRU New York to Moscow, 19 July 1943; 1258, 1259 GRU

New York to Moscow, 31 July 1943; 1350 GRU New York to Moscow, 17 August 1943.

21. Bolshakov to Dimitrov, 21 August 1944, Archive of the Dimitrov Secretariat of the Comintern, RTsKhIDNI 495-74-485. No reply was located in the Comintern's records. One should note that officially the Comintern had dissolved a year earlier. Dimitrov and sections of the Comintern headquarters lived on, however, as "institute 205" and were eventually absorbed into the international department of the Communist Party of the Soviet Union.

22. For a full discussion of Josephine Truslow Adams, see Harvey Klehr, "The Strange Case of Roosevelt's 'Secret Agent': Frauds, Fools, and Fantasies," *Encounter* [Great Britain] 59, no. 6 (1982), 84–91. See also Joseph P. Lash, *Eleanor and Franklin: The Story of Their Relationship, Based on Eleanor Roosevelt's Private Papers* (New York: Norton, 1971), 702–704.

23. Adams to Eleanor Roosevelt, January 1944, Eleanor Roosevelt to Adams, 13 July 1944, Eleanor Roosevelt papers, Franklin D. Roosevelt Library, Hyde Park, N.Y. One of Adams's letters to Mrs. Roosevelt contains a link, almost certainly an accidental one, to atomic espionage. Adams told Mrs. Roosevelt that there was a Nazi agitator at a tank factory run by Baldwin Locomotive Works near Philadelphia. The White House forwarded the letter to the FBI, which investigated the matter. It turned out that one of Adams's sources for the identify of the alleged Nazi was Robert Heineman, the husband of Klaus Fuchs's sister.

24. Even in the 1950s, when Adams's mental instability was apparent, Browder had difficulty believing that he had been hoodwinked. He insisted that Adams was not sufficiently politically sophisticated to make up the messages she delivered to him.

25. John Earl Haynes, *Dubious Alliance: The Making of Minnesota's DFL Party* (Minneapolis: University of Minnesota Press, 1984); Harvey Klehr and John Earl Haynes, *The American Communist Movement: Storming Heaven Itself* (New York: Twayne, 1992), 96–100. Hugh De Lacy, head of the Washington Commonwealth Federation (WCF), was elected to Congress as a Democrat in 1944. Howard Costigan, who had preceded De Lacy as head of the WCF, had been a secret member of the CPUSA in the 1930s. Costigan later became an anti-Communist and stated that Representative De Lacy was a secret Communist, a charge De Lacy denied. However, John Abt, a friend of De Lacy, confirmed De Lacy's Communist status in his autobiography. Abt and Myerson, *Advocate and Activist,* 117.

26. Browder's 1944 reforms and the Moscow origins of the Duclos article are discussed in Harvey Klehr, John Earl Haynes, and Kyrill M. Anderson, *The Soviet World of American Communism* (New Haven: Yale University Press, 1998). See also Maurice Isserman, *Which Side Were You On? The American Communist Party During the Second World War* (Middletown, Conn.: Wesleyan University Press, 1982).

27. John Lautner and Frank Meyer, two prominent defectors from the CPUSA, reported that they had heard of a secret Browder communications link to President Roosevelt.

28. Excerpts of Adams's testimony appear in the transcripts of the hearings of 25 and 26 February 1957, "Scope of Soviet Activity in the United States," part 54, 3590–3600.

29. Louis Budenz, *Men Without Faces: The Communist Conspiracy in the USA* (New York: Harper, 1948), 252.

30. His first book was *This Is My Story* (New York: McGraw-Hill, 1947), an autobiographical work, followed by *Men Without Faces* (1948), a book that presented primarily a fifth-column interpretation of the CPUSA. Budenz's early testimony and writ-

ings were largely accurate, and some points that were questioned at that time have been confirmed by documents appearing from Moscow's archives in recent years. Budenz, however, sometimes exaggerated his direct knowledge (conflating what he had personally observed with information he had gained at second hand) and sometimes gave his accounts a melodramatic aura.

31. Wolff gave false testimony about his Communist ties to a congressional investigating committee. See Klehr, Haynes, and Firsov, *The Secret World of American Communism*, 260–280.

32. To Foster, Minor from Dimitrov, 3 April 1942, Archive of the Secretariat of the Executive Committee of the Communist International: coded correspondence with Communist Parties (1933–1943), RTsKhIDNI 495-184-5 (1942 file). Browder was serving a jail sentence for traveling on false passports, so the cable was addressed to Robert Minor and William Foster, the ranking party officers.

33. Ryan [Dennis] to Dimitrov, 10 April 1942, Archive of the Secretariat of the Executive Committee of the Communist International: coded correspondence with Communist Parties (1933–1943), RTsKhIDNI 495-184-19 (1942 files).

34. Fitin to Dimitrov, 13 May 1942, Archive of the Dimitrov Secretariat of the Comintern, RTsKhIDNI 495-74-484.

35. Ibid.

36. The KGB had equally misplaced fears about British penetration. In 1942–1943 the KGB suspected that three of its most valuable spies inside the British government, Kim Philby, Anthony Blunt, and Guy Burgess, were double agents because it had difficulty believing their reports that after the development of the British-Soviet alliance the British had drastically reduced their intelligence actions directed at the USSR. The KGB's response to the same events had been the opposite: to see the British-Soviet alliance as an opportunity to increase its espionage assault on Great Britain. Nigel West and Oleg Tsarev, *The Crown Jewels: The British Secrets at the Heart of the KGB Archives* (London: HarperCollins, 1998), 147–153, 159–168.

37. Dimitrov to Fitin, 13 May 1942, Archive of the Dimitrov Secretariat of the Comintern, RTsKhIDNI 495-73-188; Fitin to Dimitrov, 13 May 1942.

38. Ryan to Dimitrov, enclosed in Fitin to Dimitrov, 1 June 1942, Archive of the Dimitrov Secretariat of the Comintern, RTsKhIDNI 495-74-484.

39. Ibid.

40. Venona 880 KGB New York to Moscow, 8 June 1943; Carl Marzani, *The Education of a Reluctant Radical*, book 4 (New York: Topical Books, 1995), 87.

41. Marzani, *The Education of a Reluctant Radical*, book 4, 3–7, 30; Oleg Kalugin, with Fen Montaigne, *The First Directorate: My 32 Years in Intelligence and Espionage Against the West* (New York: St. Martin's Press, 1994), 48–50.

42. Venona 1195 KGB New York to Moscow, 21 July 1943; 1206 KGB New York to Moscow, 22 July 1943.

43. Venona 846 KGB New York to Moscow, 3 June 1943.

44. Venona 142(a) KGB Moscow to Canberra, 12 September 1943.

45. Ladd memo to Director, 7 December 1945, FBI Silvermaster file (FBI file 65-56402), serial 118; see also background description of Schuster in serial 248.

46. Budenz, *Men Without Faces*, 127; Elizabeth Bentley, *Out of Bondage: The Story of Elizabeth Bentley* (New York: Ivy Books, 1988), 187; Bella Dodd, *School of Darkness* (New York: Kenedy, 1954), 96, 122, 207–209.

47. Venona messages regarding Schuster are cited in appendix A.

48. Venona KGB 283 KGB New York to Moscow, 24 February 1944; 598–599

KGB New York to Moscow, 2 May 1944; 605 KGB New York to Moscow, 2 May 1944. In 849 KGB New York to Moscow, 15 June 1944, New York reported that Browder's material was going to Moscow through Zubilin. Presumably this meant that Zubilin himself was meeting with Schuster.

49. Venona 579 KGB New York to Moscow, 28 April 1944.

50. Venona 1029 KGB New York to Moscow, 22 July 1944. The problem was complicated because Grohl was pregnant and the KGB agent, a Spanish Communist exile named José Sancha Padros, had a wife in Europe. The Mexico KGB, however, thought that marriage to an American might assist their agent in getting legal travel documents; see Venona 495–496 KGB Mexico City to Moscow, 12 June 1944; 506 KGB Mexico City to Moscow, 15 June 1944; 375 KGB Moscow to Mexico City, 18 June 1944.

51. Venona 1553 KGB New York to Moscow, 4 November 1944.

52. Venona 916 KGB New York to Moscow, 12 June 1945. Rappoport, who remained a Communist until his death, is the subject of Kenneth Kann's *Joe Rappoport: The Life of a Jewish Radical* (Philadelphia: Temple University Press, 1981). From the biographical facts he is clearly the same person as Rappoport in the Venona cable. According to Kann, Rappoport was vague about his activities during World War II.

53. Venona 1400 KGB New York to Moscow, 5 October 1944.

54. Venona 1328 KGB New York to Moscow, 15 September 1944; 295 KGB Moscow to New York, 30 March 1945.

55. Venona 1340 KGB New York to Moscow, 21 September 1944.

56. Venona 94 KGB New York to Moscow, 23 January 1945.

57. Venona 1166 KGB New York to Moscow, 16 August 1944; Fitin to Dimitrov, 19 August 1944, Archive of the Dimitrov Secretariat of the Comintern, RTsKhIDNI 495-74-485. When Burns was serving with the Comintern's International Brigades in Spain, Russian authorities identified him as "a reliable and honest member of the party" who was "suitable for organizational work." "Report on Americans," 27 September 1937, Archive of the International Brigades, RTsKhIDNI 545-3-453.

58. Venona 1769 KGB New York to Moscow, 15 December 1944.

59. Venona 1410 KGB New York to Moscow, 6 October 1944.

60. Venona 1457 KGB New York to Moscow, 14 October 1944.

61. Venona 1512 KGB New York to Moscow, 24 October 1944.

62. Ladd memo to Director, 7 December 1945, FBI Silvermaster file, serial 118; Venona 1668 KGB New York to Moscow, 29 November 1944.

63. Venona 1433–1435 KGB New York to Moscow, 10 October 1944; Pravdin's reply, making no mention of the CPUSA issue, is Venona 1442, 1447 KGB New York to Moscow, 11 October 1944.

64. Venona 12, 13, 15, 16 KGB New York to Moscow, 4 January 1945.

65. Venona 1818 KGB New York to Moscow, 16 December 1944.

66. "Comintern Apparatus Summary Report," 15 December 1944, FBI Comintern Apparatus file (FBI file 100-203581), serial 3702; Folkoff's CPUSA "Application for Permission to Leave the United States" under his party name of McLee, Archive of the Communist Party of the USA, RTsKhIDNI 515-1-3875.

67. William Crane memorandum, 14 February 1949, William Crane FBI File 74-1333, serial 213. Also see FBI file 65-59549, serial 1927.

68. FBI memorandum, "Information Regarding the Subject Furnished by William Edward Crane," 15 January 1951, FBI file 65-59549, serial 3; FBI memo, Re: William Edward Crane, 18 April 1949, FBI file 74-1333, serial 3570, and FBI teletype, 10 April 1949, FBI file 74-1333, serial 3042.

69. Allen Weinstein, *Perjury: The Hiss-Chambers Case* (New York: Random House, 1997), 111n, 138, 204, 208–209, 211, 274, 281n, 361–362, 363n, 374, 466.

70. Venona 172 KGB San Francisco to Moscow, 18 April 1945; 69 KGB San Francisco to Moscow, 20 February 1946. On behalf of his second-in-command in the underground, Leo Baroway, a.k.a. Gordon Stevens, Folkoff also inquired about the fate of Baroway's brother, Pavel, a Russian citizen who had worked in the Soviet consulate in New York in 1936–1937. Venona 266 KGB San Francisco to Moscow, 18 May 1945.

71. Venona 55 KGB San Francisco to Moscow, 8 February 1944; 101 KGB San Francisco to Moscow, 5 March 1944; 117 KGB San Francisco to Moscow, 11 March 1944, where it appears the KGB is "processing" William Mackie, a longshoreman who was working under Uncle.

72. Venona messages regarding Miller are cited in appendix A.

73. Venona 450 KGB San Francisco to Moscow, 1 November 1943; 472 KGB San Francisco to Moscow, 9 November 1943.

74. San Francisco FBI report of 1 July 1945 through 15 March 1947, Comintern Apparatus file, serial 5421 and "Comintern Apparatus Summary Report."

75. On Nelson's life and career in the party, see Steve Nelson, James Barrett, and Rob Ruck, *Steve Nelson, American Radical* (Pittsburgh: University of Pittsburgh Press, 1981).

76. Nelson, Barrett, and Ruck, *Steve Nelson*, 242–243. Nelson attributed the actual theft to an Associated Farmers office worker who had a change of heart. For RTsKhIDNI documents suggesting that the theft may have been carried out by secret Communist staff members of the La Follette subcommittee, see Klehr, Haynes, and Firsov, *The Secret World of American Communism*, 96–106, 132.

77. Son to Brother with attached "Son Financial Statement for 1942," Archive of the Dimitrov Secretariat of the Comintern, RTsKhIDNI 495-74-480; Venona 31 KGB San Francisco to Moscow, 17 January 1944; 133 KGB San Francisco to Moscow, 29 March 1944; CIA memorandum, "COMRAP—Vassili M. Zubilin," 6 February 1948, reprinted in Robert Louis Benson and Michael Warner, eds., *Venona: Soviet Espionage and the American Response, 1939–1957* (Washington, D.C.: National Security Agency, Central Intelligence Agency, 1996), 105–115. Nelson's family name in Croatia, then part of the Austro-Hungarian empire, was Mesarosh. In Croatian *mesaros* (pronounced "mesarosh") means meat-eater, while in Hungarian *meszaros* means butcher. Given what the Venona messages say about Butcher and the KGB's occasional habit of making cover names a play on the subject's name, it suggests Nelson as a candidate. The authors thank Stephen Schwartz for pointing out the translation from Hungarian and Richard Miller for elaborating on the linguistic variations of Croatian and Hungarian. Schwartz devotes one chapter, entitled "Charon's Shore," of his *From West to East: California and the Making of the American Mind* (New York: Free Press, 1998) to the intermeshing of Soviet espionage and the California Communist party in the 1940s.

78. FBI summary of Nelson/Cooper [Zubilin] conversation, 22 October 1944, FBI Comintern Apparatus file, serial 3515; Nelson also mentioned Doris Silver Amatniek, a student at City College of New York, as a courier. The FBI summary of the recorded conversation is found in "Interlocking Subversion in Government Departments," U.S. Congress, Senate, Committee on the Judiciary, Subcommittee to Investigate the Administration of the Internal Security Act and Other Internal Security Laws, 83rd Cong., 1st sess., part 15, 1050–1051. See also "COMRAP—Vassili M. Zubilin" and J. Edgar Hoover to Harry Hopkins, 7 May 1943, reproduced in Benson and Warner, *Venona*, 49–50.

79. "Comintern Apparatus Summary Report." Given the swift reaction to Nelson's

complaints, Zubilin must have endorsed them and passed them on to Earl Browder or Rudy Baker.

80. "Comintern Apparatus Summary Report"; *Daily World* (25 November 1982).

81. "Interlocking Subversion in Government Departments," part 15, 1050; FBI report, "Soviet Espionage Activities," 19 October 1945, attached to Hoover to Vaughan, 19 October 1945, President's Secretary's Files, Harry S. Truman Library, Independence, Mo.

82. "Comintern Apparatus Summary Report."

83. "Comintern Apparatus Summary Report" and memo on Bransten, 31 May 1944, serial 2753, 25 October 1944, serial 3341, all in FBI Comintern Apparatus file; Venona 294 KGB San Francisco to Moscow, 31 May 1945.

84. His son, also named Vladimir, became a spokesman for the Soviet Institute on the United States and Canada, a KGB-linked think tank, and was often on American television in the 1980s as an eloquent defender of the Soviet Union.

85. Pozner memo, 23 May 1944, Comintern Apparatus file, serial 2378; Venona 1132, 1133 KGB New York to Moscow, 13 July 1943. The same message referred to Pozner's sister, Ellen Kagan, who worked for the Office of Price Administration, but there is no indication that she was also being considered for recruitment. Another message discussed a second sister of Pozner's, Victoria Pozner-Spiri or Toto, but the context suggests only that someone she knew was being considered for recruitment. Venona 1148 KGB New York to Moscow, 14 July 1943.

86. Venona messages on Map are in appendix A.

87. Lower-level CPUSA functionaries and rank-and-file members involved with Soviet espionage are listed in appendixes A and B.

88. Harvey Klehr, *The Heyday of American Communism: The Depression Decade* (New York: Basic Books, 1984), 231–232; Budenz, *Men Without Faces*, 55–58, 60–61, 252. Gebert's wife was Jewish, and in one of the ironies of history his son became a well-known religious Jewish activist in Communist and post-Communist Poland.

89. Venona messages regarding Gebert are cited in appendix A.

90. Charles Sadler, "Pro-Soviet Polish-Americans: Oskar Lange and Russia's Friends in the Polonia, 1941–1945," *Polish Review*, 22, no. 4 (1977), 25–39.

91. Venona 700 KGB New York to Moscow, 17 May 1944; 759, 760 KGB New York to Moscow, 27 May 1944.

92. Venona 1135 KGB New York to Moscow, 8 August 1944.

93. Dimitrov to Molotov, 26 August 1942, Archive of the Dimitrov Secretariat of the Comintern, RTsKhIDNI 495-73-173. All of the Ross memorandums to Dimitrov and his cover notes conveying translated copies to Molotov are found in RTsKhIDNI 495-73-173. Ross's reports may also have led to the KGB's 1944 interest in Joseph Barnes, discussed below. Ross met Barnes in Moscow in 1942 when he accompanied prominent Republican Wendell Willkie to the USSR. She reported to the Comintern that she "had a personal conversation with Barnes. He and I have an acquaintance in common—one of the officers of our party in New York, a close friend of Barnes." Janet Ross to Dimitrov, "Wendell Willkie's Discussions with Correspondents," 23 September 1942, RTsKhIDNI 495-73-173.

94. Whittaker Chambers, *Witness* (New York: Regnery, 1997), 498; Sam Tanenhaus, *Whittaker Chambers* (New York: Random House, 1997), 182.

95. Venona 1754 KGB New York to Moscow, 14 December 1944; 20 KGB New York to Moscow, 4 January 1945.

96. Venona 1681 KGB New York to Moscow, 13 October 1943; 207 Moscow to New York, 8 March 1945.

97. Venona messages regarding Laird are cited in appendix A.

98. Venona 1154 KGB New York to Moscow, 12 August 1944. This message's reference to Elizabeth Zubilin corroborates reports that she worked on the West Coast, specifically in Hollywood.

99. Stephen Laird, "Report from Warsaw," *New Republic* (3 February 1947).

100. Venona 483–484 KGB San Francisco to Moscow, 13 September 1945.

101. Walter Bernstein, *Inside Out: A Memoir of the Blacklist* (New York: Knopf, 1996), 124, 228.

102. Venona 1509 KGB New York to Moscow, 23 October 1944.

103. Bentley, *Out of Bondage,* 108. Venona messages regarding Khan are cited in appendix A.

104. Venona messages regarding Steele are cited in appendix A.

105. Venona 1039–1041 KGB New York to Moscow, 24–25 July 1944.

106. Ibid.; Venona 1097, 1098 KGB New York to Moscow, 1 August 1944.

107. Venona messages regarding Setaro are cited in appendix A.

108. Venona 1234 KGB New York to Moscow, 29 August 1944. Setaro's cover name, Gonets, translates as Express Messenger or Courier.

109. Venona 1433–1435 KGB New York to Moscow, 10 October 1944.

110. Quoted in Harvey Klehr and Ronald Radosh, *The Amerasia Spy Case: Prelude to McCarthyism* (Chapel Hill: University of North Carolina Press, 1996), 67–68.

111. Venona messages regarding Krafsur are cited in appendix A.

112. Venona 705 KGB New York to Moscow, 17 May 1944.

113. Fitin to Dimitrov, 12 September 1944, Archive of the Dimitrov Secretariat of the Comintern, RTsKhIDNI 495-74-485.

114. Jerre Mangione, *The Dream and the Deal: The Federal Writers' Project 1935–1943* (Boston: Little, Brown, 1972), 211–215.

115. *New York Times* (12 November 1971).

116. Venona 777–779 KGB New York to Moscow, 25 May 1945.

117. Oliver Pilat, *Drew Pearson: An Unauthorized Biography* (New York: Harper's Magazine Press, 1973), 45, 170, 195, 297; Tyler Abell, ed., *Drew Pearson: Diaries, 1949–1959* (New York: Holt, Rinehart and Winston, 1974), 166–168, 172–173.

118. Venona 998 KGB New York to Moscow, 15 July 1944.

119. Statement of Rep. Fred E. Busbey, *Congressional Record* (18 February 1944), A876; Statement of Rep. Martin Dies, *Congressional Record* (1 February 1943), 504–516.

120. The story of Karr's journalistic coup is in the Henry Wallace Papers: see Harold Young from Oskar Lange, 3 July 1944; *Washington Post,* 3 July 1944; *Washington Post,* 4 July 1944; Arthur Schlesinger, Jr., to Klehr, 18 April 1990.

121. On Hammer's role in laundering Soviet subsidies to the CPUSA and cooperation with Soviet intelligence, see Klehr, Haynes, and Firsov, *The Secret World of American Communism,* 26–30; Harvey Klehr, John Earl Haynes, and Kyrill M. Anderson, *The Soviet World of American Communism* (New Haven: Yale University Press, 1998), 132–135; Edward Epstein, *Dossier: The Secret History of Armand Hammer* (New York: Random House, 1996).

122. Evgeniia Albats, "Senator Edward Kennedy Requested KGB Assistance with a profitable contract for his businessman-friend," *Izvestia* (24 June 1992), 5.

123. I. F. Stone, *The Hidden History of the Korean War* (New York: Monthly Review Press, 1952). Admiring biographies include Andrew Partner, *I. F. Stone: A Portrait* (New York: Pantheon Books, 1988), and Robert C. Cottrell, *Izzy: A Biography of I. F. Stone* (New Brunswick, N.J.: Rutgers University Press, 1992). For a discussion of

how Stone's views paralleled those of the Soviet Union until the mid-1950s, see Ronald Radosh, "A 'Jewish Dissident'?" *Forward* (23 October 1992).

124. Herbert Romerstein, "The KGB Penetration of the Media," *Human Events* (6 June 6 1992), 5–6; Andrew Brown, "The Attack on I. F. Stone," *New York Review of Books* (8 October 1992), 21; Oleg Kalugin, with Fen Montaigne, *The First Directorate: My 32 Years in Intelligence and Espionage Against the West* (New York: St. Martin's Press, 1994), 74.

125. Venona 1313 KGB New York to Moscow, 13 September 1944. All Venona messages regarding Stone are cited in appendix D.

126. Venona 1506 KGB New York to Moscow, 23 October 1944.

Chapter 9: Hunting Stalin's Enemies on American Soil

1. Albert Glotzer, *Trotsky: Memoir and Critique* (Buffalo: Prometheus Books, 1989), 76–80, 186; *How the GPU Murdered Trotsky* (London: New Park Publications, 1981), 21–25, 130–136. The latter book, compiled by American and British Trotskyists, consists largely of excerpts of testimony and exhibits from the trials of Jack Soble, Robert Soblen, and Mark Zborowski, as well as excerpts from FBI and Justice Department documents obtained under the Freedom of Information Act and by court action.

2. The international association of Socialist and syndicalist organizations that was founded in 1864 and collapsed in 1876 became known as the First International. European Socialist parties formed a new association, informally known as the Second International, in 1889. When Communists split from the socialist movement in the wake of the Bolshevik Revolution, Lenin formed the third international, the Comintern, in 1919.

3. Mark Zborowski testimony, 29 February 1956, part 4, 77–101, and 2 March 1956, part 5, 103–136, "Scope of Soviet Activities in the United States," Subcommittee to Investigate the Administration of the Internal Security Act, U.S. Senate, Committee on the Judiciary, 84th Cong., 2d sess.; Herbert Romerstein and Stanislav Levchenko, *The KGB Against the "Main Enemy"* (Lexington, Mass.: Lexington Books, 1989); Dimitri Volkogonov, *Trotsky: The Eternal Revolutionary* (New York: Free Press, 1996), 334–340, 347, 356–380, 388, 399–400, 426, 441–447, 456, 462, 467; KGB documents regarding his activities prior to his coming to the United States are in "Investigation File, Zborowski, Mark Grigorievich," box 4, Dimitri Volkogonov Papers, Library of Congress, Washington, D.C.

4. Venona messages regarding Zborowski are cited in appendix A.

5. Victor Kravchenko, *I Chose Freedom: The Personal and Political Life of a Soviet Official* (New York: Scribners, 1946), 4.

6. The trial is recounted in Victor Kravchenko, *I Chose Justice* (New York: Scribners, 1950).

7. Venona messages regarding Fighter are cited in appendix A.

8. Lilia Dallin testimony, 2 March 1956, "Scope of Soviet Activities in the United States," part 5, 136–150; *How the GPU Murdered Trotsky,* 178–189.

9. Venona 594 KGB New York to Moscow, 1 May 1944.

10. Venona 600 KGB New York to Moscow, 2 May 1944. NSA and FBI analysts were never sure whether Green was a cover name or referred to Abner Green, the Communist who headed the American Committee for the Protection of the Foreign-Born and who had many sources among immigrant Russians.

11. Venona 613–614 KGB New York to Moscow, 3 May 1944.

12. Venona 726 KGB New York to Moscow, 20 May 1944.

13. Venona 740 KGB New York to Moscow, 24 May 1944; 799 KGB New York to Moscow, 3 June 1944

14. Elizabeth Poretsky [Else Bernaut], *Our Own People* (Ann Arbor: University of Michigan Press, 1969), 262–274.

15. Kravchenko, *I Chose Freedom*, 309–311.

16. Venona 1143–1144 KGB New York to Moscow, 10 August 1944.

17. Venona 1457 KGB New York to Moscow, 14 October 1944; 1803 KGB New York to Moscow, 22 December 1944.

18. Alexander Orlov, *The Secret History of Stalin's Crimes* (New York: Random House, 1953). A more accurate account is John Costello and Oleg Tsarov, *Deadly Illusions: The KGB Orlov Dossier* (New York: Crown, 1993).

19. Mark Zborowski testimony, part 5, 107.

20. Some prominent anthropologists defended Zborowski as the victim of McCarthyite witch hunts. Isaac Don Levine, on the other hand, noted that he had "left behind a trail of duplicity and blood worthy of a Shakespearean villain." Isaac Don Levine, *The Mind of an Assassin* (New York: Farrar, Straus and Cudahy, 1959), 27.

21. Venona 217 KGB Moscow to New York, 10 March 1945.

22. Venona messages regarding these persons are cited in appendix A.

23. Venona messages regarding Kurnakov are cited in appendix A.

24. Venona messages regarding Tkach and the Sidoroviches are cited in appendix A.

25. Gennadi Kostyrchenko, *Out of the Red Shadows: Anti-Semitism in Stalin's Russia* (Amherst, N.Y.: Prometheus Books, 1995).

26. Kostyrchenko, *Out of the Red Shadows*, 78.

27. Venona messages regarding Mark and Hudson are cited in appendix A.

28. Venona 640 KGB New York to Moscow, 6 May 1944; 1251 KGB New York to Moscow, 5 September 1944.

29. In the late 1950s Rand founded the Metropolitan Council on Housing, a tenant's group in New York City. She remained a Communist activist until her death, in the Soviet Union, in 1981. *Daily World* (24 June 1981), 1.

30. Louis Budenz affidavit, 11 November 1950, "American Aspects of the Assassination of Leon Trotsky," U.S. Congress, House of Representatives, Committee on Un-American Activities, 81st Cong., 2d sess., part 1, v–ix; Louis Budenz, *Men Without Faces: The Communist Conspiracy in the USA* (New York: Harper and Brothers, 1948), 123–126.

31. Venona 749 KGB New York to Moscow, 26 May 1944.

32. New York FBI memo, serial 1980, FBI Silvermaster file (FBI file 65-56402). On Straight, see chapter 5.

33. *Sylvia Franklin Dossier* (New York: Labor Publication, 1977) contains excerpts from Callen's grand jury testimony.

34. Venona 851 KGB New York to Moscow, 15 June 1944. Venona messages regarding Callen are cited in appendix A.

35. Callen's grand jury testimony is in *The Gelfand Case: A Legal History of the Exposure of U.S. Government Agents in the Leadership of the Socialist Workers Party*, vol. 2 (Detroit: Labor Publication, 1985), 526–564.

36. FBI memorandum, "Existing Corroboration of Bentley's Overall Testimony," FBI Silvermaster file, serial 4201; Margaret Browder FBI file, 100-287645, serial 153; Booker interview in *Sylvia Franklin Dossier*. Booker is not identified in the cables deciphered in the Venona Project.

37. Venona messages regarding Miller are cited in appendix A.

38. Excerpts from Miller's trial testimony are published in *How the GPU Murdered Trotsky*, 146–153.

39. Venona messages regarding Getzoff are cited in appendix A.

40. Venona 846 KGB New York to Moscow, 14 June 1944.

41. Venona 556 KGB Mexico City to Moscow, 29 June 1944.

42. *How the GPU Murdered Trotsky*, 146–153.

43. Venona 1143–1144 KGB New York to Moscow, 10 August 1944.

44. Venona 776 KGB New York to Moscow, 25 May 1945. In this message Jack Soble is code-named Czech. Analysts mistakenly attributed this code name here to Robert Menaker, who was called Czech in earlier messages. *How the GPU Murdered Trotsky*, 146–153.

45. Venona 1143–1144 KGB New York to Moscow, 10 August 1944.

46. Franklin Folsom, *Days of Anger, Days of Hope: A Memoir of the League of American Writers* (Boulder: University Press of Colorado, 1994), 46–47; Daniel Menaker, *The Old Left* (New York: Knopf, 1987). Leopolo and Luís Arenal took part in the KGB's unsuccessful armed assault on Trotsky's residence in 1940. To add to these family ties, one of Robert Menaker's nieces was married to Victor Perlo, the Soviet spy discussed in chapter 5.

47. Menaker, *The Old Left*, 22, 42.

48. Venona messages regarding Menaker and Burd are cited in appendix A, those on Subercaseux in appendix C.

49. Venona 1313 KGB New York to Moscow, 13 September 1944.

50. Venona 1470 KGB New York to Moscow, 17 October 1944

51. Daniel Menaker telephone interview with Harvey Klehr, 23 June 1997.

52. Venona messages regarding Katz are cited in appendix A. On his background, see FBI memo, 27 October 1944, serial 3392, in FBI Comintern Apparatus file; FBI memo, "Existing Corroboration of Bentley's Overall Testimony," 6 May 1955, serial 4201, in FBI Silvermaster file.

53. Stalin's institution of an antisemitic purge of his intelligence services in this period may have played some role in Katz's severing links to the KGB.

54. Boris Morros, *My Ten Years as a Counterspy* (New York: Viking, 1959).

55. FBI memo, 8 September 1944, Comintern Apparatus file (FBI file 100-203581), serial 3318.

56. Romerstein and Levchenko, *The KGB Against the "Main Enemy,"* 187–188; Katrina vanden Heuvel, "Grand Illusions," *Vanity Fair* (September 1991), 219–225, 248–256. Vanden Heuvel takes the view that the Sterns did not cooperate with Soviet espionage.

57. Martin Dies statement, *Congressional Record* (1 February 1943), 504–516; Kerr Commission analysis of evidence in regard to William Dodd, analysis of evidence on Watson and Dodd, 21 April 1943, Report of the Kerr Commission, 14 May 1943, both in box 856, Clinton Anderson papers, Library of Congress; William Dodd, Jr., testimony, 5 April 1943, "Investigations of Un-American Propaganda activities in the United States," U.S. Congress, House of Representatives, Special Committee on Un-American Activities, 78th Cong., 1st sess., vol. 7, 3366–3382.

58. Venona 748 KGB New York to Moscow, 26 May 1944.

59. Venona 1824 KGB New York to Moscow, 27 December 1944; 4–5 KGB New York to Moscow, 3 January 1945; 11 KGB New York to Moscow, 4 January 1945; 18–19 KGB New York to Moscow, 4 January 1945. The KGB sent reports on the business to Moscow. By this time the Zubilins were there.

60. Vanden Heuvel, "Grand Illusions," 248.

61. Given that the anonymous Russian letter (see chapter 2) specifically named Morros as a KGB contact and its authenticity was accepted by the FBI, it may be that Morros in his autobiography exaggerated the extent to which he volunteered his services. The FBI most likely would by that time have gathered information about his espionage activities that would have provided leverage to encourage his cooperation.

62. Annotated list of CPUSA and Young Communist League members in the International Brigades, Archive of the International Brigades, RTsKhIDNI 545-6-846.

63. Jane Foster, *An Un-American Lady* (London: Sidgwick and Jackson, 1980), 99.

64. Venona 854 KGB New York to Moscow, 16 June 1942.

65. Venona 958 KGB New York to Moscow, 21 June 1943; 1025, 1035–1036 KGB New York to Moscow, 30 June 1943; 765, 771 KGB New York to Moscow, 30 May 1944.

66. *New York Times* (7 July 1961), 9.

67. *New York Times* (14 October 1961), 10; (7 July 1961), 9; (4 November 1961), 11; Romerstein and Levchenko, *The KGB Against the "Main Enemy,"* 195–196. Brandt, a Social Democrat, became one of West Germany's leading political figures.

68. Venona messages presumably regarding Beker are cited in appendix A.

69. Venona 48 KGB New York to Moscow, 11 January 1945.

70. *New York Times* (30 November 1960), 1.

71. Venona 777–781 KGB New York to Moscow, 26 May 1943. Other Venona messages regarding Wolston are cited in appendix A.

72. Venona 1824 KGB New York to Moscow, 27 December 1944. There is a Slava in a 1945 message (Venona 325 KGB Moscow to New York, 5 April 1945); it clearly is not Wolston but someone connected to the Rosenberg spy ring. This also suggests that by that time Wolston had a different cover name.

73. Venona 193–194 KGB Mexico City to Moscow, 14 March 1944; 474 KGB Mexico City to Moscow, 6 June 1944; 555 KGB Mexico City to Moscow, 29 June 1944; 812 KGB Mexico City to Moscow, 7 November 1944; 109 KGB Moscow to Mexico City, 20 February 1944; 355 KGB Moscow to Mexico City, 9 June 1944.

74. Pavel A. Sudoplatov, Antoli P. Sudoplatov, Jerrold Schecter, and Leona Schecter, *Special Tasks: The Memoirs of an Unwanted Witness* (New York: Little, Brown, 1994), 65–86.

75. Thomas Black testimony, 17 May 1956, "Scope of Soviet Activity in the United States," part 21, 1113–1124.

76. Levine, *The Mind of an Assassin,* 190.

77. In a 1944 Venona message Moscow informed the Mexico City KGB that Neruda, then Chilean consul-general, "is being developed" as an agent. Venona 287 KGB Moscow to Mexico City, 11 May 1944. Siqueiros later became a leader of the Mexican Communist party. His cover name in Venona was Chess Knight.

78. FBI memorandum, "Existing Corroboration of Bentley's Overall Testimony," 6 May 1955, FBI Silvermaster file, serial 4201.

79. Venona 1160 KGB New York KGB to Moscow, 17 July 1943. Other Venona messages regarding Rose Arenal are cited in appendix A.

80. Louis Budenz affidavit, 11 November 1950, "American Aspects of the Assassination of Leon Trotsky"; Don Levine, *The Mind of an Assassin,* is the fullest account of the assassination.

81. When a congressional committee asked Altschuler about her activities, she made a statement denying any criminal actions but then refused to answer any questions. Lydia

Altschuler testimony, 18 October 1950, "American Aspects of Assassination of Leon Trotsky," 3354–3360.

82. "Comintern Apparatus Summary Report," 15 December 1944, FBI Comintern Apparatus file, serial 3702.

83. Venona 177–179 KGB Mexico City to Moscow, 30 December 1943; 6 KGB Mexico City to Moscow, 3 January 1944, analyst footnote vi. In his memoir of growing up in a Communist family in New York, David Horowitz remembered Anna Colloms as a family friend who served as a courier to Mexico and later was distressed that she had been involved in Trotsky's assassination. David Horowitz, *Radical Son: A Generational Odyssey* (New York: Free Press, 1997), 76.

84. Anna Colloms testimony, 19 October 1950, "American Aspects of Assassination of Leon Trotsky," 3371–3377.

85. Letter no. 4 Buenos Aires to New York, 5 July 1942; Letter no. 5 Buenos Aires to New York, 1 August 1942; Letter no. 9 Buenos Aires to New York, 1 November 1942; Letter no. 11 Buenos Aires to New York, 6 December 1942. All of these "secret writing letters" were intercepted by American authorities and made public as part of the Venona Project.

86. Venona secret writing letters: Letter no. 12 KGB New York to Buenos Aires, 1 February 1943; Letter no. 14 KGB New York to Buenos Aires, 29 September 1943. Alexander was an unidentified KGB agent who had some connection with Mexico. In the Mexico City KGB traffic there is another cable, Venona 584 KGB Moscow to Mexico City, 6 October 1944, indicating that Altschuler was still serving as a mail drop as late as 1944.

87. Venona 193, 194 KGB Mexico City to Moscow, 14 March 1944. NSA analysts did not identify "A" as Colloms, but the context clearly refers to her.

88. Jacob Epstein testimony, 18 October 1950, "American Aspects of Assassination of Leon Trotsky," 3345–3354; "Comintern Apparatus Summary Report."

89. New York FBI memo, 1 April 1948, FBI Silvermaster file, serial 3187. Mercader had the cover name Rita until December 1943, when the designation was changed to Gnome.

90. Venona 193, 194 KGB Mexico City to Moscow, 14 March 1944.

91. Venona 800 KGB New York to Moscow, 28 May 1943; 816–817 KGB New York to Moscow, 30 May 1943; 899 KGB New York to Moscow, 11 June 1943. Another message, 1142 KGB New York to Moscow, 10 August 1944, contains identification routines for contacts with Epstein and two co-workers.

92. Venona 158 KGB Mexico City to Moscow, 23 December 1943. Klarin arrived in Mexico to take up duties as second secretary of the Soviet embassy on November 23; he left on May 24, 1944.

93. Venona 174–176 KGB Mexico City to Moscow, 29 December 1943; 177–179 KGB Mexico City to Moscow, 30 December 1943, 6 KGB Mexico City to Moscow, 3 January 1944; 193, 194 KGB Mexico City to Moscow, 14 March 1944.

94. Venona 193, 194 KGB Mexico City to Moscow, 14 March 1944; 212 KGB Mexico City to Moscow, 25 March 1944; 261–262 KGB Mexico City to Moscow, 16 April 1944; 281 KGB Mexico City to Moscow, 21 April 1944; 248 KGB Moscow to Mexico City, 27 April 1944; 288 KGB Moscow to Mexico City, 11 May 1944; 256 KGB Moscow to New York, March 21, 1945. Jacob Epstein, Anna Colloms, and several other people involved in the operation to free Mercader were later subpoenaed by the House Committee on Un-American Activities. They were all uncooperative witnesses. Jacob Epstein testimony, "American Aspects of Assassination of Leon Trotsky," 3349.

See also foreword to "American Aspects of Assassination of Leon Trotsky," part 2, ix–xv.

95. Venona 193, 194 KGB Mexico City to Moscow, 14 March 1944; 218 KGB Mexico City to Moscow, 29 March 1944.

96. Venona 474 KGB Mexico City to Moscow, 6 June 1944.

97. Venona 172–174 KGB Moscow to Mexico City, 9–10 March 1945; Sudoplatov and Schecter, *Special Tasks,* 80–81. Contributing to the KGB's failure to free Mercader was the intense security provided by Mexican counterintelligence. The Mexican political leadership, which had granted Trotsky exile, was deeply embarrassed by his murder on Mexican territory and determined that his assassin would serve out his term.

98. Harvey Klehr interview with Dr. Robert Harris, 19 August 1996. The details about Harris's sisters' employment is provided in Venona 347 KGB Moscow to Mexico City, 27 May 1945.

99. James Ryan, *Earl Browder: The Failure of American Communism* (Tuscaloosa: University of Alabama Press, 1997), 32–33, 283; Klehr, Haynes, and Firsov, *The Secret World of American Communism,* 45–46; Benjamin Gitlow, *I Confess* (Dutton: New York, 1940), 329–330; Klehr interview with Robert Harris. The complaint about Harris's lack of discipline is in J. Crosby and Marion to Alexander, 30 January 1929, Archive of the Red International of Labor Unions (Profintern), RTsKhIDNI 534-4-283.

100. It is not certain, but Harris may have used the name Adelina Zenejdas Gomez while in Mexico.

101. Venona 256 KGB Moscow to Mexico City, 29 April 1944.

102. Venona 492 KGB Mexico City to Moscow, 9 June 1944.

103. Venona 63–66 KGB New York to Moscow, 15 January 1945.

104. Venona 232 KGB Mexico City to Moscow, 3 April 1944; 208 KGB Moscow to Mexico City, 10 April 1944.

105. Venona 220 KGB Moscow to Mexico City, 16 April 1944.

106. Venona 327 KGB Mexico City to Moscow, 3 May 1944.

107. Venona 283 KGB Moscow to Mexico City, 10 May 1944. There is no decrypted message indicating the outcome.

108. Venona 129 KGB Mexico City to Moscow, 6 December 1943; 200 KGB Moscow to Mexico City, 8 April 1944; 243, 244 KGB Mexico City to Moscow, 10 April 1944; 283 KGB Moscow to Mexico City, 10 May 1944; 303 KGB Moscow to Mexico City, 17 May 1944; 347 KGB Moscow to Mexico City, 27 May 1945. Harris's nephew was astounded to learn that his aunt had communicated with her sisters in the 1940s; no one in the family ever mentioned that she was still alive at that late date. One of Harris's sisters was still alive in 1997; she refused to discuss Kitty Harris at all. Klehr interview with Robert Harris.

109. Venona 553, 554 KGB Mexico City to Moscow, 29 June 1944; 476 KGB Moscow to Mexico City, 29 July 1944.

110. Venona 312 KGB Moscow to Mexico City, 11 May 1945; 659 KGB Moscow to Mexico City, 7 September 1945; 238 KGB Moscow to Mexico City, 28 April 1946.

Chapter 10: Industrial and Atomic Espionage

1. Quoted in Ronald Radosh and Joyce Milton, *The Rosenberg File: A Search for the Truth* (New Haven: Yale University Press, 1997), 29. For the story of Gold and Black as industrial spies, see pp. 20–47.

2. Quoted in Radosh and Milton, *The Rosenberg File,* 30. Smith, Ruga, Fred, and

Semenov were Soviet intelligence officers. Brothman was a source, and Smilg was a target for recruitment.

3. For a summary of Semenov's KGB career, see appendix E.

4. Venona messages regarding Gold are cited in appendix A.

5. Venona 1390 KGB New York to Moscow, 1 October 1944; 1403 KGB New York to Moscow, 5 October 1944.

6. Radosh and Milton, *The Rosenberg File,* 152–153.

7. In recent decades Congress has enacted statutes that clearly define many types of industrial espionage as criminal acts. In the 1930s, however, few criminal statutes clearly applied to the stealing of scientific information or industrial techniques from private firms. There were remedies under civil law (patent and copyright infringement and the like), but such remedies were practical only when one firm could present evidence that another was marketing a product based on stolen proprietary information. Such remedies were rarely applicable when the thief was a Soviet intelligence agency stealing the information for use within the USSR's closed internal economy.

8. For a summary of Ovakimian's KGB career, see appendix E.

9. Thomas Black testimony, 17 May 1956, part 21, 1113–1124, and Harry Gold testimony, 26 April 1956, part 20, 1020, both in "Scope of Soviet Activity in the United States," U.S. Congress, Senate, Committee on the Judiciary, Subcommittee to Investigate the Administration of the Internal Security Act, 84th Cong., 2d sess.

10. Venona messages regarding Black are cited in appendix A.

11. In part due to the success of his field work in the United States, Kvasnikov later became overall head of KGB scientific intelligence. For a summary of Kvasnikov's KGB career, see appendix E. Venona messages regarding Malisoff are cited in appendix A.

12. Venona 622 KGB New York to Moscow, 4 May 1944.

13. Venona messages regarding Odessan and Second Hand Bookseller are cited in appendix A.

14. Venona messages regarding these individuals are cited in appendix A.

15. Alleman and Steinberg are discussed in appendix B.

16. Venona messages regarding all of these names are cited in appendix A.

17. Memo on Leona and Joseph Franey, 5 August 1944, FBI Comintern Apparatus file (FBI file 100-203581), serial 2919; memo on Leona and Joseph Franey, 21 August 1944, FBI Comintern Apparatus file, serial 2989; FBI memo on Shevchenko, 30 October 1944, FBI Comintern Apparatus file, serial Serial 3379; FBI memo on Shevchenko, 9 December 1944, FBI Comintern Apparatus file, serial 3612; Leona Franey testimony and Joseph Franey testimony, 6 June 1949, "Soviet Espionage Activities in Connection with Jet Propulsion and Aircraft," U.S. Congress, House of Representatives, Un-American Activities Committee, 81st Cong., 1st sess.

18. Venona 941 KGB New York to Moscow, 4 July 1944; Venona 1048 KGB New York to Moscow, 25 July 1944; Venona 1403 KGB New York to Moscow, 5 October 1944; Venona 1559 KGB New York to Moscow, 6 November 1944; Venona 305 KGB Moscow to New York, 1 April 1945.

19. Venona 1607–1608 KGB New York to Moscow, 16 November 1944; Loren Haas testimony, 6 June 1949, "Soviet Espionage Activities in Connection with Jet Propulsion and Aircraft."

20. Larry Kerley testimony, 15 September 1949, "Communist Activities Among Aliens and National Groups," U.S. Congress, Senate, Committee on the Judiciary, Subcommittee on Immigration and Naturalization, 81st Cong., 1st sess., part 2, 806.

21. Venona messages regarding all of these persons are cited in appendix A.

22. Radosh and Milton, *The Rosenberg File,* concentrates on the atomic espionage aspects of the Rosenberg apparatus, but it also has the most comprehensive examination of the Rosenberg network's scientific-technical espionage, including the activities of Morton Sobell, Max Elitcher, Joel Barr, and Alfred Sarant.

23. Elizabeth Bentley deposition, 30 November 1945 (FBI file 65-14603); Radosh and Milton, *The Rosenberg File,* 176.

24. Venona 628 KGB New York to Moscow, 5 May 1944. All Venona messages regarding Julius Rosenberg are cited in appendix A.

25. Venona 736 KGB New York to Moscow, 22 May 1944.

26. Venona 1053 KGB New York to Moscow, 26 July 1944.

27. Feklisov appears in numerous Venona messages under the cover name of Kalistratus. While in the United States as a KGB officer, he used the name Alexander Fomin. Michael Dobbs, "Julius Rosenberg Spied, Russian Says," *Washington Post* (16 March 1997); Joseph Albright and Marcia Kunstel, "Retired KGB Spymaster Lifts Veil on Rosenberg Espionage," *Washington Times* (16 March 1997). A Discovery Channel television documentary, "The Rosenberg File: Case Closed" (23 March 1997), featured lengthy interviews with Feklisov. See also Alexander Feklisov, *Za okeanom i na ostrove. Zapiski razvedchika* (Overseas and on the island: Notes of an intelligence officer, in Russian) (Moscow: DEE, 1994).

28. Venona messages regarding Sarant and Barr are cited in appendix A.

29. Venona 1600 KGB New York to Moscow, 14 November 1944.

30. Venona 1749–1750 KGB New York to Moscow, 13 December 1944.

31. Philip Morrison testimony, 7 and 8 May 1953, "Subversive Influence in the Educational Process," U.S. Congress, Senate, Committee on the Judiciary, 83rd Cong., 1st sess., part 9, 899–919.

32. Radosh and Milton, *The Rosenberg File,* xi–xiii; Michelle Locke, "Flight to Mexico with Lover Turns into 40 Years Behind Iron Curtain," *Los Angeles Times* (23 August 1992); Elizabeth Shogren, "Scientist for the Enemy," *Los Angeles Times* (14 October 1992); Irvin Molotsky, "Joel Barr, Defector Linked to Rosenberg, Dies," *New York Times* (16 August 1998); Alexei Kuznetsov and Carla Rivera, "Joel Barr: U.S. Defector, Electronics Whiz Helped Propel Soviets into Computer Age," *Los Angeles Times* (17 August 1998); John Corry, "Replaying the Best of Nightline's History," *Washington Times* (29 June 1996). Although Barr died in 1998 in St. Petersburg, Russia, he had established residency in California and collected both a federal Social Security pension and a California state supplemental old age benefit. His collecting U.S. government pensions inspired a group of congressmen to urge that the Justice Department open an inquiry into the possibility of prosecuting him. Nothing, however, came of the effort. Robert W. Stewart, "Inquiry Urged on Associate of Atom Spies," *Los Angeles Times* (24 June 1992).

33. Venona messages regarding Perl are cited in appendix A.

34. Venona 154 KGB Moscow to New York, 16 February 1945.

35. Venona 305 KGB Moscow to New York, 1 April 1945.

36. Radosh and Milton, *The Rosenberg File,* 299.

37. Venona 1491 KGB New York to Moscow, 22 October 1944. Five other Venona messages regarding the Sidorovichs are cited in appendix A. Julius Rosenberg's cover name in KGB cables initially was Antenna and was changed to Liberal in September 1944.

38. Radosh and Milton, *The Rosenberg File,* 299–300.

39. Venona messages regarding Nile are cited in appendix A.

40. American engineers succeeded in placing inside an artillery shell a tiny and very

rugged radar unit connected to the shell's fuse. The device set off the shell when it came close to (even if it did not hit) a target, a feature that greatly increased the efficiency of anti-aircraft shells. The device was called a proximity fuse because it set off the shell in the proximity of the target aircraft. Radosh and Milton, *The Rosenberg File*, 72. See also testimony of Col. Walter Edward Lotz, Jr., statement of O. John Rogge, and statement of David Greenglass, 24 November 1953, "Army Signal Corps—Subversion and Espionage," U.S. Senate, Committee on Government Operations, Permanent Subcommittee on Investigations of the Senate, 83rd Cong., 1st sess., part 1.

41. Venona messages regarding Julius Rosenberg are cited in appendix A.

42. David Martin, *Wilderness of Mirrors* (New York: Ballantine Books, 1981); Ronald Radosh and Joyce Milton in their 1983 edition of *The Rosenberg File: A Search for the Truth* (New York: Holt, Rinehart and Winston, 1983); Robert Lamphere and Tom Shachtman, *The FBI-KGB War: A Special Agent's Story* (New York: Random House, 1986).

43. There is one deciphered London GRU message regarding the initial establishment of Fuchs's relationship with Soviet intelligence: Venona 2227 GRU London to Moscow, 10 August 1941. This message is from a period antedating the Soviet duplication of one-time pads. Its decryption was made possible because the London GRU station in 1941 ran out of one-time pads and used its emergency back-up cipher system based on a standard statistical table to generate the additive key. British cryptanalysts working with the Venona Project recognized it as a nonstandard and vulnerable cipher and solved it, but not until well after Fuchs's arrest.

44. Venona messages regarding Fuchs are cited in appendix A.

45. Venona 345 KGB New York to Moscow, 22 September 1944; 1397 KGB New York to Moscow, 4 October 1944; 1403 KGB New York to Moscow, 5 October 1944; 1606 KGB New York to Moscow, 16 November 1944.

46. Quoted in Radosh and Milton, *The Rosenberg File*, 44.

47. [Lamphere to Gardner], "Study of Code Names in MGB Communications," 27 June 1950, National Security Agency, Venona Collection 50-025, box D045, reproduced in Robert Louis Benson and Michael Warner, eds., *Venona: Soviet Espionage and the American Response, 1939–1957* (Washington, D.C.: National Security Agency, Central Intelligence Agency, 1996), 153. Venona messages regarding the Greenglasses and the Rosenbergs are cited in appendix A.

48. Quoted in Radosh and Milton, *The Rosenberg File* (1997), 58–65.

49. There is no evidence that Greenglass's assignment to Los Alamos was anything but the chance working of the Army's personnel system.

50. Venona 1340 KGB New York to Moscow, 21 September 1944.

51. Quoted in Radosh and Milton, *The Rosenberg File*, 66.

52. Venona 1600 KGB New York to Moscow, 14 November 1944.

53. Venona 1657 KGB New York to Moscow, 27 November 1944.

54. Venona messages regarding Quantum are cited in appendix A.

55. Venona 972, 979, 983 KGB New York to Moscow, 22–23 June 1943.

56. Richard Rhodes, *Dark Sun: The Making of the Hydrogen Bomb* (New York: Simon and Schuster, 1995), 39.

57. Venona messages regarding Fogel/Pers are cited in appendix A.

58. On the intelligence information the KGB turned over to Soviet scientists in 1944, see Joseph Albright and Marcia Kunstel, " 'Did the United States Have *Any* Secrets?' " *The Bulletin of the Atomic Scientists* (January/February 1988), 53–54, and V. Merkulov to Lavrenti P. Beria, 28 February 1945, reprinted in *Voprosy Istorii Estestvoznaniia i Tekhniki*, Russian Academy of Science, no. 3 (1992).

59. Hall's name is given in clear text (no cover name) in the earliest message regarding him.

60. Michael Dobbs, "Code Name 'Mlad,' Atomic Bomb Spy," *Washington Post* (25 February 1996), and "Unlocking the Crypts: Most Spies Code Revealed Escaped Prosecution," *Washington Post* (25 December 1996); Joseph Albright and Marcia Kunstel, *Bombshell: The Secret Story of America's Unknown Atomic Spy Conspiracy* (New York: Times Books, 1997). *Bombshell* also contains extensive coverage of the espionage activities of Morris and Lona Cohen.

61. Venona messages regarding Hall are cited in appendix A.

62. Kurnakov's KGB career is discussed in chapter 6. Hall told Albright and Kunstel that he attempted to reach the Soviets by talking to staff members of Amtorg and was also directed to Kurnakov. The deciphered Venona cables refer only to Sax's approach. The decrypted parts of the Venona cable suggest that it may have been Nicola Napoli, head of Artkino, the distributor of Soviet films in the United States, who directed Sax to Kurnakov. Venona 1699 KGB New York to Moscow, 2 December 1944.

63. Venona 1585 KGB New York to Moscow, 12 November 1944.

64. Allen Weinstein, "Bombshell," *Los Angeles Times* (28 September 1997), 6.

65. Venona 298 KGB Moscow to New York, 31 March 1945.

66. Albright and Kunstel compare what is known of Hall's access to the secrets of Los Alamos with documents in papers of Igor Kurchatov and other Russian archives about espionage reports given to Soviet scientists. See *Bombshell,* chaps. 14–16.

67. Robert K. McQueen memo of 31 March 1951 on FBI interviews with Hall 16 and 19 March and with Sax 16 March, FBI file 65-3404 [65-3403], text available at *bombshell-1.com* website.

68. Vladimir Chikov, "How the Soviet Secret Service Split the American Atom," *Novoe Vremia* 16 (23 April 1991) and 17 (30 April 1991).

69. The Cohens' role in espionage against Great Britain is described in Rebecca West, *The New Meaning of Treason* (New York: Viking, 1964), 281–288, and in Albright and Kunstel, *Bombshell,* 244–253.

70. The FBI investigation of the Cohens can be followed in the FBI Morris and Lona Cohen file, 100-406659.

71. Russian Federal Foreign Intelligence Service, "Veterany vneshnei razvedki Rossii" (Veterans of Russian foreign intelligence service) (Moscow: Russian Federal Foreign Intelligence Service, 1995).

72. Chikov, "How the Soviet Secret Service Split the American Atom."

73. Michael Dobbs, "How Soviets Stole U.S. Atom Secrets," *Washington Post* (4 October 1992). Dobbs referred to the Perseus story when describing Yatskov's confirmation of the Cohens' role in atomic espionage, which has led some to think that Yatskov confirmed the Perseus cover name as well. Dobbs, however, says that Yatskov did not use the cover name Perseus. For a summary of Yatskov's KGB career, see appendix E.

74. In an earlier book the authors discussed Morris Cohen's background and his activities in Spain as well as a report written by Rudy Baker, head of the CPUSA's underground arm. Baker's report described the work during 1942 of a covert network, one that included a covert radio operator with the cover name Louis. Cohen was trained as a covert radio operator and, according to Chikov, had the cover name Louis in 1942. This led the authors to conclude that the Louis in Baker's report was Morris Cohen. Since that time the authors have found a document in the archive of the Communist International that disproves this identification. Specifically, in 1943 Earl Browder, head of the CPUSA, sent a coded message to the Comintern stating that he was sending Louis

to Mexico to establish a new clandestine radio station. This Louis was clearly the same one as in Baker's report, but it cannot have been Cohen, who by that point had been drafted into the U.S. Army. Harvey Klehr, John Earl Haynes, and Fridrikh Igorevich Firsov, *The Secret World of American Communism* (New Haven: Yale University Press, 1995), 205–226; Browder to Comintern, 15 January 1943, Archive of the Secretariat of the Executive Committee of the Communist International: coded correspondence with Communist Parties (1933–1943), RTsKhIDNI 495-184-7 1943 file.

75. Pavel A. Sudoplatov, Anatoli Sudoplatov, Jerrold Schecter, and Leona Schecter, *Special Tasks: The Memoirs of an Unwanted Witness* (New York: Little, Brown, 1994); Rhodes, *Dark Sun*, 71; *Voprosy Istorii Estestvoznaniia i Tekhniki*, Russian Academy of Science, no. 3 (1992), document 4; Albright and Kunstel, *Bombshell*, 76–77, 317n–318n.

76. Venona 50 KGB New York to Moscow, 11 January 1945.

77. Venona 239 KGB New York to Moscow, 30 August 1944; 50 KGB New York to Moscow, 11 January 1945.

78. New York FBI to Director, 8 May 1957, FBI Morris and Lona Cohen file, 100-406659, serial 33; Transcript of videotaped interview of Morris Cohen by a historian of the KGB oral history project in Moscow, 19 July 1993, and shown by the Russian Foreign Intelligence Service to Joseph Albright and Marcia Kunstel on 15 July 1995, *bombshell-1.com* website.

79. On the Smyth report's impact on the Soviet bomb program, see Rhodes, *Dark Sun,* 182, 215–17, 221–22.

80. Venona messages regarding Erie and Ernest are cited in appendix A.

81. Venona 619–620 KGB San Francisco to Moscow, 27 November 1945.

82. Venona messages regarding Hiskey are cited in appendix B.

83. Venona 619 KGB New York to Moscow, 4 May 1944.

84. Venona 1020 KGB New York to Moscow, 20 July 1944.

85. Venona 1332 KGB New York to Moscow, 18 September 1944.

86. Venona 1715 KGB New York to Moscow, 5 December 1944.

87. While it is most likely that Rose Olsen/Phlox is Roselyn Childs and that Jack Childs was designated to approach Hiskey, an alternative would be that Rose was the cover name for Morris's wife and that it was Morris himself who was picked to approach Hiskey.

88. Venona 580–581 San Francisco to Moscow, 13 November 1945.

89. Testimony of James Sterling Murray and Edward Tiers Manning, 14 August and 5 October 1949, U.S. Congress, House of Representatives, Committee on Un-American Activities, 81st Cong., 1st sess., 877–899.

90. Excerpts From Hearings Regarding Investigation of Communist Activities in Connection with the Atom Bomb, U.S. Congress, House of Representatives, Committee on Un-American Activities, 80th Cong., 2d sess., 1948; Testimony of James Murray and Edward Manning.

91. FBI memo, "Soviet Activities in the United States," 25 July 1946, Papers of Clark Clifford, Harry S. Truman Library.

92. Venona 1276 GRU New York to Moscow, 2 August 1943.

93. "Report on Atomic Espionage (Nelson-Weinberg and Hiskey-Adams Cases)," 29 September 1949, U.S. Congress, House of Representatives, Committee on Un-American Activities, 89th Cong., 1st sess., 1–15; San Francisco FBI report of 1 July 1945 through 1 March 1947, Comintern Apparatus file, serial 5421.

94. Report of 11 January 1944, serial 3378, FBI Silvermaster file (FBI file 65-56402); "Comintern Apparatus Summary Report," 15 December 1944 "Comintern Apparatus Summary Report," 15 December 1944, serial 3702, FBI Comintern Apparatus

file; "The Shameful Years: Thirty Years of Soviet Espionage in the United States," 30 December 1951, U.S. Congress, House of Representatives, Committee on Un-American Activities, 39–40.

95. Venona 1328 KGB New York to Moscow, 12 August 1943. The Venona message gives the professor's name in clear text, but the NSA chose to black it out in its release. Internal and other evidence suggests that the name was that of Ernest Lawrence, in which case the New York KGB most likely soon learned that Lawrence was not recruitable. This cable erroneously located the radiation laboratory at Sacramento rather than at Berkeley.

96. San Francisco FBI report, 22 April 1947, serial 5421 and "Comintern Apparatus Summary Report," 15 December 1944, serial 3702, both in FBI Comintern Apparatus file. Pinsky also had a brother-in-law who was a physicist and who worked at Los Alamos on the bomb project. In 1944 Pinsky may have traveled to New Mexico to contact him. Pinsky himself later became research director for the California CIO while it was headed by Harry Bridges, a concealed Communist.

97. Venona 340 KGB New York to Moscow, 21 September 1944.

98. Venona 132 KGB San Francisco to Moscow, 18 March 1944.

99. Venona 580–581 KGB San Francisco to Moscow, 13 November 1945.

100. Oral transcription of interview between Lt. Col. John Landsdale, Jr., and Dr. J. Robert Oppenheimer, 12 September 1943, inserted in hearing of 3 May 1954, "In the Matter of J. Robert Oppenheimer," U.S. Atomic Energy Commission, 871–886. In 1949 Bohm refused to answer congressional committee inquiries about his relations with the CPUSA. He moved to Brazil in 1951 and became a Brazilian citizen in 1954. Having lost his belief in communism, in the early 1960s Bohm applied for and got an American passport, stating that he had not intended to repudiate his American citizenship. He also told American authorities that he had been a CPUSA member while at the radiation laboratory during World War II. F. David Peat, *Infinite Potential: The Life and Times of David Bohm* (Reading, Mass.: Helix Books, 1997).

101. San Francisco FBI report of 1 July 1945 through 15 March 1947, Comintern Apparatus file, serial 5421. Chevalier later wrote *Oppenheimer: The Story of a Friendship* (New York: Braziller, 1965).

102. Venona 1773 KGB New York to Moscow, 16 December 1944; 580–581 KGB San Francisco to Moscow, 13 November 1945.

103. Venona 799 KGB New York to Moscow, 26 May 1945. The identification of the Reservation as Los Alamos comes from matching up the information (from a deciphered message) that Klaus Fuchs was working at the Reservation and the fact that at the time, February 1945, Fuchs was at Los Alamos. Venona 183 KGB New York to Moscow, 27 February 1945.

104. Venona 259 Moscow to New York 21 March 1945. Arnold Kramish, a physicist who was at Los Alamos, has offered an alternative set of identifications. He suggests that the Reservation was not Los Alamos but rather the Manhattan Project's Argonne Laboratory at Chicago, and that Veksel was not Oppenheimer but Enrico Fermi. Fermi, one of the Manhattan Project's key scientists, headed much of the scientific work at its Chicago facilities until he moved to Los Alamos in September 1944, but he retained the his post at the Argonne Laboratory. Kramish adds to this the suggestion that Huron was the cover name for Bruno Pontecorvo, a refugee Italian physicist who was part of the British atomic program and spent most of the war at the British-Canadian nuclear research facility at Chalk River, Ontario. Pontecorvo was a Soviet spy, probably recruited in 1943. After the war he continued to work for the British atomic program and

fled to the USSR in 1950 when British and American security officials uncovered several Soviet atomic spies. Pontecorvo had been a friend of Fermi in Italy in the 1930s and indeed visited the Chicago Metallurgical Laboratory in May 1944. Arnold Kramish, "The Manhattan Project and Venona," 1997 Cryptologic History Symposium, 29–31 October 1997, Fort George Meade, Md.

105. On the Soviet atomic bomb project and the role of espionage in it, see Rhodes, *Dark Sun;* David Holloway, *Stalin and the Bomb* (New Haven: Yale University Press, 1994); German A. Goncharow, "Thermonuclear Milestones," *Physics Today* 49, no. 11 (November 1996), 44–61. Some of the Soviet documents on World War II atomic espionage are reproduced in appendixes 1–4 of the Sudoplatovs and the Schecters' *Special Tasks* and in *Voprosy Istorii Estestvoznaniia i Tekhniki,* Russian Academy of Science, no. 3 (1992), 107–134.

106. Sudoplatov in his memoir describes both Oppenheimer and Fermi as persons who turned a blind eye to Soviet espionage, but his discussion of the two is ambiguous and vague compared with his detailed discussion of other Soviet intelligence operations in which he was involved. In December 1943 FBI listening devices in Steve Nelson's residence picked up a conversation between Nelson and Bernadette Doyle, organizational secretary of the CPUSA's branch in Alameda County, which included Berkeley. Nelson and Doyle spoke of both Oppenheimer brothers as CPUSA members, but Nelson referred to Robert as having become inactive. J. Edgar Hoover to Maj. Gen. Harry Vaughn, 28 February 1947, President's Secretary's Files, Papers of Harry Truman, Harry S. Truman Library. A February 1944 KGB memo quoted in Allen Weinstein and Alexander Vassiliev, *The Haunted Wood: Soviet Espionage in America—The Stalin Era* (New York: Random House, 1999), identifies both Oppenheimer brothers as having been secret members of the CPUSA. This memo also indicates that Frank had been a more active Communist than Robert, that Robert was a target for recruitment by the KGB and the GRU, but that, in part because of the heavy security around him, nothing had been achieved.

Chapter 11: Soviet Espionage and American History

1. Stalin and his inner circle placed a high value on information gained by espionage. See Vladislav Zubok and Constantine Pleshakov, *Inside the Kremlin's Cold War: From Stalin to Khrushchev* (Cambridge: Harvard University Press, 1996), 14, 40, 101, 105–107.

2. The value of the stolen secrets does not affect the inherent nature of the acts of espionage themselves, any more than a burglar is less a burglar if he makes off only with the everyday tableware rather than the sterling silver.

3. See, however, the discussion of the murky matter of Robert Oppenheimer's cooperation with American security officials in chapter 10.

4. M. J. Olgin, *Trotskyism* (New York: Workers Library, 1935), 148–149.

5. N. Slutsker, "Lenin, Stalin and the Communist Youth Movement," *Clarity* 1 (April–May 1940), 70, 72. Capitalization in the original.

6. Donald MacKenzie Lester, "Stalin—Genius of Socialist Construction," *Communist* 20 (March 1941), 257–258.

7. V. J. Jerome, "The Individual in History," *New Masses* (18 May 1943), 19.

8. Alexander Bittleman, "Stalin: On His Seventieth Birthday," *Political Affairs* 28 (December 1949), 1–2.

9. These and a plethora of other citations regarding the CPUSA's Stalin worship

are found in Aileen S. Kraditor, *"Jimmy Higgins": The Mental World of the American Rank-and-File Communist, 1930–1958* (New York: Greenwood Press, 1988), particularly chapters 5 and 6.

10. Michael Dobbs, "Unlocking the Crypts: Most Spies Code Revealed Escaped Prosecution," *Washington Post* (25 December 1996).

11. America's bureaucratic regime of Cold War secrecy is described in Daniel Patrick Moynihan, *Secrecy: The American Experience* (New Haven: Yale University Press, 1998).

Appendix A

1. Venona 588 KGB New York to Moscow, 29 April 1944; 687 KGB New York to Moscow, 13 May 1944.

2. Venona 335 GRU New York to Moscow, 18 April 1941; 1276 GRU New York to Moscow, 2 August 1943.

3. Venona 14 KGB New York to Moscow, 4 January 1945. Sachs is identified as Adler in Allen Weinstein and Alexander Vassiliev, *The Haunted Wood: Soviet Espionage in America—The Stalin Era* (New York: Random House, 1999).

4. Venona 1202 KGB New York to Moscow, 23 August 1944; 1322 KGB New York to Moscow, 15 September 1944; 1515 KGB New York to Moscow, 25 October 1944; 1584 KGB New York to Moscow, 12 November 1944; 1766 KGB New York to Moscow, 15 December 1944; 18–19 KGB New York to Moscow, 4 January 1945; 49 KGB New York to Moscow, 11 January 1945; 239 KGB Moscow to New York, 17 March 1945.

5. Venona 812 KGB New York to Moscow, 29 May 1943; 846 KGB New York to Moscow, 3 June 1943; 871 KGB New York to Moscow, 8 June 1943; 925 KGB New York to Moscow, 16 June 1943; 958 KGB New York to Moscow, 21 June 1943; 991 KGB New York to Moscow, 24 June 1943; 1000 KGB New York to Moscow, 24 June 1943; 1025, 1035–1036, KGB New York to Moscow, 30 June 1943; 2013 KGB New York to Moscow, 11 December 1943; 278 KGB New York to Moscow, 23 February 1944; 283 KGB New York to Moscow, 24 February 1944; 380 KGB New York to Moscow, 20 March 1944; 588 KGB New York to Moscow, 29 April 1944; 687 KGB New York to Moscow, 13 May 1944; 769, 771 KGB New York to Moscow, 30 May 1944; 776 KGB New York to Moscow, 31 May 1944; 854 KGB New York to Moscow, 16 June 1944; 918 KGB New York to Moscow, 28 June 1944; 928 KGB New York to Moscow, 1 July 1944; 973 KGB New York to Moscow, 11 July 1944; 975 KGB New York to Moscow, 11 July 1944; 1009 KGB New York to Moscow, 19 July 1944; 1052 KGB New York to Moscow, 26 July 1944; 1065 KGB New York to Moscow, 28 July 1944; 1114 KGB New York to Moscow, 4 August 1944; 1155 KGB New York to Moscow, 12 August 1944; 1208 KGB New York to Moscow, 23 August 1944; 1215 KGB New York to Moscow, 25 August 1944; 1388, 1389 KGB New York to Moscow, 1 October 1944; 1393 KGB New York to Moscow, 3 October 1944; 1442, 1447 KGB New York to Moscow, 11 October 1944; 1463 KGB New York to Moscow, 14 October 1944; 1465 KGB New York to Moscow, 14 October 1944; 1481–1482 KGB New York to Moscow, 18 October 1944; 1613 KGB New York to Moscow, 18 November 1944; 1634 KGB New York to Moscow, 20 November 1944; 1635 KGB New York to Moscow, 21 November 1944; 1636 KGB New York to Moscow, 21 November 1944; 1691 KGB New York to Moscow, 1 December 1944; 1757 KGB New York to Moscow, 14 December 1944; 1791 KGB New York to Moscow, 20 December 1944; 1798 KGB

New York to Moscow, 20 December 1944; 1803 KGB New York to Moscow, 22 December 1944; 1818 KGB New York to Moscow, 26 December 1944; 1824 KGB New York to Moscow, 27 December 1944; 12, 13, 15, 16 KGB New York to Moscow, 4 January 1945; 14 KGB New York to Moscow, 4 January 1945; 18–19 KGB New York to Moscow, 4 January 1945; 21 KGB New York to Moscow, 8 January 1945; 26 KGB New York to Moscow, 8 January 1945; 50 KGB New York to Moscow, 11 January 1945; 71 KGB New York to Moscow, 17 January 1945; 79 KGB New York to Moscow, 18 January 1945; 82 KGB New York to Moscow, 18 January 1945; 143 KGB Moscow to New York, 15 February 1945; 179, 180 KGB Moscow to New York, 25 February 1945; 195 KGB Moscow to New York, 3 March 1945; 221 KGB Moscow to New York, 11 March 1945; 248 KGB Moscow to New York, 19 March 1945; 253 KGB Moscow to New York, 20 March 1945; 292 KGB Moscow to New York, 29 March 1945; 328 KGB Moscow to New York, 6 April 1945; 337 KGB Moscow to New York, 8 April 1945; 1822 KGB Washington to Moscow, 30 March 1945 ("A." in this message was judged to be the initial of Albert, then Akhmerov's cover name).

6. Venona 448 KGB Moscow to New York, 9 July 1942; 899 KGB New York to Moscow, 11 June 1943; 148 KGB New York to Moscow, 29 January 1944.

7. Venona 1322 KGB New York to Moscow, 15 September 1944; 1586 KGB New York to Moscow; 12 November 1944; 243 KGB New York to Moscow, 18 March 1945; 163 KGB Moscow to New York, 19 February 1945; 239 KGB Moscow to New York, 17 March 1945. In connection with the other messages about Eugénie Olkhine, 1322 KGB New York to Moscow suggests that *Aleksandrov* was her father.

8. Venona 584 KGB Moscow to Mexico City, 6 October 1944. Also see "Comintern Apparatus Summary Report," 15 December 1944, FBI Comintern Apparatus file (FBI file 100-203581), serial 3702.

9. Venona 984 KGB New York to Moscow, 23 June 1943; 588 KGB New York to Moscow, 29 April 1944; 769, 771 KGB New York to Moscow, 30 May 1944. NSA and FBI analysts indicated that Arena may have been a cover name for Mary Price, along with Director. Documents in Weinstein and Vassiliev, *The Haunted Wood*, confirm that Director is Mary Price but indicate that Arena was used for an unidentified source working for the Civil Service Commission.

10. Venona 1403 KGB New York to Moscow, 5 October 1944; 1559 KGB New York to Moscow, 6 November 1944; 793–794 New York to Moscow, 25 May 1945.

11. Venona 626 KGB New York to Moscow, 5 May 1944; 864 KGB New York to Moscow, 16 June 1944.

12. Venona 1146 KGB New York to Moscow, 10 August 1944.

13. Venona 652 KGB New York to Moscow, 9 May 1944.

14. Venona 1327 KGB New York to Moscow, 15 September 1944.

15. Venona 927–928 GRU New York to Moscow, 16 June 1943; 1026 GRU New York to Moscow, 30 June 1943; 1027 GRU New York to Moscow, 30 June 1943; 1030 GRU New York to Moscow, 1 July 1943; 1123 GRU New York to Moscow, 11 July 1943; 1171 GRU New York to Moscow, 19 July 1943; 1249 GRU New York to Moscow, 29 July 1943; 1250 GRU New York to Moscow, 29 July 1943; 1324 GRU New York to Moscow, 11 August 1943; 1329 GRU New York to Moscow, 12 August 1943; 1350 GRU New York to Moscow, 17 August 1943; 1365 GRU New York to Moscow, 19 August 1943; 1488 GRU New York to Moscow, 15 September 1943; 1385 KGB New York to Moscow, 1 October 1944.

16. Fitin to Dimitrov, 22 May 1942, RTsKhIDNI 495-74-484. The Venona messages with Son/Baker are Venona 1043 KGB New York to Moscow, 25 July 1944; 1286 KGB New York to Moscow, 8 September 1944.

17. Venona 865–866 KGB New York to Moscow, 8 June 1943.

18. Venona 975 KGB New York to Moscow, 11 July 1944.

19. Venona 914 KGB New York to Moscow, 27 June 1944; 1251 KGB New York to Moscow, 2 September 1944; 1429 KGB New York to Moscow, 9 October 1944; 1600 KGB New York to Moscow, 14 November 1944; 1657 KGB New York to Moscow, 27 November 1944; 1715 KGB New York to Moscow, 5 December 1944; 1749–1750 KGB New York to Moscow, 13 December 1944.

20. Venona 3706 KGB Washington to Moscow, 29 June 1945.

21. Venona 1169 GRU New York to Moscow, 19 July 1943; Venona 1258–1259 GRU New York to Moscow, 31 July 1943; 1350 GRU New York to Moscow, 17 August 1943.

22. Venona 1954 KGB New York to Moscow, 27 November 1943; 864 KGB New York to Moscow, 16 June 1944.

23. Venona 958 KGB New York to Moscow, 21 June 1943.

24. Venona 780, 792, KGB New York to Moscow, 25 and 26 May 1945.

25. Venona 1341 KGB New York to Moscow, 21 September 1944.

26. Venona 592 KGB New York to Moscow, 29 April 1943; 725 KGB New York to Moscow, 19 May 1943; 810 KGB New York to Moscow, 29 May 1943; 952 KGB New York to Moscow, 21 June 1943; 974 KGB New York to Moscow, 22 June 1943; 1430 KGB New York to Moscow, 2 September 1943; 1452 KGB New York to Moscow, 8 September 1943.

27. Venona 618 KGB New York to Moscow, 4 May 1944; 1050 KGB New York to Moscow, 26 July 1944; 1351 KGB New York to Moscow, 23 September 1944.

28. Venona 2011 KGB New York to Moscow, 11 December 1943; 2013 KGB New York to Moscow, 11 December 1943; 278 KGB New York to Moscow, 23 February 1944; 588 KGB New York to Moscow, 29 April 1944; 687 KGB New York to Moscow, 13 May 1944; 973 KGB New York to Moscow, 11 July 1944; 1065 KGB New York to Moscow, 28 July 1944; 1353 KGB New York to Moscow, 23 September 1944; 1464 KGB New York to Moscow, 14 October 1944; 1673 KGB New York to Moscow, 30 November 1944; 1802 KGB New York to Moscow, 21 December 1944; 954 KGB Moscow to New York, 20 September 1944; 275 KGB Moscow to New York, 25 March 1945.

29. Venona 927–928 GRU New York to Moscow, 16 June 1943; 938 GRU New York to Moscow, 17 June 1943; 948 GRU New York to Moscow, 19 June 1943; 1103 GRU New York to Moscow, 8 July 1943; 1325 GRU New York to Moscow, 11 August 1943; 1348 GRU New York to Moscow, 16 August 1943; 1448 GRU New York to Moscow, 6 September 1943.

30. Venona 1509 KGB New York to Moscow, 23 October 1944.

31. Venona 874–875 KGB New York to Moscow, 8 June 1943; 1197 KGB New York to Moscow, 22 July 1943; 1207 KGB New York to Moscow, 22 July 1943; 695 KGB New York to Moscow, 16 May 1944; 1508 KGB New York to Moscow, 23 October 1944. The NSA has redacted the identification of Bibi.

32. Venona 1064 KGB New York to Moscow, 3 July 1943; 927–928 GRU New York to Moscow, 16 June 1943; 938 GRU New York to Moscow, 17 June 1943; 948 GRU New York to Moscow, 19 June 1943; 989 GRU New York to Moscow, 24 June 1943; 1348 GRU New York to Moscow, 16 August 1943.

33. Venona 1370 KGB New York to Moscow, 27 September 1944; 1403 KGB New

York to Moscow, 5 October 1944; 1429 KGB New York to Moscow, 9 October 1944; 1430 KGB New York to Moscow, 10 October 1944; 1557 KGB New York to Moscow, 6 November 1944; 1055 KGB New York to Moscow, 5 July 1945; 83 KGB Moscow to New York, 28 January 1945; 259 Moscow to New York, 21 March 1945.

34. Venona 1804 KGB New York to Moscow, 22 December 1944; 86 KGB New York to Moscow, 19 January 1945.

35. Venona 1579 GRU New York to Moscow, 28 September 1943.

36. Venona 726–729 KGB New York to Moscow, 22 May 1942.

37. Venona 1934 Naval GRU Washington to Moscow, 11 August 1943.

38. Venona 705 KGB New York to Moscow, 18 May 1943; 943 KGB New York to Moscow, 4 July 1944; 1403 KGB New York to Moscow, 5 October 1944; 1559 KGB New York to Moscow, 6 November 1944.

39. Venona 132 KGB San Francisco to Moscow, 18 March 1944.

40. Venona 1390 KGB New York to Moscow, 1 October 1944; 1403 KGB New York to Moscow, 5 October 1944; 1797 KGB New York to Moscow, 20 December 1944; 18–19 KGB New York to Moscow, 4 January 1945. Brothman is identified as Chrome Yellow in Weinstein and Vassiliev, *The Haunted Wood*.

41. Venona 774 KGB New York to Moscow, 26 May 1943; 820 KGB New York to Moscow, 31 May 1943; 846 KGB New York to Moscow, 3 June 1943; 1047 KGB New York to Moscow, 2 July 1943; 1163 KGB New York to Moscow, 18 July 1943; 1164 KGB New York to Moscow, 18 July 1943; 1430 KGB New York to Moscow, 2 September 1943; 1999, 2000 KGB New York to Moscow, 10 December 1943; 2011 KGB New York to Moscow, 11 December 1943; 588 KGB New York to Moscow, 29 April 1944; 598–599 KGB New York to Moscow, 2 May 1944; 605 KGB New York to Moscow, 2 May 1944; 687 KGB New York to Moscow, 13 May 1944; 823 KGB New York to Moscow, 7 June 1944; 849 KGB New York to Moscow, 15 June 1944; 973 KGB New York to Moscow, 11 July 1944; 1065 KGB New York to Moscow, 28 July 1944; 1328 KGB New York to Moscow, 15 September 1944; 1410 KGB New York to Moscow, 6 October 1944; 1433, 1435 New York to Moscow, 10 October 1944; 1457 KGB New York to Moscow, 14 October 1944; 1512 KGB New York to Moscow, 24 October 1944; 1818 KGB New York to Moscow, 26 December 1944; 14 KGB New York to Moscow, 4 January 1945; 236 KGB Mexico City to Moscow, 1944 April; 1258–1259 GRU New York to Moscow, 31 July 1943.

42. Venona 11 KGB New York to Moscow, 4 January 1945.

43. Venona 196 KGB New York to Moscow, 9 February 1944; 11 KGB New York to Moscow, 4 January 1945.

44. Venona 1559 KGB New York to Moscow, 6 November 1944.

45. Venona 492 KGB Mexico City to Moscow, 9 June 1944; 526 KGB Moscow to Mexico City, 2 September 1944; 985 KGB New York to Moscow, 23 June 1943; 1000 KGB New York to Moscow, 24 June 1943; 1044 KGB New York to Moscow, 2 July 1943; 1088 KGB New York to Moscow, 7 July 1943; 786 KGB New York to Moscow, 1 June 1944; 889 KGB New York to Moscow, 23 June 1944; 943 KGB New York to Moscow, 4 July 1944; 1102–1103 KGB New York to Moscow, 2 August 1944; 1163 KGB New York to Moscow, 15 August 1944; 1239 KGB New York to Moscow, 30 August 1944; 1313 KGB New York to Moscow, 13 September 1944; 1336 KGB New York to Moscow, 18 September 1944; 1353 KGB New York to Moscow, 23 September 1944; 1470 KGB New York to Moscow, 17 October 1944; 1509 KGB New York to Moscow, 23 October 1944; 1741 KGB New York to Moscow, 12 December 1944; 1821 KGB New York to Moscow, 26 December 1944; 25 KGB New York to Moscow, 8 January 1945; 37 KGB New York to Moscow, 9 January 1945; 63–66 KGB New York

to Moscow, 15 January 1945; 77 KGB New York to Moscow, 17 January 1945; 95 KGB New York to Moscow, 23 January 1945; 329 KGB Moscow to New York, 7 April 1945.

46. Venona 1166 KGB New York to Moscow, 16 August 1944.

47. Venona 1619–1620 KGB New York to Moscow, 20 November 1944.

48. Venona 31 KGB San Francisco to Moscow, 17 January 1944; 133 KGB San Francisco to Moscow, 29 March 1944.

49. Venona 580–581 San Francisco to Moscow, 13 November 1945.

50. Venona 899 KGB New York to Moscow, 11 June 1943; 926 New York to Moscow, 16 June 1943; 670 KGB New York to Moscow, 11 May 1944; 751–752 KGB New York to Moscow, 26 May 1944; 851 KGB New York to Moscow, 15 June 1944.

51. Venona 722 KGB New York to Moscow, 21 May 1942; 854 KGB New York to Moscow, 16 June 1944.

52. Venona 865 KGB Moscow to New York, 26 December 1942.

53. Venona 82 KGB New York to Moscow, 18 January 1945.

54. Venona 769, 771 KGB New York to Moscow, 30 May 1944.

55. Venona 1905 KGB New York to Moscow, 17 November 1943; 776 KGB New York to Moscow, 31 May 1944.

56. Venona 1003 KGB New York to Moscow, 18 July 1944; 1328 KGB New York to Moscow, 15 September 1944; 1430 KGB New York to Moscow, 10 October 1944; 1523 KGB New York to Moscow, 27 October 1944. Chef is identified in Weinstein and Vassiliev, *The Haunted Wood,* as Franklin Zelman, which may be a garbled translation of Zalmond Franklin.

57. Venona 860 KGB New York to Moscow, 6 June 1943; 1398 KGB New York to Moscow, 26 August 1943. In 1944 Chen is the cover name used by the KGB for Zalmond Franklin, but this 1943 Chen appears to be a different person.

58. Venona 1207 KGB New York to Moscow, 22 July 1943; 682 KGB New York to Moscow, 12 May 1944; 1251 KGB New York to Moscow, 2 September 1944.

59. Venona 1243 KGB New York to Moscow, 31 August 1944; 1838 KGB New York to Moscow, 29 December 1944; 179–180 KGB Moscow to New York, 25 February 1945.

60. Venona 1239 KGB New York to Moscow, 30 August 1944; 50 KGB New York to Moscow, 11 January 1945.

61. Venona 50 KGB New York to Moscow, 11 January 1945.

62. Venona 704 Naval GRU Washington to Moscow, 1 April 1943; 1934 Naval GRU Washington to Moscow, 11 August 1943; 1969 Naval GRU Washington to Moscow, 13 August 1943; 2933 Naval GRU Washington to Moscow, 14 November 1943; 115 Naval GRU Moscow to Washington 20 January 1943; 1194 Naval GRU Moscow to Washington 10 July 1943.

63. Venona 193–194 Mexico City to Moscow, 14 March 1944. Also see "Comintern Apparatus Summary Report," 15 December 1944, FBI Comintern Apparatus file, serial 3702; Colloms testimony, "American Aspects of Assassination of Leon Trotsky," U.S. Congress, House of Representatives, Un-American Activities Committee, 82nd Cong., 1st sess., 1951.

64. Venona 1014 KGB New York to Moscow, 20 July 1944; 1050 KGB New York to Moscow, 26 July 1944; 1385 KGB New York to Moscow, 1 October 1944; 1587 KGB New York to Moscow, 12 November 1944; 1637 KGB New York to Moscow, 21 November 1944; 1714 KGB New York to Moscow, 5 December 1944; 1845 KGB New York to Moscow, 31 December 1944; 27 KGB New York to Moscow, 8 January 1945; 55 KGB New York to Moscow, 15 January 1945; 76 KGB New York to Moscow,

17 January 1945; 992 KGB New York to Moscow, 26 June 1945; 1053 KGB New York to Moscow, 5 July 1945; 268 KGB Moscow to New York, 24 March 1945; 284, 286 KGB Moscow to New York, 28 March 1945. Coplon may be the subject of Venona 1522 KGB New York to Moscow, 27 October 1944, in which the KGB agent Joseph Katz, who had liaison responsibilities for Coplon at one point, reports the arrival of "our source in the FBI."

65. Venona 1791 KGB New York to Moscow, 20 December 1944. The NSA redacted Cora's identity.

66. Venona 1053 KGB New York to Moscow, 2 July 1943.

67. Venona 257 KGB Moscow to New York, 21 March 1945.

68. Venona 823 New York to Moscow, 7 June 1944; 1275 KGB New York to Moscow, 7 September 1944; 1403 KGB New York to Moscow, 5 October 1944; 1754 KGB New York to Moscow, 14 December 1944.

69. Venona 928 KGB New York to Moscow, 30 June 1943; 1317 KGB New York to Moscow, 10 August 1943; 1431 KGB New York to Moscow, 2 September 1943; 900 KGB New York to Moscow, 24 June 1944; 1243 KGB New York to Moscow, 31 August 1944; 1463 KGB New York to Moscow, 14 October 1944; 1634 KGB New York to Moscow, 20 November 1944; 143 KGB Moscow to New York, 15 February 1945; 253 KGB Moscow to New York, 20 March 1945.

70. Venona 619, 620 KGB San Francisco to Moscow, 27 November 1945.

71. Venona 1031 KGB New York to Moscow, 1 July 1943; 1045 KGB New York to Moscow, 2 July 1943.

72. Venona 1557 New York KGB to Moscow, 6 November 1944.

73. Venona 708 KGB Moscow to Mexico City, 8 December 1944; 1714 KGB New York to Moscow, 5 December 1944; 55 KGB New York to Moscow, 15 January 1945.

74. Venona 1195 KGB New York to Moscow, 21 July 1943; 1206 New York to Moscow, 22 July 1943.

75. Venona 748 KGB New York to Moscow, 26 May 1944.

76. Venona 1776 KGB New York to Moscow, 26 October 1943.

77. Venona 834, 846–848, Naval GRU Washington to Moscow, 18 April 1943.

78. Venona 1456 GRU New York to Moscow, 8 September 1943.

79. Venona 871–872 KGB New York to Moscow, 6 June 1945.

80. Venona 1025, 1035–1936, KGB New York to Moscow, 30 June 1943; 380 KGB New York to Moscow, 20 March 1944; 744, 746 KGB New York to Moscow, 24 May 1944; 916 KGB New York to Moscow, 17 June 1944; 1015 KGB New York to Moscow, to Victor [Fitin], 22 July 1944; 1114 KGB New York to Moscow, 4 August 1944; 1251 KGB New York to Moscow, 2 September 1944; 1613 KGB New York to Moscow, 18 November 1944; 1636 KGB New York to Moscow, 21 November 1944.

81. Venona 726–729 KGB New York to Moscow, 22 May 1942; 865, 866 KGB New York to Moscow, 8 June 1943; 1132–1133 KGB New York to Moscow, 13 July 1943; 1148 KGB New York to Moscow, 14 July 1943; 1930 KGB New York to Moscow, 21 November 1943; 853 KGB New York to Moscow, 16 June 1944.

82. Venona 853 KGB New York to Moscow, 16 June 1944.

83. Venona 894 KGB New York to Moscow, 10 June 1943; 627 KGB New York to Moscow, 5 May 1944; 864 KGB New York to Moscow, 16 June 1944; 1053 KGB New York to Moscow, 5 July 1945.

84. Venona 894 KGB New York to Moscow, 10 June 1943; 627 KGB New York to Moscow, 5 May 1944; 864 KGB New York to Moscow, 16 June 1944; 1053 KGB New York to Moscow, 5 July 1945; 1182 KGB New York to Moscow, 19 August 1944; 1508 KGB New York to Moscow, 23 October 1944.

85. Venona 1055 KGB New York to Moscow, 5 July 1945.

86. Venona 823 KGB New York to Moscow, 7 June 1944; 881 KGB New York to Moscow, 20 June 1944.

87. Venona 1557 KGB New York to Moscow, 6 November 1944.

88. Venona 749 KGB New York to Moscow, 26 May 1944.

89. Venona 1388–1389 KGB New York to Moscow, 1 October 1944; 1403 KGB New York to Moscow, 5 October 1944; 1635 KGB New York to Moscow 21 November 1944.

90. Venona 104 Naval GRU Moscow to Washington 17 January 1943; 155 Naval GRU Moscow to Washington 26 January 1943.

91. Venona 1934 Naval GRU Washington to Moscow, 11 August 1943; 2278 Naval GRU Washington to Moscow, 10 September 1943; 2346 Naval GRU Washington to Moscow, 15 September 1943.

92. Venona 651 KGB New York to Moscow, 9 May 1944; 943 KGB New York to Moscow, 4 July 1944; 972 KGB New York to Moscow, 11 July 1944; 1403 KGB New York to Moscow, 5 October 1944.

93. Venona 1220 KGB New York to Moscow, 26 August 1944.

94. Venona 800 KGB New York to Moscow, 28 May 1943; 816–817 KGB New York to Moscow, 30 May 1943; 899 KGB New York to Moscow, 11 June 1943; 1142 KGB New York to Moscow, 10 August 1944; 174–176 KGB Mexico City to Moscow, 29 December 1943; 193–194 KGB Mexico City to Moscow, 14 March 1944; 212 KGB Mexico City to Moscow, 25 March 1944; 261–262 KGB Mexico City to Moscow, 16 April 1944; 281 KGB Mexico City to Moscow, 21 April 1944; 553–554 KGB Mexico City to Moscow, 29 June 1944; 893 KGB Mexico City to Moscow, 28 November 1944; 237 KGB Moscow to Mexico City, 20 April 1944; 248 KGB Moscow to Mexico City, 27 April 1944; 288 KGB Moscow to Mexico City, 11 May 1944; 511 KGB Moscow to Mexico City, 24 August 1944; 626 KGB Moscow to Mexico City, 29 October 1944; 634 KGB Moscow to Mexico City, 5 November 1944.

95. Venona 912 KGB New York to Moscow, 27 June 1944; 1403 KGB New York to Moscow, 5 October 1944; 989 KGB New York to Moscow, 26 June 1945; 164 Moscow to New York, 20 February 1945; 619–620 San Francisco to Moscow, 27 November 1945.

96. Venona 1192 Naval GRU Washington to Moscow, 4 June 1943.

97. Venona 115 Naval GRU Moscow to Washington, 20 January 1943; 360 Naval GRU Moscow to Washington, 26 February 1943; 366 Naval GRU Moscow to Washington, 28 February 1943; 849 Naval GRU Washington to Moscow, 20 April 1943; 901 Naval GRU Washington to Moscow, 27 April 1943; 393 Naval GRU Moscow to Washington, 5 March 1943; 427 Naval GRU Moscow to Washington, 11 March 1943.

98. Venona 656 KGB New York to Moscow, 9 May 1944; 939 KGB New York to Moscow, 18 June 1943; 823 KGB New York to Moscow, 7 June 1944; 881 KGB New York to Moscow, 20 June 1944; 905 KGB New York to Moscow, 26 June 1944; 1275 KGB New York to Moscow, 7 September 1944; 1403 KGB New York to Moscow, 5 October 1944; 275 KGB Moscow to New York, 25 March 1945.

99. Venona 854 KGB New York to Moscow, 16 June 1942.

100. Venona 1397 KGB New York to Moscow, 4 October 1944.

101. Venona 287 GRU Moscow to New York, 4 May 1942; 1348 GRU New York to Moscow, 16 August 1943; 1351 GRU New York to Moscow, 18 August 1943; 1448 GRU New York to Moscow, 6 September 1943; 1498–1499 GRU New York to Moscow, 17 September 1943.

102. Venona 1769 KGB New York to Moscow, 15 December 1944.

103. Venona 823 KGB New York to Moscow, 7 June 1944; 1275 KGB New York to Moscow, 7 September 1944.

104. Venona 865 KGB Moscow to New York, 26 December 1942; 939 KGB New York to Moscow, 18 June 1943; 165 KGB New York to Moscow, 2 February 1944; 823 KGB New York to Moscow, 7 June 1944; 881 KGB New York to Moscow, 20 June 1944; Elizabeth Bentley FBI deposition, 30 November 1945, FBI file 65-14603.

105. Venona 588 KGB New York to Moscow, 29 April 1944; 687 KGB New York to Moscow, 13 May 1944; 769, 771 KGB New York to Moscow, 30 May 1944; 179, 180 KGB Moscow to New York, 25 February 1945.

106. Venona 588 KGB New York to Moscow, 29 April 1944. Flato is a candidate for the partially decrypted Char.... in Venona 769, 771 KGB New York to Moscow, 30 May 1944.

107. Venona 1155 KGB New York to Moscow, 12 August 1944.

108. Venona 212 KGB New York to Moscow, 11 February 1944; 854 KGB New York to Moscow, 16 June 1944; 1251 KGB New York to Moscow, 2 September 1944; 1749, 1750 KGB New York to Moscow, 13 December 1944.

109. Venona 429 KGB San Francisco to Moscow, 23 October 1943; 450 KGB San Francisco to Moscow, 1 November 1943; 55 KGB San Francisco to Moscow, 8 February 1944; 101 KGB San Francisco to Moscow, 5 March 1944; 117 KGB San Francisco to Moscow, 11 March 1944; 136 KGB San Francisco to Moscow, 2 April 1945; 138 KGB San Francisco to Moscow, 3 April 1945; 143 KGB San Francisco to Moscow, 6 April 1945; 172 KGB San Francisco to Moscow, 18 April 1945; 238, 239 KGB San Francisco to Moscow, 7 May 1945; 266 KGB San Francisco to Moscow, 18 May 1945; 310 KGB San Francisco to Moscow, 9 June 1945; 320 KGB San Francisco to Moscow, 13 June 1945; 69 KGB San Francisco to Moscow, 20 February 1946.

110. Venona 854 KGB New York to Moscow, 16 June 1942; 958 KGB New York to Moscow, 21 June 1943; 1025, 1035–1036, KGB New York to Moscow, 30 June 1943; 769, 771 KGB New York to Moscow, 30 May 1944.

111. Venona 749 KGB New York to Moscow, 26 May 1944.

112. Venona 629 KGB New York to Moscow, 5 May 1944.

113. Venona 768 KGB New York to Moscow, 25 May 1943.

114. Venona 700 KGB New York to Moscow, 17 May 1944; 759–760 KGB New York to Moscow, 27 May 1944; 761 KGB New York to Moscow, 27 May 1944; 763 KGB New York to Moscow, 29 May 1944; 823 KGB New York to Moscow, 7 June 1944; 928 KGB New York to Moscow, 1 July 1944; 956, 957 KGB New York to Moscow, 6 July 1944; 1229 KGB New York to Moscow, 29 August 1944; 1410 KGB New York to Moscow, 6 October 1944.

115. Venona 865 KGB New York to Moscow, 18 June 1942; 925 KGB New York to Moscow, 16 June 1943.

116. Venona 472 KGB San Francisco to Moscow, 9 November 1943.

117. Venona 826 KGB New York to Moscow, 7 June 1944; 851 KGB New York to Moscow, 15 June 1944; 907 KGB New York to Moscow, 26 June 1944; 942 KGB New York to Moscow, 4 July 1944; 292 KGB Moscow to New York, 29 March 1945.

118. Venona 823 KGB New York to Moscow, 7 June 1944; 881 KGB New York to Moscow, 20 June 1944.

119. Venona 1195 KGB New York to Moscow, 21 July 1943; 1206 KGB New York to Moscow, 22 July 1943; 588 KGB New York to Moscow, 29 April 1944; 769, 771 KGB New York to Moscow, 30 May 1944; 79 KGB New York to Moscow, 18 January 1945; 179–180 KGB Moscow to New York, 25 February 1945; 1759 KGB

Washington to Moscow, 28 March 1945; 3598 KGB Washington to Moscow, 21 June 1945; 3600 KGB Washington to Moscow, 21 June 1945; 3645 KGB Washington to Moscow, 23 June 1945; 3688 KGB Washington to Moscow, 28 June 1945.

120. Venona 1398 KGB New York to Moscow, 26 August 1943; 144 KGB New York to Moscow, 27 January 1944.

121. Venona 12, 13, 15, 16 KGB New York to Moscow, 4 January 1945; 18–19 KGB New York to Moscow, 4 January 1945.

122. Venona 195 KGB New York to Moscow, 9 February 1944; 912 KGB New York to Moscow, 27 June 1944; 1233 KGB New York to Moscow, 29 August 1944; 1345 KGB New York to Moscow, 22 September 1944; 1390 KGB New York to Moscow, 1 October 1944; 1397 KGB New York to Moscow, 4 October 1944; 1403 KGB New York to Moscow, 5 October 1944; 1536 KGB New York to Moscow, 28 October 1944; 1606 KGB New York to Moscow, 16 November 1944; 1749, 1750 KGB New York to Moscow, 13 December 1944; 1797 KGB New York to Moscow, 20 December 1944; 183 KGB Moscow to New York, 27 February 1945; 257 KGB Moscow to New York, 21 March 1945; 275 KGB Moscow to New York, 25 March 1945.

123. Venona 918 KGB New York to Moscow, 28 June 1944; 12, 13, 15, 16 KGB New York to Moscow, 4 January 1945; 79 KGB New York to Moscow, 18 January 1945.

124. Venona 325 KGB Moscow to New York, 17 May 1942; 959 KGB New York to Moscow, 8 July 1942; 725 KGB New York to Moscow, 19 May 1943; 810 KGB New York to Moscow, 29 May 1943; 846 KGB New York to Moscow, 3 June 1943; 928 KGB New York to Moscow, 30 June 1943; 1052 KGB New York to Moscow, 2–4 July 1943; 1143 KGB New York to Moscow, 14 July 1943; 1163 KGB New York to Moscow, 18 July 1943; 1253 KGB New York to Moscow, 30 July 1943; 1430 KGB New York to Moscow, 2 September 1943; 1431 KGB New York to Moscow, 2 September 1943; 1586 KGB New York to Moscow, 29 September 1943; 2101 KGB New York to Moscow, 29 December 1943; 588 KGB New York to Moscow, 29 April 1944; 769, 771 KGB New York to Moscow, 30 May 1944; 1076 KGB New York to Moscow, 29 July 1944; 1221 KGB New York to Moscow, 26 August 1944; 1388, 1389 KGB New York to Moscow, 1 October 1944.

125. Venona 1579 New York GRU to Moscow, 28 September 1943.

126. Venona 927–928 GRU New York to Moscow, 16 June 1943.

127. Venona 600 KGB New York to Moscow, 2 May 1944; 601 KGB New York to Moscow, 2 May 1944; 694 KGB New York to Moscow, 16 May 1944.

128. Venona 1340 KGB New York to Moscow, 21 September 1944; 1549 KGB New York to Moscow, 3 November 1944; 1600 KGB New York to Moscow, 14 November 1944; 1749, 1750 KGB New York to Moscow, 13 December 1944; 1773 KGB New York to Moscow, 16 December 1944; 28 KGB New York to Moscow, 8 January 1945.

129. Venona 1340 KGB New York to Moscow, 21 September 1944; 1549 KGB New York to Moscow, 3 November 1944; 1600 KGB New York to Moscow, 14 November 1944; 1749–1750 KGB New York to Moscow, 13 December 1944; 1773 KGB New York to Moscow, 16 December 1944; 28 KGB New York to Moscow, 8 January 1945.

130. Venona 1585 KGB New York to Moscow, 12 November 1944; 1749–1750 KGB New York to Moscow, 13 December 1944; 1773 KGB New York to Moscow, 16 December 1944; 94 KGB New York to Moscow, 23 January 1945; 799 KGB New York to Moscow, 26 May 1945; 298 Moscow to New York, 31 March 1945; 709 Moscow

to New York, 3 July 1945. Venona 1699 KGB New York to Moscow, 2 December 1944, does not mention Hall, but its text very likely is a report delivered by Hall.

131. Venona 880 KGB New York to Moscow, 8 June 1943; 887 KGB New York to Moscow, 9 June 1943; 921, 922, 924 KGB New York to Moscow, 16 June 1943; 931 KGB New York to Moscow, 17 June 1943; 993 KGB New York to Moscow, 24 June 1943; 1019, 1021, 1024, 1034 KGB New York to Moscow, 29 June 1943; 1106 KGB New York to Moscow, 8 July 1943; 1162 KGB New York to Moscow, 17 July 1943; 1189 KGB New York to Moscow, 21 July 1943; 206 KGB New York to Moscow, 10 February 1944; 611 KGB New York to Moscow, 3 May 1944; 694 KGB New York to Moscow, 16 May 1944; 748 KGB New York to Moscow, 26 May 1944; 993 KGB New York to Moscow, 13 July 1944; 1214 KGB New York to Moscow, 25 August 1944; 1325, 1326 KGB New York to Moscow, 15 September 1944; 1333 KGB New York to Moscow, 18 September 1944; 1437 KGB New York to Moscow, 10 October 1944; 1438 KGB New York to Moscow, 10 October 1944; 1453 KGB New York to Moscow, 12 October 1944; 1484 KGB New York to Moscow, 19 October 1944; 954 KGB Moscow to New York, 20 September 1944.

132. Venona 627 KGB New York to Moscow, 5 May 1944.

133. Venona 1999–2000 KGB New York to Moscow, 10 December 1943; 129 KGB Mexico City to Moscow, 6 December 1943; 232 KGB Mexico City to Moscow, 3 April 1944; 243–244 KGB Mexico City to Moscow, 10 April 1944; 327 KGB Mexico City to Moscow, 3 May 1944; 343 KGB Mexico City to Moscow, 5 May 1944; 553–554 KGB Mexico City to Moscow, 29 June 1944; 893 KGB Mexico City to Moscow, 28 November 1944; 167 KGB Moscow to Mexico City, 17 March 1944; 200 KGB Moscow to Mexico City, 8 April 1944; 220 KGB Moscow to Mexico City, 16 April 1944; 256 KGB Moscow to Mexico City, 29 April 1944; 283 KGB Moscow to Mexico City, 10 May 1944; 303 KGB Moscow to Mexico City, 17 May 1944; 476 KGB Moscow to Mexico City, 29 July 1944; 533 KGB Moscow to Mexico City, 7 September 1944; 653 KGB Moscow to Mexico City, 15 November 1944; 312 KGB Moscow to Mexico City, 11 May 1945; 347 KGB Moscow to Mexico City, 27 May 1945; 472 KGB Moscow to Mexico City, 4 August 1945; 559 KGB Moscow to Mexico City, 7 September 1945; 238 KGB Moscow to Mexico City, 28 April 1946.

134. Venona 974 KGB New York to Moscow, 22 June 1943; 977 KGB New York to Moscow, 22 June 1943. NSA redacted the identify of Havre.

135. Venona 764, 765 KGB New York to Moscow, 24 May 1943; 1056 KGB New York to Moscow, 3 July 1943.

136. Venona 55 KGB San Francisco to Moscow, 8 February 1944; 101 KGB San Francisco to Moscow, 5 March 1944.

137. Venona 1822 KGB Washington to Moscow, 30 March 1945.

138. Venona 1019, 1021, 1024, 1034, KGB New York to Moscow, 29 June 1943; 1056 KGB New York to Moscow, 3 July 1943; 1428 KGB New York to Moscow, 9 October 1944.

139. Venona 1166 KGB New York to Moscow, 16 August 1944.

140. Venona 640 KGB New York to Moscow, 6 May 1944; 823 KGB New York to Moscow, 7 June 1944; 1275 KGB New York to Moscow, 7 September 1944; 1403 KGB New York to Moscow, 5 October 1944; 1754 KGB New York to Moscow, 14 December 1944.

141. Venona 912 KGB New York to Moscow, 27 June 1944; 1403 KGB New York to Moscow, 5 October 1944; 1429 KGB New York to Moscow, 9 October 1944; 164 Moscow to New York, 20 February 1945; 259 Moscow to New York, 21 March 1945.

142. Venona 193 KGB New York to Moscow, 8 February 1944.

143. Venona 3711 KGB Washington to Moscow, 29 June 1945.

144. Venona 210 KGB New York to Moscow, 10 February 1945.

145. Venona 847 KGB New York to Moscow, 14 June 1944.

146. Venona 294 KGB San Francisco to Moscow, 31 May 1945.

147. Venona 1148 KGB New York to Moscow, 14 July 1943; 1930 KGB New York to Moscow, 21 November 1943.

148. Venona 927–928 GRU New York to Moscow, 16 June 1943; 989 GRU New York to Moscow, 24 June 1943; 1116 GRU New York to Moscow, 9 July 1943; 1456 GRU New York to Moscow, 8 September 1943.

149. Venona 917 KGB New York to Moscow, 28 June 1944; 943 KGB New York to Moscow, 4 July 1944; 971 KGB New York to Moscow, 11 July 1944.

150. Venona 1275 KGB New York to Moscow, 7 September 1944.

151. Venona 1427 GRU New York to Moscow, 1 September 1943.

152. Venona 880 KGB New York to Moscow, 8 June 1943. Bella Joseph is identified as Colleague in Weinstein and Vassiliev, *The Haunted Wood*.

153. Venona 880 KGB New York to Moscow, 8 June 1943; 1454 KGB New York to Moscow, 13 October 1944; 1464 KGB New York to Moscow, 14 October 1944.

154. Venona 975 KGB New York to Moscow, 11 July 1944.

155. Venona 652 KGB New York to Moscow, 9 May 1944; 1403 KGB New York to Moscow, 5 October 1944; 1716 KGB New York to Moscow, 5 December 1944.

156. Venona 1000 KGB New York to Moscow, 24 June 1943; 1136 KGB New York to Moscow, 13 July 1943; 1205 KGB New York to Moscow, 22 July 1943.

157. Venona 1403 KGB New York to Moscow, 5 October 1944; 1429 KGB New York to Moscow, 9 October 1944; 1557 KGB New York to Moscow, 6 November 1944; 1818 KGB New York to Moscow, 26 December 1944. The NSA redacted Karl's identify. There is also a cover name Karl, also redacted, in the 1945 message traffic of the San Francisco KGB: Venona 433 KGB San Francisco to Moscow, 11 August 1945.

158. Venona 998 KGB New York to Moscow, 15 July 1944.

159. Venona 1694 KGB New York to Moscow, 16 October 1943; 221 KGB New York to Moscow, 12 February 1944; 486 KGB New York to Moscow, 11 April 1944; 546 KGB New York to Moscow, 20 April 1944; 605 KGB New York to Moscow, 2 May 1944; 618 KGB New York to Moscow, 4 May 1944; 638 KGB New York to Moscow, 6 May 1944; 676 KGB New York to Moscow, 12 May 1944; 749 KGB New York to Moscow, 26 May 1944; 942 KGB New York to Moscow, 4 July 1944; 976 KGB New York to Moscow, 11 July 1944; 1015 KGB New York to Moscow, 22 July 1944; 1020 KGB New York to Moscow, 20 July 1944; 1050 KGB New York to Moscow, 26 July 1944; 1087 KGB New York to Moscow, 30 July 1944; 1190 KGB New York to Moscow, 21 August 1944; 1196 KGB New York to Moscow, 22 August 1944; 1220 KGB New York to Moscow, 26 August 1944; 1251 KGB New York to Moscow, 2 September 1944; 1266 KGB New York to Moscow, 6 September 1944; 1313 KGB New York to Moscow, 13 September 1944; 1328 KGB New York to Moscow, 15 September 1944; 1332 KGB New York to Moscow, 18 September 1944; 1337 KGB New York to Moscow, 19 September 1944; 1351 KGB New York to Moscow, 23 September 1944; 1370 KGB New York to Moscow, 27 September 1944; 1410 KGB New York to Moscow, 6 October 1944; 1411 KGB New York to Moscow, 6 October 1944; 1457 KGB New York to Moscow, 14 October 1944; 1470 KGB New York to Moscow, 17 October 1944; 1512 KGB New York to Moscow, 24 October 1944; 1522 KGB New York to Moscow, 27 October 1944; 49 KGB Moscow to New York, 19 January 1944.

160. Venona 326 KGB Moscow to New York, 5 April 1945; 3614–3615 KGB Washington to Moscow, 22 June 1945.

161. Venona 1234 KGB New York to Moscow, 29 August 1944.

162. Venona 726–729 KGB New York to Moscow, 22 May 1942; 1234 KGB New York to Moscow, 29 August 1944; 325 KGB Moscow to New York, 17 May 1942.

163. Venona 823 KGB New York to Moscow, 7 June 1944; 864 KGB New York to Moscow, 16 June 1944; 928 KGB New York to Moscow, 1 July 1944; 956, 957 KGB New York to Moscow, 6 July 1944; 1146 KGB New York to Moscow, 10 August 1944; 1337 KGB New York to Moscow, 19 September 1944; 1509 KGB New York to Moscow, 23 October 1944.

164. Venona 1337 KGB New York to Moscow, 19 September 1944.

165. Venona 1462 KGB New York to Moscow, 9 September 1943; 913 KGB New York to Moscow, 27 June 1944; 1016 KGB New York to Moscow, 20 July 1944; 1039–1041 KGB New York to Moscow, 24–25 July 1944; 1397 KGB New York to Moscow, 4 October 1944.

166. Venona 1251 KGB New York to Moscow, 2 September 1944; 1332 KGB New York to Moscow, 18 September 1944; 1582 KGB New York to Moscow, 12 November 1944; 1636 KGB New York to Moscow, 21 November 1944; 1803 KGB New York to Moscow, 22 December 1944; 50 KGB New York to Moscow, 11 January 1945; 1052 KGB New York to Moscow, 5 July 1945; 275 KGB Moscow to New York, 25 March 1945; 337 KGB Moscow to New York, 8 April 1945. Koral is identified as Berg in Weinstein and Vassiliev, *The Haunted Wood*.

167. Venona 1251 KGB New York to Moscow, 2 September 1944; 1524 KGB New York to Moscow, 27 October 1944; 1582 KGB New York to Moscow, 12 November 1944; 1636 KGB New York to Moscow, 21 November 1944; 1791 KGB New York to Moscow, 20 December 1944; 1052 KGB New York to Moscow, 5 July 1945; 337 KGB Moscow to New York, 8 April 1945.

168. Venona 705 KGB New York to Moscow, 17 May 1944; 734 KGB New York to Moscow, 21 May 1944; 738 KGB New York to Moscow, 23 May 1944; 789 KGB New York to Moscow, 1 June 1944; 847B, 848 KGB New York to Moscow, 15 June 1944; 998 KGB New York to Moscow, 15 July 1944; 1178 KGB New York to Moscow, 17 August 1944; 1291 KGB New York to Moscow, 9 September 1944; 1312 KGB New York to Moscow, 14 September 1944; 1313 KGB New York to Moscow, 13 September 1944; 1433, 1435 New York to Moscow, 10 October 1944; 1506 KGB New York to Moscow, 23 October 1944; 1535, 1537, 1538 KGB New York to Moscow, 28 October 1944; 777–779 KGB New York to Moscow, 25 May 1945.

169. Venona 588 KGB New York to Moscow, 29 April 1944; 687 KGB New York to Moscow, 13 May 1944; 1015 KGB New York to Moscow, 22 July 1944; 1163 KGB New York to Moscow, 15 August 1944. NSA and FBI analysts list the cover name Mole as unidentified, but the fit between the information reported by Mole and Kramer's activities at the time is extremely tight. Mole also appears only after Plumb, Kramer's prior cover name, disappears. Venona 3612 KGB Washington to Moscow, 22 June 1945; 3640 KGB Washington to Moscow, 23 June 1945; 3655 KGB Washington to Moscow, 25 June 1945; 3706 KGB Washington to Moscow, 29 June 1945; 3709 KGB Washington to Moscow, 29 June 1945; 3710 KGB Washington to Moscow, 29 June 1945.

170. Venona 613–614 KGB New York to Moscow, 3 May 1944; 654 KGB New York to Moscow, 9 May 1944; 724 KGB New York to Moscow, 19 May 1944; 1145 KGB New York to Moscow, 10 August 1944; 1403 KGB New York to Moscow, 5 October 1944; 87 KGB New York to Moscow, 19 January 1945; 229 KGB Moscow to New York, 15 March 1945.

171. Venona 833 KGB New York to Moscow, 10 June 1942; 929–930 KGB New York to Moscow, 17 June 1943; 936 KGB New York to Moscow, 17 June 1943; 952 KGB New York to Moscow, 21 June 1943; 985–986 KGB New York to Moscow, 23 June 1943; 1120 KGB New York to Moscow, 10 July 1943; 1251 KGB New York to Moscow, 2 September 1944; 1322 KGB New York to Moscow, 15 September 1944; 1404 KGB New York to Moscow, 5 October 1944; 1438 KGB New York to Moscow, 10 October 1944; 1449 KGB New York to Moscow, 12 October 1944; 1584 KGB New York to Moscow, 12 November 1944; 1585 KGB New York to Moscow, 12 November 1944; 1586 KGB New York to Moscow, 12 November 1944; 1699 KGB New York to Moscow, 2 December 1944; 1714 KGB New York to Moscow, 5 December 1944; 18–19 KGB New York to Moscow, 4 January 1945; 94 KGB New York to Moscow, 23 January 1945; 243 KGB New York to Moscow, 18 March 1945.

172. Venona 851 KGB New York to Moscow, 15 June 1944; 928 KGB New York to Moscow, 1 July 1944; 1154 KGB New York to Moscow, 12 August 1944; 1198 KGB New York to Moscow, 23 August 1944; 433 KGB San Francisco to Moscow, 11 August 1945; 483–484 KGB San Francisco to Moscow, 13 September 1945. Venona 1136 KGB New York to Moscow, 8 August 1944, reports confidential information from Laird's office, and he is the obvious source, but the message does not clearly state that he is.

173. Venona 580–581 San Francisco to Moscow, 13 November 1945.

174. Venona 700 KGB New York to Moscow, 17 May 1944; 759–760 KGB New York to Moscow, 27 May 1944; 761 KGB New York to Moscow, 27 May 1944; 956, 957 KGB New York to Moscow, 6 July 1944; 1000 KGB New York to Moscow, 15 July 1944; 1135 KGB New York to Moscow, 8 August 1944; 1229 KGB New York to Moscow, 29 August 1944.

175. Venona 1103 GRU New York to Moscow, 8 July 1943.

176. Venona 782 KGB New York to Moscow, 26 May 1943; 880 KGB New York to Moscow, 8 June 1943; 887 KGB New York to Moscow, 9 June 1943; 830 KGB New York to Moscow, 9 June 1944; 1325–1326 KGB New York to Moscow, 15 September 1944; 1354 KGB New York to Moscow, 22 September 1944 (does not mention Lee by name but is a follow-up to Venona 1325–1326); 1353 KGB New York to Moscow, 23 September 1944; 1437 KGB New York to Moscow, 10 October 1944; 954 KGB Moscow to New York, 20 September 1944. In addition to these, in Venona 726–729 KGB New York to Moscow, 22 May 1942, the KGB reports on those sections of the OSS of chief interest to the Soviets and mentions in a partially deciphered but garbled section the name Lee. This may be a reference to Duncan Lee, who was about to join the OSS and was already in touch with Golos through Mary Price.

177. Venona 975 KGB New York to Moscow, 11 July 1944.

178. Venona 512 KGB San Francisco to Moscow, 7 December 1943.

179. Venona 31 KGB San Francisco to Moscow, 17 January 1944; 133 KGB San Francisco to Moscow, 29 March 1944.

180. Venona 1031 KGB New York to Moscow, 1 July 1943.

181. Venona 3616, 3617, 3619, 3620 KGB Washington to Moscow, 22 June 1945.

182. Venona 373 KGB Moscow to New York, 3 June 1942.

183. Venona 602 KGB New York to Moscow, 2 May 1944; 982 KGB New York to Moscow, 12 July 1944.

184. Venona 981 KGB New York to Moscow, 23 June 1943; 1239 KGB New York to Moscow, 30 August 1944; 154 KGB Moscow to New York, 16 February 1945.

185. Venona 1132, 1133 KGB New York to Moscow, 13 July 1943.

186. Venona 882 GRU New York to Moscow, 8 June 1943.

187. Venona 1050 KGB New York to Moscow, 26 July 1944; 1403 KGB New York to Moscow, 5 October 1944; 1557 KGB New York to Moscow, 6 November 1944; 1706 KGB New York to Moscow, 4 December 1944.

188. Venona 1582 KGB New York to Moscow, 12 November 1944; 1635 KGB New York to Moscow, 21 November 1944; 11 KGB New York to Moscow, 4 January 1945; 275 KGB Moscow to New York, 25 March 1945; 337 KGB Moscow to New York, 8 April 1945.

189. Venona 952 GRU Washington to Moscow, 4 May 1943.

190. Venona 939 KGB New York to Moscow, 3 July 1944.

191. Venona 1934 Naval GRU Washington to Moscow, 11 August 1943.

192. Venona 117 KGB San Francisco to Moscow, 11 March 1943.

193. Venona 1337 KGB New York to Moscow, 19 September 1944; 71 KGB New York to Moscow, 17 January 1945.

194. Venona 629 KGB New York to Moscow, 5 May 1944; 687 KGB New York to Moscow, 13 May 1944; 769, 771 KGB New York to Moscow, 30 May 1944; 179, 180 KGB Moscow to New York, 25 February 1945. Magdoff is identified as Tan in Weinstein and Vassiliev, *The Haunted Wood*.

195. Venona 1276 GRU New York to Moscow, 1943; 193 KGB New York to Moscow, 8 February 1944; 620 KGB New York to Moscow, 4 May 1944; 622 KGB New York to Moscow, 4 May 1944; 1077 KGB New York to Moscow, 29 July 1944; 1403 KGB New York to Moscow, 5 October 1944; 1680 KGB New York to Moscow, 30 November 1944; 1706 KGB New York to Moscow, 4 December 1944; 1755 KGB New York to Moscow, 14 December 1944.

196. Venona 450 KGB San Francisco to Moscow, 1 November 1943; 472 KGB San Francisco to Moscow, 9 November 1943; 161 KGB San Francisco to Moscow, 13 April 1944; 136 KGB San Francisco to Moscow, 2 April 1945; 138 KGB San Francisco to Moscow, 3 April 1945; 167 KGB San Francisco to Moscow, 16 April 1945.

197. Venona 676 KGB New York to Moscow, 12 May 1944; 1196 KGB New York to Moscow, 22 August 1944; 1337 KGB New York to Moscow, 19 September 1944; 1351 KGB New York to Moscow, 23 September 1944; 1370 KGB New York to Moscow, 27 September 1944; 1411 KGB New York to Moscow, 6 October 1944; 1429 KGB New York to Moscow, 9 October 1944; 1430 KGB New York to Moscow, 10 October 1944.

198. Venona 766 KGB New York to Moscow, 24 May 1943; 1055 KGB New York to Moscow, 2 July 1943; 823 KGB New York to Moscow, 7 June 1944; 881 KGB New York to Moscow, 20 June 1944; 958 KGB New York to Moscow, 7 July 1944.

199. Venona 221 KGB Mexico City to Moscow, 31 March 1944; 327 KGB Mexico City to Moscow, 3 May 1944; 283 KGB Moscow to Mexico City, 10 May 1944.

200. Venona 1116 GRU New York to Moscow, 9 July 1943; 1456 GRU New York to Moscow, 8 September 1943.

201. Venona 694 KGB New York to Moscow, 15 May 1943; 1044 KGB New York to Moscow, 2 July 1943; 1185 KGB New York to Moscow, 21 July 1943; 1031 KGB New York to Moscow, 24 July 1944; 1143–1144 KGB New York to Moscow, 10 August 1944; 1313 KGB New York to Moscow, 13 September 1944; 1337 KGB New York to Moscow, 19 September 1944; 1430 KGB New York to Moscow, 10 October 1944; 1470 KGB New York to Moscow, 17 October 1944; 1512 KGB New York to Moscow, 24 October 1944; 1522 KGB New York to Moscow, 27 October 1944; 1613 KGB New York to Moscow, 18 November 1944; 1637 KGB New York to Moscow, 21 November 1944; 1716 KGB New York to Moscow, 5 December 1944; 77 KGB New York to Moscow, 17 January 1945; 55 KGB Moscow to New York, 10 January 1943.

202. Venona 854 KGB New York to Moscow, 5 June 1943; 1100 KGB New York to Moscow, 7 July 1943.

203. Venona 727 KGB New York to Moscow, 20 May 1944; 751–752 KGB New York to Moscow, 26 May 1944; 826 KGB New York to Moscow, 7 June 1944; 846 KGB New York to Moscow, 14 June 1944; 851 KGB New York to Moscow, 15 June 1944; 1143–1144 KGB New York to Moscow, 10 August 1944.

204. Venona 450 KGB San Francisco to Moscow, 1 November 1943; 472 KGB San Francisco to Moscow, 9 November 1943; 511 KGB San Francisco to Moscow, 7 December 1943; 539 KGB San Francisco to Moscow, 31 December 1943; 147 KGB San Francisco to Moscow, 27 March 1944; 68 KGB San Francisco to Moscow, 27 February 1945.

205. Venona 1131 GRU New York to Moscow, 12 July 1943; 1348 GRU New York to Moscow, 16 August 1943; 1350 GRU New York to Moscow, 17 August 1943; 1373 GRU New York to Moscow, 23 August 1943; 1456 GRU New York to Moscow, 8 September 1943.

206. Venona 842 KGB New York to Moscow, 3 June 1943; 1179 KGB New York to Moscow, 20 July 1943; 1625 KGB New York to Moscow, 3 October 1943; 1681 KGB New York to Moscow, 13 October 1943.

207. Venona 1681 KGB New York to Moscow, 13 October 1943; "Comintern Apparatus Summary Report."

208. Venona 1325 GRU New York to Moscow, 11 August 1943.

209. Venona 2505–2512 Naval GRU Washington to Moscow, 31 December 1942; 1016 Naval GRU Washington to Moscow, 10 May 1943; 1040–1041 Naval GRU Washington to Moscow, 13 May 1943; 1080 Naval GRU Washington to Moscow, 19 May 1943; 1209 Naval GRU Washington to Moscow, 5 June 1943; 1252 Naval GRU Washington to Moscow, 10 June 1943; 1271 Naval GRU Washington to Moscow, 12 June 1943; 1348 Naval GRU Washington to Moscow, 19 June 1943; 1600 Naval GRU Washington to Moscow, 12 July 1943; 1902 Naval GRU Washington to Moscow, 8 August 1943; 1983 Naval GRU Washington to Moscow, 14 August 1943; 2124 Naval GRU Washington to Moscow, 27 August 1943; 126 Naval GRU Moscow to Washington, 22 January 1943; 394 Naval GRU Moscow to Washington, 5 March 1943; 452 Naval GRU Moscow to Washington, 16 March 1943; 484 Naval GRU Moscow to Washington, 20 March 1943; 611 Naval GRU Moscow to Washington, 8 April 1943; 835 Naval GRU Moscow to Washington, 12 May 1943; 846 Naval GRU Moscow to Washington, 14 May 1943; 863 Naval GRU Moscow to Washington, 17 May 1943; 1006 Naval GRU Moscow to Washington, 10 June 1943.

210. Venona 895 GRU New York to Moscow, 10 June 1943; 927–928 GRU New York to Moscow, 16 June 1943; 987 GRU New York to Moscow, 24 June 1943; 1014 GRU New York to Moscow, 28 June 1943; 1295 GRU New York to Moscow, 6 August 1943; 1456 GRU New York to Moscow, 8 September 1943; 1008 KGB New York to Moscow, 26 June 1943; 985–986 KGB New York to Moscow, 23 June 1943.

211. Venona 1579 New York GRU to Moscow, 28 September 1943.

212. Venona 943 KGB New York to Moscow, 4 July 1944; 1341 KGB New York to Moscow, 21 September 1944.

213. Venona 1824 KGB New York to Moscow, 27 December 1944; 4–5 KGB New York to Moscow, 3 January 1945; 18–19 KGB New York to Moscow, 4 January 1945.

214. Venona 513 KGB San Francisco to Moscow, 7 December 1943; 268 KGB San Francisco to Moscow, 21 June 1944.

215. Venona 1699 KGB New York to Moscow, 2 December 1944.

216. Venona 172 KGB San Francisco to Moscow, 18 April 1945; 69 KGB San Francisco to Moscow, 20 February 1946.

217. Venona 1009 KGB New York to Moscow, 19 July 1944; 1465 KGB New York to Moscow, 14 October 1944.

218. Venona 846 KGB New York to Moscow, 3 June 1943; 854 KGB New York to Moscow, 5 June 1943; 880 KGB New York to Moscow, 8 June 1943; 917 KGB New York to Moscow, 15 June 1943. There is also a Ruff in a 1945 KGB message, but that is clearly a different person from the Ruff of 1943. 876 KGB New York to Moscow, 6 June 1945. The identification of Neumann as Ruff is in Weinstein and Vassiliev, *The Haunted Wood*.

219. Venona 863 KGB New York to Moscow, 16 June 1944; 1251 KGB New York to Moscow, 2 September 1944; 1657 KGB New York to Moscow, 27 November 1944; 200 Moscow to New York, 6 March 1945; 325 Moscow to New York, 5 April 1945.

220. Venona 943 KGB New York to Moscow, 4 July 1944. Separately there was also a Nina in KGB traffic who was a clerical worker in the KGB office.

221. Venona 1031 KGB New York to Moscow, 1 July 1943; 1045 KGB New York to Moscow, 2 July 1943; 1053 KGB New York to Moscow, 2 July 1943; 1582 KGB New York to Moscow, 12 November 1944.

222. Venona 846 KGB New York to Moscow, 3 June 1943; 1644 KGB New York to Moscow, 9 October 1943; 336 KGB Moscow to New York, 8 April 1945.

223. Venona 801 KGB New York to Moscow, 28 May 1943; 1054 KGB New York to Moscow, 5 July 1945.

224. Venona 1002 KGB New York to Moscow, 17 July 1944; 1203 KGB New York to Moscow, 23 August 1944; 1251 KGB New York to Moscow, 2 September 1944; 1275 KGB New York to Moscow, 7 September 1944; 1336 KGB New York to Moscow, 18 September 1944; 1430 KGB New York to Moscow, 10 October 1944; 1829 KGB New York to Moscow, 28 December 1944; 14 KGB New York to Moscow, 4 January 1945.

225. Venona 993 KGB New York to Moscow, 13 July 1944.

226. Venona 1438 KGB New York to Moscow, 10 October 1944; 1586 KGB New York to Moscow, 12 November 1944; 20 KGB New York to Moscow, 4 January 1945; 239 KGB Moscow to New York, 17 March 1945. The link to Aleksandrov is suggested in Venona 1322 KGB New York to Moscow, 15 September 1944.

227. Venona 619 KGB New York to Moscow, 4 May 1944.

228. Venona 1324 GRU New York to Moscow, 11 August 1943; 1350 GRU New York to Moscow, 17 August 1943; 1362 GRU New York to Moscow, 19 August 1943. NSA redacted the identities of two candidates for Oppen.

229. Venona 854 KGB New York to Moscow, 5 June 1943; 934–935 KGB New York to Moscow, 17 June 1943; 952 KGB New York to Moscow, 21 June 1943; 613–614 KGB New York to Moscow, 3 May 1944; 725 KGB New York to Moscow, 19 May 1944; 750 KGB New York to Moscow, 26 May 1944; 163 KGB Moscow to New York, 19 February 1945; 239 KGB Moscow to New York, 17 March 1945; 767 KGB Moscow to New York, July 1945. On Orloff's attempt to gain OSS employment, see Nicholas W. Orloff autobiography and offer of service, attached to Horace W. Peters of OSS X-2 branch to Darwin Marron, 11 August 1944, Office of Strategic Services records, record group 226, entry 171, box 25, folder 370, National Archives and Records Administration, Archives II, College Park, Maryland.

230. Venona 151 KGB San Francisco to Moscow, 1944 March 30.

231. Venona 943 KGB New York to Moscow, 4 July 1944; 1052 KGB New York to Moscow, 26 July 1944; 1251 KGB New York to Moscow, 2 September 1944; 1403

KGB New York to Moscow, 5 October 1944; 1661–1662 KGB New York to Moscow, 28 November 1944.

232. Venona 1517 KGB New York to Moscow, 25 October 1944.

233. Venona 1465 KGB New York to Moscow, 14 October 1944; 1661–1662 KGB New York to Moscow, 28 November 1944.

234. Venona 864 KGB New York to Moscow, 16 June 1944; 1206 KGB New York to Moscow, KGB New York to Moscow, 23 August 1944; 1828 KGB New York to Moscow, 28 December 1944.

235. Venona 717 KGB New York to Moscow, 10 May 1944; 732 KGB New York to Moscow, 20 May 1944; 854 KGB New York to Moscow, 16 June 1944; 1048 KGB New York to Moscow, 25 July 1944; 1251 KGB New York to Moscow, 2 September 1944; 1314 KGB New York to Moscow, 14 September 1944; 1491 KGB New York to Moscow, 22 October 1944; 1536 KGB New York to Moscow, 28 October 1944; 1797 KGB New York to Moscow, 20 December 1944; 954 KGB Moscow to New York, 20 September 1944; 154 KGB Moscow to New York, 16 February 1945; 224 KGB Moscow to New York, 13 March 1945; 305 KGB Moscow to New York, 1 April 1945.

236. Venona 588 KGB New York to Moscow, 29 April 1944; 687 KGB New York to Moscow, 13 May 1944; 769, 771 KGB New York to Moscow, 30 May 1944; 1003 KGB New York to Moscow, 18 July 1944; 1015 KGB New York to Moscow, 22 July 1944; 1214 KGB New York to Moscow, 25 August 1944; 79 KGB New York to Moscow, 18 January 1945; 1823, 1824, 1825 KGB Washington to Moscow, 30 March 1945; 3707 KGB Washington to Moscow, 29 June 1945; 3708 KGB Washington to Moscow, 29 June 1945; 3713, 3715 KGB Washington to Moscow, 29 June 1945.

237. Venona 232 KGB San Francisco to Moscow, 1944 May 25.

238. Venona 995 KGB New York to Moscow, 24 June 1943; 1403 KGB New York to Moscow, 5 October 1944; 1559 KGB New York to Moscow, 6 November 1944; 154 KGB Moscow to New York, 16 February 1945; 305 KGB Moscow to New York, 1 April 1945.

239. Venona 882 GRU New York to Moscow, 8 June 1943; 1325 GRU New York to Moscow, 11 August 1943; 1393 GRU New York to Moscow, 25 August 1943; 1456 GRU New York to Moscow, 8 September 1943.

240. Venona 69 KGB San Francisco to Moscow, 20 February 1946. The cover name Philip also occurs in a number of Venona KGB San Francisco cables from the first half of 1945, but that Philip was clearly a KGB officer working at the Soviet consulate.

241. Venona 1930 KGB New York to Moscow, 21 November 1943; 853 KGB New York to Moscow, 16 June 1944.

242. Venona 619 KGB New York to Moscow, 4 May 1944; 1020 KGB New York to Moscow, 20 July 1944; 1332 KGB New York to Moscow, 18 September 1944; 1715 KGB New York to Moscow, 5 December 1944; 295 KGB Moscow to New York, 30 March 1945.

243. Venona 1715 KGB New York to Moscow, 5 December 1944.

244. Venona 621 KGB New York to Moscow, 4 May 1944; 853 KGB New York to Moscow, 16 June 1944.

245. Venona 1328 KGB New York to Moscow, 12 August 1943.

246. Venona 941 KGB New York to Moscow, 4 July 1944; 943 KGB New York to Moscow, 4 July 1944; 1403 KGB New York to Moscow, 5 October 1944; 1559 KGB New York to Moscow, 6 November 1944.

247. Venona 1151 KGB New York to Moscow, 12 August 1944.

248. Venona 864 KGB New York to Moscow, 16 June 1944; 1341 KGB New York to Moscow, 21 September 1944.

249. Venona 1132–1133 KGB New York to Moscow, 13 July 1943; 1930 KGB New York to Moscow, 21 November 1943.

250. Venona 786–787 KGB New York to Moscow, 26 May 1943.

251. Venona 868 KGB New York to Moscow, 8 June 1943; 1065 KGB New York to Moscow, 28 July 1944.

252. Venona 682 KGB New York to Moscow, 12 May 1944.

253. Venona 961 KGB New York to Moscow, 21 June 1943; 972, 979, 983 KGB New York to Moscow, 22–23 June 1943; 1405 KGB New York to Moscow, 27 August 1943.

254. Venona 640 KGB New York to Moscow, 6 May 1944; 1251 KGB New York to Moscow, 2 September 1944.

255. Venona 1074–1075 GRU New York to Moscow, 5 July 1943; 1172–1173 GRU New York to Moscow, 19 July 1943; 1243–1244 GRU New York to Moscow, 28 July 1943; 1312–1313 GRU New York to Moscow, 9 August 1943; 1456 GRU New York to Moscow, 8 September 1943; 1498–1499 GRU New York to Moscow, 17 September 1943; 1523 GRU New York to Moscow, 21 September 1943.

256. Venona 975 KGB New York to Moscow, 11 July 1944.

257. Venona 1557 KGB New York to Moscow, 6 November 1944.

258. Venona 943 KGB New York to Moscow, 4 July 1944.

259. Venona 1221 KGB New York to Moscow, 26 August 1944.

260. Venona 1579 New York GRU to Moscow, 28 September 1943.

261. Venona 1047 KGB New York to Moscow, 2 July 1943; 918 KGB New York to Moscow, 12 June 1945.

262. Venona 1410 KGB New York to Moscow, 6 October 1944.

263. Venona 227 KGB Moscow to New York, 13 March 1945.

264. Venona 1553 KGB New York to Moscow, 4 November 1944.

265. Venona 1810 KGB New York to Moscow, 23 December 1944.

266. Venona 1340 KGB New York to Moscow, 21 September 1944; 1657 KGB New York to Moscow, 27 November 1944.

267. Venona 628 KGB New York to Moscow, 5 May 1944; 736 KGB New York to Moscow, 22 May 1944; 845 KGB New York to Moscow, 14 June 1944; 911 KGB New York to Moscow, 27 June 1944; 976 KGB New York to Moscow, 11 July 1944; 1053 KGB New York to Moscow, 26 July 1944; 1251 KGB New York to Moscow, 2 September 1944; 1314 KGB New York to Moscow, 14 September 1944; 1327 KGB New York to Moscow, 15 September 1944; 1340 KGB New York to Moscow, 21 September 1944; 1491 KGB New York to Moscow, 22 October 1944; 1600 KGB New York to Moscow, 14 November 1944; 1609 KGB New York to Moscow, 17 November 1944; 1657 KGB New York to Moscow, 27 November 1944; 1715 KGB New York to Moscow, 5 December 1944; 1749–1750 KGB New York to Moscow, 13 December 1944; 1773 KGB New York to Moscow, 16 December 1944; 1797 KGB New York to Moscow, 20 December 1944; 28 KGB New York to Moscow, 8 January 1945; 200 KGB Moscow to New York, 6 March 1945; 325 Moscow to New York, 5 April 1945.

268. Venona 927–928 GRU New York to Moscow, 16 June 1943; 987 GRU New York to Moscow, 24 June 1943; 1116 GRU New York to Moscow, 9 July 1943; 1456 GRU New York to Moscow, 8 September 1943.

269. Venona 917 KGB New York to Moscow, 28 June 1944. NSA redacted the identify of S-2.

270. Venona 186 KGB Moscow to New York, 2 March 1945.

271. Venona 942 KGB New York to Moscow, 4 July 1944; 1015 KGB New York to Moscow, 22 July 1944; 1087 KGB New York to Moscow, 30 July 1944; 1220 KGB

New York to Moscow, 26 August 1944; 1266 KGB New York to Moscow, 6 September 1944; 1313 KGB New York to Moscow, 13 September 1944; 1370 KGB New York to Moscow, 27 September 1944; 1523 KGB New York to Moscow, 27 October 1944; 1649 KGB New York to Moscow, 25 November 1944; 29 KGB New York to Moscow, 8 January 1945; 130 KGB Moscow to New York, 11 February 1945; 446 KGB San Francisco to Moscow, 31 October 1943; 55 KGB San Francisco to Moscow, 8 February 1944; 298 KGB San Francisco to Moscow, 13 July 1944.

272. Venona 232 KGB San Francisco to Moscow, 25 May 1944.

273. Venona 628 KGB New York to Moscow, 5 May 1944; 1600 KGB New York to Moscow, 14 November 1944; 1715 KGB New York to Moscow, 5 December 1944; 1749–1750 KGB New York to Moscow, 13 December 1944.

274. Venona 1585 KGB New York to Moscow, 12 November 1944; 1699 KGB New York to Moscow, 2 December 1944; 94 KGB New York to Moscow, 23 January 1945.

275. Venona 579 KGB New York to Moscow, 28 April 1944; 1661–1662 KGB New York to Moscow, 28 November 1944.

276. Venona 283 KGB New York to Moscow, 24 February 1944; 598–599 KGB New York to Moscow, 2 May 1944; 605 KGB New York to Moscow, 2 May 1944; 619 KGB New York to Moscow, 4 May 1944; 749 KGB New York to Moscow, 26 May 1944; 911 KGB New York to Moscow, 27 June 1944; 939 KGB New York to Moscow, 3 July 1944; 1020 KGB New York to Moscow, 20 July 1944; 1029 KGB New York to Moscow, 22 July 1944; 1166 KGB New York to Moscow, 16 August 1944; 1221 KGB New York to Moscow, 26 August 1944; 1313 KGB New York to Moscow, 13 September 1944; 1328 KGB New York to Moscow, 15 September 1944; 1332 KGB New York to Moscow, 18 September 1944; 1337 KGB New York to Moscow, 19 September 1944; 1340 KGB New York to Moscow, 21 September 1944; 1400 KGB New York to Moscow, 5 October 1944; 1410 KGB New York to Moscow, 6 October 1944; 1430 KGB New York to Moscow, 10 October 1944; 1457 KGB New York to Moscow, 14 October 1944; 1512 KGB New York to Moscow, 24 October 1944; 1522 KGB New York to Moscow, 27 October 1944; 1553 KGB New York to Moscow, 4 November 1944; 1637 KGB New York to Moscow, 21 November 1944; 1668 KGB New York to Moscow, 29 November 1944; 1715 KGB New York to Moscow, 5 December 1944; 1803 KGB New York to Moscow, 22 December 1944; 1818 KGB New York to Moscow, 26 December 1944; 94 KGB New York to Moscow, 23 January 1945; 49 KGB Moscow to New York, 19 January 1944; 14 KGB New York to Moscow, 4 January 1945; 194 KGB Moscow to New York, 3 March 1945; 295 KGB Moscow to New York, 30 March 1945.

277. Venona 1456 GRU New York to Moscow, 8 September 1943; 1579 GRU New York to Moscow, 28 September 1943.

278. Venona 726–729 KGB New York to Moscow, 22 May 1942; 1681 KGB New York to Moscow, 13 October 1943; 207 KGB Moscow to New York, 8 March 1945.

279. Venona 823 KGB New York to Moscow, 7 June 1944; 881 KGB New York to Moscow, 20 June 1944; 1203 KGB New York to Moscow, 23 August 1944; 1275 KGB New York to Moscow, 7 September 1944.

280. Venona 50 KGB New York to Moscow, 11 January 1945.

281. Venona 49 KGB Moscow to New York, 19 January 1944.

282. Venona 764, 765 KGB New York to Moscow, 24 May 1943; 886 KGB New York to Moscow, 9 June 1943; 967–968 KGB New York to Moscow, 22 June 1943; 1234 KGB New York to Moscow, 29 August 1944; 1403 KGB New York to Moscow, 5 October 1944.

283. Venona 1589, 1590 KGB New York to Moscow, 30 September 1943; 886 KGB New York to Moscow, 22 June 1944; 943 KGB New York to Moscow, 4 July 1944.

284. Venona 210 KGB Moscow to New York, 9 March 1945.

285. Venona 1491 KGB New York to Moscow, 22 October 1944; 1536 KGB New York to Moscow, 28 October 1944; 1609 KGB New York to Moscow, 17 November 1944; 1797 KGB New York to Moscow, 20 December 1944; 210 KGB Moscow to New York, 9 March 1945; 224 KGB Moscow to New York, 13 March 1945.

286. Venona 928 KGB New York to Moscow, 30 June 1943; 1057 KGB New York to Moscow, 3 July 1943; 1081 KGB New York to Moscow, 6 July 1943; 1317 KGB New York to Moscow, 10 August 1943; 1243 KGB New York to Moscow, 31 August 1944; 1463 KGB New York to Moscow, 14 October 1944; 12, 13, 15, 16 KGB New York to Moscow, 4 January 1945.

287. Venona 1508 KGB New York to Moscow, 23 October 1944; 1635 KGB New York to Moscow, 21 November 1944; 12, 13, 15, 16 New York to Moscow, 4 January 1945; 337 KGB Moscow to New York, 8 April 1945.

288. Venona 678–682 KGB New York to Moscow, 14 May 1942; 746–748 KGB New York to Moscow, 25 May 1942; 763–765 KGB New York to Moscow, 27 May 1942; 833 KGB New York to Moscow, 10 June 1942; 732, 735 KGB New York to Moscow, 21 May 1943; 794–799 KGB New York to Moscow, 28 May 1943; 888 KGB New York to Moscow, 9 June 1943; 977 KGB New York to Moscow, 22 June 1943; 1017, 1022 KGB New York to Moscow, 29–30 June 1943; 1057 KGB New York to Moscow, 3 July 1943; 1176, 1177, 1178 KGB New York to Moscow, 20 July 1943; 1189 KGB New York to Moscow, 21 July 1943; 1431 KGB New York to Moscow, 2 September 1943; 278 KGB New York to Moscow, 23 February 1944; 588 KGB New York to Moscow, 29 April 1944; 655 KGB New York to Moscow, 9 May 1944; 687 KGB New York to Moscow, 13 May 1944; 827 KGB New York to Moscow, 7 June 1944; 918 KGB New York to Moscow, 28 June 1944; 927 KGB New York to Moscow, 1 July 1944; 973 KGB New York to Moscow, 11 July 1944; 1003 KGB New York to Moscow, 18 July 1944; 1155 KGB New York to Moscow, 12 August 1944; 1243 KGB New York to Moscow, 31 August 1944; 1388, 1389 KGB New York to Moscow, 1 October 1944; 1463 KGB New York to Moscow, 14 October 1944; 1469 KGB New York to Moscow, 17 October 1944; 1481–1482 KGB New York to Moscow, 18 October 1944; 1483 KGB New York to Moscow, 18 October 1944; 1508 KGB New York to Moscow, 23 October 1944; 1606 KGB New York to Moscow, 16 November 1944; 1619–1620 KGB New York to Moscow, 20 November 1944; 1634 KGB New York to Moscow, 20 November 1944; 1635 KGB New York to Moscow, 21 November 1944; 1691 KGB New York to Moscow, 1 December 1944; 1751–1753 KGB New York to Moscow, 13 December 1944; 1787, 1788 KGB New York to Moscow, 19 December 1944; 1789 KGB New York to Moscow, 19 December 1944; 1798 KGB New York to Moscow, 20 December 1944; 1821 KGB New York to Moscow, 26 December 1944; 12, 13, 15, 16 KGB New York to Moscow, 4 January 1945; 14 KGB New York to Moscow, 4 January 1945; 21 KGB New York to Moscow, 8 January 1945; 55 KGB New York to Moscow, 15 January 1945; 71 KGB New York to Moscow, 17 January 1945; 79 KGB New York to Moscow, 18 January 1945; 82 KGB New York to Moscow, 18 January 1945; 83 KGB New York to Moscow, 18 January 1945; 205 KGB New York to Moscow, 10 February 1945; 143 KGB Moscow to New York, 15 February 1945; 173 KGB Moscow to New

York, 22 February 1945; 179, 180 KGB Moscow to New York, 25 February 1945; 186 KGB Moscow to New York, 2 March 1945; 195 KGB Moscow to New York, 3 March 1945; 248 KGB Moscow to New York, 19 March 1945; 253 KGB Moscow to New York, 20 March 1945; 268 KGB Moscow to New York, 24 March 1945; 292 KGB Moscow to New York, 29 March 1945; 328 KGB Moscow to New York, 6 April 1945; 336 KGB Moscow to New York, 8 April 1945; 337 KGB Moscow to New York, 8 April 1945.

289. Venona 1824 KGB New York to Moscow, 27 December 1944.

290. Venona 912 KGB New York to Moscow, 27 June 1944; 1267 KGB New York to Moscow, 6 September 1944; 1332 KGB New York to Moscow, 18 September 1944; 1370 KGB New York to Moscow, 27 September 1944.

291. Venona 943 KGB New York to Moscow, 4 July 1944; 976 KGB New York to Moscow, 11 July 1944; 1251 KGB New York to Moscow, 2 September 1944; 50 KGB New York to Moscow, 11 January 1945.

292. Venona 992 KGB New York to Moscow, 24 June 1943; 1086 KGB New York to Moscow, 6 July 1943; 625 KGB New York to Moscow, 5 May 1944; 851 KGB New York to Moscow, 15 June 1944; 1146 KGB New York to Moscow, 10 August 1944; 1251 KGB New York to Moscow, 2 September 1944; 1353 KGB New York to Moscow, 23 September 1944; 1449 KGB New York to Moscow, 12 October 1944; 1754 KGB New York to Moscow, 14 December 1944; 48 KGB New York to Moscow, 11 January 1945; 776 KGB New York to Moscow, 25 May 1945.

293. Venona 791–792 KGB New York to Moscow, 27 May 1943; 1118 KGB New York to Moscow, 9 July 1943; 1146 KGB New York to Moscow, 10 August 1944; 1353 KGB New York to Moscow, 23 September 1944; 1517 KGB New York to Moscow, 25 October 1944; 1553 KGB New York to Moscow, 4 November 1944; 1789 KGB New York to Moscow, 19 December 1944; 48 KGB New York to Moscow, 11 January 1945; 776 KGB New York to Moscow, 25 May 1945.

294. Venona 1405 KGB New York to Moscow, 27 August 1943; 1403 KGB New York to Moscow, 5 October 1944; 1509 KGB New York to Moscow, 23 October 1944.

295. Venona 1016 KGB New York to Moscow, 20 July 1944; 1042 KGB New York to Moscow, 25 July 1944.

296. Venona 882 GRU New York to Moscow, 8 June 1943; 986 GRU New York to Moscow, 23 June 1943; 1084 GRU New York to Moscow, 6 July 1943; 1433 GRU New York to Moscow, 3 September 1943.

297. Venona 1456 GRU New York to Moscow, 8 September 1943.

298. Venona 812 KGB New York to Moscow, 29 May 1943.

299. Venona 583 KGB New York to Moscow, 28 April 1943; 867 KGB New York to Moscow, 8 June 1943; 194 KGB Moscow to New York, 3 March 1945.

300. Venona 998 KGB New York to Moscow, 24 June 1943; 943 KGB New York to Moscow, 4 July 1944; 1403 KGB New York to Moscow, 5 October 1944; 1559 KGB New York to Moscow, 6 November 1944; 780, 792 KGB New York to Moscow, 25 and 26 May 1945.

301. Venona 669 KGB New York to Moscow, 11 May 1944; 981 KGB New York to Moscow, 12 July 1944; 1142 KGB New York to Moscow, 10 August 1944.

302. Venona 734 KGB New York to Moscow, 21 May 1944; 1039–1041 KGB New York to Moscow, 24–25 July 1944; 1393 KGB New York to Moscow, 3 October 1944; 1814, 1815 KGB New York to Moscow, 23 December 1944.

303. Venona 704 Naval GRU Washington to Moscow, 1 April 1943; 1934 Naval GRU Washington to Moscow, 11 August 1943; 1969 Naval GRU Washington to Moscow, 13 August 1943; 115 Naval GRU Moscow to Washington, 20 January 1943; 155

Naval GRU Moscow to Washington, 26 January 1943; 1194 Naval GRU Moscow to Washington, 10 July 1943; 1251 KGB New York to Moscow, 2 September 1943.

304. Venona 1824 KGB New York to Moscow, 27 December 1944; 4–5 KGB New York to Moscow, 3 January 1945; 11 KGB New York to Moscow, 4 January 1945; 18–19 KGB New York to Moscow, 4 January 1945.

305. Venona 854 KGB New York to Moscow, 16 June 1942.

306. Venona 927, 928 KGB New York to Moscow, 3 July 1942. "Stevenson" in 1681 KGB New York to Moscow, 13 October 1943, is probably an error for "Stevens." See also Fitin to Dimitrov; 8 July 1942, and Vilkov memo on Stevens, 21 July 1942, both in RTsKhIDNI 495-74-485, and Harvey Klehr, John Earl Haynes, and Fridrikh Igorevich Firsov, *The Secret World of American Communism* (New Haven: Yale University Press, 1995), 299–303.

307. Venona 687 KGB New York to Moscow, 13 May 1944; 769, 771 KGB New York to Moscow, 30 May 1944.

308. Venona 500 KGB San Francisco to Moscow, 27 November 1943; 26 KGB San Francisco to Moscow, 17 January 1944; 39 KGB San Francisco to Moscow, 22 January 1944; 104 KGB San Francisco to Moscow, 5 March 1944; 725 KGB New York to Moscow, 1944 May 19.

309. Venona 132 KGB San Francisco to Moscow, 18 March 1944; 257 KGB San Francisco to Moscow, 7 June 1944; 270 KGB San Francisco to Moscow, 22 June 1944.

310. Venona 1048 KGB New York to Moscow, 25 July 1944; 71 KGB New York to Moscow, 17 January 1945.

311. Venona 756 KGB New York to Moscow, 27 May 1944; 769 and 771 KGB New York to Moscow, 30 May 1944; 940 KGB New York to Moscow, 4 July 1944; 1118 KGB New York to Moscow, 4 August 1944; 1352 KGB New York to Moscow, 23 September 1944. Tenney was not identified as Muse until the appearance in 1999 of Weinstein and Vassiliev, *The Haunted Wood*.

312. Venona 1403 KGB New York to Moscow, 5 October 1944; 1559 KGB New York to Moscow, 6 November 1944.

313. Venona 1056 KGB New York to Moscow, 3 July 1943; 823 KGB New York to Moscow, 7 June 1944; 881 KGB New York to Moscow, 20 June 1944; 1076 KGB New York to Moscow, 29 July 1944; 202 KGB New York to Moscow, 10 February 1945; 116 KGB Moscow to New York, 9 February 1945; 143 KGB Moscow to New York, 15 February 1945.

314. Venona 622 KGB New York to Moscow, 4 May 1943.

315. Venona 927 KGB New York to Moscow, 1 July 1944.

316. Venona 700 KGB New York to Moscow, 17 May 1944; 761 KGB New York to Moscow, 27 May 1944.

317. Venona 928 KGB New York to Moscow, 30 June 1943; 1081 KGB New York to Moscow, 6 July 1943; 278 KGB New York to Moscow, 23 February 1944; 590 KGB New York to Moscow, 29 April 1944; 656 KGB New York to Moscow, 9 May 1944; 927 KGB New York to Moscow, 1 July 1944; 1122 KGB New York to Moscow, 8 August 1944; 1214 KGB New York to Moscow, 25 August 1944; 1243 KGB New York to Moscow, 31 August 1944; 1251 KGB New York to Moscow, 2 September 1944; 1325, 1326 KGB New York to Moscow, 15 September 1944; 1388, 1389 KGB New York to Moscow, 1 October 1944; 1481–1482 KGB New York to Moscow, 18 October 1944; 1634 KGB New York to Moscow, 20 November 1944; 1721–1728 KGB New York to Moscow, 8 December 1944; 1822 KGB New York to Moscow, 27 December 1944; 1836 KGB New York to Moscow, and to 8th department, 29 December 1944; 12, 13, 15, 16 KGB New York to Moscow, 4 January 1945; 71 KGB New York to

Moscow, 17 January 1945; 210 KGB New York to Moscow, 10 February 1945; 211–212 KGB New York to Moscow, 10 February 1945; 289 KGB Moscow to New York, 28 March 1945; 328 KGB Moscow to New York, 6 April 1945. Although unnamed, Ullmann may be the source of stolen documents discussed in 1751–1753 KGB New York to Moscow, 13 December 1944. See Robert Louis Benson and Michael Warner, eds., *Venona: Soviet Espionage and the American Response, 1939–1957* (Washington, D.C.: National Security Agency, Central Intelligence Agency, 1996), xxi.

318. Venona 884 KGB New York to Moscow, 8 June 1943.

319. Venona 846 KGB New York to Moscow, 3 June 1943.

320. Venona 846 KGB New York to Moscow, 3 June 1943; 1248 KGB New York to Moscow, 29 July 1943.

321. Venona 880 KGB New York to Moscow, 8 June 1943.

322. Venona 1000 KGB New York to Moscow, 24 June 1943.

323. Venona 1351 KGB New York to Moscow, 23 September 1944.

324. Venona 2693 Naval GRU Washington to Moscow, 15 October 1943.

325. Venona 2693 Naval GRU Washington to Moscow, 15 October 1943.

326. Venona 1522, KGB New York to Moscow, 27 October 1944.

327. Venona 1204 GRU New York to Moscow, 22 July 1943.

328. Venona 1804 Naval GRU Washington to Moscow, 31 July 1943.

329. Venona 1557 KGB New York to Moscow, 6 November 1944.

330. Venona 1324 GRU New York to Moscow, 11 August 1943; 1456 GRU New York to Moscow, 8 September 1943.

331. Venona 959 KGB New York to Moscow, 21 June 1943.

332. Venona 853 KGB New York to Moscow, 16 June 1944.

333. Venona 500 KGB San Francisco to Moscow, 27 November 1943; 515 KGB San Francisco to Moscow, 7 December 1943; 26 KGB San Francisco to Moscow, 17 January 1944; 39 KGB San Francisco to Moscow, 22 January 1944; 104 KGB San Francisco to Moscow, 5 March 1944; 167 KGB San Francisco to Moscow, 15 April 1944.

334. Venona 1324 GRU New York to Moscow, 11 August 1943.

335. Venona 823 KGB New York to Moscow, 7 June 1944; 881 KGB New York to Moscow, 20 June 1944; 958 KGB New York to Moscow, 7 July 1944.

336. Venona 769, 771 KGB New York to Moscow, 30 May 1944; 1325, 1326 KGB New York to Moscow, 15 September 1944; 1354 KGB New York to Moscow, 22 September 1944; 1388, 1389 KGB New York to Moscow, 1 October 1944; 954 KGB Moscow to New York, 20 September 1944.

337. Venona 590 KGB New York to Moscow, 29 April 1944; 1119–1121 KGB New York to Moscow, 4–5 August 1944; 1251 KGB New York to Moscow, 2 September 1944; 1271–1274 KGB New York to Moscow, 7 September 1944; 1388–1389 KGB New York to Moscow, 1 October 1944; 1634 KGB New York to Moscow, 20 November 1944; 79 KGB New York to Moscow, 18 January 1945; 83 KGB New York to Moscow, 18 January 1945; 248 KGB Moscow to New York, 19 March 1945; 292 KGB Moscow to New York, 29 March 1945; 328 KGB Moscow to New York, 6 April 1945; 230 KGB San Francisco to Moscow, 4 May 1945; 235–236 KGB San Francisco to Moscow, 5 May 1945; 259 KGB San Francisco to Moscow, 13 May 1945; 312 KGB San Francisco to Moscow, 8 June 1945.

338. Venona 823 KGB New York to Moscow, 7 June 1944; 863 KGB New York to Moscow, 16 June 1944; 881 KGB New York to Moscow, 20 June 1944.

339. Venona 1714 KGB New York to Moscow, 5 December 1944; 76 KGB New York to Moscow, 17 January 1945; 1137 KGB New York to Moscow, 17 July 1945.

340. Venona 1146 KGB New York to Moscow, 10 August 1944; 1714 KGB New York to Moscow, 5 December 1944.

341. Venona 256 KGB New York to Moscow, 21 March 1945; 193–194 KGB Mexico City to Moscow, 14 March 1944.

342. Venona 3, 4, 5 KGB San Francisco to Moscow, 2 January 1946; 25 KGB San Francisco to Moscow, 26 January 1946; FBI report, "Soviet Espionage Activities, 19 October 1945," attached to Hoover to Vaughan, 19 October 1945, President's Secretary's Files, Harry S. Truman Library, Independence, Mo.; FBI report, "Soviet Activities in the United States," 25 July 1946, Clark M. Clifford papers, Truman Library.

343. Venona 777–781 KGB New York to Moscow, 26 May 1943; 893 KGB New York to Moscow, 10 June 1943; 325 Moscow to New York, 5 April 1945. It is not clear that the Glory in the 1945 message is Glory/Wolston as in 1943.

344. Venona 1589, 1590 KGB New York to Moscow, 30 September 1943; 144 KGB New York to Moscow, 27 January 1944; 1014 KGB New York to Moscow, 20 July 1944; 1050 KGB New York to Moscow, 26 July 1944; 1155 KGB New York to Moscow, 12 August 1944; 1321 KGB New York to Moscow, 15 September 1944; 1385 KGB New York to Moscow, 1 October 1944; 1397 KGB New York to Moscow, 4 October 1944; 1587 KGB New York to Moscow, 12 November 1944; 1637 KGB New York to Moscow, 21 November 1944; 1714 KGB New York to Moscow, 5 December 1944; 1716 KGB New York to Moscow, 5 December 1944; 1845 KGB New York to Moscow, 31 December 1944; 55 KGB New York to Moscow, 15 January 1945; 76 KGB New York to Moscow, 17 January 1945; 221 KGB Moscow to New York, 11 March 1945; 227 KGB Moscow to New York, 13 March 1945; 229 KGB Moscow to New York, 15 March 1945; 268 KGB Moscow to New York, 24 March 1945; 284, 286 KGB Moscow to New York, 28 March 1945.

345. Venona 446 KGB San Francisco to Moscow, 31 October 1943; 457 KGB San Francisco to Moscow, 2 November 1943; 1266 KGB New York to Moscow, 6 September 1944; 1523 KGB New York to Moscow, 27 October 1944.

346. Venona 1435 KGB New York to Moscow, 4 September 1943; 864 KGB New York to Moscow, 16 June 1944.

347. Venona 1325 GRU New York to Moscow, 11 August 1943.

348. Venona 790 KGB New York to Moscow, 27 May 1943; 1184 KGB New York to Moscow, 21 July 1943; 594 KGB New York to Moscow, 1 May 1944; 740 KGB New York to Moscow, 24 May 1944; 799 KGB New York to Moscow, 3 June 1944; 851 KGB New York to Moscow, 15 June 1944; 907 KGB New York to Moscow, 26 June 1944; 1143, 1144 KGB New York to Moscow, 10 August 1944; 1145 KGB New York to Moscow, 10 August 1944; 1251 KGB New York to Moscow, 2 September 1944; 1353 KGB New York to Moscow, 23 September 1944; 1449 KGB New York to Moscow, 12 October 1944; 1457 KGB New York to Moscow, 14 October 1944; 1500 KGB New York to Moscow, 20 October 1944; 1548 KGB New York to Moscow, 3 November 1944; 1803 KGB New York to Moscow, 22 December 1944; 87 KGB New York to Moscow, 19 January 1945; 954 KGB Moscow to New York, 20 September 1944; 323 KGB Moscow to New York, 5 April 1945.

349. Venona 1251 KGB New York to Moscow, 2 September 1944; 1328 KGB New York to Moscow, 15 September 1944.

Appendix B

1. Elizabeth Bentley FBI deposition, 30 November 1945, FBI file 65-14603.
2. See chapters 6 and 10.

3. Joseph Albright and Marcia Kunstel, *Bombshell: The Secret Story of America's Unknown Atomic Spy Conspiracy* (New York: Times Books, 1997), 193–195.

4. See chapter 9.

5. FBI report, "Soviet Espionage Activities, 19 October 1945," attached to Hoover to Vaughan, 19 October 1945, President's Secretary's Files, Harry S. Truman Library, Independence, Mo.

6. Albright and Kunstel, *Bombshell,* 193–195.

7. See chapter 9.

8. See chapter 6.

9. See chapter 8.

10. See chapter 9.

11. See chapter 8.

12. See chapter 9.

13. See chapter 6.

14. See chapter 9.

15. See chapter 9.

16. See chapter 8.

17. See chapter 8.

18. Bentley deposition.

19. See chapter 3.

20. See chapter 3.

21. See chapter 6.

22. See chapters 3 and 6.

23. See chapter 10.

24. Ann Kimmage, *An Un-American Childhood* (Athens: University of Georgia Press, 1997).

25. See chapter 10.

26. FBI report, "Soviet Espionage Activities, 19 October 1945"; New York FBI report, 5 April 1946, Comintern Apparatus file (FBI file 100-203581), serial 5236.

27. See chapters 3, 5, 7, and 9.

28. See chapter 8.

29. See chapter 8.

30. Inserted statement of Nicholas Dozenberg, hearings 8 November 1949, U.S. Congress, House of Representatives, Committee on Un-American Activities, 81st Cong., 1st and 2d sess.; Herbert Romerstein and Stanislav Levchenko, *The KGB Against the "Main Enemy": How the Soviet Intelligence Service Operates Against the United States* (Lexington Books, 1989), 16.

31. See chapter 6.

32. "Comintern Apparatus Summary Report," 15 December 1944, FBI Comintern Apparatus file, serial 3702; see also memo of 1 November 1944, serial 3378; see chapter 10.

33. U.S. Department of State Passport Division brief on a conspiracy charge against World Tourists and the CPUSA, reprinted in "Scope of Soviet Activity in the United States," appendix 1, part 23-A, U.S. Congress, Subcommittee to Investigate the Administration of the Internal Security Act, Senate Judiciary Committee (Washington, D.C.: GPO, 1957), A110–111; Harvey Klehr, John Earl Haynes, and Fridrikh Igorevich Firsov, *The Secret World of American Communism* (New Haven: Yale University Press, 1995), 296–297.

34. Whittaker Chambers, *Witness* (New York: Random House, 1952), 382; Scheidt to Director, 31 January 1947, FBI Silvermaster file (FBI file 65-56402), serial 1976.

35. See chapter 3.

36. Hede Massing, *This Deception* (New York: Duell, Sloan and Pearce, 1951), 139, 182–183, 195, 202–204, 218–19.

37. Harvey Klehr and Ronald Radosh, *The Amerasia Spy Case: Prelude to McCarthyism* (Chapel Hill: University of North Carolina Press, 1996).

38. See chapter 10.

39. Gennadi Kostyrchenko, *Out of the Red Shadows: Anti-Semitism in Stalin's Russia* (Amherst, N.Y.: Prometheus Books, 1995), 78–79.

40. Elizabeth Bentley, *Out of Bondage: The Story of Elizabeth Bentley* (New York: Ivy Books, 1988), 108.

41. See chapter 4.

42. Bentley deposition; Ladd memo to Director, 7 December 1945, serial 118, Ladd memo to Director 12 December 1945, serial 235; FBI Washington Field Office report, 11 March 1946, serial 674, both in FBI Silvermaster file.

43. See chapter 8.

44. See chapter 6.

45. Robert Lamphere and Tom Shachtman, *The FBI-KGB War: A Special Agent's Story* (New York: Random House, 1995), 143, 164–165, 171.

46. See chapter 10.

47. See chapter 8.

48. Allen Weinstein, *Perjury: The Hiss-Chambers Case* (New York: Random House, 1997), 96, 146, 280, 342.

49. See chapter 3.

50. Chambers, *Witness,* 41, 422–424; Weinstein, *Perjury,* 208, 210, 226–227, 444–445.

51. Weinstein, *Perjury,* 106.

52. Klehr and Radosh, *The Amerasia Spy Case.*

53. Bentley deposition.

54. See chapters 3, 5, and 6.

55. Bentley deposition. Also see Venona 247 KGB San Francisco to Moscow, 14 June 1946, for an ambiguous mention of Kahn in the clear.

56. See chapter 6.

57. Report of 11 January 1944, FBI Silvermaster file, serial 3378; "Comintern Apparatus Summary Report"; "The Shameful Years: Thirty Years of Soviet Espionage in the Untied States," 30 December 1951, U.S. Congress, House of Representatives, Committee on Un-American Activities, 39–40.

58. Bentley deposition.

59. Bentley deposition.

60. Ray Bearse and Anthony Read, *Conspirator: The Untold Story of Tyler Kent* (New York: Doubleday, 1991).

61. William Crane memorandum, 14 February 1949, William Crane FBI File 74-1333, serial 213.

62. See chapter 6.

63. Bentley deposition.

64. Klehr and Radosh, *The Amerasia Spy Case.*

65. See chapter 10.

66. Bentley deposition.

67. Elizabeth Bentley testimony, 13 May 1949, "Communist Activities Among Aliens and National Groups," Subcommittee on Immigration and Naturalization of the Committee on the Judiciary, U.S. Senate, 81st Cong., 1st sess., part 1, 106–

123; FBI Washington Field Office memo, 26 August 1948, FBI Silvermaster file, serial 3430.

68. Klehr, Haynes, and Firsov, *The Secret World of American Communism,* 131–132; "Comintern Apparatus Summary Report."

69. Testimony of Maxim Lieber, 13 June 1950, U.S. Congress, House of Representatives, Committee on Un-American Activities, 81st Cong., 1st and 2d sess.; Chambers, *Witness,* 280–291, 408–413; Sam Tanenhaus, *Whittaker Chambers: A Biography* (New York: Random House, 1997), 80–83, 100–102.

70. See chapter 10.

71. See chapter 6.

72. See chapter 9.

73. Oleg Kalugin, with Fen Montaigne, *The First Directorate: My 32 Years in Intelligence and Espionage Against the West* (New York: St. Martin's Press, 1994), 48–50.

74. Massing, *This Deception.*

75. Ibid.

76. See chapter 9.

77. Elizabeth Bentley testimony, "Communist Activities Among Aliens and National Groups."

78. Bentley, *Out of Bondage,* 107.

79. See chapter 4.

80. See chapter 4.

81. Klehr and Radosh, *The Amerasia Spy Case.*

82. See chapter 3.

83. Son to Dimitrov, 19 April 1943, Archive of the Secretariat of the Executive Committee of the Communist International: coded correspondence with Communist Parties (1933–1943). RTsKhIDNI 495-184-5 (1942 file).

84. Nigel West and Oleg Tsarev, *The Crown Jewels: The British Secrets at the Heart of the KGB Archives* (London: HarperCollins, 1998), 112–113.

85. Ronald Radosh and Joyce Milton, *The Rosenberg File: A Search for the Truth* (New Haven: Yale University Press, 1997), 153–156.

86. See chapters 3, 8, and 10.

87. See chapter 3 and 5.

88. See chapter 6.

89. FBI memo, 23 December 1946, Silvermaster file, serial 1938.

90. Romerstein and Levchenko, *The KGB Against the "Main Enemy,"* 17.

91. Bentley deposition; Ladd to Director, "Underground Soviet Espionage Organization (NKVD) in Agencies of the United States Government," 21 February 1946, serial 573, and Scheidt to Director, 31 January 1947, serial 1976, both in FBI Silvermaster file.

92. Ibid.

93. See chapter 3.

94. Weinstein, *Perjury* (1997), 206, 209, 211, 214–215.

95. Dorothy Gallagher, *All the Right Enemies: The Life and Murder of Carlo Tresca* (New Brunswick, N.J.: Rutgers University Press, 1988), 170–176; Bentley deposition; Bentley, *Out of Bondage,* 108, 176–177; Chambers, *Witness,* 36. The FBI conducted an extensive and fruitless investigation into Poyntz's disappearance: FBI Poyntz file 100-206603.

96. See chapter 4.

97. See chapter 9.

98. Bentley deposition; "Underground Soviet Espionage Organization (NKVD) in

Agencies of the United States Government," serial 573, and FBI Washington Field Office report, 21 April 1947, serial 2349, both in FBI Silvermaster file.

99. See chapter 5.

100. Weinstein, *Perjury,* 206, 209–11, 214, 279.

101. Bentley deposition.

102. "The Shameful Years," 15–16.

103. See chapter 3.

104. Klehr and Radosh, *The Amerasia Spy Case.*

105. Hoover to San Francisco FBI, 22 November 1944, FBI Comintern Apparatus file, serial 3474.

106. FBI memorandum, "Existing Corroboration of Bentley's Overall Testimony," FBI Silvermaster file, serial 4201.

107. See chapter 9.

108. Weinstein, *Perjury,* 98, 105, 109, 111–114, 208, 273–274, 288, 361.

109. See chapter 9.

110. See chapter 9.

111. Radosh and Milton, *The Rosenberg File* (1997), 152–153.

112. See chapter 9.

113. West and Tsarev, *The Crown Jewels,* 112–113.

114. Chambers, *Witness,* 421n.

115. See chapter 9.

116. See chapter 9.

117. Inserted statement of Nicholas Dozenberg.

118. FBI report, "Soviet Espionage Activities, 19 October 1945"; FBI report, "Soviet Activities in the United States," 25 July 1946, Clark M. Clifford papers, Harry S. Truman Library, Independence, Mo.

119. New York FBI report, 19 January 1945, Comintern Apparatus file, serial 3899.

120. Inserted statement of Nicholas Dozenberg; Romerstein and Levchenko, *The KGB Against the "Main Enemy,"* 16.

121. See chapter 6.

122. Michael Straight, *After Long Silence* (New York: Norton, 1983); John Earl Haynes, "Speak No Evil: Michael Straight and *After Long Silence,*" *Chronicles of Culture* 7, no. 11 (1983); Sidney Hook, "The Incredible Story of Michael Straight," *Encounter* (December 1983); Robert King, "Treason and Traitors," *Society* 26, no. 5 (July/August 1989); Weinstein, *Perjury,* 183–184; West and Tsarev, *The Crown Jewels,* 112–113, 116, 130, 133–134, 174.

123. See chapter 6.

124. Weinstein, *Perjury,* 107.

125. Bentley deposition; "Existing Corroboration of Bentley's Overall Testimony"; "Underground Soviet Espionage Organization (NKVD) in Agencies of the United States Government." Taylor's points are discussed in detail in Hayden Peake's Afterword to the 1988 reissue of Bentley's *Out of Bondage,* and the principal part of the FBI analysis of Taylor's attack on Bentley charges is reproduced in appendix B of the same book.

126. Inserted statement of Nicholas Dozenberg; "Comintern Apparatus Summary Report."

127. See chapter 3.

128. Weinstein, *Perjury,* 107–108, 110, 138n, 204, 281.

129. Albright and Kunstel, *Bombshell,* 49; Aleksandr Feklisov, *Za okeanom i na ostrove. Zapiski razvedchika* (Moscow: DEE, 1994), 76; Vladimir Chikov, "How the

Soviet Secret Service Split the American Atom," *Novoe vremia,* no. 16, 17 (23, 30 April 1991).

130. See chapter 9.

131. Bentley deposition; "Underground Soviet Espionage Organization (NKVD) in Agencies of the United States Government," serial 573, and New York FBI to Director, 13 February 1947, serial 2466, both in FBI Silvermaster file.

132. Weinstein, *Perjury,* 57, 102–103, 137, 172, 204–206, 225, 228, 247, 293, 346, 466, 515.

133. Klehr, Haynes, and Firsov, *The Secret World of American Communism,* 142; Louis Budenz, *Men Without Faces* (New York: Harper and Brothers, 1948), 126–129.

134. See chapter 10.

135. Bentley deposition; "Underground Soviet Espionage Organization (NKVD) in Agencies of the United States Government"; Ladd memo, 15 December 1945, serial 367; New York FBI to Hoover, 6 February 1946, serial 452; Ladd to Director, 21 February 1946, serial 573; last three in FBI Silvermaster file.

136. See chapter 2.

137. See chapter 3.

138. Weinstein, *Perjury,* 137, 192, 209–210, 214–215, 246, 342, 357, 386.

139. Romerstein and Levchenko, *The KGB Against the "Main Enemy,"* 193–194.

Appendix C

1. See chapter 2.

2. Venona 13 KGB Moscow to London, 16 September 1945.

3. Venona 2227 GRU London to Moscow, 10 August 1941; 195 KGB New York to Moscow, 9 February 1944; 645 KGB New York to Moscow, 8 May 1944; 850 New York to Moscow, 15 June 1944; 1049 KGB New York to Moscow, 25 July 1944; 1345 KGB New York to Moscow, 22 September 1944; 1397 KGB New York to Moscow, 4 October 1944; 1403 KGB New York to Moscow, 5 October 1944; 1606 KGB New York to Moscow, 16 November 1944; 183 KGB Moscow to New York, 27 February 1945; 298 KGB Moscow to New York, 31 March 1945; 349 KGB Moscow to New York, 10 April 1945.

4. Venona 915 KGB New York to Moscow, 28 June 1944; 1105, 1110 KGB New York to Moscow, 2–3 August 1944; 1114 KGB New York to Moscow, 4 August 1944; 1146 KGB New York to Moscow, 10 August 1944; 1263 KGB New York to Moscow, 5 September 1944; 1271–1274 KGB New York to Moscow, 7 September 1944; 1788 KGB Washington to KGB Moscow, 29 March 1945; 1791 KGB Washington to KGB Moscow, 29 March 1945; 1793 KGB Washington to KGB Moscow, 29 March 1945; 1808–1809 KGB Washington to KGB Moscow, 30 March 1945; 1826 KGB Washington to KGB Moscow 31 March 1945.

5. See chapter 2.

6. FBI report, "Soviet Espionage Activities, 19 October 1945," attached to Hoover to Vaughan, 19 October 1945, President's Secretary's Files, Harry S. Truman Library, Independence, Mo.

7. "The Report of the Royal Commission, Appointed Under Order in Council P.C. 411 of 5 February 1946, to Investigate the Facts Relating to and the Circumstances Surrounding the Communications, by Public Officials and Other Persons in Positions of Trust, of Secret and Confidential Information to Agents of a Foreign Power, 27 June 1946" (Ottawa: Edmound Cloutier . . . Controller of Stationery, 1946); Robert Bothwell and J. L. Granatstein, eds., *The Gouzenko Transcripts* (Ottawa: Deneau, 1982), 74, 97;

U.S. Joint Committee on Atomic Energy, 82d Cong., 1951, *Soviet Atomic Espionage,* 58.

8. Richard Rhodes, *Dark Sun: The Making of the Hydrogen Bomb* (New York: Simon & Schuster, 1995), 127–128.

9. Elizabeth Bentley FBI deposition, 30 November 1945, FBI file 65-14603.

10. Venona 424 KGB Moscow to New York, 1 July 1942; 894 KGB New York to Moscow, 26 June 1942; 846 KGB New York to Moscow, 3 June 1943; 1032 KGB New York to Moscow, 1 July 1943; 1107 KGB New York to Moscow, 8 July 1943; 1137 KGB New York to Moscow, 13 July 1943; 1197 KGB New York to Moscow, 22 July 1943; 1198 KGB New York to Moscow, 22 July 1943; 847B, 848 KGB New York to Moscow, 15 June 1944; 1453 KGB New York to Moscow, 12 October 1944; 1741 KGB New York to Moscow, 12 December 1944; 447 KGB San Francisco to Moscow, 31 October 1943.

11. Venona 448 KGB San Francisco to Moscow, 31 October 1943; 523 KGB San Francisco to Moscow, 14 December 1943; 538 KGB San Francisco to Moscow, 31 December 1943; 1 KGB San Francisco to Moscow, 2 January 1944; 212 KGB Moscow to Canberra, 29 August 1944.

12. Venona 317 KGB Moscow to New York, 15 May 1942; 722 KGB New York to Moscow, 21 May 1942; 719–720, 722 KGB New York to Moscow, 19 May 1943; 764–765 KGB New York to Moscow, 24 May 1943; 804, 805 KGB New York to Moscow, 29 May 1943; 821, 823, 825 KGB New York to Moscow, 31 May 1943; 899 KGB New York to Moscow, 11 June 1943; 904–907 KGB New York to Moscow, 12 June 1943; 908–910 KGB New York to Moscow, 12 June 1943; 916 KGB New York to Moscow, 15 June 1943; 965–966 KGB New York to Moscow, 21 June 1943; 967–968 KGB New York to Moscow, 22 June 1943; 1011 KGB New York to Moscow, 27 June 1943; 1979 KGB New York to Moscow, 4 December 1943; 722 KGB New York to Moscow, 19 May 1944; 747 KGB New York to Moscow, 25 May 1944; 851 KGB New York to Moscow, 15 June 1944; 1142 KGB New York to Moscow, 10 August 1944; 1234 KGB New York to Moscow, 29 August 1944; 1470 KGB New York to Moscow, 17 October 1944; 1821 KGB New York to Moscow, 26 December 1944.

13. Venona 327 KGB Moscow to Mexico City, 17 May 1945.

14. Venona 768 KGB New York to Moscow, 25 May 1943; 1088 KGB New York to Moscow, 7 July 1943; 747 KGB New York to Moscow, 25 May 1944; 1142 KGB New York to Moscow, 10 August 1944.

15. Venona 827 KGB New York to Moscow, 1 June 1943; 1182 KGB New York to Moscow, 19 August 1944; 1333 KGB New York to Moscow, 18 September 1944; 1431 KGB New York to Moscow, 10 October 1944.

16. Venona 860 KGB New York to Moscow, 6 June 1943; 974 KGB New York to Moscow, 22 June 1943; 1094, 1095 KGB New York to Moscow, 7 July 1943; 1207 KGB New York to Moscow, 22 July 1943; 1209 KGB New York to Moscow, 22 July 1943; 1435 KGB New York to Moscow, 4 September 1943; 1461 KGB New York to Moscow, 9 September 1943; 1039–1041 KGB New York to Moscow, 24–25 July 1944.

17. Venona 833 KGB New York to Moscow, 10 June 1942; 925 KGB New York to Moscow, 2 July 1942; 830 KGB New York to Moscow, 1 June 1943; 857, 863–864 KGB New York to Moscow, 5 June 1943; 860 KGB New York to Moscow, 6 June 1943; 952 KGB New York to Moscow, 21 June 1943; 1070 KGB New York to Moscow, 4 July 1943; 1209 KGB New York to Moscow, 22 July 1943; 1398 KGB New York to Moscow, 26 August 1943; 1776 KGB New York to Moscow, 26 October 1943; 725 KGB New York to Moscow, 19 May 1944; 726 KGB New York to Moscow, 20 May 1944; 1183 KGB New York to Moscow, 19 August 1944; 1370 KGB New York to Moscow, 27 September 1944.

18. See chapter 9.

19. See chapter 9.

20. Venona 55 KGB Moscow to New York, 10 January 1943.

21. Venona 445 KGB San Francisco to Moscow, 31 October 1943.

22. Venona 445 KGB San Francisco to Moscow, 31 October 1943.

23. Venona 1954 KGB New York to Moscow, 27 November 1943; 1039–1041 KGB New York to Moscow, 24–25 July 1944; 1097–1098 KGB New York to Moscow, 1 August 1944.

24. Venona 810 KGB New York to Moscow, 29 May 1943; 833 KGB New York to Moscow, 2 June 1943; 1207 KGB New York to Moscow, 22 July 1943; 699 KGB New York to Moscow, 17 May 1944; 817 KGB New York to Moscow, 6 June 1944; 847 KGB New York to Moscow, 14 June 1944; 1385 KGB New York to Moscow, 1 October 1944.

25. Venona 952 KGB New York to Moscow, 21 June 1943; 1207 KGB New York to Moscow, 22 July 1943; 1016 KGB New York to Moscow, 20 July 1944; 1042 KGB New York to Moscow, 25 July 1944; 1397 KGB New York to Moscow, 4 October 1944.

26. Venona 952 KGB New York to Moscow, 21 June 1943; 612 KGB New York to Moscow, 3 May 1944; 617 KGB New York to Moscow, 4 May 1944; 639 KGB New York to Moscow, 6 May 1944; 695 KGB New York to Moscow, 16 May 1944; 1042 KGB New York to Moscow, 25 July 1944.

27. Venona 1012 Naval GRU Washington to Moscow, 9 May 1943.

28. Venona 1207 KGB New York to Moscow, 22 July 1943.

29. Venona 6 KGB Moscow to London, 15 September 1945.

30. Venona 911 KGB New York to Moscow, 12 June 1943; 916 KGB New York to Moscow, 15 June 1943; 1207 KGB New York to Moscow, 22 July 1943; 1777 KGB New York to Moscow, 26 October 1943; 669 KGB New York to Moscow, 11 May 1944.

31. Venona 976 KGB New York to Moscow, 11 July 1944; 1286 KGB New York to Moscow, 8 September 1944; 17 KGB New York to Moscow, 4 January 1945.

32. Venona 1251 KGB New York to Moscow, 2 September 1944; 1267 KGB New York to Moscow, 6 September 1944; 1332 KGB New York to Moscow, 18 September 1944; 1582 KGB New York to Moscow, 12 November 1944; 1636 KGB New York to Moscow, 21 November 1944; 1803 KGB New York to Moscow, 22 December 1944; 50 KGB New York to Moscow, 11 January 1945; 1052 KGB New York to Moscow, 5 July 1945; 275 KGB Moscow to New York, 25 March 1945; 337 KGB Moscow to New York, 8 April 1945.

33. Venona 1207 KGB New York to Moscow, 22 July 1943; 1435 KGB New York to Moscow, 4 September 1943; 864 KGB New York to Moscow, 16 June 1944.

Appendix D

1. Dimitrov to Fitin, 20 November 1942, RTsKhIDNI 495-74-484. See also Harvey Klehr, John Earl Haynes, and Fridrikh Igorevich Firsov, *The Secret World of American Communism* (New Haven: Yale University Press, 1995), 318–319.

2. Venona 1433, 1435 KGB New York to Moscow, 10 October 1944.

3. Venona 705 KGB New York to Moscow, 17 May 1944; 738 KGB New York to Moscow, 23 May 1944; 777–779 KGB New York to Moscow, 25 May 1945.

4. Venona 726–729 KGB New York to Moscow, 22 May 1942; FBI report of 31 May 1944, FBI Comintern Apparatus file (FBI File 100-203581), serial 2753; Comintern Apparatus Summary Report, 15 December 1944, FBI Comintern Apparatus file, serial 3702.

5. Venona 227 KGB Moscow to New York, 13 March 1945.

6. Venona 259 Moscow to New York, 21 March 1945.

7. Venona 1116 GRU New York to Moscow, 9 July 1943; 1456 GRU New York to Moscow, 8 September 1943.

8. Venona 1759 KGB Washington to KGB Moscow, 28 March 1945.

9. Venona 1053 KGB New York to Moscow, 26 July 1944.

10. Venona 1464 KGB New York to Moscow, 14 October 1944.

11. Venona 1340 KGB New York to Moscow, 21 September 1944.

12. Venona 1754 KGB New York to Moscow, 14 December 1944; 20 KGB New York to Moscow, 4 January 1945.

13. Venona 1692 KGB New York to Moscow, 1 December 1944.

14. See chapter 10.

15. See chapter 10.

16. Venona 916 KGB New York to Moscow, 12 June 1945.

17. Venona 1791 KGB New York to Moscow, 20 December 1944. The NSA redacted Cora's identity.

18. Venona 1350 GRU New York to Moscow, 17 August 1943.

19. Venona 1313 KGB New York to Moscow, 13 September 1944; 1433, 1435 KGB New York to Moscow, 10 October 1944; 1506 KGB New York to Moscow, 23 October 1944.

20. "Report on Americans," 27 September 1937, RTsKhIDNI 545-3-453; Dimitrov to Fitin, 27 March 1943, RTsKhIDNI 495-74-485.

21. Fitin to Dimitrov, 6 May 1943, RTsKhIDNI 495-74-485. On Thompson's relationship with the CPUSA and the KGB vetting message see Klehr, Haynes, and Firsov, *The Secret World of American Communism,* 303–305.

22. On Traugott's OSS career, see Klehr, Haynes, and Firsov, *The Secret World of American Communism,* 307–308. On her postwar career see Traugott to National Citizens PAC State Coordinators, 19 April 1946, and Traugott to Steefel, 19 July 1948, box 1, Minnesota Progressive Party (Genevieve Steefel) Papers, Manuscript Division, Library of Congress, Washington, D.C.

23. Venona 767 KGB Moscow to New York, 17 July 1945.

24. Venona 1340 KGB New York to Moscow, 21 September 1944.

Index

This is an index to persons, organizations, and concepts in the text. There are names of persons in the alphabetical entries of the appendixes that are not listed in this index.